The Domino Conspiracy

Also by Joseph Heywood
THE BERKUT
TAXI DANCER

JOSEPH HEYWOOD

The Domino Conspiracy

RANDOM HOUSE

New York

To Sandy

Published in the United States by Random House, Inc., New York and
simultaneously in Canada by Random House of Canada Limited, Toronto.

Library of Congress Cataloging-in-Publication Data
Heywood, Joseph.
The Domino Conspiracy / by Joseph Heywood.—1st ed.
p. cm.
ISBN 0-679-41557-2: $23.00
I. Title.
PS3558.E92W65 1992
813'.54—dc20 92-3227

Book design by Collin Leech

Manufactured in the United States of America
24689753
First Edition

Comrade Khrushchev is well aware that the borders of Albania are inviolable and sacred, and that anyone who touches them is an aggressor. The Albanian people will fight to the last drop of blood if anyone touches their borders. . . .

They spend millions to recruit agents and spies, millions of dollars to organize acts of espionage, diversion, and of murder in our countries. U.S. imperialism has given and is giving thousands of millions of dollars to its loyal agents. . . .

No, the time has gone forever when the territory of Albania could be treated as a token to be bartered. . . .

> —*Excerpts from a speech given by Enver Hoxha, First Secretary of the Albanian Workers Party in Moscow on November 16, 1960.*

I

Hibernation

FRIDAY, SEPTEMBER 16, 1960, 5:10 P.M.
The Vuoksi River Region, Near the Soviet-Finnish Border

The two soldiers squatted in icy ankle-deep marsh water scanning the horizon. It had been hours since they had left the river and made their way through a thick coniferous forest to the flat marshes. Both men carried double-barreled, rifled shotguns that had been custom-made in Belgium. The bullets were Czech-made, with exploding tips pushed by three hundred grains of flashless gunpowder—not very sporting, but there was nothing sportive about chasing a wounded elk. The idea was to kill a seven-hundred-kilo beast in its tracks, and damage to the meat be damned.

Marshals Rodion Y. Malinovsky and Tikhon Serduyakov had been hunting since early morning and both were tired, but they neither complained nor hinted at their discomfort. Each had suffered much worse, and at their ages they welcomed the pains of physical labor as a reminder of the life still in them. Too many former comrades were long dead.

They had seen the animal minutes after entering the swamp, a huge bull elk with a wide, flat sweep of antlers two meters across, a sagging black bell of hair swinging from side to side under its chin and a swollen brisket, an excellent specimen in the rut and more than they had hoped to find so close to the border. The Finns tended to keep the elk population thinned out and brutes like this seldom escaped to Soviet territory, but there was no doubting their eyes. This was a worthy prize. They had stalked him all day, but the bull was wary and moved steadily to keep nearly a kilometer ahead of them.

It was now well past the time when they should have summoned the helicopter, and at least an hour since they had last seen the magnificent animal. Since then Malinovsky had aimed them 45 degrees west of their quarry's course, and now the sun was lower and at their backs as they reached a low island of granite boulders and climbed out of the water.

Serduyakov, commander of the Siberian Military District, immediately slipped off his insulated boots and two pairs of wool socks and rubbed his feet. An old infantryman looked out for his feet first. The defense minister of the Soviet Union moved a few meters higher, propped himself on his immense belly and scanned a line of low firs with his binoculars. Serduyakov took a flask of brandy out of his kit bag, uncapped it and tapped Malinovsky's foot. "Fuel for the weary," he said.

Malinovsky accepted the bottle, took a long pull, swished it around in his mouth, swallowed with an audible gulp, smacked his lips and passed it back. "It's begun," he said.

"The elk?" Serduyakov asked, craning his neck.

"Operation Aurora," the defense minister said. He had the raspy voice of a smoker, though he had never acquired the habit; and unlike too many of his Red Army colleagues, he drank sparingly. He liked the symbolism of Aurora, the name of the Soviet ship that had fired the historic shots in Leningrad as the Revolution got under way.

Serduyakov did not respond immediately. At the age of sixty he had served forty-two years as a soldier in one army or another, and he had ascended the ranks by his prudence as much as by his skills. To Serduyakov words were like precious gems: it took only a few to have great value. "Projections?" he asked after a suitable pause.

"Too soon to tell," Malinovsky said, his attention still riveted on the tree line. "But Khrushchev will fall," he added. "If not now, then later."

"In chess the outcome is apparent after the opening moves."

"Only when an amateur challenges a master. In any event, this is no game," Malinovsky reminded his colleague. The Soviet defense minister harbored little doubt about Khrushchev's ultimate fate. His plan would ensure that. It was intricate, subtle, complex and dependent on too many factors to recall now, but he had thought it all through, gauged every angle and concluded that he could control the critical parts. Luck would have to do the rest, but that didn't bother him. Every military operation required luck—always had, always would, and this plan was no different. The idea had come to him while he watched a colleague's grandchildren playing dominoes; he had immediately imagined a huge expanse of black tiles standing on end, laid out in tight rows, files and sweeping curves. Just one tile could trigger the whole lot, send them all falling, looping and snaking this way and that, but within the graceful patterns there was a single, direct and unrelenting line aimed inexorably at Nikita Sergeievich Khrushchev, who had been born Khrush the Beetle, a roly-poly, hard-backed little bug who had grown into the insect king. Now it was time to crack his back and squash the pulp from his thorax. Probably he would detect the fall of the first tile, but he would not see that he was the target of it all. It was a subtle plan and nearly invisible, which in Malinovsky's mind placed it in the category of brilliant—not perfect, but brilliant, which was the most men could hope for. In the end it would come down to mere luck, and either it would swing their way or it wouldn't. Serduyakov was right that it was like chess, not the game played languidly by old men in Moscow's parks or the flashy, heady mathematical game of the grandmasters, but chess with flesh-and-blood pieces, each with a precise role. In chess you predicated your attacks on precise knowledge of what your pieces could do. Mask the attack, hide it, disguise it, mislead your foe: these were the rules of engagement. They had let the Nazi hordes advance to the portals of Moscow, then counterattacked with armies that German intelligence didn't know about. The most effective attack was the one that came from nowhere, the kind he had carefully arranged in this scenario, and it all began with the toppling of a single tile.

"The army must not be implicated," Serduyakov said.

That's the point, Malinovsky thought: To bring Khrushchev down and preserve the army they had spent their lives creating, an army so powerful that no foe dared challenge it. It had been a long haul, weeding out the cowards and incompetents, fools and weaklings, in learning how to coexist with bureaucrats and party hacks, then manipulating them to acquire what was needed. They had created their own supply infrastructure, their own raw-material sources, their own manufacturing, built their own factories, trained their own work force, created a distribution system that got parts where they belonged when they were needed and made themselves independent of the fools who purported to make goods for peasants. The Defense Ministry had shown the Kremlin how a production system could work if you knew how to manage workers with penalties that were real, severe and inexorable, but despite all this, the civilians in the industrial sector refused to learn and still wasted their time in committees bogged down by inane five-year plans and grand schemes driven by the ghosts of Lenin and Stalin. The Red Army had shed blood and sacrificed a generation of boys out of a common interest; it came first, the *old* army that had saved the Motherland not once but twice, not an army of missiles and gadgets made by intellectuals and scientists but an army of boys turned into men by hard discipline and sleeping with their bellies in the mud. Khrushchev did not understand, or would not—who was to say what went on in the little bastard's twisted mind? After all, he had been a political officer, not a true soldier.

It was clear now that the army meant nothing to Khrushchev. The General Secretary had decided that it cost too much; based on this he had proposed a drastic reduction in troop strength; entire divisions would be mothballed. We must keep the peace with the West, he lectured the Politburo, but he was alone in seeing it this way and he had already started the cutbacks. He claimed he would use the savings to fund a missile force and direct the remainder to boost production of consumer goods. All at the expense of the Red Army, Malinovsky thought, the people's army, *his* army. That little Ukrainian prick! He had argued with him about the strategic value of conventional forces, but Khrushchev had only laughed. "You don't understand modern thinking. You're an old war horse. You must trust me." Khrush the Beetle had laughed at him, and in that instant he had realized that the Ukrainian peasant had to be eliminated—not for him, but for the Motherland, for the twenty-five million dead at German hands, for the sake of future generations threatened by American imperialism. It was a matter of honor.

What Serduyakov referred to, of course, was his own skin because what they viewed as honor others would see as treason, clear and simple. "The essence of honor is sacrifice," Malinovsky reminded his colleague.

Serduyakov shuddered and tried to guess the defense minister's thoughts, but Malinovsky seldom telegraphed his feelings. At Stalingrad there had been bodies as far as the eye could see, corpses frozen into contorted, grotesque death statues, and Malinovsky had walked among them listening to an accounting of ammunition reserves. In Byelorussia the retreating Nazis had impaled peasants on pine trees and Malinovsky had led his staff heedlessly through the forest of corpses while reminding them that spring would soon arrive and that their tanks would need extra treads. In Berlin he had come upon several of his men torturing a captured SS junior officer and had intervened, saving the German and ordering his own men executed for unsoldierly conduct. He was the hardest, coldest man Serduyakov had ever known and the only man he would follow down the path of treason. Nevertheless, if the army was implicated the whole point of the enterprise would be compromised.

"It's too complex," Serduyakov insisted. "Simplicity is the key to a successful military operation. We learned that against the Nazis."

Serduyakov's fears were understandable. He didn't know all of it; as the plan's designer, Malinovsky knew fate had supplied a certain man to start the fall of the main line of dominoes, but to share this was to risk it all, so he kept it to himself, just as he had in the war. An American agent had come into their hands. It had been serendipitous to find such a man, unimaginably lucky, but it was he who saw the opportunity the American represented. The man was French-born and of Albanian descent, a wolf in sheep's clothing. The CIA had sent him to Paris, but he was pursuing his own agenda, leading a secret life, and it had been simple enough to use this for their ends. Lumbas, another Albanian, had been the bait. The American dreamed of unseating the Hoxha regime in Albania; his parents had passed on this obsession to him. It had been risky to extract Lumbas from the missile base after the immense risk of putting him there, but it had been done, and while he fed the American missile information he also led him down a parallel path, helping to create a mythical invasion of Albania by the United States as a provocation.

When Hoxha learned that he had been targeted he would react predictably. Vengeance was the central Albanian value, revenge their theology. Hoxha and Khrushchev loathed each other; Khrushchev had been cozy with the Americans, pursuing the policy he called peaceful coexistence. Hoxha would see that the American intervention could happen only if the Soviets approved it, if not openly, then tacitly, which for him would be the same. Hoxha would strike back at Khrushchev, and even if his attempt failed, the Politburo would see that their General Secretary no longer commanded respect. A mere flea of a nation, a suppurating boil on Communism's backside, a collection of backward brigands daring to challenge the leader of the Soviet Union? Even if Khrushchev escaped with his life, his peers would see the truth. Could the Soviet Union afford to have such a weakling commanding the Politburo? Not with the Chinese and the Americans pressing in on two sides.

Of course it would be best if the Albanians succeeded; then they could bury the little prick with honors, erect the customary statues and forget him. But even if the brigands failed, the attempt alone would be enough; this was the beauty of his plan, the ultimate political simplicity that Serduyakov would never understand. The trick was to make certain that nothing interfered with the Albanian retaliation, and this would not be easy. Despite his flawed Russian and penchant for earthy proverbs, Khrushchev had survived this long because he had a long reach and ears everywhere; he had the survival instincts of a cockroach. He had engineered Beria's death in the wake of Stalin's passing; the entire country had feared the secret police chief but it had been Khrushchev who had moved against him, then consolidated his power by eliminating his remaining political rivals, not in Stalin's way with an ounce of lead to the backs of their heads, but through remarkable political maneuvering. He had taken power without shedding blood, and that had to be respected. To fight him head-on was not practical. It had to come from the outside, and from a source so ludicrous that it would shock the Party to its very foundations. The Albanians would be David to the Ukrainian Goliath, and he, Radion Malinovsky, would be the savior of the army.

"You worry too much," Malinovsky said. "Whatever happens, we'll be safe if we keep our wits." Even if Khrushchev managed to deflect the assault before it happened, there were others to take the blame and stand the punishment. It had all been arranged.

"I still don't like it," Serduyakov grumbled.

Malinovsky knew his colleague was no coward and was committed to the cause, but he was like all subordinates; he allowed himself to doubt. Those in command could not afford such luxuries.

Suddenly the dark brown elk appeared, its snout submerged in a mass of floating plants. It was less than forty meters away, its mind on food. Malinovsky wrapped the sling of his rifle around his left forearm and braced his weapon against the rocks. "Watch this," he whispered to his colleague.

Serduyakov slithered into position beside the defense minister. "Magnificent," he whispered.

Malinovsky began to grunt rhythmically, which made the elk lift its head and grunt a reply; water cascaded from its huge snout.

The sudden explosion beside Serduyakov caught him by surprise. For hours they had been enveloped in a silence broken only by their own whispers and movement. He was surprised that Malinovsky let fly with both barrels simultaneously. The elk's head and massive antlers exploded and left the headless creature standing momentarily before it toppled sideways into the water with a great splash.

"When you hunt for survival," the defense minister said softly, "you do not concern yourself with trophies."

2 WEDNESDAY, NOVEMBER 16, 1960, 10:00 P.M. *Moscow*

Enver Hoxha, Albania's First Secretary, had said his piece at the gathering of Communist and worker parties with more than his usual flair for incendiary rhetoric, attacking Khrushchev and the Russians directly and vehemently as hundreds of delegates from eighty-one countries looked on. Having spoken, he hurried the Albanian delegation out of the cavernous meeting hall through a gauntlet of derisive whistles and angry shouts from pro-Soviet representatives. Only the Chinese had been silent.

Now Hoxha and Mehmet Shehu, the former defense minister recently elevated to premier, had been summoned to Nikita Khrushchev's office, which came as no surprise to either of them. Hoxha was a baby-faced man of medium build and moist, feminine eyes. Shehu was tall and gaunt with long, narrow hands, rounded shoulders, a wild nest of black, curly hair that tended to resist a comb and long, thin slightly bowed legs. By any standard he was a striking man, but this polished façade hid a remarkably brutal personality.

"Let us speak clearly," Khrushchev began. He had shed his suit coat, his shirt showing large sweat lines; the fringe of white down that remained of his hair stuck to his head with perspiration. "You were out of order, out of bounds."

"We're not your puppets," Hoxha said, but Shehu sensed tentativeness in his response. This came as no surprise; Hoxha was best on a stage where there was no chance of give-and-take. He had always been the theoretician and scholar, while it fell to Shehu to make things work, which meant shedding the blood of their enemies.

"It's time to put your national affairs in order!" Khrushchev thundered. Translation: Support us, not the Chinese. Or else.

"Only when the Soviets share their wealth and only after they put their own affairs in order," Hoxha answered. Translation: There would be cooperation only if the Soviets shared atomic-weapons technology with the Chinese and if Khrushchev retracted his long-standing condemnation of Stalin.

Khrushchev immediately leaped to his feet, shook his beefy little fist at them and screamed, "You are *pissing* on me!"

"Take back your allegations," Shehu demanded before Hoxha could speak.

"Where shall I put them?" the Soviet leader shouted.

"Up your fat Ukrainian ass!" Shehu snapped.

This exchange ended the meeting. Comrade Hoxha nearly ran out of the paneled office, but Shehu stopped, reversed course to Khrushchev's desk and stuck a finger in the General Secretary's face. "You think you can throw stones at us, but I warn you that your stones will fall only on *your* head."

These were the last words spoken directly between the Albanian leaders and Khrushchev's revisionist renegades. Within hours Shehu and Hoxha had fled Moscow and taken a train through Czechoslovakia and Austria; one of their own aircraft came to fetch them from Italy. Hoxha had cowered in their compartment the entire journey, fearful that the Khrushchevites would retaliate, but they arrived home without incident.

Malinovsky was pleased when word of this confrontation reached him. The split was assured; now the Albanians would sit seething in their mountain fortress contemplating ways to get even. Khrushchev had already dispatched high-level emissaries to Tirana to find ways to bring the Albanians back into the fold, but it would not work. At stake was the Soviet submarine base under construction at Vlorë; Khrushchev would try to keep the installation, but Malinovsky knew from his own sources that the effort would be futile. The plan was on schedule, but the defense minister kept this to himself. Winning a skirmish was not the same as winning a battle, much less a war, and despite this encouraging development there were many impediments ahead. Khrushchev had put a special investigator on the trail of Villam Lumbas, and if this man began to get too close something would have to be done, even if it triggered the General Secretary's highly suspicious nature. In chess you had to anticipate your opponent's moves, then remove his options. Now that the Albanians had declared their separation from the Soviets it was time to provoke the divorce.

3   SUNDAY, NOVEMBER 20, 1960, 3:20 A.M. Durrës, Albania

Mehmet Shehu stood at the end of the whitewashed stone room and watched Haxi Kasi work on the spy, who was of a rare type. Once revealed, most spies eagerly traded information against the illogical hope that they could save themselves. A minimum of pain usually started the flow of information, but not this time. Having been captured, the prisoner assumed he would die and had done all within his power to force his captors to accelerate the process so that what he knew would die quickly with him. Shehu and Haxi Kasi had dealt with such men before and knew information could be gotten from them, but it was an ever so delicate process requiring the interrogator to suspend the subject on the edge of the abyss of physical destruction. The human brain was an interesting organ; sometimes, when Shehu was in a reflective mood, he thought the mind might be the soul the Christians worshiped with such faith and fanaticism. That the mind worked in mysterious ways, however, was not as interesting to him as how it worked. If you guided a man to the brink of death, some inner mechanism of his brain would override the rational part and give you what you wanted. In the face of death, the inner mind seemed to act on its own behalf in a biochemical response rather than a rational one, but without due care and considerable luck the body could expire before the mechanism had a chance to work. To be successful with this type of man, you had to be as precise and patient as a surgeon, then hope the subject was gifted with a resilient natural constitution, something that body size could not predict. You never knew about a man's ability to cope with pain until you methodically started hurting him.

The prisoner was short and wiry with olive skin, curly black hair, several old diagonal scars on his belly, narrow hands and feet, and an extraordinarily long penis. Throughout the interrogation they kept him unclothed, in part to humiliate him but more to have immediate access. He had given his name as Adriatik Constantin, which might or might not be legitimate; he had been arrested in Lescovic near the Greek border, but thus far they had been unable to trace any family ties and nobody in the village acknowledged knowing him. They had picked him up on an anonymous tip, plucking him out of an area that traditionally harbored Greek infiltrators; some were saboteurs, but more often they crossed the border merely to collect information and disseminate anti-Hoxha propaganda. Seldom did such tips lead to anything, but this time they had gotten the Greek. Constantin's government had long coveted southern Albania, just as the Yugoslavs constantly plotted to annex the north. The prisoner had gone silent as soon as he was taken; the Sigurimi detachment that arrested him was immediately suspicious of the man's professional demeanor and had alerted Kasi, who called Shehu.

The interrogation was now in its third day, and while Kasi looked as fresh as when they had begun, the Albanian premier was exhausted. He stood outside the glare of the arc lamps, dropped his sweat-soaked shirt on the floor, toweled himself dry and put on a fresh shirt. It would have been easier to bring in other interrogators, but Shehu's instincts told him they had hold of something unusual; because of this they decided to limit access to the prisoner until they had a better idea of what they were dealing with. So far the two men knew nothing except what their time-honed instincts told them, which was that this dark little pig was more than a simple infiltrator.

The Greek's tolerance for pain was remarkable, which was typical of the race, Shehu thought. It was the trait central to Greek legends and most respected by their enemies. An hour ago Kasi had dumped Constantin facedown, braced his boot against the man's spine, lashed his elbows together, then pulled his elbows back until both shoulders dislocated with loud pops. Despite the damage the prisoner had not made a sound.

Now Kasi had the man on his back in a spread-eagle position; he stood beside him, talking softly in a friendly voice. This was an integral part of the technique that he and Shehu had first learned from Spaniards, then perfected over many years of trial and error. When you racked certain men with pain, you should address them politely as if you were engaged in a conversation over afternoon tea, and you must never lose your temper. This created a contrast that the brain had difficulty dealing with, especially as the pain mounted and the prisoner weakened.

Thus far they had been extremely patient, but now Shehu sensed that it was time to escalate the violence. He rejoined Kasi and nodded toward the table where there was a siphon and a length of rubber hose.

"We've been rude," Shehu told the prisoner. "Some pure Albanian water will refresh you."

"Albanians bathe in shit," the prisoner muttered. "Your women gave birth to syphilitic turds with limbs and call them children." Shehu was impressed. The man wanted to make them so angry that they would kill him quickly, and lesser interrogators might have done so. But not this time.

Kasi slid a wooden yoke over the man's neck, pushed his head into a slot and tied a leather strap across his forehead to immobilize him. Then they pulled him across a cot on his back so that his upper body hung down, clamped the siphon over his mouth, connected the hose to a faucet and turned it on.

"No doubt our guest is thirsty," Shehu said. "It would be impolite to neglect him."

The prisoner's eyes flashed as his belly filled with water and began to swell. From time to time Kasi extracted the siphon and whacked the prisoner's stomach with a truncheon, causing him to vomit. After each blow they reinserted the hose.

"Please," Kasi said as he removed the siphon, "kindly tell us your business in Lescovic."

"Fucking your mother's mouth," the Greek hissed.

"My mother thanks you for your many kindnesses," Kasi whispered. He replaced the siphon and this time dropped a wet cloth over the man's nose. With water pumping into his stomach through his mouth the prisoner was forced to inhale air through his nostrils, but now the wet rag hindered his air route and approximated a sensation identical with drowning. Immediately his chest began to heave violently.

"Has your thirst been quenched, comrade?"

After a time they removed the cloth and siphon and Constantin gasped as fresh air spilled into his lungs. "I would have had your mother sooner, but a rabid dog was already fucking her," he gasped.

Kasi looked at his superior, shook his head, then drove the truncheon into the man's mouth, shattering his teeth and lips. "I thank you on Mother's behalf. Our Greek is obstinate," he said as they repeated the process and the prisoner's shoulders started slapping the stone floor as he struggled for air.

Kasi started to remove the wet cloth, but his superior stopped him. "Leave it."

"Could kill him," Kasi said matter-of-factly.

Shehu shrugged. "Give him a close look at death."

While the man choked, Kasi pulled a hand-driven generator over to the body, knelt, twisted two electric wires around the man's penis, then stood and began cranking. The man's body lifted violently and shuddered while the room filled with the fumes of burning flesh. Shehu disconnected the water hose and drove his heel into the prisoner's stomach while Kasi kept cranking current into him.

After twenty more minutes of alternating shocks and water, Shehu lifted the wet rag off the man's face and saw in his eyes that his resistance was broken. They left him on the floor and questioned him slowly. He gave them five names and a brief outline of his role.

Afterward the Albanian premier walked outside with Kasi. The sea air was warm, the sun rising. "I'll make the arrests myself," Kasi said.

"Do it quietly," Shehu said. "Each of them is a step upward."

TUESDAY, NOVEMBER 22, 1960, 9:15 P.M.
Moscow

Roman Trubkin was the sort of man Nikita Khrushchev liked: smart, resourceful and openly ambitious. Best of all, Trubkin had a positive attitude; he was the sort of man who searched constantly for ways to assist the General Secretary to achieve his goals rather than listing reason after reason why and how a particular endeavor might fail. Despite this, Trubkin was no toady. He could be blunt and ardent in his opinion even if it put him at loggerheads with or risked the displeasure of his superior. Khrushchev thought, This one has balls, and so far Trubkin had shown this assessment to be true.

As so often was the case, Khrushchev had recruited the man to his service at the precise moment when Trubkin's prospects seemed most bleak. Nothing created indebtedness like rescue from oblivion. Having been among the pilots selected to train as cosmonauts earlier in the year, Trubkin had moved quickly to the forefront and had become the odds-on favorite to be the first man in space. Soon after, he had developed an inner-ear problem that left him disoriented at six G's or more. When his ailment didn't respond to therapy, Trubkin was removed from further consideration. As soon as he was informed of the development, Khrushchev recognized an opportunity and recruited him.

That he needed his own source inside the Soviet rocket program irked the General Secretary no end. Were it not for his own vision, Soviet rocketry would still consist of no more than engineering blueprints and expensive wooden models. In the wake of Stalin's death he had focused on concentrating his power and support inside the Party, but he did not neglect longer-range goals. The Great Patriotic War had left its imprint, and he would make sure that no foreign power would ever again have the nerve to attack the Motherland. The key to this, he was certain, was the development of rockets, which the Germans had pioneered and the Americans were taking to new levels. To counter the Americans, the Soviet air force was pressing for its own long-range bomber force to match what their enemies had, but it was apparent that Soviet designers could not give the air force what it required. This being evident, Khrushchev decided to look at rockets, and the route to Soviet rocket superiority, he decided, resided in the mind of one Sergei Pavlovich Korolev, a longtime bad boy and resident of Stalin's gulags, an aeronautical engineer distinguished by a sharp tongue to match his brilliance.

But where Khrushchev's interest in rocketry had been solely military, Korolev had his heart and his slide rule fixed on the stars. Roman Trubkin had uncovered Korolev's secret—indeed, he had suspected the truth from the moment he saw Korolev's R-7 sitting on the gantry—but he had no one to tell and no interest in doing so as long as he was likely to be the one to ride the gigantic rocket into space.

The day Trubkin told Khrushchev the truth was etched in the General Secretary's mind. "Would you use a battleship to defend coastal waters?" Trubkin began. "General Engineer Korolev has built a rocket that will take us to the far reaches of space, but will never rain warheads on our enemies." There were many reasons for this, he explained: the volatile propellant meant fueling could not be done until just before launch, which meant there would be no fast-launch capability; the system itself was too large to hide and move around, so it would have to be dug in; and the R-7 could not reach a target on the other side of the earth without mid-course corrections from land and sea-based tracking units, which meant that if these stations were destroyed, the rockets would be next to useless. Conclusion: Korolev had created something to satisfy his own interests, not the Soviet people's. The R-7's strategic military value was marginal at best.

Khrushchev had raged for days, then after regaining his self-control had dispatched other agents to verify what Trubkin had told him. Their opinions were unanimous: Korolev had duped him! Despite his crowing over Soviet rocket superiority after the Sputnik triumph, he was faced with the naked truth: there was no Soviet superiority, no "missile gap," as Western reporters called it. What to do? It was a delicate and dangerous situation. Quietly he mobilized several new military-rocket efforts, all of them intended to develop an effective ICBM purely for military use. Meanwhile, he maintained his propaganda effort and pushed Korolev to get a man into space. There had been enough unmanned flights, and an entire kennel of dogs had produced nothing but expensive extraterrestrial turds; what he needed was a Soviet man in orbit. If this could be accomplished, the propaganda value would be incalculable, especially with Kennedy due to move into the White House. The new president would inherit a bad situation; American journalists were hammering away at the missile gap. If he could put a man in space, Khrushchev reasoned, he would gain a huge bargaining advantage over the new president. A man in space would suggest superiority where none existed, and the Western press would seal this perception, which would buy time.

Now they were within months of seeing man's age-old dream come to fruition. Most important, Nikita Sergeievich would get all of the credit unless something went wrong. Then Khrushchev had gotten a message from Trubkin that deeply disturbed him, and he had summoned him to Moscow.

In October there had been an accident at the Tyuratam rocket base. More than a hundred men and women had died and the General Secretary had sent Trubkin to investigate. His verdict coincided with the experts': ignition malfunction. When the launch sequence reached zero, nothing had happened and hundreds of technicians scrambled prematurely out of their protective bunkers to find out what had gone wrong. Minutes later the ignition had engaged without warning and caught everyone in the open. The disaster had been effectively hidden from the West, but dozens of key personnel had been killed and Khrushchev demanded to know why. The two-word message from Trubkin had been decoded by the General Secretary himself. It read: "Human error."

Trubkin was a slight man with the curly black hair of a Jew, a receding hairline, and the dull eyes and flat face of a serf. The former pilot moved slowly and talked with great difficulty, these behaviors masking an exceptional analytical mind and superior political instincts. He stood stiffly at attention, awaiting orders from his supreme commander.

Khrushchev held up the message. "Explain." He left the man at attention; it was important for him to understand the seriousness of the situation.

"There is an engineer called Lumbas," Trubkin began, "Villam Pavelovich Lumbas. His expertise is in ignition-sequencing circuitry."

"Never heard of him," Khrushchev said, who prided himself on knowing the key rocket people.

"Nor had I, and in many ways he is purely a minor figure, but in the aftermath of the accident his role is taking on major proportions."

"He fucked up, did he?" Then Khrushchev quickly added, "Was it sabotage?" The West was forever trying to recruit Soviet citizens to work against their government.

Trubkin shrugged. "I can't judge that."

"Then what?" the General Secretary asked, his impatience obvious.

"Comrade Lumbas was removed from the project before the ignition circuits were fully tested."

Khrushchev's eyebrows raised to a sharp angle. "By whom?"

"In the aftermath it was said repeatedly that if Lumbas had remained with the project, he might have prevented the problem."

"Did General Engineer Korolev try to get this Lumbas back?"

Trubkin nodded. "But Comrade Lumbas could not be located. He had been reassigned."

"To what?"

The former cosmonaut shrugged. "Undoubtedly you would know better than I, Comrade General Secretary."

Khrushchev leaped to his feet. "What the hell is that supposed to mean, Major?"

Trubkin removed a document from his tunic and handed it to Khrushchev, who unfolded it and slowly read the official form used by the military to transfer its personnel. The document ordered Lt. Col. Villam Pavelovich Lumbas to report to an address in Moscow for reassignment. The new organization was not named; there was only an address. When the General Secretary's eyes reached the bottom of the document, his face suddenly whitened. The signature at the bottom seemed to be his, yet he had signed no such order. "It's a forgery," he said angrily.

"I thought it highly unusual," Trubkin said, "so I took the liberty of checking the address. It doesn't exist."

The General Secretary collapsed into his chair and fought to control his anger. It seemed that his whole career had been marked by challenges from lesser men trying to dislodge him from power, but this—*this* was unprecedented, and the nakedness of it sent a chill through him.

"You have orders for me?" Trubkin asked.

"Get out," Khrushchev said. "I need time to think." First the Albanian fiasco and now this.

5   WEDNESDAY, NOVEMBER 23, 1960, 10:20 P.M. *Moscow*

Malinovsky sawed off a piece of tough beef, chewed it slowly, then washed it down with a swig of red wine imported at great expense from France. Such indulgences made little impression on the defense minister, who tasted no appreciable differences between wines or vintages. There was red and white, and Malinovsky preferred red even with fish.

Colonel General Andrei Semenovich Gubin, on the other hand, was a connoisseur of wine, food, clothes and especially women. Gubin was a trim, slightly built man who always looked fresh, and other officers sometimes joked behind his back that the fastidious general ordered others to sweat for him. A famous paratroop officer with more than five thousand jumps, he had a medical chart listing more than twenty broken bones. Currently he served as commander of infantry for the Moscow Military District and was acclaimed as one of the Red Army's most innovative strategists. At present he was devising a scheme to convert all Soviet infantry into airborne cavalry, using helicopters to lift them into battle. The plan was a solid one, Malinovsky thought, but not feasible because the army budget had been trimmed so drastically by Khrushchev, with the rubles shifted to rockets and an entirely new and separate branch of the military.

Gubin knew that Malinovsky had not invited him to dinner at his private mess to discuss his plan. "You've hardly touched your food," the defense minister said, poking the air with his fork.

"An overweight paratrooper becomes a bomb," Gubin said. The beef was gray, dry and overcooked; he would eat later.

"It's time for the next phase," Malinovsky said as he chewed.

"The Albanians have interdicted the mission?"

Malinovsky nodded. "We dropped it in their laps, and now it's time to erase our connections."

Gubin had guessed as much. "Lumbas and the American?"

"Kill both of them as soon as is feasible."

"They're both in Belgrade. It can be done almost immediately."

"Does Lumbas suspect anything?"

"No." Gubin was certain of this.

"If you're not going to eat," Malinovsky said, waving his knife, "you can go."

When Gubin was gone, Malinovsky refolded his linen napkin and laid it over his plate. So far everything was progressing smoothly. Gubin had been a good choice. Over the years he had enjoyed his share of women, but he had shown good judgment in selecting married females whose interests did not include long-term expectations. It was common knowledge that he had once run six women for nearly a year, all of them friends of one another. Whatever else, Gubin was an impressive organizer and knew how to keep his mouth shut. He had been flattered when the defense minister had confided in him, but before approaching him Malinovsky had thoroughly checked out his sympathies and found him to be vehemently anti-Khrushchev. Now Gubin labored under the misconception that he alone served the defense minister, whereas Malinovsky had split the scheme into compartments and avenues, none of which would lead back to him. Lumbas and the American would be eliminated, and while Gubin saw to that another colleague would see to the former cosmonaut that Khrushchev was using as a bloodhound. All of this would take place far afield from him, just as it had in wartime. The trick, Malinovsky reminded himself, was to be able to clearly visualize all parts of the battlefield even when you were a long way off.

FRIDAY, NOVEMBER 25, 1960, 4:30 P.M.
Belgrade, Yugoslavia

Albert Frash was so astonished to see the signal that he did a double take, then stopped and stared at the marker on the electrical pole. Normally he passed markers left by assets, reading them with an imperceptible glance, but this time he had stopped and gawked like a rank amateur before realizing his error and quickly stumbling on. What he had seen was a red thumbtack with a diagonal scratch on it—an emergency signal requiring an immediate and unexpected meeting.

Using extra caution, Frash walked at varying speeds through two department stores, entering each from one direction, crisscrossing several floors, then exiting in a different direction in a process called "dry cleaning." When he saw there was no tail, he headed directly to Navo Groblje, Belgrade's New Cemetery, and entered it through the wooden gate at the entrance for gravediggers. An unlocked shed near the entrance held tools and work clothes; Frash took a tattered black coat, wide-brimmed straw hat and a long-handled shovel with a badly dented blade.

There were two meeting sites in the huge cemetery and a place from which Frash could watch both. Moving west along paths of dead brown grass he followed a line of lichen-covered mausoleums, reached his observation point and hugged the shadows of a pyramidlike tomb with a winged cherub on top.

It was not long before he saw Lumbas, but caution made him hang back. In his time with the Central Intelligence Agency, his instincts had served him well. His cardinal rule was that nothing is as it seems to be. Once understood and heeded, this principle kept you alive. Villam seemed to be alone, but despite the emergency nature of the meeting he looked almost serene. Very odd. Frash considered approaching but stayed where he was and watched Lumbas light a cigarette. Whatever caused Villam to summon him must be damned serious, yet he was smoking, something he avoided except in circumstances in which he was certain of security. Presumably this was not one of those times, yet Lumbas looked as if he hadn't a care in the world. It didn't add up. The meeting signal had been urgent and meant that they should rendezvous on the half hour, wait five minutes and if there was no contact, leave, return in an hour and try again. If there was no success on the third try, they would move everything back twenty-four hours. But a half-hour mark had already passed, Villam had not moved away and alarms were sounding in Frash's head. He was trying to decipher the puzzle when he saw two men trotting along an iron fence toward Villam, who obviously saw them but did not react until they were nearly on top of him. Frash saw him pull a pistol from the back of his belt and run, but a shot sent him crashing into a third man coming from the opposite direction. Villam and the man scuffled briefly, there were two muffled pops, and then the man was standing over Lumbas. Frash needed to see no more and left immediately, walking slowly with a fake limp, his shovel on his shoulder. Kill them, a frantic voice begged; Flee, a second voice said.

As soon as he was out of the cemetery Frash got into a crowded bus, rode two blocks, got off, caught a bus in another direction, rode several kilometers, disembarked, and walked an S pattern through a park until he was sure he was not followed. Had the ambush been meant for both of them? The trees in the park had no leaves. Fall, the dying season. This had been his mother's expression. Why did he remember it now?

He had been too far from the assailants to see more than that they were big and burly. The one who had killed Villam might have been Asian, he thought. Who were they? It doesn't matter, he told himself. Priorities. Something is wrong, but now's not the time to think about it. Figure it out when you're safe. Right now you have to concentrate on getting out.

Frash kept three separate sets of identity papers in three different dead drops. He made for the nearest one, picked up his package, flagged a cab, and within forty minutes of arriving at the airport was airborne. His ticket was one-way, Belgrade to London, with a stopover in Paris, but he had no intention of going to England.

What had gone wrong? In one week the full operation would have been launched. Months of planning and work were reduced to seven days of anticipation. Villam was not supposed to contact him again until the operation had begun, but he had. Now it was all finished; Villam had been the link, the link was dead and soon he would be persona non grata. Villam had been relaxed and smoking even when they ran toward him, so he must have known the assailants, otherwise why hadn't he reacted sooner?

The frustration was overwhelming, and as Frash sat in his seat trembling with rage, a flight attendant came up and knelt in the aisle. "Are you all right?" She had short brown hair, small dark eyes and a soothing tone developed with practice. When she touched his leg with her hand he stared at it until she moved it. "I just wanted to help," she apologized. When he looked at her, her eyes widened and she fled down the aisle.

Villam had set him up. The trap had been intended for both of them, and that told him all he needed to know. The whole thing had been a setup right from the start. Did his brother know? Frash could barely contain his rage.

His mother had recounted the events so often that Frash sometimes imagined he had been there. She always referred to it as the Black Day; it lay on him like a shroud. Not that he was fixated, but it was always there just under the surface, gnawing silently like worms eating away at wood.

The aspiring congressman wore a navy blue suit, tailored carefully, Mother said, with a blue silk tie, knotted perfectly. He was thin but relaxed, a man-boy with a golden tan and protruding eyes that made him seem sad and angry at the same time; he stood by while the patriarch of the Kennedy clan sat on the front of a wooden chair, his legs crossed, hands joined in his lap, like a closed and independent circuit, Mother said. The meeting had been arranged by Monsignor Salvatore Milani, a longtime power broker among the hordes of Italians who, in the decades before the war, had pushed the Irish out of Boston's North End.

John F. Kennedy, late of the U.S. Navy and a brief stint as a journalist, was about to enter the political arena and his father, the former ambassador to the Court of St. James's, was using his influence and money to help the effort, a feudal lord settling the fief. Father Milani had said that this was the time to make a deal and Mother had believed him. A priest. The ambassador, she said, had cold, hard eyes and the countenance of a man accustomed to deciding the fate of others.

His father had opposed his mother's plan, but when she set her mind there was no way to turn it. Milani led her to the Bellevue Hotel and took her up to the suite of rooms where the younger Kennedy was assembling his campaign.

"This is Mrs. Frascetti. She's a professor at BC and a good Catholic like us. She has connections," Milani added before leaving her alone with the two men. She had dressed carefully that day, picking a conservative gray dress and black shoes with not-too-high heels. A serious dress for serious business.

"I'm Albanian," she told them. "My husband was in Zog's regime, a leader of the Catholic faction. We left before Mussolini came and went to France. We left there because of the Nazis. Now we are here. We have a network: priests, soldiers, scholars, intellectuals, people of substance. We intend to take back our country."

The ambassador's tone was razor-sharp. "Get to the point." He checked his watch, then tightened the knot of his tie. Humiliating, she told her son later.

"I can deliver votes," she said. "My husband and I know Albanians up and down the East Coast."

"How many do you know in the Eleventh Congressional District?" the ambassador asked. He looked past her, she said later, or through her. It was hard to tell. She wanted to check a mirror to reassure herself that her reflection had not been stolen; her eyes had been puffy and red when she confessed this to her son. "We're people without shadows," she sobbed. "They mocked us."

"Two hundred," she told her inquisitor.

"Of voting age," he growled.

"Sixty or seventy."

"Sixty or seventy," the ambassador said, his face a pinkish-gray mask. "Fascinating." A long pause followed. "How many are actually registered to vote?"

How could such an emotionless old man sire children? she wondered. "All of them," she said too quickly.

"Democrats?"

She said later that her mouth moved, but it was filled with cotton and no sound came out. She nodded, her mind a blank. Party labels meant very little in Albania; what mattered were convictions and how you built a coalition. "Some," she said with a croak after a long silence. "It's irrelevant."

"Explain," the ambassador ordered.

"It doesn't matter because I can deliver them all. You can rely on that."

"I see," he said. "Sixty or seventy people of voting age, some of whom may be registered Democrats and you can deliver them all to my son." At this the son turned away from his father. "Is that it?" Was the son laughing? Why had he walked away? Earlier she was certain that he had been staring at her breasts. She felt naked before such men.

"Yes, that's it." She crossed her arms to shield herself.

"Sixty or seventy votes can make a difference," the Ambassador said. She thought his tone playful. "And what is it you expect in return for delivering this—bloc?"

"Your son will be in Congress and his position will give him the means to influence the coming debates over sovereign lands taken illegally by the Communists."

"I see," the ambassador said. "For sixty or seventy votes, an unknown number of which may be Democrats, you expect access to the United States Congress."

"You have my word."

He had tried a smile at this juncture but it was obviously not something he used often and it came out a sneer. "Thank you for coming by." No hand was extended; the eyes were fixed on a far wall.

The son had hold of her arm; it was over before it began and she had *trouble sorting her thoughts. "When will I hear from you?" she asked over her shoulder.*

"Father Milani," the younger Kennedy said as he slipped her into the other room. "The ambassador would like to see you for a moment." He gave her a wide smile and a reassuring pat on the back of the hand. "Thanks."

The door was not completely closed. The voices behind it were not particularly interested in confidentiality. She heard the ambassador's voice above the other two. "Jesus, Sal. Sixty or seventy votes? Where the hell did you find that one?" Their laughter drove her from the hotel.

She told her son everything. Over and over. Almost a mantra. Kennedy: the name was marked now, not by the mother, but by the son. By him. An insult was a crime and the penalty was death. Family honor was now on Albert Frash's shoulders. One day he would find a way to even the score. Do it now, a hard voice said deep inside him.

"What's with 23A?" a stewardess asked the one who had talked to Frash.

The dark-haired attendant hugged herself and shook her head. She had seen the eyes of a maniac.

7   MONDAY, NOVEMBER 28, 1960, 2:10 P.M.
Paris

Ramiz Kristo tapped his foot to funnel off nervous energy. It had been his idea for the group to meet in the woman's flat, but now she was complicating matters. Paula Gide-Lemestre was twenty-eight, a short, gaunt figure with auburn hair and snow-white flesh covered with rust-colored freckles. The daughter of a former member of the Resistance and minister of education, she had been schooled in Switzerland and America; she was French, but she spoke English with a perfect American accent and put off would-be suitors with proclamations of sexual liberation and right-wing politics. Paula believed in monarchies, and because none remained in France she had loosely allied herself with those Albanians who served the exiled King Zog I.

In some ways this was a legacy. Paula's mother had been a longtime supporter of artistic and émigré causes, and had had more than a few flings with the men who populated such groups. Like her husband, Jarelle

Gide-Lemestre had served in the underground, was supported by her own inheritance, and had raised her only daughter to be fierce in spirit and to think and act for herself. When Zog and his entourage abandoned Cairo in the wake of a tax dispute with the Egyptians, she had stepped forward to welcome the exiles to France. To her mother the Albanians were exotic pets; to Paula they were potential collaborators, and though she suspected that she seemed flighty to them, her ardor for the Albanian cause was earnest. The problem with counterrevolution aimed at a distant place was that it was boring. All they did was hold meetings. God, how they could talk.

Zog and his beautiful wife were not attracted to the fawning French society, but many of the king's intimates were, believing that their lavish treatment in France was their due, their rightful status in their own country having been usurped first by Mussolini and then denied by the Communists under Enver Hoxha and Mehmet Shehu. After six years, however, the love affair with French society, which in the best of times tended to be fickle about fringe political causes, had abated, leaving the majority of the Albanians to their own devices.

Kristo had met Paula when he was eighteen, become her lover at nineteen and for two years depended on her generosity for the financing of various projects, which until recently mostly involved feeble attempts to print leaflets calling attention to the royalist cause. Paula was anxious to do more, but Kristo lacked both vision and discipline; the affair had begun with him as the aggressor, but the dynamic had shifted.

When Ramiz told Paula that he needed a secure place for a meeting, she quickly suggested that they use her flat on the rue de Seine, two doors from the flat where the author Colette had slaved in an attic to produce stories published under her husband's name. Paula often thought about Colette, whose life had been a lesson to all women: Fight or die the slow, sure death of inequality. The flat was a walk-up, on the sixth of seven floors, and had nine rooms, including four with canopied beds and a bizarre mixture of furnishings from fashionable periods of four different centuries. It was not her residence but her hideaway, a place where she could be alone with friends, cavort with lovers or meditate.

The other flat on the sixth floor was owned by a Hungarian sculptor, whose studio was one floor above. Paula had confessed to Kristo that from time to time she posed nude for the sculptor in his cluttered studio. Now she was leaning against a bed. She wore Italian-made flats, a black leotard, a blue skirt, red lipstick and long silver earrings from Algeria. "I want to participate," she said, "to actually be part of everything."

"Impossible," Kristo told her. They'd had this discussion before, but never in such close proximity to his superiors.

24

"I give you money, places to meet, entertain you and your friends. . . . *Fuck* you: Why not?"

"It's not our way," he said, wanting to avoid what was sure to follow.

"Ah," she said softly. "A woman is anybody's daughter. You damned Albanians, you still live in the Dark Ages. A woman has no rights. You make no such distinctions when you want me in your bed."

"Please. It's not the right time for this."

"I give you money, my loyalty, my pussy, but I can't be part of it, not a real part. It's unfair."

He leaned toward her. She was barely five feet tall, and he more than six. "It's impossible. To be part of a cause as important as this requires self-discipline and training. It's designed so that everyone knows only a small part of what is happening; it's a matter of security. Your parents would understand from their experience during the war."

Though she was independent, Paula was proud of her parents' role in the Resistance, and he hoped to appeal to this. "That was different," she said quickly. "The enemy was here and the whole damned world was fighting."

"Our enemies are as real here and they watch us. They put pressure on friends and relatives."

Paula shook her head. *"Non, chéri.* You are twisting the truth because you cannot accept a woman as your equal. I *hate* this in you—in *all* of you."

"It won't be like this always." Kristo wanted to appease her. "There will be a day when we will all step into the light together."

She crossed her arms and pouted. "Maybe I should throw my resources over to the opposition. At least the Communists provide equal opportunity for their women. I have a girlfriend in the Party; she leads her cell and writes editorials for *L'Humanité.* She doesn't have to produce a penis as an admission fee."

This was an entirely new tactic and Kristo was dumbfounded. "You can't talk like that," he said quietly. "If *they* hear you. . . ." He didn't finish the sentence.

"Nevertheless it's true. Your side can't hope to win by ignoring half the available resources. It's inefficient. A woman can do anything a man does."

"We're not ignoring anything." He was flustered now. "All we're doing is compartmentalizing operations."

"Semantics! I call it exclusion."

"Call it what you will, but that's the way it is, and it is not intended to demean you. Can't you accept this?"

"Intellectualize or rationalize it all you want, Ramiz, but I *feel* demeaned, and my feelings are important to me."

It was time to end this. "You can't attend the meeting."

Paula threw herself on the bed, then propped herself on her elbows. "What's to stop me? I could just walk in. After all, it *is* my place."

Kristo approached the bed and tried to summon a stern voice. "I'm going to go into the meeting now; you're going to stay here. That's all I have to say. Do as you're ordered."

"I'm accustomed to leading my own life and making my own decisions."

"If you value that life, you'll stay here and keep quiet. The people in there have very strict rules."

She stared at him. "They would dare threaten me?"

"They would do more than threaten," Kristo warned her. "This is not a game."

"Just because I saw them? They would do that?" Her voice reflected fascination, not fear.

"With no remorse. Remember, we are at war."

Paula threw her legs over the edge of the bed and sat up. "I've never thought about the possibility of being killed," she said. There was an edge to her voice. "Have you ever thought about dying?"

"No." It was the truth. The war was more a philosophical contest in his own mind.

"They would kill me for no other reason than that I saw them." Her voice trailed off to a whisper.

When Kristo emerged from the bedroom he was immediately confronted by the others. "Why is the girl here?" Lazer Kryeziu demanded.

"It's her place," Kristo said. "It's normal for her to be here. Alone we would raise suspicions." First the woman had wanted to argue, now Kryeziu, and he was in no mood for it.

Kryeziu was in his late sixties, the eldest son of one of the most powerful tribal leaders in northeast Albania. He had left Albania before Mussolini invaded in 1939, had graduated from Sandhurst, fought as a British commando in the war and afterward entered private business. To the outside world he was a wealthy restaurateur with successful establishments in New York, London, Paris and Rome, but nearly all that he made went to the cause and to his dream of returning to his homeland and assuming the rightful leadership of his clan. Only this mattered.

The man with Kryeziu was known to Kristo only by reputation, which was a considerable one. Kristo considered telling them what Paula had said to him, but restrained himself.

"Zog is ill again," Kryeziu announced. "The ulcers are bleeding."

"Prognosis?" the other man asked.

"Who knows? He's frail and there's no fight left in him. He spends all his time on his memoirs; a man who wallows in his past has no interest in his future."

"What about Leka?" Kristo and Prince Leka were the same age, and though Kristo did not know the prince well, the few times they had met he had been impressed by his bearing.

"He's still a cub," Kryeziu said. "He has a good record at Sandhurst, but it remains to be seen what he's made of."

"I think he'll do well," Kristo offered.

Kryeziu frowned. "What do *you* know? You're still a cub yourself. When you have scars, you'll be entitled to an opinion."

"I'm a soldier in the cause," Kristo said defensively.

"Soldiers take orders and keep their mouths shut," the third man said. "For now we keep the crown prince out of it. Our sole objective is to cut our losses. The operation is destroyed and we have to start over."

"There's nothing that can be salvaged?" Kryeziu asked. How could this be? They had been so careful this time.

"Shehu is in a frenzy. There have been many arrests. He knows we got close this time," the stranger said. "The pieces were in place."

"Another week," Kryeziu said. "Ten days at the most. That's all we needed."

"Next time will be different," Kristo said confidently.

"First we must survive in order to *have* a next time," the stranger reminded him.

"You think Hoxha will move against us?" Kristo asked. "Here?"

"Not Hoxha. This is Shehu's kind of work. We have to assume that his retribution will have a long reach. We must disband and leave no loose ends. If we leave that bastard the tiniest opening, he'll follow it all the way to our throats. Even to you, boy." The stranger pulled up his shirt; his chest was crisscrossed with swollen, shiny scar tissue. "Shehu is a maniac. I was lucky."

Kristo stared. The stranger worked for Admiral Pinajot Pijaku, who had fled Albania and now coordinated loyalist operations against the Albanian regime from the Kosovo district of Yugoslavia. The stranger was called only the Major, and it was said that he had sworn one day to kill Shehu with his bare hands. The scars helped to explain why.

"How would Shehu find us?" Kristo asked.

"He has agents here, sympathizers among the French Communists and the Chinese. Their ambassador is close to Hoxha's ambassador. In this sort of business geography and political borders are meaningless. Shehu's people are like the tracking dogs raised by the mountain tribes. They need very little to work with."

The Major's words rang in Kristo's ears: sympathizers among the French Communists. Have you ever been close to dying? Paula had asked. "The girl," Kristo said suddenly, and the rest was out before he could stop himself.

Neither man reacted visibly to the information. It was the Major who finally spoke to Kryeziu. "Get him out of here. The network will be reactivated when it's time; in the meanwhile, if you value your lives, don't deviate from the plan."

Kryeziu stood up. "Let's go," he said to Kristo. *"Now."*

"What about Paula?"

The Major had already moved toward her bedroom door, a knife in his hand.

Kristo followed Kryeziu down the stairs. His legs were weak and he felt bile rising in his throat. Was this what it felt like to be at war? Birds were singing in leafless trees along the street and the air was soft. An old man urinated against a brick wall.

 THURSDAY, DECEMBER 1, 1960, 10:00 P.M.
Moscow

Someone was whimpering in a nearby flat and the couple across the hall was arguing over a pair of socks as bits of music wafted through loosely fitted doors; down below several dogs were yowling with the same tone of hopelessness as their owners. Roman Trubkin sat at a small table watching a sliver of lemon float in lazy circles in his tea and tried to block the sounds of real life and its petty miseries. He had lived high, and now low, and having seen bottom, he wanted to be back up where clawing hour by hour was unnecessary. In his years as a test pilot and short time as a cosmonaut trainee he had met a lot of people and made a lot of contacts; at the time it had seemed that they would always be there, but now he realized this had been an illusion.

Lumbas had proved impossible to track, and the man's records provided by Rocket Force Personnel had turned out to be fiction, which had necessitated another journey to the cosmodrome in the desert. He had not let on there was a problem but asked who had responsibility for security checks on Rocket Force personnel, and was told, as if he were a moron or had just arrived on the planet, that this duty fell to the KGB. How long had Lumbas been part of the R-7 project? They referred him to the bogus records. Did they have a photograph of the man? See the records, they said, but there was no photo in the folder; when he asked how this could happen, his answer was a bureaucratic shrug.

An audience with General Engineer Korolev had been more fruitful.

How had Lumbas come to the project? The stout, bullet-headed leader had the demeanor of a Red Army sergeant. "Sent to us," he said.

"You knew him previously?"

The general frowned. "I just said he was *sent*." Korolev had spent the better part of his years in the gulags for reasons known only to Stalin.

"But I had the impression that all your people are handpicked."

Korolev laughed. "They are, but not by me. I take what's sent."

"Then Lumbas was transferred."

"We went over this during your last visit," Korolev said as he glanced at some papers on his desk, his attention invariably returning to his only interest in life. "Moscow sendeth and taketh away, all of which is beyond my control."

How was it that the chief of such an important project did not have the power to pick his own people? Was this by Khrushchev's design? "Lumbas was competent?"

The general mulled this over before answering, in part because his eyes had settled on a sheet of paper with a column of numbers written in red and green ink. "He had skills and a good mind, but his heart was never in the project. He did what was required, no more, no less." Suddenly he reached into his desk and pulled out several stacks of three-by-five cards held by gray rubber bands, broke a stack apart, fanned the cards, found one, stared at it briefly, then sailed it over the desk to Trubkin. "Forever mixing names and faces. Somebody came up with the idea that I needed to be more personal, whatever that means. I'm supposed to look at these pictures before my meetings to help me to match names and faces."

Trubkin studied the face in the photo. It was round, almost babyish, with close-together eyes and a pouting mouth. "Did it work?"

"Don't know," Korolev admitted. "Always forget I've got them."

When Trubkin got back to Moscow he had the photograph wired to all Soviet security agencies with a request for information on the individual in the photograph, the order going out over Khrushchev's name. There was no response, but he told himself that it was only a matter of time. When the General Secretary asked for a progress report, Trubkin gave him an ambiguous answer and made a point of staying out of Khrushchev's way until he had something substantial to tell him. The whole affair was beginning to make him nervous. He couldn't bear the thought of another failure.

SUNDAY, JANUARY 1, 1961, 12:05 A.M.
Novosibirsk Region, Siberia

The room was narrow, twenty meters long by six meters wide, with walls of flat-faced black logs and a low bark ceiling patched with pieces of stiff, shellacked canvas, now yellowed. The two narrow windows on each side were nailed tight; pages of ancient copies of *Izvestia* had been pasted over them to seal them against the winter winds, but they were poor insulation. Thirty-seven men were seated in a U pattern on plank benches; two more men sat on dried cedar stumps in front of the others at the open end of the U. Another man was bound, gagged and blindfolded in the middle of the bare floor. From time to time he rolled around trying to slip his bindings; whenever he got too far, two or three men dragged him back to the middle and kicked him several times in the stomach to keep him still. Mostly, however, the assembly ignored the man's struggles; instead, they riveted their attention on the two men in front. This was a dangerous situation and all of them knew it.

Several bottles of *spirt* made their way from man to man. The clear alcohol was 192 proof and they sipped prudently. Later the blood brotherhood of the *lyudi*—the people—would drink to celebrate the new year, but now they had business to transact that demanded clear heads: a life hung in the balance. They called themselves *lyudi* because they lived by their own laws, separate from normal Soviet peoples, and in Special Regime Camp No. 9 their own laws and customs pertained, not the nonsense of the apparatchiki. *Lyudi* to themselves, they were *urki* to others, the Soviet Union's professional criminals and fiercely proud of their status, even of their captivity.

Melko, their leader, was much the larger of the two men in front. He was six feet four inches tall, broad-shouldered, with curly brown hair and thick, well-muscled arms connected to broad hands that danced in front of him when he spoke. He had a high, flat forehead and pale blue eyes that seemed to deepen to sapphire when he was angry or perplexed. Normally Melko wore a thick vest of brown bear fur over his wide-striped prison shirt, but tonight he had stripped to the waist. Dozens of tattoos stretched from his neck down, front and back, including his arms all the way to his wide wrists. Many of the designs were intricate geometric patterns, but there were also ornate Rubenesque women with flowing hair and full, rounded breasts with prominent nipples.

Though he was one of the brotherhood of criminals now, Melko had come to the *lyudi* from a legitimate past. He had been a graduate engineer from Leningrad; during the war he had been an officer in the tank corps, seriously wounded twice and decorated twice as a Hero of the Soviet Union. After the war he left the army and worked as an engineer in Moscow at a plant making special alloys for military use. But the work was unchallenging, and after his wartime experience he needed a stimulus in his life, not the boredom and whining of incompetent colleagues and harassment from the sort of Party bosses who flourished in the dirty factory. After a thorough analysis of possibilities, Melko decided to become a professional thief—not a petty thief but a great and famous thief, one who used a combination of intelligence, specialized information and exquisite skills in precise and demanding ways. It was an essential part of Melko's character to want to be the best at whatever he did.

Among Soviet thieves there is a pecking order from bottom to top: those who attack drunks, women, the elderly or handicapped; common armed robbers; murderers; pickpockets; bunco artists; and at the pinnacle safecrackers, whom the brotherhood called *medvezhatniki* or "bear killers." To prepare for his debut, Melko began an exhaustive study of his chosen field. By the time he judged himself ready for his initial venture, his knowledge of safes and their locking mechanisms was unparalleled, so that when he began his new career, he was an immediate and consistent success. For eight years he averaged more than one major theft a month, stealing hundreds of thousand of rubles and personal valuables. His victims were always selected from the elite of Soviet society, not because he viewed himself as a modern Robin Hood but because the Soviet elite were the only people with anything worth stealing. Melko was an educated man with a normal upbringing; he knew right from wrong, but he did not view his thievery from Party bigshots as stealing per se; he took what he saw as his due, and always from those who could afford it. There was nothing chivalrous in this; these upper echelons of the Party and government were taking care of themselves, so why shouldn't he do the same? What he stole he kept. Had Marx not written, "From each according to his ability, to each according to his need"? Melko's need was intense.

It was his weakness for women that had brought him down. During a break-in he had unexpectedly encountered a young woman, nineteen-year-old Annochka. Her father was a member of the Central Committee and a candidate member of the Politburo, a specialist in industrial production. Annochka was typical of the children of senior Soviet officials: spoiled and protected, accustomed to having what she wanted because of her father's position, but at the same time fiercely resentful of the closed system that provided for her. Headstrong, daring and sexually assertive, she had nearly raped Melko, or so he claimed, then shown him her father's safe and given him the combination. When he left, she went with him and for several months lived with him, helping him to plan other thefts. Annochka knew the Soviet elite as he never could, and steered him to one lucrative haul after another. For Melko it was an arrangement beyond his wildest fantasy.

But as much as Annochka loathed her father, she adored her mother, and in a moment of weakness she called home and arranged a visit. When the girl arrived, she was arrested; her mother prized her husband's position, and no stupid daughter was going to jeopardize what they had worked so hard to attain. In her day the mother had also been headstrong and had her flings, but no matter how great the fire, one needed to exercise judgment. After a single night in Lubyanka Prison Annochka broke down and admitted her connection with Melko. A deal was struck by her father; in return for revealing the location of Melko and his safe house, she would be released, her record purged. Melko was arrested within hours, and since 1955 had moved down step by step in the gulag, finally arriving at Special Regime Camp Nine.

Camp Nine was a terminal camp, the end of the line. Built in a small canyon sixty kilometers east of Ubinskoe and four hundred kilometers north of Novosibirsk, it was the frigid repository for the worst of the worst, most of them under life sentences and all judged too dangerous to be held elsewhere. Unlike most camps where there was a mixture of professional criminals and politicals, Camp Nine had only one political, he who now sat quietly beside Melko coughing lightly.

"My brothers," Melko said, "we have trouble in our family; therefore I have convened the court. At our feet is the dog Pavel Cyzalopovich. I accuse him of violating the code by which we've all sworn to live. A thief's word is his bond; we have all sworn to this. I accuse Pavel Cyzalopovich of having voluntarily performed manual labor on behalf of the state. Six days ago he helped the *lagershchiki* unload provisions. I don't care why he chose to do this. The *lyudi* recognize no authority other than our own and we shed no sweat for the state. By our code one man must be right and one man must be wrong. I ask for judgment against him, but as his accuser it's not proper for me to oversee this process. Therefore I choose Petrov to sit in judgment." He glanced at the small, dark man who sat beside him.

"He's not one of us," one of the men immediately protested.

"Petrov is here. He lives as we live, and that's enough for me," Melko countered. "In here we are all the same."

"But he has not taken the oath," the man complained, looking for support. "Our brother Pavel Cyzalopovich deserves to be judged by one of his own kind. This, too, is the law."

Melko knew better than to retreat from his position, which he had earned not by election but by virtue of his skill as a thief and held through intelligence and, when necessary, brutal action. Among this group—indeed, among all thieves in the Soviet Union—he was judged to be without equal, and his status enabled him to hold power. To show weakness now would begin an inexorable erosion of his authority. "As your leader, Melko decides such matters," he reminded the group. "This is not a normal camp. All of us will die here, which means that Petrov's fate is our fate, and ours his. We don't know why Petrov is here, and Comrade Petrov does not say, which is his right. But for a political to be among our lot signifies great power on his part and great fear on the part of the state. Therefore, he is like us *in their eyes*. We all know him to be a man who has great knowledge and who always speaks the truth, so I say let Petrov judge."

Most of the men in the room nodded agreement.

"But he has not taken the oath," the dissenter persisted.

Melko did not look at the man again; instead, he addressed the group, gesturing with his hands, his eyes darkening. "It is said that Petrov was close to Stalin. When Stalin died, Petrov was sent into the system and they sent him here *first*." Melko had heard this from a sergeant of the guard but did not reveal his source. "There is a connection. I don't know what it is, but I know that Stalin was a man to be admired; he crushed the Germans like insects and gave no quarter to his enemies. I say that if Stalin accepted Petrov, that's enough for me." It was ironic that the *urki*, while feeling no allegiance to the Soviet bureaucracy, nevertheless considered themselves to be loyal and patriotic citizens, especially when it came to hating Germans. They lived outside the Soviet mainstream and by their own rules, but in their minds and by their peculiar values they were still Soviets and especially loyal to Stalin's way of harsh, direct action. After all, it had been Stalin who had turned back Hitler. Those politicals who had come into the camps under Stalin's regime were, in the eyes of the *urki*, guilty of whatever they were accused of, but politicals who came into the system *after* Stalin's death might not be guilty of anything. And one who came into the system apparently *because* he served Stalin was surely worthy of their trust. Such was Melko's reasoning, and the brotherhood accepted it.

Petrov stood and clasped his small hands in front of him. At sixty-three he was bent and frail-looking, but this was his eighth year in Camp Nine and he had survived the system longer than most. Like many of them, his teeth were rotten, most of his hair had fallen out and his dark eyes were sunk deep in his bony skull.

"I speak for myself," Petrov said with an even voice. He put his hand on his stomach and leaned forward for a moment, then straightened up. In the past year the pain had become constant.

Melko looked around the room for objections, but there were none.

"It is true I have not taken your oath and I will not do so," Petrov continued. "But I live among you and I respect your ways. In life, there must be rules or there will be chaos. Your rules are as good as any. Melko asks me to judge because I have my own views on the implications of the alleged crime. Pavel Cyzalopovich has been accused of a transgression against the *lyudi*. I don't know if he is guilty; I've heard no evidence, but Comrade Melko has asked me to hear the case. What I do know is this: if he *is* guilty and if you wish to preserve your brotherhood, you must take action against him. Stalin is gone, Beria is dead, Bulganin, Malenkov, Molotov and Kaganovich have all been consigned to oblivion. Khrushchev has the power now. He makes speeches about morality. Managers of state farms and industrial plants are being accused of cheating the system. Khrushchev intends to eliminate corruption from society. *All* corruption."

Petrov paused to let his words sink in. "The authorities have plans for you. They will try to take you one at a time; the idea is to corrupt your code so that you will tacitly accept theirs. They do this by finding one of you who is weak, and enticing him to work. This man then feels alienated, threatened by his failure, so he works to bring others over, to compromise them so that he is not alone. It's a natural reaction; few men can stand alone; this is the essence of *lyudi,* the reason you declare yourself brothers. Those who adhere to the code then make war on those who do not. In the end two forces are created from one, and inevitably these forces destroy each other so that eventually there is no brotherhood. By crushing the *lyudi* the state demonstrates its power over you and therefore any group, and it starts with one man and his capitulation."

His speech finished, Petrov sat down. Pavel Cyzalopovich rolled around wildly, banging his heels on the floor in an attempt to get attention. The others ignored him.

"Fuck it," said the man who had complained initially. "Let him judge."

Petrov remained seated and surveyed the men. "Are there any witnesses?"

A man in the back stepped forward. "I saw our brother unloading the crates."

Two other men immediately corroborated this testimony.

"These crates were the property of the state?" Petrov asked, his voice nearly a whisper. His pain was extreme.

"Salted meat and tins from the main camp in Raisino," the first witness told the group. "They had official markings."

"Might it have been attempted theft?" a man asked.

"That's irrelevant," Melko answered. "Our code requires that he steal directly from the truck or from the store room. He may not unload cargo in order to steal it later. The means are not justified by the end."

"How many crates did he unload?" Petrov asked, ignoring Melko's outburst.

"I didn't count them," the witness snarled. "I saw only that he was there for a long time. Many trips."

Silence. "Does anybody have anything to add?" There was no response. "Guilty," Petrov said. "Because Pavel Cyzalopovich has stolen nothing from the family, there is no restitution that can be made. Because he has violated the code and threatened the existence of our society, there can only be one sentence: death."

The pronouncement was met with silence.

Melko rose slowly, then pushed forward the stump he had been sitting on. One of the men brought him a hatchet while others pulled the condemned man to his knees and pressed his head against the block. Melko's first blow drove into the back of the man's skull, killing him. Then he hacked off the head, held it in front of him, walked the length of the room and through the door into the snow, across the poorly lighted yard to the four-meter-high fence, threw Pavel Cyzalopovich's head over the wire, shouted to get the attention of the guards in the towers and returned to the barracks past the headless body, which had been dumped into the snow. Petrov knew there would be no retaliation by the guards; this was the first skirmish. The authorities had begun a process, and time was on their side. That Pavel Cyzalopovich was dead was unimportant. The state had found a man who was weak; now it knew that eventually it would find others, even here. The state's greatest allies were time and human frailty.

When the barracks doors were closed, *spirt* was poured from earthenware crocks, and when everyone was served Melko lifted his tin cup. "Happy New Year," he declared.

Later, when the *lyudi* were drunk and gambling with dice made from bones, Melko came over to Petrov's sleeping platform and sat beside him. "In the old days they left us alone," he said. "This is shitty business; in the end we will be erased."

"You are a threat to their order," Petrov said.

"As you are?" Melko asked quietly.

No, Petrov thought. It is not the same. The *lyudi* are parasites; they could never have value to the state. His own circumstances were far different; had the state meant to rid itself of him, it would have done so eight years ago. Someone who followed Stalin knew Petrov had been close to him; his time in the gulag was penance, no more. It was true that the eight years had been difficult ones, and that he had nearly died several times, but they had kept him out of the uranium mines and other camps where death was a certainty. This alone told him that he had a future. There was only one mystery: who was his mysterious protector?

Petrov knew that there had been political upheaval west of the Urals. Khrushchev had gained power, but those who fell, even those who had tried to oust the crude Ukrainian in 1957, still lived. There had been no mass liquidations and few bloody reprisals. From this Petrov guessed that Khrushchev ruled by balancing power, by creating and manipulating factions in the Politburo in order to maintain equilibrium. The army's power had been reduced. Even life in the gulag had changed subtly: fewer work hours, reduced rules, better food—not nearly enough, but *better*. Petrov was certain that the absolute power held by Stalin was now sundered; Khrushchev had to rely on guile, not terror, and his primary weapons were his own enthusiasm and the ability to bluff in the face of insurmountable odds.

It was impossible to know precisely what was going on outside, but certain things seemed clear to Petrov. The people called the General Secretary Kukuruznik, the Corn Man. He was a dreamer, the architect of grandiose schemes that promised great returns but seldom delivered. He was of a type, naturally intelligent, but with neither education nor patience, a man with more velocity than direction, a child reaching forever for new confections; *nye kulturny,* a man without culture, a peasant, an accident of Party history whose reach would eventually outstrip his grasp, and this would eventually bring him down. Khrushchev was a dinosaur, the last of his kind, and in this Petrov felt a vague kinship for the fat little Ukrainian.

10 SATURDAY, JANUARY 7, 1961, 10:30 A.M. *Tanga, Buryat Autonomous Soviet Socialist Republic*

It had taken two days to ride north from the hunting camp to Tanga. Pyotr Ezdovo could have made the journey faster by guiding his horse up the frozen Ingoda River, but river ice never froze uniformly and the Ingoda often had soft spots and holes camouflaged by slush. The decision was not a matter of fear but of prudence. No matter where a man lived or what he undertook, there were risks, though most people did not recognize them, much less calculate them. For those who understood risk and respected danger, life could be productive and full; those who didn't understand perished; those who survived didn't mourn them. This was the Russian way.

It had been a month since Ezdovo had been home to hold his wife and hear her laugh. Now, as he walked his shaggy brown gelding over the final saddleback, his heart was pounding with anticipation. Talia, his amazing, wonderful Talia! Whenever he thought of her, which was often during his days in the taiga, he reminded himself how lucky he had been to find and marry her. Their only disappointment was that they had never had children. Still, they had the boys, Sergei and Aleksei, by her first marriage, and what marvelous young men they had become! "Without you, my love, they would not be such fine men," Talia often told him, and always it made him proud. It was not entirely true; Talia's influence on her sons was immense, but it was her way to praise Ezdovo, taking no credit even when it was due. In return, he treated her as an equal, and in this way they both knew that it was their partnership that had served the boys and their marriage well.

At a pass above Tanga, their village, Ezdovo halted the horse to let him rest, and stiffened his legs in the stirrups to stretch his back. He patted the horse's neck gently. "Four hours more and you'll have fresh hay." A home-cooked meal would be welcomed by him as well, *after* he and Talia had held each other close. Their lovemaking was as passionate now as the first time they had held each other sixteen years before. Talia, ever calm, was anything but calm when he was inside her.

"You two are too old to carry on so," Sergei had teased before he left their camp. "You should leave such activity to the young." The elder at twenty-two, he was tall like his mother, with black hair, dark eyes, an excellent mind and an easy way with people. Everyone liked Sergei.

"Love is too important to be wasted on the young," Ezdovo answered as he tightened the cinch of his saddle.

"Everyone in the village gossips about you two. They make jokes and say you should act more respectably." This was Aleksei, the younger, now twenty-one, built low and wide like a small bear. Of the two of them, Aleksei was more determined, more accustomed to *doing* than talking. In the village he was recognized as second only to his stepfather in his ability to hunt and fish in the dangerous, hostile Yablonovy Mountains. In this instance, Aleksei's allusion was to an afternoon the previous summer when several villagers had seen Ezdovo and Talia making love in broad daylight on a flat boulder beside the Ingoda. Their sons had been embarrassed by this event, but the principals thought it funny and laughed it off, while the elders of the village welcomed it as a gift, a juicy morsel to whisper and cluck about during the hard winters.

"What's between husband and wife is their own business," Ezdovo told his sons. Then he held out his arms and the three embraced.

"Tell Mother we're taking good care of you," Aleksei said as Ezdovo swung into the saddle.

"Don't burn down the camp while I'm gone," he warned them. The log storehouse, which stood five meters aboveground, was jammed with fine pelts; it had been a severe winter, which was exactly what hunters hoped for. The snowfall had been about normal, but it had been the coldest winter in thirty years, reaching down to sixty below for a solid week in January. The conditions were ideal; such weather created thicker, richer furs on the animals, and with a normal snowfall the horses could get around with only minimal difficulty. Most hunters worked in pairs, but Ezdovo liked being with both of his sons; because of this they had developed a routine that gave them time to work together and still provided that Talia would have either her husband or a son with her for eleven days each winter month. When the boys went home they stayed three days, whereas Ezdovo stayed five. When it was time to return to the taiga, it was always difficult because as much as he loved his time in the forest, Ezdovo's time with his wife was the most important part of his life. He always returned to camp with bite marks on his neck and shoulders.

"Don't forget more ammunition," Sergei yelled at him.

"If you two could shoot straight, we wouldn't need more," Ezdovo shouted as he dug his heels into the gelding. It was a joke. The three of them were renowned for their marksmanship; each year the two boys got better, and Ezdovo told himself that when age began to take its toll on his eyes, as it surely would, they would become his masters. Perhaps then he would remain at home and let them hunt on their own. He could go out to visit them from time to time, but he would leave it to them to harvest the furs. With luck, however, there remained many more years with life as it was. He was fifty-two years old, technically too old for this strenuous life, but he was strong, fit and in perfect health. Talia was forty-one but looked younger, and soon they would fuse again and take strength from each other, as they had for sixteen miraculous years.

Tanga had a population of four hundred, about half of them children. Most of the villagers were of Cossack descent and proud of their heritage. Many of them could trace their ancestors back to the Cossacks posted to what was now Ulan-Ude in 1666; they treasured the knowledge that Cossacks, male and female, were hard, reliable people, more interested in personal independence than in a sense of community. But when faced by an outside threat the people of Tanga were a fierce lot, and Ezdovo and Talia were pleased to be among them.

The village was built in a sprawling valley eight kilometers west of the river. Unlike most frontier villages, where buildings tended to be packed together, Tanga was spread out. Most houses were within hailing distance of each other, but no closer, the only exception being several in the town's center built around provision stores and a large log meeting hall that in summer was the scene of the richest fur auction in the Buryat Autonomous Republic. Unlike most Soviet hunters in Siberia, who worked under an arrangement that gave them a base salary from the state and a fee for the pelts taken, the fur hunters of Tanga were independent, negotiating each year with the government to establish the season's prices. Two summers ago, when its prices for their furs were too low, the Tangans had refused to sell their pelts, which had provoked an angry response from Moscow.

"Bullshit," Ezdovo said to his colleagues. "The state is our only customer. If it won't meet our prices, then we won't sell. There are always the Chinese." This position had started an argument that ended in several fistfights. It was common knowledge that Chinese buyers waited on the borders to buy prime Russian pelts, but usually they dealt with individual hunters. Never had an entire village threatened to make illegal sales to the Chinese. It was a serious threat, and when the fighting was over, the state's buyers retreated to Ulan-Ude to seek direction from Moscow.

Many people in the village were torn. They could take furs legally only if the government renewed their annual licenses, but it had been exhilarating to see the frightened government scabs flee with their tails between their legs. It was risky, but at least they had acted as Cossacks, and what was more important than that? Moscow could stick its rubles up its ass.

The government men returned in late August, this time led by two men from Moscow, one of them a deputy minister of agriculture; they also brought two dozen armed men with them. KGB, Talia said when she saw them. They wore new clothes and looked nervous. In cities KGB men were accustomed to respect and fear, but in Tanga the people openly ridiculed their appearance and the way they stuck together like frightened boys.

The government officials were unexpectedly polite and respectful. They wanted to talk. Their bearing and soft voices said Let's use logic. Talia was chosen to represent the hunters, which unnerved the men from Moscow. How could a woman speak for these crazy Cossacks? No conference was held among the hunters to map strategy; Talia knew how her people felt and she understood what was expected of her. She put on one of her two dresses, waited until the government men were seated in the community hall and then staged a grand entrance. The dress was bright red with no sleeves, and cut short so that her long, tanned legs showed amply above white open-toed, high-heeled shoes. The government men were stunned by her beauty. The townspeople grinned at one another.

The state had reconsidered, the two men began. They went through their list, reciting revised prices for various qualities and sizes, which were 20 percent higher than the original offer but still 20 percent below the previous season's, and exactly half of what the hunters of Tanga had calculated the value of the pelts to be.

Talia greeted their effort with a wide smile followed by the kind of laugh reserved by adults for children who have been naughty in a cute way. "We appreciate your generosity," she told the men, "but these prices are unacceptable. You give us no choice. Our livelihoods depend on the prices, and we reject these. Do better or do without."

The deputy minister was a short man with reddish-blond hair and a freckled face. "These prices are better than others get."

"They should be; our furs are better."

"Some income is better than no income," he argued.

"Not here," Talia said. "This is not a city. Everything we have we must get for ourselves. Either the price is adequate or we have no reason to sell. The furs will not melt, and there is always next year; perhaps prices will be higher then. In any event we have had our best sable harvest in several years."

The rich black fur of the Barguzin sable was the most valuable in the world. At one time the state had tried to raise the animals on farms, but they had proved temperamental and refused to breed. The program had failed miserably, and once again it fell to hunters to fulfill most of the world's demand for this precious fur. Either they sold their furs or the world went without, which meant that the government lost a valuable source of foreign currency. Talia knew that her people had the advantage.

"You are backward, stubborn people," the man from Moscow told her. His good nature had faded.

"In some ways of life, stubbornness is a virtue, not a fault."

"I am not authorized to negotiate beyond the stated prices," the man said defensively. "I will have to discuss your position with my superiors."

"Tell Nikita Sergeievich," one of the hunters called out. "He's one of us."

The ministry official glared at the hunters. "I should tell you," he said, his voice deepening, "that it has been proposed that individual licenses be abolished and that all fur harvesting become exclusively a state venture."

Talia's smile did not waver. "It is one thing to pass an edict in Moscow and quite another to enforce it in the Yablonovy Mountains. You could deny us our licenses, but you cannot stop us from taking furs. Here God is on high and the Kremlin is far away."

The official raised his voice. "It could become an issue of force."

"Your words are wasted," Talia said. "There are few of us and many of you, but the Yablonovy Mountains are ours, and like you we understand the essence of direct action. How could you use force? Do you have men enough to guard every rock in these mountains? Can the KGB trap a cloud?" She laughed and the room erupted with laughter.

The government man was red in the face. "Uncooperative citizens can be dealt with."

Talia's voice turned hard. "I repeat, this is not Moscow, comrade. There are no roads, no trains, no airports. You cannot approach in force without our knowledge. Even paratroops would be ineffective; the mountains would separate them and make concerted activity impossible. To employ force, you would require huge resources, all of which we could negate with little effort."

"Your words might be judged in some quarters to be seditious."

"No, comrade," Talia said. "We are true citizens and as loyal as you. We speak only facts; our sole interest is in justice and fairness. We are resolved in this matter; there will be no sale this year. Perhaps next summer we can meet to discuss this again."

"You cannot blackmail the state," the man said angrily. He was clearly having great difficulty controlling himself.

"And you, comrade, will not blackmail *us*," Talia said. "Let us declare a stalemate; take the winter to reconsider your position."

"You will starve over winter," the deputy minister's associate blurted.

"That is entirely possible," Talia said, "but we will still have the furs and you will not." She stood then and clasped her husband's arm. "We have differences," she told the men from Moscow, "but here we offer food and drink to visitors even when we don't agree with them. We invite you to join us." The tables in the hall had been laden with food.

The officials declined the invitation and left immediately for Ulan-Ude, but the people of Tanga celebrated with a night-long feast. The next day most of the adults were still drunk or in the initial phases of excruciating hangovers.

That fall the Soviet government announced to the West that a virus had overwhelmed the Barguzin sable population, so Western buyers found less than a quarter of the normal supply. By summer prices had skyrocketed; when the government buyers returned to Tanga they paid even more generously than the villagers had anticipated and all was well again. By standing their ground and withholding their furs, the Tangans had helped not only themselves but increased the profit and foreign currency that came to the U.S.S.R. from pelt sales. The standoff that had nearly become a revolt had turned out well, and virtually no one outside Tanga and some high-placed government officials in Moscow were aware of what had happened.

This episode increased Talia's stature in the village, but it also pinpointed her as a troublemaker with the authorities. Talia and Ezdovo recognized this danger, but life today was so demanding and full that to worry about tomorrow was foolish. Done was done.

That had been two years ago. Now even Ezdovo's horse was excited and pressing to gallop, but he reined him in. When your heart is pounding and your head light with anticipation, he told himself, it's important to maintain composure.

Their house was built in a clearing on a small rise. The cedar trees around it were massive, some of them more than seventy meters high, with girths over three meters. Below the log house were larch trees and a stand of silver firs. When it was exceptionally cold the pitch in the pines sometimes exploded like grenades, a sound Talia called "winter music."

Though he was anxious to see his wife, Ezdovo did not go directly to the house. Instead he unsaddled his horse, checked the animal's legs for cuts from the snow's crust, wiped him dry, covered him with a heavy blanket, filled the grain bucket and checked the water trough. In the Yablonovy Mountains one survived by attending to detail and doing first those things that needed doing, even if your own desires had to be delayed. There was a thin layer of ice across the water trough, but Ezdovo broke it with slight hand pressure and knew the horse would be all right. He had designed the trough to collect water from a spring that came from a rocky formation above the barn; because the water moved constantly under tremendous force, it rarely froze in the pipes and formed only surface ice in the trough.

Returning to the barn, Ezdovo hoisted his gear and turned to find Talia standing two meters away. Her black hair was loose and fluttered in the winter draft that blew through the barn. She wore a heavy robe and knee-high sealskin boots. She untied the robe and let it fall, then threw her arms around his neck and kissed him hard. "Here," she said. "*Now.* A month is too long to be apart."

11   SUNDAY, JANUARY 8, 1961, 1:05 A.M.
Moscow

Situated in the stern section of a barge moored permanently in the Moscow River, the club was illegal and, like many semisecret establishments in the Russian capital, had its own peculiar clientele, in this instance fliers and Aviation Ministry people.

Trubkin arrived just after midnight and ordered a glass of straight gin. Better than vodka, he reasoned. He loathed gin, which meant he'd nurse this one glass and keep his senses. The main room was paneled with varnished white cedar and dimly lit. Three young men with scraggy beards sat cross-legged on the floor tuning their guitars. Two bartenders sullenly stacked tall glasses behind a plywood bar. Several young women sat at a table talking in low tones; Trubkin noted that they were a younger lot than usual and considerably more attractive than the regulars. Secretaries or students looking for some fun and a few extra rubles—whores, not pros.

Colonel Sergei "Snake" Mandrich sauntered in an hour later, his topcoat open and dripping melting snow. The two men embraced and sat down. "The Snake now flies a desk," Trubkin said, "but he looks fit." Mandrich had a diamond-shaped head and bulging eyes. When he spoke, his tongue flicked in and out as he constantly wet his lips. As a pilot he had been emotionless, his appearance and demeanor accounting for his nickname.

"Can't say the same for you," Mandrich shot back good-naturedly. "No word in two years, and suddenly you want to meet. You look like shit. I heard about your medical problem, and I'm sorry. You were the best."

The two men had known each other off and on for twelve years. They had met while in flight school, then taught North Korean pilots to fly MiG-17s during the Korean War; later they had served together in a MiG-21 interceptor group on the Kamchatka Peninsula. Both had been test-pilot-program graduates and cosmonaut trainees, but Mandrich had been eliminated early on, then rewarded with a flight squadron command. Now he was in Moscow as Air Force liaison to the Mikoyan Aircraft Works, where a new delta-wing interceptor was in development.

"We're born into our bodies," Trubkin said disconsolately. "In my experience they seem to fail when we need them the most."

"You lived hard," Mandrich said. "Maybe too hard."

Trubkin raised his glass to his old friend and nodded. "Direct as ever. I need information."

Mandrich called a waiter over and ordered a glass of vodka for himself. The band began to play soft jazz, an off-melody with lots of chording and discordant notes.

"It has to do with your current assignment."

"Classified," Mandrich said with a smile.

"Not details. I'm only interested in security issues. I need to be educated."

The waiter brought vodka and Mandrich leaned forward. "Such as?"

"How were you selected?"

"Based on my background."

"Not that. What mechanism is used to make selections? There must be many candidates for any job; how do they cull the lists?"

"Committee," Mandrich said. "Each service has its own, but for high-level assignments there's a mixed group, including the KGB and the Ministry of Aviation."

"To whom does this group report?"

Mandrich did not answer right away. "Nice," he said, nodding toward the women who were now mingling with purpose.

"The selection group," Trubkin said, turning his friend back to the question.

"What business is it of yours?"

"Don't press," Trubkin said softly. "Leave it at I have a need to know and that we've been through a lot of living together."

Mandrich took a drink of vodka and grunted. "Dual reporting to the General Staff and the Politburo."

"You have full responsibility for your project?"

"That's a matter of semantics," Mandrich said wistfully. "The Mikoyan people have the engineering responsibility, but directions, policy and administration reside with me."

"How many people on your staff?"

"A hundred, more or less."

"You select your own people?"

"I can say who I want. You looking for a job?"

"I have more than enough to do right now." But it was an interesting thought, and Trubkin tucked it away. "Are your requests honored?"

"Sometimes. If I make an issue of someone I can usually get him, but mostly I ask for certain qualifications, and then the selection committee sends me somebody who matches the request."

"You accept this?"

"You mean the lack of control? Of course, but the people they send are competent, and that's what matters. Even in a single-seat interceptor control is an illusion. It's the Soviet way."

"But if the project fails, you get the blame."

Mandrich grinned and raised his vodka in salute. "That's how it is."

Later Trubkin negotiated a price with two of the women whom they took to a forward cabin. Initially the women objected to being in the same room, but Trubkin sweetened the price and they reluctantly agreed.

At 7:00 A.M. the two men dressed, left the women, walked the narrow gangway to shore and shook hands. "An interesting night," Mandrich said with a grin. "It was like old times."

Trubkin doubted that his life would ever again be like old times.

"Does the selection committee report to a particular individual or to the group at large?"

"There are co-chairmen," Mandrich said. "Malinovsky and Khrushchev, but Shelepin is the liaison for both groups. The KGB is always the glue."

Trubkin stared at the Moscow River and turned up his collar. Why did Khrushchev's name keep turning up? But Shelepin was a new name and a troublesome one. The former cosmonaut walked along the river with snow spitting at his back. Shelepin was said to be Khrushchev's man, moved to the KGB three years before. Was he engineering something? Or had Khrushchev started an initiative to implicate Shelepin or others of high rank? Anything was possible, which meant he had to go carefully from here on. Only one thing was certain now: Malinovsky could be ruled out. He was a Khrushchev man; the defense minister's mouth, cynics quipped, was a perfect fit for the General Secretary's dick.

12   TUESDAY, JANUARY 10, 1961, 7:00 A.M.
Galveston, Texas

Beau Valentine was sprawled on the floor beside the bed, his bare legs covered by a tan raincoat that smelled faintly of perfume. On the floor next to him were two boxes of fried chicken, a carton of runny coleslaw on its side, several slices of dark green jalapeños and a plastic cup of red pop. There was an odd blend of aromas: perfume, rancid chicken, slaw, hot peppers, semen and sweat, the last two a familiar part of mornings-after. He rolled slowly onto his left side and stared at two empty green bottles under the bed. Where the hell was the third one?

With considerable effort he crawled onto the double bed next to the sleeping woman and examined her. Was she Hispanic? Mexican? No, Cuban, or maybe Venezuelan. Sylvia something. Sandy, Sally, Sarah. Probably she had told him, but the previous night's events were fragments without pattern, nothing linear, more a slide show with no order and randomly placed blanks. She was a customer; that much he could remember. From Miami, she had told him. It was an interesting order: six cases of fragmentation grenades, three BARS with ammo, twelve customized M-1s with Bausch & Lomb sniper scopes. She had also pressed him for several boxes of .22 caliber ammunition with subsonic loads, but he had turned her down on this because such ordnance smacked of assassination work, which he avoided on principle.

The shipment was to be sent to a warehouse in New Orleans. There was little doubt that it was the CIA that was backing her organization. Funny how life twisted in repetitive patterns. Valentine had left the OSS in 1946, and as soon as he bought his military surplus business in 1956 the CIA had sent emissaries to visit him, not payroll employees but sanitized intermediaries, people who for a fee would do as they were asked but who could not be easily traced back to the Company, their deniability based on the careful construction of layers. These emissaries let him know that certain business would come his way, and that they would provide assistance in acquiring certain difficult-to-get matériel. It had been a lucrative arrangement; he made a nice profit, and the Company's selected clients received what they needed. Yet he was not devoid of principles; he would not sell silencers or special ammunition. They could obtain these for themselves elsewhere.

Valentine rarely saw such customers more than once. Usually they came alone, or sometimes in pairs, but never in threes. He dealt with certain groups several times, but generally with different people each time. Almost always they were men, so it had been a pleasant surprise when this woman had shown up the previous afternoon. They'd argued about price, compromised, completed their business, talked, gone for a drink and ended up in his three-room suite in the Hotel Galvez.

Now he wondered who she was. Her skin was tanned but without luster, like stagnant backwater in the Atchafalaya Swamp. She had long, straight black hair that had twisted and matted during the night; now it lay against her oversized pillow like a wispy halo. Her short, muscular arms were stretched out straight, her legs apart. Tiny ankles and feet. Small breasts, but perfectly formed, gravity pulling them flat. A small shaft of light reflected back to the bed from the mirror on the opposite wall, illuminating a thick, dark mass of pubic hair. There was a line of thin, soft hair from the navel down. Had she been an enthusiastic lover or catatonic? He had no idea and didn't care, but maybe she knew where the other bottle was.

It's the slivovitz, he told himself. Plum brandy: he had acquired a taste for it during the war. He had supervised a joint operation, combining his Italian partisans with a Yugoslavian group, and afterward they had gone on a three-day binge. Since 1948 he had gotten several cases a year from an importer in Miami who had a connection in Havana. Why the Cubans had slivovitz was a mystery, but now that Castro was running the show he assumed his connection was broken. Fidel had the scent of a moralist, as all revolutionaries did, and he guessed he would be a dangerous pain in the ass for the U.S.

The woman, he remembered, had drunk her brandy too fast. Vaguely he remembered her vomiting out the fifth-floor window. Or was that another woman and another night? Since Ermine's death there had been a lot of women and he seldom remembered faces, much less names.

The woman looked to be in deep sleep. He debated awakening her. He was certain there had been three bottles of slivovitz, but now he saw only two empties. She was attractive but of indeterminate age, which was not unusual for Hispanics, if that's what she was. She might be twenty-five or forty or anywhere in between. Some remained firm and young forever; others turned into wrinkled hags when barely out of their teens. Had they finished the third bottle, too? Shit.

"Hey," he said, poking at the woman's left shoulder. "Hey . . ." What was her name? In the future, he promised himself, he would write down their names and stuff the note in his pocket for later reference. It would make mornings less clumsy. "C'mon . . . Miss." He poked harder this time.

When she awoke, it was with her eyes alone, and he had a sudden sense that she was coiled to repel an attack, yet her body was not tensed. Only her eyes moved, and when they reached him they stopped. "You want to do it *again*?" she asked. Peculiar accent. What was it?

He shook his head. "Not that," he said, trying to smile, but his head hurt too much. What he needed was a drink from the third bottle.

"Thank God," she said. "Last night I was afraid you were incapable of getting enough." There *was* an accent. Very slight. Dutch? German? But she looked Hispanic.

He grimaced and held up one of the empty bottles. "Where's the other one?"

"A good thing," she said. "I'm sore down there." Her eyes showed the way. "You really ought to see a doctor about your problem," she added.

Valentine shifted automatically to defense. "I don't need a doctor. I don't have to drink. I *like* to drink, and right now I'd like to find that other bottle. It's my last one. Maybe forever," he said disconsolately, which was overly dramatic, perhaps, but true.

"I wasn't referring to your drinking," she said calmly. "Priapism. Abnormally prolonged erection. Usually there is no libido connected to it; often there is excruciating pain. Neither of these symptoms seems to pertain to you. It can be caused by injuries to the spinal cord. Have you ever hurt your back?"

Valentine stared incredulously at her. "Who are you, Florence Nightingale?"

"I'm serious," she said. "You should see a doctor. It could be your back or an obstruction in the urinary tract. There are medicines and surgical treatments to repair the damage. It can be fixed."

His temper started to flare, but he checked himself. "I've never had complaints before."

"I'm not complaining." She stretched leisurely, starting with her ankles; he watched as she methodically flexed her muscles and joints. Again he had a sense that there was more to her than his first impression, an air of self-discipline that most people lacked. Had it been reflected in their lovemaking? He tried to remember, but couldn't. It didn't matter; in an hour she'd be stale air. "The fact is," she said as she rolled her shoulders forward, "that it was an exquisite night. You gave me great pleasure, and I hope I did the same for you."

"Sure." Where was the other bottle? He looked around.

"I didn't mean to insult you," she said, "but such conditions can be dangerous."

"It's always been that way," he told her, wondering why he felt the need to offer an excuse.

"In any event, I remember only two bottles, and they were more than enough. I think I was sick."

"I'm certain I had three." He made a face and looked around the room again. "You puked," he added.

"Sorry," she said. "Do you always drink so heavily?"

"*That?* That was just social drinking. Sometimes I really tie one on."

"What time is it?"

The switches in their conversation were intensifying his headache. "Almost seven," he told her. Or was it six, or eight?

"Got to get home before my husband finds me." When he recoiled she laughed at him. "A little joke," she said. "No husband. But I do have to go catch a plane in Houston."

She closed her eyes and moaned, then rolled across the bed, planted her feet solidly on the floor and disappeared into the bathroom. Her muscular buttocks rippled as she walked. She showered, emerged a few minutes later with a small towel wrapped around her head, gathered her clothes into a pile and began dressing. As she pulled on one of her nylons she paused, tilted her head to the side and smiled at him. "One more time before I leave?"

"Like one for the road?"

"That's the general idea."

"I think I'll pass," Valentine said. "No offense."

She shrugged, fastened her garter belt, dropped a gray shift over the top, wiggled it into place, speared her shoes with her toes and went to the mirror to examine herself. "Horror show," she said over her shoulder.

"Want some advice?" he asked.

"Part of the overnight service?"

"Just this once. If you're hooked up with the Company, be damned careful. They tend to promise a hell of a lot more than they deliver. Take it from me."

She stared at him for a moment, then came over, kissed his forehead lightly, walked to the door and opened it. "A confession," she said. "The third bottle's on the ledge." She pointed to the window. "Sorry, but another bottle of that stuff would have killed us both, and if I'm going to die I want it to count for something."

Valentine moved quickly to the window and leaned out. The bottle was on a narrow ledge tucked neatly against the sandstone wall. When he turned back, she was gone. He sat down on the bed, opened the last bottle, poured a small quantity into one of the water glasses they had used last night and thought of Ermine. No matter how many women he slept with, his mind retreated to Ermine when they were gone. Today, however, the memories seemed dimmer than usual.

They had married in 1947, and she had drowned in 1951 while they were fishing for bass in the Atchafalaya, a remote bayou in southern Louisiana filled with cypress stumps and crawdads. He had gotten out of the pirogue and made his way across several logs in order to reach a dark hole. He pitched a dozen casts, working the surface lure back to him with a wiggling motion, but there were no takers. When he turned around, the pirogue was empty and there was no sign of his wife.

At first he thought it was another of her practical jokes. She was forever sneaking up on him, trying to scare hell out of him. But it wasn't funny this time, and after thirty minutes he knew something was seriously wrong. He began diving, ignoring the water snakes and black-backed cottonmouths that wiggled wildly away from him into thick patches of floating white-water hyacinths.

He found her body just before sundown and realized what had happened. She had slipped into the water intending to pop to the surface in front of him, only she had gotten tangled in some submerged cypress roots, which became a webbed prison. It took great effort to dislodge her body and get it into the boat.

There had been a cursory investigation by the parish coroner, who had ruled it accidental drowning. Then he had buried her in New Orleans in the family vault in what remained of old St. Louis Cemetery No. 1 on Rampart Street. A priest and two Negro altar boys officiated. There was no need for pallbearers; he'd cremated her, which was what she had wanted.

Ermine had relished the fire of slivovitz as much as he did. She liked everything he liked, and he loved her. "Widower," he said out loud. "Stupid word." He raised his glass in salute, took a sip, then set the glass down. On June 2 she would be dead ten years. Where had the time gone? Wasted, mostly. Suddenly his need for a drink was gone. He put the bottle back on the ledge and took a shower.

Later he went downstairs and checked the desk for messages. The desk clerk was named Bobby Something, from the Big Thicket country north of Houston. He had bowlegs and a cowboy's gaunt face. "Not looking so good, Mr. V."

Valentine did not like Bobby Something. Hotel people were supposed to be invisible, especially in a classy place like the Galvez. People who patronized old-line hotels like this expected privacy and paid for it.

"Messages?"

"I'll look," the clerk said. "Heard you had the company of a fine-lookin' woman last night. Amazin' how you find 'em, Mr. V. What's your secret? Me, I been in Galveston five years and I never seem ta' find 'em, but you seem ta' have 'em all the time. Like fishing, I guess. They say five percent of the fisherman catch ninety percent of the fish." Bobby checked the pigeonholes behind him. Valentine imagined that his lips moved when he read the numbers on the small brass plates above each box. "Hey! You got something." When he returned to the chest-high counter, he held the envelope back, forcing Valentine to reach for it. "You ever got too many split-tails to handle you might could toss one my way," he said.

"Learn to fish first," Valentine said. He snatched the message away with a quick motion, then retreated several feet into the lobby to read the message. There was a tiny note inside the envelope. He read it and froze. It said, "Call Arizona ASAP." The area code was Washington, D.C.

"Hey, Mr. V," Bobby Something called out from behind the desk. "You see a ghost or what?"

13   MONDAY, JANUARY 16, 1961, 7:40 P.M.
Vinnitsa, Ukraine

His was a soldier's room, Colonel Taras Ivanovich Bailov reminded himself. Small and devoid of decoration, it was a place to store clothing and tools and to sleep. Soon he would again be with Raya in Moscow, and then he could bask in the spaciousness of her accommodations. And bask in *her*. The mere thought of the slippery, warm sleeve between Raya Orlava's legs provoked a response that made him laugh at himself. Here he was preparing to make a night parachute drop from two hundred meters and his independent-minded member was standing stiffly at attention with no more stimulation than a memory. He taught his Spetsnaz troops the importance of self-control, yet he could not control his own appendage. Shame on you, Taras Ivanovich, shame.

Soon, however, thoughts of Raya faded as Bailov focused on the task ahead. His head and face shaved clean, he stood beside his bed, which was neither a real bed nor the standard-issue cot, but a wooden box two meters long and a half meter high. Early in his Spetsnaz career Bailov had decided that to live comfortably on base rendered living primitively in the field unnecessarily difficult; to shift from a softer setting to a harder one created natural psychological resentment, especially early in a mission before the body accustomed itself to privation. This response, he reasoned, would most often occur early in a mission or exercise, which was always the most dangerous time. Because of this, he decided to live in such a way that any psychological adjustment would be minimal, which meant eliminating creature comforts away from the field. Thereafter he slept in a hard wooden box, using only his sleeping bag for bedding and his pack for a pillow. He had begun this practice early in his military life, and as he rose in rank the men who served with him copied him not because he demanded it but because they respected him and understood the purpose. By now all the officers in the First Independent Spetsnaz Brigade slept in wooden boxes, which they called Bailov Coffins. Between missions their commander kept his head shaved clean and did not allow his hair to grow. This, too, the men of the First Brigade copied, and over time their shaved heads became their trademark.

Standing beside his narrow box, Bailov pulled on two pairs of thick gray wool socks, stepped into porous linen underwear and then put on a net vest that hung loosely over the undergarments to create a layer of insulating air. Fatigues next, their seams stitched several times with heavy thread to provide extra strength; they were padded at the elbows, knees, and shoulders to make them more durable. Boots, his old friends, soft, reaching up to midcalf with numerous straps and wide, soft soles of special material resistant to fire and nearly impossible to penetrate. His gray leather helmet was shaped precisely to the dimensions and contours of his head and fit like a mask. It was snug; he would not remove it until the mission had ended. Next, a fur jacket with a black silk lining, and over this a special poncho that hung to his knees, its outer surface raspy to provide traction on snow and ice. Over all of this he donned a white winter smock for camouflage.

When Bailov dressed for a mission he imagined himself to be a gladiator preparing to enter the arena. He had talked so much about gladiators that his troops called the regiment The Gladiators, which pleased him immensely. They had even presented him with a reproduction of a golden helmet with red plumes that they had liberated from a movie company while they were on maneuvers in Czechoslovakia. The helmet was now displayed in the mess hall; Bailov wore it only when the regiment was celebrating. Unlike other Soviet military units, the First

Brigade had a mess hall that doubled as its recreation center. Enlisted men and officers always ate and played together, which instilled a sense of belonging.

Bailov checked his watch and equipment. Flat gray pack; he would attach this to his waist for the jump. A 180-gram flask for water. Water-purification tablets; his men called them anti-shit pills. Three kilos of specially packaged food. Four boxes of matches that would ignite even when wet. A supply of fuel tablets that could be used to heat food, like the Americans' Sterno but more concentrated and reliable. An array of medicines and antiseptics. One small towel, a plastic toothbrush, toothpaste, foldable razor, liquid soap in a metal tube, fishing gear, needle and thread. Weapons: P-8 pistol with silencer and sixty-four rounds of special ammo; a Kalashnikov AK-47 automatic rifle with one hundred and twenty rounds; on his right calf his black Spetsnaz knife, worth a fortune on the black market. The knife was spring-loaded with a button trigger; the blade could be shot like a bullet and at forty-five meters would bury itself deep in its target. He carried four extra blades in a leather case strapped to his left calf.

Satisfied that he had everything, Bailov slid his AK-47 into its black-leather case, turned off the single naked bulb overhead and headed for the briefing room two kilometers away. In other branches of service the men were transported, but Spetsnaz moved by its own power, which meant everyone walked, officers included. Fitness was paramount.

Four groups of twelve men each, called sticks, would make a jump from four small aircraft in trail formation. Bailov sat with his own stick and let his regimental staff officers conduct the briefing. The men around him were attentive but pumped with adrenaline, so a lot of snide comments were aimed at the briefing officers. Bailov liked it that the men did not alter their behavior in his presence; he had earned their respect and they his, which removed the need for artificial behavior. They were tough, coarse and wild. What's got a black heart, two legs and would fuck a snake? Spetsnaz! They would follow the orders of any officer, of course, but they respected only those who demonstrated that they had equal competence and greater aggressiveness than themselves. Bailov was the hardest officer they had ever known, and the fairest. *Their* colonel.

The aircraft were small, two-engine, prop-driven models, parked only a few meters from the briefing facility. Parachutes were strapped on in the ready room; then each stick moved as a unit to its aircraft and climbed aboard.

"Cold as fucking Siberia," one of the men in Bailov's group complained as they sat in the cabin's web seats. "Freeze off a Yakut's tool."

"Wrong, Russian," another man said. "Just cold enough to make it good and hard." He was a Yakut.

Everyone laughed. Unlike other elite Red Army units, Bailov's Spetsnaz brigade had been drawn from every race and nationality in the U.S.S.R.; here, and perhaps only here, they were true equals. Still, they took enormous pleasure in teasing one another about ethnic and racial differences, usually in fun; when it threatened to get out of hand, Bailov and his senior officers would intercede.

Aloft, the noise from the engines was too loud to allow conversation. Each man had his own way of preparing himself; Bailov's was to empty his mind of all thoughts except those required to complete the jump. This did not include emergency procedures; at two hundred meters a parachute malfunction meant death. Nothing could be done, which put a certain psychological edge on doing things right, especially in packing your own parachute. The one thing that they had learned in Spetsnaz was the importance of the human mind in the physical organism's ultimate success, which for Spetsnaz meant doing the impossible. The regular army concentrated more on the body; Spetsnaz focused on the mind and on selecting the right kind of men. There had been a lot of injuries and deaths along the way, but the price had been worth it. Now they knew how to select the candidates most likely to succeed; more important, now they knew how to train them. It would have been less costly in time, money and lives to have trained, competent psychologists and psychiatrists to guide the process, but Soviet psychiatry was the domain of political punishment. Bailov had met only one doctor worthy of his respect, and that had been long ago.

When the aircraft leveled off at jump altitude, Bailov stood and attached his D-ring to a steel cable running the length of the fuselage and terminating at a U-shaped bar over the jump door. As the heaviest man in the stick, he would jump first, the lightest man last, so that the bigger jumpers wouldn't cascade into the silk canopies of the lighter ones below them. Now the jumpmaster gave the hand signal to prepare; the jump light over the door turned from red to yellow and began flashing. Bailov made his way past the others to the door opening and crouched with his right leg forward; the other eleven men squeezed into position behind him. The next man's belly was snug against Bailov's back, his right leg in the V made by the colonel's right leg. The stick had become a snake.

The light changed from a flashing yellow to a steady green. The jumpmaster whacked the back of the colonel's left thigh and Bailov propelled himself out, followed by the eleven other men, one by one. Cold air slammed into his face as soon as he leaped out the door; soon he felt a sharp pain in his crotch and a sense of rising, a misreading wrought by the fluids churning in the inner ear. Look up. Chute good. Arms extended up the risers, legs together. Relax, now. No sight line at night, nothing to help gauge altitude, relax, wait for first touch, now! He hit, then rolled, collapsing his legs, falling sideways, hitting the outside of his right knee, then his right hip and shoulder, a somersault and quickly to his feet, hands out on the risers. No wind, that's good. Release one riser, spill the air out. Disconnect the canopy, grab the shrouds, pull everything toward you quickly, roll it into a ball, bury the chute in the snow. Harness too, get it off. Dump the chemical on the pile to keep dogs away. Done. Pat everything down, tramp it flat, hurry.

The snow was thigh-deep and soft, with pine trees all around. How many of them were hung up? No crust. Bailov took his special skis out of their carrying case and clamped them onto his jump boots. Only a meter long and very wide, their undersides were covered with a layer of fox fur, which was better than wax. The skis would slide forward with little effort but would not slip backward. On crusted snow they would leave no tracks, and they were better than snowshoes because they were easier to use and conserved energy. All right, last clasp secure. One final check. Touch each binding to be sure it's fastened; trust your hands because your eyes are useless in the darkness. Satisfied, he moved his pack from his waist to his upper back, slung his Kalashnikov over his shoulder and tightened the strap so that it would not slip. Looking around, he saw that the others were ready and strode forward with long strides, using arm swings for balance. For most able skiers the journey ahead would require four hours; Bailov and his men would do it in less than two.

Ninety minutes later they saw the glow of the lights from the base, and while they continued to glide forward, the radio operator used his radio to alert perimeter security of their approach. Bailov heard him ask, "Are we the first?" but couldn't hear the answer.

"All four groups have called in, Colonel," the man yelled ahead to his commander. "We're all close." This news sent the stick into a sprint for the fence. In Spetsnaz, to be first was paramount. "All but first are last," was their motto. Bailov's lungs were burning as the chain-link and barbed-wire fence came into view; at the same time he saw three other lines of scrambling troops hell-bent for the finish point.

"Ondatra!" Bailov shouted. Muskrat was the nickname of their fastest man, an Evenk from the Vilyui River area. Immediately Ondatra sprinted past his colonel and the others, opening a space between them as he drove across the line, barely edging out a skier from another group; this immediately set Bailov's men to cheering while the other groups cursed the victorious Evenk. "Get their speed from fucking reindeer," a voice bellowed.

"But not the ugly ones," the Evenk responded.

Having reached the perimeter, the exercise was complete. Bailov and his men stripped off their skis, carried them on their shoulders and marched in cadence in a column of twos while heat from their bodies rose into the night air.

Colonel Taras Ivanovich Bailov walked quietly and proudly at the front of his troops through the light snow that engulfed them and wondered what mere mortals were doing on this snowy night.

14 WEDNESDAY, JANUARY 18, 1961, 7:00 P.M. *Krujë, Albania*

Mehmet Shehu stood beside the crumbling white brick walls of the ancient temple and sucked the crisp night air deep into his lungs. After a lifetime of warfare his body remained lean and hard, but at forty-eight the spring in his step was gone and his joints were often stiff. Arthritis, the doctors said, but it would be a slow degeneration, an inconvenience for a robust man but not crippling for many years. Here in the limestone outcrops of the Krrabë Mountains the thin winter air took a toll, but it rejuvenated his spirits and cleared his mind as no other place did.

In these deep crags, the heroic Gjerj Kastriotei Skenderbeg had repelled the assaults of a hundred thousand Turks commanded by Sultan Murad II. With a force of fewer than eighteen thousand poorly equipped herdsmen, Skenderbeg had kept the powerful Ottoman Turks at bay for nearly a quarter of a century, facing the enemy twenty-two times and winning each time. In May 1450 Skenderbeg's disciplined mountain fighters killed twenty thousand Turks, and in 1467, a year before he succumbed to a fever, they routed the enemy for the final time. For nearly twenty-five years the great Skenderbeg had been invincible, but soon after his death the Turks returned again and this time conquered the mountain people. Shehu was certain that one day his fame would equal Skenderbeg's.

His thoughts were interrupted by Haxi Kasi, who wore a dark green coat and a black wool hat. "She's inside, Mehmet." Kasi was a colonel in the Sigurimi, the Albanian secret police, Shehu's closest companion since their days in the French Shock Brigade and his only friend. When there were special tasks, Haxi Kasi would do whatever was required, no questions asked.

"Any problems?"

Kasi shook his head. "We found her with her mother; she offered no resistance and said nothing during transport."

"Your assessment?"

"At first she looks soft. Too much pampering, a weak mouth, no eye contact. But my belly says she's tough inside."

"We'll see," Shehu said as he brushed past his colleague and entered the poorly lit interior of the old temple. The girl was sitting on the barren floor, unclothed, knees drawn up, arms wrapped tightly around her legs, her face down. Shehu recognized the submissive position. In these situations, women always reacted more powerfully to their nudity than men did.

"Good evening," Shehu said softly. The girl did not look up. "My name is . . ." Be gentle, he cautioned himself. Create a contrast between what she knows is happening and what she perceives to be happening.

"I know who you are," the girl said. Her voice was husky and firm, but Shehu heard it waver.

"What is your name?"

"I have no doubt you already know it."

Defiance? Interesting. Shehu circled her, calculating. The first moments were always the most important. "We have arrested your father."

"I know."

"He is a traitor."

"I know nothing of such things."

"He is a traitor to you as well."

"He is my father. I know only that." Her head remained down.

"You have a choice," Shehu said. "You can help your father. Would you like that?"

She nodded slightly. Her long hair was tied back with a blue ribbon. She had strong back muscles, thin calves and thick thighs that tapered to the knees. An athletic physique, like a dancer's. He sensed that she had quick reflexes.

"Your father has been charged with treason, and the evidence is irrefutable." He made a fist and held it in front of her face. "The case is like this, you understand? There is no hope. If he's brought to trial, he'll be executed." He waited for her reaction but got nothing. She was holding back, measuring the situation. Kasi was correct in his instinct; she was not as soft as she appeared.

The girl's father, Hajredin Llarja, was a hard man, born a Dukagjin Gheg of the northern mountains, now a diplomat. He too had been a partisan and had served on the Central Committee of the Albanian Workers' Party for fifteen years. For nearly ten of those years he had been attached to the Albanian delegation at the United Nations. He was rumored to be a longtime friend of the traitor Admiral Sejku, and now he had been named by the Greek infiltrator as an integral part of the conspiracy. Perhaps he was even the contact with the CIA, Shehu thought. The girl's name was Lejla, aged twenty-four, born in Tirana, but a graduate of Columbia University in New York, where she had lived during her father's UN assignment. New York was a dangerous assignment for Albanians; the city was full of Zogites and other expatriates and counterrevolutionaries who formed pathetic little groups aimed at overthrowing Comrade Enver's government. Had her father known these people? Had *she*? These questions needed answers.

"A cooperative attitude on your part would be in your father's best interest," Shehu told her. "It is possible that if you are cooperative—I say if—we might be able to arrange a more favorable outcome for him. We have uncovered a plot against our government by the Americans, Yugoslavs and Greeks. He is linked to the Americans; we know this. His mission was to provide communications support for enemy troop landings."

"My father could never betray his country," she said without emotion.

His country, not *our* country, Shehu noted. Semantics were clues to subconscious choices. "Your father has betrayed our country, and now he must pay. The question is, what price? If it pleases you, we can consider this meeting to be a negotiation on his behalf. Quite official, I can assure you."

"I have done nothing," the girl said suddenly.

Shehu smiled. Another interesting assertion, the strongest sign yet. With this simple statement the girl had separated herself from her father, and in doing so had declared a subconscious priority for her own fate. Very promising, Shehu decided. She had defended her father only mildly and already was distancing herself from him. Despite this, it was unlikely that she understood what was taking place in the recesses of her mind. Mehmet Shehu had interrogated hundreds of suspects of virtually every imaginable crime, and usually he understood their thoughts long before they did.

Lejla surely believed that her father was innocent; this, too, was normal. Why not? A father would never share his treason with a daughter; with a son, perhaps, but never with a daughter. Shehu was certain that she had no knowledge of the elder Llarja's perfidy, so she would trust that an investigation would only reveal what she knew to be true in her heart. Despite this she would harbor doubt; such was the power of the Sigurimi. Even to be suspected of a crime was dangerous; this they had learned from the Russians. Under Soviet law, suspicion and arrest were proof of guilt; though Albanian law was less rigid in this regard, the Sigurimi was as sinister and threatening as the KGB. People internalized such things; Shehu had seen to it that they did so because the security of his country depended on it. Lejla was afraid for herself; the purity of her feelings for her father was one thing, but her own fate was another matter because only she knew her own thoughts and crimes. Everybody had such feelings.

Shehu broke the silence. "I do not believe in God, but were I a religious man, my philosophy would be much different from the Party's. Males and females are equal. Both must work to live. We make allowances for each other's shortcomings. This is what we offer you, girl. You have a chance to compensate for your father's errors. Few individuals have such an opportunity."

For the first time Lejla looked up. She did not speak, but watched nervously as Shehu went to the door and opened it. Haxi Kasi entered quietly with a small lacquered box, which he placed on the whitewashed floor in front of her.

"Do you understand the Lek, the old laws?" Shehu asked. Now she was giving him her full attention. "In the mountains, where your father was born, people do not take an affront lightly. Even the smallest insult must be avenged. All members of the injured family are bound by the Lek to defend their relative's honor to the death. Retribution in kind is required. To shirk family duty is to commit the worst sort of treason. It's a hard law, but life itself is hard and the law must equal it."

"The Party renounced the Lek long ago," the girl said. "With everything else that was archaic."

There was a hint of resolve in her voice; Shehu sensed that she was probing him and smiled. "The code itself was abandoned, but not the principles. Albania is a single family now; wrongs against one require righting by all. What is important now is that you understand the implications of the decision you must make."

"I could help my father?"

Again she separates herself and retains a choice. Not can, but *could*. Theory without intent. "And yourself, but it must be a complete decision. The Lek requires total commitment." Shehu rubbed his chin. It would be a long, cold ride back to Tirana, and tomorrow morning there would be another endless meeting with Hoxha to discuss the latest negotiations with the Chinese. "You must understand the precariousness of your father's position." He pointed at the box on the floor.

The girl looked down but made no move to open it. There was no need to remind Kasi of what needed doing. He knocked the box over with his boot. For a split second the girl stared, then a scream erupted from deep inside her and echoed from wall to wall. There was a finger on the floor, and on it was a delicate ring of woven gold. It was her father's wedding ring.

15   SATURDAY, JANUARY 21, 1961, 2:00 P.M.
Ocracoke, North Carolina

It was late afternoon with a low, soot-colored sky and a pelting rain out of the northeast. Valentine stopped on the pocked macadam, watched gumdrop-sized raindrops ricochet off the pavement, and tried to get his bearings. On a sweeping right curve to the southeast just ahead, white frame houses hugged both sides of the road, their shutters closed, with red and green shingled roofs and chimneys of softball-sized stones. To the east were low dunes with wind ridges, sea oats, eelgrass and panic grass, several patches of evening primrose, their tiny yellow flowers the only color among the gray, all the vegetation chattering and snapping in the wind like spooked reptiles. To the west were more ocher sand dunes, low pygmy oaks with splotched bark, windswept loblolly pines, two dark cottontails sitting on their haunches. Arizona had sent an address but no directions, and in any event this section of the village looked deserted, so there were no local inhabitants to confer with even if he had wanted to advertise his presence.

Valentine was not surprised by the isolation. It was in character for Arizona to choose an out-of-the-way meeting place, and this was about as far off the beaten track as you could get, especially at this time of year. On the other hand, an island was the worst possible place for a meeting with an agent; it meant limited access, which meant easier surveillance. Maybe Company thinking had changed. Arizona's note had said only, "14 Cove Road, Ocracoke, North Carolina." The return address showed the name of Cordell M. Harker, which he recognized as one of Arizona's many pseudonyms. He had never known his old supervisor's real name and guessed he never would. The *d* in Cordell had a small line underneath. It was a simple code: the meeting day would be four days after the postmark date. It was their old system and Valentine had picked it up immediately.

It had been a long, uncomfortable journey. He had left his pickup at Hobby Airport in Houston, flown through Atlanta to Norfolk, rented a year-old brown Ford Falcon with black-wall tires and headed south on two-lane roads to the 125-mile strip of sandy fingers that North Carolinians called the Outer Banks. He didn't give much thought to what he would find in Ocracoke. It might be a safe house, or someone's cottage. It was more than sixty miles from Nag's Head and nearby Kitty Hawk to the ferry that yawed and rolled across Hatteras Inlet, then another fifteen miles south from there to Ocracoke. Most of the drive took him past isolated beaches and through several semideserted settlements. Once on the Outer Banks, he had seen only half a dozen cars, all of them northbound, and there had been no vehicles since leaving the ferry.

Cove Road turned out to be a crushed-shell-and-hard-sand lane near the center of the village. He guessed and turned right, saw that the number sequence was right and crept through several tight curves in a loblolly pine grove until he reached a white three-story cottage with a screened porch on three sides. A white Jeep with a blue hood and broken left headlight was parked nose out under a flat-roofed carport. A metal basket was welded to a small platform on the grille and several metal surf-rod holders were attached to the basket, the same rig used by surf fishermen along the Texas Gulf Coast.

Valentine touched the hood of the Jeep with the palm of his hand. Cold, and no fresh tracks under the lip of the carport. Either the driver of the Jeep had been there a long time or this was a permanent beach car. He stepped onto the porch. There was no lock on the door; the floor was bare gray wood in desperate need of paint. Rattan carpets were rolled against the inner walls and encased in plastic; wooden deck chairs of several hues were stacked on top of each other. Inside was a generous foyer and a tall, narrow hall; surf fishing rods were mounted vertically on a floor-to-ceiling rack, the dowels covered with green felt; the rods and stainless steel reels were dust-covered.

At the end of the hall there was a splash of gray-white light, and there he found a huge den with two-story-high windows and a massive fireplace. He dropped his duffel and moved toward the kitchen area at one end. There were two six-packs of beer in the refrigerator. He opened a can.

Several magazines were stacked on the table in the den. The top one was a four-year-old edition of the *American Journal of Legal History*. One article was marked with a black paper clip: "The Procedure for the Trial of a Pirate." He skimmed the piece, then put the magazine down. There were paper clips in all the magazines. A scholar who likes to fish, he decided. Arizona? Maybe. He had been a brilliant law professor before joining the OSS. There was no sign of the man. Had he misread the code? But a few seconds later he heard footsteps on the porch and Arizona shuffled into view. He was wearing a Washington Senators baseball cap, a new, stiff denim jacket, faded jeans and scuffed brown cowboy boots. He was heavier than Valentine remembered and there were red veins in his cheeks. He looked tired and needed a shave.

"Beginning to think you'd stood me up," Valentine said.

"Pain in the ass to get down here. My sister's place. I parked one road over and moseyed through the woods." He nodded his head southeast. "Always wonder if there's snakes in there, so I took it slow. My sister always says, 'No snakes on Ocracoke.' I must have been here fifty times before I learned the place is crawling with cottonmouths and rattlers. They're supposed to be hibernating this time of year, but a body can't be too careful." He reached out and shook his old friend's hand vigorously. "Remembered the code?"

"I'm here."

"Man never forgets that sort of thing. Like riding a bike or pokin' your best girl's sweet-meat. Pockets of memories and skills in the brain. Soon as you need something, you get it back, slam-bam. We've got shrinks studying how it works. Seems to be some correlation with language ability—left-brain, right-brain stuff. Read anything on it?"

Valentine shook his head.

Arizona opened a beer for himself, pulled the cover off a rattan chair, sat down and waved a hand at the window. "You know anything about Ocracoke?"

"Well, it's a long way from anywhere."

Arizona grinned. "Pirate hangout. Blackbeard. Tough bastard." He pointed to the bookcase. "Books about pirates. My brother-in-law teaches history at William and Mary. World's foremost expert on Blackbeard."

"That's why I'm here? A history lesson?"

Arizona took a long pull on his beer. "We've got a problem in your old stomping ground."

"Louisiana?"

Arizona smiled. "Yugoslavia, buckeroo. We had a man in Belgrade."

"*Had?*"

"Now you see him, now you don't. Disappeared."

"What's that got to do with me?"

"*Nada, amigo,* which makes you the ideal choice."

Valentine watched several seabirds circle over the pines. "You're movin' a little fast."

Arizona shook his head, took a pack of cigarettes out of his denim jacket and lit one with a wooden match. The smell of sulfur hung in the room while he inhaled deeply. "I need help."

I, not we, Valentine noted. "Company's a big operation with beaucoup assets."

"This ain't your average bear," Arizona said, blowing a perfect smoke ring that glided upward. "Yugoslavia's a special situation, a crossroad between East and West, spy heaven, the ultimate maze in several dimensions, a listening post on the bubble. One of my people was running a very special asset, and now my man's gone—and presumably his asset as well. I'm not talking about some slob checking the skid marks on a second-level bureaucrat's drawers. This is a most righteous, music-making asset. From others we get notes, a few bars. This guy has given us an opera."

"As I said, you've got lots of options."

"If I had options you'd still be sitting in Galveston with a hangover," Arizona said softly. He looked directly at his old colleague. "I need help, Beau."

Valentine walked to a window and stared out for several seconds. "I don't know. I've been out of that shit for a long time, and I've got a pretty good idea that it's a lot more complicated now than in the old days."

"It is a hell of a lot more complicated now, a war of smoke and mirrors. Cold War, partner, but you can burn your ass on dry ice."

"And I'm a dinosaur."

"Right," Arizona said. "*Tyrannosaurus rex,* the baddest mother-fucker in the valley. You were the best. A pain in the ass, undisciplined, insubordinate and brutal, but the best damned agent in the OSS. Lots of people had lots of problems with your methods, but not with your results. My man's name is Frash, Albert Frash. I want you to find him."

Valentine thought about his business in Galveston, the long afternoons in a stifling warehouse, and the long line of nut cases buying modified M-1s and surplus fatigues. "If I agree, what happens next?"

"You go to New York, then to Belgrade."

"Then what?"

"That's your call."

"Sounds pretty open-ended. Doesn't that bother you?"

"Nope. It'll be *your* ass on the line." Arizona grinned and sucked on his cigarette. This was not exactly the truth, but the CIA man liked the direction the meeting had taken. Sylvia's assessment had been correct; Valentine was bored and ready to rejoin the world. That she thought he couldn't cut it was irrelevant; she had never seen Valentine in action and he had.

"Do I get more than a name to work with?"

"Of course," Arizona said, placing a stack of papers on the table. "Take a load off your feet and let's get to work."

62

16 SATURDAY, JANUARY 21, 1961, 2:20 P.M.
Dinant, Belgium

The window of Albert Frash's fourth-floor hotel room looked directly into a yellow window in a turret of a soot-stained cathedral. Hovering above was a medieval citadel on a limestone and granite outcropping that would provide an occupying force with command of the Meuse River. Fixed positions no longer provided defense; you had to keep moving, Frash reminded himself.

His stop in Paris had been short-lived; the network built up by Myslim seemed to have evaporated, which meant trouble. Was this connected to the assassination of Lumbas? There was still not enough evidence and too many loose ends for him to know. What *was* clear was that Villam had tried to set him up, then died as a victim of his own trap. It had been intended as a double takeout, which suggested that the invasion had been a ghost all along. If not real, then what? And why? The goddamned Russians: everything was a chess game, with rules and strategies that only they understood. Europeans with Asian minds, the legacy of four centuries of Mongol occupation and indiscriminate cross-breeding of masters with slaves. The Turks had given a similar legacy to Albania.

There was a restaurant on the ground floor. He had eaten a tasteless fish soup, smoked ham from the Ardennes and freshly baked bread, but tasted none of it while the Walloons around him gorged themselves like there was no tomorrow. Eating was what the Belgians did best, he told himself, which was why it had taken centuries for them to become a nation, and then only as a buffer against the Germans.

The waitress had shown a more than usual interest in him. She was tall and thin, with a long neck and cascading black hair. He had tried to ignore her, but Ali had been restless and had left her a tip equal to the cost of the meal, setting his room key on the table next to the money. Her smile told him she would soon follow.

"This is foolish," he had scolded Ali. For as long as he could remember there had been this conflict inside him, Ali versus Albert, both him, neither him, both real, each wrestling for ultimate and complete control.

"You're the celibate; Ali needs something more than his hand."

"We can't take the risk."

"No risk," Ali countered. "A simple transaction, service for a fee, the essence of capitalism, the driving force for the oldest profession."

"She's a waitress, not a whore."

"Money tells," Ali said.

When the girl came to the door, she quickly pushed her way in and connected the chain lock. "I could lose my job if anyone sees me." She dropped her clothes in a heap and flopped on the bed, making the springs squeak. "The whole floor will hear our music," she said in French.

Albert closed his eyes; Ali got into bed. Several times the girl urged him to hurry so she could get back to her job, but Ali took his time. "I paid," he said, moving slowly to make it last. By the time he had finished the girl was angry; she stalked into the bathroom, which was separated from the bedroom by a curtain instead of a door.

Ali took a 9 mm automatic out of his satchel and checked the fit of the silencer.

"No!" Albert said. He forced Ali's hand back into the bag and made him release the weapon.

When the girl reappeared, her eyes were cold. "You owe more," she said.

"I paid too much already," Ali snapped back.

Albert fought to keep Ali's hand off the weapon. "How much?"

"Two hundred francs," she said. "They'll give me hell downstairs."

Albert paid while Ali seethed.

"I thought you'd be nice," she said from the door.

"I'm sorry," Albert said.

"Bitch," Ali blurted out.

The girl gave Frash a peculiar look, then slammed the door in his face.

"You shouldn't have stopped me." Ali said.

"I should have stopped you permanently a long time ago," Albert answered.

Someday we'll find out who stops whom, Ali thought.

"We have to concentrate on Myslim for now. We can't allow ourselves to be diverted," Albert said.

"Will you stop me when we find him?"

This was a question Albert couldn't answer.

Frash stared across at the church as the stained-glass window turned gold under the sun's reflection. The Church had money and power and yet it had failed. It had failed him, failed his country, let the Fascists in and then the Communists. It had abandoned Albania because it was poor and turned its attention to richer pastures, even while the Germans had Hitler at the helm. Myslim had set him up, but that was to be expected; Myslim was only a man, and all men were imperfect. It was the Church and its agents like the Kennedys who were the greater failure. The Kennedys were puppets. Mother knew the truth. Neither Albert nor Ali could understand these thoughts. In time, they knew, one of them would understand. "Myslim," Frash said, watching the sun intensify on the cathedral's glass.

---

17 SATURDAY, JANUARY 21, 1961, 3:00 P.M. *Moscow*

The meeting with the American ambassador had been a delicate dance, and Nikita Sergeievich had thoroughly enjoyed himself. So that there would be virtually no opportunity to communicate with Washington, he had given the American only thirty minutes' notice of the meeting; Thompson had hurried over with a second secretary named Gleystein in tow, and though the Americans had not had an audience since September, the trim ambassador was calm as if this were part of his daily routine.

In Stalin's day they had been forced to watch American westerns; Thompson reminded Khrushchev of a cowboy film hero. He was serious but not pompous, unflappable, certain of his abilities but not arrogant, and dedicated to his country and his leaders even when they made stupid decisions. He favored well-tailored suits and also had an easy sense of humor, a rare quality in a diplomat of any nationality.

Dobrynin and Kuznetsov also attended the two-hour meeting, not to speak but to listen. Each had dealt with Thompson before, so if there were subtle changes in his positions and responses they would detect them.

By design Khrushchev began quietly. What Eisenhower had done was done. Kennedy was new and therefore the slate could now be wiped clean, which would be to their countries' mutual benefit. The world was in too delicate a condition for the two superpowers to be clawing at each other's throat. When elephants fight it is the grass that suffers, Khrushchev reminded the ambassador, who smiled and nodded.

They discussed Berlin in broad terms. A reunified Germany was morally and politically unacceptable to the Soviet Union, but Berlin legitimately belonged to the German Democratic Republic, by simple geography if nothing else. This issue was important both to the U.S.S.R. and the East Germans. Laos was a different matter, an internal affair, a revolution from within; Khrushchev assured Ambassador Thompson that the Soviets had not intervened in Laos, which was not true, but until the Americans verified it there was no value in admitting it. Neither man made mention of the Chinese. There were other positive things he pointed to as evidence of improved relations, most notably the nuclear-test moratorium, which was being honored by both sides.

Thompson was polite and listened carefully but made no attempt to debate because the new president had not yet formulated policies on many issues. Khrushchev understood; until the ambassador had formal instructions he could only listen. Such instructions required time and careful thought; the democratic process in the United States was slow. In time, Thompson said, he expected that they would be ready to talk seriously with the Russians about a wide range of issues, but not now. It was too soon; Kennedy had just taken office.

It was unfortunate that the summit had been destroyed in Paris last year, Khrushchev said, but Eisenhower had been a shortsighted and stubborn fool. The president should never have taken personal responsibility for the U-2 incursions; he could have—should have—publicly put the blame on the CIA. Here Khrushchev's emotions temporarily got the better of him. He had fashioned an understanding with Eisenhower, or so he thought until Eisenhower announced that he was personally responsible for the U-2 flights. Why hadn't the president appreciated *his* position? Eisenhower had symbolically slapped him in the face, which left the Soviet leader no alternative. This sort of honor was fine for generals, but statesmen required a degree of deniability. His colleagues in the Politburo had openly ridiculed him for Eisenhower's unexpected stance. Nikita Sergeievich has a friend in the White House, they mocked, but with friends like that who needed enemies? He'd had no choice but to disrupt the Paris summit as a quid pro quo for the president's insensitivity.

At this point Khrushchev calmed himself and took a softer tack. "The leaders of our two countries, Mr. Ambassador, must work with each other, trust each other. Such a relationship requires serious discussion, give-and-take, man to man, across a small table, do you understand?"

Thompson replied that he understood the General Secretary's perspective and appreciated his candor, but it was premature to discuss such a meeting. Unlike his predecessor, President Kennedy believed that diplomacy should be conducted through traditional channels based on thorough preparation. Privacy was paramount. At a summit everything was public, more a circus than an environment conducive to serious and meaningful discourse.

Yes, yes, all this was true, but leaders must lead; we have the authority to act on behalf of those who elect us. He reminded Thompson that contrary to the endless distortions in the Western press, Soviet officials were elected, just as American officials were.

Thompson deflected this misrepresentation adroitly; the difference was that the General Secretary was not *newly* elected, and certainly not by the narrow margin that had brought the new president to office. Mr. Kennedy needed time to form his government, and then an interval during which he could carefully consider policy. Certainly Mr. Khrushchev could understand the delicacy of the position of a new leader with such a precarious balance of power, this being an allusion to the Soviet leader's near fall in 1957.

Khrushchev agreed that this was reasonable, but he wished the ambassador to convey to the new president not only his warmest personal regards, but his fervent hope for the earliest possible meeting so that they could get to know each other.

At this point the General Secretary unleashed his surprise. There was no need to perpetuate the rancor that had marked the final months with the Eisenhower administration. To this end, he had decided to demonstrate his good intentions: the two Air Force RB-47 crewmen shot down over Soviet territory last July would be released immediately and without strings attached. He hoped President Kennedy and the American people would accept this gesture for what it was.

If Thompson was surprised by this announcement, he concealed it well.

The two fliers would be released on Wednesday morning and transported to Spasso House in Moscow. They would be repatriated by commercial air service and the U.S.S.R. would pay their expenses; Khrushchev quickly added that he would allow Mr. Kennedy to make the announcement, then immediately repeated his position that an early meeting with the president would be in the best interests of both countries. The whole point of the release was to put the onus on Kennedy.

When Thompson and his lackey had gone, Khrushchev clapped his hands, then poured vodka for his subordinates. Neither Dobrynin nor Kuznetsov said anything, but both were thinking the same thing: Khrushchev was acting on his own, following his peculiar urges. Why did he behave this way? In 1956 he had attacked the cult of personality that Stalin had created for himself; now he was doing the same thing and there were rumblings in the Presidium. This latest stunt would just make matters worse.

"We have no hold on them anyway," the General Secretary said suddenly as if he had read their thoughts. "We took them down over international waters as a retaliation for Powers. We stopped their U-2 flights, then made them wary of operating even along our borders. It was a necessary gamble. But you see how it has worked to our advantage? They were intruders, but now we release them as a gesture of peace. To get a harvest you must first put your seeds in the earth."

Neither Dobrynin nor Kuznetsov responded to this, and as soon as their vodka was finished they departed. Nikita Sergeievich knew that they did not approve of his course of action, but he was accustomed to less than enthusiastic responses to his ideas. Eventually they would see that he was right. He always was.

| 18 | **Saturday, January 28, 1961, 11:30 p.m.** *Moscow* |

Roman Trubkin was in a holding pattern of little sleep and deep concern. The information from Mandrich had given him a new direction but he had suddenly turned cautious. He had ruled out going directly to Shelepin and instead concentrated on his staff, all the while reminding himself that he was in a minefield. If Shelepin caught wind of his snooping he knew he would soon be locked away in Le Fortovo or worse. Would Khrushchev back him then?

Shelepin ran a tight ship, meaning he had a small personal staff, but Trubkin was able to find out that the KGB director sometimes employed secretaries from the agency's central pool and that this list was a short one: an elderly woman who typed budget statements and two younger women who transcribed shorthand notes taken by his regular secretary, a man named Velak who had come over to the KGB with Shelepin from Komsomol. One of the two younger women was said to be romantically involved with Shelepin, but the other one seemed unencumbered. Katya Dirikova was thirty-two, with the plump face of an angel and short blond hair. He followed her for nearly two weeks before making his move, and even then he opted for a gradual approach, though he could see that she was openly impressed to have dates with a famous cosmonaut and glowed when they dined together in small cafés.

One night he took her to dinner again and only as they were putting on their coats invited her to spend the night with him. She blushed but quickly accepted, then confessed to a lack of experience in such matters. When they reached his flat he gave her a brandy, which she drank in loud gulps, all the while averting her eyes. When he told her it was time to go to bed she undressed with her back to him, turned out the lights and got under the covers, but she made up for her inexperience with her enthusiasm and kept him awake most of the night.

She rose at 5:00 a.m., sponged herself, went to work and was back again that night and several more, each time shedding a little more shyness.

Her head was on his chest now, her hand tracing his pectorals, her breathing slow and relaxed. "Someone at the office asked me today if I had a boyfriend. She said I was glowing."

"What did you tell her?"

"Nothing! What I do on my own time is my business."

"That's sensible," he said, waiting for a reaction, but she simply nodded agreement.

"That was my thought. I've always had common sense."

In the time he had known her Katya had proved to be quite talkative and Trubkin had gotten considerable information about the inner workings and petty politics of Shelepin's staff. The director was well-organized and efficient, and readily delegated decisions to his deputies. "He's not at all like Serov," she said of the previous KGB chief. "Serov had to put his scent on every detail."

Each night she chattered about the minutiae of her day. "Today I nearly had a row with Shelepin," she whispered.

"Over what?"

"He didn't understand some of my transcriptions. The selection group has been meeting for most of the week. They talk and talk and waste page after page while saying nothing."

"You attend such meetings?"

"Never. Velak sometimes goes to take minutes and I transcribe them later. When Velak isn't there, they use a tape recorder, and each time someone speaks he's supposed to identify himself, but they often forget and then it falls to me to figure out who said what. I know all their voices, but it's still confusing, and this particular meeting was more confusing than most. There was an argument and I transposed several names. Shelepin berated me and told me to pay more attention to my work. I wanted to tell him that if the big shots followed the rules, this would never happen. If he attended the meetings he could see to it."

"Shelepin doesn't attend?"

"Almost never. He delegates it to his deputy Perevertkin. But of course I simply apologized and promised to be more diligent. It does no good to correct your superior; good positions are so difficult to find, and if you're tossed out of the KGB, who dares hire you?"

Shelepin did not attend the meetings and sent a deputy in his place. "What sort of man is Perevertkin?"

Katya laughed and held out her arms to him. "A rabbit, but not the cuddly sort. He says little and does exactly what Shelepin wants, so we call him the Rubber Stamp. Come back to bed."

"Perhaps you should talk to Perevertkin and ask him to remind the committee of proper procedure."

"Just like a pilot to be so direct. In the KGB you learn that indirect is safer. Here," she said, lying back. "Enough boring talk. Let's do something more interesting."

"It doesn't seem fair," he said as he crawled back onto the bed. "If Shelepin reviews the minutes of everything he ought to see how difficult it is for you to create the reports."

She smiled, then kissed him hungrily. "I don't do all of them, so what does he care what I think? If I were beautiful he'd care, but I'm not. He reviews everything and maintains files, but all he cares about are results. How a report was botched is not his concern."

"So you get to clean up their mistakes."

"The whole section does," she said as his penis came to life in her small hand. "We have to work together." She giggled.

"You probably have to maintain the files as well," he said as she guided him inside.

Perevertkin was Shelepin's stand-in, and there were minutes of the meetings Shelepin rarely attended. Did this provide opportunity for mischief? While Katya made love to him Trubkin tried to think of ways he could get access to the committee's minutes.

---

19 | WEDNESDAY, FEBRUARY 1, 1961, 4:00 P.M.
Greenwich Village, New York

The Broadway Central Hotel on Bleecker Street was nine decades old and looked more. There had been a fresh coat of snow during the night and the soot-covered exterior was temporarily white; dozens of gray and green pigeons were huddled on the ledges above the sidewalk alert for food and targets. Valentine scooped up a handful of wet snow, packed it firmly into a ball and hurled it at the birds, coming close enough to send several of them fluttering for safer perches. "Winged rats," he muttered.

The lobby was gray and tired, carpets threadbare, light bulbs burned out, furniture soiled. To the right was an entrance to an unnamed lounge with five small oak tables and an ornate but chipped marble bar. Valentine took a table that put his back to a wall papered with a pattern of pink roses. The bartender was an obese black man with white hair, gold teeth, rings on both little fingers and minimal conversational skills.

"Drink?"

"Bottle of beer."

"Flavor?"

"Rheingold."

The man carried the bottle by its long neck and set it heavily on Valentine's table. The bottle was beaded with moisture.

"How about a glass?" Valentine asked.

"All dirty. Two bits. Pay as you go, no tabs, house rule."

Valentine gave him a quarter and felt better when the man retreated behind the bar to resume staring at the entrance. On the wall behind him was a brass-and-wood plaque that read NATIONAL BASEBALL LEAGUE ORGANIZED IN THIS ROOM, 1876.

The whole thing was preposterous. Had he made a mistake? After his meeting with Arizona, Valentine had gone back to Galveston, arranged for the business to be looked after by his assistant and then had flown to New York. Arizona had told him to check into the Algonquin Hotel. He was to expect contact there and follow whatever instruction he received by someone with the code name Karageorg, which translated loosely as Black George. That had been two days ago.

Yesterday a note had been left for him at the desk overlooking the hotel's lounge. He was to come to the bar of the Broadway Central Hotel at four o'clock and wait until seven. If there was no contact, he was to keep returning every day until someone appeared. It was a simple plan.

At four-thirty-five, Valentine went to the toilet; when he returned there was somebody at his table.

"You?" he said when he saw the woman's face.

"Karageorg," she said.

"You came to Galveston to check me out," Valentine said, not sure how he felt about this.

"Arizona said you'd be quick on the uptake." She smiled. "I'm going to be your partner," she added, holding out her hand. "Sylvia Charles."

He ignored the hand. "I've always worked alone."

"Right tense," she said. "Wrong concept. From this moment on we work together."

Valentine pushed back from the table and gave her a big smile. "Just like Galveston?"

Though her voice went cold, Sylvia kept smiling. "Not a chance," she said. "What was, was. What is, is. And what the Company wants is your standard Company relationship, meaning this is strictly business and no hanky-panky. We make decisions together, we keep each other tuned in, and we play it by the book. That's the deal."

"Doesn't seem like much fun."

"Finding our man isn't about fun," Sylvia said, placing an envelope on the table. "Our tickets."

"Belgrade?"

"To start with," Sylvia said. Arizona had insisted that Valentine was the right man for the job, but she had serious doubts. The man she had met in Galveston was charming in a peculiar way but lost in his own existence, mired in self-pity, bored. She had reported all this to her superior and recommended they pass on him, but Arizona had ignored her recommendation. "He's a little rusty" was all he had said. She hoped now for her own sake that the rust had not attacked his vital parts. "You got a problem with this?"

"I'm game."

We'll see, Sylvia thought. It was an inauspicious beginning.

WEDNESDAY, FEBRUARY 1, 1961, 7:00 P.M.
Moscow

Katya Dirikova was only a clerk typist in the KGB director's central secretarial pool but she was imbued with the same suspicious nature as her fellow employees and had a sense of self-survival second to none. The recent nights with Roman Trubkin had been a welcome respite from a dull existence, but she had realized soon after their first time in bed that he was using her to get information; she was using him as well, she knew, but in a different way. The realization had come as a shock, but when she thought further she was certain her assessment was correct. What would a cosmonaut want with the likes of her? Not that the decision was so easy; after all, her nights had been enlightening as well as enjoyable, but there was no doubt that he was using her for some scheme. The big decision was not so much to disclose what was happening as deciding whom to tell. In the end she had rejected going to Shelepin or Perevertkin and chose instead to confide in the white-haired Velak, who was a gentle and sympathetic sort and always came to her after her tiffs with Shelepin to tell her not to worry. "Think of me as your father," he had said. "Always available when you need me." When she told Velak about Trubkin he told her that she had done the right thing in confiding in him, and having told him, she should stop seeing Trubkin and put him out of her mind. She had half expected Velak to make a pass at her but he had been a perfect gentleman. Maybe this would come later; if so, she decided it would be a small price to pay for a clear conscience and a pristine security record. She had no regrets about her decision; done was done. If Roman had nothing to hide there would be no problem; if he did, then justice would be done. Velak had said as much and assured her that there was probably nothing to the whole episode other than the usual male need to take advantage of an honest girl.

21   WEDNESDAY, FEBRUARY 1, 1961, 9:30 P.M.
Moscow

The Asian sat high in the arena among a sparse crowd. The Red Army team had taken a five-goal lead over Moscow Spartak midway through the second period; the previous year's Olympic upset by the Americans had turned the Soviet ice hockey federation upside down, and all of the major teams in the first division except Red Army had been infused with young legs and inexperience as the federation began its drive to develop a new cadre of players. For now the Red Army team would dominate on experience, but next season and thereafter youth would prevail, and when the Olympics came again in 1964 the Soviet national team would be ready to resume its place on top. Though his fellow officers talked enthusiastically about the federation's plan, Okhlopkin had no sense of how ice hockey supremacy would contribute to Lenin's predictions of world political dominance. Better to leave such scheming to great men, he decided. His own role was more practical.

Toward the end of the second period Okhlopkin saw his contact limp slowly up the stairs. An envelope was passed in silence, then the man was gone. He himself left soon afterward and opened the envelope only when he was in his automobile. The face in the photograph was unremarkable; the instructions were typed and said that the death was to look accidental and was to take place as soon as possible. The back of the photo had a name and an address; nothing else was necessary. To kill a man you needed only a starting point; thereafter, the options revealed themselves. None but the most powerful men contemplated the possibility of assassination, which was what made it so easy, but only a specialist understood such matters, he told himself.

22 | FRIDAY, FEBRUARY 3, 1961, 12:40 A.M.
Moscow

What was wrong? Suddenly Katya had to work long hours and had no time for him. When he called she sounded the same, but she had excuse after excuse for not being able to meet him.

No snow had been predicted, but there had been a heavy fall and it was up to mid-calf since he entered the Praga Restaurant earlier in the evening. Even though the snow was dry, Trubkin was having a difficult time staying on the sidewalk. He had been drunk before, but never had it felt quite like this. His stomach was on fire, as if he were in the early stages of flu. To be drunk, said his fellow countrymen, was to be bitten by the green snake, whose venom was vodka.

This Lumbas business had started with plenty of thrust; initially Trubkin had been excited at the prospect of solving the mystery, especially the rewards such success might bring, but high promise had faded to dangerous options. Almost a cosmonaut, almost a hero, almost to the heart of the Lumbas mystery. Always it was almost. He wondered if there had been a Saint Almost.

If it had not been Khrushchev who'd had Lumbas transferred, then who and why, and who had sent him there in the first place? Korolev hadn't asked for Lumbas; he had been assigned. It would take somebody with power and connections and balls. Malinovsky. Shelepin. Perevertkin. Probably not Malinovsky, he reminded himself; that just didn't make sense. And not Khrushchev. What would he have to gain by putting together some scheme and then bringing me in to investigate? It came down to Shelepin or Perevertkin or both. Even with a bellyful of cheap vodka, the possibilities had a sobering effect, but he had a hunch he was close. If only he could find a way to see the minutes of the selection committee meetings. If Lumbas was listed, then he would have been sent legitimately and the record would say where he had come from so that Trubkin could backtrack. And if Lumbas had *not* been approved by the committee, that would tell him something else. Whatever the result, it had to come out of this committee or its periphery. But Katya was not helping. What was her game?

These thoughts cluttered his mind as he discovered himself in front of the Bolshoi Theater. He had no memory of intending to go there—or had he? He had learned that Perevertkin frequented the ballet, but was there a show tonight? Difficult to sort thoughts. Generally vodka made his head hurt, but never before had it clouded his memory. Strange reaction, he thought. Zia? Could Zia be the reason?

He had not planned to come tonight, but here he was. The building was dark; he went slowly to the rear entrance used by the performers and found an old man blowing on his hands to keep warm. He had known Zia years ago. Perhaps she would be receptive. Drunk or not, pain in his gut aside, he needed a woman. "Has everyone gone?" he asked the man. The ache in his stomach was getting worse, and though it was exceptionally cold he was sweating. Maybe the vodka was bad.

"They clear out fast," the old man said. "Backstage lacks the elegance of the theater itself; it's a shithole."

"Did you see Zia?" Trubkin unbuttoned his overcoat and loosened his tie.

The old man rubbed his chin. "Zia?"

"She's blond and beautiful."

The old man smiled. "They're all blond and beautiful. Even the boys." He had several missing teeth and dark eyebrows connected over a bulbous nose.

"She has a unique voice."

The old man nodded several times. "That one? She broke her leg, I think."

Trubkin tried to imagine one of Zia's perfectly shaped legs askew. "Is she all right?"

"She'll live, but not as a dancer. Perhaps she can teach now. That's what most of them do. A few whore for the KGB, but there's no future in that. She was too tall, I think. The tall ones always get hurt. Too much twisting on too-long legs. A dancer should be short and compact."

"Is she in Moscow?"

The watchman shrugged. "I'm not her father."

Circling back to the front of the theater, Trubkin encountered a young man in a red overcoat who fell in step with him and tried to hold his hand. The former cosmonaut backhanded him across the ear, sending him sprawling, then stomped him several times between his legs, leaving the man writhing and whimpering in the snow. "Degenerate," he said, then spat on the figure in a final expression of disgust. Stalin knew how to deal with homos; Khrushchev was too lenient.

It had been hot and steamy in the Praga, nearly as stuffy as the public baths, and though he had felt drunk as he chugged vodka after vodka, the effect seemed worse in the cold air. Oxygen-starved blood, he told himself, and bad vodka. There had been an officer there, an ugly Asian who said he recognized him from his cosmonaut days and kept bringing him tall glasses filled with vodka. He had been glad for the recognition and accepted the drinks even though the man was repulsive. At one point the moron had fallen and driven Trubkin backward, his ass striking something sharp. It hurt like hell for a while but now all he had was the pain in his gut. It was this Lumbas thing that was fucking him up, he told himself. Flying was the only thing in his life he had ever done well, and now fate and a substandard constitution had taken that away. To be human was to face losing those things you wanted most. To be Russian was an added burden. He could live with not being the first starman, but not to be able to fly added insult to injury.

Stopping to get his bearings, Trubkin chided himself for his self-pity. Whining pilots augured their machines into the ground. A pilot had only himself to depend on, and now, just as when he was in the cockpit, he was alone. Zia understood this. He hoped she still had her flat. Where was it? Arbat Street? No, but near there in a puke-green building.

Though he had once been a heavy drinker, Trubkin had modified his habits; this was the first time in months he had gone over the edge, and it felt uncomfortable and unfamiliar at the same time. Vodka had never given him a pain in his stomach before. Maybe he was falling apart. He had gone to the Praga because it was a favorite hangout for officers, because there was a red-haired Estonian girl there and because Katya had ignored all his calls. Previously the Estonian had eagerly entertained him no matter when he showed up, but tonight she had been cool. "I've got my period," she announced.

"I don't mind," he said.

"I do," she snapped.

So he had settled for the vodkas the crazy Asian kept sending over. Now he was confused; though he seldom remembered street names, he navigated well by landmarks, and right now he needed to find the metro because he didn't have enough left to pay for a cab. Maybe Zia would be at her place so he could kiss her broken leg and tell her not to worry.

"Hey, you!" a voice called out.

The man was in the shadows, and though Trubkin could not focus he saw that he had a uniform. "Fuck off," he snapped instinctively.

"You're weaving. The snake's got hold of you."

"I'm exercising," Trubkin said. When faced with a uniform it was best to fend it off with brashness.

"You should get yourself to a sobering station," the man said, keeping his distance.

"And you should mind your own damned business."

"I wash my hands of you," the man muttered. "A drunkard gets his due."

Trubkin grimaced and stepped into the street, the pains in his stomach stabbing now and coming in fast waves. After a few steps he doubled over to try to relieve the pressure.

Seconds later the uniformed man heard a sickening crunch and turned to see Trubkin crumpled in the street and a small dark truck racing away with its lights out. The policeman knew before he felt for a pulse that he had a stiff on his hands. A hit-and-run, maybe; it more or less depended upon who did the hitting before a crime could be attributed to the event.

There was no pulse. The policeman exhaled and gave the body a kick. "Drunkard." Now the rest of his night would be spent making out reports. Why did deaths require so much more paperwork than births? He was trying to light a cigarette with his frozen hand when he heard a sound, looked up and saw the grille of a truck nearly on top of him. His last thought was, Are Asians allowed to drive in the Chaika lane?

23 FRIDAY, FEBRUARY 3, 1961, 8:45 A.M.
Moscow

Though his days as a full-time pathologist had long since passed, Dr. Mikhail Gnedin used the dingy mortuary in the Heart Institute's basement as his personal laboratory. The Heart Institute included a large hospital, some of whose beds were inappropriately filled by Party officials and other notables needing routine care, but mostly it was the central receiving point for interesting, difficult and perplexing cases from all over the Soviet Union and its satellites. Hanging over the entrance to the laboratory was a piece of parchment in a glassed frame whose Latin words meant little to most of those who saw them. *"Taceat colloquia. Effugiat resis. Hic locus est ubi mors guadet succurrere vitale."* Gnedin not only understood the words but lived by them. "Let conversation cease. Let laughter flee. This is the place where death delights to help the living." It had been this that had first attracted him to pathology, and now as a heart specialist he found that he still learned more from cold bodies than from warm ones.

Gnedin's status entitled him to ultramodern facilities in one of the new wings, but he chose to remain in the old basement; surroundings didn't count for much with him. His colleagues considered him a genius, not merely because of his hands during surgery, but, more important, because of his intellectual capacity. Currently he was studying the hypothesis that an unknown chemical fraction of blood regulated the clotting process. His less able colleagues considered the theory far-fetched to the point of foolishness, but they also knew better than to doubt his oft-proven scientific instincts. The man had the nose of a bloodhound. What the others didn't know was that Gnedin had learned that two scientists, one English and the other American, were close to determining the structure of deoxyribonucleic acid, DNA; this discovery, he believed, would open the door to the eventual delineation of a complete "map" of human genes. Through this, scientists would be able to isolate and identify substances now unknown, and with these, or modifications of them, they would be able to conquer diseases in dramatic ways. As yet he had no evidence that his theoretical clotting factor existed; rather, he deduced its existence. Eventually, he was certain, such a substance, or even a family of them, would be revealed, and then it would be possible to reduce the high mortality associated with heart disease in the U.S.S.R. His countrymen had the worst dietary habits imaginable, and were paying the ultimate price for it.

Gnedin had been looking forward to this morning. For the first time in weeks there were no meetings to attend; originally the entire day had been committed, but inexplicably all appointments had been canceled and he found himself with the rare gift of free time. Before starting work, he boiled water in a glass beaker over a Bunsen burner; with a fresh cup of tea in front of him, he opened a journal to read, then heard a woman's high heels in the hall.

His secretary came stumbling in. Her straight skirt was so tight that she had to hike it above her knees in order to walk. Her face was flushed, there was sweat on her forehead, and she was wild-eyed. Normally Frumkina was a nonstop talker, but now she appeared tongue-tied and flustered. Gnedin liked the change. "What do you want?"

She pointed down the hall, then burst into tears and ran out of the laboratory. Gnedin was long past the point of being surprised by her antics; nothing his harebrained secretary did surprised him. Still, something or someone had addled her.

Soon there were more sounds in the hall indicating the approach of more than one person. Two large men in black leather overcoats and fur shapkas strode purposefully through the entrance together and stepped apart. A short, fat man wearing a heavy overcoat and carrying a gray fedora entered between them. "Good morning, Comrade Doctor. Your secretary said you were hibernating in your laboratory. She's much more emotional than the sort I would expect a noted scientist to select."

Gnedin had known Nikita Khrushchev for several years. At one point he had done an evaluation of the health benefits of corn oil for the Soviet leader. A countrywide plan to install corn in previously untilled areas had been prepared, but Khrushchev had been concerned that the Soviet people would not accept corn and its by-products as staples. He asked Gnedin to evaluate the nutritional value of the oil; with this he could herald the products and ensure their use. Gnedin's report showed that fats in corn oil would contribute to atherosclerotic and cardiovascular disease. Khrushchev's people did not alter the report; instead it simply disappeared. Such was the expedience of politics.

"She wasn't my choice," Gnedin answered.

Khrushchev sat on a stool; he had short, wide feet hidden in brown oxfords buffed to a bright sheen. "That is as it should be. Our scientists shouldn't be bothered with such mundane tasks as hiring office personnel."

"Poor choices reduce productivity."

Khrushchev shook a stubby finger at the doctor. "But you are one of the most productive scientists we have."

"I would be even more efficient with competent support."

"She has beautiful legs."

"And a brain the size of an almond."

"Don't complain," Khrushchev scolded. "I need your services again."

"Another report to be ignored?" Gnedin asked sarcastically.

Khrushchev brushed the remark aside. "I'm told that before you got interested in hearts you were a first-rate pathologist."

"The two interests often intersect." Petrov had once told Gnedin that he had become a pathologist in order to defeat death, but that if he wanted to truly serve mankind he would do better to focus on life. In part it was this that had turned Gnedin's interest to cardiovascular circuitry. The Latin saying had been a gift from his former leader and mentor.

"Two bodies are being brought in. I want autopsies."

"The city medical examiner is better qualified."

"But I want you to personally take care of it. I want the truth."

"So it can be ignored again?"

Khrushchev stepped toward the door and lowered his voice. "Self-righteousness is a luxury, comrade. It's one thing to know the truth and disregard it for a higher purpose; it's yet another to be *ignorant* of the truth. Just give me the facts. That's your job, and it's enough for any man."

Gnedin was in no mood to argue; in any event, if the General Secretary wanted him to do autopsies, he would do them. "To do it correctly will require time."

"Do what is necessary," Khrushchev said. "The men were struck by a vehicle."

"When?"

"Sometime last night. They were found this morning by a snow-removal crew."

"If you know that much, then autopsies are unnecessary," Gnedin said.

"I'll decide what's necessary. You give them your best professional attention." Perhaps the death of Trubkin was a simple accident, but a lifetime of intrigue had created an innate sense of caution in the General Secretary. To stay alive you learned to question everything. Trubkin had been his man in the Lumbas investigation. There had been virtually no progress in uncovering the identity of the person who had forged his signature; now his man was dead, and Trubkin was not the sort to get run down in a snowy street. An autopsy would either put his mind at ease or confirm his suspicions.

The corpses were in a mortuary room down the hall from Gnedin's laboratory. Their clothes had been removed and they rested side by side on marble tables. A man in a dark gray militia uniform was standing between the tables, his arms crossed. "This is not according to procedure," he whined to Gnedin. He had oily black hair and a thick mustache.

"You found the deceased?"

"I'd just gone off duty. Can you imagine? They called me back. My girlfriend and I had the flat to ourselves for the first time since Stalin was a Catholic. This was to be a day off. Her parents are on a retreat. So what happens? I get called back to baby-sit stiffs. The one on the left is one of ours. A real horse's ass, holier-than-thou, probably a damned closet Baptist. Couldn't get along with anyone. Better dead than Red," he added, quoting a joke that was said to be in vogue in the West.

"And the other one?"

The militiaman shrugged. "We have his identity card. A major in the air force. A pilot. Looks like he flew a bit too low this time." He waited in vain for a reaction to his joke.

"Site photos?"

"In the envelope." The man pointed to a brown packet on a wooden desk in the corner.

"Was the medical examiner called?"

"The names were called in to the station. Later we were told to bring them down here." The militiaman had known enough not to question such departures from established procedure.

Gnedin looked briefly at the photographs, then turned to the bodies. Massive trauma was obvious, and it was equally evident that a vehicle not only had struck them but had run over each of them.

"Any idea why they were together?"

"None," the militiaman said. Probably Dimitri was being his usual interfering self, putting his nose where it didn't belong, but he had no intention of offering this opinion. His job was to deliver the bodies and he had done so; now all he wanted was to get back to Galya, who had taken the interruption personally and screamed at him. If this took much longer she would lose patience and find company with one of her other boyfriends. There were lots of them; Galya was not much to look at, but she knew how to please men.

Gnedin dismissed the militiaman, then put on a full-length rubber apron, pulled on his rubber gloves, made sure that the recording system was on and began the autopsies by describing the obvious facts about the condition, size and appearance of the two bodies. At first he found nothing unusual, but then he noticed something about one of the bodies. The flesh was splotched and slightly blue. Instinct took over. The external examination was complete; it was time to look inside and take blood and tissue specimens for analysis, but something told him to be cautious and call for assistance. Another set of eyes always helped. A phone call brought Boris Topolar shuffling into the laboratory twenty minutes later.

Topolar was a toxicologist whose professional skills Gnedin respected. He was nearly seventy years old, an obese man who had survived a stroke and ten years in a psychiatric clinic, not because of mental disease but because the Stalin regime had ruled him politically unreliable. He used two sturdy oak canes to help move his bulk around. His face was always red and the slightest exertion left him gasping for breath. A diabetic, he had lost a toe to gangrene, and now he wore canvas shoes with the tips cut away.

Topolar lowered himself onto a stool and breathed hard. "This had better be interesting," he said. "I nearly killed myself getting down here."

"With all your problems you should have been dead long ago."

"Attitude, my dear Gnedin, attitude. I live because I have will. What little puzzle do you have for me? Have you killed another of your patients?"

Gnedin pointed to the taller of the corpses. "What do you see?"

"An immovable object that encountered the proverbial irresistible force. Messy. Truck or bus?"

Gnedin ignored the question. "Is that all?"

Topolar pulled a handkerchief from his trouser pocket and blew his nose loudly. "Epidermal cyanosis."

"What would you guess?"

"I make it a practice not to guess," the toxicologist said testily. "I leave hypotheses to the young. My world is analysis. Chemistry tells all." He used his canes to stand, then bent close to the body and sniffed like a dog. "Ethyl alcohol. I'd guess high blood levels. Our cold friend here was no doubt soused. Alcohol-induced cyanosis. The color of the flesh suggests it."

"That's your professional opinion?"

"Um," Topolar said. "I'm thinking aloud. When I have a conclusion, I'll label it so." He moved to the other side of the table. "Can we roll our friend onto his stomach?"

Gnedin turned the corpse over and Topolar poked the buttocks with his finger. "Um," he said again. "Fetch me a scalpel."

The instrument looked like a butter knife in Topolar's fat hands, but he deftly scraped the flesh in several places. As he worked, he muttered unintelligibly to himself from time to time, until finally he smiled, took off his glasses, blotted at the lenses with the same handkerchief he had blown his nose into, replaced the eyeglasses and looked up at his colleague. "*Voilà,* my dear Gnedin."

"What do you see?"

"An injection site, I would think, but your hands are steadier than mine. If you will kindly come over and cut here, I believe we can make short work of your little mystery."

Gnedin made a vertical incision into the gluteal tissue and peeled back the muscle with forceps. Topolar was correct. There was a clearly marked needle path.

"Aminazine," the toxicologist declared. "Intramuscular injection. The skin discoloration is typical. An overly generous dose, no doubt. Our friend here must have been in agony. The tissue should be tested, but I'm certain it's aminazine."

"Muscle relaxant."

"Technically a major tranquilizer. Once upon a time it was used in abdominal surgery, but there were too many side effects."

"I've used it," Gnedin said.

"But you are conservative with drugs and many of our colleagues are not. What you see is the result of a very liberal dose typical of certain psychiatric practices."

"It's used to treat schizophrenia."

Topolar laughed. "You're an interesting man, my dear Gnedin. Worldly, yet naïve. The drug is used to induce a stupor. It can turn a vital man into a zombie; I personally can attest to its efficacy in this regard."

Gnedin pondered this information. "Could a man walk after such a dose of aminazine?"

The toxicologist energetically scratched his left thigh. "Ordinarily I'd say no, but it depends on several factors. Individual tolerances vary. Food and other substances can affect pharmacological action, slow it, speed it, block it."

"Vodka?"

"The combination would knock a normal man flat on his bloody ass, but each human being is different."

"Could you kill a man with such a combination?"

"Without question. Aminazine and vodka? That would do it for most mortals, even a Russian."

"But this man was apparently walking around under his own power."

"Sometimes I think to myself that biological diversity within the species is proof of a higher power. He may have been ambulatory, but I suspect chemical analysis will show that this would have been temporary."

"Certainly he would have been impaired."

"Hammered, to use the American idiom."

"So it's not unreasonable that an individual in this condition might wander out in front of a vehicle."

Topolar smiled and held up his hands. "Toxicology is my specialty; I concern myself only with molecular behavior." He made his way toward the door, wheezing as he moved, then paused. "It's not every day that the country's top cardiologist can be seen doing autopsies of victims of vehicular mayhem. Be careful, my friend. The moth who flies too close to the flame may get his wings singed."

Gnedin waved him out but the fat man stopped and pointed a cane at him. "Aminazine: confirm that and perhaps I'll think you know enough to warrant listening to advice from a political unreliable."

 MONDAY, FEBRUARY 6, 1961, 11:00 A.M.
Belgrade

The American embassy consisted of several unremarkable structures surrounded by a tall stone wall topped by three strands of concertina wire that angled streetward. There were no trees near the wall and only one entrance, a stone arch with a guardhouse on the left. Two unsmiling Yugoslav soldiers in gray-green uniforms were standing outside, their Czechoslovak rifles slung barrel-down over their left shoulders. At the gate behind the Yugoslavs and inside the compound's perimeter was a U.S. Marine staff sergeant in dress blues, his .45 in a patent-leather holster. Valentine's and Sylvia's credentials were examined at both checkpoints. To enter the building they passed between two short Marine corporals, also in dress blues, frozen at attention, their eyes so unblinking that Valentine wondered if they were real or an unknown taxidermist's ultimate triumph.

The CIA station chief's office was on the second floor of the largest building in the compound. Predictably, his office faced the inner courtyard rather than the street; there was no honor among intelligence services, which unabashedly peeked in strangers' windows with telescopes and long-lens cameras.

A small wooden fence around the receptionist's desk outside Gabler's office had three horizontal bars with evenly spaced vertical posts. Inside were two banks of file cabinets, battleship-gray, with five drawers each, and an adjustable footstool nearby. The secretary had boyishly short hair, a high, shiny forehead, plucked eyebrows, no makeup and long fingernails. Her desk was neat, with yellow pencils laid side by side like ships along a pier, but the length of her fingernails suggested she did little typing. Was she a receptionist or something quite different? In embassies nothing was as it seemed to be; people often had window-dressing titles, masks for their true work. Embassy cover with its entitlement to diplomatic immunity was the ultimate shield.

Sylvia was reading what she saw. Maybe the receptionist was a case officer's wife. Nowadays the Company liked to deploy married couples in deference to the all-too-human need for companionship. The enemy specialized in entrapment—juicy boys and women, take your pick—so the agency gave people their sex on a platter, which was supposed to keep them from wandering to other beds. Still, some needed more than others, so things still went awry despite the soundness of the principle.

"Valentine and Charles," Beau announced to the secretary.

The woman reached for the phone without looking up and punched a button on the console. "They're here." When she reached under the desk a gate in the wooden fence sprang open.

Valentine carefully studied the station chief's office, searching for clues to his personality, but his room was devoid of knickknacks and personal mementos. From this he read the station chief as a careful man who followed regulations and kept everything compartmentalized. On the desk a small lamp with a flexible neck was bent to shine down on a single document. Interpretation: the man liked to focus on one thing at a time. Like most spies, he would keep important facts in his head, not on paper.

"You're a difficult man to see," Valentine said. They had been trying to get an appointment for two days and had met polite resistance from the station chief's secretary.

"Priorities," the man said wearily. "Harry Gabler," he added without offering his hand. He had slicked-back silver hair and a ruddy complexion. "Welcome to the armpit of the world," he went on. His voice was gravelly, he had a nervous tic and he needed a shave. "Wet, miserable Belgrade, where everybody hates everybody. They call it the White City, which is a joke. Gray city, gray people, gray sky. Yugoslavia's not a country; it's a goddamned zoo without cages. Only two kinds of people get sent here: career diplomats who know how to listen and the rare birds who get paid to kick ass. You two would be of the second type."

"We're looking for information," Sylvia said, placing her credentials on the desk.

"Aren't we all." Gabler grunted. "Frash again?"

Valentine checked Sylvia's reaction out of the corner of his eye. "Why do you say 'again'?" she asked.

Gabler leaned back in his chair and crossed his arms. "You're not the first."

"How many?" Sylvia asked.

"Two, back in December."

"Together?"

"Separately. Two, three weeks apart."

Arizona had given them copies of Frash's records. Gabler was sitting rigidly now, and it seemed clear that Albert Frash was not one of his favorite topics. Go slowly, Valentine cautioned himself. "How long have you been here?" he asked.

"Four years."

What was it about Gabler's tone? Pride mixed with anger? Lack of attention from his superiors? Arizona had emphasized the importance of Belgrade as an East-West intelligence crossroad. Valentine sensed an opening and took it. "All four as station chief?"

"Yes."

"Impressive. Big job in a sensitive country."

"Our assets are limited. There are a hell of a lot more substantial operations elsewhere."

"True, but size isn't everything, and sometimes the most sensitive stations have small staffs by design."

"I've accurately described its magnitude. You can draw your own conclusions."

"Frash was assigned here after your arrival."

"Yes."

"He was in Paris as station chief only five months before he was sent here. Any idea why the shift?" The records had told them this much.

"People come and go," Gabler said. "Priorities and assignments change."

"Was Frash a replacement?"

"Not exactly."

"What's that mean?"

Gabler was evasive. "He was here on a special assignment."

"Did he tell you what it was?"

Gabler shook his head slowly. "Only that we would serve as his base."

"Who told you that?"

Gabler jerked his thumb toward the ceiling. "Shit runs downhill."

"You didn't think it unusual?"

"Unusual but not unprecedented. This division spawns a lot of strange shit."

Sylvia interrupted. "But he came out of France, which is in an entirely different division, right?"

"It happens."

"So they sent you an extra man you didn't ask for," Valentine continued.

"I had requested additional resources repeatedly."

"But they turned you down, and then suddenly Frash shows up?"

"More or less."

"He reported to you on this special assignment?" Sylvia asked.

"I won't discuss that." Which probably meant that Frash was independent. Gabler sounded perturbed. Was this a sore point with him?

Valentine raised an eyebrow. "What sort of special assignment?"

"Can't discuss it."

Switch directions. "What kind of a man is he?"

"Quiet."

"That's all? Just quiet?"

"That's it."

Wrong tack. "He showed up same way we did—out of the blue, right?" Gabler was silent. "I don't blame you for feeling jerked around. You have a job to do. Suddenly you have an asset that's not an asset and nobody tells you jackshit. I know, I've been there."

"Save the bullshit," Gabler growled. "In this business you don't expect to know everything."

"Still, I can sympathize. The station chief is responsible for everything. If an asset goes down, you have to reconstruct it. But with Frash they told you nothing, and this is a small operation where people have to back each other up. Am I right?"

Gabler was staring at the wall. Was he reacting to this approach? Keep going, Valentine told himself. Build rapport, level with him. "We're in the same boat; we share the same problem. It's our job to find Frash, but they haven't told us diddley shit either. Feels like our feet are stuck in the mud. We can't move."

"I don't know anything about your mission," the station chief said. "Not my venue."

"We're supposed to find Frash. It's as simple as that."

Gabler didn't look like a believer. "I think there's more to it than that. We got unusually fast visa clearances for you through the Yugos, and from their top echelons. Why all the curveballs for such a straightforward job? It smells."

"I see your point, but maybe the Yugos also want to know what happened to Frash." Arizona had intimated this.

"The whole thing stinks, that's what I say."

Go easy now. "Look, we're in a tough spot. Our people gave us very little to go on. We can't do our jobs unless we have your help."

Gabler made brief eye contact with Valentine and Sylvia, then inhaled deeply. What was there to lose? "Frash kept to himself. He almost never came here. He had a flat in the city, but I think it was only a cover."

"Why do you say that?" Sylvia asked.

"I needed to get hold of him several times and tried calling. Couldn't reach him. After that, I set up a systematic call procedure and worked it thirty days, but never got him even though he was supposedly in and out of the embassy several times."

"Was he close to anyone?"

"Nope. Quiet but intense, like he was wired too tight. Yet cool, with no visible emotions. Good-looking sonuvabitch."

"Any idea what he was doing?"

"As I said, that was none of my business, but several times I heard him refer to Titograd."

"He was working on something there?" Where the hell was Titograd?

"I just heard him mention it. That's all."

"To whom?"

"On the telephone."

Think. "They sent him in to free-lance. Didn't you press for clarification through channels? Weren't you afraid he'd fuck up your own operations?"

"I pressed," Gabler said, his face reddening. "I was instructed to brief him on all ongoing operations, keep him updated and stay the hell out of his way."

"But *you're* the station chief," Sylvia said. It was odd that Gabler would be ordered to share such information; this was way outside normal operating procedure.

"I thought so."

"Strange setup," she said.

"Unique," Gabler agreed.

"When did he disappear?" she asked.

"The last time I saw him was early November of last year."

Three months ago. "Did you conduct your own investigation?"

"Technically he wasn't mine, so his status wasn't my business. But

I looked and filed a report, which was the best I could do under the circumstances; I had no jurisdiction, no idea where to start looking."

"Except Titograd," Valentine said.

"I tried that and got nothing. All we managed to turn up was that he may have made some flights to Paris."

"In November?" Sylvia asked.

"Before that," Gabler said. "I wanted to establish a pattern."

"Evidence?"

"A description of him from assets at the airport. Might have been him, might not. I passed what I had up the line, and that was that. I got two visits in December, and now the two of you show up, which tells me the book's still open."

Arizona had said nothing about any of this, and they had seen no report from Gabler. "This guy is like a shadow," Valentine said.

Gabler rolled his eyes. "Aren't we all?"

25   MONDAY, FEBRUARY 6, 1961, 6:20 P.M.
Mat District, Albania

The sun had dipped behind the jagged ridges of the Qafe e Shtamke mountains to the west, but there remained a distant lavender glow and a current of cool air curling up from the darkness in the gorge. Lejla Llarja could see her breath. Behind her was a slate lip; she had no way to gauge depth but she sensed a precipitous drop and the footing was poor. In front of her were two krulles, mountain houses made of rough stones mortared with mud and reinforced dark crosstimbering. There was a small door in each, ideal for a dwarf, which by design made entry difficult for a normal-sized man. The only windows were more than ten meters aboveground; these were only large enough to accommodate rifles and were easily closed off from the inside with stone plugs. The houses were three-story-high cylindrical towers with their fronts facing the flat ground where Lejla Llarja stood. An Albanian's home was literally his fortress.

She was tired and nervous. Kasi had placed her in this open area and given her clipped instructions, more tactical reminders than clues about what to expect. Examine the area, find solid footing at least one body length in every direction, keep your center of gravity low, your muscles loose and defend your ground no matter what. "Your father's fate rides on your ability, girl."

It was an unnecessary reminder. Since her last meeting with Shehu, Kasi had been working her fourteen hours a day. She had bruises all along her left side from being slammed to the ground during hand-to-hand combat training. Once in a while she managed to use leverage against his superior size and flip him, but such reversals were few and most days he knocked her around until her thoughts were jumbled. It had been different with knife training. He had taught her to parry and thrust and how to reverse roles from target to attacker. She learned slowly and had several superficial nicks on her shoulders and arms as reminders of her deficiencies, but when she had the knife now he was a lot more careful.

Nearly every day they worked on her shooting, the emphasis entirely on rapid fire from the chest with both hands on the weapon, not aiming carefully but blasting away at a straw mannequin eight paces away, trying to get all nine rounds into a paper circle pinned to its chest within ten seconds. When she shot poorly Kasi slapped her to the ground, then picked her up, immediately gave her another clip and ordered her to do it again. "Zen," he said. "Train the body and the mind will obey." She had never been through anything like it.

Twice a day he ran her through the mountains, kicking and slapping her backside with his boot when she began to lag. "How long does this go on?" she screamed at him one afternoon. His answer was a sharp fist to her ear that left her dizzy and nauseated for an hour. With all she had been subjected to, there was no longer any doubt about what would be required as payment for sparing her father's life. She was being trained to kill.

Now she stood in the darkness with a 9 mm automatic pistol in her right hand and a double-edged dagger in a scabbard strapped to her left calf. The pistol felt cold and heavy. Somewhere in the distance she heard dogs being unchained for the night; then she tensed as she heard low growls and sharp barks. She had grown up in cities, but she knew that in the mountains certain dogs were raised brutally, mistreated, starved, chained during the day and set free at night to attack anything that moved. This was the old law: the land belonged to the unchained dogs from an hour after sunset until an hour before sunrise. Anything and anyone that moved in their territory at night was fair game. A dog at night is the same as a man, the law said.

She had no idea where Kasi had gone, though she suspected he was watching from nearby. "You're on your own," he'd told her. "To live or die, I don't care which." Was Shehu here too?

The first attack came from a single animal. It loped toward her from downwind and stopped to growl menacingly, just beyond her sight. A dog's voice, she knew, was no measure of its size or ferocity, though most night dogs tended to be large, muscular and bred to overpower a man with a frontal assault. When the animal became quiet, she knew it was studying her, trying to decide how to attack. She blocked the wind from one ear with her hand in order to hear better and bent her knees to receive the assault. The dog did not announce its charge; rather, it began to circle at a trot, then tightly pivoted and leaped. It was not quick enough. When it jumped, she dropped to one knee, tucked her left elbow into her side, pulled the knife from her boot and held it firmly. She was surprised that the attack seemed to be in slow motion; there was plenty of time for reaction. By comparison, Kasi's moves seemed faster and more frightening. Some days he seemed to be able to strike her at will, but the dog was not as fast.

The animal misjudged her position and came floating in too high. Lejla was certain she could feel its body heat and smell its foul, matted coat as it came closer. When it was nearly over her, she twisted her left shoulder away and delivered a waist-high slash with the knife, striking something solid. The animal landed hard to her left and squealed once before she struck again with the knife, this time at the throat.

For a second she stared at the steam rising from the dead animal's fur, but the next assault came almost immediately. This time there were three dogs side by side, and only a growl by one of the attackers saved her. She stepped toward them, fired the pistol four times, aiming at their sounds, but was knocked down by a heavy blow to her right side. The dogs howled and snapped and she felt pain in her right shoulder, but she managed to roll away and get back to her feet, maintaining her crouch. An animal with glowing red eyes was beside her, looking up. She shot once at the eyes and they disappeared. She backed up and felt pain in several places, but oddly enough it seemed distant, as if it belonged to someone else. Strangest of all, she felt calm.

Were they all down? How many more? She kept turning her head to look for movement, trying to compensate for poor night vision. What did dogs see in the darkness? Details? Heat outlines? Black and white?

There was a new sound now from her left, the opposite direction of the initial charge. Whining. No, she corrected herself, it was whimpering. A whimpering dog. Moving? Yes, but slowly. Crawling? Did she wait or go for it? Attack the attacker, Kasi had thundered. *You* set the rules, reverse roles. Don't wait; go toward it.

She moved toward the sound, then saw a lean, light-colored cur on its belly, inching forward, its bushy tail swinging rhythmically from side to side. Submission? She relaxed and stepped toward the animal, then stopped. There were nothing but enemies in the dark, Kasi had said. How many shots were left in the automatic? Kasi's voice again: Always count. Four the first time. Then one. Five total. Four left in the clip; a second clip in her left jacket pocket, left side. Keep spare clips in high front pockets, not low or in trousers; the higher they are, the less likely they are to be lost. Change clips now? The dog was closer now, panting, wiggling with anticipation, the movements of a young animal, but when she feinted toward it, it lifted its head suddenly, snarled and gathered itself for a leap. She calmly shot twice, killing it in place, then removed the clip, shoved a new one into the grip, chambered a round and listened for more attackers. The night was silent. She moved toward the bodies of the other animals and found one of them trying to drag itself away. She killed it with the knife, not wanting to waste bullets, then squatted to get a better view of the area.

"To kill a beast in the darkness is easier than killing a man in daylight," Kasi said from the shadows. "A dog has no ability to plan or to develop alternatives. The human mind is always superior to animal instinct."

"Is it finished?" she asked.

"It's never finished," Kasi said. He sounded amused.

Lejla collapsed. When she regained consciousness she was on a wooden table in a cold room. Her shoulder felt heavy, her left leg stiff. She looked at her left thigh and saw a line of jagged flesh pulled together with crisscrosses of black thread, the ends of the sutures snipped off and standing up like new shoots in a garden. The sheet under her was blood-soaked and damp. Where were her clothes? She was sleepy. Had they drugged her?

"She did well," she heard Kasi say.

"With dogs," Mehmet Shehu whispered back. "What about infection?"

"Always possible, but I cleaned her wounds thoroughly. They're deep but clean, and there's no muscle damage. She's young and she'll heal fast, but there'll be a scar."

"Unimportant."

"A shame to ruin such young flesh."

Shehu ignored the comment. "How long until she can function again?"

"Two weeks."

"Make it ten days. You're going to take a trip."

"More training?"

"No," Shehu said. "It's time we began sending some signals to our enemies."

26 TUESDAY, FEBRUARY 7, 1961, 10:15 A.M.
Moscow

When the telephone rang, Nikita Khrushchev stared at the several telephones on the credenza behind his desk and tried to figure out which one to pick up. There were seven of the devices, but only the black one had a receiver and body that matched. One a week went on the blink and the replacement parts were always a different color. How was it that capitalist engineers could route multiple telephone lines into a single device but Russian specialists could not? When the army was reduced he would build up production of consumer goods, and telephones would have a high priority.

"What?" He said into the receiver. There was a buzz. There was always a buzz on the line.

"Gnedin. Your man was injected with what should have been a lethal dose of aminazine. His blood levels of the drug and of vodka were enough to mummify Amenhotep."

"This was the cause of death?"

"Should have been, would have been. Who can say? The cause of death was a broken neck and massive trauma. A vehicle, I would say. Maybe he stumbled into the Chaika lane."

"Odd coincidence," the General Secretary said.

"Coincidence is a political concept," the doctor said, "not medical. You wanted the cause of death, and now you have it."

Khrushchev replaced the receiver and rubbed the mole on his cheek. In the Soviet Union there was no such thing as coincidence. Trubkin had been murdered, clear and simple. The Lumbas business had been one thing but with this death it was something more, and he was sure in his gut that it was the start of something, not the end point. A wolf pack began its hunt long before its prey could detect the stalk. In his belly he knew now that he was being targeted for something, but the hunters and their game were hidden. Who? he asked himself. *Who?* Why was obvious; somebody else wanted power. It was always so. But there were ways to deal with such problems, he told himself. Stalin's ways.

27 | TUESDAY, FEBRUARY 7, 1961, 12:45 P.M.
Belgrade

They were installed in a first-floor flat in a nondescript block of apartment buildings in the northern part of the city. It was a cramped apartment with a short entry hall, a kitchen, two narrow bedrooms and a bath. The flat was poorly furnished and dimly lit with fringed red shades. There were no chain locks on the door, so they rigged a chair for security. It wouldn't stop anyone, but it might slow them down. Valentine wondered if he still had the reflexes necessary to react. It was too late to worry now; in time, he would know.

Gabler had given them two black shaving kits containing two .32 caliber automatics with no serial numbers, several twelve-shot clips and four screw-on silencers. These were a professional's tools, the silencers made of ordinary washers glued together, good for only a few rounds each. Sylvia explained, "After you use the silencer for a few rounds, you bash it on the wall, then scatter the washers so that there's no evidence." They set the weapons aside, unpacked their suitcases, opened their briefcases and reviewed what they knew.

Frash had an interesting but unremarkable record. Born in 1929 in Boston. Attended Brampton Academy in Massachusetts and graduated from Lafferty Academy, an exclusive Manhattan prep school. A degree in Balkan history from Boston College, cum laude. Recruited into the Company in February 1951; assigned to West Germany that fall. Transferred to Cyprus in the spring of 1953, then back to Washington, D.C., that same summer. Short tour also unusual. Several assignments over the next four years: Holland, Belgium, Rome. In January 1960 moved to Paris as CIA chief of station—young for that, only thirty-one; five months later went to Belgrade as a legal resident, not station chief. Demotion? Single, apparently never married. Expert in judo and jujitsu. Fluent in French, German and Russian, with passable Italian. Parents deceased, no known siblings. Bank savings of $17,000 and four hundred shares of IBM common stock, substantial but not excessive.

"Nothing much," Sylvia said. "Obviously smart, well-educated, good record, but no detail on the sorts of things he's done for the Company. A few months in Germany and a few months in Cyprus. Doing what?" She made a note to herself. "Then a string of unremarkable assignments before the promotion to Paris, a real plum even with de Gaulle in place. But only five months there, then a transfer to Belgrade. Why? And not as chief of station. His choice or the Company's? Did he screw up in Paris? Then after fifteen months in Belgrade, poof, he disappears."

Valentine frowned and tapped his pencil against his cheek. "We need more details on this guy. Who were his parents? What were his politics? Never married. Did he have girlfriends? Or boyfriends? That could be an angle."

"Being single is not exactly abnormal," Sylvia said. "Single does not mean homosexual."

"He's thirty-two and has never married. Okay, not abnormal but not common either, so we flag it."

"Maybe he likes the freedom."

"If it's that simple, fine. The point is, we need to know one way or the other. Who in the Company knows him? What kind of a man is he? When I look at this"—Valentine held up the typed biography—"I get a lot more questions than answers. Our job is to find him, but we don't even have a lousy photo. With what we know right now we couldn't locate him if he was sitting on our crapper."

"I suppose I get to do the legwork?"

Valentine laughed. Sylvia was wearing a black sweater and straight gray skirt that tended to ride high when she crossed her legs. "You said it, not me."

She ignored the innuendo. "Arizona can help get us more information. Given the time Frash has been missing, we have to assume he's been taken out, but as it stands now, we don't even know where to start looking. You can't find a needle in a haystack until you at least find the haystack. We need to know why he was in Paris such a short time. It's strange to promote a man, then move him so quickly."

"What did Arizona tell you before we left?" Valentine asked.

"That Frash had been sent here to run a very special asset," Sylvia said.

"I heard the same line, but when I pressed him he clammed up."

"To pull him out of a station-chief position suggests it was something fairly spectacular."

"It would help a bunch if we had some details."

"Security of the asset comes first," she said.

"My only rule is that there ain't no rules."

"It's a different trade now. Boxes within boxes, nothing ever in focus for very long."

"All the more reason not to be saddled with rules," Valentine answered. "If you have rules, you can be damned sure that the other side knows them, which puts us at a disadvantage. If Frash is so all-fired important, why send us? It would make more sense to send somebody in his chain of command, somebody already in the operational stream."

"Arizona sent others," Sylvia said in his defense.

"Fine, but why not keep them on it?"

"Maybe they are. Maybe we're redundant: one team within channels, one outside. There's some logic to that, and it wouldn't be unusual."

"He didn't tell us about the others, or that there had been evidence of Frash going back and forth to Paris, or that Gabler filed his own investigation report."

"Maybe he already knows and our job is to verify—like a blinded experiment. It boils down to compartmentalization."

Valentine opened his last pack of cigarettes. "You a big believer in logic?" he asked Sylvia.

She nodded. "Aren't you?"

"Hardly ever."

28	WEDNESDAY, FEBRUARY 8, 1961, 9:30 P.M. *Moscow*

For two years the monthly journey from Vinnitsa to Moscow had been a drudgery that Colonel Bailov accepted as part of the job. During most of this time he resented the trips because they took him away from his troops, but that was B.R. Before Raya. As commanding officer of the First Independent Spetsnaz Brigade, Bailov had landed the dream job of a professional soldier. With the exception of his monthly journeys to Moscow to confer with his superiors in the Fifth Directorate of the GRU, his time belonged to himself and his regiment, and what a regiment it was! *Before* Raya. Not that the regiment had lost importance since she came into his life, but he now understood that a life that was only work left a lot to be desired. Raya provided something that had been missing for too long.

In 1947 Bailov had been recruited by the Glavnoye Razvedyvatelnoye Upravlenie (military intelligence), and three years later he was sent to the Military Diplomatic Academy in Moscow. There the "elephants," as the instructors were called by their students, imparted the basic education needed by those who would divest the enemies of the Soviet Union of their military secrets. Much of what he learned in the program was new and interesting, but from time to time he was reminded of what he had been through with Petrov. In 1952 he graduated, and after another year of special GRU training, he was posted to Spetsnaz, a new organization.

The First Brigade was an experiment. Ordinarily such units were attached as companies or battalions to regular Red Army divisions or embassies, but various wars of liberation in the world had persuaded Soviet military leaders that elite, independent brigades might one day prove useful in foreign interventions. In his new career, Bailov had acquitted himself with confidence, enthusiasm and intelligence, and under his leadership the First Brigade was quickly molded into a hard-bitten elite unit, envied by other Spetsnaz groups and loathed by the regular army.

As commanding officer of the First Brigade, Bailov was required to be in Moscow one week of every month. Usually he departed on a Sunday, worked at GRU headquarters in Moscow Monday through Wednesday and caught a return flight on Thursday or Friday. For two years these monthly trips had been without incident, but seven months ago fate had intervened.

It had been a Thursday in a week without rain; the parks were filled with scantily dressed Muscovites soaking up the rare sun, and elderly members of fishing clubs were on their wooden perches in the Moscow River. Bailov even remembered the time: 10:00 A.M. He had planned to return to Vinnitsa on an afternoon flight, but some idiot in the Fifth Directorate had convinced the GRU hierarchy that Spetsnaz training should include a specially developed survival course, and parts of the study had been given to several officers, including Bailov. Rather than wait for his next trip to Moscow to begin the assignment, he delayed his departure till Friday night. He had learned long ago to finish promptly all tasks from Moscow Center; many of them never panned out, at least not into anything he could detect, but he always got his job done in less than the assigned time. It had occurred to him that some of the tasks might be tests of his dependability, so he took them seriously; those at the top were always looking downward, suspicious of ambitious subordinates. It was not that he hoped for a higher position; all he wanted to do was hold on to what he had, which was more than most Russians could dream of.

It was pure chance that he had met Raya at all; normally she worked at the library on Tuesday mornings and all day Wednesdays. But someone was ill, or claimed to be ill, which was more likely, and she was at the library at a time when she normally wouldn't have been. His task was to compile a list of all the edible birds in southern Russia. He guessed that a dozen men in his brigade could give him the information, but why take a chance even with a half-witted assignment?

Bailov's first impression of Raya Yermolaevna Orlava was nothing

96

dramatic. She stood behind an oak counter. Short brown hair, unbecoming glasses with heavy, dark frames. A sleeveless black dress of lightweight cloth, no jewelry, no cosmetics, her fingernails trimmed straight across like a man's. He was wearing a summer-weight uniform, his tunic covered with ribbons, and above these his paratroop wings. When she looked up at him he had the feeling that her mind was still partly on the journal she had been reading. "The military section is in another building," she said. Her voice was strong, accustomed to exercising authority.

"Birds," he said.

"Birds?" Her eyebrows lifted almost imperceptibly.

"I'm interested in birds indigenous to southern Russia."

She pursed her lips and stood, her chair creaking as she rose. "A field guide?"

"I don't know exactly. Something comprehensive. I'm assigned to make a report on edible species."

She grimaced. "Very few ornithological studies address the edibility of species."

"There must be something"—he lifted his hands in a sweeping gesture—"among all this."

"Size is not an indication of quality," she said flatly as she moved around the desk. "How much time do you have?"

"I leave Moscow tomorrow night."

"I have my own time constraints," the woman announced. "I'm not a librarian."

"But you were behind the desk."

"I am the curator of the ornithological collection, comrade, and a professor."

He apologized. If she would point him to a librarian, he would take no more of her time.

"There is no one else," she said. "I'm alone. If you wish to be helped, it will have to be me." She eyed his epaulets. "Colonel, isn't it?"

"Bailov," he said. "Communications."

"A colonel of communications with parachute wings who has an interest in edible birds?"

When he laughed at the description she smiled back. "I didn't choose the task; it was given to me. A soldier takes orders."

Her mood suddenly seemed more relaxed. "Could you come back this evening, Comrade Colonel? At six? I cannot get to this immediately, but perhaps there will be some time this afternoon. I will try, that's all I can promise. Meanwhile, you can visit some bookstores. The government publishes a variety of excellent field guides; I have edited several myself, though my specialties lie beyond southern Russia."

When Bailov returned he found her at her desk, which was still covered with piles of papers. "Any luck?" she asked.

He showed her the palms of his hands. "Shopping for books is like shopping for meat: long lines and sad tales of 'You should have been here last week.' "

"I'm not surprised, but there is an alternative," she offered, her voice taking on a sudden edge.

"What would that be?"

"I don't want to inconvenience you."

"Tell me the alternative and let me assess the degree of inconvenience."

"I have a collection in my flat."

"Won't your husband mind?" A contrived question, but he needed to know; he didn't involve himself with married women, which was more a reflection of his pragmatism than a moral stand.

"I have no husband. Under other circumstances you could pick them up tomorrow, but I have classes to teach in the morning at the university and it would not be possible for me to come here first and arrive at my class on time."

He agreed to go with her, thinking that his bird search had taken an odd twist.

Her flat was on the edge of the Zemlyanoi Gorod, in a seven-story apartment building, one of hundreds of characterless tenements built by Khrushchev, and still so new that there was no stench. A walk-up, naturally, and she lived on the top floor, but he noticed that she was not winded by the climb. She was more fit than he would have guessed, and this piqued his interest, though he was not sure why. Certainly not because she was his type; she was too scholarly, too accustomed to control.

The size of the flat stunned Bailov. As a brigade commander, his own quarters were generous, five meters by six, but her flat was at least twice that, a space that ordinarily would be occupied by two or three families. There was a shallow balcony across the front and a kitchen, parlor and bedroom. There was even a private bath; most of Moscow's buildings had community latrines. The furniture was of modern Finnish design, and there were thick throw rugs everywhere. Two walls of bookcases were stuffed with volumes, and more books and journals were stacked on the floor. Scores of potted plants filled the room and balcony—the effect was that of a dense, flowering jungle seven stories above the polluted city air.

"You live *alone*?"

"Of course." She seemed amused. "I am a candidate member of the Academy of Sciences. You are a colonel; surely you understand perquisites. I've always understood that high military rank carries many privileges."

"It does, but not like this."

"Make yourself comfortable," she said. "There is champagne in the refrigerator—French, not Armenian. And vodka, of course."

The refrigerator was nearly as tall as he was, and it was full! What sort of perverse system enabled a professor of birds to live in such luxury? And a woman at that!

If all this was not enough, Bailov was stunned when his professor reappeared. Gone were the harsh clothes of a curator; standing before him was the most beautiful woman he had ever seen. She wore a white silk blouse with puffed sleeves, a triple strand of large pearls and a full red silk skirt, hemmed at the knees. Her lips were painted red, and a gold brooch in the shape of a peacock nestled at the base of her neck.

"Metamorphosis complete," she declared. "In the avian world females generally lack the flamboyance of males. Much better to be Homo sapiens, where the contrary holds true." She made eye contact with him and grinned. "I assume by your silence that you approve, Colonel."

They drank Stolichnaya vodka, the brand reserved ordinarily for export to the West and with none of the odor of cheaper brands, which clung to your breath for days. Then she filled his lap with books, pivoted so sharply that her skirt floated briefly up to her thighs and went off to the kitchen.

The meal she served was unusual, like everything else about her: steamed carrots with morels, paper-thin slices of dark bread, small medallions of venison sautéed in real butter, a French Burgundy, Georgian cashews covered with clear, fruity dressing and brandy that scoured his tongue. It was more food and drink than he had taken at one sitting in years, yet he felt neither bloated nor stuffed. Afterward she stacked the dishes in the sink, then led him onto the balcony, where they watched the sun set in a pink sky.

They did not talk until it was dark. At last she rose from her canvas chair and moved to the doorway. "Are you married?" she asked.

"No."

"Do you visit Moscow often?"

"At least once a month."

She disappeared into the bedroom. "Brief trips?" she called out. Her voice had taken on an entirely different tone.

"A few days at a time."

"Do you mind all of these questions?"

"No."

There was a long silence. "Colonel, do you have a name?"

"I am Taras Ivanovich Bailov."

"A sturdy name, Taras Ivanovich. Your age?"

"Forty-three this year."

"Ah," her voice said. "Lucky for me: men don't become interesting until they're at least forty."

Then she was in the doorway, barefoot and clad only in black underwear, her figure much fuller than he had envisioned. "Raya Yermolaevna Orlava, age thirty-four. Where do you stay in Moscow?"

"A barracks for senior officers."

"Will you be missed if you don't return tonight?"

"No."

She moved to him and gnawed lightly on his upper arm, her tongue hot. "Good," she said, imitating his guttural manner of speaking.

They had been together eight times since that night, nearly eight weeks of living as husband and wife, which is how he had come to think of it. Raya never said how she viewed it, but it didn't matter. She never met him at the airport when he arrived and never accompanied him there when he departed. When he was in Moscow they usually spent most evenings in her flat listening to jazz, dancing, eating, talking, making love. She had a wide range of knowledge and interests and had lived an entirely different life than he had.

With Raya's help Bailov finished his report on edible birds and in the process earned a written commendation from the chief of the GRU's Fifth Directorate.

Now he was approaching her building on a Monday, her day off. He ran up the stairs and used his key to let himself inside. He was six hours behind schedule because the plane had encountered an engine problem; he knew she'd already be in bed. He undressed quickly and got under the covers with her. As her arms slid around his neck and pulled him toward her, she licked his chest and shoved her pelvis toward him. He tried immediately to enter her, but she pushed him away. "Slowly, Taras Ivanovich, always slowly. Only Homo sapiens is capable of prolonging pleasure."

 THURSDAY, FEBRUARY 9, 1961, 2:00 A.M.
Frankfurt

The Kaiserhaus hostel was ideal; situated across the river from what remained of the old city, it was full of students with wrinkled shirts and canvas trousers, as well as a motley assortment of other drifters traveling more on wits than on financial resources. To check in all you needed was a name, not even your own. Frash paid extra for a room to himself; this momentarily seemed to raise the clerk's suspicions, but he quickly explained that he was a travel writer working on a book about low-budget travel in Germany and wanted privacy to work.

"*Sehr gut,*" the clerk said, "but if you entertain in your room, will you please inform me; I will be obliged to charge double occupancy."

"I need privacy," Frash repeated.

"Privacy serves many needs," the clerk said with a straight face.

The room was on the corner of the fourth floor and overlooked a busy boulevard strung with *Apfelwein* taverns. A routine asserted itself. He awoke early and walked the streets before the Germans were up. He read several newspapers each morning and evening in different taverns, listening to the Germans debate politics—not Hitler because all the Nazis had evaporated in 1945, but modern politics, their fear of the Russians, and especially their concerns about the ability of the new American president to effectively counter the unpredictable Khrushchev. Their skepticism about Kennedy was strong; who better than Germans would know the insidiousness of Rome and its puppets? His mother knew it too.

Frash slept a lot and dreamed intermittently. He was six when Ali had killed for the first time. The dreams had a full ration of passion, including the fear of being discovered, but this had never happened. Sometimes the dreams seemed too real to be mere dreams; they were more like memories, full ones lacking no details. The fear of killing was worse than its actual doing; the act itself was quite simple. In some dreams he buried stained underwear in soup cans. His mother was naked, standing with her hands flat against a white marble wall, a red hood over her head, legs apart, rump presented. A long line of strangers took turns with her; he was way back in the line and never seemed to get closer, but he tried to be patient. A priest said a Mass from a pulpit built of human skulls with the initials J.F.K. painted on them. God's will, the priest intoned. Will what? Frash asked the dream, but there was no answer. He sweated through his sheets every night. Why had Myslim forsaken him? A half-brother is no brother at all, he reminded himself.

30   SUNDAY, FEBRUARY 12, 1961, 7:45 P.M. *Falls Church, Virginia*

Arizona held a cocktail party at his farm in Falls Church every Sunday at 5:00 P.M. A small herd of Asian spotted deer wandered the grounds like delicate ghosts, begging handouts. The guests represented a wide assortment of friends and acquaintances from diverse backgrounds; what they all had in common was that each represented some degree of power and influence, which meant that each had information to be traded or stolen outright. At these gatherings Arizona wore a string tie, western-cut suit, a shirt with turquoise and silver buttons, a Stetson hat and rattlesnake-skin boots with genuine western toes and heels. He worked his parties like a pickpocket, snatching bits and pieces of information he would later lace together.

It was no secret that Arizona was CIA, but his title was vague and suggested that he was some sort of mid-level personnel administrator. In truth he was the number three man in the Directorate of Operations, or DO, and was tied to virtually every covert action undertaken by the Company. Specifically he was charged with coordinating operations that required the resources of more than one of the directorate's geographic divisions—the sort of missions he called "mixers." He was a man with the most lethal form of power: that which is unknown.

Arizona had two things to accomplish tonight. The first he took care of almost immediately. Richard Warwick was fifty-eight, bald, thin, with feline features; he looked more like a high-school physics teacher than the *Washington Post* reporter responsible for intelligence reporting, a new beat established in the wake of the U-2 disaster. Warwick had an impressive academic background: a B.A. in history from Dartmouth, Harvard Law, a master's in journalism from Columbia. He had been a war correspondent for *Life* in Europe, and had been with the troops that liberated Dachau. After Korea he had written a series of articles for the *Post* on brainwashing, which was based on interviews with dozens of former prisoners of war. The pieces were later expanded into a book that won him a Pulitzer and rode the bestseller lists for nearly a year. He was also an ardent liberal, which meant that the new administration could exploit him.

When the Russians had shot down the U-2 a year before, Warwick had assailed the Eisenhower administration with an acrimonious eight-part series on the CIA. Until then the Company had enjoyed virtual anonymity. Because of Warwick, the agency's initials were said to stand for "Caught In the Act." With Kennedy in office Warwick's attitude toward the Company had softened, though Arizona suspected that the reporter might be reserving judgment only until he was convinced that Kennedy could handle his new responsibility. Warwick had even made noises about a "partnership" between the press and the government in matters of national security. He and the president's press secretary were buddies from way back; Pierre Salinger had been instructed to keep his lines of communications open so that when the need arose they could funnel information to Warwick. They had arranged to have him invited to one of Kennedy's private White House soirees. For now the reporter was playing along, but if he suddenly tried to revert to his predatory ways

Arizona was certain that Kennedy could easily corral him. If nothing else, the president could charm people, especially women, but he was no slouch with men either, and in particular he could work journalists like a maestro.

Arizona took a fresh martini to Warwick, who was in a corner of the den scanning the other guests. "Fresh fuel, Richard."

"Nice party. Appreciate the invite."

"No problem, pard. Lots of good folks here."

Warwick looked tense. "Is there someplace where we can talk privately?" he asked.

Arizona led him to a side patio. Warwick held the martini glass but did not drink from it. "I have it from good sources that you people are training Cuban expats in some sort of brigade. Word is that they're going against Castro soon. Code name's Operation Zapata." The reporter watched for a reaction.

Arizona grinned. "Lots of rumors in this town." Warwick had a solid source, but the information was dated, which meant his source was outside the stream. The operation's name had been changed to Trinidad several weeks before and would soon be changed again to Pluto. The man was fishing.

"Infantry training in Guatemala, a squadron of B-26s in Nicaragua and a radio station on Swan Island, which is in Castro's backyard," Warwick said. "Will there be air support for the invasion?"

Shit. He had most of it right. Where had he gotten this information? "I just push paper, Richard. I'm an accountant, actually. It's donkey work but somebody's gotta do it. If you've got questions you ought to direct them to the White House or the agency's public information people."

"You can count on it," Warwick said. As an afterthought, "Off the record I'm opposed in principle to such interventions, but not if Jack thinks it's essential and if it's not some half-ass Robin Hood operation. I say do it right or don't bother."

Warwick was a pompous ass, hooked without even knowing it. "Talk to the White House," Arizona repeated. He'd have to get word to the president's people right away. When Warwick swooped in, it would be up to Kennedy to deflect him.

"We ought not to involve ourselves in other people's wars," Warwick continued. "Korea should have taught us that. The difference here is that we're talking about a situation much closer to home, so there are extenuating circumstances."

"You write it the way you see it, Richard. That's your job." Reporters made the intelligence game a lot harder than it needed to be. He grabbed the arm of a woman who lived up the road and pushed her at

Warwick. "Ask him about brainwashing," he told her. Though it was cool, she was dressed in pink pedal pushers, black pumps and a strapless top designed to display maximum cleavage. If Warwick showed the slightest inclination she'd drag him into the nearest bush and bang his brains out, her proclivities for such sorties having been well established in the neighborhood.

Warwick was jabbering with animation when Arizona looked back, and his martini was nearly gone. He made a mental note: when Warwick is fishing he doesn't drink. He had a catalog of such behaviors in his head. Kennedy tapped his teeth when he was angry; Hoover looked people in the eye when he lied, which was as often as he told the truth. The Dulles brothers tugged on their earlobes when they wanted presentations speeded up. When you learned to read them, such behavior spoke louder and more clearly than words.

So Warwick was digging into the Cuban operation. Depending on how insistent he was, Dulles could suggest to Kennedy that he pull the reporter inside and offer an exclusive in return for holding the story. One way to neutralize a journalist was to make him part of the game. You could always count on the greed to get a big fat story.

Arizona checked his watch, then walked out to the stable behind the house. The meeting was scheduled for 9:00 P.M. in the tack room. Several of the horses nickered as he passed their stalls. The man in the tack room was blond, fit, an even six feet and 160 pounds, built like a swimmer, his physique flat rather than angular. At thirty-nine Dr. Lewis Venema looked like an advertising executive or the leading man in a soap opera. He wore a charcoal-gray three-piece suit, and his black shoes gleamed. He was the sort of man cursed with the kind of sheer physical beauty that made it difficult for others to take him seriously.

"Lew," Arizona greeted him. "Glad you could make it."

Venema raised his glass of champagne in mock salute. "Couldn't miss one of your legendary parties," he said. "Fascinating social dynamics. Like predators sizing up each other at a water hole. A gathering of mind-fucks."

"I'm not interested in that shit," Arizona snapped.

"Insight is where one finds it," Venema answered pleasantly.

"We've got a problem with Frash."

Venema was a psychiatrist who taught at Georgetown, maintained a private practice and, most important, was a special consultant for a handful of high-ranking officials at the Company. It had been Venema who had developed the so-called instruments used to assess the suitability of candidates for CIA employment. More and more these written and oral tests were seen as key tools in hiring decisions, and in one case, that of Frash, had been the *only* basis.

Arizona had found Frash and seen potential, but it had been Venema's idea to do only a minimal background investigation and to rely almost exclusively on the psychological instruments he had created. These tests focused on various situations designed to predict the behavior of candidates in certain situations. Venema's professional opinion was that past behavior counted for more than motivation did. Most people couldn't articulate *why* they acted in certain ways, only that they *had,* so why waste time groping for motives? If the agency could hire on psychological testing alone, it could save millions of dollars now dedicated to background investigations. This would enable them to apply the saved resources to operations, and to bring new blood into the Company without touching base with the FBI and various police agencies. This approach, Venema argued convincingly, could give the Company added insulation for its personnel, which in turn meant increased security. It had been too tempting to pass up, and Arizona had agreed reluctantly to hiring Frash as the test case for this unorthodox hypothesis.

In any event the CIA's interest in psychology had historical roots. During World War II the OSS had used psychiatrists and doctors to construct a profile of Adolf Hitler, and it had proved itself as a predictive instrument. By comparison, the tests Venema was using made the OSS effort look childish, a Model T next to a Jaguar.

"What sort of problem?"

"Can't find him."

"Not necessarily a problem. What evidence is there?"

Arizona tapped his belly. "The only evidence I need is rumbling around in here."

"Why call me?"

"He's your creation."

The psychiatrist smiled. "When there's pressure, pronouns get altered. *Our* creation," he reminded his host, "not mine alone."

"Which is why we're going to do something about it. Frash is gone and we need to find him. You're going back and vet the bastard, but this time by the book."

"You have investigators who specialize in such things. It's not my field."

"If he's gone sour, we have a problem. You said to hire him, so you find out who and what he is." Arizona was shaking.

Venema set down his glass. "I can't just drop everything. I have other obligations."

"Find the time," Arizona barked as he stalked out of the tack room.

WEDNESDAY, FEBRUARY 15, 1961, 10:25 A.M.
Belgrade

The Prince Marko coffee house had a certain Texas style, meaning that it defied most standards of good taste, which was why Valentine liked it. It had high ceilings and narrow, lead-glass windows, but little light came in because sleet was falling from swirling gray clouds. Inside the front entrance was a five-foot-high statue of the establishment's namesake. The bronze and enamel likeness of the famous prince had a bushy mustache, black eyes, heavy eyebrows, prominent cheekbones, a fur hat and a tunic of gray wolf skins.

A bearded waiter came over and said something in a language Valentine did not understand. "American," Valentine said.

The man nodded and shifted to a crude English. "Legend," he said. "Prince Marko and spirits are the same. His horse has name of Sarac and can speak. Marko and Sarac drinking wine happily together many times. Sarac is fastest horse of all. Together they fight Turks." The waiter snarled as he spit out the name of the historical enemy of all Balkan peoples. "Marko," he concluded by holding up three fingers, "three hundred years when he die. Very old," he added; then, making a fist and stiffening his forearm, "but still very good with womans."

Valentine smiled. In truth Marko had been overwhelmed by the Turks and had become their vassal. Later he led military operations for them against Christians, just as some Serbs had joined the Nazis and turned on their own countrymen, yet he was credited with providing the example that spawned Serbian independence. Somehow the statue reminded him of the elusive Albert Frash. How much of a gap would there be between what Frash was and what he was supposed to be?

Valentine sat in an upholstered chair near a window and nursed a cup of Turkish coffee. Sylvia had gone to the embassy to find out about access to the Company's computer. Every piece of information collected by the CIA was in the central data bank; the Russians had their own device, which served the same purpose, but theirs was considerably larger, originally bought from IBM. Sylvia hoped the computer would cough up more data on Frash, but she also suspected that only Arizona could access the information.

There were holes in Frash's service record; all the time was generally accounted for, but the details were sparse. Were all records like this? Sylvia didn't know; she had never seen her own. Frash had been in Paris for five months, then moved to Belgrade and an entirely different division, the most secret and powerful Soviet–East Europe group that Company people called "S.E." What sort of asset would warrant such attention? A related question: Who was Frash's case officer? Given the circumstances, Sylvia was certain that the control would be special and high in rank—maybe Arizona himself, given his interest in Frash, but he had neglected to tell them this. Why? Most important, why did the Company—or at least Arizona—want a retread like Valentine to investigate Frash's disappearance? It didn't make sense.

Valentine was on his third cup of coffee when Sylvia walked into the café and looked around. Her hair was wet and matted, and she blew on her hands to warm them. Spotting him, she walked over and slumped in a chair next to him.

"Get through?" he asked.

She shook her head. "I saw Gabler. Said he doesn't have access to the computer; all requests have to go through the home office. He also said he's been doing a lot of thinking about us and has decided that it looks to him as if we're just as out of it on Frash as he is. Our lack of information sticks in his craw because it goes against SOP. It's his view that Frash somehow never added up. It's not like the Company to give somebody such a long leash."

"You agree?"

"Most of my experience is in a different theater of operation. We're usually on short lines, with back-up and control always nearby. Frash's freedom is entirely outside my experience, but that doesn't mean anything. S.E. has its own ways and runs a closed shop."

"Which means?"

"That Gabler's decided to get off the fence." She put a standard business envelope in front of Valentine. It contained a typewritten document with handwritten editing marks. "Filed today by Reuters based on an Albanian Press Agency report broadcast on Radio Tirana."

Valentine read slowly. Enver Hoxha, the General Secretary of the Albanian Workers Party, had alleged U.S. complicity in a plot to overthrow his regime. According to Hoxha, the governments of Yugoslavia and Greece had conspired with the American Sixth Fleet and groups of Albanian traitors, all of whom had been arrested and would be tried according to Albanian law. The dictator accused President Kennedy of "preparing for the Third World War." The coup attempt was said to have occurred "recently," but the report offered no specific date.

"So?"

"A gift from Harry," Sylvia said.

"Harry?" Valentine arched an eyebrow.

"You can wipe that look off your face," she said with disgust. "Harry says the Albanians make this sort of wild-ass claim from time to time; usually it's rhetorical fog used as an excuse to kill Hoxha's latest political foes."

"Why tell us about this one?"

"Last summer Harry's people reported a buildup in weapons in Kosovo Province, which is right on the border. Nearly a million Albanians there, a natural conduit for trouble in both directions."

"Related to this?" Valentine asked, pointing to the wire story.

"Someplace between maybe and probably. Usually, Harry says, the would-be invaders have loose tongues. Last summer their usual sources disappeared or went mute. This was the tip-off that maybe something was simmering."

"What's all this got to do with Frash?"

"Timing. He showed up, and shortly after that there was action in Kosovo. You can't ignore the obvious."

"Coincidence."

"What have we got to rule it out?"

Valentine mulled it over. They knew Frash was handling an important asset, either sent from Paris to do the job, or, he suddenly realized, perhaps because it began in Paris and moved to Yugoslavia. "Would the Company back that sort of thing?" he asked, pointing at the story.

Sylvia knew about Cuba and what was scheduled there. "Wouldn't rule it out," she said, though the strategic significance of an Albanian operation eluded her.

"The Albanians are just a bunch of pissants."

"They fought Hitler to a standstill," Sylvia reminded him.

Awakenings

It was a clear, blue day, the temperature so low that snowflakes sparkled like gemstones and snapped underfoot. Petrov was in the exercise area, his arms parallel to the ground, flapping and twisting like a flightless bird. He exercised every day, two hours in the morning, two hours in the afternoon. Sometimes Melko joined him for the afternoon session, but the other *urki* regarded exercise as purposeless and avoided it on principle.

Once in a while Lt. Col. Kurile Valinchuk, the camp commander, walked with Petrov. Valinchuk was in his late forties, badly overweight, an alcoholic, short, with his head shaved bald, bad teeth and a low voice that sounded as if it were filtered through coarse gravel. He had been a hero at Stalingrad, and for this the Red Army kept him on, the military's version of patronage to those who delivered when it mattered most.

But Petrov preferred to exercise alone. Compared with most facilities in the gulag system, Camp No. 9 was spacious, its population small for the available space. In some camps two hundred men were packed into a barracks no bigger than what they had for a mere three dozen.

This morning was especially beautiful. Several ptarmigan in their winter-white plumage were lined up under the bottom strand of the barbed wire. The guards in the corner were apparently sunstruck because ptarmigan foolish enough to venture into the open were usually shot immediately and cooked and eaten soon thereafter.

Petrov was within ten minutes of finishing his walk when he sensed distant vibrations in the air. Melko immediately sauntered out of the barracks and approached, his eyes toward the sky.

"You feel it?" Melko asked. He was wearing a black wool shapka, earflaps up, an oversized shirt, no coat and high canvas boots wrapped with felt strips.

"Helicopters," Petrov said.

"Strange. Winter maneuvers?" Melko was driven by curiosity and always seeking explanations for even the most minor phenomena.

"Perhaps," Petrov said quietly. Other prisoners began to emerge from the barracks to watch the horizon.

Soon the vibrations turned to sound, and Petrov saw a line of dark specks over a low ridge. "Eight," he said. Melko grunted. Though the craft were still too distant for men with ordinary eyesight, the two men had counted the same number.

When the helicopters got closer, they began circling overhead and spread out. Petrov saw that they had black canisters attached to the inside of their starboard skids and no markings anywhere. The lead machine dove hard and set down in a clearing near the commandant's cabin. When Valinchuk stumbled off his porch toward it, he was met by two armed men in fur shapkas and black fatigues who gestured at him to retreat. Seconds later a short figure in a bulky dark coat emerged from the belly of the helicopter. As Petrov watched, the solitary figure traipsed through the snow toward the cabin, stomped his feet on the porch and disappeared inside.

By now all the prisoners were in the yard, standing behind Melko and Petrov. "What the fuck's going on?" one of them asked.

"Shut up," Melko growled over his shoulder. "What the fuck *is* going on?" he whispered to Petrov, who simply shook his head. "Whatever it is, it's unofficial, off the books."

"I saw." Melko watched the seven airborne machines bank slightly as the line hovered over the tree line to the west. "Experienced pilots," he said. "They hold position without flaw. I don't like the smell of this," he added. Melko was suspicious of everything the authorities did.

Minutes passed; then Valinchuk came trotting through the snow, screaming for his guards to open the gate to the compound. "Petrov!" he screamed. "Hurry, for Christ's sake!"

"What do you want?" Petrov asked calmly, holding his ground.

"Don't ask stupid questions," Valinchuk shouted, his chest heaving, breath exploding in small clouds of vapor. "Just move your ass, move your ass." He windmilled his left arm as a signal for Petrov to follow him.

"Whatever it is, it seems to have gotten Comrade Valinchuk's attention," Melko said. It was amusing to see the commandant so flustered.

"Just come." Valinchuk grabbed Petrov's sleeve and began pulling him forward. Melko tried to follow, but the commandant stepped between the two men to block his path. "Only Petrov."

"I'm the boss inside the wire," Melko said.

"Asshole!" Valinchuk roared, still pulling Petrov toward the gate.

"Hey, Melko," one of the prisoners shouted. "Maybe the commandant's wife didn't give him any pussy this morning." The men laughed until Melko glared at them.

"What's going on?" another prisoner called out.

Melko didn't know and didn't like the feeling that was beginning to ripple along his spine.

When Petrov reached the porch of the commandant's cabin, two huge men were waiting, their Kalashnikovs at the ready. Valinchuk accompanied the prisoner only to the base of the plank steps, then stopped.

"Up here," the wide-shouldered guard on the left side said. His face was covered by a black knit ski mask; his uniform had no insignia. "Three feet from the wall, spread your legs, lean forward, heels of your hands flat on the wall," he ordered in a voice accustomed to being obeyed.

Petrov walked slowly onto the porch and did as he was instructed. The second guard slung his rifle and frisked him. It was a thorough, professional job; the man missed nothing, even pushing his finger into Petrov's boot tops. "Clean," he announced to his partner.

"Stand up, parasite," the first man said. "Inside."

Petrov entered and the guards followed. The room reeked of urine, cabbage and wet fur. There was a wooden chair in the center of the room. A short man stood with his back to Petrov, urinating into a low wooden barrel.

"Sit," one of the guards said; then both of them stepped outside and closed the door.

The man in the corner turned, shook his penis several times, tucked it in, buttoned his trousers, moved to the only upholstered chair in the room, sat down, peeled off his ski mask and used it to wipe sweat off his face.

Petrov stared. The man was fat and bald, save for a few tufts of white hair near his ears; there was a gap in his front teeth and moles and warts all over his face. "You remember me?" he asked in Russian with a heavy Ukrainian accent.

"You were younger," Petrov said.

"So were you," Nikita Khrushchev said with a laugh. "We have no control over the passage of time. In this regard we are all equals."

"Some are more equal than others. Time has been generous to you."

"And you, Citizen Petrov. You're still alive."

"A matter of luck."

Khrushchev laughed. "Bullshit. It's a matter of planning. There are only a few individuals who are true assets to their country. In the old days we punished indiscriminately, but now we are wiser and life is not so disposable. Things have changed while you've been contemplating your sins against the state."

"You must have a good reason to come so far."

The General Secretary eyed the dark little man, who seemed unintimidated. This was a good sign, but it was important to impress upon him who was in charge. "Your rehabilitation is complete. It's time for you to return to a productive life."

Petrov said impassively, "I feel no different now than I did when I was sent here."

Khrushchev stood and stretched his short legs. "The helicopter is a wonderful device, but the vibrations twist my muscles into knots." He patted his neck with the ski mask. "What you feel is irrelevant. There's never been any question of your patriotism. You simply had the wrong benefactor."

"It was my impression that in the times you allude to we shared the same benefactor."

Khrushchev laughed. "Technically speaking, you're correct, but politics require clear-cut winners and losers."

"I'm not a politican."

"We're all politicans, Petrov. Stalin fell, so you fell. It works that way. I had the foresight to distance myself from the bastard before it was too late, and I had the support of the army, which was a matter of foreplanning. Now it's time for your return. Your services are required."

"I'm an old man."

"As am I."

"I will listen."

Khrushchev laughed. "Of course you will listen, but now let's get into that infernal machine. It's a long ride to Novosibirsk and I have important meetings to prepare for."

"I would like to hear the proposition now." Petrov crossed his arms calmly.

Khrushchev smiled. "The proposition, as you call it, is as follows: if you remain here, you will no longer be able to listen to anything." His tone was friendly, in direct contrast to the message. "Camps such as this drain our national resources. The inhabitants are worse than parasites. Keeping them alive is expensive when a bullet costs only a few kopecks. This camp is about to be decommissioned. Today. This morning." Khrushchev gripped Petrov's arm and leaned forward. "Don't be sad. Even our capitalist friends execute their parasites. It's a good policy."

"And if I choose to remain?"

Khrushchev smiled. "It's entirely up to you, comrade. I offer the gift of choice; what you do with it is your own business, but when my machine lifts off, that will be it."

"What would I do?"

"What you do best."

"Which is?"

"Follow orders."

Petrov paused for effect, but his decision had been made months ago when he suspected that there would be a moment such as this. "I would like to take one man with me."

Khrushchev studied Petrov and said nothing for several seconds. "Who?"

"Melko, a comrade in misery."

"A criminal?"

Petrov nodded.

"For what purpose?"

"He possesses certain skills."

Khrushchev grunted. "I can imagine." He yanked his mask down and straightened it so that the eye holes were properly aligned. "Done. Fetch the bastard, then. This place is too cold for me." He pushed open the door, stepped outside and stomped his boots on the porch. "Comrade Colonel," he shouted. "You have a man in there." He motioned toward the fence. "Name?" He looked back at Petrov.

"Melko."

"A zek called Melko. Fetch him and be quick about it." As Khrushchev started walking toward the helicopter its rotors began to turn slowly.

Valinchuk ran toward the gate screaming for Melko, who had already moved toward it. A huge sign hanging over the fence read EXPECT NO JUSTICE HERE. Petrov walked toward the helicopter, then stopped to wait.

"What's going on?" Melko asked when he caught up.

"I'm being released."

Melko grinned and shook his head. "You're insane. Nobody gets released from this place."

"You're coming with me."

Melko stopped and looked puzzled. "You mean they'd release me too, just like that?"

Petrov nodded.

Melko backed away. "What do they want?" There was fear in his voice.

"There is work for us."

Melko acted as if he'd been poisoned. "Work! Melko does not work for government swine; this I have sworn."

"Words."

"No."

"Then remain and—"

Melko lurched forward. "And what?"

Petrov pointed at the camp. "Goners. Imagine a field of wildflowers here, no evidence that a camp ever existed."

Melko contemplated this briefly, then grabbed Petrov's arm and began pulling him toward the helicopter. "Hurry."

When the helicopter lifted off, Melko peered through a square window in the door. Valinchuk and several guards were below, at attention, holding rigid salutes as the rotor-driven snow swirled over them. "Assholes," Melko shouted, his words lost in the whine of the engine.

A second helicopter accompanied them. When the two were a mile away, the other six spread out, flew a long arc on a downwind leg, turned, then swept over the camp trailing clouds of lethal gas that blanketed the area and killed quickly.

33 · SATURDAY, MARCH 4, 1961, 8:50 P.M. Paris

For more than a month Ramiz Kristo had lived in the darkness of the sewers of Paris. According to the newspapers Paula's death had been attributed to an intruder; the police had no suspects and no substantial leads. Judging by the way she had been mutilated, a police psychologist told reporters he was of the opinion that there would be similar murders. Single women were warned to take care.

The Café Cristobal was in the area near the avenue du Maine, a weatherbeaten, working-class district south of the boulevard du Montparnasse, an area filled with immigrant Arab laborers and their families, more like Marseilles in appearance than the parts of Paris that Kristo favored. At the café Kristo was to seek a red-haired bartender and ask him if there was a surgeon nearby. If the answer was yes, it would be safe to resume normal routines, the threat past; if negative, he was to go back into hiding without delay.

Kristo had made two previous trips to the café; the first time the red-haired man had given a negative answer; a week ago he had not been there. Not knowing what to make of this, Kristo had immediately retreated to his hiding place in the sewers.

There were nearly two thousand kilometers of tunnels under Paris, the product of six centuries of engineering, and though there were street signs at all major underground intersections, there were hundreds of narrow, uncharted waterways and rooms, some still in use, many abandoned for decades or even centuries. Ironically it was Paula who had introduced him to this obscure part of Paris. Her name still stuck in his throat. If he had kept quiet, perhaps she would still be alive, he told himself. But she had been a threat to the movement, hadn't she? The Major had killed her because she was unstable, potentially a danger to them all. Would she have actually gone over to the Communists? He passed through alternating moods of depression about her death and self-righteous resignation about having reacted responsibly for the collective interests of the Albanian royalists. To do great things sometimes required great sacrifices. But mostly he was depressed and lonely.

The café was narrow, with high ceilings and a bare cement floor. Once there had been paint, but traffic had worn it away. It was always packed with people, mostly men in dirty clothing; an acrid cloud of cigarette smoke floated in the air like smoke on a battlefield. There was no red-haired man; instead the bar was tended by a fat woman with a narrow mouth. "What do you want?" she asked when he approached.

"The other bartender. He has red hair." Kristo's words came in bursts, betraying his frayed nerves.

"I've seen you before," she said, "but you're not one of my regulars." She had a mustache of fine black hairs and a scabbed fever blister at the corner of her mouth.

"I'm new," he said, compelled to answer her challenge.

"What do you want with Thomas?"

"Is that his name?"

"Why do you want to see him if you don't know his name? I know *all* of his friends and I don't recognize you as one of them. You were in here once before but I don't think you're his friend. Are you police or another bum?"

"I'm new to Paris. A friend asked me to see Thomas."

"You didn't know his name." She studied him with hard eyes.

"I'm terrible with names. I was lucky to remember the name of this place." The fat bitch. Others were watching them now. Perspiration made his shirt stick to his back. "When will Thomas be back?" He tried to smile; usually women softened at his smile, but not this time.

"He comes on at nine," she snapped. "But if you're going to wait, you'll have to order. There's no room in here for people to loiter. Eat or move on. Maybe I should call the cops," she added. "You have shifty eyes."

Kristo considered leaving, but stopped himself; to run now would draw more attention to himself. His heart was pounding. "I'll eat."

She put her hands on the bar. "What will it be?"

"Bread," he said. "And some cheese."

"What kind?"

"Surprise me," he said, trying to make another joke.

The fat woman suddenly smiled and shook her head as if she had just solved a complex puzzle. "Just like Thomas. Can't even decide what kind of cheese you want. He's exactly the same. I have only one nephew; you'd think a merciful God would have given me a smart one. Instead I have Thomas, who attracts shiftless fools like you. My brother's dead, poor soul, and I had to pick *his* cheese, too. Want me to pick a wine as well?"

"Please."

She grinned, showing a gold cap. "There's only one," she scolded. "This is not the Champs-Élysées. You take what we have and like it, understood?"

"Yes," Kristo said, wishing he had stayed in the sewer.

She grunted and yelled at a waitress with a blue apron. Five minutes later he had white cheese and a loaf of stale bread. The Beaujolais was decent. He ate slowly, trying to decide whether to nurse the food until Thomas arrived or to leave now.

"She's a nasty old hag," a voice said in English. It belonged to a girl with short black hair. She had dimples when she smiled. "How's your cheese?"

He held the plate out to her and she sniffed tentatively. "Better left in the goat."

When she laughed, he laughed with her. How long had it been since he had been with Paula? This girl was attractive and did not look like other women in the district.

"Come here often?" he asked.

"First time," she admitted.

"Student?"

She laughed. "Does it show?"

"I have an instinct for such things." It made him feel better to know he had read her correctly. Kristo was certain that he had a gift for understanding women. Somehow he always knew what would motivate them even before they spoke. "Wine?" He caught the attention of the waitress and ordered. The girl slid her chair over to his table. When her wine came, she sipped it, then touched his arm. The warmth of her hand made him dizzy.

"I'm Ramiz," he said.

"Not French," she said. She looked into his eyes while she drank her wine.

"Not French," he echoed.

"Lilly," she said. "American."

"I guessed as much," he lied. She looked French. American would have been his last guess.

"Here on vacation," she told him. "Taking some time off from the university. I had this idea that I could have some fun in Paris."

"You haven't?" His voice betrayed his surprise.

"French men push too hard, and that turns me off. I prefer the slow and easy approach. I can't stand it when a man seems desperate. Or too sure of himself."

What was she trying to say? "Hmm," he said.

"I'd rather have a man who's humble and not in such a hurry to get to it," she said. It felt as if her eyes were burning holes in him. She touched the palm of her hand to the small of his back, causing it to arch with a sharp jerk.

"I didn't mean to frighten you," she apologized. Her voice was soft and rich. Her hand stroked his back gently. "I like vulnerability in a man."

"Am I vulnerable?" For the first time in a long while he did not feel vulnerable. An erection pressed against his trousers.

"Aren't you?" Her hand found the back of his neck.

"As much as any," he answered, his voice betraying the truth.

"Do you have a girlfriend?"

"No." Why did women always ask this?

"Jilted?"

He didn't understand the word.

"She found somebody else?"

Kristo nodded. "She left me." Technically this was true, but it was Paula's own fault that she was dead.

"Now you're afraid you'll find another woman and she'll leave you too, is that it?"

"It's been difficult," which was the truth.

She squeezed his neck. "A woman would be a fool to leave a man such as you."

Kristo was inflamed by desire, nearly out of control, when he saw the red-haired bartender behind the counter.

"Do you have a place?" she asked. "We can't use mine." Her hand kneaded the inside of his thigh.

The bartender was smiling; he looked like the sort who never had worries. How could he behave like this when the whole movement was in trouble? Was he part of it? Why was everything so unclear?

"Let's get out of here," the girl said. She squeezed his hand anxiously.

The bartender put his arm around the fat woman, who pushed him away and wagged a finger at him while he laughed. Maybe everything was all right, Kristo thought. "Would a hotel be all right?" he asked, watching the bartender light a cigarette.

"Don't you have your own place?"

"Mine wouldn't do," he told her. "It's not a very proper place."

"You're not married, are you?" She drew back slightly.

"No," he said, still watching the bartender.

When Kristo got up from the table, the woman clung to his hand and followed. For a moment he considered abandoning her, but he needed her. Maybe Kryeziu and the others could live like monks, but he couldn't.

When Kristo reached the counter the bartender made eye contact with him but showed no recognition. "Can I help you?"

The fat woman intervened. "He's the one who says he knows one of your friends. Couldn't select his own cheese." She spat on the floor and grinned.

"Is there a surgeon nearby?" Kristo asked.

Thomas's expression did not betray anything, but his eyes flashed. "No, not for a long time." His voice was even, his smile unbroken.

"Thank you," he said, pulling the woman toward the door.

"I hope there's a hotel close by," she said when they were outside. It was drizzling.

"I have to go," he told her, but when he tried to pull away she refused to let go of his hand. "My place isn't suitable. You would be uncomfortable."

"You said we could go to a hotel."

"That's not possible."

She laughed. "No money, is that it? Don't worry, I have plenty of francs."

"It's not a question of money."

"Then what?" She looked at the front of his trousers. "That part says 'yes,' but your voice says 'no.'"

"It's complicated."

"You can trust me."

When Kristo saw a police car parked several doors down, he led her in the opposite direction.

There were several ways to enter the sewers, and over time he had learned the many routes in and out of his lair, but this time he took a long, circuitous way so that it would be difficult for her to retrace it. It took them two hours to reach the place, much of the journey in dim light or darkness, but she kept up easily, didn't complain and asked no questions.

The room had once been a storage depot for the tools of sewer workers. It was twenty steps above a three-meter-wide canal. Light came from two kerosene lanterns he had stolen, and there was a cot and a table made from wooden spools that had once held telephone cable. Several blankets were on the floor around the bed.

When the lanterns hissed into life the woman examined her surroundings.

"I'm sorry about this place," he apologized.

"Are you in trouble?"

"I'm a writer. Hugo found his muse down here. I thought I might too."

She laughed. "Sounds like a line, but it doesn't matter." She sat on the cot and began to undress. Her breasts were well shaped and firm and there was a nasty scar on her left thigh that looked fresh. She dropped her clothes in a small pile and placed her shoes on top. When she lay back on the cot, she held out her arms to him. It had been so long that he came after a few hard thrusts, then collapsed into her arms. "I'm sorry," he said.

She patted his forehead. "It's all right." she said. "You're too tense."

"I have reason to be," he confessed.

"Tell me."

"I can't."

Her hand found his testicles. "I'll take very good care of you," she told him. "Share your troubles with me. Everyone needs a sympathetic ear."

A blow knocked him onto the floor. Instinctively he curled into a ball and held his hand in front of him while he shook his head, trying to clear the dizziness away. Then he saw the woman standing on the other side of the cot, a powerfully built man behind her. She had a small automatic pistol with a thick black tube on the front. He had never seen a silencer before, but he knew immediately what it was.

"Do you have questions for him?" Her voice was cold, her face expressionless. She spoke Albanian.

Kristo cowered and began to cry. "Don't hurt me."

She cocked the weapon and locked her elbows, waiting for instructions.

The man asked several questions about the movement; Kristo tried to answer him but couldn't stop sobbing.

"He doesn't know shit," the muscular man said. "Finish it."

Lejla Llarja shot Kristo once in the mouth. The sound was like a muted cough. The bullet passed through his skull and ricocheted against the wall with a sharp whack. She offered the pistol to Haxi Kasi and sat down on the cot, her legs shaking.

"Keep it," he told her. "This is only the beginning."

She dropped the pistol onto her clothes. The blood pooling under Ramiz Kristo's head looked black. She felt like vomiting, but a voice inside said, You hold your father's life in your hands.

34   SUNDAY, MARCH 5, 1961, 7:30 A.M.
Tanga, Buryat Autonomous Soviet Socialist Republic

The light streaming through the windows was unexpectedly bright; last night it had snowed that familiar kind of heavy, wet snow that typically came in late winter to ravage the Yablonovy Mountains for several days, but this time the storm had quickly dumped its load and moved on. The fresh layer of snow reflected the morning sun and intensified its glare.

Ezdovo had gotten out of bed at daybreak while Talia lay in bed listening to the distant ping of his sledge against a metal wedge. He split firewood at an even rhythm, seldom needing more than one blow to a piece; as she listened she closed her eyes and imagined him working. Whatever her husband did he did thoroughly and neatly. When the wood was split, he would stack the pieces in precise layers, his own order superimposed on minor and major chaos. Not at all like her. When he was near her she could see the compulsive urge eating at him; sometimes he ground his teeth when he saw the disarray in which she worked.

After listening to him for a while, Talia got up, splashed cold water on her face, drifted into the kitchen and smiled. He had already heated water for tea. How had she been so lucky to find him?

Ezdovo heard the helicopter as it cleared the jagged ridges north of the village, set the sledge on a stack of logs and hurried into the house. "Helicopter coming," he said.

Talia was slow to react, which was not unusual; mornings were difficult for her. She turned slowly and blinked several times, trying to return to the present from wherever it was she had been, but he could see in her eyes that she was preparing herself. "For us," she said. "I can feel it."

Ezdovo nodded. "Ten minutes," he said. "We can still get to the mountains. There's enough time."

"No," she said softly. "If we leave, our people will suffer. We've already discussed this. We've started a fight and now we must finish it. We have obligations."

He wanted to tell her how much he loved her, but could not find the right words. Why was it that he could not openly express his feelings to her?

Talia came to him, kissed him softly on the neck, squeezed his arm and laughed. "I *know,* my husband."

When the helicopter landed in the snowy meadow below the cabin, Ezdovo and Talia were already on the porch. A man emerged and struggled slowly toward them through the thigh-deep snow. "Pyotr Ezdovo?" The hunter nodded. "Talia Pogrebenoi?" She stepped forward. "You will come with me, please."

35 MONDAY, MARCH 6, 1961, 9:10 A.M. *Moscow*

The lobby was jammed with its customary mishmash of uniformed officers and bureaucrats in the process of putting on or taking off heavy wool coats and winter footwear. The reception area stank of wet fur, sweat and disinfectant. Floors harbored small, shallow eddies of diluted mud and slush, their unevenness a testament to the impossibility of leveling cement floors when workmen labored with heavy blood levels of cheap vodka.

A set of steel doors in the basement led to a huge complex that housed the headquarters of the most powerful military-intelligence organization in the world, the GRU; its denizens called it the Aquarium because everyone and everything in it was under constant scrutiny. There was something comical about entering so powerful a place through so seedy an establishment; surely it fooled none of their enemies. Bailov hated going into the Aquarium, but it was the price he paid to keep his job in Spetsnaz. In Vinnitsa he was in command; here he had limited power. Out there everything was clear and simple; here it was turgid and twisted. There his men counted for everything; here nobody counted for anything. Except Raya, of course.

He moved through the steel entrance doors into a room with a narrow opening between brick and mortar walls; a queue of people was waiting patiently to go through a security station rigged with metal detectors. In the GRU's inner sanctum no metal was allowed except what was already there: no belt buckles, keys, rings, watches, pocket knives or cigarette lighters. As a result, most of the men in the Aquarium paraded around in colorful suspenders rather than belts.

When Bailov reached the checkpoint, he put his toes on a white line painted on the floor and showed his Certificate of Officer's Identity, a small green booklet with a gold star on the cover. The armed guard took the booklet, opened it, examined the photograph, compared it with him, repeated the process, grunted, returned the booklet to Bailov and nod-ded—the signal that he could proceed through the sensors. Before step-ping through he felt himself tense in an involuntary response to the test the device symbolized. No matter how many times he went into the GRU's inner sanctum, he feared that somehow he would fail and be humiliated. How was it that in case of war he could be relied upon to parachute behind enemy lines to kill enemy political leaders and sabotage their factories, bridges and water supplies, yet in peacetime had to pass a loyalty test every time he entered his own building? Worst of all, Soviet technicians had built the sensing device, which meant it was probably as unreliable as the building's uneven floors.

No alarm sounded. On the other side he was met by two more guards; the one who hovered beside a hard-spined book was squat and well muscled, with small eyes and a bent nose. Guardsmen were unedu-cated reptiles in human form, impervious to pain, expected to do what-ever was required of them, showing no fear and probably not feeling it either, which made them different from his own troops. Both organiza-tions put a premium on brutishness, their missions requiring it, but guards were too stupid to be afraid and his own men too proud to give in to it. No doubt this particular animal could barely read what was written in the ledger, which made the procedure another of Moscow's many charades. After Bailov signed in, the man beside the door pushed it open and let him pass.

The narrow halls of the Aquarium had tan-colored linoleum floors and were well lit by powerful bulbs in small cages of black wire; the walls were pale green and there were no signs to guide newcomers; here you were expected to know your way.

As usual the elevator was out of order; Bailov took the stairs to the third floor, walked quickly to the far end of the building and pushed open the door to the Fifth Directorate, which had responsibility for "opera-tional intelligence," meaning Spetsnaz as well as a number of other special and clandestine missions.

The head of the Fifth Directorate was Lieutenant General Igor Yepi-shev, a forty-nine-year-old Russian with short blond hair, pale, translu-cent skin that never tanned because he rarely went outside, ape-like arms that hung nearly to his knees, oversized ears that stuck out like radar antennae and the thick neck of a weight lifter. Unlike many generals who grew fat from too little exercise and an excess of food and drink, Yepi-shev was fit; he ran several kilometers daily, and played handball with officers twenty years his junior. He also seldom bathed, and because of his peculiar personal hygiene personnel of the Fifth Directorate referred to him as the Goat, a term also used by the KGB for its informants. Despite Yepishev's offensive body odor, Bailov liked the man. Whatever else he might be, Yepishev was a good soldier and a true professional, something the GRU and Red Army were both short of. And though he was certain the general had similar respect for him, the Goat was not the sort to share such feelings.

Bailov slipped past Yepishev's office into an open bay filled with nicked and discolored wooden desks. After he was seated, a clerk fetched a carton of files and Bailov spread out his work; it was not true work, of course, merely paper exercises designed to reinforce the tenuousness of his position in the chain of command. By requiring his presence every month, his superiors, all the way up to Khrushchev, reminded the strong-willed young colonel and those like him that they were serving at their masters' pleasure. This was the sort of thing the czars had done; now those who had overthrown the czars behaved similarly. The aristocracy remained; only its name had changed.

Today Bailov would continue his analysis of the proposition that Spetsnaz troops at the squad level should be cross-trained in individual technical specialties, which was how American and British commando units operated. As he thought about the problem, Bailov sensed a presence, then smelled it, and looked up from his notes to find the Goat standing beside his desk.

"Good morning, Comrade General." Was Yepishev so accustomed to his own odor that he couldn't smell it? Other officers left their desks to give the two men space. Yepishev dropped an envelope on his desk. "Confidential" was hand-stamped in red ink across the front and it was sealed, which meant little because there were countless specialists in the GRU who could open and re-seal envelopes in such ways that nobody, including other experts, would know. Even so, Bailov assumed Yepishev would know the contents because nothing happened in the Fifth Directorate without his approval or knowledge.

"What's this?" Bailov asked. "Another bird study?"

Yepishev looked paler than normal. "It came by messenger from the Kremlin."

"You're joking," Bailov said with a smile.

"I don't make jokes," the Goat growled before yelling at another officer across the room and moving away.

Strange behavior, Bailov thought. He peeled open an end of the envelope, popped a document free and unfolded it. He was ordered to report as soon as possible to an address in Odessa, there to await further orders. Nikita Khrushchev's name was typed under the message and his initials scrawled in the space above. When Bailov looked up he saw that Yepishev was watching him with questioning eyes.

TUESDAY, MARCH 7, 1961, 7:15 P.M.
Belgrade

Belgrade was gray and depressing, its people seldom smiling, the sulfurous stench of factories permeating everything.

It was nearly dark when Sylvia began to cross the narrow street; the flicker of automobile lights fifty meters away caught her eye. When the vehicle was abreast of her Harry Gabler leaned out his window. "Get in," he said.

"This town has all the charm of a cement factory," she said as she squeezed into the seat next to him. They drove north out of the city onto a flat plain, passing several dark villages surrounded by long rows of fruit trees. "Cook's tour?"

"Something like that," Gabler said. He seemed preoccupied. After about forty minutes he slowed the vehicle to a crawl. "Ought to be a road to the right someplace along here. Fucking Yugos don't mark anything."

The road was a dirt two-track between rows of apple trees with gnarled trunks and contorted branches. Gabler turned off the headlights and eased the car down uneven ruts to a barn at the end of the road. There he stopped the car and flashed his lights once. The barn doors swung open immediately. A small dark Volkswagen was already inside, and when they pulled in behind it, the doors swung shut behind them. Gabler got out without speaking; Sylvia followed, moving slowly, not wanting to trip in the darkness and feeling more than a little uneasy about the station chief's secretive behavior.

Ahead of him a door opened, revealing a dim yellow light. "This way," Gabler called back.

The room was small, furnished with a hand-hewn table and several chairs. Light came from a kerosene lantern hung on the wall.

A tall, thin woman followed them into the room. She had extremely short blond hair and wore a shiny black raincoat and no makeup. Black mud caked her boots.

Gabler unbuttoned his coat and sat in a chair. "Meet Inspector Peresic," he said.

Sylvia extended her hand. The blond woman had a masculine grip and maintained the contact for an unusually long time before pushing the door shut with her heel. She was more handsome than pretty and her teeth were crooked, with a severe overbite. "I'm *Chief* Inspector Peresic," she said with a pronounced English accent. "Did you have difficulty finding the place?"

"It would have been easier to meet closer to the city," Gabler said.

"Easy is not in our domain," Peresic said as she sat down. "Harry likes things simple," she told Sylvia. "It would be difficult to explain why a homicide inspector and the CIA have legitimate business together."

"She knows who you are?" Sylvia asked Gabler, her surprise apparent.

The woman smiled. "Call me Vicki. I am homicide, not political, understand? Harry and I trade information from time to time. We think of it as professional courtesy."

Sylvia wondered if they exchanged anything else and the woman seemed to read her mind. "We're professionally related, nothing more." She smiled, took off tight black-leather gloves and slapped them on the table. "You Americans are not accustomed to women in positions of authority. In a socialist state we evaluate talent, not genitals."

Gabler chuckled. "Go easy on her, Vicki."

The inspector took a small notebook from her pocket, then put on a pair of wire-rimmed glasses. "Unidentified male, late thirties to early forties, slight stature, five foot eight by your measure, fifty-five kilos, brown hair, brown eyes, no scars or birthmarks. The body was discovered in the New Cemetery November 15, 1960, at 1800 hours. Three gunshot wounds: head, chest, left thigh. The leg wound was a rear entry, the others frontal. Apparently he tried to run, but the leg wound knocked him down. The headshot killed him instantly, though the chest wound would have sufficed." She flipped the page. "Discovered by the cemetery superintendent. Several workmen were in the area at the time but nothing was heard or observed."

The woman was confident, almost arrogant, but Sylvia also felt something else, maybe anger. Or frustration. She looked at Gabler. "Did I miss something?"

Gabler plopped his elbows on the table. "I asked Vicki to do a little checking for me."

Peresic removed her glasses. "Unsolved homicides over a six-month period with cross-referencing to missing-persons files."

Sylvia wanted to question Gabler but she had no idea if the woman knew about Frash or their search for him.

"Our record keeping doesn't compare with the West's, but we are not without some competence," Peresic said. "The deceased has not been identified. No papers. No distinguishing scars or birthmarks. Not a cavity in his mouth."

"What about his clothing?" Gabler asked.

"Like any other man in the street. No foreign labels." She took a small photo out of her notebook and slid it to Gabler. The black-and-white photograph had poor resolution, the angle from directly above the corpse, the sutured Y-shaped autopsy incision an ugly scar. The bullet holes in the chest and head were small and neat. The leg wound was gaping. Gabler passed the photo to Sylvia. "Morgue photography leaves a lot to be desired," Inspector Peresic said apologetically.

Gabler shook his head. "Can we keep this?"

"We have others."

"Never seen him before," Gabler said. "Got a best guess?" he asked the inspector.

Sylvia saw that the face had fine, almost feminine features.

Peresic paused before speaking. "Guesses only. An Albanian, perhaps; the face is a classical type. Definitely not a Serb or Croatian."

"It's not much," Gabler said.

The woman smiled. "We are both in professions where not much must often be enough."

Gabler nodded. "Is the case still open?"

"Only technically. We don't have the resources to indefinitely investigate cases such as this. I have only eight people in my section. Someday perhaps we will acquire some information that will enable us to solve it, but probably not. It rests on serendipity's shoulders."

The earmarks of the killing were clear to Gabler. "Assassination is a political act," he said.

"Our country is rife with killings. Violence is in our blood, and our people practice the Christian principle of an eye for an eye but little else. This could be politically motivated or it might be far more mundane."

"What about robbery?"

"He still had dinars in his pocket."

"Silencers must have been used," Gabler said. "Nobody heard the shots, yet workmen were close by."

"A silencer is easy enough to manufacture. It's quite simple, really. Obviously the killing was done efficiently, but this alone doesn't make it a political act."

Gabler did not ask if Yugoslavian intelligence was aware of the killing; it routinely reviewed all capital crimes. "That's it, then?"

"I will keep you informed," Peresic said.

"Same from our end," Gabler said.

The Americans left first and drove back to the city.

"One of Frash's contacts?" Sylvia asked, tapping the photo on the dashboard. The wipers clicked monotonously against the windshield.

"Maybe," Gabler said. "This guy bought it about the same time Frash vanished. There might be a connection. I've gone as deep with my sources as I can."

"What connection?"

"You and your partner are looking for Frash," Gabler said. "My wife hates my work," he said out of the blue. Then he added, "So do I, but what else can I do? Once you're in, you're in."

"I assume there's a point to this," Sylvia said.

"It's like I told you and your partner," Gabler said. "I looked for Frash. Nothing elaborate, but an effort nevertheless. Two investigation teams came through but I heard no follow-up and nobody asked for my help or opinion. I figured then that Frash had been ordered out, moved to new duty. Then you show up and your being here says this Frash thing is a real mess, so I tapped Vicki. Would've done it sooner, but I wasn't asked. See?"

"And your lady friend digs into her files out of the goodness of her heart."

Gabler nodded and turned onto a fog-shrouded bridge. "Vicki? Hell no. She owes me, and now I've called in some interest, but in the long run this will cost me."

"Previous investigations didn't take the same route?"

"You tell me," he said. "I assume you were briefed before you were sent in."

Both she and Beau had been briefed by Arizona, but it had been done separately and now, it seemed, not as thoroughly as she had assumed. She looked at the stone walls of the bridge. There were no pedestrians. Arizona had said nothing about Company contacts with the Belgrade police.

Gabler took her silence as an affirmation of what he already felt. "Who knows what angles were looked at? Not me, so I got hold of Vicki, decided it's time for me to satisfy some curiosity, fill in a few squares. I asked her to sweep her files and see what popped up."

"Is that Frash in the photo?"

"Nope."

"So we've got nothing."

"Maybe, but I've got a hunch Frash was doing something with the Pixies."

She looked at Gabler. "Pixies?"

"Company jargon for Albanians."

"Why tell me and not Valentine?"

"He's an amateur," Gabler said. "You're not. I saw that right off. I ran into Frash a couple of times; he was carrying Albanian newspapers. They've got a big group in this country, maybe a million or more in a region called Kosovo; it was annexed by Tito after the war. What the hell's Frash reading that shit for? I asked myself. Another time I heard him say something about Albanians, and another time my secretary heard him talking in Albanian. We ran an op with the Brits against the Pixies in the early fifties; I figured that maybe a replay was in the works."

Sylvia knew nothing of a previous operation, but in the old days the Company had engaged in all sorts of cockamamy paramilitary operations against the Soviets and their satellites. "More likely that all these things are unconnected, but you never know until you take a hard look."

"Right," Gabler said, "but when you try to assemble a puzzle you take the pieces you have and look for a fit. If there isn't one, that tells you something too. I believe in starting with what I have, not what I don't."

"And now your inspector friend gives us a dead body that's maybe Albanian. Maybe a dozen Albanians were murdered in the same time period. One corpse gives us nothing."

"Frash tried to hide the newspapers from me, but I saw him reading one of them." He glanced at her to see if she was taking in all this.

"Could've been left by somebody else," she insisted.

"Two places, two different times, same behavior, and Albanian rags are not exactly regular fare in Belgrade." Gabler stopped the car down the block from her building.

"Why all the sudden help?" she asked as she got out.

"Been in this business too long," he said. "Seen loose ends hang more than a few of our kind. Until you write the ending to this Frash thing my entire operation is in jeopardy. The sooner you get your job done, the sooner I can get on with mine."

She found Valentine waiting in the flat. "You ever hear of a Company operation against the Pixies?" she asked.

"Only in *Peter Pan*," he said with his infuriating grin.

37 FRIDAY, MARCH 10, 1961, 1:00 P.M.
Odessa

The car that came to fetch Bailov was a black Pobeda taxi driven by a man with white hair and liver spots on his hands. The driver dropped him at a sanatorium on the outskirts of the city. Though it was a clear, sunny day there were no bathers and no activity around the building.

The front door opened as he reached for it and Gnedin grinned from inside. "You're older," the doctor said.

"I see your diagnostic skills are as keen as ever," Bailov said. The two men embraced and exchanged kisses. Spying Ezdovo and Talia in the hallway beyond the doctor, Bailov said, "One senses the pulling of some very strong strings."

Ezdovo and Talia embraced Bailov at the same time. She seemed more beautiful than the last time he had seen her. "How does an old bear like Ezdovo hold on to such a treasure?" he asked her.

"Rope," Ezdovo said. "A short one." Talia beamed. She had once been as fond of Bailov as her husband had been.

The four of them sat in white rattan chairs in a sort of parlor, all of them knowing only one man could account for such a reunion.

Melko came in first. Because it was warm and humid he had stripped off his shirt. The others stared at his tattoos, which immediately marked him as a professional criminal.

Petrov entered a moment later. He wore a black fedora with a wide brim, a dark raincoat, khaki trousers and new black shoes. He looked gaunt, tired and in need of a shave.

"This is Melko," Petrov said. The others introduced themselves. "History sometimes repeats itself."

"If that's the case," Bailov said laughing, "there should be a bottle of pertsovka." In the old days they had always celebrated with the spicy pepper vodka.

Petrov opened his coat and placed two bottles and five metal cups on the floor, then filled each cup slowly and stepped back. "Rivitsky is dead," he said. "Complications from diabetes. Father Grigory, too. His heart gave out."

The four old team members raised their cups in silent salute to their dead comrades and saw that their former leader and the stranger called Melko did not drink with them.

"I assume there's a reason for such a reunion," Talia said.

Petrov nodded but said nothing.

The others knew that when he was ready he would explain. Whatever their mission, they knew it would be dangerous, and they wondered if they would be as lucky this time around, for to travel with Petrov was to travel with death. Oddly enough, this made living seem more real.

38 FRIDAY, MARCH 10, 1961, 9:30 P.M. *Belgrade*

Pixies! The word still made Valentine smile. He had listened to Sylvia's story about the John Doe and looked at the photograph. Gabler seemed to think there was some connection between Frash and Albania, but what kind of connection? It seemed farfetched to think the CIA would attempt to dislodge the Albanian government, but the papers back home had been filled for months with stories about a probable and not so secret effort to unseat Castro in Cuba. In fact the media seemed to consider the Cuban operation a foregone conclusion; only the timing was in question. If true, it had to be the CIA's worst-kept secret, but except for the Reuters stories he had gotten earlier from Gabler, there had been no media mention of any U.S. interest in Albania. Gabler himself said you couldn't believe anything the Albanians said publicly; they were full of shit. Hell, who even knew where Albania *was*? Unlikely or not, however, he understood covert strategy well enough to know that any operation that might put an enemy at a disadvantage would find sympathetic ears in the Company. What puzzled him was Arizona's reticence about telling him the nature of Frash's asset. All he had was the code name REBUS and an impression that the man was providing information of a technical nature. Hunting Pixies, he told himself. Serves you right for letting yourself get talked into this.

Sylvia had been gone most of the day doing something unspecified with Gabler; she was to meet him in thirty minutes at a café a couple of blocks away. By the time he got downstairs he had come to a decision; as soon as he could arrange it, he was going home to Galveston. Arizona could find some other chump to do scut work.

It was raining again, forcing him to take cover in a doorway until the downpour relented. As he waited a black Volkswagen jerked to the curb less than a meter away. A blond woman stared at him with hard eyes, then rolled down her window. "I'm Peresic," she said. "Get in."

"We haven't been formally introduced," Valentine said.

"Don't play games," she said. "Foreigners are not invisible in this place. I've met your partner."

Peresic was more attractive than Sylvia had let on, and he wondered why. "What happened to security?" he asked.

"I'm not being followed," she said, "but if you insist on standing there I'll have to move on. In or out?"

He got in.

"No need to worry," she said.

"Curious, not worried. Where are we going?" It occurred to him that this could be a setup, but something in her voice told him she was wired tight. The windows immediately fogged up and she wiped at the windscreen with the back of her hand. "The Germans exaggerate their engineering prowess," she complained.

"We going to your place?" She smelled of soap.

Their route twisted through the old quarter, then over a sharply angled bridge and river. The rain was hard now, and thunder drowned out the chatter of the air-cooled engine behind them. There were few street lights in the city, and apartment buildings were dark. When they reached a hilly area where houses had been built among stands of large hardwood trees, she pulled into a sloping driveway beside a house, cut off the motor and let the machine coast down a grassy incline. At the end there was a building with a door. "Open it," she said.

She pulled the Volkswagen into the garage and latched the door behind them. He followed her upstairs and through a low, arched door, which required both of them to crouch to go through. She locked the door behind them, then lit a small lamp that sat in the middle of a table.

"Your place?" Valentine asked.

"Ownership is irrelevant in a socialist state," Inspector Peresic said. "If we're disturbed, you go out that way." She pushed open a window. Rain blew in, whipping the curtains. "There's a tree to the right. Climb down, keep to your right until you intersect a brick lane, then right to the intersection and left down the next street. Walk until you reach the river. There's plenty of cover the whole way."

Valentine unbuttoned his coat and grinned. Suddenly she seemed very tense as she stepped toward the table and kicked off her boots. Her hooded coat crinkled when she laid it over a chair. "Is this an official meeting?" he asked.

"Was my information of interest to your colleagues?"

"Libraries are filled with interesting information. What we need is *useful* information. There's a big distinction."

"Perhaps there's more," she said. She unbuttoned her blouse, dropped it on her coat, bent her thin arms behind her, unhooked her brassiere, let it fall, cupped her small breasts and let her hands trace the line of her flat belly. The zipper on her skirt made a sharp sound as she stepped out of it, then slid her panties down and tossed them in the air with one foot. Balancing on one leg and then the other, she removed her garter belt and stockings. Her thighs were thin and her hips on the bony side. Not a bad package, though.

"Do all homicide detectives here work this way?"

"Get on the bed," she ordered. The bed was low and narrow and had been pushed into the corner.

Valentine was in no hurry to comply; he needed more time to evaluate the situation. "You mentioned something about more information?"

"I said *perhaps*."

She sat on the edge of the bed and patted the mattress. "I propose what lawyers call a quid pro quo," she said. "But first I suggest we find out how well we communicate."

"Fucking is only one form of communication and not exactly brimming with information," Valentine said. "Flattered as I am, it might be better for both of us if we talked first."

She shrugged, got a cigarette from her purse and lit it. "As you wish, but I assure you that I'm very skilled in such matters."

He didn't doubt it. "You have a wedding ring," he said. The storm outside was intensifying, the thunder nearly continuous.

"Do married women in America not have occasional affairs?"

"Most affairs have longer warm-ups. American women prefer to ease into such situations, which gives them a sense of having been seduced, which in turn protects their sense of moral righteousness." How many times had he been through this scene or something like it since Ermine's death?

"Copulation is not a moral event," the inspector said. "In our country there's no time for contemplation. One acts or loses the opportunity forever. Socialism requires decisiveness." Her voice was low. "My husband is in the government and much older—seventeen years, to be precise. Time passes, people change, our bodies decay. There are certain amenities he can no longer provide, do you understand? We have been married eight years now. I am thirty-nine, he is fifty-six, and now he takes pleasure from power, not sex. The marriage is one of convenience."

He sensed a familiar story. "So you take care of your needs in other ways."

"Of course. I am responsible for myself and do what I must." Her nipples were small but hard. "I must get to America," she said. "I think you can arrange this." It was a statement, not a question.

Valentine smiled. The rain had let up for a moment. "I'd say you've overestimated my influence."

"Not at all. I have carefully analyzed the situation. Gabler is station chief, but he defers to your colleague."

"So we hop in the sack and then you get the ticket. Is that the idea?"

She carefully extinguished the cigarette in a cup on the stand beside the bed. "The sex would be for my benefit, the information for yours."

"You do this sort of thing regularly?"

"Less frequently than the need. Such matters are not taken lightly."

"No long-term complications?"

"Exactly."

"You're a careful woman."

"Exceptionally careful." She picked up her panties but did not put them on.

"I sense something more," Valentine said. Nothing else made sense.

"There was a newspaper stuffed in the dead man's shoe," she said. "It was dated four days before his death. From Tirana. The Albanians do not export their newspapers. I concluded from this that the dead man had come from Tirana to Belgrade shortly before he was killed."

Another Albanian connection, but no more than an interesting tidbit and not nearly significant enough to warrant what she wanted in trade. "*That's* what you propose to trade?" He guessed that she would be as good in bed as she claimed, which made him regret his quick decision.

Inspector Peresic stuffed her underwear in her purse and began to pull on her blouse. "Albanians rarely venture this far north. For many years Tito and the Albanians have been engaged in a very quiet but deadly war. There have been many unsuccessful attempts to unseat Hoxha's regime, and at times there has been considerable bloodshed on both sides. I believe that the dead man was involved in such an intrigue."

"I'm listening." First Harry had produced wire stories about Albania, and now the woman was talking about Albanians. Coincidence? "Does Harry know about this?"

"He knows about the conflict but not what was found on the dead man," she said. "Tirana Radio recently announced that the Sigurimi had uncovered a plot against Hoxha."

"We're aware of that."

She pulled her skirt up backward, zipped it, then rotated it into place. "Albanians are creatures of habit, more so than my own countrymen or yours. They would make no allegations about such a plot until the conspiracy had been thoroughly investigated and crushed."

"You want to give me a history lesson, is that it?"

"I want you to hear me out, then judge the value," she snapped. "There is an individual in my country who knows more about what goes on in Albania than anyone."

"Who?"

The homicide inspector stared briefly at him, then smiled. "Duzevic," she said.

A clap of thunder was followed by a surge of wind that made the candle flicker, but it sounded like the rain had stopped.

Valentine had known a Duzevic a long time ago when the Germans were a common enemy. Could it be the same man? Probably not. Duzevic was an old coot then; surely he was dead by now.

"There are nearly a million Albanians in Kosovo province," Peresic said. "Most are devout Muslims who want nothing to do with Hoxha or his Sigurimi psychopaths. But with so many ethnic connections to connect with, Hoxha has built up his own network of agents and informers. It is General Duzevic's mission to counter Hoxha's intrigues. Duzevic reports to my husband."

Jesus, he thought. "Your husband must be an important man."

"He is," she said. "And equally dangerous."

"But you want to leave him."

"I've had enough."

"Divorce is a simple procedure in most socialist countries."

"The aftermath would be too complicated. My husband has great power. He is with Tito in Africa now and will be away for some time. If I'm to act, it has to be now. You have to help me."

"Fly to Rome, present yourself at our embassy and ask for political asylum. It happens all the time. You don't need me."

"I have to disappear, understand? *Completely*. I have great knowledge to share with the CIA. My husband has been with Tito since the war."

"It's a pretty big gamble." What was she holding back?

"You don't gamble? I thought this was an integral part of the American character."

"Only when we like the odds."

"I see. The capitalist need for collateral."

"That's about the size of it." She was quick on the uptake.

"If I provide the collateral you require, how do I know I can trust you?"

"That's *your* gamble. What it comes down to is that you need me more than I need you."

He could see her mulling this over. Finally she went to her coat, opened an interior pocket, took out an envelope covered in plastic and handed it to him. "Payment on account."

The envelope contained a photograph of two men. One of them seemed to be the dead man he had seen in the grisly photo Sylvia had shown him. There were gravestones behind them. Valentine didn't say anything. "The one on the left is the man known as Frash," Peresic said.

A photo of Frash *with* the dead man. Valentine's pulse surged.

"The one on the right is a Russian," she said.

"You told my colleagues that he looked Albanian."

"He does. It was not to my benefit to disclose everything to them last night."

"But now it is?"

"You tell me."

Was this Frash's asset? "Does this dead Russian have a name?"

"It can be acquired," she said.

"How quickly?"

"For now price is my main concern," she said. "The timing depends."

"On what?"

"A trip to America, with no trail to be followed."

SATURDAY, MARCH 11, 1961, 7:00 P.M.
Odessa

Talia was as interested in how Petrov looked as in what he had to say. He had aged, of course, but not in a linear sense; it was more as if he had suffered a massive implosion. His hair was gone, the skin taut on his face, eyes rheumy, his back bent. There was a ghastly quality to his appearance, but his voice was unchanged; high-pitched, sharp, his words came out crisp and clean like bolts from a crossbow.

"We have a new benefactor," Petrov told the group. Melko had already related to the others how the General Secretary had plucked them from an icy prison camp near Novosibirsk.

"Benefactor" was an odd choice of words, Talia thought. In the old days their orders had come directly from Stalin, whom Petrov had always referred to as the Boss. Now it would be Khrushchev who gave orders. Did this signal a different sort of relationship? Stalin's power had been absolute, his word law, and all of them, even Petrov, she suspected, feared him. With Stalin the penalty for failure was death, and the mere thought of the dictator's name gave her a chill. It was not the same with Khrushchev, and Petrov's use of the word "benefactor" seemed almost benign. Was he suggesting that the Ukrainian was not the mad Georgian's equal?

Last night the group had socialized and drunk their fill, but Petrov had left them alone, which also seemed to signal a change; in the old days he would have stayed with them, not imbibing with the same enthusiasm, but with them spiritually, and invariably within arm's length. If the others had been bothered by Petrov's absence from the reunion, they had not said anything, and when she had mentioned it to Ezdovo he had dismissed it and reminded her of her overactive imagination.

"Fact one," Petrov began. "An accident at Tyuratam with two hundred and fifty dead. Cause: ignition malfunction in an R-7 booster.

"Two, a key technical specialist was transferred from the project a few weeks before the accident. There was subsequent speculation that had the specialist remained with the project, there would have been no accident.

"Three, Khrushchev assigns a special investigator to look into the project and the accident.

"Four, the investigator discovers that the specialist in question was

138

transferred by orders signed by Khrushchev, but Khrushchev denies this, ergo, Five, the papers were forgeries and the transfer engineered by parties or persons unknown.

"Six, Khrushchev instructs his investigator to find the missing technician.

"Seven, the investigator is killed in an apparent hit-and-run accident in Moscow, and an autopsy reveals high levels of blood alcohol and aminazine."

Finished, Petrov nodded to Gnedin.

"The combination of aminazine and alcohol is lethal," the doctor said. "In this case, however, the victim was struck and killed by a vehicle before the chemical reaction had time to work."

"Observations and questions?" Petrov asked.

"The man would have died if he hadn't been run down?" Bailov asked.

"Yes," Gnedin said.

"One hundred percent probability?" Ezdovo asked.

"Nothing is one hundred percent. Individual tolerances vary, but working backward from the blood level we can say with certainty that the dose was well above what's generally accepted as lethal."

"What about the hit-and-run driver?" Bailov asked.

"Unknown, and there were no witnesses," Petrov said.

"Two people were killed," Gnedin interjected. "Khrushchev's man and a policeman."

"What's the connection?" Bailov asked.

"None known," Petrov said.

"Where is the technician transferred from Tyuratam?" Talia asked.

"Missing," Petrov told the group. "Vanished."

"His records?"

"All false, if the investigator is to be believed."

"No leads?"

"None we know of," their leader said.

Talia sensed that Petrov was enjoying himself. "The technician's name?" she asked.

"Lumbas," Petrov said, "Villam Lumbas. At least that's the name we have. It could be false."

"And the dead investigator?"

"Roman Yegorovich Trubkin."

Bailov sat up when he heard the name. "An air force major?"

Petrov nodded. "You know him?"

"Met him once at a GRU reception. He was with a striking woman—an actress, dancer, singer, something like that. He was a test pilot, and a rather important one, I gathered from the interest in him."

"Perhaps *the* best pilot in the Red air force," Petrov said. "Illness knocked him out of the cosmonaut program. He was to be the first into space, and instead was struck down by an automobile."

"What's the connection between the poisoning and the hit-and-run?" Ezdovo asked.

"That's the wrong question," Talia said too quickly. She saw the surprise on her husband's face, then a deeper emotion, which he masked immediately; she knew she had hurt him, but to her own surprise she continued. "We should ask, '*Is* there a connection?' "

"Yes," Petrov said almost dreamily. "Exactly."

"We can ask that all we want," Gnedin said, "but there are no witnesses."

"Speculate," Petrov said. "What options do we have?"

Gnedin crossed his legs and leaned back. "Party A attempts to poison Trubkin, but before the poison does its work Party B unintentionally strikes and kills Trubkin, panics and drives away. Coincidence, no connection between events."

"In which lane was the body found?" Bailov asked.

"The center lane," Gnedin said, understanding the implication of his colleague's question. In Moscow the center lane was reserved for the automobiles of high officials; those entitled to use it were not bound by laws governing other traffic, the center lane being more or less a no-man's-land where pedestrians had no rights. Gnedin went on. "In which case Party B simply drove away, Trubkin's accident being his problem alone and in this scenario Party B being someone entitled to the Chaika Lane."

"Or someone with access to an automobile licensed for the lane," Talia suggested.

"Other options," Gnedin continued. "Parties A and B are different persons with a shared objective. Or it's possible that the two parties are the same person."

"The dead policeman could likewise be involved or not," Bailov added.

Melko listened carefully to all of them but was having trouble concentrating. In a little more than a week he had gone from a zek with no future to a spa in Odessa, and the others had apparently likewise been plucked from their previous circumstances. He was not sure what to make of it, but Petrov had rescued him from certain death, and this was reason enough to listen. Whatever this was all about, he was now a part of it, which beat hell out of the alternative, no matter what the eventual outcome. As a leader of the *urki* he had survived by being flexible and adaptable, traits that he suspected would continue to serve him.

"I'm interested in the technician," Gnedin said to Petrov. "Villam

Lumbas? You said there was speculation that his absence from the project contributed to the accident."

"The speculation was that if Lumbas had been there, the accident *might* have been avoided," Talia said, this time correcting the doctor.

Again Petrov gave her a peculiar look. "She's right," he told the group. "Talia listens carefully; all of you must emulate her."

Talia regretted her forthrightness and immediately went to Gnedin's defense. "Your question, however, is appropriate. Did Lumbas's absence contribute to the accident?"

"More than likely it was not causative," Petrov said. Trubkin had told Khrushchev as much.

"But we can't say his removal from the project was not *intended* to affect its outcome," Talia said.

"I agree," Petrov said and suddenly he barraged her with questions, none of which had answers. Who is Lumbas? Why was he there? Who moved him and why? And why that particular timing? Where was he sent afterward? Where is he now?

"He was moved on Khrushchev's apparent orders," Talia said. "If we consider the timing of the transfer we could conclude either that somebody wanted to make it appear that his absence contributed to the accident, or—a simpler possibility—that he was needed elsewhere more urgently." She paused. "At this point neither case pertains. We need to find Lumbas either on paper or in the flesh." She looked to Petrov for some sign of support.

"Khrushchev wants Lumbas found," Petrov told them. "Trubkin claimed to be developing leads but shared few details, so we don't have the advantage of his findings."

"Assuming he had anything," Melko said in his first foray into the discussion. "Every investigator claims he has something in the works even when it's not true. It keeps his bosses off his back." The comment drew stares from the others and Melko wished he had kept silent.

"Thank you," Petrov said. "Melko has a good mind and experience different from ours. We can benefit from his abilities and knowledge."

Talia remembered a time when Petrov had introduced her to a skeptical team with a similar speech. "Light draws the moth," she said, and again she saw Petrov staring at her. Thinking aloud, she continued. "Who would have the power or audacity to transfer a man in the General Secretary's name and from a project of the highest national importance?" She did not mention the KGB, but the allusion was understood. "We can safely assume that whoever is responsible is not alone, and has both access to and the cooperation of powerful people."

"If you're suggesting a conspiracy," Petrov asked, "who can be ruled out?"

"Only God," Ezdovo said. "Some say he's left this country to ruin itself."

Bailov and Melko smiled, but Talia answered, "We rule out us, only us."

Melko stepped forward and bowed to the group. "Begging your pardon, your worships, but when one speaks of conspiracy one thinks of crime—hand-in-glove. As it happens, I know something about crime, by the looks of it considerably more than any of you. When cops look at a crime they go for motive first, so I ask, who profits most from this act? Let's start there."

"Melko and Talia are both correct," Petrov said. "We rule out ourselves, and we must determine a motive."

"Without names motives are speculative, a creative exercise with no potential return," Talia said. "It comes back to finding Lumbas."

"And knowing what Trubkin was up to," Gnedin added.

Talia nodded. "It might be possible to work backward from Trubkin's death."

"And Lumbas?" Petrov asked.

"Everything is connected in our country," Talia answered. "Parents inform on children, children on teachers, teachers on administrators and so on, everyone pressured to tell the authorities something about someone, and every word is written down. This is our system, and somewhere in all this paper there will be trails to Lumbas. Perhaps there is a conspiracy, perhaps not. First we solve Trubkin and Lumbas and then we reassess."

Petrov leaned slightly forward and pressed his hand to his stomach. It was a fleeting gesture, but Talia caught it and wondered what was wrong.

"Let's sleep on this," Petrov said, motioning for Melko and Gnedin to remain as the others filed out.

40   SUNDAY, MARCH 12, 1961, 1:20 A.M.
Belgrade

Sylvia was in the flat and seemed ambivalent about his no-show for their dinner. "Miss me?" he ventured. For one of the few times in his life he had overridden his baser instincts and he wanted her to know about it, though he was not sure why.

She shook her head. "By your age most people have learned that the world doesn't orbit them. When you didn't show I figured you had a reason."

Not the response he had hoped for. "I got picked up," he said.

"Spare me the details," she said, turning away.

"By your pal Inspector Peresic. I was on my way to meet you but she shanghaied me downstairs."

"Why?"

He handed the photo to her. "That's Frash on the left. Gent on the right is the stiff from your photo. Seems like our detective wants out and she's willing to trade. She claims that the dead man's a Russian who was connected to Frash, but we get the man's name only if we help her disappear." He then explained who Peresic's husband was and the connection to Albania.

"Why?" Sylvia repeated.

"I just explained that." He was pissed off.

"I mean why did she come to *you*?"

He weighed his answer. "It started out as a more traditional sort of deal," he said, "and I don't think she likes girls."

She ignored the inference. "She knew who you were?"

"And that I was with you."

"Maybe she's setting us up."

"Could be," he said as he sat and kicked off his shoes. "But if she's not and if this snapshot is legit, then just maybe this is a break. It seems worth the risk."

"I'll call Harry," she said. "He can confirm Frash's identity, but he'll have to agree if we're going to try to move her."

The conversation and her tone were strictly business, which disappointed him.

41 SUNDAY, MARCH 12, 1961, 2:00 P.M.
Paris

The Major entered the Père-Lachaise Cemetery through a gate off the avenue by the same name, walked slowly along cobblestone lanes through the confusing maze of tombs and monuments down to the main entrance more than a kilometer away, then backtracked to a pedestrian roundabout with a statue on a ten-meter-high pedestal. This position gave him easy access to the sprawling cemetery's three exits and placed him in the middle of one of its only open areas, a perfect location from which to monitor the spot where he was to meet Lazer Kryeziu. It had been two and a half months since he had dispersed the organization, and though he still had some uneasiness about it, he had called for a meeting in order to assess the situation.

Setting down his wooden box, the Major took out his painting supplies and assembled a portable easel. He smelled incense burning nearby and saw mourners and tourists moving along the roads and paths and between the graves, maps or flowers in hand.

Nearby there were three other painters and a young photographer posing a child against a gray tomb discolored by pigeon shit. There were always people near this spot, which was why he had chosen it. With so many people packed into a cluttered landscape there would be several escape routes.

In recent weeks he had carefully tapped every source he had in an effort to get a line on what Shehu and Hoxha were up to; arrests had apparently ceased in Albania, but so far there had been no known retaliation outside the country. That Shehu would retaliate was not in doubt; it was only a matter of when and where. He would aim his blow at the movement itself, and if the past was a predictor, he would go for the maximum body count as a blunt message to others who dared challenge his power.

Normally for a clandestine meeting the Major liked to arrive at a rendezvous at the same moment as those he would meet, but in this business it wasn't good to get set in your ways. This time he was in place and making an effort to look like a painter a full two hours early. Probably there was no need to worry, but survival demanded attention to detail. People died as easily on a sunny day with the birds singing as on any other. Too many people had a false perception of death, expecting it to telegraph its awful arrival. It seldom did.

The Major spotted a potential problem several minutes before Kryeziu was scheduled to arrive. He had never seen the man before, but as soon as he saw the muscular frame, alarms sounded in his head. The man had a passive face but intense eyes and he was sweating heavily. Why? It was sunny but still cool. Running? Nerves? Whatever the cause, it wasn't normal. The Major dabbed his brush in a dollop of burnt umber, rolled it until the bristles formed a fine point, then carefully drew a thin line along a shadow on his paper. The stranger had his hands in his pockets and stood perfectly still, but he could see that the man was watching for someone, looking without looking, the sign of a professional.

Eventually Kryeziu came into sight, making his way directly to the meeting place, but the stranger seemed to pay no attention to him and this relieved the Major for an instant; the man had probably been hurrying to be on time for a tryst. Ruled by his dick, he decided, typically French.

Kryeziu pushed up a shirtsleeve, nervously checked his watch and lit a cigarette. Below him in the roundabout, a young woman in a long tan coat and red boots approached. The Major saw him smile; then the woman apparently said something that froze his colleague's expression. He tried to not look directly at them as an old woman on crutches came up beside Kryeziu, stopped and wiped her eyes with a white handkerchief. Then everything seemed to shift to slow motion. The woman with red boots took a step toward Kryeziu. The Major saw a pistol come up. No silencer. The young woman held the weapon in two hands and crouched slightly, knees bent, legs apart for balance. The heavyset stranger moved several feet closer to the Major as the first of three quick shots echoed through the area. Initially the Major looked the opposite way of the shots, then glanced back over his right shoulder. Kryeziu was down on his back, one leg bent, the other wiggling violently as the young woman stood over him, looking down, her pistol held high over her head with both hands; then she walked slowly in the direction from which she had come. Onlookers threw themselves on the ground or ducked behind mausoleums as she passed.

The muscular man walked quickly downhill, paralleling the woman's path, while the old woman beside Kryeziu poked his body with a crutch, then shrieked, which panicked people as much as the shots.

The Major abandoned his painting gear, walked to the east entrance of the cemetery then down the rue de la Réunion and south toward the Seine. Two police sedans raced past him toward the cemetery, their sirens caterwauling. Shehu had struck; now to find Ali and finish what had been botched in Belgrade.

42   SUNDAY, MARCH 12, 1961, 4:20 P.M.
Belgrade

Harry Gabler looked as if he had not shaved since the last time they had seen him, and he was clearly perturbed that they had used a priority signal to fetch him back to the embassy. "This better be good," he said from behind his desk. "My wife hit the roof when I told her I had to come back to the office."

Valentine put the photograph in front of him. "Frash?"

The station chief picked up the photo. "Where the hell did you get this?"

"Is it Frash?"

"Does Uncle Miltie like gingham dresses?"

"Recognize his companion?"

Gabler contorted his face in concentration.

Valentine placed the mortuary photograph in front of the CIA man. "This help?"

Gabler placed the photos side by side and studied them. After several seconds he grunted and looked up. "Vicki's stiff. The Albanian, right?"

"Russian," Valentine corrected.

"Says who?"

"Peresic."

Gabler looked at Sylvia. "You saw her again?"

"She approached him last night," she said with a nod toward her partner.

Valentine interrupted. "She wants a one-way ticket to the Land of the Big PX, and a new identity."

"In exchange for what?"

"This photo and the Russian's name. We get the name when we tell her it's a go."

Gabler scratched his chin. "It's not that easy. Have we got other options?"

"She says all the way or no way. She wants a new name, no trail and gimme a life on the lone prairie."

"Is it worth it?"

Sylvia said, "We've got nothing else."

"Hell of a lot of work to set up something like this. You can't just turn a key, and we've got to consider the fact that her husband is a honcho. I've got to think about political balances here, measure how this affects everything."

"You know about her husband?" Valentine asked.

Gabler looked surprised as he nodded. "Small country like this, you get to know a lot about everybody—especially the main players."

"You've got to expedite this," Sylvia said.

"Her husband's on the road with Tito and she wants out," Valentine explained.

Gabler rubbed his cheek. "This sort of defection could fuck up operations here, knock the status out of quo big time. Right now everything's going smoothly with the Yugos."

"When she gets her ticket out, we get the name of the dead Russian; that's the deal," Valentine said. "If this jaybird was Frash's asset, we've got to find out who he is and why he was killed. We need that name."

"This is getting complicated."

"It's our only lead, Harry," Sylvia said in her partner's defense.

Gabler leaned back in his chair and pursed his lips. "I probably could get her to Turkey on my own, stash her there for a while, then move her on after I make other arrangements. Would she buy an intermediate stop?"

"We didn't talk details, Harry, but she's desperate. My guess is that she'll buy anything with an exit sign."

"If we had to, we could probably stash her in Israel temporarily," Gabler said to himself. "We've got a solid working relationship with the Mossad. If it went smoothly it would look like their operation, which would help reduce the heat here; they could help us repatriate her later on. Either way, though, there'll have to be an intermediate stop. I can't send her straight through to the States until they're ready for her on the other side. Maybe I can sell it on the basis of her old man being close to Tito; she's probably got information the Israelis and we could both use."

"Will you need to clear this up the line?" Valentine asked.

"Not all the way, at least not initially. I can move her to Turkey on my own authority, but after that the deputy director for operations will have to clear the transfer to Israel or Stateside."

"What's the time frame?"

"If we get in gear now, I can be ready to move her out in seventy-two hours and I mean so thoroughly that it will look like Martians lifted her off the planet. Impress on her that there mustn't be any change in her routine, no sloppy good-byes and no damned suitcases. We'll pick her up between breaths, and poof, she's gone. She tell you how to contact her?"

"She said she'd get back to me."

"Don't like that," Gabler grumbled. "I'd rather have control at this end."

"Can't be helped. We play the cards in the order they're dealt."

"No shit," Gabler said. "We'll need a pick-up point."

"Name it," Valentine said.

Gabler described the place and circumstances of the pick-up. "Tell her that if she varies one iota from our instructions, she's on her own." I hate this shit, he thought. For now it would be all right, but when it was over there would be diarrhea again. That and the shakes. This time his wife would walk for sure; she had begged him to quit for years, but now the begging had turned to threats: either he quit or she would. It was his choice, she had screamed. But it was no choice at all; you did what you had to do. Twenty years eliminated choices, and the Company's clout outweighed hers.

43   SUNDAY, MARCH 12, 1961, 5:00 P.M.   *Odessa*

The day was overcast, with high humidity and no breeze; the inside of the sanatorium was sweltering but Petrov looked comfortable with a wool blanket draped across his lap. When the team came into the room they saw six black leather wallets arranged in a line on a small table. The first was open, revealing the Red Badge inside, a red circle with a silver hammer and sickle in the middle. The power afforded the holder of such a device was awesome; no Soviet citizen could deny him anything, the penalty for noncompliance being death. For the possessor of the Red Badge there was allegiance only to the individual who had bestowed it, and only the most powerful man in the federation had that power. The Red Badge had been invented by the czars and was but one of the many things the Communists had adopted from the royal regime. Under the czars badges had looked different, but the concept was identical and the power so immense that the Red Badge took on mythical proportions.

"Time to begin work," Petrov began. Melko, Bailov, Gnedin and Talia would go to Moscow; Ezdovo would remain with him.

Talia would report to Khrushchev, move into his household and assess and manage his personal security. Bailov and Gnedin would attempt to track Trubkin and Lumbas, while Melko would open an old and improbable connection to the KGB, and see to the team's accommodations. They would work together and report to Talia, who in turn would report back to him, her position in the General Secretary's retinue providing access to secure communications.

"Where will you be?" Talia asked when Petrov had finished.

"Here," he said. "You don't need an old man's interference."

This brought glances among the old team members. Petrov had almost always been with them and at the center of their activity, but now he would stay behind. This change worried Talia.

Each of them left the meeting carrying a Red Badge, its psychological weight greater than that of a loaded weapon. And more lethal.

44   MONDAY, MARCH 13, 1961, 3:00 P.M.
Lamoura, Franche-Comté, France

The cabin was thirty kilometers north of Geneva, not an elaborate place, but isolated and well situated at the end of a limestone valley reachable only by foot, all of which made it ideal for what he had in mind. Frash had moved cautiously through the rocks and found a place from which he could watch. There were still large patches of crusted snow and translucent blue ice among the rocks on the northern slopes; a stream flowed below the cabin, a twisting, cascading silver rivulet of clear water filled with smooth boulders, deep pools and long stretches of riffles. Idyllic, Albert thought; for an execution ground, Ali chimed in.

Albert had done a lot of thinking since Belgrade. Back issues of Parisian newspapers had offered as much misinformation as information; to get answers he had to read between the lines and think backward. Now he knew he had some of the pieces of the puzzle—not how they fit, but that eventually they *would* fit, and that the main piece was Myslim.

A bastard product of their mother's affair with an Italian diplomat, Myslim had been thought dead in Europe's postwar chaos. Their mother's indiscretion had come before the marriage to Frash's father and was not something she discussed. Before Ali's birth the new stepfather had adopted Myslim and given him his surname and the legitimacy that came with it. During this period the Italians had put Zog on the throne and created modern Albania in the process; that Mussolini would depose his puppet seemed certain, so the elder Frascetti took his wife and stepson to France, where Ali was born. If not for the Nazis, Myslim might have gone to America with his family, but he had true Albanian fire, meaning that vengeance overrode more reasonable values, honor and revenge being eternally linked in the Land of the Eagles.

In America the family name was changed from Frascetti to Frash, and in keeping with this Ali was christened Albert, his Americanization complete. His parents were intellectuals; his father's foray in Albanian politics notwithstanding, their true habitat was the university. After brief stints at CCNY and Bard College the professors Frash found positions at Boston College, and there they remained until four years ago when they died less than six months apart. Frash felt no grief over their passing. He harbored no great interest in death or a fantasy afterlife. As a boy he had explored such concepts, using various domestic animals and his mother's hat pins. It had been these experiments that led to his sojourn at Brampton Academy, where they had packed him away like a rare specimen and watched him around the clock. But he had found ways to subdue his turmoil there, learned the importance of appearances, all of this with not a single thought for Myslim, who was a presumed casualty in the war against the Nazis. Thinking back so far is unfruitful, he reminded himself; it opened pockets of memory better left sealed.

But the gates had already been opened and the memories flooded back.

Maine a long time ago. He remembered switchbacks up a mountain of black pine forest and a wooden shack in a meadow. A morning when the dew was heavy. A wicker basket filled with eight beagle pups, soft, wiggling, clumsy creatures not yet weaned from their mother's teats. A revolver in his hand, too heavy for a toy and shiny as a new dime. A familiar hand stroked his neck, patiently instructing, urging him on. Then there was the smell of gunpowder in the air and eight lumps of tan and black fur, still as statues but warm. Then his mother's voice. "Yes, that's good for the first time but you must keep your eyes open. It will get easier," she had promised, and it was true. Mother was never wrong. The pups were buried in a common grave without prayers.

She was forever talking about Albania and Zog, the jackal and dog, pseudoelitist, betrayer of their people. Thrones belong only to the strong, she often said, but the getting is less difficult than the keeping. Your father had the stomach for neither, Zog only for the easy part and then only because the Italians backed him. "Your father wanted to join Zog—to fight them from the inside was his rationale, but you can't fight from the inside and still be a man. Your father failed, Ali. We fled. Will you?" Mother's dream, ill drawn, fuzzy but full of promise and carefully inculcated in her son, her stories repeated over and over until they were his, as real as his own memories, the vicarious indistinguishable from that which he had lived. Even at Brampton she had been there whispering, reinforcing the dream in him, trying to will him to freedom. When the CIA opportunity came she pressed him to take it, and later gave him the names of men in Paris who could be relied upon.

Think, he urged himself, play it all back, dissect it. Still no sign of Myslim at the cabin. Would he just walk in or approach cautiously? Myslim was a professional and a survivor; he would come like a stalking cat, he guessed, sniffing the wind, watching everything; if not, he would know that Myslim was an instrument. But in whose orchestra?

Like all people, Venema and Arizona had seen only what they had wanted to see. Professionals were human and therefore weak. Mother had taught this: give them what they want, then take what's yours. He had met Arizona at BC, introduced by a Jesuit septuagenarian who saw government service as a calling nearly as sacred as his own. Crown and Church, hand in hand, as it had always been, Loyola's Soldiers of God. A week spent in Atlanta with Venema taking test after test and then the results: high intelligence, independence, strong self-image, self-reliance, language competency, focused thought, analytical skills; he had passed them all, knew he had beaten their system even as he neatly scratched marks on paper with a No. 2 pencil. It had been more thorough than he had anticipated for a preliminary psychological screen. Only later did he learn why; it was not a preliminary but a final exam, and soon thereafter intensive one-on-one instruction at the Farm in Virginia, a whore brought in every Saturday night at nine, a Tex-Mex puta with no name, a mustache and a tattoo of a coiled red-and-blue rattlesnake on her left breast. I suck but I don't swallow, she said.

Mother said there was no need to fear background checks; his bona fides would hold up, had been seen to, false birth certificate and all, with no possible link to France or Albania. But tell them about Brampton; that, too, had been covered. She gave him a name to use. Ours, she explained, and loyal. So easy because it was what they wanted and needed. He guessed that he was some kind of experiment, but exactly what and the reasons for it were not clear to him. Once among them he had risen, learned his lessons, angled for Paris with a goal rather than a plan. Ali Frascetti, Albert Frash, Ali and Albert, the two, the one, rising together to fulfill a mother's dream.

Then Myslim had appeared. Unexpectedly, illogically, suddenly.

Still no life around the cabin. Mother's words: "Leave your mark on our enemies. Keep both eyes open. Those who die deserve it. Do what your father could not. If only Myslim had lived; together the two of you would be unstoppable." Now Albert knew she was wrong about that, and he wondered what else she had been wrong about.

Zog no longer mattered; Hoxha and the Communists ruled now; they were the enemy, and his people were awaiting their deliverance. The Kennedys had looked through his mother, made her into nothing, just as Hoxha had turned their country into a nonentity. A man needed to remember such things if he was indeed a man. Mother understood this.

How would Myslim come to him? Still too early. It would not happen until dark.

45 MONDAY, MARCH 13, 1961, 7:02 P.M. *Belgrade*

Vicki Peresic had given Valentine the addresses of six public telephones. He was to be at the first one at 7:00 A.M. on Monday, wait three minutes, and leave if there was no call from her. If a phone rang he was to answer it only after the second ring. He was to repeat the same procedure with a different phone two hours later and so on until all six locations had been covered, and after that there was another cycle of six in the same order as the first. If there was no contact after two full cycles, he would know she was no longer interested. Or worse.

This was the first station of the second cycle; there had been no contact in the first cycle, which came as no surprise. Gabler had told Valentine she would probably call in the evening when the streets were filled with crowds of home-bound government workers. Now he was in a decrepit train station next to a public toilet that stank and the sound of the phone was so feeble that he nearly missed it. He picked up after the second ring and said, "It's on."

"When?" Peresic asked. Her voice was hard to hear.

"Seventy-two hours after delivery."

"Not fast enough," she said, and he heard fear in her voice. "I have an unexpected guest coming."

Her husband. "When?"

"Thursday morning."

"I'm not sure we can accelerate that much."

"There's no choice," she answered sharply, but she did not beg and he admired that.

"Is this line secure?"

"Not really."

"I'll do my best," he said. "How do I get details to you?"

"Shorten the sequence to one-hour intervals and I'll keep calling," she said; then the line went dead.

Sylvia did not like the suddenness; there was too much room for error. When he asked, "What's the alternative?" she had no answer.

46 MONDAY, MARCH 13, 1961, 9:20 P.M.
Lamoura, Franche-Comté, France

He could not see the crows but he could hear them in the distance, their lookouts yapping at a main group, their sharp eyes recording details their tiny brains couldn't process; anything they saw that didn't fit their meager memories or suspicious natures would be assumed foreign and therefore dangerous. Or interesting. Sometimes it was hard to tell the difference. Mother said Kennedy's campaign office had been guarded by young men in dark suits. *His* crows. Frash felt no kinship to the crows; he had been in control, with everything going smoothly, and then Villam had been murdered and in that instant everything was rendered suspect. Since then anything that didn't fit what he knew with certainty was dangerous, and Myslim was the epitome of something that no longer fit. His mother had had the same experience in the Bellevue Hotel. His brother had trudged purposefully up the valley floor before sundown, neither circling nor being circumspect but going straight on, shoulders squared with resolve, or resignation perhaps. The fact that he walked openly in the light was enough; it told Frash what he needed to know. Actions speak louder than words, Mother's voice warned from the memory bank; your father is proof of this. A half brother was no brother at all, an insight proven correct once again. Villam was dead, and it had been Myslim who had delivered Villam to him. A brother's gift, he had said, and Albert had taken it at face value, seen what he wanted like a common mortal. Kill the bastard, Ali growled menacingly, but for the moment Albert had more strength. No killing until we get what we need. There is duty to be done even in a containment operation.

At the time Myslim had come to him, it had seemed like fate, though Frash had never believed in such a force: one made one's own fate. An informer on the fringe had come to him with the story of a Russian named Ivanov said to be six months out of the Motherland via Helsinki and now officially cloaked in asylum, a French bestowal, the Frogs well known for not being picky about who they let in. Ivanov had royal blood, French kin and self-touted knowledge of certain classified tidbits about improvements in Soviet air defense radar. He was skeptical; only the rare Russian émigré had anything of value to offer, and most of them were unabashed bullshit artists, but you never knew until you checked them out. The

Communists had done a thorough job of convincing their subjects that capitalism was a process that allowed bullshit and fantasy to be traded at even par for hard currency.

The meeting was set for a room above an obscure bookshop in the Latin Quarter. The simple arrangements demanded by the Russian both encouraged Frash and inflamed his more suspicious nature; amateurs preferred to make things hopelessly complex. Frash was to ask the clerk if he had any of Chekhov's journals; if the meeting was on, the answer would be "In the special section above." Any other response meant it was off, a simple-enough plan that suggested a professional hand. Perhaps Ivanov would be the rare find, or else something entirely different. The KGB made an art of using émigrés to entrap and compromise Western agents; as the CIA's chief of station in Paris he had no doubt that the Soviets had made him. No fear, of course, but he had been professionally cautious in approaching the rendezvous, and more curious than usual. The bookstore clerk was male, young, balding, effeminate. French culture embraced extremes; so, too, did America's, but the difference was that the French knew themselves while the Americans did not. Except for the Kennedys, who gave thumbs up or down.

Ivanov was supposed to be a graybeard, sixtyish, short and stocky, as Russians tended to be. They were a diminutive people, but novelists and Hollywood had enlarged them in the collective psyche.

The room above the bookstore had shelves of dusty books with faded spines. Frash had entered to find a man's broad back; having seen it, an alarm sounded in his head and he made for the door. "Wait," a voice said in high-speed Parisian French and he had turned to find a tall, muscular, dark-eyed figure with hair the color of obsidian. The man wore the soiled coveralls of a common laborer and a spreading grin. The eyes were vaguely familiar. "You don't recognize your own brother?" the stranger asked, opening his arms. "Come give me a proper greeting or I'll turn you over my knee."

Frash was dumbfounded. His brother? "We thought you were dead."

"So I am," Myslim said, "to most, and would be to the rest if they had their way." He laughed.

It had been too much to take in. "How do I know that you are who you say you are?"

His brother gave him a photograph identical with one in his mother's albums and a small card with a black double-headed eagle and crossed sabers above it, the symbol of the Albanian Freedom Front.

"We thought you were killed in the war."

For days Frash had grilled Myslim about his past in an unbrotherly way. In retrospect, sitting here among the rocks, he now realized that

Myslim had been circumspect in his answers, professionally evasive, yet seemingly forthcoming. But it was information that only seemed to be. Myslim had spent his life at war: with the French underground, then with Tito against the Nazis, soon thereafter with Hoxha against the Nazis, and eventually with the AFF against Hoxha. In the front he was known as the Major, a rank he had never held. Frash did not immediately embrace Myslim's story, but he later used the Front to establish that such a person existed; then his contacts identified Myslim as the man, and eventually he had accepted it.

By then Myslim had brought him Villam Lumbas, late of the Soviet Rocket Force, who was in Belgrade. A brother's gift to his only brother, the half notwithstanding. There had been a quick trip to Belgrade to evaluate Lumbas and a long interview at a place on the Adriatic in Italy, then a call to Arizona. What Lumbas passed along had checked out. Where had this come from? Arizona pressed. We need bona fides. Move me to Belgrade, Frash implored. Let me work this one myself; he won't talk to anybody else. All right, but no mistakes, his handler advised. This was the long-awaited Midas asset, purest of pure, and let's keep it so. We don't get these very often. By then Myslim had revealed his network in Kosovo Province, where there were a million Albanians waiting to be led home, a ready-made army for the right leader. Lumbas would be a perfect diversion for Frash's masters and allow Frash to pursue what was deep in his heart. It had gone well, nearly flawlessly. The Belgrade chief of station was nosy but could be sidestepped because a Midas asset required a short chain of command: Arizona and him, and only he knew Lumbas. Arizona had a name but no face and no details. Only he could work Lumbas, which was how Frash wanted it. Alone he could move when and where he wanted, with a perfect cover for his true work.

The lights were on in the cabin now, billowing smoke silhouetted against the sky. Let him sit awhile, Frash cautioned himself.

It was Myslim who had suggested the focus on Kosovo, a province in southern Serbia filled with Albanians who had fled their homeland during the thirties and forties, and descendants of those who had fled Zog, the Nazis, and later the Communists. The Albanians were the province's majority but were ruled by Serbs, whom they loathed; the area was a powder keg which with careful provocation might make them rise against their Serbian masters or strike across the border at Hoxha, who ruled what was once theirs. Where else can we find a ready-made army? Myslim had argued.

His brother shared his dream, and in mutual interest a plan was born. While information about Soviet rocketry flowed from Lumbas through Frash to Arizona and CIA analysts, Frash and his half brother concentrated on their plan to unseat Hoxha. At each turn Myslim seemed to have a ready-made answer, and not once had he been wrong.

In the course of this Frash asked Myslim how he had come to know Lumbas.

"His parents are also Albanian," Myslim revealed. "He wants all the things we want."

At first Frash resisted Lumbas's involvement in their true work but Villam had his own contacts in Kosovo, and in the end the three of them became the heart of the new alliance; from this grew their plan, sketchy at first, but quickly taking shape. No, Frash said, revising the thought. Not *their* plan. *Myslim's* plan. His and Villam's. Sitting in the dark crevices above the cabin, he now saw how the two had led him to believe that it was his own, but it had been theirs from the start.

Myslim was well connected inside Albania and got them information indicating that 35 to 45 percent of the mountain tribes would rise if they could be assured success. Tito, in fact, had helped establish these sympathies through his own covert operations led by General Milos Duzevic, a partisan hero now officially retired but responsible to Tito for counterintelligence operations against the Hoxha regime. Duzevic's main lieutenant was Admiral Pinajot Pijaku, formerly of the Albanian navy and himself a refugee from Hoxha's wrath. The Yugoslavian effort, however, was aimed solely at keeping Hoxha off balance, not toppling him from power. What the brothers intended was considerably more ambitious: a land attack from the north by Kosovo-based Albanians and a second front in the south by the Greeks, who were tired of Albania's support for Greek Communists. With the battle committed, Hoxha's opposition would rise up and link with the invading forces. To gain acceptance, Frash had convinced the various parties that as support for the attack the U.S. Navy would cruise the Albanian coast, pouring gunfire onto mainland strongholds. There was no way to actually involve the Navy, but if Albania was to be his, he had to convince them that it was true, and eventually they had believed him. This too had been Myslim's idea.

"How will the Soviets react?" he had asked his brother.

Don't worry about the Soviets, Myslim assured him. The Albanians were already on the verge of a split with the Soviets. Hoxha was forever reminding Soviet officials that the Albanians had freed themselves of Nazi oppression without Soviet assistance and therefore the relationship was one of equals, not master and vassal; thus Albania was a sister state, a full member of the socialist family, and with this they insisted on full and equal rights. There's a schism, Myslim told him. The Soviets think they're losing Albania to the Red Chinese; if Khrushchev thinks Tito can annex the bastards, he'll stay clear. Stalin and Tito hated each other, but now Khrushchev wants Tito back in the family and he's willing to give him Albania as a dowry. Don't worry about the Soviets.

It had all been set, the arrangements made, promises given, money collected, arms purchased and distributed and the plan initiated; then Lumbas had been killed. Frash went over Villam's killing again and again. Villam had given the emergency signal for the rendezvous, but he had been calm in the cemetery. Only later had Frash understood that this behavior revealed more than words. Villam didn't balk when he saw the killers because he *expected* them to be there. Explanation: Lumbas had attempted to set him up but had been killed in his own trap. Why? There was only one reasonable conclusion: Villam had been used to draw him in, but the killers had intended all along to take out both of them.

Myslim came out on the porch, lit a cigarette, took several puffs, looked around several times, flicked the butt into the darkness and went back inside. Frash decided to stay put a while longer.

The assassins in Belgrade had been Russians; there was no mistaking their style. But why? Despite its reputation for brutishness the KGB was a professional and competent organization, killing only when it was logical, when no other option existed, or when it was an essential tactical component of a scheme. Syllogistically: Lumbas the Russian was leaking rocket information to the CIA; the Russians used Lumbas to set him up; therefore, the Russians knew about the leak and about the operation to unseat Hoxha. But if they knew, why had Villam been killed? Procedure would require them to interrogate Lumbas in a process that would entail months, perhaps years, the Russians being incredibly meticulous in such matters. Against this well-established standard they had not bothered to plumb Villam's perfidy and they had summarily executed him. Why? The killing was counter to established procedure on both sides.

Tired now, concentration faltering. Stay with it. You're closer now.

If they killed Lumbas and were not worried about determining what he had passed to the West, this meant they already knew what he had leaked and perhaps had dismissed its value. Or what he had was of no value in the first place, or if it was valuable, its passing had been intended, the information expendable. Valuable or not, his murder meant that Villam was not what he was purported to be. It had been Myslim who had led him to Lumbas and vouched for him. A brother's gift! He could feel Ali's rage growing inside him. The Russians wanted both him and Lumbas dead because they were pawns in something larger, and Myslim had engineered it. If the Soviets tried to set him up in Belgrade, they would try again. Such a decision would not be turned on and off. His own death had to be one more move in a grander scheme; yet there had been no pursuit, so alternatives must exist, and now Myslim had called for a meeting just as inexplicably as Lumbas had. Who could reach him? Only his brother. There was no other way to read it: Myslim had double-crossed him.

Myslim moved in and out of Albania with impunity when even top Yugoslav agents could not achieve this with any regularity. The conclusion was inescapable: Myslim was a Soviet agent. His brother had given him Lumbas because the Soviets *wanted* him to have Lumbas. But why? So they could take down Hoxha? No. If that had been the intent, they would have allowed the operation to take place, but Villam's death had shattered the operation just as it got rolling. Why?

When Frash stepped through the door of the cabin his 9 mm automatic was in his left hand and he saw a grinning Myslim seated by the fireplace, a blanket over his lap, his hands underneath.

"You look tense, my brother," Frash said.

"It's a disaster," Myslim said. This was not going to be easy. His brother was spooked and he was a professional. They had missed him in Belgrade, so now it fell to him to finish the job. The orders had been explicit: after the Albanians had been helped to uncover the plot, both men were to be eliminated. Their parts had been played and they were to be removed so that there was no chance of interference and no way to backtrack the events that had been set in motion.

"What's a disaster?" Frash asked, keeping his distance.

"The plan. Shehu knows what's going on. He's sent his people to Paris; they're killing our comrades."

"*Our* comrades?"

Myslim stiffened. "The movement." He nodded at a manila envelope on the table. "Newspaper reports," he said. "Read them. You'll see how it is."

"I've seen them," Frash said coolly. "How does Shehu know where to look?"

Myslim raised his eyebrows. "The Sigurimi must have infiltrated us. Or perhaps the Greeks cut a deal with Shehu. You can't trust Greeks," he grunted. "We should have anticipated that."

"Perhaps the Russians betrayed us," Frash said. It wouldn't be the first time. He knew that an earlier CIA-Brit operation had been launched from Crete and been crushed over a three-year period; it had been the Russians who somehow got wind of the mission and alerted the Albanians then.

Shit, Myslim thought. Did his brother know or was he guessing? "The Russians are not our worry. Remember? What have the Russians got to do with this?"

This was the same question Frash had. He backed up slightly to open more space after pushing the door closed with his heel. "Why did you call for a meeting? This was to be only a last resort."

"The whole thing was crumbling; I tried to find you in Belgrade but you and Villam had disappeared. I thought: Ali will see that it's gone badly and he'll know what to do, so I left."

Frash paused a long time before answering. "Yes, brother, I *know*.

I saw Villam killed." Myslim tensed. "Let me see your hands," Frash said softly. "Slowly."

"Is this a joke?" He *knew*.

"Tell me about Lumbas," Frash said. "And Kennedy."

The wide grin faded from Muslim's craggy face. "I don't understand." Kennedy? What the hell was he talking about?

"Put your hands on top of your head and stand up."

Myslim struggled to maintain composure. "A parlor game?"

"Up," Frash repeated. When his brother stood, a revolver thudded to the plank floor.

"Expecting a problem?" Frash asked. Did the new President expect problems?

"I'm a cautious man."

"Not cautious enough. Squat." Frash moved carefully and kicked the pistol away. When Myslim glanced over his left shoulder Frash struck him hard over the opposite ear, then searched his clothing. In his breast pocket he found a small glass ampule; it was cyanide in the form favored by KGB illegals, as good as an engraved calling card. When Myslim revived he was bound to a wooden pillar. Frash flicked the ampule into the fireplace.

"You'll get nothing from me," Myslim said, his grin steady.

"My dear brother," Frash said, "I'll get everything."

 47 MONDAY, MARCH 13, 1961, 10:40 P.M.
Barvikha, Russia

The room felt comfortable and lived in but had more furniture than Talia had ever seen. There was a modern record player and a tall wooden case filled with albums, several vases filled with fresh flowers, and on one wall two small icons in gilt frames. Beside a chair was a wooden box overflowing with paperbacked books and colored crayons. She picked up one of the books and thumbed through the pages; they were filled with outline drawings of smiling animals. What sort of book was this? She looked through several more and found some with the pictures colored in. How odd to have the outline of the animals already drawn; wasn't that part of the artist's function?

"You see what my grandchildren do for amusement," Nikita Khrushchev boomed as he entered the room. "At least it's better than the jazz music my daughter's husband amuses himself with. You come from Petrov?"

"Yes, Comrade General Secretary." She held out one of the books. "What is this?"

"They're from America. Gifts from President Eisenhower's grand-children to my grandchildren."

"I don't understand their purpose."

"It's ironic," Khrushchev said. "Americans put great value on inde-pendent thinking, yet they teach their children to stay within the lines." The General Secretary sat down in an upholstered chair and put his feet up on a leather footstool. He wore a silk robe and scuffed brown leather slippers with crushed heels. "If such books existed in our country the Americans would chastise us for mind control." He laughed, showing a gap between his upper front teeth. His voice was pleasant and younger than his appearance, and she could sense his energy.

Talia returned the books to the box and sat down.

"Petrov sends a woman to me and asks me to cooperate fully." Khrushchev grinned. "He has audacity. What would my colleagues say if they knew I was taking instructions from a woman?"

"They might guess you were married."

Nikita Sergeievich's grin widened. "Your tongue is as sharp as Pe-trov's."

"As is my mind," she said, and immediately regretted her retort.

"Let's hope that your resolve equals your intellect," the General Secretary said sharply, his pleasant grin suddenly gone.

"For the moment," Talia said, "my needs are simple. First you must tell me everything about your personal security organization. I must know exactly how things are done. Every detail."

"And then?"

"You will be taken care of."

The General Secretary was intrigued by her. Tall, with dark hair and high cheekbones, she wore a gray suit that looked new but didn't fit well; even so, she was elegant and obviously confident. Her voice was soft and feminine, but there was something in her demeanor that suggested a reservoir of inner strength. Most people who had to deal with him let their anxiety show, but this tall woman seemed entirely at ease, and he was impressed.

"I'm called Talia."

"A beautiful name." Would her strength endure over time? It was one thing to be strong outside Moscow, but life and power in the Kremlin exacted an inevitable price on those who managed to rise. Those who sat at the pinnacle became targets whose eventual fall was the sole objective of those below them. Most who managed to get this far had exquisite skills and unshakable confidence, but longevity required much more, especially for a woman. It would be interesting to see how she fared.

Talia was also measuring Khrushchev. He was short and fat, with a round face and thick lips, but there was a certain grace in his movements. Still, his presence was ordinary; if he were removed from Moscow and deposited in Tanga he would look as if he had always been there. With his plump peasant's face, he would seem at home in a shapka and dog coat, perhaps even more at home than in his present surroundings. By and large he seemed to be an ordinary man who had achieved extraordinary success. That this was possible suggested that the Soviet system was not so bad. Talia also knew that whatever Khrushchev's current image and her first impressions were, he had once been one of Stalin's most ruthless lieutenants. To rise so high under the old regime, she decided, required a peasant's brutish view of the world. But if Nikita Sergeievich were starting his career now, would he be as successful? Remember that he is a sort of predator, Petrov had advised her; those around him are scavengers and much less predictable. They had spent only a few moments together, but already she felt that she could work with the General Secretary. Had Petrov also sensed this when he sent her here?

It had been just before dusk when her train pulled into the station at Kievsky Vokzal Square. Petrov had told her to hire a cab and given her an address in a suburb built along the Moscow River. Her driver was the gregarious sort who kept up a lively monologue; several times he tested her availability, but with caution. Suggestive remarks were followed immediately by laughs in case she reacted badly. Talia took no offense from such overtures; like many men, he was an emotional child. Like love, anger was much too valuable to waste on life's petty moments.

The twilight drive afforded her a fleeting view of Moscow. After sixteen years the predominant color was still gray, but there had been a massive amount of new construction. The modern buildings were dreary multistory boxes, one identical with the next, standing where there formerly had been row upon row of traditional wooden houses. Though it was getting dark, the buildings were poorly lit; when she had last been in the city it had been blacked out at night, and now it looked nearly so. Muscovites still moved with their distinctive shuffle, their walk a product of long winters and sidewalks seldom clear of ice. The roads were packed with green trucks filled with young soldiers; they seemed to be everywhere. She absorbed everything as if it were fresh air. Tanga was now her home, and in sixteen years away from the capital she had seldom thought about the city that Soviet citizens called the Center. Now that she had returned, she felt unexpected nostalgia; whatever she was now had been forged here, and she promised herself that she would pay attention to every detail so that she could tell her sons about the city where they had been born.

The taxi driver went silent when he stopped in front of her destination. "How much?" she asked.

"Whatever you want," he said quickly. There was heavy perspiration on the back of his neck. While she looked for rubles in her purse, three soldiers came down to the cab and peered inside.

"Never mind," the driver said. "It's not necessary."

"I insist," she told him. "After such pleasant conversation I want to be sure you're adequately compensated."

The driver produced a strangled sound. "God will reward me," he gasped.

"I think not," she said, passing the fare to him.

One of the soldiers tapped his gloved hand on the driver's window and motioned for him to move on. When Talia got out, the cab shot forward with its rear door still flapping.

Now the General Secretary rose and signaled her to follow him. "Petrov asks that we billet you here," he said with a grin. "An outrageous man. He has large balls," he added.

"So do I," Talia added, at which Khrushchev's explosive laugh filled the room.

 ## TUESDAY, MARCH 14, 1961, 8:30 A.M.
Moscow

Gnedin had gone to the Heart Institute while Melko went to arrange quarters for them. Bailov arranged to meet them later and rushed off to find Raya. She blinked once when she saw him in front of her desk, but it was the only indication that she was surprised. He was dressed like a common laborer: gray coat, brown sweater, heavy canvas trousers, mud-spattered boots. "Interesting costume," she said coolly.

He looked for some sign that she was glad to see him, but found none. "I have some time on my hands," he said.

"What has that got to do with me?" There was a hard edge to her voice.

"Is there somewhere we can talk?"

"I'm on duty."

162

Bailov moved around her desk, grabbed her by the arm, pulled her to her feet and led her between a stack of books toward a study room. "We have an appointment," he explained to a male librarian who peered down from a ladder as they passed. When they were inside, he jammed a chair under the doorknob and tested it to be certain it was secure.

"This is outrageous," Raya said. "Let me out."

"I was called away on special duty. It was very sudden and there was no time to let you know."

"And now your duty has ended, so your leisure takes precedence over *my* duty, is that it?" Her eyes were on fire, her checks flushed.

"I'm sorry," Bailov said.

The muscles in her jaw tightened. "If I remember correctly, we began our—acquaintance—on an identical note."

"Acquaintance?"

Her hand swung before he could react and caught him flush on the jaw. "*That's* reality," she snapped. "How do you like it?" He rubbed his cheek. "I won't have you walking in and out of my life without warning," she said. "I won't. Do you understand?"

He stepped back. "I'm sorry, but when a soldier receives orders he obeys. That's my reality."

"I knew it was a mistake from the beginning," Raya said. "I've known other soldiers. You're all alike." His stomach churned at what he took as an allusion to previous lovers. "Why should I expect any more from you?"

"Because I care for you, Raya."

"I care for my birds but I know them for what they are," she snapped.

"I'm not one of your damned birds," he shot back.

"You're always flying away from me." Suddenly she was in his arms sobbing. "I thought you were dead," she said. "Or worse."

In the middle of the night he awakened to find her on her side, her head propped in her hand, staring at him. "Was I snoring?" he asked.

"I was just reminding myself what a fool I am," Raya said. "I thought I'd lost you; now that I have you back I'm not sure it's what I want."

"You seemed sure enough a couple of hours ago."

She slapped his chest gently. "I'm serious, Taras Ivanovich. Before I met you I was content; my life was full. If I needed a man it was easy enough to arrange. You'd be surprised how easy it is in Moscow. We were compatible, I knew that, and there was none of the tediousness afterward that normally goes with such relationships. From the beginning

I knew it was different, but then you were gone and I didn't know what to feel." She bit him gently on the lower lip and her hips pressed against him. "How long do I get you this time?"

Bailov had no idea.

4 9	WEDNESDAY, MARCH 15, 1961, 10:15 A.M. *Odessa*

Living in the sanatorium was like being kept in an elegant brothel with a prepaid tab. In the Yablonovy Mountains one had to work hard every day simply to stay alive. You built your own shelter, made your own clothing, and if you were to eat you had to go out into the forest and gather the food or kill it. Here it seemed that all you had to do was let a desire creep into your mind, then reach for what you wanted because, whatever it was, it would be there magically. Ezdovo hated it. Talia and the others were gone and he had been left behind. He expected Petrov to keep him busy with tasks, but it had not turned out that way.

In the mornings Petrov stayed in his room; Ezdovo remained close by in case he was wanted, but his leader never called. In the afternoons Petrov sat on the veranda in the shade, facing the Black Sea, bobbing in a wooden glider, his eyes half closed. When he spoke, it was only to complain about the wind (too much or too little), the sun (too bright or under clouds), the black sand (it got into the food and bedding), or the food (too much, too little, too spicy, too bland). On and on it went, with Petrov grumbling and Ezdovo thinking more and more that the resort was a prison. After so many years in the taiga and winters of fifty below, the warm sun and salty air soothed him initially, but in no time at all this passed and he became restless. It was not just the idleness; he could handle that if there was a goal looming somewhere ahead. In the taiga with his sons, nature sometimes demanded idleness, but always in the context that the delay would be temporary, part of a larger plan. This was different; here there appeared to be no expectations or future, and Talia and the others had gone to Moscow. Damn Khrushchev! Since the war Ezdovo's entire life had revolved around his beloved wife and her sons. They were the center around which he orbited. Life was full and there was purpose. Without her he withdrew into himself, his mood growing darker by the hour.

Today he had walked along the beach for nearly three hours and returned to the sanatorium shirtless and sweaty. As he climbed up the steps he saw Petrov on the veranda. His head was tilted to the side, his flesh was yellow, and dark blood was trickling from both nostrils.

In an instant Ezdovo had the employees of the facility scrambling to his orders. Petrov was taken up to bed, a doctor called, his leader's bloody clothes changed, wads of cotton inserted in his nose and ice packs applied to stem the nosebleed.

The doctor who came was young, in her mid-thirties, a short, slightly built woman in a full skirt with a flower pattern. She carried a small carpetbag and wore a wide-brimmed straw hat. Her examination was over in minutes, but she had a concerned look as she wrestled a cigarette from her skirt pocket. "There will have to be tests," she said.

"Then take him to the hospital."

"Not here. In Moscow," she said. "Here they dip arthritics in mud baths, treat tuberculosis with sunlamps and induce abortions with coat hangers."

"It will take time to get him there."

"Tests can be done anywhere, comrade. It's the therapy that counts, and Moscow, I fear, is superior to Odessa. Marginally better, but an improvement nonetheless." The doctor dropped her cigarette in a vase. "Soviet medicine is like Soviet democracy: a contradiction in terms."

"You criticize your own profession?"

The doctor smiled crookedly. "I'm Russian and I speak truth. If it insults you, don't listen. If you need to worry about patients, go ahead. I prefer to worry only about whether the day will be sunny and the sea trout is cooked properly." She took several steps down the hall, stopped, looked back over her shoulder and said, "When you get to Moscow, find a butcher who knows something about cancer."

The word played over and over in Ezdovo's mind as he entered Petrov's room. His leader was awake.

"I'll call Gnedin," Ezdovo said. "He'll know what to do. Khrushchev will send a plane."

Petrov blinked. "Why?"

"The doctor said we should move you to a hospital in Moscow."

"I'll decide when we move," Petrov said, his high voice firm. "Have you forgotten who commands?"

"But she mentioned cancer."

Petrov waved his hand in dismissal. "A word, no more."

"Cancer is . . . serious."

"Life is serious," Petrov said. "Cancer is merely terminal. We stay here and let our comrades do their work."

50 WEDNESDAY, MARCH 15, 1961, 10:00 P.M.
Belgrade

Inspector Peresic was dressed in loose black trousers and black wind-breaker, her blond hair brushed back and held in place by a small comb. She leaned down to look into the taxi that was parked in an alley between warehouses along the Danube. Gabler motioned for her to get into the backseat, where Valentine was curled up on the floor. What's going on?" he asked her as Gabler drove them away.

"My husband's coming back."

"Why?"

"I don't know. Tito uses him for a variety of tasks. If he's coming back, it's Tito's idea."

"It's going to be dicey," Gabler said from the front. "There hasn't been time to tie up all the loose ends."

"But you can get me to America?" It was clear that she was worried.

"Eventually, but there's going to be an intermediate stop."

Valentine saw her tense. "Where?"

"If it's not good enough you can get out now."

"No," she said. "I no longer have a choice."

"The name of the dead man?" Valentine asked.

"Lumbas," she said. "Villam Pavelovich Lumbas."

"Embassy staff?" Gabler asked.

She raised her eyebrows. "There is no more. You asked me for a name and now you have it. I expect you to keep your part of the bargain." She was visibly nervous now.

"Where did the information come from?"

"What does it matter?"

"It matters," Gabler said.

"From an . . . associate of my husband."

"How would this associate know this particular name?" Valentine asked.

"He was involved in the investigation. It was from him that I first learned that the dead man was a Soviet. My husband's associate was instructed to officially inform me that the death was no longer a police matter. Later the case reverted back to us."

"After another investigation had been completed?"

"Presumably."

"But you didn't reopen your own investigation?"

"I've already explained that there was no reason. We had already looked at it, and when it was remanded to us again we simply carried it in our open file; there was nothing more for us to do. When I pressed my husband's associate for details, he told me that the dead man was Russian, and that this should serve to dampen the enthusiasm of the homicide unit. It was a warning I heeded."

"Nevertheless he gave you the name."

"I think he wanted me to know," Peresic said.

"Why?"

She shook her head. "He didn't say. It's only a feeling I had."

"Did the Russian embassy report a missing person to the police?"

"No."

A dead Russian that the embassy doesn't miss. This was as strange as everything else. The Russians were particularly careful to keep track of all of their citizens in a foreign country, even that of a quasi-ally. Either the Russians knew he was dead or they didn't. Or perhaps he was an illegal. But if he was in the country legally the embassy would know, so why hadn't they inquired? Unless he was someone special and they were afraid to risk disclosure. No. If he was theirs and they had not inquired, then they knew the man was dead; if they didn't claim the body, they didn't want it. *Unless they knew nothing about him.* The KGB did not tell its secrets to embassy people. Sylvia said that only the rezidents, or legal agents, had credentials. Lumbas could have been off the books. Valentine had seen firsthand how thorough the Russians had been after the war; they left nothing to chance. If they knew Lumbas and didn't want the body, they wanted him dead and anonymous. He repeated the dead man's name to Inspector Peresic. "Villam Pavelovich Lumbas."

"Yes."

When they crossed a bridge, Gabler stopped the car. "Here's where we lighten the load."

"Lie down," Valentine said as he opened the door. As he sat up and made a show of passing the fare to Gabler, he asked, "Anything we should do?"

"Be conspicuous for the next couple of days. Be tourists until you hear from me again."

"What about her?"

"She's my problem now. Let's hope she's worth the effort."

"Can you handle it?"

Gabler smiled, pressed the clutch and put the vehicle into gear. "No choice," he said as if to himself.

51   THURSDAY, MARCH 16, 1961, 5:00 P.M.
Bastogne, Belgium

The Hôtel le Sud was a four-story anachronism, battered but not broken during the Nazis' last-gasp offensive into the Ardennes, now refurbished with comfortable beds, clean floors and community toilets on each floor that were stocked with American magazines. Frash had a corner room on the third floor with a window looking down on a gravel parking lot, and below and beyond that a sunken rail line with two sets of tracks.

There had been heavy rain at noon, but now the dark skies had lightened and the rain came in brief, soft showers. Across the hall a couple made love, the man grunting with workmanlike regularity, the woman ranging from squeals of delight to urgent commands, which Frash understood more by the tone than by the garbled words. He had seen them arrive that morning; the man was short and thick across the chest, immaculately dressed in a houndstooth sportcoat and forest-green tie; she was taller and full-bodied, with long red hair, dangling earrings and thick red lips. He reeked of money, she of followers of the same. Madame had given them the room directly across the hall. Only three guests and all of them placed together; Frash guessed that Madame cleaned the rooms herself to save the cost of a maid and put them close to each other to make her work easier. The couple had paid in advance for five days' lodging and would have their meals elsewhere. From their glow, Albert guessed a tryst. After a while their lovemaking took on a cadence that left his mind clear to think.

His brother had been tougher than he had anticipated, but in the end the truth had come tumbling out. Myslim had been a Soviet agent. He had known Lumbas since their days at university in Moscow; both of them had served the KGB most of their adult lives. As Frash had surmised, the trap in Belgrade had been set for both of them; Lumbas was bait, trigger and target, and had seen only the part he had wanted to see. Myslim had been instructed to provoke the Albanians, so he had asked for Lumbas and his superiors had delivered him. But his brother was more tool than architect and had no sense of the operation's strategic purpose, or how far up the chain of command it had originated; he had simply been asked to put an operation together and had done so. Finding Frash had been serendipity, pure and simple, and having found him and plumbed his passion for the Albanian cause, Myslim had the perfect foil.

The Soviet rocket information had been legitimate and complete, a calculated giveaway, which meant that the operation had been cleared at the highest levels, perhaps even by the Politburo. Myslim needed Frash to believe in Lumbas down to his soul, so what they had given him was stunning. Space and the Soviet defense rocket program were not compatible; the Kremlin had been duped by its own scientists. This was known by a few now, but eventually would be widely known, Myslim said, so giving it to the West made no difference ultimately.

Myslim had died hard but he had died broken, spilling everything.

Why did the Russians want to provoke Albania? Myslim didn't know; of this Frash was certain. It had been messy at the end, and he had been forced to burn the cabin to disguise the torture. Later he regretted not taking Myslim into the mountains, dismembering him and disposing of the pieces separately. Motion was safety and a whole night in the cabin had been nerve-racking, so he had used this shortcut. Ali's hand had seen to everything, but he was sated now, which made it easier for Albert to think without interference.

What was Khrushchev thinking? Where was the logic in all this? There would be no internal uprising, Myslim had admitted. The hill tribes were docile now, entirely broken by Shehu and the Sigurimi. Children were separated from their parents, wives from husbands, brothers from sisters, mountain people sent to cities and farms on the coast, city people to mountain villages, the old beliefs prosecuted and crushed, relatives set against relatives, suspicion and fear the driving forces of individual life, Communism and Marxist principles the cement of society, the government's power paramount in all matters, the Albania that Frash had dreamed of lost forever, his father's failure magnified. A stronger man than Zog might have resisted Mussolini and altered history, but his father had fled; now he could see truth in his mother's words. His father could have turned history but he had failed. Why had justice forsaken him?

Sleep came. When Albert awoke, he was disoriented, his heart pounding. There was a houndstooth sportcoat hung over a chairback, a man on his back by the bed, his left eye gone, the red-haired woman cowering on the bed.

"No," Albert called out to Ali, but he could not bring the man back. The woman on the bed was crying silently.

"She's mine," Ali said. It was an old pattern and Albert let him go.

When Ali finished with the woman, he made her dress and then they went downstairs. Madame was in her quarters behind the bar; Ali shot her once in the face, then tore two pages out of the registry, hung the CLOSED sign, locked the door and left in the dead man's Mercedes, the woman driving.

They made their way through the rain and darkness along winding, narrow roads amid pine forests. Before midnight they found a crèche at the intersection of two dirt roads. The lights of the Mercedes illuminated the stone structure built to protect the statuary. Ali took the woman inside and made her undress. Tendrils of fog snaked through the trees.

"Do you believe in God?" Albert asked her.

"*Oui*," she whispered. "More than ever."

"Say your prayers," Albert advised. There was no more he could do for her. It had to be.

Ali took her in the long wet grass at the base of the crèche. When he had finished, Albert knelt beside her and began a prayer. "You know these words?"

Her eyes were wide, her face streaked with mud, her hair matted. "Extreme unction," she whispered. "Last rites." When the words were finished, he pointed the 9 mm at her face. Ali wanted to pull the trigger, but Albert held him off. "You would steal her temporal life. I give her eternal life," he said.

"There's only this," Ali scoffed. The forest and heavy air swallowed the silencer's cough.

Beside the crèche Albert saw water tumbling into a stone basin from an oxidized copper pipe. The inside of the crèche was filled with wilted flowers and small cards with prayers to the spirits of Lourdes, the leavings of pilgrims. Below the water spigot was a sign: WATER UNPOTABLE. Albert studied the crèche, the cards, the dead woman's face, the water. People sought miracles, but there were none left. There was only reality and it was obscene. Did the Kennedys' money build shrines for the faithful and neglect greater needs? What sort of God would create such a world?

 FRIDAY, MARCH 17, 1961, 1:50 P.M.
Moscow

Lieutenant General Igor Yepishev was a physical-culture enthusiast who exercised at least twice each day. One of these workouts always began at noon, the routine never varying. He warmed up with stretching exercises for fifteen minutes, then played handball for forty-five minutes, followed by a fifteen-minute torture session with a twelve-kilo medicine ball, and finished with thirty minutes with free weights. Afterward he toweled dry, put on his uniform and returned to his office, a twenty-minute walk, his body odor leaving a rancid trail.

The Fifth Directorate's physical-culture endeavors were concentrated in a warehouse that had been crudely remodeled into a sports club. It was common knowledge that Yepishev had used Directorate funds to refurbish the warehouse, but nobody challenged him. In Moscow individuals with power were expected to use it; if they didn't, they were suspected of weakness, and where there was weakness the predators swarmed like sharks crazed by bloody water.

When Bailov arrived, Yepishev was standing in front of a full-length mirror, grimacing as he did slow curls with six kilos of iron disks on a stainless steel bar.

"You're looking fit, Comrade General," Bailov greeted him. And smelling as foul as ever, he thought.

"Fitness requires commitment," the chief of the Fifth Directorate grunted.

"I would like a word with you," Bailov said.

"I'm listening," Yepishev said.

Bailov held up his Red Badge. When Yepishev saw it, he froze in mid-curl, exhaled slowly and then lowered the bar to the floor. "You were always capable of irrefutable logic," he said. "What can I do for you?"

"What we have to say to each other stays between us, do you understand?"

Yepishev nodded.

"I need information about a certain individual, but I don't want anybody to know that an inquiry has been made."

"For most inquiries this is quite possible," Yepishev said, "but for others it is quite impossible."

Bailov slid his arm around Yepishev's shoulders and smiled. "Then you must do the impossible, Comrade General."

53 SATURDAY, MARCH 18, 1961, 7:00 P.M. *Belgrade*

Harry Gabler had been gone for nearly three days and Sylvia Charles was alternatingly angry and worried. For seventy-two hours she had been railing at her partner; they had been sent as a team to find Frash, but Valentine had gone his own way with the Yugoslavian detective. This was not the old days; the enemy often did not show itself openly. You had to move slowly, analyze, be certain. Who was this woman to bargain for asylum? Had they made a mistake in meeting her terms?

"It doesn't matter. She gave us Frash's picture and Lumbas's name," Valentine said.

"You don't *know* that," Sylvia said. Couldn't he see that what looked like one thing could be something else entirely? "The woman may have used you to get to Gabler. You make a noise about hunches as if the world drew true north from you."

Valentine considered a comeback, but decided against it. "Harry introduced you to Peresic first. Don't you trust him?"

"You don't get it," Sylvia answered, her voice rising. "This isn't a scavenger hunt at the country club. There's no big prize waiting for the winner. All there is, is this, or more of it. You track carefully, examine all possibilities before you commit, and tie up every loose end you can find."

He held up the photographs of Lumbas and Frash. "But we've got these."

She raised her eyebrows. "Those? Frash and somebody your Yugoslavian detective says is Russian."

"We know that Frash was working a Russian asset in Belgrade."

Sylvia's temper seemed to recede, but her words were sharp. "An asset, but not necessarily our corpse or REBUS. We don't know what or who he is. We don't know *anything*." Then she stalked out, slamming the door behind her. Valentine assumed she was going to walk it off and give herself time to cool down. That had been early afternoon. Now it was evening and he was beginning to worry. When the phone rang, he waited for the second ring to finish before picking it up. "Yo."

"Clear the nest," Sylvia said. "Use four," she added, referring to one of several escape routes they had worked out. Her voice was calm but forceful; he hung up immediately, grabbed his bag and hers and fled.

54   MONDAY, MARCH 20, 1961, 11:58 A.M. *Moscow*

Marshal Rodion Malinovsky walked slowly around the triangle park that separated the Council of Ministers Building from the Arsenal. It was nearly noon and warm for this time of year, the sun reflecting off the pavement to bake fur-clad passersby, even though there were still piles of snow along the curbs and under the trees. The marshal wore a tailored greatcoat, unbuttoned, and walked with his hands clasped behind him, a pose his subordinates called his Napoleonic strut. Even without such posturing, he was an imposing figure. Groups of Russian tourists with box cameras scattered from his path and looked away, fearing eye contact with such an imposing old boar.

Malinovsky was brooding. The populace still believed that the military held sway inside the Kremlin, but this was false and growing more so by the day. Most of his colleagues on the General Staff considered him Khrushchev's yes man, which was not true, but this perception was the price for having gained the General Secretary's trust. Nikita Sergeievich had given himself the title Supreme Commander in Chief, so there was no choice but to obey in public. As in America, Soviet soldiers were subordinate to civilians. However, the marshal's private behavior was entirely different, and sometimes he wished his colleagues could see him give the Ukrainian toad some of his own medicine. But when responsibility sat square on your shoulders, the load had to be carried; if his colleagues didn't understand, so be it. In time they would know the truth.

Gubin was standing to the side of one of the arched entrances of the ocher-colored Arsenal, close to one of the cannons taken from Napoleon in 1812 and now displayed as reminders of the inevitable fate of invaders of the Motherland. Malinovsky often said that Napoleon's mummy in a glass case would have been even more effective.

"Andrei Semenovich," Malinovsky called out. "It looks like an early spring. Perhaps we can get in some fishing. There are salmon in Siberia as long as a man's leg."

How could the man be so nonchalant? "I apologize for interrupting," Gubin said.

"It's a welcome diversion," Malinovsky lied. He had been looking forward to a lunch at the Praga, across the street from the Ministry of Defense, where a shipment of American T-bone steaks had arrived from Germany. "I've spent my morning listening to a proposal to standardize the uniforms of the branches of the service. Some members of the Presidium believe that if we all wear the same costumes, interservice rivalry will be eliminated. If that precept holds, I told them, perhaps we should have all citizens walk about in the raw and trim their penises to a standard length."

Gubin smiled. The Marshal's reputation for sarcasm was well deserved.

"I believe some of those fools actually took me seriously. We are surrounded by idiots, Andrei Semenovich. It's no wonder that nothing gets done. Khrushchev wants to put a man in space and struts for the Western press, but our enemies understand what such stunts cost." Malinovsky glanced at the blue sky. "They will overtake us up there, but not at the expense of their growing arsenal down here."

"Our Ukrainian friend has a female visitor in his nest, and she's not a relative," Gubin said, tired of the small talk.

"I know," Malinovsky said.

"Who is she? Perhaps we should take steps to protect ourselves," Gubin said. Several teenaged girls stared at them, then giggled nervously and trotted on.

"Tourists in the Kremlin," Malinovsky grumbled. "Soon we will be giving them rides in our tanks so they can see how well their leaders spend their rubles." The Marshal touched Gubin's sleeve. "A thrown rock cannot be called back. In any event it's not possible for an investigation to lead to us. You must learn to relax, comrade. Life's too short to worry about things that can't be controlled."

"I've been informed that Red Badges are in use," Gubin said as they neared the Presidium.

Malinovsky grunted, then smiled. "Next Nikita Sergeievich will try to resuscitate Beria," he said, shaking his head. "The man sends rockets into space while reverting to antiquated practices. Stalin had a man who carried the Red Badge, and even Beria feared him."

"What happened to him?"

"I would guess that he met the same fate as Stalin's other lieutenants." Malinovsky drew his finger across his throat.

"All but Khrushchev," Gubin reminded him.

"Let us hope that this historical oversight will soon be rectified." Khrushchev's new baby-sitter, if that was what she was, was already under surveillance.

55 MONDAY, MARCH 20, 1961, 12:10 P.M.
Bakovka, Russia

At the height of his criminal career Melko had thought of the white pine forests of Bakovka as his private hunting ground. The entire area was ringed by a high stone wall with black iron buttresses, stainless-steel teeth along the top and frequent road signs: AUTHORIZED ENTRY ONLY. TURN AROUND AND GO BACK. In six years the number of signs had multiplied like dandelions.

The intersections of roads leading into the exclusive dacha community were manned around the clock by heavily armed militiamen who checked passes and turned back those who didn't belong. Once inside there were additional checkpoints and, depending on the importance of a dacha's current resident, private entry gates and security forces to each estate. The area looked idyllic, but to a practiced eye the trappings of power and security were obvious.

Melko climbed over the wall at the same place and in the same way he had always gone in. He had regaled Petrov about Annochka during their days in Camp Nine, but in Odessa it had been Petrov who raised her name. "We need to get a window into the real politics of the Kremlin," he said. "Unobtrusively. Perhaps your Annochka can help us, but only if she hasn't changed. Rebellious children sometimes lose their fury. Be sure she has retained hers."

"She was nineteen," Melko had said in his own defense. "Not a child." She was certainly not a child now.

Petrov had ignored him. "Test her. If she's still an adventuress, we can use her. If not, then we must pursue other avenues."

Melko wondered how his former girlfriend would greet him. Less than enthusiastically, he imagined. Annochka's father was Sergei Denisov, head of the small but important KGB Finance Department, a step up from the old days when he had been a high-level transportation expert with Sovintrans. Denisov now reported directly to Boris Shelepin, director general of the KGB.

Melko had staked out Denisov's estate for four days without luck, though he had seen Annochka's father several times. Every morning his chauffeur drove off at eight-thirty sharp, and they returned each evening at eight. This pattern had held for three days and the man had left on time again this morning. Now it was midafternoon of the fourth day and a light drizzle was falling, the sky low and yellow-gray, with ragged wisps of black clouds passing overhead. More snow, Melko guessed. Russian winters were not known for an easy capitulation to spring. Just before 2:00 P.M. a small black Volga slowed on the road, turned into the driveway and accelerated quickly up the small hill toward the house, trailing clouds of blue-gray exhaust. There was a uniformed driver and somebody else in the backseat but he couldn't see who. He crossed the road, climbed a small tree and jumped over the stone wall that protected the estate. Like all walls in the area, this one was painted dark green, the same color of the interrogation rooms in Lubyanka Prison, an unpleasant memory. Once over the wall, he raced quickly through the trees and reached the front of the house in time to see the back of a woman herding two small children up the steps into the open arms of an older woman. When the four were inside, the chauffeur returned to the Volga, unfolded a newspaper, spread it out on the steering wheel, put a foot up on the dash and hung his hat on the rearview mirror.

As he had years before, Melko went into the house through the cellar. In one of the many rooms he found some dry rags, which he used to clean his shoes. There were four sets of stairs leading up; one set was very narrow and steep, and heavy dust showed that the route had not been used in a long time. The stairs terminated in a small room with no doors, but a ladder built into the wall led upward, exactly as it had years ago. Like many others in the area, the house had been built nearly a century before, and such structures invariably had several emergency escape routes, including a tunnel leading under the grounds from the southeast corner. The czarists had been paranoid with good reason, not from fear of their miserable serfs, whose resistance they had methodically crushed over the centuries, but from wariness of each other. At the top of the ladder was a small platform and the outline of two hatches cut into the walls. The second was the one he wanted. Several taps with the heel of his hand popped it open; he squeezed through the opening into a long closet filled with dark suits and cloth pockets filled with shoes. The closet opened into a sitting room; beyond that lay a bedroom. He paused briefly to listen but heard nothing and stepped out.

He explored the upper floor one room at a time, eventually finding the one where he had first met Annochka. He was tempted to pause and remember, but pushed on. There would be time for memories later.

In the center of the upper floor was a wide spiral staircase curling downward. He had just reached it when he heard voices below. "The children are asleep," a woman said. "You should also take a nap. You are overdoing it these days. You must learn to pace yourself."

When a familiar voice said, "I'm capable of making my own decisions," Melko felt a surge of desire. "You aren't my mother, so don't tell me what to do. We're nearly the same age, and I don't accept orders from my peers." His Annochka still had fire in her voice.

"I'm your stepmother."

"You're a quarter century younger than my father," Annochka shot back. "If he wants to call you his wife in order to legitimize fucking you, that's his business, but don't try the stepmother charade on me. I see you for what you are, a whore who got lucky." She laughed and took several steps up the stairs.

The other woman's voice was shrill. "A whore, is it? You of all women would know about such things, you who ran with a criminal!"

Annochka's voice calmed. "I'm now a properly married woman with children, my dear Helen, while you are still what you always were."

"Don't call me Helen!"

"I give my husband children. What do you give yours?"

"Bitch," the woman hissed as her stepdaughter trotted upstairs.

Melko ducked into a room and saw Annochka walk past. She had a triumphant smile on her face, which had matured; she was not as gaunt as when he had last seen her. After a few minutes, when he was certain nobody would follow her he went to her suite, let himself in quietly, latched the door behind him, sat in a chair just inside the doorway to the bedroom and watched her, his heart pounding. "You still sleep like a little girl," he called softly.

Annochka rolled over and sat up, her eyes wide. *"You?"*

"Melko."

"You're dead." She pointed her finger at him. "Father said they executed you."

"As you can see, I am alive and well. Your father lied."

Her mouth was open, her fists clenched. "No!"

"But I've asked for nothing," he said. "Do you answer no to nothing?"

"They wanted to try me, to send me to the gulag, but my father stopped them."

"Bullshit," he said. "Dependents of the privileged don't suffer such treatment. Your father simply wanted to reassert his control—for his benefit, not yours."

"I was younger then," she snapped. "And foolish."

"Ah," he said. "I see. Melko was a stupid mistake of youth and now you are ashamed of him. Is that it?"

Their eyes locked. "They nearly sent me to the camps," she said. "Can't you understand?"

"I told you that you were never in such danger, and in any event the camps aren't so difficult. I enjoyed their hospitality for six years."

"You broke out?"

"In a sense." He smiled. "And as good as ever."

"How?"

"Why is more important than how. As always, it pays to have powerful friends."

"*You?* You're nothing."

"Even the *urki* can have influence. That's the wonder of our society. One day you're on the bottom and the next day on top. Like magic."

She drew back against the pillows and balled her legs under her. "I'm married now. I have children and responsibilities."

"I heard."

"Things have changed. I have a husband. He's just been promoted to lieutenant colonel in the KGB. Do you know what that means?"

Melko understood: lieutenant colonel was the critical rank to attain in a man's career with the KGB. The promotion moved him into the inner sanctum for the genuine perquisites of power. "So you are satisfied with your life? A husband with promise, children, the continuation of power. Your father must be pleased."

"My father is my father. I'm older now. I understand things better."

"For me as well, Annochka. The camps afford survivors an excellent education. No other institution provides such insight, not even the Kremlin."

There was fear in her eyes. "You're a criminal."

Melko smiled. "Who is to say who is a criminal in our country? Stalin wasn't and now he is. You see how it works? Definitions are ambiguous. I was the best and you helped me to be even better. Do you help your husband with the same ardor?"

"I embrace my duty," she said tentatively.

Melko nodded his understanding and crossed his arms. "A wife *should* understand her duty, Annochka. Even a thief's woman has duties."

"Go away," she said. "My stepmother will be up here at any moment. She always looks in on me when I nap."

"Yes, I heard you talking to your stepmother. It's clear that you have great affection for each other."

"Fool!"

"One might argue that I am worse than a fool for getting mixed up with you," he said, "but all that's behind us. My only concern now is the future."

"I thought the *lyudi* lived solely for the present."

Melko stood up and took a step toward her. "The importance of the present is assumed."

She drew back against the headboard, but he stepped back to the doorway. "What do you want?" she demanded.

"Only a look at you." He pivoted into the parlor and heard the springs of the bed as she got up.

"That's all?" she asked, following him into the other room. "To look? What kind of shit is this? What are you up to?"

"What more can there be? You have your duties, and as a lieutenant colonel's wife you should mind your paranoia."

"Just like that? You disappear all these years, then come back to *look*? For only ten minutes!"

Melko checked his watch. "More like five, which has been more than adequate."

She rushed past him and blocked the door. "What the hell does that mean?"

"It means I made a mistake," he said, and gave her an exaggerated bow. "I hope the lieutenant colonel's wife will forgive me."

She was shaking her head violently. "No."

He reached for the doorknob, but she pushed his hand away, threw her arms around his neck and kissed him hard, her mouth open, tongue extended and demanding. "Tell me what you want," she whispered. She was shaking as she twisted one of her arms behind her back and fumbled with the mother-of-pearl buttons that stretched the length of her dress, but she was too excited to manage them and in frustration ripped the dress downward and let it fall. "I thought you were dead," she whispered as she embraced him again and pushed her hips against him.

Melko slid his hand against the silk fabric between her legs and felt the wet.

"The bed," she said, arching her back, her eyes closed, but he pushed her away and opened the door. Her eyes popped open. "What?" Then, understanding, she grabbed at him. "No!"

"Why did you marry into the KGB?" he asked. "Your father's idea?"

"Survival," she said as she desperately tried to pull him back.

He stared at her with hard eyes. "Think about your duties, Annochka. Think *very hard* about them. I'll be back, but you must decide if you're willing to lose all that you think you have." He opened the door, looked into the hallway to make sure it was clear, then stepped out of the room.

She stared at him, disbelieving. "What about *me*?"

"That's exactly what I want you to think about," Melko said.

 MONDAY, MARCH 20, 1961, 5:18 P.M.
Dubrovnik, Yugoslavia

Valentine had taken a cab to the railway station in Belgrade, caught the first available train to Sarajevo, changed to Titograd, and there switched again, this time to Dubrovnik on the Dalmatian coast of the Adriatic. The trains stopped frequently and the passengers made such a din that he couldn't relax. At one point the train sat on a siding for nine hours. In Dubrovnik he caught a cab to the isthmus of Lapad and got out on a small street lined with houses with orange-tiled roofs and whitewashed limestone walls. When the cab was gone he backtracked to a street that paralleled Sumartin Bay and checked into a small hotel called the Blue Madonna.

Sylvia was in the lobby when he arrived; he ignored her as he checked in, then went up to his room and left the door open a crack. She slid in five minutes later, eyes weary, hair plastered down, looking drained.

"Harry's dead," she said. "Peresic too, both of them asphyxiated in his car. Their bodies were discovered at the airport two days ago. The official story is that he was giving her a lift and that the deaths were an accident. Unofficially the embassy is saying it was a double suicide. Harry's married, his wife wouldn't divorce him, and he was due for a transfer. He couldn't take his lover with him, so they killed themselves rather than be separated."

"Horseshit. Do they know the truth?"

"Part of it. They know it was neither accident nor suicide but beyond that they're lost. I think Harry was handling this alone because it had to be done so fast."

"Jesus," Valentine said.

He looked miserable and she was sure he was having the same thoughts. "It's not our fault. These things happen. Nature of our business," this as much for herself as for him.

For a moment she thought there were tears in his eyes, but they never fell. "Could it have been an accident?" he asked.

She shook her head and sat down in a canvas-back chair. "You and I know what was going on; the embassy doesn't. Somebody took them, worked them over, dumped the bodies at the airport, and tried to make it look like a suicide."

"Where are the bodies now?"

"The Yugos have them; they refuse to release Harry's until their investigation has been completed."

"Autopsies?"

"They're not saying."

"How do you know they were worked over?"

"Harry's secretary and one of the embassy Marines identified the body."

"You talked to them?"

"Briefly. The secretary saw one of Harry's wrists; she said the hand was angled in an odd way, the skin discolored. Lividity, she said, a sign he had been tied up. The sergeant said he got a good look at both bodies before the Yugos came in and sent him packing. He said the marks on the wrists showed that they had been tied up with wire, not rope, and that there were a lot of cigarette burns on Peresic's stomach. Brutal, he called it. Said he'd seen similar stuff in Korea; he was a POW for fourteen months."

"That makes him more credible than most. Your opinion of the secretary?"

"Definitely not secretarial. She's one of us, I'd guess, maybe even Harry's number two."

"Is the embassy pressing the Yugos for the body?"

"More like going through the motions. Harry was CIA, so they're being circumspect. If Harry died in the line of duty they'll leave that determination to the investigating officer."

"He's here?"

"Got here fast and he's very uptight."

"Did he know about us?"

"I told him I was here on a special assignment outside Harry's purview. He told me to seek guidance through my chain of command. No, I didn't contact Arizona," she added quickly, anticipating Valentine's next question.

"Did the officer ask about me?"

She shook her head. "I let him believe I'm alone."

"Where does that leave us?"

"Given the circumstances, I think that Arizona would have told the investigator we were here, if for no other reason than to avoid crossing wires during the investigation."

"Maybe there wasn't time."

"You don't believe that," she said, her voice tired.

"No. I assume Arizona knows Harry's dead and that he chose not to reveal our presence. Which means we're further into the black than we thought, and that makes my skin crawl." Then, "The deaths weren't reported in the Yugoslavian newspapers?"

"Nothing. The Yugos are holding back, either because they don't want any interference with their investigation—"

Valentine interrupted. "Or because they already know what happened."

"We have to assume that Peresic's husband was involved and that the Yugos know about us.

"So how do we get them off our backs?"

"We don't," she said. "First thing tomorrow we get the hell out of the country."

In the middle of the night he heard water running. "You all right?" he asked through the door.

"No," she said softly, "but thanks for asking."

"You want company?"

"You think that would make me feel better?"

"It would me," he said.

"I'm not sleeping with you."

"I didn't ask."

"Good." He heard her slosh water over the side of the tub.

"But I thought about it," he added.

"You're hopeless," she said.

He suspected that she was right.

57   TUESDAY, MARCH 21, 1961, 8:40 A.M. *Segue River, Montana*

The investigation was like a board game that kept sending Venema back to the starting line. He had spent considerable time following leads on a man named R. R. Jeruby, who had been listed by Frash as a personal reference from something called Brampton Academy, but the man had died in a one-car accident in 1957 in northern Maine. The Massachusetts State Board of Education provided a short list of faculty names, which was all they had; Brampton had closed in 1950 and the state building containing most of its records and those of the state's other private institutions had been destroyed in a fire classified as probable arson. The school itself was gone as well; it had become a thirty-six-hole golf course and retreat for the faculty of Boston College. The list of former faculty members led nowhere; the nine men on the list had all died in automobile accidents between 1957 and 1959, which was counter to all actuarial probabilities, and put him on edge. In one sense it was an impressive set of findings, but it led nowhere. What he needed was a live body to tell him about Albert Frash.

The break came when he discovered that the village near the old Brampton site had once had its own newspaper for a three-year period in the late forties. The former publisher-editor now lived in Champlain, New York, where he ran a French-English weekly that listed boats for sale. The man turned out to be the anal-retentive type, with a full file of every issue of the defunct newspaper, each of which carried a weekly but scanty roundup from the school. From these Venema gleaned a list of names which the IRS and Social Security then processed for the Company; all but one of the names were in the deceased file, but one was all he needed.

Now Venema was standing on a granite outcropping watching an old man fish in the middle of a gray river while snow cascaded from dark clouds rolling in from British Columbia. The man wore a battered green crusher over a black stocking cap, a black mackinaw and green waders. Venema watched him rollcast a red streamer into an eddy along a snow-covered bank, then methodically strip away line on the retrieve.

By the time he got down to the riverbank, the old man had crawled ashore and pulled his waders down to his waist, leaving the suspenders flopping while steam rolled off him. "You're not much on wood lore," the old man called out. He had dazzling white hair. "Heard you comin' a half mile off. Indians used sound as an early warning system, except against each other, which is ironic. Could hear just about anything except each other." The man grinned.

"Dr. Frederick Missias?"

"Just plain Fred nowadays," the man said as he wiped sweat off his face with a blue bandanna. "Title's retired." Fish flopped in a hickory creel at his side.

"I'm trying to find out something about a former student of yours," Venema said, flashing the credentials of an Office of Special Investigations agent. The CIA often used OSI cover for domestic investigations.

Missias sat down, kicked off his patched green waders, peeled off two pairs of gray wool socks and studied his toes, "Goddamned water's cold as Kelvin till July and then the trout stop biting. You want trout you gotta pay the price," he said. "This a joke or a screwup?"

"No joke," Venema said. "It's a federal security check, deep but routine, part of the drill. Walk, talk and verify."

"You've come a long way for a drill." This part of the river was a good six miles from the nearest macadam.

"Routine doesn't mean unimportant. Vetting is the heart of security. You're not the easiest man to find."

"Didn't stop you." Missias had good-natured eyes and a half-smile that always seemed on the verge of spreading.

"My job."

"Good at it, are you?"

"Found you."

Missias chuckled. "Important for a man to know he's good at his job. Work is culture's glue; it gives man his identity. Then one day you hit the magic birthday and it's revoked. Now I fish. They can't take *that* away. Not that I'd go back anyhow," he added. Missias seemed mildly bitter but his tone made it seem a joke.

"Can I ask you a few questions about R. R. Jeruby?"

"You want coffee? My place is a short hike upriver."

It was also uphill. Venema followed the old man along a narrow track to a log cabin built on a bluff fifteen meters above a bend in the river. "Belonged to my wife's grandfather, but she's dead and him too. We had no kids and now there's just me, which is how I like it. More time to think, though mostly I think about fat rainbows."

Missias made coffee in a battered pot on a wood stove. On one wall of the room there were several bamboo fly rods and a lethal-looking high-powered rifle with a scope. "Varmints," Missias said, reading Venema's eyes. "Lots of beauty out here, but where there's beauty there's usually ugliness too. Fact of life, no matter where you are or how you cut it."

"About Jeruby?" Venema wanted his questions answered and to get on with his work. "You were together at Brampton?"

"Yep."

A decision needed. The focus of his investigation was Frash. Jeruby was only a reference and Brampton Academy was not part of Frash's background. But Jeruby was dead and there was no way to tell what his connection was to Frash. When in doubt, go direct. "You ever hear of an Albert Frash?"

Missias gave him a hard look and took a long time before answering. "I remember him, if that's your question."

"Good student?"

"Wouldn't know."

Venema didn't understand. "But you were headmaster."

Missias grinned. "What's this nonsense about being headmaster?"

"Brampton Academy."

"Where'd you hear that?"

It had been a hard assignment; everything about Albert Frash seemed to float just out of reach in a mist. You could sense the outline of a picture but there were no details except the easy ones that seemed to corroborate Frash's background. Yet Venema had a strong feeling that he was seeing only what he was supposed to see, that everything had some-how been masterfully arranged for his benefit. What didn't jibe was that Brampton Academy—if the small-town editor could be believed—was some kind of junior West Point for brats in custom-made khakis. Sorry little bastards, the man had said. Missias was described in newspaper accounts as the school's headmaster; IRS and Social Security records showed that he had been employed for six years by the Boston-based Brampton Foundation, which had been founded in 1934 by an industrial-ist of the same name. A retired official of the state department of educa-tion had described Brampton as an experimental program but knew nothing more about it. Venema had traced Social Security checks to Missias at his postal box in Segue River and learned that the man picked up his mail only once a month. That left him no choice but to hike out to the cabin through crusted, ankle-deep snow. "Read it in the newspa-per; we located you through Social Security."

"The eagle shits monthly," Missias said. "Don't much like it that I can be tracked down, especially for *that* one."

"Then he was a student?"

"You said you wanted to talk about Jeruby, but Bob's dead. Which means your real interest is Frash. That about right?"

"Yes."

Missias poured two coffees and sat down with an amused expression. "Why do you think he was my student?"

"You were headmaster at Brampton Academy."

"I was chief administrator and chief of the medical staff."

Now it was Venema who didn't understand.

"Brampton wasn't a school in the traditional sense. Our students had problems."

"A military school."

"You're not picking up on this, son," Missias grinned. "Brampton was that, but we also had an arm that was a psychiatric program for juveniles—an experiment, when you get down to the pulp. Back then people wanted to bury their mental and behavioral problems, but asylums were nothing more than holding tanks. Still are, I guess. The Brampton Foundation had an idea that a well-designed school setting might turn some kids around by showing them how to do right. If they follow the rules, reward 'em; if not, make them do it again. The principle was that we really couldn't understand the source of their problems, but we could see their disorders manifested in certain behaviors. If you change their behavior, maybe you alter the state of the disease. The idea was to work upstream from the symptom rather than worrying about the cause, which was the standard approach. Back then we thought we had some successes, though nowadays I'm of the opinion that those were not true disease states. For all the progress medicine hoots about, we still don't know squat about the brain, and Dr. Freud, bless his troubled soul, seems to me to be mostly hogwash. Severe mental disorders are most likely the result of chemical imbalances, but we don't know enough about brain chemistry to intervene intelligently. We've got drugs to knock people on their asses and drugs to settle people down so they can have some semblance of normal life, but that's all. Not much progress when you get down to it."

Venema did not volunteer his own medical credentials. "Was Frash one of your successes?"

Missias shook his head and pursed his lips. "Quite the contrary, and why do you call the boy Frash? That was his parents' name. He was Ali Frascetti, though his mother sometimes called him Albert. Never saw the father. Just his mom. Not that it mattered to him what anybody called him."

"Tell me."

"Fact you're here at all amazes me. Really, it's quite remarkable. He was schizophrenic in the extreme. Figured he'd be dead or locked away permanently by now."

"Split personality?"

"More like two separate entities in one body. One of the worst cases I ever saw."

"You couldn't treat him?"

"Couldn't communicate with the little bastard; then one day he woke up as normal as Jello."

"Spontaneous remission?"

Missias shot a curious glance at Venema. "That was the opinion of my staff."

Venema sensed something. "But not yours?"

Missias grinned. "Read people like a book, do you? No, it *wasn't* my opinion. I think it was a charade."

"An A-segment override of B."

Missias was impressed. "You seem to know something about dual personality disorders."

"Some. What happened to the boy?"

"He was twelve then, nearly thirteen. This would be in '42. He'd been with us two years and completely dysfunctional; then one day he's more normal than Ike and no apparent residue. That's what was suspicious. That severe a case and suddenly a spontaneous remission; it just didn't add up. Two plus two equaled five or three, but not four."

"You'd never seen a spontaneous remission before?" Venema had.

Missias stretched his legs straight out. "Seen them, but not often and never in such an extreme case. He had classic symptoms. At six he was telling his mother that God and the Devil were inside him. Odd logic and associations all over the place, A to Z and back to M with no apparent sequence. Didn't talk for long periods; thought others could read his mind, so he had no reason to converse. Nearly continuous masturbation while he shouted his mother's name. The mother was a devout Catholic and devoted to the boy. Can't say about the father. He never came around."

"Paranoia?"

"You do know your stuff. No apparent psychosis, but he was young and that sort of symptomatology usually shows up later, though I've no doubt that's where he was headed. Like I said, one day he turned up sane as a parson, if I can use that term, and while everybody else took the reversal at face value, I didn't. Have you seen him?"

"No," Venema lied. Actually he had spent considerable time with Frash, but had never seen any indication of mental illness. "They gave me a name, some facts and asked me to confirm. He listed Jeruby as a reference."

"No subsequent episodes?"

Venema shook his head. "The record says he's entirely normal."

Missias stared for a while. "I would have sworn it was all an act."

"Why?"

"Like I said, it was too perfect. No backsliding, no symptomatology, no baggage, so to speak. A whole year more and no sign. It told me that the cure was an act."

"But there could have been an override, or assertion by one segment over another, a resolution between the personalities?"

"Well, yes, of course. That was my colleagues' theory, but I sensed more of a standoff, some kind of truce made consciously between A and B. It's my opinion that this sort of disorder is biochemical, so you just don't will it away. Can't run a Chevy on willpower alone."

"Puberty could have altered his biochemistry."

"Granted, and that's what my colleagues focused on, but there were no signs of puberty until months after the transformation began." Missias leaned forward. "Can I ask what sort of government job he's after?"

"Classified," Venema said quickly. Missias got up, poured a tumbler of brandy and held it out to Venema, who shook his head. "Too early."

"When you're a retired gentleman, artificial standards no longer apply. Drink when I want, fish when I want. Fact is trout are illegal right now, but that sort of law doesn't apply to locals. Game warden fished with me last week. Caught some beauts. You ought to give it a try."

"Someday."

"Someday could be too late, son. You ought to try listening when an old fart rambles."

"I'll do that. If Frash is still behaving normally, does that mean you were wrong?"

The old man downed his brandy and grimaced. "Doubt it. Felt I was right then, and that I'm right now. He's controlling the balance but one of these days—" Missias snapped his fingers. "Then the game will be on again, and this time for real."

"What sort of situation would cause it?" Venema already had a pretty good idea.

"Impossible to say. Like flies and trout. Never know for sure what sets them off. A bright color, a sunset, a word association, a dog's bark—no way to predict. Something emotional, probably, something to fuel the paranoia. Stress could do it. What's he doing nowadays?"

Venema grinned. "I really can't say," he apologized. "I don't make the rules."

"That's the problem in this world. Nobody makes the damned rules but everybody cites them. That's always struck me as a couple of degrees the other side of peculiar." Missias stared out the window again. "Curious, I guess. He wanted to be a priest. Tried to pray his troubles away. Jacking off and screaming his mama's name between Hail Marys. Pathetic little creature, I'm here to say. Never saw another like him before or since, and got no doubt I'll still remember him on my deathbed."

"When did you leave Brampton?"

"Resigned right after they released the kid. It was a matter of principle for me. I figured we'd cut loose a problem and I didn't want it on my conscience."

"Did you keep track of your colleagues?"

"Didn't bother. I was pretty ticked off when I left. I heard Bob Jeruby was killed in a car wreck, but I don't know about the others. If you talk to them I'm sure they'll tell you they were glad to be shed of me. I tended to ask questions they didn't want to hear. Organizations can't handle that. I moved a lot after that, decided to settle here after the wife died. Miss her, but that aside it's a great way to live." Missias suddenly stared hard at his visitor. "Want some advice from an old man?"

Venema didn't respond.

"No need to say anything. My guess is that you're a doctor, probably a shrink. If you have this boy on the payroll, get him off. If you're thinkin' about puttin' him on, don't. I don't care if he's been the world champion in deportment. Frascetti is a time bomb."

Venema felt a chill. Suddenly their problem with Frash had taken on a new complexion. If Missias was right, their experiment was a bomb waiting to detonate, and maybe already had.

The old man followed Venema down the trail. "Sure you won't stay a spell and try your luck?"

"No, thanks," Venema said. He had another kind of fish to catch.

"Too bad," Missias hollered. "They bite right in the middle of the day. Like they can't wait to get caught."

Venema doubted that Frash would be as accommodating.

58   WEDNESDAY, MARCH 22, 1961, 10:40 A.M. *Paris*

They came to Paris by train, arriving at the Gare de Lyon on a sleeper that smelled of wine, perfume and suntan oil because the station was the arrival point for trains from the Alps and the Riviera. They had been thrown in with an odd assortment of passengers, some carrying skis, others toting beach baskets, snorkels and swim fins, it being a season on the cusp, between windburn on the white slopes and sunburn on the white sand. They had taken a cab from the station to the area called the Marais in the third arrondissement and gotten out at place de la Bastille.

Sylvia looked briefly at the monument, mumbled "Phallic," and walked briskly north. Before the Revolution the Marais had been home to French nobles and rich merchants; now it was distinctly blue-collar, dilapidated and tacky, which in Paris gave it an illogical romantic luster. The streets were crowded with jaywalkers and horn-honking drivers switching lanes like Grand Prix hopefuls. There was a queue in front of a shop that specialized in horsemeat and the east–west streets in the area were narrow and dark, set between solid rows of five-story buildings with sloping roofs and red tiles. Fresh water coursed along the gutters, washing away yesterday's debris.

"A lot of traffic," Valentine complained to Sylvia as they walked north into the Marais.

"Around the clock," she answered. "Which makes it ideal. We'll be within walking distance of three major metro stations. Easy in, easy out, and plenty of people to mingle with."

She led him to the Hôtel Agneau, a thirty-four-room mausoleum on a quiet street lined with storefronts. The lobby was tiny and badly worn, everything covered with dust. There were threadbare Oriental carpets on the floor and flocked velvet wallpaper peeling off the walls. When they arrived, Sylvia asked to see the *patron,* who turned out to be a hunchbacked Chinese dressed in black tie, tails and a red cummerbund. He looked eighty or more, had gold fillings, a face spackled with black moles, yellowed eyes, thin lips and long, bony hands shaped like talons. He supported himself by a blackthorn cane with a silver dragon's head as a knob. When he saw Sylvia, he bowed, not in the herky-jerky Oriental way but elegantly, and stepped forward, took her hand in his withered claws and touched the tip of his nose to the back of her hand.

"My heart swells," he said. His accent was not Chinese. German? "You do me great honor."

"Father," Sylvia said, "this is Mr. Valentine. Beau, this is Mr. Li."

The word knocked Valentine off balance. Her father?

Li took Valentine's hand and held it. "Are you her husband?"

"No," Sylvia said, smiling.

"Her lover?"

"No," she answered just as quickly. "He's a colleague and you should stop prying."

The *patron* stared at Valentine for a long time before releasing his hand. "She is a woman of substance," he said, and though the words were spoken softly Valentine interpreted them as a warning. "How long will you stay?" he asked Sylvia.

"We're not sure."

"It's an unpredictable business," he said and she nodded. Mr. Li looked at Valentine, then turned back to Sylvia. "His eyes show past strength." Then "You shall have my very best, dear girl, my very best."

He went behind the reception desk and fetched a massive brass key attached to a long black velvet cord and gave it to her. "Left at the top," he said, looking up. "Take the lift." Leaning close, his voice low, he added, "Two sets of stairs, front and back. Also a fire escape and a buzzer."

Sylvia hugged him affectionately, kissed his forehead and pushed the button for the lift.

They ascended in jerks and fits, the pulleys wheezing and squeaking, the cage finally stopping three inches below the floor line. There was a door at each end of the short hallway and Sylvia turned left.

When Valentine stepped into the room he was amazed to see that they had a suite consisting of several rooms, a long balcony and a bank of skylights facing south. The carpets were rich, the furnishings antique and exquisite, and there wasn't a speck of dust. "Shangri-la?" he asked.

"Li was my father's business partner in Jakarta. He fought against the Japanese, and after the war was a deputy chief of intelligence for Sukarno in the struggle against the Dutch. In 1950 there was a new constitution and Sukarno offered him the government's top intelligence position, but Li turned it down because the man was politically unreliable. People like Sukarno are good at bringing people together against a common enemy, but once they've achieved victory they can't govern the peace. Such people become paranoid, see enemies everywhere, and eventually it all falls apart." Valentine followed her onto the balcony. "Li worked for a while as a translator for the UN in New York, then came to Paris in 1956. He's the most reliable man I've ever known. He's my godfather, and now that my parents are gone, he's my only family."

It was the first time since they had met that Sylvia had revealed anything of her past. He wanted to know more, but she had made it clear that the Company owned her, and that was that.

"Get that wounded-calf look off your face," she said coolly. "You asked about Li, so I told you. It's information, nothing more."

God, she was beautiful. "He knows what you do?"

"Of course. He's godfather and mentor, which is the Chinese way. You don't keep secrets from your mentor."

"And now he runs a hotel. That's all?"

"For now," she said. "Nothing is forever in this world. Life is transient."

"An existentialist."

"A realist," she said. "We'll be secure here. If Li detects trouble, he'll buzz a warning."

"He can't be on duty all the time."

"His sons can," Sylvia said with a smile. "He has beaucoup sons; think of this as Fortress Li."

"You've used it before?"

"I've kept it in reserve. I alerted him before we left the States. Forewarned is forearmed."

To what end? he wondered. Did they have a chance? Would she even consider a different sort of life? Would the Company allow it? He decided to banish such thoughts. The train ride from Yugoslavia to France had left him on edge and given him time to start sorting things out. He had intended to give up the foolish chase and go home, but Harry's death had changed that. If it hadn't been for him, Harry would still be alive. He had wanted to talk to Sylvia about his feelings but found he couldn't.

While she took a bath Valentine poured a brandy and opened the door onto the balcony. Frash and Lumbas were connected; the photograph proved that. Frash had disappeared, Lumbas was dead, and Inspector Peresic had intimated that Albania and the U.S.S.R. were common denominators. Harry had also pointed them at Albania, but Valentine had decided he would bet the ranch that there was another connection and that Lumbas was the asset passing Russian secrets; yet the Albanian connection was too persistent to ignore.

Valentine pushed the bathroom door open and walked in without announcing himself. Sylvia let out a gasp and slid deeper into the tub. "I knew it," she said with obvious irritation.

He furrowed his brow. "Knew what?"

"This," she said.

"What?" he repeated, enjoying her predicament. "I've been thinking."

"That's a scary thought."

"I'm serious. For argument's sake let's say that Frash was tied to Albania. Let's also say that he was probably initially connected to the Russian here in Paris. How do these two things fit?"

"Why assume the connection began here?"

"Because Frash left the station chief job here, then shifted divisions with a loss in rank. There had to be a good reason for this, and if he recruited the Russian here, then moving to Belgrade to run him just might be the reason."

"You can't jump to conclusions like that," Sylvia said with a sigh. "Can I have a towel?" Frash's brief stint in Paris had also bothered her, but she had kept this to herself.

He looked at the shelf above her. "You're closer."

"Don't be a jerk."

"What's the big deal? As I remember, it's familiar territory." He smiled for effect. He had startled her, but she was calmer now and he sensed she was protesting more out of protocol than conviction. Or was this a miscalculation on his part? With most women he usually knew right away, but it was turning out that Sylvia was not like other women. He got a towel, handed it to her and turned away. "Understand what I'm getting at?"

She stood up and wrapped the towel around her. "You're not exactly the world's greatest mystery." She put her hand on the small of his back and shoved him toward the door. "Paris has a substantial Albanian expatriate community," she added.

When he turned to say something more she let the towel drop, smiled, stood still for a second to give him a good look and then closed the door in his face.

"You did that on purpose," he complained.

"It didn't look like you were seeing familiar territory," she called through the door.

When she emerged a few minutes later she was dressed in a robe and her hair was wrapped in a towel. "Li will help us," she said. Then she saw that he had a peculiar look on his face. "What's with you?"

"You actually *like* me," he said with mock astonishment.

She closed her eyes, grimaced and collapsed backward on the couch.

59 | WEDNESDAY, MARCH 22, 1961, 1:00 P.M. *Moscow*

In the old days Melko had operated out of the Marina Roscha district northwest of the Moscow River near Timiryazev Park. Then, as now, the area was known simply as the Zone, a gathering place for criminals, dregs and toothless counterrevolutionaries, a center within a center, a sort of counterbalance to the Kremlin. It was a place the Moscow police avoided, and when they did go there, it was always in force and then only briefly. No authority prevailed in the Zone except what could be exercised hour to hour and day to day inside the five square kilometers of dark twisting streets that reeked of garbage, dog shit, boiled cabbage, urine, open sewage and human sweat. As it had been in Stalin's heyday and long before, the Zone was part of the Soviet state, but the Soviet state was not part of the Zone. It was a place foreigners might hear about but never saw. The district had not changed since the civil war. A neighborhood long past its prime, it had no factories, no majestic war memorials or schools, no Young Pioneers or trade union halls, no flower stalls, state stores or schools. Its colors were earth tones, with none of the flamboyance of the Arbat; houses and buildings changed color only as years passed and grime and soot from the rest of the city built up layer by filthy layer. The Zone's denizens tended to be stunted, dark-skinned, swarthy creatures with predators' eyes, the flotsam of nearly every Soviet republic; they savored all possible addictions, fought to the death over insults real and imagined, and adhered to their own loose rules. Simply put, the Zone was Moscow's no-man's-land, and the ideal place for Melko to meet undisturbed with Annochka.

The place Melko had selected was a third-floor garret over a coffee house owned by a one-legged Armenian. Georgian homosexuals called Black Asses controlled the second floor, which stank worse than the camps. The Black Asses were not criminals in the traditional sense; theirs was a violation of party-sanctioned morality, but unlike the foppish, effeminate Russian homosexuals who cruised near the Bolshoi, the Georgians were a fierce and violent lot.

The front of the brown building had a hand-painted sign proclaiming FRESH MUSHROOMS, though nothing served by the Armenian was fresh or edible, even by Russian standards. The garret consisted of a single room with a low ceiling in desperate need of repair. There were several holes and exposed beams, and day or night small pairs of red eyes peered down from the darkness. The room was furnished with a sagging brass bed turned green and black by oxidation; an unpainted door set across two sawhorses served as a table. There were two ways into the building on the ground floor, a single set of stairs leading up to the third floor and an easy jump down to a nearby rooftop, which in an emergency would be their way out.

Melko's note had instructed Annochka to change taxis three times, then take the metro to a station one kilometer from the flat, walk past her destination and take a city bus back to a drop-off where Bailov would monitor her arrival, then trail her to the rendezvous to make sure there was no tail.

Melko had paid the Armenian and his Georgian neighbors a fee for making sure that no unauthorized personnel entered the building when Annochka was there; as long as the payments continued he was fairly certain they would be secure. If she was disturbed by the condition of the flat, she never let on. They met for an hour every other day, made love and talked. Melko recorded their sessions on a small tape recorder.

Annochka undressed as she walked to the bed, leaving a trail of garments from the door. He turned on the recorder, set it on the chair by the bed, and joined her; she sat on top of him, pressed the palms of her hands against his shoulders and moved her hips slowly as she talked. It was odd how she could be passionate and matter-of-fact in alternating moments.

"Not even a kiss?" he said.

"I don't do this for your kisses."

"I'm an old-fashioned boy. Making love begins with kisses and embraces."

"I'm a modernist," she said. "Fucking is not the same as lovemaking."

Melko laughed. "One must be true to one's values. What does a modernist believe in?"

"I'm sitting on it." She shifted her hips, lowered her right knee to the mattress and began a rapid forward thrusting.

"How is your lieutenant colonel?"

"Haunted," she gasped. Petrov wanted Melko to use Annochka to ascertain the current mood in the KGB, and she had already revealed that Shelepin's appointment as KGB chairman had created a nasty backlash among the apparatchiki who had worked their way up through the ranks. Shelepin's predecessor, the foulmouthed, crude General Ivan Serov, was no favorite either, but at least he was one of them, a former deputy of Beria in the classic mold. By contrast Shelepin was polished and glib, but he was an outsider and worst of all an amateur, his career having been forged in the Komsomol, the Communist Youth Organization. Serov was now the head of the much smaller GRU, its mission considerably narrower and less politically important than his previous position. For as long as anyone could remember, state and military security had been at each other's throat, each working to infiltrate the other; despite this, there was now apparently a regular but informal exchange of information between the competing agencies. Oddly enough, these contacts were between the echelon of deputies that reported to Shelepin, the same people that he and Khrushchev had installed since 1958. Bailov said that this was surprising; assuming old loyalties, it would have been more likely that the contacts would be with Serov's former appointees, not Shelepin's, but this apparently was not the case. Did this signify that Shelepin did not have ironclad control of his organization?

"My husband is obsessed with making his mark in the way our fathers did, but poor Yeroslav doesn't have our fathers' instincts," she said. Melko lay back and let her talk.

"A little harder, please," she said, shifting her weight. "Yeroslav is not his father, but he's loyal to the state and he works hard. His father's strength was in grand schemes, but Yeroslav is more like an accountant," she said with a moan, "a master of details and small tasks."

After they finished she rolled off him onto the bed. Melko went to the window, lit a cigarette, inhaled once and put the butt out against the wall. "Yeroslav has discovered a series of accounts," she said. "They're open-ended and apparently not earmarked for particular departments or projects. Such unassigned accounts are strictly forbidden by policy, yet he's found them, and having discovered them, it's his duty to report them. But to whom? He says to me, 'If I make the report to my superior, he will take credit or he will blame me. Either way there is no advantage to my doing my duty.'" She sat on the side of the bed, stretched her legs out and rubbed her neck. "We're not finished, are we?"

"In a minute," he said. "What will your Yeroslav do about his discovery?"

"I advised him to talk to my father; he always knows what to do. Yeroslav spoke to him off the record last night and my father advised him to ignore what he has found and to keep his mind on his own direct responsibilities. My father said that the special accounts are called *kadrirovannye*, skeletons, used to finance special KGB initiatives. Only one department uses them."

"Which one?"

"Department Five, First Directorate."

"That's it?"

"The skeletons are marked with a sequence of numbers that are coded in the same way that special files are coded in the Third Directorate, where Yeroslav is assigned." Annochka got off the bed, walked over to him and bit him hard on the upper arm, but got no reaction. "You still feel no pain. I like toughness in a man. If I nipped Yeroslav like that he'd whine for a week." She stared out the window for several seconds, then ran her hand along the wall. "Why do you suppose there's such a close connection between pleasure and pain?" When Melko didn't answer she went on. "Because the coding of the skeletons is the same as in the Third Directorate," she continued, "Yeroslav has concluded that they are tied to the Odessa Military District. The chief of the Third Directorate is Menkov, who reports to General Perevertkin, who is one of Shelepin's people. The general's brother is in the Foreign Ministry." Annochka traced her finger along the tattoos on Melko's chest.

"Menkov's brother or Perevertkin's? Which one has the Foreign Ministry connection?"

"Perevertkin's brother, but he's just a flunky."

"What does all this mean?"

"You asked for information; I brought it. What it means is your business. Now, can we do something more than talk?"

WEDNESDAY, MARCH 22, 1961, 7:30 P.M.
Tirana, Albania

Mehmet Shehu walked slowly across Victory Square, paying little attention to the packs of bicycles that swarmed around the huge space during the compulsory public recreation period. Kasi was sitting on a stone bench at the edge of the square eyeing several jackdaws strutting in the grass. "You've seen Hoxha?" he asked.

"Kennedy will agree to meet with Khrushchev," Shehu said. "Our sources in France say the American will visit de Gaulle in late May. The Americans are practical. He'll meet Khrushchev during the same trip."

Kasi tried to envision the two enemy leaders standing side by side. "The girl did well in Paris?"

"She followed orders without hesitation," Kasi assured him.

After a long silence Shehu got up. "Don't let up on her; there'll be only one opportunity."

"She'll be ready."

 THURSDAY, MARCH 23, 1961, 8:15 P.M.
Moscow

The train from Odessa was a soot-covered, battered derelict hauled by an ancient black locomotive that got up to fifty kilometers an hour on infrequent stretches of stable track, but averaged far less. The trip included numerous stops for passengers and long delays on sidings so that angry or confused dispatchers could resolve schedule conflicts—firsthand testimony to the inefficiency of the Soviet rail system. "Miserable Reds couldn't build a privy," Ezdovo sputtered during the journey. "They pack us together like ants on a dunghill. How can they run a country if they can't run a bloody railroad? If we had flown," he added, "we'd be there already—or dead. Either result would be an improvement on this."

These complaints did not amuse Petrov, who hated to fly; every time

Ezdovo mentioned airplanes the color drained from his jaundiced face. As far as the Special Operations Group knew, flying was Petrov's only fear, and it seemed to be worse now than in the old days.

Ezdovo hated the trip. In the Yablonovy Mountains people talked of European Russia as if it were some sort of utopia; this train proved that it was anything but. The fifty-year-old cars, called wagons, were made of wood; the air inside stank of unwashed human bodies, and the latrine was a malodorous cubicle wedged into the end of the car, fine for someone of Petrov's stature, but a torture chamber for the muscular Siberian, who had to sit with the door open. Their compartment was classified as a soft sleeper, which translated into two hinged platforms covered with thin canvas pallets stuffed with lumps of old straw; with all their gear there was barely enough room for them. There was no dining car, so from time to time Ezdovo jumped out at stops in small villages and bought sandwiches or meat pies. Petrov ate nothing and drank little.

During the trip Ezdovo pulled steadily on a bottle of fiery cognac. "Best go easy on that," Petrov warned. The Siberian's separation from his wife seemed to be causing him some distress. He made a mental note to talk to Talia about this; if her husband could not concentrate on the mission, he would have to be dropped, a decision he would not like to make, but would if it became necessary. The man's emotional state was ample evidence of the destructive power of romantic human attachments, Petrov observed.

By midnight Ezdovo was drunk and shouting from the latrine at the end of the aisle. "Look at me! I'm a bloody czar. Where are the servants to strip down my trousers while I fertilize Ukrainian soil with royal turds!" Once he stumbled back to the compartment and lowered his voice to a whisper. "It's just shit," he confided. "Living cells out with the dead. Every shit is one shit closer to death. Remember that," he said, poking his chief with a thick finger.

When Ezdovo slept, his mouth hung open and he made sounds like a pig, his snores enormous and unpredictable.

Petrov sat with folded arms. Right now the pain was faint, but eventually it would intensify. For a year he had been learning its cycle. "It's not death that's ugly," he said out loud at one point. "It's the dying."

"What?" Ezdovo mumbled.

"Go back to sleep."

It was cool and still dark when they disembarked at a station in a southern district of Moscow. Bailov was waiting in a windowless van with red crosses. Ezdovo looked around anxiously for Talia, but neither she nor Gnedin were there. Bailov understood and patted his comrade on the shoulder. "She's fine," he said softly; then, looking toward Petrov, "How is he?"

"Not the old Petrov."

They helped their leader into the back of the van. When they got to the top step Petrov sniffed the air. "Red Rome," he said to no one in particular. "Before the fall."

Bailov raised an eyebrow and looked at Ezdovo, who wiggled a finger by the side of his head and shrugged.

 FRIDAY, MARCH 24, 1961, 10:00 P.M.
Kosino, Russia

Gnedin wanted to put Petrov in a hospital, but the old man stubbornly refused. Melko had been instructed to take possession of a certain house in Kosino, and here they delivered him. The unpainted structure sat a few meters from the reedy shore of Holy Lake, where a youthful Peter the Great had often come to sail his wooden boats and dream of a royal Russian navy. The oval lake had once been far outside the city; now it was an easy twenty-minute walk from Ring Road, the city's current border. The lake itself was a shallow body of brackish water choked with stunted fish and ringed by small weathered shacks under stands of leafless oaks and diseased elms.

It was a cold night, with paper-thin surface ice jamming the shoreline. Petrov asked Melko to break a hole in the shallows, then lowered himself into the dark water, which for centuries had been linked to miraculous cures; nowadays few Russians believed in such miracles and the old ways and beliefs were fading fast. From where they stood they could see the lights from banks of apartment complexes being built by the Khrushchev regime. Like a patient predator, each month the city crept closer; eventually it would engulf the village.

Petrov sat in the lake with only his small head protruding from the water.

Talia watched briefly, then jerked Gnedin away from the others and unleashed her fury. "You approve of this? You let him sit in the water like a fool? You know about the cancer!" she snapped. "Get him out of there and into a hospital and do it *now*."

The doctor pulled away from her. "It's his decision. He refuses a hospital, and yes, he told me about the cancer, but he ordered me to keep it to myself." He paused for a moment to collect his thoughts. "There's nothing I can do. At the end I can blunt the pain with morphine, but that's all. My options are strictly palliative. If he believes in the curative power of the lake, who are we to tell him he's wrong?"

"He'll catch pneumonia," she complained.

"It's what he wants," Gnedin said. "And he *is* the leader."

"Superstitions don't cure cancer," she snapped, keeping her voice low so that the others wouldn't hear.

"They work as well as anything else at our disposal," he said. "With cancer and any other serious illness the patient's mental attitude is crucial."

"What about surgery?"

"He rejects everything but this." Gnedin had debated this with Petrov in Odessa, and again this morning, but their leader's mind was set. "Leave it alone," he told her. "He's made up his mind."

Eventually Petrov asked to be lifted out. Melko hustled him into the house, placed him in front of the fire and tried to dry him with a towel, but the old man snatched it from him and stiff-armed him in the chest. "I can take care of myself," he snapped.

The Special Operations Group gathered silently around their leader. "How is Nikita Sergeievich?" Petrov asked Talia.

"Consumed by his interest in the new American president."

"Describe his security arrangements."

She had expected the question and was prepared. "Everything is orchestrated by the Operod, which technically reports to the KGB's Ninth Directorate, but in fact takes its orders from Khrushchev and the Politburo. General Nalepin heads the Operod."

"Nalepin was appointed by Stalin," Petrov said. So he was not the only one of Stalin's intimates to survive.

"There are nearly two hundred men and women on Khrushchev's staff, and they manage every detail of his life. He's virtually surrounded," Talia went on. "The chief of this detachment is a Colonel Litovchenko, who takes orders only from Khrushchev. The guards are well trained, alert, suspicious, attentive to detail and handpicked. I detect strong loyalty for him among them. Dr. Bizzubik is his personal physician. General Tsybin handles the General Secretary's flights and always flies with him; he's a perfectionist. Tsybin and Litovchenko work well together and seem to know what their man requires at all times. He has many secretaries and personal assistants, but Shuisky and Lebedev are the main ones. Shuisky is a cold fish, with no opinions of his own, while Lebedev seems to genuinely care, not in a fawning way but attentive and considerate beyond simple professionalism."

Petrov glowered at her. "Replace them all."

She looked at the team for help, but the others, including her husband, were all staring at the floor. She was on her own. "Who?" she asked.

Petrov's lips tightened. "Get rid of Litovchenko if you like, but definitely get rid of his men. It's one thing for his security chief to form a personal attachment, but fondness among the guards invites sloppiness. You should have seen this on your own and taken action," he added. After a pause for effect, he added, "And don't replace them with more of their kind." He looked at Bailov. "Bring in your people."

Bailov glanced at Talia, then back at Petrov. "They're not trained for such duty."

"Good," Petrov said. "That will make them all the more vigilant. Fear of failure and punishment are reliable motivators."

Bailov nodded. "As you wish," Talia said meekly.

"Not as I wish, but as the mission requires and circumstances dictate," Petrov corrected her. "You were sent here to take control of Nikita Sergeievich's security," he said with obvious irritation.

Why was he criticizing her? She had done exactly what he asked. He had told her only to assess the situation. Had the authority to act been implicit? She felt her neck redden.

"What have we got on Trubkin?" Petrov asked next.

"Nothing," Bailov said too quickly. "Yet," he added as a hedge.

Petrov stared daggers at the Spetsnaz colonel. "Don't lie to me!" he roared. "I'm not one of your GRU stooges." He paused. "What do we have on Lumbas?"

Talia felt her stomach tighten; their leader was on the attack now and angry beyond anything they had seen in the old days. Was the cancer affecting his thinking? This was entirely out of character.

"Nothing," Gnedin said in a voice barely above a whisper.

The leader of the Special Operations Group sat back in his chair and closed his eyes. "I expect action," he said. "Understand that there is nothing personal in this. This is not a reunion to relive a glorious past. What's done is done, over and finished. The past counts only for its predictive value. Your strength is in each other, not in independent action. Lumbas and Trubkin are mere men, which means that they have pasts. Every life produces tracks, and you must find them together by cooperating, by sharing. The Chinese say that one and one make three. Each alone is one thing for a sum of two, and the two together make a third. Look for connections. Our country is a web of transparent strands. Find the ones that lead to these men. I have no patience with incompetence and self-service, and our country has no need for them either. I feared this sort of performance, and now my fears have been realized." His eyes opened and he looked at each of them. "Those who do not produce will be discarded," he said, his black eyes hard. Then, turning to Melko, he asked, "What about the girl?"

"Exactly as you anticipated," Melko said. "She still has an itch for the old game. Her husband is a lieutenant colonel in the KGB's Third

Directorate; he's involved in some sort of low-level liaison work with the military and is ambitious. He's recently stumbled across some special funds linked to the Odessa Military District. The funds are called skeletons."

Petrov nodded. "A term as archaic as the concept. Money is appropriated without a written plan and can be used by whoever has the key. What will our colonel do with his discovery?"

"Annochka says he's evaluating his options. Apparently the KGB is not what it used to be. Shelepin holds the office and the power, but his predecessor Serov retains informants inside Dzerzhinsky Square."

"That's to be expected," Petrov told them. "Serov was often Beria's stalking horse, so he knows how to hedge his bets. You're sure the girl is willing to cooperate?"

"Yes," Melko said.

"Good," Petrov said. "That's a start. The girl's husband will help us evaluate the security apparatus. You've done well," he added. He turned to the others. "Take Melko's lead. He brings something to the table, while you're all empty-handed." He stared at the fire. "Petrov does not fail," he said after a long time. "You've wasted two weeks that we can never recoup. Now you have ten days to do something constructive. Ten days," he repeated as he rose and shuffled out of the room.

When they heard the bedroom door slam Bailov said, "Shit," and wiped the sweat off his forehead. In the old days the price of failure had been death. What was the price now?

"We have a lot to discuss," Talia said, determined never to give Petrov another reason to criticize her or the team again.

63 SATURDAY, MARCH 25, 1961, 8:50 A.M. *Moscow*

Khrushchev didn't bat an eye when Talia told him that Petrov wanted his bodyguard changed. Within minutes the chief of the General Secretary's personal security detachment came into the office and stood at attention. Guard Colonel Litovchenko was tall and broad-shouldered, with a massive head, a flat Slavic face and the unblinking eyes of a reptile. When Khrushchev told him that all personnel were to be replaced, Litovchenko's crooked smile evaporated and his head drooped like a scolded dog's. If the General Secretary sympathized he didn't show it, and Talia was suddenly overwhelmed with dread. Litovchenko was obviously fond of his master and loyal to a fault, yet in an instant none of this counted for anything.

"Nalepin will protest," Khrushchev told his chief bodyguard," but the Operod serves me, not vice versa." The organization's sole function was the protection of key personnel.

"My people will be replaced by Operod personnel?" Litovchenko's gray eyes pleaded for answers to soften his professional shame.

Talia interceded. "You've done nothing wrong, Colonel. The decision in no way reflects badly on you, and neither does the selection of replacements. It's precautionary, not disciplinary."

"But only Operod troops are properly trained for this work," Litovchenko protested mildly.

"Granted," Khrushchev said, "but the decision has been made and that's the end of it. Inform Nalepin and tell him not to come whining to me."

Litovchenko knew that his dismissal would mean an end to his career; in the Operod one served a senior official until his death or dismissal, and reported solely to him. He had been with Khrushchev for a long time and was not a favorite of Nalepin, so the Operod chief would not be sympathetic. When Litovchenko turned to leave, Talia stopped him. "Wait," she said. "This order applies only to your people; you will be retained."

"Is this true?" the colonel asked the General Secretary, who was watching Talia with what appeared to be amusement.

"Of course," Khrushchev said. "Tell Nalepin and then report back to Pogrebenoi. Take your orders from her."

When Litovchenko was gone Khrushchev popped up from his desk. "If security must be changed, why does he remain?"

"Because he knows the routines better than anybody else."

The General Secretary's eyes were intense. "Petrov said to keep him?"

"That decision was mine."

"Sympathy is a sign of weakness," he reminded her.

It's also a sign of humanity, she thought.

64   SATURDAY, MARCH 25, 1961, 2:30 P.M.
Paris

The church was old, small and cramped, its high-back pews worn by decades of pious buttocks, the kneelers padless, stone floors scratched. The pallbearers were forced to raise the wood coffin chest-high in order to get it down the center aisle. There were a dozen elderly mourners, all packed together up front. After placing the coffin on its stand, the pallbearers went outside to smoke and pass around a bottle of red wine. Smoke from a nearby factory hung over the street. An old woman in a cane-back wheelchair sat in the center aisle, listening to the priest say Mass in a monotone; the mourners dipped and bobbed on cue, but their genuflections were more approximate than precise. The old woman in the wheelchair did not cry; Sylvia supposed that she had used up her sorrow simply by living so long.

When the Mass ended, the people shuffled out, leaving the old woman at the front of the church. A young nurse in a navy-blue cape adjusted a blanket on her lap. Sylvia made her way to the front, blocking the aisle.

"Madame Celiku?"

The woman stared up with alert eyes. "I don't know you."

"I'm a reporter," Sylvia said. "For a newspaper."

"You're not French."

"American."

The woman nodded sharply as if her suspicions had been confirmed.

"I'm writing about Albanians forced out of their own country."

"I wasn't forced out."

"But you would like to return?"

The old woman shook her head. "I'm French now, and I have the papers to prove it," she croaked defiantly.

"I want to write about what it's like to be uprooted from your country."

"It was my choice," the woman said defiantly. "Take me outside," she snapped at the nurse. "Churches make me ill."

A priest appeared and tried to console the old woman, but she waved him off. "You should be ashamed," she said with a wagging finger, and the priest retreated. "Production-line funerals," she muttered to herself.

Outside there was a hearse with dented fenders. The mourners and pallbearers were gone—to the cemetery, Sylvia supposed.

"I only need a few moments of your time."

"When you're my age you have all the time in the world and none at all. Funerals become the center of social life. It's pathetic."

"There is a generation of Albanians in France who know nothing about their country."

"Lucky for them," the woman said. "Leave me alone."

Sylvia considered her situation. Since arriving in Paris, Beau had been guilt-ridden over Harry's death; if anything was to be done, she had decided, it was up to her. Last night he had gotten so drunk that he had spent the night on the bathroom floor. This morning he tried to apologize, but she was in no mood to forgive. "You've lost whatever you had in the old days," she had told him. No rancor, no anger, just a statement of simple fact.

"Right," he had answered, not bothering to defend himself. "Maybe I ought to move on."

"Your choice," she had said coolly before departing for the church. Now she regretted it and didn't understand why. Beau was one of the walking wounded, a type she had never been able to resist. She had abandoned her medical career because she couldn't let go of the most helpless cases, and now it seemed she had another one on her hands. Dead or alive, Frash had turned into a ghost, and Valentine was not much better. For now, however, she put her personal problem aside and concentrated on the task at hand. Madame Celiku was reputedly well connected in the Albanian community; the funeral today was for a man who had once been some sort of consultant to King Zog. Sylvia hoped that the old woman would be her window into their world. Stay focused, she reminded herself.

The Farm, the Company's training facility in Virginia, had been a frustrating experience, with tradecraft taught as a science when it was more an art, and a vague one at that. One instructor, a man twice her age, had finally given her the right perspective when he had likened investigative work to collecting butterflies. Most of the time you ran and ran, with nothing to show for the effort, but if you were in the right area, and when you least expected it, a fine specimen would land within arm's reach and wait obediently to be netted. Sylvia hoped that the old woman in the wheelchair would prove to be just such a specimen.

Paris had been neither a random choice nor a product of panic. This had been Frash's last post before Belgrade and it had a large Albanian expatriate community. Also, Gabler had suspected that after he arrived in Belgrade Frash had made some flights to Paris. What this meant was

204

unclear, but with Harry and Peresic dead it made no sense to remain in Yugoslavia.

Sylvia was using every avenue she could think of to infiltrate the royalist community. At the Farm they taught you to dissect a problem with the thoroughness of a surgeon. She recalled in particular one tenet: An enemy often knows more about you than an ally. Everybody she had talked to had pointed her to Maria Celiku.

"I'm sorry to have bothered you," Sylvia apologized. Cats were drawn to people who showed no interest in them. Some people were like that as well.

The old woman twisted her head at an angle and watched her walk away.

There was a small park down the street. Sylvia sat down on a low wall and tried to think. When she looked up, the nurse was holding out a piece of paper folded once. "Next Thursday at ten," she said. "In the morning." Inside was an address.

<h2>65   SUNDAY, MARCH 26, 1961, 11:00 A.M.
Moscow</h2>

Bailov stood on a sidewalk above a bend in the Moscow River where it looped suddenly from southwest to northeast to meander past Gorky Park and the red walls of the Kremlin. Though the European Nordic skiing competitions were finished for the year, the Soviet national team was hard at work on the steep Lenin Hills; as he watched, Yepishev struggled up the birch-covered slope among the athletes, his breath coming in visible bursts, a gray hood pulled tightly over his head, his upper body drenched in sweat. Bailov trotted down a series of wooden steps and angled into the woods to intercept him.

"In wartime a general is tied to a desk and in peacetime it's the same," Yepishev panted. "It's no way for a real soldier to live." The Goat had not been a true field soldier for many years, and though he was fit Bailov doubted that he could measure up to current Spetsnaz standards. They began a long, slow descent to the river while skiers with teammates on their backs chugged up the steep incline. When they reached a small clearing halfway down the hill, Yepishev collapsed on a log and wiped his neck with a black kerchief. "There's a rumor going around that Khrushchev has replaced his personal guard detachment."

"It's true," Bailov said.

"And the guards will be replaced by Spetsnaz?" Yepishev asked, eyeing the young colonel closely.

"Have been."

Yepishev stared at his colleague for a long while. "Your men?"

Bailov grinned. "The General Secretary deserves the best."

"Don't get me started on what that one deserves," Yepishev said. "You wanted information on Lumbas. It seems that there was an official request from Khrushchev to all ministries and agencies for information on him." Yepishev dug into the elastic in the back of his sweatpants and pushed an envelope at Bailov. "A wire photograph of your man. He's Foreign Ministry property, a technician of some kind."

"Source?"

"How I obtained the information is my concern, comrade. It was risky enough to get this much."

"And his whereabouts now?"

Yepishev shook his head. "A request from Khrushchev himself got no answer to that."

Bailov guessed how Yepishev had probably interpreted this lack of response, silence sometimes being as much an answer as a flood of words. It was not possible to be an unknown in the U.S.S.R. Births were as carefully recorded as marriages, divorces and deaths. All citizens were required to carry an internal passport identifying them by nationality, plus another document that reflected their complete work history. Soldiers carried a separate set of credentials, and all of these were duplicated by various government bureaus and agencies, which had their own requirements. The request for information about Lumbas should have brought several responses, but there had been nothing. If so, Lumbas did not exist in the Soviet bureaucracy, which made him unique and suggested the hand of the KGB. Who else had the wherewithal to make somebody disappear without a trace? Yet if Yepishev's information was correct, the man was attached to the Foreign Ministry. Probably he was KGB and had been assigned there; every ministry was filled with KGB operatives who served as its eyes and ears.

"No response from the Foreign Ministry either?"

"None."

"You're certain?"

"Quite."

Bailov reflected on this, then pursued another line of questioning. "Which ministries would *not* be required to respond?"

"Each one has some kind of security apparatus, so all would receive it and none would be immune."

"But some might not have enough information to respond," Bailov said, thinking out loud. "Some security units are strictly perfunctory. Health, for example, or Education."

"Security for such operations is under the umbrella of the KGB."

"But perhaps there are records held by some who would never have heard of the request?"

"Possibly," Yepishev said, "but it's hardly likely. The KGB's tentacles are everywhere. Begin with what you know, but keep me out of it. I've done all I can for you, comrade. This is shitty business for soldiers."

---

66 SUNDAY, MARCH 26, 1961, 7:25 P.M. *Moscow*

Trubkin's flat was in a dilapidated building in an industrial district in the city's northwest suburbs. A factory across the street belched black smoke that rained particles and covered the area with black dust. Ezdovo and Melko made their way up a dark stairwell past a young man who was asleep on a landing; on the next level they stepped around a young couple so engrossed in their embrace that they hardly noticed the two strangers. The door to the flat was one of four on the fifth floor and marked with a police sign that forbade entry.

"In my day such a sign would stop no one," Melko scoffed as he picked the padlock with a small steel awl. "Of course, if the police have already been here we can be sure that anything of value is long gone."

As the lock popped open a shrill and elderly female voice assaulted them from behind. "You there! What do you think you're doing?" She was short and fat, with white strawlike hair, a face covered with warts and a broom that she brandished like a cudgel. "Can't you read? The police put up that sign."

"We can read, Baba," Melko said pleasantly. "You can put away your weapon."

"I'll do no such thing," the woman said. "You think I don't know what you are?"

"Appearances can be deceiving," Ezdovo said softly. He was beginning to lose his patience. "Leave us to our business, granny."

"You don't frighten me," the woman shot back. "I lived through the Germans, and Stalin too. There's a militia station just up the street," she added. "They know me by name down there. One call and there will be policemen all over this place."

Ezdovo waved her away. "Then call them, Baba. Perhaps we'll have them haul you off to Lubyanka and tear out your interfering tongue."

The woman sucked in her breath, retreated and slammed her door.

Trubkin's one-room flat was surprisingly clean. There was an icon on the wall, a bureau with some socks and shirts in the drawers, a battered leather jacket on a hook on the wall, a pair of rubber boots piled in a corner and an empty refrigerator. "That's the first thing the cops steal," Melko said. A small cupboard held an assortment of dishes and teacups that didn't match. Several knives had keen edges. Against a window was a small wooden desk with a piece of cardboard for a pad and a small lamp with a burned-out bulb. A double bed was unmade in the corner, the blankets wadded on one side. One of the desk drawers contained more than a hundred black-and-white snapshots of Trubkin in various uniforms; another held two new light bulbs, several medals with faded ribbons and a set of pilot wings.

"Tin baubles," Melko said, fingering the medals. "Not much to show for risking your life."

"Pay attention," Ezdovo said. "He was working for Khrushchev, so he wouldn't operate without having taken notes. Also he was a pilot, and they believe in records. Names, addresses—something—but the cache won't jump out at us. We have to use our brains and think like him." Somebody had killed Trubkin; did he suspect that it was coming? Probably not, but he would have been cautious and left a second record. This sort of business made everyone paranoid. Ezdovo tried to concentrate. What in the room was out of place? Or did everything fit *too* well? Let your mind be a camera; record everything, then analyze it. Overlook nothing. There were three clocks, all showing different times; he examined each of them, checking for scratch marks, but found none. The bed had one leg shorter than the other three. "Turn the bed over," he told Melko, who only grinned and folded his arms.

"Why? Look, we can tear the place apart or we can do it the easy way," he said. "Remember, finding things that people don't want found is *my* specialty."

Ezdovo sat on the edge of the bed and gestured with his hand. "Show me."

"First of all, this fellow may have been a hotshot pilot, but in more unsavory matters we can assume he was an amateur. Only a professional thief is clever enough to conceal something safely. An amateur thinks, Out of sight, out of mind, whereas a professional puts things in plain sight. The amateur sticks things in his shoes, or in folded socks in a drawer, behind a book, on a string down a drain pipe, or"—Melko sat down at the desk, took hold of the light bulb in the lamp and began to unscrew it—"in a burned-out light bulb." The bottom twisted off easily, and when he tapped the bulb against his hand a small roll of paper slipped out.

At that moment a militiaman burst into the flat, followed by three other uniformed men. The man's face was flushed, his tunic unbuttoned. "What have we here? Two illiterates who can't read a simple sign? Or is it a political protest?"

"They're the ones," the old woman said as she pushed between the police. "I warned them, but they refused to listen and now they'll pay! Now do you believe me?" she cackled at Melko.

The sight of so many police at such close quarters put Melko on edge, but Ezdovo stepped forward.

The militia leader looked surprised as he wiped his face with his sleeve. "This is a posted area and you two are violating an ordinance of the criminal code. There's no admittance here without a pass issued by central headquarters."

Ezdovo smiled benignly. "You want to see our pass, is that it?"

"I've already radioed to headquarters," the man said smugly. "No passes have been issued."

"Haul them off," the old woman cried. "Teach them proper respect for authority."

When Ezdovo reached into his coat pocket two of the militiamen suddenly produced revolvers and he held up his hands. Melko backed out of the line of fire waiting to see what would happen next. The door was the only way out and it was blocked, but his companion seemed relaxed.

"Have the police taken to idly threatening citizens?" Ezdovo asked. "I only want to show you my pass."

"Easy," the leader cautioned his men; then to Ezdovo, "All right, comrade. I would advise you to give great thought to what you do next."

Ezdovo flashed a moronic grin, reached into his pocket, extracted the leather case, held it out and let it fall open in front of the leader's face.

"Christ," the man squawked as he took a step backward into one of his officers. "Please stay as long as you like. We had no intent of intruding, but how could we know? If you had called—no, what am I saying? You have the right to be here, of course." He was nearly babbling. When one of his officers questioned what was happening, he backhanded the man and set off a chain reaction, knocking him against another man who stumbled and inadvertently grabbed the old woman, who began to shriek as the leader herded all of them into the hall and slammed the door, leaving Melko and Ezdovo alone. "It's the Red Badge!" they heard the militia leader shout at his people.

Melko looked dumbfounded.

"What was in the light bulb?" Ezdovo asked.

Melko unclenched his fist and unfolded the piece of paper. "A telephone number. No name."

They searched Trubkin's flat further, but found nothing else. On their way out the old woman peeked at them from her door but slammed it when Melko dangled his Red Badge in her direction. When they reached the street he was almost giddy. This Red Badge was the ultimate license.

"You're impressed with the power of the badge?" Ezdovo asked.

"They nearly clawed each other's eyes out getting away from us."

"The badge confers absolute authority. No one may refuse you anything."

"And all I have to do is show it?"

"That's all."

"Only a Russian could conceive of such a thing."

Or need to, Ezdovo thought.

 ## MONDAY, MARCH 27, 1961, 11:45 A.M.
Pacific Trail, California

The cottage was small and tidy, with stucco walls painted blue, green shutters, a blue-tiled roof and a white wooden veranda on three sides. There were clusters of browned palms and cacti with small purple flowers along a narrow gravel two-track that led in from the road. Circling the house at a distance Venema saw a wooden walk built through a V in the dunes. Beyond the mounds of white sand he could hear the surf; seabirds called softly to one another but he couldn't see them.

Carla Foli Calvin had not been easy to find. A source at Boston College said she had been an acquaintance of Frash. Married and divorced five times, she had moved frequently since leaving Boston. Her latest IRS statement showed her to be a composer-in-residence at San Diego State, but the dean of faculty affairs told Venema that she had resigned months before and left only this address. A dented red Cadillac convertible was parked near the house and a broken surfboard stuck in the sand like a grave marker. When he got no response to the doorbell he peeked through the windows and saw that the house was sparsely furnished.

At the end of the wooden walk there was a cove of translucent green water whose mouth was blocked with a steel-mesh shark net attached to pylons anchored by cement in the dunes. At the water's edge was a white canvas cabana. He approached cautiously and saw that someone was sitting in the shadows, Venema watched for a while but saw no move-

ment. In the distance incoming waves broke against the top of the shark
net, spewing a fine froth into a soft wind. He took off his shoes and socks
and rolled up his trousers. "Mrs. Calvin?" He repeated the name several
times as he approached the shadow like a supplicant, shoes in hand, the
hot sand cooking his feet.

"What is it?" a voice asked in a low monotone.

Not who, but what? "Carla Foli Calvin?"

An oversized black-and-white silk scarf was draped loosely around
her body, another scarf covered her head, and she wore huge sunglasses
with mirror lenses. "A previous life," she said. "Foli before, Foli after,
Stieglitz, Corhartly, White, Lantana and Calvin, the latest incarnation."

Venema had never heard a voice so bereft of emotion. Her whole
presence was eerie—a dark figure hidden in the shade. Foli before, Foli
after; what the hell did that mean? "I just flew in from the East Coast."
She drew back at this. Damaged goods, he told himself. After a lifetime
with such people he had an instinct about how to handle them. At least
before Frash. But then Frash was still a question mark, at least technically. In this instance the symptoms were apparent.

"We die a little each day," she said, "or so I've heard, but you can't
put much stock in the news."

"I want to talk to you about Albert Frash."

She cringed at the name. "No V's today," she said, scanning the sky.
"Consider it an omen."

The letter V? "Of what?"

"To be a man is enough," she droned. "V's can fly away," she
added. "Without tickets or reservations. The rest of us are less fortunate."

"I see," Venema said in an effort to be both ambiguous and supportive. She was in her own world. He knew he would have to be careful not
to push her into even darker recesses, but there was no doubt she had
reacted to Frash's name. He guessed the V's referred to geese or seagulls.
What was she trying to say?

"What are you?" she suddenly asked, her eyes locking into his.

Again, not who, but what, an abnormal point of reference. "You
mean age, religion, political leanings, profession?"

"It's not important what I mean," she answered. "The question
focuses on you."

He held out his ID, but she didn't seem to notice. "I'm looking for
information about Albert Frash, a.k.a. Ali Frascetti."

This time her recoil was accompanied by a long, distinct hiss. "Refer
all calls," she said. "Nobody home. There may be a rip in the shark net,"
she added. "I knew it wouldn't hold forever. There's safety only in
movement. You must dance out of harm's way constantly."

"This will require only a few minutes," Venema said, trying to reassure her.

"The dead should stay where we put them," she said. "Coming back is extremely unsanitary. And it's rude after flowers and all the costs."

"You knew him in Boston," he said, hoping to prompt her.

"The girls in the dormer slept with their nipples pointed north," Carla Foli Calvin said. "Multiply times two to get the sum. For a woman there's something soothing about so many bare breasts. Safety among your own kind is one possibility, but there are other schools of thought. I turned to music after that. Sound affords the best peace of mind. Did I already tell you that?" she asked as she got up and shed her black scarf, which floated like a parachute to reveal a nude chalk-white body, spectacular in its lines and angles. She loomed like an Amazon above the squatting Venema.

"Count my V's," she ordered, her brown eyes staring down at him.

"Maybe I should come back another time," he said, but suddenly there was a nickel-plated, snub-nosed pistol barrel against his head. It felt icy cold.

"Start at the bottom," she said. "Marksmanship is not an issue at this range."

Venema stared at her feet. After a while he saw that where her toes joined there was a sort of V made by her flesh. "Eight on the bottom," he reported, and thought, What the hell. I've played even crazier games with other nut cases.

"Excellent," she said. "An auspicious debut," she added in a tone he took to be encouragement. "I can circle my wagon if memory fails you."

She paraded slowly around him; small grains of sand sparkled where sweat adhered them to her skin. Now and then she stopped to strike an exaggerated pose, but she did not speak.

"Twenty-seven," Venema announced after a while.

"Are you certain?"

"You want me to count again?"

"Not *that*," she snapped. "About Ali. I don't want him coming back from the dead. He was the first to count twenty-seven," she added.

"He's not dead."

She tapped her cheekbone with the pistol barrel. "He's in here. For me. Death has only partly to do with biology."

It struck him that her eyes didn't track properly.

"Glass," she said, interpreting his silence. "Except for size they're identical to the marbles children play with. They turn cold in northern climates and create unbearable headaches. This forces me to be a creature of the sun."

She waded ankle-deep into the ocean and pivoted to face him. "One should never swim beyond the barrier," she told him. "Sharks are as indiscriminate as they are omnivorous, but their god is efficiency, not malice. They view the world as food to support them. It's an egocentric existence, don't you think?"

Looney Tunes, her connections askew, yet even among the balmiest there was logic. "Frash is a shark?"

She grinned. "Less noble. We were political then, but the movement rejected him, so he took me instead. Too much a loner, a nontalker, adjudged unreliable, but very good in bed, especially for a first lover. I saw him as heroic, the lone figure against the world and fearless in the face of rejection. I couldn't have taken it, but he seemed to thrive."

"What sort of political movement?"

"Free the Eagles," she said. "A sham, but I was taken in on all counts. I admit to naïveté, but I was barely eighteen. At first I thought we were trying to save the habitat of eagles in the Balkans, but I was wrong. He raised money to buy weapons for Albania, fifty thousand dollars at one point, but the movement refused it when he tried to give it to them. They said he was too unstable."

"Was he?"

"It was never a healthy relationship. I gave, he took, and the longer it went on the more miserable I was, but when misery is all you have, you think of it as normal. I finally told him, No more. He never said a word, just grabbed me and pushed his thumbs into my eyes. I could feel his fingers in my brain, and then I was in the hospital with my parents, police, everybody wanting to know what had happened. He came to see me in the middle of the night and said if I told anybody the truth he'd kill me. I knew he meant it."

She related all this without emotion. Venema was nauseated. "So you left Boston?"

"Back to Indiana and good old Goshen College, got a degree in music, which created a stir because of my eyes, but I made a career out of that and husbands. You don't need eyes for music or fornication. Where is he now?"

"Out of the country," Venema answered evasively. "A long way from here."

"Too close," she muttered. "Much too close."

She strode back to the cabana, dropped gracefully to her knees and began pawing for her scarves. He retrieved them for her and touched her arm gently. "He's no threat to you," he said.

"Leave your card," she said. "There can be no further discussion until science confirms the finality of death."

Venema left the card beside her right foot. "You can reach me night or day."

"Sharks have the same power," she said. "I told the police nothing. Make sure he knows that. Principles are meaningless when survival is at issue. An altered state is still a state."

When Venema left she was sitting on the sand, her legs stretched stiffly in front of her, her expressionless face lifted to the sun. By the time he reached his car he had made several decisions. First, it was imperative, for his reputation as much as for the agency's security, that the use of his vetting instruments be suspended. If someone like Frash could slip through the net, the mesh was much too coarse. Second, the doctor in Montana had called Frash a paranoid schizophrenic, but based on what he had heard from Carla Foli he suspected that the man was a sociopath and would do whatever pleased or moved him without remorse. A value system would be in play, but it would be one understood only by Frash. Third, Arizona had to find Frash; a thwarted sociopath was a bomb, and it was virtually impossible to predict the behavior of such people. Fourth, even if the Company found Frash alive, Venema wanted nothing more to do with him. He was too dangerous to deal with, and if Arizona was smart he would see to it that Frash remained among the missing. He was a terrible mistake that neither of them could afford ever to have come to light.

When Venema reached the San Diego airport, he tried to call Arizona but was told he was unavailable, which in CIA parlance could mean anything from being dead to taking a crap.

68   TUESDAY, MARCH 28, 1961, 2:00 P.M. *Moscow*

The gaudy central spire of the dormitory of Moscow State University was wholly out of character for an academic institution, even a Russian one, Bailov thought. At night it was lit with thousands of small lights, like a Western Christmas tree, and by day looked like New York's Empire State Building. Outside the main entrance was a polyglot of pale-skinned men from the Baltic states, blue-black Africans in caftans, short Congolese with kinky reddish-brown hair and pale palms, a Yakut in oilskins, the ever-present Chinese, who moved in clusters, never alone, Russians, Georgians and Ukes, who stared with hatred at one another, Hungarians and Czechs, even East Germans, who stood apart but not together, each trying to be more arrogant than the next.

"Like a zoo," Bailov said. "A menagerie of exotics from the far reaches of the empire."

Gnedin smiled. There was more truth to this than his colleague could know. Most students here were selected for their connections and commitment, not their brainpower. A willingness to commit mayhem for socialist causes was a sure ticket to a Soviet education.

The university records section on the third floor of the main building was a windowless warren of large rooms connected by narrow halls stacked with cartons overflowing with papers. "Chaos," Bailov complained. In the First Brigade records were meticulously kept. "Our primary resource is people," he would tell his clerks. "Records represent people; treat them with respect." They did.

The chief administrator was a dwarf named Miss Yezhov, her name crudely painted on the outer door. She reached hardly to their waists, a bent young woman like no one either had seen before, a living ogre with a giant head, long frizzy brown hair, black high-buttoned shoes, no cosmetics, a huge nose, bowed bird legs, square-cut fingernails, intense green eyes and a falsetto voice. "*I* am Miss Yezhov," she proclaimed. "Did you come to admire my body, comrades?" She chuckled.

The two men looked at each other, then turned away trying to stifle laughter.

"Pity," she said. "If not my body, then my mind will have to suffice. I can read your faces," she croaked. "Chekists." She held up a hand, which was normal size and therefore all the more incongruous in contrast to her stunted body. "You saw my name and you wonder, can this Yezhov be related to the Yezhov who was Stalin's monster?"

All Russians were well acquainted with the name of Nikolai Yezhov, who for a brief but bloody period had reigned over Stalin's purges. A dwarf with a crippled leg, Yezhov, the Bloody Dwarf, had in only eight months ordered the killing of three thousand NKVD men—*his* men. He had been a hideous creature who fancied tall, beautiful women, ballroom dancing and torture. It was said that in Lubyanka he spent his nights stalking the forest-green torture cells, moving from one to another, inflicting pain, teaching techniques, immersed in his work, drunk on blood. Predictably, in 1938 Stalin accused him of being a foreign spy, and he was tried, sentenced to death and shot by the same men he had trained. Yezhov had been but a brief interlude in Russian history, yet he had done more than anyone else to instill intense fear of the security apparatus.

"Yezhov was my father," the dwarf proclaimed. "The likeness is undeniable. I was illegitimate, my mother normal—quite beautiful, in fact—but inexplicably she succumbed to him. I was born in 1938, six months after his death. My brains come to me from my mother, rest her pitiful soul, my body from my father, may dogs shit on his grave. My mother was executed in 1940. Her crime? Fucking Yezhov. I can't argue with that. What was I to do? The Bolshoi has no roles for dwarves, and who wants damaged goods for a wife? Education," she said. "Education was my way out. If the body offers no hope, use the mind, and that's what I did. Library sciences. I've been here since I was sixteen, the director at twenty-one, proof that the Party rewards competence. I have this position because I'm smarter than the rest of them. I work harder, too. No diversions. Don't be fooled by my appearance or that of my children," she warned, gesturing at the musty rooms behind her. "It's all here, every line, every form, all the secrets. Whoever passes through this university is my child. I own the facts of their lives, comrades." Despite her appearance and strange voice, she had fire inside her. "So what will it be? A Presidium member who diddles boys? A general caught masturbating in his tank? A chief engineer who failed math and chemistry? A spy, defector, drunkard, cheat? Tell me; my children await." She stood with her hands on her hips, challenging.

"A student, last known surname Lumbas," Gnedin told her.

Miss Yezhov pressed her forefingers to her temples and closed her eyes. Seconds passed; then her eyes popped open and she grinned. "Got him! Vilco Laz, later Villam Lumbas. Albanian-born, educated here. His parents were diplomats. Adil and Nora Laz."

Bailov was impressed. "You have them all memorized?"

"All the memorable ones and most of the rabble, but the damned African names give me trouble. However, in time I shall conquer our chocolate guests, you can be assured of that." Then she was off, rooting through boxes in a nearby room, mumbling to herself. When five minutes turned to thirty her mumbling faded to silence. Boxes were handled roughly and several crashed, raising clouds of dust that wafted through the doorway. When she finally returned she was carrying a thin manila folder with a single sheet of paper.

"Impossible," she said, slapping the folder on her desk. "Outrageous!"

"A problem?" Gnedin asked.

"I read this file one year ago and it was much thicker then. Now there is only a sanitized summary. I do not permit sanitization here. Never! It violates Miss Yezhov's principles."

"I don't understand," Bailov said.

She held the sheet of paper up for them to see. It had only the man's name and a red stamp that proclaimed, RECORDS TRANSFERRED TO SECURITY STATUS.

"What's it mean?" Bailov asked.

Miss Yezhov was on the verge of explosion now, her words issuing in tight bursts. "It means, *comrades*—that—one of my—children—no, I—have been raped."

"Stolen?"

"Removed, transferred, stolen—it's all the same. Violated!" She flung the paper down in disgust, then plopped into a backless chair with several thick books stacked to provide elevation, opened a desk drawer and extracted cigarette papers and a pouch of strong-smelling tobacco. She rolled a cigarette faster than they had ever seen anyone do, propped her tiny feet on the edge of the desk and leaned back in an impossible position, seeming to levitate over the floor. "Can't offer you one," she said. "Might stunt your growth!" Her giggle turned into a deep racking cough; then her feet hit the floor and she snapped back into a sitting position. "There, a smoke calms the nerves and allows the brain to function. The brain is no more than a network of chemical connections, but you have to let it have its own way, and now mine has. They have the file, but I have the information. You can steal one of my children, but not my memories." Her eyes snapped shut. "1949–1952. Chemical and electrical engineering. Laz was a near genius; he picked up where the Nazis left off with plastics called polymers and had some interesting ideas about electrical microcircuits. Komsomol member. Floor commissar. Performed at the highest levels in all academic subjects. Exemplary deportment. Selected by the Foreign Ministry in 1952, but stayed on to finish his studies here. Much in demand. One of our prized graduates."

"And then?" Gnedin asked.

She pursed her lips and raised her bushy eyebrows. "Not my child any longer."

"That's it?"

"Let me think." She closed her eyes again. "His roommate was also Albanian. In those days they tried to pair students by race and nationality. That's changed," she added with obvious disapproval. "Now we have Asians, blacks, Arabs, Russians all mixed together. Men sleep with women, men with men, women with women, all in broad daylight and on the same floor. A lot of abortions. Moral disintegration."

"The roommate's name?"

She grinned. "Frascetti, Myslim. A brute with brains. Not of his friend's magnitude, and older, but another one in great demand by the Chekists. A partisan during the war and a wrestler afterward, I believe. Never defeated. Broke an opponent's neck once—an Armenian, I think; the boy died. It was a match, not a brawl, and all within the rules, so there was no trouble. Frascetti went to the KGB, a perfect choice for them."

"Is there a way to trace them now?"

"Nothing I can do. A mother's children always leave her. It's an immutable law of nature."

They thanked her and turned to go but she followed close behind. "Yezhov," she said. "*Miss* Yezhov. Remember that name. My father was a monster. Come back soon. I'm always here with my children."

⌷⌷ THURSDAY, MARCH 30, 1961, 10:00 A.M.
Paris

It was a neighborhood full of mature oaks, high flagstone walls around the properties, and not at all what Sylvia had expected. Last Saturday's funeral had been modest and the mourners were shabbily dressed, but the house in front of her suggested wealth. The grounds were immense, the trees pruned and wrapped, flower beds spaded and weeded, the grass trimmed.

An Arab maid in black showed her into a library with high ceilings and books in several languages. Madame Celiku was seated in her wheelchair near a bay window. "Sit," she said. "Let's skip the nonsense. You've been asking around. Such things are never secret in Paris." There were hard lines around her eyes. "I'm French," she said. "*Now*. Once I was one of them, but no longer. They waste their lives making air castles, and for what?"

"They want to go home," Sylvia ventured.

The old woman cackled. "To what? Enver Hoxha? I know *that* one. Or Shehu the butcher?"

Sylvia let her talk. "I left Tirana in '32. I'd studied here and gone home to teach. But you can't teach that sort. Tribes, you know. They wear clothes, of course, but beyond that they are no different from the savages that live along the rivers of central Africa. I saw what was coming. Zog!" She hissed. "A sergeant playing king, licking Italian boots and worse. I said, To hell with them all, came back to Paris, married well, raised my children and left all that behind me."

"Why did you agree to meet me?"

The woman's head bobbed several times. "I'm not senile. Only my body fails me." She paused to catch her breath. "You're intelligence. You worked your way to me."

"Certain people suggested that you might be of assistance."

"No," the woman said. "You were told I opposed the royalists; based on this, you thought I would tell you things the others would not."

"Is that true?" Sylvia sensed an open door. She had been told no such thing.

The woman smiled. "That I opposed them? Of course. But what else you get from me will depend."

"On what?"

"You've been asking questions about the deaths," Madame Celiku said, evading the question.

"Murders," Sylvia corrected her.

"The police think it's a local affair," the old woman said, "but I still read the newspapers."

"You disagree?"

"Revenge is the Albanian raison d'être, but the tamed Albanians of Paris no longer have any fire. They sit in their cafés and lie to each other. They are cowards, not patriots; the good ones stayed on to resist and have paid with their lives."

"*You* fled."

The woman cracked a smile. "True enough, but unlike the others I haven't spent my life looking backward. When the Nazis came here I fought them as hard as any native Frenchman. Had I remained in Albania I would have fought the Nazis *and* the Communists, but it was my decision to leave and I don't regret it." She gazed into space briefly. "Ten years ago the Americans and British tried to unseat Hoxha. Did you know that?"

"No." Was this what Harry had alluded to?

"They recruited Albanian refugees from DP camps, trained them on Cyprus and sent them in to make a counterrevolution. It was a complete failure because the Russians compromised it. Hundreds were killed, perhaps more; certainly only a few escaped."

This reminded Sylvia of the news stories Gabler had shown them, and she saw a possible connection. Maybe Valentine's conclusion had substance. "It's been said that not to learn from history is to risk repeating it." Frash's record had also said something about Cyprus, hadn't it?

"Sound advice," the old woman said. "Very sound indeed. You know about the new American initiative?"

A surprise here. "I'm aware of nothing of the sort." If there was anything like it, she was certain she would have heard rumors. Perhaps years ago the Company could hide covert military operations, but not anymore; the sloppy security around the Cuban operation proved that. "There is no plan," Sylvia repeated. "There have been news reports based on Albanian radio broadcasts, but it's well known that the Albanians make groundless allegations when they're suppressing internal political opposition."

"Ummm," the old woman said. "I see." Her tone said she disagreed.

Sylvia passed a photograph of Frash to her. "Do you know this man?"

The woman adjusted her glasses. "Why do you want to know?"

"I can't go into that."

"He's missing, is that it?" Then to herself, Of course he's missing. Why else would she be here? He's gone and you can't find him. His network here has gone to ground and Shehu has his thugs here killing them. The French don't understand, but you do, don't you, girl?

She was beginning to. "His name is Albert Frash," Sylvia said, impressed by the woman's intensity.

"No," the old woman said. "His name is Ali Frascetti, and he was born in France in 1923. I knew his father. He's dead now, like most of the old ones. He was posted in France when Albania fell to the Italians but he moved to America and tried to keep the dream alive, and for that he was a damned fool." Again her gaze went blank.

Frash was Frascetti? There was nothing of this in the records. The file they had said Frash had been born in Boston. Had Arizona given them a legend rather than an actual history? "Please," Sylvia said. "Have you ever seen the man in the photograph?"

"His father married the whore with a child; later this one was born," Madame Celiku said, tapping the photograph. "He was a boy when they left Paris for America. They were diplomats, then academics—you know, professors. The whore was smart, I'll give her that, but he was a fool to marry her, a fool to leave France, a fool in all ways. She was the true zealot."

"Frash's father?" The old woman was rambling. Get her back to the point and keep her focused.

"How well does any woman know any man?" Madame Celiku asked. "You care for them, worry about them, cry with them, sleep with them, but do you ever really know them? I knew him well enough, but he chose the whore. Said he was sorry, that it was love. What was it we had? I asked him. Also love, he said, but different, and he begged me to forgive him and to understand. He came back to Paris after the war, supposedly to attend scholarly conferences, but he always met with the others and sometimes I saw him. I had a husband by then and my own family, of course, but I went to him anyway. That's what a man can do to you if you're not strong, understand?"

Sylvia had known such men, one of them her current partner, but so far, Galveston notwithstanding, she had resisted him.

"It was the usual sort of affair, obsessive, centered on sex and romance. Then he asked me for money. My husband is from an old family and was very successful in his own right. I refused, of course, and told him to go away. He called me and wrote to me after that, but I never saw him again."

"What about his son?"

"He was here, sat right where you're sitting—to pay his respects, he said."

"When was this?"

"Just over a year ago. He said he knew of me through his parents, and since he had just moved to Paris he was looking up their old friends."

"Did he also want money?"

"No, nothing like that; it was merely social, he said. He claimed that his company had transferred him to Paris but I think he was evaluating me. He had his mother's eyes, her intensity too. It was only a small surprise to me when he appeared. I had already heard that he was in Paris initiating contacts with the so-called Albanian Freedom Front."

"But he didn't tell you about this."

"He didn't have to. As I said earlier, there are no secrets in Paris, and I have excellent contacts. Albanians are notoriously bad with secrets, especially when their self-esteem derives from them. My sources said he was with the CIA, sent here to help the royalists, but this part I heard after he came here to visit me."

"What do you think he wanted?"

"As I heard it, he was gauging opposition to Hoxha. Later I heard that a new operation was being mounted."

"Against Hoxha?"

"Presumably."

"Do you think that the recent murders are connected to this?"

"It's an old pattern. Shehu has a long reach."

"If that's true, why haven't the authorities made the connection?"

"In part because French ethnocentricity precludes their understanding anything that's not exclusively French. But the French are also weary of trivial Albanian plots. They are concocted in cafés and there is always a new one, like hatches of newborn insects lifting off ponds, never to be seen again. Nothing comes of all this scheming, you see, and the French have grown tired of it, so they pay no attention. The émigrés tell the Sûreté that this bogey man or that one is after them, and it is like the little boy crying wolf."

"But you think it was real?"

"I heard that weapons were sent from Marseilles to Trieste. A lot of weapons—small arms, mortars, land mines, grenades. At least this is what's being said."

"And you agreed to meet me in order to tell me."

"No, I want you to stop this nonsense. I want the killing to end."

"Whose?" Sylvia was having trouble following her.

"I never expected to see that one," Madame Celiku said, returning the photo. "His parents were dead and I assumed it was over, but the whore—his mother—was smarter than I reckoned. They said he was insane, put in an institution when he was a child. A hopeless case."

"Who?" Sylvia was really losing track now.

"The son," Madame Celiku said. "*That* one," this said with a finger waved at the photo.

"Institutionalized?" Albanian, crazy? Were they talking about the same man?

"When he was young, just after they moved to America—during the war. This came from his father's own lips. We were in bed, which is always where these secrets come out. He wept—said it was hopeless. He loved his son and couldn't come to grips with the boy's insanity. The French handle such things better."

"Yet the son visited you?"

"Last winter. He was a handsome man, nearly the likeness of his father; he had the same gestures, same eyes, even the voice. He'd have an easy time with women."

"How many times did you see him?" Sylvia wanted to ask more but something held her back.

"Just once."

"Then what?"

"I have no idea," the old woman said, pivoting her wheelchair. "He never came back."

"But you wanted me to know that he had been in an institution?"

"Of course," the old woman said, tugging a satin cord that brought the maid at a trot.

"I don't understand why."

The woman stared over her shoulder. "Because I sensed that you would know what must be done."

Sylvia needed to talk to Valentine. Did Arizona know any of this? If he did, why had Frash been recruited into the Company? "Do you still think that?"

Madame Celiku followed Sylvia to the door; when she opened it, the old woman grabbed hold of her arm and pulled her back. "Kill him," she whispered. "Before others die."

---

70 **FRIDAY, MARCH 31, 1961, 12:35 A.M.**
   Paris

There were no floodlights on the spires of Notre Dame, but the lights of passing traffic played tricks and made it seem as if the cathedral's flying buttresses were swaying. Valentine and Sylvia sat on the quay that ringed

Île St.-Louis; it was cool and threatening rain. A couple had wrapped themselves in blankets at the base of the wall behind them. A convoy of barges passed by and sent small waves slapping against the concrete embankments while Sylvia recounted her meeting with Madame Celiku, taking care to repeat the old woman's precise words.

"You're sure she said there was something between her and Frash's old man?"

"Unvarnished," Sylvia said, "which is unusual. Even woman to woman, most of us wouldn't be so explicit."

"And she made a point of the fact that at one time Frash's dipstick might have been a little short of oil?"

"She blames Frash's mother for his condition. Both parents were mixed up with the Albanian liberationists, but apparently Frash's mother was the driving force."

Vallentine shrugged. Albanians again. "She's old. Age plays tricks with memories." He had noticed this in himself—a sign of his own mortality, he supposed—but he seldom let such thoughts linger. "If Frash was a rubber-room alumnus he'd never have made it through the CIA screening process. I don't buy it."

"The Company is fanatical about screening candidates. We're required to take a polygraph every year, part of the institutional paranoia about possible infiltration by the Russians. It's possible, I think, that there could be misjudgments made in various psychological and emotional analyses, but not in a background check. You can't believe what sort of resources are directed at this," Sylvia said. "It's the cornerstone of the selection process. If Frash was in a booby hatch when he was a kid, there would be no way to hide it, and no way the Company would hire him."

"Maybe the old bat's just beating her gums."

"That's one way to look at it," she said. "But—"

"But nothing about Frash has been reasonable so far," he said, finishing her thought.

"The father married another woman. Madame Celiku is obviously still jealous. Frash was close to his mother, so maybe she told me the story to make trouble for Frash."

"Do you buy that?" he asked.

She shook her head. "Jealousy doesn't have much to do with logic."

The couple behind them were passing a cigarette back and forth. "We really don't know a hell of a lot about Frash," Valentine said. "But what we do know smells more and more like two-day-old catfish."

When they got back to the hotel they went directly to their respective bedrooms. Later he heard the shower come on; the water hissed for a long time.

Later still he found himself standing in her doorway. "Get out," she warned from the darkness.

"I think it's time we had ourselves a chat with our friend back in the home office," Valentine said.

"We can discuss it in the morning."

Only later did it occur to him that she had been as awake as he was, and he wondered what this meant.

71 FRIDAY, MARCH 31, 1961, 8:15 P.M. *Fulks Run, Virginia*

The estate was right out of a high-rolling realtor's dream: sculpted green pastures, a dozen sleek brown Morgan horses grazing free, a long white gravel driveway with crocuses poking up on either side, a red-brick house with eight white Doric pillars, Negro servants in black uniforms, beagles in small kennels beside a white barn, the whole place contained by white-slat fencing laced with photoelectric cells and monitored by several lookouts with 30.06s and German-made scopes. It was a fortress in disguise, and now that the day's meetings had ended and the sun had set, the perimeter was awash in floodlights while armed guards in black kept to the shadows. Arizona stood at the window in his room and stared out into the white light that washed the grounds.

The entire day had been spent discussing the Cuban operation, and he had been pressed to confirm that Cuban pilots would receive new MiGs at the end of May. It was true, he had assured the group. The information came from a high-level asset called REBUS—Frash's asset—but he had volunteered no details and the others had accepted it because sources of this magnitude were not customarily revealed in such a mixed group. Despite his assurances, his colleagues and a liaison man from the White House had grilled him about the dates and the facts; he had stuck with what he knew. Cuban pilots were being trained to fly MiG-17s in Czechoslovakia; by the end of May they would be back home and with them would come a squadron of Soviet-built jets. Once the MiGs were in place an invasion would be impossible without full-scale—meaning American—air support.

This single piece of intelligence from Frash's asset was pivotal to the timing of the operation; the White House man had whined several times that the CIA was trying to force an executive branch decision without giving the president full information. Arizona had wanted to slap the arrogant little bastard in his three-hundred-dollar suit, but he had repressed the urge and calmly explained again that Cuba was not his venue, that it was mere chance that one of his people had learned this, and that as a team player he had simply passed it along. If he hadn't, he would be back in the office rather then getting the third degree in the Shenandoah Valley. What the White House *should* be doing, he argued, was thanking their lucky stars that the CIA was so efficient and that one of their not-inexpensive assets had paid off. Without this break they risked sending Cuban expats and some World War II–vintage birds into a squadron of modern jet fighters. After this reply the White House man had sulked, and Arizona had congratulated himself.

The White House man was thirty-five at the most, but had zeroed in on the most crucial factor of the plan. All the while he was urging the man and his own colleagues to not worry, Arizona knew that there was no justification for such advice. Frash had slid into parts unknown, so there was no way to get confirmation. Venema was still investigating. Valentine and Sylvia had not reported from Yugoslavia in some time, the damned Belgrade station chief had gotten himself snuffed over some Yugo dame, and now his widow was all bent out of shape. To top it all off, he had gotten a cable from Mossad liaison in Washington, D.C. saying that the Israelis were set to receive the special shipment in Istanbul and would transfer it to Tel Aviv, not Haifa. Would Washington please confirm final disposal of the shipment? What the hell did *that* mean? Be calm, he urged himself throughout the day; chaos is only a state of mind.

When the phone rang Arizona expected it would be Bissell wanting yet another assurance about the MiGs, but when he answered, a female voice said, "Please confirm by voice, then pick up line five."

When Arizona said his name into the phone a special device in the telecom center verified his identity and emitted an approving tone. He pushed 5 on the console. "Yes?"

"Venema here."

"It's about time. What have you got?"

Ever the consultant, Venema described his travels, the meeting with Dr. Missias and the encounter with Frash's ex-girlfriend in California. Only then did he lay out the possibilities. "One, Missias is right all the way. Two, Missias was correct with his initial diagnosis, but wrong about his reading of the spontaneous remission. Three, Missias is wrong all the way."

"And the winner is?" Arizona asked impatiently.

"The ex-girlfriend corroborates Missias."

"Meaning Frash is a nut case?"

"Certifiable, and chances are that if I keep digging I'll find more. The Calvin woman is not likely to be the only downstream victim."

"No," Arizona said. "As of now you're out of it."

"We should formally review the instruments," Venema protested.

"This has to be viewed as a temporary setback. We need to do some more fine-tuning, that's all. We both know that the principle of paper vetting is the wave of the future—"

"Fuck the future," Arizona said and slammed the receiver down. Great, he thought. Frash was a psycho, and today he had used his mysterious asset's information to set the timing of the Cuban invasion. Jesus, schizoid *and* violent. How the hell had an apparently severe nut case faked Venema *and* him? Forget the past, he cautioned himself. If Frash is alive he's a serious risk not only to you but to the Soviet–East Europe division and the Company itself. What if he's wrong about the MiGs? Or lied about them? Was this Soviet disinformation? The big question now was whether Frash was alive, and if so, where? It was going to be a sleepless night.

A second call came an hour later. "This is Crawdad, remember me?"

"I'm glad you called." It was the truth.

Valentine said, "Your boy's asset was a Russian named—"

"No names," Arizona said, cutting him off. *Was?*

"This line isn't secure?"

"More a matter of prudence. We need a meet."

"We've had similar thoughts over here," Valentine said.

"You'll have to come west," Arizona said. "I can't leave the country just now."

"Say where."

"New York. Same drill as last time; I'll leave instructions."

"You know about Gabler?"

"We'll talk." Of course he knew about Gabler; to nobody's surprise his widow was threatening to talk to the media about her husband's death. Arizona felt caught in a whirlpool pulling him downward at an increasing rate. "What about your primary objective?"

"A Kiowa Indian once told me that the secret to hunting buffalo is finding the damned things. So I asked him, 'How do you find them?' He says, 'Follow their turds. When you find a wet one you'll know you're close.' In this case I'd say the turds over this way are getting wetter."

"Get to New York fast." What did they have?

"Right, *Jefe*," Valentine said and hung up.

72   SATURDAY, APRIL 1, 1961, 4:30 A.M.
Moscow

Talia dialed the telephone number that Ezdovo and Melko had found in Trubkin's apartment. It was early morning, a time ideal for catching somebody off guard. The phone rang several times before it was answered by a sleepy male voice. "Mandrich here. Who the hell wants to talk at *this* hour?"

"I'm sorry to call so early, but I want very much to see you."

"Who is this?"

"A friend of Roman Trubkin." Talia had a naturally enticing voice, but when she made an effort she could be irresistible and now the charm was turned all the way up.

"Trubkin?" She could hear Mandrich struggling to clear the cobwebs from his mind. "Poor bastard was killed in a traffic accident. I saw his obituary in *Soviet Air Force*. Have we met?"

"No, Colonel, but I would like to remedy that."

"Of course," he said too eagerly, but just as quickly his defense instincts kicked in and he backed off. "Why?"

"You were his friend."

"I have many friends, but their women don't call me out of the blue."

"Trubkin was murdered," she said, "and I'm not his woman."

There was no delay in his reaction this time. "Who are you?" he asked in a whisper. Then, "Is this some kind of joke?"

"You can call me Talia, and I assure you that your friend was murdered. He was injected with a lethal dose of a drug."

"The paper called it a traffic accident."

"Do you believe what you read in Soviet newspapers?"

"We weren't close friends," Mandrich said in an obvious effort to distance himself from the potential trouble that Trubkin now represented.

She had expected this. "He had your telephone number."

"He probably knew lots of people. Call one of them."

"No, Colonel, he had *only* your number."

"I saw him recently," Mandrich confessed.

"I want to meet you," Talia repeated.

"My schedule won't permit it," he said weakly.

"Then you must change your schedule to accommodate us." Us, not me; give him a sense of a group, she told herself. Let him guess which one.

"I have important meetings."

"Call in sick. It's a time-honored practice."

"I'm sorry," he snapped, "but I don't make it a habit to engage in verbal jousts with the mentally ill. You need help, young lady." Mandrich was adept at tactical switches; he had moved quickly from defense to attack.

"I'll send a vehicle. Say in one hour?"

"Impossible," he persisted.

"Would Lubyanka be more convenient?"

There was a long pause this time; she guessed that he was weighing nonexistent options. "I'll be waiting," he said with resignation.

"Your address?"

"You don't have it?"

She sensed a glimmer of hope in his voice and countered it with a preemptive laugh. "Don't be difficult, Colonel. I can have it in minutes, so let's not play childish games. I want to talk to you and that's all. You have nothing to fear from me."

"You're certain he was murdered?"

"Yes."

He gave her the address and hung up abruptly.

"Well?" Melko asked after she set the phone down.

"He'll be there," she said. "He has no choice."

73 SATURDAY, APRIL 1, 1961, 5:45 A.M. *Moscow*

Colonel Sergei Mandrich lived in a brown apartment building in a nest of similar buildings surrounded by pockmarked streets and narrow sidewalks buckled by hard winters. There were no trees or parks nearby, and the nearest metro station was three kilometers away. The colonel was standing by the curb checking his watch when Melko eased the Volga to a stop. Talia opened the back door and watched Mandrich ease himself in as if he would be sitting on eggs. He was short and muscular, with a neatly trimmed blond mustache, a thick neck and straight white teeth. His head was an odd shape and his eyes set in such a way as to give him the appearance of a snake.

228

"Thank you for coming," Talia began.

Mandrich tried to smile but couldn't manage it. "Let's get this over with," he said grimly.

She noticed that he avoided looking at her. "You saw Trubkin before his death."

"It was a month before that, maybe more. Who remembers details? We met and had a few drinks."

"You invited him?"

"No, no, it was Roman who called me."

"Why?"

Mandrich pondered this for a while before answering. "The two of us go—*went*—back a long way. We met a couple of girls that night—you know, the usual sort of thing," blushing when he said it.

From his demeanor Talia understood exactly what sort of girls and night it had been. "But you hadn't seen him in a long time."

"It had been at least two years. He lost his position in the cosmonaut program and dropped out of sight. Trubkin didn't like to lose and this wasn't his fault. His inner ear wasn't right and that was the end of it. An act of God." He looked to see her reaction and seemed relieved when she said nothing.

"You've still not told me why Trubkin wanted to see you. You leave me to infer that it was purely social, but I can tell that you were surprised by his call."

"It was mostly social."

A hedge. "Mostly?"

Again Mandrich paused to gather his thoughts. "He asked some questions about how personnel are assigned to sensitive projects."

"Why?"

"He didn't volunteer, and I didn't press him. His questions weren't anything earth-shattering, so I saw no harm in answering."

"I see," Talia said, letting the silence work for her. Few people under stress could keep quiet; it was as if a sheer volume of words could stave off danger.

"We flew together, had been through a lot together, and he asked for nothing that put me on dangerous ground."

"Tell me about the conversation."

There no pause this time. "I told him that for secret military projects each branch of service has a committee of senior officials to screen candidates and make selections. When a project requires personnel from several branches, or when it's of national importance, there's a mixed group that includes the KGB and the Aviation Ministry. Marshal Malinovsky and Khrushchev co-chair this interservice group, but Shelepin of the KGB is the primary liaison and serves as its secretary."

"You have no idea why he wanted this information?"

"Absolutely none."

"And you never saw him again?"

"Just his obituary, but it didn't surprise me. When I last saw him he looked terrible and seemed under considerable stress."

Talia tapped Melko on the shoulder and the car stopped. She extended her hand to the colonel. "Thank you."

"That's it?"

She smiled. "I told you there was nothing to be concerned about."

"I thought there would be trouble."

"Over what?"

"Since when has justification been a prerequisite for causing trouble in Moscow?"

Talia opened her purse and displayed the Red Badge. "We'll expect you to keep this conversation strictly between us," she said.

Mandrich nodded, his eyes locked on the badge. "It never took place," he croaked as he scrambled out of the Volga and fled down a nearby metro entrance.

"I'm surprised that the state entrusts valuable aircraft to such a nervous man," Melko said as they drove away. "Did you get something from him?"

"Maybe," Talia said. She had no intention of asking Petrov for help. Had Lumbas's assignment to and transfer from Tyuratam been effected by the interservice group that Mandrich had just described? Obviously this was what Trubkin had suspected, but had he been able to confirm his suspicions?

74 SATURDAY, APRIL 1, 1961, 10:00 P.M. *Barvikha, Russia*

On most nights Nikita Khrushchev took a brisk walk; when he was at his dacha this meant a full circuit of the grounds, with a stop here and there to investigate whatever struck his fancy. Tonight Talia walked at his side, with two alert Spetsnaz men in combat gear trailing at a respectful distance. "I like the night air when the seasons are changing," the General Secretary confided. "It purges the mind. A man can't live a proper life with his ass glued to a desk. What is it you want?"

"Perhaps I simply relish your company."

He grinned. "If I were ten years younger I'd order you into the bushes to test your sincerity, but I am who I am and I understand such matters better than you. You're here to pick my brain, so get on with it."

"Am I that transparent?"

"That focused," he muttered.

"You're chairman of a committee that selects personnel for national security projects."

"I seem to spend all my days in committee meetings," Khrushchev complained. "A camel is a horse built by committee," he joked, but got no reaction. "Which group are you asking about?"

"Marshal Malinovsky is the co-chairman and Shelepin is the secretary."

Khrushchev acknowledged this with a grunt. "What about it?"

"Do you personally oversee the deliberations of this group?"

"I delegate. There are dozens of committees and just one me. Others run them on my behalf."

"Who conducts the meetings of this group?"

"The reports and recommendations come from Shelepin. The responsibility of that group is security, so ultimately it's the KGB's concern." He stopped suddenly and faced her. "You're thinking that the Lumbas selection came from this group?"

"I'm only considering possibilities."

He shook his head. "Malinovsky is an old cow and Shelepin is my man."

Translation: Neither man had the imagination or the nerve to undercut the General Secretary. "I'm not interested in them." At least not yet, she thought. "I'm more interested in the committee itself—how it works, what records it keeps, what the records show, who staffs it."

"It won't be easy to get you access to the records."

He's afraid, she thought. Technically he has the authority to do virtually anything, but he hedges. Still, she had anticipated this and was prepared. "Not all the records," she explained. "Just those for a certain period. You could request them for review."

"It would be unprecedented."

"Ask for records from half a dozen committees at the same time. In this way no particular request will stand out. You can say that you're concerned by the proliferation of committees, and that you want to evaluate their value to the state in order to consider combining or eliminating some of them. While you're retrieving records we'll interview the committee's staff."

"All committees?"

"That won't be necessary. We'll retrieve records from several, but interview only this one group. After a decent interval you can send the records back and declare that there is no need to change anything. This will put everyone at ease and nobody will be the wiser. All the records should be delivered to your office. You should take at least one hour a day to pretend to study them. Seal yourself away so that nobody will know exactly what you're doing. At night you'll bring the records we need to the dacha, where we'll examine them."

"And if I don't agree to this?"

"Do you want us to find out what happened to Lumbas and Trubkin?"

The General Secretary grunted, then attempted a smile. "You've thought of everything."

Talia ignored the compliment. "We'll interrogate the people on Monday night. A location will be arranged tomorrow. They'll be picked up at their residences and taken there. We'll work on them individually."

"Done," Khrushchev said. "Now let's finish our walk and enjoy the night's sounds."

75   MONDAY, APRIL 3, 1961, 11:50 P.M.
Nagatino, Russia

Nagatino was ten kilometers southeast of the Kremlin; here the Moscow River had been redirected, dammed and reshaped to create a domestic seaport that teemed with traffic. The area was packed with ancient warehouses in dire need of repair, crumbling wharves and jetties, fleets of dark barges and small cargo ships lashed side by side six deep, and all sorts of abandoned and rusting equipment. The river itself was filthy, a mixture of human waste and industrial sludge under a multicolored oil slick.

In an abandoned warehouse in the middle of all this Melko and Ezdovo had rigged a series of spotlights under which one man and four women from Shelepin's office sat together in silence. None of the five had resisted when they were picked up at their homes, but all of them were visibly shaken as they sat under the lights. As in the old days Bailov took the lead in asking questions while Gnedin looked on. Talia waited in a separate area, and from time to time her colleagues reported their progress to her.

When Katya Dirikova's turn came to be shown into the battered office that served as the interrogation room, she was so frightened that she collapsed, and they were forced to carry her the last few meters.

"You know why you're here?" Bailov began.

Dirikova shook her head and avoided eye contact.

"There may have been certain irregularities in your branch," Bailov said. "The law mandates punishment for those who sabotage the work of the state."

"I'm just a stenographer," she said in a wavering voice.

"No position is less important than another," Bailov said. "A stenographer is no less accountable than the director general of the KGB."

Katya's mind raced. Was Shelepin under investigation? Or had he initiated this? If he was the focus, then she had nothing to fear because she had done nothing wrong. If not, then she had to be careful and evaluate her circumstances. If only there had been a moment to talk to Velak; he would have been able to advise her. She decided to remain silent; if you didn't talk, nothing could be twisted, and she was not very good with words even under ideal conditions.

Bailov placed a photograph of Roman Trubkin on a stool in front of her and saw her stiffen.

Her mind raced to find an appropriate response. She had seen Trubkin's obituary and had attempted to talk to Velak about her former lover's sudden death, but he had simply said that men with drinking problems often met with untimely, violent deaths. Several days passed before it had occurred to her that she had never told Velak that Roman had a drinking problem; in fact, she had not known of it. From then on she had avoided Velak, fearing that he would want to collect on the favor he had done her. It would be stupid to refuse him, she had decided, but she would not put her heart into it and perhaps that would limit his demands. But he had never bothered her and never mentioned the incident. Now she was faced with Roman's death again. Since she had seen the obituary she had suffered pangs of guilt that were now transformed into terror. Should she acknowledge having known Trubkin or play dumb? Why did life force so many difficult choices?

"I knew him," she admitted. "I read about his accident."

"He was murdered," Bailov said.

The color drained out of her, the room spun and she looked as if she would faint, but neither man stepped forward to help her. "Velak," she gasped.

Bailov glanced at Gnedin. "What about Velak?"

She told them about Trubkin and her suspicions, how she had confided in Velak and been told not to worry, and to see Roman no more. They seemed uninterested in Velak but intensely interested in her relationship with Trubkin. They threw questions at her for three hours; always the focus was Trubkin and his interests and how he had methodically tried to wheedle information about the committee from her. With each question and answer she felt more lost, until suddenly the two men stopped and left the room.

Talia was directly across the hall. "Trubkin asked Mandrich about the committee, then apparently took up with the girl, who was one of three people responsible for transcribing the minutes of the meetings," Bailov said.

"She identified Trubkin?" Talia asked.

"They were lovers. If she's telling the truth he was her first. She's a plain girl and never expected romance, much less from the likes of Trubkin. Then she began to suspect his motives and, fearing for her position, confessed to Velak. He told her she had acted responsibly, and a couple of days later Trubkin was dead. She didn't draw the conclusion for us, but it's obvious: she believes that Velak had something to do with Trubkin's death."

"How long after she told Velak did Trubkin die?"

"Forty-eight hours."

"Which makes it an unlikely coincidence," Talia said. "Was Velak the focus of Trubkin's questions?"

Dirikova had related her conversations with Trubkin in detail. "It's not certain who he suspected," Bailov said, "but it probably wasn't Velak. It might have been Shelepin, or perhaps Perevertkin. She went to Velak only because he seemed sympathetic."

"Trubkin was careful," Gnedin chimed in. "Apparently his questions were circumspect. The girl is high-strung, so he probably didn't want to alarm or focus her on any single area; most of his interest seemed directed at the disposition of committee minutes."

"We'll see those soon," Talia said.

"What do we do with our guests?" Bailov asked. "We can't hold them indefinitely."

"Hold Dirikova to protect her," Talia instructed, "and let the others go. I'll put someone on Velak. It's possible that the timing of Trubkin's death is coincidence, but if not let's see where Comrade Velak leads us."

"He'll probably become suspicious when he learns that five of his co-workers were picked up," Bailov said.

"I doubt that Velak himself killed Trubkin," Talia said. "If he's involved it's more likely he acted as a go-between. The KGB has too many specialists in wet matters to use someone like him. It's also unlikely that a decision to kill Trubkin would be his alone."

"He's close to Shelepin," Gnedin pointed out.

"Only as a servant," Bailov said. "If he had the qualities for direct action he wouldn't be where he is."

"I agree," Talia said. "Bring him back here, but don't share what

Dirikova gave you. Go hard on him, then let him loose around midday. By then I'll have surveillance arranged."

"My men?" Bailov asked.

"No," she said. "I have in mind someone with different qualifications." She guessed that Melko would know where to find the sort of individual she had in mind.

76 TUESDAY, APRIL 4, 1961, 5:20 A.M.
Moscow

Leonid "Lenya" Sarnov was a man of many accomplishments and faces: pickpocket, enforcer, forger, counterfeiter, black-marketeer and pimp. But it was just this range of interests that made Moscow's hard-core criminals wary of him. Everyone agreed that he had courage and imagination, but he was also unpredictable and too much of a loner to trust. Worse, it was rumored that he had unusual political beliefs and a link to the Russian Orthodox Church; if either was true, he had too high a profile to risk associating with him. About his talents, however, there was no question. Lenya could do just about anything. He had once stolen a Red Army tank, stripped it and shipped the parts to some Armenians; it was said that there was no better man in a fight, especially with a knife; he had a tremendous network of informants to help him liberate government supplies; he could make a virgin beg him to undress her in Red Square; and if you needed somebody tailed, he could slide into his quarry's shadow and never be seen. When Talia explained her need, Melko thought immediately of Lenya, and hoped he was alive and in Moscow.

Finding Sarnov was not difficult; for years he had operated out of a metro station in southwest Moscow; where he lived was uncertain, but if you were the sort who needed his services you had only to go to his station and wait. With his unerring instincts for people wanting to do business, he would find you.

It was not yet 5:00 A.M. when Melko rode the nearly vertical escalator into the underground. The station had several levels, most of them empty at this hour, but he found a bench on the third level and took a seat. Thirty minutes later a tall man with a black cape swooped down beside him. Lenya was now about forty and as strange-looking as ever. For some reason he had never been able to grow any hair other than a narrow scalp lock that hung in a braid down the back of his skull. His pointed head was shiny, and the lack of eyebrows and his pale skin gave him a ghostlike appearance. "I heard that the great Melko had returned from the dead," he said. "And suddenly here he is in Lenya's place of business. What brings you here? The last I knew they had given you life, an oxymoron of the first magnitude."

"Debt," Melko said.

Sarnov had light brown eyes that were almost yellow; now they seemed to darken. "A man who doesn't honor his debts is not a man," he said, "but not all debts are collectible to infinity."

"Some are."

The two men had met in a penal camp east of the Urals. Lenya had been scheduled for release, but had made too many enemies, and with his release at hand they had tried to set him up. A fight ensued, and during it Lenya had killed a man. Melko had taken a liking to Lenya; as a thirty-year man, he had nothing to lose by stepping forward to take responsibility for the death, so he did. Lenya had gone free, while Melko's sentence had been increased to life and landed him in Camp Nine. Such an act put Lenya in his debt, but it was clear now from his expression that he had expected this to be one debt that would never be collected. Lifers didn't come out of the gulags.

"What is it you want?" Lenya asked.

"A straightforward matter," Melko told him. "I want you to follow a man and report his movements to me."

Sarnov seemed to think about this for a long time. "One doesn't equal the other," he said. "It's not an even transaction."

"The one who is owed decides equity."

"Bullshit," Lenya snapped. "Were it not for you I'd still be in the camps. Or worse."

"Later we can discuss any further balance due," Melko said. "The mark's name is Velak. He works for Shelepin."

"You want me to tail a KGB man?" An infectious grin covered Lenya's thin face.

"Do you think you're up to it?"

"Lenya could strip the condom off a mark while he's using it, but since he's KGB I don't feel so bad about the exchange of favors. Where do I find this Velak?"

Melko gave him the address. "He'll come out around noon. From then on, he's yours."

"I'll count the hairs on his ass for you."

"That's why I came to you."

By the time Melko had crossed the corridor and looked back, Lenya was gone. He bought a small flower from an old woman, stuck it in his lapel and caught the escalator up to the street. It was going to be a pleasant morning; the bite of winter was fading from the air.

TUESDAY, APRIL 4, 1961, 5:30 A.M.
Stuyvesant Falls, New York

Stuyvesant Falls was a two-hundred-year-old village in Columbia County a hundred miles north of New York City. In the nineteenth century there had been a cloth mill on the lower falls of Kinderhook Creek, but now the old mill was owned by a New Jersey chemical company and the river was filled with yellow froth that left the area reeking of sulfur. The village itself was built on a gentle incline and consisted of a dozen houses, an old stagecoach inn, a general store–barbershop and a walk-in post office. People kept chickens, ducks and goats, all of which ranged freely. Though it was in upstate New York, Valentine saw immediately that Stuyvesant Falls was like a hundred Texas towns where women worked two jobs and raised broods of dull-witted kids while their menfolk whiled away their lives drinking warm beer and jack-lighting corn-fed deer.

Sylvia was asleep when he turned off the highway and waited at a one-lane bridge while a white Wonder Bread truck lumbered across. Their destination was a small white house that sat on the point of a ridge south of the bridge. As promised, an envelope had been left for them at the Algonquin Hotel in the city: it contained the key to a safe-deposit box at a Chase Manhattan Bank branch at Forty-sixth and Madison. The box contained directions to Stuyvesant Falls and the keys to a Ford sedan that was parked in an underground garage on Fifty-second Street. They weren't supposed to meet Arizona until tonight, but Valentine insisted on arriving early in order to look over the meeting site.

"You don't trust him?" Sylvia had asked.

"Do you?"

She had shrugged and curled up to take a nap.

Valentine cruised slowly past the house, made a one-eighty beyond the village and came back for a second pass. The house was dark and there were no vehicles in the two-track dirt driveway. Just east of the bridge he found a gravel road, followed it down to the river's edge, backed into a sumac grove and cut the lights and engine.

"Where are we?" Sylvia asked sleepily.

"Some kind of lovers' lane."

She cursed at him and bunched her coat like a blanket. "Are we going to spend the rest of the night in the car?"

"Romantic, isn't it?"

	TUESDAY, APRIL 4, 1961, 7:00 P.M.
78	*s'Hertogenbosch, The Netherlands*

s'Hertogenbosch was more village than city, a maze of well-maintained brick and wooden tenements with white shutters on the windows, gingerbread trim, cobblestone streets and polluted canals of still, brown water. In the town square there was a half acre of blood-red tulips, a memorial to those who had perished during the disastrous Arnheim raid. British and American paratroopers had fluttered down under their silks or crashed their plywood gliders into muddy fields and been bottlenecked by the Germans because of weather and too few bridges to get them across strategically important canals. The Arnheim raid had been a Brit show turned bad by factors beyond its planners' control, Frash reminded himself; this described his own situation as well.

Kennedy was coming to Europe. The newspapers said he would visit France and perhaps England. Neither of these was a surprise; American politicians found it difficult to visit Europe without paying homage to their former masters. The question was, Would Khrushchev meet with Kennedy? European media led by the Germans speculated that it would happen, but so far the White House and Kremlin were silent on the question. He would like to catch them together.

Frash could not remember the woman's exact address, but landmarks were etched in his memory and these led him to a brick house with blue-and-white shutters and a brass nameplate on a blue door. It was precisely where he remembered it; the place had not changed in three years. It was a law office, but the names on the brass plate meant nothing. It was her first name he remembered: Ina. "I work here," she had told him. A secretary or clerk, he assumed. He let himself in without knocking. A small woman was putting on a black raincoat. The sky had threatened rain all afternoon.

"Ina?"

"You have an appointment?"

"I'm an old friend." What could be a more accurate description of twenty-four hours of intimacy?

The woman looked him over, trying to make a judgment, then reached for the telephone. "Let me ring her for you."

Frash tried to charm her with his smile. "Actually, I'd rather it was a surprise."

The woman shrugged and pointed. "Upstairs to the right."

Ina was sitting on a loveseat, her legs folded under her. There were papers all around her and a half-eaten sandwich on the corner of a large desk. Her eyeglasses were suspended by a gold chain and rode between her small breasts. She wore a white sweater with the sleeves pushed above her elbows; her shoes were off. She did not look up when he closed the door. "Lock up on your way out, Marie," she said. "I've got a lot of work tonight and I don't want to be bothered."

"But I've just arrived," Frash said, his voice startling her.

She clutched at her glasses and stared at him. "*You?*"

"I'm flattered that you remember me."

Her eyes were wide, her body rigid. "I never even knew your name."

"You never asked."

She had short reddish-blond hair and pale skin covered with freckles; a blush crept up her neck. "What is it you want?" She pressed herself back against the loveseat.

"You told me you worked here. You didn't tell me you were a lawyer."

"I'm not. I'm the accountant."

There was no pride in her voice; it was a mere statement of fact. Was she unhappy? Bored? "A scorekeeper," he said in English.

She didn't understand the word. "Why are you here?" She seemed frantic.

"Why are you so nervous?"

"You know why," she said, uncurling her legs and tugging her skirt down. "It's not Carnival," she added. "The circumstances are different; this is not permitted."

"I simply wanted to see you again," he said. "I need some advice." He had met her during the town's annual Shrovetide carnival, a three-day event during which all of society's restraints were cast off without guilt. He had never experienced anything quite like it.

She closed her eyes, removed her glasses, set them on the cushion beside her, then folded her hands in her lap and looked directly into his eyes. "What sort of help?"

"Why don't we get reacquainted first?"

She rose, walked to the window and looked down dolefully. "You're a dangerous man," she said. "I knew it then and I feel it now. You frighten me."

"Is that a problem?"

He tried to put his arms around her, but she squirmed away. "I don't know," she whispered. She smelled of talcum powder and strong soap and was trembling.

He smiled apologetically. "I'm sorry." Ali urged Albert to force the issue, but Albert kept him at bay. "I only wanted to surprise you, but now I see that it was a poor joke. If I had known it would upset you, I would have phoned instead."

She turned to face him again. "It's not as bad as all that," she said. "I suppose I'm overreacting."

"Dinner to start afresh?"

"I really shouldn't."

"Is that a yes?"

She smiled. "What harm can there be?"

 TUESDAY, APRIL 4, 1961, 7:40 P.M.
Stuyvesant Falls, New York

Valentine saw immediately that Arizona was under stress. "Thought maybe you two had run off somewhere to play doctor and nurse," the CIA man said. "What happened to Gabler? He wasn't supposed to be part of your act."

"Our script had a lot of blank pages," Sylvia said. "If somebody had helped us we might not have needed to involve Harry."

"The State Department is frosted. The dead woman was married to a Yugo VIP, which means there'll be repercussions."

"We think Frash's asset was terminated by the Soviets," Sylvia said. "His name was Lumbas. The dead woman was named Peresic; she was a Belgrade cop, a homicide inspector. She was a collaborator of Gabler's."

"Soviets?" How had they found out the identity of REBUS? Even he had not known that. "You're sure?" Had the asset been blown before or after he passed the info on the Cuban pilots?

"We have autopsy photos. Peresic said that the Russians took him out. She wanted to trade the information for a ticket to the West."

Which explained the frantic messages from the Israelis, but if the Soviets were on to Lumbas why would they kill him? It made no sense.

"What did Frash have going?" Valentine asked. "And no bullshit this time around."

"Lumbas *was* his asset. He had been in the Soviet missile program, and still had contacts there, which gave us an exceptionally clear window into the program."

"Did everything he gave you check out?"

"Not everything is verifiable with this kind of information, but nothing he gave us was disputed by our analysts. The man knew his subject cold."

"His motive?" Sylvia asked.

Arizona laughed. "Cash."

"Life's most reliable motivator," Valentine said.

"Bona fides?" Sylvia was pressing.

"There are two schools of thought about situations like this. In one you establish the bona fides of the source as a precursor to accepting information; in the second the quality and legitimacy of what you're getting establishes its own bona fides. We accepted Lumbas on the second principle, partly because he was too valuable to risk alerting the other side by digging into his background, but, more important, because his information was so damned fertile."

"But the Yugoslavs claim the Soviets blew him away," Valentine said. "If he was legit, why didn't the Ivans put him on ice and squeeze till his balls popped out his ears?"

Arizona allowed that this was perplexing, but since he had just heard about it he was not prepared to speculate. This would be assessed in due course; in the meanwhile, what had they learned about Frash?

Sylvia did the talking while Valentine sat back to watch their superior's reaction. "Harry and the Yugos thought Frash had something going in Albania," she began. What little color remained in Arizona's face drained as he fumbled to light a cigarette. "We also have a source that leads us to believe that Frash had networked with Albanian expatriates in Paris," she went on.

"*Hard* evidence?"

"You judge," she answered. "First, he was born in Paris, not Boston. Second, his parents were Albanian. Third, our source says that he was mixed up in some scheme to invade Albania. Fourth, the source claims that there was an earlier operation against the Pixies about ten years ago. The operation involved Cyprus, which fits the timeline bio you gave us. He was there in '53. Was he part of that show?"

"Briefly," Arizona admitted, "but only tangentially. Tell me about this so-called new scheme."

"He had money in Paris and bought arms, which were sent to Trieste. It may be that the Yugos thought the Company was bankrolling the deal, so they committed to it; so did the Greeks. Certainly the Albanian expatriates in Paris believe it was our op—and maybe even under way." She related the news stories about Albania. "The evidence says Frash was playing director and maybe screenwriter as well. Were you the producer?"

Arizona felt tired. "Not a chance," he said, shaking his head slowly.

"His job was the Russian and nothing more. I cut him loose from Paris so that he could concentrate on REBUS."

"Was that move your idea?" Valentine asked.

"No, his," Arizona said. "I agreed to send him to Belgrade because it made sense. The asset was based there. He was a marginal station chief, but a whiz in the field."

"How did he get the Paris job?" Sylvia asked.

"He was due a promotion and had requested Paris; he spoke the lingo like a native. We sent him as a test to see if we could move him up the Soviet–East Europe Division ladder. S. E. is the major league, but not everybody's cut out for it." He paused. "Where is he now?"

"He's Houdini," Valentine said. "Maybe the Russians grabbed him instead of Lumbas."

"Maybe," Arizona said, but he doubted it.

"If the Russians don't have him and he hasn't checked in with his own people, what does that tell us?" Valentine asked.

"Listen up," Arizona answered, almost relieved that at last he was going to have to explain what he had been living with since Venema's call. "There are some things about Frash that have just come to light and that you two need to know."

80 WEDNESDAY, APRIL 5, 1961, 7:25 A.M.
Barvikha, Russia

Talia and Gnedin worked through the documents methodically. The files were thicker than anticipated, containing not only finished documents— minutes, agendas and special reports—but also notepads used by various committee members, rough drafts and the tapes used to record their rambling deliberations. In all, the files amounted to seven large cartons. As she anticipated, the boxes had been packed haphazardly, which meant that before they could analyze and evaluate their contents, they had to reorganize everything chronologically. Once this had been done, they examined every piece of paper from oldest to newest. Gnedin read official minutes of a meeting while Talia listened to the raw tape; then they swapped. This done, they went through all the supplementary information connected to a particular meeting before moving on to the next. Throughout this process they each made their own notes; there was no discussion because they had agreed it would be best to develop their own ideas and hypotheses, then compare when they had control of the information. To think out loud together before they had formed their own opinions might risk losing an important insight.

Khrushchev came in several times to find out if they had made any progress, but each time he found them deep in concentration and left without disturbing them.

They worked straight through for twenty-four hours, then ate, took showers and reconvened to compare notes.

"Sloppy work," Gnedin began. "There's nothing about Lumbas in the notes or final reports."

Talia's search had yielded the same result. "Even so," she said, "it seems to me that the deliberations and record keeping are so loose that there was plenty of room to conceal something." She had also noticed that at the end of the meetings there was a rush to approve various transfers that needed committee approval; for these there was little if any committee discussion.

"Shelepin rarely attends the sessions," Gnedin said, "which bears out what Dirikova told us. Khrushchev delegates to Shelepin, who delegates to Perevertkin."

"But Malinovsky seldom misses a meeting," she added.

"Which adds up to very little; he rarely says anything," Gnedin said. When Malinovsky did speak, it generally was to brag about some military official he had served with or nurtured in some way, but for the most part he was silent. On those few occasions when he did enter a debate he spouted so much ideology that the discussion seemed to drown in trivia. "The minister of defense is a doddering old fool," the doctor concluded.

"Perevertkin is the one who controls the committee," Talia said. "Whatever the committee approves has to be followed up by him."

"But all transfers go to Khrushchev and Malinovsky for signature. To move a man requires both."

They were silent for a long time. "If there is no information, then we look at behavior," Talia said at last. "What is consistent or inconsistent?"

This time they concentrated on the tapes, but as the hours passed Talia's frustrations grew. "What the hell was Trubkin looking for?"

"He never got this far," Gnedin reminded her. "His focus was the committee itself because he guessed there was information there, but he had no chance to confirm whatever suspicions he harbored."

"His questions to the woman showed an interest in Shelepin and Perevertkin, but now we know that it was Perevertkin who shouldered the lion's share of the work. There has to be *something* in the tapes," she said with growing exasperation.

Gnedin put the first reel on the tape player again and slumped in a chair.

The doctor was the one who caught it. Rewinding a tape he said, "Listen to this." It was the end of a meeting and Perevertkin was speaking. "We're running late," he said. "If there are no objections I'll take care of the remainder of the agenda items." Gnedin then stopped the tape, rewound it, took it off and put another on. This time Perevertkin said, "We're running late. What's the committee's desire with regard to the remaining agenda items?" An unidentified voice said, "You take care of them." Several other voices chimed assent and the tape ended with the shuffling of papers and the sound of chairs scraping the floor. Gnedin put on another tape and advanced it to the end of the meeting. Talia sat with her head back, arms crossed, eyes closed. The end of the new tape was nearly identical with the last one, and on each subsequent tape the meetings ended the same way. "Hear it?" he asked. "In all the tapes but that one he's strictly reactive. Only that once did he volunteer to take care of what hadn't been covered. It's an exception."

Talia found the file of papers that related to this particular meeting and examined the agenda again. Several items were unchecked. Perevertkin's own copy contained the notation "Handle," and arrows were drawn from the word to several items. One man was to go to the Office of Technology Exchange, whatever that was, two more were headed to a submarine project at Kamchatka, another to assess problems at a radar installation on the Kola Peninsula, two more to come from Siberian installations to Moscow for special training assignments in project security, another man to attend a London conference on television microwave transmission, and a final man to go to Belgrade on loan to the Yugoslavian Aviation Ministry to serve as a technical consultant. "Check the original paperwork on these," Talia said, but Gnedin was already searching. They laid the papers out side by side and studied them.

By now Talia's concentration was flagging, but Petrov had pressed them and there was no time now to sleep or eat. After a while she flung up her hands. "Nothing," she cried. "Not a goddamned thing!"

"Wait," Gnedin said. "Wait a minute." He had one paper in his hand and picked up others. "Top right," he told her. "Top right." Each application had a box in the corner, and in each was a handwritten three-letter designator and a typed number. All of them showed the letters "V-P-S," but none of the numbers were sequential.

Talia picked up the committee's cloth-bound logbook and flipped through the pages. "The initials are for Velak, Perevertkin and Shelepin," she said. "They have to initial each set of papers before it goes to the committee."

Gnedin placed one of the pages in front of her. "But this one's different. All three letters are the same, but it looks to me like one hand wrote them."

She stared at them for a while. "I see it," she said, "but whose hand?"

"Each time we get closer," he said, "it seems we drift farther from the answers."

"When you walk through the forest," Talia said, "you often don't see your destination until you're on top of it, but you can't let your inability to see it stop you from going ahead." Petrov's criticism still burned, and she was determined that if reaching their destination meant pushing the team to its limits she would do so. If Petrov could push, so could she.

81   WEDNESDAY, APRIL 5, 1961, 2:00 P.M.
Moscow

Experience had taught Leonid Sarnov that a good tail needed determination more than skill; over the long haul energy ground talent into dust, so it was the determined tracker who invariably had the advantage, especially if he had a little luck. Not that he would need much luck with this Velak fellow, who moved like a hundred-year-old tortoise. No fast movements, no mysterious destinations, no backtracking or crossovers, nothing unpredictable. It was hard to believe he was KGB; in fact, it was hard to believe that someone like Velak could be of the slightest interest to Melko, much less so important that he would erase a debt just to have the man followed. Eventually he decided that it didn't matter; if this was what Melko wanted, this was what he would get, even though it was laughably easy.

It had been forty-eight hours since Velak emerged from the warehouse in Nagatino, went straight to the KGB complex on Dzerzhinsky Square, stayed until 6:00 P.M., then took the metro home and spent the night. Yesterday he had come out at 8:00 A.M., taken the metro to work, again appeared at six and come straight home. Today had started the same way but this time he had unexpectedly emerged at noon and taken the metro home. Lenya had been suspicious immediately, but he was not the sort to assume the worst; maybe Velak couldn't stomach the food in the KGB's canteens for three days running. A few weeks earlier, workers in the Foreign Ministry had rioted over their food and used their forks to stab cooks, one another and security guards in a bloody melee that lasted for hours. A woman showed him sets of fresh tine marks on her left arm and said that workers in the Foreign Ministry now had only spoons as utensils. Perhaps conditions were the same at the KGB.

When Velak entered his building at noon, Lenya engaged a sewer repair crew across the street in conversation; like most good Russians, they preferred a lively chat with an odd-looking stranger rather than work, so they poured a cup of vodka for him and hunkered down to enjoy the respite. Lenya regaled them with stories of women he had known, but all the while he had a perfect vantage point; there were only two entrances to Velak's building and he could see them both. In the two hours since Velak had gone in nobody else had entered or left the building. A muscle-bound Asian in a too-tight suit had walked past twice in a forty-minute span, but neither Lenya nor his newfound comrades paid any obvious attention. Even so, he had seen the man seem to glance at the door on his first pass, then pause briefly and look up the next time, and this behavior made Lenya edgy. The Asian wore a suit with all the confidence of a nun in a bathing suit, and one of his pant cuffs was stuck in the top of a high black boot. Every Muscovite knew that Asians were the most backward of people, but what sort of lout wore boots with a suit? It was *nye kulturny*. Mongols were not welcome in Moscow, especially in an area such as this. Probably nothing, Lenya cautioned himself, but if Velak had come home just for lunch, what the hell was taking so long? How could he follow someone who was sitting as tight as a constipated goose, and if he couldn't follow him, how could he erase his debt? It was time for a decision. What life taught, if one cared to learn, was that one's emotions and intuitions should not be ignored. Knowledge and reason were adequate for civilized pursuits, but tracking someone on the sly was an uncivilized act.

The trick to getting into places where you didn't belong was to pretend that you did. Lenya went to the door to the lobby and stood so that the day watchman could see him, but after several minutes the door had not opened, and when he leaned close to look through the glare he saw that the console was vacant. Circling to the service entrance he tried again, but still got no response. Something was wrong. His instinct was to break in the door, but Velak was KGB and the building might be wired to a nearby security center; if an alarm was tripped, the place would be quickly swarming with armed and nervous KGB personnel, and if it turned out that Velak was all right, he would know that he was being followed and that would end it. Be smart, Lenya cautioned himself; perhaps the watchman has stepped away to piss. But after a few more minutes the man had not returned, so he decided to call from a public phone across the street.

"Stay put," Melko said after hearing a brief summary of the situation.

Ten minutes later Lenya was in the rear of a black panel truck recounting events to Melko and two muscular men with hard faces. Bailov was the one with extremely short hair—a soldier, he guessed. The other one had a wild beard and hard eyes, and he knew immediately that this was not the sort of man to trifle with. He was introduced as Ezdovo. Lenya related every detail, including the peculiar behavior of the odd-looking Asian wearing boots and a suit, and he apologized for not acting sooner, but Melko dismissed his self-reproach and congratulated him for exercising caution.

"How do we get past the alarm?" Bailov asked.

Melko smiled. "We go over it."

With Lenya guarding one end of the alley and Ezdovo positioned at the other, Melko and the soldier disappeared. After a few minutes Bailov whistled at them from the service entrance. There was no sign of the security man. Lenya was left to guard the entrances while Ezdovo hunted for the doorman and the other two went upstairs to check on Velak.

Lenya sat at the console and memorized the layout for future reference. Information was life's treasure; what had no meaning now might have great significance later. After a while a grim Ezdovo reappeared and went past him without speaking. Another half hour passed, and then the truck pulled up to the service entrance. Lenya dialed Velak's room. "The truck's outside."

"Open the door," Melko said softly.

A few minutes later a covered body was carried downstairs on a blanket by Melko and Ezdovo. Then another body was then brought up from the cellar and loaded on the truck, which immediately departed with Ezdovo and Bailov, leaving Melko and Lenya alone.

"Velak is dead," Melko said, and then added, "It's not your fault. In any event, your debt is erased."

"No," Lenya snapped. "I failed."

Melko patted his shoulder and left him stewing. What the hell was going on? If Velak was dead, the debt could not be erased. He decided that he would not rest until the account was settled to *his* liking.

The sewer repair crew had returned to work after their lunch break, and Lenya strolled over to join them. "How big is the sewer system?" he asked. The place where they were standing was at least two meters deep, but he could see smaller tunnels and pipes intersecting the main below them.

"All fucked up," one man said. "Several centuries of systems, all jerry-built. You can drive a truck through some of the tunnels; in others only a starving snake can wiggle through."

"Could someone get into the building across the street from down there?"

"Why do you want to know?" one of the men asked; the question triggered predictable Russian paranoia.

"There's an eager woman on the fifth floor, but her husband is KGB. She told me that if I could get into her flat she would give me a time to remember, but I'm no fool; that building is probably rigged with alarms."

The men smiled, any doubts they had harbored now transformed by the universal male bond. Their new friend was a man with a mission, and men had to stick together, especially when it came to hanging horns on some KGB shit. "Come on," one of the men said as he started down a ladder. "We'll show you how to crawl through our holes into hers."

A metal ladder led up from the tunnel to the basement of Velak's building. "These hatches aren't locked?" Lenya asked.

"No need," one of the men said. "Only unfortunates like us come down here. It stinks, there are poison-gas pockets, cave-ins, armies of rats, and it's such a maze that half the time even we get lost. Once a month we find bodies or skeletons. It's enough to keep all but the worst fools out. Besides," he added with a sarcastic laugh, "there's no crime in Moscow," this being the Kremlin line.

"But if the building's wired," Lenya argued, "it makes no sense to leave the bottom open."

"It's not open," the man corrected. "The hatch is hard-wired into the security system." He held out a long black wire with alligator clips on each end. "We have to notify the KGB if we're going to work in one of their playhouses. Years ago they always had a man come with us to supervise, but these days even the KGB has limits to its manpower. Now we simply bypass the connection and attach a seal when we're done."

"So I can't get in this way either?"

The man smiled. "What are friends for?" He climbed the ladder and motioned for Lenya to follow. When they were at the hatch the man attached one alligator clip to the hatch frame, the second to the hatch itself, and opened it. "See? When the wires are in place you can open it and the circuit is preserved; the wire's long enough so that it won't get in the way. When we're done we loop a new seal through the frame and wire it into place." He showed Lenya where.

"Shouldn't there be a seal on there now?" Lenya asked, craning his neck.

The man shone his light around the hatch, then down the ladder. "Is there a seal down there?" he called to his comrades below.

There were sounds of movement below. "Nothing," a voice called up.

"Bastards," the man muttered as he took a new one from his pocket and gave it to Lenya. "Nobody gives a shit anymore. They hire new people, teach them nothing and expect old-timers like us to clean up after them. It's a fucking disgrace. When you come out, make sure you put this on," he said with a nod toward the seal in Lenya's hand.

When they descended into the tunnel again the men slapped their newfound friend on the back, gave him a flashlight and the wire with the alligator clips and went off to finish what was left of their workday. "Leave everything behind the ladder," the sewer gang leader said. "We'll pick it up tomorrow. And give her a few pumps for us."

As soon as he was alone Lenya searched around the base of the ladder and found a broken seal looped over a valve behind it. He picked it up and stuffed it into his pocket, then turned his head slowly to let the light cover the area in a slow sweep. It would have been better if the workmen had let him come alone, but done was done: the thin layer of muck around the ladder was obliterated by their footprints. Five different mains intersected a few meters away; two of the channels were man-sized and the other three were smaller but navigable. Along the curved sides of the tubes were narrow cobblestone curbs that soon petered out. Thirty meters down one of the smaller tubes he found what he was looking for: a single set of fresh footprints made by a short, wide shoe with an unusual rippled pattern. A boot print.

Three hours later Lenya emerged in a neighborhood he didn't recognize. It was an old area interspersed with small, newer apartment buildings and minor estates gone to seed, probably the homes of doctors and merchants who had fallen from grace in the civil war. It was typical that such fine places had gone unoccupied for all these decades, but his countrymen were a superstitious lot; houses retained spirits and accumulated their earthly misfortunes. Some people laughed at superstitions, but he didn't. What was God if not a spirit?

There was a small park near the exit from the sewer. Lenya found a bench and sat down, his back aching from being doubled over for so long. The prints, he guessed, belonged to the odd-looking Asian he had seen. There was the broken seal for evidence that somebody had entered the building, and the footprints were fresh. It was possible that somebody had gained entrance through the sewer, dispatched the security man, killed Velak and escaped underground. The tracks showed that the man had made his way confidently; there were no signs of hesitation, no wrong turns; he had come straight as a crow to this exit. Why? Lighting a cigarette, Lenya sat back to study the area. Melko might think that his debt had been discharged, but it hadn't been, at least not yet.

WEDNESDAY, APRIL 5, 1961, 9:00 P.M. *Stuyvesant Falls, New York*

82

During a lifetime in the trade Arizona had worked with or against the top echelon of intelligence professionals on both sides of the Iron Curtain. Some contacts recurred over many years and formed the basis of rudimentary relationships, a few of which were shaded with a sense of trust but most were antagonistic. In Arizona's mind his foes fell into distinct categories. Wolf of the East German Stasi was a brilliant strategist but an archenemy, pure and simple; Holicik of Czechoslovakia was at the other extreme, a muddling, dull-eyed bureaucrat who needed written orders to know when and where to take a shit and was no threat to anyone, except perhaps to himself; Yepishev of the GRU was somewhere in the middle of the spectrum. Somehow the Russian had never seemed as ideologically fire-hardened as some of his colleagues; he discharged his military intelligence responsibilities with apparent efficiency, but Arizona had sensed in the man the resentment of an old-line soldier saddled with unsavory duty, resigned to doing what was required, but loathing it at every turn.

The last time he had seen Yepishev it had been a one-for-one trade: an American-educated Czech taken in Prague for an Estonian netted in Las Vegas. The Czech had been caught trying to photograph a new Soviet tank during Warsaw Pact maneuvers; the Soviet agent had tried to recruit a McDonnell Douglas engineer in order to buy information about a new interceptor prototype. The trade had been made in Helsinki, which was the preferred venue for such exchanges; Berlin was often painted by writers as the capital of East–West exchanges, but getting in and out of that city was fraught with staging difficulties. The Finnish capital was easier for all involved, and the Finns were politically predisposed to minding their own business. Yepishev was stiff, taciturn, efficient and confident; yet in Helsinki he had unexpectedly opened an avenue so frightening that Arizona had not allowed himself to think about the implications. Without even a preamble the smelly Russian had proposed the unthinkable.

"We have similar problems," Yepishev had begun. "We both dance to the tune of politicians who put their own fortunes ahead of their country's. By law you and I must obey our civilian bosses, so we're not so different, but we're also professionals, which means that we can act reasonably when necessary. We look to common sense, not ideology."

Arizona let the Russian talk, sensing a proposition in the offing.

"Our individual objectives are not dissimilar. Each of us is charged with maintaining national security through national strength. We protect our nations' secrets."

Not quite true, but almost. In practice the Soviets were far more aggressive in stimulating trouble as a way of depleting American resources and prestige. Yet Yepishev was essentially correct, and Arizona acknowledged this with a nod.

"I think a day might come when you and I need to talk with the sort of candor that our political leaders would neither comprehend nor condone."

Arizona knew that there was no suggestion of treason in this proposal. It was just what it seemed to be: one professional opening a communications channel to another, and the politicians be damned. Right now there was reason to remember the Russian, Yepishev's position in the GRU making the growing notion even more attractive. As the Soviet Union's smaller intelligence service, the GRU was an acknowledged poor second to the KGB. In the West the rivalry between the two organizations was well known; only the true depth of the animus and exactly how the rivalry affected their operational cooperation was in doubt. Given the long-standing trouble between the two, Yepishev might be receptive to an overture, especially if Lumbas represented a KGB effort gone sour. The Russians' alleged execution of Lumbas without careful damage assessment strongly suggested that there were some problems on the other side. If Lumbas had been a danger and had given the West accurate information about the Soviet missile program, Yepishev would want to know, and if he was appreciative he might use the contact to help them trace Frash. The key was to move as quickly as possible; the invasion of Cuba was only a couple of weeks away.

Pouring himself a brandy, Arizona reminded himself that Yepishev had made a gesture; now it was time to reciprocate.

83   WEDNESDAY, APRIL 5, 1961, 11:50 P.M.
Moscow

Talia needed a long, deep sleep but could not afford the time. Two of Bailov's men had driven her to the Heart Institute and she had napped in the backseat; when they arrived she was still groggy, her legs as heavy as cement as she trudged along the dark corridors of the hospital.

The two bodies were laid out on tables. The watchman was fiftyish, with short white hair on his chest and protruding ribs; Velak was short and pudgy, with thin legs and wide shoulders, an assembly of ill-fitted parts. Both bodies had been opened with a Y-shaped incision; their viscera were in stainless steel pans.

Ezdovo was in a corner, his head against the wall; Bailov and Melko sat on the edge of a metal desk. Gnedin was standing between the bodies, still wearing a rubberized black apron and elbow-length gloves splashed with blood.

"You look like a dead fish," Talia said by way of announcing her presence.

Gnedin peeled off a glove, tossed it into a sink and rubbed his neck. "This one fell down the stairs," he said with a nod toward the watchman, "and our friend Velak died of an embolism."

"Plain language."

"Air bubble in his heart. Sometimes happens naturally, but not in this case. Not in either case. This one's neck was broken before he went down the stairs; Velak was injected with the same gauge needle as used on Trubkin, and expertly applied. Both died instantaneously." Gnedin tried to explain the medical evidence, but his colleagues were too weary for technical trivia. "Murders," he summed up.

"I've heard enough," Talia said wearily. Petrov would accept this as progress. Not that they knew any more now than before, but the interrogation of Shelepin's staff seemed to have stimulated some countermoves. "Tomorrow at noon," she said and left.

Ezdovo followed her and caught up with her outside the hospital. "You look exhausted," he said as she fell into his arms.

---

84   THURSDAY, APRIL 6, 1961, 1:30 A.M.
          s'Hertogenbosch, The Netherlands

Frash had learned early in life that above all other human conditions, human beings most feared being alone, and that this fear was the root of the awe and trepidation inspired by death. Fear of loneliness drove people to endure the most desperate circumstances for the illusion of companionship, and even to mistakenly characterize it as love. To discover a person's innermost secrets one had only to listen, which was a greater skill than conversation but less understood and inadequately developed in most people. Years before, he had spent a night and a day with Ina VanderLeyden; yet in that twenty-four hours he had plumbed her as thoroughly as if he had injected her with sodium pentothal. It was not animal magnetism that made this possible; rather, it was his ability to listen that encouraged her to reveal her every secret, mistaking his listening and her self-interest as intimacy. The more a person talked, the greater the attraction of the talker to the listener. Sex was a product of listening, yet few people understood this dynamic.

Part of what Ina VanderLeyden had revealed that night three years before was that one of her firm's clients was a South African shipping company whose vessels were registered in Liberia. The company specialized in cargos she referred to as "of a dubious nature," so they needed to hire crewmen willing to take risks. The Dutch law firm's principal was a former ambassador to Jakarta and Johannesburg who, through a combination of influence and well-placed guilders, had gained access to blank Dutch passports, which he then supplied to the shipping company at a substantial profit. Ina had even shown Frash the safe, opened it and revealed the documents. She had also told him that soon they would have blank passports from many countries: Belgium, Germany, Norway, Greece, even the Soviet Union.

These and the relative obscurity of s'Hertogenbosch had combined to reunite Frash and Ina; he needed new papers, and the attractive Dutch woman was a potential source. Despite his goal, he did not move directly toward it; she was too skittish, and his unexpected arrival had spooked her. Ali wanted to press ahead, to break into the safe and be done with it, but Albert still had control, and this time he wanted to accomplish his mission with surgical precision. He was on his best behavior and used his skills to get her talking. She told him straightaway that she was now married to a man fifteen years her senior; he traveled a lot because he owned a firm that manufactured components for high-frequency radios for tanks used by NATO; their marriage was one of convenience. Ina stayed on with the law firm because it gave her "something to do," which translated to not being alone.

Frash took a room at an inn on the east edge of town next to a canal with water muddied by the runoff from adjacent farmlands. In the morning old men gathered along the canal to fish with long cane poles and gaudy, hand-painted cork bobbers. Last night he had not pressed her; as he knew she would, tonight she had come of her own accord. She was thirty-seven, brunette and thin, with the firm breasts of a much younger woman and long legs with perfectly shaped calves and thighs that flared upward, then tapered suddenly and unexpectedly inward at the top. She wore expensive clothes from Amsterdam and diamond jewelry, her husband having part interest in a diamond-trading firm in Antwerp.

They spread a quilt on the ground beside the canal. Ina had brought champagne and a wicker basket filled with fresh bread, cheese and pâté. They sat half clothed under a partial moon hidden by haze. Across the canal an occasional lorry or Volkswagen raced by, but mostly they heard only the clatter of bicycles or frogs peeping from the banks. Last night there had been a chaste kiss at their parting; tonight she had shed her clothes and was on him even before they had smoothed the wrinkles from the quilt. Afterward she clung to him, the tone of her voice telling him that it was time to set the hook. "I've never forgotten you," she whispered.

"You got married," Frash reminded her. Tease a little, don't be too eager, make her reach.

"What does that matter? Perhaps you're married too."

"No." It was true; there were too many important things to accomplish and life was too short for a long-term relationship. There had been someone once, but she had abandoned him, just the way his mother had died and left him alone. "I'm not well suited to marriage." Also true.

"Someday?"

"I never say never," Frash said. This was the tricky moment. Part of her needed the illusion of uninterrupted companionship, but she also required excitement, a sense of danger, immediate gratification, the insistence of the id. She was at an age where she was beginning to sense her own mortality and the loss of her youth; it was a fragile period, which meant it could be used to manipulate her.

"Are you going to leave me again?" Ina asked, her voice wavering.

"You have a husband."

"He's not important. I want you."

This was what he had been waiting for. "You couldn't go with me," he said. Work her now: anticipate her intent, deny it, increase the intensity, block her logic with emotion.

"I have money," she said. "A lot of it."

He caressed the back of her neck. "You mean your husband's money."

"My own. I've planned for myself."

"Your husband would interfere."

"He wouldn't even notice," Ina said with a touch of anguish.

"Businessmen are collectors, which means they can't stand losing their possessions. In time he would make it difficult for you." Open the door to possibility gently, he warned himself. Listen to her, Albert said, while Ali whispered, "Get the combination from the cunt."

"He doesn't own me," she snapped back.

Indignation? Good. "All merchants are the same. He has the means, so no matter where you go, he could find you. Our lives would be miserable. There would be endless legal entanglements. In my business I travel a lot and I can't afford that sort of problem. I only have one passport and I can't risk losing it, even for us."

Ina rolled onto her back and stretched her arms above her head, mulling it over; he could almost hear the desperate logic as she swallowed the bait. "But the legal problem would be temporary," she said. "In time it would be resolved and then we would be free."

"I don't have the patience for all that."

"Would your business allow me to travel with you?"

She had complained that her husband would not allow her to join him on his trips. "Of course. That's the point, isn't it? To be free *together*."

She sat up. "What if we had different identities?"

Albert felt the glow of success. "Possibly," he said. "It might work." He had told her that he was an independent insurance investigator, a specialist in fraud working for a percentage and expenses. "But how?"

Ina was watching him now, trying to come to a final decision. "I can arrange it," she said confidently.

He shook his head. "It's not likely."

"My firm," she said. "Don't you remember?"

"I don't understand."

"The company has certain credentials. I showed you the safe that night."

"All I remember is you," he lied. It was important that she think of herself as the author of the idea.

"The safe," she repeated. Then she reminded him of the firm's secret business, just as she had the first time they had met.

"I vaguely remember," he said, "but I had only you on my mind that night." He slipped his hand between her legs to emphasize the point.

She moaned and shifted her weight, then pushed his hand away and rolled over. "It's a good thing one of us can think clearly."

"We'd need several identities to stay clear of him."

"How many?" she asked, not catching the shift in momentum.

"At least six for each of us."

"It can be done."

"But the firm will discover the loss."

"Of course," she said, "but who will they report it to? It's illegal for them to have such documents. It's safest to steal from thieves."

Her cynicism impressed him. "It's a big risk for you." Set the hook deeper.

"There's no risk," she replied. "Can't you see how easy it is?"

He could. "If it's to be done, it has to be soon."

"I can get them tonight," she volunteered.

"I don't want you to get hurt."

She reached for her clothes and began to dress. "I'll get them right now and bring them back."

"I know somebody in Amsterdam who can fix them for us," he said. Another lie; he would do it himself. The CIA had given him a higher education in the use and preparation of false documents. "It will be expensive."

She licked his lips and nuzzled her check against his. "Do you have enough?"

"For the documents, yes, but we'll need some money to travel on. My funds are in an English bank. I could have them wired to Amsterdam, but it might take an extra day."

"We'll use my money," she said. "I don't want to waste even one day."

As good as her word, she was back before daylight, gave him the passports and money, made love to him eagerly and left before sunrise. The plan was for him to go to Amsterdam, get the documents prepared, then meet her at the airport. Where were they going? she had asked. Let it be a surprise, he said. As soon as she was gone, he checked out of the hotel, drove to Brussels, bought supplies in a printshop and caught a bus to the Ardennes. He had twelve blank passports now and a substantial sum of cash. By the time she discovered the truth he would have disappeared, and who could she tell? She had said it herself: it was safest to steal from a thief. As he sat in the bus he felt disgust for her weakness. All women were the same, and most men—including Khrushchev and Kennedy—were not much better.

---

85   THURSDAY, APRIL 6, 1961, 5:30 A.M. *Moscow*

Bailov had given Yepishev an emergency telephone number. Now, as they stood in a field west of the city, the Goat's expression told him that there was a problem.

"You've been flying high these past few weeks," Yepishev began. "The greater the altitude, the weaker the lift. Eventually you risk a stall."

"This unexpected get-together is not for discussing aerodynamics."

Yepishev stared off into the rising sun. "When you reach the edge of the atmosphere you need the power to blast clear, or else you're sucked down by gravity. And as difficult as it is to get clear, the reentry is an even greater danger."

"Get to the point," Bailov said.

"Some years ago I had occasion to confer with a high-ranking official of the CIA," Yepishev said. "We talked candidly about mutual needs and problems. He is a soldier of sorts and, like us, is constrained by an unwieldy political superstructure. We agreed that a day might come when his service and ours might need to talk openly and off the record. This morning I received a message from the American; that day has come."

"Why tell me?"

"He wants to talk about a traitor the Americans call REBUS. The traitor is ours, or shall I say yours?"

"Lumbas?"

"He was passing information to them, but they claim he's dead now and that our people terminated him. Shot him out of hand, so to speak, in Belgrade."

Bailov's heart was racing, his need for sleep suddenly gone. "What does this code name mean?"

"A rebus is a puzzle composed of pictures; they say that Lumbas gave them photographs of classified materials from Tyuratam."

"You agreed to the meeting?"

"I have no interest in Lumbas," Yepishev said, evading the question.

"But you can arrange such a meeting."

"If that's your wish, but if it goes sour, it's your problem and yours alone."

"Then you expect trouble?"

Yepishev grinned. "I *always* expect trouble, my friend, and if you value your worthless skin you'll do the same."

With this they shook hands and Yepishev handed him an envelope. "What's this?" Bailov asked.

"Confirmation of your promotion to brigadier general, effective July 1. Khrushchev is retiring old dogs, moving his own people in and up. The list came yesterday afternoon. *Do svidanya,* Comrade General Bailov. I'll inform the Americans that we accept and let you know the arrangements."

"When?"

Yepishev shrugged. "That's up to the Americans." Which meant there was no way to predict. The Party taught that Americans were one-dimensional, but professional soldiers didn't rely on political rhetoric to form military strategy. Bailov knew otherwise; like his own people, the Americans were a paradoxical race and exceptionally unpredictable.

On his way back to the city he drove slowly in order to think. Lumbas was dead and had been an American agent. What did it mean?

More important, what did he tell the team? The American request put him in a quandary because Yepishev was sticking his neck out for him. If he told the others about the American initiative, there was some chance that Yepishev might be compromised before the meeting could take place. In the end he decided to keep the information to himself and to alert the team only when all the arrangements had been made; still, having made this decision, he was uneasy.

Raya welcomed him with more than usual ardor, but soon after they were in bed she began pressing to find out what was wrong.

"I've only got a couple of hours," he snapped. "Are we going to waste it talking?"

Raya raised an eyebrow and took him into her arms. "Your tenderness is overwhelming," she whispered, but he was too lost in himself to hear the sarcasm.

86   THURSDAY, APRIL 6, 1961, 7:00 A.M. *Moscow*

The Third Tank Guard Regiment had earned its place in Russian history at Stalingrad when a Guards captain named Apahkin had refused food offered by the city's starving people and said, "Give it to the women and children. The Third Tank Guards will eat iron." For effect he had snatched up a bolt, popped it in his mouth and swallowed. From then on the men of the regiment were known as Iron Eaters; later they had participated in the assault on Berlin, but the already legendary Apahkin was not with them; the swallowed bolt had lodged in his stomach, where it ripped a hole and started an internal hemorrhage that couldn't be stopped. He died forty-eight hours after his historic moment, not in battle but sitting in his tank while it was being refueled. Now there was an impressive bronze statue of the famed Apahkin at the regiment's training ground north of Moscow, and every new recruit who joined the Iron Eaters was required to stand before the statue and swear allegiance to Apahkin, the Iron Eaters, the General Staff and the Motherland. At the conclusion of the sunrise ceremony the new men swallowed a plastic bolt; when it was excreted a few hours later they would attach the memento to the chain that held their metal ID tags and wear it with honor.

A dozen black and gray tanks were lined up in front of the bronze Apahkin, their crews at attention in front of their machines. Marshal

Malinovsky and Colonel General Gubin stood off to one side as witnesses to the ceremony. When it had concluded they saluted the new men, marched silently past the line of vehicles and got into a staff car for the ride back to Moscow.

"Silly tradition," Malinovsky complained.

Himself a former Iron Eater, Gubin still carried his memento in a pocket over his heart. "It binds the men to their history."

"If that asshole Apahkin had been one of mine and lived, I would have shot the fool as a traitor," Malinovsky said. "All we had then were the people, and by losing his own life he jeopardized the Motherland."

The marshal had been in a foul mood since Gubin had picked him up around midnight. Not that he was ever the jovial sort, but usually he was more considerate of others, and never had Gubin heard him denigrate military rituals. Something was obviously eating at the defense minister, but the general knew better than to question him.

"Things are happening," Malinovsky said suddenly. "First that sniveling Trubkin stuck his nose where it didn't belong, and now Khrushchev has some sort of special team conducting an inquiry."

"The woman in Khrushchev's retinue?"

"Retinue, my ass! She's living with the bastard."

"Even Furtseva didn't have that sort of gall," Gubin said. Ekatarina Furtseva had been Khrushchev's longtime mistress, a onetime member of the Central Committee and the only woman to ever have the honor of reviewing the troops at the May Day parade in Red Square. Now she had lost her Central Committee position and been banished to the Ministry of Culture to brood out of the Kremlin's limelight.

"Would that it were that simple," Malinovsky said. "Earlier this week several people from Shelepin's staff were picked up and interrogated."

Gubin was stunned. "Who dares pick up the staff of the director of the KGB?"

"Those with Red Badges. One of Shelepin's secretaries was not released."

"Trubkin's girlfriend?"

Malinovsky nodded grimly. "Velak is dead."

"How?"

"Never mind," Malinovsky said. "Things are moving too fast. We have to slow them down."

"I thought you told me not to worry," Gubin said. It was infuriating to listen to Malinovsky's righteous preachings when events were unfolding in ways the defense minister had said were not possible.

"Don't misread me," Malinovsky growled back. "It was inevitable that an investigation take place. We don't want to stop it; we simply want to slow it down and send it off in the wrong direction. The Albanians need time to mount their response."

"Assuming that they will."

"I know what they'll do," Malinovsky said. He also had an idea of what else needed doing now. When a opponent was deployed in line you broke him by attacking his flank, then wheeling 90 degrees to deplete the enemy a few at a time. It was time to give Khrushchev's new friends reason to worry about their own health.

87 THURSDAY, APRIL 6, 1961, NOON
Kosino, Russia

When Talia and Ezdovo arrived, Melko was sitting on the stoop staring into the distance, and she saw immediately that something was wrong. Gnedin and Bailov were in the bedroom with Petrov, whose flesh was ashen, his eyes swollen. "Is he . . . ?"

"Not yet," Gnedin said. "Cancer spreads, invades the organs, shuts down systems. With radiation we can try to kill the cancer cells faster than the healthy ones, but at best it only retards the process."

"You said he refused radiation," Talia reminded the doctor.

"He can't refuse now," Gnedin said. "The decision is ours to make."

"No," Talia said. "It's his life and he told us what he wanted. No X rays and no drugs. He's still the chief."

"Morphine for pain," Gnedin said.

"Nothing," she said firmly.

"At least let me move him to a hospital," he pleaded.

She glanced at Bailov and her husband, who nodded. "All right," she said, "but no intervention."

"He'll die," Gnedin said.

"In his own way and by his own choice," Talia said. "We owe him that."

88   THURSDAY, APRIL 6, 1961, 8:30 P.M.
Lamoura, Franche-Comté, France

This time Arizona's orders to Valentine and Sylvia had been explicit: Return to Paris, track down Frash's Albanian contacts and stay in touch. If they could backtrack his involvement with the Albanian expatriates they might be able to make some educated guesses about where he was. Though not knowing how the meeting with Arizona would turn out, Sylvia had anticipated something like this and in their absence had put Mr. Li on the case. On landing at Orly Airport they took a cab to the Marais and walked to the hotel.

After they showered and changed into fresh clothes, Li brought tea to their flat and sat down. "There is a gentleman at the Sûreté," he began. "He is associate director of the domestic intelligence branch, and by all accounts is a competent man and exceptionally ambitious." He paused. "Yet Monsieur Barrie is not without vices. He is both an enthusiastic gambler and consistently unlucky in games of chance. At present he is also unable to repay certain individuals, and has approached an acquaintance of mine for a loan to consolidate his debts. But as fate would have it, my colleague is not sufficiently capitalized, so I have agreed to finance Monsieur Barrie's loan if certain stipulations are met. Barrie has been involved in investigations focusing on what some have characterized as a war between Albanian expatriate factions. I've had a good chat with him, and it seems that our friends at the Sûreté have been suppressing information. For example, Monsieur Barrie has reason to believe that certain recent events in the village of Lamoura are related to the events here." He handed Sylvia a slip of paper with a telephone number on it. "I have informed Barrie that when you are satisfied with his cooperation, his fiscal problem will be ended."

"Just like that?" Valentine asked.

"He has no alternative," Li said solemnly.

Sylvia dialed the number and asked for Barrie.

"A moment, please," a woman said.

"Barrie here."

"Li gave me this number," Sylvia said.

The voice shifted from satin to burlap. "*Oui*," he said, and a long pause ensued. Was he trying to collect his thoughts? "Lamoura is a village north of Geneva," he said in bursts. "Franche-Comté. It may be of interest. Historically," he added in a conspiratorial whisper. "Concentrate on late March. Ask for Constable Grave; he will help you. Tell him I directed you to him."

"Thank you," Sylvia said.

Barrie lingered on the line. "You will tell Li that we have spoken?"

In other words, is my debt canceled? "We'll let you know how it works out," she said and hung up.

"Well?" Valentine asked.

"We're taking a short trip," Sylvia said, retrieving her coat and heading for the door.

Li took them to a garage behind the hotel; there was a new Jaguar under a black tarp and he gave Sylvia the keys. "A windfall," he explained. "It's yours for as long as you need it."

Sylvia flirted with the red line on the tachometer, but the Jaguar clung solidly to the road; after a hundred kilometers Valentine admitted that she knew what she was doing and leaned back to sleep. They stopped once for petrol and covered the five hundred and fifty kilometers in four hours flat.

Constable Grave, who worked out of his home, was bearded, five feet tall and wide-waisted, with sunburned cheeks and chapped lips. He came to the door with his trousers unbuttoned and a shirt in his hand. "Yes?" He had small eyes set close together, a thick, protruding mouth and a chestful of gray hair that grew onto his shoulders like furry epaulets. He resembled a species of East Indian monkey.

Sylvia explained that she was a journalist from the Paris bureau of the Associated Press. She flashed a card from her purse and earned a grunt from the constable. She had covered several murders of Albanians in Paris and had been directed to Lamoura with the suggestion that there might be a connection here.

"Who sent you?" the constable asked.

"Monsieur Barrie of the Sûreté."

Grave flashed a smile. "My wife's second cousin," he explained. "I read about the Paris killings and told him that I had a possible link between his stiffs and mine."

"You had a murder here?"

Grave began buckling his belt. "We found the body on the morning of March 14. A fire had been started but rain put it out before it could get going." The constable grinned. "At first I thought it was a prank, but when I got up there and smelled the place, I knew. You can always tell *that* smell. Not at all like a sheep or a cow—or anything else, for that matter. Sweeter. You never get used to it. That's why I left Paris: too many stiffs. Here death is seldom violent, but there are exceptions."

"You say you notified the Sûreté?"

Grave rolled his hand. "As a matter of procedure. I may live in the country but I'm no bumpkin. I trained in Paris and have seen the worst it has to offer. I could tell you stories."

"The Sûreté wasn't interested?" Sylvia asked.

"Here we say that Paris is interested only in Paris. Understand?"

She smiled encouragement. "But you suspected something."

"Certainly." Grave slid his shirt over his head as he led them around the house to a brick garage. His office was up a set of steep wooden stairs built along an outer wall. A fat Siamese cat was asleep on the window ledge. "We aren't complicated here," he said. "If one of the villagers goes awry I pick him up and set him straight. Country people still feel shame, so you can talk to them and settle them down. It's not like Paris. Up there. . . ." He didn't finish.

Grave fetched a green folder from a battered wooden file cabinet and set it on a table. The grainy photos displayed black-and-white gore. The corpse's death mask distorted its features and there was some bloating, but the fire damage was not extensive.

"Did the newspapers report this?" Sylvia asked.

"Locally, yes, but only here, and it was, shall we say, homogenized. There are lots of tourists around here and we depend on their generosity, so we can't have our newspapers scaring them off. We characterized the cause of death as a probable suicide."

"But it was murder?"

"Look at the photographs and read my report. I wrote it with care—so that one could conclude that it was suicide or murder, a necessary blurring of distinctions, but an expert would see right off what I suspected."

"Fingerprints," Valentine said, picking up a small card from the folder.

Grave bowed. "Procedure."

The Americans were impressed. The little constable was thorough, confident and perhaps considerably more competent than appearances suggested. "Why are you telling us this?" Sylvia pressed. "I'm a journalist."

The constable fumbled in a desk drawer and spoke to them while looking for his pipe. "Simple. You're not."

"You saw my credentials."

"Ink is cheap." Grave smiled. "American intelligence, I would guess. Barrie sent you, is that not so?"

"Yes."

"There," the little man said with conviction. "Despite his many flaws he's not a stupid man. He knows what went on so he wouldn't send a genuine reporter because then he might be embarrassed, and my wife's cousin does not like to be embarrassed." Grave lowered his voice. "Bad for the career. Besides, he sits high in the domestic intelligence branch. I conclude, then, that you are trustworthy, so we talk as one professional to another." He lit his pipe and waited for his visitors' reaction.

"Okay, straight talk," Sylvia agreed. "It will make our work easier. Why not suicide?"

Valentine spoke up. "Shot in the eye."

Grave nodded. "Exactly. Suicides shoot into their mouths or a temple, but never into the eye. Not once can I remember such a thing, and in Paris I saw many suicides. Perhaps they don't want to see it coming," he joked. "Nine millimeter: small hole in, substantial hole at exit, what the gentlemen in forensics call splattering. It's caused by a soft-nosed bullet in a steel jacket. Quite effective. I have what's left of the slug."

"How does this connect to the killings in Paris?"

"Professionally done and, as I understand it, a 9 mm was used there as well. These would appear to be earmarks. The Paris killings were assassinations and there was a wad of newspaper clippings about them in the cabin where the body was found. They were singed by the fire, but most are still readable." He went to the file cabinet and took out a box filled with charred paper.

Valentine was still skimming Grave's report. "No weapon found."

Grave smiled. "Does a suicide eat his weapon after shooting himself?"

Sylvia was still not satisfied. "But there's no actual link to the Albanian émigrés."

"Technically the connections are only circumstantial, but I have a body killed by the same caliber weapon and there were clippings about the previous murders. A lawyer might fret over circumstantial evidence, but I'm not a lawyer, so I don't worry so much about such things. All I care about is what I have, and what I have seems to connect—or at least raise suspicions. It doesn't matter to me what the evidence adds up to; a cop feels these things, and this one feels strong to me."

"Does Barrie concur?"

"Not in so many words. He said that publicity about Albanian feuds would only serve to further sully the reputation of Paris, so it remains a suicide, case closed. You know how the press handles such matters. Personally I don't see Paris as being anything except an aging whore well past her prime, so how can her reputation be sullied?"

"We'd like to get copies of your records," Valentine said, tapping the folder.

"You're in Lamoura, not Paris. Take them, and the slug as well."

"That leaves you with no record."

"Country constables are forever misplacing things," Grave said with a laugh. "I don't need them and you do; otherwise Barrie wouldn't have sent you to me. Call it professional courtesy; besides, I don't like unsolved murders. Now you can finish it and I can forget about it, whatever *it* is."

"Identification?" Sylvia asked.

"The dead man? I have only the fingerprints, which is less than some leave and more than others."

"Didn't the Sûreté run them?"

Grave shook his head. "Barrie said it wasn't advisable. I think that he was afraid that it would raise suspicions. Especially when I told him about this." The constable opened the desk and took out a small plastic bag. "This was in the fireplace."

Sylvia took the bag and saw the remnants of a glass ampule. The glass shards were covered with dark soot. "You know what this is?"

Grave nodded solemnly. "Some Nazis carried them at the end of the war."

Sylvia was sullen as they raced through greening foothills on their way back toward Paris. "Not a planned killing," she shouted over the straining engine.

"Why?"

"Tried to cover it with a fire but didn't stick around to make sure."

"Maybe we can convince Barrie to run the prints," Valentine suggested.

"I expect he'll be real happy to help," Sylvia said as she shifted into fifth gear and accelerated still more.

"What was in the plastic bag?"

"Suicide pill," she yelled. "Cyanide. Soviet agents carry them."

He thought for a moment. "The stiff was a Soviet agent?"

"Somebody is," she said through clenched teeth.

89   FRIDAY, APRIL 7, 1961, 2:40 A.M.
Tirana, Albania

The interior of the prison was painted black, the intersections of the narrow stone corridors lit by small red bulbs. The Albanians had learned from their KGB mentors how to design a facility to keep every prisoner isolated. When inmates were moved they were sandwiched between two guards, and escorts snapped metal clickers to let others know that they had priority. Those without the right of way turned their prisoners face first into specially built alcoves in the corridors so that they couldn't see anything. It seemed to Lejla Llarja that the prison was overrun by boisterous crickets.

She was taken into a long room with heavy glass windows that looked down on the prison cells. Even in the poor light she could see bent limbs and fresh scars, evidence of torture on the naked prisoners below. But the end cell was different; it was well lit and decorated like a parlor, with a bed, a desk, an easy chair, two lamps, a radio and a bookcase filled with books. Newspapers were stacked along a wall. Her father was sitting in the chair, reading. He wore a robe and slippers and looked thin, but the bandage on his left hand was clean. The memory of his severed finger made her shudder.

After a couple of minutes she was led away, steered again through the black corridors and taken outside, where Haxi Kasi was waiting in a Russian automobile, the motor revving. She got in beside him and looked straight ahead.

"You saw him?" he asked.

Lejla nodded.

"Good," Kasi said. "We're keeping our part of the bargain, and you must keep yours."

The killings in Paris had not been difficult because they had no connection to reality. She had convinced herself that it was just a game. The dead men had been strangers, nameless men—targets, not people. It was easy to shoot a target if you ignored the blood. The important thing was that her father was alive and that she was the reason. There had been a time when she had considered herself independent, but now she realized that this had been an adolescent illusion. One's blood inexorably connected one to family, and there was nothing to be done about it. As a little girl she had studied the Ten Commandments and thought of them as a list with priorities. *Honor thy father and thy mother. Thou shalt not kill.* The former took precedence over the latter.

90	FRIDAY, APRIL 7, 1961, 11:00 A.M.
	Moscow

How did one come to grips with the whims and thoughts of great men? Captain Eduard Boryavich Okhlopkin did not understand; even when he got things right they invariably were used against him. First it had been the man with the iron constitution. He had filled the bastard with vodka, then injected the aminazine just as he had been instructed, but the man had carried on as if unaffected, and Okhlopkin had worried that something was wrong with the drug. This left him no choice; he had waited until the man was in the street, then run him down. Was it his fault that a militiaman had somehow wandered into the street before his second pass? It had not been his intention to run over the fool, but he was there and might be a witness, so what choice did this leave? The great man's representative had raged at him. The drug and alcohol would have worked, but how was he to know? Gaponov had assured him that the aminazine would be quick and foolproof, yet the man had walked several kilometers after he had stuck the syringe in his ass. Had *he* made the drug? Had it been *his* idea to use it? No, but it remained his fault. The militiaman was bad luck, and he had taken him out to prevent the possibility of a witness, so why was the colonel so angry? He had done what Gaponov had asked; couldn't he see that?

Now there was another mess. It must look natural, the colonel had reminded him, and it had nearly turned out that way; the one called Velak had been easy enough, but the security man had spotted him on the way out and demanded to know how he had gotten in. He had not been briefed on this possibility and had handled it the only way he could think of—by making it look as if the man had fallen down the stairs. A natural death and an accidental one in close proximity might provoke some unusual interest, but he had been careful; in any case, what other choice had there been? The important thing was that the people the colonel wanted out of the way were dead, so why all the fuss over minor details? They asked him to take care of things and he did so, but Gaponov's unwillingness to see what was so obvious was exasperating. An hour ago he had been dressed down by the colonel, who recounted his shortcomings while writing prissy little notes to himself. He congratulated himself for taking Gaponov's crap with a grin, which seemed to irritate the colonel, but he was smart enough to keep his mouth shut and let the man ramble on. His superior had warned him that no more errors would be tolerated; Okhlopkin was to send his men into the Zone to "squeeze" some scum, while he himself would take care of more important business, and this time it must be done perfectly.

As he emerged from the metro Okhlopkin paused to straighten his overcoat, then cut through the park near where his troops were billeted. It was Friday and the weather pleasant, so the streets were jammed, and it seemed that every Muscovite was watching him. When the great men had brought him to Moscow they had told him how exciting the city was, but they had not mentioned the open hatred for Asian people. This he had learned the hard way. Even whores spat on him and refused his rubles.

At the far side of the park a man suddenly confronted him. "Cigarette?" he begged. He was tall and thin, with a bald head and a scalp lock of the sort people wore in the East, but he was too effeminate to be a real man and Okhlopkin was disgusted to be so close to him. If it had been dark or if there was more time he would have pulled this disgusting excuse for a man into the shadows and rid Moscow of a dreg, but Gaponov had demanded that everything happen tomorrow, and he was not a patient man. He pushed the parasite aside and walked on, not looking back to see that the man was following him.

91   FRIDAY, APRIL 7, 1961, 3:20 P.M. *Vinkeveen, The Netherlands*

Monsieur Barrie was not happy to hear from Sylvia again, but he understood that to refuse her was to invite his own destruction, so he readily agreed to process the fingerprints from Lamoura. Like all government agencies in France, the Sûreté had an enormous workload, he explained, but after making this point he pledged to see to it personally that the prints were processed quickly. If Mademoiselle would ring back on Monday he would have the results for her.

The next task was to have the slug and ampule pieces examined. She had discussed this with Valentine; the Sûreté had the expertise for ballistic tests, but the FBI was the best in the world at this sort of thing. She called Arizona, who told her to deliver the bullet to the embassy in Paris and ask the station chief to tag it for FBI liaison in Washington; the glass fragments were to go in a separate bag addressed to Langley. When she got to the embassy there was a phone call waiting for her. It was Arizona again. "Amsterdam," he said with uncustomary excitement. "Go to the KLM flight crew desk at Schiphol Airport and ask for Mr. White."

"Why?"

"You'll find out when you get there," Arizona said. Actually it was not clear to him what they would find when they got to the airport. After putting Venema on Frash's track he had cabled MI5 and asked the Brits to alert him to any unusual goings-on that involved American agents, their suspected contacts, money washing or problems with credentials. It was a long shot, but in the shadows of intelligence work a lousy horse was better than no horse at all. Police work was the equivalent of fishing with a line, whereas intelligence was more like the deployment of nets—in this instance a rather coarse one. Now MI5 had called back to request a meeting; Sylvia and Valentine were closest, and with the Cuban operation so near there was no way he could leave Washington right now.

It took them just over six hours to get to Schiphol, park the Jaguar, find the KLM crew desk and inquire about Mr. White. They were shown into a room with a wooden table and several sturdy chairs. Fifteen minutes later a tall man with white hair and a pronounced limp greeted them with a stern nod and cold blue eyes.

"Identification?" he asked, stretching the word to twice its normal syllables. After studying their papers he gave them back and said, "Cumming."

Sylvia had heard about the legendary Sir John Cumming, and looked at him with interest. He was the grandnephew of Sir Mansfield Cumming, the founder of England's Secret Intelligence Service, MI5, never smiled and so rarely betrayed his emotions that his harsh countenance had earned him the nickname of Sunny John to CIA officials who had to work with him. Nowadays he served as a senior liaison officer at No. 10 Downing Street, but despite his breeding and influential position he was a battle-hardened agent, a first-rate field man who had risen through the ranks.

"What have you got?" Valentine asked immediately, but Sir John pivoted and led them to a Mercedes waiting in a no-parking zone just outside the terminal.

Thirty minutes later they passed through the village of Vinkeveen and up a long gravel lane that led to a stone farmhouse surrounded by a two-meter-high stone wall. Two men in gray coveralls and muddy black gum boots opened the gate for the Mercedes, then closed it and took up positions nearby. Sylvia realized that despite their intended appearance the farmhouses were part of some sort of elite security unit; no doubt the farm was an MI5 safe house.

Sir John led them to an upstairs room where two women waited: one sitting by the window, her attention directed outside; the other, a thin but attractive blonde with swollen eyes, at a dressing table. The woman by the window surrendered her seat and left, closing the door quietly behind her.

"Mrs. VanderLeyden," Sir John said softly. "Please tell these people what you told me earlier."

Ina VanderLeyden's face radiated hope. "Then you *believe* me?"

Sunny John was noncommittal. "Please."

The woman described a man with such precision that Sylvia could clearly visualize him; she was sure it was Frash.

"Her paramour," Sunny John said when she had finished. His description made the woman wince.

"Albert Frash?" Sylvia asked. No reaction. "Ali Frascetti?" Still none.

"He said his name was Albert Frijk," the woman said, barely able to hide her anger.

Sylvia smiled: old training, ingrained habits, never change the whole name. Loose ends often came together in unexpected ways. Could it really be Frash? She tried to calm herself but it was no use; the scent had been cold and now it was warming again. She wanted to know everything. "When did you last see him?"

Before the woman could answer, Sir John crossed between them and motioned for the Americans to follow. They descended to a study on the ground floor where the Englishman shed his trench coat, straightened his red-and-black striped tie, patted the lapels of his gray suit, poured two jiggers of straight vodka from an unlabeled bottle and passed them to his guests. "A bloody accident we got onto this at all," he said. "Think it's one of your lads?"

Apparently Arizona had asked the Brits to watch their nets for any unusual catches; it was equally obvious that he had given them few details, which was why Sir John was trolling. Ambiguous favors like this were traded regularly by friendly intelligence agencies. Sylvia nodded. "Could be." She drained the jigger and let the fire bloom in her stomach. "We'd like to show her a photo."

"Yes," Sir John said, drawing the word out. "That should do nicely." He held up his jigger, said "Cheers," and swallowed. "Here it is, plain and simple. If it's one of your people he's made a complete fool of her and hurt us in the process. Can't say that I blame him. She's a lovely creature but a bit of a twit. Reap what ye sow and so forth. She's employed as an accountant by a solicitor in s'Hertogenbosch, a longtime employee who is quite competent, by all reports, and has been extremely reliable until now. Gets sticky here; my people established this firm in 1947 to broker certain credentials to a network of Allied cold warriors. That's the sole reason for the firm's existence; has its public clients, of course, but they're only fronts to assure legitimacy. The woman was part of that front and not part of the covert operation, but somehow she got onto the existence of the credentials. Apparently that's what attracted the man. At first she was going to keep her mouth shut about what happened, but then she figured that the firm had enough muscle to go after what they'd lost, and in the process would take care of the man who had played her for a fool. So she confessed the whole lot to her employers, never understanding that they weren't who she thought they were all these years."

Cumming poured another vodka for himself, swallowed it and resumed. "Several years ago, this fellow and Mrs. VanderLeyden, then unattached, became, shall we say, acquainted, then involved in the strictest biblical sense, all in astonishingly short order. Fast worker, that boy. Must say I envy him; never had that sort of knack with the girls myself.

Had themselves a fling, your countrymen would call it, and she told him about the firm's private holdings. The little vixen even had the combination to the shop's safe. Wanted to impress him, one could assume. This was three years ago, and apparently the man tucked the information away for a time when he needed it. Time passes, circumstances change and now he needs a new identity, something untraceable. What better than pristine passports?"

Sir John was playing all the parts in a morality play, his voice resonant. "The man returns unannounced and the lovebirds take up where they left off, the power of lust being ever so durable. She is infatuated, bored, unhappily married, in need of a diversion, and, no doubt with his subtle prompting, proposes an elopement of sorts. Impossible, he counters. Too bloody troublesome because her husband is much too powerful, a man of considerable influence who would track them down. Match point here. She racks her pitiful mind for a solution. Eureka! The safe. She suggests new identities. Freedom in new names, new pasts, which no doubt was his intent from the outset. Elementary, my dear Watson! He agrees. She pinches the documents and passes them to him to take to Amsterdam, where they can be expertly forged, but of course she never sees him again. Buggered on all counts," Cummings said with a snort. "He has his new identity, she has a broken heart, and I have debris that has to be properly disposed of. There you have it."

Sylvia fought an urge to cut him off so that she could take the photo upstairs.

"The heart is a durable organ. Pure muscle." The Englishman paused to light a pungent Gauloise. "She'll never appreciate the irony. She's labored all these years under the illusion that her employer is engaged in illegal activity, confesses to her superior in the belief that the firm will do anything to recover its precious property, in so doing hoping they will become the instrument of her revenge. Cold-blooded bitch is rather reptilian, but not altogether unclever. We must grant her that, her amateur status notwithstanding."

"But her employers are your people, so they alerted you," Valentine said.

"Straightaway," Sir John said. "Bloody shame to see an effective operation end over such a silly thing, but all good things must end, and end they do. Mustn't bowl stones in the land of mirrors, eh?"

"When did this happen?" Sylvia asked.

"Two days ago," Sir John said.

Sylvia's heart jumped. Two days! Compared with November this was like yesterday.

"The man is clever. He now has a dozen blank passports, and one presumes he can forge them without outside assistance."

"Piece of cake," Valentine said.

"Quite."

"What happens to the woman?" Sylvia asked.

"Sacked. The firm will be closed after a decent interval. She'll be properly debriefed and returned to her husband. Turns out that he's an old chum, you see—RAF during the war, Battle of Britain and all that. He'll have to deal with the creature."

When they finally were able to show Frash's photograph to Ina she sobbed and smacked her hands against her thighs.

When Sir John drove them back to the airport he gave Sylvia a piece of paper. "The passport registration numbers and nationalities," he said. "They're legitimate and worth a fortune in the right hands."

Valentine considered the implications. "Which means they can be traced through immigration services?"

"Piece of cake," the Englishman said, deadpan. "Now do you think you might let us in on your problem?"

"Talk to Washington," Valentine said as he and Sylvia got out of the Mercedes.

92 SUNDAY, APRIL 9, 1961, 2:06 P.M. *Moscow*

Ezdovo sat by the window, not moving, still as as hunter along a game trail, occasionally checking his watch, while Melko looked on with amusement. "We have more than enough eyes watching our asses, and they're paid to be reliable."

But Annochka did not come at the appointed time and now an hour had passed; though both men were worried, they did not speak of it.

A little after two o'clock there was a ruckus on the stairwell and Melko heard a familiar voice mixed with those of the Georgians he had hired to protect them. Seconds later a frantic Leonid Sarnov burst into the flat, saw Ezdovo's revolver pointed at him and threw himself on the floor. "Don't shoot," he shouted. "It's me, Lenya."

Ezdovo immediately triggered his walkie-talkie. "Scout One?" No answer. "Scout One, are you there?" There was still no answer, and none from the other two Spetsnaz men who had been posted as lookouts. Melko saw the concern in his colleague's eyes.

"Did you think you could be shed of me so easily?" Lenya said as he dusted himself off.

"What are *you* doing here?"

"Came to warn you," Lenya chirped just as Ezdovo suddenly flattened himself against the wall by the window and tried again to make contact with their lookouts. "Just in time," Lenya added as he hurried to the window for a look.

"What the hell is going on?" Melko demanded.

Ezdovo saw several men advancing down the street in loose formation. "Trouble," he growled.

"Of course it's trouble," Lenya added. "Do you think I'd push my way through those damned Georgians without good reason?"

Muffled pops stopped any further conversation. Lenya moved to the far window and jumped to the roof; Melko started to follow but paused astride the sill. "This way," he said to Ezdovo, but the Siberian had moved to the door.

More shots sounded below; they seemed closer now. At least two shotgun blasts were outgoing. When he looked back Ezdovo saw Melko perched in the window, waving for him to follow. He went into the darkened hallway and got down on his belly. Two armed men came bounding up the stairs; he let their heads get to his level, took careful aim, hit each man in the chest, darted to the bodies, searched them, took their wallets and papers, fired three rounds at more men at the bottom of the stairwell, scrambled upstairs, ran to the window, jumped to the roof below, rolled over, got up and ran. Melko was ahead, waving for him to move faster. Shots came from the window behind them but snapped harmlessly over their heads; Melko fired several answering rounds as Ezdovo reached him, and the two of them ran along the roof's edge to the sounds of a full-fledged firefight erupting in the Armenian's place behind them. The noise subsided after a grenade burst.

The three of them fled the Zone at a point near where they had left one of their lookouts and saw that he was down, his head in a pool of dark liquid. After a long run they ducked into an alley and stopped to catch their breath. Lenya knelt and splashed his face with water from a puddle.

"What's happening?" Melko gasped.

"I'd like to know who, not what," Ezdovo said.

"No questions now," Lenya said. "We have to put distance between us and them."

With one lookout dead and the other two presumed to be, there was no way to return to their vehicle. "Move," Ezdovo ordered. "Keep apart, but maintain visual contact. No more than ten meters apart; head for the metro and don't look back."

A steep escalator carried them underground to an ornate marble platform with floodlights, chandeliers and alcoves jammed with statues depicting the nameless heroes of the Bolshevik Revolution. The platform was not crowded. A man in a leather coat was asleep on a bench with a shoe perched on his chest. Several babas tightly held the hands of young children. An air force sergeant embraced and fondled a fat girl in skin-tight slacks. Two militiamen appeared at the far end of the platform; they were smoking and talking with great animation and seemed interested only in each other, but Lenya knew their ways; they would be scrutinizing everyone in the area. As he suddenly walked toward the two men, Ezdovo stepped back to get a better firing angle, but one of the policemen smiled as he lit Lenya's cigarette and soon the three of them were carrying on like old schoolmates.

When the train arrived Lenya boarded at the last possible moment and slumped into the seat beside Melko.

"You've got nerve," Ezdovo said.

Lenya shrugged off the compliment. "They're trained to look for people skulking away. The direct approach throws them off every time."

They rode to the southwestern section of the city and got off at a station called Ocakovo. The area was old, with only a few modern apartment buildings amid a sprawl of crumbling older places.

"How did you find us?" Melko asked.

Lenya grinned. "You found me, I found you. Men like us can always find each other."

"Why?"

"The Asian."

Melko's nostrils flared. "The one you saw at Velak's?"

"The same. Something about him just didn't sit right, and my life depends on my ability to sniff out things that don't fit," Lenya said. "He got into Velak's apartment house through the sewer. I found tracks and followed them, which was no great accomplishment because he has feet as wide as a duck's and boots with rippled soles. I lost his trail when he surfaced, but I'm not one to give up. I thought, he came here for a reason, and his tracks showed that he knew where he was going. Old dogs piss on the same trees. I told myself, if he came here once maybe he'll come again, so I made myself comfortable and sure enough, there he was."

"You could have been wrong," Melko said.

Lenya only smiled. "When I'm stumped I always tell myself to try something, which is better than doing nothing, though doing something often looks exactly like doing nothing, which was the case this time. I went around the neighborhood. Hey, old man, have you seen an Asian the size of a musk ox? Baba, there's a sinister-looking Mongol lurking around the area; have you seen him? Ask questions and you'll get answers. Sure, they said. He's an ugly one and not very friendly. He's been around here for several weeks, but we don't know where he lives. That was enough for me. I waited, and sure enough he came back and I spotted him, the same guy I saw at Velak's, no mistake about it. I followed him to a building and tried to get close, but that wasn't possible. He has a lair filled with confederates, and they watch the place like mothers with virgin daughters." He paused and grinned. "If you want to get at a virgin you don't go to her house. You've got to be patient and get her alone, so I settled back to wait. This morning the Asian came out with his play- mates, loaded them onto two trucks, and fled with me following in a taxi. The fare I paid was criminal, but what's a few rubles when a friend's interests are at stake? The Asian unloaded his comrades near the Zone, then went off on his own in a cab, which left me with a decision: follow him or the group? I chose the pack, and at first I thought I'd made a mistake. They spread out and set their security, but made no effort to move in until suddenly they shot a man. They did it from behind; his hat flew off. He had a shaved head like the soldier who was with you at Velak's. I remembered reading somewhere that Spetsnaz troops shave their heads. My logic was that the Asian killed Velak; you brought a soldier with you to Velak's; the Asian brought his people to the Zone; they killed a man who reminded me of the soldier; then they move into the Zone, which I remember was once the self-proclaimed kingdom of Melko. By God, I thought, they're going after my benefactor. Luckily they moved cautiously and I flew past them." Lenya paused to catch his breath. "A long time ago you told me about your connection to the Armenian, but you never mentioned those damned Georgians. I said to myself, Find a common language, Lenya, or your goose is cooked, so I waved my dick at them, and while they were licking their lips I got past them. You can fill in the rest." Another pause. "It was God's will that I didn't fall or they'd still be putting it to me." He roared with laughter.

"You're insane," Melko said with as much admiration as apprecia- tion.

"It makes life more interesting."

"If you live."

Lenya thumped his chest in mock defiance. "I'll outlive you, com- rade."

Which might not be such a noteworthy achievement, Ezdovo thought. The unprovoked attack in the Zone meant that the Special Operations Group had touched a raw nerve. But whose? "We've got to call Talia and the others."

As they cut through dark streets he tried to look at the papers he had taken off the two assailants. Each man had an ID card that looked normal except for a huge red X stamped across its face. He passed the cards to Melko, who handed them on to Lenya. "Wolf tickets," Sarnov said as he led them toward a monastery.

"KGB?" Ezdovo asked.

"Border guards," Lenya said. "If one of them fucks up too often or at the wrong time he gets shot. A few are spared and given wolf tickets. The X across the card means that the holder of the card is officially dead, but is being given one final off-the-record chance to redeem himself. If he fails again—" Lenya drew a finger across his throat as he led them to a small office near the entrance to the monastery. "There's a telephone in here."

It occurred to Melko that Petrov and his team also had wolf tickets.

93   SUNDAY, APRIL 9, 1961, 8:00 P.M.
Paris

The first item of business after their return to Paris was to get the blank passport numbers to the embassy. The station chief agreed to notify Interpol that the holder of any of the documents was wanted for questioning in the United States and should be detained. Names were to be ignored; all that mattered were the numbers. The CIA man was happy to help but doubted that anything would come of it because most immigration officers were not likely to be attentive to passport numbers unless there was a payoff for them. "Tell them he's suspected of killing children," Sylvia said. "They might be a little more careful if they think they're passing a murderer over their border."

"I'll add hotels to the request," the station chief added. "Call it a second line of defense."

Sylvia placed her telephone call to Barrie from a secure phone in the embassy. "The prints belong to an unidentified male whom we know only as the Major," Barrie reported.

"A man without a name has known prints?"

Barrie stammered. "There's an explanation. We believe that he's linked to several Albanian groups, but his precise role and of course his identity are unknown. Four years ago we got the same prints at the site of a murdered informer. Subsequent information described the Major as an enforcer-courier with ties to Albanians in a score of European cities. We've had several descriptions of the sorts of things he's done, or is alleged to have done, but nobody has come forward to corroborate any of it. The Albanians seemed to be afraid of him, but their fears can now be put to rest. The prints prove that he's dead, and that's all we require to close his file."

"That's all you have?"

"You might try your own resources," Barrie said curtly. "You have everything from me."

"Did you do ballistic tests on the Paris shootings?"

"Naturally."

"They matched?"

"I believe so," Barrie said vaguely. "The files are in a different office."

"We'd like copies of your ballistics photos and data sent to Washington."

Barrie paused to consider the implications and then became defensive. "You question our technical competence?"

"Just send them to the embassy tonight," Sylvia said sharply. She was tired of being nice. Frash had been close, but now he was gone again and this asshole was concerned about the honor of the Sûreté. What had happened to old-time cops who cared only about results? It was a pain in the ass to wade through evidence that might not pertain, but the only way to make sure you didn't miss anything was to cover everything.

"May I ask if you have talked to Mr. Li?" Barrie asked sheepishly.

"You may ask anything you like," she said and hung up.

They ate dinner at a small restaurant near the hotel where waiters screamed out orders and drowned out each other and their customers' conversations. Sylvia stared at a plate of snails. "He went to the woman for the passports," she said as she traced the spiral of a shell with her finger.

"Reasonable thinking on his part," Valentine said. "The passports give him more flexibility, but the fact is that Europe's borders are like sieves. A blind man on a donkey could make his way across without being detected."

"Lumbas was killed and Frash disappeared. Why didn't he check in?"

"Maybe he thinks the Company is part of the problem, not part of the solution."

Sylvia made a face at him. "Help me with this. If he thinks the Company is a threat to him, why does he stay in Europe? And if he can go virtually anywhere in Europe without a passport, why go to the trouble of getting them from the woman?"

"Frash is crazy. You can't use logic on a nut case."

"So we just give up?"

"That's not what I said." Valentine sipped his coffee. Since Ermine's death it had seemed that nothing made much sense and there had been times when he had thought that if he had just one worthwhile thing to focus on, his life would have meaning again. But all he had was an army-surplus business, which was the sort of thing that you left to a son of diminished capacity. When Arizona had approached him about Frash he had hoped that this would be what he needed, but it was not working out.

Sylvia saw Valentine's hangdog look but tried to ignore it. Why had Frash told the VanderLeyden woman that cockamamy story about his money being tied up in a London bank? More to the point, how was he living if he was no longer drawing a government check? "Money," she said out loud.

"How much?" Valentine asked, thinking she meant the restaurant bill.

"Not that," she said. "He needs money for expenses."

"Most of us do."

"Dammit, listen to me. He's been on the run since November. What's he living on? Arizona said that REBUS was working for money. Given the sort of information Lumbas had, the amounts could be substantial."

Valentine's eyebrows crept toward each other. "In the old days we kept stashes for times like this."

"We need to get to his banks to freeze his accounts." She threw a handful of wrinkled francs on the table and headed out of the restaurant with Valentine trailing behind. "Zurich," she said.

"Gnomes," he said. It was the first word that came to mind.

"Exactly," Sylvia said.

 TUESDAY, APRIL 11, 1961, 2:30 P.M.
Moscow

The candlelit church had been packed with crook-backed old women with their heads bowed reverently and chanting off-key in response to a line of priests singing Mass in an alcove filled with faded icons in gold-leaf frames. The nave smelled of incense, aged bodies and hundreds of tallow candles. Lenya wedged his companions through the worshipers and down a side corridor where they encountered a priest with a square black beard and wild eyes seated on a thronelike wooden chair at the end of the hallway. "My friends wish to pray with Brother John," Lenya told the priest, who kept his eyes on the prayer book in his lap.

After passing through several rooms and up a steep set of steps,

Lenya stopped on a landing and did something to the underside of a handrail which caused a panel to open in the wall. When the three of them were inside, the panel closed and they were engulfed in dark, stale air.

"Where are we?" Melko asked.

"No talking," Lenya answered. His voice had lost its lilt and had taken on an unexpected somberness.

The room began to rise, stopped, shuddered, slid sideways, stopped, shook and began to descend, the downward journey taking several minutes. All the while the temperature rose, leaving the three of them sweating. When at last they stopped they crawled into a dark room and Melko immediately stumbled and sent something clattering. "Bones," Lenya said quickly. "Mind your step." They walked for nearly fifteen minutes through a maze of passageways turning left and right, this way and that, moving away and doubling back—or had they? Melko had no sense of direction down here. Eventually they reached another room and were led down a long, curving stairwell dimly lit with small kerosene lanterns and so narrow that Melko's shoulders rubbed both walls. Tunnels at the bottom led off in several directions but Lenya ignored these, turned to a wall and pointed to indentations in the stonework. "Handholds and footholds. We climb up about four meters onto a floor. Crawl away from the edge and wait. There are vertical shafts everywhere. When we move, touch the shoe of the one in front of you."

When they were up Lenya crawled past them. Now and then Melko felt around with his hands and located one of the shafts they had been warned about. After a while Lenya said, "Careful, there's a hole here. There's a ladder, but you have to lower yourself onto it. Go down feet first, rest on your forearms, stabilize, then lower yourself with your hands. When you're fully extended, feel around with your toes for the holds, get a foot seated, then slide your hands along the edges of the stones. The footholds alternate, but it's only a meter until you get to the ladder and it's easy from there. It feels trickier than it is."

The ladder was where Lenya said it would be, but he had not said that it would take another fifteen-minute, nonstop descent to negotiate it. The bottom was bathed in darkness, and once again they traveled horizontally, this time along a tunnel with wooden timbers that Melko felt with his hands. "Fresh timber."

Ezdovo said from ahead, "I can smell it."

Eventually the tunnel veered left and ended at a metal door, which Lenya opened and locked behind them. Then he flicked on a light switch and announced, "We're in."

Now they saw that they were in yet another complex of tunnels. They walked through a large recess filled with tall stacks under canvas tarps and finally reached a small room with bunk beds and other furnish-

ings, including a sanctum with a gilt crucifix and a set of icons. Lenya shed his coat, blessed himself and knelt before the crucifix, then turned to them. "You're safe here and welcome to stay as long as you need to."

"Where is here?" Ezdovo asked.

Lenya lit a brass samovar. "Some would say we're under the Church of St. John, though to expect anyone to find us with such vague directions would be foolish." When the tea was brewed he poured for them. "I'm sure you're thinking that now the debt has been paid," he told Melko, "but it's not. Secular debt is one thing, but here our debts are only to the Almighty. This is His refuge for all true believers, but it's only temporary. The true refuge comes with death."

"I believe in nothing," Melko said, "except preserving my carcass for as long as I can."

Lenya laughed. "If you believe in your own survival you believe in something. All people believe in something; they can't help it. To wait for the bus is to believe that it will come and that it will deliver you to your destination." The former gulag inmate seemed a different man here from the one in the streets above.

"I mean I don't believe in God or an afterlife or any of that," Melko persisted.

"There's no good reason to believe now." Lenya smiled. "At the moment of death all doubt will be mercifully removed."

Ezdovo wondered what this fellow Sarnov had led them into. He had the air of a priest, but in the darkness he had moved with the confidence and surefootedness of a veteran scout. Ezdovo had tried to telephone Talia, Gnedin and Bailov outside the monastery, but had not reached any of them. He had been on the verge of panic but had not let on to Melko. In the Zone the former *zek* had hovered in the window as the attack began, and only later did Ezdovo see the gesture for what it was; Melko had covered for him, and in that simple act had declared his commitment to the team. But real trust required time, so he kept his concerns to himself and refused to let his worries about Talia's well-being undercut his ability to think clearly. The lack of contact with the others suggested that the entire unit had been assaulted, but he knew that imagination could be worse than reality. When he had been unable to reach the others Lenya had offered them refuge, but Ezdovo was uneasy about hunkering down for too long. The best tactic against a surprise assault was immediate counterattack. When he had called the hospital and inquired about the condition of the patient in Room 301, he had been told with no hesitation that no such room existed, which left no choice but to lie low. By now they had been underground for twenty-four hours and he felt a growing anxiety about Talia and their comrades.

For much of the night Lenya had left them alone and they had slept fitfully. From time to time they heard muffled voices in the larger ante-room, and once the crying of a child that went on for what seemed like hours.

Now it was early afternoon and they were anxious to move on, but Lenya had not returned, and without him there was no way to get out.

Melko went into the larger room, found a pile with a tear in the canvas, peeled back the flap and saw stacks of Bibles.

"We call this our armory," Lenya said from behind him. Melko turned to find him in a brown cassock with a belt of wooden beads attached to a small cross.

"You're a priest?"

Lenya smiled. "That's a hotly debated question in certain circles."

"Bibles," Melko said, looking back at the stacks around them.

"The basic ammunition of our revolution."

Melko was not sure what to say. "The Revolution is long over, and those who won have a different view on the question of God."

"You can dictate policy and declare whoever you want persona non grata, but you can't expunge the love of God from the human heart."

"You fight to preserve the Church?"

Lenya smiled. "Russian generals think in terms of defense and pres-ervation; the lessons of the Khans, Napoleon and Hitler are their prece-dents. We fight to win, which requires risk. This is the fortress of the Brotherhood of John the Avenger. In the world above we are known by other names and bound by the rules of the Party; down here we live by more enduring principles and by what the Party can never give—genuine hope. We are one million declared believers: Orthodox, Roman, Jew, Baptist, a dozen denominations. In the end we will prevail."

"A million is nothing. Hitler sent twice that and they were con-sumed." Not to mention that they were armed with more than Bibles.

"Our numbers are increasing. We are like a persistent disease that spreads slowly but eventually kills the organism. Khrushchev is the begin-ning of the end."

This was a crazy man's rambling, nonsensical, without logical refer-ence points. Melko was at a loss for words.

"Listen to me," Lenya said. "The Communists will pass, the Party will evaporate and the statues of Lenin will be toppled and smashed, just as the statues of Stalin now lie on their backs. Khrushchev has opened the door."

"Khrushchev?" This made even less sense. "He's part of your revo-lution?"

"He's a peasant with a peasant's instincts. Stalin was one of the czars, concerned only with himself; Khrushchev is opening us to the West. His vision is glasnost, openness. He's denounced Stalin and the purges, and now he looks west toward capitalism. The world is smaller now and isolation is impossible. How long can the old ways continue when more and more of us know what exists beyond our borders? Missiles," Lenya said, "these will be the instruments of our resurrection."

Melko could no longer look at his old gulag friend. Bibles as ammunition in a war that would lead to resurrection through missiles? Was Lenya in the opium trade and sampling his own wares?

"It's like this," Lenya continued. "How many centuries did it take to replace the club with the spear and the spear with the bow and arrow?"

"Don't know," Melko said.

"A missile built today will be obsolete tomorrow, which means more money has to go into research and production, an overlapping of obsolescence driven by paranoia. To build the first missile puts us in a cycle that will eventually choke us. Khrushchev whets our appetite for Western goods but wants his missiles as well. In the long run the sheer cost of trying to do both will create an economic implosion, the house of cards trying to support an anvil will fall flat, and it will have been Khrushchev who started us down the road. If he were to fall now, all this might be reversed, but if he retains power for three or four more years the way back will be impossible. Eisenhower and other Western leaders have pushed us into an arms race, which we can't win. Can a cobbler outproduce a factory?"

Lenya preached with such ardor that his words gave Melko a chill. Sensing his friend's uneasiness, Lenya took his arm. "I've made arrangements for you and your comrade," he said. "The monastery has a truck that delivers mail between churches in the city. We're faster than the government and there are fewer eyes to see what passes between us. The government takes three days to do what we do in three hours."

"They allow this?" Melko asked.

"They tolerate it. Our Patriarch keeps our flock outwardly calm, and in return we get to keep a few churches open, have our own mail service and so forth."

"But they must know you're trying to bring down the system."

"They see what they want to see. In a prison camp there are two chains of command. One is open, declared and led by a senior official—in our case the Patriarch. This hierarchy deals exclusively in the present and with the obvious. The second chain of command is private, secret, looks at the long term, does all it can to advance the cause and operates with neither the blessing nor even the knowledge of the leader of the first chain. The Patriarch plays for balance, the second chain foments change. If nothing else, the Church is rich in the art of surviving; for most of our history we have had to operate under the scrutiny of one enemy or another. Sometimes I fear that legitimacy might destroy us. Do you have any idea how many of our priests are KGB stooges?"

"Who *are* you?" Melko asked again.

"One believer among a million."

"And I'm Czar Nicholas's hemophiliac grandson," Melko said sarcastically.

"Out there I am Lenya; down here I am not. All men have several existences, but few have either the conviction or courage to act on their secret thoughts."

"How can a thief be a priest?"

Lenya laughed. "Perhaps it's the priest who is the thief. We all steal in one way or the another. What matters is intent." Then he was gone.

When he returned in a few minutes his cassock had been replaced by one of his peculiar costumes and he was once again Lenya of the street. The route out was different from the way they had come, and when they eventually reached a cellar Lenya told them to go on alone.

Melko had begun to walk away when he remembered the papers Talia had given him. He gave one of them to Lenya.

"What's this?"

"There are boxes in the upper corner. Each of them has been initialed."

"So?"

"Look at them. Are they written by three different hands?"

The sometime forger and counterfeiter took a metal case from his pocket, fastened his wire-rimmed spectacles around his ears, adjusted their placement on the bridge of his nose, took the paper, tilted it toward better light, seemed barely to glance at it, refolded it, pushed it back to Melko, removed his glasses, returned them to the case and put it back in his pocket. "Two, not three."

"You're sure?"

Lenya grinned. "Child's play."

Melko looked him hard in the eyes. "It's necessary that you be certain."

"If I asked Melko about a safe, could I rely on his answer?"

Point made. "Which two?"

"The first and the second were initialed by your friend Velak. See, he has signed a notation on the bottom."

Melko looked at Ezdovo, who said, "Show him the other one."

Lenya studied the second sheet. "This is not Khrushchev's signature."

"How do you know?"

"To be Russian and not know the General Secretary's signature is to be blind, or else stupid. Let me have that first one again," Lenya said. He laid the documents side by side and pursed his lips. "Now *this* is interesting," he said after a few moments. "Same hand."

"Velak?"

"It's amateurish, but an experienced eye can see that it's Velak."

Melko refolded the papers, slapped them against his open hand and stared at the gaunt face of the mysterious Leonid Sarnov. "Now the debt is paid," he said.

"That's for me to decide," Lenya answered firmly.

"Best you stay clear of us," Melko said softly as he extended his hand.

"Have it your way," Lenya said, "but if you have need of my magic again you know how to reach me."

95   TUESDAY, APRIL 11, 1961, 3:00 P.M.
Zurich

Sylvia telephoned Arizona from the Swiss border and again when they reached Zurich. During their first contact he was elated that Frash had finally shown himself, and angry that he had disappeared again, then irritated when she pressed him with questions about Frash's finances. Did she think he was a goddamned fool? He had already put a stop on his known bank accounts and assets, which meant they couldn't be released unless the Company was notified first. Sylvia persisted. What about paychecks? Since he was officially missing, his checks were still being cut and forwarded to his bank. Was there any way that Frash could draw on the funds set aside for Lumbas? This seemed to stump Arizona. Probably not, he said, but he would double-check. "What's your point?" he asked.

"I'm not sure," Sylvia admitted. "I just want to cover all the bases." She had in mind some kind of trap, but she had not worked out the details. Frash had access to at least a dozen new identities now, and this might leave him feeling safer than he was. They knew the numbers of the stolen passports and Frash didn't know they knew, which was for now the only advantage they had. "What's the name and address of the banker we deal with in Zurich?"

"Jesus," Arizona said. "I can't give you that."

"Do you want Frash or not?" she asked.

There was a pause. "This is going to take a little time," Arizona said finally. "Check back with me when you get to Zurich."

When they arrived she called again and Arizona gave her the information she had asked for. Horst Schiller was the CIA contact at the Zurich bank handling payments to REBUS. The money went from a

Company front in Memphis to Brussels to Munich to Zurich, where it went into a numbered account. At each stop the money's apparent source changed, which made backtracking nearly impossible unless you knew the players and the route.

The bank was in the old city, in a tidy, venerable building that bespoke tradition and trust. Sylvia entered when the bank first opened at 10:00 A.M., asked to see Schiller and made no mention of her connection to the Company. Instead she passed herself off as an American looking for a place to salt away a substantial sum of cash, source unspecified; she mentioned something in excess of a quarter of a million, but was deliberately vague beyond this. Schiller was businesslike and obviously eager to please; it would take twenty-four hours to make the paperwork ready. Could he deliver it to her hotel? No, she was staying with friends at Lake Como in Italy, but she would be back in three days to complete the transaction. If she was satisfied she hinted that there would be additional deposits later. He clicked his heels together and bowed when she left.

They watched the bank for the rest of the day. Schiller emerged at 7:45 P.M., lit a long, narrow cigar, walked to the river, bought a newspaper and crossed a bridge to a park that sat on a peninsula between the swift-running Limmat and Sihl rivers, which split the city roughly in half and looked like quicksilver in the evening light.

Schiller checked his watch as he walked but showed no interest in reading.

"Looks like he's in a hurry," Sylvia said.

"Now's the time," Valentine said, moving toward Schiller. When he reached him he pushed him backward toward a bench, then sat down uncomfortably close to him as Sylvia slid in from the other side, trapping the banker between them. When he tried to get up Valentine pinned him against the backrest with a beefy arm. "You've obviously got some sort of hot date, so let's skip the foreplay," Valentine said with a smile that belied his tone of voice. "You've been handling dirty money, podnah, and if that were known, it might not be so good for business, especially yours."

"Who are you?" Schiller asked, his head swiveling. He wore a dark suit and dark tie, black shoes and French cuffs. The rims of his glasses were colorless, his eyes gray, his skin pink.

"We're a very troublesome pair," Valentine said. "No ethics, you could say, which should put us at even par with you. You're nursemaid to certain funds routed by the CIA to you via Memphis, Tennessee, Brussels and Munich." Valentine gave him the account number. "Now, before you get to thinking we're common thieves, we want to make it clear that all we want is information, and to show you that we're not barbarians, we're going to reward you for your trouble."

Schiller was frozen. "Why should I listen to you?"

"If you don't, the newspapers will. Either we get what we want and you earn your fee, or tomorrow every newspaper in Switzerland will receive documented evidence of your dealings with the CIA. Of course it will come as no surprise to anyone that an august Swiss bank is handling dirty money; that's a given. What *will* interest newsmen is your name and your exact connections. Your dealings with the CIA will destroy your anonymity, and that will more or less finish your career. You'll be hounded for details, especially when American journalists get onto the story—and I assure you they will. Your employers may keep you on, but whatever assets you've attracted to the business will dry up. Anonymity is all you have to sell. Am I right?"

"Your logic has some merit," Schiller admitted. He fished a pressed handkerchief from his breast pocket and dabbed delicately at his forehead.

"Good," Valentine said brightly, slapping the man heavily on the back. "We want to look at the account. Our interest is in knowing if any of the funds have moved. If it will ease your pain, think of us as auditors."

"Perhaps it would be better if I retrieved the information for you and brought it back."

Valentine laughed. "We insist on seeing for ourselves."

"When?"

Valentine made a show of checking his watch, then grinned. "Let's say right now."

"I have a previous engagement," Schiller said.

"Had," Valentine said, lifting the man to his feet and walking him through the park.

An hour later they were back on the street. Frash's asset had drawn nothing from the account; neither had Frash, and Schiller assured them that if Frash were in the city there was no way he could get the money, especially with a stop-order issued, unless he came to the bank. As they parted company, they warned him that if any movement took place in the account they were to be notified. If he failed they would blow his cover.

The two Americans walked on a tree-lined street near the bank. "Maybe we're ahead of the bastard," Valentine said. "For once."

"And maybe he's not headed here at all. That's the problem with hunches."

"I don't think so. Let your feminine intuition focus on this: Arizona says the asset worked strictly for cash, but I've never known a man with that orientation to squirrel it away. Yet Lumbas never touched the money, which I'd bet is no accident. Conclusion: the money wasn't the point. But if not the money, what?"

Valentine was vaulting a huge chasm of missing facts, but Sylvia got what he was driving at. If the asset was cash-motivated, why hadn't he withdrawn the money? Was it possible that Lumbas had never been interested in payment at all, and that his interest in feeding Frash information had another motivation? "All right, I see it," she said. "But that doesn't mean Frash is going to show up here. He knows how the Company works."

"If he needs money, he knows that there's a nice little nest egg right here."

"You agree with me?"

He didn't answer the question directly. "When a scientist doesn't have all the facts, what does he do?"

Sylvia gave him a funny look. His mind was unlike any she had ever encountered, and despite her irritation with his brooding, she knew that she was strongly attracted to him. "He looks at what he knows, pieces proven facts together to form a hypothesis, then backtracks to fill in theories as a way of testing his hypothesis."

"Bingo," he said, and before she could react, much less defend herself, he swept her into his arms and crushed her with a powerful hug. Later she admitted to herself that she had not wanted to push him away, though at the time she nearly knocked him down getting loose.

"You're a loose cannon," she said, "but you handled Schiller pretty smoothly."

"And you thought I was just a pretty face."

Why did he always have to bring everything back to some sort of personal reference point? He *had* handled Schiller well enough, but bankers were gamblers if nothing else, and money was a disease with them. The successful ones knew how to hedge their bets. Maybe they had caught Schiller unawares, but she was not convinced that he would simply roll over. They had gone right to his professional core and it was unlikely that he would meekly accede. He was no fool; in one way his cooperation put him in their power, but it also put his back to the wall, and people like Schiller, no matter how soft they looked, would not tolerate loss of control without a fight. "You want first watch?" she asked.

Valentine seemed disappointed. "No problem. Call Arizona and tell him what's going on. If Frash shows, I've got a hunch we're going to need help."

"You'll be all right?"

"You mean on my own?" he asked. "It's more or less my natural state." He sounded sad.

96 TUESDAY, APRIL 11, 1961, 6:50 P.M. *Moscow*

Petrov was seated on the edge of the bed retching into a stainless steel pan held by Talia, who sat beside him and used her other arm to keep him from falling forward. Their leader's skin was the color of an onion, his eyes red and sunken, his chin dripping pale green sputum. Talia held him as steadily and tenderly as she had her sons when they were young.

"Annochka never showed," Ezdovo said.

"Bailov found the bodies of his men," Talia said as another spasm wracked Petrov and doubled him over. She waited until he recovered, then turned to Melko. "Your Georgian comrades also paid the ultimate price," she said, "but they bought you time. When we couldn't find you or the attackers we hoped that you had gotten safely away."

"Wolf tickets," Melko said as Bailov came into the room with a tray heaped with warm hand towels.

"What about wolf tickets?" Bailov asked as he passed the tray to Talia.

"Our attackers," Melko said with a nod to Ezdovo, who handed the identity cards to the soldier.

After a brief look Bailov passed the cards to Talia. "They're useless," he said. "It's standard practice to use nonexistent names—usually the names of prominent czarists long dead. A man with a wolf ticket is already dead, so it doesn't matter what name he goes by. If he's lucky he'll get his real identity back after a time, and if he's smart he'll toe the line from then on. A wolf ticket is a preview of purgatory, and when a man's in such a state there's no way to trace him."

"Perhaps the cards themselves tell us something," Talia said. The others waited for an explanation. "Who uses such things?" It suddenly struck her that the Special Operations Group could be carrying wolf tickets as easily as the dead men.

"The KGB," Bailov said.

"Which tells us all we need to know for the moment," she said. "Either Melko's girlfriend has engineered this through her husband and father, or she and her family are in grave danger." She slid off the bed and waited for Gnedin to take her place.

"Too late," Petrov suddenly croaked. He had pulled loose from

Gnedin and now steadied himself, his long, thin toes sticking out of the bottom of his dressing gown like withered talons. "Diversion," he gasped. "Diversion," he repeated, and then he began to gag and collapsed on the floor.

"Go," Gnedin said, waving them out. "I've got him."

97 TUESDAY, APRIL 11, 1961, 8:50 P.M. *Zurich*

At 7:45 P.M. Frash saw a man and a woman intercept Schiller in the park and push him roughly to a bench under some trees. After a while the three walked back to the bank and the woman went inside with Schiller while her companion remained on the sidewalk. He was tall and large-framed, an obvious lookout, but he seemed to know how to move around just enough to blend into the scenery. Still, he didn't seem to be the type favored by the Company. She was; he wasn't. What did it mean?

When the banker emerged an hour later he headed back through the park and Frash followed at a safe interval, timing his intercept for a point several blocks from their agreed-upon rendevous. "You're late," he growled at Schiller when he caught up.

"I came as quickly as I could. It couldn't be helped."

"You had unexpected visitors," Frash said.

"Some of your lot," the banker complained, then explained what had happened. "Did you send them?"

Albert needed to ask questions, not answer them, and Schiller's arrogance irked him. "Did you tell them I was here?"

"I'm not stupid. I gave them only what was necessary. I knew that if there was a problem I could count on you for the appropriate solution."

Frash grinned. "You want me to clean your dirty laundry?"

"I would not characterize it so crudely. Their threats necessitated my fulfilling certain obligations, but not so as to jeopardize our arrangement. In banking one must learn how to balance conflicting demands."

Not to mention greed, Frash thought. "Where do we stand?"

"It is arranged, of course, as we agreed," Schiller said with a self-important bow. "The account is like a cabinet that can be opened from two sides. Different numbers, different access codes, but against the same funds. It's possible because of accounting practices and the relative freedom that banks enjoy here."

"Can the funds be traced?"

"That's the wrong question," the Swiss said. "Anything tangible can be traced. What you want to know is if there's any way that you can be stopped from making a withdrawal, and the answer to that question is no. This particular sort of transaction is based on accounting misdirection. To detect it would require a gifted auditor with immense patience and enough time to devote himself solely to the task for weeks. The money is quite secure until you want it, and then it is yours. Nothing can be done to prevent that."

"What did they want?"

"Your colleagues? They wanted to know if any of the money had been withdrawn."

"And you told them."

"It's easy to tell the truth, and of course the ledger entries were evidence. They told me to report any attempt at withdrawal. In accordance with their request I've put a hold on the funds—frozen them in place."

Frash stiffened. "Then how—"

Schiller cut him off. "Remember, the cabinet opens two ways, but the freeze applies only to the numbers and codes on, shall we say, the front side, and only if you try to move the funds through the Swiss system. In Italy there will be no problem."

"But the ledger will reflect movement?"

"It will show movement, but I'm assuming you will make only one withdrawal, and by the time it shows up there will be nothing they can do about it. From their perspective it will look as if water has evaporated. Who can trace vapor in the clouds? In any event, if you make the withdrawal at the time I've specified there will be no record for forty-eight hours, by which time you can be well on your way."

"Where does that leave you?"

Schiller seemed surprised by the question. "A good architect builds a house that will withstand the most severe weather. If your compatriots are willing to invest a great deal of time and effort to learn how it was done, they will eventually learn the secret, but it will not point to me." He paused and lowered his voice. "The Italians are *such* a messy people," he said. "Even a clever auditor will find nothing to incriminate me; it will look like a coincidence, an accident bred by the coming together of two banking systems. I will remain credible and will have served my client of record in accordance with the established traditions of my profession."

Frash thought about this briefly. "You're sure you've told them nothing that would lead them to suspect I'm here?"

"The money is untouched and frozen as per their instructions. What would motivate me to tell them more?"

The arrangement had been that both he and Schiller could draw from the account, and while the lion's share would go to Frash via an Italian bank, the remainder would be Schiller's, his fee for engineering the arrangement.

"There's absolutely nothing to fear," the banker said. "I've covered every contingency."

"All but one."

"What is that?" Schiller asked as Frash pushed him backward to the top of a stairwell that led down to a cellar entrance, placed the barrel of his 9 mm against the banker's left eye, squeezed and let the body fall backwards. Then he took Schiller's wallet, watch, pocket money and wedding ring and hurried back toward the park. Partway through he caught his heel on a crack in the sidewalk and fell on his left side, but recovered quickly. When he saw the Jaguar again with the silhouette of the American inside he skirted south along the river. Don't hurry, he reminded himself. They're watching the bank, and when they find Schiller it will look like the work of a common thief. By tomorrow you'll be in Italy. If Kennedy comes to Europe, will he stop in Italy? Powerful Catholics are as drawn to the Pope in Rome as Muslims are to Mecca. It would be interesting to get Kennedy alone. Stay out of this, Albert said.

98   TUESDAY, APRIL 11, 1961, 9:30 P.M. *Moscow*

Bailov's men had been too long in Moscow and were eager for anything that would take them away from the boring grind of guarding the General Secretary, so an assault on the building identified by Lenya was a welcome diversion. Even Bailov saw this task as real, which made it a lot more satisfying than the ghost hunt that had occupied the team for weeks.

Yet when they had taken and secured the place they found that it had been abandoned. Melko and Ezdovo had returned less than six hours before and the operation had been mounted quickly, but apparently not quickly enough.

"What now?" one of his Spetsnaz asked.

"We do what soldiers do best," Bailov said. "Sit on our asses until we are called." His gladiators laughed. The mission had been a zero, but at least they were with their commander and together.

TUESDAY, APRIL 11, 1961, 9:45 P.M.
Moscow

Melko and Talia used their Red Badges to gain admittance to Annochka's building. When they reached her floor they knocked but got no answer, and Melko quickly picked the lock. He was first into the bedroom, and after one look tried to block Talia's way, but she pushed past him. Annochka and her husband were facedown on the bed, their hands bound behind them, their lower legs bent back to their buttocks and tied securely to their wrists. Like pigs ready for slaughter, Melko thought. Each had been shot once in the back of the head.

Neither of them said anything for a long while; Melko felt queasy as he touched Annochka's cold hand and realized she would never be warm again. "Don't touch anything," Talia said. "Where are her children?"

Melko found them face down in the bathtub and vomited when he realized that someone had drowned them. He lifted the tiny bodies out of the water and began wrapping them in towels. "I can't leave them like this," he apologized to Talia, who patted him on the back and immediately knelt to help. They carried the children into their bedroom and laid them gently on their beds.

When Melko came out of the room Talia was surveying the damage to the apartment. "What do you make of this?" she asked.

"Not what it appears," he said softly. "It's been made to look like amateurs did it, but whoever was here knew how to take a place apart."

"Her husband's files?"

"She was supposed to bring them to us and never showed up. What sort of animal drowns babies?" he asked, his voice cracking.

Talia touched his arm. "Keep your mind on the mission," she whispered. "Help her by helping us."

"I'm all right," he said. Annochka had said that her husband had brought the files home where he could study them safely. Presumably he had looked at them more than once, which ruled out permanent concealment. Annochka was to have brought them on Sunday, which also meant that they must have been here. He moved through the rooms like a hunter, taking a step, pausing, letting his eyes work, trying to think like the dead man. Closet: the clothes bar had been removed, examined and cast aside. The doors had been unhinged so that they could be checked for hollow places. The carpets and bedding were slashed, pipes broken, the back of the toilet lifted off, an oversized wooden chest smashed, the pieces scattered like so many fallen soldiers. Where would you hide them, he asked himself as he sat down beside Annochka's body and stared at the blood that had soaked into her robe. He saw that all but two of her toenails were freshly painted. Was this what she had been doing when the intruders arrived?

Talia followed him into the bathroom. "What is it?" she asked, but he was too lost in his thoughts to answer.

Soiled towels were heaped on the floor. There were some rubber toys in the tub and an open bottle of shampoo on the ledge under the faucet. Where was the nail polish? He leaned down and found it tucked beside the base of the commode. The cap was loose, as if the applicator had been hurriedly pushed into the opening and not tightened.

"What is it?" Talia asked again.

He closed his eyes and waited for a scene to unfold. The children are playing in their bath, but Annochka is not concerned. She is beside them, painting her nails. They are safe, within arm's length. Probably she does not hear the watchman ring the apartment to tell them that visitors are coming up. Her husband waits for the doorbell, then goes to the door and peeks through the eyehole. He sees the intruders, senses what is about to happen, shouts at his wife and rushes into the bathroom. The children are out of the tub; their mother is watching them wiggle in their towels. No time, he says. He shoves the folders at her; Quick, hide them. She drops the applicator into the polish bottle and pushes it out of the way. Quickly, my little ones, back into the tub; I can still see some dirt behind your ears. What's wrong, Mommy? Quiet, quiet, I just want to give you a little more soap. Here, let me scrub. Then the holocaust, which was more a series of sounds than pictures in Melko's mind because he refused to let himself see the babies being murdered. Where were the files? He slid to his knees and stared into the gray water in the tub. He rolled up his sleeve, fished for the plug and pulled it loose, watching the water drain away, curling finally into a tiny whirlpool that gurgled like a tiny death rattle. On the floor of the tub was a white rubber mat with ridges to keep the children from slipping. Annochka was a careful mother. "There," he said to Talia with a nod of his head.

She leaned past him, lifted the rubber mat and saw the papers encased in plastic. When she looked up, Melko was weeping silently. Annochka had shielded the papers with her children's lives.

100   TUESDAY, APRIL 11, 1961, 10:35 P.M. *Zurich*

Sylvia was elated; Arizona was getting reserves to help them and this had been a boost. Now she felt sure that Frash was coming to Zurich and that it would end here. As she hurried through the park she felt a pebble in her shoe and stopped to get rid of it. A man was hurrying down one of the walkways about ten meters away. She saw him stumble and fall, then jump to his feet, glance in her direction and hurry on. When she reached the Jaguar she looked back but could no longer see the man; she wondered if he had hurt himself. Valentine was sitting with his feet crossed over the gearshift. She tapped on his window.

"Next time can we get something a bit bigger than a toy?" he complained.

She started to say something but suddenly stiffened and fled back into the park with her pistol unholstered and held over her head. Valentine struggled out of the Jag and sprinted to catch up. "Dammit," she shouted. "Goddammit!"

"What?" he asked, but she was spooked and angered and obviously didn't hear him. "What the hell is going on? You took off like somebody pinched your ass."

"Frash," she hissed. *"Here."*

"In Zurich?"

"Here," she said as she began to stomp the cement. "Right here. I saw him. He slipped and fell down and I saw him get up."

"You're sure?"

"Less than three minutes ago. He looked right at me, then went that way," she said, pointing to a path along the river. When he started in that direction she caught him by the arm. "No! We're not going to screw this up. It's a small place. We'll get help. Between our people and the locals we can close this place down."

"And if he's on his way out right this minute?"

"We'll get him."

Valentine didn't share her optimism.

101 TUESDAY, APRIL 11, 1961, 10:45 P.M.
Bakovka, Russia

The front door of the stately dacha was standing open and Ezdovo knew immediately that something was wrong. There were two bodies in the study on the ground floor. Annochka's father was in a chair and had been shot once through the back of the head; the impact had snapped him forward and knocked over an inkwell, whose contents had mingled with his blood. The woman had been shot in the mouth and was on the floor beside the chair. She had white-blond hair, but her death had caused a chemical reaction and turned the peroxide a ghastly pinkish-brown. A revolver was on the floor beside her, and Ezdovo saw quickly that the situation was intended to be misread as a murder-suicide. He rejected the obvious. Women seldom shot themselves. Poison, asphyxiation, slashed wrists—these, not guns, were the methods of escape taken by women.

102 WEDNESDAY, APRIL 12, 1961, 12:35 P.M.
Brennero, Trento Province, Italy

There was still crusted snow on the limestone outcrops along the Brenner Pass, but Gino Knauer no longer climbed that high. At sixty he lacked the stamina and strength that had let him board trains and steal whatever struck his fancy, but after nearly forty years at the game he had learned a few tricks to offset the deficits of aging. Old age tended to turn your bones to chalk, but if you were lucky your mind could more than compensate. Not that a great deal of thought was required to do what had become second nature. In 1948 he had discovered a place where the trains moving between Italy and Switzerland had to slow almost to a dead stop because of a dangerous series of curves and grades. From here he could simply step down, do his shopping and get off when the train slowed again twenty kilometers down the line. In the old days he had boarded earlier, from the steep rocks in the Brenner Pass, and ridden the full forty kilometers into Bressanone; with that amount of time he had been able to clean out a train, especially when his sons were along, but nowadays he worked alone and there were only enough minutes and energy to root through half a dozen cars, or even fewer when padlocks had to be forced. It was more a hobby than a vocation now.

This afternoon Gino sat at his usual place listening to the hoot of the whistle to the north. The sun was high and warm, the rocks alive with clear rivulets of water from melted snow, the air a soft caress that tempted him to ignore the train and enjoy the weather. Yet a man could not walk away from what he was, and above all else Gino was a thief, perhaps the best who had ever challenged trains in the mountains.

Practically speaking, there was no need to keep stealing. He was a widower now and his eleven children were grown and on their own, his livelihood having given all of them a life much better than any of them had any reason to expect. Even so, a man needed purpose, and if you let sloth get its claws into you it would be the end to your edge.

The train would arrive in ten minutes; in earlier times he had gauged by the smoke of locomotives, but now there were diesels along the line and only their whistles gave them away at a distance. Because of this it was now necessary to climb up several meters to watch the tracks below. A hundred meters north of him there was an odd little plain of grass. Engineers used it as a marker and when the engines passed it, the trains began to slow for the two sharp curves ahead. When the train began to decelerate he would climb back down to his ledge, remain in the shadows, count the cars after the engine passed and step down to the one he had chosen. The dismount was nearly as easy.

Centuries before, a king of Portugal had tried to send an elephant across the Alps as a gift to a Hapsburg emperor. An inn in Bressanone was now called the Elephant in commemoration of that long-ago event, and Gino thought of boxcars as his elephants, and their contents as ivory to be poached. What interesting booty would he find today? A case of watches, perhaps, for his granddaughters, or sturdy German boots for his sons and sons-in-law? He enjoyed not knowing what each car would hold.

When the engine reached the grass plain Gino began counting cars, but was interrupted when he saw something tumble onto the grass from the train, roll several times and stand up. A man? After the war there had been dozens of refugees on every southbound freight, but nowadays such vagabonds were rare. He was so astounded by the man's athletic dismount that he lost his count and his chance to board, and instead watched the stranger quickly climb into the rocks. Had he been so graceful in the days when he leaped from moving trains? It was almost like watching himself.

| 103 | **WEDNESDAY, APRIL 12, 1961, 2:30 P.M.**
Zurich |

The Swiss had used neutrality to carve their niche in the world community, yet for all their declared interest in peace they were more than happy to turn themselves inside out in the search for Albert Frash, and also to demonstrate herd behavior beyond anything Valentine had ever seen. All of this was triggered by the powerful but unseen hand of Arizona. By sunrise the border services of Switzerland, France, Germany, Austria and Italy had photographs of Frash to go along with the registration numbers of his twelve passports. The Zurich police had sent his photograph to airports, train stations, bus depots and taxi services. The women who directed traffic in the city's busiest intersections had them and day-boat services on the lake had them, as did hospitals, newspaper kiosks, post offices and virtually everyone in any position to make contact with the renegade American. Yet by midmorning their net was still empty. When Schiller failed to appear at his bank at his customary time, policemen were immediately dispatched to his house. He had not come home the previous night, his wife reported, but this was not unusual and she was not alarmed; her husband had a wide range of customers with peculiar notions about business hours, and after all Swiss bankers had built their reputations on their willingness to satisfy their customers. Eventually he would show up, she told the police; he always had.

Sylvia did not take Schiller's disappearance so lightly; within minutes of learning that he had not come home she was on the phone to the bank's managing director, advising him that there was a high probability that Schiller might have been forced to engage in certain improprieties with the bank's assets. She suggested that he order an immediate audit, but the man did not make any commitment over the phone. Instead he listened attentively, thanked her for the information and hung up. She guessed that he would have auditors at work within minutes. Swiss banks lived not only on their discretion but also on their reputations for reliability. In such a small country gossip traveled like lightning, and the mere suggestion of a scandal could bring a run on deposits and an almost immediate crash. Ironically, the same state-mandated secrecy that attracted depositors would send them into a panic if there was even a whisper of impropriety. Because of this Swiss bankers were quick to squelch rumors. Reputation counted for everything.

Sylvia and Valentine had talked to Schiller in the park, and she had seen Frash in the same place only an hour later; because of this she suspected that the banker had gone directly from them to Frash. Of course it was possible that it was a coincidence, but she thought this unlikely. Schiller and Frash must have worked out some sort of deal that only auditors would be able to detect.

Valentine could not cope with sitting in the American consulate while all of official Switzerland looked for Frash. Sylvia found him outside in the Jaguar. "Schiller's still missing."

There was no response. His eyes were red, his hair oily, his face rough with several days of whiskers. He stared out the window.

"I called the bank," she continued. "I talked to the managing director and suggested he audit Schiller before word leaked out that there was a problem."

"It won't matter," Valentine said. "The only time you ever see a fox is on his way out of the hen house. He's moved on."

"He can't," she said with less conviction than she meant to convey. "It will end here."

"If you say so," he said arching his back to stretch. He let out a long sigh and leaned his head back. "Guys like him always seem to find a way out."

She fought an urge to argue. "I'm optimistic."

"So was Jesus when they were nailing him to the cross," Valentine said. "If optimism and enthusiasm counted for anything, we wouldn't have to remember the Alamo."

"So quit," Sylvia snapped.

"Nope. I've always had a thing about finishing what I start."

"Most people would say that's a virtue."

He rolled his head toward her. "Most people have never taken anything to the far end of the line," he said grimly.

104 WEDNESDAY, APRIL 12, 1961, 3:00 P.M. *Moscow*

Yepishev stared at the telephone for a long time before trying again. The Americans wanted a meeting in Geneva on Sunday. It was an interesting choice. The International Red Cross was headquartered there, as was the International Labor Office, and the city had a regular flow of Russian diplomats. That they had asked for a meeting at all told him that they had a serious problem, and the selection of Geneva confirmed his suspicions. Neutral ground, neutral city, former home of the League of Nations, Geneva was a place where dangerous situations could be defused through talk. It was a choice that called for help, and he had agreed, then found it difficult to contact Bailov. With each unsuccessful attempt he grew more uneasy. Where was he? Why didn't the man answer his phone so that he could wash his hands of the whole affair? The thought made him smile. Could one wash away treason so easily? I like you, Taras Ivanovich, but you're testing me. He considered aborting the plan, but Bailov already knew about the American connection and no doubt had told his confederates, which meant that the secret was out. There was no choice but to see it through. The time for retreat had passed.

When the phone was finally answered he asked for Bailov and felt his pulse quicken. When he came on the line, he said, "I've been trying to reach you."

"Not now," Bailov said immediately. "Not on the phone. I want you to meet me."

"This line is secure."

"Can you say the same for my end?" He did not wait for an answer. "Go to the west end of the Borodinsky Bridge. I'll join you in an hour."

Yepishev replaced the receiver and slumped forward in his chair. Bailov's voice had been firm but without emotion, his statements clipped but complete, exactly the way a commander talked in the swirling vortex of battle. Yepishev wondered if he would soon be drawn into the same maelstrom that was engulfing his younger comrade.

105 WEDNESDAY, APRIL 12, 1961, 3:50 P.M. *Zurich*

Sylvia stared at Schiller's gray face and exploded left eye, then asked the morgue technician, "Was a bullet recovered?"

"Just pieces," the man said apologetically. "You can never tell with a head wound. One time the projectile passes cleanly through, another time it enters at just the right angle and spins round and round in the curvature of the skull. More often it separates on impact. This one is more the rule than the exception."

"We want the fragments," she said in a tone that offered the man no alternative, but he was accustomed to dealing with the Swiss authorities and parried easily with an invocation of rules. "Only the police can release evidence," he said with no hint of apology. "I have no authority."

Shortly thereafter they encountered the head of homicide for the city and found him equally obstinate. "It is clear," he said, "that Herr Schiller was in a locale where a gentleman of his station should not be. His watch has been removed, along with his billfold and his wedding ring, and his pockets were turned inside out. Like all cities, we have our problems, but Schiller was a banker and one of us and he should have known better." The captain emphasized the word "banker" in the way that a parish priest might refer to his bishop. His meaning was clear; if a man such as Schiller put himself into the path of dangers that he knew about, then the outcome was on his own head.

"We need the bullet fragments," Sylvia repeated.

"It is a sad thing," the policeman said, "and a tragic loss, but this is not your affair. You have no jurisdiction over matters such as this."

"I'll remind you that your government has pledged its full cooperation."

The captain shrugged. "Cooperation is a nebulous concept with no legal standing. Zurich is my venue, and I am empowered by the city to investigate and file criminal charges. I am responsible for evidence, and even the city would not dare intervene against my duly constituted authority."

Sylvia looked at Valentine for help, but he was staring out the window, grinning. "There's no need for confrontation," she said, trying to conciliate him. "We're trying to help. We want the same thing."

"That may be so, but I know my duty. You have no authority to seize evidence, and I have no intention of giving it to you. I believe that this leaves us with nothing further to discuss."

She moved to block the door. "I don't mean to challenge your authority," she said, "but we need to establish connections." The policeman's stubbornness made the hair on her neck stand up, but she understood what was going on. The city council had instructed him to stonewall them until the bank could finish its audit. It all boiled down to money and the protection of private interests.

"I am well aware of your interest," he said. "Perhaps I can even sympathize professionally. You have lost a suspect, and now you ask us to do what you could not. Very well: consider it done, but we shall do it our way and in our own time and we will tolerate no interference. If the suspect is in Switzerland he will be found, but there is no evidence to connect him to Schiller. I know my business, young woman, and I suggest that you let me get on with it."

Valentine was still grinning mindlessly when Sylvia turned to him. "Do you think you might render some assistance here?"

He seemed surprised. "Me?"

She rolled her eyes.

"Should this be assistance with finesse or without?"

"Think in terms of speed," Sylvia said.

Valentine nodded, turned to the captain and draped a big arm over the smaller man's shoulder. "She's a woman," he said in a conspiratorial tone. "Ours is men's work." The captain glanced at Sylvia, then smiled just before Valentine slammed him against the wall and pinned him with his feet off the floor. "The problem with women is that they're too damned polite," he told the wide-eyed captain. "Men know how to cut through the shit and get to the point." He turned to smile at Sylvia. "And here's today's point. In the States we say that there are two ways to do things: the hard way and the easy way. We want to borrow the bullet fragments. We promise to return them. We will sign all the paperwork you require and pledge the souls of our firstborn children. Now, the easy thing for you to do is to blink your eyes real fast to tell me that this is a deal. The hard way is for you to keep playing tough-cop and make me break both your collarbones. That's for a start. And I would remind you that even under Swiss law two witnesses carry more weight than one, so all we ask is a little cooperation. Now, what will it be?"

The captain blinked wildly, his face blue from lack of oxygen. Valentine let him drop, rifled his briefcase and flipped a plastic bag to Sylvia, then jerked the man to his feet and dusted him off with several friendly, open-handed whacks on the chest and shoulders.

When they were outside Valentine put his arm around her. "And you thought I couldn't be persuasive."

"I didn't like that crack about men's work."

"Did we get the fragments?"

She pulled away from him. "Would you have broken his collarbones?"

He grinned. "The first law of poker is never to show your hand unless you have to."

She got into the driver's seat of the Jaguar. "This is a poker game to you?"

Valentine crossed his arms and leaned back. "Getting to be a pretty damned good one, I'd say."

106 WEDNESDAY, APRIL 12, 1961, 4:30 P.M.
Moscow

Yepishev stood stiffly in the center of the group, his eyes downcast, not wanting to see them individually.

"Tell them," Bailov said softly.

"The Americans claim that Lumbas was passing rocket information to them and that he was murdered in Belgrade in November."

"How do you know this?" Talia asked.

"Some years ago I proposed to a counterpart in the CIA that a day might come when our sides might want to meet privately and unofficially—in the shadows, one might say."

"This happens often?"

"It's the first time," Yepishev said.

"Why would they tell us?" Gnedin asked.

"I'm not clairvoyant," the GRU general said.

"Don't be modest," Bailov said. "You've watched the Americans for years, competed against them, and know them better than any of us."

"It's said that Russia cannot be comprehended with pure intellect," Yepishev said. "To know Russia is to feel it, to have it flow through your veins. It's the same with them."

"What this one spouts we'll need shovels to pick up," Melko grumbled, but Yepishev ignored him.

"The Americans say that Lumbas was theirs, and that our . . ."—he paused to find the right words—". . . our fellow countrymen murdered him. They say that they want to talk, but I see their reasoning as follows: if Lumbas was theirs alone and we discovered it, why did we not take him into custody and interrogate him thoroughly? If he had been my responsibility I would have clamped his balls in a vise and squeezed them for a year. When I was finished I would know precisely what damage he had done, and then I would have to decide whether to shoot the bastard or turn him. This presupposes that he was theirs. But what if Lumbas was mine from the outset and they only *thought* he was theirs? That changes everything. If he were ours and only pretending to be theirs and we suspected that they had discovered the truth, then his death might have more value to us than his continued existence." Yepishev paused. "But only if he were mine from the start, and only if he had no other value."

"The Americans think that we gave them Lumbas deliberately?" Talia asked.

"They're neither stupid nor naïve," Yepishev cautioned. "If you were them, how would you read it?" The Special Operations Group was silent. "The meeting will be on Sunday in Geneva," he continued. "I accepted on your behalf, but whether or not you keep the appointment is up to you. They will see to all the arrangements, which means that you must trust them. They have a place on the lake close to the airport. I'll give Bailov the directions if you wish."

Talia stood directly in front of him. "If it were you, would you go?"

Yepishev answered quickly. "It's not me."

Bailov walked the Goat to the elevator. "You can find your own way from here?"

"We all must find our own way, Taras Ivanovich. Mind your tail feathers," Yepishev said as the door slid closed between them.

When Bailov rejoined the others Petrov was standing in the center of the room, his eyes dark, his emaciated body trembling, his hand raised in Bailov's direction. "You knew," he croaked. "You knew and said nothing!"

Bailov felt light-headed. Petrov's rage consumed the room, swallowed the very air and electrified it. "Yepishev has taken great risks for us. The meeting was not confirmed. I felt I owed him protection."

"What do you owe *us*?" Petrov hissed.

"Competence," Bailov shot back. "That, effort, my life if need be, but not the needless betrayal of a comrade."

"You were different in the old days," Petrov said.

"We were all different then," Talia interceded.

"I say he has failed us," Petrov snapped, glaring at her.

"I say he used judgment. He was caught between conflicting obligations and did the best he could." She stepped to Bailov's side. "In his place I would have done the same."

Ezdovo joined his wife. "Me as well."

Gnedin rose from his chair and joined the others. "The mission is all that matters," he said. "Bailov has given us more than we had, and the Americans may tell us more. It was you who once told us that only results matter."

"I said that?" Petrov said. He looked amused.

"Even in the camps," Melko chimed in as he took his place among the group.

"You forgive this bastard too?"

The team members looked quickly to each other for support. "We all do," Talia said with conviction.

"And you would meet the Americans in Geneva?"

"Yes."

Petrov gathered his robe around him and sat down in a chair. "Trubkin?"

"He was important only as a connection to Lumbas," Talia said. "But now we have another possible route to Lumbas. If the Americans are of no help, we can always go back to him."

"Velak?"

"Another link, and perhaps a more important one, but we can't assess him any further at this moment. We know he signed the orders that transferred Lumbas from Tyuratam."

"Which suggests what?"

"Nothing until we know more about Lumbas, and only the Americans can help us with that."

Petrov eyed Ezdovo. "You were assaulted."

"It was a futile attempt," Ezdovo reminded him.

"Half-assed," Melko chimed in. "The Asian dumped his men in the Zone and then went his own way."

"We can guess where he went," Gnedin said. "The girl, her husband, her—"

"Children," Talia said. "We have her husband's files. She told Melko that they're connected with the Odessa Military District, and we'll follow that lead, but for now we concentrate on the Americans."

"Who goes?"

"Me," Talia said immediately, and then after looking at the others, "and Bailov."

"You can't trust him," Petrov said.

"Like Yepishev, Bailov has studied the Americans. He's GRU, which will give him more in common with the CIA contact than we can offer."

"And what do the rest of this shiftless lot do while you're in Geneva?"

"They wait."

"That's how you see it?"

"That's how *we* see it," Gnedin said.

"Then who am I to change your minds?" Petrov asked as his head drooped.

When the rest of the group was gone Gnedin helped his patient into bed and covered him with a blanket. Petrov's eyes were closed, but Gnedin sensed that it was an act. "Did you get the result you expected?" he asked.

"Always," Petrov said without opening his eyes.

107 WEDNESDAY, APRIL 12, 1961, 9:10 P.M.
Zurich

The hotel was only a couple of years old but was already showing signs of stress from too many guests and too little maintenance. Valentine sat by a window and listened to the panes shudder as jet airliners wallowed down the glide slope toward the airport two kilometers away, passing directly overhead. He had the clippings from Paris spread around him, but the lines of print had become a blur and the image in his mind was a collage of expressionless faces with obliterated left eyes.

Sylvia returned to the hotel later than he had expected. She brushed past him, tossed her purse on the floor, kicked off her shoes and collapsed on the sofa. "I need a drink," she said in a voice he could not quite peg. "A stiff one," she added with her eyes closed.

A waiter with slicked-down black hair and a black uniform with frayed cuffs brought them a bottle of slivovitz and two plastic water glasses. Valentine filled them both to the brim and handed her one.

She held the plum brandy in her mouth like mouthwash, then swallowed it with a loud gulp. "Awful."

"You were gone a long time."

"Was I?" she said. "The fragments are on their way to the States." She seemed to be in a fog and curiously detached. "The thing is," she said wearily," that the slugs from Paris and Lamoura don't match. More," she said, holding out her empty glass. "It's not fair. All this time and no match. Both came from a 9 mm but not the same weapon, which pisses me off," she added. "Does it piss you off?" she asked, looking him in the eyes. "Are you getting any of this?"

"One of us has to keep a cool head."

"I don't like to lose," she said.

"Can't win all the time."

Sylvia gave him an overly sweet smile. "That's crap. Only losers lose."

"Very instructive." Could she be hammered on so little slivovitz?

"No matter what happens, there's always something else that can be done. You lose all options only when you're in the ground. I saw him last night," she said. "You don't believe me, do you?"

"If you say you saw him, then I'm sure you think you saw him."

"He slipped, fell, got up and looked in my direction, but didn't see me. I saw his face."

"It was dark."

She sipped the brandy, then held up her glass to admire the amber liquid, rolling the glass left, then right. "I can see my fingers," she announced.

"Bad news for optometrists."

"He grabbed hold of a railing. I didn't remember that until today. I saw him grab the rail with both hands and pull himself up. Our people went there today and brushed it for prints."

"That's good," he said. "They'll be processing the prints of half the population of Zurich."

"A lot you know," she said. "The FBI can do it. The prints will go to them by wire tonight."

"You've been a busy girl."

"Don't patronize me," she snapped, and held out her glass for another refill. "He's set up a meeting for us with the Russians," she said.

Valentine froze. "Arizona?"

"Sunday in Geneva," she said, chewing her lower lip.

"Did he tell you what the hell we're supposed to do with them?"

She used a finger to lower the neck of the bottle and stuck her glass under the opening. "He said we should tell them the whole story."

"Just like that?"

She shrugged. "Every fact, every speculation, every fear—everything, including the warts on your asses. His words, not mine," she added as she let her empty glass drop to the floor.

"You don't tell your enemy you've been in his knickers," Valentine said.

"You have an unusual way of putting things, have I ever told you that?" She took the bottle away from him and tossed it to the other end of the sofa.

"It goes against all the rules."

Sylvia smiled. "Screw the rules," she said. She held her hands out to him, led him into the bedroom, pushed him backward onto the bed and began to undress while he watched in a state of shock.

"Do I get to take my clothes off?"

"Shut up," she said. "I'm making the rules tonight."

"But what if I'm not that kind of boy?"

"You will be when I'm done with you," she said, biting his shoulder.

108   SATURDAY, APRIL 15, 1961, 11:50 A.M.
Geneva

Valentine stood outside the front door of the cottage and watched the volleyball game limp along. "Hot game?" Sylvia asked as she came up beside him.

"The endomorphs are slaughtering the ectomorphs," he muttered. "The fat ones can't move but they take up so much space that the skinny ones can't get a ball past them."

They were in a nudist camp called Sun Bird, which was built in a grove of stunted pines north of the city along the rocky south shore of Lake Geneva. "I remember an old saying about there being no secrets between naked people," she said, kissing his shoulder and leaning against him.

He pulled away. "I'll never be able to go outside as long as you're around," he said.

"Think of it as an exercise in self-discipline," she said with a soft laugh.

109   SUNDAY, APRIL 16, 1961, 9:30 A.M.
Geneva

The cabdriver flashed a knowing grin when they gave him the address, but neither of the Russians made anything of it. Even when he dropped them at the gate and left them standing on the grass with their suitcases they didn't understand. There was a high wall of gray stones and a gate for automobiles, but Talia saw that it was chained and that pedestrians had to pass through a gatehouse with a red-tiled roof. Several people in blue shirts and white trousers were just inside the gate. They were greeted inside the gatehouse by a man with a silver mustache and horn-rimmed glasses. "Reservations for Grundheim?" Talia asked.

The man had a practiced smile, which he flashed dutifully as he paged through the registry. "Here it is, Cottage Eleven. Your friends are next door in number twelve." He gave them a small map, showed them the route and tapped a bell.

A young woman in blue and white appeared, bowed and asked them to follow. She took them to a larger gatehouse set into a brick wall. It was surrounded by tall red pines and thick rhododendrons. "Leave your things here for inspection," she said. "You can undress in there." She pointed to a room with a door.

Bailov tried to say something but Talia elbowed him and pushed him forward. When the door was closed she pushed a chair against the wall under a high window and stood on it to look out. "It's a nudist colony," she reported.

"What?"

"A nudist colony."

"There must be a mistake."

She shook her head and climbed down. "You're the one who said the Americans were unpredictable. Even you must admit it's an interesting choice," she said with a mischievous smile.

"We can't—"

"They have important information about Lumbas," she reminded him as she slid her dress over her head.

He pulled off his shoes, tossed them across the room, sat down and peeled off his socks.

"You can wear the shoes," she said.

"Should I be consoled by that?"

"I offer it only as information, comrade." They were giggling like schoolchildren.

When they emerged, their guide pointed to the open suitcases. "Everything is in order," she said. "The forecast is for warmer weather and continued sun."

"Isn't that wonderful?" Talia asked Bailov, who rammed his clothes into his suitcase and held it in front of him to shield his groin.

"You're acting like a priest in a brothel," she whispered as they walked.

"With justification," he snapped.

"Be brave, Taras Ivanovich," she said, fighting back a smile.

Cottage Eleven was made of cedar with a fresh coat of green paint. The interior was sparsely furnished, a single room with ancient uphol-stered furniture and several posters proclaiming the benefits of sun wor-ship. There was only one bed. "How do we manage *that?*" Bailov asked disgustedly.

There was a basket of fruit on the table and an envelope underneath. Talia opened it and read the message. "Time to attend to business," she said.

When they knocked at the door of Cottage Twelve they were ush-

ered inside by a small woman with black hair, olive skin and the narrow-
est waist Talia had ever seen. As they stepped inside the woman handed
them towels. "These arrangements were imposed on us," she said
apologetically. On the far side of the room was a large man in a towel.
He was considerably taller than Bailov, with huge shoulders and long,
heavily muscled arms. He seemed vaguely familiar and gave her a look
that seemed to suggest a similar feeling. Had they met before?

"Is English all right or would you prefer German? I'm afraid our
Russian is not very good," the woman said apologetically.

"English," Talia said after another glance at the man.

"Shall we get directly to the point?" Sylvia asked.

"Please."

Bailov and Valentine traded stares across the room while Sylvia
followed Arizona's orders and laid out the history of the Lumbas arrangement, the still-ambiguous relationship to the Albanians and their search
for Frash. Throughout this the Russians gave no hint of their thoughts.

"This is an unprecedented meeting," Talia said when Sylvia had
finished.

"All the more reason for us to speak openly," Sylvia answered.

"You say that Lumbas is dead."

Sylvia opened her purse and took out some photos. "The first has
Lumbas with Frash. The second was taken in the morgue."

Talia looked at the photos, then passed them to Bailov. "Your
source claims that Lumbas was killed by our people?"

"Yes."

"Is it a reliable source?"

"She traded the information for political asylum."

"We would want to question her."

"She's dead," Sylvia said. "Murdered along with our chief of station. We're assuming it was a Yugoslav response, but that's speculation
at the moment."

"What do you expect of us?"

"The fact that you're here at all suggests that you have your own
concerns," Sylvia pointed out.

Talia paused for a long time before answering. Petrov had given no
instructions, not even guidelines, and there had been no time to talk it
through with the team. No time even to take Ezdovo aside and hear his
advice, which over and over had proved to be insightful. No, she was
alone in this, forced to weigh the decision on her own; now she understood the sort of pressure that weighed on their leader. Taking charge in
Tanga was one thing; this was something entirely different. What to do?
The Americans appeared to be in earnest. They had answered every
question she had thrown at them, but it was clear that their primary

interest was in their own man, not Lumbas. Go with your instincts, she thought.

"We have been searching for Lumbas," she said. "With no luck."

"Until now," Bailov interjected, returning the photographs to Sylvia.

"Lumbas was inexplicably transferred from Tyuratam," Talia began, and seeing that the name made no impression, she added, "It's our Cape Canaveral. Lumbas was a scientific technician with expertise in electronic ignition systems. Last October there was an accident at Tyuratam. Many people were killed and there was the customary investigation. Initially it was suggested that had Lumbas still been there the accident might have been averted."

"We've heard nothing about an accident," Sylvia said.

"It's not national policy to announce our failures," Talia said. "The Soviet people have been led to expect perfection in all technical matters. As it turned out, Lumbas's absence was *not* a contributing factor, but the investigation revealed that he had been transferred illegally. Our own investigation has led us to conclude that the technical aspects of his transfer were engineered by an individual in the KGB." How far did she dare take this?

Sylvia interrupted. "You said an individual in the KGB. Does this mean that Lumbas was KGB?" The Russian woman had said "our investigation." Separate from others?

"That's what you Americans would call a loose end," Bailov said. "It is like your man. His relationship with Lumbas was supposedly CIA-inspired, but can you say that their Albanian interests, whatever they may have been, were also CIA?"

"Correct," Talia said. "Our guess is that Lumbas was not involved in an *official* KGB operation, but we haven't entirely ruled it out. Do all the top officials in your CIA have knowledge of every covert operation?"

"No," Sylvia said. "It more or less depends on the sensitivity of a particular situation. There are times when our top people need to be able to deny certain events for political reasons."

Bailov smiled. "In this regard we are different. Nothing may occur officially unless it is approved from the top, and liquidations must always have before-the-fact approval at the Politburo level, including the General Secretary."

"Did the Lumbas killing have such approval?"

Talia glanced at Bailov and shook her head. "Like your man, Lumbas simply disappeared. Until now we had no idea of his fate. Or his whereabouts," she added.

Valentine tightened the towel around his waist, pulled a chair between the two women and sat down. "The espionage connection keeps getting in our way," he said. "Frash and Lumbas may have used it to cover whatever it was they were up to in Albania. If not, Frash wouldn't have disappeared after Lumbas was killed. That he ran tells us that he thinks he has a problem with the Company, but why he has chosen to stay in Europe is a mystery."

110   MONDAY, APRIL 17, 1961, 7:00 A.M.
The Lido, Venice

The Lido is a narrow spit of sand a twenty-minute boat ride across the polluted lagoon from Venice. Although it was only mid-April, the city was already beginning to swell with tourists. Frash relished Venice; here virtually anything was permissible with no questions asked. You could do as you pleased and anyone could become invisible. Other people came here to have their little adventures; the Venetians who could afford it crossed over to the Lido and indulged their fantasies quietly and privately. It was Venice's pressure valve, an escape hatch, which was precisely what he needed. The mornings were cool and sunny. Breezes swept in from the Venetian Gulf to be absorbed by low, pastel-colored buildings. Unlike Venice, which remained a sort of boisterous fish market, the Lido represented a higher order.

Frash's successes in Holland and Switzerland had pleased him, and the banking transaction had gone flawlessly. Just as Schiller had promised, the bank in Genoa handed over the cash with not so much as a single question. With money and passports he now had the flexibility to do what needed doing. Mother would be proud. Even so, all was not well; the Company's agents had been waiting for him in Zurich, which meant they wanted him. But how much did they know? With them on his back he'd have to be extra careful now, which would be difficult because it was becoming increasingly difficult to keep Ali at bay. He could not afford a serious loss of control now, another downward spiral driven by volcanic internal fires that defied reason or logic. Ali had triumphed in Belgium, Albert in Holland, and the killing in Zurich had been necessary for both of them, which meant that the ledger was still more or less even. Albert thought his way through and around life's obstacles; Ali destroyed them. For years Albert was convinced that Ali was contained, sealed off by his strength, but the assassination of Villam in Belgrade seemed to have cracked the seal. Could Ali be endlessly restrained? Myslim had been a shared outcome; Ali had wanted vengeance, pure and simple, while Albert judged coolly that Myslim was a dangerous thread in need of cutting. Brother or not, Myslim's death had been the result of a rational decision. France, Belgium, Holland, Switzerland. Three of them in Albert's favor. This comforted him.

The Hotel Excelsior was the right choice: old and distinguished, with three-star ambience and the usual stiffness that went with such exclusiveness. The hotel itself was not perfect, but the rich paid for service and attitude, not appointments. There were gaps under the doors, offering the free movement of sound, but guests took care to make love in muted tones and the hotel staff tried to quietly satisfy their guests' needs. Albert guessed that the recalcitrant Ali could be tamed here, but only by regimentation. He awakened early every morning, walked three kilometers and ran several more, finishing with a hard kick, then moved to his balcony to cool down and do his daily ration of push-ups and half sit-ups, the latter making his rippled belly strong and lean. Sometimes Ali made his presence felt during the adrenaline surge of the final sprint, but the cool-down effectively banished him.

In the afternoons Frash went to the beach to read and rest. The weather was still too cool for the locals, so he usually had the sand to himself. In the evenings he walked the narrow, tree-lined streets and ate in small restaurants, never the same one twice. Albert ate for nourishment; Ali ate to satisfy his needs for textures and flavors. Albert limited alcohol to one glass of Barolo at each meal, while Ali craved glasses of chilled vodka. Albert bought two suits in traditional styles; Ali forced the purchase of new Italian briefs and relished asking a female clerk how his penis should be arranged to keep it in check. She had smiled and offered to help Ali in the fitting room, but Albert had declined politely and gotten them away before there was a scene.

Last night Frash had read about speculations from Washington that Kennedy would soon meet Khrushchev, and he thought about this as he undressed for bed. Kennedy claimed heroic deeds during the war. Would he be so brave with a 9 mm in his rich Catholic face? The knock on his door did not alarm him, but it put him on guard. His papers were impeccable and his appearance had changed. He had peroxided his hair and let his beard grow, and he now wore heavy-framed glasses. His passport said he was Adolf Van Geer, a German schoolteacher. He opened the door to find the woman from the tailor shop holding a blue-cloth hanging bag out to him.

"Final fitting," she said. "I'm Sultana Fregosi." She was short, with close-cropped black hair, large brown eyes and a grayish-black mole on her left cheekbone. She wore a blue silk blouse with puffed sleeves, a dark skirt that hung almost to her ankles and sandals with modest heels.

"I can come down to the shop in the morning," Albert told her politely. "This isn't necessary."

The woman stepped past him and looked around the room. "A gentleman should always have a final fitting in private," she said. "Especially a gentleman who stays at the Excelsior." She was businesslike as she draped the suit bag over the chairback, unzipped it and laid the suits side by side on the bed. During the actual fitting she worked silently, asking only if each adjustment was to his satisfaction. When she had finished she put the suits back into the bag, informed him that the tailor would require one more day, and that she would deliver the suits on Thursday.

"It's no trouble for me to come to the shop," Albert repeated.

"I insist."

"Then I insist on buying you dinner," he said with a quick look at his watch. It was out before he could weigh the consequences.

"It's late," she said. "Everything closes early here."

"Room service, then."

"It's really not necessary."

"And perhaps not proper?"

She smiled. "Propriety is a personal matter. It's just that I'm really not that hungry."

"Something light, then, and a glass of wine?"

Now it was morning and he was late for his workout, his eyes still filled with sleep. As he always did after waking he remained still for several seconds in order to clear his mind, and only then realized that he was not alone. The woman's leg was draped over him. "You're a deep sleeper," she whispered.

"I'm late for my workout," he said, trying to pull away.

Her hand closed gently on his penis. "You won't need that sort of exercise this morning," she said. "I have a much better idea." Frash was surprised to discover that Albert and Ali both agreed to the proposition, but even as they began to make love he wondered if this would turn out to be a mistake.

111   MONDAY, APRIL 17, 1961, 11:30 A.M.
Arlington, Virginia

Like any large organization, the CIA had its own rules, values, prescribed behaviors and its own distinct culture; and after so long in the business and having lived through the transition from the OSS and a hot war to the CIA and a cold one, Arizona could read the organization in subtle ways. Today the signs were clear. Only a small number of people knew the specifics of the Cuban invasion, but everyone could sense that something important was afoot. George Zezulka, the third-floor security supervisor, had quit smoking a year ago but today he was chain-smoking Lucky Strikes. Edwin Razornik, a China analyst and impeccable dresser, was wearing one brown penny loafer and one black one. Wilma Washington, a secretary whose life away from the CIA was wrapped up in some sort of evangelical church, was wearing a red silk dress cut so low that her breasts nearly fell out when she breathed. Normally she wore drab dresses with high collars and complained about declining American morals; now she looked like a ten-dollar hooker on a Baltimore street corner. None of these people knew about Cuba, but all of them sensed that something was about to happen, the mass anticipation like a virus floating from person to person.

Arizona had never romanticized the Company or its work. What they did was essential, dangerous and often dirty by normal standards. Cuba was a piece seated on the periphery of the world's playing board, a cancer that some argued had to be surgically removed, and it was this assumption that made him doubt the mission's objectives. Motives counted for nothing if an effort failed, as he suspected this one was bound to. Many of the invasion's assumptions were flat-out false, but the architects of the operation were blinded by righteousness and a compulsion to revenge themselves against Castro, who had screwed them after they helped him defeat Batista. The landing site was poorly chosen, the air cover plan inadequate, and there was no hard or recent evidence that there would be a popular uprising to support the invaders. The expatriates would go in, the Cubans would react frantically, the Russians would condemn the act, and the U.S. would counter with a denial of involvement. He sensed that there had been too much concern about political cosmetics and not enough focus on the mission's purely military aspects.

Castro might be an amateur soldier, but his raggedy-ass troops had eventually done the job against Batista. The whole mission was a throwback, a step backward to the days of larger-scale military intervention. This had been Sylvia's view, and she had shown poor judgment by making her opinion known outside her own chain of command. Had he not moved to extract her from the Cuban operation, her career would have been finished. Once a decision was made, the Company's culture demanded enthusiastic cheerleaders, not skeptics, especially outspoken ones. Most especially, outspoken women.

Arizona checked his watch. Were the invaders on the beach yet? Not that Cuba matters, he reminded himself; all that matters now is finding Frash. The timing of the invasion was predicated on information that came from Frash. When the operation failed, the inevitable hunt for scapegoats would begin, and if doubt settled on the veracity of Frash's information, the searchlight would settle on him. He had no desire to be charged with altering information, so Sylvia and Valentine had to find the bastard. When that was done he would see to it that no trails led backward; officially Frash would be gone and would stay that way. Ironically, Gabler's death had been transformed into an advantage. He had the logic worked out: someone had moved against the Company in Belgrade and two men had perished, along with a Soviet asset. He could weave a story out of this, patch the pieces together, sell it and make it stick—but only if Frash could be found and eliminated. Elsewhere in the Company the men in charge were entertaining visions of victory, of a parade through old Havana with Castro's head on a bayonet. Arizona's vision was solely on damage control. To win at chess, one ignored the current situation and examined the board in order to chart the next ten moves. Chess was played in the future, not the present.

Wilma Washington brought him a pot of hot coffee and lingered to put sugar and cream in his cup. Her breasts strained to escape. "Nice dress," Arizona said.

She smiled. "Woke up this morning with the strangest feeling," she said. "It was as if this dress insisted I put it on. Must be something in the air. Maybe it's spring fever."

More like a plague, he thought as she marched out of his office swinging her hips.

112 MONDAY, APRIL 17, 1961, 6:35 P.M.
Geneva

The couples had separated to talk. Valentine opened a bottle of mineral water, turned on the radio and sat down to listen to a news bulletin.

"Cuba claims that it has been invaded by American forces," an announcer said. "A spokesman in the Cuban embassy in Paris has announced that a hostile force landed on Cuban soil early this morning with American naval and air support. The Cubans claim that these forces were stopped quickly and destroyed. There have been many news reports in recent months alleging that the Americans were training a secret army of Cuban expatriates, but there is no comment so far on today's events from the United States."

Valentine looked up to see Sylvia in the doorway of the bedroom, her eyes dark, mouth open. "Stupid, stupid, stupid, stupid assholes," she whispered.

"We have to tell the Russians," Valentine said. "Right now." He went next door and entered without knocking. The Russians were seated at a table, talking animatedly. "We've just heard on the radio that the Cubans are claiming they've been invaded by the U.S., or at least by a U.S.-supported military force."

"Which is probably true," Sylvia said, stepping past him. "An operation has been planned for some time; I doubt that it will be a surprise to your people, but we felt you should know."

"Cuba doesn't concern us," Talia said quickly. "Our own interests remain paramount. Leave it to our governments to sort out Cuba. We need to concentrate on Frash and Lumbas, and nothing else must get in our way."

The Americans joined the Russians at the table again and the discussion lasted until early the next morning. In the end they agreed on a course of action. The Americans would concentrate on Frash, while the Soviets would focus on Frascetti and his connection to Lumbas. Communications between the two sides would be through the channel that had brought them together this time.

TUESDAY, APRIL 18, 1961, 7:30 A.M.
Arlington, Virginia

Arizona's ashtray was overflowing and the desk was a chaos of stacks of handwritten notes, pencil stubs, twisted paper clips and dirty coffee cups. The reports from Cuba were fragmentary, but in Arizona's mind the military issue had already been decided; Operation Pluto was a disaster of the first magnitude. Pluto, the arrogant, scheming god of the underworld, had turned out to be more like his Disney namesake. The Cuban expats were getting their asses kicked and the president was seething. It was a bad scene about to get worse. The only good thing about the whole fiasco was that he did not have to be at the White House. He had drawn communications relay duty and was on a secure telephone helping to pass the latest reports and developments to the Cabinet Room several miles away, where Kennedy's people were alternating between grousing and pontificating.

Nothing had gone right. The preemptive air strike had been intended to cripple Castro's twenty-nine-bird air force, but bomb-damage assessment from U-2 photos showed that less than 20 percent of the dictator's aircraft had been destroyed. Of all that could go wrong, this was the worst. Pluto had been predicated upon elimination of all Cuban warplanes; this would have limited the decision to the ground, where the fourteen-hundred-man invasion force could move against Havana with a reasonable margin of safety as their own air cover took out the tanks and troop concentrations ahead of them. Now, Arizona guessed, all bets were off.

As soon as the analysts saw the U-2 photos, only one decisive option was possible: an immediate and comprehensive second air strike. But Kennedy had refused, reminding the CIA of their own caveat—that this had to look like a Cuban expat operation. No second strike would be authorized until the invaders secured an airfield, declared their government to be in place and formally called for assistance. Only with a democratic government on the ground could the invaders assume the role of patriots requesting help from their American friends.

The president's stubborn refusal was the invaders' death sentence. Arizona found this decision difficult to accept. The invasion's cover story was already blown, so why was Kennedy refusing to face reality? One of the attacking B-26s had been painted to look like one of Castro's aircraft. While the other air attackers struck Cuban targets, the decoy was flown to Miami, where the expat pilot told reporters that he had defected to join the cause. This event had gone as planned, but then one of the attacking B-26s had encountered engine trouble, turned around and landed at the municipal airport in Key West and the newspapers had photos. Who were these Cubans flying unmarked aircraft? The cover was shot.

Arizona had been tracking the battle from radio reports, and what he heard was a nightmare. The initial target was three small beaches connected by tidal swamps. No escape routes, no safety valves. The original plan had called for an old-fashioned, full-scale amphibious assault near Trinidad on Cuba's southern shore, but Kennedy's people questioned this because it might deteriorate into a beachhead defensive action and force premature U.S. intervention. This logic had come to the fore early in March, so mission planners had been given only ten days to develop an alternative. They had settled on an area called the Bay of Pigs, which would require three separate landing forces to fight their way inland to link to a battalion of paratroopers who would be dropped ahead of them after sunrise. But unlike the Trinidad site, which offered the nearby Escambray Mountains as a refuge if the operation went sour, the Bay of Pigs provided no escape hatch. It was up and inland or die, with no margin for error.

Problem after problem cropped up after the brigade landed. The reefs along the Bay of Pigs were supposed to be inconsequential, but coral tore the bottoms out of some of the little fiberglass boats used to land the troops, and waves capsized others. Some men drowned; many others had to swim ashore. Then Castro's aircraft sank the USS *Houston* and another ship; the invasion force's supplies and munitions were on the *Houston,* which meant that the invaders had only the equipment and ammo they carried ashore. Castro's troops were supposed to be nowhere near the invasion zone, but on one of the three beaches the expats immediately ran into a heavily armed Cuban infantry company and got trapped in a deadly firefight. The plan called for guerrilla forces and anti-Castro insurgents to join the invaders, but none showed up. Every piece of information confirmed what Arizona had already concluded: the Bay of Pigs was inadequately planned and poorly executed. The only question now was how many of the fourteen hundred invaders would die in the effort. There would be hell to pay over this, and he guessed it would be the CIA that paid, especially when Congress learned that the $13 million it had authorized for the effort had burgeoned to more than $100 million.

Ike had given approval to the initial plan, but Kennedy had inherited it and gone along with it because the planning was so far advanced. He had pressed for a one-year delay to study the situation better but had been advised that this was impossible; Cuban pilots were finishing flight training in Czechoslovakia, and by June 1 would return to Cuba with a squadron of Soviet MiG 17s. If the operation was delayed, the MiGs would annihilate the expat B-26s. It was now or never. Okay, Kennedy said, but this had better work. Not to worry, Mr. President.

With one notable exception, Arizona's role in Operation Pluto had been minor, but that exception put him and his career at risk. The intelligence on Cuban pilots training in Czechoslovakia had come from Lumbas. Now that Frash had disappeared there would be reason to question the Cuban pilot story; if it wasn't true, then Arizona was responsible for the hurried attempt to bring Castro down. Frash was gone, Pluto was a disaster, and unless Valentine caught up with Frash, Arizona himself was in deep trouble. Kennedy's opinion of the CIA was already negative; he had trusted the agency to be right, but it had been wrong. Last year's U-2 situation had created a political storm, but before Powers was shot down the flights had at least confirmed that Khrushchev's claims of Soviet missile superiority were so much hot air, and his recent stunt of putting a man into space changed nothing. REBUS had further confirmed that the Russian missile lead was so much air. But what intelligence success could be salvaged from the Bay of Pigs failure? Castro would retain power, fourteen hundred patriots would be lost, and the U.S. had demonstrated that it could not handle a two-bit dictator in its own backyard. N.F.G., Arizona told himself. No fucking good.

114 **WEDNESDAY, APRIL 19, 1961, 11:20 P.M.**
Moscow

The General Secretary had been raging all day at his aides, his secretary, Politburo members, and various messengers and officials of the KGB, GRU, armed services and the Foreign Ministry. Now his throat was raw, his voice hoarse, his temper frayed. It was not that they lacked information; the problem was that the sheer volume of it was overwhelming them. Despite this, Khrushchev had no coherent assessment of what had happened, much less what was at stake. Castro had cabled that he was facing an all-out American invasion, while American newspapers were reporting that the attackers were Cuban expatriates armed by the United States and trained in Central America. Soviet embassy people in Havana had no idea what was going on, yet they cabled every thirty minutes with a new message that said, in effect, "We are analyzing the situation." Idiots!

Despite his ignorance of the real situation, and though it was couched as a message of support to Castro, Khrushchev shot off a message to the American president. The Soviet Union was prepared to render all necessary assistance to Castro to help their gallant socialist brothers and sisters repel the invasion. Kennedy had quickly replied that the Soviet Union should stay out of it. Tough talk; was he prepared to follow through on the threat? There was no way to tell, which was why they had to meet. Face-to-face he would know once and for all if Kennedy had what it took to play on the world stage. Meanwhile he had to get this sorted out.

There were some facts to go on, but they were disconnected, so the General Secretary ordered translations of American newspaper reports containing a number of related facts: unmarked B-26s had ineffectively attacked Cuban airfields; there had been landings in at least two locations by a force of one thousand to five thousand well-armed men; no tanks or artillery were involved; Castro had issued a statement claiming that the invaders had been stopped near the beach and that some of their boats had been sunk; he was rounding up political opponents in order to forestall a popular uprising.

Khrushchev guessed that the reports from the American papers were close to the truth, but facts aside, what was Kennedy thinking of? In this regard he examined his own experiences. In Hungary he had smashed the uprising ruthlessly. History taught that if you were going to make a show of force for reasons of survival or as an instrument of foreign policy, there could be no limits. Strike suddenly, hit hard, crush the opposition before it can get organized. Hungarian students had been no match for Soviet tanks. One went all the way or did not go at all. Did the American president not understand this elemental strategic principle? In one month against Hitler's invaders the Motherland had swallowed nearly two million casualties, but they had made the Germans pay an even higher price for every kilometer of ground gained. Anytime a trigger was pulled, the battle had to be to the death.

It was unthinkable that the United States, with the most powerful military machine in history, could not swat Castro like a pesky sweat bee. Yet it seemed that the Americans had made what could only be viewed as a halfhearted, half-assed attempt to rid themselves of Cuban Communism. Why had Kennedy held back? It was a critical question, his first chance to evaluate his new opponent. For long-term Soviet interests, specifics were not as important as an American leader's motives. In this lay the clue to Kennedy, his motives the measure of his scrotum's capacity: big balls, little ones or none at all. These events needed thorough, thoughtful assessment, not the sort of sniveling, undisciplined analysis that would trickle slowly out of the Foreign Ministry in the ensuing months.

The General Secretary left his office at 10:00 P.M. and went to his flat on Granovskiy Street, a place he had only recently acquired and which had not yet been fully furnished. The building was only a ten-minute drive from the Kremlin and more convenient than the dacha, but for now it looked like an empty hall.

Pogrebenoi, his acting chief security adviser, was gone without explanation and had left a muscular, bearded man in her place who objected vigorously to the General Secretary's decision to go to the flat. "There can be no assurance of security there," the man snapped at him.

"I don't want to hear what *can't* be done," Khrushchev countered. "People are forever telling me what can't be done; I'm here and I intend to stay, so do your job."

The man was uncowed. "We were not aware of this place. It hasn't been properly cleared."

"An oversight," which was the truth.

"Oversights are opportunities to be exploited by an enemy. The seams of life are its weak points."

"Don't lecture me."

The man was persistent and outspoken. "We have a job. We can't do it unless you cooperate. You want security, but then you run here and there like a perpetual motion machine."

"It's closer to the Kremlin."

"How many more oversights will we have to deal with?" The man was peeved but in control of himself, and he had the leader of the Soviet Union on the defensive. Khrushchev was impressed. How did Petrov find such people?

"This will be the last time."

"How can we be sure?"

"Are you trying to bully the General Secretary of the party?"

"I'm trying to bring some order to an old man's sloppy thinking." The words were out before he could stop them, but having said them he did not regret them.

Khrushchev stared at him for a long time, then grinned and showed him the palms of his hands in a gesture of submission. "What's your name?"

"Ezdovo."

"You have the courage of your convictions, Comrade Ezdovo. I like that in my people."

"I have a job to do, no more, no less."

"Tomorrow I will dictate a complete list of locations. Will that satisfy you?"

"It should have been done weeks ago."

Another rebuke. "Have you no sense of caution?" Khrushchev's voice was up an octave and his face was red, but he was amused, not angry.

"It is a sense of caution that motivates me. Caution on *your* behalf, comrade."

The General Secretary raised his hands above his head. "I surrender."

"I ask for trust, not surrender."

"They're the same thing."

"Perhaps in the Politburo, but not elsewhere."

Khrushchev went over to the lone couch and sat down heavily. "Get us some coffee, lots of coffee. And some dark bread and hard butter. I need to chew on something and fill my belly."

That had been half an hour ago. Now Ezdovo was back with two Spetsnaz men who put trays draped with linen towels on the floor and departed. Unlike the General Secretary's former guards, who avoided his gaze, the new men regularly made direct eye contact and kept it. These Spetsnaz fellows were clearly a different breed and a force to be considered in the future. Men like this could be enemies as easily as allies; in the future he would see to the welfare of Spetsnaz because one day they might prove to be valuable assets.

Ezdovo lingered after the men departed. "Will you require anything more?"

"Yes. Sit with me." Khrushchev patted a cushion. "Don't worry," he said. "I simply want to talk, one comrade to another." Ezdovo draped his coat over the couch and sat down on the floor. Khrushchev poured coffee, gave him a cup, stretched his short, thick legs out in front of him and kicked off his shoes. "You believe my thinking is sloppy?"

"Only in personal security matters."

"Don't retreat."

Ezdovo took a deep breath. "Pogrebenoi says that you jump around and that there is no continuity to your thoughts. You are like a frog among endless lily pads, never long on any one, always moving."

"But she seems to be able to follow me perfectly well."

"Most around you do not. They fear your power."

"My power is an illusion. To be with Stalin was to see real power and be petrified by real fear." He sipped his drink. "But you are not afraid of me?"

"No." It was true, Ezdovo realized. Wary, yes; afraid, no.

"Why not?"

"I don't analyze my feelings. I'm not, that's all."

"Do you understand what has taken my attention today?"

"Bits and pieces. Cuba is under attack."

The General Secretary smiled. "You were outside my office."

"There is often more to be learned outside an office than in it."

"You've been eavesdropping on my advisers?"

"My mission is your security. I take information where and when it's available."

"Meaning?"

"To your people I'm merely a guard. If I'm present, then that is what I must be. Prejudices can be turned to advantage. People see what they expect to see: a guard is like a piece of furniture."

Khrushchev was impressed. How many of his colleagues had such powers of logic? "Say that you had an enemy and that one day this enemy sent mercenaries to wipe you out. Your enemy has its own army and vast resources, yet it chooses to attack with a small force of intermediaries. How would you interpret that?"

"As a wish to maintain anonymity. From the perspective of others it would appear as if we had simply suffered misfortune, an act of God, but this is no hypothetical situation. You're talking about Cuba."

"Why would the American president choose a strategy that could fail? Cuba is in his backyard and Castro is a political amateur, a nothing."

"The Americans have always been sensitive about maintaining a particular image among other nations. They want Cuba to fall, but they don't want to be accused of direct intervention. We acted the same way in Laos and in the Congo."

"But not when it was really important and close to the Motherland." Khrushchev countered with the examples of Poland and Hungary. "It is their flaw," he decided. "The American president must live in two worlds and justify every action in each. Eisenhower understood this. So did Roosevelt and Truman. There is always more meaning in actions than in words. Kennedy shows me weakness and I keep asking myself why? To govern, one must exercise power, sometimes subtly and other times forcefully, but always in view of the whole world. If one doesn't exercise the necessary power when the need is obvious, there must be a reason. Why does Kennedy act as if he's impotent? Nurturing an image is not an adequate explanation."

"I lack the information to make such a judgment."

"One never has all the information one desires," the General Secretary said. "One takes what is available and extrapolates. Kennedy fears us. That's the secret heart of the matter. If he has not taken direct action, it's because he fears our intervention."

"Would we?"

"Too difficult to supply and support," the General Secretary said quickly, "but we could exert pressure elsewhere." Berlin, he thought. "Castro is a nothing, a banana-republic opportunist. When he was in the mountains fighting Batista, the Americans supported him and made it possible for him to prevail. I'll tell you something: Castro is not even a Communist."

Ezdovo did not understand. "Then what is he?"

"See, you didn't know! A socialist, yes; a Communist, no. The Americans never understood this and pushed him into our camp. Fidel is a revolutionary, which means he needs total control. Lenin was the same. Because the Americans helped Castro, they felt this entitled them to control and influence like their other Latin American puppets, but Fidel balked at such interference. We saw this and used it. We're both socialists, I told him. I won't accept interference, only assistance, he said. Now he calls himself a Communist and the Americans are frantic to be rid of him. Thus, an invasion was not unexpected. We saw it coming, though the timing was uncertain. The Cubans are hot-blooded, and Cuban capitalists even more so because Fidel swallowed their assets, just as we relieved the Czar of his. The Cubans are like the Albanians, forever imagining insults and swearing blood oaths of revenge. But unlike the Albanians, who live in isolation like Neanderthals in their caves, the Cuban expatriates have American power to support them. They created a small army—bakers, accountants, lawyers, gigolos. Not much of an army, but an army nevertheless."

"And now that army has attacked."

"Yes, but virtually alone, not with direct American involvement. That's what makes no sense to me. If Cuba is a true threat to American security, then why not remove it permanently? Castro wanted missiles but I put him off. Without missiles what threat can the Cubans be? Would Fidel invade Florida in his fishing boats? No. Yet the Americans sponsor a veiled invasion."

"Which seems to have failed."

"Which *might* fail. We don't have all the facts, but it appears that actions could have been taken to give the invasion force an increased chance of success."

"Such as?"

"Air support. It seems that there were only two attacks beforehand, and only with ancient aircraft. Fidel's few jets survived. Kennedy could have stationed one of his carriers off the island and created absolute air cover. This young president neglects to understand that any action or failure to act can create more than one image. He worries about his image among nonaligned nations, not how *we* might view his failure. He has miscalculated."

"If the Americans have not been directly involved, then the failure is not theirs."

"*I* see it as their failure." Suddenly Khrushchev rose and crossed the room to a window that looked out on the city's few lights.

"Get away from the window," Ezdovo told him. "There are no curtains and your silhouette makes a good target; even a nearsighted sniper would have no trouble picking you off."

The General Secretary's eyes were hard. "At this moment I can clearly see Kennedy," he said. What he saw was a man trying to look like a leader rather than leading, and it was a critical difference. "He thinks his image is intact," Khrushchev said, "but I see him for what he is."

"Get away from the window," Ezdovo repeated.

"Where's Pogrebenoi?" the General Secretary asked as he stepped back.

"Working."

"What's your relation to her? Second in command?"

"Something like that," Ezdovo said. "I'm her husband."

115	THURSDAY, APRIL 20, 1961, 8:45 A.M.
	The Lido, Venice

Sultana Fregosi was thirty-six, had never married, and held two degrees in anthropology from the University of Padua. Her grandfather owned a tailor shop, the smallest of many business holdings in Venice, real estate in Genoa and Milan, and a villa at the base of Mt. Vesuvius near Naples, where he now lived under round-the-clock nursing care, with four sons counting his every breath in the hope that the end would come soon, and their inheritances immediately thereafter. Sultana had tried anthropology, but her skin reacted to the sun and she hated teaching; in front of a crowd her legs turned to jelly and her voice fled. She had tried other jobs but abandoned them all for one reason or another, and in the end her grandfather had given her responsibility for the tailor shop. She had surprised him and her father and uncles by doubling sales and tripling profits in less then four years. Eventually the shopkeepers on the Lido had accepted her as one of them, though she was aloof, while her grandfather held her up to his sycophantic sons and brothers as an example of what he expected from his kin.

Adolf Van Geer was only her second lover. The first had been when she was seventeen; he had been fifty and virile. The relationship had lasted only six weeks and the sex had not awakened her libido; it was pleasant enough, but she laughed when she thought how ludicrous the act itself must look; it was difficult to understand why people made such a fuss over such an insignificant matter. It had been nearly twenty years since "all that," as she now thought of it, but Van Geer stirred something anew in her and she had given in to it without much analysis or anguish.

During her second night with Van Geer she told him how the men on the Lido called her the Virgin. Many had made a play for her, but they had given up, some sooner than others, all of them eventually concluding that she was unconquerable. She had slept with Van Geer for the past three nights; tonight she took him to a large stucco house with twenty rooms that was connected to her shop by an underground tunnel.

"You should move in with me. When business is slow, I can pop over. Besides, it will save money." Above all else, Sultana Fregosi believed in frugality. Frash agreed; in the hotel there was always a chance that he might run into somebody he didn't want to see.

The hotel's cashier held court over a narrow gray marble counter. He was a young man in a well-cut double-breasted suit and slicked-back hair that looked as if he had just stepped out of a shower. "Was everything satisfactory?" His voice suggested that it would be impossible for Frash not to have been satisfied; here nothing less than complete satisfaction was allowed.

"How much?" Frash asked.

The cashier passed the bill to him on a small silver plate. Frash paid in cash.

"You're leaving Italy?" the man inquired.

"No—" He didn't finish the sentence. Ali cursed Albert's stupidity. Tell him nothing.

"May I see your passport?" the clerk asked.

Frash stiffened. What the hell was going on? He smiled and began patting his pockets. "I must have left it in my briefcase."

The cashier smiled. "I'll wait." This new rule was unnecessary because it disturbed the guests, but the directive had come from the general manager, and a rule was a rule. The passport numbers of all guests were to be recorded and forwarded to the police. He guessed that they were searching for someone, but why at the Excelsior? This was not a place where undesirables congregated. The Excelsior had three stars and was a special place for only the best people. It was an insult to irritate guests with this sort of nonsense. Tawdry and regrettable, to be sure, but it was required.

It's nothing, Frash told himself. He could try to wheedle his way out, but he saw that the young cashier was the sort of dutiful employee who did what he was told. Ali wondered if the man would scream just before his neck snapped; Albert overrode the impulse. No scene, it's nothing. This is routine; besides, the passports are untraceable. Frash pulled the document from an inside pocket and slapped it on the marble counter. "Must have missed it."

The cashier bowed, slid the passport off the marble top, disappeared through blue curtains, and was back in less than five minutes. When the document was returned to him Frash stuffed it in his pocket and walked downstairs.

The cashier went to the window that faced the street and saw the man walking with a woman pushing a bicycle; she glanced backward as they walked. For a moment he thought it was the Fregosi woman, but how could this be? She was a confirmed man hater. Impossible, he concluded; your eyes played a trick on you.

---

116 · THURSDAY, APRIL 20, 1961, 11:50 P.M. *Alexandria, Virginia*

Earlier in the evening Arizona had spent two uncomfortable hours with Allen Dulles. A cable had arrived from the Brits and he was anxious to follow up on it, but when Dulles marched into your office you were there for as long as he wanted. The CIA director was tall and distinguished-looking, with pink skin and rimless spectacles that barely covered his eyes; he had a receding hairline with short white hair on the sides brushed neatly back like wings, a neatly trimmed white mustache, a prominent chin and a Scottish briar pipe that hung straight down from the corner of his mouth. A flap of skin hung over his Adam's apple and showed his age. His customary dark suit and polished black shoes created a funereal impression.

"I offered the president my resignation," Dulles said matter-of-factly.

"His reaction?"

"None, which is tantamount to acceptance." Arizona offered no commiseration. These things happened, and Dulles understood it better than any of them. "Dick Bissell will have to go too. Ultimately this was his show. The fundamental plan was sound, but the president wouldn't authorize the necessary air support, and that doomed us. Nevertheless we made enough errors of our own, and for this our critics will exact a price. Our information about the level of opposition among the natives was wrong; they were not ready to revolt. The people may loathe Castro and his regime, but not enough to risk their lives. In any event we failed to alert rebel leaders of the invasion times, so there was no possibility of a coordinated uprising even if they were so inclined. Too many serious errors in analysis and execution. Our Cubans fought beyond expectations, but the landing sites were poorly chosen and we gave them no escape option."

"By design," Arizona reminded him. "There's no better motivation for going forward than the sea at your back." Normandy was the classic example.

"I understand the reasoning, but I reject the philosophy; it grew out of prejudice, not strategy. We feared that the Cubans would be less brave than white boys."

"The Cubans are amateurs."

"We defeated the Nazis and the Japs with amateurs," Dulles reminded him. "Congress and the press will have a heyday with the Bay of Pigs. I expect lots of investigators to use this sad event as a way to probe into our organizational marrow. There are a lot of people who can't or won't understand the nature of clandestine conflict; they argue that covert operations violate the spirit of the Constitution."

What Dulles was saying was true. Arizona tugged a drooping sock up his leg. When Dulles wanted a reaction, he would look at him. The director believed in orderly, sequential communications, not sloppy give-and-take.

"The timing of the invasion is being questioned by the president's brother," Dulles said. "There is something both honorable and frightening about that man. 'Why now?' he asked me. 'Couldn't we have waited?' "

Arizona cringed inwardly. The answer was because REBUS had led them to believe that MiGs would soon be deployed, information that could not be reverified now that Frash had disappeared and Lumbas was dead.

Allen Dulles rubbed the back of his neck, exhaled a smoke ring and looked for the first time in Arizona's direction.

"Bobby Kennedy is a zealot," Arizona said.

"Worse," Dulles responded. "I suspect he has his own political agenda." The director set his pipe on the desk. "What about the asset who provided the information on the Cuban pilots? REBUS?"

"I don't understand." Arizona's stomach was tightening.

"The timing of the operation was based on your asset's information."

"It was and is accurate. Cuban pilots will rotate from Czechoslovakia in early June. The Russians are giving them MiG 17s." Dulles knew nothing about Frash or the identity of his Russian asset, and Arizona wanted desperately to move the discussion off this subject.

"The information needs reverification," Dulles said. "Bobby Kennedy is saying that there was not enough time to examine the invasion plan; he alleges that we pressed the administration. That timing could become a focal point of the failure, which means that *you* could have a problem."

Arizona did not volunteer his own resignation; clearly Dulles and Dick Bissell would bear the brunt. They would go, others would remain and this would ensure the continuity of the Company. The director's visit was a professional favor; Dulles was warning him before there was an official inquiry that his source of information should be sanitized. What this meant was left open to Arizona's interpretation.

"Khrushchev will take advantage of the Cuban failure," Dulles went on. "He'll probe everywhere, which means that operations in Western and Eastern Europe will take on increased importance. We'll need every man we have with experience in those theaters." He seemed almost relieved that he was leaving the fray. Translation: Save your own ass, and the Company's with it.

The meeting ended with an unenthusiastic handshake. There were no regrets, no nostalgic remembrances, only the business at hand, which was to clean up Operation Pluto's offal. Arizona did not care for Allen Dulles; he admired what the man had built and accomplished, but not the man himself. He was from old money, old connections and old values based on his own caste, which amounted to three or four hundred families in a dozen enclaves around the country. Not that Arizona was driven by the fires of egalitarianism, but in his philosophy people of merit could move up. In the director's world you were either born into the elite or you weren't. People like Dulles lived in a sort of velvet cocoon. He would resign and that would be that; he would still see the same people, think the same thoughts, have the same discussions. But if Arizona fell, it would be a long drop back to a cactus law practice in Phoenix and teaching an occasional course at the law school. It was a fall he intended to avoid, no matter what the cost, and the first step was to answer the coded wire from Sir John Cumming.

He made the call from a telephone booth on Highway 1. Two hundred meters away stood the Appomattox Confederate Memorial. Robert E. Lee had killed more Americans than Hirohito and Hitler combined, yet there was a fucking statue of him standing in the same city he had attacked. The United States was full of maniacs.

The phone rang several times before it was picked up. "Cumming here," a sleepy voice said.

"Got your wire."

"Didn't expect such a prompt reply," Sir John said. "Rather suspected that our cousins might be busy mopping the decks. Bloody bad luck with our bearded friend. I read a report once that said he was protected by voodoo. Do you suppose there's any truth to it?"

"Nothing would surprise me. What's up?"

"One of the passports has shown up. Thought you might like to know. It was in the possession of a gentleman who checked out of the Excelsior Hotel in Venice. It's on the Lido."

He knew the place. It was a hideaway for the wealthy. "When?"

"Cheeky to live so high. He checked out this morning. The hotel reported the number to the carabinieri, who passed it on to Interpol. Their computer spit it out this afternoon. Reassuring to know that our Continental allies can follow a simple procedure."

"They were supposed to process the numbers at check-in."

"Yankee optimism."

"Where was he headed?"

"Sorry, old boy, haven't heard anything, but if he crosses the bloody border again, we'll nick him. Thought you might like to have the first crack at following up on this." Cumming then offered the use of what he called a speciality unit, but Arizona politely refused. "You'll make sure that my people have a chat with this desperado when you apprehend him? Don't know your angle, old chum, and wouldn't pry—professional respect and so forth—but he did cost us an important asset. A matter of form, you know. Need to assure ourselves that it amounts to simple theft and nothing more sinister. Left to me, I wouldn't even raise the issue, but we all have our procedural goblins. Can we count on your cooperation?"

"Your position is crystal clear," Arizona said by way of evasion. What he really wanted was to tell Cumming to go fuck himself. British intelligence had been crawling with Soviet agents and Commie sympathizers for at least twenty years. The fact that the Russians rarely defected to the Brits suggested that would-be defectors knew that Her Majesty's Secret Service was badly compromised. "We'll stay in touch."

"Good hunting," Cumming said before hanging up.

As soon as he could find his hunters.

FRIDAY, APRIL 21, 1961, 7:15 A.M.
Moscow

Talia and Bailov made straight for the hospital, where Talia immediately called Ezdovo and asked him to join the team there.

Bailov went to Petrov's room and found Melko snoring loudly on one of the beds, but there was no sign of the patient or the doctor. He gave the bottom of Melko's left foot a sharp whack and backpedaled to a safe distance; the former criminal instantly bolted out of the bed cursing, his fists chopping the air with lethal intent. "Where's Petrov?" Bailov asked.

Melko shook his head in an effort to clear it and stared at the bed where their leader had been.

When Talia joined them her eyes also went directly to the empty bed, then to Melko and Bailov. "Where is he?"

"He was here when I fell asleep," Melko sputtered.

"You bray like a bloody ass when you sleep," Petrov complained from the bathroom door. "A dead man couldn't stand such a racket." Their leader was fully dressed and standing under his own power. His coloring was still poor and his eyes were sunken, but otherwise he looked improved. "Call me Lazarus," he said.

Gnedin arrived moments later and was followed almost immediately by Ezdovo, who looked drawn and tense. He moved to his wife's side but made no attempt to embrace her. "I'm glad you're back," he whispered.

"Miss me?"

"Don't leave me with that one again."

She knew he meant Khrushchev and understood his frustration. Guarding the man was like trying to keep a blanket on a dervish.

Petrov stared at Bailov. "It's gratifying to see you return to us." Bailov started to protest, but Petrov's wry smile stopped him. "What did the Americans have to say?"

"Lumbas is dead. Their agent called Frash was born Frascetti. That's the same surname as the Albanian who was Lumbas's comrade at the university."

"They had proof that Lumbas is dead?"

"He was killed in Belgrade," Talia said. "The Americans showed us a photograph of their man and ours together, and another photograph of Lumbas in a Belgrade morgue. The Americans believe that Lumbas was killed by Russians. He was passing classified information to the Americans, but they believe that this may have been secondary to his primary interest."

Petrov was listening carefully. "Which was?"

"The Americans have evidence that Frash and Lumbas tried to mount an operation against Albania. Frash's parents were Albanian expatriates involved with groups sworn to overthrow Enver Hoxha. The son may have tried to continue this."

"You told them that Lumbas and his university comrade were Albanian?"

"We withheld that information," she said.

One of Petrov's eyebrows moved ever so slightly. "Why?"

"A mixture of instinct and logic," Talia admitted. She couldn't explain it any better than that.

"Logic separates man from animal," Petrov said.

"Man *is* animal," she came back. "Our logic sometimes obscures this."

Petrov nodded. "An interesting perspective."

"The Americans asked for a meeting. They laid out the whole thing, and it was our impression that the exchange was straightforward." She looked at Bailov and got a supportive nod. "We felt that they held nothing back from us."

"Yet you held back from them," Petrov said.

"Truth is often the perfect lie," she said. "We believe they were being open, but what if they knew only what their superiors wanted them to know? If Lumbas passed them information about the rocket program, why would they tell us? Even if he's dead, why reveal the secret? Why give up what nobody knows you have?"

"Paranoia is a powerful force," Petrov said. "It's also what keeps people like us alive." He turned to Gnedin who had been looking into the Albanian situation from another perspective.

Gnedin took a deep breath, then spoke softly. "There were radio reports out of Tirana of an attempted coup last year. They claimed that the Americans, Yugoslavs and Greeks were involved."

"The Americans say they have a source in Paris who claims that Frash was the architect of such a plan," Talia said.

"The Albanians say they have arrested all the conspirators," Gnedin said.

"Expatriates were murdered in France," Talia added.

"How did the Albanians discover the operation?" Petrov asked. The group was silent. "We need to know this." He looked at Talia. "Was it your thought that the Americans mounted an operation, and when it was discovered perhaps tried to implicate the Soviet Union?"

"Lumbas is dead, and presumably the Americans have already absorbed and analyzed what information he passed to them," she said. "To disclose that they had penetrated such a classified operation requires a comprehensive security revaluation on our part; such a critical loss requires a strong reaction. People, procedures, everything would have to be re-vetted and reexamined. More important, this could create a level of paranoia that might slow down our missile development. As for Albania, if there was a legitimate attempt to overthrow the regime and it failed, what better way to cover it than to make the Albanians think that we were partners in the effort? Lumbas is dead and their man is missing, so there is no way to confirm anything. Telling us that there may have been a combined effort by one of their people and one of ours has the same effect as unmasking Lumbas as a traitor. If we try to investigate officially any activity against Albania, it's likely to simply reconfirm the Albanians' suspicions. We thought it best to discuss it with the team before revealing that Lumbas and Frascetti were Albanians."

"I agree with what you've done," Petrov said, "but not necessarily with your assessment."

"What if Lumbas was *sent* to the Americans?" Melko suggested. "Let's say for the purpose of discussion that there was in fact a plan to provoke Albania, and that this came not from Lumbas but from those who pulled him out of Tyuratam."

"If the Soviet Union wanted to crush Albania militarily, it could do so in a matter of days," Gnedin interjected.

"I didn't say 'crush,' I said 'provoke,'" Melko said. "There were once three rival gangs in Georgia. The first arranged a provocation against number three so that it seemed to come from the second group. The third gang reacted by declaring war on the second, and when it was finished the real provocateurs stepped in and destroyed what remained of the two rival groups. Now this group controls Georgia."

Petrov stared at the wall for a long time. "It's plausible," he said finally, "but for the analogy to apply, the second and third groups would have to be nearly equal in strength to the first group."

"They were," Melko said.

"Which is not true if we name the gangs U.S., U.S.S.R. and Albania," Petrov said.

"What if we call them Albania, a faction in the U.S. and a faction in the U.S.S.R.?" Talia asked.

"The Americans believe that Lumbas was murdered by Soviets," Bailov said. "Which is not exactly standard procedure."

"Khrushchev knew nothing of a wet operation against Lumbas," Petrov said, picking up Bailov's point. "Yet *someone* in the Soviet Union moved him from his duties at Tyuratam and sent him to Yugoslovia. There is ample reason to conclude that the real enemy is inside our borders," he concluded. "What do the Americans plan to do?"

"Continue to search for their own man," Talia said.

"What do they expect from us?"

"Consultation," Bailov said. "If they can find and capture their man, they promise to share what they learn. I believe them."

"As do I," Talia said.

"Where do we focus?" Petrov asked as he reached for a towel. Talia saw that he was prespiring heavily. "Who killed Lumbas? Who and where is the Frascetti in his past, and is he connected to this in some way?"

"We've already tried to backtrack Lumbas and our Frascetti," Gnedin reminded the group. "It's as if they never existed in the Soviet Union. What traces remain lead nowhere."

Bailov coughed quietly and chewed his lip. He had protected Yepishev and drawn Petrov's ire. Now there might be reason to protect somebody else, somebody so dear to him that his mouth seemed filled with cotton. "Perhaps we've been looking in the wrong place," he said mysteriously.

The others looked to him for an explanation. "Would you care to amplify that statement?" Petrov asked with an edge to his voice.

"Not at this time," Bailov answered.

118   FRIDAY, APRIL 21, 1961, 10:30 A.M.
Geneva

It was a blustery, sunny day with a clear blue sky and whitecaps snapping energetically on Lake Geneva. Valentine stood inside the door of the cottage and watched people prowling the grounds wearing gloves and scarves. He grinned and motioned for Sylvia to look. When she saw the nudists so attired she smiled too.

"Crazy," he said. "Why do people come to a place like this?"

"Good way to tell if your man has a wandering eye," Sylvia said. "Not fair."

"It's men who wander," she answered. "Not women."

A knock at the door sent Valentine scrambling for the bedroom.

When Sylvia returned she was carrying an envelope. "Maybe a love note from a secret admirer," she teased. "Could be somebody likes what he's seen."

Valentine wrapped his arms around her and pulled her into bed. "Let's play plumber," he whispered.

"I should read the mail first," she said, pushing him away. "Business before pleasure." She tore open the sealed envelope and seconds later was up and grabbing for her clothing.

"What is it?" he groaned.

"It's from Arizona," she said, tossing the message to him.

The note read, "One of twelve has shown up at the Excelsior Hotel, Venice. Assess ASAP." He stared at the note and watched her as she pulled on her sweater. "Frash," he said.

"Pretty good guess," she said, buttoning her skirt.

"I'm really starting to hate that son of a bitch," Valentine grumbled as he rolled off the bed and searched for his clothes.

119   FRIDAY, APRIL 21, 1961, 8:55 P.M.
Moscow

Bailov arrived first and waited in the lobby. Raya came in a few minutes later. She wore a long overcoat, a dark print dress and flat black shoes, all of which were part of her professional disguise. "I assume you have a good reason for such a public meeting," she greeted him icily.

He took her coat and traded it for a red plastic claim check. The Peking was one of Moscow's finest restaurants and there was a large crowd in the cavernous, poorly lit lobby. He took Raya by the arm and led her through the crowd to the headwaiter, a tall Oriental with a shaved head and a goatee. "No room tonight," he said before Bailov could speak. "Full up."

Bailov smiled and slipped a one-ruble note to the man, who immediately changed his attitude. "Right this way," he said with too much enthusiasm. "Best table in the house." Which meant the best for the price.

The dining room was twenty meters high and dimly lit. Brightly painted dragon heads stared down from the top of square columns; the room was filled with the blue haze of cigarettes. "I don't like this," Raya said when they were seated. "Our relationship is private."

"We need to talk."

She smiled and shook her head. "Even a lunatic knows you can't talk in a Russian restaurant." As if on cue, a five-piece band struck up a song, sending the sound bouncing around the room to obliterate a hundred conversations.

Bailov waved at a nearby waiter who refused to make eye contact.

When he held up a folded five-ruble note the man immediately came over to the table and bowed. "There will be more if the service warrants it," Bailov said as the man palmed the bill.

The dance floor was filled. Half a dozen men in air force uniforms used a red blanket to toss a small woman into the air. She squealed, the airmen cheered, dancers clapped, shouts rose from tables, vodka flowed, food came slowly, the smoke thickened. "I need help," Bailov said over the noise.

Raya kicked off her shoe and stuck her foot up his trouser leg. "You're all the way across the table," she complained.

"I'm serious," he said.

"Me too."

"You once told me about Albania," he said. She had been there many times to study her beloved birds.

"I've told you many things about my life. I can't say that my openness has been reciprocated."

He ignored the complaint. "There was something specific about a man you met at a reception. A historian, I think. He claimed he was compiling a list of traitors, sympathizers of Zog, the former king."

She gave him a hard look. "I don't think I'm going to like this."

"Do you remember?"

She wished she didn't. Her Albanian friend Debra said that the man was affiliated with Sigurimi, the Albanian secret police, and that in public trials he had often served as a state's witness, his knowledge leading to several executions. Dozens of people were in jails or concentration camps because of him, and he used his power immorally. Debra herself had been forced to sleep with him several times and loathed him, but her teaching position at the university was important to her and she was resigned to doing whatever was necessary to keep it. It's not so much, she had rationalized. On meeting him Raya had behaved as she was instructed and had praised Stalin several times at the reception. The Albanians had loved the Soviet dictator, and Khrushchev's denouncement of him in 1956 had angered them. After the party the history professor had cornered her outside and tried to force his hand up her dress, but she was menstruating and this had saved her.

"Vaguely," she lied. She wanted no part of the memory. "Why are you interested in some dull story? Albania is drab and depressing. Only its birds warrant interest."

"I have to ask you something."

She sensed something terrible in the offing and it twisted her stomach into knots. "*Have* to? You've been ordered to ask me something?"

"It's my idea, just mine. If you say no, it will not change what we have together."

"Life is hard, Taras Ivanovich. A simple question can alter relationships. Is what you have to ask me worth such a risk?"

Their eyes locked. "It's a matter of duty."

"To whom?"

Bailov was not certain. "Duty is always a matter of individual choice," he said finally.

"Duty is imposed by circumstance," Raya said. The band had taken a break and the restaurant had quieted to a low buzz of voices.

"I want you to go to Albania," he said. "The historian you met may have certain records of critical importance."

"To whom?" She was tense now, her jaw set.

"National security."

"You're a Chekist," she said, her horror undisguised.

"No, I'm only a soldier."

"Soldiers do not ask civilians to perform tasks unless there is a war."

"Not all wars are openly declared."

She pushed back from the table and flung her arms up in frustration. "I have no choice."

"It will be dangerous," he said. "I want you to know that before you decide. If you say no, I'll understand."

"It's not possible for me to refuse you."

"You don't understand."

"No, it's you who don't understand," she whispered. "I can't say no to the man I love."

Her answer made him queasy. It was the worst moment of his life.

| 120 | FRIDAY, APRIL 21, 1961, 10:20 P.M.
Murano, Italy |
|---|---|

The police on the Lido were unexpectedly efficient. They had the passport number from the Excelsior and the name of the man who had phoned it in.

A thunderstorm had delayed their landing at the airport in Venice; the bay was foggy and water taxis crawled along tooting their foghorns. It was late afternoon when they finally reached the Excelsior.

The cashier's name was Bellini, the general manager told them; normally he worked the day shift, but because of today's weather he had not reported in. "He lives in Murano," he said. "It's an island." He waved his arm in the general direction and assured them that Bellini was a dependable employee. The general manager obviously sensed a serious problem and wanted to protect the Excelsior's reputation; he was red-faced and sweating heavily.

"We'll need a launch," Valentine said in a tone that suggested the general manager would provide the boat.

The man sighed. "Of course. I'm certain we can arrange something."

Murano is a small island with ancient stucco and brick buildings, a medieval hump looming in the fog and darkness, and surrounded by putrid black water. Its streets are narrow, barely as wide as the hallways in a small American house, and smell of age, mildew and raw sewage. The address was in an unlit alley with stone steps that led upward into the darkness. The lips of the steps were worn in the center and seemed to sag. How many feet and centuries had it taken to erode stone? Valentine wondered.

The apartment was several levels up. The young man who came to the door was short and thin. He wore a black silk robe and leather slippers. "*Si?*"

They showed him a photograph, but the light was poor and he had to step back to get a better look. It was a small place, one room with a black iron stove, several anemic plants in clay pots and a hammock for a bed. "What do you want to know?" he asked nervously.

"Do you recognize him?" Sylvia asked.

Bellini passed the photo back. "I see thousands of people every year. It's their wallets I remember. My job is to see that they pay. The concierge remembers faces; that's *his* job." He raised his arms and tried to shoo them toward the door. "Please excuse me," he said.

"You forwarded his passport number," Sylvia said. She held up the photo again. "We don't want to cause trouble for you," she said, turning on her charm.

"Faces mean nothing." The anonymity of guests was the cardinal rule of the Excelsior.

Suddenly Valentine grabbed the man's face and squeezed his cheeks. "Even your own? Faces are delicate things. Bone, tissue and millions of nerves. Injure a muscle and it recovers, but not a face. Damage persists."

The cashier reached for the photograph again.

"We're waiting," Valentine said.

"The face is familiar. I see that now."

"You remember him?"

The man shook his head slowly. "Familiar, that's all. I'm sorry." He remembered the man, of course, though he had changed since the photograph had been taken. He was light blond now, with a short, neatly trimmed beard and heavy glasses, but it was him. He made it a practice to memorize faces; he wouldn't always be a cashier. Someday he would be the general manager of a fine establishment and then it would be his job to remember faces, at least the important ones. Also to practice discretion, this being an equally essential value. "I'm sorry," he repeated, averting Valentine's angry eyes.

Sylvia made eye contact with Valentine, who in releasing Bellini gave him a hard shove. "We're registered at the Excelsior," she said. "As guests of the general manager," she lied. "We're meeting him tomorrow at eight A.M. If you remember anything, please see us." She left the photograph on a table.

Valentine stopped at the door and pointed at the cashier. "It's important that we find this man," he said. "Extremely important. Your general manager understands this and is helpful. We wouldn't like to report that one of his people is uncooperative, or . . ." He smiled and said *"Arrivederci"* as they left.

"He recognized Frash," Sylvia said. "It was in his eyes."

Valentine grinned. "I know."

"Would you have hurt him?"

"Don't know," he said. What he didn't add was that in the old days he would have cut off the little bastard's head if it meant getting what he needed.

121   FRIDAY, APRIL 21, 1961, 11:40 P.M.
Tirana, Albania

"One more time," Haxi Kasi said. "Go." He started the stopwatch.

Lejla brought the weapon to her chest with both hands and rapidly fired nine rounds into the carcass of a goat suspended on a rope. All nine rounds struck the chest, five in a tight cluster, the other four slightly scattered. With these explosive bullets any of the hits would have been lethal.

"Rest," Kasi said. "Weapon down." She did as she was told. "New target." She slid the shattered carcass to one side and swung another into place. The room was cold and the girl was nude, her lips blue. Numb all sensations, Kasi had told himself, gut her values, keep her confused. It was going beautifully; whatever he asked she did without hesitation, and her shooting was consistent now. Her ears were unprotected, but she no longer flinched. He wanted her accustomed to the sound of the shots and slugs smashing real bone and tissue. "Back up," he said. "Kneel." When she was down he picked up a can filled with fresh goat's blood and dumped it over her head. No reaction. He held out a new clip. "Load." She pulled out the empty clip, let it fall to the floor, inserted the new clip and locked a round in the chamber. "Just under ten seconds that last time," he said. "We need to have you under eight."

Steam rose off the blood that covered her. She folded her right index finger, mopped her eyes clear and raised the pistol.

122 SATURDAY, APRIL 22, 1961, 7:00 A.M.
The Lido, Venice

The bell to their suite sounded a sequence of harplike notes. Valentine answered the door. The cashier's hair was slicked back, his cheeks pinched with color, his charcoal-gray uniform crisp and pressed, brass buttons sparkling and black shoes freshly shined, but he looked drawn and his eyes were red as if he had not slept. *"Buon giorno,"* Valentine said.

Bellini thrust the photograph and a carbon copy of a hotel bill at him. The man's name was Albert Van Geer, Dutch passport, from Amsterdam, here as a tourist. Valentine saw that the passport number matched one on their list. "He's changed," the man continued. "He's no longer the same as in the photograph, but I recognized him. His hair is blond and he has a beard, a small one. Dark glasses with thick lenses."

Sylvia came out of the bedroom wearing a white terrycloth robe with the Excelsior crest over her left breast.

"He checked in late the afternoon of April 15 and checked out the morning of April 20."

"Did he have a reservation?" Sylvia asked.

"No."

"But the Excelsior is an exclusive establishment," she said. "Can anybody just walk in and get a room so easily?"

"There are exceptions, but our business here is basically seasonal. Even at peak we hold a few rooms open. Signor Van Geer asked for one of our better rooms."

"Did he pay cash?"

"Yes, in lire."

Sylvia and Valentine exchanged glances. As elsewhere, money talked at the Excelsior.

"What did the money look like?" Valentine asked. The cashier seemed puzzled. "Was it rumpled, well used?"

"Crisp," Bellini said after a moment. "As if it were new."

Banks often paid large withdrawals with new bills, Valentine thought. "Where did he go?" he asked.

"He didn't say."

"Was he alone?"

"Yes," the cashier said. "Just him."

"Did he act funny?"

Again the man looked confused. Sylvia interceded. "Was there anything about his behavior that seemed odd or unusual?"

"Only when I asked for his passport. He said it was in his briefcase but then he found it in his pocket."

"What was odd about that?" Sylvia asked.

Bellini paused. "He seemed upset. Perhaps confused is a better word, but I didn't really think about it. People with money don't like to be bothered with details, so it seemed normal that he would not like to be asked for his passport."

"Still, it caught your attention."

The man shrugged. "For a moment I had the feeling that he would walk away without giving it to me."

"He tried to walk away?"

"No, it was only a feeling, but I insisted on having the passport and then he found it in his jacket."

"How much baggage did he have?" Sylvia asked.

"One suitcase of dark leather. Very expensive. It looked new. No scars or blemishes."

"He left as soon as he paid?"

"Yes. He went down the front steps."

"Did somebody take his bag for him?"

"He carried it himself."

"You're sure he was alone?"

"Yes."

"Did he take a launch or a cab? Did anyone pick him up?"

"He just walked down the street," the cashier said. "There was a woman beside him, pushing a bicycle."

Sylvia jumped on this. "You saw him walk down the street?"

"From the window."

"With a woman?"

The cashier wrinkled his brow. "I thought for a moment that I knew her. I thought it was a local woman, Sultana Fregosi. She owns a tailor shop not far from here. But that couldn't be."

"Why not?" Sylvia asked.

"I'm not sure it was her, and in any event it's impossible. She doesn't like men. Everyone in the Lido knows this."

Sylvia's intuition was in high gear. "But initially you said you thought it was her. That was your first impression."

"But when I saw the face I knew it was impossible."

"You saw her face?"

"It was more a profile, a flash of the side of her face."

"But you thought it was the woman who runs the tailor shop. What's her name again?"

"Fregosi. Sultana Fregosi. She's very striking, but as I said, she's not a man's woman."

"All right," Sylvia said. "Anything else?" she asked Valentine.

"That's all for now."

"You'll tell the general manager I cooperated?" the cashier asked.

Sylvia smiled. "You've been very helpful."

"One last thing," Valentine said.

"Anything," Bellini said, clearly glad that his business with them was nearly finished.

"Check with the concierge and everyone else to find out if anything was delivered to Van Geer while he was here." Valentine knew that exclusive tailor shops the world over provided personal service to customers who stayed in places like the Excelsior.

"Right away."

Bellini was back in an hour. "One of our domestics saw Fregosi in the hotel on Wednesday morning," he reported.

"What time?" Valentine asked.

"Early."

"Business hour early or earlier?"

"Much earlier," the man said. It was astonishing, but the maid was adamant that it had been Fregosi.

"Where is her shop?"

Bellini gave them directions.

The façade of the building was fashionably shabby, but the inside was plushly carpeted and the walls filled with pigeonholes stuffed with bolts of expensive cloth. Sylvia went in and pretended to look at the merchandise; Valentine followed several minutes later and asked to see the manager.

Sultana Fregosi wore a white blouse and a pale blue linen skirt. Her short black hair was slightly damp and she had sunglasses propped on top of her head. Immediately she sized him up. "A large frame," she said.

"We can make a nice suit for you and give you a good price." She reached for a bolt of tan cloth. "For summer," she said. "Italian wool. It breathes and keeps you cool."

She was aggressive in a pleasant way. "No suits," Valentine said. "Just looking."

"A double-breasted blazer, then? Or some shirts? We have very reasonable prices and guarantee our workmanship."

"No, thanks," Valentine said with a friendly smile. Sylvia was hunched over several bolts of cloth, but he saw her studying the layout.

American, Sultana Fregosi told herself, but not a rich one. His shoes said he was middle-class—a salesman, perhaps. You could always judge people by their shoes. "There must be something I can help you with." Adolf had been especially passionate this morning. She had intended to be in the shop at nine but he had been randy again, and after she had finished her bath and dressed he had coaxed her back to bed. So much passion! She had always thought of the Dutch as a stolid people, but not Adi. If she could get rid of the Americans and return to the house he would be ready again. What was it in men that made them so? She liked the idea that she excited him.

The American took a photo out of his coat and showed it to her. "Do you know this man? His hair is blond now, and he has glasses and a beard. He's an old friend of mine. He's supposed to be vacationing here and I'd like very much to see him. He'll enjoy the surprise."

"Why ask me?"

"He has a fetish for clothes," Valentine said. Pretty lame, he thought. You're losing your touch.

She tried not to show her surprise. It was Adolf in the photo; he was thinner now and his hair was different, but it was him. "No," she said. "Sorry." Could this American really be her Adi's friend? Something inside her urged caution. Was he in trouble? He had said virtually nothing about his past, and she had not pressed him because for now it didn't matter. Then it struck her. What if he went away? It dawned on her that she had assumed he would be permanent, like a favorite chair, a possession; his departure would bring terrible loneliness. His libido was overwhelming, but it was a small price to pay for company; besides, most of the time it felt rather pleasant. To be single was to be alone; having found Van Geer, she had no desire to return to her old life, but how should she tell him about this? She turned on her charm for the American. "If there's nothing else, I have work. You're certain you don't want a suit? We do excellent work."

Valentine thanked her for her time, went outside and crossed to the grassy median on the boulevard. Sylvia joined him a few minutes later. "She's seen him," she said. Valentine waited for an explanation. "She has the look."

"Which look is that?"

"Give me a break," she said. "I saw it in her eyes when you showed her the photo. She knows him."

"We'll wait," Valentine said, sitting down.

"For what?"

"Until she comes out. Then we'll follow her. This close to Frash, we pursue every possibility. The sooner we nail this asshole the sooner we can say adios to all this shit."

Sylvia sat down on the grass and hiked her skirt up to her knees. "Going to be hot," she said. The air was heavy enough to cut.

"I'll take the back," Valentine said.

She watched him dart between two red automobiles and disappear down the block, not bothering to look back. When this was over would he also disappear without looking back?

---

123   SATURDAY, APRIL 22, 1961, 11:00 P.M.
The Lido, Venice

Valentine appeared out of the darkness and sat down on the grass beside Sylvia. The shops in the area had closed two hours earlier. "Did we miss her?" she asked.

"Maybe she's still inside."

"No lights, and the rest of her employees left two hours ago. One of them locked the doors."

"Maybe she lives above the place."

"No lights up there either, and no curtains. If there was somebody up there we'd know."

He saw that she was right. "Maybe she turned into a bat and flew away." They both smiled.

"I'm starved," Sylvia said.

There was a café at the end of the block with a blue-and-white tile floor and sepia photographs of gondolas tacked to the wall. They ordered antipasto and pasta with clams. A dry red wine puckered their mouths.

Their waiter was friendly. "Tourists?" he asked.

"For a few days."

"Good time to be here. Too hot in the summer." He rolled his eyes and snapped his hand like a whip for added effect.

When Valentine asked about the Fregosi woman, the waiter made a face. "*That* one," he said, not finishing his sentence. "But she makes good suits if you can afford them."

"We were supposed to meet her tonight, but we were late. What time does she get to the shop in the morning?"

"She opens up at ten, just like the rest of us."

"Does she come in from Venice?"

The waiter grinned. "She walks."

Valentine looked confused and the man seemed amused by this. "She lives close by?"

Another nod, and a raised eyebrow. "Ninety seconds."

Valentine pointed up. "Above the shop?"

"Behind it," the waiter said. "It's her grandfather's house. There's a passageway under the alley. It's not unusual on the Lido; in the old days there were smugglers here, especially after the war."

"Convenient," Sylvia chimed in.

"Not for me," the man said. "Too close to work. But for her, work is all she has. God's will, I think, that she's alone, since she's not hard on the eyes. Me, I live an hour away. When I close up, I'm finished." He brushed his hands together. "I don't think about work when it's over, and even if I did it's too far to come back."

"A tunnel," Valentine repeated.

"Directly under the shop," the man said. "A hundred meters long."

They could see the house from the alley. It was surrounded by a high wall with pieces of broken glass on top. "You climb," Sylvia said.

She circled to the side that fronted on the lagoon; on the far shore of the bay the lights of Venice twinkled seductively and she saw the lights of boats on the water. Valentine found the ground-floor patio door closed and locked. He got in from an oak tree, crossing to the second-floor balcony with a short leap, and explored for ten minutes, then came out the front door and trotted down to the shore. A seawall held back waves. There was a cement building with a flat roof. He looked inside; it was a boat slip. There were fresh gasoline fumes and the sea doors were open. He opened the gate and Sylvia joined him. "They're gone," he said. "By boat."

"Maybe she likes midnight rides."

"There were whiskers in a bathroom sink and a space in the closet, as if somebody had pulled out a bunch of clothes. Two cups and plates. Only one cup had lipstick."

"We'd better get help," Sylvia said wearily.

124   MONDAY, APRIL 24, 1961, 12:38 P.M.
Tirana, Albania

By Party edict there were no streetlamps after dark, and the lights in all buildings were blacked out in the same paranoid way that Moscow was darkened. This practice was a legacy from Stalin, now fallen and, like Tirana's lights, only a dark memory. In Albania a siege mentality still reigned.

By 9:00 P.M. everything was dark, but it was still too early for her task. Taras Ivanovich had been explicit in his instructions: Give them time to get to sleep. She still did not understand why she had agreed to do this. Love, that accursed word again! Lust is a better motivation, she reminded herself; at least it's short-term, over and done with and no looking back—or ahead. Love made you think in terms of the future, which was always a mistake. *Now* was the only time frame with power. It was her own fault, she knew; she could have refused him, and she had wanted to, but he had made it impossible by not pressing her. At night when they lay pressed against each other in the darkness she had told him of her research trips to Albania and about her friend Debra; Taras Ivanovich had listened more attentively than she had realized. Mostly she had talked about birds but sometimes had drifted to other subjects: the lack of automobiles in the backward little country, its bland food, the lack of recreation, distorted Albanian values, little laughter, sex only for procreation, the pervasive drabness.

Her friend Debra Jelisu had taken her to official receptions at the university and to an occasional gathering of friends and colleagues. These were afternoon affairs, and by and large polite. Albanian academics lacked ardor; even in small groups of established friends opinions seldom strayed from what was politically correct, which struck Raya as odd. At home, especially in private, Russian academics were quick to criticize the system and its failings, but in Tirana she heard no such criticism; even Debra, who was more sister than colleague, refused to engage in such talk unless they were outside, and then only when they were alone.

Despite Albanian circumspectness, Raya had heard bits and pieces about life in the backward country. She did not remember telling Bailov about the historian who was cataloging events of the pre-Party days and had compiled a list of traitors who supported Zog; schoolchildren, he had proclaimed with righteousness, would use his work to memorize the names of their sworn enemies. She remembered similar lists from her youth; getting even was a new regime's first order of business. Certainly she had no more than mentioned the man as one more gull in a cacophonous flock of scavengers, but Bailov had remembered, filed it away and played it back. Though she had agreed to come to Tirana, she still did not understand the real reason why it was important. It's too dangerous, Taras Ivanovich had told her; it's better you don't know.

He had questioned her closely. Did she know if the man had an office? Yes, she thought it was in the same hall with the other members of the social sciences department. How difficult would it be to get into his office? Nothing is locked, she reminded him; it was the law. Officially there was no crime in Albania, so locks were not only unnecessary but an open refutation of the Party's declaration. He asked her to get information from the historian's file and she had agreed, then wondered if this was the start of just what she had always feared. She had friends and colleagues who had been stupid enough to be drawn into the darker corners of the system, and at a terrible price. Once you were in, there was no way out.

There was no moon when Raya finally slipped into the night air dressed in black. Lone security men patrolled the area but did not enter the university offices—another edict. It was three hundred meters to the building that housed the social sciences department. Once she had to stop and duck into the shadows while a guard lit a cigarette, the flame briefly illuminating his features. She was acutely aware of her frayed nerves. Were there people who did this sort of thing all the time, or did it fall to innocent citizens to do their dirty work for them? Her anger had not yet dissipated—anger with herself as much as with men, who were forever using women in their games. Why had she thought Taras Ivanovich would be different?

She got into the building without being detected and began her search immediately. Names were not painted on the office doors because individuals had no importance. She had no choice but to go from room to room and hope that there were no academicians with nocturnal habits. The office she sought was at the far end of the first floor, one above ground level. She could not remember the professor's name until she found his appointment book. The room's walls were lined with black metal filing cabinets, which gleamed under her flashlight beam. The cabinets were locked. She fought her anxiety and tried to think. In the basement she found a maintenance room with tools scattered, as if somebody had walked away in mid-task. She took a screwdriver. The drawers resisted but with some effort she opened them. The files were alphabetical within each drawer, but there was no system from drawer to drawer. The front of the alphabet was next to the back. She found the one she wanted in the fourth drawer, a thick folder marked FRASCETTI. The elder Frascetti had been married once; his wife had delivered a bastard before marrying him. Myslim was the first, Ali the second, both hers by different partners. There was a big age difference between the two. She photographed the papers, returned the folder to the drawer, put the screwdriver back and made her way out.

It was after 4:00 A.M. and the sky had clouded over. Aeroflot's special flight to Albania operated only twice a week, but Bailov had told her that this time there would be flights on three consecutive days, which would give her some options. He did not say it, but she sensed that he had the authority to arrange this, which heightened her fear. Who *was* he?

Returning to her hotel, Raya changed into a dress and fretted about the weather. How long would it be before someone discovered that the locks on the drawers had been forced? What if the weather made it impossible for her to fly? Though it was cool in the room, she spent the rest of the night worrying and perspiring heavily. When she got back to Moscow, she promised herself, she would take a long hot bath and give Taras Ivanovich a piece of her mind. Were there monsters who did this kind of work willingly? She felt nauseated. Damn him.

When she reached the airport the weather was marginal and deteriorating but there was no problem with her exit check. An older man in a gray uniform glanced at her passport and gave it back. "You should have stayed in your hotel," he said. "Even Soviet pilots can't fly in this soup." He grinned good-naturedly and picked up his copy of the Albanian Workers' Party newspaper.

There were three other passengers in the lounge, all males in ill-fitting suits. Two of them looked fresh, while the third needed a shave and had a fresh scratch down his left cheek; his light blue suit was badly wrinkled and the knees of his pants were soiled. Eventually an Aeroflot stewardess came in and motioned for them to follow her. She was short and heavy, with greasy brown hair and muscular calves.

They were halfway to the aircraft when four armed, uniformed men suddenly materialized from the mist and trotted toward them, their rifles angled upward. Raya froze. Had they discovered the break-in? Behind her she heard footsteps and turned to see the passenger in the blue suit running away. More armed men appeared and intercepted him; one of them calmly stepped forward and knocked the man down with a slow-motion sweep of his rifle butt. The man rolled over and over, holding his head. Albanian soldiers dragged him toward the terminal, and after they disappeared into the fog she heard shouts and a single gunshot. Her heart was racing and she had difficulty breathing as more soldiers led her and the two remaining passengers back to the terminal.

A handsome Albanian wearing a charcoal-gray sweater and black slacks came into the lounge and stared penetratingly at her and the other passengers. He was tall and slender, with dark hair graying on the sides. After a few moments he limped away. Then another Albanian in a black uniform entered and announced that no flights could leave because the weather was below minimum visibility. He did not offer an explanation of what they had just seen. Raya felt light-headed. Next an Aeroflot pilot arrived and began a hushed debate with several airport officials. The discussion lasted ten minutes; during this time the officials looked increasingly angry, until finally one of them threw up his hands in frustration and stalked away, slamming the door behind him.

The pilot grinned, then motioned for Raya and the two men to follow him. The clouds were now so low that she could no longer see the tower. The pilot fell into step with her. "Comrade Orlava?" he asked in a low voice.

"Yes," she said, her voice betraying her fear. "How can we fly in this?"

"Would you rather remain here?"

"No," she said with conviction.

When the man slipped his arm around her shoulders, she instinctively pulled away, but he held her tight and leaned close to whisper, "Relax. My colonel would skin me if I let anything happen to you now."

"Colonel?"

The answer was an acknowledging squeeze.

The aircraft was an antique trimotor with dents in the fuselage and faded decals. Wires hung off the left wing, a landing light was broken, and it was damp and cold inside. Raya tried to strap herself in but the seat belt was broken. She hoped that the engines were in better shape than the rest of the plane.

The pilot sat down beside her and lit a cigarette. "Shouldn't you be up there?" she asked, pointing at the cockpit.

"I'd only be in the way," he confessed. "A costume," he said, touching his tunic. "I'm not a pilot." He grinned. "Not even an officer," he added with pride.

She tensed when the aircraft began its takeoff and did not relax until one of the real pilots came back to fetch a cup of tea. When he passed he smiled at her. Raya turned her head away and tried to will herself to sleep; her relief at rescue was fast turning to anger at Taras Ivanovich.

125	**MONDAY, APRIL 24, 1961, 7:20 A.M.** *Venice*

Antonio Spinola sat on the foredeck of the *Palazzo*, puffing his pipe and enjoying the fresh morning air. The barge ahead of the tug was filled with chunks of shiny black coal. Was it really possible that coal could be squeezed down to diamonds? With a barge filled with diamonds he could buy a real boat, go to sea and be a real sailor. But wishes paid no bills or fed seven children, and his was not such a bad life, he reminded himself, especially with his son in the wheelhouse. The boy was only sixteen, but already he handled the tug with the confidence of a veteran. Spinola counted himself a lucky man.

"Papa," his son called down, waving to starboard.

Spinola followed the line of his son's arm, saw what appeared to be an empty boat in the distance and signaled the boy to steer toward it. There was no wake behind the derelict; another drifter, he grumbled. Damned pleasure boats; they were forever crapping out and getting in the way of working craft. Once he had found one filled with drunks asleep in their own puke. Another time it had been a big-bosomed woman and three naked men; they had thrown their clothes overboard, then run out of diesel fuel. He didn't bother to ask why. People—who could understand them? Sailors were different. They knew when to work and when to play, and they always respected the water.

The drifting boat was long and narrow, the sort of craft favored by old-time smugglers, but now toys for the rich who gunned them up and down the coast, spewing rooster tails. This one wallowed helplessly in soft swells. Spinola looked up at his son and drew a hand across his throat; the engines backed off, the transmission grinding as the boy reversed them, then idled in neutral. As his son maneuvered, the elder Spinola looped a heavy line over one of the drifter's chrome mooring posts and slowly pulled the two craft together. When the bow of the cigarboat swung around, he tightened the forward line and went aft to secure a second one. Capture complete, he told himself.

Spinola had always been fond of cigarboats, and this one was a beauty, well cared for, with a fresh coat of varnish. He stepped into the cockpit and yelled down the narrow passageway, "Anybody in there?" There was no answer. He moved forward, bending low to keep from striking his head. The front end had once been a hold, but now it contained a small stateroom. The bed had been used. He searched the remainder of the boat, including the tiny head, but found nothing. When he returned topside, he told his son to call the harbormaster on the ship-to-shore radio.

"Anybody?" the boy asked.

"Ghosts," Spinola said. "Only ghosts."

126   **MONDAY, APRIL 24, 1961, 6:50 P.M.**
Moscow

It was cool, but the air felt good after being cooped up on such a long flight. Raya Orlava eased her way down the crew ladder, hoping to find Bailov; instead she was confronted by a tall, striking woman with black hair and penetrating eyes. "Raya Orlava?"

"Yes."

"Taras Ivanovich sends his regrets."

Did the woman imply intimacy in the way she said his name? "I expected *him* to be here," she said. Fool! She knows that. Am I jealous? Best hide it.

The woman seemed to read her thoughts. "We're colleagues, that's all." Her smile seemed sincere, tuned perfectly to the voice. Raya countered with her own smile.

"Please come with me," the woman said, her tone suggesting that she was accustomed to being obeyed. Raya wanted to resist, but despite her position at the university, she was accustomed to listening to the voices of authority. One kept what one had by knowing when to submit.

The woman took her to a Pobeda parked near the airplane and they sped into the city using the express lane reserved for the Kremlin's big shots, ignoring traffic signals along the way while white-gloved traffic militia chased inattentive pedestrians out of their way. Eventually they reached a multistory building with a small sign that said CLINICAL ANNEX. Raya scanned the façade, but saw no bars or grates on the windows. At least it wasn't a psychiatric hospital; she had heard rumors about such places, which made them out to be even worse than Vladimir or Lubyanka. If you weren't crazy when they took you in, you would be when you got out—*if* you got out, which was the exception, not the rule. She gripped the railing to steady herself and followed her escort up the steps.

An elevator delivered them to a floor whose cleanliness amazed her; she had been through three abortions, all in places called hospitals, but run more like abattoirs. How was it that Soviet women marked their lives by abortions instead of by babies with fat, healthy faces? Abortion clinics were not painted white inside; they were built of cinder blocks, with cement floors like bunkers. This place sparkled; it was obviously intended for patients of a privileged class, and it intimidated her. Did those below her feel the same way in her presence? Probably, she decided. To be Russian was to live with fear inspired by differences. Did Taras Ivanovich fear anything? Control yourself, she ordered.

There were several men in the corridor. They had similar builds and haircuts and were all short, even by Soviet standards; white lab coats hung to their ankles. The men stepped out of her way, and despite her beauty made no lewd remarks. Very un-Russian. Were they eunuchs? They certainly weren't doctors.

The journey ended in a hospital room where a little man in a black robe sat on the edge of the bed staring at a plate of cabbage and a bowl of thick white pudding. He looked up. "You were successful?" He looked like a Gypsy, or perhaps a Jew.

Be careful, she thought. Use the old tricks; when faced with authority, play stupid. "Pardon?" Deafness was even more effective than ignorance.

The little man stared her down. "You were sent to Tirana to obtain certain information for us. Bailov says you are an intelligent and reliable woman. We're his colleagues and trust his judgment, and if you're his friend, you must also trust it. What you've done has been in the interests of national security."

What should she say? The little man looked drained, but his eyes were powerful. She took a deep breath, exhaled slowly and told him what she had found, then gave him the film.

"The two men were half brothers?" he asked.

"Yes."

"You're certain?"

"I'm trained to remember facts; the pictures will prove it."

There were no further questions. The tall woman led her to the door, where two men fell into step on either side of her. She felt small and powerless. "These men will escort you to your flat and stay with you until Taras Ivanovich can come."

"I can find my own way," Raya protested weakly. "This is Moscow, not Tirana."

"We can't allow you to be alone."

"I don't understand." Was there danger? Nothing made sense.

"Just do as we ask and everything will be fine," the woman said reassuringly.

When the elevator doors closed and it descended, Raya was overwhelmed by a sense that she was plummeting into a black void.

127

MONDAY, APRIL 24, 1961, 7:30 P.M.
Venice

Bartolomeo Tomme had made a fortune in the antique business, not because his offerings were superior to those of his competitors but because he knew how to merchandise his wares. Instead of Venice or Ravenna or Florence, Tomme operated from the relatively obscure town of Ancona on the Adriatic coast and employed elderly women to monitor the traffic of antique collectors in other cities. These grandmotherly women approached customers in their hotels and advised them that in Ancona there was a trove of antiques as good as anywhere else but less expensive. They explained that important Italians, having made their fortunes in the late nineteenth century in Italy's cities, retired to the Adriatic coast, where they had built huge villas and furnished them luxuriously. Now these people were gone and their descendants had fallen on hard times, which made magnificent antiques and paintings available. In a few years such items would make their way to big-city emporiums, where prices would be beyond all but the wealthiest collectors. The message was subtle but clear: Buy now or lose the opportunity. It was a pitch too compelling for bargain-hunting collectors to resist, so the old women pushed customers south while Tomme scoured the country for junk, which he sent to Ancona to be sold at inflated prices. It was a lucrative living, particularly because Tomme owned most of the hotels and several restaurants in the coastal town two hundred and forty kilometers south of Venice.

What gave Tomme an edge was not just his understanding of the psychology of bargain hunters, but his unerring instincts about all facets of his operations. It was this instinct that sent him to the navy's coastal service when a tug called *Marie III* was only four hours overdue from Venice. The tug was loaded with rolled canvases, sixteenth-century religious paintings by a sect of women who had lived in the Dolomites and painted them as an expression of their devotion to Christ. The works were hideous beyond belief but would net him a huge profit, which meant that he was not about to risk losing them. If anyone else had called the coastal service, he might have been ignored, but Bartolomeo Tomme was a much respected and powerful man who made sure naval officials received regular bribes.

Before the sun came up on the morning following the discovery of Sultana Fregosi's cigarboat, a patrol craft found the *Marie III* aground just south of the Po River delta. While the paintings were recovered, there was no sign of the crew. Having got the paintings back, Tomme had no further interest in what happened, but the coastal service and the police launched its customary search for survivors, the hunt concentrating on the area north of where the Po entered the sea. By midafternoon three bodies had been found and flown by helicopter to Venice in gray rubber bags.

Valentine and Sylvia had been summoned to the city morgue while the bodies were en route. The two dead men were employees of Bartolomeo Tomme; the dead woman was Sultana Fregosi. The last time they had seen her she had been flushed with life. Now her skin was blue-gray, with dark splotches; sea creatures and salt water had accelerated decomposition. Like the two men, she had been shot in the left eye by a 9 mm; all three had been split down the middle and their viscera removed. An old smuggler's technique, the police explained; if you remove the stomach and lungs the body stays down longer. In this instance, however, the killer or killers had not counted on the tides, and the bodies had been discovered in the tidal flats. Had they been dumped a few kilometers offshore, they would never have been found. Whoever did it, the police speculated, had been in a hurry.

Sylvia telephoned Monsieur Barrie at the Sûreté in Paris. Ballistics from the Lamoura corpse were wired to Venice, and by midnight they had a match. The prints recovered from Sultana Fregosi's house, her boat and the antique dealer's tug matched Frash's.

They had to guess at what had happened. Probably Fregosi had told Frash about their visit to the tailor shop, whereupon he persuaded her to go for a boat ride. In the lagoon he shut off the motor, pretended they were disabled and begged a ride from the passing tug. Farther down the coast he killed Fregosi and the two sailors, dumped their mutilated bodies overboard, beached the tug and went ashore.

Frash's trail had led from Belgrade to Lamoura to s'Hertogenbosch to Venice, with bodies as markers at most of the stops. They had been close this time but he was lost again, and for now there was no way to track him. Police agencies now had his photograph and immigration officials on the borders had the passport numbers; all they could do was pray that he didn't slip through a crack in the network.

354

128

MONDAY, APRIL 24, 1961, 8:25 P.M.
Moscow

Okhlopkin fidgeted in the front seat of the automobile and checked the two-way radio. The illuminated green light told him that it was on and operating properly. Often it wasn't. Surveillance was boring work, but what choice was there? Images of his Korean girlfriend tried to push the present aside, but he resisted. An officer should concentrate solely on his mission, he lectured himself.

His people had reported that the tall woman had escorted another woman into the hospital, and that they were still inside. If they came out, his men would see them and let him know. *His* men? They were wolf tickets and this was their last chance, soldiers who had tried to back out of their commitments to the Motherland or had screwed up and had toppled into the abyss, only to come crawling back to beg for a final chance. Gaponov argued that their desperation made them reliable for dirty work, but Okhlopkin doubted it; they were dog shit.

How long had it been since the women had gone inside?

"Sable One, Pup One. Are you receiving?" The voice on the radio sounded frantic.

The call signs were his creation and he liked hearing them over the radio. The sable was a smart, tough animal like himself, and these men were his children, his stupid pups. "Sable One hears you. Don't shout."

"The short woman just came out the back exit with two Spetsnaz. They got into a gray Pobeda."

"Tell me when they move," Okhlopkin said as he fumbled to start the motor.

"Do I follow them?" the voice queried.

"Stay where you are," Okhlopkin snapped. How many times had he been over the procedure with them? "You stay with the tall woman." The smaller woman had come as a surprise; she was not one of the regular group that visited the hospital or orbited Khrushchev, and he hoped she would be easier to follow than the rest of them, who moved like spirits.

"The Pobeda is moving west, Sable One."

Okhlopkin accelerated down a parallel street, then veered right, reaching the intersection in time to see the vehicle pass. Although the traffic signal was against him he floored the accelerator, cut across oncoming traffic and fishtailed into a lane two hundred meters behind the car, which continued west, taking no evasive maneuvers. The men in the Zone had been Spetsnaz, Gaponov told him. Be careful, he had said. The important thing now was that even though his men had screwed up, they had learned that these Spetsnaz were human. Perhaps they were better at offensive operations, but now they were on the defensive, even if they didn't know it. Tonight he would show Gaponov how a real soldier performed.

"Pup Seven, this is Sable One. I'm moving west." He gave the street name and a landmark, a synagogue that had been converted to a Komsomol hostel. "I want you to parallel me on my north flank, understand?"

"Pup Seven is moving now."

Okhlopkin sent another vehicle west on a parallel street two blocks south. It was like tracking a wounded animal, with him as the point of a small triangle and the others trailing on his flanks in case the quarry tried to double back or make a break.

What was this all about, anyway? Gaponov said that the General Secretary had replaced his personal security detachment with Spetsnaz. He had given no explanation for this; Gaponov said it was their job to find out what was going on, establish patterns of movement and record them. The group that went in and out of the hospital was some kind of elite commando unit, but what went on in there was still a mystery. Gaponov had said not to worry about that; his job was merely to watch and report. Even so, Okhlopkin had some ideas of his own. Perhaps Khrushchev was the captive of a bandit element. Or infiltrated by Jews. The Spetsnaz troops were directed by a small liaison unit whose members had been virtually impossible to follow for any distance; hardly surprising, since Gaponov's wolf tickets were stupid, unskilled men who couldn't find each other in a one-hole shit house. If this mission was so important, why were no real troops assigned to it? Or the GRU?

He had ordered his men to hang back during the operation in the Zone, but they hadn't listened and he hadn't been there to stop them because Gaponov had sent him off to Bakovka. The old man and his young wife had been easy kills. It had been a shame to not have a few minutes with the woman before he killed her, a real waste, but his orders had been explicit; it had to look like a murder-suicide. The couple and their brats hadn't been easy, but he'd done the job and that's what counted. After he finished the jobs and got back to the Zone he found bodies everywhere: his men, several bearded Georgians and the three Spetsnaz. A real mess, and nothing to show for the carnage, which had happened more or less spontaneously. He had written in his report that his men had been attacked by Georgian criminals while attempting surveillance and had had no alternative but to return fire. He had personally

356

executed the man he had left in charge as an example to the survivors, but it was a nagging failure and Gaponov had been crazy with anger. It was frustrating; how could he honor the great men if his own men could not follow simple orders? This time he would be sure there was no screwup.

Gaponov had eventually accepted the report, but there was no doubt that his superior knew it was a lie and had accepted it only to cover his own ass, which made them partners in deception. This gave him an advantage; Gaponov could no longer denounce him without denouncing himself. Since coming to this realization Okhlopkin had been alert for an opportunity to demonstrate that neither Gaponov nor his troops could do what he could do. An Evenk could follow a butterfly's shadow on a cloudy day, and tonight he would do more than follow. If Khrushchev was in trouble, he needed help. This woman was new. She had been brought to the hospital by one of the conspirators and taken away by a Spetsnaz escort, which he guessed signaled her importance, though he would not know how or why until he interrogated her. When it came to extracting information he was an expert; in the past he had made his victims sing whatever song he or his superiors had chosen, but this one would sing the song of truth, and then he would know what to do.

Okhlopkin was lost in the possibilities of his grand plan when the Pobeda ahead of him suddenly swerved to the curb and stopped. He was past them before he realized what had happened, and was forced to park two hundred meters beyond. By the time he ran back to the building they were inside.

129   MONDAY, APRIL 24, 1961, 9:45 P.M.
Moscow

It had been Petrov's idea to bring additional Spetsnaz reinforcements to Moscow; Bailov had made the necessary arrangements while Raya was in Albania and was glad to have the assignment. Without it he would have thought about nothing but her; as it was he had been forced to push her out of his mind. He was worried in a way that generated emotions he had never felt before. When she returned he was elsewhere deploying his men. After getting them settled he telephoned Talia.

"Everything's fine," she said right away. "Your Raya did very well, but she's a bit frayed by the experience. She has some fine mementos of her holiday, which are being developed. We took her home."

"And left her alone?" His heart raced.

"Two of your associates are with her," she said reassuringly.

When Bailov arrived at Raya's apartment he cautioned himself to behave properly in front of his men, but when he got to her flat he saw that the door was standing open and that it was dark inside. Bailov froze on the stairs and listened. A low sound. A moan? The hair on the back of his neck bristled. He chambered a round in his automatic and moved in cautiously. The floor was slippery. He hugged a wall for stability and tried to adjust his eyes to the darkness. Another moan rose; it was low, nearly inaudible and from deep inside the flat, but he recognized it as an expression of pain. Further along he saw the silhouette of a form against the wall. He toed the body, got no reaction, stepped over it and kept moving until he reached the living room, where some light bled in from the outside. Another body was sprawled on the carpet; he knelt and rolled it over. The eyes were open, the face still, and he saw that it was one of his men, a boy from Minsk named Aleksei who had been afraid before his first parachute jump but had eventually made sergeant.

He thought he detected movement near the door to Raya's bedroom. Crouching, he started to take a step forward when plaster exploded near his head and showered him. He dived left, rolled and a split second later heard the low snap of a silenced round demolish a pane of glass to his right. "Fuck!" a voice complained; this was followed by a moan from the bedroom. "Stay back," the voice ordered.

"Don't shoot."

"Who's there?"

He recognized the voice. "Dudek, is that you?" Another of his men. "Where's Raya?"

"Unlucky," Dudek said matter-of-factly. "Who else but me would have had such bad luck?"

Bailov pictured his soldier; he was a man of skill and currently a private but would soon be a corporal again if he stayed off the bottle and curbed his unfortunate habit of punching anyone who disagreed with him. He was a damn fine soldier when it counted. "Stay calm," Bailov said softly. "Is it safe to put the lights on?" He stepped over Aleksei's body, flicked on the switch and saw Dudek propped against the jamb of the bedroom door, his shirt and a pillowcase stuffed into a gaping belly wound. The point of his left shoulder was shattered, but not bleeding heavily; exit wound, he thought.

"Shot from behind," Dudek complained.

"Better than *in* the behind." Bailov said, stepping past him. "You've still got your balls." There was another moan from the bedroom and he saw a blood trail leading to the bed. There were dark stains on the cover. He read the signs; someone had fallen on the bed and tumbled over the far side. "Who was it?" he asked Dudek.

"We had no idea we were being followed," Dudek said apologetically. "The woman was tired, so we took our time coming up the stairs. We were closing the door when the attack came. It was confusing. Aleksei got shot straight off. I was hit before I could react but I managed to push the woman ahead of me. We exchanged rounds in the dark and then it was quiet. Did we get them?"

Bailov's heart sank as he reached the far side of the bed. Raya was on her back, covered with blood, her left leg mangled at the knee, the lower leg sticking out at an unnatural angle. She had taken off her blouse and brassiere and used a wooden hanger to make a tourniquet which her left hand still clutched tightly.

"Said she was hit," Dudek called from the living room. "I told her how to stop the bleeding."

Raya was somewhere between conscious and unconscious. Her eyes followed him, but she said nothing as her free hand moved some strands of hair off her forehead.

Bailov used the telephone by the bed to call the hospital. Talia answered. "I need help here," he said. "We have two cold, two warm."

Her voice was calm. "Raya?"

"Warm," he said, looking down at her. "Barely," he added.

"Help is coming," Talia said and hung up.

"I don't want to die," Raya Orlava whispered to him. Bailov knelt and loosened the tourniquet. The leg color was bad, the damage extensive. In the field he would have cut the remaining tissue to get the useless leg out of the way, but Raya was not one of his soldiers.

"Will I lose my leg?" she asked, straining to see, but he pushed her back gently.

"No." His concern now was that she might not live long enough to worry about a lost limb. They could argue about cosmetics later.

"Guns sound just like someone gagging. Did you know that?"

"Yes," he said. "Silencers compress the air."

She smiled weakly and her head lolled to the side. "Very good, Taras Ivanovich. Your technical explanation is a great comfort to me." She extended an arm to him. "Come here and hold me, please."

He re-tightened the tourniquet and lay down beside her, gently sliding his arm around her shoulders and drawing her close.

"Who would think that a career in ornithology could end so terribly," she whispered. "You said it would be dangerous there, not here."

"Hush." Why had this happened?

Talia and Ezdovo arrived minutes later with an armed Spetsnaz escort; Gnedin followed and looked first at Dudek, then at Orlava. Her pupils were dilated, her skin clammy. "She'll probably lose the leg," he declared without looking up. "There's not much I can do."

"I know," Bailov said.

Talia and Ezdovo searched the clothing of the dead assailant by the wall, but he carried no identification. They found a hundred rubles in one pocket and a condom and forty kopeks in the other. There were three extra ammunition clips in his jacket pocket. His weapon was several feet away; it was Soviet military issue, an officer's sidearm with a homemade silencer. "Don't touch it," Talia told her husband. "Fingerprints. Yakut," she added, looking at the dead man's face.

"Tungu," Ezdovo said, quickly correcting her. Then, "Evenk." Tungu was the name used by the old Cossacks. "Evenk," he repeated, as much for himself as for her. Talia's sudden prominence in the group was affecting his mind. "Evenk," he said again, "not Yakut."

"I heard you the first time," she snapped. Why was he angry with her? She needed his help, not resistance. Couldn't he understand that?

The soldiers helped carry Dudek and Orlava down to an ambulance. A small crowd had gathered, but when Bailov emerged in his blood-spattered uniform the crowd dispersed and melted into the night. Four men scrambled out of an unmarked truck, one of them stepping into Bailov's path immediately. He wore a black raincoat, a dark tie with a huge knot, and a cigarette hung from his bottom lip slightly left of center. He showed Bailov his militia credentials. "What's going on here?"

Bailov held up his Red Badge, then shoved the man so hard that he tripped against one of his henchmen, causing them both to fall unceremoniously. Then he got into the ambulance with Raya and Gnedin and pulled the doors closed as the ambulance raced away without lights or siren.

Ezdovo picked up the Evenk's pistol by catching the trigger guard with the blade of his pocketknife and carried it downstairs. He was amazed to see that the serial number had not been filed off.

"Taras Ivanovich looked shaken," Talia said.

Ezdovo grunted. "He's afraid of losing his woman." It was a familiar feeling.

---

130   TUESDAY, APRIL 25, 1961, 1:00 A.M.
Moscow

In his sixteen-year career Colonel Anton Gaponov had grown accustomed to being obeyed. In the beginning he marveled at the way enlisted men jumped at his words; now he expected such compliance and was no longer impressed by his own authority. He had also become accustomed to telephone calls in the middle of the night. During a trip to Helsinki he had bought a telephone that chimed softly when it rang, and now the chimes were singing their muted song. When he rolled over to answer, his wife, Yelena, draped a muscular leg over his hip and hooked him with a wrestling hold that was the first signal of the stirring of her on-again, off-again libido. Yelena was a former two-time European shotput champion, and though she had a naturally compact build, she had added to her strength through a combination of hormone injections and weight lifting. Her years of rigorous training had altered her menstrual cycle, her libido, and worst of all, her timing. Most of the month she had no interest in sex, but when she was within a few days of her period she came alive. Gaponov worked his way loose and slid off the bed. "Your biology is showing," he scolded her.

She made her way across the mattress and balanced on the edge like a massive, hairless cat. Why was Anton blushing? She pawed at him, but he pushed her arm away as he talked into the telephone.

"Say that again," he said, his voice wavering.

She raised an eyebrow. "Who is it?" she demanded.

"Why would he do that?" Gaponov asked, his voice rising. He grimaced at the answer. "You saw the body?" He bit his lip. "Shit."

"Who is it?" Yelena insisted. "Your latest sweetie?" Her altered libido also included the worst sort of jealous streak. For several days of the month she raged at his imagined infidelities; the rest of the time she acted as if she couldn't care less whether he was dead or alive. Her jealousy was unfounded; Gaponov's sole mistress was his career, and because of it he now felt stabbing pains in his chest.

The crazy Evenk had been shot while breaking into a woman's flat. "His orders were explicit," he hissed into the telephone. "Surveillance only." Why was he telling this to the cretin on the other end of the line? "Assholes!" he shouted. What to do now? Get the unit out of Moscow; he had planned for this, but had never expected to have to put it into action.

"All right," he said, "all right. Be calm, comrade. Implement the recall plan." He listened for a moment, then hissed, "Yes, idiot, I mean *now*!"

The look on her husband's face told Yelena that there would be no lovemaking tonight. Something was very wrong. "What is it?" she asked tenderly.

"Work," he told her, his standard response to most of her questions.

She made a face and rolled her eyes as he began getting dressed. "You're going out at this hour?" She leaned back to look at the alarm clock on the nightstand. "Why tonight, Anton? Send somebody else."

Gaponov ignored her as he put on his field clothing and strapped his service revolver to his hip. It felt foreign to him. Though he was a soldier, he had forged his career on his ability to think, not to fight in primitive ways.

"Anton?"

He sat in a chair to slip on his knee-high boots. "If there are any more calls, tell them you haven't seen me tonight," he told her. "I went to work yesterday and didn't come home."

"But I have and you did."

He glared at her. "Do as I say."

She could not hide her fear. "I'm your wife," she said. "I have a right to know if there's a problem."

He left without answering her. The Evenk had fucked up badly, and now he had to set things right. Wolf tickets led by an Evenk; it had been a crazy combination from the start, and not his idea, but what choice had there been? An officer followed orders and did not question motives, especially if the officer was interested in a long career.

An hour had passed since Gaponov left Yelena. The thirty men had arrived at the airport in several groups, including the one who had gone up the stairs behind Okhlopkin in time see the muzzle flashes that followed the Evenk's unexpected charge into the flat, but he couldn't explain why it had happened. He simply mumbled "Evenk," which implied an innate unpredictability and left it at that. Evenks, Yakuts and the others with slant eyes were all Mongols and therefore savage and unreliable, worse than wolf tickets.

The men gathered in a hanger where a three-decade-old twin-engine transport was parked, its pilots in the cockpit waiting for their passengers to climb aboard. Gaponov could see the glow of the red light on their faces as he checked his list one final time. The men waited in a loose formation, sharing cigarettes, their faces tense. "Mount up," Gaponov ordered.

Unlike regular soldiers, these men dared not question orders, especially now. Their situation was too precarious; they were trying to earn their way back into the system, not to challenge its authority. They boarded in silence.

As Gaponov waited for the last man to get inside he was surprised to see the deputy director of the KGB enter the hangar.

"I wanted to see you before you got away," Perevertkin said.

"There was no need," Gaponov said. Why had he come?

"Are all of them accounted for?"

"All but Okhlopkin."

"Let me worry about him. You followed the recall procedure?"

"To the letter."

"Your wife?"

"I told her nothing. I instituted the recall, notified you from a public phone and came directly here."

"Well done," Perevertkin said. "Don't worry. Everything has been arranged."

The two men shook hands, Gaponov disappeared inside and the hatch closed. Perevertkin signaled with his hands for the pilots to wait, ducked under the wing, opened a small panel, reached inside, then closed the door, relatched it, trotted back to the front of the plane, gave the pilot the engine-start sign and headed for the hangar door without looking back.

Gaponov made sure his men were strapped in, climbed into the cockpit and knelt on the jump seat between two sleepy-eyed pilots. The engines had not started. "What's the delay?"

"Your friend out there saw an unlatched door," the pilot in the left seat said. "We're ready to go now." The man stank of cheap vodka.

"File a visual flight plan and leave the transponder off," Gaponov told them as he handed them a chart. "We'll take care of our own navigation." He gave them the destination and course. This way air-traffic-control radars would not be able to track them.

"Cherepovets?" The copilot looked puzzled as he lit a cigarette and studied his chart through blue smoke.

Gaponov went back to strap in. Their people in Cherepovets would be waiting. He had been told that there would be a court set up there. The men would be charged as antisocial elements, then shipped to uranium mines in the east. These were sentences of death, but not instantaneous, which was better than the scum deserved. When it was done he would remain in Cherepovets for several days, then return to Moscow. In his absence, others would be conducting damage control, though he had no idea how they would dissociate Okhlopkin from him. All he knew was that it would be done efficiently and thoroughly; secure in this and glad to be close to being shed of his wolf tickets, he told himself to put it out of his mind; he was part of the party's sword and shield. He would be protected; assurances had been given. The system rewarded loyal service. As the aircraft began to taxi, he finally allowed himself to relax. It would be all right.

<table>
<tr><td>**131**</td><td>**TUESDAY, APRIL 25, 1961, 5:30 A.M.**
Moscow</td></tr>
</table>

Raya was under heavy guard at the hospital, in critical but stable condition. Gnedin had been forced to amputate her mangled lower left leg, and had carefully crafted a flap and stump that could later be fitted with a prosthesis; his Soviet colleagues had no access to such technology, but Western devices could be acquired through diplomatic channels. It was ironic, Gnedin thought, that while Khrushchev boasted about his spaceman, most Soviet amputees still hobbled around on homemade wooden stumps, just as they had in czarist days.

For now, however, Orlava's lost limb was not his primary medical concern. The blood loss had induced shock; the tourniquet had saved her, but her life was still in jeopardy. She had the classic symptoms: low blood pressure, soft, erratic pulse, clammy skin, cold hands and feet, no color, blue splotches on her extremities and hyperventilation. He put her on oxygen, cross-matched her blood and replaced 40 percent of the lost volume with saline, which was all that was available on short notice. He knew there was danger of edema with the salt solution, but there was no alternative. He had started her on two units of whole blood, O positive. No need for corticosteroids; they would only hinder peripheral vascular function, which was important to the health of the stump. He had done all he could; if her heart was strong and there were no clots, she would recover. Bailov wanted to stay with her, but Gnedin forbade it; responding quickly, Talia sent him with Ezdovo to identify the dead assailant.

When Bailov appeared at Yepishev's quarters, the general simply shook his head and opened the door with a look of resignation on his haggard face. "You again. Will I never be rid of you?"

"We need help."

"Obviously," Yepishev said, stepping back.

Wrenches, benches, gauges, shovels, gaskets, boots—all these and more routinely disappeared from government inventories, but the Red Army did not misplace or lose weapons. Ever. Because they had a weapon with a serial number they had a good starting point for tracing Raya's assailant.

It was easy to see how Yepishev had been promoted. He not only had many contacts, but also an uncanny understanding of military administrative procedures. Within two hours he came up with Okhlopkin's name, as well as fingerprints that matched those on the weapon and a photograph taken in 1958. Captain Eduard Boryavich Okhlopkin was the bastard son of a Russian mother and Evenk father, a half-breed assigned inexplicably to the Soviet Rocket Force. Administratively he was attached to the political branch under a Colonel Anton Gaponov, but his current duties were unknown. Yepishev told them that until July 1960 Gaponov had been adjutant to Lieutenant General Babadzhanyan, who commanded the Odessa Military District. It made no sense that a nobody like the dead Evenk would be in the Rocket Force's political section; such assignments were usually reserved for native Russians who were Party members and on upward career tracks. Okhlopkin's record showed no evidence of a Komsomol background or Party membership. His fitness reports might tell more, but Yepishev said that obtaining these would require time, and might not be available at all.

In the old days Petrov had taught them that the art of investigation was sequential. One started at the end of a chain and worked one's way through the links one at a time. With Okhlopkin dead, Gaponov was the next apparent link. Bailov and Ezdovo did not overlook the fact that the murder of Melko's ex-girlfriend and her family had also been linked to the Odessa district through the mysterious KGB accounts Annochka's husband had stumbled onto. They doubted that this was a coincidence.

Yepishev's contacts produced Gaponov's office number; a call to his office gave them his home address. Melko was sent to the office while Ezdovo and Bailov went to the colonel's residence, which was on the second floor of a five-story apartment building. The woman who opened the door was short and mannishly muscular, but not unattractive; Bailov thought he recognized her, but he couldn't put a name to her face. Her brown hair was trimmed short, she wore a plaid shirt for a nightgown and she was barefoot. Her pink nail polish was a badge of her husband's rank; such cosmetics were impossible to find in Moscow unless one had access to exclusive state stores or traveled outside the country. "What do you want at this hour?" she challenged. She wore her husband's rank with confidence.

"Is Colonel Gaponov at home?" Bailov asked politely.

"Who wants to know?" she demanded.

"Where is he?" Ezdovo pressed, his voice hard.

"I haven't seen him since yesterday morning. He left at eight."

"He works nights?"

"Sometimes."

They could see that she was nervous, but doing her best to hide it. "Does he call in when he's going to be out all night?"

She smiled. "I'm his wife, not his commanding officer. May I tell him who called?"

"That won't be necessary," Ezdovo said.

"As you wish, but he's very reliable. I could ask him to call you when he returns." The appearance of the two men had shaken her. The one with the red hair looked like a soldier, but not the other one, who had intense eyes. Why had Anton gone out so suddenly? Was he in trouble? If so, then she was in trouble.

"Forget we were here," the wild-eyed man said.

Yelena Gaponov pushed the door closed, listened to them go down the stairs, went to the phone and dialed her husband's office.

At the office there were three clerks on night duty, two females and a slightly built young male who looked as if he had yet to have his first shave. When the phone rang, he reached for it, but Melko caught his arm. "What's your name?"

"Nestorev, Junior Lieutenant," the boy said nervously.

Melko pointed him to a chair, motioned for him to sit and picked up the receiver. "Junior Lieutenant Nestorev," he announced.

"This is Mrs. Gaponov," Yelena said. She tried to remember Nestorev's face. He was young and smooth-skinned; that was all that she could recall. Why did his voice seem so much older? "Is my husband there?"

"No," Melko said. He heard the panic in her voice. "Is the colonel coming in?"

How much should she tell a junior lieutenant? "I think so, but maybe I misunderstood."

"Shall we have him call you when he arrives?"

"Please. If it's convenient for him," she added.

Her voice betrayed her frayed nerves. "When do you think he'll be here?" Melko asked.

Why didn't Nestorev just take the message and shut up? Suddenly she wished that she had not called, but the two men at her door had frightened her and she felt she had to do something. "Any moment."

"May I ask how long it's been since he left?" Melko tried to sound sympathetic.

What if something had happened to Anton? "A couple of hours ago, perhaps a little longer." Actually it had been before midnight, which was more than enough time for him to get there. Anton had told her to say nothing, but Nestorev was one of his men.

"Ah," Melko said. "Perhaps he had other stops to make. You're certain he said he was coming to the office?"

"Not in so many words."

Melko looked at the duty board. Several personnel were signed out to various locations, including four who had gone to something listed only as B-4, TTC. He cupped the receiver and pointed at the board. "What's B-4?" he asked Nestorev.

"Tactical Training Course. Small arms," the young officer told him, his eyes locked on the Red Badge that Melko had left lying open on the desk.

"How far is it?"

"Just outside the city. Near the airport."

"Which one?" Melko asked.

"Vnukovo."

Melko uncovered the phone. "Mrs. Gaponov?"

"Yes?"

"Perhaps he went to TTC. Several of the officers are there for training."

His field dress! That would explain it. "Yes," she said. "Perhaps I misunderstood. He was dressed for the range."

"Then that's where he must be," Melko said. Then in a whisper to Nestorev, "Draw a map for me and be quick about it."

"What's that?" the woman asked.

"Nothing," Melko said. "We'll have the colonel call when he comes in."

"It's really not urgent." The fact that she had called at all would tell him that it was. She hung up.

Junior Lieutenant Nestorev shoved a map toward Melko. "Restricted area," he said. "You can't get in."

The *urka* smiled and retrieved his Red Badge. "With this I could fuck your sister on Lenin's tomb during the May Day parade," he growled as he picked up a telephone and dialed a four-digit number. Though it kept ringing, he acted as if he had gotten through to someone. "Recorder on?" he asked the phone, then nodded. "Yes, all outgoing and incoming traffic. Was that last one clear enough?" The phone was still ringing when he hung up. "Let me caution you," he told Nestorev, "that all calls from this building are being recorded." He guessed that this would delay any attempt by his comrades to warn Gaponov.

When Bailov and Ezdovo arrived several minutes later, Melko climbed into the truck grinning. "His wife called in," he told them.

"She told us he left yesterday morning at eight," Ezdovo said.

"She told me he left a little over two hours ago in his field uniform, and she's edgy. Gaponov's people have some sort of restricted training facility near Vnukovo," he added, and held out the hand-drawn map. "Several of his comrades are there. Maybe he's with them."

Ezdovo made a U-turn and accelerated.

TUESDAY, APRIL 25, 1961, 7:17 A.M.
Kashkin, Kalinin Oblast, Russia

The Red Star collective farm was Pavel Abramov's pride and joy—and, with the right blend of sun and rain, his future. Khrushchev demanded corn from state farms and Abramov had grown it; this fall he was certain this planting would produce a record yield, which surely would earn him not only a medal but promotion to manager of a larger operation. It was a sunny morning with low, fast-moving cumulus clouds racing overhead. Yesterday's rain had been just enough to wet the rich black earth and perfume the air with its distinctive scent.

Abramov half heard the aircraft approaching, but paid no attention. His interest resided solely in the earth. Life was now and on the ground, not in some imaginary kingdom in the sky after death. "I believe only in what I can touch and see and smell," he sometimes said to reaffirm the principles that guided his life. The earth was real, heaven debatable.

It was a muted pop that finally caught Abramov's attention, and though he had never heard such a sound before, he instinctively flinched before looking up. The aircraft had been approaching from the south and was nearly overhead, but when he looked up he saw two pieces, a wing and the rest of the plane spinning end over end in a steep downward arc, trailing heavy white smoke, the whole thing in slow motion. Abramov threw himself to the ground and covered his head, his only thought for his field. He would plant soon and the earth was perfect. Debris rained on him; there was fire everywhere and he was engulfed in a pall of suffocating black smoke.

Abramov struggled to his feet. He was shaking, but he didn't seem to have been hit. When he looked around him, it was not the carnage that struck him initially but the massive destruction to his field. Pieces of bodies lay everywhere and a fire poured heavy black smoke under a firm wind. He ran toward the farm buildings screaming orders.

Abramov called his superior in Kalinin to report the accident, then joined his people who were already slapping the fires down with wet burlap sacks and shovelfuls of black dirt. Without bad luck a farmer would have no luck at all, he told himself.

One of his people approached him. "Comrade Manager, what should we do with the dead?"

"Put them in the ice house." Why had such misfortune visited him at the very moment when his future seemed so bright? He felt like crying.

 TUESDAY, APRIL 25, 1961, 9:30 A.M.
Moscow

Even with the map they had gotten lost several times and been forced to go through several guarded checkpoints. The small-arms range was in a windowless building on the perimeter of Vnukovo Airport. Several men were inside drinking coffee; the smell of gunpowder and strong tobacco lingered in the room.

"We're looking for Colonel Gaponov," Bailov said.

"How did you get in here?" a captain asked. When he reached for a pistol on the table in front of him Melko knocked him out of his chair.

Bailov's Red Badge gleamed in the artificial light. "It's been a long and tedious night," he said. And Raya had only one leg, which was *his* fault.

"We haven't seen him," said a junior lieutenant with a tight face like a chipmunk and a sparse black beard.

"How long have you been here?" Ezdovo asked.

"I've been here all night," a sergeant said in a weary voice. "He hasn't been around and he isn't scheduled."

They had parked near a grove of white birch trees. "Every time we get a lead it disappears," Melko said as they climbed back into the truck.

THURSDAY, APRIL 27, 1961, 5:00 P.M.
Kashkin, Kalinin Oblast, Russia

Officially the Soviet Union had a near-perfect air safety record; that is, it did not report accidents unless they happened so publicly as to be undeniable, meaning outside the country or in plain view of too many foreigners. Despite its official position, however, the government maintained civil- and military-accident investigating teams, in part to determine the cause, but, more important, to sanitize the sites, warn survivors to keep their mouths shut and settle the damage claims of local residents.

Captain Viktor Kostromin led his Moscow-based team to the Red Star farm. The carnage was considerable, but Kostromin had seen so many crashes in recent years that such scenes no longer affected him. Soon to be twenty-eight, he worried that such work was slowly destroying his ability to feel anything in the normal range of human emotions.

The idiotic state farm manager greeted Kostromin with demands for payment of damages. Thirty-three men dead, and all he could think about were his fields. Unfortunately, he had been the only one to see the aircraft come down, so Kostromin was forced to interview him at length. Abramov was certain that there had been an explosion that separated the port wing and engine from the rest of the craft, and that he had seen two pieces falling. When his examination of the wreckage verified this, Kostromin's interest increased. Most crashes were caused by pilots, or sometimes rivets popped loose or sheet metal collapsed, but it wasn't often that one was sabotaged by a bomb with a sophisticated timer. What was even more interesting in this instance were the personal belongings that had survived, especially several identity cards with red slashes across them, and a wallet belonging to one Colonel Anton Gaponov.

Kostromin did not linger at the site. By now his technicians knew how to take care of the details without supervision; what he needed for his report would come from what he had already seen and the photographs that would arrive in Moscow tomorrow. Basically it was a clean site. He wished Abramov's people had not collected the bodies and their parts before he arrived, but done was done. A casket needed only a piece or two; fragments were enough to satisfy the living. For his part, he had seen what he wanted.

His work complete, Kostromin drove to Kalinin and flew his own aircraft back to Moscow. Bombs were planted with intent. This one was a small one, ingeniously placed to make the crash look like material failure. It had been placed, he felt sure, inside the wing at the joint where the engine was attached to a main spar. Whoever had put it there was a virtuoso with explosive devices. Such experts were rare, and all of them no doubt worked under the protection of certain government agencies, the sorts of organizations connected to shadowy power centers in the Kremlin itself. Every artist had his own signature, and in this regard bomb makers were no different.

135   FRIDAY, APRIL 28, 1961, 10:45 A.M.
Moscow

Melko and Ezdovo split time at Gaponov's office, each taking six-hour shifts. They had found no evidence at the Vnukovo facility or vicinity, and the colonel still had not returned home. His wife was under around-the-clock surveillance by Bailov's men, her phone tapped. They had checked aircraft departures, but all had been accounted for. It seemed that Gaponov had vanished.

Ezdovo had reported everything to Talia, who urged him to be patient, this advice intended to have personal as well as professional meaning. "Everything will be fine," she said, as much for herself as for him. She tried to think what Petrov would do, but she wasn't Petrov, and though he seemed to be getting stronger, he was still too weak to help. Gnedin continued to insist that there was no hope. Talia sensed that everything had gone wrong and that they were still focusing on the wrong areas, but how could she redirect them? For his part, Khrushchev was busy preparing for the unofficial summit with the new American president. The meeting had not been officially announced, but the United States had tentatively agreed to it. Details were yet to be worked out, but it looked as if it would be in Vienna.

Earlier in the day she had met briefly with the General Secretary. "Progress?" he had asked. He seemed to be in an unusually good mood, but disturbed. She had briefed him quickly, omitting their contact with the Americans. "Everything points to the Rocket Forces, is that your view?"

"So far," Talia said.

Khrushchev grunted. "Wrong. Nobody in the Rocket Forces has anything to gain. Nothing at all." The Ukrainian pulled back a curtain and looked out. "Perhaps I've made a mistake. Perhaps you were the wrong choice to take charge of this."

"Petrov is in charge," she said.

"He's an old man," Khrushchev said, watching for her reaction. "Filled with cancer."

How did he know? "He is Petrov."

"He was Stalin's lackey," Khrushchev said. "You move too slowly. I need people with energy around me."

"We need your plans for Vienna," she answered. "Once you're outside our borders it will be more difficult to protect you."

"If you do your job, I won't need you in Vienna. I want things settled *before* I meet the American."

"You'll be exposed in Vienna."

"The Foreign Ministry and the KGB are more experienced in such matters," the General Secretary replied sharply. "Besides, there will be Austrian security, and the Americans will have their people as well."

"The Americans will concentrate on their own man."

"Since I will be with him most of the time, they will also concentrate on me. That's exactly my point."

"We still need to review the security planning."

Khrushchev closed the curtain. "I'll think about the request," he said, ending the meeting.

When Captain Viktor Kostromin arrived at Gaponov's office, he asked who was in charge and was taken to Melko, who had just come on duty.

"Where's your uniform?" Kostromin challenged.

"In your wife's closet," Melko snapped. This duty was too much like being a camp guard. The captain looked angry. "What is it you want, comrade?"

"Information."

Melko smiled. "That can be a precious and rare commodity in the Motherland."

Kostromin laid Gaponov's charred identity card on the desk. Melko read the name and asked, "Where did you get this?"

"From the mud," Kostromin said.

136	FRIDAY, APRIL 28, 1961, 2:00 P.M. *Moscow*

The team was silent. Melko had brought the accident investigator to Talia, who had interrogated him for nearly two hours; when he departed his face was ashen. The bombing led upward, all right, too high. Talia had been blunt with Kostromin; he was to drop his investigation and forget everything he had seen; all records and files on the accident were to be delivered to her. "My mind is a blank," he assured her.

Now she had finished recounting the details to the team: Gaponov's sudden and mysterious departure, now verified by his wife; the crash; Kostromin's bomb theory and supporting evidence; his draft report, photographs, the remains of several identity cards, including Gaponov's; a hand-drawn diagram of the crash site and of an aircraft wing showing how and where the investigator believed the lethal bomb had been attached. Kostromin was adamant: a bomb this sophisticated could have been assembled only by an extraordinary technician. How many such people could there be in the country? Such skills were too highly prized to go unnoticed by the authorities.

Talia posed the question to Petrov, but it was Bailov who answered, the word out even before it registered in his brain. "Odessa. Special demolition development," he said. "A modern-day Kamera."

In the old days the NKVD had a special branch called Spetsburo whose sole mission was assassination. The Kamera, or Chamber, was Spetsburo's laboratory, which had the single purpose of developing more efficient methods of killing. The Kamera had been so shoddily run that legend said its operators feared to walk around it for fear that an accidental touch could bring instant death. Over the years there had been stories about equally bizarre operations. The Kamera was defunct now, abolished by Khrushchev, but Department 13 of the First Chief Directorate of the KGB had a similar operation said to be more scientific in its approach.

"Why Odessa?" Talia asked. "Why only one facility?" It seemed an unlikely place for such an operation. Normally special installations were kept close to Moscow, where they could be regularly observed and tightly controlled. It was one thing to authorize such operations, quite another to make sure you didn't become their target.

"The weather is nice for bomb makers," Bailov said. "Nice beaches, women in their underwear and blue sky to contrast against the black smoke." He turned serious. "It's an anomaly; its founder is a pilot who lost his leg to the Germans; when he couldn't fly anymore he started experimenting with explosives. Why only one place? Soviet doctrine requires central control and a rigid chain of command. If you decide to create a special operation you put it out of the way and organize it so that only the most reliable people are employed there and at every level of control in its chain of command. There is only one plant in the country making rubber boots, only one making washing machines and only one manufacturing secure radios. Should we be surprised that there is only one laboratory producing special explosives? This place developed what Spetsnaz calls a vibration charge, an all-plastic mine that metal detectors can't find. Pressure from above pushes a plastic fuse into the device; the fuse pierces a pocket of chemicals that heat it and ignite the charge. It weighs half what a standard mine weighs and delivers several times the punch. Anyone who can make something so insidious would have no trouble with the type of explosive used to kill Gaponov, and I remind you that the chief designer there is a former pilot, which means that aircraft hold no mysteries for him."

"How many people know about this place?" Gnedin asked.

"To my knowledge, not many. We had problems with the nine prototypes and I raised hell about it. The chemical reaction was supposed to occur almost instantaneously, but some of the devices took an hour; in the heat of summer we had several explode before they were primed. I was sent to meet a man named Chelitnikov. I spent a day in Moscow with him and described the flaw. After that we got new mines that worked as they were supposed to." Bailov shook his head. "He was not what I expected, and seemed to talk more than listen. A very peculiar man. He told me all about his base, which is near Odessa."

Petrov thought for a moment, then turned to Talia. "Gaponov's former assignment?"

She thumbed through the dead colonel's dossier and found the entry. "Odessa Military District," she said. "There's no other detail." Petrov had seemed only to glance at the file earlier; had he picked up such a detail with so little effort?

"Lieutenant General Babadzhanyan commanding," the little man said with a grandfatherly smile. "It's on the next page."

Talia found it exactly where he said it would be.

"Chelitnikov invited me to visit him," Bailov said. "I'd say it's time to accept his invitation."

"It may be another blind alley," Talia said.

"Perhaps. But if he didn't make this bomb he may know who did. He's an artist, and every artist knows who the up-and-coming competition is."

III

Alert

Frash spotted the woman in the morning, and from time to time during the day he came back to see if she was still there. Thirtyish, with curly black hair, a dirty face and dangling copper earrings, she wore a faded red dress, no shoes and carried a fat infant in her arms. She had taken up a position under the central dome of the Galleria Vittorio Emmanuele and played the role of beggar well, but she and the baby were too healthy; her panhandling was a job rather than an attempt to survive. Twice he saw carabinieri escort her out of the glass-roofed mall, but each time she made her way back. Frash admired her persistence as much as her gall. He guessed that she was a Gypsy.

He had moved constantly for a week, walking and hitchhiking by night and sleeping in abandoned buildings by day. Along the way he had thrown away his clothes and stolen some blue coveralls from a cement factory before purchasing new clothing in Milan. He realized that something was wrong with the blank passports. It had been a surprise to have his first one checked by the hotel clerk when he had left the Excelsior, for shortly thereafter the Americans had come snooping. He doubted that they were on his trail now, but it seemed likely that they had some sort of a net out for him. In a pinch he could stay in transient hotels, but it would be safer to find someone to take him in, somebody who knew how to live in the seams of life. The gypsy seemed a possibility.

At about 9:00 p.m. the arcade's shops began to close, the crowd thinned, and the woman began to pack up. The infant was androgynous, filthy and silent, making pitiful sounds from time to time, usually when a mark was near. Trained and programmed like Pavlov's dog, he guessed. Did she use pain or pleasure?

"Hey, *gadjo*," the woman said as he approached. "You been watchin' me all day, eh?" She spoke with an accent he couldn't place. Her voice was soft, though there was no doubt about the challenge she had hurled at him. "Nosy or what?"

"Just interested."

She raised her eyebrows. "In what, a starving woman fallen on hard times? You look like you got enough trouble taking care of you." She extended her hand in an age-old gesture.

"Likes attract," he said. "You won't get something for nothing from me."

"Hey, you want a prostitute, go to Central Station. Plenty of them over there. Real beauties." She contorted her face in a hag's mask.

"Do I look like the sort to pay for it?"

She stood up, set the baby on her hip and smiled. "Every man pays for it. Most don't know it, but they always pay." She dismissed him with a wave of her hand.

"You're a hard woman."

"Life is severe, *gadjo,* and we have to be equal to it." When she walked away, he followed. It was raining outside, the downpour coming in heavy sheets, the gutters filled with rushing water, the dark streets shiny, with few streetlights. The woman shielded the child's head with a newspaper and walked steadily at a brisk pace.

After two blocks she pivoted without warning and tried to sweep his legs with a low judo move, but Frash stepped over the kick, grabbed her by the arm and pushed her against the wall, only to find a knife point set firmly against the soft flesh under his chin. Her smile showed perfect white teeth. He raised his hands to show he was not resisting. "You have pretty good reflexes, *gadjo.*" She was watching his reaction. "What's your game?" The pressure of the knife point increased.

"A place to sleep and eat," he said. "I can pay."

"You know what I am?"

"Rom," he said. "Just about anything for a price." He had known Gypsies in Boston.

She lowered the knife, pushed him away and grinned. "You have nerve for a *gadjo.* You got a problem with the law, eh?"

"Does that mean yes?" he asked.

"You can pay cash?"

"Of course."

"I'll think about it. First I have to return the child."

"Not yours?"

"Leased," she said. "Cheap."

After nearly two kilometers they turned into a street filled with soot-covered tenements. "Wait here," she said as she went inside. The area was strangely silent, and she was gone more than half an hour. When she returned, the baby was gone, as was the dirt; she was wearing clean clothes. "Worried, *gadjo?*"

"I'm still here."

They walked another block and got into a new black Fiat. "The life of a Rom is not so bad," he said, admiring the automobile.

"Outside the majority's rule, you understand?" She smiled.

He did. It was his credo as well.

They drove north out of the city, and after passing through an area of small farms pulled into a grove of trees, stopping beside a small Airstream caravan. She went in first and flicked on the light.

She may be a Gypsy, Frash thought, but her standard of living is in the modern world. "No horses?"

"The Rom must live in the world as it presents itself."

"Do you have a name?" he asked.

"Would it matter?" She motioned for him to enter. "I have a hundred names but they mean nothing. If it makes you feel better, call me Kenya."

"Like the country?"

"Yes, a primitive country awaiting exploration."

"Perhaps I intend to steal your national secrets." Albert knew that European Gypsies frequently made illegal border crossings. It was Ali's job to find a way to benefit from such knowledge and get them closer to Kennedy. The only question now was where.

"A secret is nothing more than a ploy to increase the price," Kenya said.

138   WEDNESDAY, MAY 3, 1961, 7:40 A.M.
Odessa

Perevertkin saw Chelitnikov in gray coveralls on top of the helicopter. Neither man acknowledged the other. They had already had their conversation.

The helicopter's copilot was squatting about fifty meters in front of the craft, smoking a thin green cigar, tracing circles in the dust on the tarmac with his forefinger. "What's the problem?" Perevertkin asked by way of a greeting.

"Just another precautionary check," the lieutenant colonel said. "These heaps have a habit of coming apart in flight. If Moscow replaced the defective parts, this shit would be unnecessary."

"We're not like the Americans," Perevertkin said. "We must make do with what we have."

"If the rotor housing gives way while we're flying, you may sing a different song, comrade."

The deputy director of the KGB tried to shift the conversation. "It looks like good flying weather."

"Fair, foul, who cares?" the lieutenant colonel said without looking up. "They pay me to fly when it has to be done, not just when I'm in the mood."

"You know who I am?" Perevertkin whispered.

"To my great misfortune."

Perevertkin smiled. "Black-market violations are punishable by death."

"I sold cigars, not national secrets."

"You rationalize, but I deal with facts. Principles count. You sold five thousand cigars stolen from the state, but you're a lucky man. When the crime came to my attention we thought your general was behind it."

"Babadzhanyan is an honest man," the copilot growled. "What I did was by and for myself."

"Thanks to your candor, we now know that with certainty. Is that so bad? You're your general's guardian angel. If he knew, he'd thank you for keeping his record spotless."

"If he knew I had trouble with the KGB, he'd chop off my head and spit into my neck."

"But you're married to his niece."

"I am where I am because I'm a good pilot. If I was a bad pilot and his eldest son it would get me nowhere. My general rewards performance, not wet kisses on his ass."

Perevertkin put his hand on the copilot's shoulder, but he pushed it away. "Your general is lucky to arouse such loyalty in his men."

"Fuck off. I gave you what you wanted, but I don't have to pretend to like it."

Perevertkin changed tones. "This thing eats at you."

"Like a cancer in my belly."

"Would you like to be free of it?"

The copilot looked at the KGB general. "How?"

"One final favor and you'll hear no more from us. Your record will be pristine."

"What is it this time?"

"We believe that the Americans are monitoring our surface-to-air missile tests," Perevertkin said. "We've devised a way to verify it. Today's test has been arranged to find out once and for all."

"What's that got to do with me?"

"Before your second flight today we want you to set your radio to a certain radio frequency. Make two transmissions." Perevertkin gave him the frequency.

"That's all?"

"As clear as the palm of one's hand."

"When do I make these calls?"

"At any time during your second flight. When is entirely up to you."

"No special interval?"

"It's not necessary."

"And for this I'm off the KGB's horns?"

"You'll have a clean bill of health, your political cancer will be gone, and your general will never be the wiser."

The copilot stood up. "How do I know this is the truth?"

"You don't."

An honest response. "Agreed."

Perevertkin was pleased. General Babadzhanyan was linked to the KGB's special funds, which meant he had to die. When the general was ready to return to Odessa tonight, he would find an excuse not to be with him. When Babadzhanyan's helicopter departed, the general's personal copilot would unknowingly serve as the instrument of death. It had been an intricate dance to get this far, but perhaps the end was now in sight. Babadzhanyan would die and that would tie up another loose end. When Perevertkin returned to Odessa, he would make sure that Chelitnikov the bomb maker was also permanently removed. Malinovsky had assured him that all of this was designed to bring Khrushchev down, and that in return for his services he would have Shelepin's top position at the KGB. Better late than never. The position should have been his before Shelepin, who was an amateur. If all this worked out, what was rightfully his would finally be his for real. The surprise was that Malinovsky seemed to be the architect of the plot. Like everybody else in Moscow, Perevertkin had been certain that Malinovsky was Khrushchev's handpicked yes man—which, he reminded himself, showed once again that nothing in the Kremlin was as it seemed to be. He would remember that when he was head of the KGB.

"Fly carefully," Perevertkin told the copilot, who simply grunted as he sought to relight his cigar.

"You," the copilot bellowed to the mechanic climbing down from the chopper. "Is this going to take all day?"

The mechanic held up two fingers and smiled. "Two minutes, Colonel, and you're on your way."

139   WEDNESDAY, MAY 3, 1961, 1:00 P.M.
Odessa

Bailov dropped a parachute and harness at Melko's feet. "What's that?" the *urka* asked.

"Vertical transportation," Bailov said. "Think of it as a kind of elevator."

Melko studied the parachute for a moment, then pushed it away with his foot and looked up at the Spetsnaz colonel. "Not me," he said with a nervous grin.

"Put it on," Bailov ordered.

Loose ends sometimes came together in mysterious ways. Perevertkin, the KGB deputy director, was scheduled to attend a missile test at the Nikolayev SAM Proving Ground today. His host would be General Babadzhanyan, former commander of the late Colonel Gaponov. Perevertkin, they knew, was part of the special interagency committee that reviewed and approved all high-level special assignments, and Trubkin, Gaponov and Okhlopkin had no doubt all been cleared by it. Today Talia would confront Shelepin with these facts. Ezdovo would take control of the KGB bomb-making factory outside Odessa, and Bailov would lead a contingent of his men against Perevertkin's contingent at the proving ground. The grand plan had been mapped by Talia, and neither Khrushchev nor Petrov had been informed. "Until now we've tried to fill the basket one fruit at a time," she told the group. "Now we'll to shake the trees and see what falls out."

When Gnedin answered, "It may be us," none of them laughed.

General Babadzhanyan was not in Odessa. He had flown his helicopter east to Nikolayev to observe the missile firing at the range; Perevertkin was with him. Bailov had three aircraft in formation, with two hundred men in them ready for a parachute drop. It was the real thing at last, and he could see by the faces of the men in his group that they were ready. Yepishev had come up with a map of the isolated proving ground. The place was too spread out and most of the terrain too jagged to make a surprise ground assault, so he had decided to do what his troops did best. The men would zero in on the main observation bunker at the center of the complex; they would jump at an altitude of one hundred and fifty meters and overwhelm the target before those on the ground even knew that there was an assault. They would grab Babadzhanyan and Perevert-kin, put them on one of the helicopters flying behind the drop birds and spirit them away. The planes would return to Odessa to wait for them there. While Bailov's group assaulted the proving ground, Ezdovo and fifty men in trucks would secure the demolition laboratory outside Odessa.

All the briefings had been completed. From now on there would be radio silence. Bailov moved among his men, helping them check their equipment, giving words of encouragement, reminding them of their specific tasks ahead.

Melko had put on his harness and chute but had not sufficiently tightened his straps. Bailov showed him how to do it. "Is this really necessary?" the *urka* asked.

The colonel patted him on the back. "Don't worry, comrade. If it doesn't work, we'll give you another one."

Melko was not amused.

 WEDNESDAY, MAY 3, 1961, 2:35 P.M.
SAM Proving Ground, Nikolayev Oblast

Babadzhanyan thought Kolpakchi's idea typically stupid, but Kolpakchi was chief of combat training for the General Staff and this missile firing was a political exercise, not a military one. The SA-3 surface-to-air missiles had been fired hundreds of times, but when General Perevertkin, deputy chairman of the KGB, suddenly expressed an inexplicable interest in a personal demonstration, Kolpakchi had seen an opportunity to make political hay, and it had fallen to Babadzhanyan to arrange the show. A prop-driven drone would be sent over the course at four thousand meters; for the SA-3 a hit on a slow-moving target like this was a 100 percent probability, no more difficult than trying to hit a barn wall with a howitzer placed inside it.

Though it was a needless imposition, the commander of the Odessa Military District had taken great pains to ensure the demonstration's success, but now Kolpakchi had suggested that they get a better view; he wanted to go up in the helicopter to observe, and this concerned the general. During the flight from Odessa to Nikolayev, Babadzhanyan had noticed an odd vibration in the main rotor. All the instruments had functioned normally and the controls had responded properly, but he could sense a problem about to assert itself. Good pilots learned to anticipate trouble before it materialized. All old pilots were good pilots, and Babadzhanyan was among the oldest and most experienced in the Red Army. He argued briefly with Kolpakchi about the need for an unscheduled flight, but in the end he acquiesced. It was within his right as aircraft commander to refuse to fly an unsafe vehicle, but what could he say was wrong? The problem was in his instincts, and these would not suffice. The odd thing was that Perevertkin seemed to share his concerns because Kolpakchi's suggestion made him turn white and he began making excuses. In the end, however, Kolpakchi had pushed the KGB man aboard.

Babadzhanyan checked his watch as the rotor began turning. The drone would be in the target area in seven minutes; the missile would be launched one minute later. He turned to his copilot. "How long since our last autogyration?"

"January, Comrade General. You made the landing. Permission to switch frequencies?"

"Why?"

"Static on this one," the lieutenant colonel lied. "I'll inform the command post that we're going off primary." Perevertkin had instructed him to change frequencies during the second flight, which meant now. It would be good to get the KGB off his back once and for all.

The general's earphones seemed clear, but it was a routine request. "Go ahead, but if we lose power I'll take it." The rotor was cutting the air with heavy whacks now, the helicopter bouncing against its shock absorbers. "Clear our right."

"Starboard is clear," the copilot shouted across the cockpit.

"Ready for takeoff," he radioed to the command post. One radio call done, one to go and he would be free.

The general glanced left. "Also clear to the left. Here we go." The helicopter vibrated as the copilot shifted the rotor's pitch and began a slow, forward assent.

Suddenly Perevertkin appeared between the two pilots, screaming, "Don't use the radio!"

"Airborne," the copilot broadcast, and then was engulfed in white light.

WEDNESDAY, MARCH 3, 1961, 2:38 P.M.
SAM Proving Ground, Nikolayev, Oblast

Bailov was floating under his canopy when the helicopter lifted off. He watched the silver craft start a climb up a low ridge, then assumed his landing position and struck the ground. The sky was filled with chutes and the clatter of equipment. He heard the scream of the target drone just before the missile drove into its port engine and turned the ancient aircraft into a cascading fireball. As debris was blown into fiery arcs there was another explosion above the ridge and Bailov saw another fireball, followed by a curl of thick black smoke from the trees.

On the ground his men shed their canopies and ran off in files to secure their objectives as he used hand signals to move them.

Melko was beside Bailov when he smashed through the door of the observation building. Inside they found a dozen surprised civilians and military personnel. "Where's Babadzhanyan?" Bailov shouted, brandishing his Kalashnikov.

"In the helicopter," a major said, pointing at the fire-covered ridge.

Bailov held out his hand and his radioman handed him the mike. "Gladiators, this is Centurion. Stick Five, secure the observation building; Stick Six, provide cover. All other groups converge on the ridge and set up a perimeter around the crash area. The downed chopper is our objective. Move now. Centurion out." He handed the microphone back as they ran out of the building. *Shit.*

There were no survivors. The wreckage was not badly scattered, but there had been a flash fire inside. One section had seven bodies still strapped in their seats, their flesh black, their clothes burned away. The stench was overpowering. Parts of other bodies were stuck to aircraft parts.

"Dig in," Bailov told his men over the radio. "If anybody tries to move anything out of this area, shoot him. Nothing is to be touched until I say so." One disaster after another.

Melko returned to the observation building with him. "Who was in the helicopter with Babadzhanyan?" he asked a nervous colonel.

"There's no manifest," the colonel said. "It was an unscheduled flight. We'll have to call the roll."

"Then do it," Bailov snapped. "Now!" They had been *so* close.

The accounting took an hour. The thirteen missing included Babadzhanyan, his crew of three, five officers from the proving grounds and three Moscow VIPs: General Kolpakchi, the General Staff's chief of combat training; Perevertkin, deputy chairman of the KGB; and General Gaffe, a deputy of Varentsov, marshal of the tactical missile forces.

Bailov's first call went to the unit assigned to take out the demolition laboratory, which was located in a forested area above a stretch of isolated beach forty kilometers east of Odessa. "Moon Strike, this is Centurion."

"This is Moon Strike," Ezdovo replied immediately. "Mission complete here. No casualties. The facility is secured, so you can take your time out there."

Finally some good luck. Bailov allowed himself to relax. "Hold it until I get there. Nobody gets out. Detain any visitors."

His second call went to Talia in Moscow via a communications relay in Odessa. "One out of two," he reported. "We have the explosives facility, but we weren't so lucky at the proving ground." Quickly he explained what had happened.

"Survivors?"

"None."

"Assume that the crash was no accident," Talia said. "Be thorough," she added before hanging up.

 WEDNESDAY, MAY 3, 1961, 9:20 P.M.
Moscow

Boris Shelepin's reputation for womanizing was a well-kept secret outside the Kremlin; he was discreet, but in his position as director of the KGB he kept his personal security unit informed of his whereabouts even when he visited his consorts. Yepishev had learned that tonight Shelepin would visit a Romanian woman who lived on the same street as the offices of the Patriarch of the Russian Orthodox Church. The building was not far from the Foreign Ministry and was leased to the Romanian government for use as a guest house. Shelepin's hostess would be the twenty-year-old daughter of the deputy director of the Romanian secret police.

Talia parked her car near the church offices, walked slowly around the gentle curve of the narrow street and stopped in the shadows of the street's only light. A black Zil was parked near the gate to the house, with two men in black leather coats lingering in the entryway and two smaller vehicles parked farther down the street.

She stopped within a hundred meters of the house, turned her back to the security people and took a walkie-talkie from her coat. "This is Talia," she said. "Three vehicles. Two men on the sidewalk immediately in front by the Zil and two black Pobedas down the street to the west. Copy?"

"Copy," a voice said. "That's all?"

"All that I can see. Start now."

"One minute," the voice said. "Keep your head down in case they're not cooperative."

A man got out of the Zil and began walking toward her. She turned her face to him and made a flame with a small lighter. The man stopped and looked back at the Zil, as if he were expecting instructions.

Ropes slapped against the sides of buildings up and down the street and black-clad Spetsnaz silently rappeled down to the dark street. Twenty of Bailov's soldiers sprinted along the walls, and within seconds had the security detachment under control. Down the street she saw the interior lights flicker on, then off, in the Pobedas. She never heard the doors open or shut but she knew that Bailov's men now had control of the area. She was impressed at how quickly and quietly they had attacked.

The young woman who came to the door had piled her shiny black hair hurriedly on her head. She had dark brown eyes that betrayed fear as she looked out at Talia and the two uniformed Spetsnaz behind her. "I've come to see Comrade Shelepin," Talia said as she pushed her way in. "Tell him I'm waiting."

The girl ran up the winding wooden staircase, clutching a red robe around her.

Shelepin appeared moments later, stopping on the landing to adjust his tie. He was forty-three but looked much younger; he was trim and handsome, with thick black hair and an easy, disarming smile. It had been Khrushchev who had moved him from the Komsomol to the KGB and ordered him to repair its public image—part of the General Secretary's cosmetics to make the Soviet Union more palatable to the West. When he got to the bottom of the stairs Talia held the Red Badge out to him.

"Very impressive," he said, "but hardly necessary. An appointment could have been arranged. I'm a simple civil servant."

"I don't like to be patronized," she said. "Please follow me."

"This is not an opportune moment," he said with a glance over his shoulder. The Romanian girl had crept down to the landing and was watching.

"That's a matter of perspective."

"Shall I fetch my overcoat?"

"No need. We'll bring you back to your . . ."—Talia paused—"engagement."

A sedan was waiting outside. "Tell your dogs to behave while we're away," she told Shelepin as they passed his security people. The Spetsnaz commander had collected his men in the garden beside the front walk.

"Everything is under control," Shelepin said to his men. "I'll be back." He got into the backseat beside Talia. "Now," he said in a weak attempt to assert control, "what's this all about?"

"It's a matter of state security."

The KGB director smiled. "State security is my concern."

"Not when *you* are the focus." Talia thought she saw him tense, but he recovered quickly and hid his emotions well.

"Whom do you represent?"

"An interest in the truth. Where's Perevertkin?"

"I'm not certain."

She guessed he was stalling in order to assess the situation. "Then you're not doing your job, comrade." She took some papers from her purse, turned on the overhead light and handed them to him.

"What are these?"

"Read."

Shelepin was visibly nervous now. "What about them?" he said after a quick scan of the documents.

"You initialed them."

"I sign hundreds of papers every week."

"Look closer."

He pulled the papers nearer to his face. "This light is poor in here," he complained. "They look like my initials."

"They're not."

His confident demeanor was gone now. "Say what's on your mind."

Was he fighting anger or fear? Both, she guessed. "These were forged by the late Comrade Velak. They were the cause of his death."

"Nonesense. Velak died of a heart attack."

"He was murdered. He engineered the transfer of a man named Villam Lumbas, now also dead. The investigator assigned to find Lumbas found his way to Velak and was himself murdered. The investigator had made contact with Katya Dirikova—"

"Dirikova?" The name seemed to stump Shelepin.

"She's a secretary in your central administrative section; she transcribes the tapes of the security selection committee meetings. She didn't know what the investigator wanted, but she was suspicious of his motives and informed Velak, who told her he would take care of it. Two days later the investigator was dead, and soon after Velak as well."

"This is some sort of crazy fairy tale."

"Comrade Denisov was also murdered," she went on.

"Suicide-murder," Shelepin said quickly. "His wife was much younger than he and unstable. The family has a history of certain instabilities."

"Denisov's daughter, son-in-law and children were murdered the same day."

"There was a robbery. Our investigation concluded that they came home during the crime and were killed."

"It was an attempted robbery," Talia said, "but their fate was sealed from the outset. Denisov's son-in-law had stumbled on a series of special accounts that were connected to the Odessa Military District, off-the-books accounts used to fund certain sensitive operations. When the original investigator on the Lumbas case was killed I took over."

"What operations?"

"That's what you're going to tell me."

"Why should I? You have no clearance for such information."

"My badge gives me all the authority I need. I believe Velak forged your initials. Your frequent absence from committee meetings made it easy for him. He wanted Lumbas transferred, and you gave him the opportunity to do it."

"I don't know anything about these fantasies of yours."

She stared at him for a long time, then turned off the overhead light. "For now I will accept that, but in my estimation Velak was not the sort to work on his own."

"He was Perevertkin's man," Shelepin said.

"In what way?"

"Velak was his administrator. Perevertkin is more the type for grand schemes, but only if the risks are low."

"He was Serov's longtime deputy. How did he react when you replaced Serov?"

"Perevertkin could teach the Chinese to kowtow. He has no ambition for greater power."

"Had," she said. "He was killed today in a helicopter crash at the Nikolayev Proving Ground."

Shelepin stared at her for a long time. "He told me that General Babadzhanyan asked him to attend a missile demonstration," he said.

"The general was in the same helicopter. Is it normal for a deputy director of the KGB to attend such events?"

Shelepin was visibly shaken and shook his head solemnly. "They were old friends. I took it to be an excuse to spend time with a friend. That sort of thing is not unusual."

"I have a line of bodies that suggests otherwise. Every time I move the line of investigation in a new direction, bodies pile up. I don't believe in multiple coincidences."

"What is this all about?" Shelepin asked, his voice weak.

"I'm not at liberty to say. What I expect from you is complete details on these." Annochka and her husband had died while saving the records of the Odessa accounts. Talia placed copies of them in Shelepin's lap. "I also want complete dossiers on Perevertkin, Babadzhanyan, Lumbas and Velak."

The KGB director didn't look at the files. "How do I reach you?"

"Collect them and I'll reach you." She could smell his sweat.

When they returned to the Romanian woman's house, Shelepin lingered in the backseat. "I know nothing about any of this," he whispered.

"That's a poor testament to your fitness to hold such high office," Talia said. She was pressing hard, she knew, but the entire team had gone too far to turn back now. "Enjoy your evening," she called to him when he got out and stood on the sidewalk, blinking wildly.

---

143 THURSDAY, MAY 4, 1961, 3:50 A.M.
Odessa

As the chopper let down the occupants could see where Ezdovo's trucks had crashed through three rows of electrified concertina wire. The Siberian and several Spetsnaz were waiting outside a low, cinder-block building. "You won't believe this place," he said by way of greeting Bailov and Melko.

"It went smoothly?"

Ezdovo laughed. "There's only one man here. No security. Television cameras monitor the fence, and the grounds are one big minefield."

"But your trucks got through?"

"The mines are electrically controlled from inside, and luckily the switch was off. Comrade Chelitnikov was lost in his work when we came through."

"Chelitnikov." Bailov remembered the day he had spent with the bomb designer years before. He was tall, with shaggy brown hair, hollow cheeks and a strap-on artificial leg—when he sat down for any length of time he removed the leg and used it as an ashtray.

As the three of them walked through the building Bailov saw that the various rooms were filled with wooden crates, metal tubes with shredded paper packing, long workbenches covered with timers and detonators, ammo cases and an entire wall with shock-resistant nitro containers; the place was like a museum of explosives and munitions. When they reached the laboratory they found Chelitnikov sitting on a stack of ammo cases, his artificial leg off, a cigarette in hand, butts all over the floor, a technical manual on his lap, his eyeglasses perched on the end of his nose.

"Good," Chelitnikov said with a smile; then his expression changed. "I remember you. Spetsnaz, right? You had some vibration charges that weren't working. It was the chemical core. I changed it and it solved your problem, right?"

"We didn't come here to talk about the past."

The explosives expert pointed his cigarette at them and laughed. "All talk is about the past. As soon as you make a sound it's not the present anymore. Something went wrong with the device I made for Perevertkin, is that it?"

"You made a bomb for him?"

"Device, not bomb. A bomb is stupid, but a device is an extension of my intelligence. I installed it myself on the helicopter. I wired it to the radio."

"Why?"

Chelitnikov shrugged. "None of my business. I don't concern myself with reasons, just what, how and when."

"Perevertkin was on the helicopter when it exploded."

"A pity, I'm sure, but not my fault. The detonator was rigged to activate the device the second time a certain radio frequency was used on the second engine-start of the day."

"Perevertkin ordered the device?"

"Actually my main contact was Colonel Gaponov. When devices were needed, he usually provided the specifications and I did the rest."

"Gaponov ordered the device you installed on the helicopter?"

Chelitnikov stared at his cigarette and grunted. "Sometime back."

"You have records of this?"

The bomb maker dropped his cigarette into the artificial leg, lit another and tapped his head. "I work alone, so I keep everything up here. It's safer that way. No need for records, which could fall into the wrong hands, and it's less expense for the state. Perevertkin came here last night—or did I already tell you that?"

The three men exchanged glances. "For what?" Ezdovo asked.

"He told me he wanted the new device installed on the helicopter this morning and I explained how it worked."

"That was it?"

"Thirty minutes. He seemed extremely nervous, but if you ask me that's not unusual for political types."

"Did you see him today?" Bailov asked.

"This morning while I installed the device, but we didn't talk. I just did my job."

Bailov tried to think. It didn't make sense that Perevertkin would kill himself, so something had to have gone wrong. Had the KGB man intended the bomb for Babadzhanyan? "Is there a way such a device could malfunction?"

"None," Chelitnikov said confidently.

"The vibration mines didn't work correctly," Bailov reminded him.

Chelitnikov looked annoyed and glared at him. "They were not my design. You called me to fix someone else's problem, and I did. This device was set for the second flight of the day, and I assume that's when it detonated."

"It *was* the second flight," Melko said suddenly. "Someone told me that the flight was the idea of the man called Kolpakchi."

"Chief of combat training for the general staff," Bailov said.

"Apparently he wanted a closer look at the missile intercept," Melko said. "I heard this from several people in the bunker. Perevertkin didn't want to go and made a fuss, but Kolpakchi prevailed."

"Where was Perevertkin's body found?" Bailov asked.

Melko took a notebook from his pocket, leafed through the pages, passed it to Bailov and pointed at a crude diagram. "What was left of him was hung up on the copilot's control column. There was part of a leg stuck in the ladder that probably led up to the crew deck. We never found his head."

Bailov was familiar with this model of helicopter. "There are no jump seats in choppers. Could he have been standing on the ladder behind the pilots?"

"No way to tell," Melko said. "But all the others were either still strapped in, or there were harness fragments embedded in their torsos."

"We know that Kolpakchi wanted a closer look, and Perevertkin was apparently forced to go along. But he knew about the bomb, which left him no choice but to try and stop the general and his copilot from using the radio."

"At the risk of alerting the others to the bomb," Melko reminded him.

"He knew he'd die if he didn't. Why did Kolpakchi want the flight?" Bailov passed the notebook back.

"We'll never know," Melko said. "Live generals rarely give reasons, and dead ones not at all."

"So," Chelitnikov said, "if we're finished, I'd like to get back to my work."

"Did you ever make a device with watch gears?" Bailov asked. There was something about this man that made his skin crawl.

Chelitnikov nodded with obvious pleasure. "Just one, and it was a masterpiece. A quarter kilo of plastique with a double switch, the whole thing no bigger than two packs of cigarettes."

"Installed on an aircraft?"

"That was the one. Ingenious. The detonation was designed to push the engine down into the slipstream, which in turn would cause the wing to separate. A pop more than a bang. Very subtle. I had to be careful to brace the device's supports properly or the aircraft's vibrations might have disconnected it, or worse."

"You installed it yourself?"

"Of course."

"When?"

Chelitnikov pursed his lips and mumbled to himself while he counted on his fingers. "Six weeks ago."

The bomb that killed Gaponov had exploded on April 25. "Where?"

"Moscow."

"Vnukovo?"

"No, it was at some sort of special airport north of the city. Just a small place, with no fighters. Mostly old stuff, twin-engine scows."

"How did you keep it from activating for six weeks?"

The bomb maker raised an eyebrow. "I made a new stem for the watch. It worked like a safety pin. As long as the stem was pulled out and safetied there was no danger. Once the stem was in, the timer started."

"But somebody had to disconnect the safety. You?"

"I only installed the device."

"Who was your client for that one?"

"Perevertkin, which was a surprise. As I said earlier, I usually dealt with Gaponov. They were my only customers. This is a KGB installation dedicated solely to manufacturing devices for them."

Bailov evaluated what he had heard and told Ezdovo, "Call Talia. Tell her we need to know Perevertkin's movements from early evening April 24 to daybreak April 25. We also need to know if Shelepin knows about this place."

"I have work to do," Chelitnikov said, making no effort to hide his growing irritation.

Melko said, "We have two of Perevertkin's security people at the proving ground. Lucky bastards. There wasn't enough room for them on the flight. Two others were killed in the crash. The survivors may be able to help us pin down his movements that day."

Ezdovo returned soon after. "Talia says she can't get that information right away."

Chelitnikov clapped his hands together, brushed away ashes, seated the artifical leg in its housing and began buckling the straps. "So, that's it?"

"Yes," Bailov said, "that's it."

"Excellent," the demolition expert said. "Excellent."

Bailov stopped at the door of the laboratory.

"What do we do about this place?" Ezdovo asked softly. "Blow it?"

"Too dangerous," Bailov said. "We've got no idea what's here. We'll leave people here to keep it secured and send in demolition teams later to remove the explosives a few at a time."

"What about him?" Ezdovo asked.

Bailov opened the door and called two of his men inside. "That's Comrade Chelitnikov over there. Take him outside the perimeter and shoot him."

144   THURSDAY, MAY 4, 1961, 8:40 A.M.
Rome

It had been ten days since the discovery of Sultana Fregosi's body and four days since they had learned that despite the trap they had set in Zurich, Frash had gotten his money through a complicated banking arrangement with a partner institution in Italy. Zurich had no way of knowing this until auditors caught it in a debit report that was traced to Genoa. Sylvia and Valentine had moved to Rome and checked into a hotel near the American embassy a block from the Tiber. The city would give them better flight possibilities if and when Frash surfaced again. The Italian police had issued a national alert that had triggered an onslaught of alleged sightings, but so far none of them had checked out, and they did not have a lot of faith in the Italians' motivation to stay the course.

Valentine was sitting on the balcony nursing a cup of espresso. "He has to know now that his passports are worthless," he said. "He'll drop even further under our radar from now on, same as he did coming out of Zurich."

"We don't *know* that," Sylvia said.

If Frash didn't know, he soon would. They had talked the authorities into sending a photograph to Italian newspapers. It was appearing every other day and would keep running until the news organizations were told to stop, or until the CIA money stopped flowing. Nothing was free in Italy; it was good to know that its people had not changed much since the war. "He'll know it when he sees his face in the funny papers."

"All it will do is spook him," she said. "I'd rather have him thinking he's in the clear. This way he'll keep looking over his shoulder. We're not a posse," she added, "and you're not some Texas Ranger reading tracks in the badlands."

"Be a lot easier out there."

"There's got to be a pattern," Sylvia said. "We know that at least part of the time he's not moving randomly. He got passports from the Dutch woman, arranged for money in Zurich, picked it up in Genoa and went to ground in Venice."

Valentine got up, went back into their room, took a map of Europe out of Sylvia's bag, spread it on the bed and pulled a chair over. "All right. Let's try it your way. We know he started out in Belgrade."

"We *assume*."

"All right, but we know he was in France." He pawed through her purse looking for a pen but found only an eyeliner pencil. He circled Lamoura, then Amsterdam, drew a heavy line between the two and added lines to Zurich, Genoa and Venice.

"Add Paris," Sylvia added. "Before Lamoura. Gabler said he thought he'd made some flights to Paris, and we know that this all started there. When you build an escape plan you use a familiar route, then break off it unexpectedly."

"That makes you predictable." Valentine's training had been different.

"*If* the other side knows that you're moving. If not, familiarity provides control, which in turn assures security. If you use regular patterns you understand where the opportunities are. In any event, the whole thing began in Paris, and when it fell apart in Belgrade he would have headed back. It's logical."

Valentine nodded, drew a line from Paris to Lamoura and stood up to get a better perspective. "Nothing," he said after a while.

"The lines don't cross," she said after studying the map. "If Paris was the starting point, he went south, north, south again to Zurich, then farther south to Genoa, then north to Venice." After another pause she asked, "Does that mean he'll go north again?"

"We can't predict on the basis of this pattern."

"He's not wandering aimlessly," Sylvia said slowly. "Credentials, money, asylum. The money wasn't the objective; it's just a tool, like the passports. He went to Venice to hide. He goes only where he has a reason to. Intent," she added.

Valentine tried to humor her. "Maybe he wants to go back to Yugoslavia."

"He'd need a visa to get in. His passports wouldn't help."

Valentine prowled around the room. "He's crazy. How do we apply logic to that?"

"He's schizoid, which means that part of the time he's perfectly logical, maybe even obsessively logical. Since Holland he's moved steadily east, and every step has had a purpose. He's not moving aimlessly."

"Without visas he's gone about as far east as he can go. And he can't cross red borders the way he can in the West," Valentine pointed out.

"If he'd planned to leave Europe he could have gotten out from Venice. He had plenty of time and the means; instead he chose to hunker down there. His next move has to be to the east."

"All that's left is Austria."

"I have a feeling," Sylvia said.

145   FRIDAY, MAY 5, 1961, 11:50 A.M.
En Route to Moscow

Most of his men were sleeping as the plane droned northward, but Bailov couldn't join them. Perevertkin's surviving security men said they had driven him to a special airport north of the city on a night that might have been the twenty-fourth of April. He had gone into a hangar, stayed a short time, and then they had returned him to his residence. Bailov thought about the long, bloody trail that seemed to point to Perevertkin, but if this was the end, why did it feel unfinished? What was Perevertkin's link to Lumbas and the American named Frash? Until this loose end was tied it wasn't over, he told himself.

Melko broke his concentration. "Whatever you're thinking about," he said with a smile, "I hope it doesn't include parachutes."

146   FRIDAY, MAY 5, 1961, 5:30 P.M.
Milan

Kenya appeared frazzled when she climbed into the trailer after dark and threw her purse and a newspaper on the couch. "You look tired," Frash said.

She sat down, kicked off her shoes and let her head flop backward. "Cops," she said. "They grabbed me this morning and put me in a truck.

Four of them, led by a Fascist lieutenant who says they're thinking about charging me with kidnapping. I said, 'It's my sister's baby. He likes crowds.' It's an old routine; they threaten charges and I counter with alibis. In the end it comes down to money. The pig wanted fifty thousand lire. I told him I had thirty thousand, and if they'd only let me do my work I'd have the rest. The swine says, 'Okay, thirty thousand and a blow job.' I say, 'Fine, pull it out and let's get on with it.' He says, 'For all of us.' I need a swim," she said disgustedly as she stomped out of the trailer.

Frash followed her down to the clear creek behind her place and watched her undress. She had the lean, hard muscles of a swimmer and small buttocks shaped like an inverted heart. He sat on the moss-covered rock and scanned the newspaper while she splashed around. On the bottom of the front page there was a short article with a headline that read SUMMIT IMMINENT? Several Italian diplomats were quoted as saying that Khrushchev and Kennedy had agreed to a meeting in Europe, but as yet no time or location had been announced. The reporter ended the piece with a speculation; his sources had reported that Austrian security forces had been notified of leave cancellations during the last week of May and the first week of June. His stomach tightened when he read the report and felt himself drawing nearer to Kennedy.

Deeper in the front section Frash stared at himself in a one-column photo captioned, "Wanted for Questioning." The brief piece below described a multiple homicide. There was a physical description, but no name or nationality was mentioned, and there was nothing about a reward. He should have taken the bodies farther out to sea and weighted them with chains, but he had been spooked by the Americans' appearance and had not been thinking clearly. The piece listed a local telephone number to call with information. The photos had to be the Company's work, which meant they had lost his trail and were trying to flush him out. He knew that they would keep running the photograph and that eventually the woman would see it. "Goddammit," he cursed softly.

"What?" Kenya asked. She was directly in front of him, brushing her hair.

"Nothing. Seems like there's nothing but bad news in the paper these days."

"That's why I never read them. Only *gadji* need somebody else to tell them life is hard. You should do what I do."

She's a risk, he told himself. The police will harass her again and she might betray me to get them off her back. He would have to move on. Whoever had placed the photograph was counting on his connecting with someone, and understood how he worked.

"I need help crossing the border," he said. "Undetected."

"Which one?"

"Into Austria."

"I thought you were happy here."

He saw that she was upset. "You knew it couldn't be permanent."

She draped the towel over her shoulder and gave him her hand so that he could help her up the bank. "I didn't think it would be so short."

"Some things are beyond our control."

She laughed. "Do you care how much it costs to get across?"

"No." He folded the newspaper and flicked it into the stream, then fell into step beside her.

"It's risky," she said.

"There's danger everywhere. Most people don't recognize it for what it is."

There was no more conversation while she made dinner. Afterward they went to bed. She was on her knees and bent forward, pushing her hips backward to receive his thrusts, gasping, reaching back to claw his legs with her long fingers. "Do it hard, *gadjo*. Use me," she said between moans.

Later she sat in a chair in the corner and smoked a dark cheroot whose ember glowed. "If you want to go," she said, "there's only one condition. You'll have to take me with you."

"Why?"

"You smell dangerous to me, *gadjo,* and I like how that feels."

"Are you Catholic?"

She laughed. "As much as any Gypsy can be Catholic. I've learned to appreciate more earthy idols."

Catholic and pagan. He liked that. "Shall we shake to close the deal?"

The ember disappeared and she crawled back into bed. "I have a better idea."

147   SATURDAY, MAY 6, 1961, 8:45 A.M. *Moscow*

"Eat," Khrushchev told his unexpected visitors. He was clad in a faded flannel robe and scuffed leather slippers and looked groggy, but Talia knew from experience that this was one of his many guises. Like peasants everywhere, he awoke alert and ready for the day's work. The table was covered with sliced meat, cheeses, pickled vegetables, hard-boiled eggs and loaves of bread. A samovar hissed at the end of the table. Talia, Petrov and Gnedin had no interest in eating, but when Khrushchev got something in his head it was impossible to dislodge it.

The General Secretary smeared a layer of lard on a thick slice of black bread and picked through a pile of tomato wedges with his fork. He had listened to Talia's briefing without interrupting, but he seemed to be more interested in his breakfast than in what she had to tell him. Even Petrov, who had insisted on coming along, looked more intent on the back of one of his bony hands than on her report. "The lesson seems to be that you can never tell where a threat will come from," Khrushchev said finally. "Who would have imagined Perevertkin at the center of anything other than his own farts?"

Talia glanced at her leader. Having dealt alone with Khrushchev for the past few weeks, she was suddenly unsure about how to proceed in Petrov's presence. Bailov had insisted that while Perevertkin seemed to be at the center of something, they still didn't know what it was. Now Petrov was gazing at a wall. "Everything began with Lumbas," she said. It was impossible to tell where Petrov had drifted off to, but there was no time to wait for his return.

"He's dead," Khrushchev said with his mouth full. "Or did I hear incorrectly?"

"That's not the point," Talia said.

"Perevertkin took him out of Tyuratam, and now both of them are dead."

"But *why* did he pull him out?" Gnedin always looked past the disease to its manifestations. "Until we know that, nothing is settled."

Unexpectedly, Petrov stirred to life beside Talia. "A conspiracy is contagious," he said. "When winter comes, malaria abates and no more cases are reported. But is it finished? Spring comes, the ice melts, the air warms, the mosquitoes rise and the epidemic resumes. To end it you must eliminate the conditions that gave rise to it."

"The Russian soul encourages conspiracy," Khrushchev said. "It's our true religion, but it can't be sustained without leaders. Perevertkin is dead, and with him any potential conspiracy."

"Certainty is a trap of small minds," Petrov said.

"A fox has an instinct for traps."

"Old foxes and old men indulge themselves."

Khrushchev sat back and crossed his short arms. "Age is more than an accumulation of birthdays. Old men know where they want to go and how to get there."

Petrov nodded solemnly. "Conditions and men change. Consider Stalin and yourself. Who were his advisers? Whom did he trust?"

A weak laugh issued from the General Secretary. "That bastard trusted no one. He was his own man, and his word was law. What's your point?"

"Is your hold on power as absolute?" Khrushchev stared at Petrov but did not answer. "If Stalin wanted the Winter Palace painted in zebra stripes the scaffolds would have been up and the ground floor done before he had finished talking."

"That time is gone."

"Precisely," Petrov said. "You can't drive the counry alone. You took Stalin's seat but not his power, and now you are forced to create alliances with this faction or that individual, and with every issue you face the alliances change, depending on who gains or loses."

"It's no longer the thirties," Khrushchev muttered.

Petrov's voice was barely audible, but his listeners were mesmerized. "You are to be congratulated for what you have accomplished. The gulags are empty, you've opened windows to the West, the people are with you for now, and all this by virtue of your wits rather than the strong arm of the apparat. Better than anyone else, you understand that power here is no longer absolute; yet there's security in the delicacy of a balancing act. Just as you rule by shifting alliances, those who would unseat you must seek the same equilibrium. It follows that Perevertkin, given his level and assuming he was what he appeared to be, could not have operated without ties to those above him. Only when we understand his alliances can we know for certain that our work is finished. To ignore such realities is to encourage conspirators to adjust to their losses and renew their efforts."

Khrushchev leaned toward the small dark man. "Let's assume for the moment that your assumptions are correct. Would you then agree that if Perevertkin represents a broader threat, his death diminishes that threat in the near term?"

"I never said that the threat was broad," Petrov said. "In fact it's likely to be narrowly focused."

"There's no evidence pointing to me as the focus."

"True, but your instincts launched our investigation. You felt threatened enough to turn to me, someone outside the power structure and therefore not beholden to anyone."

"Everything you've done points to Perevertkin, and now he's dead." The General Secretary was losing patience.

"We don't yet understand the architecture of the conspiracy. What were his intentions? While everything points to him, it's possible to see all the events from Lumbas and Trubkin onward as a kind of covering action. Trubkin intervened and was murdered. We intervened, so there were attempts directed at us, and when these failed, everyone in our path was destroyed before we could interrogate them."

"We want to take it to the finish," Talia said.

Khrushchev pushed his hands into the pockets of his robe. "You can continue for now," he said over his shoulder as he left the room, but Talia sensed that change was in the wind.

148   SATURDAY, MAY 6, 1961, 7:20 P.M. *Melago, Italy*

"Let me do the talking, *gadjo*," Kenya warned. On the tree line Frash saw several wagons and three large fires burning, their embers rising in the dusk. "Stay here," Kenya whispered, and kissed him lingeringly before slipping away.

Frash saw people near the fires and heard female voices, loud and contentious. The language was Romany, which he had often heard in Boston; an argument was under way. He squatted in the high grass and made sure he was alone. So far Kenya had proven trustworthy but with Gypsies you had to be alert at all times. She had assured him she could get him across the border if he took her with him. "Why should I take you?" he had asked.

Her eyes flashed as her hand closed on his neck. "I like taking care of you," she said with a little squeeze.

The discussion in the Gypsy camp was animated and continued for nearly an hour. Eventually Kenya returned, fumbling to light a cigarette. When the match illuminated her face he saw that she was anxious. "There are several wagons," she said, pointing back at the camp. "We get into the one on the far right. Get in, sit down and keep still. No talking. When we leave here, follow me and keep your eyes down. Watch the backs of my legs and look at no one, understand?"

He tried to embrace her, but she pulled away roughly and struck his chest with a fist. "This is no game, *gadjo*!" she hissed.

Frash followed closely behind her as she led him through the field. Several horses in rope hobbles nickered softly as they passed. When they reached the wagon, she swung open the bottom half of a Dutch door, crawled up a small ladder and disappeared inside. "Hurry," she said. Frash started in behind her, glanced back and saw a man in a green tunic glowering at him. The man had long hair, a heavy mustache and an eye that seemed to be all white.

"Shit," Kenya said as she reached out, pulled him inside and slammed the door. "Fool!" she cursed as she began pounding him. Her voice was angry and desperate. "Idiot," she said over and over.

The wagon lurched awkwardly throughout the night. Several times Frash thought it would topple onto its side, but each time it righted itself and continued on. He sat in the darkness, bracing himself. "This is crazy," he told Kenya at one point. She answered by pressing a finger to his lips. When Ali tried to put his hand under her blouse she pushed him away. "Later," she said. "If we live."

When the light began to seep through the cracks in the shuttered windows, the wagon slowed on a steep incline. Kenya crawled past him and tried the door, but it wouldn't budge. She moved back toward a small window but the wagon lurched suddenly and knocked her down.

"What?" Frash asked, crawling toward her.

"Locked in," she said. The wagon seemed to be speeding up, the ground leveling.

Frash tried the rear door with the same result. "Kick it out," Kenya said. She sounded frantic.

It took several blows but the wood around the latch finally gave way and the upper door popped open. Kenya climbed over, stood on the small ladder and leaped, rolling to her left. Frash followed. "Quick," she urged as he hit the ground. They crawled into the trees, then got to their feet and ran. He heard the wagon still moving and the horses snorting. Moving through the pines like a deer, Kenya led him down a rocky slope to a trail. They ran for a long time. By the time they finally stopped, they were soaked with sweat and dew, their chests heaving from exertion and altitude.

Frash unbuttoned his shirt to let air circulate. "What the hell's going on?"

"You saw his face."

"Meaning?"

"They would have killed us."

"Seems extreme." He was more interested than anxious.

"They're a crossover clan. They carry people across, but *gadji* may not see their faces. For security."

"Which explains the unscheduled exit."

"Better than the alternative," she said grimly.

When they regained their breath, Kenya led him along a narrow canyon with a silver creek far below. A flock of white birds glided below them and the rising sun cast a yellowish glow on the snow-covered peaks all around them.

"Are we in Austria?" Frash asked from behind her. She was moving at a steady pace.

"We were almost at the border when we started last night."

"Then let's rest here." Kennedy was close now; he could feel his presence.

"Better keep going."

"There's always time for life's sweetest diversion."

She cocked her head and studied him. "Not here," she said. "Patience is a virtue."

"Now and here," he repeated. His voice froze her in place.

They were on the lip of a nearly vertical rock wall. When she looked down she instinctively pulled away. "Down the trail. There will be better places farther on." She didn't care if it sounded like pleading; this was too dangerous.

"Here," he insisted.

She undid the red scarf from her waist and dropped it. The white silk blouse and lavender skirt followed, forming a pool of cloth at her feet. "You always have to have everything your own way, don't you, *gadjo?*"

Ali smiled and lay down on his back. The earth felt cool and moist. She lowered herself onto him, but made love tentatively. "Don't hold back," he growled. Their bodies quickened.

When she threw her head back and arched her spine, Ali grabbed her right arm just above the elbow and pulled it down and to his left as he simultaneously drove his right leg up and vaulted her over his head. She fell silently, turning end over end and ricocheted off two rock outcroppings before crashing into a grove of aspens.

Albert wanted to bury her clothes, but Ali wouldn't allow it. "We have to hurry," he reminded his brother.

 SATURDAY, MAY 6, 1961, 8:50 P.M.
Moscow

Marshal Malinovsky's wife shopped every other Saturday night at Yeliseyev's on Gorky Street. Yeliseyev had once run a popular Moscow restaurant, but he had disappeared in the wake of the Revolution; now the former restaurant was a food shop officially known as Gastronom No. 1, but such was the former proprietor's reputation that his name endured. When he could, Malinovsky accompanied his wife, in part to restrain her spending, but also because it was good for other privileged people to see that the minister of defense took his domestic duties seriously. Left to her own devices, she would shop every day among the treasures of Yeliseyev's.

While his wife stood in line for English biscuits, sweet spongy crumpets and jellied fruits, Malinovsky moved on to find Colonel General Gubin.

Yeliseyev's was always crowded at night when privileged clientele could use darkness and plain packaging to mask its greed. One needed rank to have access here; the shelves were packed with goods from throughout the world and resold at sums only the elite could pay, but they were cheap compared with Western prices. People here even looked different. The women wore foreign dresses and high-heeled shoes. The men's haircuts were always fresh and their suits fit. Colognes and perfumes permeated the air. The ceilings and walls were covered with off-white plaster and ornate designs in bas-relief, everything gaudily accented in gold leaf; light beamed down from three chandeliers resembling fiery clusters of grapes with golden stems. Here, more than anywhere else in Russia, Malinovsky sensed what an aristocrat's life had been like during czarist times. As a peasant's son he had dreamed of such luxury, but he had never in his wildest dreams imagined that one day he would be entitled to such privileges.

It was an appropriate place to meet Gubin. Legend had it that Rasputin had sometimes used the room at the back of Yeliseyev's to deflower young nuns taken from the city's numerous convents. His henchmen brought the little sisters here and tied them to his bed. Rasputin labored all night on his victims, then threw them naked into the street in the morning. Rasputin, the outsider, had gained control over Czar Nicholas II. In the end there was only one way to stop him. Some St. Petersburg noblemen had poisoned the Antichrist, then shot and castrated him, and thrown his body into a hole cut in the ice of the Neva River. Which was a reminder that difficult men were not easy to kill; Malinovsky knew that the removal of Nikita Sergeievich would be no less difficult.

Gubin was hovering near the meat counter; he had selected two large lamb chops, which an elderly clerk was wrapping in brown paper. Malinovsky knew immediately what his friend was up to. Andrei Semenovich was no longer married. His wife had been an unpleasant actress named Angelique, who got fat soon after their marriage. Gubin was a handsome and vain man; going out in public with a fat woman was impossible for him to accept, so he had divorced her (rumor said with her father's assistance), and now moved from girlfriend to girlfriend. Judging by the lamb chops, he was on his way to another rendezvous.

"Dinner for two?"

Gubin shrugged. "She adores lamb."

"Perevertkin is dead," Malinovsky whispered.

"We were lucky." The general had already heard the news from his own sources.

"Pessimist," the defense minister said. "Luck is a natural force. It was supposed to look like an accident."

Gubin studied Malinovsky's bulldog face. It *had* been an accident, but not precisely what had been planned. The explosion was supposed to take place *after* the SAM test, but Perevertkin had somehow botched it and paid with his own life. They had designed everything to point toward Babadzhanyan; instead it had ended up pointing to Perevertkin, which might well bring the trail back to Moscow.

"It's just as well," Malinovsky went on. "He was weak. Eventually we would have been forced to do to him what he did to himself; he saved us the trouble."

Malinovsky was so matter-of-fact about the death of the deputy director of the KGB that Gubin wondered if Perevertkin's death had not been the stupid accident it seemed. The thought made him light-headed. Had Malinovsky planned accidents for others as well? "All the KGB needs is a name. They can build palaces out of air."

"Not when one of their own is in question. Nobody dares look left or right inside the KGB. Khrushchev installed Shelepin as a way to return control of it to the Party. Shelepin is not one of them, and because he's an outsider the rest of them must act in their own self-interest. It ends with Perevertkin because it's in the KGB's interest for it to end there."

The colonel general accepted his package of lamb chops and a receipt. To pay he had to take the paper to another line where a cashier was waiting with an abacus.

The marshal's wife bulled her way through the crowd to the two men and held up a bulging shopping bag. "It's like a treasure hunt," she said greedily. Twenty-five years younger than her husband, she was not quite forty, but was beginning to thicken in the waist; even so, she still had luxuriant golden hair and strong legs that tapered to delicate ankles.

"Andrei Semenovich," she greeted her husband's colleague, who smiled and bowed. She rolled her eyes and elbowed her husband. "You'd better watch this one, Rodion. Such eyes are meant for the bedroom. No woman but me can resist them."

As the three of them merged with other shoppers carrying armloads of packages and inched their way forward in a queue that snaked its way toward a fat cashier with blue hair, Gubin watched Malinovsky's passive face and wondered if the defense minister was feeling as secure as he appeared. If so, was his calm due to events yet to unfold? All of the plan's contingencies up to now had been hastily constructed and sloppily executed. The Albanians were supposed to strike against Khrushchev, but so far had shown unexpected patience.

When Gubin reached the cash register he put down the lamb chops and receipt, told the cashier he had changed his mind and hastily departed. The latest developments had dampened his desire for a night of lovemaking. Malinovsky watched him go and wondered if he was losing his nerve. Perhaps the exercise in damage control was not yet complete.

150   MONDAY, MAY 8, 1961, 10:30 A.M.
Tösens, Austria

Frash was tired, dirty and hungry, but he was determined to get out of the area before indulging his needs. It had been more than twenty-four hours since he had eliminated the Gypsy; without her he had become disoriented and found his way out of the mountains only by shadowing a group of hikers who had led him to a village, which he had skirted. Since yesterday he estimated that he had walked thirty kilometers. His feet were blistered and his leg muscles afire, but he made up his mind not to try for a ride until the situation felt right.

When he saw the red Mercedes truck, he made his move and stepped onto the shoulder, waving his arms. The truck's brakes squealed as it stopped, so that he could smell the rubber. The vehicle had Italian plates and an oversized bed, with its cargo secured under a black canvas.

"Have a problem?" the driver asked in Italian, his eyes scanning the tree line behind Frash.

The dialect was from somewhere in the south—Naples, Frash thought. "My girlfriend brought me up to her chalet, her husband showed up unexpectedly, and I had to make a run for it."

The Italian smiled and motioned for Frash to climb in. "At least you got away with your trousers," he said with a laugh as he worked through the gears.

"I would have gladly given up the trousers to keep what I carry in them," Frash answered.

The driver laughed again. "One time I got caught by a husband in Livorno. He was a stevedore with a nasty temper. He walked in just as his wife had her legs wrapped around me. We never heard him. First thing I knew, the bastard was bashing me in the head with a coal shovel. I was lucky he didn't break me in half." The man lifted a forelock of hair to show off a wicked scar. "I couldn't work for three months."

"Did you swear off married women after that?"

"Only my own," the driver said.

"Was the woman worth it?"

The driver snapped his right hand several times. "What's a little pain for the sweets of an eager woman?"

Before entering the village of Tösens, Frash asked the Italian to pull over. "I have to piss."

"There's a village just ahead. We can get some coffee and you can go there. Piss it out, put it back."

"Can't wait," Frash said.

The Italian grunted, checked his rearview and side mirrors and steered the rig onto the shoulder of the road.

They got out on opposite sides. While the Italian stood next to a set of wheels behind the cab, Frash circled around the long side and charged him, driving his head against the door. The man managed to get in a weak punch as they fell, but he was off balance and Ali was too strong; when they hit the pavement the driver was underneath. Ali grabbed the man by the hair and pounded his head against the pavement until he was unconscious.

The body was heavy, but Frash managed to drag it through the woods to where they opened onto a steep boulder field. He shot the man once, emptied his pockets and rolled him into a crevice in the rocks below. "Too much pasta," he complained to the corpse, then ran for the truck, released the parking brake, shifted into low gear and drove off.

In Landeck he stopped and bought a newspaper, then turned east toward Vienna. Let them try to track him this time.

151 **MONDAY, MAY 8, 1961, 3:00 P.M.**
Rome

Valentine was tired of reading police reports. Publishing Frash's photograph in the newspapers had sparked an endless stream of sightings, most of which the police rejected out of hand and only a few of which they followed up. The likelihood of such reports producing a capture seemed remote at best, but a courier delivered a batch of reports twice a day and he went through them diligently. Frash was reported as far south as Brindisi and as far north as Turin, where he reportedly asked a priest about a private viewing of the church's famous shroud. One report had him trying to get work as a gondolier in Venice; in another a woman from Pisa had called to say that her sister had spent the night with a man answering Frash's description. She wanted her sister arrested for adultery, assuring the authorities that she had a long history of such encounters and deserved to be punished.

Sylvia found Valentine on the balcony. He had used stones as paperweights to hold down the stacks of reports. She dropped her purse and leaned against the wrought-iron railing. "I talked to Arizona." Valentine perked up. "The Russians want another meeting, and this time they've picked the site."

"I hope it's someplace where people wear clothes in public."

152 · MONDAY, MAY 8, 1961, 4:00 P.M.
Innsbruck, Austria

When Frash pulled into a truck stop west of Innsbruck, he checked the cargo in back and found eight ornate wooden coffins. The vehicle was registered to a Naples company and the load was assigned to a mortuary in Vienna. He was tempted to keep the truck, but the information in the paperwork was scant and, given the Italian propensity for paying little attention to clocks or calendars, there was a good possibility that the delivery was overdue. It was safer to dump the vehicle, he decided, but not until he had gotten some rest. There was no sleeping compartment attached to the cab, but the driver had built himself a nest between the two rows of coffins.

It was dark when he awoke. The temperature had dropped and he stepped out into a light mist, climbed to a path above the parking area and started walking toward the faint glow of Innsbruck in the sky. A whiff of garlic reminded him of how long it had been since he had last eaten. He went into the first place he came to, ordered a dish of noodles, ate quickly and left. The town was empty; the skiers had cleared out and the summer gentry would not arrive until late June. He went to several bars, bought a beer in each, but left them untouched and saw little to interest him. The sight of the Gypsy woman spinning silently end over end played over and over in his mind, but Ali was satiated for the moment and Albert was determined to keep the upper hand now. Be smart, he cautioned himself. Khrushchev's photograph was on the front page of a paper he bought after changing a small amount of money.

At a tavern in the center of a village there was a crowded dance floor with a loud, slightly off-key rock 'n' roll band with too much percussion. He slithered his way between women jitterbugging together and couples clinging to each other under the spell of the beat. The light was poor and the air heavy with the scent of sweating bodies and cheap perfume. A red-haired girl ran her hand across the front of his trousers and smiled in encouragement, but when he kept moving she glowered at him and raised her fist in anger. A local, he guessed, which was not what he had in mind, at least not yet.

He saw a man with black hair and the stubble of a beard sitting at a corner table with a woman with long blond hair pulled back into a ponytail. "Sirini," the man was saying drunkenly. "I am to a camera what Michelangelo was to a paintbrush," he said, thumping his chest. "You've heard of Michelangelo?"

"Every Italian thinks he's someone important," the woman said wearily.

"Sirini *is* an artist," he repeated vehemently.

When Frash walked beyond the table he saw that Sirini was trying to wedge his hand between the woman's legs, but that she had clamped her knees together. There was a camera bag under his chair. Frash acted drunk and lurched into the Italian, breaking his hold below the table. "Sorry," he mumbled as he lay across the drunk and watched the woman scramble into the safety of the crowd. When she was gone, he delivered a crisp blow to the Sirini's throat and got to his feet as the man began to gag. A bouncer in a black leather coat came over and stood beside Frash as Sirini partially recovered his wind and vomited. "Your friend?" the bouncer asked.

"Never saw him before," Frash said.

The man helped Sirini to his feet and led him outside. Frash followed with the camera bag and handed it to the unsteady Italian. "Can't go to Vienna without that," the drunk said out loud to himself and started down the street. Frash followed and saw him stop at a Fiat, get a suitcase from the trunk, cross a small square and enter a hotel.

Frash returned to the tavern and saw the blond woman at the edge of the dance floor. She had luxuriant hair, a square build with rounded shoulders and a face that seemed to be off-center. She was one of those women, he decided, whose sum was inexplicably greater than her parts. When she saw that he was looking at her she gave him an encouraging smile and made her way toward him. "My rescuer," she said. "I think I should thank you."

"It's not necessary. He was drunk."

"What prompted you to rescue me?" Her voice was firm yet inviting, perhaps open to possibilities.

"I didn't think your legs would hold out."

Even in the poor light he could see her blush. "Italian men," she said disgustedly. "They refuse to accept no for an answer. I'm in your debt."

"He was really going on about his photography. Is he famous?"

"He's nobody. He's going to Vienna to work with some woman on the Russian-American summit. I've heard of her. She reports dirt—I'm sure you know the kind."

"Yes." Every country had them: professional shit-stirrers.

"The Italian says she hired him because nobody in her circle will work with her anymore."

"Why him?"

"He's been a Vatican watcher for years. She saw some of his shots of the Pope mingling with his flock this past Easter and thought his work was good. He also told me that this woman was man-crazy and probably had heard what an accomplished lover he is."

"Whereupon he invited you to sample his wares before he bestowed them on his new employer in Vienna?"

She smiled. "Something like that, but more crudely put. Can I buy you a drink to show my gratitude? There aren't many men these days who will rescue a lady in distress."

He pretended to weigh her offer. "Just coffee," he said finally.

They found a table in the shadows near the entrance, nursed their coffees and said little. "You don't drink?" she asked after a while.

"Only when I intend to get drunk, and then only in private. Public drinking invites trouble."

She nodded. "Forgive me. I didn't take you for the cautious type."

He smiled. "You believe in types?"

"Of course. It's a matter of intuition."

"What do these intuitions tell you about me?"

She wiggled her forefinger at him. "One can feel intuitions, but it's bad luck to explain them. One drinks coffee at this hour only to sober up or to remain awake. You obviously haven't been partaking, so why do you want to stay awake while the rest of the world sleeps?"

He laughed. "Maybe not everyone here intends to sleep tonight."

Her chin lifted defiantly. "An Italian uses drink to help him build his courage to overpower women, whereas you use your sobriety as a weapon. Doesn't that make you alike?" Her voice was playful, not scolding.

"I never impose."

She looked at the dance floor and waved her hand like an auctioneer awaiting an opening bid. "Many options are close at hand. Who will it be?"

He studied the dancers, then turned back to her. "You."

Her smile was unwavering. After a long pause she said, "I live ten minutes from here. I'll leave first and get my car. Give me a few minutes."

"Are you trying to fool a husband or a boyfriend?"

"Neither, but why let people know what you're doing when it's none of their business?"

"And if I come out and find that you've flown away?"

She touched his cheek softly. "It's the unknown that puts a little spice in our lives." She rose and slid past him.

He heard the Jaguar before he saw it. It was white and low and looked ghostlike in the mist.

"A lot of machine for mountain roads," he said as he got in.

She shifted into first and accelerated sharply. "Risk is relative," she said as they quickly wound their way up the mountain. "If it's clear in the morning there'll be a wonderful view of the river."

The house was built on stilts against a sheer rock wall; the rooms inside were paneled. She turned on a floor lamp, then draped her raincoat over a chair. One wall was covered with small watercolors and the floors were shiny with varnish.

"You live here?"

"Visiting. My brother owns it, but it's mine whenever I want it."

"He's a generous man."

"Not by choice. Our parents left us well off, but I got the investment portfolio and he got the property. From time to time I serve as his private banker, so he has to be nice to me."

"What else do you do?"

She raised her eyebrows. "Is that open-ended?"

"I was thinking of work."

"Hydrologist," she said as she went into the kitchen, opened a bottle of beer and held it out to him. When he shook his head she took a long pull. "Not exactly the most romantic work. I work with a small private institution that is studying the effect of industrial operations on groundwater. Pretty boring, when you think about it. And you?"

"Professionally?"

"It's your call."

"Assassin," he said and watched her carefully for a reaction.

She cocked her eyebrow and smiled. "Am I to be your next victim?"

He looked around and smiled. "There seems to be no alternative."

She finished the beer, set the bottle on a table, slipped her arm around his waist and guided him through a door.

"What's this?"

"The killing ground," she said as she led him toward a canopied bed.

Later Frash sat in a high-back chair beside the bed and studied the body. There had been no reason to kill her and he'd had no intention to do so, but now she was on her back on the wooden floor, her left eye gone and her nose shattered where the heel of his hand had driven cartilage into her brain. He doubted she would have caused a problem for him, but he had to be sure, which signed her death warrant. Her legs were spread and bent, and her arms were up as if she were poised to jump to her feet. For a moment the dead woman reminded him of his mother, but it was a fleeting image soon forgotten. Although she had lived in Cologne, she was Swiss, not German, here on leave to write a scientific paper. With luck it would be weeks before she was discovered; she had told her brother that she would stay until the end of June, and had made it clear to Frash that she and her brother stayed away from each other as much as possible.

He left the body in the cellar by a wall nearest the cliff, figuring that it would be coolest there, set open boxes of baking soda around the body like votives and sealed the only door with masking tape, everything designed to retard the odors that would soon be emitted by the decaying corpse. Before departing, he ransacked the areas of the house that might be the targets of a professional burglar and emptied her purse.

It took twenty minutes to get back to Sirini's automobile. The mist had turned to rain but the temperature seemed to be rising. He opened the hood, disconnected the wires to the distributor cap and sought refuge under a balcony in a nearby alley. Sirini came out of the hotel at 7:00 A.M., went straight to the Fiat and tried to start it. When he failed he rested his head on the top of the steering wheel.

Frash rapped his knuckles on the driver's window. "Looks like you've got trouble. Want me to take a look?"

Sirini nodded without looking up. Frash reconnected the wires and told the Italian to try again. This time the engine came to life and Sirini looked relieved. "Can I pay you?"

"Where are you going?"

"East. I have to be in Vienna tomorrow."

"I'm going there too. Mind if I ride along?"

Sirini smiled. "Not at all. If this piece of junk gives me trouble again, maybe you can be useful."

Not as useful as you, Frash thought as he got in.

153 TUESDAY, MAY 9, 1961, 5:15 P.M.
Vienna

The Alitalia turboprop floated momentarily, then dropped hard on the runway and lurched as the pilot stood on the brakes. Several passengers grumbled about the rough landing, but Lejla Llarja sat impassively with her hands folded in her lap. Kasi was two rows back and she could feel his eyes watching her.

How long had it been? A week? The Sigurimi brought the men in one at a time and made them sit; an executioner stepped behind them, placed the barrel of his revolver against the back of their heads and squeezed off a single round. The first victim pitched forward. The second one's head snapped backward and his left arm flew up as he tumbled off to his right, his last sound an audible grunt when he hit. No sentence had been read and no statements were made. They had simply brought in the condemned men and shot them, informally, Russian style, without fanfare. No pulses were checked afterward and no pronouncements of death made. The fifteen observers included Shehu and Kasi. The two men had been tried for treason, convicted of spying for the Soviets, their capital crimes consisting of telling several Russians at a reception in Moscow that conditions were poor in Albania.

After the executions, Kasi had made Lejla scrub the floor and pick up pieces of hair, bone and brain with her bare hands. When she was finished she was taken to her father, who was in the same building. He was thin and gaunt, his eyes listless; when she embraced him there was little response. "I heard shots," he whispered.

"It's your imagination," Lejla lied.

"I smelled gunpowder," he said with a thin smile. "You can't save me," he whispered as she pulled him close. There were tears in his eyes.

She had to try.

154   TUESDAY, MAY 9, 1961, 5:20 P.M.
Going, Austria

Benedetto Sirini was a compulsive talker, but despite a nasty bruise on his cheek he had no memory of the previous night's adventure. Within thirty minutes Frash had heard the Italian's abbreviated life story and future plans. The photographer was going to Vienna to meet a woman called Mignonne Mock; with her connections and reputation his pictures of the coming summit would be seen around the world, and afterwards he would be showered with offers.

"Perhaps your employer will send you packing when she gets a look at that face," Frash said. Reporters would have more access to the summit than the general public.

Sirini craned his neck to see himself in the rearview mirror. "She's never seen me. She'll think this is normal."

"You've never met her?"

"We played tag on the telephone but never made contact. The whole thing was arranged by telegram. Can you imagine?"

"Odd." Possibilities were mounting quickly.

"Determined is a better word. That's how she's made her reputation. She manages to get stories others can't."

Frash smiled. "Sounds like you'll make a great team."

"I have no doubts," Sirini crowed.

When the Italian turned east at Wörgl onto a road that would cut across a small piece of Germany, Frash guessed that the border was less than eighty kilometers away, which meant that it was time to take control. They were about the same size. "I need a piss."

"Hang it out the window," Sirini suggested with a laugh.

"I'm serious."

"All right," the photographer grumbled as he downshifted, steered to the side of the narrow road and slowed.

"Not here," Frash said. "Look for a side road. I need a little privacy." The Italian shook his head and accelerated. A few miles on he swerved onto a dirt road and raced up a steep hill trailing a low plume of dust. The countryside was rocky, with no houses or farms. "Here is good," Frash said.

"Be quick," Sirini said as he looked at his watch and stopped.

Frash drove the heel of his hand into Sirini's windpipe, and as the man clutched at his throat his passenger got out, walked around the vehicle, opened the driver's door, pulled him out by the hair, locked his arms around his head and neck, and twisted hard to snap it. "Is that quick enough?" he asked as he dragged the body into the rocks.

155   WEDNESDAY, MAY 10, 1961, 5:50 A.M. *Durrës, Albania*

For Methat Dishnica freedom was only a word in the dictionary. Every aspect of his life was constrained by obligations, which were often conflicting and required him to move cautiously. At thirty-five he was a lieutenant colonel in the Sigurimi, Albania's secret police, but the higher he climbed, the greater his obligations seemed to be and the less his power. His people had a saying: The higher the stone, the greater the fall. At his current rank he was now among the elite, which meant that the dangers were greater and increasingly difficult to see. This came as no surprise, of course; he had known from the outset how the game was played, and throughout his career he had kept alert for insurance. Now an unexpected obligation required him to do something he had never expected.

Dishnica squatted in the gray dunes and stared at the silhouette of the fortresslike house built into the rocks above the Adriatic. Haxi Kasi's stronghold reflected his personality: strong, self-sufficient, resilient, unfeeling as stone. Yet Dishnica had heard that in recent weeks Kasi had been seen several times with the same woman. He had tried to get details, but most of his colleagues in the Sigurimi had been closemouthed. Kasi and his patron Shehu didn't tolerate loose talk among the secret police, and harshly enforced their rules. Even so, some people were careless and shared what they knew, so that he had been able to piece together a picture from a variety of shards. The woman had been taken to visit a political prisoner named Llarja, who was said to be one of the cabal that had engineered last year's plot against Hoxha. A cousin added another tidbit: the woman had faced dogs in the mountains, a test usually reserved for Shehu's assassins. Several contacts reported that she spoke English, and a fisherman had seen her several times outside Kasi's place, once in the nude. In fact, she had been seen here more often than anywhere else, and always with Kasi. Now there was a rumor that she and Kasi had left the country, and he sensed that this was the opportunity he needed. Dishnica doubted that there was a romantic connection between the two of them; Kasi didn't seem to need that. If she was under his wing it was purely business, something special in the offing. The answer might be his safe passage out of Albania.

When the false dawn began he approached the house and concentrated on the object at hand, blocking the mixed emotions that bedeviled him. If any guards were here, they would be groggy from sleep; even the best sentries lost their concentration at this hour, which made it the ideal time to break into a place where you didn't belong.

156   WEDNESDAY, MAY 10, 1961, 4:00 P.M. *Washington, D. C.*

In more than three decades of intelligence work Arizona had made few errors either in the selection of people or in evaluating events and their implications. What counted most was instinct, the fiery ball in your stomach that was not 100 percent accurate, but nevertheless was more reliable than cold logic, which was bound by assumptions built on prejudice. The heart of intelligence was collecting people, not information, and in this belief, which was fast becoming a minority view in the CIA, he was more like a Russian than an American. The emphasis in the U.S. intelligence community was shifting to the electronic collection of information, ELINT and SIGINT which was like pressing your ear to a keyhole five thousand miles away. The new view sanctified free-standing information, while the Russian paradigm was Let us know the man who gives us information; then we'll know the information. The Russians wanted another meeting on Friday. Did they know something about Frash? The missing agent was a mistake he intended to rectify, and though the outlook was bleak at the moment, everything in life was transient. A break would come.

Because of the impending summit, the Austrians had issued a special bulletin to all border units. Any unusual events, however minor, were to be reported directly and immediately to a security liaison unit in Vienna. Ever mindful of their national reputation for thoroughness and precision, the Austrians did not intend to have their reputation sullied by an accident, especially one growing out of carelessness.

The body of a young woman had been discovered by German hikers on Saturday afternoon. When they reached the border village of Nauders, they dutifully reported the find to the local police chief, then led him back to the site. He had notified Vienna on Sunday.

An American named Briarly was on duty in the liaison unit when the report came in. The Austrians discussed it briefly, decided it was unimportant and consigned the information to the appropriate file. As one of the CIA's liaison officers to the presidential Secret Service detachment, Briarly was trained to question everything. Having read the report, he called Washington; Arizona had thought about little else since then.

He poured a double shot of whiskey, stared at the wall map of Europe and imagined lines between the sites where Frash had appeared. Why the hell was he sticking to the Continent? With the money he had now he could disappear into the Middle East or Africa and never be found. The living would be bad but he would be free and clear, and with money you could buy a lot of comfort in either region. If he can go so easily, why does he stay? Why did Briarly see spooks in some podunk Austrian town? He knew why; it was Briarly's job to see patterns in shadows. Briarly had once been one of his people: once one of his, always one. Except Frash, who had never really been one of his; he had Venema to thank for that. And Valentine; only God knew who he belonged to. Austria, for Christsake, a good country for a nut case. Hitler had leaned heavily on his own kind to erase the Jews because he imagined they had treated him badly, rejecting him as an aspiring artist in Vienna. Or maybe it wasn't something that real; a nut case didn't need real reasons. Like Frash and that woman in California. He had blinded her for trying to do something sane, getting the hell out of his life. Venema's report made it clear that even now, years later, she was still scared shitless of Frash. It's a sign of good mental health to be afraid of things that can hurt you. Especially in Austria, which gave us Hitler, who stuck to Europe with the persistence of Frash. Or was it vice versa? A dead woman in Austria wasn't much to go on, but in this business you have to play your hunches.

Venema's report lay open on Arizona's desk. "The late-stage paranoid schizophrenic may be driven by voices imploring him to kill. Most patients with advanced symptoms are intent on righting an imagined wrong." He read on, closed the folder and put his feet up on the desk. Austria. "The Vienna summit," he said out loud. Sylvia and Valentine had learned from the Yugoslavs that the Russians had killed Frash's contact. A payback for an imagined wrong. Lumbas was a Soviet agent. Vengeance? It would be crazy with so much security, but if you were a fruitcake maybe it made sense. But the dead body in Austria just as easily might have nothing to do with Frash. Briarly said the local police report called it an accident, probably a fall. All right, don't get worked up. Check it out. Lean on Briarly's instincts. If he thought it important enough to call, the least you can do is have it checked out. Cover your ass.

Valentine answered the telephone halfway through the first ring. Bored or edgy? It was hard to tell, but either way it was good.

"This is your fairy godfather," Arizona said.

"Send us back to Kansas," Valentine shot back.

"How about Austria instead? I presume by the long silence that you two are dead in the water."

"You've heard from the Russians?"

Had his voice perked up? "Yes, but this is a separate matter. There's a place called Nauders; it's spittin' distance from the Eye-tie border. They've got a body up there."

"Left-eye signature?"

"Don't know. Fell off some rocks is how I heard it. A female. Nobody with her. Some Kraut hikers found her. No ID. Weird for a woman to tramp around in the mountains all by her lonesome. What do you think?"

"Wild goose chase. What about the Russians?"

"They're headed for Vienna. Should arrive tomorrow and they want a meeting the next day." Arizona read off two telephone numbers. "Tell them you're with Eagle Casualty of Miami. Meanwhile, get your asses up to Nauders. Head cop there's named Petermann. Tell him you're with the summit security team. Our Vienna unit will provide the cover."

"We'll drive up and get there before morning."

It was probably nothing, Arizona told himself after hanging up. It didn't make sense that Frash would elude them so that he could go to Vienna amid what would be the heaviest security concentration in the world. It made no sense at all, even for a man on a long walk down Looney Tunes Lane.

157   THURSDAY, MAY 11, 1961, 1:05 A.M.
Bajraku Hotit, Albania

Lt. Col. Methat Dishnica moved slowly along the man-high coils of concertina wire, feeling his way through the rocks, his duffel bag over his left shoulder. This was risky, he knew, but there was no choice; family honor was at stake, an oath to his dying father.

Dishnica guessed it was another kilometer to the rendezvous point. The army guards captain he had rousted at the border station had been so shocked to find a Sigurimi officer beside his bunk that he had been unable to talk for several seconds. Dishnica had explained that an illegal border penetration was expected. Where were the Sigurimi troops? the captain stammered. A unit from Tirana was on the way, Dishnica lied. They would be along at any moment; meanwhile the captain should concentrate all of his men in a position 1.5 kilometers east of the official crossing point, but they should take no action until Dishnica arrived with his team. "There's no need for you to take risks others are trained to handle."

The captain was a good officer, which translated to a frightened one; he immediately suggested that they also station a token force west of the border road, but Dishnica dismissed this idea; in matters of this sort it was the Sigurimi who gave orders, not border guard captains. Cowed, the officer called his men in by walkie-talkie. Dishnica saw that they were young, no more than boys, and for a moment he felt ashamed. When Shehu discovered his defection, the guards would pay for it. But he reminded himself that honor was at stake, blood honor, and this took precedence over the lives and the suffering of strangers. If they were truly competent in the discharge of their responsibilities, they should have known that he was violating established procedures and challenged him. If they suffered, he rationalized, it would be their own fault.

When he reached the crossing point, Dishnica quickly checked the nearest bunker to be certain it was empty, saw that it was, slipped downhill to the wire, stood on a boulder, pointed his flashlight into the darkness and blinked it three times. The answer came from the right. One blink, then two more. He replied with a single and got three more in return. As arranged, they were waiting for him on the other side. He felt unexpectedly calm.

Using a chart of the minefield and a small light, he slowly made his way north into the frontier; the border guards would wait a long time before realizing that something wasn't right, and longer still before their captain got up his courage to do something about it. Discipline built on fear obliterated tactical flexibility, which made such people easy to manipulate.

The crossing of the mined area required forty minutes. When Dishnica finally emerged from it he flashed his light once and waited. For six months he had vacillated, but when word had come from his cousin that his father was dying, the issue was settled; a son had no choice in such matters. He had gone into the mountains to see the old man, who looked more worn out than terminally ill. His father reminded him that years ago he had arranged a marriage for him, and that a good son did not question such decisions. The bride's family had gone over the border to Kosovo after the war. Dishnica had tried to reason with his father; if the bride was in Yugoslavia, the arrangement was null and void. In any event, the girl was now a thirty-year-old woman and no doubt already married or even dead. His father raged at him. Political borders did not affect commitments of honor. The girl had been promised; he had promised; the union must occur or there would be a blood feud. Every life was connected to others. But he was Sigurimi, he argued. You are family and clan first, the old man countered. Dishnica argued, If I leave, then you and everyone here will be in danger; Shehu will retaliate. The old man laughed. Let the bastard try. He had always relished a fight, and often bragged that during the war he had personally killed forty Nazis. If Shehu comes into the mountains we'll feed his balls to the dogs. A son should do what he's told and keep his family's honor intact; nothing else matters. Besides, if the marriage was to be a good one, there must be children. As an only son it was Methat's duty to ensure the continuation of the family name.

In the end Dishnica swore an oath to his dying father, and it was this that decided the outcome. He would have to defect, and now he had the information to trade for sanctuary and a new identity in Yugoslavia.

Though there was no moon, he now saw two silhouettes moving toward him. He recognized Admiral Pijaku by his height and peculiar gait.

"Not very often that the Sigurimi loses such a distinguished cog in its machine," the old officer said, his voice still strong. A long time ago when he had been a cadet officer, Dishnica had been one of Pijaku's students. He had distinguished himself and Pijaku had predicted he would have a fine military career. He had not seen the admiral since, and in the interim the man had been declared an enemy of the state by Enver Hoxha, forcing him to flee Albania. Now Pijaku was collaborating with the Yugoslavs and had sworn to bring Hoxha down. It had not been difficult to get a message to him.

"Some decisions make themselves," Dishnica answered.

"We had an agreement," the admiral said. "You got this far on your own, but to get any further you need me, and I require payment."

Dishnica quickly laid out the information he had gathered: Shehu's henchman, Haxi Kasi, had left the country.

"You can confirm this?"

"He was seen at the airport in Tirana."

"He was alone?"

"No, there was a woman with him."

"His wife?"

"You know he never married. The woman is the daughter of a political prisoner named Llarja, who is said to be one of the conspirators."

"In what?"

"You should know. You've been identified by Shehu and Hoxha as the architect."

The admiral laughed softly. "Shehu sees me as the architect of all his nightmares. What about the woman?"

"Mid-twenties, dark hair, trim. She speaks English."

"Kasi's lover?"

"Not likely. She faced the dogs."

Pijaku nodded to let Dishnica know that he understood that this was the sort of test given to assassins. "What makes you think such information is worth sanctuary?"

"To get Kasi would be to rip off Shehu's right arm. You can do serious damage to the regime. He can't be replaced."

He's correct in his assessment, Pijaku thought. They had been after the brutal Kasi for a long time; perhaps now they would finally get him. "This information is of interest, but Shehu's man could be anywhere."

"Vienna."

"You're certain?"

Dishnica handed an envelope to the admiral; it contained a receipt for a fortune in Austrian schillings from the Sigurimi paymaster, a hand-scribbled flight itinerary and a photograph.

"Where did you get these?"

"From one of his hideaways."

The admiral stared at Kasi's photograph; he had aged, but he still had the eyes of a night dog. "You didn't get these papers without great risk."

"Risk is offset by need. Only Kasi and Shehu have the minefield charts, and there was no way to cross without them." He gave the chart of the northern sector to Pijaku.

"They'll discover they're gone."

"By the time they realize it, I'll be beyond their reach."

"You have family?"

"Only cousins, and they're in the mountains. Shehu doesn't have enough manpower to dig them out of the rocks."

"Who knows that you're defecting?"

"Only my father, and he's dead."

"You've planned well," the admiral said solemnly. "I said a long time ago that you would be a competent officer, and you've proven me right." He took a step to the side. The man with him raised a revolver and fired three times into Dishnica's chest, the muzzle flashes traveling almost as far as the bullets, then bent down and put a round through his head. Gunpowder hung in the night air. "It would have been more prudent to have taken him in for interrogation," the man with the revolver said.

No, the admiral thought. If Dishnica were allowed to defect there would be an investigation and Shehu might discover that Kasi had been compromised. "Get the charts and take him back to the other side. This way it will look like he encountered a border penetrator."

At daylight the guards found Dishnica sprawled on a coil of concertina wire on the Albanian side of the frontier. Later he would be given a hero's burial.

158   THURSDAY, MAY 11, 1961, 10:05 A.M.   *Nauders, Austria*

Nauders was a small, neat town with wooden houses and brightly painted balconies. The police station was in a red-brick building in the center. A small arched gate and wall ruin marked a onetime Roman outpost. Valentine glanced at the arch as they went into the building. "Duty here must have been like a transfer to Greenland," he muttered.

Petermann was a small blond man who smoked fat cigars, parted his hair in the center and spit-shined his knee-high boots. His voice was soft, his choice of words economical, and he tended to bow his head sharply after making a point. "I gave complete information to Vienna," he told the Americans. "Everything was correct and in accordance with the directive."

"Bah," Valentine whispered, mimicking a sheep. Sylvia elbowed him gently and began asking questions. Had the woman been identified? No. Were there any leads? Nothing.

"What about hunches?" Valentine asked.

The Austrian didn't understand. "Theories," Sylvia said.

"Ah," Petermann said with a nod, "hypotheses."

They waited for him to gather his thoughts. He led them to a wall map and showed them a red pin. "The woman's body was found there. This area is frequently used by Gypsies to make illegal border crossings."

"Since when do Gypsies recognize borders?" Valentine asked.

"In the past they moved around, but circumstances are different now," Petermann said. "Most Gypsies don't move from country to country anymore. They're nationalized, a nation within nations, not like the old times when nobody claimed them." He tapped the map. "There's a clan of Italian Gypsies who make a business of escorting *gadje,* non-Gypsies, across the borders. It's a lucrative undertaking. Their customers are mostly criminals or men trying to escape bad marriages."

"Is there some way to talk to these people?"

Petermann smiled. "One can talk, but about what? They don't advertise such services. Clients are referred to them by other Gypsies."

"Can we see the body?" Sylvia asked, shifting the direction of the conversation.

Petermann looked at her impassively. "If you wish."

The morgue was in the same building. It had six metal drawers in two rows of three. The police chief pulled out one of the middle drawers and unzipped the gray bag that contained the remains.

The dead woman had black hair and dark skin blanched by death. The left side of her head was shattered and bones stuck out of her upper left arm. Sylvia lifted the sides of the bag, examined the rest of the body, looked at Valentine and shook her head, which meant there were no bullet wounds.

"Her spine was broken in the fall," Petermann said. "Death was more or less instantaneous."

"You've classified it as an accident?"

"Preliminarily, but there are many possibilities ranging from simple accident to suicide."

"Or homicide," Sylvia said.

Petermann executed a crisp bow. "Of course nothing has been ruled out, but neither is one more probable than another. These mountains are experienced, dispassionate killers. We have no medical examiner here; the body was handled by our mortician, whose clients are mostly old people. However, her injuries are consistent with a fall."

"Unless she was pushed," Valentine said. "Did you get photos at the site?"

The police chief spread them out on the table. They were Polaroids, not 35 mm, and fuzzy, with poorly defined details. Petermann seemed to sense potential criticism and moved to blunt it. "We're a small town with no crime. We took more professional photographs, but they require more time for processing. The Polaroids are insurance," he explained. "My idea," he added with obvious pride.

Sylvia picked up one of the photographs. "She was unclothed?"

"Yes. Her clothing was found on a ledge approximately one hundred meters above the body."

"That seems a bit unusual," Valentine said. "I wouldn't think that nude hiking would be the rage here."

"Of course not, but in and of itself her nudity proves nothing. Suicides sometimes do bizarre things, and our mountains attract some peculiar people."

"Was there evidence of intercourse?" Sylvia asked.

"There appeared to be semen, but there was no evidence of violence."

Valentine bored in immediately. "Doesn't semen suggest that she had company up there?"

"To be candid," Petermann said after a cough, "suicide is not the best conclusion."

"Why?" Sylvia asked.

Petermann smiled. "Gypsies drive others to suicide, not themselves."

"The woman is Gypsy?"

"Of course," the police chief said, surprised that they had to ask.

"How do you know?"

He fetched a cloth bag and emptied the contents on the table. There was a white silk blouse with smudges and a red silk scarf. The lavender skirt was of heavy material, embroidered ornately at the hem; no brassiere, white cotton panties and flat red shoes with small buckles. Petermann held up the scarf. "A Gypsy emblem," he said. "Single women wear red, married women black."

Valentine frowned. "A red scarf is hardly conclusive."

Petermann gestured to the body. "The Gypsies are an old race, largely free of other genetic influences because they rarely breed with *gadje*." He obviously enjoyed lecturing. "Look at her hair, the size and coloring of her eyes, flesh color, head shape, her size, her clothes. Gypsies are small people, always small. The scarf simply confirms what my eyes and experience tell me."

"An Austrian Gypsy?" Sylvia asked.

Petermann smiled. "There are no Austrian Gypsies," he said. "Credit Hitler with that." It was difficult to tell if he approved.

"Blame would be a better word," Valentine growled.

Before leaving, they pressed the policeman for a way to find the Gypsy clan that made its living moving people across the border. Petermann pointed again to the map and with his finger made a small circle on the Italian side. "They're usually somewhere in this region, but it would be like looking for air."

"If you know what they're doing, why don't you arrest them?" Sylvia asked.

"To arrest them you need to catch them in the act," the Austrian said. "They've had centuries to hone their skills. Their services are secured through intermediaries. If a client sees them they're killed. Even when we catch an illegal, which sometimes happens, they can't identify anyone. Simplicity and deception are the essence of all their schemes."

"You think this is Frash's work?" Valentine asked when they were outside.

"No gunshot wounds and both of her eyes are intact."

"You buy it that she was rock-hopping alone?"

"Not with semen in her."

"Could have been with somebody, then gotten separated. Could have been with one of the German hikers who found her, I suppose."

"To me separated followed by dead spells missing. If somebody lost her, how come nobody's asked? The semen says that somebody should have."

Valentine stared off at the dark peaks to the south. "If you know you're being hunted and that normal routes over the borders are being watched, you've got to find an escape hatch. You can try on your own—and our boy has experience—but there's some risk in that. Then you hear about a neat little Gypsy scheme—crossing for cash, no questions asked. Maybe you learn this from a nice Gypsy lady who volunteers to be your go-between. What the hell, you like female company and she's got to make the contact, so why not take her along? You can always dump her later."

"I hate this guy," Sylvia said.

"You've got to admire his ingenuity," Valentine said.

"*If* it's Frash," she cautioned. "We don't know that yet."

He rubbed his hands together and took a deep breath of mountain air. "Then the sooner we find that Gypsy outfit, the sooner we can fill in this square."

"Are you proposing a posse of two?"

"Nope. We're going to call in the cavalry."

"Come again?"

"Make that Cossacks," Valentine answered.

159   FRIDAY, MAY 12, 1961, 6:12 A.M.
The Italian-Austrian Border

Bailov had twenty men in four teams of five, all with standard Spetsnaz arms, their weapons having been sent to Vienna in diplomatic containers over a period of years and stored for the eventuality of war. Valentine lay on a bed of wet pine needles beside the colonel, while a few meters away Sylvia sprawled beside the tattooed Russian called Melko. She was whispering to the man, who smiled enthusiastically.

Bailov craned his neck to look at the sky through an opening in the treetops and checked his watch. "Dawn soon," he said, as much to himself as to the Americans. A radio operator was hunkered down beside him, his radio pack giving him the silhouette of a hunchback. The colonel picked up the receiver-transmitter and depressed the transmit button. "This is Gladiator. Where are my children?"

"Brother One is in a grassy area south of the camp. There are seven wooden caravans down this way, horse-drawn. No motorized vehicles, no movement inside the perimeter, no one in sight and no dogs. The horses are on rope hobbles."

"It's quiet in the camp," Bailov told Valentine.

"Orders?" the radio voice asked.

"Hold where you are," Bailov said.

Valentine saw that the Russian was calm, his breathing slow and normal. He seemed to listen carefully and pause before talking, obviously allowing himself time to think and to ask for information efficiently, all the signs of a professional.

"Brother Two?"

"We've been all the way through the camp. Nothing but snores," the voice reported.

"Sentries?"

"*Nyet,*" Brother Two said. "The henhouse awaits the fox with open arms."

Bailov grinned and nodded. "No sentries," he said in English to Valentine. "Brother Three?"

"We're approximately twenty meters east of the easternmost caravan. All quiet here. We've heard at least two babies cry, one in the caravan closest to us and another two wagons west."

Bailov looked up at the sky again and rechecked his watch. "Brothers, this is Gladiator. The time is zero-six-twelve. We move in five minutes. Brother Three, take targets seven and six. Brother Two, you've got numbers three, four and five. Gladiator will harvest the first two. Remember, no sound; go in fast, get them out and on the ground. Quickly. Silencers and knives, but only if necessary. If anybody fucks up, in a week he'll be mining uranium with a spoon." He winked at Valentine.

The two Americans had contacted the Russians in Vienna and asked for help. They had met outside Nauders, the Russians arriving in two unmarked trucks; though they were armed, they wore civilian clothing. Sylvia noted that their disguises were much better than those Soviet agents usually employed. They were learning.

The group drove to an area near the border and crossed on foot. Five scouts, operating well ahead of the main force, had located the camp at zero three hundred. It took two more hours to reconnoiter the encampment and develop a plan. The two Americans were exhausted from the pace and altitude, yet the Russians seemed to handle the exertion effortlessly. Valentine saw that they were careful in their preparations and not anxious to rush into danger without a solid assessment, which was in sharp contrast to their image in the U.S.

"Let's hope it's the right bunch," Valentine whispered.

"We'll secure them first and establish identities later," Bailov replied.

At six-seventeen Bailov took his P-8 pistol out of its holster, chambered a round and clicked the safety off. "Silencers and knives only," he repeated into the radio. "Go *now*."

By the time he could react, Valentine found himself several paces behind the Russians, who bolted forward in a crouch.

It took less than fifteen minutes to empty the caravans, with no shots fired. The Gypsies were assembled and made to sit on the ground, legs in front of them, their hands clasped on the back of their necks. The captives consisted of seventeen adults, only five of them males, and nine children. Four infants were left sleeping in the caravans. The soldiers shone their flashlights into the captives' faces as the sun began to rise. The Gypsies were attentive but did not seem overly concerned.

"Which of you is the leader?" Bailov asked in German.

No response. He nodded to Melko, who came forward and spoke to them in Romany. "The leader will identify himself or in thirty seconds I will begin cutting off testicles." He pulled out a knife and made a show of stropping the edge on his trousers.

A wide-shouldered man stood. "I lead."

Melko approached him, then regarded the people around him. "He's the right one," he said, seeing it in the others' faces. "A few days ago you took a *gadjo* across the border," he went on

"You speak our language well," the Gypsy said.

Melko smiled. The *lyudi* had frequent contact with Russian Gypsies, whom the Soviet government had tried unsuccessfully to assimilate into society. In some camps in the gulag there had been two factions vying for power: Gypsies and *urki*, professional criminals. Gypsies were as familiar to Melko as the ways of his own people. Their patterns of behavior were predictable: first they would try charm to disarm you, then move on to lies; if these failed, they would shift to anger and threats. Violence was the desperate last choice, seldom used. "Where is the *gadjo* now?"

"We're simple shepherds," the man said earnestly. "Who do you think you are, barging into our camp? We've done nothing wrong."

Melko smiled. "You shear your own fleece?"

"Of course," the man said.

Melko grabbed one of the man's hands and examined it. "The only sheep whose fleece you seek are *gadje*." Melko turned to Bailov. "Check all their hands. Fleece contains lanolin, which makes the skin smooth and removes calluses."

There were no smooth hands among the adults.

"Tell us about the man," Melko said politely as he returned his attention to the Gypsy leader.

"A curse on you," the man said. He spat at Melko's feet.

Melko picked up four large stones and placed them at the corners of a rectangle. The Gypsy was staked to the ground and his wrists and ankles placed over the stones. He didn't struggle, but his dark eyes flashed hatred.

Melko searched the fire pits, hefting several stones before finding the one he wanted; it weighed three or four kilos and was wedge-shaped. "Tell us about the *gadjo*," he said again. His voice was soft and encouraging; no threats were made, or even implied; one reasonable man was talking to another.

"I curse the grave of your mother," the Gypsy said in an equally reasonable tone.

Without warning, Melko raised the stone over his head and brought the pointed edge down hard, smashing the man's left wrist. His scream shattered the morning silence and his people immediately began to curse and weep.

"The *gadjo*," Melko repeated.

"Your mother was a whore," the Gypsy said through clenched teeth. Pieces of bone stuck out of the crushed wrist.

"Sad but true," Melko said. When he smashed the second wrist, the man passed out. "Find water," he told one of the soldiers, who emptied a canvas bucket on the leader.

When the Gypsy revived, Melko knelt on his right leg. "You'll pick no more *gadje* pockets," he said regretfully, "but you can still walk. Reduce your losses while you can."

"I would crawl on my belly like a snake to spit on your grave," the man howled.

Melko looked at Bailov and his men, raised an eyebrow, shrugged and struck downward again, this time smashing the Gypsy's right ankle, which bled heavily.

Still the leader would not relent, so the Russian broke the other ankle, causing the Gypsy to convulse.

"More water?" the soldier with the bucket asked.

"*Nyet*," Melko said.

They waited for the man to regain some semblance of consciousness.

Valentine had seen scores of men tortured during the war, but never one with this sort of tolerance for pain. He felt ashamed when the bile rose in his throat, forcing him to swallow several times. When he looked over at Sylvia, he saw that she was staring back and forth between the man on the ground and Melko. What was she thinking? What had the two of them been so buddy-buddy about earlier?

Melko squatted and drew his knife across the Gypsy's cheek. A small cut spilled a trickle of dark blood. Then he inserted the knife in the waistline of the man's trousers and cut them away. The Gypsy tried to squirm but the effort rekindled his pain and forced him to lie still. Melko pressed the flat of the knife between the man's legs. "When does a man stop being a man?" he asked in Romany.

The Gypsy's eyes glazed over and tears ran out of his eyes as he described Frash in near-perfect detail.

Valentine handed Melko a photograph. "Ask him if this is the man they took across."

When asked, the man shook his head.

Valentine held the photo out to Sylvia. "Lumbas," he said. He handed Melko a second photo, this one of Frash; the Gypsy nodded.

"Where did you take him?" Melko asked.

"He got out before the end," the man gasped. "With the whore."

"What whore?" The man described a woman he called Kenya, his words coming in spurts. Melko looked up at Valentine. "A woman acted as go-between. They got out of the wagon before they reached their destination."

Sylvia came forward and held the Polaroid of the dead woman so that the Gypsy could see it. He spat at the photograph and turned his face away. She looked at Valentine and said, "Bingo."

"Your man is in Austria," Bailov said.

"Looks like," Valentine said.

"Why?" the Russian asked.

"We're not sure," Sylvia said.

Bailov checked his watch: zero seven fifty. "Let's go," he told his men.

Melko grabbed Bailov's sleeve and said, "We should finish him."

"There's no reason. We've gotten what we came for and he's in no shape to cause trouble."

Melko kept his hold. "He's lost face. A Gypsy leads until he fails. They'll pack up and leave him just as he is."

Bailov understood and nodded to one of his men, who stepped forward and fired a round into the Gypsy's forehead. The bullet hit with a dull, cracking sound, like two stones struck together.

The group began the return march at the same pace they had maintained on the way out. "Jesus," Valentine complained, struggling to keep up. Birds sang in the trees and there was the smell of rain in the distance.

After a while the Russians stopped, fanned out and lay down among the trees on the side of a hill covered with small white flowers. "Why are we stopping?" Valentine asked, his lungs burning.

"Last night was difficult," Bailov said. "When it's time to push, we push. When it's time to rest, we rest."

430

160 FRIDAY, MAY 12, 1961, 1:00 P.M.
Vienna

Lejla and Kasi sat in a coffee house. He had wrapped two towels in brown wrapping paper, and it sat on the bench beside him.

A woman in a gray raincoat with a long face and narrow lips came to the table. "It's crowded today. May I join you?"

Kasi pointed to the bench beside him. The woman sat down, unbuttoned her coat and set an identical package next to Kasi's. "So much rain," she said, "but it's good for the flowers." She ordered a Turkish coffee and a small cream cake but ate only a couple of bites before picking up Kasi's package and leaving.

Ten minutes later the two Albanians left.

When they reached the flat, Kasi opened the package and held a garment out to her. "Try it on. You have to look natural in it." Given her looks, it was going to be a long reach.

161 FRIDAY, MAY 12, 1961, 8:00 P.M.
Vienna

Sirini was surprisingly well organized; an oversized briefcase was loaded with labeled film canisters and held an envelope containing the exchange of several telegrams with the Austrian journalist. Sirini's meeting was supposed to have taken place on Wednesday night, but Frash was in no hurry. The briefcase also held a portfolio of photographs, mostly skin shots of a woman with huge breasts, not particularly well framed or even in focus. If the Austrian woman was in such a bind that she had to hire Sirini, he guessed, she would be desperate enough to wait. He had driven to the outskirts of Vienna, taken a room at a small hotel near the airport east of the city and slept until he got his strength back. When he finally telephoned the reporter late in the afternoon there were equal portions of sharpness and relief in her voice. He let her ask for a meeting.

As it had been for centuries, Rotenturmstrasse remained the center of Vienna's red-light district, an area where all things were possible and prices negotiable. The wide street stretched out behind St. Stephen's Cathedral, an eight-centuries-old landmark with a single gaudy tower and a tiled roof in a garish zigzag pattern. Frash liked the idea of the city's prostitutes working in the shadow of the church, the whores stopping to confess between tricks or on their way home from the cabarets.

The Rotenturm's haunts were varied, old with new, sacred with the openly profane. The tavern was on a side street. It was dark inside, the walls bristling with dozens of small deer skulls with shellacked antlers, the tables crammed with men in plaid sportcoats drinking beer from pewter mugs. Most had their plates heaped with chunks of pork; eating kept conversation muted. He found a table that afforded a good view of the rectangular room and ordered a pils.

Mignonne Mock had long, straight hair the color of paprika and freckles, and wore small gold loop earrings, a red skirt hemmed above her knees, high heels with open toes and no wedding ring. She came to his table and stood in front of him, obviously trying to come to a decision. "Sirini?"

"A little late," he said, motioning for her to sit down, but she didn't move.

"Let's not misunderstand each other," she said. "I'm the boss, and you've got this job only because of me. I decide the assignments, tell you where to go, and when and what to shoot. Deviate once and you're fired."

Frash grinned and bowed his head in obeisance.

"Where are your bags and equipment?"

"At my hotel."

"We'll pick them up," Mock said. "You're going to stay at my place. This is hard news now, not the paparazzi garbage you're used to. When I get a lead, I move fast and I want you close. Have you got an automobile?"

Frash shook his head. He had left it in a car park, where it would keep until needed again. Better to let her think he was without means. "I flew in and took a cab."

When they were outside she wheeled suddenly and poked him in the chest with a finger. "This is a working arrangement, not a screwing arrangement. Understand?"

He held up his hands. "Whatever you say, *Duce.*"

Mock's stern gaze melted to a rare smile. "Good."

Ali wondered how it would feel to wring her scrawny neck.

432

162   FRIDAY, MAY 12, 1961, 10:40 P.M.
Moscow

"This is Zakharov," Khrushchev said without preamble. "He'll be officially responsible for security in Vienna."

The general was thin and handsome, his appearance that of a soft and overly fastidious man, but he was a much decorated veteran of the Great Patriotic War and most recently the commander of Soviet forces in Berlin. Among generals, he was reputed to be a brilliant strategist; that he had suddenly been pulled out of Berlin to head security for the summit suggested that the whippetlike general was KGB and much closer to the top than anybody imagined.

"I can't accept this," Talia said firmly.

"If we alter normal security," the General Secretary said, "the Americans will know it, and we can't show any weakness in Vienna. That's crucial. Vienna will be like a theatrical production—only the stakes are greater."

"No doubt the Americans already know that there have been drastic modifications in your security arrangements here in Moscow," Talia countered.

"What they see and what they know are often different. The West has great difficulty reading what goes on here," Khrushchev answered. "If everything appears normal in Vienna, they'll assume it's normal. Americans are most comfortable with the obvious."

"And our role?" Talia asked.

Khrushchev sat down behind a small desk and put on his wire-rimmed spectacles. She knew that he didn't need them, but he sometimes wore them to make himself look more grandfatherly, one of his many little subterfuges. "You'll travel with me," he said. "We'll let it be known that you're a relative."

"What about the rest of the group?"

"No change in its mission, but Zakharov will be officially in charge. He'll provide whatever you need."

"Petrov will never agree to this," Talia said. "Our sole concern is your safety."

Khrushchev smiled and patted her arm. "The old ones like Petrov never accept anything. He wants to keep chasing shadows? So be it. Let him chase." He smacked his belly. "Down here I sense that everything is finished. All I want now is to think about this Kennedy fellow."

Ezdovo was waiting for her, glad to have some time alone with his wife, but when he saw her face he knew there was trouble. "Did you tell him about your contact with the Americans?"

"Just drive," she said coolly. "I need to think."

She had not told Khrushchev about the Americans and wasn't sure why. Because of Zakharov's presence? Perhaps. The general had said nothing and shown no emotion, which made him impossible to read. "If he knew, he would be worried, and his mind must be clear in Vienna. There must be no distractions."

"I would have told him," Ezdovo said.

"It wasn't your decision," she snapped. Her husband's hands tightened on the steering wheel as they drove through the darkened city. "A general named Zakharov will be responsible for the General Secretary's safety in Vienna."

He stared at her. "And us?"

"We can do whatever is necessary. He'll assist us." She wondered how willingly.

Ezdovo shook his head. "If the general is in charge, then we're out?"

Talia turned to face him. "No, this frees us to do what we have to do." Her husband's look told her that he thought she had failed; she wanted desperately to tell him he was wrong but it would only provoke an argument, and right now there were more important things to think about. Zakharov could complicate their work; Ezdovo was right about that. Did Khrushchev doubt Petrov's ability? The team's? Or was it her? These thoughts made her feel inadequate, and she knew she had to put them aside. Khrushchev had said repeatedly how critical the summit would be. This was not a slap in her face, she reassured herself; the General Secretary was simply compartmentalizing his life so that he could concentrate. If it was important for him that everything seem normal in Vienna, they would do everything possible to make it so.

"I don't like this," Ezdovo said as he turned up the street to the hospital.

"Everything will be fine," Talia answered. She did not like to think in terms of failure. Could Zakharov be trusted? By the time they were parked at the hospital she had decided that it didn't matter. "Say nothing about this to Petrov," she said as they got out of the automobile.

Ezdovo stared at her as if she had proposed treason.

"I mean it," she said as they approached the entrance.

163   MAY 14, 1961, 4:10 A.M.
Vienna

The Russians had established themselves in a long, rusty barge anchored along a stone jetty in the Danube. The interior was battered and dented, the wood devoid of varnish, the metal flooring warped, and when the wind came out of the west the stench of the bilges was nauseating. The Americans saw that one cabin was jammed with communications gear, none of it bolted down, which suggested a temporary setup. After the encounter with the Gypsies they had slept in the forest, then made their way back across the border at night and driven straight to Vienna in the rear of one of the Russian trucks, leaving their vehicle in Nauders. It had been dark when they boarded the barge. For the past twenty-four hours they had been left alone in a small, dank cabin with filthy net hammocks for beds. Each time they tried to leave the cabin Russian guards gently herded them back inside with a whispered, gentle *nyet*.

By the time Bailov summoned them to the galley amidships Valentine was fuming. "My apologies for keeping you penned up like this," the Russian said, "but we needed to confer with Moscow."

"Where's the woman who was with you in Geneva?" Valentine asked.

"In Moscow."

Which could mean she was the leader of the group, or one of them; with the Soviets it was hard to know how far any individual's authority stretched.

Bailov drew a deep breath and let it out slowly in order to choose his words. "Do you agree that the Gypsy confirmed that your man has moved into Austria?"

"Probably," Sylvia said.

"He's here," Valentine said, thumping the table heavily with the palm of his hand. "Or coming here."

"Vienna?" the Russian asked, leaning forward.

"It doesn't make sense, which in Frash's case means it's perfectly logical."

"Why?"

"Revenge, the universal motivator."

"Against whom?"

"That's where I draw sort of a big-ass blank," Valentine said. "I had the peculiar notion that you fellas might have a few ideas along that line."

Bailov spoke slowly. "Your Frash may be the half brother to the one called the Major. The family name is Frascetti."

"Tell us something we don't already know."

"The brother came to Moscow during the war. He was a close associate of Villam Lumbas, who was also Albanian-born. After university Lumbas went to the Foreign Ministry and Frascetti to the KGB, but both of them were paid on the twentieth of each month. Do you understand?"

Sylvia spoke up. "December 20, 1917."

"Exactly," Bailov said, impressed by her knowledge.

"Will somebody clue me in?" Valentine asked.

"It's the date the Cheka was founded," she said. "Nowadays KGB officals carry identity cards with the sword-and-shield emblem of the Cheka, and they're all paid on the twentieth of each month."

"So Lumbas was a KGB man assigned to the Foreign Ministry, but not as a diplomat?"

"You've got the idea," she said.

Valentine looked back at the Russian. "What about the fingerprints?" They had given the Lamoura prints to the Soviets in Geneva.

"Nothing," Bailov admitted. "The records were purged, and neither Lumbas nor Frascetti exists in the state's official memory bank. However, we know that Frascetti's parents emigrated to America through France. Same mother, different father."

"Where in America?"

"Boston, Massachusetts."

"All right," Valentine said, thinking aloud now, "let's forget the brothers and concentrate on Frascetti-Lumbas. You say they were connected a long time ago; are you saying you think they maintained contact all those years?"

"An investigator seldom has all the facts he needs," Bailov said. "The craft is in gathering facts, the art in tying them together. You connected Frash and Lumbas in Belgrade; we connected Frash's half-brother and Lumbas in Moscow. That's too much coincidence to ignore. Besides, in my country there is a saying: 'Better to have a hundred friends than a hundred rubles.' This means that Russian people create their own networks, little personal states within the big official state. Family, friends and comrades are valuable, even essential to survival. You get ahead by whom you know, or whom your friends know. We can assume that Frascetti and Lumbas maintained contact because they were at university together, because they were Albanians, because both went to the KGB, and because it's our way."

What kept nagging at Valentine was the Russians' interest in Frash. It should tell me something, he thought, but he couldn't pin it down. "We think that Frash and Lumbas attempted something against Albania, but Frash wasn't acting on our orders. He was free-lancing."

"Nor was Lumbas acting on our orders."

"But Lumbas was eliminated by your side."

"Not by us. By Russians possibly, even probably, but not by us."

"Let's assume that somebody in your camp wanted Lumbas dead," Sylvia said.

"Such a killing would indicate action by someone outside the system. We would have required a thorough and lengthy debriefing."

This made sense. "Which means that whoever was running Lumbas wanted him out of the way?" Sylvia asked.

"Perhaps. Lumbas was at Tyuratam last year. At the university he showed a high aptitude for electronics."

"But he went to the Foreign Ministry," Sylvia reminded him.

"I have a university degree in mechanical engineering," Bailov said, "but I'm not an engineer. In the Soviet Union we keep track of people with special aptitudes, and when the state needs them they're recruited. We believe that Lumbas was assigned to the rocket program for legitimate reasons, and we know that while he was there he contributed much to the effort. In fact, our attention wasn't drawn to him until the accident. When there's a big problem in Russia everyone accuses everyone else in order to obscure the issue. With Lumbas gone, fingers pointed to him, so we started looking for him and discovered that his transfer had occurred under highly unusual circumstances."

"We heard most of this in Geneva," Valentine snapped. "You thought this was a KGB operation, but there were some loose ends to tie up. You weren't certain then that Lumbas was KGB."

Bailov ignored this and continued. "As I said, we began a quiet investigation because of the possible implications. One investigator was murdered, and after that more people died."

"What implications?" Sylvia asked. It seemed to her that the Russian was working his way around to something. "Nothing you did brought you any closer to Lumbas, is that it?" she asked.

"We took our investigation to a conclusion."

Sylvia heard something in Bailov's voice that suggested they were not satisfied with the outcome. "You know who transferred Lumbas?"

"We know how it was done and who signed the papers."

"But not why," Valentine said. "You have it all and nothing at all, a closed case that isn't."

"Lumbas is a line touching the circle in only one place, but is he the target or the central figure? We've taken it to what appears to be a logical conclusion, but something in here"—Bailov touched his hand to his heart—"says Don't stop. When the weather's bad a pilot trusts his instruments, but which instrument is best now, the mind or the heart?"

"Why did you pick Vienna for our meeting?" Sylvia asked.

"Because of the summit."

She glanced at Valentine but he was staring at a wall, seemingly oblivious. "You think the summit is connected to Lumbas?" Her words seemed clumsy and forced.

Suddenly Valentine made an odd face. "You work for Khrushchev," he whispered. Sylvia looked from one man to the other. "The investigation began because Khrushchev had the willies about Lumbas." His voice was louder, more sure. "Lumbas was a threat, but you haven't been able to nail it down, so you're assuming that whatever this is all about will happen here."

Bailov cleared his throat. "Lumbas was transferred over Khrushchev's signature. It was forged."

Jesus, Valentine thought. "Which explains your willingness to meet us. The first time we met you were fishing too."

"We knew nothing about your Mr. Frash," Bailov admitted.

"Which now makes Frash a worry for you."

"Yes," Bailov said. "If he's coming here."

"He's coming," the American said.

"We agree," the Russian said. "As you said earlier, revenge is a universal motivation, but who's the target? If your man believes he was used by our side, which is possible based on the information you gave us in Geneva, it's now likely that he realizes that Lumbas was sent as a provocateur."

"What you're telling us is that you've run out of possibilities in Moscow."

The Russian nodded. "He would appear to be the last surviving thread. Is that how you would say it?"

"Only metaphorically. How much leverage do you have to make things happen on your side?"

"Enough," Bailov said, though after last night's talk with Talia he was not certain any more. Zakharov was an unexpected complication.

"What we're doing here is forming a partnership, right?"

Bailov nodded and floated his hand over the table. "With everything above the surface."

"For as long as it takes."

"Agreed," Bailov said with a firm nod.

"Is there a customary way of sealing a deal in Moscow?"

Melko placed a bottle of vodka on the table. "Will this do?"

438

SUNDAY, MAY 14, 1961, 3:30 P.M.
Moscow

The sun was out but there was a cold wind, and Yepishev had pulled up his collar. "Winter dies as hard as some men," Talia said as she approached him. He had sounded relaxed when he called and asked her to meet him, but now that she could see his eyes she knew that he was deeply troubled.

"For you," he said, handing her a small envelope.

She read slowly. "Where did you get this?"

"It's reliable; that's all you need to know."

"Who is Kasi?" she asked, checking the name to be sure she had it correct.

"A fanatic who works for Shehu and takes care of certain unpleasant tasks."

"A killer?"

"That's one of many labels that could be applied."

"So he's left Albania. What of it?"

"I have other sources who report that he and his female companion were in France earlier this year."

"When?"

"At the same time that certain Albanian expatriates were being killed in Paris."

"The French said that a young woman was involved in at least one of the murders."

"Yes, I thought of that. It's unusual for the Albanians to employ a woman."

"How unusual?"

"I know of no instance since the war."

Talia stared at the paper. "What is this?" she asked, looking at a list of five addresses.

"Kasi and the woman flew to Vienna from Rome. They went to Italy by diplomatic shuttle. They may be at one of those addresses."

"You've confirmed that they're in Vienna?"

He nodded.

"How does this connect to Lumbas?"

"They're Albanians, and Kasi is Sigurimi. I leave final solutions to you. My expertise is in collecting information, not in its analysis."

"Nothing in this situation seems to come together neatly," Talia said.

"Which suggests that your adversaries have planned well."

She smiled. "You said your forte was not analysis."

"I point to the obvious. There's no great analysis required."

She looked at the addresses again. "You didn't happen to have these places checked out?"

"Your job. I didn't want to tip any balances. It's best to respect boundaries."

"We're indebted to you."

"Perhaps," Yepishev said, added, *"Do svidanya,"* and was gone.

When she emerged from the birch forest Talia saw her husband and went to him. "You're going to Vienna," she said. "Today."

---

165   SUNDAY, MAY 14, 1961, 4:40 P.M. *Vienna*

Albert was in a talkative mood, with Ali compliant. "Besides the obvious news value, what is it about this summit that interests you so much?"

Mignonne Mock poured coffee into two bowls, added cream and pushed one to her new photographer. "Breathe a word of this and I'll cut your balls off," she said. "Reuters has asked me to follow up a lead that could be extremely important. If I can confirm the story there will be a correspondent's position for me in Berlin, and I want that job badly. In this life you have to go after the things you want."

"As good a philosophy as any," Frash said. "You're more direct than most."

"News is a vulture's business. I'm not good at sharing and I can't trust my fellow Austrians."

"Which is why you chose me. Are you good at your work?"

"If you mean am I prominent, the answer is probably, but most of my competitors would describe me as notorious. And a bitch. They always include that."

"You thrive on notoriety?"

Mock flashed a hard smile. "On the contrary, but I accept it when it means that people fear me and give me space. In my kind of journalism having space to maneuver is critical, and now it's particularly so. Until recently a General Major Zakharov was in charge of Soviet forces in East Berlin. He's disappeared. An informant told Reuters that Zakharov will come to Vienna as the head of Soviet security."

440

"It's not unusual for officers to be transferred. It happens in all armies."

"Shut up and listen," Mock said. "Zakharov has had extensive contact over recent months with an East German named Honecker, and a source close to him claims that the Soviets and East Germans have been gathering blueprints of buildings in all sectors of Berlin—street maps, sewer routes, all sorts of things that seem to point to something extraordinary."

"I'm missing the point." Which was not exactly true. Obviously the Soviets and East Germans were up to something. Lumbas had said several times that the Kremlin was concerned about the flow of educated East Germans to the West. Perhaps a decision had been made, and he wondered if the Company had any inkling of it.

"The Reuters people believe that the Soviets are preparing to seal off East Berlin this summer," she said. "What do you think of that?"

There was some logic to this; Khrushchev had shown the Hungarians how the Soviets handled perceived threats to their national interest; Frash had no doubt that if the Soviets thought that isolating Berlin would be in their interest, they'd do it. He decided that his life as an Italian photographer was going to be useful. Whatever information Mock gathered, he would have access to it. "What you've got is worthless." Especially if she was going to get him close to Kennedy.

"It won't be when I confront the Russians with it publicly."

"And how do you plan to do that?"

"You get paid to take pictures," she snapped, "not to think."

166 SUNDAY, MAY 14, 1961, 8:15 P.M.
Vienna

The flat was in a gray building on a short, narrow street off Linzerstrasse, nine blocks east of Auer Welsbach Park and ten blocks west of the city's western rail terminus. The park sat at the foot of the 1,441-room Schönbrunn Palace, which had once housed a brooding Napoleon and would soon host the American and Soviet leaders. Canvas-top green trucks filled with Austrian security troops raced past the end of the street several times, but Kasi paid no attention. The Austrians were toy soldiers, better suited to gassing Jews than fighting man to man, a country of clerks and chocolate eaters with rotten teeth.

Kasi had been over the plan with Shehu so many times that it was now a part of his unconscious. It was daring and simple in concept but would require him to make countless on-the-spot decisions. His entire life had been a preparation for this moment, the key being to get the girl in so close that she could do her job, then eliminate her when she had served her purpose. They counted on the sheer size of the security force to guarantee access and success. The Austrians would be stepping on one another's feet, a two-legged Maginot line. Hitler had already proven that fixed offensive positions were easily breached. In Vienna history would repeat itself. It would be no great feat to get the girl inside, but could he maneuver her face-to-face with the target?

"The girl can't survive," Shehu warned before they left. Kasi needed no reminder. She would die, even at the cost of his own life; he was comfortable with his own expendability, his entire career having been based on this assumption.

Since 1951 Shehu's agents had been acquiring Viennese real estate under the cover of a Belgian company. They had thirty properties now, five of them in the city itself, all intended to be used briefly, then abandoned. This particular flat apparently belonged to a French-born architect named Shank; the contract provided not only the purchase price, but an extra clause paid the owner of record a handsome bonus to abandon the place on twenty-four hours' notice. Large and well furnished, it was on the second floor and had two bedrooms and a small balcony that overlooked the street. In an emergency they could jump to the street or go down the stairs to an inner courtyard, from which there were ample escape routes in either direction. Of the Viennese sites this one was the best suited for their needs.

The girl seemed serene. How could she be anything else? He had stripped away her illusions. She had no idea what lay ahead, but he supposed she assumed that this would be a repeat of the Paris mission. If she knew the truth too soon she might balk. He had seen such reactions before in less momentous circumstances, and had learned that it was better to keep people in the dark. In Paris she had performed with near perfection, but eliminating soft-bellied expatriates was not the same as killing someone whose face was recognized the world over. The sheer magnitude of the act would give pause even to a seasoned assassin.

The girl came out of the bathroom dripping water, sat at a dressing table and dried her hair. She was so accustomed to having him around that she no longer paid any attention to him. When she bathed, she left the door open and sometimes went around without clothes. He saw that the scar on her leg was dark but cleanly healed. He had been surprised and pleased at how easily she had handled the dogs, and felt bad about the scar. When her hair was dry, she began brushing it. It had grown out now and reached down to her neck.

"Tomorrow you'll have new clothes," Kasi told her. Lejla glanced at him in the mirror and kept brushing methodically. She had a tiny waist, too small for the rest of her body, and a long torso. "A manicure, perhaps," he added. "Would you like that?"

He saw her look at her left hand. "Whatever you say," she said.

She was a remarkably handsome woman. Kasi had been close to her for months now and had sometimes felt desire, but he had pushed it away with tricks of self-discipline. Before there had always been a tomorrow, another test for her, intensified training, continuous monitoring of her attitude. But now they were at the end, and what went on between them was their secret.

He was shaking as he undressed. He arranged his clothes on the floor and got into bed, sliding his automatic under his pillow. "Turn off the light," he said.

The girl got up and walked soundlessly to a switch along the wall. "You want to sleep now?" she asked. "I'll finish in the other room."

Kasi thought of Shehu. If something went wrong and Shehu learned . . . "Yes," he said. "You do the same. We need to be rested."

Lejla Llarja went into the other bedroom and sat down on the bed. Her father's voice still said, "You can't save me," but she still had to try.

167   **MONDAY, MAY 15, 1961, 4:50 A.M.**
Klosterneuburg, Austria

The newest Russian was named Ezdovo and seemed to the two Americans to be on a par with Bailov and Melko rather than with the others, who seemed to be soldiers of lesser rank. The three conferred for some time before asking the Americans to join them.

"In Switzerland you told us about several murders among Albanian expatriates in Paris," Bailov said.

"Why are we going back to this? They were officially classified as political infighting, but we also heard that they could have been the work of Albanian execution teams," Sylvia said.

"One of the victims was shot by a young woman. Have I remembered correctly?"

"What are you getting at?"

"We have information indicating that an important Albanian named Kasi flew to Vienna last week. He was accompanied by a young woman."

"That doesn't mean—"

Bailov cut her off. "Kasi is a senior officer in the Sigurimi, but more important he's close to Shehu, closer than Hoxha himself. Shehu is Hoxha's iron first and Kasi is Shehu's. It's unlikely he's here on holiday."

"In other words, he's here on business," Valentine said.

"That's the guess, but your Western logic won't explain it. When Khrushchev denounced Stalin five years ago, the Albanians were miffed. Stalin had sent them arms during the war with Germany. A fallout began with the denunciation, and it has worsened since. Now the General Secretary has also fallen out with the Chinese, and Chairman Mao is attempting to maneuver our country into a position where we would have to support him." It had been Petrov who explained the nuances and intricacies of the Sino-Soviet problem to the team.

"Even the Chinese can't make the Soviet Union do what it doesn't want to do," Sylvia said.

"You don't understand," Bailov said. "Mao wants Khrushchev and the Soviet Union to accept the role of leadership of the world socialist movement. If Nikita Sergeievich allows this to happen, then we must regard the movement as a single entity, and therefore must support whatever our brothers do."

"If China goes to war, the Soviet Union goes to war," Sylvia said. "Like that?"

"That's the extreme," Bailov said, "but it is also precisely the concern. Khrushchev had to reject the Chinese initiative because he knows that they are headstrong. We can't afford to support their adventures."

"Which means that Khrushchev is allowing the socialist movement to become fragmented," Sylvia said.

"Let's stick to facts and forget geopolitics," Valentine said. "You don't know that this Kasi character had anything to do with the events in Paris. With Frash here we can't afford to divert our attention."

"Hear me out," Bailov said. "The trouble between Khrushchev and Hoxha is deadly serious."

"A rip in the Iron Curtain," Valentine said, but the Russians didn't laugh at his joke.

"The rip, as you put it, is ideological," Bailov answered. "Attempts have been made to smooth it over, but the Albanians are recalcitrant."

Valentine didn't get it. "A big old dog doesn't fear the fleas on his back."

"Khrushchev is simply acknowledging reality. No less than democracy, Communism works differently in different parts of the world. It's incredible to us that the West has never seemed to grasp this. Khrushchev seeks reform, but change isn't possible if we have to stand on ideology."

"Let's say for the moment that we buy this," Valentine said. "We still don't see how this links up to what happened in Paris."

444

"We're relatively sure that Kasi was in France when the killings took place," Ezdovo said. "We think it's possible that the Albanians believe that the Frash-Lumbas plan was a Soviet response to the ideological rift."

"But you're saying that it isn't?" Sylvia asked.

Bailov nodded. "We accept that your CIA wasn't engaged in a special operation, and we hope you'll believe that Lumbas wasn't part of an official Soviet action."

"Do your sources in Moscow offer an explanation for the Albanians being here?" Sylvia asked.

Ezdovo opened his hands to express futility. "We have to assume that he's here, that the girl is with him, and that whatever else they have in mind, they won't stray far from the Lek."

"The Lek?" Valentine asked.

"That is the name of the Albanians' old tribal law whose central tenet is revenge. Under the Lek virtually every insult requires death as a response. Kasi made his reputation as an assassin."

"Nice. So if you know they're here you must have some idea where they are."

Bailov laid a piece of paper on the table. "This may help us."

Valentine saw that there were five addresses on the page. "You wouldn't happen to have one for Frash, would you?"

168   MONDAY, MAY 15, 1961, 8:30 P.M.
Vienna

It was irritating how the echo of telephone scramblers seemed to stack words on top of each other. "Where are you now?" Arizona asked as he heard the echo that seemed to repeat his question. Where I am is in purgatory, he told himself, awaiting direction from forces beyond my control. "What the hell has taken so long?"

"Frash is in Austria," Sylvia said wearily. "He crossed under the radar."

"Confirmed?"

"Good enough to act on it," she said. "We think he's headed for Vienna."

Naturally, Arizona thought. The bread was about to land peanut-butter side down. "Why?"

"Nothing else makes sense. He's stuck to Europe for a reason."

She was right on that count. He pictured Frash as a missile on course to a target. Somehow they had to intercept him and worry about his motives later. "Who else knows?" he asked.

"The Russians," she said.

Which complicates matters, Arizona told himself, but without the Russians they could never have confirmed the Frash-Lumbas connection. What was important now was how they dealt with the future, rather than the past.

"Do you want us to alert the Secret Service team?" Sylvia asked.

This was the last thing Arizona wanted, but he warned himself to go easy so that she wouldn't catch on. "Good idea," he said. Then after a pause, "Wait . . . it's probably better that I do it. You two are out of the loop and liable to get tied up if you walk in cold turkey." Give her support, then withdraw it gently. Let her believe that it was a fifty-fifty call on who would make the contact. "I'll take care of it. Leave the details to me and I'll be on the next plane. I want you two to stick close to the Russians, and I don't want our people to know about that relationship. It may give us a bit more room to act." Their independence meant leverage; at least he hoped so.

Sylvia was quiet after she hung up the phone.

"Burr under your saddle?" Valentine asked.

"More like systemic skepticism."

"That's my line," he said with a laugh. "But it ain't paranoia when somebody's really out to get you. What's the word from our mountain?"

"He's coming to Mohammed."

"Should we be comforted by that?"

She patted his hand. Technically Arizona was correct; if they made contact with the Secret Service it might raise too many questions. But if it was so logical, why was she so antsy?

169   MONDAY, MAY 15, 1961, 11:00 P.M. *Klosterneuburg, Austria*

The main task was organizing the team to check the five addresses. Maybe the Albanians were at one of the five locations, maybe not; in any event, they would soon know. Frash was a different matter. Thus far he had slipped through every net; this time they would have to use a finer mesh.

"We have time," Bailov told the others. "We have more than two weeks to find them." He had already subdivided his men and assigned them to watch embassies and other public places where the leaders would meet. Concentrate on adjacent areas, he had instructed. Overlook nothing. Watch who comes and goes and when they're there. Write it down. Take photographs. Look for patterns but avoid them yourselves. See but don't be seen, which he helped ensure by assigning only a few men to a given area. When the leaders arrived his men would serve as an inner screen, the line behind the security the rest of the world would see; because of this he wanted them to know as much as possible about the terrain where they would operate. However, the immediate problem was the five addresses.

"We don't have enough people to move against all five at once," Sylvia reminded the Russians. "We have to assume that the five are linked—safe houses, perhaps, or offering short-term travelers' aid. If we concentrate on one and it's the wrong choice, we risk alerting the Albanians. We have some time, but we need to use it constructively. Who owns the properties? Who lives in them? Any recent changes or new residents? We need phone numbers, tax records, anything that will give us more information and help us narrow the search."

"We're looking at everything," Bailov said. "Moscow wants us to examine the same ground being covered by security." Sylvia had a feeling that when these Russians referred to Moscow it wasn't the same Moscow the CIA tried to track. "The key is access. Who will be close to the General Secretary? Security, police, embassy employees, government employees, reporters. All of these people and others will have more access than the public at large."

"With a rifle and a telescopic sight, a sniper could be a threat from a long way off," Sylvia pointed out.

Bailov rubbed his forehead. "Security forces will have to take care of threats from the street. All routes will be swept ahead of time and monitored. Automobiles with armor will be used, and there will be tight crowd control at all entry and departure points. A moving target presents too many uncontrollable factors for a sniper, so security will concentrate on the areas that present stationary opportunities."

"Back home," Valentine said, "ranchers shoot the ears off jackrabbits running thirty miles an hour."

"I'm not arguing it can't be done," Bailov answered. "Only that if you're a sniper, you try to pick a shot at a stationary target from the best possible angle and a maximum distance of sixty meters. A professional plans for two rounds, no more, and we can assume that amateurs are not a concern here."

Valentine nodded.

"What are your people monitoring specifically?" Sylvia asked.

"The Austrians have vetted everyone who will or may get involved. The backgrounds of janitors, dishwashers, electricians, caterers, plumbers and so forth have been investigated. If there is a need for emergency services of any kind, only those people who have been cleared ahead of time will be allowed into any of the sites," Bailov said. "As a safeguard, all these names have been sent to Moscow to be checked against our own lists."

"Tidy," Valentine said. But Frash had shown an uncanny ability to go where he wanted, and the Albanians might be better prepared and less wild-eyed than the Russians made them out to be. He had a feeling that everything was going to get even more complicated than it already was.

170 TUESDAY, MAY 16, 1961, NOON
Purkersdorf, Austria

Vladimir Rakimov had been installed on the first floor of the Soviet embassy, a stone's throw from the Belvedere Palace complex. While his cover was second deputy director of the Foreign Ministry's Department of Information and Propaganda, he held a second and more important position as U.S. sector chief of Section K of the KGB's First Chief Directorate. In this role Brigadier General Rakimov was responsible for penetrating foreign intelligence services and for monitoring Soviets living outside the U.S.S.R. But now he was in Vienna as part of the tripartite security apparatus, his job being to review press credentials. Technically it was the Austrians who gave authorization to reporters wanting to cover the summit, but in practice all requests were reviewed by Soviet and American officials at their respective embassies. Any of the three could blackball any request, which meant that every journalist who passed muster had been cleared by all three intelligence services.

Rakimov was sixty, short, obese, ruddy-cheeked and a heavy smoker, the sort who exuded a remarkable natural affinity and affability for anyone he encountered. The holder of three university degrees, he spoke English with a Midwestern American accent, and could talk knowledgeably about American culture, from the lackluster sales of the 1959 Edsel to National Football League standings and the accounting practices of the Hollywood studio system. Raconteur, eclectic, linguist, he was that rare individual who would rise to the top no matter where he was born.

Ezdovo first met Rakimov on Sunday to arrange a twice-daily review of incoming requests for press credentials. The Siberian's authority derived from a letter from Khrushchev, which Rakimov barely glanced at. Ten minutes into their initial meeting he asked Ezdovo to call him Volodya, and proceeded to relate how he had recently divorced his wife of thirty-four years and married a woman who would turn thirty-five in mid-June, adding that he was anxious about having left his beautiful bride alone in Moscow. "Zhenya had lots of boyfriends, legions of them," he said, "but she chose me. Who can understand women?"

Ezdovo was not deceived by Rakimov's breezy style. If the woman had picked him over so many others, no doubt she had done so in part because she wanted access to his power. His looks and age certainly had not attracted her.

The plan was for the Siberian to come to the embassy at noon and again at 7:00 P.M. each day. On each visit the KGB man would have a new list ready for him.

This morning Rakimov was his usual ebullient self. "I had a telephone conversation with Zhenya last night," he said immediately. "She misses me terribly and says she needs no birthday gift other than my safe return. Can you imagine?" He lowered his voice. "I worry about our—compatibility," he confessed. "Right now it's fantastic, but I'm no longer a young man. Is your wife younger than you?"

Ezdovo recognized that Rakimov was fishing. Reveal a few personal details that may or may not be true, then use them to troll for information. It was like priming a pump, but even though he recognized it for what it was, Ezdovo was impressed. Volodya was so friendly and open that you had to fight the desire to tell him what he wanted to know. Stalin's people had been much different, using brute force rather than charm. In this regard there had been changes in the sort of men who held power in the Kremlin, and in how they operated. The old ones had been iron-fisted party hacks whose major qualification was a willingness to do Stalin's bidding. The new ones are different, the Siberian thought, and probably more effective, though their goal—to preserve the status quo—is identical. He decided that the best way to handle Rakimov was to ignore his questions.

"Where's the list?"

"Nothing exciting," Rakimov said, paying no attention to the rebuff. This was also his style. Cast and retrieve, cast and retrieve; no matter what happens, keep the bait in the water. "It's no wonder Americans can't protect their secrets. Too many reporters, each following his own scent. Even so, they're an interesting lot. Enterprising as hell, which no doubt is a product of capitalism. Or," he went on, casting again, "perhaps they're capitalists because they're enterprising, the system re flecting the people rather than the other way around. What do you think?"

"What's the total now?" Ezdovo asked as he scanned the new list.

"Just under one thousand. Ever been in the States?"

"No."

"In America you have to have a strong sense of self-interest, otherwise you perish. The Americans maintain that we're no different." He was fishing for some indication of political reliability. "Perhaps they're right."

"Our people are unique," Ezdovo said.

"Remarkable place," Rakimov prattled on. "Absolute chaos. They're like pack animals at each other's throat. To have too much freedom is to have no freedom at all. If we were to pluck an ordinary citizen out of—" Rakimov paused. "Where did you say you were from, comrade?"

"I didn't," Ezdovo said coolly.

"As I was saying, pluck an ordinary citizen from a Byelorussian collective, put him in New York and he would think he had been abducted by aliens from outer space. Trust me on this. I've seen it. Spent eight years in New York. My first wife loathed it, all but the food. She was fat as a prize sow."

Ezdovo slid the folder back across the desk. "Thank you," he said.

Rakimov tapped the folder with his pipe. "If I knew what you were looking for, comrade, perhaps I could be of more help."

Ezdovo smiled. "Where did you say *you* were from?"

Rakimov's grin faded. "I'll have an update for you tonight," he said, turning to pick up the telephone.

171   TUESDAY, MAY 16, 1961, 6:15 P.M.
Georgetown

Venema's office was in a stone building in Gothic style on the periphery of what served as the Georgetown University campus. The ground level contained two laboratories and a small conference room. The sign outside read INTERVIEW RESEARCH INSTITUTE. Arizona wondered how the Jesuit powers would react if they knew that IRI had been wholly financed by the Company. With a yawn, he decided. Georgetown had built its academic prowess around international studies, and probably had more government consultants than any academic institution in the country. The Jesuit order had lost its once-immense power because the various governments they served came to fear them; in time the fear passed, the order had been rechartered, and now the Jesuits were back on familiar ground, hand in glove with politicans. Some things never change.

Arizona was escorted to Venema's upstairs office by a heavyset brunette who spoke English with a Polish accent. Venema was behind a mound of papers at a huge oak desk, tipped back in a swivel chair, a folder in his lap, feet up, a pipe clenched in his teeth. Arizona had called him after talking to Sylvia. "That his file?" the CIA man asked as he sat down.

"I'd say that our Mr. Frash is coming unglued," Venema said. "You think of him as a rogue, but I see him as something else. People like this have their own patterns. We know he's schizophrenic, with two personalities battling for superiority in the same brain."

"Spare me the medical bullshit," Arizona growled.

"The bullshit, as you put it, is essential to our being able to predict his behavior. Schizophrenia is not unusual in killers like this who strike randomly."

"Fuck random. The bastard knows what he's doing."

Venema paused to regroup. "Let's not play semantic games. The killings are random. In this type what you find are two distinct personalities and conflicting value systems. Two for the price of one. Statics is afforded by a crude but efficient division of labor, each personality taking on certain roles and functions split along some arbitrary line of demarcation, often a moral one."

"Like one likes sweet, the other likes sour?"

"It's not that clear cut or simplistic, but that's the general idea. In this case our man appeared to be fixated on overthrowing the present Albanian regime. His father was cast out by those who held office. Frash carries the stigma, the father's sins inherited by the son, probably with the mother as the conduit, which again is predictable."

"The Albanian fixation *causes* the schizophrenia?"

"You're looking for sin when you ought to be looking for chemistry," Venema said. "A tiger is born a tiger. Frash was born with schizophrenia, just as he was born with a certain eye and hair color. A lot of people don't buy that but I do. It was there from the start. The Albanian trigger came into play later. A father fails at something; the son tries to succeed as a means of atonement. These things exacerbate rather than cause. Failure can motivate everything in its wake, especially where there is a perceived higher order of morality. Royalty often engages in such fanaticism; in fact, one could argue convincingly that royalists are the products of such a force. As evidence we have Russian expatriates protecting the myth of the identity of Anastasia for decades. Or networks of ex-Nazis dedicated to reestablishing Aryan supremacy. Irish Catholics and Protestants in America buy weapons for factions in Northern Ireland. Our Jews send money to Israel and provide information to the Mossad. Armenians in Detroit seek revenge against Turks and Russians. Kurds bide their time for revenge against Iraq, Syria, Iran, Turkey and the Soviet Union. Latvian expatriates are raised on their native language and customs, the idea being to preserve the culture until the country can be reclaimed. These motivations take on lives of their own, but as time passes the first-generation passion tends to ebb. For most members of such groups there's token support for the perceived holy mission, a shared vision that helps keep them together in an environment seen as essentially foreign and hostile. It's only a small number of these fires that burn brightly, and these people become the priests of the cause, the true believers."

"Frash's parents?"

"From what I could assemble, it was primarily the mother," Venema said, "but I'm dealing with bits and pieces, so I have to interpolate. We know that the progeny of such people tend either to reject the basic premise entirely, or else take it to new extremes. In the latter case the child feels guilt for not having suffered as extensively as the parent has, so he embraces the cause with greater intensity as a way of demonstrating his worthiness. As time goes by the elders adapt to new realities, but the neophyte doesn't, and therefore he tends to become an isolated soldier in the cause; factions often sprout from such seed. Depending on the time of onset, the process of adolescence complicates matters. In the case of males, there's the natural complication of adolescent rebelliousness, a figurative killing of the father so that the boy can pass into adulthood. As part of this, he may begin to assign blame to his father."

"Frash begins to think that Zog fell because of his father's inadequacies, so the group shame becomes his individual shame? Therefore he decides to do something about it?"

"That's pretty much how it works. It would seem foolish to normal folk, but it's quite real to a believer."

"Meaning that the Albanian operation was real in his mind?"

"I'd say it was his raison d'être. He was its spiritual head, architect and general, and eventually he would be its primary beneficiary."

"But he was also running the Russian agent."

"This is schizophrenia hitting on all cylinders. Because of his parents' dual lives the man-boy has an overdeveloped sense of responsibility. He strives to achieve, and whatever he undertakes, he does well; that is, he ran the Russian agent effectively because it was his job, what you expected. One part of him concentrated on reality while the other part focused on the mythical cause. Both parts serve different masters and serve them well until the moment comes when one must be chosen over the other."

"The killing of Lumbas."

"Possibly," Venema said, "but it doesn't really matter. What we do know is that something provoked a crisis; whatever it was has now knocked him off balance, so there's probably a war between his competing personalities. He's probably oscillating back and forth; first one personality gets control, then the other, with frequent and unpredictable reversals. The result is an escalating internal combat to see which will ultimately prevail."

"How can you know that?"

"Patterns," Venema said. "Both parts work as one to acquire confederates. One part uses them—to wit, the Dutch woman—and leaves it at that. The other part uses people, then kills them, as in Venice, and again in Austria. From what we've seen we can surmise that our Mr. Frash will undoubtedly recruit another female to help him resolve his morality play. Gender is crucial. Because he's at war with his father, his mother becomes his ally. He clings to her because she's the opposite of his father, and because she provides a way to reject the father, yet maintain loyalty to the family unit and therefore to the cause. Women are tools to be employed in his quest; if Frash is in Vienna you can bet there'll be a woman with him. Find her and you'll find him."

Most of the foregoing was mumbo jumbo to Arizona, but this last bit might be useful. "What sort of woman?"

"I thought you'd never ask," Venema said. "She'll be a risk taker, aggressive I would think, somebody looking to change her own circumstances in some way. I expect that she'll have some degree of competence—a career, perhaps. She'll be attractive but not easily swayed by just any man who comes along. Don't look for hotel maids or hausfraus. Whatever environment she's in she'll stand out in some way, perhaps negatively because she's not likely to conform to the community's expectations for women."

"Will he kill her?"

"When he's finished with her."

"We should look for the woman rather than him?"

"It's an option. My guess is that he'll use her as a shield, so only she will be visible."

"Say we find him, how do you suggest we approach him?"

Venema dumped his pipe into an ashtray. "That's more in your line of expertise."

172   WEDNESDAY, MAY 17, 1961, 9:20 A.M.
Vienna

Every journalist requesting accreditation had to visit the summit press center in the ministry offices near the Schönbrunn Palace, but Mignonne Mock was not the sort to be hemmed in by details; her own credentials had already been vetted and now she wanted speedy approval for her new partner. To avoid bureaucratic entanglements she went directly to the Hofburg Palace to see an old friend, the senior press aide to Austrian president Adolf Schärf.

Richard Wehrmann was thirty, blond, tall, square-jawed, outgoing and known to his closest friends as Dickie. In 1956 he had been a favorite for a downhill medal in the Winter Olympics, but he had taken a catastrophic spill in a practice run and now had several steel pins holding together his right leg. Always a media favorite, Wehrmann's appointment to the president's staff had been widely applauded. He wore nicely tailored double-breasted dark suits and walked with the assistance of a cane whose handgrip was a brass skier.

"My favorite meddler," Wehrmann greeted Mock. He took her hand and touched his nose to it. "Radiant," he said, looking at her sleeveless white cotton dress and wide-brimmed straw hat. He knew she had dressed up for him, which meant that she was after something. They had been friends for several years, and though both had once considered the possibility of an affair, they had each decided that it would ruin their friendship, and because of this they had rejected intimacy. Now Wehrmann was married to an attractive woman who played the cello in the Vienna Philharmonic.

"You look well, Dickie. You must make sweet music with your wife. It shows on your face."

Wehrmann laughed and waved her to a high-backed chair by his desk. His office looked as if it had been lifted from the nineteenth century. One wall held a sepia study of a nude by Gustav Klimt. "The life of a musician is worse than a skier's," he said. "Practice, practice. I tell Ann-Sophie not to be so driven, but she counters, 'As you were not driven?' " Wehrmann had been known as a perfectionist who practiced relentlessly while his teammates soaked in spas and partied. He laughed at his wife's words. "She knows me too well."

"As do I," Mock said. "I have myself a photographer, a brilliant Italian. He's unknown for now, but he does exquisite work. I need credentials for him."

"Previous press experience?"

"None. He thinks he's an artist," she answered with a laugh.

Wehrmann smiled, returned to his desk and took a piece of stationery from a lacquered box. Mock opened her purse and put Sirini's identity papers on the leather desk pad. The press aide scanned them and jotted down the necessary information. "You should request credentials through normal channels," he reminded her as he wrote.

"You know very well that I hate standing in lines," she said. "I want to put him to work right away—which reminds me, any interesting tidbits to share off the record?"

Wehrmann grinned. Good friend or not, Mock's reputation as a journalistic shark was legendary. "I can process the application, but you understand that your Italian will have to be vetted by both the Americans and the Russians. However, there should be no problem as long as I vouch for him. I'll ask them to hurry. Come back tonight at six."

She pretended to pout. "So late?"

Wehrmann pushed the papers back to her and shook his head. She never let up. "All right, make it four. I'll take care of this personally."

"And once again I'll be in your debt, Dickie."

"Which, like all the others, will never be repaid," Wehrmann said with a laugh as he walked her to the door. "Is the Italian also sharing your bed?"

She kissed him on the cheek. "You're a naughty boy to ask such a personal question. You had your chance."

Frash was waiting on the street. "Any problem?"

"I have to come back at four."

"It's that easy?"

"It pays to have connections," Mock said, getting into the automobile.

Dickie Wehrmann was standing on the balcony outside his office savoring his morning cigar when he saw her emerge from the entrance and fall into step with a man. Her car was parked where it didn't belong, of course. Was that her photographer? Probably not; he looked only vaguely like the photograph on the passport she had given him. It would be an inconvenience to take care of her request, but one's duty to a friend ranked second only to obligations to one's family.

173 | WEDNESDAY, MAY 17, 1961, 6:00 P.M. *Vienna*

Bailov went to the summit security center and roused the Soviet duty officer, a clean-shaven Red Army major with burn scars on the left side of his face. The major was a by-the-book sort; the authorization letter from Khrushchev did not satisfy him, and in the end Bailov was forced to show him his Red Badge, which made him more cooperative but not happily so. Within minutes he produced an Austrian police officer, but when Bailov dismissed the major, he showed his displeasure by slamming the door as he left. It occurred to the Spetsnaz commander that life in the Soviet Union was changing and that the days of the Red Badge's unquestioned authority were disappearing. After learning what was required, the policeman made two telephone calls, then directed Bailov to the Zoning and Deeds Office in the New Town Hall on Rathausplatz. The Soviet major turned his back as Bailov passed him in an outer office.

The Americans were waiting in a truck. A low front was passing over the city, creating a thick haze that made the New Town Hall's exterior lighting glow in the distance. A young woman in a black raincoat waiting for them on the steps of the front entrance introduced herself as Birgit Nestroy, head of the deeds section; she explained that though the offices were closed she had been asked to assist them. Her section was located off a subterranean tunnel, and both the office and records storage area were neat and uncluttered. "The law requires us to maintain physical records for thirty years," she explained. "Everything earlier than that is on microfilm but cataloged and easily retrieved."

Valentine gave her the list of addresses, and true to her word, she was back in five minutes with file cards.

While Valentine read, Sylvia asked Nestroy if her records would show who the current occupants were, in the event that owner and resident were different. No, she said, but this information could be gotten quickly from another section in the same building. Phone numbers? Yes, of course, those as well. Sylvia asked her to get them.

Valentine rubbed his eyes. "This is strange. All properties last changed hands in 1958. All five transactions took place over a two-week period in June of that year."

"What about the purchasers?" Bailov asked.

"All different, but all five are held jointly by couples, husband and wife."

"Prices?" Sylvia asked.

"Each seems to be about fifty percent over the previous sale price."

"Inflation?"

"Ask the clerk," Valentine said. "All five couples paid cash," he added.

"That's not extraordinary for Europe," Sylvia said. "Forty percent cash down payments and higher are routine here. It's not like the States."

"*All* cash," Valentine said. "Not just the down payments." He did a quick conversion of Austrian schillings to dollars. "All five buys were in the neighborhood of seventy thousand U.S. How many people have that much ready green to sink into real estate?"

Bailov shook his head. "A Soviet knows nothing about such things." Especially a Soviet soldier, he thought. On his pay it would take half a century to accumulate the equivalent.

When Nestroy returned, Valentine said, "All of these properties changed hands in June 1958. Was there inflation then?"

The woman tugged her chin. "There is invariably some, but I have been here since 1956, and that was not a period of particularly high inflation."

"How many Viennese pay the full price in cash? Is this normal?"

"More now than a few years ago," she answered, "but it's still unusual. Only a few of the very rich would find it possible, but such people would think it senseless to tie up so much cash. The rich don't accumulate wealth by stupidity."

Valentine had already reached the same conclusion. "Are these properties in exclusive areas?"

Nestroy squinted at the list of addresses, then moved to a huge city map mounted on the wall. "Three are in middle-class areas, two in poorer districts."

Valentine looked at his companions. "We can rule out the rich-man angle."

"They could be investments," Sylvia said. "Did you get the other information?" she asked the Austrian woman.

"Of course." She handed them an envelope with an embossed city seal on the flap.

Valentine compared the names of the owners with the current residents. All five were the same. "That rules out the investment angle," he observed.

"Who handled the financial transactions?" Sylvia asked.

"A bank must act as a fiduciary agent," Miss Nestroy said. "That's the law."

"Even if there's no borrowing?"

"The bank's financial gain is not the point," she explained. "The law ensures that the government gets an accurate accounting of all transactions for taxation purposes."

All five purchases had been handled by the same bank. "The Royal Hapsburg," Valentine announced. "Big?" he asked.

"Solvent but relatively small," the Austrian woman said.

There were too many coincidences, Valentine thought, and he suspected that Sylvia was thinking the same. "Maybe we need to talk to somebody at the bank. What I'd really like to know is where all these folks do their regular banking, and what their financial situations are. Would anybody expect them to have this much cash?"

"That would require time," Nestroy said. "It would also require the intervention of a court; you must show evidence of criminal activity in order to open personal financial records."

Valentine grimaced and opened the second set of records. "All the phone numbers except one are the same as in 1958. That one was changed the next year."

Nestroy looked at the wall map. "In 1959 there were readjustments in the city's districting," she said as she walked to the map. "See? The address in question is on the periphery of three districts. That address may have been assigned to a new district, which would require a new exchange. Such changes are dictated by the law governing redistricting; telephone subscribers have no option."

Valentine looked at the wall map. "Show me the city's railroad stations," he asked without explaining why. The woman walked to the map and used a pencil as a pointer. If the Albanians were here they would need an escape route. If the hit took place in the city, it would be difficult to get all the way to the airport, much less catch a plane. A train would be a handier alternative, but only one of the addresses was close to a terminal. "I need help, people."

"You could check with the postal service," Miss Nestroy said.

"Why?" Sylvia asked.

"Hypothetically it is possible that there has been a recent sale that has not yet come through the system to us. Or the residents might be on holiday."

"How long does the paperwork for a sale take?"

"One day," Nestroy said. "That's the law."

"That makes a sale pretty unlikely. Why would their being on holiday be relevant?"

"They would have to notify their post office, which would then collect and hold their mail for their return."

Valentine shrugged. "If they chose to."

"It's not a matter of choice," Miss Nestroy said disapprovingly.

"Law?" Valentine asked.

"Of course. Why should the mail carrier make unnecessary deliveries? The postal union sponsored this law. It's been in force less than a year."

"Slim," Valentine said.

"Even a thin line may catch a fish," Bailov said. He was impressed by the rational way the Americans were attacking the problem.

"Are the postal service offices here?" Valentine asked Nestroy.

"There is a central administration here," she answered, "but a decentralized system with a different post office for each district. The law requires notification of the local office, not the central authority."

"Can we call the postmasters for these districts?" Sylvia asked.

"The law forbids any queries before the opening time of eight A.M., and no business is done over the phone. In any event, they will not disclose this information to you."

"This is an emergency," Sylvia said.

"The postal service is independent by law and required to protect the privacy of those who use their services. Even our national security interests may not override individual privacy."

"But we have to try," Valentine told her.

She got the names and addresses of the postmasters for them within a few minutes. When they reached the street the haze was thicker. "The Austrians have a lot of laws," Bailov said glumly.

"There's probably a law that requires it," Sylvia said wryly.

174   WEDNESDAY, MAY 17, 1961, 7:05 P.M. *Vienna*

Rakimov was stretched out on the couch in his office snoring, a nearly empty bottle of vodka on the floor beside him, the fumes floating upward, the floor littered with papers as if he had been stricken.

Ezdovo poked the inert form. "The green snake claims more victims than Stalin, comrade."

Rakimov rolled his head and half opened one eye. "Cuckolded," he mumbled.

"Cuckolded?" Ezdovo repeated.

"The horns," Rakimov said with a moan, "the horns." The eye closed.

"Where's the list?"

"Talked to her this afternoon. She said it straight off, like a man. *I went with him,* she says. *Went.* What kind of a word is that?"

Ezdovo sat in Ramikov's chair behind the desk and thumbed through several three-by-five cards with handwritten names.

"Said she couldn't help it. He wore her down," Rakimov said as he grimaced with pain and clenched his fists. "I said, he wears you down in days? A few hours, she answers. *Hours?* I treat her like a princess for a year and this bastard gets between her legs in hours?" The little KGB man moaned, then sighed.

Ezdovo stacked the cards in alphabetical order and began transferring information to a pad of paper. There were no Soviet names, and it struck him that there were few among the requests so far. "Why so few of our people?"

Rakimov struggled to sit up, and held his head in his hands. "Nikita Sergeievich always hedges his bets."

"Explain."

"What is it about women that lets them break a man's balls?" Rakimov leaned down and tried to grab the bottle, but missed.

"You said something about Khrushchev hedging his bets," Ezdovo prompted.

The other man stared blankly at the Siberian, puffed his cheeks and exhaled. "Information alone is unimportant," Rakimov said. "What matters is how it's presented, you see? *There's* the true power. A dictionary is only words. How you put them together is the art, and Nikita Sergeievich is a master craftsman."

Ezdovo understood. No matter how the summit went, it would be Khrushchev who defined the results, which meant that Soviet reporters were unnecessary. A proverb said that Russia's history was harder to predict than its future.

Rakimov collapsed back on the couch while Ezdovo resumed his list making. Before writing down a name, he questioned the other man. Though still drunk, Rakimov stated a few details about each; Ezdovo was astonished by how many Western reporters he seemed to know.

"Díaz?"

"Mexican, Columbia graduate, European correspondent for *El Diario del Sol,* tennis player, socialist. The Americans wanted to veto him because they think he's one of ours," the Russian said with a pained look.

"Is he?"

Rakimov shook his head.

"Meier?"

"A fat Texas Jew; his family owns cotton mills. CBS Chicago bureau, recently moved to New York. Superficial, but handsome and glib in social situations. No apparent personal political ideology. Never drink with him," Rakimov warned, shaking a finger. "Holds it too well. Like a Russian."

"Pelosi?"

Rakimov tried to sit up again and this time made it. "First name Dawn. Changed her name from Brown. She's from Pittsburgh. Now works for a syndicate, don't remember what it's called."

"Unger News," Ezdovo read from the card.

"Unger, *da*. A new organization looking for sensational stories. Right-wing but moderate and easy to misdirect; they'll go with a rumor, seldom check anything. Dawn Pelosi is a very beautiful woman with hair the color of fire," Rakimov said. "Like my wife," he added wistfully.

"Jensen?"

"Eric James Jensen. *The Times* of London. Well educated, astute, respected, served in Moscow in the late forties. Stalin hated his guts, maybe even feared him, which was the closest he ever came to respect. Jensen served as a British agent with the French Resistance during the war. Decorated. Doesn't smoke, drinks only socially, has a stable marriage: he's unimpeachable. Some say he senses information through his pores. Eventually there'll be a 'K' for him. He's acceptable to all parties. A remarkably honest man. You'd like him."

The next two cards were stuck together. Ezdovo peeled them apart. "Sirini?"

Rakimov stared blankly. "Again?"

"Sirini, Benedetto."

The Siberian handed the card to Rakimov, who dug his eyeglasses out of his suit pocket. The lenses were covered with lint and dust as he plopped them crookedly on his nose. "Sirini," he said, tapping the card against his leg.

"Sirini," Ezdovo repeated.

"New to me," Rakimov said with a shrug.

"You approved him." The team had agreed that anything unusual should be thoroughly investigated. Turn over every stone, Bailov had said.

"*Da*," Rakimov said. "Now I remember. It was a favor."

"To whom?"

"Dickie."

"Dickie?"

"Austrian president's press officer. Richard Wehrmann, Dickie. He was a famous skier a few years ago. You must have heard of him."

"This man submitted the Italian's name?"

"Came to see me this afternoon. After you were here."

"Normal procedure?"

"*Nyet.*"

"You know nothing about the Italian, but you approved him?"

"As a favor to Dickie." Rakimov looked for understanding.

"But you said yourself he's unknown."

"Irrelevant," Rakimov said. "A favor now *for* Dickie, a favor *from* him later. Small compromise today, large gain tomorrow. Like wooing a woman. We must be patient and give to get, you see?"

Ezdovo picked up the telephone. "Call him," he ordered.

"Who?"

"The Austrian. Find out what he knows about the Italian."

"Won't be in the office now. It's late. Austrians arrive and leave on time. They live by the clock; punctuality is their master."

"Then call him at home," Ezdovo said, thrusting the telephone at him again.

Rakimov hobbled to his desk, opened a drawer, took out a fat notebook, thumbed through it, held a finger on a page and dialed the number with his free hand. Ezdovo picked up a second receiver and cupped his hand over the speaker.

A woman answered on the second ring. "Sorry to bother you," Rakimov said, "but is Dickie there?"

"One moment, please."

"Wehrmann," a smooth male voice said.

"Rakimov."

"You're working late tonight, comrade," the Austrian said, his tone friendly.

"Unavoidable these days," Rakimov said. "My people insist on having more information about Sirini, the man we talked about this afternoon."

"Giving you a hard time, are they?" The voice seemed tighter this time.

"Nothing so dramatic. It's a question of procedure, that's all."

"I've never met him," Wehrmann admitted. "I did it as a favor for a friend. She'll be working with him. She tells me he's quite talented but has no significant journalistic experience."

"She?"

"Mignonne Mock—you know her?"

Ezdovo scribbled the name on the card. " 'You know her?" the Austrian asked again.

"Yes, yes," Rakimov said, "of course. Is there any truth to the rumor that she's going to work for Reuters?"

Wehrmann laughed. "I'd expect you'd know better than I. You're the collector of rumors, comrade. Anything else?"

"Her address," Ezdovo whispered.

"Where does she live?" Rakimov asked.

Wehrmann's voice suddenly communicated caution. "Are you certain there's not a complication, Vladimir?" Ezdovo clearly heard the edge in the voice this time.

"You mustn't worry," Rakimov said. "You know how my comrades can be sticklers for detail."

Wehrmann gave him the address. "Top floor. On Blutgasse. She's an old friend, a bit flamboyant but not unmanageable." This was not true, but Wehrmann wanted to cover himself.

"Thank you for your help, my good friend. Consider the matter closed," the Russian said.

When he hung up, Ezdovo asked, "Who is Mock?"

"An Austrian bitch who asks difficult questions, has an excellent network of contacts and is openly anti-Soviet—a vestige of our glorious occupation, no doubt."

"She's already been approved?"

"Absolutely," Rakimov said. "Not that I wanted to, but if we denied her credentials she would raise the roof. We don't worry about the enemies we know."

"Really? You approved the Italian without knowing a thing about him."

"There are no absolutes in these matters. Do you have an alternative?"

Ezdovo started to say yes, then stopped himself. If the Italian was not what he was supposed to be, it would be better to leave everybody thinking that everything was all right. "*Nyet.* That's your responsibility. I'm simply trying to understand."

Rakimov relaxed, smiled weakly, slumped into his chair and put his head down on the desk. "There will be another list tomorrow, comrade."

Ezdovo tucked Sirini's card in his pocket and left.

175 | **THURSDAY, MAY 18, 1961, 10:25 A.M.**
Vienna

Kasi was certain that he dreamed because sometimes he awakened with strange thoughts and atypical emotional surges. The frustrating part was that he could never remember what stimulated such feelings. Today, however, he knew; it was the girl and the temptation, and he cautioned himself to guard against his lust. As a precaution he stopped talking to her except to give instructions, which she obeyed and did not question. It was not clear if she felt any of the urges that had seized him. He hoped for some encouragement, but none came and finally he put her out of his mind. All that mattered was that she do what she was told when the moment arrived.

While Lejla was in the bathroom Kasi laid the garment on the bed. The dress was made of dark material, similar to what Albanian women wore year round in the mountains. When she emerged from her bath, he told her to try it on.

"Again?"

"It has to look right." The Austrians were taking great pains to make sure that their role in the summit was played flawlessly; the essence of his plan resided in their ability to be invisible, to be there but unseen.

The girl pivoted once to show him. "It's hot," she said.

She wondered if there had actually been a time in her life when she actually cared how her clothes fit. She had rebelled over her parents' recall to Albania; she couldn't understand how they would willingly return to such an awful place. New York City was filthy and dangerous, but at least there was freedom. She had begged her father to defect, but he had said it was impossible, and now he was in a Sigurimi jail cell.

Kasi pinched the fabric at her waist. "Too loose. It needs to be taken in some more."

"I don't sew," Lejla said, slipping the dress over her head.

"I do."

She remained silent, trying to banish the anger that threatened to erupt. How could she chastise her father now when his life depended on her? Feel nothing. Kasi's trousers bulged. How long would it be before she had to endure that too? Do as you are told, she reminded herself.

176   THURSDAY, MAY 18, 1961, 11:00 A.M.
Vienna

They had gotten nothing at their first four stops. The fifth postmaster was a tall man with an aristocratic bearing and a gray pallor, his skin so thin that it was transparent and showed crisscrossing matrices of small blue veins.

Sylvia had convinced the others that the approach to the postmasters would be best handled by her and with each stop she had grown more confident in her routine. She smeared on lipstick, doused herself with perfume, smiled at Valentine, marched into the man's office, held out her hand and started talking before he could react.

"We've just now arrived from America," she announced. "We intended to surprise our friends, but when we got here we discovered that they were gone. We're on holiday, an entire month in Austria. Most Americans rave about London, Paris or Rome, but we love Vienna."

"We welcome tourists in our country," the postmaster said hesitantly. "Do you have an appointment?" He glanced at his calendar.

Sylvia ignored the question. "It's a silly problem, you see, entirely our fault to think that our friends would be here to show us around, but they're not here, so we're at a loss." She gave him a long face to underscore her disappointment.

"Perhaps you should have informed your friends before you came," he said cautiously.

She had guessed there would be a little I-told-you-so and countered with a smile. "You're quite right, but that would have ruined the surprise, which was the whole point of not calling."

"Some people do not relish surprises," the postmaster said. Which was undoubtedly his view on the subject, since she was clearly an unwelcome surprise as well, exactly what she intended to be.

"No, no, you don't understand. Our friends *love* surprises," she said, trying to reassure him. "Last year they came to Chicago," she said. "Did I tell you we're from Chicago?" She didn't give him time to answer. "Filthy place, too many people, foul air, noisy factories everywhere, no history, totally unlike Vienna. Anyway, they surprised us last year and we're here to return the favor, so you've just *got* to help us."

The postmaster nervously checked his watch. If he didn't do something, she would talk the morning away. "How may I assist you?" He even managed a smile.

"You're so kind," Sylvia said. "I don't know how to thank you."

"It's not necessary," he assured her and checked his watch again, hoping she would get the hint, though in his experience Americans were not good at social conventions, even obvious ones.

"I don't even know if it will help."

"*What?*" Anything to get rid of her.

"It's really a wild idea, more hope than anything else, but we Americans are known for playing hunches, aren't we?" She saw by his face that she had stretched him to the edge of his patience.

"I really don't know about such things," he said. "I've had very little interaction with Americans."

"You *should*," she bubbled. "Really, we're not the bores some make us out to be. Chicago is a dreadful city but if you were to visit you'd find the people quite friendly. We *love* to have foreigners visit. Our friends couldn't get over how open Americans were."

"You were saying your friends were gone," he said, trying to steer the conversation back.

"Yes," she said disconsolately. "So disappointing. You look forward to something and poof! then it goes wrong. Not fair, but then my husband always says we should expect it. Do you agree?"

"I'm not sure that I understand," the postmaster said. It was time to get rid of her. "I'm sorry," he added, "but I have another appointment." He tapped his watch to confirm it.

Sylvia clasped her hand over her mouth, then reached suddenly to touch his hand, which he pulled away as if she were a poisonous snake. "Oh, I'm *terribly* sorry! You must forgive me. My husband says I ramble on, and I suppose he's right, though I don't think I ramble on that much, do you?"

"Not at all," he said. What sort of man was the husband who would put up with this ridiculous female?

"Do you think you could help?"

"*How?*" Finally she was going to get to the point.

"We had an idea—" she said, then stopped and began again. "My husband had the idea that perhaps our friends went on a trip. When we do that we always ask our post office to hold our mail until we get back. We used to ask a neighbor's son to collect the mail, but he was a teenager and unreliable, and we found out that he was bringing his girlfriends into the house—fornicating in our bed, drinking our beer if you can imagine it—so now we do what we should have done in the first place and let the post office handle it."

Now he understood; what she wanted was against the rules, but this was an instance where an exception could be made for his own peace of mind. "You want to know when your friends will return, is that it?"

"Yes," Sylvia said, clapping her hands to show him how pleased she was. "If we know when they'll be back then we can go ahead with other plans and return to Vienna when they do." Suddenly she changed expressions and leaned forward. "You don't think they'll be gone the whole month, do you?"

"I don't know."

She giggled and fluttered her eyes. "How stupid of me! Of course you don't know. I don't understand where my mind goes sometimes."

"The names of your friends?" He gave her a pencil and paper.

She printed the names and the address.

The postmaster took the slip of paper, left the office and returned five minutes later. "Your friends left on May 8 and asked that their mail be held until we receive further instructions from them."

"How odd," Sylvia said.

"Not at all. It is perfectly normal for people who are in the process of changing residences." He held up the card for her to see.

"This may be the one," Sylvia told Valentine and Bailov. "They cleared out the day before the Albanians arrived and left no forwarding address. They'll send it after they get settled." She was proud of herself.

"They stopped the mail but not the phone," Bailov said. "That makes no sense."

"It does if they knew the phone was going to be used," Valentine said. "By somebody else."

177   FRIDAY, MAY 19, 1961, 9:30 A.M.
Vienna

The hotel was small, the front walk lined with beds of geraniums planted in black soil. The woman behind the reception desk was middle-aged, with smooth white skin, frizzled brown hair and eyes that assessed him as he looked around the tiny lobby. "I'm looking for Sirini," Ezdovo said.

"Are you a relative?"

"A friend."

"He checked out."

"When?"

"Yesterday."

"Alone?"

"I'm not his keeper."

Ezdovo showed her the photograph that the Americans had provided. "This him?"

She looked at the photograph, then at Ezdovo. "You're Russian," she said. "Your people took everything when they were here before."

He placed a roll of schillings on the desk. "The photo."

She counted the money, folded it, slipped it into her dress, opened the guest book and turned it so Ezdovo could see. "There," she said, pointing to Sirini's name. "He's the one—same as the photograph, though his hair is shorter and darker now."

178   FRIDAY, MAY 19, 1961, 9:45 A.M.
Vienna

The streets were jammed with slow-walking people, some of whom congregated in groups around several flower stalls and a bakery, examining and admiring more than buying. On the corner a dark-haired young girl with ringlets snapped a tattered red parasol open and closed like a three-dimensional klieg light, oblivious to passersby who flowed by her like water around a boulder in a stream.

The two men in the truck dropped Sylvia just beyond an intersection where a narrow cobblestone street met a boulevard several lanes wide. They had not discussed the next step in detail, but both of them had warned her to take care. There was no time for discussion, and it was obvious what needed doing: somebody had to house-watch. Sylvia thought she would be the least obtrusive and had volunteered, certain that her surveillance skills were superior to Valentine's. She kept this opinion to herself, however, and the Russians didn't object.

When she got out of the truck, she melted into the midday crowd without looking back. People were dressed in clean but drab work clothes, not the splashy styles of the Kohlmarkt and wealthier districts. Most of the women wore sleeveless blouses, but had substantial sweaters draped over their shoulders. When the Viennese sun went down it got cold quickly even if the day had been sunny. Today the sun was in and out of moving banks of clouds and the air had a bite to it.

The address led her to a narrow, multistory building with a shiny stone façade. There were steps up to the first floor and black iron bars covering the ground-floor windows, evidence that the neighborhood had its share of crime. There would be no unlocked doors here. Several apartments had flower boxes filled with yellow and white flowers. The buildings on either side of the address were shabbier, their fronts blackened, the stone sills chipped. The target building was better cared for than those around it, but it was difficult to believe that property anywhere in this area would sell at the prices listed at the city hall.

Sylvia walked up the steps into the entryway and checked the mailboxes, four rows of two, eight in all, stacked like tiny file drawers. Only one was labeled; it said ROMONA, written with a thick crayon. She peeked into the letter slots and saw envelopes in two of them. Incoming or outgoing? There was no way to tell. The numbering on the doors showed odd-numbered apartments to the left, even numbers to the right.

The flat in question was on the second floor. There were only two flats to a floor, each taking one side of the building, each facing both front and back, meaning that there were at least three ways out. There was an exit at the back of the entry hall on the first floor; she walked to it and looked out into a courtyard of fine gravel interrupted by a single mottled linden tree with stunted white blossoms. The building at the far side of the courtyard had brick walls with mud stains.

Without more people to cover all the possible exits, the building might as well be a fortress. Moving back to the street, Sylvia went into an adjacent building and climbed to the roof, which had a low wall around the perimeter; the center was filled with sagging clotheslines. The roofs of the buildings abutted each other, with no space between. She estimated there were ten to twelve buildings on each side of the street, and that there would be no difficulty going from roof to roof, which meant they would need somebody up here as well. She unpinned some clothes, taking a tan long-sleeved blouse, an indigo skirt and a threadbare gabardine coat, peeled off her own clothes, including her stockings, put on the new ones, and looked for somewhere to stash her things, but found nothing suitable. In the end she stole a towel and wrapped her clothes in it. The Albanians, she told herself, might be alert, but so far there was no reason for them to suspect that anyone was watching them. Because there was no way to cover all the exits, she decided to sit on the front steps of the building next door. If they came in or out she hoped they would use the front entrance. By sitting on the same side of the street she could not be seen from the flat above, and with her borrowed clothing she would blend in except for her shoes, which she kicked off and tucked under the fold of her skirt. She hoped the owner of the clothes wouldn't discover her loss for a while.

Thirty minutes after she took up her post, an old woman with a shopping bag lurched to a halt in front of her, stared at her bare feet and flashed a disapproving look. "A proper lady wears shoes when she is in public," she croaked. "This is Vienna, not the farm." Sylvia slid on her shoes until the woman disappeared down the street, then removed them again.

179   FRIDAY, MAY 19, 1961, NOON
Vienna

It was no surprise that Mignonne Mock liked having her orders followed without question; this had been his mother's way as well. The more you got to know a woman, the more their physical attributes seemed to fade. The more beautiful the woman, the greater the ugliness inside. They were all demons at heart, and whores eager for men with big money. Mock wanted him to go to the railroad station and look it over in anticipation of Khrushchev's arrival.

"Talk to people," she said. "Learn which track he'll arrive on and find a place where you'll be able to get some clear pictures of Zakharov." Whatever was brewing in Berlin, the mysterious Zakharov would be at the center of it, and while the summit was today's story her intuition told her that Berlin was the future news.

"You don't even know whether I can take a picture."

"I have faith," she said, which was not exactly true.

"What if my credentials are challenged?"

"They won't be. I've taken care of everything," Mock said, and gave him an irritated look. "The help should be careful about questioning their superiors."

"I'm not accustomed to being categorized as mere help."

"Just get the station scouted. If there are guards, shoot a roll of them. The public needs to see how much it costs for Khrushchev to be guarded when he leaves his own country."

"The Austrian guards also protect the American president."

"That's not my story."

"I thought journalists were supposed to be objective."

She laughed. "There's no objectivity in a war."

"War?"

"The ideological shadow boxing that invariably precedes the real fight. Ideas lead to words, and words lead to acts. It's an old formula."

"You think the Americans and Soviets will fight each other?"

"Their histories prove that both are inherently violent. To tell a story, you have to pick a slant, which means that you've already made a judgment."

"Your slant being that the Soviets are inherently evil?"

"They *are* evil. The so-called Soviets are Russian slaves, just as some Austrians were Soviet slaves after the war."

"So it's personal, is that it? A vendetta?"

"I grew up with them," Mock snapped. "What does an Italian know about such things?"

"I know that it's not a good idea to have you for an enemy," Albert said, trying to ease the tension. This sort of talk was a waste of time.

"The worst."

"I'll try to remember that."

"Good. Remember it while you scout the station."

"Photos of armed guards."

"Pick those that look the most menacing. Like you."

Frash left ten minutes later, taking Sirini's cameras with him. He would do what she wanted, then tend to some of his own business. Let *her* worry about Khrushchev.

FRIDAY, MAY 19, 1961, 9:00 P.M.
Vienna

Mignonne Mock's address led Ezdovo to a flat over one of the city's most popular coffee houses. Even to his eyes the area looked worn and not the sort of place to attract a woman who reputedly considered herself one of the city's most important people. A few subtle questions in the coffee house brought blank stares and an unspoken message that people here minded their own business. Circling the block, he found that all the buildings were connected and that all the entrances were public and right on the street, which left no choice but to wait until dark.

There was a shed built off the back of the coffee house, and above it hung a rusty fire escape. When he was sure he was alone Ezdovo used a parked truck to reach the shed roof, from there grasped the metal ladder and climbed as quickly and quietly as he could. Mock's window was locked, which came as no surprise. Those who tried to unlock others' secrets were generally fanatical about safeguarding their own. A careful look told him there was no alarm, and in less than a minute he had jimmied the lock and was inside, careful to shut the window behind him. It was dark, but after a few minutes his eyes adjusted.

It was a large flat, as big as their stable in the Yablonovy mountains, the air thick with scents of perfume and soap. The kitchen was clean, with no dirty dishes and a scoured coffeepot left upside down to drain. There was a small refrigerator with some food, all of it carefully aligned. In Tanga they still depended on blocks of ice cut from the frozen river in winter and stored underground in straw. The dishes in the cabinets and the flatware in the drawers were lined up as neatly as a surgeon's tools, and in the bedroom Mock's dresses were evenly spaced on hangers in a cedar armoire. Here was a woman who liked order and was attentive to detail. It meant she was a slave to her habits.

Ezdovo used a small flashlight to search the place. There was a huge color photograph of a redhead stretched out on the same sofa over which it hung. Too thin for his taste, he thought. Talia was muscular and curved. The redhead was covered with freckles. The photo was an odd decoration for a woman's flat. There was no sign of a man anywhere, now or in the past, and nothing in the bathroom but a woman's things.

There was a locked desk in what appeared to be a study. He picked it easily, but examined it cautiously and was glad he had when he found two slivers of mica on either end of the edge of the drawer; she was as suspicious as she was organized. There were no notes in the desk, no records, no addresses—nothing. Paper clips were sorted by size and in separate containers. Was she as compulsive in her work as she was in her tidiness?

Where was her private cubbyhole? He went through the flat again, this time concentrating on those places that were not meant to be found, coming finally to the bathroom, which had a toilet, bidet and a tub on claw feet, all of them surrounded by red-and-white tile and terrazo, installed by somebody who knew his craft. Talia said that a woman felt most like a woman in the refuge of her own bath. There was a new diaphragm in the medicine cabinet, its box still sealed. If a new one was here, there must be a used one elsewhere—with her, he guessed. But there was no hiding place. A woman who took no chances. She had another place, he decided, but not her own; she would be too careful for that. It would be borrowed, transient, a moving target, and the American was with her, posing as a photographer. The woman at the hotel had identified Frash as Sirini. Why? Credentials would get them close to the main players, but just how close would be determined by security. Surveillance here would be a waste of time; she would not return here until her work was complete.

181 FRIDAY, MAY 19, 1961, 11:35 P.M.
Vienna

Richard Wehrmann lived in an impressive neighborhood in the hills above the city. Ezdovo guessed that the mousy woman who came to the door was his wife. She seemed confused by his presence, but when he told her he was from Soviet security she led him into a study where he found a coatless Wehrmann bent over a pile of paper, writing with a silver fountain pen.

"Comrade Rakimov sends his regards," Ezdovo said in Russian from the doorway.

"Have we met?" Wehrmann replied in perfect Russian.

"I've come about the Italian,' Ezdovo said. "Sirini."

"It's after hours," Wehrmann said, setting his pen aside. "Is there a problem?"

Ezdovo saw beads of sweat on the man's forehead. "Comrade Rakimov said he explained it to you. It's a question of procedure."

"Serious enough to bring you to my home."

"Please," the Siberian said. "I must apologize, but I only follow orders. We would like very much to talk to Miss Mock. It's important that we talk to her now; otherwise this could get blown out of proportion. I'm sure you understand."

"I see," the Austrian said. "But you already have her address."

"She wasn't there."

So that was it. They had lost her, which was not really a surprise. Mignonne tended to flit from one friend to another, gathering gossip and information under the guise of fellowship. "I have only the one address," Wehrmann said apologetically. "In any event, she was properly vetted through the agreed-upon system. Rakimov himself cleared her for your side."

"Actually it's the Italian who interests us," Ezdovo admitted. "We need her in order to reach him."

"He was also vetted. I spoke personally to Rakimov about this."

"Comrade Rakimov was not thinking clearly." Like twenty million of their countrymen at any given moment, he had been blind drunk. The Austrian was off balance now; it was time to shift gears. "Please," Ezdovo said. "Don't take offense. I don't mean to be argumentative; we both want the same thing. We all have an interest in seeing that the summit goes smoothly."

Wehrmann exhaled and said quickly, "I'm happy to cooperate with my Soviet colleagues."

"The Italian is not at the hotel listed on his application. It's some distance from the city, so perhaps he's moved to the center for convenience. We simply want to talk to him."

Were the Russians checking the addresses of all reporters? Damned odd. "I don't see how I can help you."

"You've met Sirini?"

Wehrmann eyed the Russian. "Actually, I haven't."

"If Miss Mock calls, could you ask her to get in touch with us?"

"I doubt she will, but I will of course ask her."

"How well do you know the woman?"

"Superficially."

Ezdovo studied the small room; two sides were filled with bookshelves and there were three framed photographs on the paneled wall. One of the photographs was of Wehrmann holding a huge, gleaming trophy. A redhead with a microphone stood beside him, the same woman as in the photo at Mock's flat. "You were a skier," Ezdovo said.

"A long time ago." The Russian was staring at the photograph. Did he know it was Mignonne holding the microphone? If so and I don't say something he'll think I'm covering up. If I confirm it's her and he doesn't know, will it hurt her? God, what a pain in the ass. What did the Russians want? The bastards never told the truth. She's anti-Communist, but they already know that. It's the Italian, then, which figures. She's gotten herself mixed up with an unsavory character. Probably she's sleeping with him. It was her pattern; colleagues became lovers, and she dominated them until they were smothered. How many men had she enticed away from their wives, then cut loose because the challenge was ended? She really was a barbarian. Combativeness was the essence of her nature, and she vented it in every way possible, one of those people hated in life who would be mourned heavily in death as an original free spirit. "That's Mignonne in the photograph," Wehrmann said after considerable deliberation. "She was interviewing me after a downhill in Switzerland."

"She's quite stunning," Ezdovo said. It had taken the man a long time to identify her but he was smooth.

"I suppose," the Austrian said. The other photographs were of gondoliers in Venice. "She shot the other pictures herself."

The photos looked as if they had been shot through gauze. In one of them a woman with a scarf sat with a gondolier. Her blouse had been pulled back to reveal a perfect breast. Ezdovo stepped closer. "That's her as well, isn't it?"

Wehrmann laughed nervously. Even those who knew her rarely could identify her in that shot, which was the whole point, she had told him. People see the breast and the gondola and not much more, and she

474

had been right. The Russian, however, had zeroed directly on her. "Yes. She's an accomplished photographer, but a bit narcissistic."

"Taken with a timer?"

"I have no idea. She processes her work as well, but all that business is too technical for me."

A very self-centered woman, and technically adept, so why does she use another photographer when she could do it herself? "Why does she work with Sirini?"

Wehrmann had anticipated this question. "Photography is her hobby and journalism her profession. It's an important distinction. When she works, she insists on having an equally professional photographer along. To do her own photography, she says, would be as stupid as a doctor diagnosing his own medical problems. At least that's what she says." Wehrmann didn't tell the Russian that Mignonne had said that the Italian had no journalistic experience; it would simply raise more suspicions. When he talked to Mignonne again they would get it all sorted out and that would be the end of it. He chastised himself for letting her use him, then reminded himself that it was not the first time, and not likely to be the last either.

"It's necessary for us to talk to both of them," Ezdovo said as he made his way toward the door.

"Of course I'll do what I can, but as I've explained I have only the one number. She uses her flat for an office."

"Where's her laboratory?"

"Somewhere in the cellar, I think. Below the coffee house. She used to have it in the flat, but she said the chemical fumes ruined her clothes."

"Call Rakimov if you hear from her or Sirini."

"You may count on Austria's full cooperation."

"We are," Ezdovo said as he backed out, nodded politely to the woman who had let him in and slipped back into the night.

182 SATURDAY, MAY 20, 1961, 3:20 A.M.
Vienna

Melko cursed the drizzle as he made one sweep down the short street to look for the American woman and saw her huddled in the entrance of a soot-blackened building adjacent to the target address. She motioned for him to cross at the end of the block, then double back. He didn't hurry.

"Anyone in there?" he asked, bounding up the steps in two leaps.

"I haven't seen anybody, and there are too many ways out to cover them all," she told him. "Street, courtyard, roof. It's a maze."

"Go stand in their doorway," Melko said. "You look like you belong; even if you don't, nobody will question your wanting to escape the rain. People aren't suspicious of the obvious. I'll be on the roof." He handed her a thermos. "Tea. You look like you can use it."

183 SATURDAY, MAY 20, 1961, 6:45 A.M.
Vienna

Just before first light Ezdovo made his way back to the storage shed behind the coffee shop under Mock's flat, picked the lock quickly, then closed the door behind him and relocked it. The shed was filled with crates and boxes of supplies, and blue smocks hung on a row of hooks along one wall. He took a smock, put it on and set to work springing the next lock.

The coffee-house kitchen was dark and sterile. There were stairs to the cellar next to a huge refrigeration unit. The cellar had two levels, the first one consisting of an office and several supply rooms, the second considerably deeper, with old brick and mortar walls, including a bricked-over arch at the end of the corridor. At the end of the second level he found the darkroom, which was small and well equipped, with stainless steel basins, an enlarger and a clothesline to hang freshly processed film and prints to dry. A huge metal wastebasket was empty.

A small refrigerator was in one corner. Inside he found twenty rolls of 35 mm film, but there was no indication of where it came from. If she bought so much, she probably used a single supplier. In the Soviet Union there was no such thing as a discount, but here every shop seemed to advertise a reduced price for quantity purchases. If her flat served as her office and the darkroom was here, wouldn't it make sense that she made purchases nearby? There was not a lot of hope in this, but it gave him an angle to work on. Petrov had always taught them to follow every possibility, no matter how insignificant it seemed.

When he got back to the storage room the back door was open and a truck was backed up to it. Two men stared down at him from the tailgate as he hung his smock on a hook. "Who are you?" one of them asked. He was bald, with salt-and-pepper mutton chops.

"Electrical inspector. Had a power failure last night."

"Shit," the man said. "We'd better check the cooler before we unload this stuff."

184 SATURDAY, MAY 20, 1961, 9:50 A.M.
Vienna

Kasi sat at the front window, watching sheets of drizzle undulate along the street in graceful waves. The rain had continued unabated since yesterday and he had a stiff neck from sitting at the window—a sign of age, he reminded himself. In his youth there were no sore muscles, no strains, no lingering aches, but now his body seemed to resist him at every turn; he accepted this as inevitable and tried to compensate by working harder to maintain fitness, but it seemed more difficult every day. Despite the soreness in his neck, he liked watching the rain; it made the dust disappear and washed the streets. And if the stiffness in his neck was a sign of aging, the stiffness in another part reaffirmed that at least one essential fire still burned hot. Lejla's sinewy body had been on his mind all night. Now she was nearby and he wanted her. He stood. "Come over here." When she got to him he began to undress her; there was no resistance. When she was undressed he pushed her to the wall beside the window and pulled her hips back. Instinct made him look out the window. As soon as he saw the man on the far side of the street he knew that he was a Russian and that they had been discovered. He was tall and strong, with curly brown hair and dark, sinister eyes, reflecting the darkness all Russians carried in their souls. Kasi had worked with all sorts of Russians in his life, from White émigrés in Paris to military advisers in his own country, all of them swaggering like conquerors. They were competent soldiers but unimaginative, like musk oxen plodding forward, single-minded creatures, thinking alike and feeling little. They even seemed to walk identically, and it was precisely this peculiar gait that gave the man away. Kasi quickly guessed that this was a surveillance, not an assault. How had they found them? This place was supposed to be untraceable. He regretted now that they had traveled light, with no weapons, but he realized quickly that this was also an advantage; without weapons there could be no temptation to stand and fight. He pushed the girl away. "Get dressed," he said.

"What is it?" Lejla Llarja asked; what had he seen?

"Dress," he snapped. "We're leaving."

She did as she was told.

On the first floor they had a glimpse of a woman leaning against a wall by the front steps. She looked vaguely Asian, Kasi thought; it was possible that she was with the Russian, who was still on the far side of the street. How many others were there? He nudged the girl down the steps to the interior courtyard; they walked to the far side and into the facing building, raced up several flights of stairs to the rooftop, crossed several roofs until they were near a corner, then went down into the street, catercorner into another building, up to a roof again, and used streets and roofs in this way until they were four blocks away. Along the way he snatched an umbrella from an elephant-foot holder in a hallway and held it over her, not out of sympathy but because appearances were important.

As they crossed the street he was tingling with the adrenaline surge that came with action and the fresh memory of what had almost been. Suddenly the wind whipped up, causing the girl's skirt to flutter, and he saw the firm white flesh underneath. When they reached the far side of the street he pulled her into an alley and pushed her down a series of steps into a recessed entry. From here they could monitor passersby and not be seen.

Later he hailed a cab at a stand. The Russians only complicated matters; they made it a contest, after all. The cabdriver wore a stained red fez. "Allah be praised for the rain," he said as the American-made Checker pulled away from the curb. "Where to?"

"Just drive," Kasi said. He needed time to think. Get your mind off the girl, he chastised himself.

---

185 SATURDAY, MAY 20, 1961, 1:00 P.M.
Vienna

There were a dozen places near Mock's flat that sold film, and Ezdovo visited them all. "I met a woman last night," he told the clerks. "Red hair, beautiful. She lives nearby and asked me to pick up some film for her from the usual place, only she forgot to tell me the address. Do you know her?" There had been negative replies or blank stares at every shop, and now only one remained, on the corner of a square opposite a huge church. A sign in the window read PROFESSIONAL DISCOUNTS. The door tripped a bell when he entered.

A man with crooked yellow teeth emerged through a set of black curtains and bowed. "Terrible weather," he said, "but good for the flowers."

Ezdovo was barely into his story before the man nodded and said, "Mignonne."

"Yes, Mignonne Mock."

"You're a lucky fellow. Do you work with her?"

"No, it's a personal favor."

The man grinned and raised his eyebrows. "Lucky dog."

"She said I should pick up the film and handle it the usual way, but she didn't say what that meant."

"It's not like her to be so imprecise."

Defuse his suspicions. "It was actually a request made in passing. We were engaged in other activities at the time. I thought it would be nice to surprise her."

"Other activities. Lucky dog," the man said again.

"You know how it is when there's good chemistry."

"I can imagine." He leered. "You want the customary order?"

"Yes."

"Do you want to pay, or shall I handle it the normal way?"

"What's that?"

"I bill her."

Ezdovo opened his wallet. "How much?" The clerk named a figure. "I don't have that much," he said apologetically.

"Not a problem," the clerk said. "I always bill her. Which address this time?"

This was what he had hoped for. "Where do you usually send it?"

The clerk leafed through a box of invoices and read off one of the addresses.

"Send it there."

"The film's out back," the man said as he slid through the curtain. When he returned several minutes later, he saw that the shop was empty and laughed. "I'd run to that, too, if she were mine." He didn't notice that the box of invoices was not where he had left it.

186   SATURDAY, MAY 20, 1961, 3:45 P.M. *Vienna*

Bailov found Melko on the edge of the roof between puddles of standing water. "We're going in," he said.

"Seen anyone?"

"No."

"Better to wait."

"It's too quiet. We need to know for certain. This could be a waste of time."

Melko shrugged and followed Bailov downstairs, thinking how easy it might be to die in this crazy game. Petrov had saved him from Camp Nine, but he had not asked for help, which meant there was no obligation. Or was there? Petrov was in Moscow; the others were strangers. He liked them well enough, but he was the outsider; what would happen to him when Petrov died? Look out for yourself. He had given considerable thought to his options. It would be easiest to slip away after the General Secretary arrived and while they had more important things to worry about. Khrushchev was not scheduled to leave Vienna until Monday after the summit, which Melko guessed would give him the two full days during the meetings to disappear. A destination was no problem. In the old days he had traded with the Turks. He was certain there would still be an organization in Istanbul, and it would be easy enough to find. They would help him make contact with the Armenian Brotherhood; with them as partners he could work a black-market operation from outside Russia that would be far more lucrative than safecracking.

A touch on the shoulder brought him back to the present. "You take the door," Bailov said.

"And you?"

"In the street with the Americans. Give me ten minutes to get down there. I'll cover the front."

Melko waited a few steps above the landing wanting a cigarette, but he knew from experience that it was better to keep both hands free. Earlier he had checked several locks on his way up to the roof; they were all the same. He estimated ten seconds to get one of them open, maybe less. He gave Bailov twelve minutes to get into position, approached the door, listened for a while, heard nothing and turned his attention to the lock, sensing that the place was empty.

When the lock clicked open, he inhaled, rotated the knob slowly, pushed gently on the bottom of the door, let it swing open and ducked back. If the Albanians were inside, the hall light would make him an easy target. Had the others picked him for this task because he was expendable? Another good reason to think about a future apart from the group.

The flat was empty. Going to the window, he called down, "Get the others."

Damp towels in the bathroom, unmade beds and a half-eaten loaf of bread in a paper bag on a kitchen counter told them the place had been occupied.

"Did we spook them?" Valentine asked.

"It would have been easy enough for them to get out when I was here alone," Sylvia said. "I couldn't watch everything."

Valentine wondered if she had fallen asleep, but kept this to himself. They went over the place methodically. Melko saw thread and two small strips of black fabric next to a table leg. He had looked at the spot several times but had not seen it until he was in the right position for the light to reveal it.

"Could be off something the owners took with them," Valentine suggested.

"Or not," Sylvia said, examining the cloth. "Odd texture."

It appeared that whoever had been there had departed in a hurry. "It's like looking for air," Melko said.

"We were close," Valentine said.

"Close isn't good enough," Bailov said curtly.

 ## SUNDAY, MAY 21, 1961, 1:10 A.M.
Klosterneuburg, Austria

Valentine snored evenly, his mouth open, arms at his sides. The Russians had given them space in the winery that served as their headquarters north of the city; the small, unpainted room had two cots and smelled of fermented fruit. Sylvia saw that he slept diagonally to minimize the amount his legs hung over the end; he looked uncomfortable. The world wasn't made for him, or perhaps it was the other way around.

There had been no conference when they got back to the winery and no interest in eating; they each had gone their own way, but tired as she was, Sylvia couldn't sleep. She *had* fallen asleep outside the Albanians' flat—not for long, but perhaps long enough—and she was still sore and cold from more than twenty-four hours outside. The issue was not self-pity but trust, and she was ashamed. Beau's life—indeed all their lives—depended on each of them doing their jobs, and she had failed them.

"You think too damned much," Valentine growled softly from the other bed.

His voice startled her. "I fell asleep," she said.

"That's usually why people go to bed."

"Last night on the steps."

"We all did," he said. When he rolled onto his side the cot squeaked.

"You're just saying that. In any event, if it's true, then we're all too dangerous to be worth a damn to each other."

"You're right," he said. "I made it up."

"Don't patronize me," she snapped. "It's unprofessional."

"Downstairs," Valentine said as he shifted his weight again.

"What?"

"Lumber, hammers, nails, a do-it-yourself crucifixion kit. Every-thing you need."

"Don't make jokes."

"You want to wallow in the Boo Hoo Sea, go ahead; just don't keep me awake. If you stretch your endurance, sooner or later your body takes a hike. It's happened to me plenty of times. What you did is normal, so get it out of your head that you're special."

The way he said it made her believe him. "It's never happened to me before."

"And you probably got all A's on your report cards too. Some people can go longer than others, but nobody can go indefinitely without sleep. Welcome to the human race. You just hope that these little lapses don't happen at the wrong time."

"They could have slipped away while I was asleep."

"They also could have cut your throat, but they didn't. What's done is over. Concentrate on the future."

"I can't get it out of my mind."

"You will after it happens enough times."

"I want to sleep," she said, "but my mind won't shut off."

"There's ways to handle that," he said, his voice low and tantalizing.

"Guaranteed?"

"Money back, but you'll have to come over to my place. I don't make house calls for common insomniacs."

"There's nothing common about me," she whispered as she crossed to his bed. "You're awfully noisy," she added as he shifted to make room for her.

"Let those Russians bastards eat their hearts out."

"How do I know you're not just making this up?" She put her hand on his bare chest and held him back.

"You don't."

"And if it doesn't work?"

"I'll administer the second treatment free of charge."

She slid her arms around his neck. "Can we start with a hug?"

"That just happens to be the first step in the cure."

188   SUNDAY, MAY 21, 1961, 4:00 A.M. *Vienna*

Ezdovo had watched people move in and out of the building earlier in the evening, but now it was quiet and there was no more traffic. He had recognized Mignonne Mock right away from her photograph. More attractive than he had expected, but she moved with confidence and an air of being in control. He had seen her twice, the first time at 3:30 P.M., then an hour later, both times alone. There had been no sign of the American masquerading as the Italian. The flat was on the fifth floor and a light was on, but she had the shades pulled and was staying away from the windows. The nameplate in the lobby said RAGOTZY, A.

At least the rain had stopped. He sat cross-legged on the wet ground in heavy rhododendron cover in the park across the street from her building. The night reminded him of fall hunts, when the leaves were down and before the tracking snow fell. What were his boys doing? In the morning he would call the others, but for now it was enough to be patient, to watch, and to remember a simpler life.

189   SUNDAY, MAY 21, 1961, 4:30 A.M. *Vienna*

Frash was stretched out on the sofa, neither awake nor asleep, but somewhere on the fringe of consciousness, trying to see through the walls with his ears. A train's whistle moaned in the distance and he sensed the movement of air pushed by the occasional vehicle in the street. It occurred to him that these were imaginings rather than reality, but how could one be sure? The woman was in the bedroom; she was real. There had been a single muted telephone ring snatched up immediately, and then her whisperings. He went to investigate.

She wore a robe and was curled up on the bed, protecting the telephone as if it were a suckling infant. There was no direct light, only reflections from outside the building, barely enough to illuminate her freckles. He watched her ease the phone back onto its cradle and fumble to light a cigarette, cupping the match in her hand to shield the glow.

"Odd hour for a phone call," he said. He saw her jump at the sound of his voice.

"It's nothing," she said. "A wrong number."

"Do you always have such long conversations with wrong numbers?"

She mashed her barely smoked cigarette in a glass ashtray. "It was Dickie."

"He's your lover?" Ali stirred at the thought of her warm flesh.

"Don't let your imagination run wild, Sirini. The Russians have been asking questions about you. Dickie was simply alerting me."

"At this hour?"

"Did you have problems with the Russians in Rome? You told me you were clean. It was part of our deal."

The Russians again. "There must be a simple explanation," he said, but the time of the phone call contradicted this.

"It's about your credentials."

Curious. "They've already been issued."

"They're just being paranoid," Mock said. "It's their nature." She stretched her legs out and let her robe fall open.

"They want to revoke them?"

"No," she said too quickly. "Their security people are nervous. I've seen them in action before. They need somebody to push around in order to justify their overdeveloped sense of self-importance. Dickie thinks that once their main delegation arrives they'll settle down. They've got a case of the jitters, that's all."

Frash saw it differently. "What does your Dickie advise?"

"They want to talk to you. He thinks you should cooperate."

"You think I should do that?" There was no way; she was simply a cover. If the Russians had concerns, it was time to move on.

She chewed on the edge of the sheet. "I didn't say that." Then, "I don't know."

"If I talk to them they might try to make an example of me and revoke my credentials."

"I've already considered that. As long as you stay away from them until Khrushchev gets here, we should be all right. Dickie says they'll settle down, and I think he's right. We simply have to keep out of their way until they have more important things to think about."

It sounded as if she was trying to reassure herself. "Maybe they'll pull your papers as well." It was not like the Russians to let go of anything so easily.

"I'm going to get my story no matter what," she said through clenched teeth. "We're not going to overreact to this."

"This isn't your place," Frash said, changing the subject. The flat was barely furnished and had no feminine touches. This had bothered him since they arrived.

"What's your point?"

"Your friend Dickie knew how to reach you here. If he can find you, perhaps the Russians can too."

"Nonsense," she said. "The number's not written down. A friend of mine owns it, and he only uses it for entertaining."

"Does this friend know we're here?"

"He's in London until next month. I have my own key. I don't have to ask permission."

A deflection. How long had she been on the telephone? Three minutes, five? Perhaps long enough for a trace, and if two people knew about the hideaway, then others might also know. "He shouldn't have called you here."

"Now who's being paranoid? Dickie was simply trying to help us."

More like protecting his own ass.

"What are you doing?" she asked nervously.

When his hand moved up the inside of her leg she smiled and put her head back on the pillow. "You might be getting more than you've bargained for," she said as his fingers plunged into her.

"I was thinking the same thing," he whispered.

190 SUNDAY, MAY 21, 1961, 5:55 A.M.
Vienna

The others arrived thirty minutes after Ezdovo's call, spilling out of two panel trucks onto the street that ran behind the park; they spread out and joined him under the trees.

"You've seen him?" Valentine wanted to know.

Ezdovo stared at the building. "Her. She's in Number Eleven, Apartment 5D."

"What about Frash?"

"I've only seen her."

"Then he may not be there."

"He's there." A hunter knew such things.

"Is there a back way out?"

"A service drive with open land behind it. Both sides are open as well. Unless they can fly we'll catch them."

"It's a big building," Valentine said. He counted seven stories.

"We have enough people," Bailov said.

"We want them alive," Sylvia reminded them.

"We'll have to surprise them," Bailov said.

Valentine doubted that Frash ever dropped his guard. "This might be a bitch," he whispered to Sylvia.

"We need him alive," she repeated loud enough for all of them to hear.

The fifth-floor hall was poorly lit, the walls cracked, and there were thick spiderwebs in the corners. Melko knelt at the door, listened for a while and shook his head. Bailov signaled with a twist of his hand and Melko tried the knob, which turned easily.

"Open," he mouthed without speaking.

Ezdovo and Bailov chambered rounds in their automatics and checked the safeties off. Melko eased the door open and froze when it squeaked, but still there was no sound within.

Bailov squeezed through the opening and disappeared into the dark flat. Three minutes passed; then a light snapped on inside and he came back and waved them in. "Bedroom to the left," he said wearily.

Mignonne Mock was on the bed, which was soaked with her blood. Her left eye was gone, not shot through, but cut out, and she had been severely mutilated in other ways. Her mouth was stuffed with a blouse. One of her hands had been cut off and placed on her chest, all the fingers except the middle one tied down with a bloody scarf, leaving the middle finger fully extended, mocking them.

"What does it mean?" Bailov said.

"It's a lunatic's declaration of war," Valentine said.

486

SUNDAY, MAY 21, 1961, 10:30 A.M.
Nussdorf, Austria

Though Lejla was exhausted, Kasi kept her moving throughout the night.
The Russians had disrupted the plan, and now he needed to make some
adjustments. If they had found the safe house, it meant that the others
were also blown. He wondered how this was possible, but there was no
time to think about it now. Perhaps they had been spotted in Rome, or
else Soviet agents in Tirana had learned of their departure. Assume that
the operation is compromised and revise the plan, he told himself. No
doubt there would be trouble this morning, and he hoped the girl would
be up to it. This option had not been part of the plan.

The small white house had a steeply pitched roof of red and black
ceramic tiles and a lawn that stretched around the house and sloped down
to a whitewashed high wall topped with embedded glass shards. Thick
lilac bushes grew down the sides, and climbing roses on wooden trellises
covered both ends of a small veranda. They were above the city and could
see its landmarks and the Danube, which looked like a ribbon of chocolate.

The man who answered the door was of average height, slope-
shouldered and entirely bald. His goatee was a small gray spot over his
chin, his eyes yellow. He wore leather slippers, wrinkled green trousers,
black suspenders and a red vest over a white silk shirt with the sleeves
rolled above his elbows. He looked calm and unfettered by worries, his
skin unlined and smooth, too youthful for his apparent age.

"Too much rain for the flowers," Kasi said in French.

"The blossoms suffer but the roots grow deeper," the man said after
a pause to look them over. He stepped back to let them in, looked toward
the street, closed the door and locked it. "Why are you here?" he asked
as his eyes locked on Lejla.

"You have a package for me," Kasi said.

The man was nervous as he led them into the parlor, where an
enameled grandfather clock counted cadence in the corner. There were
antimacassars on the furniture. Four shotguns sat in a glass-and-wood
cabinet with a carved stag on top. "This is not what I agreed to," the man
said. "This is my home."

"You are paid to provide," Kasi said, "Details are not your concern."

"This puts me at risk."

"Relax," Kasi said. "We won't be here long. My associate would like a hot bath, and we need something to eat."

"I'll show her the way," the man mumbled. He got up and motioned toward the stairs with his hand.

"Avoid drafts," Kasi called out as Lejla followed the man up the stairs.

Kasi was warning her; she began to regulate her breathing. The bathroom was large and white, the floor tiled in blue-and-white diamonds.

"Let me get you a fresh towel," the man said.

She placed herself between the open door and a mirror and turned her back. Your back is a weapon to buy time, Kasi had repeatedly told her during training. All but a true professional will pause when faced with a back, so use it to your advantage. She took off her blouse and dropped it on the floor.

Kasi stood at the bottom of the stairs. The man peered down, his arm draped with towels. "Have some wine," he called down. "I won't be a moment."

In the mirror Lejla saw that the man had a revolver under the towels; she watched his eyes. When his stare switched from her back to her image in the mirror she straightened up to make her breasts easier to see, paused to let him peek, then bent forward, took a quick step backward, pivoted, drove both her hands into his forearm and knocked him off balance. Despite the suddenness of her attack, he got off two erratic shots as he stumbled. He tried to regain his balance but she bent her knees, drove her fist into his throat, snapped an elbow into his solar plexus, grabbed his shirt collar, pushed her hip out and flipped him onto his side.

As soon as the man entered the bathroom, Kasi had started up the stairs and was halfway when he heard the two muted pops. He found her with a pistol in both hands, crouching over her attacker, who was on the floor clutching his throat, gasping for air. "Not good enough," he said, examining the man on the floor. "The blow should crush the trachea; when it swells, suffocation is quick." He made his fist into a sort of claw, drove the heel of his hand into the man's throat and backed away. The mouth opened wide and there was muted gurgling, followed by convulsions and stillness.

Kasi sat on the edge of the bathtub and turned on the water, which he tested with his hand. "Clean yourself," he told her as he hoisted the body onto his shoulders. It would have been better to show restraint, but this was the sort of behavior to expect when remuneration was the sole motivation. Only honor was incorruptible.

"How did you know what he was going to do?" Lejla asked.

"The same way you did," he said. She sponged a small spot of blood from the floor before stepping into the hot water.

192   SUNDAY, MAY 21, 1961, 3:00 P.M.
Vienna

A nameless tavern around the corner from the stables of the Spanish Riding School. Bailov, Ezdovo, Melko and the two Americans sat at a round table with a leather top covered with dust. The room was hexagonal, with heavy wood paneling and an unusual drop ceiling. A waiter popped in and out of the room with plates of greasy pork and carafes of heuriger, but the collective mood was sullen and little was eaten.

"Bunch of zombies," Valentine grumbled. "We look like somebody barbecued our pet longhorn. These are setbacks, comrades, just setbacks. We found them once and we can do it again."

"Ezdovo found your countryman through Mock, and now she's dead," Bailov said. "The Albanians were not at the safe house, which suggests they knew we were coming. They'll avoid the other safe houses, which means we have nothing."

"Even nothing has structure," Valentine answered. "We can't see molecules, but they still exist." The Russians gave him puzzled looks and Sylvia stared as if he had gone off the deep end. He didn't blame them. Given what Frash had done to the Austrian woman, it was difficult to think of him as capable of even a shred of rational thought, but the gesture with the severed hand was unmistakable; he had issued a challenge. *Catch me if you can.* "We don't know where they are, but we've got a damned good idea where their interest lies and we've spooked them, which can work to our advantage."

"Spook?" Melko asked. "You speak of ghosts?" The other Russians looked equally confused.

"He means that we've frightened them," Sylvia explained. "Frash has press credentials, but I can't believe he thought they would get him through security. He knows that all of Europe has been looking for him."

"Exactly," Valentine said, "but if he never intended to use them, what was his purpose? Does he see a hole in security that we've overlooked?"

"Even if he tried to use the credentials we can make it impossible for reporters to get near our leaders," Bailov said. "We can close the meetings and make information available only at briefings by press secretaries."

"No," Valentine said. "If our leaders shut themselves off, the whole world will get the jitters. Besides, I doubt that either of them would agree. They came here to stand in the spotlight. My point is, we know in detail everything that will go on. If we think like Frash and the Albanians, we may see opportunities. What would we exploit?"

"Or," Bailov said, getting into the spirit, "we alter the itineraries to make them *think* there are opportunities." The American's point was well taken. "We need to examine the itinerary again."

"And have another look at every site they'll use," Valentine added. "We need to think like assassins."

Melko placed a flat strip of black cloth on the table. "This was in the flat."

"This whole goddamned thing has been a roller-coaster ride, but now we can see the end of the run," Valentine said.

193	SATURDAY, MAY 27, 1961, 4:30 A.M.
	Klosterneuburg, Austria

The Americans had worked hand in glove with the Russians for nearly a week, the two parts operating together efficiently as they monitored the list of reporters that grew longer by the day, examined meeting sites, drove routes and timed them, poked into nooks and crannies of the railroad station where Khrushchev would arrive and the airport that would receive Air Force One, analyzed security maneuvers and reviewed the personnel files of hundreds of police, maids, cooks and other support personnel who would provide seamless service to the visiting dignitaries. They also instituted a new sign-in procedure for reporters, and as a precaution asked the Vienna police to stake out the Albanian safe houses.

The team convened each night after Ezdovo's return from Raki-mov's office and went through their information like bookkeepers, one entry at a time. Having covered everything each of them had done during the day, they separated to their respective quarters.

Sometimes Sylvia awoke in the night to find Valentine staring at the strip of cloth from the safe house, his legs crossed Indian style and rocking ever so slightly; at such times she pretended sleep and wondered what was going through his mind. In the last week he had become more withdrawn.

The Americans guessed that their Soviet colleagues called Moscow every night because they seemed unusually knowledgeable about Khrushchev's latest moves. By contrast there were no such calls to Arizona. At this point there seemed to be nothing that he could contribute; they also feared that his involvement might upset the current balance. Besides, both of them remembered that Arizona had sent them out blind, which had cost Harry Gabler his life.

Tonight Beau was at it again, rocking, his arms folded around his legs, staring at the swatch of cloth found in the safe house. "I know you're watching," he said.

"You've got eyes in the back of your head, or is it ESP?"

"You breathe differently when you're asleep."

"Very observant."

They had visited a dozen or more fabric shops, including a mill, but had drawn a blank. "A piece of cloth is not like the alloy off a damned UFO," Valentine said. It occurred to him that the FBI ought to start an evidence collection for investigators—cloth, screws, doorknobs, fibers, paint, metals, every detail of human existence, though it would take a warehouse the size of Oklahoma to house it, a Smithsonian for spies. "The thing is," he said intensely, "I know I've seen this stuff before."

Sylvia pulled his shoulder and he fell back gently. "It will come to you," she said.

194	FRIDAY, JUNE 2, 1961, 5:05 P.M.
	Vienna

As the five-car train moved slowly into the station, Talia scanned the platform for her comrades but couldn't pick them out of the crowd. Austrian soldiers and security men were shoulder to shoulder along both sides of the concrete platforms, their automatic rifles at the ready. Such receptions were normally ceremonial, but this time troops were twitching nervously. More soldiers were on the steep roof over the platform, the glint of their scopes betraying their positions. She was relieved to see that the Austrians were taking their responsibilities seriously.

Khrushchev and his entourage stopped outside Talia's compartment. He wore a dark suit and gray hat but no overcoat. He looked into her compartment but didn't seem to see her; his public smile was strained, his eyes distant.

Zakharov was in front of the General Secretary, wearing a navy blue suit rather than a uniform. He had a small walkie-talkie that squawked now and then, but she heard no voices. Two men came up the aisle and whispered briefly to the general. They were young, also in blue suits and carrying radios. He nodded and dismissed them with a wave of his hand.

After they were gone he approached Khrushchev. "Everything is ready. The Austrian president is waiting."

Talia and Gnedin wedged into the aisle outside the compartment, the doctor moving out first to open a path for her.

"What the hell is Schärf doing here?" Talia heard Khrushchev ask. The presence of the president of Austria seemed to irritate the General Secretary.

"It's a courtesy," Zakharov said softly. "The Austrians want to please you."

"And Kennedy," Khrushchev asked, with an edge in his voice, "will he get the same treatment?"

Zakharov ignored the cynicism. "We're still scheduled to go from the station to his palace for the formal ceremony."

"The Austrian politicians boast of democracy and live in palaces," Khrushchev grumbled. "Eventually their people will see the truth and throw them out."

"He works in the palace," Zakharov answered. "It's not his residence."

Talia was surprised at the general's forthrightness. Few people had the nerve to confront Khrushchev with facts, especially when he was in one of his moods. Was this integrity or contempt on Zakharov's part? During the journey he had kept to himself except when duty required his presence. That Khrushchev was irritated at the Austrian president's unscheduled visit was no surprise to her; he frequently violated itineraries, but raged when others dared to do so.

"We have a schedule to keep," Zakharov politely reminded the General Secretary.

Khrushchev grunted, pushed back a sliding door, went out onto the platform between cars and descended the steep metal steps. A square-jawed Russian security man offered him a hand, but he slapped it away and smiled at the crowd.

The Austrian president was dressed formally, his top hat making him seem twice the General Secretary's height. The two men shook hands, and then Khrushchev moved on to greet several Russians waiting on the platform.

Talia pressed forward to keep up, but Zakharov blocked her with his shoulder. "Remember your place," he said under his breath.

"I know mine," she snapped. "Do you know yours, comrade?" She pushed slightly ahead where she could see the General Secretary and those waiting in line to greet him. She was not worried about threats from afar; she concentrated on the people on the platform. Most assassins liked to get in close.

Everything seemed to proceed normally until Khrushchev got to the end of the line. It took a second for Talia to realize that something was wrong; then she saw that the Soviet leader's face had turned bright red. Whatever he had seen had caused him to stiffen and stop in his tracks. Where was Gnedin?

After a brief pause Khrushchev extended his hand to a taller man with a round face and swept-back black hair. While their hands were joined, the General Secretary leaned forward and said something to the man, then moved on to finish his obligatory greetings, glancing back briefly after he reached the end of the line. Talia caught Gnedin's attention and pointed to the dark-haired man. The doctor acknowledged with a nod and followed.

The crowd inside the station was huge, but people were standing quietly. When the Soviet delegation entered, there was a smattering of polite applause beyond the barricades. A few let loose catcalls but Khrushchev smiled dutifully, ignoring them. In the corridor leading to the vehicles more Austrian soldiers presented arms. The General Secretary suddenly veered left, opened the door to a public rest room and barged inside. Zakharov followed, then returned quickly. "Seal the corridor," he instructed an aide, who relayed the information to an Austrian officer, who barked commands that sent soldiers scurrying to both ends of the hall. "He wants to talk to you," Zakharov said to Talia.

When Gnedin tried to follow her the general stopped him with an arm. "Just the woman," he said, but Talia reached back, caught the doctor's arm and pulled him along with her.

"Where I go, he goes," she told Zakharov.

Khrushchev was standing in the middle of the room with his hat in front of him. Gnedin was amazed at the latrine's cleanliness; Moscow's public facilities were still little more than privies, especially in the hospitals where sepsis was as normal as vermin. Here even the urinals glistened.

Khrushchev gestured to Talia with his hat. "I'm returning full responsibility for security to you," he said.

Zakharov's mouth opened, but he said nothing.

Khrushchev turned to the general. "You'll be the figurehead and act as official go-between with the various agencies, but her decisions are binding."

"I advise against this," Zakharov said.

"The decision is made," Khrushchev said, "so do your damned duty. A soldier has no function but to follow orders; now we'll see what kind of soldier you are."

Talia started to say something, but Gnedin caught her arm. "That was Molotov on the platform," he whispered.

The name said all that Talia needed to know. Molotov was the former Soviet foreign minister and premier who four years ago had led the attempt to oust Khrushchev. The clever Ukrainian had outflanked the plotters at the last second and retained his power by pressuring the Politburo and demanding that the question of his power be put to the full General Assembly, which had sided with him. This had never been done before and proved that Khrushchev could outthink his opposition. Afterward he had sent Molotov into exile. The list of guests had said nothing about the former premier and Nikita Sergeievich's meeting the man face to face must have been like seeing a ghost, a reminder of how fragile his political position was. Talia understood what had happened. Lumbas was somebody else's tool; Molotov's unexpected presence had jarred Khrushchev back to reality, and he had returned power to the Special Operations Group because of it.

"Find out why that bastard was here," Khrushchev growled to Talia as he stalked out the door.

The General Secretary got into a new white Ford convertible with the top down and waved to the crowd that stared silently at him as if he were a man from Mars. There were police cars ahead of and behind the convoy and a phalanx of dark green motorcycles surrounding his vehicle, their riders wearing uniforms with heavy gold braid and shiny leather boots. Circus Cossacks, Talia thought.

One of Zakharov's people pointed Talia to a car behind the General Secretary's, but a whistle from someone in the crowd caught her attention and she saw Bailov waving for her to cross through security and join him. "Go talk to him," she told Gnedin. "I'm supposed to be Nikita Sergeievich's relative; I'll have to remain with the group for now. Take whatever initiatives are necessary, but keep me informed." More and more she felt the isolation that came with leadership.

She saw Bailov and Gnedin embrace briefly, then disappear behind a line of civilians with closed umbrellas. They looked like carbines to her and made her clench her teeth.

195   FRIDAY, JUNE 2, 1961, 8:50 P.M.
Purkersdorf, Austria

The Soviet embassy in Purkersdorf was a dreary survivor of the last century, a sprawling brick box of forty once-grand rooms set in a forest of spike-topped pines and walking trails cleared with hand scythes. The coming of the General Secretary was viewed by the ambassador as an opportunity to impress the ebullient Ukrainian; contingency funds had been depleted to give the old place new paint and new Swedish furniture to replace the garish junk that found its way there over the years. The house, which had been built by a world-famous glassmaker, now housed Soviet embassy personnel and a steady stream of visitors from Moscow.

Security was predictably heavy. Even in normal circumstances Khrushchev moved with a phalanx of armed personnel clinging to him like a second skin. Soldiers from an Austrian Alpine regiment were stationed outside the residence walls, and Talia saw two gray panel trucks with revolving-loop antennae near the entrance. Several armored personnel carriers were parked at intervals along the street. Inside the walls Zakharov's people patrolled in pairs, their Kalashnikovs slung over menacing black suits. She saw no dogs but could hear them on the grounds.

Talia's room was on the top floor, next to Khrushchev's; his wife, Nina Petrovna, was in a separate room on the other side of her husband. Talia draped her raincoat over a black chair, kicked off her shoes and went to the window. A set of blueprints of the embassy had been placed on the desk, the corners of the documents held down by small glass paperweights with red stars inside them. From her window she saw a kidney-shaped swimming pool and three grass tennis courts with bare spots along the service lines. The grounds were illuminated by small spotlights mounted on wooden poles; several of the lights were improperly aligned and left gaps. Soviet workmanship, she reminded herself, was a contradiction in terms. Fumes of fresh paint and turpentine engulfed her. All the lights inside the villa were on, which added to the peculiar feeling of the place. Moscow was dark, in part because of inadequate power, in part because the blackout mentality of the war persisted, but mostly because the Russian soul was inherently dark. Artificial light unnerved her people because it made them easier to see. The Mongols, the czars, Stalin—no matter who ruled—the people were kept in darkness. The system could not tolerate light. Sharp nails get the hammer first, a proverb warned, a lesson that seldom strayed from her countrymen's minds. Reduce your profile and erase your shadow; these actions and luck were the paths to a long life.

Khrushchev came into her room through a connecting door. Sweat stains reached from under his arms to the center of his chest. He folded his arms and watched two guards stop in the middle of the nearest tennis court to pass a cigarette back and forth over the net. "You saw Molotov?" he asked.

"Yes."

"He sought rarefied air," Khrushchev said, his voice low and distant, "so I shipped the treacherous bastard to Outer Mongolia. I told him, At least I let you live; Stalin would have dumped you in a hole in the ground."

"Why is he here?"

"The Mongolian air disagreed with him. I underestimated the collective sympathy for him. He's not a man to attract blind adulation, but he's admired and he has a weak heart. The Eastern winters were killing him, so I transferred him to Vienna, where he represents us at the Atomic Energy Commission. He sought power, and now he manages it," Nikita Sergeievich said with a chuckle. "They all feared Stalin and cursed his ways until he was dead. Then each of them wanted to *be* Stalin. Molotov, Malenkov, Saburov, Kaganovich, Shepilev, Bulganin—they tried to throw me out, attempted the unspeakable, yet they lived because I chose to let them live." He stretched and turned to face her.

It wasn't like the General Secretary to talk like this, and it made Talia uneasy. "Molotov has no connection to Lumbas," she said. "Perevertkin was the engine."

"That's the point. Molotov and his kind fought by the old rules. Leaders chose leaders; this was the way from Lenin through Stalin, but now I've changed it. They stacked the Politburo against me, but I outflanked them by pushing the question of my leadership down to the full Central Committee. It was unheard of, but it was legal, and Molotov and the others hadn't thought of it, so they had to give in when the Central Committee backed me. But because the full committee made that decision, they now have the power to make it again. It altered everything," he added. "Why do I demand changes in our economy? The common people don't yet understand, but their leaders do, at least intuitively. The Central Committee is the people's body, its arm, and it has power for the first time. The people ensured my survival, and in time they'll see that they can also bring about my fall."

"This has nothing to do with Perevertkin."

"It has everything to do with what he represented."

"Perevertkin was nothing."

Khrushchev answered, "That's exactly my point. Though he was nothing more than a high-level apparatchik, Perevertkin *became* someone by daring to try to bring me down." His voice was lower as he continued. "Our people are ignorant; yet in their ignorance they have true knowledge. They nod their heads at the Party's words, but they read reality like scholars. They understand symbols; they live by them and take their lead from them. If Perevertkin dared, then others will, and each time somebody tries, it closes the gap between the symbol and the act and brings power closer to the masses. Eventually it will occur to some drunken reindeer herdsman or half-assed Party lawyer that he can change things, and he'll brood about this until he believes it, and then he'll tell his family and friends and they'll tell theirs. One day all the reindeer herdsmen or lawyers will not only believe it but accept it as their right, because if you say something enough times it will be assumed to be true. I outflanked Molotov and the others, but in doing so I fear I may have outflanked myself. In winning I've lost, which is brilliantly Russian," he said bitterly. "One day I'll fall but they'll let me live, and by my living and my letting Molotov and his bunch live, all that has gone before will die. Somewhere some young bureaucrat is watching Moscow, and one day he'll understand all this, see what's been spawned and will make his own bid for immortality, but he won't dare move backward. The Cossacks say that when a big horse begins to run, a rider can do nothing more than hang on. The smart Cossack spurs the horse faster and faster until the animal begins to sense that it's approaching its limits; then and only then, the Cossack may carefully turn the horse." The General Secretary wiped his forehead with his sleeve. "Perevertkin's act tells us that the Soviet horse has begun to run, and I'm depending on you to make sure I'm not thrown off."

"But Perevertkin has been stopped," Talia reminded him. "He failed."

"Maybe he needed only to try. One who leads makes a bridge for others; Molotov's presence today reminded me of this. I haven't seen the bastard in four years, and even though I transferred him here, I was stunned that he had the balls to show himself. If one with so little power can be so bold, what will those with the real power do?"

"Perevertkin is dead."

Khrushchev nodded solemnly. "True, but is what he set in motion equally dead?"

A crossroad. "Listen to me," she said. "There's something you need to know, comrade."

196   SATURDAY, JUNE 3, 1961, 10:45 A.M.
Vienna

The Boeing 707's tires spit small puffs of smoke, even though the runway was speckled with puddles of standing water. Arizona stood in the crowd watching the soldiers unroll a red carpet while Secret Service agents raced around the parked jet like ants feasting on fresh carrion—an unsettling image, he reminded himself. An honor-guard detachment in white toy-soldier costumes was positioned fifty meters from the passenger ramp.

Kennedy's hair ruffled in the breeze as he emerged from the aircraft, and he was squinting. There was cheering throughout the airport. Kennedy's wife's hair defied the breeze; she walked stiff-legged and looked rigid and self-conscious, even from a distance. Yet people were fascinated with her, and with them as a couple. It made no sense; lousy senators don't become great presidents, especially senators whose brains reside in their dicks.

Now Kennedy read a short statement into a small forest of microphones. Arizona couldn't make out the words, but the crowd applauded enthusiastically.

Secret Service agents in dark suits and dark glasses studied everything and everyone except the president. The White House's Swiss Guard, Arizona told himself, which was to say that they were single-minded and conspicuous. He had known a lot of them over the years; they tended to be colorless men with few outside interests, which he supposed reduced the incidence of wandering minds. Robots, really, but highly motivated and exquisitely trained; you couldn't deny that. They understood their jobs and did them well; for a moment he wished his own people were as good, but did not let himself dwell on this. The CIA's job was much more complex than simple protection and far more murky in its mission.

Arizona studied the area dispassionately and decided that even if Frash was in Austria to cause trouble there was no way he would strike here. In any event, there was no reason to think that Kennedy was the target. He had given considerable thought to this; it had been the Soviets who set up Frash, and it was they who were most at risk.

A gust of wind caught the umbrellas of three onlookers, ripped them free and shot them into the sky like small rockets. As he craned his neck to watch the presidential delegation move toward a line of limousines he sensed someone behind him and turned to find a glowering Valentine. "Thought you might show up here," Arizona said. "Where's Sylvia?"

"Doing her bit for hands-across-the-Iron-Curtain. Our newfound Russian colleagues have themselves in an uproar."

"Frash?"

"He's *our* problem. What they're worked up over is a possible Albanian hit on Khrushchev. They've got a lead on a pair of Albanians, one of them a big shot in the Albanian secret police who's traveling with a woman. The Russians think they whacked Albanian expatriates in Paris. The way they see it, Paris was a prelim for the main event here."

"You think they're right?"

Valentine shrugged. "Considering the circumstances and timing, they're assuming the worst. No other way to play it. Sylvia and I have been helping them."

"What are the chances that Frash is linked to them?"

"If the Russians are right, he's not with them—if that's what you mean—but the Albanians they took down in Paris were probably part of his network. The way I see it, that puts them on opposite sides."

The crowd had thinned out. Arizona moved to the railing and pushed up the collar of his coat. Could it be that Frash had stayed in Europe to counter the Albanians? Did he know something about an assassination plot? No, that didn't fit Frash's pattern. Don't grasp at straws, he told himself. "Where is he?"

"Here," Valentine said, "and still up to his old tricks. He used Gypsies to get into Austria, then snuffed his escort."

"The dead hiker?"

"Natch. After that he hooked up with an Austrian reporter and posed as an Italian photographer. The Austrian woman helped him get summit press credentials, but the Russians got onto him and traced him through the woman."

"Where?"

"Here, but he got wind of us, killed the woman and skipped again."

Arizona's heart was racing. Were they ever going to catch up with this maniac? "What did he want the press credentials for?"

"The Russians think that's the sixty-four-thousand-dollar question."

Arizona sensed something in the former OSS agent's voice. "But you don't?"

"I'm not sure. Your boy has shown an uncanny ability to stay invisible. We've flushed him a couple of times, but by and large he's still calling the dance. He's done it by keeping in the shadows. I can't see that he'd be so stupid as to think he could blend into the journalist corps without our picking him out. If I had to guess I'd say that the credentials are irrelevant. The Austrian woman he killed was well connected. My hunch is that he was using her to gather information and to lie low. What I don't get is why the bastard's here. My gut tells me that somehow he's tied to the Albanians, but I can't work it out. It's like one of those bizarre pictures where you see one thing when you first look at it and something entirely different if you cock your head or turn it to one side."

Arizona opened his briefcase and took out a large envelope. "We've updated his psychological profile."

"Anything new?"

"Not that I can see," he said, closing the briefcase. When he looked up Valentine was gone. "Asshole," he muttered and then smiled. Beau had gotten his intensity back. In the old days that meant success was as good as in the bag. He wondered what it meant now.

197 SATURDAY, JUNE 3, 1961, 12:45 P.M.
Vienna

A Spetsnaz lieutenant drove the black touring car that carried the General Secretary to his meeting with Kennedy. Talia and Zakharov rode in back with Khrushchev while the rest of the delegation followed in other limos. The convoy was accompanied by motorcycle police and a carload of Spetsnaz personnel.

"You should be aware that there's a potential problem," Talia said to Zakharov.

They were passing a huge bed of red and lavender poppies. "Life is a potential problem," the General Secretary interrupted. "Beria once initiated a project aimed at sedating a village through its water source in Estonia, but several people died because the drug was too concentrated and because some couldn't tolerate it. Even with careful planning, death is a random event." Khrushchev had spent the whole night and morning with advisers. Even so, he felt fresh and rested. "My only concern is Kennedy; all else is secondary for the next two days," he said. "Pogrebenoi's group suspects there are assassins in the city," he told Zakharov without emotion.

"There's always such potential," the general answered without apparent concern. "Our security is tight."

"Effort means nothing. I want results. Nothing must get in the way of this meeting."

"Then you must stick to your itinerary," Zakharov said.

"I will do what my instincts tell me," Khrushchev said. "Protection is your concern," he told both of them.

The convoy slowed as it approached a police barricade outside the American embassy residence. The grounds were covered with weeping willows, dark firs, lindens, oaks and rhododendrons. The building was the color of sculpting clay, a squat modernistic box with chocolate-colored columns and harsh right angles; the overall effect was depressing, almost exactly the opposite of the natural splendor surrounding it.

"You see?" Khrushchev said, shaking his head. "They let the architect express his individual taste, so there is no harmony. Chaos is the price of capitalism."

The building reminded Talia of the gray tenements being built around Moscow. Austrian police were everywhere, many of them with muzzled Alsatians on short choke chains. The animals looked as tense as their handlers.

The meeting was scheduled to begin with a luncheon in forty-five minutes. It had been Khrushchev's idea to arrive early to demonstrate that even in the enemy's camp he could seize the initiative and force the Americans to play by his rules. Flashbulbs lit the gray day as the limousine passed through a heavily guarded checkpoint, then skidded slightly on the driveway as it stopped at the front entrance. A Spetsnaz man was beside the car immediately and Zakharov motioned for him to open the door.

More flashes popped as the General Secretary got out. Kennedy was waiting on the embassy steps, his suit a perfect fit; the shorter Khrushchev looked like a troll beside him as they shook hands. The General Secretary's smile looked forced. Talia was surprised by the racket made by the cameras behind the press barrier. When the two men at last went inside she felt immediate relief; now protection became the Americans' responsibility.

"So far so good," Bailov said to Melko as they stood among the photographers and journalists some distance from the principals.

198   SATURDAY, JUNE 3, 1961, 3:25 P.M. *Vienna*

The subterranean area was narrow, dark and cramped, exactly what Frash needed for cover and access. It was dry but chilly belowground, but he was dressed entirely in black and wore two sweaters to help cut the cold. The 9 mm was strapped to his chest, where he could reach it quickly and he had a double-edged knife in his boot. He had moved beyond the point where tourists were allowed, and now he searched methodically for a place to settle. If anybody came along now he would act first, identify second. In the meantime he would make a nest. It would be a long night, but when he was finished he would fly to Las Palmas through Madrid, find a woman and reward himself with a few days in the sun. The wait wouldn't be bad; he had once sat ninety hours straight waiting for someone, and this would be a snap in comparison. Ali decided that he would wink at Kennedy's woman before killing both of them.

199 SATURDAY, JUNE 3, 1961, 4:20 P.M. *Vienna*

Sylvia and Bailov explored the Schönbrunn Palace, where in less than four hours there would be a glitzy dinner hosted by the Austrian president for the two summit delegations. After nearly two hours she said, "This is like trying to seal off Texas." The palace was yellow, and seemed to stretch forever. As with the others she had seen, it was difficult to understand how such wealth could be accumulated, much less concentrated in a single family.

Gnedin and Melko approached, the tattooed Russian freshly shaved, clad in a tuxedo that looked too small and tugging at his collar every few seconds. "Come," Gnedin told her. "We've found something interesting."

In a room off the Great Gallery a symphony orchestra was rehearsing a waltz. The musicians, including several women, wore an odd assortment of clothing; behind them were two stacks of battered instrument cases and two clothing trolleys filled with black bags bearing the orchestra's emblem.

The two Russians led her behind the musicians as the conductor rapped his baton on a metal music stand. "Again, again," he said in a tone that suggested he would never be satisfied.

Gnedin took her to a small sitting room whose walls were lined with oil paintings of naked women being fondled by huge swans. Sylvia shook her head. Swans were surly creatures; only a painter could fantasize such nonsense. A pale green dress lay over the back of a red chair, and new shoes were in a box on the floor. "We had to guess your size," the doctor said before letting himself out and pushing Melko ahead of him.

Tonight there would be a formal dinner for the two delegations, with entertainment to follow. Everyone but Valentine agreed that if something was going to happen this was the ideal setting. The palace was massive, with hundreds of rooms, most of which had been closed for years. There would also be hundreds of guests, along with musicians, the opera company, caterers and others, all melding together in a splendid setting. Valentine had come along, briefly walked the grounds and departed with one of the cloth swatches in his hand like a talisman, leaving without a word to her or the Russians. She assumed he would be back, but there was a fluttering in her stomach. No matter how hard she tried, she couldn't fathom his thought processes.

200 SATURDAY, JUNE 3, 1961, 5:00 P.M.
Vienna

Cabdriver Dieter Hinz was the talkative type, eager to share his life story. A onetime medical student at Heidelberg, he had been conscripted into the Luftwaffe medical service, been sent east, deserted at the first opportunity and now claimed to have once watched a colleague remove a splinter from Adolf Hitler's ass. For two years he had lived on the run, dodging retreating Nazis, charging Russians and vengeful DPs. After the war he made his way to Greece, where he worked as a fisherman; when the Soviets left in 1955, he moved to Austria, settling first in Linz, only recently moving to Vienna. Twice divorced with no known children, he admitted to antisocial tendencies and an insatiable hunger for money. Valentine liked him immediately.

What Hinz did *not* have was a strong work ethic. Valentine wanted another look at tomorrow's meeting sites; the Russians were nervous about tonight's festivities, but he didn't buy it, at least not as far as Frash was concerned. Each time he returned to the cab, Hinz had the radio turned up, his head leaning back against the door, his feet stretched out, a foul-smelling cigarette in his nicotine-stained fingers. "I could use some help," Valentine complained.

"I was hired to drive," Hinz said. "Tours are extra."

"What you're doing is mostly sitting on your ass."

"The essence of my profession," the German driver said with a mischievous smile. The air was damp and heavy and Valentine had walked so much that sweat rolled off him, fogging the windows.

The next stop was an address on Blutgasse. "Tough district," Hinz said as he crowded the Mercedes into the traffic stream amid several dissenting horns.

"I'm not worried," Valentine said. "I've got you for a bodyguard."

Hinz grinned in the mirror. "That will also cost you extra. Basically I'm a pacifist."

Valentine went up to Mignonne Mock's flat, picked the lock and spent nearly two hours looking around. When he passed through the coffee house, Hinz waved at him over the day's *Frankfurter Allgemeine*. When he reached the cellar he was surprised to see Ezdovo sitting in the corridor outside the photo laboratory watching smoke curl up from his cigarette. Valentine took a quick look at the laboratory, then settled onto the floor beside the Russian. "Thought you'd be at the palace with your comrades."

Ezdovo tapped his chest. "I don't feel it in here," he said in German.

"Me either. But damned if I know what I *do* feel. I've been over tomorrow's route so many times I could walk it in my sleep."

The Siberian smiled and held out a cigarette pack. "Russian," he said. "They taste like shit."

Valentine took one and tapped it against the heel of his hand. "It's becoming my favorite flavor."

201 SATURDAY, JUNE 3, 1961, 7:40 P.M.
Vienna

The gown was gray-green satin, the hue of distant pines on a cloudy day, with a cramped bodice that pushed her breasts together to form an unnatural cleavage. It had no straps and the back dipped far down to bare her spine. Sylvia had no idea where the Russians had gotten it, but it was exquisite. The stockings were real silk. The shoes were a size too large, which was better than a size too small; they were new, with unmarked soles and pencil-thin three-inch heels. There was no opportunity for a shower, much less a lingering soak in a tub of hot water and bubbles, but it didn't matter. The clothes were enough to sanitize her spirit for what was likely to be a nerve-racking night.

As part of the security setup, the six hundred guests would all file through a door at one end of the building, and most were already filtering in; the help and entertainment would enter at the opposite end. As a precaution the Russians were paying special attention to the employees who would cook, serve and take care of the numerous behind-the-scenes tasks required of such an affair, and would be especially alert to any last-minute developments such as late arrivals or somebody calling in sick. Every worker had an identity badge that had to be checked against a master photo in the security unit. Each face was to be matched, and each person had to sign in so that signatures could also be checked.

After dressing, Sylvia joined Gnedin in the room where the help had entered. Half a dozen Viennese police officers were there in their dress uniforms. "Anything?" the doctor asked one of them.

"No problems," the man reported.

Sylvia left Gnedin with the Austrians and went to the ceremonial room, where many of the early arrivals were hovering in anticipation of the arrival of the stars of the show. There would be no receiving lines; the guests would gather in one room for cocktails, then move to another for the dinner. They stood in small groups, generally separating themselves by nationality. Typical cocktail behavior, she thought. Waiters in tight-fitting eighteenth-century costumes and plumed hats carried trays filled with glasses of champagne. Most of the waiters were young and trim and seemed to float unobtrusively between the guests, their demeanor suggesting that this was not their first exposure to the glitterati.

Sylvia saw Bailov among the guests; dressed in a dark suit and tie, he made brief eye contact with her, but kept moving. After a while it was easy to pick out the various security people; their eyes moved constantly, while the legitimate guests chatted and smiled. Illuminated chandeliers made the room glow. By and large the women were young and dressed elegantly, while most of the men were older. Sylvia felt strangely calm as the room filled, but she wondered what Beau was doing.

| 202 | SATURDAY, JUNE 3, 1961, 8:10 P.M. *Vienna* |

Hinz found them in the cellar. "The meter is running," he announced. "It's my duty to remind you."

It was not the helpful act Hinz made it out to be, Valentine thought; he was afraid his fare had skipped.

"Cool down here," Hinz said. "More comfortable than upstairs."

"We think better in the darkness," Valentine said.

The cabdriver stepped past the two men, examined the bricked-over arch at the end of the hall and kicked halfheartedly at the structure. "Relatively new bricks," he said. "Usually these things are falling apart."

"What things?" Valentine asked.

"Plugs," Hinz answered, tapping the wall lightly.

"Plugs?" Ezdovo asked, his first words since the cabbie had joined them.

Hinz turned to face them. "To keep the tramps, children and other undesirables out of the underground."

"A subway system?" Valentine asked. He didn't remember the city having a subway.

Hinz laughed. "The old city had catacombs."

"Here?" the Siberian asked.

"Underneath most of the central district. In some places it stretches all the way to the river."

Ezdovo and Valentine looked at each other. "How extensive?" the American asked.

Hinz rolled his eyes and shrugged. "Never been down there." Then, seeing their sudden interest, "and I have no desire to see its mysteries. The authorities deal severely with intruders," he added.

"How do you get down there?" Ezdovo asked.

The two men were fluent in German, but both had accents. The fare was American, but what was he doing with a Russian, and why all this interest in the underground, which was a mere sewer that even the cops avoided. "I don't, and I would like to be paid now," Hinz said. "Please."

"I'll double your fare if you show us how to get down below," Valentine said.

"I don't need the money," Hinz said, backing up.

"Triple," Valentine came back.

"Paid now?"

"Half now, half after you show us."

"I won't go down there for any reason."

"Just show us."

Hinz led them up to the street and into a square before a huge cathedral. "Stephansdom," he said. "You can get into the catacombs through the burial vault in the church. There are guided tours every day."

"I don't understand," Ezdovo said as he scanned St. Stephen's Cathedral.

"Catacombs," Hinz said, holding out his hand. "People say that everything is connected below. It's easiest to get in through the church."

"Wait here," Valentine yelled as he began to trot toward St. Stephen's with the Russian beside him.

"What about my fare?" Hinz called after them.

"When we've finished," the American shouted. "Stay put."

<table>
</table>

203   SATURDAY, JUNE 3, 1961, 8:15 P.M.
Vienna

Khrushchev and Nina Petrovna were the first principals to arrive. He wore a dark business suit and tie with a muted checkerboard pattern. He looked small but beamed his infectious smile, shamelessly showing the gap in his front teeth. Sylvia thought he looked younger than sixty-seven; photographs tended to make him look older and to round off a surprisingly sturdy frame.

The Kennedys entered ten minutes later, the president tall, tanned and seemingly aglow with good health, a man in his prime. Mrs. Kennedy looked equally tall but undernourished, more fashion model than First Lady. She wore a sleeveless pink dress and white gloves that fit tightly above her elbows. Her smile looked manufactured and she moved with her back straight and chin up. Shy, Sylvia thought. Bird legs, narrow hips, an aloof air.

The two leaders and their wives were taken into a small room, where they remained for several minutes. When they reappeared, Kennedy stayed in one place, letting others pay homage, while Khrushchev restlessly worked the room, laughing and telling stories. The contrast in their styles and appearance was striking. She wondered what the two leaders had talked about during the afternoon session. In the space of six hours it would be difficult to avoid substance, she guessed. Had the Soviets criticized the Cuban fiasco?

At eight-thirty the guests moved into the massive room called the Great Gallery, which had vaulted ceilings and floor-to-ceiling windows with arches. The head table stretched nearly fifty meters. There were glittering chandeliers and huge sconces between the windows. The walls were white, and everything in the room was gaudily accented with gold leaf. The parquet floors had been polished to a mirror sheen, which seemed to multiply the effect of the gold. When the multitude was seated, waiters immediately began to serve the first of five courses, while a forty-piece orchestra played flowing waltzes against the rhythm of flatware clinking softly against bone china. The conductor looked relaxed and confident as he smiled at the head table and let his baton guide the musicians through the score.

Sylvia had no appetite. While the soup was being served on the imperial china of the Hapsburgs, she crumpled her napkin, excused herself and went into the hall, where Gnedin and Bailov were talking in hushed tones with Melko. "No problems so far," she heard him say. He carried a walkie-talkie on a strap slung diagonally over his back, and acknowledged her with a nod.

"The entertainers are warming up," Bailov reported. "When dinner is finished everyone will be moved to the other room while the Great Gallery is reconfigured."

Bailov checked his watch, then motioned for Melko to go back outside. "If I go back to stealing, maybe I'll wear a monkey suit like this," he joked as he left. "They'll call me the most elegant thief in Moscow."

Sylvia and Bailov remained in the hall while Gnedin returned to the main security room. When she looked again she saw that the guests were eating thick, dark, beef fillets covered with a sauce of wild mushrooms.

Most of the dancers were stretching in the back room. The women wore white tights; the men's were pale blue. The men were shorter than she expected, with narrow waists and massive thighs, their toe shoes scuffed and badly worn. One of the women warmed up with a dark cheroot dangling from her lips. Another had peeled down her top and an older woman was rubbing a pungent liniment into her back, leaving the air heavy with wintergreen. A male dancer was taping his right ankle in a figure-eight pattern, while another man held a small blond woman above his head, spinning slowly, seemingly without effort, but Sylvia saw that he was perspiring heavily; grace hid his effort. The girl over his head was stiff and looked as if her back had been cemented to his hands. Intermittent bars from a waltz wafted in from the Great Gallery; the revolving dancers in the rehearsal room were not in step and suddenly looked awkward.

In the corridor there was a trolley filled with gaudy costumes and lace petticoats. There were a dozen doors along the hallway, all closed. Behind them she heard muted voices, male and female, singing musical scales as warm-ups; each in their own world, she thought.

Halfway down the hall sat a corpulent man in a pleated white silk shirt with a scarlet cummerbund, his bow tie undone, his jacket draped over the chairback; he was talking to two women in red dresses. "I don't care what that cunt Minari says, or how she feels, or if she has her period. No understudies for this, and to hell with her fucking contract. She pulls this shit before every performance. Just ignore her."

Sylvia watched the two women trot down the hall and duck into a room. Soon there was a burst of shouting, which abated quickly.

"What is it?" the man asked when he saw Sylvia. "Can't you see I'm busy?"

"Just looking around," she said.

"Try the damned zoo," he snapped. "At least the animals there have justification for their behavior. This bunch—"

"Security," she explained.

He made a face and opened his briefcase.

She drifted back to watch the dancers and saw men in brown overalls crouched against the hallway walls; when dinner was finished they would transform the Great Gallery into a theater. The dancers' faces looked as distracted as a photo she had once seen of Marines riding toward a beach in an LST.

204   SATURDAY, JUNE 3, 1961, 8:57 P.M.
Vienna

The American and the Siberian drifted slowly through the huge cathedral. For some reason it made Valentine think of the Alamo, a lousy place for a showdown. There had been a priest stationed at an iron gate that led down a set of stairs, but when they approached he said, "No more tours tonight." Now he was gone and the heavy brass cage that surrounded the stairs was locked.

The two men followed the north aisle back to where it connected with one of the cathedral's towers. Several people were standing in the nave with bowed heads; compulsive worship, Valentine thought. He sat down on the floor and leaned back against the wall to think. The Siberian squatted some distance away, surveying the shadowy vaults high overhead. Odd that Ezdovo was not with his people; what was eating him?

Valentine had spent a lot of time poring over the updated Frash profile along with the original report, hoping for new insight, but the words seemed to blend into meaningless mush and he had eventually pitched them aside. In the old days he had never had the patience for the scholarly approach, preferring instead to let his intuition rule. Right now even that seemed to have abandoned him. Sylvia had forced him to go with her to the palace, but he had stayed only briefly and moved on. It didn't feel right there, but was this any better? He moved closer to the Siberian. "Why aren't you with your comrades?"

"I found the Austrian woman, and now I intend to find the American as well. We need to find a way to the underground. Why aren't *you* there?"

"Dunno," Valentine said. Frash was in Vienna; no doubt about that. But why? Something to do with the Albanian operation, but not necessarily the Albanians. To intercept Shehu's people? Not likely. The Russians had sent Lumbas to Frash, and perhaps with him the plan for the Albanian operation. But then the Russians had taken Lumbas out. Why set something in motion, then stop it? Not *your* Russians; *their* Russians. He smiled at this thought. The war had been a lot more clear-cut about who your enemies were. Does Frash want his pound of flesh? Maybe. If so, then the Russians are under the gun. But Frash is deranged, which means his logic isn't necessarily yours.

"The underground," Ezdovo reminded him again.

They found Hinz outside the cathedral's west entrance. Several gray army trucks had backed into the square, and Viennese police were supervising the unloading and setting up of white wooden barricades. "Well?" the German cabdriver asked.

"Locked tighter than a chastity belt," Valentine said.

"When do I get paid?"

"When you're finished. You want to earn another bonus?"

Hinz was hesitant. "For what?"

"An errand, that's all." Valentine went over the instructions several times with the cabdriver before he was satisfied that he understood what had to be done. Security at the Schönbrunn would be heavy, but if Hinz did as he was told, he should be able to make contact with Sylvia and the Russians.

205 SATURDAY, JUNE 3, 1961, 9:00 P.M.
Vienna

Melko had just come outside when he heard a series of sharp popping sounds. At night it was hard to pinpoint their location precisely, but he looked instinctively toward the north perimeter and walked quickly in that direction to investigate. As he got closer he heard more pops which seemed to come from the security entrance directly ahead.

A Spetsnaz man was nearby and had a walkie-talkie next to his face. "What was it?"

"Just firecrackers," the man said. "Probably political malcontents," he added. Before the guests began arriving for the reception a large crowd had gathered outside the main entrance to the Schönbrunn; the Viennese police estimated it at four to five thousand people. Most carried placards criticizing the American president's presence. Some signs alluded to Yalta, which was seen by some as America's postwar giveaway of Eastern Europe to the Soviets. "It's nothing," the soldier said. "Just politicals. They actually tolerate such shit here."

Melko continued toward the main entrance and was joined along the way by Bailov, who jogged toward him out of the darkness and passed him, forcing Melko to run to keep up.

The guards at the entrance were laughing. "I nearly shit my pants," one of them said. "I thought they were shooting at us."

Whatever real shots were fired tonight would sound more like coughs than thunderclaps, Bailov knew. "What happened here?" he asked in German.

"Just a prank," one of the policemen said. "A car went by and somebody threw out some fireworks. With so many journalists here everybody wants attention tonight."

"You saw the vehicle?"

None of the policemen had seen anything.

The two Russians went through the gate and met two policemen coming toward them with a paper bag. "Just firecrackers," one of them said. "See?"

Melko shone his flashlight into the bag. There was a blackened matchbook among the fragments of firecrackers. He saw that all of the matches had been ignited. Bailov studied it and saw that one stuck out at an angle from the rest. More than once in the old days he had seen matchbooks used this way as crude timers. You lit one match, and when it burned down it ignited the others, a simple and effective way to give you time to get away.

They went back to the entrance. "What happened?" Bailov asked again.

"Firecrackers," a policeman said.

"No, after that."

"Most of us ducked." The man laughed. "A natural reaction," he added defensively.

"Who was here? Was anybody coming through?"

"We were here," the man said. After a second he added, "A woman was just checking in when the fireworks went off. I think one of our lieutenants took her through."

"You checked her identification?"

"Yes." Then, "No, we were in the process. We sent them through when the disturbance began."

"Why did the lieutenant go with her?"

The policeman smiled sardonically. "We value our women here; we don't put them on tractors." Several policemen grinned as the Russians walked off.

"Suspicious bastards," one of the Austrians said. "That was a fine piece, though. Maybe the lieutenant will get lucky with her."

"Keep your mind on your work," a sergeant said sharply.

"Where the hell is Ezdovo?" Bailov asked.

Melko shrugged.

Bailov looked grim as he ran toward the palace.

SATURDAY, JUNE 3, 1961, 9:10 P.M.
Vienna

Brother Johann Schmidt had been the curator of St. Stephen's catacombs since the last year of the Great War. He had seen the breakup of the Austro-Hungarian empire, the rise of Hitler, the Anschluss, the Nazis' fall and the start and end of the Soviet occupation. Through it all he had gauged every event solely by its potential for affecting the sacred remains in his care. Compared with past events this summit between the Americans and Russians was but a small ripple, yet their security forces had been as nervous as novitiates meeting the archbishop for the first time. They had wanted tours stopped three days before the meetings but he had stood his ground and the archbishop had backed him. Who else would do what he did, living his days among ghosts? The order had trouble attracting the young, and no priest would accept such menial duty. The security people had wanted to check the underground, but he had fought this as well. Beyond the area where tourists were allowed the tunnels were sacred; he would have no infidels traipsing in there, especially Communists.

It had been the archbishop who had proposed a compromise. "Brother Johann will personally search the catacombs," he assured the visitors, his voice syrupy. But despite the archbishop's assurances Johann did not alter his routine, touring the catacombs every night at the same time and making his way to his own private chapel built with and among the sacred relics.

The catacombs were cool, the temperature constant, the air in the upper levels slightly humid. Brother Johann was as aware as anybody of events in the world above but he was more comfortable belowground where he could count on everything being in place, and where whatever organic change there was would be more easily measured in time frames that were magnitudes of his life span. Down here he had some sense of the control that God must feel. Sometimes he even confessed his arrogance.

Despite the thousands of times he had traveled his twisted and confined world Brother Johann never took his rounds for granted. As insurance that his refuge remain undisturbed he employed sprinklings of a mixture of talcum powder and cinnamon at shadowy intersections, threads strung at various heights and angles in the corridors, slivers of black paper inserted in door hinges and strips of foil tucked into burial chambers, each designed to help him guard this holy ground. Most intruders came on four legs, but every few years somebody tried to violate the sanctuary, usually as a prank or lark. Nevertheless, his caution paid. The tunnel system under the city was frequented by tramps and rough elements, and their potential for desecrating his beloved sanctuary was never far from his thoughts.

"Let them come," he whispered as he made his way down a tunnel toward the Y-shaped forks. If people made their way in they would find a few surprises. There were surprises down here that only he knew about.

Brother Johann was close to the crossing when he saw a heel print in the powder-cinnamon he had spread along one of the walls. Kneeling beside it, he saw that the print had a tread, which meant that it was not one of the other brothers, who wore sandals at this time of year, and not Father Martin, the only priest who had ever shown any genuine interest in his relics. Father wore a laceless shoe he called a penny loafer that he had acquired during his sojourn in America. This print had not been there this morning or at midday, which meant that somebody had been here in the past eight or nine hours.

Brother Johann squinted as he stared along the corridor floor looking for more prints. He was surprised when something struck him in the head and sent him sprawling backward. Bless me, Father, for I have sinned, he prayed as he lost consciousness.

207   SATURDAY, JUNE 3, 1961, 9:12 P.M.
Vienna

The last woman to enter was some sort of performer in the opera company; though he wasn't sure why, Gnedin rechecked her signature after she had gone through security. She was attractive and nervous, and he wondered what part she would play in the performance.

There was no more traffic now in the security office, and there wouldn't be until the festivities were over. Then all the guests would file through and repeat the same procedure they had undergone when coming in.

Gnedin stepped outside to breathe some fresh air and saw stars twinkling above.

"Did a woman just check through?" Bailov asked as he approached.

"A few minutes ago. I think she's part of the opera company."

"Identity verified?"

Gnedin nodded. "Photograph, signature, the whole thing."

"Was she alone?"

"Came in with a police lieutenant. Middle-aged, with a black mustache."

"Where is he now?"

"He left her here and came back outside." Gnedin looked at the sky again, then at the pebbled walks, which were dry. He thought for a moment, then said, "He had an umbrella."

"There's no rain," Bailov said, looking at the clear sky.

"He said, 'Here you are, Miss. Not a drop on your hair.' "

Now Melko joined his comrades in looking at the sky. "It hasn't been raining," Bailov said. "Not even a sprinkle." He pushed Melko. "Get back to the entrance and find out if those idiots checked the lieutenant's identification. See if they know him; get me a bloody name." He turned to Gnedin: "Find the woman."

"Detain her?"

"Yes."

Melko ran off, his walkie-talkie banging against his hip.

"What about you?" the doctor asked.

"I'll look around out here."

"Maybe it was nothing," Gnedin said, but Bailov had already disappeared down the walk.

 ## SATURDAY, JUNE 3, 1961, 9:20 P.M.
Vienna

The monk on the tunnel floor was the one who had led the tour earlier today. Frash had blended into the middle of the group, and as they climbed a set of nearly vertical stairs he had thrust a hip back, caught an elderly man off balance, and knocked him down the stairs, setting off a chain reaction. Like a good samaritan, he had been first to reach the fallen man, apologizing profusely for his clumsiness. The monk and others helped to carry the injured man up to the surface, and in the confusion Frash had backtracked into the tunnels; even if they were counting heads above there would be no way for them to get an accurate count in the chaos he had created.

He had only meant to stun the monk, but the man had been too old, his bones too frail. One blow with the butt of his pistol had left a gaping hole in his skull. Had he gone to Heaven? Without baptism the souls of infants were consigned to Limbo, a room filled with cotton wads and soft towels fresh from the clothesline. Zog: No name for a king. Mother had large breasts, even when she read the *Boston Globe*. Use me, the bitch said. Mother's cunt or was it Mother Cunt? Was there a special neighborhood set aside for monks and priests in Heaven? Surely there was such a place in Hell. It had been their kind's idea. Ali felt good, strong.

There was a copperhead under the table in the kitchen at the cottage; it was short and fat, with a head shaped like a trowel. "Papa can't kill it," Mother whispered. "Don't make a mess, I just cleaned the floor." The .22 rifle held Remington longs. Did copperheads have brains or go to Limbo? There were more questions than answers. One round at the bottom of the left eye and only a small amount of blood thereafter, the small bullet cutting a skip mark in the linoleum and lodging deep in a knotty pine cabinet. "Papa would be proud," said Mother, "if he could stand the sight of blood."

Salt poured into an open wound. No lie there, the cunt. Collectively you could sometimes believe what you heard, but odds were bad on individual items. A dog couldn't bite with its left eye blown out. The devil's eye, that left one, radiating evil. No left eye, no lifeline; it severed the umbilical cord to Lucifer. Hoxha's left eye dominated; Mother's too, but she denied this.

To shoot well, you had to think the bullet into the target. Someday missiles would use the same principle, but it would take practice, not to mention engineering. Why didn't maggots eat bone? He had hated lima beans as a child; same principle, he supposed, but principles mattered only to kings and a few priests, never to politicians. And not to Mother. Erasing a blackboard did not make it clean; you had to wash it as well. Only then could you start anew. Trust no one, Mother said. Including her? The Gypsy woman had a soft mouth that swallowed everything. Had Mother?

It was exciting to find a will of your own, satisfaction in knowing you had equals, even when they were few and far between. Knowing too much made it impossible to keep facts straight. There was only so much storage.

"You'll never be a scholar," Papa had said. "You lack focus and discipline." Such as abandoning your own people to left-eye dominance. Hitler knew how to lead, but had a low aptitude for common sense.

Past is present, Ali thought, or was it the other way around? Who controls them? he taunted Albert. Mother's voice: "Jesus, Sal. . . . where the hell did you find that one?" Do it now, Ali said.

---

209 | SATURDAY, JUNE 3, 1961, 9:22 P.M. *Vienna*

Melko searched for the man they had talked to earlier, but couldn't find him. He described him to several policemen, but drew blanks; he guessed they were taking some pleasure in playing dumb for a Russian. Eventually he found a sergeant who told him he had just relieved several of his men for a smoke.

"Where?"

"Over there," he said, motioning to a line of trees where a couple of red embers glowed in the shadows.

He found the policemen squatting with their backs braced against tree trunks, and shone the light on each of their faces, moving down the line slowly. "Turn that fucking thing out," one of them complained. "You're ruining my night vision."

"Which wasn't much to begin with," another man joked.

The first policeman was the one he was looking for. Melko turned the light on him and saw a lighted cigarette go tumbling into the darkness. "Hey," the man complained. "I told you about the light once. Now shut it off or I'll have to teach you some manners." Several of the other men snickered.

Melko put his hand around the man's throat and hoisted him violently, banging his head against the tree. The other Austrians scrambled to their feet, but Melko ignored them. "You said a lieutenant took the woman through the entrance just after the firecrackers went off."

"Fetch an officer quickly," one of the other men told a mate, "before this damned Ivan breaks Kurt's neck." None of the men tried to help their comrade.

The man clawed at Melko's arm, but couldn't break the grip; when he began to gag, the Russian loosened his grip and let the man tumble heavily on his side.

Melko heard footsteps moving away. "That lieutenant who took the woman through: did you know him?" He kept the light in the man's face.

"Never saw him before. Never seen most of these people before," the man croaked as he rubbed his neck.

"Did you check his identification?"

There was no answer; Melko saw in his eyes that he had not. "Fool," he muttered. When his own men failed in such basics, he had executed them on the spot.

He heard people running toward him, their slung weapons rattling, the beams of their lights dancing across the lawn. There was a conversation on his walkie-talkie. "Clear the frequency," Melko said in German. Then in Russian, "Team One, are you there?"

"What's going on?" an Austrian demanded.

"Shut up," Melko snapped.

"I hear you." It was Gnedin's voice.

"The lieutenant was never checked and nobody here can identify him. Is One with you?"

"No," Gnedin radioed back, his voice clear and crisp.

"Tell him I'm coming."

"I demand to know what's going on here!" the sergeant said, raising his revolver toward Melko.

Three Spetsnaz men stepped quietly out of the darkness and flanked the Austrian. "Trouble, sir?" one of the soldiers asked Melko.

Melko waved them off and pointed a finger at the sergeant. "Seal the grounds. Let nobody in or out until further notice. Do it quietly." He liked being called sir, he decided as he trotted toward the palace.

<hr/>

210   SATURDAY, JUNE 3, 1961, 9:31 P.M.
Vienna

<hr/>

The Archbishop's Palace faced the north side of the cathedral. A nun with a hawk nose and missing lower teeth opened the door and frowned at them. "No visitors," she said with a croak and attempted to close the door, but Valentine got his foot in, caught the door with his hands and pushed past. The nun retreated several steps and began looking around the foyer. Frantically looking for a weapon, he guessed; he was impressed that she was ready to sacrifice herself in the defense of church property. He held up his hands as a sign of peace, then slowly pulled his wallet out of his jacket and took out a card. "Show this to your superiors."

211   SATURDAY, JUNE 3, 1961, 9:40 P.M.
Vienna

Gnedin found Sylvia with the ballet dancers. "A woman in a dark coat and a large bag?"

"I saw her," Sylvia said. "She was wearing a long black dress underneath."

When his walkie-talkie came to life, Gnedin stepped to the side and talked to Melko. His face told her that they had a serious problem. "Find her and hold her," he told her. "I have to get Bailov."

"Didn't she clear security?" Sylvia asked.

"She did but her companion didn't, and now nobody can identify him." He vaulted over a dancer who was doing a split on the floor.

Sylvia went over to where the opera people had gathered and found a heavyset police lieutenant on the stairs at the intersection of two halls. The men in brown coveralls were up and moving, blocking her way. She checked her watch; by now dinner would be finished.

"Did you see a woman in a dark coat?" she asked the policeman.

He seemed to think about it, then shook his head. "Not since I came on duty an hour ago."

"How long is your shift?"

"Three hours, which is standard."

She moved on and began opening doors to the private practice rooms, but the fat man in the red cummerbund saw her and began shouting as he ran toward her. "What the hell do you think you're doing?"

Inside the first room was a heavyset woman in a black gown. She was sitting on a love seat, bent down, trying to buckle the thin straps to her shoes. "Is it time already?" she asked.

When Talia caught up she found Sylvia kneeling beside the singer holding her dress in one hand and the swatch of cloth from the Albanians' flat in the other. "It's a match," she said excitedly.

212   SATURDAY, JUNE 3, 1961, 9:44 P.M.
Vienna

The nun led them into a library where several folding tables were set up. A man with thick glasses and a Notre Dame sweatshirt was perched on a stool beside one of them. He had slicked-back brown hair and wore plaid Bermuda shorts and penny loafers with no socks. "You've given Sister Mary-Helene quite a scare," he said with a touch of amusement. The table in front of him was covered with various shapes of balsa wood and a bolt of cheesecloth. "The archbishop is at the Schönbrunn tonight," he said, "which gives me a chance to work on my model airplanes. They fly on a tether, which is analogous to the human condition. We think we're free, but the Hereafter awaits us all." He pushed his glasses up on his head, picked up the card Valentine had given to the nun and slid it across the table. "American Legion," he said. "Should this mean something to me?"

"It got us in," Valentine said.

The man waved the glowering nun out, held out his hand and shook his head. "Most of the world hates American impetuousness, but I find it refreshing. When an American gets something in his head there's no stopping him and all rules go out the window. Father Martin Good," he added. "But Marty will suffice."

"Our names don't matter," Valentine said.

"Not a fellow countryman by the looks of him. Russian?" the priest asked, looking at Ezdovo.

"Something like that," Valentine said.

The priest lit a cigarette and sat down. "Is your American Legion chapter a good one?"

"It's got a great bar. Lots of chicken-fried steak and Lone Star beer at bargain basement prices."

"Shit kickers dancing the two-step."

"It's that kind of place," Valentine said. "You seem to know a lot about the States."

"Ten years in South Bend, Indiana. Professor of history. Medieval architecture—churches mostly. My superiors felt I was drifting too far from my order's values. They sent me here for a refresher in the pastoral life, which is not so bad, though Vienna hardly resembles South Bend on a football weekend. But I guess you're not here for cross-cultural small talk. A matter of security, I presume?"

"We need to get into the catacombs." Ezdovo showed the priest his official security credentials.

"Brother Johann's purview," the priest said. "He's old now and a bit past his prime, I'm afraid. He even sleeps down there. Thinks of it as his private domain. I doubt that he'll open up, even for me."

"To come right to the point, we don't really care whether he gives permission or not." As Father Marty smiled and nodded, he reminded Valentine of one of those plaster dolls with bobbing heads that cowboys back home glued to the dashboards of their pickups.

 SATURDAY, JUNE 3, 1961, 10:07 P.M.
Vienna

The circle of cloth was caught on the hedge between the walk and the palace wall. Gnedin was not sure what it was, but there was no litter of any kind in the area, which meant that anything they found could be significant.

Bailov saw the doctor staring up the wall. "What is it?"

"Maybe nothing," Gnedin said, holding up the fabric. "I don't even know what this is, but this whole area is clean." Bailov examined the material while the doctor probed the wall with his hands. "This can be climbed," he said. "Maybe somebody dropped something." Before Bailov could reply Gnedin had moved up into the darkness.

214 SATURDAY, JUNE 3, 1961, 10:17 P.M.
Vienna

After accounting for every member of the cast, Sylvia and Talia came back down the hall and found a different policeman on the stairs smoking a cigarette. "What happened to the man you relieved?" Sylvia asked, showing him her credentials.

He shrugged.

"How long ago did you come on duty?" She showed him her ID card.

"This morning," he said. "But it feels longer."

"I mean here—this post."

The man looked puzzled. "I'm not on a post. I'm taking a smoke break. We're supposed to go outside to a special area, but it's a long walk and I only have a few minutes." '

"What's up the stairs?" she asked, looking past him.

"Everything above is sealed off. The only entrance open is at the far end of the building, and we have people there."

She moved past him, hitched her dress above her knees and went up the stairs three at a time, with Talia close behind. At the top she tried a tall white door; when she pushed, it squeaked softly and opened several inches.

Talia caught her by the arm. "Stay here until I get help," she whispered, and then ran down the stairs.

Sylvia slid through the door into the darkness, crossed a thick carpet runner to the far wall and crouched, pausing to remove her revolver from her purse.

Within minutes she saw Talia and Bailov beckoning her to come back. "That policeman came up here," she whispered to them. "It must have been unlocked from the inside. When I talked to him earlier he said he was on a three-hour shift, but the man downstairs now says there's no post here, that the upper levels are sealed and locked, that the only way up is at the other end of the palace and is heavily guarded. I think they're up here."

Talia crossed the hall first, then Bailov and Melko followed. Down the hall a door opened, spilling light onto the floral-patterned carpet and Gnedin stuck his head out. "Up here." The room was narrow and unfurnished; a carpet had been rolled against one wall. Gnedin took them into a white marble bathroom. There was a large purse behind the toilet, and a police lieutenant's uniform and long rope had been stuffed into it. The rope was attached to a small umbrella frame. "Steel," the doctor said. He showed them how the cloth he had found in the hedge fit over the frame. "Grappling hook made to look like an umbrella."

"The woman I saw was carrying a handbag like that," Sylvia said.

"The window was closed but unlatched," the doctor added. "It took me a while to climb up. It would have been faster for him."

They went back into the hall, which was lit with small overhead lights every twenty meters.

"Where does it lead?" Talia asked.

Bailov pulled a diagram from his coat pocket and spread it on the floor. "More light," he said and one flashed on over his shoulder. "Guards here," he said, tapping his forefinger on the paper. "But they're below. Everything above ground level is supposed to be sealed off."

"What's this?" Talia asked, pointing toward a stairwell.

"It's on the other side of the ballroom," Bailov said. There were two red circles inside the doors to the ballroom near where the stairs descended. "Security," he added.

Talia traced the line of a corridor that ran parallel to the main hall, then dog-legged left. "And this?"

"Anteroom to the stage," Gnedin said. "It's not in use tonight. There's one on the other side as well, which connects to the rehearsal rooms. The two areas aren't connected, which allows the stage manager to move the acts in and out without traffic problems."

"You two go below and cross the ballroom to here," Bailov said to the women, pointing. "We'll sweep this level and meet you there. If they're up here and trying to get into that far rehearsal room we may be able to trap them between us."

"Alive," Talia whispered, grasping Bailov's sleeve. "If possible."

215   SATURDAY, JUNE 3, 1961, 10:30 P.M. *Vienna*

Father Good had treated their exploration as if it were a fraternity prank, which suggested that his recall from Notre Dame had more to do with his judgment than anything else. He gave them flashlights, a hand-drawn map, some loops of electrical wire and a small sledge. "The wiring below is old," he explained. "The current seems to attract rats—not in the tourist area, but farther in. The wires are set into the ceiling. The rats jump to it, or maybe they can walk the ceilings like flies. The point is that if the lights go off, don't worry. Find a dead rodent and the break should be just above it." He gave them a roll of electrical tape for splices.

"Where's the switch?"

"Just beyond the tourist area. There are doors everywhere but don't be alarmed. Look for the one with four crosses on the corners. It's black, I think, or deep gray." He drew an X at the approximate position.

"Why the sledge?" Valentine asked. They were standing in a cellar coated with coal dust.

"You go up the coal chute from here. There's a metal door into the side; it has a steel-bar lock, and there are more doors between here and the cathedral. The sledge will get you through. It's an emergency route."

"You've thought of everything."

"Not everything," the priest said, suddenly turning serious. "I can't imagine why you want to do this."

Me either, Valentine thought as he and Ezdovo crawled on their bellies through a tunnel so small that their shoulders rubbed the walls.

216   SATURDAY, JUNE 3, 1961, 10:50 P.M. Vienna

Talia and Sylvia tried to be unobtrusive as they made their way between the guests crammed together in the makeshift theater, but there was no way to avoid stepping on toes as they moved. Out of the corner of her eye Sylvia saw dancers at the corner of the stage spinning like ghosts, defying gravity.

When they reached the far side Talia flashed her ID at one of the two guards and went through the double doors; both women kicked off their shoes, took out their pistols and threaded silencers into place. The light in the area was poor, but there was enough to get a sense of the layout.

The Russian padded her way to the staging door, found it open, slid in and emerged a few seconds later shaking her head. Sylvia crossed the hall to the far side of the curving stairwell and started up cautiously. When she reached the top, she waved Talia up. "This doesn't feel right," Sylvia whispered. She lay just below the top step watching the darkened upper corridor ahead, with Talia several steps below her. Somewhere ahead there were doors, but it was impossible to see them clearly.

"What do you mean?" Talia asked.

"Too dark," Sylvia said. "We might hit our people."

"They're prepared to take the risk," Talia said coolly. "They'll do what they have to, and we'll do the same." Suddenly she was overwhelmed with the need to know where her husband was.

They had gone over the schedule repeatedly. The idea was to strike late during the final act when the guests were most likely to be tired and thinking about how they were going to get out. It was critical, Kasi had decided, to make the assault in one fluid move, with no stops along the way. The blueprints showed an alcove beyond the stairs, and here they lay, watching the place where the steps emerged. The girl seemed calm, but her breathing was shallow and fast. Nothing to worry about, Kasi reassured himself; the nerves will keep her alert. "Remember," he whispered. "I'll create the diversion. You walk onto the stage, go to the edge, pick out the target, empty the clip, drop the weapon and walk off the same way you came in. Understand?"

Lejla clutched his sleeve. "My father," she said.

He heard the urgency in her voice, pulled her hand loose and touched the palm of his hand to her mouth. "Once we start down the stairs you have to keep going," he told her. "No matter what happens, get to the stage and do what you've been trained to do." He checked his watch.

"My father," she repeated.

"He'll soon be free," Kasi said.

Sylvia was startled by the swishing sound behind her and immediately let herself slide down the carpet runner that covered the marble stairs. Talia had no idea what had caused her companion's reaction, but as the American slid by she saw that she had her pistol in both hands pointing up the dark stairs. Taking the cue, she also moved down the stairs and ducked behind a post at the bottom.

The three Russians moved quickly through the upper halls, leapfrogging their way, taking turns on the point, hugging the walls, perspiring under the stress.

"The stairs should be through there," Bailov said as they saw a massive double door looming ahead of them. It was ajar. Bailov signaled for Melko to go first and to the right. He would go next and to the left. Gnedin was to move to the door and sit tight unless he heard something.

As soon as Melko got through the door he saw a woman's silhouette ahead and relaxed as he leaned against the wall. Was it Talia or the American? It was impossible to tell. It struck him as funny that though they were hunting for the Albanians they kept finding each other. It reminded him of the days when he had led the cops through Moscow; until Annochka betrayed him the closest they had ever gotten was the stale scent of a shit he had left hours before. He stepped toward the center of the hall. "So you didn't find them either?" he called softly to the woman at the head of the stairs. She glanced over her shoulder and started down. Strange behavior, he thought, and took a step forward.

He had the night eyes of a cat, Shehu had always said of him. Kasi saw the sliver of light at the door and a dark form move through it, the voice calling with familiarity, unsuspecting. He froze immediately behind the girl; she was on her way down. Let her go; there's time. Be calm.

· · ·

Sylvia saw the figure on the stairs and heard the rustling of her dress. She seemed to float down the stairs, her eyes straight ahead, her face serene. A pretty girl, and young, the same one she had seen sign in. She was wearing a black dress like the opera singer's. Had she herself ever been that young? The pistol grew heavier in her hands. You've never killed, she reminded herself. Some firsts were not worth waiting for. There wasn't enough light for a good shot. No matter, she thought; she'll come closer.

What was Melko thinking? Bailov saw the woman, immediately flicked his eyes left and right looking for the man, saw motion and lunged toward Melko, hoping he was not too late.

The head of the stairs lit with muzzle flashes. At least three, maybe more; it was impossible to count. A minor fireworks display without appreciable sound, only a whine of something nicking stone. The girl on the stairs paused and looked back. Sylvia started to get up but Talia flew past and crashed into the girl's legs, toppling her, wrestling with her as they rolled down the stairs. Sylvia threw herself on them and began pounding with the butt of the revolver. She had no idea who or what she was hitting.

Bailov heard Melko grunt as a slug struck him, and then the big man was down and both of them were firing at the muzzle flash ahead. Bailov fired, rolled left, fired again, rolled right and heard a silencer coughing from behind him as Gnedin moved up. There were no more muzzle flashes in front of them. He lay on the floor, breathing heavily.

"Shit," Melko swore from somewhere in the darkness.

Gnedin ran past them, approached the body at the top of the stairs, kicked it and got no reaction. At the bottom of the steps Talia and Sylvia were sitting on someone.

"Clear up here," he called softly.

"Everything's under control here," Talia answered. "Ours is alive."

Gnedin felt the throat of the man beside him. "This one's dead."

217   SATURDAY, JUNE 3, 1961, 10:52 P.M.
Vienna

Dieter Hinz had no idea what had gotten into the police, but they were in a foul mood, and given the proximity of such important guests, in a dangerous state of mind. The American had said it would be risky and he had been right. He wondered how long he had been here but there was no way to tell; the security man had taken his watch.

He had done exactly as Valentine instructed and driven to Schönbrunn, where he had asked the police to fetch a woman called Sylvia Charles. He had parked a kilometer away and worked his way through an unruly crowd, which included plenty of loudmouths carrying placards and shouting political slogans. You could always count on Americans to find something to bitch about—at least when it was safe.

When he got to the main gate he had asked for the woman and had been told to go away. When he persisted, he was blindsided by a policeman, handcuffed by another and dragged face down to a truck. They struck him several times with a leather sap, threw him inside and slammed the door shut. The inside of the truck was dark and had a lingering stench of piss. Hinz's knees were bloody, there were bits of gravel in his skin and the salty taste of blood in the back of his throat; his lower lip was split and swollen. All in all, not an auspicious way to to earn the money he had been promised. A number of times he had lain on his back and driven his feet into the thick rear door to create enough noise to get somebody's attention, but only once had he gotten a reaction, and it was not the one he had hoped for: a brute in a white helmet had climbed inside and kicked him several times with steel-toed boots.

Pain notwithstanding, Hinz knew there was no permanent injury. The police might brutalize him, but they wouldn't kill him; a corpse meant too much red tape. Circumstances be damned, he told himself. The American's money would soothe a lot of hurt, and in any event he was blessed with a hard head and had always healed fast. He began kicking the door again.

526

SATURDAY, JUNE 3, 1961, 11:20 P.M.
Vienna

Melko was lying along a wall chewing the end of an unlit cigarette, a fresh bandage wrapped tightly around his midsection, his shirt off, his tattoos glowing in the low light. The Albanian was dead; he had been hit four times. The body was covered by plastic left by the painters in the upper-level room. The Albanian girl was unconscious, her eyes swollen shut, several lacerations taped closed by Gnedin. Sylvia's pistol had done most of the damage. Talia had a swollen left eye as well and a small cut where she had been struck by the American's revolver during the scuffle.

General Zakharov sat on an antique chair surveying the scene. He had arrived only minutes before, looked at the Albanians and sat down. The General Secretary, the president and their retinues had departed the palace none the wiser. Talia's people had moved the dead and wounded and sealed off the area, and Spetsnaz men were already cleaning the hallway to remove any evidence.

Talia rubbed an ice cube on her eye. "They nearly got through," she told Zakharov. "She was dressed as one of the singers—a nun, of all things. He got her through the security lines in a police uniform, brought her into the building and left. The upper doors were all locked from the inside; he climbed up the outside wall, opened the door from the inside and led her up. He changed into a tuxedo; we think she was going to make the assault through the rehearsal room." Talia pointed at a small package on the floor. "Thermite with a three-second fuse. I think he probably planned to drop it as a diversion. Then the woman would come across the stage—"

"Think? You *think*?" Zakharov said, wiping his chin with the back of his hand.

Talia shot him a hard look. "Show him," she told Bailov, who handed the general an envelope.

"It's a rough seating chart," he said. "It shows the front row."

When Zakharov unfolded the drawing, a photograph slipped to the floor. He bent to pick it up and saw the smiling face of Nikita Khrushchev staring up at him.

"Each of them had a copy," Talia said softly.

219   SUNDAY, JUNE 4, 1961, 12:23 A.M.
Vienna

Hinz saw the outlines of people gathered over him, but couldn't make out their features. His eyes were nearly swollen shut from the beatings, but his spirit was intact. Their attitude in standing between him and the American's money had become a personal matter; they threatened to silence him permanently, but he kept insisting on seeing Miss Charles. As long as he had a voice the game was on, he reasoned.

Voices. "What's going on here?" a woman asked.

"Claims he has to talk to a woman named Miss Charles."

Melko eyed the muscle-bound policeman he had tangled with earlier. There was a bruise on the man's neck. He avoided Melko's grin and the bloodstain on his jacket. The man on the floor of the panel truck was a mess, not in any true danger, but they had really worked him over. A Russian cop would never mark a face like that, Melko thought; better to give a man hidden wounds. He had been on the receiving end in the camps often enough to know.

"We'll take over," Sylvia told an Austrian police sergeant. "I'm Miss Charles."

"He's our prisoner," the man insisted.

"Has he been charged?" she asked.

"Unlawful gathering."

"He was part of the demonstration?"

"Close enough."

"We'll take responsibility for him."

The police sergeant glanced at the man on the floor. "We've got his name. We can always take care of him later."

Fuck you, Hinz thought. He had left his identification in his cab and given them a false name. He supposed that the lack of papers had added to their hostility, but he had not stayed alive this long without understanding the fascist mentality. Would the woman be able to pay? If not, he decided that when he got back to the cathedral he would insist on immediate payment in American greenbacks, then get away from these crazy people.

Melko followed the police outside and blocked their view while Gnedin helped Hinz sit up.

"You asked for me?" Sylvia said.

"I want to see identification," the cabdriver said. It felt like several teeth had been loosened. She showed him a card with a photograph and he wished he could see more clearly. "Your friend says he would like to take you to Mass."

Gnedin and Sylvia looked at each other, not understanding. "At Saint Stephen's," Hinz added.

220   SUNDAY, JUNE 4, 1961, 12:28 A.M. *Vienna*

Valentine was exhausted by the time he and the Siberian reached the public sector of the catacombs housing the Ducal Vault. Their clothes were torn, their hands, elbows and knees raw, their faces black with coal dust that had mixed with sweat to form a kind of grease. The area had a neatly laid black-and-white tile floor—too neat, he guessed, to satisfy tourists with their hearts set on the macabre. "Nice atmosphere," he whispered to Ezdovo. The place reminded him of a cross between a Galveston barbershop and a New Orleans graveyard. The area near the vent tunnel was cluttered with stone biers and the Hapsburg burial vault containing copper urns filled with the intestines of several centuries of the royal line, their hearts and bodies being buried elsewhere; the logic of such separation escaped him, but the variety of human behavior was infinite, especially in its treatment of the dead.

"We're wasting time," Ezdovo said. He slipped into one of the robes supplied by the priest and moved ahead.

The area beyond was open but they moved cautiously when they found the door with four crosses; it was just beyond the entry to a small chapel with red cushions on its kneelers. The door was ajar, and there were lights in the dusty tunnel beyond. Valentine slid behind his companion and checked his pistol. "No silencers," he told the Siberian. "If there's a problem we can use the sound to locate each other."

Ezdovo nodded and dropped his silencer into his pocket.

A few yards down the tunnel they saw the switch for the lights, and along the ceiling they saw the wire the priest had described; it was threaded through grommets cut from stone. Valentine took a coin from his pocket, flipped it, caught it and pressed it against his hand. "Heads or tails?"

"For what?" the Siberian asked.

"To see who takes the point."

"I'll go first."

"Call it."

"Why?"

"It's an old American custom."

"Tails," the Siberian said.

Valentine lifted his hand just enough to peek. It was tails. "Heads," he said. "You lose."

He returned the coin to his pocket and started to move forward, but Ezdovo caught his arm. "I didn't see it," he growled.

The American twisted free. "That's another wrinkle of democracy," he said. "Secret ballot."

---

221   Sunday, June 4, 1961, 1:00 a.m.
Vienna

Bailov drove the truck while Gnedin worked on Hinz, who sat between them. He was conscious but battered, giving directions with hand signals and an occasional word to guide them to the center of the city and a location behind the archbishop's palace.

"What's this?" Melko asked as they turned into a pitch-black alley.

"I've brought you where I was told to."

As soon as the truck stopped and Sylvia and Talia had jumped down from the back a priest emerged from the darkness. "How many of you?" he asked.

"Four," Bailov answered.

"Where's my money?" Hinz asked. What did the priest have to do with these people?

"When we're done," Bailov said. "Remain with the truck."

The group descended a set of stone stairs to a cellar; there the priest pointed to a rack of hooded black robes. "Take what you need."

Father Good showed them the base of the coal chute and gave them flashlights and a hand-drawn map. "Years ago the catacombs were used as an escape system," he said. "They would enter from the center of the church—the current tourist entrance—and from the towers and altar. Your friend asked me to tell you that."

Sylvia stepped forward. "Why?"

The priest looked at his watch. "Your colleague said that I should remind you that in eight hours President Kennedy and his wife will arrive at St. Stephen's for Mass."

Sylvia kicked off her shoes and climbed into the coal chute. When she got to the vent tunnel she called down to the others, "It's really tight. We'll have to crawl."

Bailov took Melko's arm. "You're in no condition for this."

"He's right," Talia said, removing her shoes and turning to the priest. "Is this the only way in?"

"Until Brother Johann opens the tourist gate in the cathedral at ten A.M."

"Brother Johann?" Talia asked.

"The caretaker."

"Where is he?"

Father Good smiled. "Only God and Johann know. He sleeps somewhere in the tunnels."

When the team had disappeared up the chute Melko sat on the floor and lit a cigar. He would give them some time, then follow. Only Melko decides what Melko can't do, he told himself. The bullet had only nicked his side.

222   SUNDAY, JUNE 4, 1961, 1:25 A.M. *Vienna*

Albert wondered whether he had dozed off. He was moving slowly through the tunnel, which seemed to stretch to infinity. It doesn't go up, he told Ali; it doesn't feel right. He sensed that the tunnel had angled gently away from the end of the cathedral and that it would not connect with the sacristy, but Ali refused to listen, which was how it had always been.

223	**SUNDAY, JUNE 4, 1961, 1:30 A.M.** *Vienna*

It had been interesting to see Kharlamov and Salinger, the official Soviet and American spokesmen, sitting together on a stage at the Hofburg Palace. In previous summits the two sides had issued individual statements, usually from separate locations. Sometimes the opposing briefings were held at the same time, which made for head-to-head competition and gave each camp a rough idea of who had captured the most press interest. But yesterday afternoon there had been a thousand journalists jammed together in the same theater, crawling all over one another like shrimp in a basket, the noise unbelievable, the reporters' manners barbaric—par for the course, Arizona reminded himself.

Neither spokesman had said much of substance and both had smiled a lot in an effort to demonstrate genuine goodwill for the other. It was pretty convincing, Arizona admitted to himself; even the most skeptical journalists seemed filled with optimism. A very good show indeed.

Now he was back in the CIA office in the embassy with so much caffeine in his system that it kept him awake only in the technical sense; his thoughts were skipping and jumping haphazardly. Dinner at the Schönbrunn Palace had gone off with no major hitches; he had heard that someone in the Soviet delegation had been taken ill, but the Russians had assured everyone that it was nothing serious, which might or might not be the truth. The bastards tended to distort even the most inconsequential facts, a practice that the Company understood to be Soviet strategy; if you lied about everything all the time your enemy had to work twice as hard to sort out what was really happening. But now the day was over, there were no signs of Valentine, Charles or their Soviet pals, and everyone was on his best behavior. It was downright bizarre.

532

224 · SUNDAY, JUNE 4, 1961, 2:45 A.M.
Vienna

The air was cool but their robes were heavy and made them sweat. They took turns leading, each of them sticking close to the walls. The corridor led them past bins filled with chalky bones, containers cut into the earthen walls like sleepers on an overnight train. Several times huge brown rats leaped out and ran squealing down the tunnel. When the bins ran out they found rooms cut into the sides. These were three meters square and packed with remains. One room contained rows of skulls stacked like bottles of vintage wine; others contained other parts, but most of them were a mixed jumble. In some places bulbs were burned out, and whenever they got to a dark stretch they slowed down. They had just passed through such an area when the Siberian sank to one knee and held up a hand. Valentine edged his way forward and kept to the far wall. "The floor's been dusted," Ezdovo said.

Valentine saw that his companion was tense. "This whole place is a dust bin," he whispered.

The Siberian touched his fingers to the floor, brought them to his lips and grimaced. "Talcum and cinnamon," he said. "Part of a security system. Primitive but effective." He reached forward, poked at a thread dangling along the wall and held it up for Valentine to see.

Further on Ezdovo stopped again, knelt and touched the dirt.

"More cinnamon?" Valentine asked.

"Blood," the Siberian said, sniffing like an animal. "Fresh."

225 · SUNDAY, JUNE 4, 1961, 3:20 A.M.
Vienna

The tunnel ended abruptly at a concave wall made of gray cobblestones fitted tightly together. No cement, which suggested that it was more than one layer deep. Albert tapped the stones with a human femur, the sound an unresponsive click. There was no way through; it might as well be Hoover Dam. It was a dead end, like the inside of a stone condom. He retreated a few meters and squatted, holding the femur out like a golfer gauging a difficult putt. The stairs to the sacristy had been cut off. No way up, Ali wailed softly, no way up. Albert felt Ali's adrenaline kick in and tried to resist. Don't panic, he cautioned himself. Control your breathing, stay calm, think.

Talia's left eye was swollen shut, every exertion sending a searing pain through her head, but she hid this from the others. The bothersome thing was that they had no indication that the renegade American was here, but Ezdovo and the American called Valentine had called for help, which meant they suspected something. How had her husband ended up with the American? Hunters, she guessed. Similar instincts and a need for solitude. The group had been impressed at how Ezdovo had tracked Mock to her flat, and they had all seen his rage at finding the Austrian woman dead and Frash gone. Teamwork had been neater under Petrov's leadership, she chastised herself. The catacombs were eerie and cramped. Until she found Ezdovo she would worry. Two units without coordination were a threat to each other.

Sylvia moved to Talia's side, sensing her concern. "We should keep moving."

Talia put the priest's map on the floor. The basic pattern of the tunnel system under the cathedral was a Y, with the right branch the path to the blocked-off sacristy and the left one stretching away to uncharted tunnels that eventually connected to Vienna's underground. This area, the priest said, was the most dangerous because it was not part of the original catacombs and suffered frequent cave-ins. Ezdovo would wait at the intersection of the Y she guessed; if Frash was trying to get to the sacristy he would be in the right branch and could be trapped there until the force reunited.

Sylvia touched Talia's back. "They'll wait for us," she said.

Albert felt his control slipping as he ducked in and out of the burial vaults, desperately searching for another way forward rather than retreating back through the tunnel.

By the time they reached the intersection even Valentine could see that somebody had tried to brush the blood trail clean. Ezdovo found faint footprints. They were as clear to him as if he were reading a book. "Deeper here," he said, pointing to a print. "The weight has shifted to the heel, which means he's carrying something heavy." A wounded man? The blood suggested someone was hurt.

Valentine wanted to go on, but the Siberian stopped him. "We'll wait here for the others. If he's ahead we have him trapped."

"He's there," the American said. "I can feel him."

As soon as he got into the vault Ali knew something was different, but it took a while to sort it out. The floor was cluttered with neat islands of human bones, some of the piles as high as his waist. There was room to move, not a lot but enough. Some skulls had dried flesh and pieces of hair still stubbornly clinging to them, like his clinging to the dream. Or was it a nightmare? The truth of the room opened to him like a gradual sunrise. Its dimensions were different, not in size but in shape. Even the bone piles had new meaning, islands in a small sea. He skirted them slowly, knowing there was a through passage here, but he discovered it only when he brushed against a pile of bones that didn't rattle and give like the others. When he got hold of it and pulled, it raised up. Shining his light on the pile, he saw that the bones had been secured together and that the mass attached to a small trapdoor. Instincts intact; the Church taught the one true path to its flocks but never closed all its own options. Disguise them, yes; obliterate them, no. He shone the light into the hole. Solid earth, polished by use. He moved in, leaving the trapdoor open behind him.

Talia made the soft clicking sound of a ptarmigan, heard it repeated ahead and saw Ezdovo step out of a shadow. She wanted to run to him but knew better; discipline counted now. She saw his concern when he looked at her. "The Albanians," she said. "Finished."

Valentine heard shuffling behind him; then the Siberian appeared, leading the others. Sylvia came last, her face streaked with coal dust. "He's here," he told her as she slid her hand to his waist, let it linger briefly and withdrew it. "We were at Mock's laboratory and saw how the cellar was walled off. There's an underground beneath the old city and it's connected to the cathedral. It hit me when we were in it. Kennedy will be here tomorrow."

"Today," she said, checking her watch. "In six hours."

"It's ideal," he said. "There's no way for security to search it thoroughly even if they had been allowed to, and the archbishop apparently put the kibosh on that."

"Seems almost obvious," she told him. "Too easy. How would he have known?"

"How does an animal know anything?" Valentine said. "Besides, we don't have him yet."

Albert smiled when he emerged into another room; this one had a small altar in the corner, a bed, an empty bookcase and several kerosene lanterns. The monk's private hideaway, he guessed, and best of all, another tunnel, smaller than the main one, but running parallel, a possible way around the dead end, the Church's predictability not disappointing him. An institution couldn't survive nearly two thousand years on absolutes. Mother would appreciate how well he had learned to read their foes. His heartbeat was normal, his pulse slow and regular, whereas Ali's adrenals were as fierce as fire storms; his own were slower to ignite and once lit, fast-burning, over and done with, and in that sense more human. What to do when the secret voices were yours but not yours? Mother never appreciated this; she wrote it off to late maturity, as if a full allotment of testosterone would stiffen his manhood and silence his wretched voices. Use me. He saw her face, sweaty, eyes rolled back, lips drawn tightly over her teeth. Deeper, she said as he stared into the tunnel. Not yet, Albert said.

The tension was heavy. Talia knew that safety dictated posting someone at the intersection, but when she told the group none of them was interested in volunteering. She understood; they needed action now to finish what had been started. She wanted this as much as any of them, but repressed her feelings, understanding now how Petrov must have been torn when he sent them out and remained behind. They were gone, leaving her with her thoughts. If they ran into trouble they would use the walkie-talkie.

Back in the main tunnel Frash saw nothing. It was time to hide his trail. He pushed a bone under the electrical wire and pulled down softly. The bulbs along the corridor flickered before he broke the circuit and ducked back into his newly found escape route.

When the lights surged Valentine looked toward Sylvia, but they were in darkness before her face registered. The team froze. "The switch is back near the entrance," Valentine said loud enough for all of them to hear.

"Be still," Ezdovo said with a growl. "I heard something ahead. Scraping."

The walkie-talkie crackled and Bailov fumbled to turn down the sound. "Is there a problem?" Talia asked. Even at low volume her voice seemed to echo in the close confines.

"Maintain radio silence," Bailov said quickly. "No contact unless there's imminent danger." Tight fits like these tunnels wouldn't allow much room to maneuver.

Albert heard the radio and knew he was no longer alone. Fuck them, Ali said, we have to push on. Careful, Albert countered weakly, there's no room for error now. Who was he talking to? He had trusted Mother and Lumbas. My way now, Ali said. He had a picture of Kennedy in his mind.

Using his light, Ezdovo saw the bone along the wall; above it was the broken wire. Why here? he wondered as the rest of the group caught up; the end was nowhere in sight. He shone his light on the wire long enough for them to see it, then clicked it off. He remembered the long journey under the monastery in Moscow, and how it included blind alleys, false leads and traps. Were Russian Orthodox minds any different from their Roman kin's?

"Why've we stopped?" Bailov asked.

The Siberian flashed his light again, this time illuminating the bone by the wall. "Not an accident," he said as he moved into the closet ossuary, came out, went into the next one and was gone nearly ten minutes. When he emerged from the second one he switched on his light and waved for them to follow.

It had taken him no time at all to see the signs that led to the phony stack of bones and amateurishly disguised trapdoor. The others seemed bewildered when he showed them. "He went down here."

"What about the main tunnel?" Bailov asked. "This may be nothing."

"Talia has the intersection blocked," Ezdovo pointed out.

"If you're wrong we could be trapped down there," Bailov told him.

"You shouldn't worry, your worships," a familiar voice boomed from the entrance to the room.

Sylvia was closest and snapped her light on. Melko's face was contorted in pain but through it he managed a crooked grin. "Talia told me I should stay with her, but I don't like being left behind. Follow Ezdovo," he said, sitting down heavily and clearing away some rubble. "If someone is down the main tunnel they'll have to pass me." Then, "Go on. All this talk is noisy. I've gotten used to the silence down here."

The small tunnel twisted left at a 90-degree angle and opened into the main tunnel a few meters beyond where it had been walled off. A quick look told Frash that the wall that had initially blocked him was two meters thick or more; that he had so easily bypassed it was a reminder that not all things are as they seem to be. If the schedule he had gotten from Mock was accurate he had three hours to reach his objective. Plenty of time, even with company.

Ezdovo eased his head into the inner chamber and listened for a long time to be sure there was no ambush. Valentine covered him from the hole in the floor while he made a quick circuit and found the exit tunnel. There were fresh marks on the floor and dangling pieces of cobwebs where someone had passed through.

Albert trotted through the tunnel, his light bobbing as the dirt floor sloped gently upward.

The other three followed him out of the bypass into the main tunnel, dropping quietly from the opening to the hard-packed floor. The Siberian flicked his light off and on, barely long enough to do more than ruin the group's night vision, but long enough for him to see the trail in the dust. There seemed to be no side rooms in this area. "No lights," he whispered. They moved forward, two to a side, one behind the other, Valentine ahead of Sylvia, Ezdovo leading Bailov.

The iron door was more hatch than door, and old, held in place with a flat iron bar. Two ancient padlocks hung open on pegs beside the door, and it took him a moment to understand the rationale. An escape hatch would be locked from the inside to slow pursuit. There would be no locks on the other side, though dummy ones were possible as camouflage. He tried the bar with his hands, but it was wedged tight and rusty. He thought he felt cool air along the seams. A bar this substantial could not be put in place easily. He shone his light around the end of the tunnel and smiled when he saw a small sledge suspended by a metal ring in the ceiling. So predictable. Had the Church's leaders ever considered that a way out for them could become a way in for their enemies? The thought made Ali laugh. How would Kennedy react when there was a pistol pointed at his tanned face?

The half-dozen metallic blows that reverberated down the tunnel startled the group. These sounds were followed by a shrill scream cut short, the way a cornered animal stifled its cry, Ezdovo thought. Even the most harmless creatures could be dangerous when injured, and this was the sound of a man, which multiplied the danger manyfold.

Ali writhed on the floor, stunned, trying to figure out what had happened. The last blow had loosened the iron bar. He had braced a leg against the wall beside the hatch when something ripped into his support leg and sent him crashing down. When he touched the leg he felt the bones protruding through the skin. Fuck. The leg was destroyed, useless. He pounded the ground in frustration, his rage growing. Not now, Albert's inner voice repeated over and over, but it was quickly banished by Ali, whose rage was hot and unrelenting. He dragged himself back to the hatch, pushed up on his good leg and began trying to dislodge the iron bar again.

There was an open iron door and stairs beyond, with a dull light filtering down from above. Ezdovo squatted at the hatch and studied a huge slab of stone that hung at the end of a cable on a pulley system.

"Booby trap?" Valentine asked as he squeezed next to him.

How many had he and Melko gone by in Lenya's underground maze? "There could be more," Ezdovo cautioned. He saw splashes of fresh blood on the floor, which explained the scream they had heard. "Brother Johann would have known about such surprises," he added.

"Frash," Valentine said, his heart racing. The stairs ahead were narrow, with room for only one person at a time. "We have to string out," he told Sylvia. "Single file."

Ezdovo pulled up his hood and went through first, with Valentine, Sylvia and Bailov following.

The stairs curved right. When the Siberian made a clicking sound the others halted below him and waited.

Another hatch; this one slid sideways. Ezdovo pulled it back slowly and looked through a screen into a hall with a marble floor. He eased into the opening, pulled the second cover back, rolled onto the cool marble and breathed fresh air into his lungs. Moving to the other side of the corridor he saw that he had come out of the bottom of a bulky wooden cabinet, its shelves lined with candle holders. When Valentine's head appeared behind him Ezdovo motioned him to come through. There were drops of blood on the marble. The blood led them into an octagonal room filled with built-in closets and cabinets. A metal door opened onto the square; a set of double wooden doors led to the back of the altar. There was no more blood.

Ezdovo knelt beside a wall, alert but not nervous. Different prey, but only a hunt, one more in a lifetime of them. Expect the unexpected, he warned himself.

Ali grinned at the prospects. He had the injured leg tied off now; a crucifix twisted into his belt had served to tighten the tourniquet. There were four of them. Monks. He had seen their robes. Setting up for Mass, preparing priests' tools. No hurry. Let them settle in and get busy. The sun was rising, shooting arrows of light into the room. Wait. Let the light get brighter; let them immerse themselves in their tasks. Only one was left now; the others had moved out of view. He had heard the door to the altar area open. He pulled up his hood and prepared himself. It would be difficult to get rid of the bodies, but it was not far to the place where he had come out. They would be safe there. He would have to clean the area

as well, and fix the damned leg, but time was on his side. He rechecked
the weapon to be sure the silencer was snug and admired the workmanship, his own. Such a simple thing to make, yet so deadly. Where was
Albert? You can't miss this, he said gleefully, but there was no response.
What was Kennedy doing right now?

Sylvia leaned against the wall, her body a collection of aches, her
hair matted. Just beyond the light she saw the dusty outline of where a
crucifix had hung on the wall, and where the light hit it just right a faint
trickle of something. A flaw? She touched it with her finger, saw the red
wetness and the trail her finger left. Sweet Jesus, she thought as she
turned.

Ali pushed the handle upward and eased the door open. Upward
pressure always seemed to reduce squeaks; it countered the warping, he
supposed. He felt light-headed. The monk in front of him had a broad
back. A huge man and an easy target. Take the back, not the head; less
blood that way. The monk in the tunnel had bled like a stuck pig. Aim
for the midline and offset a couple of fingers left. It would be easy. One
here, but where were the others? At the altar? Because of the leg he
couldn't pursue them; take this one now and get the others as they come
back. The altar is sacred. Keep it that way. Mother would understand.
His mother, his father, son to son, a good way to settle it. The Lek would
be honored. Kennedy would die today.

Valentine felt a bump, then heard a clatter and turned to find Frash
less than an arm's length away, his eyes wide, mouth open, shuddering,
not continuously but in surges, now, again, like a dance, his chin shaking,
his pistol spinning in slow motion across the floor, the silencer shattering,
its washers rolling free as he pivoted lazily, sinking onto his shattered leg,
popping the tourniquet, eased to the floor by Sylvia with her small arm
around his face and a knife in her other hand, the blade and her hand
glistening with fresh blood turning orange in the morning light, a deep
red wound under Frash's chin, a stain spreading like a bib. When the
Russians returned they found her sitting beside the body, holding the
knife up like an offering to the light flooding through the windows.

226 SUNDAY, JUNE 4, 1961, 6:50 A.M.
Vienna

Father Martin Good stared at the two bodies and blessed himself. Though his face was bloody, Brother Johann looked peaceful. Where were the others?

"Real sorry about this," Valentine said, "but we've got a damage-control problem here and we need help." The American had fetched him from the archbishop's palace.

"What happened?"

"Brother Johann got walloped and died instantly." Valentine toed a length of bone. "This here was the murder weapon." God made some heads stronger than others.

"I don't understand," the priest stammered, his legs rubbery.

"You want to protect the Church, right, Father?"

The priest nodded.

"Good. That's going to make this a lot easier." Valentine escorted the priest down the tunnel. "Brother Johann fell and hit his head. His death was an accident."

"I can't do this," the priest protested.

"You have no choice. Things happened down here that neither we nor the Church can afford to have come to light. Remember, it was the archbishop who blocked a proper search."

Father Marty drew in a deep breath, bowed his head and made the sign of the cross in the air.

"An accident," Valentine repeated. "For the good of the Church. Go back to the Archbishop's Palace. Wait until noon, then call for help. Tell the authorities Brother Johann didn't show up to open the tourist gates. When they get down there they'll find him. It will look like an accident."

"God help me," Father Good said as he stumbled away.

God help all of us, Valentine thought as he went to find the others.

The Russians placed Brother Johann's body at the exact spot where it had fallen, then swept the area clean of any sign of Frash. Valentine and Sylvia built a wall of cobblestones behind the iron door that led to the sacristy; if anyone ever again discovered the escape tunnel they would never get past the door. They interred Frash's remains in Brother Johann's sanctuary, filled the hole under the trapdoor behind them and scattered bones across the floor of the room to a height of four feet, leaving it looking like just another cave of yellowed remains. Someday, perhaps, someone would find Frash's bones, but who would think twice about another skeleton in an underground filled with them?

The team made their way back to the basement of the Archbishop's Palace and up the rear stairs, where they helped Melko into the waiting truck. When the Russians got in, the Americans stayed outside. Talia made eye contact with them, nodded almost imperceptibly and slid the door shut.

227 SUNDAY, JUNE 4, 1961, 10:08 A.M. *Vienna*

Arizona watched the Kennedys walk smiling from the cathedral to their limousine. A cloud of blue exhaust trailed up behind the vehicle as it sped away from the crowd that had gathered to have a look at the young president and his wife. More women than men, more young than old, he saw. Maybe Kennedy's aides had rounded them up the way they did during the primaries.

He spotted Valentine in the rear of the dispersing crowd. "Never figured you for a churchie," Arizona said as he reached him.

"Only funerals," Valentine said. "You can scratch Frash off your do-next list."

"Dead?"

"And buried."

"How?"

"Details don't matter."

"They do to me."

"They mattered to Harry Gabler and look where it got him. A man in your line of work ought to be accustomed to ambiguity."

"I had nothing to do with Gabler's death," Arizona said too quickly.

"And nothing to do with keeping him alive, which is the other side of the coin. You sent us into this thing blind, but we handled it. Frash is no longer a problem, which means end of deal." Valentine handed him an envelope filled with every scrap of paper he and Sylvia had collected along the way. "For the archives."

Arizona's eyes narrowed. "He was here?"

"He wanted Kennedy."

"How close did he get?"

Valentine smiled. "Feet and minutes," he said over his shoulder as he merged with the Sunday crowd.

228   MONDAY, JUNE 5, 1961, NOON
Moscow

Meetings were under way at the Defense Ministry, but Malinovsky had no desire now to discuss steel allotments with sweaty comrades, no interest in failures to meet production quotas at the Kharkov tank factory or the desertion of a company of besotted Tadzhiks from a garrison regiment in Vilnius. He went into his study, whose brocade curtains were closed, and sat behind the massive mahogany desk in semidarkness. When the phone rang he picked it up without identifying himself.

"The General Secretary boarded a plane an hour ago," a hushed voice said.

"To Berlin?"

"To Moscow. The change was announced privately last night. No reason was given. Air, not rail, destination Moscow, not Berlin."

Malinovsky hung up, unlocked a desk drawer, took out a dusty bottle of Armagnac and set it in front of him. Indonesia's Sukarno would arrive today for a state visit, and all the arrangements had been made for handling it in Khrushchev's absence. Now he was returning to Moscow. Obviously something had gone wrong; the Albanians had not reacted to plan. Bastards.

Nikita Sergeievich traveled by train when he felt at peace. Aircraft meant speed and a worried peasant. When the cat's away, the mice will play. The Armagnac had been bottled in 1812, perhaps in the very month that Napoleon stood on the field at Borodino thinking that the battle was won when it had only begun. What was going on now in the cloudberry mind of Khrush the Beetle? Surely the General Secretary knew now that the battle had been joined and that the enemy was close at hand. His change in plans said he knew. He was alive, but something had happened. Not as good as he hoped, but as surely as Napoleon fell, Khrushchev had begun his descent. Malinovsky opened the bottle and poured just enough of the amber liquid to cover the bottom of the champagne glass.

"Self-discipline is an enviable trait," a voice rasped from the darkness across the room.

The defense minister was startled but concealed his surprise. When a light snapped on across the room he squinted to see who it was and tapped the base of his desk to release a small drawer next to his knee.

"Petrov," the voice said.

Glancing into the drawer, he saw that the revolver was gone; in its place there was a gleaming Red Badge.

"So predictable," Petrov said. "So old-fashioned and true to the species *Homo militarus*. But I applaud your subtlety, Comrade Marshal; the pieces were carefully played."

The man under the dim light was small and dark, his eyes sunk into his head, the flesh on his skull tight and opaque, a shrunken head with the power of speech. The revolver from the defense minister's desk was in his hand.

Malinovsky considered triggering the alarm.

"Disconnected," Petrov said. "Like us, the alarm system is an anachronism. Mere wire, comrade, severed with mere scissors. A photoelectric cell would be more effective. It's time you came to grips with modern gadgetry."

"What do you want?"

"Your plan was so seamless as to be invisible," Petrov said. "Which made it predictable," the final word drawn out. "Nevertheless, I must congratulate you."

When Malinovsky shifted in his chair the revolver shifted with him. For the first time in years, he felt a fluttering of nerves, a sense of terror creeping over him like a wet cloak. "A man who enters another's house could be taken for a common thief."

Petrov smiled. "Righteous words from a man trying to steal an entire nation."

The defense minister eased back in his chair. Had he miscalculated the American or the Albanians? Was Khrushchev hurrying home as he had in 1957, when his throne was in jeopardy? "I'm a soldier," he said in a voice filled with resolve. "I don't deal in the riddles of a madman."

Petrov nodded, though not in affirmation. "Motive," he said softly. "Motive. One takes the possibilities and examines them carefully, as delicately as one handles the wings of lepidoptera. After all of the possibilities have been eliminated, that which remains would be the answer. One stands in the forest looking for the stag, but doesn't see it until its camouflage is deciphered; only then does it stand out clearly." A long pause, a shift of weight, a soft wheeze. "I see you now, Malinovsky, as clearly as that stag. Did you think you could undo what's done and turn the clock back?" A bony hand waved at his desk. "What vintage do you hoard?"

"1812."

A protracted sigh. "Borodino. Of course, it *would* be Borodino. Napoleon wins the day, but the main force of the czar flees to fight again, to find victory in defeat, the Russian way of sacrifice for the greater good. But then who is the enemy, Malinovsky, the Frenchman or the czar? Did those who fell in the imperial cause lay down their lives for nothing? Did 1917 erase what those before had given? Why is it, my dear Marshal, that we Russians make heroes out of failures? The greater the needless bloodshed, the greater a man's mistakes, the more we love him. Tell me why this is so."

The man was weak, the color of wax, but to charge him would be a foolish gesture; he was too far away. The blood that trickled from his nose was black, lacking oxygen. There was no threat here, only a small impediment. "All who fall in the defense of the Motherland fall in honor."

Vision failing, Petrov saw the truth in the old general's eyes. "The old cavalryman longs for the clatter of his troops on the march," he said. "Old-fashioned honor. There's no honor in a missile dropping silently from the sky if the cost is tradition. I understand, Comrade Marshal. Sad to say, I too live by old principles."

"To do what must be done," Malinovsky said, "what others fear to do. Not all men are capable of that."

"Fetch me a glass," Petrov said, his voice barely a whisper, blood now issuing from his mouth. "A glass of Borodino. I long for a taste of history."

Malinovsky approached carefully and held the glass out to the man, who at close range seemed even smaller than from behind the desk.

Petrov took the glass with his left hand, which shook with small tremors; the hand with the revolver remained steady. When he began to laugh, Malinovsky took a step backward. "Nikita Sergeievich is right," Petrov said. "The past has been wasted, comrade."

"You're insane."

"No argument," Petrov said. "We're all insane to someone. That's exactly the point, but I'm impressed that you see it now."

"I see nothing except you."

"The Chinese built a wall around themselves," Petrov said. Malinovsky did not react. "Do you understand the purpose of a wall?"

"To keep people in."

Petrov sighed. "You *don't* see. A wall is most useful for keeping the unwanted out. The missiles make no difference either way."

"Enough nonsense," Malinovsky said with a growl and turned, but the sound of the revolver hammer being cocked froze him in place.

"Old armies, new missiles, neither of them matter," Petrov said. "They never did. I see that now. The wall is down forever. Others will be built, but down they'll come until there are no rubles left to build them. Guns and butter, my dear Malinovsky, guns and butter, with all men equal by economic principle. Now do you see it?"

"Yes," the Defense Minister said in an attempt to shut him up. Could he roll behind the cover of the desk, bolt to the door, call for help?

"No, you don't. If you had to pick a single weapon to win the next war, what would it be?" Petrov asked. "Just one, mind you."

Malinovsky heard the pain in the voice behind him, heard the death rattle in the man's chest and turned to face him. "Tanks."

Petrov shook his head. "You have no sense of history. What single factor won the Great Patriotic War?"

"Our gallant and heroic people and the leadership of the Red Army."

"Capitalism," Petrov whispered. "Without Western production there would be no statues today, and when the war ended they switched to making toasters *and* tanks. *Now* is it clear? They grow while we tread water. Ten years, twenty, thirty, pick a time; they will have toasters and tanks *and* missiles, and we will have only tanks and missiles and no way to feed or clothe our people. We're open to the world now, all of us, open for all of them to see and understand that Lenin was wrong. I saw it during the war. I realized it then; I *knew*. Khrushchev's missiles are not the problem. It's the toasters that our people want, and the Ukrainian has opened a door that can never be closed again. The end has begun, comrade, and there is no way you can stop it."

"How did you find me?" the Defense Minister asked.

"Does it matter? What one can do, another can duplicate. You had best dwell on that."

"Khrushchev will fall," Malinovsky insisted.

"Eventually," Petrov said, "but who has won?" He gulped the Armagnac, stared at the glass, smiled and dropped the pistol, his head tipping forward.

Malinovsky remained still for a long time, then kicked the pistol away, placed his fingers on the man's throat and felt no life.

Epilogue

The birches were covered with leaves the color of ripe limes and drooped under the weight of an early morning drizzle. Six Spetsnaz soldiers in black uniforms carried the unadorned open pine coffin down a narrow gravel path in Novodevichy Cemetery, the final resting place for the Soviet Union's elite. Talia wore a black cape, which flapped in the breeze; she held Ezdovo's arm tightly, using him to shield her from the wind. Bailov wore his dress uniform and pushed a wheelchair holding Raya Orlava, who snuggled under a dark raincoat. Melko wore a baggy brown suit with no tie and walked slowly beside Gnedin, who had his hands clasped behind him. The women had black scarves tied over their heads.

Two more Spetsnaz walked behind the mourners carrying the coffin lid, which was draped in red crepe that rustled in the breeze.

The procession passed slowly through the crowded graveyard, past red enamel stars, bronze busts and life-sized marble statues. It struck Talia that only in death did her countrymen get the recognition they had craved in life. One grave was topped by a full-sized propeller hub from a Stuka; it was painted with a swirl of red and yellow lines, and the nubs of what had been propeller blades were adorned with dozens of black swastikas in small white circles. The grave of an Arctic explorer was marked by a marble snowshoe on a white pedestal; a small bronze submarine seemed to surface from another stone.

When they reached the grave, the soldiers set the casket on the ground beside the trench and backed away as the others formed a circle. Talia placed her hands on Ezdovo's shoulders and felt one of his hands cover hers. Petrov looked tiny in the wooden box, the Red Badge on his chest gleaming in the morning light.

They were not sure what had happened. No one had seen him slip away from the hospital. City sanitation workers had found the body the next morning sitting open-eyed on a bench, staring out at the Moscow River, close to the place where Talia had first met the leader of the Special Operations Group more than sixteen years before. He had been as enigmatic then as he looked now, his hands clasped across his tiny stomach. The autopsy had attributed the cause of death to stomach cancer. "Filled with it," the pathologist told them.

Why had he left the hospital? Talia wondered, knowing they would never know.

She placed her own Red Badge on Petrov's chest and leaned down to kiss his cold flesh. Ezdovo, Gnedin, Bailov and Melko followed; then Bailov placed the lid on the coffin and nailed it down. When he had finished, the soldiers lowered the box into the grave and each member of the Special Operations Group threw a handful of black dirt onto the red crepe in the darkness below.

230   FRIDAY, JUNE 21, 1961, 1:10 P.M.
 Galveston, Texas

It was a scorcher, the air thick, the white sand searing, a violet wall of heat shimmering menacingly on the muddy green horizon of the Gulf of Mexico.

Sylvia took off her sunglasses, closed her eyes and tilted her face up at the sun, which glared red through her eyelids.

Four surf rods, upright in the sand, stood at the water's edge like black antennae; Valentine squatted between them cutting pieces of squid for bait. They had been in the sun constantly since returning from Europe. He wore a sweat-stained Stetson with the front bent up and saggy jockey shorts.

They had not talked about Vienna and had not discussed their own situation. She had gone to the airport with him in Vienna, watched him buy two tickets, taken the one he held out to her, and asked what the weather would be like on the Gulf. "So hot it makes the lizards sweat," he answered.

Sylvia rolled off the blanket and walked down to the surf. He was reeling in one of the baits and standing knee-deep in the rolling surf.

"What are we fishing for?" she asked.

"Whatever Neptune sends."

"He hasn't sent much." She smiled.

When Valentine had replaced the bait, he waded over to her and handed the ten-foot-long rod to her. "Your throw." The glare made him squint. His tan was more red than brown.

She looked at the rod, then at him. "Meaning?"

"Time we made a decision."

"I thought we were here to fish."

"I *hate* fishing."

"You want me to just walk away from the Company?" Sylvia asked.

"If that's what you want."

"And we ride off into the sunset together? Is that how you see it?"

"Pretty much," he said. Two pelicans skimmed the water twenty yards away and splashed to a landing.

"Man and wife. *That* sort of thing?"

"I reckon."

"We just forget about Vienna and get on with our lives?"

"That's about the size of it."

The pelicans were joined by a third that landed between them, but they flapped their wings furiously and drove it away. "We're gonna wake up one morning and find Arizona in our faces," Sylvia said.

Valentine grinned. "You ever hear about the two armadillos that met up with a mountain lion on the trail and one of them up and spit in the cat's eye?"

She raised her eyebrows and looped her arms around his neck. "No."

" 'Why did you do that?' the second armadillo asked. 'Well,' said the first one, 'I figured that I'd get his attention while you slipped around and jumped him from behind.' 'Hell,' said the second one, 'don't you know two armadillos can't lick a mountain lion?' 'You know and I know,' said the first one, 'but does the lion?' "

231   SUNDAY, AUGUST 13, 1961, 1:25 A.M. *West Berlin*

Arizona stared down at Potsdamer Platz, where searchlights knifed the night mist as thousands of East Germans worked shoulder to shoulder along the square. The air was filled with the faint reverberations of jackhammers and picks, the roar of bulldozers pushing huge rolls of barbed wire down cobbled streets, and the unmuffled growl of tanks. After watching for several minutes he let his binoculars hang around his neck as he lit a cigarette, hiding the light of the flame in a cupped hand. Less than an hour ago he had been asleep in his hotel, secure in the knowledge that nothing was brewing in Berlin other than the usual minor one-on-one provocations and surveillance schemes. Now, from a suite of offices on the ninth story of a building owned by a West German bank, he had an excellent view of the frantic activity below.

Curtis, the chief of station, was using a Leica with a telephoto lens and fast film to snap photographs of the German work details building the wall. He was the sort of careerist who usually hid his intensity under a mask of affability, but tonight he made no effort to disguise his concern. "What the hell are they up to?" he asked as he wound in a new roll of film.

"Mitosis," Arizona said. "Two cells from one." What they were really doing was measuring the size of Kennedy's balls. Khrushchev had gotten a look at them in Vienna and now it was squeeze time. The unofficial word was that the Soviet leader had talked exceptionally tough at the summit and that Kennedy had flinched. Which might be a plausible explanation for all this, but wasn't the only one. Valentine and Charles were now watching sunsets on Galveston Island like two lovebirds. According to his informants they had shown up in Texas a week after the summit and had made no effort to contact him.

Valentine said Frash was dead, and he'd had that look which Arizona had seen many times before. If Valentine said Frash was dead, then it was true, which meant that he could relax. The Company was going to be house-cleaned soon, but he would be able to stay clear of the worst of it. Even so, he was still curious. He had even considered going to Galveston to confront the lovebirds, but had decided against it. Valentine and Sylvia were too wed to pedestrian moral principles to see the bigger picture, so they could stay where they were and good riddance. She had submitted her resignation but he had not processed it; her pay would keep going to a bank, and Valentine would move to a list called "inactive but available."

Maybe he would never need them again and maybe he would. Never say never in this business, he reminded himself.

"Do the Russians think they can get away with this shit?" Curtis asked, snapping Arizona back to the present.

"Looks like they already have," he answered.

"I can't believe that Khrushchev would risk a war over Berlin," Curtis said.

A long line of tanks was setting up along a boulevard below as foot soldiers scrambled to pile sandbags around them. The question is, Arizona thought, Will Kennedy?

ABOUT THE AUTHOR

JOSEPH HEYWOOD was born in Rhinebeck, New York, and graduated from high school the week John F. Kennedy and Nikita Khrushchev met in Vienna. He holds a B.A. in journalism from Michigan State University and did graduate work in English literature at Western Michigan University.

Mr. Heywood is a U.S.A.F. veteran who grew up in an Air Force family. He has spent more than twenty years in corporate public relations, and his travels have taken him to Russia, China and scores of other countries. He lives in Portage, Michigan, and currently is working on his fourth novel, a thriller set in contemporary Russia.

ABOUT THE TYPE

This book was set in Sabon, a typeface designed by the well-known German typographer, Jan Tschichold (1902–74). Sabon's design is based upon the original letter forms of Claude Garamond, and was created specifically to be used for three sources: foundry type for hand composition, Linotype, and Monotype. Tschichold named his typeface for the famous Frankfurt typefounder Jacques Sabon, who died in 1580.

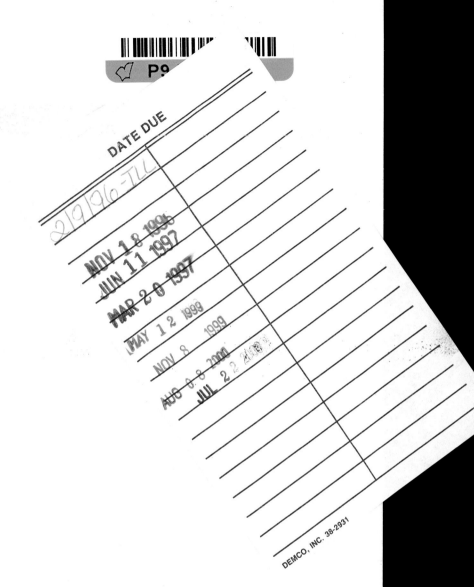

NUREMBERG
INFAMY ON TRIAL

JOSEPH E. PERSICO

NUREMBERG

INFAMY ON
TRIAL

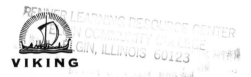

VIKING

VIKING

Published by the Penguin Group
Penguin Books USA Inc., 375 Hudson Street,
New York, New York 10014, U.S.A.
Penguin Books Ltd, 27 Wrights Lane, London W8 5TZ, England
Penguin Books Australia Ltd, Ringwood, Victoria, Australia
Penguin Books Canada Ltd, 10 Alcorn Avenue,
Toronto, Ontario, Canada M4V 3B2
Penguin Books (N.Z.) Ltd, 182–190 Wairau Road,
Auckland 10, New Zealand

Penguin Books Ltd, Registered Offices:
Harmondsworth, Middlesex, England

First published in 1994 by Viking Penguin,
a division of Penguin Books USA Inc.

1 3 5 7 9 10 8 6 4 2

LIBRARY OF CONGRESS CATALOGING IN PUBLICATION DATA
Persico, Joseph E.
Nuremberg: infamy on trial / Joseph Persico.
p. cm.
Includes bibliographical references and index.
ISBN 0-670-84276-1
1. Nuremberg Trial of Major German War Criminals,
Nuremberg, Germany, 1945–1946. I. Title.
JX5437.8.P37 1994
341.6'9—dc20   94-2879

Printed in the United States of America
Set in Adobe Janson Text
Designed by Francesca Belanger

To brother Richard and sister Annabelle

CONTENTS

INTRODUCTION

AFTER A HIATUS of nearly half a century, Nuremberg is again on people's lips. After over one hundred wars, insurrections, civil conflicts, and revolutions that have racked the world over the past forty-five years and claimed more than 21 million lives, after hardly a breath of outrage over atrocities committed in the name of ideology, liberation, independence, and religion, people at last have begun to cry out for justice that can penetrate national borders, for a Nuremberg-style prosecution of war criminals. The cry arose in 1990 after Saddam Hussein seized Kuwait, then bloodily supressed Iraq's Shiite and Kurd minorities. The cry for justice, for a new Nuremberg, became full-throated with the black-and-white images of Auschwitz and Buchenwald updated in color in Serbian concentration camps in the former Yugoslavia, with accounts of mass deportation, calculated extermination, and organized rape, with the campaign of "ethnic cleansing" of Bosnian Muslims, an echo of Adolf Hitler's call to "cleanse the world of Jewish poison."

Finally, the family of nations acted. On February 22, 1993, the United Nations Security Council voted to create an international tribunal to prosecute war crimes committed in the crumbling lands that once formed Yugoslavia. In May, the court was established. Another Nuremberg.

But what was Nuremberg? What happened in that shattered city between 1945 and 1946? Were lessons learned or lost after the trials of Nazi leaders? Why did its hope blaze so brightly and then burn out, the flame of its example reduced thereafter virtually to historic ash?

It would be convenient to say that this book was written in response to the current interest in Nuremberg, to invoke history's guidance in dealing with war criminals in our time. Actually, the book has older, more personal roots. Its impetus has been an image lodged in my memory for nearly fifty years, a photograph that appeared in newspapers in October 1946: Hermann Göring, his face contorted in death, just after he committed suicide on the eve of his scheduled execution as the leading surviving Nazi war criminal. To one too young to have fought in World War II, but old enough to have been shaped by that cataclysm, the trial and execution of the major Nazi leaders has a riveting fascination. The trial seemed to say that good must triumph over evil, a perception perhaps stronger in a boy then sixteen than in a man now in his sixties.

Through the years I dipped casually into the story. What I encountered was a considerable literature dealing with the legal dust kicked up by the trial of the Nazis before the International Military Tribunal of Nuremberg. Most of these books made a contribution to understanding. Some were outstanding in dissecting the juridical controversies. What they whetted the appetite for, but failed to satisfy, was my curiosity about the human drama that must have been unfolding in Nuremberg during 1945 and 1946. As I was to discover when I began my research, beneath the legal battle pitting prosecution against defense lay several simultaneous conflicts. Nuremberg set defendants against defendants. Hermann Göring, for example, wanted his fellow Nazis to go down with the swastika flying; Albert Speer preached confession and contrition. Speer, in turn, vied against Fritz Sauckel to see which one would have to bear the heaviest guilt for the Nazi slave labor program. Robert Jackson, the American prosecutor, on leave from the U.S. Supreme Court, battled professionally and personally with Francis Biddle, the American Nuremberg judge. Biddle, disappointed at being deprived of the chief judgeship (Jackson's doing), maneuvered the other judges to try to make himself de facto head of the IMT. The representatives of the four nations—the United States, the Soviet Union, Great Britain, and France—that made up the court fought to see whose system of jurisprudence would prevail, the Anglo-Saxon or the Continental. The prison commandant was determined to maintain an escape-proof jail, only to lose three prisoners to suicide. The prison psychiatrist and psychologist, who had unlimited access to the defendants, turned this unprecedented opportunity into a race to see who could publish the first insider book on the psyche of war criminals. In the testy relations between the staffs representing the Western Allies and the Soviet Union, we see intimations of the coming Cold War in microcosm in a Nuremberg courthouse. And outside the courthouse, while American prosecutors inside were trying defendants for the murderous consequences of Nazi racism, white GIs brawled with segregated black GIs, importing America's own brand of racism.

Overarching all these subdramas was the major theater, the Nuremberg trial itself. Was it victors' vengeance or the authentic pursuit of justice? Indeed, can a just court be created to try acts which have not been defined as crimes until after the fact? The charge of ex post facto law was to haunt the IMT from its first day to its last. How valid is the jurisdiction of a court that permits a British prosecutor to try a German national before a Soviet judge for crimes committed in Poland? If aggression was on trial at Nuremberg, then what were Soviet judges doing on the bench? Their nation had invaded Finland and conspired with Germany to divide up Poland. And, granted that Nazi atrocities dwarfed the misdeeds of other belligerents, had not war crimes been committed on all sides? Why were only those on the losing side tried?

These anomalies raise the age-old distinction between law and justice. They are not the same. If the law at Nuremberg was flawed, does it follow that the justice meted out was flawed as well? Before, during, and after the trial, respected voices argued that honest vengeance was purer and preferable to rickety legality. Winston Churchill was but one of many who wanted the top Nazis shot out of hand with minimal legal fuss.

This work is an attempt to reveal these intersecting dramas. That I was able to proceed was largely the result of serendipity. In Washington, D.C., in March 1991, alumni of the Nuremberg International Military Tribunal held a forty-fifth-anniversary reunion. The reunion answered a question I had posed to myself. What fresh perspectives could be brought to a trial that ended in 1946 and has since been written on voluminously? To my good fortune, the reunion organizers had published a directory of persons still living who had been involved in the trial. But for a few protagonists, Nuremberg turned out to have been largely a young person's game. Many participants were still available to provide firsthand accounts of their experiences. I was able to interview people who had never before talked about Nuremberg: prosecutors, interpreters, researchers, journalists, jailers, secretaries, drivers, and bodyguards, whose individual contributions are recognized in the acknowledgments section.

The most moving part of the research was an odyssey to the sites where the story took place: to work in the same courtroom where Hermann Göring displayed his perverse brilliance (a longhaired, slack-jawed drug dealer was on trial during my visit); to stand on the podium from which Hitler whipped the Nazi faithful to a frenzy during *Parteitagen* (Party Days) at Nuremberg's Zeppelin Field; to pore over letters the defendants wrote to their families on the last days of their lives and to see unpublished photographs of their executions at the Berlin Documents Center; to go through Auschwitz, the scene of events so exhaustively exposed at the trial, with a party of Austrian Jews, all of whom had family ties to the Holocaust and some of whom were survivors.

One question I pondered was how to deal with the massive and sickening evidence of atrocities introduced during the trial. Though it may not seem so to the reader, I have chosen to keep such material to a minimum, just enough to communicate the nature and magnitude of these depredations. To include more would risk numbing rather than quickening the reader's sensitivities.

Nuremberg stands as a powerful drama in its own right in its own time. But what does it say to our time? Beyond punishing the guilty, the dream of those who championed this historic experiment was to set precedents, to give would-be aggressors pause, and to hold future aggressors accountable. Until virtually this moment, that dream has failed abysmally. Does Nuremberg offer lessons, a usable matrix that can be salvaged from the bin of history and put to good service to deal with war crimes in our era? Given the UN's recent actions, we may be about to find out.

My treatment of the trial is intended for the lay reader and general student of history more than for the academic or legal historian. For that reason, I have chosen a strongly narrative style, hoping to interest a new generation in an old but important story. The style does not influence the factual foundations of the book. In light of recent controversies and court actions, there has arisen in publishing a heightened sensitivity to the authenticity of words and thoughts attributed to figures in works professedly of nonfiction. When I have described subjects of the present work as thinking, saying, or doing something, I have drawn from their own writings, letters, oral and written histories, and from other books, archival documents, contemporary press accounts, the above-mentioned interviews, and the forty-two-volume transcript of the trial itself. The account is narrative supported by historic fact.

THE TRIAL CAST

AMEN, John Harlan: U.S. colonel, associate trial counsel, head of
   interrogations.
ANDRUS, Burton: U.S. colonel in charge of the Nuremberg prison.
BALDWIN, William: assistant U.S. prosecutor.
BARRETT, Roger: lawyer who ran the documents room.
BERNAYS, Murray: War Department lawyer, drafter of the initial pro-
   posal for prosecuting international war criminals.
BIDDLE, Francis: former U.S. attorney general, American justice on
   the court.
BIRKETT, Sir Norman: alternate British justice on the court.
BORMANN, Martin: secretary to Hitler; missing, tried in absentia.
BRUDNO, Walter: assistant U.S. prosecutor.
BURSON, Harold "Hal": Armed Forces Network correspondent cov-
   ering the trial.
CONTI, Leonardo: SS "mercy killing" doctor; first suicide in the
   prison.
D'ADDARIO, Ray: U.S. Army Signal Corps photographer.
DIPALMA, Emilio: U.S. Army cell guard.
DIX, Rudolf: defense counsel for Hjalmar Schacht.
DODD, Thomas J.: associate and later deputy U.S. prosecutor.
DÖNITZ, Karl: grand admiral, commander of the German U-boat fleet,
   successor to Raeder as commander in chief of the German navy.
DONNEDIEU DE VABRES, Henri: French justice on the court.
DONOVAN, William J.: U.S. general, founder and chief of the Office
   of Strategic Services, briefly a prosecutor at Nuremberg.
DOSTERT, Leon: first head of the Language Division and initiator of
   simultaneous interpretation at Nuremberg.
DOUGLAS, Elsie: secretary to Robert Jackson.
EXNER, Franz: German law professor and General Jodl's defense
   counsel.
FABER-CASTELL, Roland and Nina: members of German pencil-

manufacturing family, owners of the castle in Stein where the Nuremberg press was housed.

FALCO, Robert: alternate French justice on the court.

FISHER, Adrian "Butch": legal advisor to the American justice, Biddle.

FLÄCHSNER, Hans: Speer's defense counsel.

FLANNER, Janet: correspondent for *The New Yorker*.

FRANK, Hans: governor general of Nazi-occupied Poland.

FRICK, Wilhelm: Nazi minister of the interior, later Protector of Bohemia and Moravia.

FRITZSCHE, Hans: chief of radio operations in the Nazi propaganda ministry.

FUCHS, Moritz: U.S. sergeant, bodyguard of Robert Jackson.

FUNK, Walther: president of the Reichsbank.

GAU, Lilli: mistress of Hans Frank.

GERECKE, Henry F.: U.S. major, chaplain for the Protestant defendants.

GILBERT, Gustav M.: prison psychologist.

GILIAREVSKAYA, Tania: interpreter for General Nikitchenko.

GILL, Robert J.: U.S. general, administrative officer for the prosecution staff.

GLENNY, William: U.S. Army cell guard.

GÖRING, Carin: Hermann Göring's first wife.

GÖRING, Emmy: Hermann Göring's second wife.

GÖRING, Edda: Hermann Göring's eight-year-old daughter.

GÖRING, Hermann: *Reichsmarschall*, chief of the Luftwaffe, Hitler's designated successor until supplanted by Dönitz.

HARRIS, Whitney: assistant U.S. prosecutor.

HAUSHOFER, Karl: professor of geopolitics, mentor of Rudolf Hess.

HESS, Rudolf: deputy führer, third-ranking Nazi until his flight to Scotland in 1941.

HIMMLER, Heinrich: *Reichsführer*, head of the SS; a suicide by the time of the trial.

HOESS, Rudolf Franz Ferdinand: commandant of Auschwitz, a witness at Nuremberg.

HOFFMANN, Heinrich: Hitler's personal photographer, a prison trusty and photograph expert for the prosecution.

HORN, Martin: Ribbentrop's second defense counsel.

HORSKY, Charles: lawyer, Washington liaison aide to Robert Jackson.

HOSSBACH, Friedrich: German general who took notes at what came to be called the "Hossbach Conference."

JACKSON, Robert H.: chief U.S. prosecutor, on leave from the U.S. Supreme Court.

JACKSON, William E.: lawyer; assistant to his father, Robert Jackson.

JODL, Alfred: colonel general, operations chief of the German armed forces.

JODL, Luise: wife of General Jodl, employed by her husband's attorney during the trial.

KALNOKY, Ingeborg: German-born countess who ran the Witness House during the trial.

KALTENBRUNNER, Ernst: head of the RSHA, the Nazi security apparatus, second to Himmler in the SS.

KAUFFMANN, Kurt: defense counsel for Kaltenbrunner.

KEITEL, Wilhelm: field marshal, chief of staff of the German armed forces.

KELLEY, Douglas: U.S. major, prison psychiatrist.

KEMPNER, Robert: German-born former official of the Prussian Interior Ministry, later an American citizen and head of the Defense Rebuttal Section at Nuremberg.

KILEY, Daniel: OSS officer, architect who restored the Palace of Justice.

KORB, Rose: secretary to the prison commandant, Colonel Andrus.

KRANZBUEHLER, Otto: German navy judge, Dönitz's defense counsel.

KRUG, Willi: German POW employed in cellblock C.

LAMBERT, Thomas F.: assistant U.S. prosecutor.

LAWRENCE, Sir Geoffrey: British justice and president of the court.

LEY, Robert: head of the German Labor Front.

MARGOLIES, Daniel: assistant U.S. prosecutor, husband of Harriet Zetterberg.

MAXWELL-FYFE, Sir David: de facto head of the British prosecution, nominally under Sir Hartley Shawcross.

MITCHELL, William: U.S. general, administrative officer for the justices.

NEAVE, Airey: British major, lawyer, aide to the justices.

NELTE, Otto: defense counsel for Keitel.

NEURATH, Konstantin von: Germany's foreign minister before Ribbentrop; Protector of Bohemia and Moravia, 1939–41.

NIKITCHENKO, Ion Timofeevich: major general of jurisprudence; Soviet justice on the court.

O'CONNOR, Sixtus: Catholic priest, chaplain for the Catholic defendants.

OHLENDORF, Otto: SS general, commander of Einsatzgruppe D; a witness.

OWENS, Dorothy: secretary to Francis Biddle.

PAPEN, Franz von: German chancellor before Hitler, vice chancellor under Hitler, ambassador to Turkey.

PARKER, John J.: alternate U.S. justice on the court.

PFLUECKER, Ludwig: German POW employed as physician for the defendants.

POKROVSKY, Y. V.: deputy Soviet prosecutor.

POLEVOI, Boris: *Pravda* correspondent at the trial.

POLTORAK, Arkady: documents officer for the Soviet staff.

RAEDER, Erich: grand admiral; until 1943 commander in chief of the German navy.

RIBBENTROP, Joachim von: Nazi foreign minister.

ROBERTS, Geoffrey Dorling "Khaki": leading counsel under Maxwell-Fyfe for the British prosecution.

ROHRSCHEIDT, Gunther von: Hess's first defense counsel.

ROSENBERG, Alfred: Nazi minister for the Occupied Eastern Territories and head of Einstab Rosenberg.

ROWE, James: former Roosevelt aide and naval officer, legal advisor to Biddle.

RUDENKO, Roman A.: lieutenant general, chief Soviet prosecutor.

SADEL, Gunther: U.S. counterintelligence agent on the staff of General Watson.

SAUCKEL, Fritz: head of the German conscript labor organization.

SAUTER, Fritz: Ribbentrop's first defense counsel; also Funk's and Schirach's counsel.

SCHACHT, Hjalmar Horace Greeley: president of the Reichsbank prior to Funk, and former minister of the economy.

SCHIRACH, Baldur von: head of the Hitler Youth, later governor and *Gauleiter* of Vienna.

SCHMIDT, Paul: Hitler's personal interpreter, held as a material witness.

SEIDL, Alfred: Hess's second defense counsel, also Frank's defense counsel.

SERVATIUS, Robert: Sauckel's defense counsel.

SEYSS-INQUART, Arthur: Nazi commissioner of occupied Holland.

SHAWCROSS, Sir Hartley: formally chief British prosecutor, who delegated the day-to-day task to Maxwell-Fyfe.

SHIRER, William L.: CBS correspondent covering the trial.

SMITH, Howard K.: CBS correspondent covering the trial.

SPEER, Albert: Reich minister for armaments and war production.

SPRECHER, Drexel: assistant U.S. prosecutor, later prosecutor at subsequent war-crimes trials.

STAHMER, Otto: Göring's defense counsel.

STEER, Alfred: U.S. Navy officer and linguist, succeeded Leon Dostert as chief of the Language Division.

STEWART, Robert: U.S. major, legal advisor to alternate justice Parker.

STOREY, Robert: U.S. colonel, head of U.S. prosecution team under Jackson.

STREICHER, Julius: publisher of the anti-Semitic newspaper *Der Stürmer*.

STRENG, Otto: German POW employed as prison librarian, mailman.

TAYLOR, Telford: U.S. general, prosecutor of the High Command case, later chief prosecutor at subsequent trials.

TEICH, F. C.: U.S. major, deputy commander of the prison under Colonel Andrus.

TROYANOVSKY, Oleg: son of the first Soviet ambassador to the United States, interpreter for the Soviet justices.

UIBERALL, Peter: official in the Language Division.

VOLCHKOV, Alexander: alternate Soviet justice.

VONETES, John: U.S. housing officer for the trial staff.

WALCH, Katherine: British researcher in the Defense Rebuttal Section.

WATSON, Leroy H.: U.S. brigadier general, commandant of the Nuremberg-Furth Enclave; Colonel Andrus's superior.

WECHSLER, Herbert: chief legal advisor to the American justice, Biddle.

WHEELIS, Jack G. "Tex": U.S. officer on the prison staff, responsible for the baggage room.

WOODS, John: U.S. master sergeant, Third Army hangman.

ZETTERBERG, Harriet: lawyer on the U.S. prosecution staff, wife of Daniel Margolies.

ABBREVIATIONS

ACC: Allied Control Council. Body representing the four nations (United States, Great Britain, France, Soviet Union) that governed occupied Germany.

IMT: International Military Tribunal. The court established by the Allies to try German war criminals.

ISD: 6850th Internal Security Detachment. The military force that operated the Nuremberg prison.

NKVD: Soviet secret police at the time of the trial; forerunner of the KGB.

OKW: Oberkommando der Wehrmacht, High Command of the German armed forces.

OSS: Office of Strategic Services. U.S. intelligence service during World War II.

RSHA: Reich Central Security Office. Component of the SS that controlled the Gestapo, the secret political police, the criminal police, and the SD, or security service.

SA: Sturmabteilung. The Nazi storm troopers, or Brownshirts.

SD: Nazi security service, essentially engaged in political intelligence, counterintelligence, and clandestine operations.

SS: *Schutzstaffel.* Literally "guard detachment"; became the umbrella organization for Heinrich Himmler's empire, including SS military forces (the Waffen SS), the RSHA, and the operation of concentration camps.

CHAPTER I

PRELUDE TO
JUDGMENT

1

WILLI KRUG COCKED AN EYE at the battered alarm clock he kept within arm's reach on the floor. Five-thirty, still dark out, with only the pewter light of the moon angling down from the barred window and spilling through the open doorway of his cell. The rare sound of a truck revving and pulling out of the prison yard had awakened him. Earlier his sleep had been broken by the noise of hammers banging and the muffled shouts of GIs. He had fallen back to sleep until the truck woke him again.

Willi swung his legs out of the cot and planted his feet on the cold stone floor. He started pulling on his clothes, cast-off U.S. Army fatigues dyed black for prison staffers like himself. He left his cell and paused on the catwalk. An uneasiness swept over him. The hammering in the night, the sound of the departing vehicle. This could be the day. Ever since the sentences had been handed down, two weeks before, on October 1, the unknown had hung over the prison like a cloud.

He began making his way down a stairwell strung with chicken wire to prevent suicide leaps. He had made this dawn descent every day for nearly fourteen months, ever since the defendants had been sent here for trial. Krug was not a reflective man, or he might have pondered the odd existence he led—confined to prison yet not a prisoner, something more than a trusty, but still something less than the well-fed American jailers for whom he worked.

In the last days of the war, he had been a corporal attached to a field kitchen in General Wenk's Twelfth Army, which had been deployed to halt the Russian advance on Berlin. Willi's immediate concern had not been whether they could stop the Red Army. That hope was forlorn. His aim had been to keep himself out of Russian hands. He had eventually succeeded, along with hundreds of thousands of his comrades, thanks to a man now caged in this prison, Grand Admiral

Karl Dönitz. Dönitz had succeeded Adolf Hitler at the end, and with all lost, had determined to drag out the surrender negotiations the few precious days that allowed Germans like Willi to flee West and entrust their fate to the expectedly more tender mercies of American and British captors. Willi had once tried to express his gratitude to the old man, but something stiff and forbidding in Dönitz's manner had held him back.

After his surrender to the American Ninth Army, Willi had been herded into a cage at Bad Kreuznach near the Rhine, one of two hundred American pens holding over four million defeated Germans. They had been left out in the open, rain or shine, fed half rations and one cup of water a day. In those POW cages, Willi's comrades, who had survived the heat of North Africa and the winters of Russia, died by the thousands. And they call Germans war criminals, he and his comrades had complained.

He had survived through the cunning of the desperate. Willi had picked up a smattering of English while working as a waiter before the war, and managed to have himself selected to serve as a trusty at an improvised prison in Bad Mondorf, Luxembourg. There he was astonished to find himself among German leaders whom he would have once considered as remote as the stars. When over a dozen of them were shipped to Nuremberg to be tried as war criminals, Willi was given a choice. He could be released and go home, or else work for the Americans in the Nuremberg prison. For Willi Krug home was the bombed-out shell of what had been an apartment building in Schweinfurt, rubble that had entombed his wife and child. He had been offered what amounted to a roof over his head and regular meals—more than millions of his countrymen could now hope for. But he would have to live in the Nuremberg prison. Willi gratefully seized the offer.

On the main floor of the cellblock he looked out on a familiar scene. On each side of the corridor stood the GI guards, one to a cell, condemned to stare through a square porthole, never taking their eyes off their charges, two hours on and four hours off, for twenty-four-hour stretches. Usually they greeted him, "Hey Willi, *wie geht's*, you old Kraut," and other fractured German gibes as he passed by. His morning arrival was the signal for the guards to turn off the spotlights that they directed through the portholes onto the sleeping prisoners' faces. But this morning's air of anxiety had tempered even these brash young Americans, and they let him pass with bare nods.

He headed for the basement to fill the tin washbasins that he brought to each cell every morning. En route, he passed cell 5 and glanced in. He briefly caught sight of the *Reichsmarschall*'s square face, defiant chin, long sharp nose, and thin lips. Hermann Göring lay there, hands resting outside the blankets, regulation style, so the guard could see them. Willi hurried by. He was required only to dispense cold water for washing up. But whenever he had time, he liked to heat the water for the *Reichsmarschall*, particularly this morning when he wondered if he might ever perform this small kindness again. The corporal posted at the end of the cellblock waved him down the basement stairway to the kitchen. Willi smiled. He always smiled, even at their taunts. The truth was that he did not much like the guards. They were like badly brought-up children. Their behavior toward the prisoners, addressing once-powerful leaders of the Reich by first names, even nicknames, shocked him.

He checked the stairwell carefully as he descended. It was the GIs' habit to grab an unauthorized smoke on the stairs, and it was a rare morning on which he did not find a treasured butt or two.

Hermann Göring had not been asleep when Willi Krug passed by. He had slept fitfully that night. The Amytal and Seconal pills that Doctor Pfluecker always gave him had failed. He too felt the foreboding, and with far more reason than Krug had. The guard snapped off the hated light and Göring allowed his eyes to open. His exposed hands felt cold. He felt scant desire to rouse himself, and closed his eyes again.

He might well have been recalling the last days of the other war, the war of his early manhood. One memory always stood out as crisply as the sun on that July morning in 1918. Three months before, their squadron commander, the living legend Baron Manfred von Richthofen, creator of the Flying Circus, single-handed destroyer of eighty enemy planes, had himself been shot down and killed over France. Göring, with twenty-one kills to his credit, holder of the Pour le Mérite, the coveted "Blue Max" presented personally by the Kaiser, and with enough panache to rival the Red Baron, fully expected to be his successor. Instead, the squadron went to a by-the-book flying bureaucrat, Wilhelm Reinhardt. Göring, impatient and impetuous, had been judged lacking in the steadiness required of a commanding officer.

That July morning, he and Reinhardt had been sent to Adlershof field to meet Anthony Fokker, the Dutch-born builder of German warplanes. On the way out of the officers' mess, Göring spotted an awkward-looking biplane in a corner of the airfield. What was that? he asked Fokker. Just an experimental craft, Fokker said. He wanted to fly it, Göring announced. It had been insufficiently tested, Fokker warned. Göring insisted. After a quick explanation of the controls, he found himself bumping along a grassy runway and nursing the aircraft aloft. He beat up the field, flying at times almost at zero altitude. He looped and spinned and yawed and finally, after a breathtaking pass down the runway on canted wings, brought her in and jumped out of the cockpit before an astonished crowd.

Reinhardt's pride demanded that he too take up the plane. He was, after all, commander of the Richthofen Flying Circus. The spectators watched Reinhardt streak toward the sun. And then it happened: a resounding crack, audible from the ground. The left wing simply drifted away from the fuselage. That was how Hermann Göring, at the age of twenty-five, became commander of the Flying Circus.

Two weeks later, he stole from behind a cloud, locked his guns on a British Spad, and shot down his twenty-second plane. It was the last time he would experience the pure adrenaline joy of the kill. After that, it all fell apart. The Kaiser fled to Holland. The despised Communists paraded down Berlin's Unter den Linden. On November 11, a courier handed Göring a dispatch. Germany had surrendered. He was to turn over his squadron at a French airfield near Strasbourg. They could go to hell, he answered. His commanding officer threatened a court-martial. Göring sent a few token aircraft to the French and led the rest of the squadron back to a field at Darmstadt. As he neared the end of the field, he slewed the plane around until the wingtip struck the ground. He kept churning until the Fokker was ground to junk. The other pilots followed his lead.

A polite tapping on the cell door broke Göring's reverie and he sat up with a start. Framed in the porthole was the sad, smiling face of Willi Krug, announcing that he had brought the *Reichsmarschall* his water. Göring reluctantly threw off the covers and took the washbasin. He set it on the table opposite his cot. Despite all the power and glory that had followed, those days in the van of the Flying Circus had been the acme of his life. This day was certainly the lowest and possibly the last of the mad adventure he had lived. He had managed to cheat the victors of his planes at the end of the last war. All he wanted now was to cheat them of the vengeance they expected to exact from him. He began to unbutton his blue silk pajamas, bent over, and splashed the water over his face. It was, he noted, agreeably warm.

2

WASHINGTON, APRIL 1945

THE TRAIN OF EVENTS that put Hermann Göring into a Nuremberg jail cell had been set in motion a year and a half before, by a phone call from the White House to the Supreme Court. Samuel Rosenman, speechwriter and confidant of President Franklin D. Roosevelt, was calling Associate Justice Robert H. Jackson. Rosenman asked if he might stop by; what he had to say, he explained, was best discussed confidentially in Jackson's chambers. Rosenman's call came barely two weeks after America had been staggered by the sudden death of FDR, whose successor was an as yet unknowable quantity, Harry S Truman.

On his arrival, Rosenman, an old-fashioned man, gave Jackson's secretary, Elsie Douglas, a courtly nod and smile. Mrs. Douglas was attractive, blond, a slightly plump widow of early middle age who managed to combine a good nature with brisk efficiency. She ushered Rosenman into a wood-paneled chamber.

Jackson rose and greeted his visitor warmly. The justice's solid appearance, the banker's blue suit, the gold chain stretched across the faintest suggestion of a paunch, suited the august quarters he occupied. The two men embraced almost as members of a family still feeling a grievous loss. Jackson motioned his guest to a leather-upholstered armchair, and asked his secretary to bring in coffee and hold all calls.

They talked for a time about the death of the president. Then Rosenman, speaking in the rolling cadences that evoked the speeches he had written for Roosevelt, came to the point. He had been in England with Churchill, he said, just three days before FDR died. He had gone there to discuss what was to be done with the Nazi leaders when the war in Europe ended, as it soon must. Rosenman's eyes crinkled as he repeated a story that Churchill had told him. In his last meeting with Stalin, Churchill had remarked that whenever they captured one of the Nazi bigwigs, he ought to be summarily shot. With that, Stalin announced sanctimoniously, "In the Soviet Union, we never execute anyone without a trial." Churchill responded, "Of course, of course. We should give them a trial first." Rosenman and Jackson roared. The butcher of the Soviet show trials of the thirties insisting on due process, while a champion of Western civilization called for drumhead justice.

Rosenman was not sure what the president had really wanted—when he said "president," he still meant Roosevelt. At times, Rosenman recalled, FDR had also leaned toward shooting the Nazi leaders out of hand. But, Rosenman had argued, if it was a crime for Germans to shoot people without a trial while at war, why was it less a crime for the Allies to do so when the war was over? Finally, last February at Yalta, FDR, Churchill, and Stalin had all gone on record as favoring the law. There would be war-crimes trials soon, Rosenman announced, and Harry Truman wanted Bob Jackson to prosecute for the United States. Rosenman explained that Truman had not forgotten Jackson's earlier reputation as a formidable prosecutor.

Jackson was an old Washington hand, and he accepted that whenever a president did something, there was a good reason and then there was the real reason. Sam Rosenman was giving him a good reason. He asked if Rosenman knew of his recent speech on war criminals before the American Society of Law. He opened the door and called to Elsie Douglas to bring in a copy. Jackson had told the society, "If we want to shoot Germans as a matter of policy, let it be done as such. But don't hide the deed behind a court. The world yields no respect to courts that are merely organized to convict."

Mrs. Douglas handed the speech to Rosenman. He flipped quickly through the pages with a lawyer's practiced eye. He saw no problem, he said. What Truman wanted was a fair trial with all the protections due a defendant, not a legal lynching.

Jackson's mind was racing. This was a minefield that had to be trodden with exquisite care. Was one of his Supreme Court rivals trying to get him off the bench? Would this assignment mean leaving the court? he asked. Of course not, Rosenman replied. Jackson wanted the weekend to think the matter over. Fair enough, Rosenman answered, and rose to take his leave.

Jackson expected to put the time to good use. He was going to a dinner party Saturday evening with Senator Alben Barkley. Barkley had just returned from a trip to a recently liberated concentration camp. Just the man for Jackson to talk to about war crimes.

The man Truman wanted to prosecute war criminals was unique on the twentieth-century Supreme Court. Robert Jackson did not possess a law degree. He had been born on a farm fifty-three years before in rural Pennsylvania. His father, William, was a self-taught, self-made entrepreneur who always had his hand in something—a sawmill, a hotel, a stable of harness-racing horses. Jackson's mother, Angelina Houghwout, was descended from an old Dutch family that had been in America since 1660. When young Bob was five, the Jacksons moved to the Jamestown area of western New York State, and there he was raised in a world long since vanished, reading the Bible, singing hymns, and learning his letters from *McGuffey's Reader*. He was also absorbing, from his profane, hard-drinking father, an independent streak. The elder Jackson was a lone, outspoken Democrat in a community of rock-ribbed Republicans.

Young Bob was drawn to the law in part because his father opposed it. He spent a year at Albany Law School on money borrowed from an uncle, and received a certificate of completion, but not a degree. Thereafter, he settled in Jamestown, population 31,000, and, over the next twenty years, became a success in his small corner of the world, representing banks, railroads, industries, and wealthy estates. But a populist streak in him also propelled Jackson to defend the tiny local telephone company against the giant Bell system. He defended, without a fee, a poor black accused of stabbing a white farmer to death; his client went free. By 1932, Bob Jackson was prosperous, a Jamestown pillar, married to his law school sweetheart, Irene Gerhardt, and the doting father of a son, William Eldred, and a daughter, Mary Margaret.

In a single evening, fate conspired to remake his life. Jackson had gone to a Jamestown Democratic fund-raising dinner. In that spring of 1932, the burning issue for Democrats was the massive corruption recently revealed in the administration of New York City's bon vivant mayor, Jimmy Walker. To Jackson's dismay, not a single speaker made any reference to the Walker scandals. When it was his turn to speak, Jackson said that this omission was a disgrace: "It comes perilously close to putting the state Democratic party in Walker's back pocket," he warned.

Months later, New York's governor, Franklin Delano Roosevelt, was elected president and Bob Jackson was invited to Washington by Henry Morgenthau, a man he scarcely knew. Morgenthau, a confidant of the president, had been appointed Roosevelt's secretary of the treasury. "I didn't like your Jamestown speech," he told Jackson, "but I did admire your intentions. It took courage to say what you said. That's what the president is looking for down here."

Thus it was that Bob Jackson warily gave up the good life as "just a country lawyer" and entered the New Deal. He started in the White House, drafting tax legislation, and soon was receiving appreciative "Dear Bob" notes from an admiring FDR. His rise was swift. Roosevelt named him head of the antitrust division in the Department of Justice, then solicitor general, in which capacity he argued the government's cases before the Supreme Court. At age forty-seven, Bob Jackson became U.S. attorney general.

There was about him an almost innocent integrity. At one point, Roosevelt invited the Jacksons for a Potomac River cruise on the presidential yacht. Jackson declined, saying he had to attend his son's graduation from Saint Alban's school. His secretary was horrified. "You don't say no to the president," she advised. But he had, and a half hour later the White House secretary was back on the line saying the president wanted to congratulate young Bill on his graduation, and was delaying the yacht's departure until the Jacksons could make it aboard.

In 1940, FDR, running for an unprecedented third term, was shopping for a new vice-presidential running mate, and Bob Jackson figured on the short list. There was speculation about his succeeding FDR in the future. But, the president noted, "The trouble with Bob is that he's too much of a gentleman." That crusty and perceptive Roosevelt aide, Harold Ickes, made another judgment of Jackson that was to haunt him in prosecuting war criminals: "He has not yet learned to stand up to fire directed at him personally."

Roosevelt was nevertheless still high on Bob Jackson. In July 1941, when the Supreme Court's chief justice, Charles Evans Hughes, resigned, Jackson was a strong candidate to become Hughes's successor. Roosevelt was pressured instead to name a sitting associate justice, Harlan F. Stone, as chief. But the country lawyer from Jamestown, lacking a law degree, was named an associate justice when Stone moved up to the top spot. Jackson hoped that Roosevelt would name him chief justice when Stone left.

On Sunday afternoon, three days after Rosenman's proposal, Jackson sat alone in the study at Hickory Hill, his rambling home in the Virginia hunt country. He had seen Senator Barkley at the dinner party the night before and had pulled him aside at an appropriate moment. He confided to Barkley that he regarded these tales of Nazi horrors with skepticism. Barkley's usually amiable air vanished. Believe them, he said. He was just back from Buchenwald.

Now in the seclusion of his study, Jackson turned over the Truman offer. He recalled the attempt to punish war criminals after the First World War—a fiasco. The victorious Allies had drawn up a list of over 4,900 potential defendants, and quickly trimmed it to 901 names. Of these, twelve men were ordered to trial by a German court in Leipzig in 1922. Three of the twelve simply failed to appear. Charges were dropped against three more. The remaining six got off with laughably light sentences.

Now the president was asking Jackson to become part of an effort to try again, this time through an international tribunal. There were no precedents, no existing body of law, not even a court. The legal instruments for prosecuting a drunk driver in any county in America were better than those for prosecuting the murderers of millions during a war. The risks to Jackson's career were high, the rewards uncertain. The course of prudence was to turn Truman down. Yet the truth was that Jackson had become bored on the Supreme Court. The titanic legal battles of the thirties over FDR's New Deal legislation were over. The main arena now was abroad, in a world turned upside-down by war. Jackson had also made a formidable enemy on the court, Associate Justice Hugo Black. Black resented Jackson's assumption that he was Stone's heir apparent. Black, a former Ku Klux Klansman from the deep South, a man whose integrity Jackson suspected, was an alien figure to the upright Yankee. Their constant clashes had drained much of the pleasure out of Jackson's service on the bench. He had been thinking about resigning even before Truman's offer dropped from the blue. He remembered what his father had once told him after a horse-swapping deal. "How do you dare trade that way, Pop," the boy had asked, "when you don't know what you're getting?" The old man answered, "Bob, it's sometimes enough just to know what you're getting rid of."

Jackson picked up the phone and dialed his son, Bill, recently graduated from Harvard Law School and now a navy ensign assigned to a Washington desk job. He told Bill that he was inclined to take Truman's offer, and as his first staff appointment he wanted to hire Ensign Jackson. "Not bad for your first case," the father added. Bill hesitated briefly. It meant leaving his recent bride for an uncertain period, since the trial would be held in Europe, and wives, his father made clear, were not coming. Jackson went on, "You'll be defending me on this one long after I'm gone. That's one reason I want you there. Anyway," he added, "I expect we'll be home before Christmas."

On May 2, President Truman issued Executive Order 9547 appointing Robert Jackson as U.S. representative and chief counsel for the prosecution of Axis war criminals. Jackson planned to leave soon for London to meet with his Allied counterparts. But before he left, he made two more appointments. He named quiet, loyal Charles Horsky, a lawyer and former subordinate in the Department of Justice, as his Washington special assistant. In the treacherous Washington terrain, Jackson needed someone to watch his back, to serve as his eyes and ears with the press, the White House, and the Pentagon, and especially at the Supreme Court. He trusted Horsky implicitly. And there was one more person whom he had no intention of leaving in Washington: his secretary, Elsie Douglas.

3

TWO DAYS BEFORE Robert Jackson was named the American war-crimes prosecutor, his greatest prey escaped him. On April 30, in a bunker twenty feet below the Berlin sewer system, Adolf Hitler took his own life. That left the man expected to succeed Hitler, Reichsmarschall Hermann Göring, as the ranking Nazi. Göring had last seen Hitler in the bunker at a maudlin birthday party held for the Führer ten days before his suicide. At that point, the Russians were one mile away, yet Hitler refused to leave the doomed capital. Göring felt no such compulsion and explained to Hitler that he had to head south to organize the defense of what was left of Germany. Hitler gave Göring a cool handshake and a look that suggested he smelled treachery and cowardice.

Göring flew from Berlin to Berchtesgaden and there made a fateful decision. Hitler, by remaining in Berlin, would soon be dead or captured. Göring retrieved from his safe his copy of the Führer Decree dated June 29, 1941. Its meaning was unmistakable. In the event of Hitler's death or incapacity, Göring was to become leader of the Reich. He fired off a telegram to the bunker saying that unless he heard otherwise, he was taking over the nation's leadership. It was a rash gamble, and Hermann Göring lost. An enraged Hitler read the message as absolute proof of treachery. Göring's keenest enemy, Martin Bormann, secretary to the Führer, seized the moment to try to finish off his old adversary. He issued orders to the political police in Berchtesgaden to have Göring shot.

Göring, his wife, Emmy, and their eight-year-old daughter, Edda, were riding in a Mercedes touring car inching along an icy Bavarian road clogged with retreating troops when they learned of the broadcast out of Radio Hamburg. Reichsmarschall Göring, the report announced, was suffering from acute heart disease and had asked to be relieved of his posts. Upon discovering Bormann's execution order as well, Göring did what Willi Krug and hordes of other ordinary Germans were doing in those waning hours of the war. He headed for the American lines.

On May 6, U.S. Army Lieutenant Rolf Wartenberg, earlier a refugee from Nazi Germany, found himself stripping medals from the fleshy, heaving chest of Hermann Göring. Göring took it all with good humor. So far his captivity had been lovely, reminding him of the chivalry that had prevailed among enemy aviators on the Western front in the Great War. He recalled the time an English flier's guns had jammed. He had simply given his foe a salute and flown off.

General Carl "Tooey" Spaatz, commander of the Eighth Air Force, which, with the RAF, had virtually blown Göring's Luftwaffe out of the sky and reduced German cities to rubble, came to greet the *Reichsmarschall*. Spaatz broke out the champagne for his fellow airman. They toasted bravery and daring in the heavens. That night Göring was invited to dine in the officers' mess, where his hosts vied to buy him drinks. An American major sat down at a piano and began banging out "Deep in the Heart of Texas." Göring joined in the circle around the piano and quickly caught on to the song's clapping refrain. Sweat coursed down his puffy face. He told Lieutenant Wartenberg, remover of his medals, that in the mountain of luggage he had brought with him was an accordion. The accordion was promptly produced and soon the *Reichsmarschall*'s pudgy fingers were picking out the melody to "Ich weiss nicht was soll es bedeuten," which Göring rendered in a clear baritone. At two a.m., a tipsy, happy prisoner toddled off to bed.

But wire service photos of the famous Nazi being feted by American officers produced a howl back in the United States. An embarrassed and angry General Dwight Eisenhower, the Supreme Allied Commander, reprimanded the offending officers. Hermann Göring, Ike ordered, was henceforth to be treated no differently from any other prisoner of war.

Actually, he was to be treated much differently. He was to be transferred to a place called Bad Mondorf in Luxembourg. At first, the place presented a pleasant prospect to Göring; it was a spa, a watering hole of some repute. But why necessarily Bad Mondorf, he asked his captors? That, he was told, was where the Americans were rounding up war criminals.

4

JUSTICE JACKSON EAGERLY READ the document before him, only six pages plus a cover memo, bound in a blue folder with "Top Secret" stamped across the cover and on every page. A week had passed since his appointment as American prosecutor, and saying yes to the job now seemed to have been the easiest part. He was beginning with virtually nothing. Yet here, condensed in a few pages entitled "Trial of European War Criminals," he detected a brilliant start, a simple concept from which all else might flow. He flipped back to the cover memo to note again the author's name: Colonel Murray Bernays, Special Projects Branch, Department of War.

If prosecuting war criminals was new to Bob Jackson, Murray Bernays had been living with the issue for the previous nine months. The assignment had fallen to the fifty-one-year-old Bernays virtually by default.

Upon getting his new assignment, Bernays had given himself a crash course in the subject. In 1944, President Roosevelt had handed the War Department responsibility for figuring out how to bring war criminals to justice. But the president's old friend Treasury Secretary Henry Morgenthau, the man who had brought Bob Jackson to Washington, rushed a plan to Roosevelt's desk before the War Department could act. Morgenthau belonged to one of New York's old Jewish families, and had clear ideas about what Germany deserved.

On a sweltering Washington day in August 1944, Secretary of War Henry Stimson received a copy of Morgenthau's plan bucked over from the White House for his comments. Stimson was an old man, already in his seventies, a Republican of unbending rectitude in a New Deal cabinet. He read the proposal in the backseat of his government limousine, dabbing a handkerchief across his brow to absorb the sweat caused either by the heat or the words he was reading. Morgenthau proposed stripping Germany of all its industry and turning it into an agricultural society. He wanted to use German POWs as forced labor to rebuild a ravaged Europe, to exile Nazi party members to remote places, and to give advancing Allied armies a list of Nazis to shoot on capture. Morgenthau's plan even provided for dealing with children of members of the SS, the umbrella organization of Nazi elites. Stimson stuffed the memorandum back into his briefcase as though he wanted to forget its existence. Morgenthau's plan was virtually an eye for an eye.

When Stimson reached his office, he summoned Assistant Secretary of War John McCloy and directed him to come up with something more reasonable. But the war was still far from won, and more urgent problems than war criminals occupied McCloy's thoughts. The order was bumped down to a lower level, where, in turn, it was bumped still lower, until it finally landed in the office of a three-man catch-all unit called the Special Projects Branch, headed by Colonel Murray Bernays.

Bernays's life had been a model immigrant success story. His Lithuanian Jewish parents had brought him to America in 1900, when he was six years old. Bernays was a brilliant student, graduated from Harvard and then Columbia Law School, and eventually was associated with the prestigious New York firm of Morris Ernst. He had married Hertha Bernays, a niece of Sigmund Freud, and found it advantageous to take her name. He had left a prosperous practice to join the army.

The idea of branding Nazi atrocities as war crimes, Bernays's research revealed, had arisen even before America came into the war. President Roosevelt had been outraged to learn that the Germans had executed French hostages en masse soon after they defeated France in 1940. In 1942, the whole world learned of the obliteration of the Czech village of Lidice and the murder of 1,331 inhabitants to avenge the assassination of Reinhard Heydrich, deputy chief of the Gestapo. By 1942, the evidence was irrefutable that the Third Reich was embarked on a calculated policy of exterminating the Jews.

On September 15, 1944, a Saturday afternoon, just a week after Bernays received the war-crimes assignment, he sat in his small office on the third floor of the War Department building on Pennsylvania Avenue, a gothic stone pile next to the White House, and tore open his second pack of Camels. The chain-smoking lawyer had been working nonstop. Now he slumped back in his chair, the job done. The freshly typed draft that his secretary had just brought in, he believed, outlined what could become the single most important step in the history of international law.

He had expected the task of inventing legal machinery for bringing mass murderers, plunderers, and aggressors to justice to be monumental. Two traps especially had to be avoided. He did not want an approach that bogged down in an attempt to deal individually with hundreds of thousands of SS flunkies who had beaten a prisoner to death or loaded the gas chambers; nor did he want legal machinery that would allow the top leaders to escape simply because there was no blood directly on their hands.

The idea had struck him like a burst of light, beautiful in its simplicity. The Nazi regime was a criminal conspiracy, a gigantic plot. The whole movement had been a deliberate, concerted effort to arm for war, forcibly seize the lands of other nations, steal their wealth, enslave and exploit their populations, and exterminate the people from whom Bernays himself sprang, the Jews of Europe. If the whole Nazi movement was a criminal conspiracy, then those who created it were, ipso facto, criminals. This part of Bernays's net caught the ringleaders, the masterminds who did not themselves blow up the safe, shoot the bank guard, or drive the getaway car. Bernays's second inspiration had been to declare the organizations that made up the Nazi apparatus—such as the party, the SS, the Gestapo—criminal as well. This approach would catch the lower-level war criminals. If you could prove that the SS was a criminal organization, then you did not have to go through the near-impossible task of proving that individual members were criminals. You need only demonstrate that the man belonged to the SS and hand down appropriate punishment.

Bernays reworked a few phrases and called his secretary back. He told her to cut a stencil, run off multiple copies, and classify the document top secret. He was by now practiced in the ways of the bureaucracy and knew that just as the problem had bumped its way down to his cubicle, his solution would now have to climb its way back up to the top of the Roosevelt administration.

Secretary Stimson had a trusted friend, his former law partner William C. Chanler, who was just back from Europe, where he had been serving as a colonel in military government. Chanler had sent Stimson an idea to mix into the Bernays brew: make the waging of aggressive war a crime itself, Chanler urged. He had worked up a lawyerly rationale. Germany was a signatory of the 1928 Kellogg-Briand Pact for "the Renunciation of War as an Instrument of National Policy." Germany, by breaking the treaty, was not waging legitimate war when invading its neighbors; it was committing murder, assault, and destruction of property.

President Roosevelt liked Bernays's thesis: Nazism as a criminal conspiracy. He also liked Chanler's contribution: aggression as a crime. He wanted the combined plan circulated to a few key administration officials for their reaction.

Herbert Wechsler frowned at the folder, stamped "Top Secret," resting on his desk. Bernays's plan had come over to Wechsler's office in the Justice Department preceded by considerable fanfare. Wechsler's boss, Attorney General Francis Biddle, had passed it along to the subordinate whose judgment he trusted most. Before entering the wartime government, Wechsler had been a distinguished legal scholar at the same Columbia Law School that had produced Murray Bernays, and he found Bernays's scholarship slapdash and superficial. What was this conspiracy nonsense? Any international court was obviously going to have to include the major allies, America, Britain, Russia, and France, in a war-crimes court. Yes, Anglo-Saxon law recognized criminal conspiracy. But the concept did not even exist in the courts of France, Germany, or the Soviet Union.

And defining acts as criminal after they had been committed? That was ex post facto law, bastard law. And declaring that whole organizations—some of whose members numbered in the hundreds of thousands, some in the millions—were criminal? This meat-ax approach was fraught with potential for injustices. Bernays was ignorant of the law, his plan was full of holes, and Wechsler intended to tell the attorney general so. He felt like an art expert who had exposed a fake.

At this point, Wechsler's quarrels with the Bernays plan were largely theoretical. Neither Wechsler or Biddle yet knew that both were fated to play out roles at the future trial; nor that the flaws Wechsler believed he detected in Bernays's grand design would haunt them to the very end.

Bob Jackson still found the Bernays plan inspired. He savored the imagery of a single net flung wide and snaring all his prey. He invited Bernays to his Supreme Court chambers so that he could meet the author of this imaginative idea. Bernays sat before him, smoke rising from his ever-present cigarette and swirling around his large, handsome head. Murray Bernays was an impressive-looking man, but for his sallow complexion and tired, cavernous eyes. He spoke in cultivated tones, his speech marked by well-turned phrases that Jackson savored. After half an hour, they concluded their talk and Bernays departed.

It was Jackson's habit, before he left the office at night, to dictate into his diary the high points of the day. The final entry this afternoon was that he intended to hire Murray Bernays as his executive officer, his right arm.

5

ON THE OTHER SIDE of the world, another lawyer, Hans Frank, contemplated the irony of his existence. When Frank was a young man, his single driving obsession had been to make himself a respected figure in his profession. Instead, at age forty-five, he was sitting in a prison cell, running his thumb along the edge of a gardener's knife and hoping it was sharp enough to slit his wrist.

His body ached. Before dumping him here in the Miesbach jail in Bavaria, American GIs had formed a double line seventy feet long and forced Frank to run the gauntlet. He had staggered between their ranks, stumbling under a hail of kicks and punches, only to be hauled to his feet and shoved ahead for more blows. His tormentors were combat veterans of the Seventh Army's Thirty-sixth Regiment who, days before, had passed through the concentration camp at Dachau. Hans Frank, they had learned, was "the Jew butcher of Cracow," a man said to be engaged in a line of work similar to what they had just witnessed.

Lilli Gau, it seemed to Frank, had been the motive force behind the decisions that had led him to this fate, his body beaten to a pulp, his life forfeit of meaning. She was the beautiful, elegant, dark-haired daughter of a rich and much-respected Munich industrialist, the girl Frank had loved from boyhood. Frank's roots were not remotely similar to hers. His middle-class father was a weak, womanizing lawyer of suspect ethics. His mother came of peasant stock. While Hans was in his teens, she deserted her husband and three children to run off with another man. That scandal had soon been eclipsed by another.

Hans had just taken his law degree at the University of Munich and had joined his father's practice. Forever seared into his memory was the day when the police came and arrested Frank senior for embezzlement—for which, soon thereafter, he was disbarred and imprisoned. All this had gone on while Hans was courting Lilli. Even before the disaster, the Gau family had disapproved of the shyster lawyer's son. Now, the thought of their daughter marrying the son of a jailbird horrified them. The engagement was broken and a marriage quickly arranged between Lilli and a suitable magnate. Hans rebounded into a marriage with Brigitte Herbst, a typist for the Bavarian parliament and the daughter of a factory worker. She was five years his senior and worldly beyond her humble origins. Unknown to Hans, Brigitte managed to bring along her lover on their honeymoon.

After his marriage, Frank vowed he would expunge the stain of his father's disgrace. He would achieve recognition and respectability as a professor of law. In the meantime, with one child and another on the way, Frank had to earn a living. In October 1927, he read a classified ad in the Nazi party organ, the *Volkischer Beobachter*. A dozen storm troopers had broken into a Berlin restaurant where a party of Jews was having dinner. They proceeded to tear the place apart. The police were called and the storm troopers arrested. The *Volkischer Beobachter* was looking for a lawyer to defend these "poor party members without means." Strapped though he was financially, Frank made a rash gamble. He wrote to the paper saying that he would take the case without a fee. His offer was snapped up. He then traveled by train, third class, to Berlin and got the rowdies off with a light sentence.

After the trial, he stopped by the Nazi party office on Schillingstrasse, where Adolf Hitler himself appeared to meet this youthful prodigy of the law. "You must come and work for the party," he told Frank. "But," Frank demurred, "I'm planning an academic career." Hitler waved aside the objection, and Frank soon found himself defending hundreds of Nazis against charges of slander, libel, assault, attempted murder, and destruction of property. By the age of twenty-eight, he was the Nazis' chief counsel. His party work won headlines and soon other clients flocked to his Munich office. Hans Frank never traveled third class again.

In 1930, Hitler summoned him and thrust a list of Reichstag candidates into his hand. He had placed the name of Hans Frank on the Nazi slate. Frank was elected and, at thirty years of age, became one of the Reichstag's youngest members. The Nazis came to power in 1933, and Frank continued to prosper. By 1939 he was Germany's minister of justice, founder and president of the Academy of German Law, the highest-ranking jurist in the land, a man of undeniable respectability, all before his fortieth birthday.

But he never forgot Lilli Gau. As the nanny readied his children for school, as he sprang down the steps of his villa, as his chauffeur opened the door to his Daimler-Benz limousine, he often wondered, what would Lilli think of Hans Frank now?

When the war broke out, Frank joined his Bavarian regiment as a lieutenant. Within weeks after Poland's defeat, an orderly delivered a personal telegram from the Führer. Frank was to come to Hitler's private railway car in Silesia to discuss an assignment more suitable to his talents. After the meeting, Frank raced back home and burst into his wife's dressing room. "Brigitte," he exclaimed, "you are going to be the queen of Poland!" As Frank explained, a huge chunk of western Poland had been absorbed into the Third Reich for German settlers. The Soviet Union had taken a slice of eastern Poland. What remained in the middle, some forty percent of the original country, was to be ruled by Frank as "governor-general," exercising "supreme powers"; or almost supreme powers, since the Führer had explained that Frank would have to share some of his authority with Reichsführer Heinrich Himmler, head of the SS. Himmler's repressive apparatus was needed to run the concentration camps that would keep the unruly Poles in line. Where would they live? Brigitte wanted to know. In Cracow, he told her, in a palace.

At his first sight of Wawel Castle, the ancient seat of Polish kings, Frank behaved like a child given a huge toy. His open touring car roared through the gateway and into the courtyard of a structure dating from the tenth century. Resplendent in a personally designed uniform with flaring breeches and black boots, he bounded up the steps to the main entrance, trailed by adjutants. He entered the throne room, its walls cloaked with medieval tapestries depicting Noah's ark. Here, he decided, he would hold official receptions. Nearby he found an only slightly smaller room, its twenty-foot walls sheathed in tooled red leather. This would be his private office. In another wing he came upon the royal bedchamber, the bed raised up on a platform approached by marble steps. Over the bed a canopy of gilded brocade hung suspended on four marble pillars. He spied a jewel-like chapel off the bedroom. This would please Brigitte, who had never abandoned their Catholic faith as Frank had done in order to advance his career under atheistic Nazism.

As Hans Frank began to rule over this remaining rump of Poland, he felt uneasy only at the arrival of the intimidating Himmler. Frank well knew Himmler's priority, and was eager to please. Thus, his first official act as governor-general was to order all Polish Jews to report for assignment to German labor offices.

Nazi Jewish policy was ticklish for Frank. As an intelligent, cultivated man who could recite the verses of Heine by heart, he did not believe the Nazi party's crude anti-Semitic claptrap. More troublesome, Frank had a dark secret thus far kept from the party's arbiters of purity. Though he had been raised as a Catholic, he was part Jewish. The family name was believed to have been Frankfurter originally. Frank overcompensated with zeal. On his first anniversary at Wawel Castle, he invited his staff and their families to the throne room for a celebration. Beneath the ancient tapestries long tables were set up, burdened with Polish hams, cheeses, and bottles of vodka. Frank took the center of the floor and reviewed the year's progress, achieved in great part, he said, because so many "lice and Jews had been eliminated." "I am telling you quite candidly," he went on, "there must be a stop to them one way or another." As he spoke, a young, bespectacled officer scribbled furiously. Frank had ordered that everything he said, in public or in his office, was to be recorded for posterity. They had met their quota, Frank boasted, by deporting 1.3 million Poles for forced labor in Germany. And, "At the current level of permitted rations, some 1.2 million Jews could be expected to die of hunger." That was not enough, he went on. "We must obliterate the Jews. We cannot kill them with poison. But somehow or other we will achieve their extermination."

Afterward, Brigadeführer Strechenback came up and thanked the governor-general for a letter of commendation he had recently received. "What you and your people have done, *Brigadeführer,*" Frank had written, "must not be forgotten and you need not be ashamed of it." What Strechenback had done was to round up 3,500 prominent Poles and have them shot.

Cracow was to have been their Camelot, and in the beginning, Brigitte Frank reveled in the glittering social life her husband inaugurated, with its stream of Nazi luminaries to whom she played hostess. She relished her trips to the city's Jewish section and up to the Warsaw ghetto. She loved the craftsmanship of the hand-sewn camisoles the Jews made, the furs, gold, and carpets that, in their desperation, they would sell for practically nothing. Frau Frank was greedy, but not insensitive. The reports sent back to Germany about the improved lot of the Poles under her husband's leadership were contradicted in the wizened face of every child she saw, and by the Jewish corpses littering ghetto streets. The undisguised hatred that greeted her every appearance in Poland began to depress her. And so she retreated to her country home in Schliersee in Bavaria and had the Polish loot shipped to her.

Hans Frank became lonely. He sent for his thirteen-year-old son, Norman, and gave him the bedroom once occupied by the Polish queen Jadwiga. Norman was enrolled in a school for the children of Nazi officials. On a day in May 1941, while he and his classmates were playing soccer, they heard men singing the Polish anthem outside the school walls. The boys stopped to listen when the song was cut short by the crack of rifle fire. What was that? Norman asked the teacher. "Oh that," he said. "They're shooting Poles." After school Norman came into his father's office and asked why the Poles had been shot. The smile with which Frank had greeted his son vanished. "This is war," he said. "Don't ever ask such foolish questions again."

Later, a classmate of Norman's drew a picture of a factory with Jews entering a chute at the top and bars of soap emerging at the bottom. The teacher found the drawing amusing and passed it around the class. That night when his father came to say good night to him in the cold, damp Queen Jadwiga bedroom, Norman wanted to ask about the picture but decided not to.

Hans Frank, whatever the surface glitter of his life, was close to a nervous breakdown. On Himmler's most recent visit, the *Reichsführer* had confronted Frank with proof of massive corruption in his administration, including a fur-smuggling operation carried on by his wife. Himmler told Frank he was willing to drop the investigation on one condition: Frank was to turn over to the SS all police functions in Poland. Frank knew that this meant unfettered exploitation of the Poles and accelerated extermination of the Jews. He wrote a letter to the chief of the Wehrmacht, Field Marshal Wilhelm Keitel, asking to be returned to military duty. The lackey Keitel immediately showed the letter to Hitler, who read it and said, "Out of the question." Frank thereafter accepted Himmler's conditions. The flow of Jews to the concentration camps quickened.

Then, when all seemed hollowest, her letter arrived in a pale blue envelope. The familiar handwriting jolted him. It was from Lilli, whom he had not seen for over twenty years. It began, "My Dearest Hans," and in it she appealed to him, as a powerful figure in the Reich, to help a heartbroken mother. Her son had been killed on the Russian front and she begged him to find out the details. Frank immediately set his staff to work on the case. He flew to Germany and personally delivered his finding to Lilli at her country home in Bavaria. The electricity between them still crackled, and he found her husband surprisingly tolerant. Lilli took an apartment in Munich for their love nest and Frank flew from Cracow almost every month to be with her.

He felt as if he had been reborn. In Poland he may have signed a pact with the devil in order to maintain his station and to keep Himmler at bay—but these acts only affected backward Poles and wretched Jews. In Germany he could again be the man he had started out to be, a champion of the law. Lilli had inspired him. He was going to ask Brigitte for a divorce and marry Lilli. He was going to remake his life.

In June 1942, he went home to address the Academy of German Law. He made a speech the likes of which had not been heard since Hitler had taken power, a speech certainly that no other member of the Führer's inner circle would have dared. Germany, Frank said, must return to the rule of law. No civilized nation could permit the arbitrary arrests, the imprisonment without due process, carried out by the Gestapo and the SS. "Law either exists or it does not," Frank warned. "Where there is no system of justice, the state sinks into a pit of darkness and horror." He made three similar speeches, one at his

Munich University alma mater, to the wild cheering of the law students.

Frank was summoned before the Führer, expecting the worst. Hitler told him that he could excuse an occasional lapse of judgment, and that he intended to regard Frank's bizarre behavior as such. In the future, however, Frank was to confine his speeches to Poland and to the party line. And as for Frank's divorcing his wife, that was impossible.

Hans Frank returned to Poland and dutifully delivered up the conscript workers to the labor czar, Fritz Sauckel, and the Jews to Himmler. Most of the latter, he knew, were sent to a camp some thirty miles from Cracow called Auschwitz. He resumed his chant of hate. One month after he gave the speeches on restoring law to Germany, he pulled together a group of Polish collaborators and told them, "Jews? Yes, we still have a few of them around, but we'll soon take care of that."

In January 1943, Frank summoned his closest associates to his private office. "All of us gathered here are now duty-bound to stick together," he said. "We are on Mr. Roosevelt's list of war criminals." And, he added cockily, "I have the honor of being number one." As he spoke, the bespectacled aide took down every word, which he would later type up for the governor-general's diary, just as he had done for the past three years.

The mad round at Wawel Castle went on. An endless parade of Nazi *Bonzen*—propaganda minister Joseph Goebbels, the party's chief theorist, Alfred Rosenberg, as well as a stream of movie stars, musicians, and opera singers—continued to arrive for Frank's fabled parties, traveling in Frank's private railway car. But when he was alone, the inner torment became agonizing. He would retreat to the piano in his bedroom, where he played Chopin and Beethoven. He also began writing a novel, called *Cabin Boy of Columbus*. These distractions helped him to forget what Hans Frank had become.

In early 1945, as the Red Army thrust deep into Poland, Frank fled Cracow. He took with him, among other art treasures, Leonardo da Vinci's masterpiece *Lady with an Ermine*, stolen from a Polish museum. He also brought along his diary, now bound in forty-two red-and-gray volumes totaling 11,367 pages.

He returned to his home in Schliersee and set up a "branch office" of the Polish governor-general. He was fooling no one, least of all himself. He was simply waiting for the war to end. When the Americans found him in May, he put up no resistance, since he was convinced he had a strong hand to play. First, he led Seventh Army officers to a cellar and told them he was turning over twenty-two priceless works of art, including the Leonardo, works he said he had been protecting from the Russian barbarians. He also gave the Americans his diary. It was all there, the words that would save him, his improvement of the lives of the Poles, his fights with Himmler, his brave law speeches in Germany, his attempts to resign the governor-general's job. Certainly, the Americans would see through the pro forma anti-Semitic rabble-rousing. It was simply the lip service any Nazi official was expected to spout in order to keep his job.

Instead of receiving gratitude from the American officers, Frank had been beaten, kicked, and spat upon by their troops. They had thrown him into the back of a truck for the trip to Miesbach prison. As the truck bumped along the shell-pocked road, he had taken out an army knife and slashed at his throat. An alert GI had pried the knife from his hand. The cut was superficial. A military doctor bandaged his neck and the trip continued.

Now, he sat in Miesbach prison, a pasty, soft-looking man with thick lips, thinning dark hair, and dark-rimmed sad eyes, the gardening knife clutched in his right hand. As he drew it across his left wrist, a GI burst into the cell and flung him to the ground, thwarting his second suicide attempt. Hans Frank had been saved for eventual transport to Nuremberg, where he would face trial for war crimes and crimes against humanity.

6

ROBERT JACKSON HAD staffing problems. The Democratic national chairman wanted him to hire hack lawyers as political payoffs. A Jewish delegation from New York tried to tell Jackson which witnesses to call and which Jewish lawyers to hire. He pointed out the damage they would do if they let this become a "Jewish trial." They had to get away from the racial aspects. They were prosecuting these Nazis not because they had killed Jews but because they had killed people. The trial must not be seen simply as an exercise in vengeance.

Jackson's resources at this point were undeniably thin: a six-page master plan, a secretary, his son and a friend as aides, and a potential executive officer in Murray Bernays. Bernays impressed him, but Jackson was disappointed by the rest of the War Department. The department staff had collected only sketchy data on scattered atrocities thus far, hardly the quality of evidence that forms the life's blood of any successful prosecution.

And then Senator Alben Barkley tipped him off to where the gold lay. The key was a proud man, a power in his own right, and wooing him could be tricky, Barkley warned. Jackson was prepared to chance it. He buzzed Elsie Douglas and told her to ring up the Office of Strategic Services on Q Street and arrange a lunch date for him with General Wild Bill Donovan.

They had much in common. Both were upstate New Yorkers, boys of humble birth who had made good; both were Justice Department alumni who loved the law; and both were members of the club of influence, Jackson on the Democratic and Donovan on the Republican side.

Jackson came to Donovan like a man hungry for a crust of bread. Fifteen minutes into their meeting, Donovan seemed to have spread a banquet before him. Until now, Jackson had known little of Donovan or of his creation, the hush-hush OSS. The pudgy, modest-looking general had been the most heavily decorated American officer to come out of the First World War. He had gotten rich between the wars in a gilt-edged New York law practice. In this war, he had fought the naysayers and bureaucratic rivals in the FBI and the armed forces to build the OSS from nothing into America's first intelligence service.

The OSS, Donovan explained, had field operations throughout Europe. His people had been tracking potential war criminals since 1942, and had accumulated substantial dossiers. Furthermore, he had every imaginable specialist within his ranks: scientists, linguists, even architects who could build Jackson a courthouse if need be. Best of all, he had attracted some of America's brightest young lawyers into the OSS. Depending on the demands of the war in the Pacific, he could make many of these people available to Jackson.

As Donovan talked, Jackson considered a bold gamble. Wild Bill not only had an organization in place, but knew how to open doors throughout Washington and the military. If Jackson had Donovan at his side, the battle of preparation, recruitment, and organization would be half won. He took the plunge. He did not know how, he said, to make his offer attractive to a man of Donovan's stature—but would the general possibly consider becoming his lead prosecutor? The general's pale blue eyes gazed off briefly and then he said, "I'll think about it."

7

THE WAR IN EUROPE ended in the ancient cathedral city of Rheims in a sterile red brick building, the Boys' Technical and Professional School. On May 6, 1945, its windows were jammed with Allied military personnel eager to catch a glimpse of history. On the second floor, in what had once been a drafting classroom, General Eisenhower gazed out as a dun-colored U.S. Army command car pulled up bearing an eagerly awaited party.

Colonel General Alfred Jodl, small, trim, erect, with the pinched expression of someone weaned on a lemon, stepped from the car. Jodl began to raise his hand in a salute that was barely acknowledged by Allied officers who regarded him with cold curiosity. Jodl was escorted into a room where, before the war, French schoolboys had played Ping-Pong and crammed for exams. Jodl sat down with Eisenhower's deputies, since the supreme commander had refused to negotiate with a Nazi general. Jodl proceeded to carry out the orders given him by Grand Admiral Karl Dönitz. His instructions were simply to stall as long as possible before surrendering. Every day, every hour gained would mean more German units could escape the clutches of the Russians and surrender instead to the British and Americans.

As Jodl dragged his feet through the deliberations, Eisenhower lost all patience. He directed his aides to inform Jodl that either he signed the instrument of surrender or he would seal the Western front. Fleeing Germans would then march into gunfire instead of POW cages. The game was over. At 2:38 a.m., May 7, Jodl affixed his signature to the terms of surrender to take effect in forty-eight hours. Six years of world war in Europe were about to end. The next day another ceremony took place in Berlin to satisfy the Russians.

After the surrender, Jodl returned to Flensburg, near the Danish-German border, where Dönitz was headquartered. There he learned that the stalling strategies had allowed over 900,000 German soldiers originally facing the Russians to reach the American and British lines.

Grand Admiral Dönitz had set up his government in Flensburg just days after succeeding Adolf Hitler as führer. He had placed a plaster bust of Hitler on his dresser in the captain's stateroom of the Hamburg-American line's steamship *Patria*, where he established his living quarters. Every morning the admiral was driven in one of Hitler's Mercedes autos five hundred feet from the *Patria* to his headquarters, where the flag of the German military still flew. There he met with the government he had formed: a minister of education to deal with schools in the postwar era, a minister of war who was determining what salutes, flags, and medals would be used in the new Germany. Dönitz had named Albert Speer, Hitler's armaments chief, as minister of economics and production in this Potemkin village government. After the surrender, with the official photographer present, Dönitz had presented the Knight's Cross to General Jodl for his performance at Rheims.

Dönitz, a slight, gray man, might well have passed for a small-town pharmacist. This unprepossessing figure had, however, been the terror of the Atlantic. Karl Dönitz invented the "wolf pack" submarine strategy that had sunk 2,472 Allied ships. Hitler had called him "the Rommel of the Seas," and eventually gave Dönitz command of the entire German navy. Since he had few political convictions, other than a distaste for messy democracy and a hatred of Bolshevism, Dönitz had let Hitler become his political compass. The usually cool technocrat became mesmerized in the Führer's presence. After a few days, Dönitz admitted he had to flee the Führer's headquarters to regain his independence of mind. Why Adolf Hitler had chosen him, a simple sailor, to succeed as führer still mystified Dönitz. He was an outsider, hardly one of the old party fighters. He had accepted the appointment with the same spirit that had governed his entire naval career: obeying an order was an officer's highest duty.

On May 23, fifteen days after the surrender, British tanks rolled into the Flensburg town square. A British officer arrived at Dönitz's office and asked the admiral if he would be good enough to gather his ministers in the lounge of the *Patria*. On their arrival, General Eisenhower's personal representative, Lowell W. Rooks, announced, "Gentlemen, I am empowered by the supreme allied commander to inform you that as of this moment, the Flensburg government is dissolved. You have one half hour to pack one bag before you are taken to your respective places of detention." Rooks then drew a list from his pocket and said that the following men would be taken to Bad Mondorf as defendants in future war-crimes trials.

When his name was called, Dönitz summoned the discipline of a lifetime to mask his shock and outrage. He caught sight of an equally stunned Jodl as the general's name was called. The Flensburg net also swept up as war-crimes suspects Field Marshal Wilhelm Keitel, chief of staff of the armed forces, Alfred Rosenberg, the philosopher of Nazism, and Albert Speer.

Dönitz went to his room and began packing a black leather bag. He looked briefly at the Hitler bust and decided it was now excess baggage. In the passageway on his return to the lounge, he encountered Jodl. What did the admiral suppose all this war-criminal talk meant? Jodl asked. Were they not soldiers doing what a soldier does —Eisenhower, Montgomery, Zhukov, the whole lot of them? Dönitz gave him a mirthless smile. In his case, the admiral observed, Hitler was dead, so his successor evidently would have to do.

8

THE SUN AT Washington's National Airport was blazing the morning of June 26. The air shimmered off the tarmac, enveloping the silvery hull of an Army Air Forces C54C transport fitted out for VIP service. Justice Robert Jackson, in a dark, three-piece suit, felt his shirt collar form a damp noose around his neck. He motioned to Elsie Douglas to mount the portable staircase to the plane's hatchway. As she started up, he gave her hand a squeeze. He knew that she was uneasy. It was her first flight. The rest of the party—seventeen lawyers, secretaries, and assorted staff—fell in behind Jackson for the trip to London.

Inside the plane, an Army Air Forces sergeant suggested that Jackson take a first-row seat next to the window. Jackson turned and signaled for U.S. Army Colonel Robert Storey to sit next to him. As the transport became airborne, Jackson looked out and caught a last glimpse of the Supreme Court building below.

Colonel Storey, a Texas lawyer before the war, had paid a courtesy call soon after Jackson was appointed chief American prosecutor. A mild-mannered, balding man in his fifties, Storey fit Jackson like an old shoe. The colonel also had a useful background. Jackson was off to meet his foreign counterparts to organize an international court, including representatives of the Soviet Union. Everything he had learned thus far persuaded him that the Russians were going to be trouble. In the final months of the war, Storey had carried out an OSS mission with the Red Army, and as the Soviets advanced into Germany, he had witnessed war-crimes trials, Communist-style. Jackson valued this experience, and he liked Storey. Thus he had enlisted the man for his staff.

As the plane leveled off, Jackson began questioning Storey about his Soviet adventure. The Russians, Storey explained, would put the accused on the witness stand, convict him by confession, and execute him, usually before the sun went down. Often, the condemned were not war criminals at all, Storey had concluded, but simply opponents of Communism. Jackson should know, he warned, that the Russians understood only one language: power.

The trial of war criminals, Jackson had become convinced, must signal not simply the triumph of superior might, but the triumph of superior morality. He was in a position to fashion a future in which aggressive warfare would no longer be resignedly accepted as the extreme edge of political activity, but dealt with as a crime, with aggressors treated as criminals. That could be the greatest leap forward in the history of civilization. Surely, it surpassed anything he had yet done, including his service on the Supreme Court.

On arriving in London, the Jackson party checked into Claridge's Hotel. To one who had never witnessed war, the scene from Jackson's window was sobering. Skeletons of buildings stood silhouetted against the night, their blasted windows gaping like empty eye sockets. He watched Londoners weave around craters and along paths cut through the rubble. This brave city, pockmarked and bleeding, with thousands of innocent dead, confirmed his sense of mission. War-crimes trials were a splendid idea, Jackson thought.

Robert Jackson and Britain's attorney general, Sir David Maxwell-Fyfe, were entering Church House on Great Smith Street, which the British government had provided for the Allied war-crimes negotiations. Jackson found himself chatting with a dark-skinned man in his mid-forties, thickset, heavily jowled, with full lips, thinning hair, eyes set in deep recesses, and the self-effacing manner of a secure personality. He resembled a Syrian diplomat or an Egyptian merchant far more than the Scot that he was. "Swarthy and ugly," was how Sir David described himself, "and my waistline has launched a career of its own."

The delegations from the Big Four powers seated themselves at a table of India teak in the conference room. The others seemed to expect Jackson to take the place at the head of the table. The Americans had pressed hardest for trying war criminals; they held most of the expected defendants in custody. More to the point, in a Europe enfeebled by war, they were in the best position to pick up the tab for whatever this enterprise cost. Jackson presented the agenda. What the delegates faced was the legal equivalent of drafting the Ten Commandments, he began. Every nation had its criminal statutes. But for the world at large, none existed. They had to invent a court and give it authority. They had to agree on procedures. They had to write a statute that would describe the crimes the defendants had perpetrated and the penalties for conviction.

Jackson looked around, judging the colleagues from whom he would have to extract a consensus: Maxwell-Fyfe and his fellow Britishers—probably reasonable; the French delegation—inscrutable; the Russians—likely obstructive. General Donovan's OSS had provided Jackson with a profile of the principal Russian negotiator, Major General of Jurisprudence Ion Timofeevich Nikitchenko. Jackson had read the report at Claridge's the night before. Nikitchenko, fifty years old, had gone to work in a coal mine in the Donbass at age thirteen. The Communist revolution provided his escape. He became a Red Army soldier and fought in the Russian civil war. Afterward, he took a law degree at Moscow University and rose to his present position as vice president of the Soviet Supreme Court. Jackson knew the facts, but could read nothing beyond them in that broad Slavic face with its steel-gray, unblinking eyes.

For ten days the delegates wrangled. Jackson was looking forward to escaping, at least temporarily, to check out possible trial sites on the Continent. This evening, he was stretched out in his suspenders and stocking feet in his sitting room in Claridge's, dictating to Elsie Douglas. He wanted to get down on paper where the negotiations stood before he left London. She flipped open her steno pad as Jackson began the resonant phrase-making that always pleased and impressed her.

The greatest problem they faced, he said, was to overcome criticism that they were creating ex post facto law. *Nullum crimen et nulla poena sine lege*, the ancient Romans had said: No crime and no punishment without law. Obviously, the Nazis had committed naked aggression and unspeakable acts. But what *laws* had they broken? What statute, what chapter of what code could a prosecutor cite? Yes, Germany, along with sixty-three other countries, had signed the Kellogg-Briand Pact outlawing war. Germany had also signed peace pacts with Poland and the Soviet Union. Germany had signed the Treaty of Versailles, and the Locarno Pact. Germany was a signatory of the Hague Rules of Land Warfare of 1907 and the Geneva Conventions of 1929. Jackson read off Germany's violations of these solemn agreements with biblical righteousness: 1939, Poland invaded; 1940, Norway, Belgium, Luxembourg, and the Netherlands invaded; 1941, Greece, Yugoslavia, and the Soviet Union invaded. Four days after Pearl Harbor, the Germans had declared war on the United States. As for the accepted norms of warfare, Germany had left the Geneva and Hague agreements in tatters.

Jackson began to craft his rationale as to why the Allies were not engaged in ex post facto law, dictating it to Elsie Douglas. By creating a court and defining procedures and punishment, they were merely adding the missing element of enforcement. If no punishment followed violation, what was the point of august figures gathering in world capitals and signing all these treaties? Jackson warmed to his argument. "Let's not be derailed by legal hair-splitters. Aren't murder, torture, and enslavement crimes recognized by all civilized people?

What we propose is to punish acts which have been regarded as criminal since the time of Cain and have been so written in every civilized code."

Colonel Storey had warned Jackson about the Russians, and General Nikitchenko proved Storey a prophet. Still, the man puzzled Jackson. Nikitchenko could sit motionless as a Buddha for hours, though Jackson thought he detected in those cool eyes the fleeting bemusement of a man performing a part. Some of Nikitchenko's argumentativeness, however, was understandable. The French displayed it too, though less belligerently. To the Continental Europeans it seemed that the Anglo-Saxons were trying to ram an alien court system down their throats. Nikitchenko listened as Jackson and Maxwell-Fyfe explained adversarial law, with its opposing attorneys, direct examination, and cross-examination, before a judge who acted as umpire. That was not how it was done in his country, he said. The French agreed. Their judges did not demean themselves by prying battling lawyers apart like a referee at a prizefight. Judges took evidence from witnesses, from the accused, from the police, from the victims, sifted it, weighed it, and arrived at their decisions. Lawyers were merely to help the accused prepare a defense. They had little role in the court itself. Lawyers are not so important, Nikitchenko concluded with a lecturing tone; judges are important. And this matter of pleading guilty or not guilty: Were they really going to allow a man like Ernst Kaltenbrunner, responsible for the Gestapo and for concentration camps, to stand up in a court of law and declare himself not guilty?

When at last they adjourned for lunch, Maxwell-Fyfe invited Jackson to his club.

Jackson, whose capacity for outrage occasionally left him drained, envied Maxwell-Fyfe's self-containment. They might as well accept it, Sir David said over lunch, they were going to wind up with a hybrid, given the national differences that had to be conciliated. At least they had reached agreement on the number of judges, four principals representing each country, and four alternates. Multiple judges provided the Continental touch. Sir David regarded it as a major victory that they had finally been able to persuade the Russians and French to accept the adversarial system of opposing lawyers. Jackson mentioned

Nikitchenko's fight for easy convictions. They had won that point too, Sir David pointed out. They had agreed on three of four votes to convict, causing Nikitchenko to howl. And they had a name for the court, the International Military Tribunal—rather grand, Sir David observed.

Jackson asked what he thought they should do when the accused raised the defense that they were simply carrying out superior orders. That, Sir David said, could not be permitted; the whole prosecution case would collapse. The Germans under Hitler had operated on the *Führerprinzip*, the concept that the leader has absolute authority. What the Führer ordered, his subordinates carried out. What those below him ordered, their subordinates carried out in turn, and so on, down the pyramid of power. If they allowed the defense of "superior orders," they would be able to convict only Adolf Hitler, and he was dead.

Jackson remained uneasy. In the final months of the Italian campaign, an American GI had gunned down defenseless German prisoners and escaped punishment through a "superior orders" defense. Sir David countered with the statement printed in the paybook of every German soldier: he was not required to obey an illegal order. If that was true for a corporal in the Wehrmacht, why would it not apply to those immediately under Hitler? Jackson suggested that they at least consider superior orders in mitigation of sentence.

What surely would give them the devil of a time, Maxwell-Fyfe went on, was tu quoque, the "so-did-you" defense. If the crimes they were defining applied only to the Germans, how would they escape history's verdict that the trial was not justice but merely victor's vengeance? Atrocities had been committed on all sides. Further, they were planning to prosecute aggression as a war crime. Yet sitting in judgment would be Russians whose nation had invaded Finland in 1940 and grabbed a chunk of Poland under its 1939 pact with the Nazis.

Tu quoque, Jackson said, had to be another unacceptable defense. It implied that because some murderers went free, then all murderers must go free—a mockery of justice. The Nazi murders had been committed on an unimaginable scale. How could the world simply walk away from the deaths of from six million to ten million people? It would be hypocritical to deny that there was no element of vengeance in a war-crimes trial. Germans were going to be in the dock because

Germany had lost the war. But, Jackson pointed out, a thief or em-
bezzler is only in the dock because he gets caught. All well and good,
Maxwell-Fyfe persisted. But how did Jackson suggest that they get
around tu quoque? They would simply state in the statute that tu
quoque was inadmissible, Jackson suggested. Sir David looked at his
guest with renewed respect. He had not anticipated Yankee pragmatism.

9

ERNST KALTENBRUNNER, whose very name incensed General Nikitchenko, was what people expected in a Nazi. So many of these once-
fearsome figures were a disappointment up close—like Dönitz, with
his clerklike mien. A man like Jodl would have escaped notice in a
group of five people. Kaltenbrunner, chief of the RSHA, the Reich
Central Security Office, however, was out of central casting. His neck
rose directly from his shoulders to his head without tapering. Huge
hands dangled at his sides. His horse face was seamed by a thin, cruel
mouth and a scar that cut a purple swath across his left cheek. At six
feet six inches tall, he managed somehow to look fleshy and gangling
at the same time.

At the war's end, Kaltenbrunner had been hiding out in a chalet
in the Austrian Alps near Alt Aussee, where a patrol from the U.S.
Third Army stumbled onto him. The lumbering giant, just another
kraut officer to General Patton's GIs, surrendered meekly. Twelve
days after his capture, Frau Rosel Plutz heard on the radio that the
Americans had arrested a high-ranking SS officer. The unemployed
thirty-three-year-old mother, with a missing soldier husband, was desperate. Here was a chance to ingratiate herself with the victors. She
immediately went to the American military government office at
Nordhausen. She had been a typist, Frau Plutz told the captain in
charge, at a concentration camp called Dora-Gestapo. One of her duties had been to type death sentences. She remembered the signature
that appeared on all of them: that of Ernst Kaltenbrunner.

After his denunciation, Kaltenbrunner was placed in the military
prison near Nordhausen. A few days after his arrival, he approached
a GI guard and tried to bum a cigarette from him. The American was

reading a U.S. tabloid, and flashed the paper under the prisoner's nose. Kaltenbrunner saw his photograph and a bold headline. What did it say? he asked. It said, the soldier explained, "Gas Chamber Expert Captured." Kaltenbrunner went deathly pale. Soon afterward, he was bundled into the back of an Army six-by-six truck and taken to Bad Mondorf.

10

NOT UNTIL EARLY JULY did Justice Jackson manage to disentangle himself from the London negotiations long enough to look for a trial site. He traveled in a Dakota transport with his son, Bill, and Wild Bill Donovan, whose OSS personnel always met them with useful information wherever they landed. By July 7, they had checked out Wiesbaden, Frankfurt, and Munich, where they met with Ike's deputy, General Lucius Clay. Clay had suggested the merits of Luxembourg as an appropriately neutral site. Jackson, however, insisted that the place to drive home German criminality was Germany. The Russians, Donovan noted, would insist on Berlin for the trial. Clay frowned. The army could not find housing for the trial staff in that shattered city. He had a better alternative, he said as they reboarded the Dakota.

Jackson dozed off briefly, only to be wakened by Clay pointing earthward. That was it, the general said. Jackson gazed out the starboard window. He had seen the bomb damage in London, the ruins of Frankfurt and Munich. But nothing had prepared him for the urban corpse below. Where were they? he asked. Where Jackson would likely find his courthouse, Clay said. That was Nuremberg.

Until the war, Nuremberg had preserved its medieval aspect. Tourists, particularly well-to-do Britishers, loved scaling its eleventh-century watchtowers and walking along the banks of the gently winding Pegnitz River, spanned by bridges built four hundred years before. Some might find the gingerbread charm of the city cloying, but most delighted in Nuremberg's houses with their high-pitched, red-tiled roofs and carved dormers jutting out overhead, their gables crowned with painted wooden statuettes.

Nuremberg had given Germany its first railroad line and the

world its first pocketwatch and clarinet. It was a toy-making center famed for exquisite miniatures, perfectly replicated trains, the engine no bigger than a man's thumb, and tiny cannons that actually fired. Nuremberg had also given Germany her greatest artist, Albrecht Dürer, whose birthplace still stood on the square that bore his name. Emperor Charles IV had christened Nuremberg his *Schatzkästlein*, the treasure chest of his kingdom.

It was also in Nuremberg that the Nazis had found their spiritual home. The medieval aura suited the movement's mystical streak. And the local police could be counted on to be sympathetic. By 1933, with Hitler in power, the annual Nuremberg rallies had become the chief celebration of Nazi life, weeklong extravaganzas choreographed by Hitler's brilliant young architect, Albert Speer. The *Parteitagen* began in September with church bells tolling Hitler's arrival at the railroad station. The city's streets rumbled with the pounding of hobnailed boots. The night sky lit up like a giant bonfire as party faithful from every corner of the Reich bore their torches through the ancient streets. Their destination was Zeppelin Field on the edge of town, a massive stadium that held a quarter of a million people arrayed in ranks of hypnotizing precision, shouting themselves into an orgiastic frenzy at the words of Adolf Hitler.

This was also the city where the Nuremberg Laws had been proclaimed, statutes that deprived German Jews of their rights, their property, and eventually their status as human beings.

The treasure chest of the kingdom had been transformed into the sight that chilled Justice Jackson by men like Lieutenant Colonel Chester Cox, 388th Bomber Group, U.S. Eighth Air Force. At 7:28 a.m. on February 19, 1945, Cox and his B-17 crew had taken off from a field in England's East Anglia. Cox rendezvoused with 1,249 other Flying Fortresses and set a course for Nuremberg. At 11:11 a.m. they were over the target. Captain Hanlen, the bombardier, hunched over his bombsight, looking for the pretargeted marshaling yards, locomotive shops, and a tank factory. The bomb-bay doors swung open and the plane disgorged five 500-pounders and five incendiaries. The aircraft, suddenly lighter, shot upward as Cox banked her hard to get away from the flak bursts exploding around them, and headed home.

The day before, another 900 B-17s had struck Nuremberg, dropping 11,042 bombs. Today's raid rained 6,693 high explosives and 4,624 incendiaries on the city. From the time the RAF had first struck in October 1943 until the war's final raid, Nuremberg was bombed eleven times. In the final siege, the American Third and Forty-fifth infantry divisions pounded the city with an artillery barrage followed by five days of house-to-house fighting.

After the surrender, an American military government team surveyed Nuremberg and declared it ninety-one-percent destroyed. Of 130,000 original dwellings, only 17,000 had survived intact. Of a population of 450,000 people, 160,000 remained. The city gave off a stench from an estimated 30,000 bodies trapped beneath the rubble. Nuremberg was a city without electricity, public water, public transportation, telephone, mail, or telegraph service, and without a government. Until the occupation authorities took over, the streets belonged to looters, thieves, and rapists. The Americans declared Nuremberg "among the dead cities of the European continent." Yet there survived on its western edge a huge, frowning structure, the *Justizgebaude*, the Palace of Justice: the courthouse of the government of Bavaria.

The Jackson party landed at an airfield outside of Nuremberg designated by the military as Y28. As the Dakota taxied to a halt, a motorcade of staff cars and jeeps snaked out to the runway. Young Bill Jackson noticed an angle iron welded perpendicular to every jeep's front bumper and rising well above the hood. What were they for? he asked. A driver explained that the angle iron served as a knife to cut wires the Germans strung across the road at night. Several GIs had already been decapitated by them.

The ride into town proved a grim confirmation of what Jackson had glimpsed from the air. Shabbily dressed people wound their way through trenches of rubble, heads bent, faces vacant, movements listless. The few standing walls along the route were plastered with signs warning GIs against fraternizing with German nationals. A girl in a tight dress pointed to one such sign as Jackson's party rolled by. She slapped a shapely behind and shouted, *"Verboten!"*

The motorcade slowed and turned through a gateway in a wrought-iron fence surrounding a fortresslike structure. Their arrival put a halt to games of pitch-and-catch that GIs were playing in the yard. Jackson stared up at a three-story stone building capped by a steeply pitched roof. Most of the windows were blasted out. The yard was littered with spent cartridge cases, and the façade of the court-house pitted with bullet holes. A U.S. Army colonel approached and introduced himself as their escort. The colonel informed the party that the Palace of Justice had taken five hits, with one bomb plunging from the roof to the basement. The building seemed simply to have shrugged off the blows and gone on dominating what was left of Nu-remberg's skyline.

Inside, they entered a maze of corridors, the walls blackened by fire and the floors wet with leakage from burst water mains. Army quartermasters had strung Lister bags along the walls to provide pure drinking water. The colonel led them up a stairwell littered with scorched books. General Donovan picked one up. "Law text," he said and tossed it aside. They arrived at room 600 on the third floor, the main courtroom. Over the entry was a sculptured tablet representing the Ten Commandments.

As they entered, a group of GIs came to desultory attention. A keg of beer sat on what had been the judge's bench. Behind the bench a red-lettered sign proclaiming TEXAS BAR was flanked by several pin-ups and another sign announcing BEER TONIGHT, ½ MARK. The room was strewn with broken chairs, Coke cases, beer bottles, and candy wrappers. Wedged between two desks stood an upright piano. Only the ornate chandeliers, a huge baroque clock, and bas-relief figures of Adam and Eve carved in marble over the doorway reminded the vis-itors of the Texas Bar's previous incarnation.

There was something else they must see, the colonel said, and led the party across a driveway to a twenty-foot brick wall. Behind that wall, he explained, were four wings of cellblocks fanning out from a center core, enough cells to accommodate twelve hundred prisoners. The prison was currently full of ordinary criminal defendants. One wing, however, could quickly be cleared for war criminals. The best hotel in Nuremberg, the Grand, was also standing, miraculously in-tact, the colonel explained. In this virtually dead city, General Clay pointed out, were a courthouse with plenty of office space, a jail, and first-class hotel accommodations for top staff. That, Jackson observed, was precision bombing.

As the motorcade began its crawl back through the defiles of destruction, Jackson wondered how they could ever hope to operate amid this chaos. How would he sell Nuremberg to the British and French, and talk the Russians out of Berlin? Clay said he would make a start. He could have General Patton move in fifteen thousand German POWs in the next forty-eight hours to clear the streets.

11

LIEUTENANT ROGER BARRETT was a thirty-year-old Chicago lawyer with a knack for spotting significant documents—a trait acquired from his father, a noted collector of Lincolniana. Barrett had before him a complaint filed by a German construction official attached to a plant in the Nazi-occupied Ukraine. In it, Hermann Graebe described in detail how, out of curiosity, he had followed a German SS unit that he saw herding thousands of Jews out of the town of Dubno to an earth embankment outside the city. "Without screaming or weeping," Graebe had written, "these people undressed, stood around in family groups, kissed each other, said farewells. . . . An old woman with snow-white hair was holding a one-year-old child in her arms and singing to it and tickling it. The child was cooing with delight. . . . A father was holding the hand of a boy about ten years old and speaking to him softly; the boy was fighting his tears." An SS man standing at a pit concealed behind the embankment shouted to one of his comrades guarding the now naked Jews. The latter counted off about twenty persons and instructed them to go behind the earth mound. Graebe's report went on: "I well remember a girl, slim, with black hair, who, as she passed close to me pointed to herself and said, 'Twenty-three years old.' "

Barrett forced himself to keep on reading. The German next described how he went behind the earth mound and saw the pit "already two-thirds full. . . . I looked for the man who did the shooting. He was an SS man, who sat at the narrow end of the pit, his feet dangling into it. He had a tommy-gun on his knees and was smoking a cigarette." Thus the five thousand Jews of Dubno perished in a single afternoon. What struck Barrett most forcefully was that this report was no confession coerced by Allied interrogators from a reluctant

Nazi. It was one of thousands of ordinary documents found in the Nazis' own files.

Earlier, when he had been dependent on the War Department, Justice Jackson had worried about a dearth of evidence. Now, thanks to his partnership with Wild Bill Donovan's OSS, a river of documents was pouring in. In June, Jackson had named Colonel Robert Storey as chief of a new documents division. Storey had set up shop in Paris at 7 rue de Presbourg, near the Arc de Triomphe, while a trial site was being decided. Barrett worked for Storey.

In mid-July, Storey received an urgent phone call from an OSS ensign named English. The naval officer, in the unfathomable ways of the OSS, had been sent to scour Eastern Europe for documents. He was calling, he said, because he had come across something that might interest Storey. A German nobleman, Baron Kurt von Behr, chief aide to Nazi party philosopher Alfred Rosenberg, had offered to reveal the hiding place of all of Rosenberg's files if the Americans would reserve a part of the baron's sixteenth-century castle for his exclusive use. Baron von Behr thereupon conducted the Americans to a cellar five stories below the castle and to forty-seven crates of green ring binders. The next day, the nobleman and his baroness retreated to their bedchamber and took poison washed down with a bottle of 1918 Champagne.

Storey ordered Ensign English to fly the crates to Paris, and four days later a C-47 touched down at Orly field bearing three thousand pounds of the Nazi party's meticulously recorded past, dating back to 1922.

It was as if a dam had burst. The Rosenberg find was followed by a tip from a German Foreign Office archivist who led Storey's people to the Harz Mountains and 485 tons of diplomatic papers. Hitler's personal interpreter, Paul Schmidt, turned over twelve volumes of his notes of the most secret foreign policy conferences. In a salt mine in Obersalzburg, GIs discovered the Luftwaffe's records along with art that Hermann Göring had looted from all over Europe.

Late in July, another bombshell burst. Storey immediately put through a call to Jackson in London. The keystone of the Bernays thesis was that the Third Reich had carried out a deliberate conspiracy to commit aggression. But how to prove it? As Storey explained to Jackson, one of his researchers had found the notes of a General Friedrich Hossbach, Hitler's adjutant, recording a meeting at the Reich Chancellery in Berlin on November 5, 1937. The meeting involved Hitler, Göring, Foreign Minister von Neurath, Grand Admiral Raeder, and a handful of other top leaders. According to Hossbach's notes, Hitler told his subordinates that he was about to reveal "my last will and testament." Germany's 85 million people, he said, represented Europe's purest racial entity. The country's present boundaries were inadequate to serve this population, a condition that "justified the demand for more living space." "The German future," Hitler went on, "is therefore dependent exclusively on the solution of the need for living space, no later than 1943–45." In short, since her neighbors were unlikely to give up their soil to Germany, and since Germany's expansion was justified, the country was left with no recourse but acquisition by aggression. There it was, from the Führer's lips to General Hossbach's notes and now in Storey's hands.

The Hossbach coup, along with files containing Nazi invasion plans and material like the Graebe report that Roger Barrett had unearthed, had brought Jackson to a major decision. The Allies could convict the Nazis simply by introducing German documents in evidence. Witnesses would be far less necessary and less convincing than anything the Nazis themselves admitted.

12

HIS GREATEST ENEMY thoughout the war, Albert Speer explained to a Frankfurt symposium on "The Organization of German War Production," had been bureaucratic inertia and stupidity. The American and British officers nodded knowingly as the former armaments minister of the Third Reich described how, at one point, he could not get gasoline to the front because 180,000 desperately needed gas cans had been reclassified as water cans for use by the Afrika Korps. By then, he said, the Germans had been driven out of North Africa for two years.

Speer's participation was the high point of the two-week symposium. The forty-year-old architect was a legend to insiders on both sides of the war, the wunderkind who had increased German production of weapons seven times, ammunition six times, and tanks and other armored vehicles over five times in only three years. He had reached his peak output just ten months before the war ended, despite crippling shortages and incessant day and night bombing. The Allies wanted to know how he had done it.

Since the war's end, all had gone well for Albert Speer. Though he had initially been arrested along with the rest of the Dönitz government, he sensed early on that he held a special interest for the Allies. Soon after his arrest, he was interviewed by three members of the U.S. Strategic Bombing Survey who wanted to know how effective Allied air raids on Germany had been. His interrogators (visitors would be a better word, given their respectful behavior), were an economist, John Kenneth Galbraith, and two Pentagon war planners, George Ball and Paul Nitze.

Speer was aware that Wernher von Braun and other German rocket scientists were already saving their skins through knowledge they possessed and that the West wanted. Maybe his freedom too could be bought by what he held in his head. The fatal effect of the bombing, he had explained to the three Americans, had not been to his armament plants but to fuel production. It made scant difference that he was turning out the world's first operational jet fighters if they could not fly. Allied air attacks had cut fuel production by ninety percent. That, Speer said, had been catastrophic for Germany.

Along with intellectual brilliance and limitless energy, Albert Speer possessed charm. People were drawn to this handsome, cultivated man. His *Gauleiter* liked him; Adolf Hitler liked him; even the Twentieth of July plotters, who tried to kill Hitler, had wanted Speer in their government. The famed German filmmaker Leni Riefenstahl had once clipped Speer's photograph from a newspaper, hoping to cast him in a movie. Now the Allies seemed to be succumbing to this combination of usefulness and attractiveness. After his meetings with Nitze, Galbraith, and Bell, Speer had been transferred to a comfortable incarceration near Versailles. From Versailles he had been sent to Frankfurt to lecture his former enemies.

The first thing he had done, when Hitler appointed him armaments czar in 1942, Speer told his Frankfurt audience, was to throw out the military chiefs and put arms manufacture in the hands of professionals—industrialists, engineers, and administrators. Next, he borrowed the strategies of Walther Rathenau, the great Jewish chief of the German economy in World War I: parts standardization, division of labor, maximum use of the assembly line, dispersal of plants to reduce bombing disruptions, and total control of raw materials kept in his own hands. He had been lucky, Speer said, when his arms ministry was destroyed in a raid on November 22, 1943. The bombing had rid him of useless paperwork and paper pushers. The only factor he left out of this account of his production feats was the role of slave laborers.

The session ended on a note that left his listeners stunned. Nazi Germany, Speer claimed, had been only a year or two from producing an atomic bomb when the war ended. The delay, he added, with disarming contrition, served Germany right, since she had driven out so many of her most brilliant scientists, particularly Jewish physicists. When his talk ended, the audience gave Speer a standing ovation.

Outside the meeting room, a British lieutenant was waiting. Speer was to report to the commandant's office before returning to house custody. He felt no alarm. They were probably going to ask him to repeat his lecture somewhere else, perhaps in England, maybe even America. On Speer's arrival at the office, the commandant informed him that he was under arrest as a major war criminal.

13

LESS THAN THREE WEEKS had passed since Justice Jackson's visit to Nuremberg. The challenge now was to persuade the other countries' delegations to accept the city. He returned there on July 21, this time with Sir David Maxwell-Fyfe, French representative Robert Falco, Wild Bill Donovan, Bill Jackson, Elsie Douglas, Murray Bernays, and others who formed the latest Jackson coterie. Nikitchenko, under orders from Moscow, had refused to come. The Soviets were still holding out for Berlin in their zone of occupation.

Bernays was relieved at being included. Jackson had become a magnet for ambitious people who wanted to be part of a historic moment. Donovan would play a key role just under Jackson. Storey, who seemed to Bernays to be an amiable plodder, had sewn up the vital documents operation. Jackson had also taken on John Harlan Amen, a tough New York racket-busting prosecutor in the Thomas E. Dewey mold, to head up an interrogations unit. The operation was getting crowded at the top. Still, it was Bernays's concept that guided them all. There had to be a meaningful place for him.

Jackson was particularly relieved to have Maxwell-Fyfe along. He had recently come close to losing his strongest ally. In July, Sir David's Conservatives had lost power in the first British general election since the end of the war in Europe. Churchill was out. Maxwell-Fyfe had managed to hold on to his seat in Parliament, but was no longer at-torney general. His Labour party successor, Sir Hartley Shawcross, had been named Britain's chief war-crimes prosecutor. But, with the European war over, Shawcross was more interested in the anticipated social revolution at home than in war-crimes trials, and had asked Maxwell-Fyfe to stay on as Britain's de facto chief prosecutor.

Nuremberg looked as stricken as before, though General Clay had made good on his offer to clear the streets of rubble. Donovan's OSS had come up with Captain John Vonetes, a twenty-nine-year-old graduate of the Cornell University school of hotel management, to scout for housing and dining facilities in the battered city. Vonetes, a fast-talking Greek American from Binghamton, New York, was of the breed that every army produces, the soldier who can turn up Scotch for the party, nylons for the ladies, gasoline for the junket. Just don't ask too many questions. At Jackson's request, Vonetes arranged a luncheon at the scarred but still elegant Grand Hotel. The British and French, who had not dined so well in years, were suitably impressed. Vonetes also told Jackson that he had located nearly one hundred relatively undamaged homes on the outer ring of the city for the trial staff. For Jackson he had found a castle, the manorial seat of the Faber-Castell family, Europe's pencil magnates. Jackson took a quick tour through its rococo interior, replete with cherubs clutching pencils, and bathrooms with tubs, as Jackson put it, "not quite big enough for swimming pools." The press would be all over him for living in such splendor, Jackson concluded. They ought to use the castle to billet reporters. "They're the only ones who can live here without being ridiculed because they control the laughs," he said.

On the last night, the Jackson party attended a concert at the Nuremberg Opera House. Most of the roof had been blown off; the top of the piano was missing. The musicians, in ragtag clothes and army castoffs, performed a spiritless Beethoven's Fifth Symphony.

Nuremberg had a courthouse, a luxury hotel, housing, a prison, even remnants of culture. The British and French delegates agreed that the trial of the Nazi war criminals should be held here. As for the Russians and Berlin, they were out of luck. Jackson had a three-to-one vote.

On August 8, roughly six weeks after the Allied representatives had first assembled in Church House, they were ready to sign an agreement to try war criminals in an international court. The document defined the crimes, the structure of the court, the procedures and punishments. But what to name this new instrument? Nomenclature had been tricky. To call it a law, a statute, a code, would brand it, at the outset, as ex post facto. And so a neutral term, *charter*, was settled on: the Charter of the International Military Tribunal.

Murray Bernays took his copy of the charter back to his office on London's Mount Street. It was only nine pages, scarcely longer than his original memo. He read the document with a suffusion of pride. The heart of the charter was Article 6, three short paragraphs essentially expressing the idea born in his imagination eleven months before, that Nazism had constituted a criminal conspiracy. The charter defined four crimes: conspiracy to carry out aggressive war; the actual launching of aggression; killing, destroying, and plundering during a war not justified by "military necessity"; and "crimes against humanity," including atrocities against civilians, most flagrantly the attempt to exterminate the Jews.

At the time the Allies signed the charter, they finally agreed on who was to be tried. The Americans, British, French, and Russians had horse-traded, compromised, placated national pride and pet hates, and come up with a list of twenty-three major war criminals. Hermann Göring topped it, followed by Hitler's foreign minister, Joachim von Ribbentrop, who had managed to escape the Allied dragnet until June 13, when the son of a business partner turned him in. The last führer, Admiral Dönitz, also made the final list, along with General Jodl, signer of Germany's surrender. Others included Rosenberg, Speer, Kaltenbrunner, and Hans Frank.

The Americans held most of these men, but the Russians insisted on producing their own defendants. Two men in Soviet hands, Grand Admiral Erich Raeder and Hans Fritzsche, were thus added. Raeder had been Dönitz's predecessor as head of the German navy, but had been out of the war since 1943. Fritzsche was a third-string operative in Josef Goebbels's propaganda apparatus. They were the best the Russians could produce.

Murray Bernays walked down the hall to his office the day after the agreement was signed. Coming toward him from the opposite direction were Colonels Storey and Amen and three other recent Jackson appointees. They moved past him with a bare nod. He turned and watched them disappear into Jackson's conference room. Increasingly, he was being brushed aside.

Bernays had become a pain to the Jackson staff. He was seen as a zealot who resisted any changes in his original idea. The men now around Jackson were compromisers, adroit legal politicians. Even Jackson, with his own streak of righteousness, found Bernays's purist posture discomfiting.

Bernays stopped by Jackson's office and told Elsie Douglas that he had to see the boss, privately, as soon as possible. At the tag end of a hard day, a tired Jackson braced himself for the encounter with Bernays. A man who reveled in legal combat, Jackson dreaded personal confrontations. Bernays told Jackson that his health was bad. He hoped he might be relieved of his duties and return home to the States. Jackson was all solicitousness and understanding. He agreed instantly.

That night Bernays wrote to his wife, "I'm not to blame if these glory thieves made away with my property. They're practical men. I'm only a dreamer." He settled up his affairs and was soon on his way home. Murray Bernays was to have no further involvement in the Nuremberg war-crimes trial.

14

THE ONLY INSTRUCTION First Lieutenant Robert G. Denson had been given this Sunday, August 12, 1945, was to fly his C-47, *Jinx*, to an airstrip near Bad Mondorf to take on "classified cargo." Denson jumped from the hatch to the ground just as several ambulances emerged from a side road. The first ambulance pulled alongside his plane and an army colonel leaped out. Something in the officer's appearance and bearing brought Denson to immediate attention. The colonel wore a green, brilliantly shellacked helmet, rows of ribbons, and kept a riding crop tucked under his arm. His round face possessed a severity heightened by steel-rimmed glasses and a thin mouth under a pencil-line mustache. His posture was rigid. The colonel asked Denson if he was prepared to load. His voice was high-pitched yet authoritative, the voice of a man accustomed to being obeyed. By now, the drivers had hopped out and began opening the rear doors of the ambulances.

Denson looked on in puzzlement as several middle-aged, unshaven, haggard-looking men in disparate dress emerged and shuffled listlessly toward his plane. Only one had any bounce in his step. The stout, smiling figure gestured toward *Jinx* and said in heavily accented English, "Good machine." Denson's eyes popped. He recognized Hermann Göring. His classified cargo was obviously the Nazi war criminals he had been reading about.

The officer who had addressed Denson was Colonel Burton Andrus, recently commandant of Bad Mondorf prison. Burt Andrus liked to say that he had first gone under hostile fire at age two months while his West Point father was serving on the Indian frontier in the 1890s. Unlike his father, Burt Andrus had not managed to make the military academy, but he did earn a regular army commission during World War I. Instead of France, however, Andrus had found himself assigned to the army stockade in Fort Oglethorpe, Georgia. The jail housed the army's worst cases—murderers, armed robbers, and drug addicts.

The Fort Oglethorpe stockade, young Lieutenant Andrus quickly discovered, was a disgrace, run by a kangaroo court of incorrigibles and subject to frequent escapes. As Andrus told the story in later years, he spotted the leaders "by the defiance in their eyes," and immediately clapped them into solitary. He then clamped an iron discipline over the prison. Soon there were no further escapes from Fort Oglethorpe. In his subsequent twenty-seven years in the army, however, Andrus had had nothing further to do with prisons.

The end of World War II found him serving as a combat observer with General George Patton's Third Army in Bavaria. Andrus idolized Patton, and proudly identified himself as a fellow cavalryman.

He wrote a friend, "I will go anywhere with Georgie, anytime, for any purpose." It was on Patton that he had modeled his shellacked green helmet, the riding crop, and a penchant for the theatrical. Andrus had been on leave in London after V-E Day when his Fort Oglethorpe service caught up with him. He received orders to take command of the detention and interrogation center at Bad Mondorf, which the GIs had christened "Ashcan."

Andrus had clear opinions about his Nazi charges. He wrote a friend, "I hate these Krauts and they know it and respect me for it. I guess that's why I got this job. It's too bad we could not have exterminated them and given that beautiful country to someone who was worthy." Just before the London charter was signed, Andrus received secret orders to bring the leading Nazis from Bad Mondorf to Nuremberg and to assume command of the prison there.

The colonel provoked mixed feelings. One officer who had visited Ashcan wrote afterward that he was astonished to find "an old acquaintance, Burt Andrus, as commandant," adding that "he was generally noted for his lack of judgment, pettiness, and naïveté." Andrus was, admittedly, a spit-and-polish stickler. Some took his addiction to smart appearance as the sign of a martinet, his devotion to rules and regulations as the mark of a closed military mind, his peacock strut and the riding crop as the affectations of an insecure man. He was, at bottom, simply an old-fashioned soldier who loved his profession. Another colleague may have summed him up best: "A great guy. Maybe not the brightest, but a great guy."

Colonel Andrus surveyed his charges sitting on the canvas pull-down seats that lined both sides of the fuselage. He studied the broad back of Hermann Göring standing in the rear of the plane using the portable urinal. As Göring came back, buttoning his fly, he peered out a window. "Well, my friends, take a good look at the Rhine," he said. "It's probably the last time we'll ever see it." The gray, impassive faces laughed weakly at the *Reichsmarschall*'s joke. Sitting down, Göring caught the eye of Colonel Andrus and mutual contempt flared between them.

The antipathy had begun the moment Göring arrived at Bad Mondorf. Andrus had stared at the puffed, sweating, smiling face of his prisoner in near disbelief. Göring, at 264 pounds packed over a five-foot-six-inch frame, came accompanied by a valet and sixteen pieces of matching luggage. Andrus muttered to one of his subordinates that here was one prisoner he intended to whip into line. The luggage contained, along with a trove of jewelry, over twenty thousand paracodeine pills, of which Göring took twenty a day.

Andrus put Göring on a diet, and gradually started withdrawing the paracodeine. By the time they left Bad Mondorf, the *Reichsmarschall* was sixty-five pounds thinner and drug-free. As Göring regained his health, he regained his latent powers. He was no longer a sluggish voluptuary. His restored wit and intelligence made him a formidable adversary for his jailers. During an early strip inspection at Bad Mondorf, Göring had deliberately left a cyanide capsule in his clothes to be found and to distract the Americans from other capsules he had secreted elsewhere.

Next to Göring on the plane sat General Jodl, and next to Jodl, Field Marshal Wilhelm Keitel, Hitler's chief of staff for the armed forces. Just before they left Bad Mondorf, Andrus had stood Keitel and Jodl before the others and torn off their emblems of rank. "You are no longer soldiers," he said. "You are war criminals."

Opposite the military men on the plane sat the former foreign minister, Joachim von Ribbentrop. As Ribbentrop rose to use the urinal, Andrus watched him clutching his baggy, beltless trousers, flopping about in shoes without shoelaces. A small humpty-dumpty figure in the forward part of the plane leaned out and gave Andrus a hopeful smile. Weeks before, Walther Funk, former president of the Reichsbank, had come to Andrus, eyes brimming with tears. There was something he had to get off his chest, he told the colonel. Jews had been murdered for their gold teeth. The camp guards had tried at first to yank out the teeth while the Jews were alive. But that had proved too difficult. So they killed them and then pulled their teeth. The gold, Funk confessed, had been deposited in his Reichsbank.

Next to Funk sat Arthur Seyss-Inquart, Reich commissioner for conquered Holland. When Seyss-Inquart first took up his duties in 1940, Holland had 140,000 Jews. By the end of the war, eight thousand remained. Among the dead was a girl three months short of her sixteenth birthday, Anne Frank, who died at the Bergen-Belsen concentration camp.

The presence aboard the plane of the old man with the corded neck and imperious manner puzzled Andrus. Hjalmar Horace Greeley

Schacht had been reared in America by German immigrant parents. The family eventually returned to Germany, where the brilliant Schacht became president of the Reichsbank, Funk's predecessor. Here was a man, Andrus reflected, who had been found by the Americans in Dachau, where he had been sent for his alleged role in the Twentieth of July plot to assassinate Hitler. Why was Schacht being flown to Nuremberg to face trial as a war criminal?

One German aboard the plane enjoyed Colonel Andrus's total confidence. Dr. Ludwig Pfluecker was in his seventies, a neurologist, drafted into the German army medical service. Pfluecker had initially been brought to Bad Mondorf because he spoke English, and because the younger POW doctors had been unable to cope with their high-ranking Nazi patients. Dr. Pfluecker had agreed to come to Nuremberg under the same conditions as Willi Krug and the other POW prison workers. He was to live in the Nuremberg prison, and be available twenty-four hours a day. It was a way, for the time being, to survive. Pfluecker's presence comforted Andrus, since, above all, the colonel had one objective, to keep these men healthy and alive until judgment day.

Lieutenant Denson cut the engine speed and the plane began to descend. The prisoners twisted around to look out the windows. As the C-47 broke through the cloud cover, the carcass of Nuremberg spread beneath them. Colonel Andrus remembered the famous boast Göring had made as Luftwaffe chief: "If any enemy bombers ever make it across the German border," he had said, using an old German expression, "then my name is Meir." He studied Göring, who was calmly peering out the window.

By four p.m. on a gray, drizzly afternoon, the aircraft was on the ground at Y28. Another cavalcade of ambulances appeared. The prisoners disembarked from the plane and walked to the vehicles. The first leg of a long journey had been completed.

15

CHARLES HORSKY WENT into the men's room of the law firm of Covington and Burling, took off his civilian clothes, and put on the uniform of a Coast Guard lieutenant commander. Horsky, a Harvard lawyer who had once worked for Jackson at the Department of Justice, carried out this routine several times a week, ever since he had become the justice's man on the scene in Washington. Jackson had pulled strings to get Horsky the quickest military commission possible—in the Temporary Reserve of the Coast Guard—plus an office in the Pentagon to facilitate his work. Today, Horsky was meeting Jackson's son, who was back briefly from Nuremberg, to try to unravel a vexing challenge.

The language problem had surfaced as soon as the first talks began in London. These negotiations had been confusing enough, with English-, French-, and Russian-speaking principals trying to hammer out the charter. But what were they going to do in the courtroom when an American prosecutor's questions had to be understood by a German-speaking defendant and the German's response had to be understood by one judge who spoke Russian, another who spoke French, and a third who spoke English? Jackson had sent his son, Bill, to Geneva to find out how the League of Nations handled the situation. Bill's report was discouraging. What they did at the League, he found out, was consecutive translation from written documents. A translator read in French, then another in English, another in Spanish, and on and on. At that rate, Jackson realized, the trial would drag on forever. But while in Geneva, Bill had learned about something promising that IBM was working on in the States. How would he like a chance to get back to Washington and see his wife and check up on this system? his father had asked. Bill leaped at the opportunity.

In an auditorium at the Pentagon, Horsky and young Jackson were met by a short, dapper army colonel with a pronounced French accent. Leon Dostert was a naturalized American citizen, former head of the French department at Georgetown University, more recently an interpreter for General Eisenhower. Dostert asked Horsky and Ensign Jackson to have a seat midway back in the auditorium and proceeded to place earphones on their heads. On the stage were three men and a woman, each with a separate microphone. Off to one side, an IBM engineer stood before a control panel.

Dostert called out to the woman on the stage, who began to speak extemporaneously in English about some of the tourist attractions of

Washington. The three men began speaking into their microphones in a babel of tongues. Dostert smiled triumphantly toward Horsky and Jackson. But the smile faded instantly when he saw their puzzled expressions. "Nothing?" he asked. Dostert cursed in French and went up to the stage and conferred with the engineer. He signaled the woman to start speaking again. A piercing feedback shot through the earphones. The engineer fiddled with the terminals and dials, and Dostert gave another signal to the woman. What did they hear now? he asked his visitors. English, Bill Jackson answered. Dostert shouted an instruction to the engineer. What now? Dostert asked. French, Horsky answered. A triumphant Dostert called out again. What were they hearing now? Russian. And now? German.

What they were getting, Dostert explained, was everything the young woman had been saying in English translated, almost as she spoke, into the three other languages that would be used in the trial. Obviously, the gremlins still had to be worked out, Dostert admitted. But IBM was eager to pioneer the world's first system of simultaneous interpretation. The company believed it could perfect the technology by the time the trial began.

Horsky cabled Robert Jackson that afternoon. If IBM could make the system work, a trial in four languages could proceed almost as rapidly as a trial in one.

16

CAPTAIN DANIEL KILEY HAD one thing in common with his new boss, Robert Jackson. Neither man held a degree in the profession he practiced. Kiley had studied architecture at Harvard just long enough to know that he needed no formal education to pursue his visions. What he did best was devise the optimal use of space. This was what he had been doing in Washington as the thirty-year-old head of his own firm, developing wartime housing. Later, he was recruited into Bill Donovan's OSS. Kiley became chief of the Presentations Branch, which, among other tasks, built mockups of clandestine targets.

Kiley's appearance belied his character. He was delicate, almost elfin-looking, and had never weighed more than 130 pounds. The slight frame, however, pulsated with energy and contained a will of steel. "I never take no for an answer," he liked to say.

Late in August, Kiley arrived at Nuremberg's Grand Hotel and was assigned room 412, the Adolf Hitler suite. The army had been instructed that this mild-looking, low-ranking officer enjoyed carte blanche, for Kiley's assignment was to restore the Palace of Justice for the war-crimes trials.

The next morning, an army car and driver were waiting outside the hotel for Kiley. He had come to Nuremberg earlier, on the last Jackson trip, and now he noted that the smell of buried bodies was slowly being overcome by disinfectant. Still, he found disconcerting the sight of German women performing heavy labor, loading rubble into small cars and hauling it away on movable rails.

When Kiley arrived at the Palace of Justice, a broad-chested army colonel eyed him uncertainly, as though this were not the man he expected. The officer came forward and asked if he might be Captain Kiley. Kiley nodded curtly. The colonel introduced himself as John F. Corley, commander of the First Division's battalion of engineers, and added that whatever Kiley wanted, he would get. Kiley headed wordlessly for the courthouse.

After two silent hours of scouring the building, Kiley and Corley reemerged into the sunlight of the courtyard. Kiley turned to the colonel. He wanted carpenters, plasterers, electricians, plumbers, even chimney sweeps, recruited locally or flown in, if necessary. They would need 250 German POWs as laborers. They were going to double the size of the courtroom, vertically and horizontally. He wanted the rear wall taken out and the attic over the courtroom cut into for a visitors' gallery. Throw out all those fancy chandeliers and that gingerbread molding, he ordered, and install fluorescent lighting. He wanted office space for six hundred personnel. And they would need cabinetmakers to build office furniture. He preferred white oak. He would design the furniture himself.

Colonel Corley scribbled on a notepad. They would also need glass, tiles, brick, and plywood, Kiley went on. Corley, a man used to getting things done, nevertheless, interrupted to ask where in this ravaged city they would find these materials. There were factories around Nuremberg, Kiley said. Just put them back into operation. The glass they could fly in from Belgium. He started to head for the waiting car. When would he be back? Corley asked. In a day or so, Kiley answered. He was going to Ansbach, where he had seen some seats in a theater. They would be just right for the visitors' gallery.

17

THEY LOOKED SO FORLORN, these onetime goliaths of the Reich, Hans Frank thought. Here was Field Marshal Keitel, once the very model of a Prussian Junker officer, the discolorations visible where the insignia had been ripped off his uniform, still clicking his heels every time Göring passed by. And Wilhelm Frick, a lawyer like himself, promulgator of the Nuremberg Laws, wearing an incongruous plaid sport jacket with all the buttons done up the front. Most pathetic were Robert Ley and Julius Streicher, who had arrived at Nuremberg with only the clothes on their backs. The U.S. Army had issued them dyed black fatigues, class X, which meant "unfit for further use." One thing could be said for Ley, Frank thought. Here in prison was the only place he had ever seen the former head of the German Labor Front sober. Their belts, suspenders, and shoelaces had been taken away. On August 12, they had been marched into C wing, one of four cellblocks that radiated from a central core in the prison behind the courthouse. Cells lined both sides of the wing and ran up three tiers served by a spiral stairwell at each end.

"I have been here before, several times," said Streicher, a short, bald, powerfully built man of sixty who spoke with an air of foolish pride. Before the Nazis took power, he had indeed been jailed for slandering Jews. Of all the prisoners, it was Streicher whom Hans Frank loathed most. This vulgar little man robbed Nazism of even the pretense of respectability. Streicher was founder and editor of *Der Stürmer*, the anti-Semitic newspaper that read on a comic-book level. Frank would not have been caught dead reading Streicher's rag. "There is a plaque," Streicher said wistfully. "It used to be over my cell, number 258, in another wing." Cell 258 had been a tourist stop for faithful Nazis visiting Nuremberg in palmier days. The plaque had since been torn off by a GI souvenir hunter.

A German-speaking U.S. sergeant told Streicher to shut up. He called off their names and assigned each prisoner a cell. Frank entered number 14. What struck him instantly was the stale air, as though it too had been imprisoned. The walls were stained and unclean. The only fresh patches were where hooks, protrusions, and electrical connections had been pulled out and plastered over. Immediately to the right, Frank spotted a toilet in an alcove, with no door, no toilet seat. An iron cot with a filthy mattress occupied the left wall. Opposite it, on the other side of the cell, was a table. Frank tapped the top. It was made of flimsy cardboard. A steam pipe ran along the back of the cell and above it a small barred window exposed a patch of gray sky.

Frank was startled by the metallic slamming of an iron bolt. He walked to the door and looked out of a square porthole. A pair of GI eyes stared back. This was not going to be Wawel Castle.

Colonel Andrus tried to dictate over the cacophony of banging hammers, shouting voices, and the rumble of wheelbarrows outside his office door. Captain Kiley's restoration was in full sway. The blazon was to be on a field of azure, the colonel repeated to a GI serving as his secretary, one who was clearly unfamiliar with the language of heraldry. "The bordure is sable, charged in chief with a key argent. . . ." Andrus was determined to make of his prison staff an elite unit, and nothing, he believed, added more to unit pride than distinctive insignia and uniforms. He was personally designing a coat of arms for the 6850th Internal Security Detachment, the ISD, as his prison command had been designated. He had sketched a shield with a key at the top to symbolize prison security, the scales of justice in the middle, and, at the bottom, a broken Nazi eagle. He could envision numerous uses for the coat of arms: the ISD shoulder patch, a letterhead, a pin for female staffers. His keenest hope was to have Justice Jackson adopt his design as the official symbol of the IMT.

Andrus heard a tapping over the din. His visitor was Major Douglas Kelley, an army psychiatrist. The army had recognized that sound minds had to be produced before the IMT, along with sound bodies; and so Kelley had been assigned to the prison. Headshrinkers, as the colonel called them, were an alien species to this career soldier. He had been relieved, however, to find Kelley a genial, witty man and not some brooding behavioral mystic.

Kelley saluted casually and asked for a few minutes of the colonel's time. Once they had the prisoners settled in, Kelley said, he

believed they should set up a small library for them. They were going
to have a great deal of time on their hands. It was the kind of request
that rankled Andrus, and he reminded Kelley of his principal mission,
to keep him advised of suicidal tendencies among his charges. That
was precisely the problem, Kelley explained. They had to keep the
prisoners' minds occupied. Andrus relented. "All right, I don't want
them to go stir-crazy. A guy could go nuts in a little cell with what
some of those boys have on their minds." As Kelley started to leave,
Andrus asked him to stick around. He was going to give the guard
detachment its first briefing in a few minutes, and it might be useful
to have the psychiatrist watch.

Corporal Emilio DiPalma, a combat veteran of the First Division—
the "Big Red One"—lacked enough points to be shipped home yet.
He had been assigned, with other GIs at loose ends, to report to the
ISD. On a late August afternoon, DiPalma found himself with a dozen
other soldiers standing in the exercise yard, a plot of hard earth and
straggling weeds between C wing and a building the GIs used as a
gym. A sergeant's bellow brought them to attention. A party of officers
emerged from cellblock C into the yard. In the lead strode a colonel
whom DiPalma studied closely. The character of his new commanding
officer would determine the quality of his life from now until he got
out of the army. The officer's uniform was pressed to razor-edged
sharpness. The shellacked green helmet was something new to Di-
Palma, and that riding crop tucked under the arm did not suggest an
easygoing civilian in uniform.

Colonel Andrus ordered the men at ease, though there was nothing easy in his voice or manner. Andrus began speaking softly but
firmly in the faint drawl adopted so often by career officers. They
were, as of now, he informed them, part of the ISD, and it was going
to be a proud unit, charged with a historic task: guarding the worst
criminals mankind had ever known. The first thing that they as "sentinels" had to understand was that these men were prisoners of war.
Their rank did not matter. There was to be no exchange of salutes or
other military courtesies. When a sentinel entered a cell, the prisoners
were to stand. When an American came down a corridor, prisoners
were to stand aside.

The colonel's continual reference to them as sentinels, not guards, made DiPalma uneasy. The word had an unwelcome spit-and-polish ring to a combat veteran. Sentinels, Andrus went on, would pull twenty-four hours on and twenty-four hours off. When they were on duty, they would spend two hours on the cellblock and four hours off. A dayroom had been provided on the third floor of cellblock C. Cards, Ping-Pong, bunks, and books would be available there. Each guard was responsible for four cells, Andrus went on. No more than thirty seconds were ever to elapse before a sentinel peered through the port-hole directly into the cells to observe his four prisoners. A sentinel's chief responsibility was to keep these men alive. At no time were the prisoners ever to be allowed to talk to one another or to the sentinels. Nor were the sentinels to talk to each other. DiPalma began to imagine two-hour stints lasting an eternity.

The rest of Andrus's talk was a drone of daily routines. Breakfast at seven a.m. Afterward, defendants mop and clean their cells. Lunch at twelve, supper at six. Cold showers once a week. Library privileges in the afternoon. Lights out at nine p.m., at which time prisoners were to turn in their glasses, pens, and watches, anything that could cut or stab. Cells were to be inspected whenever prisoners were out of them; and that included the sentinel putting his head down low for a good look inside the toilet bowl. Virtually all of Andrus's pronouncements were followed by, "Failure to obey will be considered a court-martial offense."

Sentinels would be unarmed on the cellblock, the colonel said. However, a leather blackjack packed with cotton and lead pellets would hang beside each cell door. The sentinels were to carry this club only when accompanying prisoners outside the cell. If they had to use the blackjack, they were to apply it only to the elbows and shoulders. A blackjack, Andrus explained, was the ideal jailer's weapon. It hurt like hell but did not break the skin.

The voice became almost paternal. "Just about all of you men have seen combat," the colonel said. "You've seen the bodies of your buddies on the roadsides, in the woods, hanging out of burned-out tanks. You've seen the cemeteries where your friends will never earn enough points to get home. These prisoners are the men who put them there. Your job is to see that they survive long enough to be brought to justice. That is all." As Andrus turned to leave, Emilio DiPalma did not know if he liked or disliked the colonel under whom he was now to serve.

The next day, the corporal of the guard came bursting into Colonel Andrus's office in the Palace of Justice. "Dr. Pfluecker says you got to come right away," he said breathlessly.

As Andrus entered the cellblock, the old German physician explained that, after breakfast, a guard had handed Göring a mop and pail and ordered the *Reichsmarschall* to clean his cell. Göring had raged and then collapsed on his bed, breathing unnaturally. Dr. Pfluecker was called and found him in tachycardia—a rapid heartbeat, the doctor explained—two hundred to three hundred beats a minute. It could lead to heart failure. He had given Göring a shot and he was resting comfortably.

Andrus was enraged. Less than twenty-four hours had elapsed since he had issued his first regulations and already the worst of the prisoners was presenting him with an impossible choice. He went to Göring's cell and stared through the port. The bulky figure was stretched on his cot. No matter what his personal feelings, his mission was to keep the prisoners alive. Andrus accepted that he would have to make a medical exception. In the future, one of the POW prison staff was to be assigned to clean Göring's cell. Mastery of the prison was going to be a contest of wills, Andrus recognized, and round one, it seemed, had gone to Hermann Göring.

18

ON SEPTEMBER 5, 1945, Justice Jackson was back briefly in Washington for consultations with the president. Jackson was impressed by Harry Truman. Not that the man possessed a shred of the grandeur of his predecessor—quite the contrary. It was the quiet confidence with which this common man filled the shoes of a giant that had won Jackson's admiration.

What rank did he want for the Nuremberg job? Truman asked with a knowing smile. No rank, Jackson replied. Nor did he have the slightest desire at this point in his life to start wearing gold braid and epaulettes. That was not what he meant, Truman explained. Simulated rank was what he had in mind. He knew all about the military from his days as an artilleryman in the last war. Without rank, Truman said, Jackson would have trouble getting a haircut from the army, much less proper support for a major trial. How about lieutenant general? Truman asked. Jackson admitted that it had a pleasant ring.

Truman mentioned that he needed to appoint an American judge and an alternate to the court. What did Jackson think of Francis Biddle, the recently dismissed attorney general, as the principal judge? Jackson was caught off guard. He was temporarily leaving the Supreme Court to associate himself with what he expected to be a historic event in law. The appointment of less than a great jurist to sit on the Nuremberg bench would diminish the occasion. Francis Biddle had served a few unhappy months as a judge on a federal circuit court, where he had not distinguished himself, and he had gladly left to succeed Jackson as attorney general. Biddle, in Jackson's estimate, did not qualify for the IMT. Instead of responding to Truman's suggestion, Jackson raised the name of Owen J. Roberts, recently retired as associate justice of the Supreme Court. Roberts would not take the job, Truman answered; he had already asked. What about John Parker, Jackson suggested, naming a distinguished judge on the Fourth Circuit Court of Appeals. Jackson knew that Parker had missed going on the Supreme Court in 1930 by a heartbreaking single vote. The Senate had tied on his appointment, and Vice President Charles Curtis could not be found in time to break the tie. Truman said that he would happily name Parker, but as the alternate.

The next day, Jackson got a call from Francis Biddle, who asked if he could come out to Hickory Hill. The Jacksons and the Biddles had been part of a tight Washington social set. They were often in each other's homes and had gone to the Chicago Democratic Convention together in 1936 to see Roosevelt nominated for a second term. Still, Jackson did not want Biddle at Nuremberg. He had talked the matter over with Bill Donovan, and Donovan agreed. Jackson also thought that his lukewarm reaction to Biddle had dissuaded the president from naming him. He wondered what Biddle wanted.

The man who came to Hickory Hill was a lean, tanned Philadelphia aristocrat, aloof in appearance, but unaccustomedly humble this day. Jackson was obviously in the throes of preparing to move to

Nuremberg, and Biddle apologized for taking up his time. Nevertheless, he said, he thought they ought to have a chat in light of their
probable close professional relationship in the future. He had been
vacationing in Quebec province, Biddle said, when the White House
switchboard tracked him down. He had simply been killing time since
being dropped as attorney general, and the prospect of returning to
private practice in Philadelphia, after the adrenaline charge of the New
Deal, appalled him. Truman's offer had arrived like a life ring thrown
to a drowning man.

The way that Truman had fired him as attorney general had been
clumsy and painful, Biddle went on. Of course, he had worked against
Truman's nomination for vice president in 1944, and he supposed that
was the reason why Truman resented him. But to fire him by a phone
call from a White House staffer? That was poor form. After being
asked to resign, he had asked for an appointment with the president.
With the two of them alone in the Oval Office, Biddle continued, he
told Harry Truman that he had expected his dismissal; but shouldn't
Truman have called him in personally and asked for his resignation?
That was how these things were done. After that, Biddle said, he got
up to leave, and as he did so, he put his hand on the president's
shoulder and said, "You see. It's not so hard."

Jackson accepted the story, including the final touch. It was just
the sort of Main Line condescension that would have made Truman dislike Biddle. But now, at least, Jackson understood why Biddle
had been given the Nuremberg judgeship. It was Truman's bad
conscience.

Since Biddle was going to take the job, Jackson said, he hoped
that he would fly to Germany as soon as possible. Organizing a four-
power bench from scratch was going to take time. Was Irene coming?
Biddle asked. No, Jackson answered, his wife was not coming. Biddle
said that he hoped he would be able to bring his Katherine along.
Jackson rose and jammed his hands into his pockets—his favored
courtroom stance. Europe was full of GIs, he said, who had been
separated from their families for years. It would be the worst possible
blow to the morale of these men to allow VIPs to bring their wives.
General Patton had already ruled that since his GIs could not have
their spouses in the American Zone of occupation, no one else could.
He fully supported Patton's position, Jackson said. Biddle had no idea

what a sinkhole Nuremberg was. The smell of death, the plague of rats, the mood of gloom. It was no place for an American woman. Yes, Biddle said, he understood perfectly. As soon as he could put together some sort of staff, he would make arrangements to get to Germany quickly.

Soon after his conversation with Jackson, Francis Biddle called on President Truman in order to accept formally his appointment to the IMT. He took the occasion to ask if he might have the president's permission to bring his wife to Nuremberg eventually. Yes, Truman said, still wanting placate a man he had wronged. Biddle also arranged for passage to Europe, not by air, but by sea.

19

MAJOR DOUGLAS KELLEY HAD another request of Colonel Andrus. The prisoners desperately needed exercise, he warned. Andrus looked skeptical. He had earlier allowed women prisoners from another wing into the exercise yard, including the notorious Ilse Koch, wife of the commandant at Buchenwald concentration camp. As the women came out, the guards had lined up and urinated in their direction. He wanted no more such spectacles, Andrus said.

Kelley pressed on. "Exercise is important to relieve psychological stress," he explained. "The tension these men are under causes an endocrine imbalance which produces psychological debilitation and . . ." Kelley sensed that he was boring Andrus. What he meant was that exercise let off destructive steam. He would think about it, Andrus said.

On September 11, a memo to the staff crossed Kelley's desk, entitled "Exercise Yard, Regulations Governing." Kelley scanned it. No talking, no sitting down, no picking up anything, thirty feet between prisoners, twenty minutes per day. But, at least, Kelley had persuaded the colonel.

On the first day in the exercise yard, Göring, disregarding the colonel's rule, delivered a pep talk to his fellow inmates. They were in prison, he said, for one reason only. They had lost the war. But someday a grateful nation would honor them with marble sarcophagi. He himself, Göring said merrily, expected a special place in Valhalla. "Shut up and spread out!" a guard barked.

The military men walked in single file, Dönitz, Keitel, and Jodl, purposeful and silent. In another corner the untouchables milled uncertainly, like lost molecules trying to attach themselves to a larger organism: Streicher, founder of the Jew-baiting *Der Stürmer*, running in place, working up a sweat that glistened on his bald, neckless head; the towering Kaltenbrunner, lurching from group to group; runty Fritz Sauckel, labor "plenipotentiary" of the Reich, the man who had herded millions of workers from their homelands and delivered them to the Nazi war machine. The loner by choice was Hjalmar Schacht, whose haughty air made clear that he had no business among such people. The prisoner who most concerned Major Kelley these days was Robert Ley, destroyer of German labor unions and creator of the ersatz Nazi Labor Front. Ley looked disoriented, stumbling about the yard with the halting steps and furtive glances of a cornered animal.

"Time's up!" a sergeant shouted, and the ragtag collection formed into a single line to return to the cellblock that was now their home.

20

THE FIRST THING Robert Jackson observed on his return to Nuremberg on September 13 was that the nonfraternization rule was being torn to shreds. On the way in from Y28 his party drove along a street that had become a flesh market, with knots of GIs and German women engaged in intimate negotiations. They were heading for the suburbs—Jackson and his son, Bill, Elsie Douglas, housing officer John Vonetes, and Colonel Robert J. Gill, a handsome, wealthy Baltimore lawyer who was expected to relieve Jackson of the administrative duties he loathed. The party also included a bodyguard and driver. Vonetes had commandeered for Jackson a sixteen-cylinder Mercedes-Benz touring car with six forward speeds that had formerly belonged to Joachim von Ribbentrop. He would keep this car for ceremonial occasions, Jackson said, but for everyday use he wanted something less ostentatious.

And a bodyguard? Jackson protested. He had no desire to have some plug-ugly following him day and night. Still, the clean-cut young sergeant assigned to protect him, Moritz Fuchs, hardly seemed cast to type. How much did his protector weigh? Jackson asked. About 155 pounds, the five-foot-nine-inch Fuchs answered. It did not seem like much protection, Jackson observed with amusement.

They entered Dambach, a village of solid homes on the western edge of Nuremberg barely brushed by the war. The huge car slid to a stop before a buff-colored stucco home at 33 Lindenstrasse. The door was opened by a stout woman who introduced herself in English as Mrs. Hassel. "I am your housekeeper," she said. "I have lived five years in America." Her attitude was servile, except when she addressed the rest of the staff, which included a maid, a cook, a cook's helper, a waiter, and three gardeners.

Vonetes conducted them to the justice's bedroom on the second floor, then to Mrs. Douglas's room.

Each of three bedrooms had its own bath. The tub in the master bedroom was four feet deep and six feet long. Jackson noted the shower, sitz bath, tub, and bidet, which, he observed, would allow him to bathe standing, sitting, lying, or squatting, according to his mood. What did Jackson think of his billet? Vonetes asked. The house, Jackson said, combined all that was godawful in Teutonic taste; everything was heavy and gloomy. But it would do fine. That evening, he and Elsie Douglas stood looking out the picture window of the room he had chosen as his study. What did Bob guess all those sullen faces they saw in the streets thought about the forthcoming trial? she asked. People without a roof over their head and empty bellies did not much care what happened to Hermann Göring, Jackson believed.

21

JOHN HARLAN AMEN, "the Tom Dewey of Brooklyn," now head of the interrogation division, had brought a formidable reputation to Nuremberg. In civilian life, Amen had successfully prosecuted the notorious Louis "Lepke" Buchalter of Murder Incorporated, the outfit that killed for a fee. But his specialty had been nailing crooked politicians in over a hundred corruption cases. He was hard-driving, hard-living, hard-drinking, and a womanizer with a penchant for the dramatic, his favorite role being that of Mr. District Attorney. His first drink went down while he was shaving in the morning, and there was little letup all day. The alcohol appeared to have remarkably little effect on Amen. One colleague had dubbed him "the sterling knight of the bed, the bottle, and the ego." Amen was also engaged in a rivalry with the more placid Bob Storey for Jackson's favor.

Amen had gone out to 33 Lindenstrasse to discuss a sticky ethical question. To interrogate these prisoners would be the equivalent of a district attorney's going into a cell and questioning a defendant for evidence that could be used against him in a trial. To meet the legal niceties of this situation, they concluded that, since none of these men had been formally indicted yet, they were still technically prisoners of war—and POWs could be interrogated. As they parted, Jackson asked Amen if he would take his son, Bill, along the next time an interesting interrogation came up. The experience would do a young lawyer good.

On a late September morning, with Bill Jackson in tow, Amen headed for room 55, the interrogation room in the Palace of Justice, to question an obscure but promising figure. As they entered, Amen ordered the American guards to clear out a POW work party that was still putting the finishing touches of plaster on the ceiling. Amen tilted his chair against the wall and lit a cigarette. A guard appeared with one of the least appetizing prisoners the two Americans had yet seen. Albert Göring was an engineer by profession; he was a year younger than his brother, Hermann, and bore not the slightest resemblance to him. GI fatigues hung on his skeletal frame like clothes on a coat hanger. He was bald and his skin was sallow. That morning a prison doctor had counted over seventy carbuncles on his back and neck; some of them poked above his collar.

Albert Göring immediately began complaining about the injustice of his plight. He had always been anti-Nazi. He had voluntarily approached the Americans the day after the war ended, and they had rewarded him by throwing him into jail. That was no way to treat a man who had been arrested by the Gestapo four times for helping Jews and for calling Hitler a criminal. Never mind Albert's attitude toward the Jews, Amen said through the interpreter, he wanted to know about brother Hermann's attitudes.

That, the younger Göring said, was not so simple. His brother was not a deep or consistent thinker. Hermann was motivated by the whim of the moment. Was the colonel aware, for example, that Hermann had saved the lives of two old Jews after Kristallnacht? He had been badly wounded during the failed Munich beer-hall putsch of 1923—Hitler's attempt to overthrow the Bavarian government. A policeman's bullet had ricocheted off the Odeonplatz and struck Hermann in the groin. Storm troopers had carried him into the nearby house of Ilse Ballin, the Jewish wife of a furniture dealer. Frau Ballin and her sister had tenderly cared for the young Nazi, who would otherwise have bled to death. Fifteen years later, in 1938, after storm troopers had gone on their window-smashing rampage against Jewish store owners, Hermann sent a Luftwaffe aide to find the two sisters. Exit visas were arranged for them, and they got out of Germany with all their money, Albert explained, thanks to Hermann.

Amen's tilted chair came crashing to the floor. Wasn't this the same Hermann Göring, he said, who also proposed that the Jews be assessed a billion marks to save the insurance companies who would have to pay for all that broken glass? That was Hermann, Albert conceded, a bundle of contradictions.

Amen nodded to Bill Jackson to take over the questioning. Had he ever discussed the plight of the Jews directly with Hermann? young Jackson asked. A friend of his, Albert said, had come back from Poland and told him that Jews were being herded aboard trains like cattle, taken somewhere and machine-gunned, even women and children. Albert had written to Hermann reporting this matter. What happened then? Jackson wanted to know. When he got no answer, Albert said, he made an inquiry and was told that his report had been referred to the "appropriate department." Which meant? Jackson asked. Himmler's SS, Albert answered.

Albert noted that he probably could do himself good by denouncing his brother. But he just could not bring himself to do it. Hermann had bailed him out every time the Gestapo had arrested him. Hermann had gotten him a good job at the Hungarian office of the Skoda works. Though Hermann considered this brother the black sheep of the family, he had been good to him.

22

JOHN HARLAN AMEN RUSHED to Jackson's unfinished offices and told Elsie Douglas that he had to see the chief right away. Mrs. Douglas sat amid a chaos of overspilling cardboard boxes, typing at an Underwood set on a crate. She herself, however, looked crisp in the uniform without rank or insignia that most of the civilian trial staff had adopted. Amen apologized to Jackson for the interruption, but said he was sure Jackson would want to see immediately the letter he had brought.

The handwriting was cramped, the English stilted, yet Jackson found the message electrifying. Joachim von Ribbentrop had written that he was ready to take full responsibility for the actions of the leaders jailed with him. If Ribbentrop was ready to take responsibility for the crimes of the regime, then they would be acknowledged, per se, as crimes, and the prosecution was halfway home. Ribbentrop had set a condition, however. He would take responsibility, he wrote, only if the Allies dropped the trial. They would cross that bridge when they came to it, Jackson told Amen. In the meantime, he intended to interrogate this prisoner himself.

As they threaded their way through an obstacle course of scaffolding and carpenter's horses on the way to the interrogation room, Amen briefed Jackson. Ever since his arrest, Ribbentrop had been acting bizarrely, writing letters to Winston Churchill and Anthony Eden, offering to come to England to explain why war between the British and German peoples had been a tragic error. He babbled incessantly about the titled Britons he expected to call in as witnesses in his defense, including King George VI and Lady Astor. Amen reminded Jackson that Hitler, in his last will and testament, had dumped Ribbentrop as foreign minister for Arthur Seyss-Inquart. Between that shock and the subsequent blow of being cited as a war criminal, Amen said, Ribbentrop's mental stability was questionable. Jackson stopped before room 55 and braced himself for his first face-to-face encounter with a Nazi.

Ribbentrop jumped to his feet as Jackson entered. The former foreign minister wore a shapeless gray suit, a frayed shirt with no tie, and laceless shoes. His manner suggested that of a whipped dog. The two Americans sat down behind the interrogators' table, facing Ribbentrop. When one of Amen's cigarettes rolled off the table, the German started to dive for it, but caught himself at the last second. Amen picked up the cigarette and handed it to Ribbentrop, who stuffed it into his jacket pocket as Jackson posed his first question.

Jackson's annoyance was visible, his face flushed and his voice harsh. He was only in this room, he said, because Ribbentrop had written that he was ready to take responsibility for the acts of his fellow prisoners. Specifically, what was he taking responsibility for? Could Jackson finally get a straight answer? Ribbentrop continued to emit a verbal fog, as he had done for the past fifteen minutes. "Let's try again," Jackson said. "Do you take responsibility for the war of aggression?" Of course not, an injured Ribbentrop answered. What about the violation of treaties? Ribbentrop's answer was unintelligible. "Are you responsible for the shooting of American airmen?" No, he could not have done that, Ribbentrop replied. What about the deportation of slave labor? Another muddled answer. The mistreatment of Russian prisoners of war? The shooting of hostages? The destruction of Lidice? The Warsaw Ghetto? The concentration camps? No. No. No. No, Ribbentrop replied plaintively.

"Do you at least take responsibility for the foreign policy of the Third Reich?" Jackson asked. Again, Ribbentrop demurred, saying that he did not know the foreign policy. Jackson's eyes rolled in disbelief. "Do you really want me to go to my associates and tell them that the foreign minister of the Reich didn't know what the foreign policy was?" "I am sorry," Ribbentrop said. "I must tell you that the Führer never revealed his aims to anybody."

Striding angrily toward his office, Jackson told Amen this was the last time he expected to set foot in the interrogation center. The waste of time with Ribbentrop had convinced him that the documentary route was the best way to convict these people. Certainly, nothing coming out of the prisoners' mouths would help. Jackson's words troubled Amen. He had hoped this firsthand experience would hook Jackson on the importance of calling witnesses. Instead, documents, the domain of Amen's archrival Robert Storey, were winning the day.

23

THE GUARDS PREFERRED duty on the second tier of cellblock C, where the less important Nazis were held. Here, as they put it, they caught less of Colonel Andrus's chickenshit. The corporal responsible for the last four cells on the floor this Friday morning, October 5, was leaning sleepily against the stairwell when Willi Krug appeared at 6:30 a.m. with his washbasins. Willi smiled mechanically and nodded as he passed by. Seconds later, Krug let out a cry. The startled soldier came running.

Colonel Andrus was shaving when he received the call from the duty officer. Within twenty minutes he was entering cell 110. Andrus studied the bloated, purple face of Dr. Leonardo Conti, chief of health in Heinrich Himmler's SS. Conti was known as the "mercy killing doctor," specializing in quick, painless injections that eliminated inmates of asylums, jails, and homes for the aged. He was not a major defendant, but was being held for later trial. Conti had fashioned a noose from a towel, tied one end to the middle bar of his window, and jumped off his chair. "Cut him down," Andrus ordered.

The point was not to panic, to think through how this disaster had happened and to make sure it could not happen again, Andrus told himself. But first there was the galling necessity of informing his superior, the commanding officer of the Nuremberg-Furth Enclave, that Burton Andrus had lost his first prisoner.

They had not even had their breakfast yet, Kaltenbrunner complained as the prisoners filed down the stairwell to the basement shower room. The corporal of the guard ordered them to strip and face the wall. An army doctor arrived and told the prisoners to "bend over and spread your cheeks." Ribbentrop translated the order for the others. As the doctor went by, peering up their rectums, other GIs searched their clothing, producing a nail from one pocket, a broken razor from another, a tiny file from a third. After the search, the prisoners were marched into the exercise yard and told to sit on the ground, no closer than thirty feet apart. Hours went by as a crew of Dan Kiley's POW workmen ripped the bars out of the cell windows in cellblock C, plastered over the holes, and covered the windows with something the army called "cello-glass," which admitted only a blurred patch of sky. When the prisoners returned to the block, they found that they had been assigned new cells. The guards warned them that their chairs were never to be placed within four feet of any wall. Colonel's orders.

The plan agreed upon at headquarters command was that Conti would be taken to the base hospital, where he would be pronounced dead of unknown causes *after* his arrival. A report of the actual manner of his death, classified top secret, was spirited back to Third Army Head-quarters in Heidelberg. As the days slipped by and no inquiries were made by the press, the prison staff began to relax.

24

TURBULENCE OVER the English Channel tossed the RAF Anson about like a kite. Dr. Ellis Jones noticed his patient's stricken expression and shoved a pail under his chin, into which Rudolf Hess vomited. Hess felt embarrassed at getting sick in a plane. He was a skilled pilot who, just five years before, had carried out one of the most sensational flights of the war.

In 1940, Hess had been deputy führer, the third-ranking Nazi in Germany, one of a handful of old party fighters whom Hitler ad-dressed by the familiar *du.* That August, Hess had been visited by his old professor from the University of Munich, Dr. Karl Haushofer, the seminal influence on young Rudolf's thinking. The professor taught geopolitics and believed that the Anglo-Saxons and Germans, pos-sessing superior blood, were destined to rule the world. As a student, Hess had drunk deeply of the professor's wisdom. They had remained close, and Hess usually refered to Haushofer as "Uncle Karl."

One Sunday afternoon, after a vegetarian dinner that Hess had inflicted on his mentor, Haushofer suggested that they go for a walk in the Grünwald. He was unhappy, the professor said, that Germany was at war with England. War between these racial cousins made no sense. When Germany went to war against Russia, as she inevitably must, she would face a geopolitical disaster. England would bring in the might of the United States from the West. Germany would face the Bolshevik hordes in the East. The fatherland would be crushed between two jaws. Somehow, Germany had to make peace with the British. Haushofer had an idea. His son, Albrecht, also a professor at Berlin's Hochschule für Politik, was a personal friend of the duke of Hamilton, and the duke was in contact with Churchill and King George. Haushofer proposed that his son write to the duke through a woman he knew in neutral Portugal, and suggest that Albrecht and Hamilton get together in Lisbon. What did Hess think of the idea? the professor asked. Hess explained that he too had a passing acquaintance with the duke, whom he had met at the 1936 Berlin Olympics. He had invited the Briton to his home for lunch in view of their common interest in aviation. Uncle Karl's idea, he concluded, was splendid.

The letter was sent on September 23, 1940. Its contents were made known to the duke, but not as Haushofer and Hess had hoped. The letter had been intercepted by British censors. Such correspondence to an English nobleman, now on active duty with the RAF, aroused the suspicions of British intelligence. Hamilton was closely questioned about the letter and his relationship with Albrecht Haushofer.

As weeks went by and the younger Haushofer received no response, an obsession began to take root in the mind of Rudolf Hess. Hess recognized that he was being elbowed out of the Führer's inner circle by craftier players. Once, cooling his heels in the Führer's anteroom, he had complained to Felix Kersten, an aide to Heinrich Himmler, of his neglect. He was determined, he told Kersten, to do something spectacular, to make of his life "one great deed."

Flying was Hess's passion. In 1934 he had won a race around the Zugspitze; but Hitler, furious that one of his chief lieutenants had risked his life for a ridiculous trophy, had ordered Hess grounded. Secretly, however, Hess persuaded Willi Messerschmitt, the aeronautical engineer, to let him fly Messerschmitt's ME-108 and ME-109 fighter planes out of the company's Augsburg works. He then persuaded Messerschmitt to let him try the still secret ME-110. Over a cup of coffee one morning, Hess bet the engineer that he could not add two more fuel tanks to the plane without losing maneuverability. Messerschmitt took up the challenge. An ME-110 was refitted, and Hess was ready to attempt his "one great deed."

In December 1940, he went to the Augsburg field determined to embark on his solitary crusade. In order not to let even his secretary know what he was up to, Hess carried a peace proposal that he had written in longhand. The weather, however, proved unflyable. He actually got into the air in January 1941, but turned back because of a faulty aileron. Later, he made a third attempt, and again the weather defeated him.

On April 27, 1941, Hitler announced to his inner circle his intention to invade the Soviet Union in eight weeks. Hess heard the words in a confusion of fear and exhilaration. Here was Uncle Karl's nightmare come true, Germany entangled in a two-front war. Hess determined that he must reach the duke of Hamilton and talk England out of the war before Germany attacked Russia. On May 10, a quiet Saturday afternoon, he drove out to the Augsburg field, wearing a Luftwaffe uniform so that he would not be treated in Britain as a spy. He dared not confide his intention to anyone except his aide, Karlheinz Pintsch, and Professor Haushofer. Yet Hess was sure Hitler would approve of his mission. The Führer shared Haushofer's view that enmity between Germany and England made no sense. Hitler was only unhappy that England refused to see the light.

Hess had the mechanics at the Messerschmitt works roll out the ME-110 with the extra fuel tanks. He handed Pintsch a letter to deliver personally to the Führer. In it he described his intention to seek out an Anglo-German peace. Hess added that if his enterprise failed, "it will always be possible for you to deny all responsibility. Simply say that I was out of my mind." By 5:45 p.m., Hess was airborne with nine hundred miles of night flying and devilish navigation ahead of him, much of it over the North Sea. His destination was Dungavel Hill, thirty miles south of Glasgow, ancestral seat of the duke of Hamilton.

Five hours later he approached his objective. Hess doubted that he could land the plane without being shot out of the sky first. And so, from an altitude of twenty thousand feet, he made his first parachute jump. David McLean, a Scottish plowman, discovered Hess in a field of barley, trying to slip out of his chute. As the Scot approached, Hess smiled his bucktoothed grin and announced in English, "I have an important message for the duke of Hamilton." He later liked to boast that he had landed thirteen feet from his destination. It was more like thirty miles from Dungavel Hill. Still, it had been extraordinary flying.

After reading Hess's letter, a stunned Hitler was uncertain how to handle the affair. Yes, peace with England. But the number-three Nazi dropping unannounced out of the sky into the enemy camp? No one was going to take this lunatic seriously. After waiting two days, still not knowing if Hess had arrived in Britain, Hitler decided to take the man's advice. He issued a statement on May 12 that read: "Party member Rudolf Hess has set out on an unauthorized flight from Augsburg and has not yet returned. A letter he left behind unfortunately shows by its distraction, traces of a mental disorder, and it is feared that he was a victim of hallucinations."

Thus far, Hess's wild gamble appeared to be succeeding. The morning after the flight, he actually had a conversation with the duke of Hamilton, not at Dungavel Hill, but in a British army barracks. Germany's victory was inevitable, Hess said, and he hoped that the duke would persuade leading members of his party to discuss peace with Germany.

Hamilton subsequently received instructions to brief the prime minister. Churchill was staying at a favored hideaway near Oxford, Ditchley Park, an eighteenth-century mansion owned by Churchill's wealthy friend Ronald Tree. On his arrival, the duke was put off until after the prime minister had watched a movie, *The Marx Brothers Go West*. Thereafter, Churchill grilled Hamilton until two a.m., trying mostly to establish that their aerial visitor was in fact Rudolf Hess.

Hess was subsequently interrogated by British officials of escalating rank, up to Home Secretary Lord Simon. And then his fortunes began to decline. His proposal that Germany would leave the British Empire unmolested in exchange for German domination of Europe struck the British as laughable. His premise that England was soon to be defeated and therefore could ignore these generous terms only at her peril infuriated a pugnacious Churchill. Most damaging, those who met him soon came to believe that Rudolf Hess had a disturbed mind. Churchill thereafter ordered him treated no differently from any other high-ranking POW. For the next five years, Hess sat out the war. While Hitler invaded country after country, while millions were herded into Germany as forced laborers, while the gas chambers did their work, Hess occupied a succession of British jails and military hospitals, a figure judged somewhere between eccentric and mad.

Yet, on October 9, 1945, he was being flown to Nuremberg to stand trial as a major war criminal. True, he could be tried on the conspiracy count since he was an early, high-ranking member of what the Allied prosecutors considered a criminal cabal. Hess's real crime, however, had been to antagonize the Soviet Union. Through its spy in Britain, Kim Philby, then working for the BBC, the Russian NKVD had learned within four days of Hess's arrival in Scotland of the details of his mission. When, six weeks later, Germany invaded the Soviet Union, the Russians had no doubts. Hess was no crackpot acting out of quixotic impulse, they believed. He was clearly Hitler's agent in a scheme to get England out of the conflict so that the Germans could fight the Russians in a one-front war. When the Allies began negotiating the list of major war criminals, the Russians insisted that they wanted Hess in the dock. The British, in order to dispel any suspicion that they had ever considered pulling out on their Russian allies, willingly delivered him up to the IMT.

Later, accounts would circulate that British intelligence had lured Hess to England. After intercepting the first Albrecht Haushofer letter to Hamilton, MI5 was supposed to have initiated a faked correspondence between Hamilton and Hess. Yet Hess had made three unsuccessful attempts to fly to England *before* the false correspondence was supposedly initiated. There had been no necessity to lure Hess to Scotland. He was eager to get there.

Since learning that he would be tried, Hess had had plenty of time to rehearse the stance he would assume in his latest captivity. In England, after accepting the failure of his mission, he had decided that he had to protect the Führer. If Adolf Hitler had said that Rudolf Hess was crazy, then Hess would make the lie credible. Furthermore, he had to behave in a way that would reveal no Reich state secrets useful to the enemy. Finally, he wanted to enhance his chances of being repatriated in a prisoner-of-war exchange. His best strategy, he had reasoned, was to claim amnesia. The pose had served him well in England. How could the Allies try, much less convict, a man in Nuremberg who did not remember anything?

25

JUSTICE JACKSON and General Donovan dined in early October at the Grand Hotel, where the OSS chief had taken a room upon his return to Nuremberg. Jackson was furious, he told Donovan. First he had urged Francis Biddle to come to Europe as soon as possible. Instead, Biddle had chosen to take his sweet time, coming over on the *Queen Elizabeth* on one of the liner's first civilian crossings since the war. Now it looked as if Biddle had maneuvered himself to become president of the court. That, Donovan said, would never do. The Americans already dominated the show. They had picked a trial site in their zone and had provided most of the defendants—and Jackson would clearly be the principal prosecutor. They had to give the court a more international flavor. Biddle had to be derailed, the two men agreed.

The converted Lancaster bomber could scarcely have carried two less similar passengers than the judge the British government had selected for the war-crimes trial and his alternate. The unhappier of the two was the alternate, Sir Norman Birkett. Before his elevation to the bench, Birkett had been the most famous trial lawyer in England. When Radclyffe Hall was charged with obscenity for writing the lesbian story *The Well of Loneliness*, Birkett defended her. When Wallis Simpson wanted to divorce her husband so that she could marry King Edward VIII, she went to Birkett. One of Birkett's clients was found with the decomposed body of a murder victim in his room, where it had been kept for weeks; Birkett won an acquittal. A colleague described Sir Norman, now sixty-two years old, as "one of the ungainliest men ever to have been miscreated." At six feet three inches tall, with undisciplined red hair, hatchet features, and teeth like "a misaligned picket fence," he looked as if the various parts of his anatomy had been assembled from different persons. He also possessed a lively wit and effervescent charm.

Initially, the lord chancellor of England had asked Birkett to be Britain's chief judge at Nuremberg. Three days later, the lord chancellor had called with most distressing news. The Foreign Office insisted on a law lord for the post. Would Birkett be willing to take the alternate position? the lord chancellor asked. Birkett was trapped. To say no to the one post after saying yes to the other would appear unpatriotic. He accepted, but wrote in his diary that night, "I cannot record the secret anguish this has been to me: To have been selected as a member, then asked to become an alternate, merely because of the absurd snobbishness of the Foreign Office!"

The man who had supplanted him was sitting across the aisle of the Lancaster. After minimally correct English amenities, neither man had spoken another word. The twitchy energy of Norman Birkett was nowhere present in Sir Geoffrey Lawrence. He sat placidly leafing through the cattle breeders' quarterly. An unruffled calm emanated from this rotund, glowingly bald, Pickwickian figure. With his wing collar and black suit, Sir Geoffrey might have stepped from another age. He was currently lord justice of appeals, a position he came by almost as a hereditary right. His father had been lord chief justice of England.

Birkett had scant respect for Lawrence's legal talents. Yet, at Nuremberg, Lawrence would occupy a place of substance, and Birkett would serve only as his shadow.

The judges from the four nations met for the first time on October 13 in Berlin, as a sop to the Russians. As soon as they could pick a chief judge, however, they would be on their way to Nuremberg. To Francis Biddle, his expected election as president of the IMT fed a hungry ego. He had been fired as attorney general. He was nearing sixty. Nuremberg was likely his last chance. If he presided over this trial, his name would surely achieve a certain immortality. Biddles were not accustomed to being cast aside as cavalierly as Harry Truman had dismissed Francis. He was the product of two blue-blooded lines, the Randolphs of Virginia and the Biddles of Philadelphia. He had been born in Paris while his parents were making the grand tour. He spoke fluent French from childhood. As a new boy at Groton, he had looked on the sixth-former Franklin Delano Roosevelt as "a magnificent but distant deity, whose splendor added to my shyness." In later years, President Roosevelt had recruited his fellow Grotonian into the service of the common man's New Deal. Eventually, Roosevelt had appointed Biddle to succeed Jackson as attorney general.

On the transatlantic crossing aboard the *Queen Elizabeth*, Biddle had brought his chief aide, Herb Wechsler, the Columbia Law School professor, who still harbored doubts about the Bernays plan and the legitimacy of the trial itself. Biddle expected his wife to follow later. As the ship plied the ocean, Biddle and his staff wrestled endlessly with the most nettlesome issue that would face the judges, just as it had bedeviled the drafters of the charter: the cry of ex post facto law. The procedures and punishments decided on in London had undeniably been devised after the alleged crimes. The last night aboard, Biddle simply announced that the charter made no provision for challenging its authority. He must either support it, or resign before he started. And Francis Biddle had no intention of losing his main chance.

The four-power Allied Control Council that ran occupied Germany threw a cocktail party for the judges and alternates in Berlin. Robert Jackson flew up from Nuremberg, but not for the sociability. Midway into the party, he took Francis Biddle to a quiet corner. Why, he asked, had Biddle taken so long to get to Germany? Biddle admitted that he had deliberately chosen to sail rather than fly. But, he explained, he and his staff had worked hard aboard the *Queen Elizabeth*. The time spent had not been wasted.

Jackson understood, he said, that the British were prepared to support Biddle as president of the court. That would not do. The French role in the war had been too minor to merit the presidency, Jackson said; the Soviets' right to judge aggressors was already shaky; and the Americans were too dominant. Surely Biddle must recognize that. What Biddle must do, Jackson continued, was to persuade the French to throw their support to a Briton. Jackson went on to say that he had already spoken to Maxwell-Fyfe and that Sir David was working on Sir Geoffrey Lawrence to accept the presidency. Right there were the necessary three votes—British, American, and French. Biddle's disappointment was deep, but he accepted Jackson's logic. The next day, Sir Geoffrey Lawrence was elected president of the IMT. His selection rubbed more salt into the wound of his alternate, Sir Norman Birkett.

26

JOHN HARLAN AMEN DID NOT KNOW what to make of the new prisoner. Rudolf Hess, sitting opposite Amen in the interrogation room, certainly looked like a mental case. Amen studied the lipless line of the mouth, the angular head with the skin stretched taut over every hollow and cleft. It would have been a weak face, given the receding chin and sloping forehead; but the protruding brow and deeply sunken eyes gave Hess's gaze a disturbing intensity. Amen had seized the opportunity to interrogate Hess the moment the prison psychiatrist, Major Kelley, had told him that Hess was claiming amnesia. Amen had stared down hundreds of lying, forgetful, crooked local officials in his racket-busting days. He leaned so close that Hess could smell the morning liquor on the man's breath. "When did you get the idea of losing your memory? When did you think it would be a smart thing?" The American fired the question in his best break-the-witness style.

"You imagine I think it would be a good idea to lose my memory to deceive you," Hess answered.

"If you didn't remember your crimes, that would make it tougher for us, wouldn't it?" Amen said. "When you directed the murders of various people."

"I never did that," Hess objected.

"So the witnesses say," Amen added.

Hess gave him a bucktoothed smile. "Am I supposed to think because I can't remember something, that makes your witnesses more credible?"

"You say you can't remember your wife's name," Amen went on, "yet the British told us you wrote to her all the time. What kind of amnesia do you call that?"

"Ah yes, I received letters from her, so I copied the name from the envelope. In my trial, I will be fighting for my skin," Hess added, "and the only weapons I will have are my brain and my memory. Do you think I would deliberately give them away?"

The man had the cunning of a trapped rat, Amen concluded. Still, he planned a surprise for this afternoon, and it ought to prove whether or not Hess was faking.

Hess was marched back into room 55 after lunch to face his mentor, Dr. Karl Haushofer, and Hermann Göring. Göring beamed as though he had found a long-lost brother. "Rudolf, you know me," Göring said, springing forward to take Hess's hand, until a guard shoved him back into his seat. Hess's eyes were unfathomable. "Who are you?" he said dully. "But," Göring said, "we were together for years! Listen, Hess, I was supreme commander of the Luftwaffe. You flew to England in one of my planes, behind my back. Don't you remember?" "No," Hess answered. Göring reminded him of a memorable day in the Reichstag when Hitler announced Göring as his successor and Hess as Göring's successor. Surely he could not have forgotten that.

"I have lost my memory," Hess said. "It is terrible."

Amen motioned to Dr. Haushofer. The old man looked at Hess with tears in his eyes. He spoke, using the familiar *du*. He had news of Hess's family, he said. "I have seen your wife and your little boy. He is seven now, you know." Hess muttered only, "I don't remember." "The little boy is now a big boy," Haushofer went on, "a wonderful little man." Hess's eyes were fixed on the floor. His own son Albrecht, Haushofer continued, who initially wrote to the duke of Hamilton, was dead. "Albrecht was arrested because he knew some of the Twentieth of July plotters," Haushofer explained. Hess shook his head. He did not remember any Albrecht, nor did he remember the mentor of twenty-two years now standing before him.

As Amen ended the session, Göring rose and grumbled, "He's crazy."

While the Hess interrogation was going on, Colonel Andrus summoned Dr. Kelley to his office. The doctor found Andrus sketching the outfit he planned for the guards who would serve in the courtroom: white helmet, white web belt, white gloves, white leggings, and a white billy club setting off the olive drab of their uniforms. Kelley told Andrus that it looked sharp. What did the psychiatrist make of Hess? Andrus wanted to know. The Polish invasion had come as a shock to Hess, Kelley said. "His father substitute proved not to be a god, but a cruel and . . ." Andrus interrupted him. He did not want to hear any psycho-lingo. What did Kelley think of Hess's current mental state? Was he crazy? He was, Kelley said, probably borderline insane.

Hess was a fake, Andrus announced bluntly, a sham, a phony. If this fellow's memory was gone, the colonel wanted to know, how was it that he remembered how to speak English? He wanted Kelley to make a deal with Hess. If Hess would agree to testify against the others, Kelley would agree not to reveal him as a fraud, and Hess would get off lightly as an amnesiac and a crackpot. "Otherwise, tell him you'll expose him," the colonel said. Kelley gave a vague response. It was so hard to discuss these matters with a layman.

27

CAPTAIN DREXEL SPRECHER PASSED Göring coming out of Hess's interrogation. Colonel Amen was still in room 55, chatting with two aides. What did Sprecher want? Amen asked gruffly. He had come to take part in the interrogation of Dr. Ley, Sprecher said. Justice Jackson had assigned him to prosecute the former Nazi trade union chief. The short, combative Amen looked up at the six-foot-three-inch Sprecher with gleeful malice. That was exactly why Sprecher had no business here, Amen said. Sprecher was part of Storey's operation, not Amen's interrogations division.

Drexel Sprecher was an affable, energetic young officer. An OSS veteran, he had impressed Jackson by his ability to condense the essence of a prosecution case into a single page. Jackson sent his memos around as models to the other lawyers. Sprecher recognized the roots of Amen's present belligerence. Initially, Amen had assumed that because his people conducted interrogations, they would serve as prosecutors in court, and Storey's people would merely provide documentary evidence. But, as Jackson leaned increasingly toward a trial conducted via documents, Storey had risen in Jackson's stock. The justice had recently placed him in charge of the prosecutors who would go into court. Amen's people had largely been reduced to showing documents to the prisoners, having them confirm that a particular record was authentic, that the facts were correct, that Keitel's or Jodl's or Sauckel's signature was genuine. Amen had been forced into the hateful role of servicing his rival, and Sprecher was part of that team.

28

UNTIL NOW THEIR STATUS had been ambiguous. Technically, they were prisoners of war. For the military men, this state made sense. But for Funk, a banker? Or Franz von Papen, briefly Germany's chancellor? Julius Streicher, a publisher of anti-Semitic trash? On October 19, 1945, their status would become all too clear.

The instrument of change was a twenty-nine-year-old Englishman who sought to overcome a boyish countenance by deadly earnestness. Major Airey Neave was already a British legend. He had been captured in France in 1940, escaped, was recaptured and thereafter subjected to the mercies of the Gestapo. Later, Neave had led the most spectacular break of the war, out of the supposedly escape-proof Colditz Castle, from which he made his way back to England in 1942.

Neave was by profession a lawyer and had been picked by the president of the court, Sir Geoffrey Lawrence, to assist the bench at Nuremberg. He had barely settled into a room in the Grand Hotel when he received a message to report at once to the American judge, Francis Biddle, in the dining room. He found Biddle lunching with a portly, kindly-looking man, the American alternate, Judge John J. Parker, who greeted Neave in a warm North Carolina accent. Biddle was brusque: "Major Neave, is it? You look remarkably young." The voice had an aristocratic nasality, rare in Americans Neave had met. Biddle wore a chocolate-brown suit, a paisley bow tie, and a blue shirt; the flashiness of his dress contrasted sharply with his patrician manner. Biddle informed Neave that the following day he was to deliver the indictments to the prisoners and help them find lawyers.

On Friday morning, a party consisting of Neave, Colonel Andrus, Dr. Kelley, an interpreter, and two GIs loaded down with bulky copies of the indictments entered the cellblock. Andrus wanted Kelley along to note whether delivery of the charges seemed to affect any of the prisoners emotionally. The door of the cellblock clanged shut behind them and Neave felt a shiver of memory. That morning, he had put on his best dress uniform with a Sam Browne belt and polished brass. He had memorized a little speech: "I am Major Neave, the officer appointed by the International Military Tribunal to serve upon you a copy of the indictment in which you are named as defendant. I am also here to advise you as to your rights to counsel."

"I hope I shan't make a balls of it," Neave confided to Colonel Andrus as their heels clicked hollowly down the corridor. They stopped before the first cell, and Neave braced himself to meet Hermann Göring.

The public image of jolly Hermann, the fat favorite of the German masses, had led Neave to expect an evil buffoon, a malignant clown. Instead, he found a man with quick, ferret-like eyes, a body still too heavy for his short frame, but far lighter than the overstuffed voluptuary captured five months before. Neave sensed something indefinably feminine and feline about the man, not homosexual, but more like a sybaritic ancient Roman. Göring began to tell Neave that his father had been Chancellor Bismarck's commissioner for the German Empire in South-West Africa, as if appealing to Neave as a fellow imperialist. When the gambit met with dead silence, Göring looked suddenly deflated. He shrugged and began to glance through the indictment.

Neave explained Göring's right to have a lawyer. "I have nothing to do with lawyers," Göring said. He had lived as a law unto himself for years. "You find one for me," he instructed Neave. As they were about to leave, Dr. Kelley suggested that Göring might want to write on the indictment his reaction to it. He handed Göring a pen. Göring wrote in quick, bold strokes, "The victor will always be the judge and the vanquished the accused."

The party moved to the next cell. "We've had this bird a little over a week," Andrus observed. "He's a charmer, you'll see." On their entering the cell, Rudolf Hess jerked himself to attention like a robot. Neave was astonished at the gauntness of the face, the spidery wrists, as he handed Hess the indictment. Hess tossed it on the table. His eyes rolled. He began to groan and fell to the bed, clutching his stomach. "Cramps," Andrus said wearily, "that's the latest." After making his set speech, Neave started to leave. Kelley handed the moaning Hess a pen and asked him to write something on the indictment. "I can't remember," Hess wrote in a surprisingly neat hand.

They continued down the corridor to the cell of Wilhelm Frick, drafter of the Nuremberg Laws, who, in his incongruous checked jacket, struck Neave as an aging actor with a worn-out wardrobe. "The most colorless man in the place," Kelley observed. Then to Julius Streicher, who met them with hands poised arrogantly on his hips. Streicher looked at Neave's list of possible lawyers and said, "Jews, these are all Jew names, and I know the judges are Jews too."

Neave braced himself before cell 25. The brutal figure of Ernst Kaltenbrunner loomed in the doorway. Neave had long wondered what impulses drove men like Kaltenbrunner, the executive-suite officials of the factories of extermination. After his first escape from a prison camp at Torun in Poland, Neave had been questioned by a young, coldly handsome, blond, blue-eyed Gestapo officer. The grilling had been tough and conducted without a trace of recognition that Neave was a fellow human being. Then, at one point, the young officer's voice softened, and he offered Neave a cigarette. Neave was emboldened to ask, "Please tell me what you were doing before all this began." The man looked almost wistful. "I was taking my doctorate in philosophy at the university," he said. Then, as though suddenly embarrassed, he barked for a guard to take Neave away.

Neave left Kaltenbrunner's cell in disgust. The giant had flopped onto his cot, sobbing inconsolably, "I want my family!"

Dumpy Walther Funk also cried on reading the indictment. "Be a man, Funk," Andrus said, "and listen to the major." To Neave, the Hitler Youth leader Baldur von Schirach suggested a bisexual with "dansant eyes," the sort that molests little boys. Ribbentrop's untidy cell actually stank. After hearing Neave out, the onetime foreign minister handed him a scribbled list of British aristocrats. "They can give evidence of my desire for peace," he said. Dr. Ley, head of the Nazi labor unions, screeched, "Why don't you just line us up against a wall and shoot us?"

Neave found it taxing to be civil to Seyss-Inquart. The Britisher had spent the final months of the war in Holland on the banks of the River Waal. Every night, Dutch resistance fighters had crossed the river bearing tales of mass death by starvation, and of atrocities in the part of Holland still under Seyss-Inquart's control.

The military men, Dönitz, Keitel, and Jodl, behaved stoically. The admiral said that he wanted a certain German naval lawyer, Otto Kranzbuehler, to defend him. Failing that, he wanted an American or English U-boat captain. They would know that he had fought an honorable war, Dönitz said. Neave noticed that Field Marshal Keitel wore carpet slippers. He remembered standing barefoot for hours on a cold stone floor in the Gestapo prison in Plotsk, after his recapture, until his feet went numb. Neave had responded to the soldier's duty to try to escape. A fellow officer like Keitel must have understood that duty. Yet, this man, who looked every inch the soldier, had signed orders that sent brave British POWs to their deaths for doing exactly what Neave had done. Keitel had issued orders that meant death to thousands of Russian POWs as well, and mass shootings of innocent civilians as hostages. The man, in Neave's judgment, had disgraced his profession.

Cell 13 meant another emotional jolt for Neave. He had been imprisoned in Nazi jails in Poland, where Hans Frank ruled. Frank, this day, was wearing a woolen glove over his left hand to conceal the scar inflicted when he had tried to slit his wrist. Neave could see the fresh pink wound where Frank had also tried to cut his throat. Frank began speaking breathlessly: "It's as though I am two people," he began, "the Frank you see here, and Frank, the Nazi leader. I wonder how that other Frank could do those things. This Frank looks at the other and says, 'Hans, what a louse you are.'" Andrus told Frank to save his soul-baring for Dr. Kelley and to listen to Major Neave.

The prison had turned a monochrome gray with the failing of the afternoon light. Neave felt drained. There remained one more cell to visit, in the far corner: number 11, housing Albert Speer. Speer, who had only recently arrived in Nuremberg, had been distressed to discover Fritz Sauckel in cell 9. Sauckel, the conscript labor czar, represented Speer's greatest danger. Which of them would be found most responsible for what the Allies were calling the slave labor program— Sauckel, who had recruited the workers, or Speer, who had used them? Speer had to play it carefully. If he tried to dump all the blame on Sauckel, he would come across as a manipulative schemer. If he took the blame himself, it could be his neck instead of Sauckel's. Earlier, Fritz Sauckel had made a dreadful impression on Neave. The little man with the Hitler mustache had stood in his cell, sweat pouring off his bald head, whining, "I know nothing of crimes against humanity. And who will defend me? I know none of these lawyers." His mouth had trembled and tears rolled down his cheeks.

Speer, by contrast, was cool, dignified, and spoke fluent English in a cultivated voice. He read the indictment and started to speak. The first move of his survival strategy must strike just the right note. "This trial is necessary," he said. "There is a common responsibility for such crimes, even in an authoritarian state." Dr. Kelley asked politely if Speer would mind writing that sentiment on his indictment.

They were no longer a disparate collection of captives. They were now criminal defendants whose trial was scheduled to begin November 20, Neave had informed them. They would still be interrogated, but were no longer required to respond. What surprised him was how eager most of them were to keep talking.

29

MAJOR KELLEY WENT directly from cellblock C, after delivery of the indictments, to his office down the hall from Colonel Andrus. He felt frustrated as prison psychiatrist by his inability to speak German. Before the day was out, he believed he might have a solution to that problem. Kelley almost missed the officer waiting for him in a corner, thumbing through one of the psychiatrist's professional journals. The man rose gravely and introduced himself as Captain Gustav Gilbert.

Gustav Mahler Gilbert spoke fluent German, learned from his Austrian immigrant parents. Though a psychologist, Gilbert had spent the latter part of the war in intelligence, interrogating POWs. After the European fighting ended, he had been quartered in a private home where he engaged in conversations with ordinary Germans about the war. He quickly grew weary of their teary rationalizations. None of them had ever wanted war. None of them had favored persecution of the Jews. Their familiar, rhyming refrain became burned into his memory: "*Man hat uns belogen und betrogen* [We were lied to and betrayed]."

Gilbert had learned that an interpreter with a background in psychology was needed at Nuremberg, and seized the chance for a transfer. The assignment was not wholly satisfactory. Interpreting meant an underuse of his talents. Still, Gilbert sensed an unprecedented opportunity. Nuremberg offered access, as he was later to write, "to history's most perfectly controlled experiment in social pathology."

What made civilized human beings join the Nazi movement and do what they did? If he could get into those cells, he might find the answers. If the only way was as an interpreter, so be it.

Kelley found Gus Gilbert's gravity a trifle much. Still, here was someone who could interpret for him and who was a professional colleague to boot. He invited Gilbert to come with him down the hall to the CO's office. Before he could take Gilbert on board, he said, he would have to win the approval of Colonel Burton Andrus.

30

KEITEL AND JODL HAD WORKED together for so long, the former passing along Hitler's orders, the latter drafting operations, that they were closely attuned to each other's moods. As they walked the exercise yard this morning, Jodl detected a heaviness in the field marshal's step. Keitel had been interrogated the day before, and Jodl asked, in a whisper, what he had been questioned about. "The Commando Order," Keitel said out of the side of his mouth. Jodl nodded. That was bad.

When Colonel Amen had grilled him about the Commando Order, Keitel thought that his explanations must satisfy any soldier. Clearly, the colonel could understand an officer's duty to obey orders. Amen's response had stunned him. Under the London charter, obedience to orders was not an acceptable defense. How, Keitel wondered, as Amen dismissed answer after answer, could he ever make these people understand the force of Adolf Hitler's will? That August morning in 1942 was typical. They were in the Wolf's Lair, the Führer's headquarters in an East Prussian pine forest, near the Russian front. On the agenda was a recent Canadian commando raid on the Nazi-occupied French coast at Dieppe. Hitler, in a rage, fumed that these commandos were not soldiers. He had evidence that they had been recruited from the ranks of criminals. He flung a report at Keitel. Look at what these barbarians did, he pointed out. The report described German prisoners bound in "death slings," with a noose tied around the neck and the other end tied behind the back to their legs, so that with every movement, they strangled themselves. The Germans also found a British *Handbook of Irregular Warfare* on one of the commandos. Hitler read from it: "Never give the enemy a chance, the days when we could practice the rules of sportsmanship are over. For the time being, every soldier must be a potential gangster. . . . Remember, you are out to kill." With all the strategic decisions before them, Keitel was amazed at how much time Hitler spent ranting over the commandos. They were thugs. They violated the Hague Convention on Land Warfare. Gangsters, he noted, did not enjoy the protections of the Geneva Convention.

A month after Dieppe, twelve British commandos were captured in Norway on a mission to blow up a power station. Henceforth, Hitler announced, all commandos were to be shot, even if they were in uniform and surrendered willingly. "They are to be slaughtered to the last man," he said, and without a trial. Hitler directed Keitel and Jodl to get the word out to the armed forces in a formal order. Both professional soldiers understood the rashness of this act. But they had also witnessed the futility of resisting Hitler. Two fine fellow officers, Generals von Fritsch and von Leeb, had been sacked for opposing the Führer. The Commando Order was issued, over Keitel's signature, on October 18, 1942.

This order had not been the first corruption of Keitel's soldierly ethic. Earlier, in October 1941, soon after the invasion of Russia, Hitler told the senior staff that Russian guerrilla operations had to be stopped. Fifty to one, one hundred to one, that was a proper price for every German soldier the guerrillas killed. The Slavs, he said, were simply brutes, "and neither Bolshevism nor Czarism can change that." Furthermore, political commissars assigned to Russian units were unregenerate Communists who would always make trouble, even as prisoners. They were to be liquidated upon capture. Keitel was to issue orders to that effect.

Keitel had gone back to his quarters and drafted the Reprisal Order and Commissar Order. One month afterward, twenty-three hundred Russian civilians were herded together and executed in retribution for ten German soldiers killed and twenty-six wounded in a guerrilla attack. The original Reprisal Order, Commissar Order, and Commando Order, with Keitel's signature penned in purple ink, were now in the Palace of Justice documents room.

Since his arrest, Keitel thought often of how he had sunk into this pit. Martial appearance apart, he had never wanted to be a career soldier. He once hoped to be a gentleman farmer in his native Helmscherode. His fellow officers had been stunned when Hitler, in 1938, named him chief of staff of the Armed Forces. The reason soon became apparent. Hitler had taken personal command of the military, and, as he pushed the generals around like so many toy soldiers, he would mock Keitel. "I could never get away with this with Blomberg," he liked to say. Field Marshal Werner von Blomberg had been Keitel's esteemed predecessor.

Keitel, on occasion, tried to stand up to Hitler. He remembered the time he had flung his briefcase on the table and stormed out after Hitler again demeaned him in front of his colleagues. After issuing the infamous execution orders, he offered his resignation, and when that failed, he considered suicide. But he always came back, held in thrall by Hitler's hypnotic powers. He had learned to endure the taunts that he knew were made behind his back. "Lakeitel," his colleagues called him, a pun on the German word *Lakai*, a lackey; or "Nichgeselle," a toy donkey that constantly nods its head. The stenographers liked to joke that they never had to write down the first words Keitel said at a meeting: they would always be the last spoken by Hitler.

He complained once to a fellow officer about the things Hitler made him do. The colleague reminded him of the old Prussian maxim "Opt for disobedience if obedience brings no honor." Other officers had dared to disregard improper orders and had survived, his friend reminded him. They believed in the words contained in a German soldier's paybook: "No enemy can be killed who gives up, not even a partisan or a spy." Those officers, Keitel replied, had never worked directly under Adolf Hitler.

He had also paid a crushing personal price to this regime. His youngest son had been killed in action, another was missing, and the third was held prisoner, all on the Russian front, where his Reprisal and Commissar orders had taken so many innocent lives. Yet his doglike devotion to Hitler never really flagged. Keitel had been in the room on the twentieth of July when the plotters' bomb miraculously failed to kill Hitler. It was Keitel who carried him from the shattered building, crying, "My Führer, my Führer. Thank God you're alive."

"Time's up," a guard shouted to the shuffling men in the exercise yard. Back in his cell Keitel took out his copy of the indictment and reread it. Was it possible, he wondered, that a soldier could be punished simply for following orders?

31

AFTER MEETING CAPTAIN GILBERT, Colonel Andrus had to make a decision. The whole lot, psychiatrists, psychologists, left Andrus uncomfortable. Kelley, at least, with his voluble charm, did not look or act the part. But this Gilbert fellow came across as just what bothered him most, one of those deep Jewish thinkers who always looked as if he were X-raying your mind. In the end, however, the colonel went along with Kelley's wishes and approved of Gilbert as the psychiatrists' interpreter.

Soon afterward, Kelley took Gilbert on his first round of cell visits. As they entered cell 5, Hermann Göring, speaking serviceable English, asked, "Do you know what you have if you have one German? You have a fine man. If you have two Germans, you have a bund. Three Germans? You have a war!" Göring slapped his thigh and roared with laughter. Kelley mentioned that they had seen Hess earlier, and that the man was demanding that his food be tested for poison. "Ah, Hess." Göring shook his head. "When the Führer announced that he would be next in line after me, I was furious. I told Hitler, how could he give that nincompoop such a position? The Führer said to me, 'Hermann, be sensible. When you become führer, *poof!* You throw Hess out and name your own successor.' The Führer had a genius for handling men, you know," Göring said. Kelley asked what Göring thought about Hitler's committing suicide. Was that not the act of a coward? Not at all, Göring responded. It was unthinkable to imagine the head of the German state sitting in a cell like this awaiting trial as a war criminal.

Gilbert hazarded a question. What about his own death? Was he concerned? "What is there to be afraid of," Göring said grimly. "I have given orders to hundreds of thousands of men to go into battle knowing full well many would not come back. Why should I, their leader, cringe when called on to face the enemy?" He gave out a joyless laugh. "I know that I'm going to hang. But let me tell you something. Fifty years from now they will erect statues of me all over Germany. Big statues in the parks and little statues in every German home." He paused for a moment and then started laughing again. "One Englishman? You have an idiot. Two, a club. Three, an empire!"

Kelley invited Gilbert to dinner with him that night at the Grand Hotel. Through the dining-room windows, they watched sullen Nurembergers passing by; children's faces pressed to the windows as the two Americans waded into their steaks. Kelley asked Gilbert if he knew what psychological treasure was at their fingertips. Of course, Gilbert answered. He himself had been thinking of a study of the Nazis based on visits to their cells. Kelley noted that their minds were running along the same track. But there was more than an academic monograph here. They had the raw material for a book, a major book, a collaborative effort, Kelley said. He wanted Gilbert to start taking notes after the cell visits, getting down everything that was said. Gilbert did not mention that he had already recorded every word of Göring's that he could remember.

32

GENERAL DONOVAN HAD BEEN in the Far East for weeks, out of touch with Nuremberg. Nevertheless, Jackson was alarmed by the way Donovan had moved in since his return. It was not a raw power grab; rather, it was the magnetic loyalty the man generated. The OSS veterans still seemed to think that Donovan's wishes amounted to orders.

Later in October, Jackson called a meeting of the top prosecution staff. Donovan immediately suggested the priority order of business, to choose the first witness and who would examine him. That suggestion, Jackson said, started on precisely the wrong foot. He realized that Donovan had not yet had time to learn the advantages of the documents approach over the witness approach. Jackson asked one of his aides to summarize a document recently found, written by a German doctor in Kiev. The young lawyer began quoting Dr. Wilhelm Schueppe, of the "Reich medical department," telling of his work in a Kiev hospital. His assignment, Schueppe had written, was to liquidate through morphine injections one hundred people daily who were "unworthy, mentally defective, terminally ill or from inferior races, such as Jews and gypsies." This, Jackson said, was an example of the evidence available in documentary form to prove, for example, count four, crimes against humanity. Donovan ought to see the other incriminating material coming out of Hans Frank's diaries, Rosenberg's papers, and a dozen other written sources.

Donovan remained unpersuaded. He had been talking to reporters, he said, and documents struck them as deadly dull. If the people in this room wanted the world to listen, they had better put some flesh-and-blood witnesses on the stand. Jackson was not eager to have his authority challenged in a staff fracas. He brought the meeting to an early close. On the way out, he suggested that Donovan come to his place for dinner that night. He had an excellent cook.

The dinner went well as long as they stuck to small talk. Donovan ate with zest, particularly Frau Hassel's *Apfelstrudel*, but only nursed a white wine. After dinner, they retired to the music room. "This trial is going to be far more than a lawsuit," Donovan remarked. Nuremberg could provide the stage for the greatest morality tale ever enacted. And they needed live actors, witnesses. Jackson had to understand the public-relations dimension of the trial. Jackson was unpersuaded. His experience had convinced him of the preferability of documents over witnesses. Documents, unlike witnesses, did not have faulty memories or commit perjury. He intended, he claimed, to write a record that would outlive the hammer of the critics. Of course they would call a few witnesses. But by relying essentially on documents, they could convict these people with their own words. Donovan abruptly announced that it was time for him to leave.

As Jackson watched Donovan's car pull away, he accepted that he had probably alienated the general. Still, he was certain he was on the right track. What he did not admit was that it had been a long time since he had examined a witness in court. The documentary approach, along with its intrinsic superiority, seemed far less daunting.

33

IN LATE OCTOBER, with less than a month until the November 20 trial-opening date, the court members gathered in what had been designated the Judges' Room. They sat around a conference table covered with an army blanket, the room illuminated by a portable electric lamp. Alternate justice Norman Birkett was complaining about living conditions, his hawkish nose sniffing. Since Major Airey Neave was the court's liaison man, the heat of Birkett's ire fell on him. Neave sat against the wall, as one of his colleagues described him, "looking twenty, being thirty, acting forty." Birkett's voice grew more shrill as he tried to speak over the hammering, sawing, and shouting of the workmen outside. He had arrived in Nuremberg, he said, to find his house at 16 Steilenstrasse unprepared. The pillows were made of cast iron. Not a thought had been given to the most ordinary comforts. Sir Geoffrey Lawrence, sitting at the head of the table as president of the court, listened with infinite patience. He turned to Neave and asked if the major would please report Sir Norman's unhappiness to that American housing gentleman, Captain Vonetes.

Birkett said that he was not yet finished. Couldn't something be done about the dining arrangements? It might be admirably democratic to stand in line with all ranks and have one's food dumped into a tin tray by a GI, but it was hardly befitting the justices of an international tribunal. Francis Biddle, by now a friend of Birkett's, tuned out this outburst by the ordinarily charming Englishman. Instead, his attention was focused on Nikitchenko's interpreter, Tania Giliarevskaya, a small, exquisitely proportioned beauty. Though he was nearly sixty, Biddle's eye for a handsome woman was undimmed.

As Birkett went on, a flicker of annoyance flashed across Sir Geoffrey's face. They would soon be dining privately in this very room on bone china which this Kiley chap had somehow managed to unearth, Sir Geoffrey explained. Birkett slumped back in his seat, knowing that his tirades made him look petty, and that they were born of thwarted ambition.

Perhaps they could turn to more pressing matters, Sir Geoffrey suggested, particularly the need to provide lawyers for the defendants. He turned to Neave. Many of the defendants, Neave said, were asking for lawyers who had been Nazis. He needed the court's guidance on this matter. The usually impassive face of General Nikitchenko tightened. The beautiful interpreter rendered his cold anger into a colloquial American English that charmed Biddle. Nazis as officers of the court? Nikitchenko asked, disbelieving. Men who should be in the dock themselves? Surely this was some sort of a bad joke.

Biddle broke in, extracting some papers from his briefcase. Göring had requested a lawyer from Kiel named Otto Stahmer. Biddle read from a letter that a Frau Noak had written to the American occupation authorities on Stahmer. Just five months before the war ended, he had complained to his landlady that a fellow tenant, Frau Noak, was a Jew, protected only by the fact that she was married to a Gentile. If the landlady did not throw the Noak woman out, Stahmer said, he intended to denounce her under the Nuremberg Laws. Thus, Frau Noak had wound up in the Theresienstadt concentration camp. As Biddle read, Nikitchenko nodded sagely. Clearly this Stahmer was an unregenerate Nazi. Was he to be allowed to defend war criminals? Precisely, Biddle said. The London charter stated unequivocally that defendants were to be allowed the counsel of their choice. It said nothing about excluding Nazi, Communist, or vegetarian lawyers, for that matter. The point, Biddle said, was that these men must not be given the slightest excuse to protest afterward that they had been denied a fair trial. Nuremberg must not become a legal Versailles, planting a smoldering resentment in the breasts of Germans. Sir Geoffrey supported Biddle. It was agreed that Nazi defense lawyers could be appointed.

34

HERB WECHSLER, Judge Biddle's chief assistant, sat poring over an appeal from one of the defendants. General Jodl was demanding documents relating to Allied war crimes. Jodl had sent his appeal to Biddle, who bucked it to Wechsler to draft a reply. Jodl's request was just what Wechsler had feared from the first moment he had read Murray Bernays's plan. Jodl was saying, If we committed war crimes, so did you. If we are being tried for them, why aren't you? Emotionally, Wechsler wanted to see these people punished. As a Jew, he found that his sleep, since coming to Germany, had been tormented by nightmares. But he was a distinguished legal scholar to whom the law was sacred and immutable. In a world of pure justice, Jodl had a point. Yet, the charter drafters had already decided that tu quoque would not be accepted as a defense.

Wechsler was wrestling with this issue when he got a phone call from Biddle. Luise Jodl, the general's wife, had just turned up at the Palace of Justice. Would Herb please see what it was all about? Biddle asked.

The cool detachment Wechsler felt when faced with a legal riddle deserted him at the prospect of confronting the wife of an accused Nazi. He entered a small office to find a GI guard and a woman wearing a fedora of the kind favored by German women in the thirties, a mannish overcoat, and flat shoes that had seen hard use. She was not stylish or beautiful, but her unaffected dignity struck him. She rose and introduced herself in fluent English. He guessed her to be in her mid-thirties, a good twenty years Jodl's junior.

Luise Jodl had been married for only a year and a half. She had previously worked as a secretary in the German High Command and had been a friend of Jodl's first wife, Anneliese. She had nursed Anneliese through a terminal illness, until the woman's death in the spring of 1944. Dr. Kelley found Jodl the coldest man in cellblock C. To Luise, however, the general had revealed an impetuous romantic streak. He told her bluntly that the war was lost well before he dared tell anyone else. They should, therefore, marry as soon as possible and wring from life whatever brief happiness it offered.

Wechsler asked Frau Jodl to sit down, while he occupied the desk opposite her. She had walked, she told him with a self-conscious glance at her battered shoes, virtually all the way from Berchtesgaden to Nuremberg to be near her husband. She had found a room in a half-destroyed house that she was sharing with the wife of Field Marshal Keitel. She had come here to do everything in her power to save her husband. She wanted Wechsler to tell her what that might be.

Wechsler found himself responding to Luise Jodl's sincerity. He asked how she came by her command of English. Through a British grandfather, she answered. An English-speaking secretary would be a tremendous advantage to her husband's lawyer, he told her. Did Jodl have a lawyer yet? That was another matter, she said, where she asked for his help. Professor Franz Exner of the University of Munich was an old friend of the Jodl family. Could Mr. Wechsler engage him for her husband? Wechsler knew Exner; they had met when the German came to Columbia University before the war. Wechsler knew him to be a master of criminal law. He would ask Major Neave to try to track down Exner, Wechsler said. And he would try to arrange a job for Frau Jodl with her husband's lawyer. She thanked him, and they parted with a handshake.

Back in his office, Wechsler wondered why he had been so sympathetic, until he reflected on Jodl's plight. He knew the charges the man faced, particularly for his role, along with Keitel, in transforming Hitler's manias into military orders. He also knew that he would have to recommend to Biddle that Jodl's request for documents on Allied war crimes be denied because of the IMT's position on tu quoque. No, he was not doing too much for an admirable woman whose husband, he suspected, would end up on the gallows anyway.

Airey Neave spent ten hectic days locating lawyers in a country split into four occupation zones, where telephones rarely worked, mail delivery was erratic, public transportation was disrupted, and his quarry were often living in bombed-out ruins. In the end, counsel was found for all the defendants. Nearly half had been Nazi party members.

35

HANS FRANK AWOKE with a shudder, felt the eruption and sticky dampness. He had just had another wet dream. It was embarrassing to have this happen in his forty-fifth year. In some dreams, his daughter appeared, making him feel, when he awoke, depraved. He explained these nocturnal arousals to himself as the result of the passion he had been experiencing ever since he started rereading the Bible and meditating on his Catholic boyhood.

That afternoon he told Dr. Kelley and the new man, Dr. Gilbert, that he believed he was undergoing a moral regeneration. "I tell you," he said, "the scornful laughter of God is more terrible than any vengeance of man. Here we are, the would-be rulers of Germany, in tiny cells with four walls and a toilet, waiting to be tried as common crim-inals. Is that not proof of God's amusement with men who lust for power?"

What did he think of Hitler now? Gilbert asked. "If only one of us had had the courage to shoot him," Frank said, "what misery the world would have been spared." Hitler's mesmerizing gaze, Frank now believed, had been nothing but the stare of a psychopath. The man was a primitive, an egoist, contemptuous of conventional human stan-dards. "That's why," Frank went on, "he hated all legal, diplomatic, and religious institutions, any social values that restricted his own im-pulsive ego." Outside, the two Americans agreed that Frank's dissec-tion of the Hitlerian psyche was worthy of their own professions.

Saturday afternoon, October 20, Frank made up his mind. He begged the guard to summon Father Sixtus O'Connor. Tough luck, the sol-dier answered, the American chaplain was out at Soldiers Field, watch-ing his football team, the undefeated Big Red One, take on the Eightieth Division.

Father Sixtus had indeed gone to watch his old division play. The Catholic priest from Oxford, New York, had been an outstanding stu-dent before the war at the University of Munich, which he left just two days before the invasion of Poland. He had also been mad about sports since his youth—a fact that endeared him to Colonel Andrus's sentinels. Father Sixtus was currently serving his smallest congregation ever, the six defendants who had been born Catholic. The half-crazed Streicher, he feared, was hopeless. Every time O'Connor went into his cell, Streicher would tell him he was no "last-minute Christian," and launch into a jeremiad against the Jews. Streicher, however, never failed to hit up the chaplain for chewing gum, which had become his latest obsession.

When he returned from the ball game, O'Connor found a mes-sage from Hans Frank.

Colonel Andrus had barely hung up his shellacked helmet that Mon-day morning when Father O'Connor burst into his office. "Colonel!" O'Connor cried, "Hans Frank has been saved! He has returned to the faith!" Frank had asked the priest to baptize him again in the Catholic church. What did that mean as far as the man's mental stability was concerned? the colonel asked. O'Connor was puzzled. Did this mean, Andrus wanted to know, that he was more or less likely to commit suicide? The priest laughed. The Catholic church condemned suicide, he assured the colonel. Suicide meant a quick trip to perdition.

Days afterward, with Frank kneeling on the stone floor of cell 15, and with Willi Krug holding a tin washbasin of holy water, Father O'Connor rebaptized Hans Frank. The priest also urged the prisoner to start writing his memoirs.

36

ON OCTOBER 23, Gilbert and Kelley visited the cell of Dr. Robert Ley, the puffy, red-faced, alcoholic former chief of the German Labor Front. When first arrested, Ley had entertained hopes of salvation. He had written to Henry Ford, offering to share with Ford his experience in manufacturing Volkswagens. But now he appeared to live in a permanent state of distress.

Gilbert strove for a professional objectivity toward all the prisoners. But one of Ley's earlier demands had nearly shattered his composure. Ley had told him that he wanted a Jewish lawyer to defend him. He had in mind a respected man from Cologne. What, Gilbert wondered, was the likelihood of finding any Jews left in Cologne, much less an eminent attorney? This afternoon, he and Kelley found Ley unusually agitated. Flinging his indictment to the floor, Ley cried, "Am I supposed to defend myself against crimes which I knew nothing about?" He plastered himself against the cell wall and spread his arms out. "Stand us against a wall and shoot us," he said. "But why should I be brought before a tribunal like a cuh——, cuh——, cuh——" "A criminal?" Gilbert offered. "Yes," Ley said, dropping his arms. "I can't even say the word."

Afterward, Gilbert went to the prison office, an empty cell fitted out with a desk, to record the conversation. He believed that note-taking in front of the prisoners would inhibit their frankness. He always provided a copy of his notes to Kelley, who assured him that this material was pure gold for their book.

37

"JESUS CHRIST!" the guard passing in front of cell 25 groaned. "Will you look at him." He was peering through the port at Julius Streicher. Earlier, the guard had watched in disgust as Streicher carried out his customary morning routine, vigorous calisthenics in the nude, with all parts flopping about freely. Now, sweating profusely, Streicher was washing his face in the toilet bowl. The man had become a pariah, reviled by his captors and shunned by his fellow defendants. Streicher was convinced that the source of his ostracism lay across the corridor, with Hermann Göring, in cell 5.

Before the war, Streicher had prospered with his tabloid newspaper, *Der Stürmer*, filled with stories of Aryan maidens defiled by debauched Jews and pseudoscientific disquisitions on the quality of Jewish sperm. He had also possessed political power as the much feared *Gauleiter*, the Nazi party leader of Franconia. One oft-told tale concerned a Nuremberg schoolteacher jailed for insulting Streicher. The *Gauleiter* had horse-whipped the teacher senseless. Afterward, Streicher left the prison sighing—"I needed that. Now I feel relaxed."

He became notorious, even by Nazi standards, for abusing his office. Streicher forced Jews to sell him their property for ten percent of its value, then resold it at the market price. He had once ordered his subordinates to turn in their gold wedding rings so that they could buy a suitable birthday present for the Führer. Instead, Streicher used the gold to have an elaborate brooch made for his current girlfriend.

Streicher had been outraged to learn that Göring's actress wife, Emmy, consorted with Jews, and so he printed in *Der Stürmer* a photograph of her shopping at Jewish stores. Finally, he went too far. In 1940, he printed a story that Göring was impotent and that his daughter, Edda, had been conceived through artificial insemination. Göring thereafter engineered the appointment of a six-man tribunal of fellow *Gauleiter*s to investigate the cesspool of corruption that Streicher presided over. The tribunal found Streicher "unfit for human leadership." He was stripped of all party posts and banished to his farm at Pleikershof, outside Nuremberg. He continued to publish *Der Stürmer*, but otherwise, Julius Streicher sat out the war.

As defeat became inevitable, Streicher grew a beard, assumed the name Seiler, retreated to a tiny village near Berchtesgaden, and passed himself off as an artist. On May 23, 1945, he was sitting on his terrace painting a watercolor, when two American officers appeared, brandishing revolvers. Streicher's cover quickly collapsed. He later described what happened. "Two niggers," he said, stripped him, burned his nipples with lit cigarettes, and beat his genitals. They pried his mouth open and spat into it. He was forced to march around with a placard reading JULIUS STREICHER, KING OF THE JEWS.

At Nuremberg, Streicher's lawyer, Dr. Hans Marx, listened to his client ranting and asked that Streicher be given a psychiatric examination. A crackpot, Marx said, should not have to stand trial. During the course of the examination, Streicher was asked to strip. A female Russian interpreter turned her back to him, and Streicher said, leering, "What's the matter, don't you want to see something nice?" The psychiatrists concluded that Julius Streicher had a monomania, his obsession with the Jews. "But, his ideas, while false and odd," Major Kelley wrote, "cannot be classed as true delusions. He is sane."

38

ON THE EVENING of October 25, Colonel Andrus was at his living quarters writing to an old army friend. Shortly after 8:30 p.m., his phone rang. His deputy, Major Fred Teich, was calling. Something terrible had happened, Teich said. The colonel must come to the prison at once.

Second Lieutenant Paul Graven, twenty-one years old, had taken over as duty officer on cellblock C at eight p.m. A long night stretched ahead of Graven, and so he had gone to the prison office and started reading a paperback novel. Barely ten minutes passed before the corporal of the guard burst in on him. The lieutenant had better take a look at Robert Ley. Something looked fishy. Graven tossed aside the book and hurried to cell 9. He peeped through the porthole. Because the toilet was in a tiny alcove to the right, only Ley's feet were visible, with his pants around his ankles. Graven called to the prisoner, but there was no answer. He flung open the bolt of the door and went in. Ley was seated on the toilet, bent forward, his face swollen and blue-black, his eyes bulging. Around his neck he had looped a noose improvised from a strip of towel and tied it to a water pipe against the wall. Ley had stuffed a rag into his mouth to stifle any cry, and had apparently leaned forward until he choked himself to death. Burton Andrus had lost his second prisoner in less than three weeks, this time a major defendant.

The Leonardo Conti suicide had been successfully hushed up, but the nature of Ley's death would be impossible to keep from others in the cellblock. The next day, Andrus ordered Major Teich to assemble the prisoners in the corridor. "When unpleasant news needs to be published, as in this case, I myself will do it," the colonel said. "Ley has killed himself. He gained time to do this by giving the appearance of making a call of nature."

Hermann Göring whispered to Hess from the side of his mouth. "It's just as well. I had my doubts about how Ley would stand up to a trial." Colonel Andrus cut Göring short, and sent the prisoners back to their cells. He directed his staff to meet with him immediately in his office.

Andrus looked drawn and tired. Losing a prisoner was rather like a captain losing his ship, and proud Burton Andrus had lost two. Security was obviously not tight enough, he began. From now on, instead of one guard for four cells, they would post one on each cell. Two hours on, four hours off. And never during those two hours was the guard to take his eyes off the prisoner. This system would require more men, an officer noted. Andrus recognized that, he said testily, and he would take up the matter with the commandant of the Nuremberg-Furth enclave.

The next morning, Andrus was having coffee in the courthouse cafeteria when Boris Polevoi, a Russian journalist for *Pravda*, came up and asked him about the Ley suicide. That sort of thing was over now, Andrus answered. He explained to Polevoi the new measures he had taken. His jail, he said, was now suicide-proof.

39

ROBERT JACKSON SAT in his office in the Palace of Justice amid a clutter of mimeographed documents. He was speaking on the phone in a controlled rage. The officer who handled all his administrative head-aches, Colonel Robert Gill, was calling to tell him that Gill's coun-terpart, the judges' administrative officer, had just bounced some of Jackson's people from their housing. There was nothing Gill could do about it, because the court's man, General William Mitchell, out-ranked him. He would see about that, Jackson said, ending the con-versation. As far as Jackson was concerned, this was Francis Biddle's doing. Biddle might resent being deprived of the presidency of the court, but Jackson was damned if he was going to lose control over this show to him. He called to Elsie Douglas and dictated a cable to President Truman.

It was shocking, Francis Biddle told General Mitchell, the empire that Bob Jackson was building. "Do you know what my driver told me this morning?" Biddle said. "He was amazed that the prosecution needed six hundred people just to hang twenty-one." Jackson's people, he went on, "are overrunning this city. They're either monopolizing transportation and communications or else sitting around drinking in the Grand Hotel." Mitchell agreed. He had just dealt with Jackson's administrator and had taken over some of the prosecution's housing, he explained.

What Jackson understood more clearly than ever, he told Elsie Doug-las, was the fundamental difference between himself and Francis Bid-dle. Biddle was Main Line, and Jackson was Main Street. And Main Street had just outsmarted Main Line. He wanted her to summon Colonel Gill. Jackson intended to read him personally the response he had just received from the White House. Gill had been promoted by direct presidential action. Now Jackson and Biddle each had his own general. There would be no more rank-pulling by the Main Line.

40

GUSTAV GILBERT FOUND the letter painful to write. He had not seen his wife, Matilda, since the fall of 1943. He had a fifteen-month-old son, Robert, whom he had never seen. He now had enough discharge points to go home, and he was writing to tell her that, instead, he was staying on in Nuremberg.

Gilbert's character had been forged early in poverty, work, and striving. His Austrian immigrant father had died when the boy was nine. His mother, overwhelmed by the responsibility of raising him and two younger brothers, turned the children over to a Jewish welfare agency. They were sent to an orphanage in Westchester County. Quiet, studious Gustav eventually won a scholarship to the Ethical Culture School in Manhattan, and went on to the Harvard of poor but bright students, City College of New York. He earned a doctorate in psychology from Columbia University in 1939.

At Nuremberg, he had been chagrined at first to be regarded simply as an interpreter, but thanks to Major Kelley, his future looked promising. The idea of a book on the psychopathology of the Nazis, with the subjects as available to him as laboratory mice, had proved irresistible. How could he turn his back on this chance? He hoped Mattie would understand. He dropped off the letter at the army post office in the Palace of Justice and returned to his office, where he learned that the colonel was looking for him.

Gilbert, who had never been summoned to Andrus's office before without Kelley, felt apprehensive. Colonel Andrus greeted Gilbert with forced bonhomie and asked the captain to have a seat. After chitchat about the suitability of Gilbert's quarters, the colonel rose, closed the door, and resumed his place behind the desk. He appreciated, he said, that Gilbert spoke German so well. You could never know what these birds were up to if you could not understand their lingo. Yes, Gilbert was doing fine interpreting, Andrus went on. But, that was only half the job. What he also needed was "an observer," Andrus said. He wanted Gilbert to hang around with these fellows in the exercise yard, even when they took their weekly showers. Win their confidence, become a friend. Pick up whatever they said. And, if it proved interesting, Gilbert should report back to the prison commandant immediately.

Andrus wanted him to be a spy, Gilbert realized. At one time, he might have found the idea repugnant. Now, instead, his mind was racing. Of course, he would be happy to report on the defendants in the prison and the yard for the colonel, he said. But imagine what they could learn once the trial began, if Gilbert could also have access to the courtroom. Surely, a good case could be made to the bench for having a trained psychologist there to watch how the proceedings affected the defendants' psychological well-being. If, at the same time, Gilbert could gather useful intelligence for the colonel, so much the better. Andrus liked the idea and said that he would try to obtain permission from Sir Geoffrey Lawrence, the president of the court.

One more point, Gilbert said, as he rose to leave. Would not all this have a better chance of succeeding if instead of being simply an interpreter, Gilbert could be designated as prison psychologist? Andrus reached for his helmet and riding crop. He was about to conduct a white-glove inspection of the sentinels' quarters, he said. Gilbert's request was all right with him if it was okay with Major Kelley.

When the day's work was done, Gilbert suggested that he and Kelley have a drink at the Grand. It was not the kind of invitation the taciturn Gilbert ever extended, and Kelley was delighted to accept. After they had settled into a quiet corner of the hotel bar, Gilbert described his conversation with the colonel. Kelley did not instantly embrace the idea of Gilbert alone getting access to the courtroom and the new title. But, if they were going to do a book, Gilbert's observation of the defendants' behavior in court would obviously be valuable. Of course Gilbert could consider himself the prison psychologist, Kelley said.

41

ON NOVEMBER 6, Hermann Göring was delivered to the interrogation room and surprised to find there an older man, a civilian of quiet, dignified bearing, who introduced himself as Dewitt Poole of the U.S. State Department. Poole took Göring's hand, before the guard could stop him. He told Göring that he was not there to interrogate him. His interest, Poole said, was strictly in diplomatic history.

"Our studies lead us to the conclusion," Poole went on, "that among those close to Hitler, only you showed independence of thought and action in foreign relations." Göring listened warily. "Let me read from a cable our ambassador in Berlin sent on you in 1938," Poole continued, taking a paper from his breast pocket: "He is boyish, likable, and still carries with him something of the air ace out on a spree. . . . The painters and sculptors who are his friends are legion. In this respect, Göring is like an Italian prince of the Renaissance." Göring was now beaming. Here was an American gentleman among so many barbarians. Of course, Göring said, he virtually conducted his own foreign policy in the Third Reich. What about Ribbentrop? Poole asked. Göring laughed. Ribbentrop had convinced Hitler that he knew all the people worth knowing in France and England, Göring said. "We didn't fully grasp at the time that he knew the French only through champagne and the English only through whiskey." Poole laughed appreciatively.

Hitler's decision to break his nonaggression pact with Russia, Poole asked—would Göring tell him about that? He had talked to the Führer for three hours privately before the invasion. There was no end to that country, Göring had explained. Once you got to the Volga there were the Urals. Once you got past the Urals, there was Siberia. Germany was already at war with Britain; with America likely to come in, it would be madness to take on the Soviet Union too. He had left Hitler that day believing he had dissuaded him from a catastrophe.

As Poole continued his gentle probing, Göring recalled his past. On an evening in 1922, the unemployed air ace went to the Café Neumann in Munich to hear the leader of the tiny National Socialist German Workers Party. Adolf Hitler's subject was the peace treaty of Versailles. Göring could still remember that voice, shy at first, almost inaudible, building to a crescendo. "Only bayonets can back up our threats to the French," Hitler had roared. "Down with Versailles!" The next day Göring joined the party. He had provided just the ornament that Hitler was looking for—an authentic, respectable, colorful war hero.

Years of struggle followed in which Göring sank to unimaginable depths, which he was not about to describe to Dewitt Poole. In 1928, his fortunes finally began to change when he became one of a handful of Nazis elected to the Reichstag. In 1932, the party won the largest bloc of seats, and Göring became president of the Reichstag. It was he who delivered the news to Hitler on January 30, 1933, that the Führer would be named chancellor of Germany.

Hitler appointed him minister of the interior for Prussia. In this post, Göring created the Secret State Police—Geheime Staatspolizei —to eliminate political opponents. The agency's name was soon abbreviated to "Gestapo." Göring also established places of confinement for political enemies, soon called concentration camps. Both enterprises gained such notoriety worldwide that Göring feared for his reputation. He gladly let the Gestapo and the concentration camps slip into the ever-expanding orbit of the ambitious SS chief, Heinrich Himmler.

Göring's appetite for power found other outlets. The old flier became chief of the Luftwaffe in 1935. In 1937, despite a near-total ignorance of economics, he persuaded Hitler to name him head of the Four Year Plan. He was going to make the country self-sufficient, build synthetic-gas and -rubber plants, do whatever was required so that in the event of war, Germany could withstand a blockade. He had the iron and coal mines and the steel mills of the Ruhr named the "Hermann Göring Werke," and raked off millions through payoffs and kickbacks.

During the Polish campaign, Göring's shrieking Stuka divebombers knocked the Polish air force out of the war. Hitler was much impressed by the strategic potential of airpower and, in 1940, he elevated Göring to *Reichsmarschall*, the highest military rank in Germany. A year later, he formally designated Göring as his successor in the event of his death.

Göring was enjoying the session with Poole, telling him how he had befriended Charles Lindbergh in the thirties, and that Lindbergh had sent a gift of a silver dish when Göring's daughter, Edda, was born. He had presented Lindbergh, in turn, with a Nazi medal, the Service Cross of the German Eagle with Star.

Was it true, Poole wanted to know, that Göring had willingly supported German rearmament? Of course, Göring said, but not to oppress other people, only to ensure Germany's freedom after the evils of Versailles. He had told the German people, he explained, "What is the point of being in the concert of nations if Germany is only allowed to play the kazoo? I told them, would you rather have butter or guns? Shall we produce lard or iron ore?" He laughed and slapped at his still ample belly. "I told the people, butter only makes you fat!"

Poole questioned Göring about the widespread conviction that he had arranged the burning of the Reichstag shortly after Hitler came to power. The fire had been used by Hitler to justify the suspension of civil liberties in Germany and to launch the mass roundup of political opponents. This was an old chestnut, Göring said. If he had burned down the Reichstag, it would not have been for political reasons, but because the place was an architectural offense. The next thing they would be saying was that he had stood around watching the blaze wearing a Roman toga and playing the violin.

The interview went on into the night, finally ending at 10:30 p.m. Dewitt Poole was exhausted when he left. Göring had proved a fascinating combination, a quick mind, a ready wit, a student of history —and clearly an amoral man.

Göring returned to his cell exhilarated. At last he had been treated with the respect he deserved. He felt important again, a world figure to be reckoned with.

42

WITH THE TRIAL only two weeks off, the world press began descending on Nuremberg. Howard K. Smith, CBS's man, arrived in late October. Despite a boyish demeanor, Smith was already an old European hand. He had been reporting from Berlin when America entered the war and had managed to get out of Germany one hour before the border was sealed. After the war, he had succeeded the legendary Edward R. Murrow as the network's European chief. He had been delighted to get the Nuremberg assignment, until the CBS news director informed him that, once the trial got under way, Murrow would also be coming, along with William L. Shirer and maybe Eric Sevareid. What, Smith began to wonder, would be left for him?

Smith arrived at a press camp unlike any he had ever known. The U.S. Army had taken Justice Jackson's offhand remark literally. It had turned the castle of the Faber-Castell family, in the Nuremberg suburb of Stein, into a press billet. As the jeep carrying him came to a halt, Smith got out and gazed at a heavy-handed version of a fairy-tale castle, gray, massive, with stout round towers and turrets. The castle rose like a stone island in a sea of devastation. Not only had it been spared the bombing, but the source of the family fortune, the Faber-Castell pencil factory next door, was still humming, unscathed.

The GI house manager led Smith upstairs, where the pleasant prospect of palatial living collapsed. Correspondents were jammed twenty to a room and sleeping on army cots. The bathrooms were ornate, but there were only four of them to serve what would eventually swell to over three hundred correspondents. Already, Smith could detect the sour odor of overused toilets. He stretched out on an unoccupied cot, feeling lonely. After a courtship plagued by the intrusions of war, he had finally managed to marry his Danish sweetheart, Benedicte Traberg, a fellow journalist. He and his wife were scheming to get her accredited to the Nuremberg trial. In the meantime, this crowded castle was to be his home.

With the trial not yet under way, Smith was eager to get out into the city to experience the ground truth. On a Sunday morning, he started on foot from the courthouse. Outside the main entrance he watched an honor guard of forty-five Frenchmen parade by, men with the spirit gone out of their step. You could read national character, he thought, in these units. The Russian honor guard used a belligerent stomp just short of a goose step. The most colorful were the Scots, with flashing bayonets accompanied by the spine-tingling wail of bagpipes. His own Americans marched with a slouching nonchalance, some chewing gum. Smith was unperturbed. He had seen enough of what strutting militarism could do to a country.

Away from the courthouse, it was as if a curtain had descended on civilization. The first street he turned into was a trench between mounds of debris; the houses on both sides vanished. He spotted smoke from a pipe peeping above the rubble. People were living under there, he knew. Nuremberg was an upside-down city, its inhabitants occupying cellars, air-raid shelters, the basements of destroyed apartment houses and hotels. The music of Haydn issued from the ruins of the Frauenkirche, a splendid thirteenth-century Gothic structure, now looking like a tattered, windblown piece of theatrical scenery. Out of the church stepped a bride in white, clutching a bouquet, walking daintily through the debris with her groom at her side.

Some German women wore shabby coats, out at the elbows. Others sported chichi frocks, stylish shoes, and silk stockings brought back from Paris by a Wehrmacht husband or Gestapo boyfriend. Inside the Grand Hotel, guests dined on chicken and ice cream, while in the street old women ransacked garbage cans and cooked what they found on open fires. Smith passed a cart pulled by two young boys and a woman. They were hauling a piano, headed, no doubt, to the only remaining prosperous part of Germany—the farmlands. Nurembergers would gladly swap a piano for a sack of potatoes.

The last leg of Smith's tour took him past the destroyed railroad station. Here, on the few standing walls, scraps of paper hung from a nail or were held in place by a stone. "Any word of Franz Fuschl, last seen at Cassino? Inform Red Cross," one read. "Klaus Werner, father is missing. Mother at Aunt Helga's," another read. Nurembergers stood before them, faces upturned in hope. As the light began to fade, a mood of menace settled over the ruins. Smith headed back toward the Palace of Justice. Still, little violence was reported nowadays. No more GIs were decapitated by wire strung across roads. For the Germans, apathy had become stronger than anger.

43

WHAT HAD STARTED as a teapot tempest was getting more serious. Robert Jackson's administrator, General Gill, had directed Captain Kiley to have chairs made for the judges, high-backed, thronelike seats for the four principals, and modest armchairs for the alternates. Judge Parker, the American alternate, had been outraged. The ordinarily placid North Carolinian complained that the "little seat" was an insult. Furthermore, the distinction in chairs pointed up the ambiguous state of the alternates. Just why were they in Nuremberg? What were they supposed to do beyond waiting for someone to take sick or die? Not only did Parker expect an equivalent chair, he wanted an equivalent vote. Otherwise, he was going home.

That afternoon, Jackson was summoned to a meeting in the Judges' Room at which he tried to explain that the London Charter gave the alternates no vote. They became active only when their principal was absent. To Jackson's annoyance, Francis Biddle sprang to Parker's defense. Biddle insinuated that General Gill's chair policy had been deliberately designed to sow dissension among the judges. At that, Jackson stormed out. The court could do whatever it pleased about chairs and votes. He was particularly upset by Biddle's lack of support and wondered what it boded for a more serious test coming up in a few days.

One of the defendants was not on cellblock C. Though indicted, he was still living at home, an old man suffering from hardening of the arteries, incipient senility, partial paralysis, incontinence, and impaired speech. His name was Gustav Krupp, of the arms dynasty. German industrialists, Robert Jackson knew, had connived in bringing Hitler to power because they knew he would break the Communists. Without the businessmen's complicity, there could have been no Third Reich. When the war came, they willingly powered the German war machine. The very name Krupp summoned visions of huge guns rolling off assembly lines. Gustav Krupp was on the list of major war criminals because Jackson wanted the German industrialist class represented in the dock.

The problem with having Krupp personify the guilt of his class was his incapacity, already verified by a team of doctors. Jackson was undaunted. Gustav Krupp had a son, Alfried, who throughout the war had served as president of the Krupp works. Jackson had petitioned the court to indict Alfried if it could not try his father. On November 14, the issue brought the court into its first formal sitting in Nuremberg. The Krupp family lawyer argued the injustice of indicting a man because his father could not stand trial, while Jackson argued that the German industrial class bore criminal guilt for the war and must be tried.

After the hearing, the members retired to the Judges' Room to debate their decision. Sir Norman Birkett shuddered in disbelief. Jackson's argument, he said, was abhorrent. "This is not a football match. You don't simply field a reserve because one of the other players is sick." Jackson's petition was denied.

After the session, Judge Biddle asked Herb Wechsler to join him in his chamber. He had not enjoyed opposing Bob in front of the others, he said. But Jackson had behaved outrageously, Biddle believed, even foolishly. He was starting to detect, he said, a self-righteousness in the man, a fanaticism. Had Wechsler noticed this behavior? Biddle asked. "I thought," Wechsler answered, "that when the judges rejected Jackson's motion, he was going to have a nervous breakdown."

Francis Biddle himself was enjoying Nuremberg. No, he was not the de jure president of the court. That amiable plodder, Sir Geoffrey Lawrence, held that honor. Still, it was almost embarrassing, Biddle believed, the way the other judges went along with virtually everything he wanted, on the Krupp case, on the issue of the chairs, even on what they should wear in court. On the latter point, Biddle had suggested they wear whatever they pleased, within the bounds of propriety. That idea too had been accepted. It was late in the day.

Jackson was putting in a crushing day. His young assistant prosecutors, researchers, document specialists, and translators were also working sixty and seventy hours a week, preparing for the trial now only days off. What enraged Jackson about the petty power struggles, the housekeeping crises, the squabbling with Biddle, was that it detracted from the matter uppermost in his mind. It was his responsibility to deliver the prosecution's opening speech. This lover of words, this gifted phrasemaker, wanted all the time available to polish his address to an incandescent glow. Yet they were grinding him down with inconsequentials, deciding who would bunk in what house, and in what type of seat a North Carolina judge would plant his derrière.

44

"Plus vite! Plus vite!" Colonel Dostert shouted. The colonel, former interpreter for General Eisenhower, champion of the still unproven IBM simultaneous-translation system, had set up a mock courtroom in the attic of the Palace of Justice. One person was playing the prosecutor, another the defendant, another a judge. Dostert was testing a job applicant to see if she could keep up with the "witness." Speed

was the acid test. An interpreter could not delay more than eight seconds before starting to translate. Otherwise, too many words backed up. Academics might be able to interpret written passages of Nietzsche or Schopenhauer, but often fell apart when the subject was toilet arrangements in a concentration camp. One of Dostert's assistants, Lieutenant Peter Uiberall, a Viennese-born American, had developed a practical test. Uiberall would ask candidates to reel off in two languages the names of ten trees, ten birds, ten medical terms, ten automobile parts. They were looking for breadth of experience, people with curious minds as much as language mastery. Uiberall was always surprised by the number of city people who could not name ten farm implements in any language.

Dostert had made one basic decision. The best work was done when the interpreter listened in his native tongue and translated into the second language. They found that the interpreter first had to understand perfectly what was being said and then could usually find suitable words in the second language to express the thought.

Their greatest headache was German. Because the verb usually appeared at the end of the sentence, the interpreters never knew which way a thought was headed. Yet they dared not wait too long to start interpreting. The sentence in English might be, "I deny all knowledge of the existence of the death camps." But what the interpreter heard in German was "Of the existence of the death camps all knowledge I deny."

Dostert had dispatched his deputy, Alfred Steer, a navy lieutenant commander and a gifted linguist himself, to scour Europe for the talent they needed. Steer raided the League of Nations in Geneva. But he found that many interpreters there were older, accustomed to translating from written documents, and unable to adapt readily to the pressure of interpreting on the spot. Steer had better luck at the Paris international telephone exchange. The operators were used to everyday foreign conversation under time pressure. In the end, whatever the candidate's background, Steer found that only one prospect in twenty had the mental agility to listen and talk at the same time.

With the latest candidate dismissed, Dostert went searching for Captain Dan Kiley, restorer of the Palace of Justice. Robert Jackson was hounding him. Everything depended on having the interpreting system in place on opening day. Dostert found Kiley downstairs in the courtroom supervising the installation of the witness box. Had the IBM equipment arrived yet? he asked frantically. Kiley answered with an unflustered no.

45

ON A MORNING in November, the call had gone to the documents researchers from Robert Jackson's office. The chief prosecutor wanted the most compelling items for his opening speech. Jackson's request came on top of demands from other prosecutors, as well as defense counsels, all of which had turned Lieutenant Roger Barrett's documents room in recent days into organized bedlam. Steel shelves rose dizzily from floor to ceiling to house the ceaseless delivery of paper. Document clerks clambered up and down rolling ladders in quest of the one key statement a prosecutor wanted that could doom a defendant. Recently, Admiral Dönitz's staff had relinquished an additional sixty thousand German navy documents which would have to be processed and added to the already bulging inventory. Barrett had put through a call to his superior, Colonel Storey, for more space and more help. He had scant faith in the colonel's executive follow-through. He regarded Storey as pleasant enough, but in over his head. The staff liked to mimic Storey's folksy manner and colloquial locutions, particularly his referring to the papers they worked with as "dockaments."

Barbara Pinion showed up, an attractive, brisk British war widow, just back from a documents run to Berlin. These Germans were unbelievable, she told Barrett. One report she had brought back described how an enterprising SS team had filled a van with inmates of an asylum, had run the exhaust pipe into the back of the van, and then had driven to a graveyard. By the time the vehicle reached its destination, the passengers were asphyxiated and ready for burial. That had not shocked Pinion so much. By now she had read of virtually every combination and permutation of barbarism. What astonished her most were the postscripts to these reports: "Give my best to Frau Himmler and all the little Himmlers." How could they have kept this stuff? she wondered. They must never have considered the possibility of losing the war.

They faced an occupational hazard, Barrett knew. As chief of the documents room, he felt particularly susceptible to it. A report substantiating the shooting of thirty innocent hostages was not even worth translating, so much worse was available. It had taken the recent delivery of the *Todesbücher*, the "death books" retrieved from the Mauthausen extermination camp, to jolt Barrett anew. The Teutonic passion for recordkeeping required that every life dispatched there be recorded. Obviously, the truth would not do. And so SS clerks painstakingly entered into the books each victim's name and the time and cause of death; according to this record, people, during a given hour, died in alphabetical order, one minute apart, all from heart attacks, the next hour all from strokes, the next hour from another imaginary cause.

But most of the time repeated exposure to horror developed a callus on the conscience, Barrett found. The first time you read of the murder of children it was with disbelief, the tenth time with sadness, the fiftieth time with one part of the brain wondering what would be on the menu that night at the Grand Hotel. That, Barrett believed, was the worst part of the job.

46

NOVEMBER 15, five days before the trial was to begin, a team of IBM engineers landed at Y28 in a C-47 with a cargo of six crates. The simultaneous-interpreting equipment, including 550 headsets for court officials and visitors, had gone wildly astray, some of it to Peru. With the gear finally arrived, Colonel Dostert badgered Dan Kiley to get it installed. Kiley was already juggling a dozen crises. Most recently, a section of the courtroom floor had fallen through to the basement. The architect was getting by on four hours' sleep a night, usually on his office couch. He assured Dostert that his interpreting system would be in place on opening day.

47

Couldn't that woman leave anything alone! Robert Jackson bellowed. He was in the glass-enclosed conservatory upstairs at the house on Lindenstrasse. Elsie Douglas came running in and gasped when she saw the mess. Jackson had organized the documents he was drawing from for his opening speech in piles. Their busybody housekeeper, Frau Hassel, Jackson said, had insisted on opening the windows to air out the room. A storm had come up and now all his carefully ordered papers were in disarray. Mrs. Douglas was already on her hands and knees reassembling the scattered sheets. Jackson slumped into a chair and watched her deftly retrieve order from chaos. It was Sunday night, and evenings were virtually the only time he could piece together a few uninterrupted hours to work on the speech.

"Melancholy grandeur," Jackson said. That was the tone he wanted in the opener. That was the mood he envisioned for the trial. He considered this speech, he said, the most important act of his life. He wanted it to proclaim to the world "the why of Nuremberg." They retreated to his study. He took an armchair while Elsie sat at a desk. Their work patterns were so synchronized that few words were needed. Jackson drew a yellow legal pad from his briefcase and she went for her steno pad. "Germany became one vast torture chamber," he began. "The cries of its victims were heard round the world and brought shudders to civilized people." She was always surprised at how his words, inspired by a few scribbled notes, took on a finished quality as soon as he started to dictate.

He shifted from the resonant tone. He had a problem, he said. The London Charter provided for the death penalty. And when a crime was heinous enough, it was customary for a prosecutor to ask for the ultimate penalty. Yet, all his life he had opposed capital punishment. "A completely civilized society," he noted, "would never impose the death sentence." All that capital punishment did was to sanction violence. Yet, he could understand how Nazi butchery had ignited a cry for blood retribution. Did he have the right to reject the sternest and largely justified punishment that the charter allowed, because of his personal morality? What penalty did he intend to ask for?

Elsie queried. He would simply say nothing on that point, he concluded. Punishment was for the judges to decide. His role was to convict.

48

"CHAPLAIN," Colonel Andrus said, eyeing his latest staff arrival, "just remember, you are here to fulfill the requirements of the Geneva Convention. You are to provide spiritual counseling. You are not here to convert anybody." The man standing before Andrus, Major Henry F. Gerecke, was a portly fifty-four-year-old Lutheran army chaplain from St. Louis just assigned to the ISD. Raised on a farm in a German-speaking family in Missouri, Gerecke spoke an unsophisticated version of the language. He had joined the army at an age when most men would have been content to stay home and hear about the war on the radio. Two of his sons had been badly wounded fighting against the men Colonel Andrus was about to take him to meet in the cellblock.

The Protestant prisoners found the new chaplain, with his modest demeanor and everyman looks, the kind of simple clergyman that the Nazi regime would have crushed. Field Marshal Keitel, however, immediately took to Chaplain Gerecke. Keitel had a sense that Gerecke, unlike his captors and his fellow prisoners, did not despise him.

After the cell visits, Andrus asked Gerecke what he thought of the prisoners. Gerecke answered that the question of their earthly guilt was not his concern. His duty was only to look after their souls. They passed by the cell used as the prison office. Andrus stopped to introduce Gerecke to his Catholic counterpart, Father Sixtus O'Connor. O'Connor took Gerecke's hand. "At least we Catholics are only responsible for six of these sinners," he said with a grin. "Your side has fifteen chalked up against you." Gerecke laughed. He suspected that he and the priest were going to get along.

Gustav Gilbert was recording the answers of the defendants to an IQ test he and Kelley had scheduled. With the trial only days off, the two Americans realized that any distraction would help reduce the prisoners' anxiety. The test results would also make a fascinating contribution to their book.

The men were given a German version of the Wechsler-Bellevue Adult Intelligence Test, designed to measure memory, ability to think in words and figures, problem-solving, speed of mind, and power of observation. Hermann Göring attacked the test like a brash, bright schoolboy. On the memory portion, repeating increasing strings of numbers, Göring could remember up to eight numbers forward and six backward. "Oh come on, doctor," he begged, "give me one more chance." He had already done the best of all, Gilbert told him. Sixty-nine-year-old Hjalmar Schacht was worried that his years might hurt his score. Gilbert assured them that the results were adjusted for age. Schacht, ordinarily so arrogant, confessed to Gilbert that he was weak on simple arithmetic. The genius who financed the remilitarization of Germany? Gilbert asked. Schacht answered, "Any financial wizard who is good at arithmetic is most likely a swindler."

Julius Streicher confirmed Gilbert's suspicions of his intelligence. It took the old rabble-rouser a minute to figure out how much change he would get from fifty pfennigs if he bought seven two-pfennig stamps. "Don't bother me with these childish sums," Streicher said. "Try me on calculus."

On a scale in which 100 indicated average intelligence and 120 to 140 was to be expected of university graduates, Streicher scored lowest, 106. The highest raw score, 141, was achieved by quiet, scholarly Arthur Seyss-Inquart, the Reich commissioner of the Netherlands. But with the age premium, Schacht came out on top with 143. Precisely, Schacht said, what he had expected. Gilbert was surprised that the extraordinarily able Albert Speer scored only a modest 128. The test, Gilbert knew, was a limited tool, unable to plumb the myriad factors that made up ability. Hans Frank, at 130, scored considerably lower than the third-ranking Göring at 138. Still, Gilbert had dealt with both men, and Frank was clearly Göring's superior in his grasp of philosophical abstractions, social issues, and aesthetic nuance.

49

A SURPRISED ELSIE DOUGLAS poked her head into Robert Jackson's office and announced that General Rudenko was demanding to see him at once. Of course, Jackson said, he should come right over. Roman A. Rudenko, of the Soviet Judicial Service, was Jackson's counterpart, the chief Russian prosecutor, a thirty-eight-year-old Ukrainian of peasant stock with a broad, handsome face. Jackson hoped that Rudenko's visit was in response to his repeated requests for more documents from the Russians. Too much of the evidence was being provided by the American side. Thus far, the Russians' idea of documentation was a confession wrung from some Nazi by a Soviet political commissar, which hardly met Jackson's standard of objective, self-incriminating evidence. Rudenko had assured Jackson a few days before that a truckload of files fitting Jackson's request was on the way from Leipzig in the Soviet Zone; it was supposed to arrive in Nuremberg this very day.

Rudenko took a seat and glared belligerently. The documents would not be coming, he said. American soldiers had broken into the truck and deliberately burned the Soviet files. Jackson tried to suppress his annoyance. The Russians, he knew, had suffered far more at the hands of the Nazis than any other people. Their military and civilian dead totaled over twenty million. He was sympathetic, but could not fathom their self-defeating contrariness. Was this another stall? Had American GIs really burned precious Soviet evidence? Of course, Jackson told Rudenko, he would track down what had happened to the Soviet documents. But in the meantime, he said, he looked forward to seeing the general at the banquet he was giving on Saturday, November 17, in honor of the visiting Soviet deputy foreign minister Andrei Vyshinsky. Jackson's cordiality seemed to mollify Rudenko.

Justice Jackson received a report from the army on the fate of the truckload of Soviet records. A group of GIs had indeed burned the files. They had been cold and the load of paper provided the nearest available fuel. Jackson hoped that the bash he was throwing for Vyshinsky would soothe relations with the Russians. He had directed Captain Vonetes to stint on nothing. In the meantime, he had to deliver the implausible explanation to Roman Rudenko.

50

NUREMBERG HAD BECOME an emotional life raft for General Donovan. True, Donovan had returned from his long stay in the Far East to find most positions of power at the trials already staked out. And after the uncomfortable dinner at Jackson's home, he was well aware that his honeymoon with the chief prosecutor was over. Still, he was grateful to have a place to land. Harry Truman viewed a postwar OSS as an incipient American Gestapo, and had virtually killed off the intelligence agency that was Donovan's reason for being. The general's restless energies now sought a new outlet at the Palace of Justice.

Donovan, nevertheless, had little to do and spent time roving the halls making small talk with secretaries. Then his break came—a letter from Hjalmar Schacht. The wily Schacht buttered up Donovan, calling him "an officer of high standing" and a "well-deserved international reputation." The old financier went on to ask if Donovan would be interested in looking at "a brief summary of the underlying reasons and conditions of the dreadful Nazi regime, as I experienced them." Donovan, a seasoned courtroom lawyer, could smell a defendant ready to turn state's evidence a mile off. If he could get Schacht on the stand testifying against the others, that would be a major breakthrough.

When Göring learned that Donovan appeared open to offers, he too seized the opportunity. He sent Donovan word that, for a price, he was willing to testify against Ribbentrop, Kaltenbrunner, Schacht, and Speer, all of whom had crossed him through the years, and against that swine Streicher, who had maligned his manhood. Göring's price was that he be given an honorable death before a firing squad instead of a shameful death at the end of a rope. Donovan could envision it all: Schacht testifying against Göring, Göring against Speer, Speer against Sauckel. What a spectacle: the Nazi leaders consuming each other before the world. Donovan began interrogating Schacht and Göring personally.

Justice Jackson first got wind of what was happening when John Harlan Amen came complaining about Donovan's horning in on his territory. Was he or was he not the head of the interrogations operation? Amen wanted to know. Why was Wild Bill unsurping his role? Jackson faced a painful dilemma. He knew all too well his debt to

Donovan. Yet he resented the general's interference and disapproved of the direction in which Donovan wanted to take the trial. Jackson sent Colonel Storey to find out from Donovan what role, precisely, he had in mind for himself. Donovan was insulted, especially since Jackson had used Storey, an OSS veteran, to run this errand. Men of their stature, Donovan believed, did not deal through intermediaries.

Jackson thereafter invited Donovan to his office. It was still "Bob" and "Bill," but the tension in the room was palpable. Jackson did not immediately raise the sharpest point of contention. He had a preliminary complaint, information that Donovan opposed indicting the High Command of the German armed forces as a criminal organization. Not entirely true, Donovan said. He favored prosecuting individuals in the military. And he certainly favored prosecuting organizations like the SS and the Gestapo. Membership alone should be sufficient to convict those people of war crimes. But to convict top-ranking generals and admirals simply because they were top-ranking? He had led troops in combat himself as commander of the famed Fighting Sixty-ninth regiment in the First World War. He knew that his "Micks," in the heat of battle, had shot surrendering Germans. If Germany had won that war, would that have made Bill Donovan a war criminal? Hang a general because he committed a crime, Donovan said, not because he was a general. Jackson replied that he was going ahead with the prosecution of the High Command anyway.

Jackson next raised the issue of Donovan's dealings with Schacht and Göring. "I don't want any deals," Jackson said. A prosecutor might plea-bargain and turn one accomplice against another to crack an ordinary criminal case. But such courtroom shenanigans had no place in an international tribunal involving profound moral issues. Whenever a defendant was convicted on the testimony of an accomplice turning state's evidence, the conviction had a bad odor, Jackson said.

Get up in that courtroom and tell the Germans that their leaders are guilty because we say so, and they won't believe it, Donovan countered. But put the most popular man in the Third Reich on the stand and get a public confession from him, and that will convince everybody. "Bill, you may be right," Jackson said. Time alone would tell. "But it so happens that I have the responsibility. And I'm going to try this case by indisputable documentary proof."

The next day Donovan received a note from Jackson saying that he saw no further use for him in any position of prominence in the trial, "because of our different viewpoints." Wild Bill had been fired. He did not go quietly. He called on Francis Biddle and told him that the trial would be flat as Kansas with all that paper evidence. Furthermore, he had discovered that Jackson was a poor manager and that the prosecution office was a shambles. He did not want to be part of this fiasco anyway. Nor was he talking behind Jackson's back, he made clear. He had said the same things in a letter to Jackson.

51

THE STRATEGY THAT Albert Speer had settled on was to take manly responsibility for his acts and express genuine contrition for Germany's aggressions and barbarous conduct of the war. But from what he had been able to gather about the conniving between Göring, Schacht, and the Americans, he concluded it might be time to play another card. Had he not given the U.S. Strategic Bombing Survey team invaluable information after his capture? Had he not persuaded other German scientists to cooperate with the Americans? He was sure this collaboration had proved useful in the defeat of Japan. While they were in no position to admit it openly, the Americans were clearly preparing for an inevitable confrontation with the Russians, and when it came, Speer's knowledge could be priceless. He had to act quickly. It was November 17; the trial would be under way in three days. Speer asked his cell guard for a pencil and paper and began writing in neat block letters, "I am in possession of certain information as to military and technical questions that should be made known to the right persons." He was the only one, he went on, who knew what mistakes had been made in the air war against Germany, mistakes the Americans would not want to repeat. He knew how any industry could be put out of action for good. In the event of a jail sentence, he wrote, "I should not fall into Russian hands. My knowledge should stay on this side of the fence." In the event of a death sentence, he pointed out, all that he knew would be lost. He folded the paper, and wrote on the outside, "For transmission to Justice Jackson."

Jackson, his son, Bill, and Elsie Douglas left the house on Lindenstrasse and entered the army Chevrolet staff car that had replaced the
grand Ribbentrop vehicle. Jackson had hoped to spend the drive in
polishing the latest draft of the opening speech. But Wild Bill Donovan's meddling had evidently spread the word through cellblock C
that deals could be cut with the prosecution. How else to explain the
letter he drew from his briefcase? Jackson finished reading Speer's
proposition much annoyed. Speer had ended it by advising that nothing he knew should be heard by "third parties," meaning the Russians.
The only way that the Russians could be cut out was if Speer never
had to go to court. Apparently, the defendants did not yet know of
the fall of Bill Donovan and his prosecutorial machinations. Albert
Speer was going to stand trial along with the lot of them.

52

THE MONTH BEFORE, the Russians had made a social splash with an
October Revolution party. The guests had been happily stunned to
discover bowls of caviar, rivers of vodka, and delicacies flown in from
the Caucasus. Andrei Vyshinsky, the Soviet deputy foreign minister,
had just arrived in town for the opening of the trial, and now it was
Jackson's turn to repay the Russians' hospitality at the Grand Hotel.
Vyshinsky had a fearsome reputation as the chief prosecutor in the
Soviet show trials of the thirties. He supposedly had engineered the
trial and execution of a comrade named Serebrevkov in order to get
the man's pretty little dacha outside Moscow. Here in Nuremberg,
Jackson found Vyshinsky a fascinating contradiction, one minute a
dogmatist denouncing the West with all the standard Communist clichés, and the next minute an exuberant, witty companion. Vyshinsky,
Jackson concluded, was as much actor as party stalwart. When Jackson
extended his invitation to the Russian, he thought it prudent to mention that the IMT judges would also be present, and that Vyshinsky
should say nothing bearing on the trial.

During the cocktail reception, tongues wagged over what looked
like a budding and likely perilous romance. Judge Parker's chief aide
was a handsome veteran of the Battle of the Bulge, Major Robert
Stewart. Bob Stewart, like his boss a Southerner, had served as Par-

ker's law clerk in civilian life and was performing the same function at Nuremberg. This night, Stewart seemed unable to tear himself from the most attractive woman in the room, General Nikitchenko's interpreter, Tania Giliarevskaya. The petite, blond, blue-eyed beauty had made her Nuremberg social debut at the October Revolution party. She had proved charming and vivacious, talking about *Gone with the Wind*, the writings of Mark Twain, and the latest Hit Parade songs, all in slangy American English. Stewart had become the first to breach an unspoken barrier between East and West. He had asked Tania Giliarevskaya to lunch at the Grand. There, they felt the hard-eyed stare of the Russian alternate judge, Lieutenant Colonel A. F. Volchkov, rumored to be the NKVD's man in Nuremberg, the Soviet secret police watchdog. The next day, Stewart had asked Judge Biddle's advice about the propriety of what he had done, to which Biddle replied, "*Toujours l'audace*"—"Be bold, always." Now, at the banquet for Vyshinsky, Stewart was monopolizing the young woman's attention, and she seemed a willing accomplice.

Lights were dimmed, signaling that the dinner was about to begin. Between dessert and coffee, Jackson rose and made a gracious toast to the guest of honor. He closed by introducing "Mr. A. I. Vyshinsky of the Foreign Office, who I trust will say a few words." Vyshinsky rose, vodka glass in hand. Standing off to his right was a shy-looking young man who could have passed for an American college student. He was, in fact, a graduate of Dartmouth College named Oleg Troyanovsky, son of the first Soviet ambassador to the United States. Troyanovsky had been dispatched to Nuremberg as a translator for the bench.

Vyshinsky emptied his glass and said, "Vodka is the enemy of man, and therefore it must be consumed!" The guests cheered and followed his example. He then made a little speech about the brotherhood of the law and how lucky they all were to be in a profession where they could speak their minds, not like diplomats who had to behave "like a dog on a leash." More laughter followed. Vyshinsky raised a refilled glass and said, "I now propose a toast to the defendants." A stillness fell over the room. Vyshinsky went on. "Here's to the conviction of all the men who will go on trial next Tuesday." Oleg Troyanovsky looked uncomfortable, but rendered the words into English. Vyshinsky spoke again. "May their paths lead directly from the courthouse to the grave," Troyanovsky translated, and a few nervous titters were heard. Judge Parker whispered loudly to Colonel Storey, "I will not drink a toast to the conviction of any man, regardless of his guilt, before I hear the evidence."

Riding back to Lindenstrasse, Robert Jackson slumped in the backseat of his car, deep in thought. After the fiasco at the Grand, he was trying to fathom the behavior of Vyshinsky and Rudenko, indeed of most of the Soviets—by turns bombastic, self-conscious, boorish, charming, oversensitive, or thoughtless. The British and American staffs constantly joshed each other and traded good-natured barbs. The Russians could never be kidded. They immediately became defensive. All that boozing, the over twenty toasts that had been drunk this night, what was it about? Some Americans thought it was a trick to loosen their tongues for the benefit of Soviet intelligence. Jackson thought not. The Russians, with their revolution, had eradicated their aristocratic class. They had crushed the middle class and its values. What was left was a proletarian leadership. The heavy drinking was designed to lower the socializing to a level where they were comfortable, down to the trite masculine rite of seeing who could drink whom under the table. Their conduct led Jackson to one inescapable conclusion: The Russians suffered a national inferiority complex.

53

KALTENBRUNNER WAS COMPLAINING of terrible headaches, and Streicher had spat at a new prisoner in the exercise yard, Major Teich reported to Colonel Andrus on returning from a tour of the cellblock. Had a doctor been notified of Kaltenbrunner's condition? Andrus asked. Yes, Teich answered. Which prisoner had Streicher spat on? Andrus wanted to know. Hans Fritzsche, Teich said, just turned over by the Russians. Suspend Streicher's exercise privileges for a week, the colonel ordered.

Streicher had tried to cozy up to Fritzsche. After all, he said, they were fellow journalists. Streicher's *Der Stürmer*, Fritzsche replied, was a detestable rag that cheapened the Nazi movement. "Whenever I saw that muck quoted in the foreign press," Fritzsche told Streicher, "I winced." It was at that point that Streicher had spat in his face. Streicher's ensuing scuffle with the guards had distracted everyone from Kaltenbrunner's odd behavior. He had been moving about the yard unsteadily. Later, back in his cell, he collapsed. The doctors found that he had suffered a subarachnoid hemorrhage and sent him to the hospital. A blood vessel located in the membrane covering his brain had ruptured. The condition could be fatal.

Colonel Andrus was upset. Kaltenbrunner's sickness was not his fault. Still, he was going to fail to deliver another defendant to the dock on opening day. What happened? he asked Kelley and Gilbert. Fear and stress had probably raised the man's blood pressure to the bursting point, they explained. Andrus sighed. Fear and stress. These were the very conditions that a prison psychiatrist and psychologist were supposed to prevent.

54

THE DAY BEFORE the trial was to open, the Palace of Justice was a hive of crises. Dan Kiley was supervising the last-minute laying of the courtroom carpet, purchased on the Paris black market. He left the installation crew long enough to check on the press arrangements. He looked over the fluorescent lighting installed in place of the junked chandeliers. These lights would allow photographers to shoot without using distracting flashbulbs. He had built positions behind heavy, non-glare glass from which movie cameras could shoot soundlessly. He popped down to check out the pressroom he had installed on the floor below, large enough to accommodate over one hundred reporters at a time.

In the pressroom, William L. Shirer, who, with Howard K. Smith, was reporting for CBS, sat at a typewriter pounding out a story. Germany had been Shirer's beat throughout much of the rise of Nazism, and in returning for its burial he felt a satisfying symmetry. He was now reporting his impressions after touring the ruins of the city. "Nuremberg is gone," Shirer wrote, "a vast heap of rubble beyond description and beyond hope of rebuilding." He had tried to find his favorite beer garden, the Bratwurstglöcklein. It had vanished. He had hitched a ride out to Zeppelin Field and stood before the grandstand where he had heard Hitler speak in 1937. He remembered watching throngs of Germans shouting themselves hoarse as Hitler proclaimed, "The German form of life is definitely determined for the next thousand years."

Shirer was depressed by the way even the best Germans he met interpreted their present misfortune. He had asked an anti-Nazi engineer about the morality of Germany's military buildup during the thirties. If Göring had done a better job of building up the Luftwaffe, the engineer said, their cities would not now be in ruins. As Shirer wrapped up his story, he turned to a German journalist working next to him and asked how much interest his people had in the trial. "Oh, they think it's all propaganda," the German replied.

The defendants with nothing presentable to wear to court the next day were gathered in the cellblock corridor to be fitted with suits of an unappetizing blue-brown color. A conscripted German tailor measured Streicher's cuffs. Sauckel was trying on a pair of new shoes and Frank a white shirt. In the stiff, cheap, ill-cut outfits, they looked like a bunch of hicks on their first visit to the big city.

Colonel Y. V. Pokrovsky, General Rudenko's deputy, was calling Justice Jackson, insisting on seeing the prosecutor. Pokrovsky came into the office bearing the usual shield of belligerence carried by Soviet bearers of bad tidings. The trial would have to be postponed, Pokrovsky announced. Jackson eyed him in disbelief. Postponed? How long? Jackson asked. Indefinitely, the Russian answered. General Rudenko was in Berlin and ill. He had come down with malaria. Jackson experienced simultaneous incredulity and rage. This trial was not going to be derailed at the eleventh hour, he said. To start without the chief Soviet prosecutor, Pokrovsky warned, would be viewed by the Soviet Union as an affront. With that, he withdrew.

General Nikitchenko delivered a similar message to his fellow judges. Jackson got word to come to a meeting in the Judges' Room that afternoon to resolve the crisis. In the meantime, he instructed Elsie Douglas to call the army medical office and find out what the likelihood was of anyone coming down with malaria in Berlin.

Jackson's press relations man, Gordon Dean, soon learned of the latest Russian monkeywrench. He explained to Jackson that he was supposed to brief the press within minutes on trial arrangements. Should he cancel? he asked. Jackson told him that everything was to proceed as though the trial would start on time.

The crush of reporters stepped back to make way for Dean and Colonel Andrus. For most of the press it was a first look at the prison commandant, who, in appearance and bearing, seemed born to the role. What they did not know was how much Andrus hated dealing with them. Until this inescapable appearance, he had fobbed off most press contacts to his deputy, Major Teich.

Dean began describing the technical support available to the journalists. He gestured to a soldier who pressed a button. A buzzer sounded once. One buzz, Dean said, signaled something useful coming up in the courtroom. Two buzzes meant something important. Three buzzes meant something sensational. They would be able to hear the buzzer virtually anywhere in the building. Loudspeakers had also been positioned around the courthouse so that they could hear the proceedings even if they were not in the courtroom.

A cacophony of voices erupted as soon as Dean finished. Was it true, a reporter asked, that Ernst Kaltenbrunner had tried to commit suicide? Dean turned the floor over to Colonel Andrus, who explained that Kaltenbrunner had suffered a mild stroke, and that the doctors expected that the man should be able to stand trial. When could they interview the defendants? a reporter asked. No interviews would be permitted, Andrus answered. He was, however, arranging tours for small groups of the press corps to pass through the prison, where they could briefly observe the lions in their cages.

Jackson arrived at the Judges' Room, where he met Sir Hartley Shawcross, just arrived from England. Though Shawcross intended to allow Maxwell-Fyfe to conduct day-to-day prosecution business, he had, as England's chief prosecutor, decided to handle the opening. Also present was General Rudenko's deputy, Colonel Pokrovsky. Jackson informed the judges that he had it on good medical authority that contracting malaria in Berlin was near impossible, and that he wanted the trial to proceed. They need do nothing that involved the Russian prosecution, Jackson noted, until Rudenko arrived. In the meantime, could not Pokrovsky stand in for Rudenko?

Shawcross rose. Nothing in his perfectly groomed appearance or languid speech suggested his membership in Britain's Labour party. If a delay was what the Russians wanted, Sir Hartley observed, perhaps the court should grant it. Jackson looked dismayed. But, Shawcross added, Colonel Pokrovsky would have to convey to his government that the Russians must take full responsibility before the world for delaying the trial of Nazi war criminals.

Just before this meeting, Pokrovsky said, he had received good news. Because of recent medical advances, General Rudenko was making a remarkable recovery. He could be in Nuremberg in days. Pokrovsky sat down, wearing a sickly smile. In that case, Sir Geoffrey said, he was going to rule that the trial commence on schedule the following morning.

Jackson left, as baffled as ever by the Russians' behavior. Why had they tried to delay the trial? He did not understand this any more than he did their sudden decision to have Rudenko miraculously recover.

The first rays of daylight knifed between the heavy drapes of the courtroom windows. At six a.m., November 20, Dan Kiley collapsed into the chair behind his desk and began scribbling on a pad. He wanted to get it all down while it was still fresh in his mind. The restoration of the Palace of Justice was complete. It had involved an average 875 workers daily, 5,200 gallons of paint, 250,000 bricks, 100,000 board feet of lumber, a million feet of wire and cable. His pencil dropped as his head rested on his desk, and he dozed off.

CHAPTER II

THE
PROSECUTION
CASE

1

THE DEFENDANTS WERE AWAKENED, as on every other day, not by any call of reveille, but by the crashing of washbasins and raucous GI repartee during the changing of the guard. By nine a.m., they were milling about the corridor between the cells, some in their prison-made suits, the military men in uniforms with discolored patches where their insignia had been stripped away. For the first time in their captivity they were allowed belts, ties, and shoelaces. Göring wore one of three dove-gray Luftwaffe uniforms he had brought to Nuremberg. The tunic, tailored for a much heavier man, sagged at the neck.

As Colonel Andrus arrived, the duty officer assembled the prisoners and brought them to attention. "Hitch 'em up," the colonel ordered. Eventually, they might be allowed to go to the courthouse without handcuffs, but on the first day, he was taking no chances. The escorts handcuffed the prisoners, guard's left wrist to defendant's right wrist. The party marched out of the cellblock and entered a covered wooden walkway connecting to the courthouse. As the last man filed out, Andrus shouted to the remaining guards, "Search the cells."

The defendants waited by an elevator in the courthouse basement. The guards were to take off the cuffs, Andrus ordered, and bring the prisoners up three at a time.

Buses, jeeps, and command cars jammed the courthouse yard. The honor guards of four nations stood at attention as Sir Geoffrey Lawrence's black limousine arrived, glistening in the sunlight. The chief judge of the Nuremberg trials stepped out wearing a long blue broadcloth coat, a bowler, and a prim smile for the photographers. He passed by sentries checking passes and rifling through the handbags of women visitors. His short, rotund figure disappeared into the throng.

POWs were still sweeping up shavings and sawdust and the hallways gave off a bracing smell of fresh paint as the correspondents filed into the press gallery. They had a choice position, just behind the prosecutors' tables, with the dock to their left and the judges to their right. Among them were Janet Flanner and Rebecca West, covering for *The New Yorker*, the novelist John Dos Passos for *Life* magazine, Marguerite Higgins for the New York *Herald Tribune*, and Smith and Shirer for CBS. Correspondents from twenty-three nations crowded into 250 plush maroon tip-up seats that Dan Kiley had confiscated from a German theater. In a balcony above them, visitors filed into 150 similar seats.

The courtroom had achieved the "melancholy grandeur" that Justice Jackson sought. Heavy sage-green drapes, dark paneling, and thick carpeting that silenced footsteps contributed to the solemn aura. The muted effect was broken only by the harsh fluorescent lighting and a few bright touches of color provided by the flags of four nations, which a GI was smoothing out behind the bench.

A small sliding door opened in the rear of the dock and the rumble of conversation halted. Out stepped Göring, Ribbentrop, and Hess. They blinked under the bright lights and made their way uncertainly toward the dock. Behind them, against the wall, stood six American sentries, arms folded behind their backs like a basketball team being photographed for the yearbook.

Howard Smith found his attention riveted on Ribbentrop. He remembered his telephone ringing in Berlin in the middle of a July night in 1941 and a voice ordering him to come at once to the Foreign Office. After the foreign press had been left cooling its heels for an hour, Ribbentrop appeared, deeply tanned from a sun lamp, announcing imperiously, "Gentlemen, we have just invaded Bolshevik Russia." Could this dishrag in the dock be the same man? Smith wondered.

Janet Flanner started taking notes: "You look at Nuremberg, and you are looking at the result of the war. You look at the twenty men in the dock, and you are seeing the cause. . . ." She was interrupted by a voice out of the Old Bailey, that of the marshal, Colonel Charles W. Mayes, shouting, "Atten-shun! All rise. The tribunal will now enter!" The British and American judges, wearing black robes, came through a small door. The two French judges, Henri Donnedieu de Vabres and Robert Falco, wore robes adorned with white bibs, ruffles at the wrist, and a touch of ermine, as if they had stepped from a Daumier sketch. Nikitchenko and his alternate, Volchkov, were resplendent in chocolate uniforms with green trim and gold shoulderboards.

At ten a.m. sharp, Sir Geoffrey rapped his gavel, a handsome piece of oak that Francis Biddle had brought, thinking he would preside over the court. Biddle had generously given the gavel to Lawrence. "This trial, which is now to begin," Sir Geoffrey began in a precise, metallic voice, "is unique in the annals of jurisprudence." The first order of business, he announced, would be the reading of the indictment.

The voices of the prosecutors, with each nation taking turns reciting the catalogue of Nazi duplicity and barbarism, occupied the entire morning. A young French lawyer, just months out of a concentration camp, began his turn tremulously: "Out of a convoy of 230 French women deported from Compiègne to Auschwitz in January 1943, 180 were worked to death within four months," he recited. "Over 780 French priests were executed at Mauthausen. . . ." Keitel bowed his head. Ribbentrop dabbed at a sweating brow. Funk sobbed softly. Göring sat with a bored expression, occasionally writing on a piece of paper. He was keeping track of the number of times his name was mentioned in the indictment. So far, he was the clear leader, with forty-two citations.

After two and a half hours, Sir Geoffrey temporarily adjourned the court. Colonel Andrus realized that he had made no plans for the defendants' lunch. He hastily summoned his aides and ordered that the prisoners be fed in the courtroom. For the next hour, they enjoyed a treasured taste of freedom, chatting freely among themselves for the first time since their captivity. Some of them had never met before. Göring discovered a small gate in the front of the dock and soon the defendants were spilling down into the lawyers' area, luxuriating in their attorneys' comfortable seats.

What was all this fuss about breaking treaties? Ribbentrop asked Captain Gilbert. Was that not how the British had built their empire, through broken treaties, aggressive warfare, and the mass murder of subjugated peoples? Did they notice that the food was better today? Hans Fritzsche remarked. "Yes," Schirach, the Hitler Youth leader, commented, "I suppose we'll get steak the day before they hang us."

The afternoon session continued with the reading of the indictment. The room became hot and airless. Robert Jackson itched to get back to editing his address, which he would deliver the next day. As a young Russian prosecutor droned on, Jackson threaded his way through the press gallery and headed for the exit. He smiled at the sentry at the door and started to walk out. The sentry blocked his way. Did the soldier know who he was? Jackson asked. Yes, the sentry answered, but he had his orders. No one was to be allowed out until the court adjourned. By whose orders? Jackson asked. General Mitchell's, the guard replied. Jackson reddened. Were Biddle and his coterie to hound him everywhere? He heard a firm, quiet voice over his shoulder. "I outrank General Mitchell and I say open that door." Jackson turned to see Wild Bill Donovan. The guard quickly complied, and the two men stepped out. They greeted each other awkwardly. After this purely ceremonial appearance, Donovan would be flying home. Jackson wished that it had all worked out better between them.

After the court adjourned, Ray D'Addario, an army pictorial service photographer, brought his four-by-five-inch Speed Graphic down to the courtroom floor to take shots of the now-empty chamber. As he focused on the bench, another army photographer appeared in his viewfinder. The GI was stealing Sir Geoffrey's oak gavel. "Are you crazy?" D'Addario shouted. "Put that thing back. You'll get us all court-martialed." "Like hell," the man responded, shoving the gavel into his pocket. "This is history!"

2

ELSIE DOUGLAS TUCKED a snowy handkerchief into Robert Jackson's breast pocket and stepped back to examine her handiwork. Bob certainly looked splendid.

In front of the house, the touring car waited, waxed to a fine sheen and brought out for the occasion. Moritz Fuchs, the bodyguard, opened the back door for Jackson, Mrs. Douglas, and young Bill. As the car began rolling down Lindenstrasse, Jackson turned to his son with a wry smile. "This is the first case I've ever tried," he said, "where I had to persuade others that a court should be established, then help establish it, then find myself a courthouse to try the case in." Mrs. Douglas handed him a freshly typed copy of his speech with the latest corrections. She had clipped a slip of paper to the first page on which she had written in red ink, "Slowly!"

The reading of the indictment ended by midmorning. Sir Geoffrey announced that the defendants were now to enter their pleas, and called first upon Hermann Göring. Göring made his way to the center of the dock. He held a typed statement, which he began to read. He was cut off by a sharp rapping. In the absence of a gavel, Sir Geoffrey was tapping a pencil on the bench, the sound resonating through a microphone. "I have already explained," Lawrence remarked tartly, "the defendants are not to make a speech." Göring angrily snapped, "I declare myself, in the sense of the indictment, not guilty." He returned to his seat. Hess was called on next. He moved like a tin man to the microphone and uttered a single word: "*Nein.*" "That will be entered as a plea of not guilty," Sir Geoffrey said as quiet laughter rippled through the courtroom. Hans Frank, his eyes bothered the day before by the lighting, stepped forward wearing sunglasses. The unfortunate effect was to increase the resemblance of this jowly, full-lipped man to a gangster. Frank pleaded not guilty. The other defendants, in various forms, made the same plea, "*Nicht schuldig.*"

Fritzsche, the last defendant, had finished his plea, when, unbidden, Göring again headed for the microphone. Again, Lawrence cut him off. "You are not allowed to address the tribunal except through your counsel, at the present time," he said with icy courtesy. The staff, which had previously judged Sir Geoffrey as a pleasant cipher, began seeing a different man.

All eyes turned to a distinguished figure in a morning coat and striped trousers making his way to the prosecutor's stand. Robert Jackson gazed around the room with imperturbable calm. He squared the pages of his text and set them on the lectern. "May it please your honors, the privilege of opening the first trial in history for crimes against the peace of the world imposes a grave responsibility," he began. "The wrongs which we seek to condemn and punish have been so calculated, so malignant, and so devastating that civilization cannot tolerate their being ignored because it cannot survive their being repeated. That four great nations, flushed with victory and stung with injury, stay the hand of vengeance and voluntarily submit their captive enemies to the judgment of the law is one of the most significant tributes that power has ever paid to reason." Jackson's style was by turns Elizabethan, Spenserian, and Gladstonian—the oratory of a passing age, soon destined to disappear.

He wanted the legitimacy of the court recognized. "The world-wide scope of the trial has left few neutrals," he said. "Either the victors must judge the vanquished, or we must leave the defeated to judge themselves. After the first world war, we saw the futility of the latter course." He signaled the prosecution's strategy. "We will not ask you to convict these men on the testimony of their foes," he said. "There is no count in the indictment that cannot be proved by books and records." The accused, he noted with a brief smile, "shared the Teutonic passion for thoroughness in putting things on paper." He rejected criticisms that it had taken too long to launch the IMT. Courts in America dealing with comparatively limited events, he noted, seldom began a trial in less than a year. "Yet, less than eight months ago, the courtroom in which we sit was an enemy fortress in the hands of SS troops."

After he had spoken for two hours, Sir Geoffrey declared a recess for lunch.

Colonel Andrus was not about to repeat the lunchtime mistake of the day before, when the defendants had run all over the courtroom. He had arranged a dining room for them in the attic of the courthouse. Göring dominated the room, rather like a coach bucking up a losing team at halftime. He told fat little Walther Funk not to worry about any crimes the prosecution might charge him with in the financial area. He, Hermann Göring, as head of the Four Year Plan, would assume all responsibility. Funk's baggy eyes brimmed with gratitude. The defendants bolted their lunch and crowded the attic windows. They had seen virtually nothing but prison walls for too long. Today, they could look beyond the shambles of Nuremberg and see the Peg-nitz River leave the city behind and wind through forests and fields toward the mountains. Their eyes drank in the view.

Elsie Douglas had set two large chairs together to form an impromptu couch for Bob in his office. His eyes were closed and she hoped he was asleep. She waited until the last minute to shake him. As they headed back toward the courtroom, she warned him that the interpreters' red and yellow warning lights had flashed often during the morning. He was still speaking too fast when he became carried away, she warned.

Jackson took a document from Elsie Douglas's outstretched hand. He wanted to read the court, he said, a few excerpts from the diary of the defendant Hans Frank. "The Jews must be eliminated. Whenever we catch one, it is his end." Jackson turned a page and the rustle could be heard in the silent room as he continued to read, "Of course I cannot eliminate all the Jews in one year's time . . ." Frank's head lowered as his words from Wawel Castle echoed in the mouth of an American prosecutor.

Mrs. Douglas next handed Jackson a large leather-bound book. He was quoting from the report of the German general Jürgen Stroop entitled "The Destruction of the Warsaw Ghetto," Jackson explained. He read of German troops turning flamethrowers on apartment buildings, and of Jews jumping to their deaths from smoking upper stories or gunned down as they poured from doorways. The yellow light on the prosecutor's stand flashed, signaling Jackson to slow down. He paused. "You will say I have robbed you of your sleep," he went on, "but these are things which have turned the stomach of the world." The defendants, all but Hess, listened in rapt attention, eyes open wide.

Jackson turned to the bench. "And let me make clear that while the law is first applied against German aggressors, the law includes, and if it is to serve a useful purpose, it must condemn, aggression by any other nation, including those which sit here now in judgment." Jackson picked up his text and returned to his seat.

The defendants filed out of the dock and into the elevator. The force of Jackson's words was not wholly responsible for their subdued state. Frank's lawyer, Alfred Seidl, had just passed a note to his client, which Frank shared with the others. A week before, an American military court had hanged five German civilians for murdering the crewmen of a downed B-17. Just four days before, a British court had sentenced

eleven concentration camp officials to death, including the commandant of Bergen-Belsen. If minor Nazis fared thus, what must be their
own fate?

3

JACKSON WAS MOBBED. Howard Smith told him that, while he had
covered Germany for years, he had never understood until now what
had been the fate of his disappearing Jewish friends. Shirer said Jackson's words had sent shivers down his spine. Possibly the most erudite
man on Jackson's staff, Colonel Telford Taylor, concluded that Jackson's opener marked the pinnacle of legal writing thus far in the century and was not to be easily surpassed. The next day, the word from
Charlie Horsky, Jackson's man in Washington, was music to the prosecutor's ear. The speech had made the front page of *The New York
Times* and *The Washington Post*—in long stories that quoted generously
from Jackson's text.

Shortly afterward, Sir Hartley Shawcross, Great Britain's chief
prosecutor, delivered an opening address that nearly equaled Jackson's
in eloquence. Shawcross, handsome as a matinee idol, read from the
Hermann Graebe report on the fate of the Jews of Dubno. "The
people put down their clothes in fixed places, sorted according to
shoes, outer clothing, and underwear . . . they stood around in family
groups, kissed each other and said farewells . . . they went down into
the pit, lined themselves up against the previous victims and were
shot . . ." As Shawcross spoke, Fritzsche buried his face in his hands.
Göring yanked off his earphones. "I looked at the man who did the
shooting," Shawcross went on reading; "he was an SS man, who sat
with his feet dangling into the pit. He had a tommy gun on his knees
and was smoking a cigarette."

Later, Shawcross confronted the ex post facto argument. "I suppose the first person ever charged with murder," he observed, "might
well have said, 'See here, you can't do that. Murder hasn't been made
a crime yet.'"

General Rudenko arrived in time to deliver the opening argument
for the Soviet Union. The Russians had counted the pages in Jackson's
speech, and made Rudenko's speech one page longer. The moment

Rudenko took the stand, Göring and Hess tore off their earphones, as if members of one gang had suddenly found a member of a rival gang daring to accuse them.

4

ROSE KORB, Colonel Andrus's new secretary, loved her job. Just turned twenty-three, out of Hammond, Indiana, Korb suddenly had a ringside seat at history. She found Andrus, by turns, stern or fatherly, but thoughtful on the whole, and she liked him. One exception had been the time that Captain Gilbert left the office and the colonel made an anti-Semitic remark. It always hurt more, this young Jewish woman thought, when nice people did those things.

Another advantage of her job was that Rose got to meet the new men assigned to the ISD first and could report on them to her roommates in the apartment building known as "Girls' Town." She particularly liked the second lieutenant who had joined the ISD two months before, Jack G. Wheelis; he was strapping and ruggedly handsome. Wheelis had told Rose at the time, with a drawl and a grin, to call him Tex.

Colonel Andrus had plans for Wheelis. The colonel was having a deuce of a time with personnel. In his judgment, the security mission required superior people; yet the army kept sending him green second-raters. And the minute his experienced personnel reached the requisite discharge points, they went home. This brawny Texan had a commanding presence and certainly looked like a leader. Andrus was going to appoint him assistant operations officer.

On the way back from Chaplain Gerecke's Protestant service, Göring saw Father Sixtus O'Connor. What was this baseball that the priest was always talking about? he wanted to know. Was there money in it? Branch Rickey, general manager of the Dodgers, earned ninety thousand dollars a year, nearly a million reichsmarks, Father Sixtus informed him. Göring clapped the priest on the back and said, "You see, Father, you and I went into the wrong business!"

Göring was fast becoming the guards' favorite. He would ask them where they came from and whether their rations were adequate, as though he could do something about it. Privately, the young Americans' lack of decorum disgusted him, as when they addressed him bluntly as "Göring." Still, it served his purposes to win them over. This day, November 27, Göring was expecting to meet his lawyer, Dr. Otto Stahmer, in preparation for the next session of the court. The prosecution was expected to deal with Germany's annexation of Austria, in which Göring had figured prominently. He had barely returned to his cell from the chapel when one of the guards shouted, "Bring Fatso to the visitors' room."

The room was split down the middle by a mesh screen with chairs along each side. Sliding plastic slots allowed defendants and lawyers to pass documents back and forth through the screen, after a guard examined them. Tex Wheelis was on duty this morning in the room, and Göring went after him like a politician after a voter. So the lieutenant was from Texas? Good hunting there, he had heard. Did the lieutenant like to hunt? It was the *Reichsmarschall*'s passion. In fact, he had been Germany's chief gamekeeper. There was wonderful shooting around his estate at Carinhall. Too bad he could not show the lieutenant around it.

Wheelis asked Göring how the trial was going. He had the best seat in the house, Göring explained cheerily. Right in the corner of the dock. Göring looked around at the audience of guards and asked, Did they know the difference between a German and an Englishman? A German has a soft heart but a hard hand, Göring said. And an Englishman has a soft hand but a hard heart. The Americans laughed, especially Tex Wheelis, who directed the guard to remove the *Reichsmarschall*'s handcuffs.

The lawyer, Stahmer, arrived, a large man in his seventies whose appearance suggested an aging, belligerent stag. He let the guard frisk him and check his briefcase, then took his place opposite Hermann Göring. Göring told Stahmer in German that he believed Wheelis was a friend.

5

A WEARY HOWARD SMITH came out of the Stein castle into the chilly night and stumbled aboard the army bus for the trip to the Palace of

Justice. Smith felt grimy. Only on weekends could he get into the bathroom long enough to shave, and a five-day stubble spiked his chin. One week had passed since the trial opened, and he intended in tonight's broadcast to deliver a state-of-the-court report. He was having trouble, however, staying awake. Bill Shirer was down with the flu, and Smith was covering the trial alone for CBS, writing stories and broadcasting a half dozen times a day.

He fell asleep on the bus, and the driver had to wake him up as they pulled into the gate of the courthouse. Smith made his way to the third floor and the ladder leading to the attic broadcast booths. Facing a microphone that carried his voice through a chain of land lines and shortwave feeds into American living rooms, he began. Three trials were under way in Nuremberg, he said. The first was the American trial, its purpose to warn aggressors and to give the world a body of law for trying future war criminals. Second was the Europeans' trial, particularly the Russians and the French, "an enterprise of passion, a tribunal of vengeance." Finally, there was the defendants' Nuremberg, marked by the Nazis' growing awareness that the trial was fair and that "it may still be possible to squeeze out of this pinch with a prison term instead of death, maybe even with a shred of dignity." Two stars thus far had emerged at Nuremberg, Smith noted. The surprise winner was the IMT's president, Sir Geoffrey Lawrence, the sort of man who let people underrate him, and then capitalized on their mistake. The other was Hermann Göring, who was becoming something of a bellwether. Every time the prosecution sought to score a point, all eyes turned to Göring to measure the reaction of that mobile, expressive face. By the time Smith finished his broadcast and made his way back to the castle, it was nearly 1:30 a.m. He would be back at the courthouse by seven in the morning.

6

WHAT SMITH AND THE REST of the press corps did not publicly admit, since no salesman wants to disparage his product, was that the trial was bogging down. As a legal strategy, Jackson's documentary approach was unassailable. As drama, it had become stultifying. Colonel Storey had his assistant prosecutors introducing documents wholesale, often without even having them read in court. Charlie Horsky reported from Washington that U.S. press play of the trial was dwindling. Jackson grudgingly recognized that the prosecution had to come alive.

On Thursday morning, November 29, the defendants filed through the sliding door into the dock five minutes before the ten a.m. opening time. Göring took his seat in the front-row corner and looked up to meet the gaze of a short, thickset man with close-cropped gray hair. *"Guten Morgen, Herr Reichsmarschall,"* the man said in perfect German. Göring looked at him blankly and asked, "Do I know you?" Of course, the man explained; he had worked for Göring at the Prussian Ministry of the Interior years before. His name, he said, was Robert Kempner. Göring searched the face skeptically. Kempner offered to refresh his memory. In 1933, he had been general counsel to the Prussian police, and Göring, as minister of the interior, had fired him. Why? Göring asked warily. Because, Kempner said, he had successfully prosecuted storm troopers before the Nazis took over. He had also urged dissolution of the Nazi party and the arrest of Adolf Hitler for treason. And, Kempner added, he probably had been fired because he was part Jewish. Göring glared belligerently. Kempner went on. He remembered what Göring had said after dismissing him. His words had been, "Get out of my sight. I never want to see you again." Well, here he was again, Kempner said, moving down the dock.

He stopped at the eighth position. *"Guten Morgen, Herr Doktor Frick,"* Kempner said. The usually phlegmatic Wilhelm Frick looked up, startled. He remembered Kempner all too well. Frick, after succeeding Göring as minister of the interior, had deprived Kempner of his German citizenship and had him thrown into a concentration camp. Frick avoided Kempner's eyes. Kempner left and resumed his seat at the prosecution table. He had fled Germany long ago and was now an American citizen attached to Jackson's staff. He was in charge of the Defense Rebuttal Section, charged with anticipating the arguments of these men in the dock and preparing counterevidence to crush them. Kempner sat back to enjoy the morning's proceedings.

The afternoon session continued with the annexation of Austria. The prosecution introduced verbatim transcripts of Göring's virtually directing the takeover by telephone. A tale of bullying and deceit unfolded, and Göring winked, nodded, and smiled at his codefendants as it was told. During a brief recess, he turned and asked, What was the point of calling the *Anschluss* "aggression"? Didn't the Austrians pave the Führer's way from the German border to Vienna with flowers? Who had ever seen such joy?

7

DURING THE RECESS, the spectators saw a new face approach the prosecutors' stand. Navy Commander James Donovan was about to provide Jackson's answer to the complaint that his paperwork prosecution was too dry. "May it please the tribunal," Donovan began, "I refer to document number 2430 PS, a motion picture entitled 'Nazi Concentration Camps,' which the United States now offers into evidence. It was compiled from motion pictures taken by Allied military photographers as the armies in the West liberated areas in which these camps were located." The film had been ordered, Donovan explained, by General Eisenhower, and produced by one of Hollywood's leading directors, then on army duty, Lieutenant Colonel George Stevens. The courtroom went dark, except for the dock where the defendants were kept illuminated for security purposes. At one end of the dock stood Captain Gilbert.

A projector began whirring and cut a cone of light through the room, delivering images to a screen on the back wall behind the witness stand. Later generations might become hardened by repeated exposure to these sights, but scenes of bulldozers shoving moon-white corpses into mass graves were being seen for the first time by this audience. On the screen, GIs, wearing gas masks, pointed out bodies stacked like cord wood. Jack Taylor, an American navy lieutenant captured on an OSS mission behind the lines, appeared in the film and described the Mauthausen extermination camp. Prisoners were compelled to carry huge stones out of a quarry on their backs until they died of exhaustion, Taylor explained. Occasionally, bored guards amused themselves by dropping a prisoner back to the bottom of the quarry. This was called "parachuting." Quiet weeping sounded in the courtroom. A woman fainted and had to be carried out.

Film taken by the Germans themselves was shown next, most of it unearthed from hiding places by an OSS team. One reel had been shot at a camp near Leipzig. Some two hundred prisoners were shown being herded into a barn. SS men then doused the building with gasoline and set it afire. The few prisoners who escaped were mowed down by machine guns. Gilbert jotted down the defendants' reactions: Keitel wipes brow, takes off headphones; Frank trying to stifle tears; Funk blows nose, wipes eyes; Speer swallows hard; Dönitz bows head; Göring leans on elbows, yawns.

The films went on for over two hours, a phantasmagoria of broken, charred, gray bodies, ribs protruding, legs like sticks, hollow eyes gaping. When it was over, the lights went on. Silence hung like a pall over the room. Sir Geoffrey rose and left almost at a run, without adjourning the court. The defendants headed toward the elevator. Hans Frank remained seated, incapable of movement. A guard took him by the arm and led him away.

On their return to the prison, Göring noted that white enamel name plates had been placed over each cell. He was annoyed that the Americans, as usual, had neglected any civility. His plate read simply, "H. Göring," no rank, no title, as if he were a shopkeeper. He could always tell by the rearrangement of the photographs and his few personal articles that his cell had been searched during his absence. He feared most that the Americans might also have gone through his luggage stowed in the prison baggage room, two doors down from him. Two cyanide capsules were concealed there, one in a jar of face cream, another in his ultimate hiding place. He could only hope that they were still there. In order to go to the baggage room himself, he would have to be accompanied by a guard, and he did not want to draw attention to his cache.

Gilbert and Kelley waited until after supper before going to the cells to get the defendants' reaction to the films. Hans Fritzsche sat, head hung low, on the edge of his cot. For years his voice over the radio had stirred Germans to a hatred of the Jews. "No power on heaven or earth will erase this shame from my country," he said quietly. "Not in generations, not in centuries." Wilhelm Frick, who had promulgated the Nuremberg Laws, which had foreshadowed the atrocities shown, said he didn't understand how such things could have happened, then asked, Would there be time for an evening walk in the exercise yard? Göring was morose. They had all been having such a good time over the Austrian case, he said, before that wretched film spoiled everything.

General Alfred Jodl refused to talk to his visitors. But before lights out, he wrote a note for Dr. Exner, his lawyer, to pass to his wife, Luise. "These facts are the most fearful heritage which the National Socialist regime has left the German people," he told her. "It is far worse than the destruction of German cities. Their ruins could be regarded as honorable wounds suffered during a people's battle for its existence. This disgrace, however, besmirches everything, the enthusiasm of our youth, the entire German Wehrmacht and its leaders." He assured Luise that he knew nothing of such matters. He would, he said, "not have tolerated it for a single day."

While Kelley and Gilbert visited the cells, Robert Jackson was at home preparing a second surprise.

8

THE WITNESS HOUSE, a square, solid, two-story structure, stood at the end of a dead-end street in the Nuremberg suburbs. The house was run by a smokily beautiful aristocrat, the Countess Ingeborg Kalnoky. Nothing in her earlier life would have foretold the countess's present fate. Ingeborg Kalnoky, the daughter of a Prussian officer, had married into the Hungarian nobility. In the spring of 1945, Kalnoky was living in Budapest with her three young children and was pregnant with a fourth. As a German and a noblewoman, she feared for her safety as the Red Army approached. Leaving her husband behind, she had fled with the children to Germany. Her fears had had nothing to do with pro-Nazi sentiments. Once while summering in a Hungarian village, she had watched freight cars filled with Jews, packed like cattle, pass through for an entire week. She had heard their cries, glimpsed their tortured faces, and felt ashamed to be German.

The countess had found herself in a Nuremberg military hospital the night before she was to give birth to her child. She had been wondering what would befall her next when an American occupation

officer asked if she would like to manage a house that had been commandeered to lodge witnesses for the war-crimes trial. She seized the
opportunity.

On a night toward the end of November, Kalnoky answered the
door at the Witness House to find two MPs delivering a tall, gaunt,
palely poetic figure, unshaven and dressed in filthy clothes. The man
introduced himself as General Erwin Lahousen, in better times an
intelligence officer attached to the German High Command. Countess
Kalnoky found Lahousen a room, gave him soap and a razor, and left
him some GI rations.

That evening the fifty-eight-year-old Lahousen sat by the radio,
listening to classical music, his face buried in his hands, sobbing.
He was obviously a broken man, which the countess duly reported
to her American superiors. To her surprise and embarrassment, an
MP showed up the next day with a dark-haired, good-looking girl,
whom Kalnoky was directed to put up in Lahousen's room. Who she
was the countess never knew, but she visibly improved Lahousen's
spirits.

On Thursday, November 29, Hermann Göring's face displayed mingled shock and contempt as General Lahousen marched to the witness
stand. Field Marshal Keitel's face expressed terror. Documents had
already been introduced that established Germany's aggressive intentions against Poland. In one, Hitler was quoted saying, "Further successes cannot be obtained without shedding blood. . . . Poland must
be attacked at the next suitable opportunity. . . . It is a question of
expanding our living space in the east." Thus, the charge of aggression
seemed amply proved out of Hitler's mouth. Still, Jackson had become
sensitive to criticism that the trial lacked fire. Erwin Lahousen's appearance, Jackson believed, could lend a human dimension to the
charge. He had assigned the old gangbuster, John Harlan Amen, the
direct examination of Lahousen. Lahousen testified that, in mid-
August 1939, he received an odd order from his superior, the chief of
Abwehr intelligence, Admiral Wilhelm Canaris, to provide Polish uniforms, weapons, and false papers for a secret operation planned by
Heinrich Himmler. The Canaris order smelled fishy to Lahousen. He
nevertheless complied.

As soon as he heard the communiqué reporting that Polish troops had attacked a German radio installation at Gleiwitz, Lahousen became suspicious. The next day, Admiral Canaris revealed to him the full story. An SS team had forced concentration camp prisoners to don Polish uniforms and then shot the men in front of the radio station, making it appear that Poles had attacked it. Hitler had his provocation for invading Poland.

Amen introduced document 1795 PS, dated August 17, 1939, the transcript of a meeting between Keitel and Canaris. The document made it clear that the Gleiwitz scheme had originated with the SS. But it was Keitel who had approved the army's participation and who ordered Canaris to come up with the uniforms for the synthetic attack that launched World War II.

The next day, Amen questioned Lahousen about orders Keitel had given for the recapture and execution of two fugitive French generals, Maxime Weygand and Henri Giraud, before they could slip back to France. "The order to liquidate, that is, to murder Weygand and Giraud was given to me by Canaris, who received it from Keitel," Lahousen testified. But he and Canaris had connived so that the odious order was never carried out. As Lahousen spoke, Keitel's posture slackened visibly.

9

ERWIN LAHOUSEN CONTINUED on the stand, implicating Göring, Keitel, and Jodl in the destruction of Warsaw, the Reprisal Order, and the extermination of the Polish intelligentsia, nobility, and clergy. Cross-examination of him by the defense attorneys revealed their clumsiness with the unfamiliar technique. They merely elicited further testimony so damaging that they stopped questioning the general.

When Lahousen had finished, Sir Geoffrey declared a recess. The court was to be cleared of all visitors, he announced. A delicate issue was about to be decided in closed session: the competency of Rudolf Hess to stand trial. His behavior raised reasonable doubt—eating while lying on the floor, goose-stepping in the exercise yard, refusing to wear earphones, making obscene asides, and reading novels in court. Three weeks before, at the court's request, Hess had undergone examination by a ten-man panel of psychiatrists from America, Great

Britain, and the Soviet Union. The panel concluded that Hess's amnesia would "interfere with his ability to conduct his defense and to understand the details of the past." The final decision on his competence to stand trial, however, rested with the justices.

Shortly after the experts had examined Hess, Major Kelley had gone to see Jackson with an idea for restoring Hess's memory. Hess's condition was what psychiatrists called "hysterical amnesia," Kelley explained. The man might be snapped out of it by "truth drugs," Amytal or Pentothal. Kelley was familiar with the use of them in over a thousand cases with no ill effect, he said. Still, Jackson turned him down. If Hess was struck by lightning a month later, he feared, the drug would be blamed. They could not take the chance. Jackson was, nevertheless, curious to know what Kelley thought of Hess. "If one considers the road as sanity and the sidewalk as insanity," Kelley said, "then Hess spends the greater part of his time on the curb." Maybe so, Jackson replied, but he was going to urge the judges that Hess be tried.

During the recess before the competency hearing, Captain Gilbert approached Hess in the dock. Gilbert was convinced of the authenticity of the man's amnesia, but thought he ought to warn him of the likely consequences. If the judges found Hess incompetent to stand trial, "You probably won't be coming to court anymore," Gilbert advised, and he would soon be separated from the other defendants.

Hess looked stunned. In the few minutes before the court would resume, he had to make a decision. He had already spent five years in an alien, unsympathetic land. For the past two months, however confined, he had lived again among his compatriots, speaking his native tongue. Even coming into court daily represented more sociability than he had known in all those years.

The bailiff shouted, "Attention." The judges returned, and Sir Geoffrey declared the court back in session. He gestured toward Hess's lawyer, Gunther von Rohrscheidt, an older man whose previous practice had been in automobile accident liability cases. The diminutive Rohrscheidt adjusted his robe and began to explain why his client should not stand trial, quoting extensively from the psychiatric panel's report. Because of his memory loss, Hess could not follow the court proceedings, could not testify, could not challenge witnesses, in short, could not defend himself.

As the lawyer spoke, Hess ripped a sheet from a notebook and scribbled on it. He signaled to a guard to take the note to Rohrscheidt. The lawyer glanced at it but kept on talking. Hess began gesturing wildly for Rohrscheidt to stop. Justice Lawrence, unable to ignore the defendant's behavior, asked Rohrscheidt if Herr Hess might speak for himself. Hess rose and a microphone was brought to him. The court observed a Rudolf Hess not seen before at Nuremberg. His manner was calm, the voice steady. "Mr. President," he said, "henceforth, my memory will again respond to the outside world. The reasons for simulating loss of memory were of a tactical nature. . . . My capacity to follow the trial, to defend myself, to put questions to witnesses, to answer questions myself is not affected." Dr. Rohrscheidt was not a part of this deception, Hess went on. He had fooled the lawyer too. He rejected the authority of the IMT, Hess maintained. However, he was competent to stand trial. A stunned Lawrence quickly adjourned the court.

As reporters rushed to the pressroom phones to file the news, Douglas Kelley and Gustav Gilbert hurried to Hess's cell. They had believed in the man's mental impairment. Their professional reputations were on the line. They found Hess smiling calmly, the mad stare absent from his eyes. He spoke easily, answering in detail their questions about his youth, his conversations with Hitler, his flight to Scotland. Gilbert asked if Hess remembered his saying he might not be coming to court anymore. "Yes," Hess said, "that's when I decided to stop playing the game."

The two men left, subdued. Could they have been wrong and a layman like Burton Andrus right? Kelley ventured that Hess's amnesia was still real. It was this sudden cure that was the hoax. He was aware of numerous cases, he said, where amnesia patients, in order to preserve their ego, claimed that they had only pretended loss of memory.

Gilbert excused himself to duck into the prison office and write out his notes. After recording their conversation with Hess, he wrote his assessment: "Rejected as insane by the Führer, Hess seeks refuge in amnesia, then snaps out of it to avoid the same reaction by his friends." Hess's amnesia was therefore real, Gilbert concluded, but controllable at his discretion.

Gilbert next stopped by Keitel's cell. He knew that the field marshal, after General Lahousen's testimony, had been much distraught. "I don't know what to say," Keitel began, speaking of the plot to murder the two escaped French generals. "I know that an officer and a gentleman like yourself must be wondering about me. These charges attack my honor as an officer. I don't care if they accuse me of starting a war. I was only doing my duty and following orders. But these assassination stories, I don't know how I ever got mixed up in this." He had violated a sacred tenet of the Prussian officer corps: the inviolability of another general's person, whether friend or enemy. During the lunch break today, he said, the other military men, Dönitz, Raeder, even his longtime associate Alfred Jodl, had cut him dead.

The Saturday morning after Hess's turnabout, the judges announced their decision on the man's competence. Hess would stand trial. The legal definition of sanity that had guided them was a defendant's capacity to distinguish between right and wrong. In the judgment of the IMT, Rudolf Hess had moved off the curb and into the road.

10

THE GUARD ON Julius Streicher's cell motioned to the GI on Wilhelm Frick's cell to come over. What he wanted to show would only take a second. Frick's guard made sure his prisoner was asleep in the proper position, back to the wall, hands outside the covers, and came over to Streicher's cell. Streicher's guard had fashioned a tiny hangman's noose from a piece of string. He was dangling the string in front of the spotlight directed into the cell. The light projected the shadow of the noose, full size, against the back wall. Streicher's guard banged on the door. Streicher awoke, sighted the shadow of the swinging noose, and let out a bloodcurdling scream. The guards laughed uproariously.

To Colonel Andrus it seemed that not a day went by without a defendant's filing a complaint. At the top of the pile this December morning was Streicher's grievance about the noose trick. Ribbentrop was complaining that he got no sleep because the guards sang "Don't Fence Me In" all night. Rosenberg protested at having to keep his hands outside the blanket. They got cold, he said, and every time he slipped them under the covers, the guard jabbed him with a pole. Göring objected to eating in the same room with a toilet bowl. Schacht disliked having VIPs parading through the cellblock, staring at the defendants like animals in a zoo. A defense lawyer wrote complaining that the colonel addressed the defendants by their last names only. In Germany that was considered rude. At least he might refer to them as "Herr so-and-so." Andrus called in his secretary, Rose Korb, and dictated his response to the lawyer: "*Herr* is a German term. It is not my practice to speak German."

These people were a mystery to him, he told her. The United States government provided them with the pencils and paper necessary to write their complaints and fed them eighteen hundred calories a day, more than other Germans were allowed. They had a six-hundred-book library, a pound-a-month tobacco ration, and a little machine for rolling their own. Dr. Pfluecker and an American physician tended to their health needs daily. They received free dental care, as long as they did not ask for anything long-term like bridges or dentures. Yet these men who complained to him about cramped quarters represented a regime that had shipped human beings to their deaths in cattle cars. Men who complained about delays in getting mail from their wives had led a regime that snatched people from their beds in the middle of the night, people who were never to be heard from again. Andrus had an idea, one form letter for answering all complaints. He started dictating to Korb: "You are hereby informed that your protest against the treatment given you is wholly unwarranted and improper. You are entitled to nothing under the Geneva Convention, which your country repudiated. . . . Your treatment here is superior to any treatment ever accorded by Germany to any of its prisoners, foreign or domestic. . . . The kind and considerate treatment you receive in this jail is accorded to you not because you deserve it, but because less would be unbecoming to us, your conquerors."

11

THE DEFENSE COUNSELS were up in arms, Sir Geoffrey Lawrence told his fellow judges. They were objecting to the flood of prosecution documents introduced in court in English with no German translations available. The Germans were further convinced that, when they requested documents, the prosecution dragged its feet in complying. An obstructed defense would make a mockery of justice, and the trial would be seen as an extravagant exercise in revenge, Lawrence feared. He asked Sir Norman Birkett to look into the complaints. Though he disliked taking direction from Sir Geoffrey, Birkett welcomed the outlet for his energies. Robert Jackson agreed to have Colonel Storey meet with Birkett and acquaint him with all that was being done to aid the defense.

Storey and Birkett drove to the courthouse together the next day. Storey described the difference between this trial and what he had observed on his OSS mission to Bulgaria six months before. In Sofia, he had watched a war-crimes trial that began in the morning. By four p.m., the verdict had been announced. By eleven p.m., the condemned men rested in a common grave. They had received virtually no defense. Sir Norman took the point, he said, but Nuremberg was not Bulgaria.

At the courthouse, the two men entered a doorway marked DE-FENSE INFORMATION CENTER. Storey pointed out the library. Every law book the prosecution had been able to lay its hands on was here and available to the defense, he noted. The German lawyers were provided with secretaries, stenographers, and translators at no cost. The center was open until ten p.m. every night, seven days a week. Every day, the prosecution posted in this room a list of documents to be introduced the following day. They were available to the defense in German. As they left the center, Storey remarked, "I wonder what facilities the Germans would provide us if we were the ones being tried?" Birkett said nothing, but that night he wrote in his diary of the Defense Information Center: "More of the vaunted American efficiency, another expression of their superficial-ity." Soon afterward, Sir Geoffrey received another complaint from the defense lawyers. There were not enough coffee cups in their lunchroom.

12

DAVID Low had had a particularly good session this Monday morning, December 10. The artist had been commissioned by *The New York Times* to sketch and write impressions of the defendants. His spidery lines quickly caught the essence of his subjects. Hans Frank may have rediscovered religion, but Low's sketch captured Frank's fixed cynical sneer. Underneath it, the artist wrote, "The nastiest person present." Ribbentrop, with his pursed lips, struck Low as "a fussy family solicitor." The woeful banker, Walther Funk, had "a fat-sick face." Göring "looked jolly, until you noticed the cruel cut of his mouth." After the lunch recess, Low returned to his seat in the press section, and a new subject caught his eye: towering Ernst Kaltenbrunner. Kaltenbrunner, sufficiently recovered from his stroke, was making his first appearance in the dock. Low took out his sketch pad and began to limn a brute.

Kaltenbrunner had been released from the hospital and returned to his cell the previous weekend. While away, he learned from a friendly POW orderly the best news since his arrest. SS Major Franz Ziereis, commandant of the Mauthausen concentration camp, was dead. Quite possibly the most damning witness against Kaltenbrunner had gone to the grave.

Knowing that Kaltenbrunner's return from the hospital was imminent, Captain Gilbert had reviewed the man's dossier in advance of a cell visit. Gilbert found in Kaltenbrunner a classic Nazi success story. He had been born in Austria to a Catholic family in 1903 in Ried on the Inn, virtually next door to Hitler's birthplace, Braunau. Kaltenbrunner was a third-generation lawyer and liked to boast that he had put himself through school working the night shift in a coal mine and thus considered himself a friend of the workingman. Kaltenbrunner joined the Austrian Nazi party in the thirties and soon amassed useful credentials, beating up democratic Austrians, robbing to support Nazi party activities, tapping telephones, and instigating riots. He soon caught the eye of Heinrich Himmler, chief of the SS. Kaltenbrunner came into prominence in 1942, when Czech agents tossed a bomb into the Mercedes sports car of Reinhard Heydrich, head of the RSHA, the Nazi police apparatus. Himmler plucked Kaltenbrunner, then a relatively unknown provincial SS leader, to succeed Heydrich. He had substantial shoes to fill. Heydrich had masterminded the phony Polish attack on the Gleiwitz radio station for Heinrich Himmler. Heydrich had been in charge of the *Einsatzgruppen*, the extermination squads that followed the German armies into Poland and Russia. Heydrich had drafted the protocol for the "Final Solution of the Jewish problem."

Kaltenbrunner may have lacked Heydrich's icy finesse. He may often have been drunk. But he went at his duties—chief of the Gestapo, the concentration camps, the SD—with crude energy. Along the way he developed ideas that might have seemed odd to anyone except fellow Nazis. Kaltenbrunner believed that all German women of fertile age must bear children. If their husbands could not do the job, then proven fathers should do it for them. The father of three children himself, Kaltenbrunner had also acquired a titled mistress, the Countess Gisela von Westaupwolf, who gave birth to twins toward the war's end.

Even the inevitability of defeat had not tempered Kaltenbrunner's zeal. As the Allied armies plunged into Germany, he had sent out an order to the concentration camps: "The liberation of prisoners or Jews by the enemy, be it by the Western enemies or the Red Cross, must be avoided. . . . They must not fall into their hands alive." Just eleven days before the war ended, he informed Franz Ziereis, the Mauthausen commandant, that his quota was still 1,000 Jews to be killed daily. When time ran out on that schedule, he ordered Ziereis to herd all remaining prisoners into a tunnel, seal off the entrance, and suffocate them. Even Ziereis, who had supervised the deaths of 65,000 people, blanched at this last order and did not comply. When the desperation of his plight had pierced even Kaltenbrunner's alcoholic fog, he played his last card. He ordered the surrender of Mauthausen and its survivors to General Patton. It was this final order, and not the orders to the dead Ziereis, that he was counting on to save him.

Of all the papers in Kaltenbrunner's dossier, one that impressed Gilbert was a report by a doctor who examined the man after he had been appointed chief of the RSHA. Never, the doctor wrote, had he seen such a lummox, or one so stupid. "The man would have to get drunk to be capable of reasoning," the doctor concluded.

Kaltenbrunner's appearance that afternoon triggered a three-alarm press alert and a correspondents' stampede for the courtroom. The photographers were particularly pleased; Kaltenbrunner was a Nazi out of central casting. He lumbered into the dock with a lopsided smile on his long horse face. He put a hand out to General Jodl, who refused to take it. He greeted Hans Frank, but Frank turned away. He took his place next to Keitel, who suddenly felt a need to talk to Ribbentrop. Kaltenbrunner spied his lawyer, Kurt Kauffmann, a fellow Nazi. He rose, leaned over the rail of the dock, and put out his hand. Kauffmann clasped his hands behind his back and gave Kaltenbrunner a brief nod.

Justice Lawrence called the court to order. The first business this afternoon was to hear the plea of Ernst Kaltenbrunner, he announced. Kaltenbrunner rose, looking like a helpless giant. When the indictment had been served on him nearly two months before, he had written on it, "I do not feel guilty of any war crimes. I have done my duty as an intelligence operative. I refuse to serve as an ersatz Himmler." Throughout his captivity, he had taken the position that he was only nominally responsible for the Gestapo and the concentration camps. His superior, the late Reichsführer Himmler, had his own people who actually ran those operations. Kaltenbrunner merely sat on top of them in an organization chart. His true role, he intended to convince the court, had been to run the SD, essentially an intelligence service. The guard handed him a microphone. Kaltenbrunner ran his fingernail across the face of it to see if it was live. In a voice totally at odds with his brutal appearance, a voice smooth, cultivated, and reasonable, he said, "I am not guilty."

David Low sketched in Kaltenbrunner's long purple "dueling scar." Like so much about the man, the scar was a fraud. It had been earned not in a test of manliness, but against a windshield in an auto accident after a drunken spree.

13

ONE OF THE STREAM of visitors to Nuremberg that December was Major Albert Callan of the army's Counterintelligence Corps, who had come ashore on D-Day and later fought with the French resistance. Before he went home on points, Callan wanted to witness the war-crimes trial. While applying for a visitor's pass at the Palace of Justice, Callan ran into an old CIC buddy now posted to Nuremberg, who invited him to lunch at the Grand Hotel.

Their waiter spoke the lightly accented English of an educated person and seemed unusually attentive, Callan thought. As the waiter left, Callan's friend said quietly, "One of ours." "What?" Callan asked. "He works for CIC. We've got agents spotted all over town to keep an eye on the Commies. They report anything useful to us." CIC people, he explained, were also searching any cargo the Russians trucked in. Feelings were running high between the American and Russian military, Callan's friend added, and matters were getting touchy. Just a few nights before, a Red Army driver, waiting outside the Grand for his superior, had been shot to death in an argument with a GI. As Callan listened to the catalogue of friction and suspicion, he said, "There goes the alliance."

14

COLONEL ANDRUS COULD virtually hear the air crackle between himself and his superior, Brigadier General Leroy Watson, commander of the Nuremberg-Furth Enclave. From their first encounter, Watson had been antagonistic, examining the colonel's shining helmet and riding crop as if they were contaminated objects. Andrus resented the way Watson had summoned him this December afternoon. "You will report personally and immediately to explain . . . ," the memo had begun. Andrus stood in Watson's huge office, just inside the entrance to the courthouse, waiting for Watson to express the elementary courtesy of asking a fellow officer to sit down. The gesture was long in coming. The two men were roughly the same age, with the gray-haired, stocky Watson even tougher-looking than Andrus.

Watson was obsessed with security. Unfortunately for Andrus, this concern did not appear to extend to the safekeeping of the prisoners in the colonel's charge. Andrus had put in a request to Third Army Headquarters for more personnel. Watson had disapproved. Instead, he cut Andrus's roster. He was getting the dregs, Andrus complained. "I can't be held responsible for the court and the prisoners with insufficient manpower." Watson cut him off. That was not why he had summoned him. He wanted to know how two CIC agents had been able to slip into the courthouse past Andrus's guards without passes. What kind of security did he call that? Watson demanded.

Sitting outside in the general's waiting room was a cherub-faced nineteen-year-old private first class, Gunther Sadel, who could hear every word. Sadel sensed the steeliness in Watson's voice and wondered what it boded for him, since he was just reporting for duty in the Watson operation. Sadel was half-Jewish and had escaped Germany in 1939 at the age of thirteen. His Gentile mother had been forced to divorce Sadel's Jewish father and had stayed behind in Berlin. Sadel had never heard from her again. He eventually joined his father in America, and had been drafted late in the war. His command of German had saved him from becoming an infantry replacement during the bloody fighting along the Rhine. He was assigned instead to the CIC, and was now posted to Nuremberg.

Andrus left, and Sadel was summoned into Watson's office. The general spoke almost paternally to Sadel, with far more courtesy than he had shown Andrus, though he quickly got down to business. The nonfraternization policy had failed miserably, Watson explained. One only had to look at the epidemic of venereal diseases to know it. It was just as well that the army had dropped the policy. But a lot of these GIs, and officers too, Watson said, were taking out the wrong kind of girls, probably divulging secrets to them. Who knew what information these women might be passing along to the lawyers for the defense, or to the Communists? From now on, they had to be screened. Once a girl checked out okay, Watson's office would issue her a "social pass" with her picture on it. The pass would allow a girl into the various enlisted men's clubs. The social pass would not apply to the Grand Hotel. There were too many secrets floating around the Marble Room already. No German women were to be allowed there. He was giving the job of implementing the pass system to Sadel.

The day the announcement appeared that German women would need a pass to enter a GI club, Gunther Sadel feared he had unleashed a riot. A surging mob surrounded the Nuremberg Opera House, where applications were to be submitted. Sadel knew that more than a date with a GI was at stake. For a German girl, the social pass meant a decent meal, maybe a little extra food that could be slipped back to a hungry mother or kid brother. And with this winter proving the harshest in a generation, a date at a GI club meant, if nothing else, a warm night. Sadel had drafted rules for obtaining the social pass: no married women, no former Nazi party members, no members of the Bund Deutscher Mädel (the female version of the Hitler Youth), no prostitutes, and no one with a criminal record. He found the recently reactivated Nuremberg police only too willing to curry the favor of the Americans by divulging anything in their files on their women.

15

COMMANDER JIM DONOVAN, who had shown the earlier concentration camp movie, had recently sold Robert Jackson on a film that could make the conspiracy charge something more than a paper abstraction. George Stevens and the writer Budd Schulberg had compiled this film from captured German newsreels and propaganda footage. They called it *The Nazi Plan.* The morning session of December 11, the courtroom lights went out, and a projector threw a test pattern on the screen. The defendants sat resignedly, remembering the disastrous effect of the earlier film. *The Nazi Plan* opened with a familiar voice. The defendants turned to Alfred Rosenberg, who could be heard narrating scenes from the Leni Riefenstahl propaganda masterpiece, *Triumph of the Will.* Nuremberg, as it had once been, appeared on the screen during the Party Day rallies. Albert Speer could not suppress a smile as he watched the spectacle of his invention, ranks of powerful searchlights throwing an ethereal "cathedral of ice" over Zeppelin Field. Under this luminous arch, throngs of torchbearers marched to an insistent drumbeat, platoons of Hitler Youth and phalanxes of goose-stepping troops. Throaty male voices lifted the "Horst Wessel" song into the night air, and a quarter of a million Germans chanted, "*Ein Reich, ein Volk, ein Führer!* [One state, one people, one leader!]" Hitler appeared, his voice tracing its familiar cadence, almost inaudible at first, building slowly, climaxing in calculated hysteria. Gustav Gilbert studied the faces in the dock. The defendants were leaning forward in hypnotic fascination. Ribbentrop cried openly. Göring turned to Hess and said, "Justice Jackson will want to join the party now!"

The film shown in the afternoon was less pleasing to the defendants. In the aftermath of the Twentieth of July assassination attempt on Hitler, suspected conspirators had been tried by the People's Courts, some of them here in room 600. American troops had discovered eleven hours of film taken during these virtual kangaroo proceedings, of which the court was now seeing excerpts. The defendants' rapt attention of the morning gave way to restless fidgeting. Two SS men were seen dragging a defendant before a judge named Roland Freisler. The man was clutching at his beltless, falling trousers. As Freisler browbeat him, the People's Court audience could be heard laughing. Another defendant, an army officer, began describing murders he had witnessed in Poland. "Murders?" Freisler shrieked. "You piece of garbage!" The defendant sagged visibly. "Are you collapsing under the stress of your vulgarity, you filthy rogue?" Freisler went on. After the plot against Hitler, nearly five thousand Germans had lost their lives through People's Court justice.

That evening, Kelley and Gilbert made cell visits to assess the reaction to the films. They found Göring despondent. "You know what hurt me more than even the concentration camp film, bad as it was?" he asked. "It was that loudmouth, Freisler. It actually made me squirm the way he screamed at the defendants. After all, these were German generals, not yet proven guilty. I tell you, I could have died of shame." Gilbert left the cell buoyed. Something was getting through to the defendants. The difference between their trial and what passed for justice under the Nazi regime could not have escaped them.

The visit to Ribbentrop, however, was less satisfying. The man's eyes shone as he spoke of the Riefenstahl film. "Couldn't you just feel the force of the Führer's personality?" he asked. Getting no response, he added, "Well, maybe it doesn't come through on the screen." Then the eyes lit up again. Ribbentrop virtually purred: "Even though I am here in jail on trial for my life, if Hitler were to walk into this room and command anything, I would do it immediately without any thought of the consequences."

16

THE BULLETIN BOARDS POSTED around the courthouse were avidly read. To visitors, they were like a playbill, announcing what dramas would be performed next, and who would enact the featured roles. To the prosecution staff, the announcements were a starting lineup, revealing who would be getting into the game, since the goal of most of Jackson's lawyers was to appear in court. For the defense attorneys, the bulletin board revealed the opponents they would be facing. The December 11 posting indicated that the case against slave labor was scheduled next. The prosecuting attorney listed was Thomas Dodd, a former FBI man who stirred mixed feelings at Nuremberg. Socially, Dodd was a boon companion, a raconteur, enlivening an evening in the Marble Room with well-told stories. Others saw him as a born politician with a talent for maneuvering himself into the limelight. Rumors circulated that the political bosses in his native Connecticut had engineered Dodd's appointment to Nuremberg to prepare him for a run for the U.S. Congress, maybe the Senate. To his more erudite colleagues, those most at home researching law books and drafting briefs, Dodd was a lightweight who used their work to prop up his own thin legal scholarship. All were eager to observe his first performance in the arena.

As he moved to the prosecutor's stand, Dodd cut an impressive figure, his hair steel-gray, his profile classic. He stood out among the sea of uniforms in a well-tailored banker's blue suit. The most uneasy men in the dock, as Dodd spread his notes on the lectern, were Albert Speer and Fritz Sauckel. Their respective guilt for the death and suffering inflicted by the slave labor program had become a topic of hot debate in evening bull sessions at the Grand Hotel. Dodd's performance could resolve the debate.

Ernst Friedrich Christoph Sauckel, known all his life as Fritz, sat in the dock in the same state of emotional befuddlement that had marked his entire confinement. Sauckel was the least imposing figure among the defendants, a little man with a shining dome, sad brown eyes, and a silly mustache patterned after the Führer's. He was as puzzled to find himself on trial as he had been to discover that Germany had lost the war. What pained Sauckel most was that no one at Nuremberg seemed to understand his logic. How could he be guilty of crimes against working people when he himself sprang from the working class? When Airey Neave delivered the indictments in October, Sauckel had written on his, "The abyss between the ideal of a social community which I advocated as a seaman and a worker and the terrible things that happened in the concentration camps has shaken me deeply."

He was fifty-one years old, the son of a mailman and a seamstress, raised in a strict religious home. He had gone to sea as a boy of fifteen, and sat out the First World War in a French prison after his merchant ship was captured. When he came home in 1919, few berths were available for merchant seamen. Germany was convulsed by Communists and right-wingers battling for the souls of unemployed workers like Fritz Sauckel. "I could not be a Communist," he told his Nuremberg interrogators, "because Marxism states that religion is the opiate of the masses. Marxism states that private property is theft. Marxism embraces the concept of class warfare which must lead to civil war." On the other hand, he could not join the conservative political movements, "because they ignored people of my station." Then he had heard Adolf Hitler speak. "I had found a man who could create a union of all German people whatever their level, whatever their calling, workers and intellectuals." He joined the party and became an energetic if unimaginative recruiter. In the meantime, he worked as a toolmaker in a ball-bearing factory. By 1927, Sauckel was *Gauleiter*—district party chief—of Thuringia. He had risen not by flair or connections, but by tireless, plodding effort. He was uncomfortable at party affairs where other men swapped war stories and spoke of heroic deeds and medals won during a conflict which he spent in a French jail. He was uncomfortable with cultivated people. He had never read a book in his adult life. All the intellectual stimulation he needed, he said, was supplied by Adolf Hitler. Fritz Sauckel felt truly at home only within the bosom of his family, with his wife and ten children.

He remained a *Gauleiter* until a fateful day in 1942. Sitting with Sauckel in the second row of the dock, four places to his left, was the man responsible for what happened that day.

In 1942 Albert Speer, then thirty-seven, had just been appointed armaments minister. A principal task he faced was to move labor where it was most needed. But the *Gauleiters* refused to give up workers from their regional fiefdoms to send to other districts. Nominally, solving the problem should have been the responsibility of Hermann Göring, head of the Four Year Plan and presumably chief of the German economy. That, Speer knew, was laughable. Göring had become a self-indulgent sybarite barely capable of directing the Luftwaffe, much less German industry. Speer went to Hitler and persuaded him that the regime needed a labor czar, someone who could break the grip of the *Gauleiters*, preferably someone from their own ranks whom they would heed.

In March 1942, Fritz Sauckel found himself with Speer and Hitler in the Reich Chancellery in Berlin. "This has been a brutal winter," Hitler said, pacing. "We've suffered a heavy drain on our vehicles, trains, fuel. We've taken heavy manpower losses. We can only keep pace if every German enters either the military or the armaments industries." He looked directly at Sauckel. "This is a gigantic job. And you, Sauckel, are going to perform it. You have the ability. You are a party man and a patriot. Now you have a chance to fulfill your obligation as a soldier." Sauckel overcame his speechlessness long enough to ask why this honor had fallen to him. Speer spoke up. "Because," he said, "we think you've got the guts to break through the bureaucracy, to overrule the *Gauleiters* and get the job done."

Sauckel was enough of a bureaucrat to ask what authority he would have to perform this job. He was to be, Hitler said, plenipotentiary general for the allocation of labor. He would have authority to issue orders to commissioners of occupied lands, to heads of civil agencies, even to generals and admirals, to round up the labor needed. His powers in this sphere were unconditional.

Within days, Sauckel was called again before Hitler. This time there was no praise for his energy and patriotism. Hitler had Sauckel's recently proposed manpower plan crumpled in his fist. Where in it, Hitler fumed, was there provision for conscripting foreign workers? The job could not be done with German manpower alone. Sauckel was to raise 1.6 million foreign workers in the next three months, Hitler ordered. Sauckel shifted uneasily. Did not conscription of foreigners violate international law? he asked. That was not Sauckel's concern, Hitler replied. Ask for volunteers in the occupied territories; and if they did not volunteer, conscript them. Besides, the Soviet Union was not even a party to the Hague or Geneva conventions, and there were millions of able bodies there. Sauckel was to stop quibbling and start bringing in workers.

However dilatory a legal scholar, Tom Dodd was proving a dramatic courtroom performer. With well-controlled emotion, he read into the record document 294 PS, which described how a Sauckel manpower directive was carried out in the Soviet Union. The author of this report, Dodd pointed out, was Sauckel's fellow defendant Alfred Rosenberg. "You cannot imagine the bestiality," Rosenberg had written Sauckel. "The order came to supply twenty-five workers, but no one reported. Then the German militia came and began to set fire to the houses of those who had fled. . . . People who hurried to the scene were forbidden to extinguish the flames. Instead, they were beaten and arrested. They fell on their knees to kiss the hands of the policemen, but the policemen beat them again with rubber truncheons and threatened to burn down the whole village. . . . The militia went through the adjoining villages and seized laborers. . . . The imprisoned workers are locked in the schoolhouse. They cannot even go out to perform their natural functions, but have to do it like pigs in the same room. Among them are lame, blind, and aged people. We are now catching humans like dog catchers used to catch dogs."

In the beginning it had been different, Sauckel knew. He had been able to get Frenchmen, Dutchmen, Belgians, and Russians to come voluntarily to work in Germany for good wages. But after the defeat at Stalingrad, all that changed. Workers had to be dragooned, transported in handcuffs.

As Dodd went on, Sauckel waited to hear Speer's role in all this. The way the system had worked, manufacturers would inform Speer of their labor needs. A tank factory might inform him, for example, that it needed a hundred die makers, two hundred welders, and a thousand common laborers. Speer would aggregate such requests from all industries and direct Sauckel to come up with the required number of workers. Speer coordinated this task through a central planning board, of which Sauckel was not even a member. Sauckel merely saw himself as Speer's procurer.

Speer had never let up the pressure; he was forever demanding more and more workers. Sauckel suspected that Speer was hoarding labor far beyond his needs, while the army desperately sought more men. At one point, Sauckel added up all Speer's pending demands, and they totaled more workers than the entire German economy required. Complaining did no good. Sauckel knew where he stood in the pecking order. Speer had once snapped at him in Hitler's presence, "You are my man." During another squabble, Speer sent Hitler a memorandum insisting that Sauckel be treated as his assistant. Hitler himself had made clear that "Herr Speer is my main authority in all economic spheres."

A despondent Sauckel listened to Dodd pour on the incriminating evidence and wondered why nothing was said of his efforts to have foreign workers treated decently. In one directive to recruiters he had written, "Underfed slaves, diseased, resentful, despairing and filled with hate, will never yield that maximum of output which they can achieve under decent conditions." He told the *Gauleiters*, "Beaten, half-starved or dead Russians do not supply us with coal and are utterly useless for steel production."

Dodd was now describing conditions Russian workers endured in a typical armaments factory: three-quarters of a cup of tea at four a.m. when the workday started, a quart of watery soup and two slices of bread fourteen hours later at the day's end. The workers caught mice to supplement their diet. Sauckel waved to attract the attention of his counsel, Robert Servatius. Servatius must make clear that he, Sauckel, had not been responsible for working conditions. That was Speer's bailiwick. Dodd was already reading into the record further damning evidence, Sauckel's words spoken at a meeting with Speer: "I have even employed and trained French and Italian agents of both sexes to do what was done in the old days, to shanghai, to go hunting for workers and dupe them using liquor to get them to Germany."

The Führer had given him an impossible job, and one defendant in the dock knew how hard Sauckel had tried to get out of it. During the war, Admiral Dönitz had been astonished by a radio message from one of his U-boat skippers, Captain Salmann, reporting that he had found a stowaway among the torpedoes: Fritz Sauckel. Sauckel was begging to be allowed to stay aboard in any capacity. Dönitz had ordered the sub to bring Sauckel back to port.

Sauckel traced his final fall from the Führer's grace to August 4, 1944. With the Allies securely entrenched in France, with the Red Army closing in from the east, Hitler had decided that a plenipotentiary for total war was required to maximize manpower. He called a meeting of Speer, Sauckel, Keitel, and the propaganda minister, Josef Goebbels. Goebbels immediately began attacking Sauckel. Sauckel had allowed millions of Germans to stay in soft civil service jobs, Goebbels charged. He had failed to mobilize Germany's women. Why, he said in disbelief, 500,000 females were still working as charladies!

Ever since he had taken the labor job, Sauckel had known nothing but abuse from Speer and Goebbels. They would never give this little proletarian any credit, no matter how many bodies he delivered to Germany. Behind his back they called him "Saukerl," the equivalent of "jerk." Speer regarded Sauckel as in a class with the trashman— one who served an essential function, but God forbid that he should sit down at the same table with Speer.

Without these charladies, Sauckel said, who would clean all those offices in Goebbels's propaganda ministry? Most of these women did their work before the bureaucrats even arrived, and then went to second jobs to support their families. Goebbels's own bureaucracy was larded with useless people, Sauckel noted. Yet every time the army tried to get at them, Goebbels threw the army recruiting officials out. Sauckel, by contrast, had given the lives of two of his soldier sons to Germany.

Goebbels ignored him, and said that he would be happy to take on the additional burden of plenipotentiary for total war. Keitel saw Hitler start to nod, and quickly added that this was a splendid idea. Dr. Goebbels was going to be in charge of the total war effort, Hitler announced, and Sauckel had better do as he was told. Goebbels was still not through. "History," he warned Sauckel, "will find you weak, guilty of not freeing enough men for service at the front, guilty of losing the war!" Sauckel looked to Hitler, who he thought would certainly defend him from such calumny. The Führer said nothing. Instead, he closed the meeting, expressing perfect confidence in Goebbels. After that day, Sauckel had toiled as hard as ever; but he had been invited to no more high-level meetings. Every time he tried to see Hitler, the watchdog, Bormann, said that the Führer was not feeling well. Sauckel never saw Hitler again.

Dodd returned to document 294 PS. His voice filled with cold anger as he quoted a German officer's report on a labor roundup in Russia: "Recruiting methods were used which probably have their precedent only in the blackest periods of the slave trade. A regular manhunt was inaugurated."

Captain Gilbert went to see Sauckel in his cell. He found him sitting on his cot, head bowed, hands dangling between his legs, yet eager to talk. The captain must understand, Sauckel said: "About the abuse of foreign workers, I am really not responsible. I was like a seaman's agency. If I supply hands for a ship, I am not responsible for any cruelty they may experience on board. I just supplied workers. If they were mistreated, it was not my fault." The ship's captain was to blame, he said, and the captain of the German war industry had been Albert Speer.

17

THE PLACE TO ESCAPE the sullen city when the day's work was done was the Marble Room in the Grand Hotel, where the food was good, the drinks large, and both subsidized by Uncle Sam. Five dollars easily financed an evening of dining and drinking, and the waiter would be happy with a two-cigarette tip. Major Airey Neave threaded his way through the jeeps and command cars that clogged the hotel's entrance as the sounds of Kamil Behoneck's orchestra filtered out into the street. Herr Meyer, the manager, always smiling, greeted Neave, displaying his phenomenal memory for names. Neave entered the Marble Room, where Zarah Leander was singing, "*Der Wind hat mir ein Lied Erzählt.*" Leander had been a singer and film star of some prominence. Now her voice had a mechanical quality, like a piano roll played too often. Her gown, once fashionable, was now frayed and faded, like her song. Years before, even months earlier, she would have been singing the same refrain for storm troopers and party stalwarts.

Neave made his way around the dancers to a table where he

joined British friends. Under the festive disorder, the Marble Room had a traceable structure. American men dominated the room, usually sitting together, though they might have with them as many British women as Americans. The American women were easy to spot—smartly dressed, spared the six years of clothes rationing that European women had undergone. At one American table, Tom Dodd, fresh from his presentation of the slave labor case, held court in an ebullient mood.

Neave was struck by the contrast between the horror revealed in the courtroom during the day and the determined merriment of the Marble Room at night. He sat down, and his companions asked what Neave thought of Dodd's performance. Whatever their respective guilt, Neave observed, the contest between Sauckel and Speer was going to be influenced by social class. Look at the men on the bench. Then look at Speer and Sauckel. Whom would they invite to their club? A companion disagreed. The Speer-Sauckel case would revolve around another question: Who had been the motive force in the slave labor operation, Sauckel the slave trader, or Speer the slave driver? If it had been the latter, then it seemed hard to believe that Speer could suffer a lesser fate than Sauckel. Neave hoped the bench could be that objective.

18

DURING THE GLORY DAYS, Heinrich Hoffmann had often stayed at the Grand Hotel with Adolf Hitler. Now Hoffmann occupied a cell in the Nuremberg prison. As Hitler's personal photographer, Hoffmann had been shrewd enough on his arrest to bring with him a cache of photos. Since he was the only one who knew what they portrayed, Hoffmann managed to have himself made a trusty and was given the job of indexing the pictures. Hoffmann had a son-in-law in the dock: Baldur von Schirach, the youth leader, was married to his daughter, Henriette. This relationship, however, did not prevent Hoffmann from happily gathering photographic evidence against Schirach or any of his other former colleagues.

Hoffmann was supervised by lean, athletic Richard Heller, a thirty-year-old navy lieutenant and lawyer who spoke a smattering of

German. The first time Heller saw Hoffmann, the old man was lost in an oversize set of dyed army-reject fatigues. Yet, a twinkle shone in his eye as he introduced himself with a flourish as "Professor Hoffmann, doctor of fine arts."

Hoffmann constantly badgered Heller that there was no reason to keep him locked up. He was not going anywhere, and he could be far handier to the prosecution if he were free. He knew where tons of photographs were hidden, he said. Heller trusted Hoffmann, or at least recognized him as a predictable opportunist with no loyalties except to his own survival, and persuaded his superiors to allow him to take Hoffmann on a photographic hunting expedition.

Their jeep no sooner set out on the bomb-cratered road to Munich than Hoffmann piqued Heller's curiosity by mentioning that it was he who had introduced Eva Braun to Hitler. He had been running a photography shop in Munich at the time, he said, and felt uneasy about Hitler's interest in young girls, particularly in Hoffmann's seventeen-year-old daughter, Henriette. Hitler at the time had been in his forties. Hoffmann deliberately steered the Führer to another seventeen-year-old—his shop assistant Eva Braun. What Hoffmann omitted from this account was that much of his business had been in pornographic postcards and photographs of nude dancers. His models had been girls who worked in second-rate bars—including Braun, who had become both his assistant and his mistress. He had happily handed Eva over to the Führer.

Hoffmann was a shrewd businessman. He had persuaded Hitler to grant him a monopoly on selling photographs of the top Nazi leaders to the German people. He then founded a publishing house, and his turnover for the pictures and albums totaled 58 million marks in the twelve years of Nazi rule. Still, the old pornographer and court jester hungered for respectability, and he had persuaded Hitler to have the degree of doctor of fine arts conferred on him.

When Hoffmann and Heller arrived in Munich, the German indeed unearthed a photographic lode. He also hit up a friend for a feathered hat, a Tyrolean jacket, and a pair of formal striped pants several sizes too big, an outfit that was to become his everyday attire. After Munich, Heller wanted to take a side trip to Dachau. In the camp, which still exuded the odor of death, Hoffmann put on a sober face and professed his shame. His contrition, however, was short-lived.

As they hit the road again, this time for Berchtesgaden, Hoffmann began again entertaining Heller with stories of the Nazi court. The others around Hitler had been spellbound by the man, Hoffmann confided. But he was not. He knew too much about the private Hitler. Eva Braun, for example, was so coarse that Hoffmann's wife had to tell her how to dress. Heller wanted to know if Hitler's affair with Eva had ever been consummated. He was not sure about the Führer's sexuality, Hoffmann said. If he had to guess, he would have said that Hitler was probably asexual.

By the time the expedition ended, they had unearthed enough photos to fill two army trucks. On their return to Nuremberg, Heller concluded that there was no further need to cage Heinrich Hoffmann. He arranged more desirable lodgings for his traveling companion.

Countess Inge Kalnoky opened the door of the Witness House to an older man, his white hair tinted with a blue rinse. Tyrolean hat in hand, he made a sweeping bow and introduced himself as Professor Heinrich Hoffmann. He was, he said, going to be her guest.

Hoffmann quickly established himself as the house jester. Over dinner, he regaled other guests with stories of life in Hitler's entourage. Someone asked if he had known Hess. Of course, Hoffmann said. He had been with Rudolf when somebody hit him in the head with a brick at a rally in Munich. That explained why Hess was so loony, Hoffmann said. Kalnoky had lodged several men like General Erwin Lahousen, broken by their experiences under Nazism. She found Heinrich Hoffmann, however, irrepressible, a man untouched by shame, suffering, or defeat.

19

IT WAS COLONEL ANDRUS'S POLICY that his staff not talk to reporters. So why, he wanted to know, had Captain Gilbert been giving interviews? He had information, the colonel said, that Gilbert had talked to Reuters on December 12 and to the London *Daily Express* on December 13. It was true, Gilbert admitted. Day after day, the reporters saw him in intimate conversation with the men in the dock whom they were not allowed to interview. Consequently, they hounded him for insider stories. For a long time, he had resisted. Avoiding the press had seemed part of an unspoken arrangement with Kelley not to give away anything intended for their book. But Kelley himself had gone on Armed Forces Network, the most listened-to station in Europe. Harold Burson, a twenty-four-year-old tech sergeant heading the Nuremberg AFN bureau, had chosen the congenial Kelley over the deadly earnest Gilbert for an interview about Göring. On the air, Kelley had described Göring as "dominant, aggressive, merciless, yet a jovial extrovert capable of occasional tenderness. The only real leader among them." Kelley had given away other tidbits. He had described how he once told Göring that it seemed Hitler's entourage was composed entirely of yes-men. That was true, Göring had replied: "All the no-men are six feet under." On learning of the Kelley broadcast, Gilbert concluded that if one coauthor could give interviews, why not the other? That was when he had spoken to Reuters and the *Express.*

Gilbert apologized to Andrus, promised to sin no more, and left the office. He had two relationships with the colonel, as if he were two different people. In one role, he became Dr. Gustav Gilbert, practitioner of a suspect profession, to be treated warily and at arm's length. In the other role, he was Captain Gilbert, spy for the prison commandant, to be dealt with confidentially if not necessarily warmly. He had performed the latter role well. Gilbert arranged to have German-speaking soldiers among the white-helmeted GIs guarding the dock. They reported to him daily what they overheard the defendants saying to each other. He had set up a similar arrangement with the escort guards who brought the prisoners from the cellblock to the courtroom. Whatever Gilbert gleaned, he passed on to Andrus. He was also supplying the same information to Justice Jackson.

Gilbert wondered if Kelley fully appreciated him. It was not only that he could speak to the defendants in their own language. Gilbert, with his formal manner, using the old-fashioned forms of respectful address, came across to the defendants as more European than American. The confidence he enjoyed in the cellblock was now near total. All of them, except the clamlike Jodl, had opened their hearts to Gilbert. And these confidences, Kelley should realize, would be the making of their book.

Nuremberg at the time
of the trial, and after
eleven Allied air raids.
*(Walter Sanders/*Life
magazine © Time-Warner)

RIGHT: Hermann Göring, the number-two Nazi after Hitler, in the dock and some sixty-five pounds lighter than at the time of his arrest. *(U.S. Army Signal Corps)*

BELOW: Field Marshal Wilhelm Keitel, chief of staff of the German armed forces, derided by the Nazis as "lakeitel," Hitler's "lackey." *(National Archives)*

Fritz Sauckel, organizer of the conscript labor program. A key trial issue: who was guiltier, Sauckel the slave trader or Speer the slave driver? *(National Archives)*

Albert Speer, Hitler's youthful architect, who became the German arms production czar and whose life was saved by a brilliant defense strategy. *(National Archives)*

In the dock: Grand Admiral Karl Dönitz, chief of the German navy and the man Hitler chose as his successor. *(National Archives)*

Baldur von Schirach, creator of the Hitler Youth, later gauleiter of Vienna, who compared his youth movement to the American Boy Scouts. *(National Archives)*

ABOVE: Ernst Kaltenbrunner, scar-faced chief of the RSHA, whose responsibilities included the Gestapo and the death camps. *(National Archives)*

RIGHT: Hans Frank, the "Jew Butcher of Cracow," Nazi governor-general of occupied Poland, who may have shared a secret with Hitler: possible partial Jewish ancestry. *(National Archives)*

LEFT: Julius Streicher, publisher of the tabloid anti-Semitic newspaper *Der Stürmer*, a man so corrupt that even a Nazi tribunal called him "unfit for human leadership." *(National Archives)*

BELOW: Alfred Rosenberg, Nazi party "philosopher," minister of the Eastern Occupied Territories, and art thief for Hitler and Göring. *(National Archives)*

BELOW: Grand Admiral Erich Raeder, earlier chief of the German navy, who heard Hitler declare his intention to make aggressive war, yet stayed on. *(National Archives)*

LEFT: Arthur Seyss-Inquart, an Austrian who helped turn his country over to Hitler and later became Nazi commissioner of Holland. *(National Archives)*

BELOW: Wilhelm Frick, minister of the interior, who prepared some of the earliest anti-Semitic laws, described as the most colorless man in the dock. *(National Archives)*

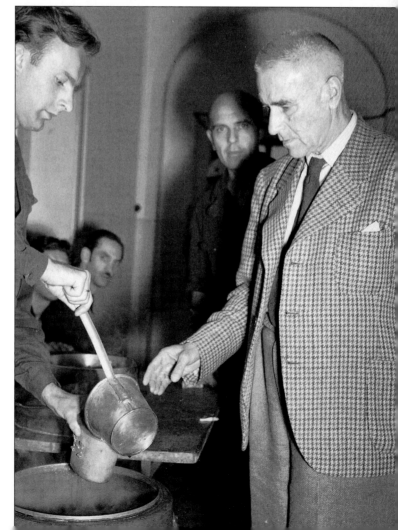

RIGHT: Colonel General Alfred Jodl, operations chief of the German armed forces, who might have suffered a lesser fate if the Russians had not insisted on including him among the major war criminals. *(National Archives)*

BELOW: Rudolf Hess, third-ranking Nazi, who made the quixotic peace flight to Scotland. Behind him is Gustav Gilbert, psychologist. *(National Archives)*

OPPOSITE: Jewish children held for medical experiments at Auschwitz. Part of the trial's photographic record. *(National Archives)*

ABOVE: Nazi roundup of Jews from the Warsaw Ghetto. Part of the trial's photographic record. (*National Archives*)

BELOW: Jewish women herded past German troops at a concentration camp in Poland. Part of the trial's photographic record. (*Lydia Chagall; courtesy U.S. Holocaust Museum*)

RIGHT: A canister of the gas Zyklon (Cyclone) B, used to exterminate inmates at Auschwitz and other camps. Part of the trial's photographic record. (*National Archives*)

BELOW: Boxes containing gold teeth extracted from murdered concentration camp inmates and later deposited in the Reichsbank. (*National Archives*)

BELOW: Two inmates at the crematorium in the Mauthausen extermination camp. (*U.S. Army Signal Corps; courtesy Air Force Academy*)

The Palace of Justice. Behind it lies the prison, comprising four buildings. The defendants were held in the right-hand wing. The small structure angled to the right of that wing is the gym, where the executions were carried out. *(National Archives)*

Cellblock C, where the defendants were jailed, with a twenty-four-hour guard posted at each cell. The wire fencing in the upper tiers was designed to prevent suicide leaps. *(National Archives)*

RIGHT: Colonel Burton Andrus (left), the prison commandant, in the walkway that joined the prison to the Palace of Justice. *(National Archives)*

LEFT: A cell, looking toward the door. The toilet was concealed from the guard's vision, an arrangement that permitted the defendant Robert Ley to carry out his suicide undetected. (*Charles Alexander*)

RIGHT: Guarding Hermann Göring's cell. A spotlight was beamed on the prisoners during the night while they slept. (*U.S. Army Signal Corps; courtesy U.S. Air Force Academy*)

BELOW: Interior of the courtroom. The prisoners' dock is at the far left, the bench at the far right, and the witness stand at the rear. Seated before the dock are the defense counsels. Seen in the far left corner are the interpreters' booths, and the prosecutors are seated in the foreground. (*National Archives*)

Mementos on the table in Hermann Göring's cell. *(National Archives)*

RIGHT: Hermann Göring in the visitors' room posing with Lieutenant "Tex" Wheelis, who befriended the Nazi and may have played a role in Göring's suicide. *(U.S. Army Signal Corps; courtesy Rose Korb Williams)*

Master Sergeant John Woods, who hanged the condemned men. *(AP/Wide World Photo)*

Captain Drexel Sprecher, who prosecuted Schirach and Fritzsche. *(Ray D'Addario)*

The International Military Tribunal (left to right): Robert Falco, Henri Donnedieu de Vabres, Ion Timofeevich Nikitchenko, Sir Geoffrey Lawrence, Alexander Volchkov, General William L. Mitchell (court administrative officer), Francis Biddle, Sir Norman Birkett. (Missing is John Parker, the American alternate.) *(U.S. Army Signal Corps; courtesy U.S. Air Force Academy)*

LEFT: Chief Soviet prosecutor Lieutenant General Roman Rudenko, who later prosecuted the American U2 spy-plane pilot Gary Powers. *(National Archives)*

BELOW: The American chief prosecutor, Associate Justice of the U.S. Supreme Court Robert Jackson, in court. To his left is Sir David Maxwell-Fyfe, the major British prosecutor on the scene. *(National Archives)*

On a December evening, the two Americans stopped by Göring's cell to find the *Reichsmarschall* in a fury. He had seen a newspaper photograph of Heinrich Hoffmann sorting out pictures for the prosecution. "When I think of the money that bastard made selling my picture!" Göring fumed. "It must have been at least a million marks, at five pfennings apiece. And now he's finding pictures to hang me!"

Kelley turned the conversation to the prosecution's charge of aggression. They did not have to show those films or read all those boring documents to prove that Germany armed for war, Göring said. "I rearmed Germany until we bristled! When they told me I was playing with war by building up the Luftwaffe, I told them I certainly wasn't running a girls' finishing school."

One of the guards had recently passed along to Gilbert a paper found on Ribbentrop's floor. In it, Ribbentrop described a conversation with Hitler one week before the Führer's suicide. According to Ribbentrop's recollection of the conversation, Hitler had said that Göring did not understand aircraft development and that the man was a fount of misinformation. When the Americans started bombing Germany with four-engine planes, Göring told Hitler that this was splendid; these planes were the easiest to shoot down. According to Ribbentrop, Hitler had considered Göring's failure in the air to be the chief cause of Germany's defeat.

Gilbert confronted Göring with this story. Göring gave out a contemptuous laugh. Did the Americans know what Ribbentrop had done when he was presented to the king of England? Göring asked. He gave the Hitler salute. "I told the Führer," Göring went on, "how would you like it if Stalin sent an ambassador to Berlin and he greeted you with 'Long live the Communist revolution'?" After the assassination attempt on Hitler, Ribbentrop had said foolish things, Göring claimed, so "I hit him with my marshal's baton. I said, 'Shut up, Ribbentrop, you champagne peddler.' And he said, 'Remember, I am still foreign minister and my name is *von* Ribbentrop.' " Göring laughed uproariously. The way that Ribbentrop had virtually bought the noble *von* was a standing joke among the Nazis, he said.

Kelley asked if Germany had not behaved criminally by breaking foreign treaties. "Just between us," Göring said, "I considered your treaties so much toilet paper."

Göring stretched Gilbert's professional demeanor to the breaking point. Gilbert was sickened that the man had developed a following among Americans and Britishers at Nuremberg. Many of them openly admired his blunt honesty, his unapologetic admission of his acts, his pungent humor. Howard Smith, the broadcaster, had reported that Göring had become a courtroom barometer. If Göring looked up in surprise at a fact, the prosecution double-checked it for accuracy. If he nodded, the prosecution knew that the defense would not challenge the fact. If Göring shook his head, it meant the prosecution had it wrong. And the court never tried to rein him in.

Gilbert had found ways to inflict his own quiet punishments on Göring. He knew it was important to the *Reichsmarschall* to board the courtroom elevator first, so he arranged with the guards to put him on last. Gilbert also knew that Göring hated to be ogled by the spectators on his way up to the lunchroom during the midday break— Göring tried to make himself less conspicuous by walking among a knot of other prisoners—so Gilbert instructed the guards to push him out front.

20

ON DECEMBER 13, Tom Dodd again demonstrated his talent for the dramatic. Some of his diffident colleagues were scandalized that Justice Jackson had approved Dodd's approach, in what looked this time like a total retreat from the documentary strategy. The evidence that Dodd planned to introduce had been kept in paper bags by Lieutenant Barrett, chief of the documents room. Now concealed by white sheets, the exhibits rested on the prosecutors' table in the courtroom. No trace of flamboyance marked Dodd's manner today; he spoke with grim matter-of-factness. The first exhibit, he explained, was the result of an order that had gone out in 1939 from Standartenführer Karl Koch, commandant of the Buchenwald concentration camp. Koch had ordered all tattooed prisoners to report to the dispensary. Those with the most interesting and artistic tattoos were put to death by lethal injection. Dodd whisked the sheet from USA exhibit 253. The exposed, pale, leathery objects with the designs of ships and hearts still visible, Dodd said, were human skin. The Buchenwald commandant's wife, Ilse Koch, now confined here in the Nuremberg jail, liked to have the tattooed flesh tanned and fashioned into household objects like lampshades.

USA exhibit 254, Dodd explained, originated with the punishment the Nazis reserved for Poles who had sexual relations with German women. Those caught were hanged, Dodd said, pulling away the sheet from the next exhibit. From a distance it was not easy to identify the fist-size, nut-brown object. It was, Dodd explained, the head of an executed Pole, shrunken and used as a paperweight by Koch. As Dodd took his seat, the stillness in the courtroom was interrupted only by nervous coughing. To some, Tom Dodd was a grandstander. One critic described him as a "photogenic phoney," another as a "glory hound." But to others, he was a formidable prosecutor and a quick study. Give Tom the right material in court, and he would make it sing.

Justice Lawrence averted his gaze from the exhibits as he called upon the defense to cross-examine. Rudolf Dix, a sixty-one-year-old Berliner, well thought of by the judges because he had defended Germans hauled before the People's Courts in the Nazi era, had been chosen this day as defense spokesman. Dix looked shaken. He would put off his cross-examination regarding the exhibits, he said, until the next day.

Commander Jim Donovan moved to the prosecutors' stand next. Donovan requested the court's permission to show yet another film, this one only ninety seconds long, and damaged by fire. It had been taken with an eight-millimeter movie camera by an amateur SS photographer and found in a barracks near Augsburg. The film was believed to have been shot during the razing of a ghetto. The lights went out and the film flickered on the screen, its images rough but identifiable: a naked woman running out of a house, her face twisted in terror; a street strewn with bodies; a soldier dragging an old woman across the road by her hair; other soldiers standing by, idly watching. So quickly had the film passed that Donovan asked the court if he might run it again in slow motion.

That night, Janet Flanner began writing her report for *The New Yorker*: ". . . naked Jews, male and female, moving with a floating, unearthly slowness and a nightmare-like dignity among the clubs and kicks of the laughing German soldiers. . . . One thin, young Jewess was helped to her feet by an officer, so that she could be knocked down again."

The next morning, Justice Lawrence asked Rudolf Dix if he was ready to proceed with the cross-examination. Dix rose gravely, wearing a dark blue robe trimmed in burgundy, emblematic of his university, Leipzig. The exhibits seen the day before, Dix began, were undeniably horrifying. But, here in a court of law, they must confine themselves to the admissibility of evidence. Mr. Dodd had based his knowledge of USA exhibit 253, the tattoos, on an affidavit by an alleged Buchenwald inmate named Andreas Pfaffenberger. But where was this Pfaffenberger, so that Dix could cross-examine him and determine the authenticity of the exhibits? If Pfaffenberger could not be produced, the evidence should be disregarded by the court.

Kaltenbrunner's counsel, the tall, combative ex-Nazi Karl Kauffmann, sprang to his feet. In a Continental court, Kauffmann argued, the prosecutor is expected to produce evidence both favorable and unfavorable to the accused. Yet, on the matter of Standartenführer Koch, the prosecution conveniently omitted one salient fact. The Buchenwald commandant had been condemned to death by an SS court.

Subsequently, the prosecution introduced evidence demonstrating that Koch had indeed been convicted by an SS court, but not for torturing, mutilating, and murdering inmates of Buchenwald. Those acts were not crimes in the SS canon. Koch had been condemned for embezzlement of SS funds and for killing a fellow Nazi in an argument.

During the lunch break the defendants filed morosely out of the courtroom, avoiding the eyes of the curious who lined the roped-off passageway through which they had to walk. They looked forward to gazing from the attic windows of the lunchroom out over the Pegnitz Valley, but today they found that the Americans had sheathed the windows with corrugated metal. They glumly took their places at five folding metal camp tables.

Gustav Gilbert circulated among them while they ate. Ribbentrop, sitting next to Frank, asked if Hitler might have known of the terrible deeds revealed in court. "It would not have been possible otherwise," Frank answered. "They were done at his orders." Göring leaned back from a neighboring table and gave Frank a murderous look. Frank went on. "Hitler got us into this," he said, and added that the Führer had then abandoned them through suicide. Gilbert observed Göring's mounting anger. Too often, the defendants were guarded in the *Reichsmarschall*'s presence. Frank had broken ranks.

Göring rose, took Gilbert aside, and spoke confidentially. "I don't want to exaggerate my love for the Führer," he said quietly. "You know how he treated me at the end. But I think in the last year or so he just, well, he left things up to Himmler." Heinrich Himmler was indeed the most chilling figure in the Hitler entourage, a remote, self-contained enigma who had accumulated terrifying power. The death camps, the Gestapo, the *Einsatzgruppen*, all the components of terror had been in his grip. Now Himmler was conveniently dead, having taken a cyanide capsule soon after British soldiers captured him, the perfect scapegoat.

"Hitler and Himmler certainly must have had an understanding," Gilbert said. "Otherwise it would have been impossible for such horrors to happen." Göring started to explain how, in the confusion of war, details could easily have escaped Hitler's attention. Gilbert walked away.

Baldur von Schirach, creator of the Hitler Youth and *Gauleiter* of Vienna, spoke to the psychologist. "After today it's all over," he said in flawless English, "I wouldn't blame the court if they just chop off all our heads, even if a couple of us are innocent. What are a few more among the millions already murdered?" Gilbert wondered if Schirach too might be ready to stand up to Göring.

21

FOR A PROSECUTION LAWYER, getting into court was a rite of passage. Many of those at Nuremberg were in their early thirties, some still in their twenties; to be at the prosecutor's stand here was, briefly, to be at the center of the legal universe. Sam Harris's turn came a few days after Tom Dodd's presentation. Harris had come to Nuremberg via the U.S. Securities and Exchange Commission. For his day in court, he had enlisted the help of Roger Barrett from the documents room.

Barrett had found Harris intelligent, thorough, well organized. As the two men had reviewed the documents to be presented, however, Harris had appeared uncertain and ill at ease.

Justice Lawrence called the court to order. Sam Harris approached the prosecutor's stand and said with a nervous grin, "The sound you hear is my knees knocking. They haven't knocked so hard since I asked my wonderful little wife back home to marry me." The awkward silence was broken only by a loud guffaw from Hermann Göring. Justice Lawrence glared over the top of his glasses. Birkett whispered, "Unbelievable." After Harris finished his questioning and the court adjourned, Gordon Dean, the IMT press officer, begged the reporters to forget the young lawyer's gaffe. Reporting it would make a laughingstock of an able lawyer and could ruin his future.

Harris's performance provided further proof of what many of the British had come to believe about their American colleagues—that they lacked the courtroom finesse, classical education, and intellectual polish customary at the British bar. Other frictions grated as well. Justice Jackson's staff, from lawyers down to mimeograph operators, approached 700. The total British delegation at Nuremberg numbered 168. A middle-ranking American civilian lawyer earned $7,000 a year at the IMT. Sir Geoffrey Lawrence, president of the court, was paid by the British government roughly at the level of an American translator, approximately $2,800 a year.

Bizarre inequities crept into the system. A British researcher working for the Americans found herself earning more money than a British judge. The Europeans pressured the Americans to adopt two pay scales, a higher one for their own citizens and a lower scale for non-Americans. This solution created new disparities. Two interpreters would be working side by side, on the American payroll, with an American earning four times the salary of a British or French employee doing identical work. Barbara Pinion, a British researcher caught in that anomaly, liked to joke that Fritz Sauckel was not the only one at Nuremberg guilty of exploiting slave labor.

Sir Norman Birkett expressed his opinions of the Americans in his diary. The Germans may have been guilty of murdering millions, he wrote, but the Americans were guilty of murdering the English tongue. He winced at the U.S. prosecutors' constant use of "privatize, finalize, visualize, argumentation and orientation." After one particularly annoying session, Birkett wrote, "Words I never intend to use again while life lasts: concept, applicable, ideology, and contact (as a verb!)"

22

ON SUNDAY, December 16, Major Henry Gerecke, the Protestant chaplain, stopped by cell 5 to invite Göring to attend church. Of course he would go, said Göring, who never missed any chance to get out of the cell. As the guard opened the door, Göring put his hand out to the chaplain, who took it. Handshakes were against regulations, Gerecke knew, but how could he win somebody's soul if he refused to touch his hand? The chaplain felt optimistic with Göring beside him. He was keeping track, and so far, he believed, he had brought half the defendants in his charge back to Christ. He was sure that he could soon enter Göring in the "saved" column. What he hoped to hear from the defendants was a clear "Yes, I accept Christ." Those exact words were not always forthcoming, and in certain cases Gerecke had been satisfied with nothing more than a promising smile.

The chapel was two cells with the intervening wall knocked down. The cold concrete of the walls had been softened by olive drab army blankets. The altar was a crate, also covered by a blanket, and in one corner stood a wooden crucifix. A former SS colonel, who was turning state's evidence, played a small, battered organ. The men assembled in the chapel were downcast. Baldur von Schirach regularly received newspapers through his American relatives, and the news that had swept the cellblock this morning was that the Japanese general To- moyuki Yamashita, the "Tiger of Malaya," had been sentenced to death for war crimes in a Philippine court. Göring responded to the news by increasing his swagger as he marched to the front pew.

Most of the staff fled the gloom of Nuremberg on weekends; but not Gustav Gilbert. He assuaged his guilt over not returning to his family by working virtually seven days a week. This Sunday afternoon, he spoke briefly to Schacht, Sauckel, and the former foreign minister, Konstantin von Neurath. He saved the best for last, indulging his grudging fascination with Göring. Göring was asleep, as he frequently was of late—a form of escapism, Gilbert concluded. With the arrival of the psychologist, he jumped to his feet and became instantly alert.

Gilbert asked Göring to talk about his relationship to Hitler. "I just can't get it through my head that he really did those things," Göring said. Gilbert thought he meant the horrors committed in Hitler's name. Then he realized that Göring was talking about how hateful Hitler had been to *him*. His troubles began, Göring said, with the famous boast he made while touring the air defenses of the Ruhr and the Rhineland—that if any enemy plane got through, you could call him Meir. On the night of May 30, 1942, 150 British bombers hammered Cologne. Göring, off disporting himself at one of his castles, had been summoned by the Führer. Hitler had pointedly refused Göring's hand on the *Reichmarschall*'s arrival, humiliating him in front of other Luftwaffe officers. "The Führer would scream about the inefficiency of the Luftwaffe with such contempt and viciousness that I would actually blush and squirm and would have preferred to go to the front to avoid these scenes," Göring told the psychologist. The raids went on. Over 250 British bombers struck Berlin, destroying twenty thousand homes and killing seven hundred people in a single raid. Soon the Americans were coming by day and the British by night, a thousand bombers at once blackening the sky, until an astonishing portion of urban Germany had turned to rubble.

Enemy aviators who destroyed homes, women, and children were not soldiers, Hitler had told Göring. They were terrorists. He ordered that Allied crews bailing out of downed aircraft be shot. Göring tried to explain that if Germany did that, the Allies would reciprocate. "I see," Hitler observed. "The Luftwaffe operates on the mutual life insurance policy. You don't hurt me and I don't hurt you."

But wasn't Göring just as hard and cruel as Hitler? Gilbert asked. What about the Röhm purge? Ernst Röhm, head of the SA, the storm troopers, had taken seriously the "socialism" in National Socialism. Röhm wanted to break the Prussian aristocracy and swallow up its army into his populist Brownshirts, so called for the mud-colored uniforms they wore. The Junkers, the Prussian militarists, had let Hitler know that if he would crush these "leftist" Nazis, he could have the army's support.

Göring hated Röhm, he told Gilbert. Röhm had accused Hitler of betraying Nazism by tolerating a corrupt reactionary like Göring.

Röhm publicly referred to Göring as "Herr Reaktion." In 1934, Göring, by then heading the Prussian police, retaliated with a vengeance. He persuaded Hitler that Röhm was plotting to overthrow him. He drew up for Hitler a list of the most disloyal Brownshirts. He showed Hitler pictures of Röhm and his SA lovers caught in their homosexual pleasures, disgracing the manly code of Nazism.

On June 30, carrying Göring's list, Hitler flew to Munich and tracked Röhm to a sanitarium where he was reportedly involved in a tryst. While Hitler's gunmen eliminated the suspect Brownshirts, including Röhm, Göring was in Berlin leading a police team to SA headquarters. He went from room to room saying, "Arrest him, and him . . . no, not him." Thirty-two Brownshirts were taken away and shot on Göring's orders. The leader of the German nation and the chief of the Prussian police had simply rounded up their political opponents and killed them. No charges had been made, no trial held, no evidence presented, and no objections raised.

Gilbert asked Göring if the killings of Röhm and the others had not been murder. Göring jumped to his feet. "Now, there was a clique of perverted bloody revolutionists. They are the ones who first made the party look like a pack of hoodlums with their wild orgies and beating Jews on the street and smashing windows. . . . They were bent on wiping out the whole general's corps, the whole party leadership, all the Jews, of course, in one grand bloodbath. . . . It's a damned good thing I wiped them out, or they would have wiped us out."

Wasn't it odd, Gilbert said, that Hitler had had to build his organization out of a bunch of hoodlums like the SA? Göring started to defend Hitler, when there was a tapping at the cell door. The guard said that it was time for supper. Gilbert glanced at his watch. He had been with Göring for two and a half hours. "We'll have plenty of time to talk these things over before the verdict," he said.

"Death sentence, you mean," Göring said glumly. "Death doesn't bother me, but my reputation in history does. That's why I'm glad Dönitz got stuck with signing the surrender . . . a country never thinks well of its leaders who accept defeat. As for death? Hell, I haven't been afraid of death since I was twelve years old."

23

THE MORNING OF DECEMBER 20 was bitter cold. Secretaries and prosecutors, translators and journalists, their breath visible in the air, filed
into the courthouse. They gratefully entered the building, well heated
by the U.S. military government. The more compassionate among
them wondered how the Nurembergers they had passed that morning
on Furtherstrasse, heads bent against the blustering wind, were getting
by in the coldest European winter in living memory. Snow had begun
falling in November and had stayed on the ground as temperatures at
times hovered barely above zero.

Two days before, the prosecution had begun the most novel part
of the original Bernays plan—the attempt to prove that seven organizations were criminal: the Nazi party leadership, the Reich cabinet,
the SS, the Gestapo, the SD (an intelligence and clandestine operations agency), the SA, and the High Command. The Americans alone
held some 200,000 potential war criminals, and individual trials of so
many were impractical. Thus, Jackson had seized on the concept of
group guilt. If the organizations they served could be proved criminal,
then the members would automatically be guilty.

Not until this new phase of the trials did an indifferent German
public wake up to what was happening at Nuremberg. The Allied
Control Council, the four-power body that governed occupied Germany, had issued Edict 10, making clear that any member of an organization found criminal would be subject to penalties ranging up to
death. Four and a half million Germans had belonged to the SA alone.
Membership in the SS numbered in the hundreds of thousands. Potentially, half the families in Germany had members who would be
touched by Edict 10. Letters poured into the Palace of Justice from
POWs, wives, mothers, fathers, and children until by the end of December they averaged two thousand a day. One day, five thousand
letters arrived. The message was virtually unchanging: Franz or Dieter
or Klaus was not a criminal, but merely a guard, or a clerk, or a cook,
doing his duty.

The organization case had an unexpected effect. Robert Kempner, head of the Defense Rebuttal Section, had surveyed Germans of
all classes and found near unanimity. They wanted the defendants

convicted and punished. As Kempner wrote to Jackson, "If the leaders are found guilty then the onus of guilt is removed from those who merely did their bidding."

The issue on the docket this morning, as Justice Lawrence called the court to order, was the role of the SS in conducting "medical" experiments for Göring's Luftwaffe. The Luftwaffe had faced a problem. Pilots shot down over the North Sea had often survived the crash into the frigid waters, only to die later in lifeboats after being rescued. The problem had been brought to the attention of Dr. Sigmund Rascher, a professor of aviation medicine, who worked out of a secret "laboratory" at Dachau.

A British prosecutor read the affidavit of a Dachau inmate named Anton Pachelogg, according to whom Dr. Rascher ordered inmates dropped naked into water tanks. Chunks of ice were then added until the water approached freezing. Thermometers were thrust into the often unconscious subjects' rectums to determine if they were properly chilled. The inmates were then plunged into hot water, warm water, or tepid water, or warmed by the bodies of naked female inmates, to see which method would best revive a freezing human being. The prosecutor read from Dr. Rascher's meticulously kept records: "It was evident that rapid rewarming was in all cases preferable to a slow rewarming because, after removal from the cold water, the body temperature continued to drop rapidly. Therefore rewarming by animal warmth or women would be too slow." Dr. Rascher added that most of the subjects of his research went into convulsions and died.

As the testimony ended, Justice Lawrence announced that court would adjourn and resume twelve days later, on January 2, 1946, after a Christmas holiday.

Justice Jackson threw a Christmas party at the house on Lindenstrasse principally for the judges, lawyers, and a few secretaries. The Russians, however, had pressed hard for an invitation for a man identified as I. V. Rasumov, carried on the Soviet roster as chief of the Russian Translations Division. From the instant the Soviet delegation arrived, his countrymen displayed unusual deference to Comrade Rasumov, who played the piano and told dreadful jokes.

General Nikitchenko stood next to Birkett, by now his good friend, joining in the group singing. The Russian was tipsy, as he usually was at parties. His ordinarily grim-set mouth was upturned in a smile as he kept time with a waving glass. Birkett had long since concluded that Nikitchenko was a decent chap and a covert liberal, but a man imprisoned behind the ideological bars of the regime he served.

Mrs. Douglas took over the piano and started to play "Silent Night." Glasses stopped tinkling and conversation faded as a short, blond Russian officer with a bell-like baritone began singing, "*Stille Nacht, heilige Nacht. Alles schläft, einsam wacht . . .*" Jackson looked out happily over the faces of his guests. The camaraderie with the Russians pleased him. Outside this oasis of harmony, relations between East and West in Nuremberg had become increasingly chilled. The GIs posted here now were youths who had not fought against Nazism. The Nurembergers told them about their sons killed fighting Communists on the Russian front and of the atrocities committed by the Red Army, the mass rape of German women in the Soviet sector. The young GIs were sympathetic. They liked these people. They were so tidy, so hardworking, so honest, just like the folks back home. The Russians, by contrast, were foreign, incomprehensible to boys from Ohio and Tennessee.

As the last notes of "Silent Night" faded, Comrade Rasumov gave an unobtrusive hand signal and the Russian guests left in a body. At least, Jackson thought, now they knew who ran the Soviet secret police in Nuremberg.

Francis Biddle resented that he had not yet been able to arrange to have his wife join him. Bob Jackson refused to buck the army's ban on spouses. Why should the brass and VIPs enjoy a privilege that occupation officials could not provide to thousands of married GIs? the army's reasoning went. Biddle was convinced, however, that personal rather than democratic impulses explained Jackson's acquiescence. Bob obviously did not want his wife there, since he had, in his secretary, all the companionship he desired. Inflaming Biddle's sense of the arbitrariness of it all was the fact that the British and French felt themselves unbound by U.S. Army restrictions. Chief Justice Lawrence's handsome, statuesque wife sat in court every day.

24

HANS FRANK SAT at his table, puffing his pipe and reading a letter. He had taken to wearing a glove while in court. But now the glove lay on the table, revealing a left hand starting to shrivel from nerve damage caused when he had slashed his wrist. In the old days, when confronted with unpleasantness, he had played the piano. Now he conjured the music—chamber pieces, whole oratorios, even symphonies—in the auditorium of his mind. The particular unpleasantness he was seeking to drive off today was news contained in a letter from his wife, Brigitte. All their homes had been confiscated, and she was desperately trying to find a place to live. She had had to send their two youngest children out into the street to beg. Minister of justice at thirty, Frank thought, governor-general of Poland at thirty-nine, jailbird and father of homeless beggars at forty-five.

He heard a tapping at the cell door. It was Gilbert. Frank quickly pulled the glove on. Gilbert came in and Frank stood at attention. Frank told Gilbert how grateful he was that he and the Catholic chaplain, Sixtus O'Connor, came to see him. If you could say "virgin" about a man without being facetious, that man was Father Sixtus, Frank said, "so delicate, so sympathetic, so maidenly, you know what I mean." Though Gilbert found Frank much too glib, he was coming around to believe that his religious reawakening and his remorse were sincere.

Göring had been after him lately, Frank said. "The fat one is sore because I turned in those forty volumes of my diaries. 'Why didn't you burn them?' he scolded me." But, Frank went on, he had heard the voice of Christ telling him, "You cannot hide the truth from God." And so he had given the diaries to the Americans, he told Gilbert—handily ignoring his original motive, his belief that their contents would exonerate him. The fat one had also attacked him for saying at lunch the other day that Hitler must have known of the atrocities. Gilbert nodded sympathetically. Any defendant standing up to Göring had to be encouraged.

It was torture, Frank told Gilbert, to sit through the trial and hear Germany's sins bared before the world. "The shame is devastating," he said. Here in court he saw such admirable figures, Justice

Lawrence and the American prosecutor, Jackson. "They sit on one side, and I sit among repulsive characters like Streicher, Göring, Ribbentrop."

How could he have been part of such an apparatus? Gilbert asked. "I don't know," Frank answered. "I can hardly understand it myself. There must be some basic evil in me. In all men. Mass hypnosis? Hitler cultivated this evil in man. When I saw him in that movie in court, I was swept along again for a moment, in spite of myself. Funny, one sits in court feeling guilt and shame. Then Hitler appears on the screen and you want to stretch out your hand to him. . . . It's not with horns on his head or with a forked tail that the devil comes to us, you know," Frank said. "He comes with a captivating smile, spouting idealistic sentiments, winning one's loyalty. We cannot say that Adolf Hitler violated the German people. He seduced us."

Was he still having troublesome dreams? Gilbert asked, alluding to Frank's earlier confessions of nocturnal emissions involving dreams of his daughter. That had ended, Frank said. In his latest dream he was conducting a Bach violin concerto. As Gilbert rose to leave, Frank added with a bitter smile, "*Mitgegangen, mitgefangen, mitgehangen* [We sinned together, we fell together, we'll hang together]."

With Gilbert gone, Frank picked up the autobiography he had begun writing. His lawyer's mind could fix the exact point at which an ambitious but basically decent man became an ambitious, corrupt man. It had been in 1934, during the Röhm purge—*Nacht der langen Messer*, the night of the long knives. He was then minister of justice for Bavaria and had received a call from the jailer at Stadelheim prison informing him that SS men were filling the cells with storm troopers, including Ernst Röhm, the SA chief. Frank rushed to the prison and went directly to Röhm's cell. Röhm had no need to fear the SS, Frank assured him. "Remember, Ernst, you are in my palace of justice."

Sepp Dietrich, a high-ranking SS officer close to Hitler, arrived at the prison and informed Frank that these men had been denounced personally by the Führer and were to be shot at once. Frank refused to release the prisoners. An angry Dietrich phoned Hitler at the Brown House, the party headquarters in Munich. He handed the phone to Frank. Hitler's voice shattered Frank's ear. "I decide the fate of criminals in the Reich, not you!" he shouted. But these were men who had marched with them in '23, party fighters whom he had defended in court, Frank argued. They had been dragged out of bed and thrown into jail with no charges placed against them. "I am a man of the law," Frank said. "You don't shoot 110 men without a trial." The conversation ended with Frank believing he had won. Then, the phone rang again. It was Rudolf Hess calling this time. The Führer had relented, Hess reported. Of the 110 men, only 19 were to be shot. On what grounds? Frank wanted to know. The Führer was getting impatient with this foot-dragging, Hess warned.

The price of standing by his principles would be exorbitant, Frank recognized—his position, the servants, the limousines, his several homes, the twin narcotics of power and wealth. In the end, he turned over the prisoners, including Ernst Röhm, to their SS executioners. "All revolutions devour their own children," Röhm had warned Frank on the way to his death. When the shots rang out that day, Hans Frank found himself defined. He was more Nazi than jurist. Hitler had known his man.

Frank finished the passage in his autobiography and glanced again at the letter from his wife. He returned the latter to the smoking-tobacco tin which he used as a file box. He needed to lift the pall of despair settling over him. The guard heard him humming Beethoven's "Ode to Joy."

25

COLONEL ANDRUS INFORMED his staff that the defendants were to be treated no differently on Christmas Day than on any other day. There would be no special meals served. Most certainly there was to be no exchange of gifts. However, since it might be their last Christmas, he would allow religious services. That was a damn sight more consideration than they had ever shown their victims, he noted.

On Christmas Eve, in the chapel, thirteen Protestant defendants listened to Chaplain Gerecke read the Gospel According to Saint Luke in his low German. His knowledge of the language had been acquired from uneducated immigrant parents. It was as if a Kentucky mountaineer were reading the Bible to the British cabinet. His lack of sophistication, however, did not matter. Since his arrival, the clergyman had won over his strange flock. Major Gerecke did not judge them; that was what they appreciated. He wanted only to reclaim their souls, an objective most of them increasingly shared. As the organist began playing *"O du Fröhliche, O du Heilige,"* they joined Gerecke in subdued voices, except for Göring, who belted out the song.

Before Major Kelley slipped away for the Christmas break, he and Gus Gilbert talked about their book. They were onto something big, Kelley said. He confided that he had received a request from the U.S. surgeon general, who wanted to study the brains of the defendants after they were executed. That request had been followed by an appeal from a group of New York psychiatrists, who wanted to interview the defendants. On Kelley's recommendation, Justice Jackson had turned down both requests. He and Gilbert had the field to themselves. They were going to produce, Kelley said, a magnum opus. Sometimes the arrangement seemed a bit lopsided to Gilbert. He was monitoring the defendants in the dock and during their lunch break, and making most of the cell visits. Kelley received a copy of every note Gilbert took after his talks with the defendants. Yet it was Kelley who was going away for the holidays while Gilbert continued to work.

Field Marshal Keitel was on Gilbert's Christmas Day rounds. The psychologist had learned from Tom Dodd, the prosecutor, that a remorseful Keitel had recently considered pleading guilty, but Göring had bullied him out of it. The old soldier, Gilbert thought, might need some spine-stiffening.

Keitel stood at rigid attention, as if he were meeting Bismarck rather than a U.S. Army captain. "I thank you from the bottom of my heart for this Christmas visit," Keitel said. "You are the only one I can really talk to." Gilbert noted Keitel's Christmas dinner, the tin mess kit containing remnants of corned beef hash, potatoes, and cabbage, which the prisoners were required to eat with a spoon. The conversation drifted to Hitler's wrongheadedness in attacking the Soviet Union in the summer of 1941. He himself had been convinced that the invasion was a blunder, Keitel said. Had he made this opinion known to Hitler? Gilbert asked. Keitel was silent.

What interested Gilbert most was not Keitel's views on military strategy, but how a member of a caste steeped in a code of honor could have drafted instruments like the Commando and Reprisal orders. In France alone, nearly thirty thousand innocent people had been shot under the latter order. Cruelest of all was *Nacht und Nebel*, the "Night and Fog" decree, intended to terrorize resistance movements. Suspects were arrested in the middle of the night and never heard of again. They were secretly shot and their families never learned their fate. As Hitler liked to put it, "They disappeared into the night and fog." Keitel had issued the *Nacht und Nebel* order.

"I am dying of shame," Keitel told Gilbert. "I only wish I had spent more time in the field. I spent too much time in Hitler's company. Please let me talk to you once in a while, as long as I am not yet a sentenced criminal," Keitel pleaded, as Gilbert rose to leave. Snapping to attention, the old soldier wished Gilbert a happy Christmas. In a sense, Gilbert pitied Keitel. He had behaved criminally, thinking he was behaving correctly. Now, with that illusion stripped away and the true nature of his acts clear to him, his mediocre mind lacked even the solace of rationalization. He stood naked before his sins.

Not so with the next soldier on Gilbert's visiting list. He agreed with Kelley that General Jodl was their most impenetrable case. The guards called Jodl "Happy Hooligan" after the sad-faced comic-strip character of the time. The gibe was on target, Gilbert thought as he entered Jodl's cell. The general was sitting erect at his desk, his face pinched, his nose a veined strawberry, his complexion blotchy, his cold blue eyes peering at nothing. He stood and clicked his heels. Gilbert was reminded again of what a small man Jodl was physically.

Gilbert asked Jodl how men of honor could have signed such brutal orders? Jodl answered that the prosecution's naïveté surprised him. All this documentary evidence with his and Keitel's initials on it meant nothing. When a directive to the armed forces began "The Führer has ordered . . . ," it meant that the command had been given orally by Hitler and that he and Keitel had merely committed it to paper, not invented it. They were little more than errand boys. If a military order is given to a lieutenant, Jodl went on, does he have the right and responsibility to say, "Just a minute, Captain, I have to consult the Hague Convention on Land Warfare to see if I am allowed to carry it out"? Their relationship to Hitler was no different. "And if we had disobeyed, we should have been arrested, and rightly so," Jodl observed.

Gilbert argued that without the acquiescence of the generals, Hitler could never have waged war. That was true, Jodl agreed. Equally true, if the infantryman did not march, if no arms maker supplied weapons, if the cooks did not cook, there would be no war. Is the soldier, the gunsmith, the cook therefore guilty of committing aggression? "I don't know how you people can fail to recognize a simple fact," Jodl concluded. "A soldier's obligation is to obey orders. That's the code I've lived by all my life."

Gilbert asked about what went on in the death camps. He had no idea about ninety percent of it, Jodl said. "It's impossible for me to understand what kind of beasts could have been in charge of the camps and actually have done those things."

Gilbert got up to leave. "Germans, obeying orders, no doubt," he said.

26

THE "WHY" STILL GNAWED at Gus Gilbert after every cell visit. They were not dealing with the denizens of some savage society. Hans Frank could spout yards of Schiller. Speer could move comfortably at any social level. Seyss-Inquart was a man of powerful intellect. Frick was trained in the law. It would be hard to pick out most of these men as war criminals from a gathering of Rotarians or accountants. If he and Kelley could not ultimately explain their behavior, then all they could present to the world in their book would be the riddle, but not the key.

Gilbert had learned that thirty-nine SS men were being held in the former concentration camp at Dachau awaiting execution after having been convicted by an American military court. The Nazi defendants at Nuremberg were able to put a protective layer of distance between themselves and the actual crimes committed. None of them had shoved anyone into a gas chamber, shot a prisoner in the neck, or injected a human guinea pig with a lethal drug. The men at Dachau, by contrast, were the journeymen of the death trade. One of them, whom Gilbert had read about, a former pastry chef named Mussfeld, had killed twenty thousand people—not supervised their killing, but killed them all by his own hand. By studying these men firsthand,

Gilbert thought, he might better understand the murderous impulses of Nazism. And so he arranged to spend part of the Christmas break at Dachau.

On his arrival, he found a sanitized charnel house where the U.S. Army now ran guided tours. Gilbert remembered stories he had heard. When the crematoria were turned on, the gas in nearby homes had gone down. Ashes spewing from Dachau's chimneys settled over the landscape for miles around. People said they had no idea what the source was.

Gilbert interviewed and administered intelligence tests to twenty of the condemned men. Their IQs, he found, averaged 107, in the "dull normal" range. Many, he learned, had been unemployed before Hitler became chancellor. After they had experienced powerlessness, the opportunity to dominate others had enormous appeal to them. What dismayed Gilbert most was their self-pity. They had simply carried out their assignments as ordered, and Heinrich Himmler, escaping via suicide, had left them holding the bag.

Two days later, Gilbert boarded a train back to Nuremberg, feeling emotionally exhausted. As the train rolled north through soft, rolling hills, the flurry of impressions began sorting themselves out. He believed that he now understood at least one piece of the puzzle. Every one of the condemned men at Dachau had confirmed it. Germany was a society where people did what they were told. You obeyed your parents, your teachers, your clergymen, your employer, your superior officer, your government officials. The German was raised from childhood in a world of unquestioning submission to authority. This compulsion to obey explained part of the riddle of "why." To produce a Dachau, an Auschwitz, a Buchenwald, required not a few sadists, but hundreds, even thousands of unquestioning, obedient people.

That explanation would account for the dull-normal minions at Dachau, but what about the sophisticated defendants at Nuremberg? One of the condemned SS men had complained to Gilbert, "We didn't dare oppose the orders of the Führer or Himmler." The excuses of the workaday killers and those of the men on cellblock C were identical.

27

ONE MORNING AFTER CHRISTMAS, Albert Speer lay on his cot staring at cracked walls covered with flowing figures and animals he had sketched with a piece of soft coal given him by a guard. Speer and Streicher had emerged as the two cellblock artists. He rose, went to the square porthole, and asked the guard to inform the colonel's office that defendant Speer would like to meet with Dr. Flächsner, his defense counsel. Speer operated at Nuremberg on a modified version of the old saw that says, "Treat a lady like a whore, and a whore like a lady." He treated everyone with courtesy. It worked. None of the guards called Speer by the derisive nicknames reserved for the others. He was always "Mr. Speer" or "Herr Speer."

Speer faced his current situation precisely as he would have handled a production bottleneck or a steel shortage in the old days. The goal of his survival was to be pursued by rational analysis, by breaking the task down into its component parts. Where was he now? Where did he want to be? And what actions must he take to get there? His last strategy, trying to trade his technical knowledge for preferential treatment, had failed when Jackson turned it down. He had to find an alternative. That was why he wanted Flächsner.

Albert Speer had always found intellectual beauty in the technical, the logical, the mechanical. His most vivid childhood memory was of being allowed to sit behind the wheel of the family's limousine, pretending to drive. Of this moment he later wrote, "I experienced the first sensations of technical intoxication in a world that was still scarcely technical."

The automobile was of a piece with the rest of the world that Albert Speer had been born into in 1905. The Speers were a leading family in Mannheim. Albert's father and grandfather before him had been architects. Speer grew up in a fourteen-room apartment furnished in the French style, attended by butlers, maids, and a chauffeur in purple livery. When he was thirteen, a fortune-teller at a fair predicted that he would win fame and retire early. He had never been entirely able to drive the seer's prediction from his mind.

One day in 1931, while Speer was teaching architecture at the

Institute of Technology in Berlin, his students urged him to come to a lecture. They proceeded to a shabby room over a workingmen's beer hall. Speer expected a roughneck demagogue. Instead, he found himself entranced by Adolf Hitler. The next day, he joined the Nazi party.

He subsequently returned to Mannheim and set up his own architectural practice. Not much business came his way in those depression years. He entered competitions, yet never placed better than third. Then, through party connections, he won a commission to design a Nazi district headquarters. Hitler, by now chancellor, found the work impressive. He chose Speer to stage the Nuremberg party rally of 1933. Speer was next asked to build the Reich Chancellery and Hitler's private residence in Berlin. During work on the Berlin commissions, the Führer invited Speer to join him for dinner one evening with other party leaders. Speer, covered with dust, begged off. Nonsense, Hitler said, and sent his valet to fetch clothes for the architect. That evening, the status-conscious Göring stared curiously. There, next to Hitler, sat an unknown young man, wearing the Führer's blue blazer with the gold party badge.

Speer became Hitler's personal architect, closeted alone for hours with the most powerful man in Europe. He sat next to Hitler at the theater and dined with him in the best restaurants—heady stuff for a man just twenty-eight. To Hitler, Speer reflected what he saw in himself, but in none of the party philistines: the soul of an artist. Hitler once told the architect that he wanted a massive grandstand built at Nuremberg's Zeppelin Field, where an old streetcar depot now stood. As the depot came down, Speer noticed how poorly modern construction lent itself to noble ruins. Ugly, rusted, twisted reinforcement rods protruded from the broken cement. Speer came to Hitler with an idea. He was going to build "ruin value" into the grandstand. He made sketches showing how the structure would look in a thousand years, crumbling but dignified. It was the sort of vision Hitler prized.

As for Speer, he occasionally glimpsed the dark side of his new master; but he was, by his own admission, "intoxicated by the desire to wield pure power, to order people to do this or that, to spend billions." Hitler made it all possible—the Führer as Ludovico Sforza, Speer as his da Vinci.

If Hitler could be described as having a friend, that friend was Albert Speer. After Speer completed the Reich Chancellery, Hitler took him into his office and shyly presented him with a gift, a water-color of a Gothic church that Hitler had painted in Vienna in 1909. Speer was flattered by the gesture, but appalled by the painting. It was, he later wrote, "precise, patient, and pedantic. Not a stroke had any life."

Speer recalled those early years with Hitler as the romantic chapter. The realistic phase began with unexpected suddenness on February 8, 1942. Speer had gone to the Wolf's Lair, the Führer's East Prussian headquarters at Rastenburg, to discuss building plans. Also present was the armaments minister, Dr. Fritz Todt. Speer intended to fly back to Berlin with Todt the next morning, but Hitler kept him up until two a.m. with a rambling monologue on the degeneracy of modern art. Speer decided to skip the flight and sleep in.

He was awakened by a jangling phone. Hitler's physician, Dr. Karl Brandt, informed Speer that Dr. Todt had been killed in a plane crash. Before the day was out, Hitler appointed Speer as Todt's successor. As minister of armaments and chief of construction, he immediately found himself in control of 2.6 million workers. As he later absorbed the naval production program, he directed 3.2 million workers. By the time he wrested aircraft production from Göring and became minister of the economy, 12 million Germans and foreigners worked under Speer. By age thirty-eight, he had fulfilled half of the fortune-teller's prophecy.

To run a country's arsenal was, by itself, no war crime. But at Nuremberg Speer might have to explain actions less easily defended. In December 1943, he had visited a plant carved out of the Harz Mountains, the manufacturing site of Germany's secret rocket weapon, the V-2. The dank limestone caverns held over fifty thousand slave laborers. Once these workers entered the caves, they remained for three months, working seventy-two hours a week, fed a daily diet of eleven hundred calories. Sanitation facilities and housing barely existed. Because of the dampness and air pressure, the workers' muscle and bone tissue deteriorated quickly. Some spaces were so low that the men worked stooped over until they could no longer stand up straight. Deaths in the plant averaged 180 a day.

Speer was appalled. Following the visit, he wrote a report that this kind of work imposed intolerable emotional strains on the SS guards who had to drive these workers. Some of the guards' nerves became so shattered that they had to be sent away from time to time.

Speer also visited the Mauthausen extermination camp, where prisoners hauled stones out of the quarry up 186 steps until they dropped dead of exhaustion. He had already explained to his American interrogators that he had gone there to inspect a site for a new railhead and had seen only a small part of the camp. He had witnessed no atrocities.

Hardest to explain away, he knew, would be his relationship with Heinrich Himmler. As procurement of workers became more difficult, Speer had gone to Himmler, who controlled hundreds of thousands of people in the concentration camps. In October 1943, both men were speakers at a meeting in Posen of Nazi party officials—*Gauleiters* running regions, and *Reichsleiters* with national posts. Speer threw the fear of God into the party functionaries. When it came to producing manpower, he said, he was not going to tolerate any obstructionism. "I have spoken to Reichsführer Himmler," Speer warned, "and from now on I shall deal firmly with districts that do not carry out these measures."

Then it was Himmler's turn to speak. The bespectacled, chinless *Reichsführer* told the *Gauleiters* that he wanted them to understand the crushing burden he and his SS carried. It was easy enough to say "the Jews must be exterminated," he said. But what did that mean to the poor rank and file who had to do the job? "I ask you only never to talk about what I tell you in this circle," he went on. "When the question arose, what should be done with the women and children, I decided to adopt a clear solution. I did not feel justified in exterminating the men, while allowing their children to grow up to avenge themselves on our sons and grandchildren. The hard decision had to be taken. These people must disappear from the face of the earth." Speer told the Allies that he had somehow missed this speech. Whether this was true or not, his interrogators found it inconceivable that its message had not reached his ears.

One of Himmler's lieutenants described Speer's demands for labor as "insatiable." In the spring of 1944, he asked for 400,000 workers from Auschwitz. Speer could hardly disclaim knowledge of the nature of the camp. Earlier, a friend, Karl Hanke, the *Gauleiter* of Lower Silesia, had warned him. He had seen death in battle, Hanke said, but never had he witnessed anything to compare with Auschwitz.

Speer should never accept an invitation to go there. Speer had not pressed for details.

His captivity had given Speer abundant time to examine how a man of his cultivation, of his station and advantages, had slipped into this moral ditch. His conscience, he concluded, had been elbowed aside in the desperate arms race he was running against the Allies. His fixation on production blurred all human feeling. The sight of people suffering affected his emotions but did not influence his conduct. He was, he admitted to himself, fonder of machines than of people.

Defending his behavior as munitions chief was near impossible, he knew. His salvation, he was convinced, lay in his actions during the last months of the war. Toward the end, Hitler had issued an order that stunned Speer. With the Allied armies advancing into Germany, Hitler had directed that everything in their path be destroyed—every factory, bridge, power plant, road, and mine. The Allies were to conquer nothing but ashes. Hitler told Speer, "If the war is lost, the people are lost too. It is not necessary to worry about the fundamentals that the people will need for a primitive future existence. On the contrary, it would be better to destroy these things. The German people have shown themselves weaker and the future belongs to the stronger peoples of the East. Those who survive the war will, in any event, be only the inferior. The best have fallen." In his scorched-earth order, Hitler had finally and fully revealed his maniacal nature to Speer.

The war was indeed lost, and Speer's practical mind was already on postwar Germany. He was a scion of the industrialist class, and he feared a long, dark, primeval night if the country's industrial base were destroyed. Hitler's dictum had to be undone. On his own authority, Speer ordered high explosives, supposed to be used for blowing up iron and coal mines, to be hidden. He had pistols issued to factory workers to defend their plants. He arranged for orders to be sent to the armed forces, directing that rail lines and bridges not be destroyed. In the meantime, he begged Hitler to rescind this policy of national suicide. By late March, he had made some headway. He persuaded Hitler that only military considerations should determine which facilities would be blown up. On April 10, Speer wrote a speech revealing the hard truth to the German people. The war was lost. No fresh armies, no miracle weapons were going to save them. They were to destroy nothing vital to rebuilding the nation. He was waiting only for the right moment, he told himself, to deliver the address over the radio.

Still, for all his disillusionment, Speer had felt an overpowering urge to see the Führer one last time. He braved Allied strafing and Russian artillery to fly into besieged Berlin, landing near the Brandenburg tower in a moth-like reconnaissance plane. He made it to the Führerbunker as Russian shells were slamming into the Reich Chancellery that he had built. Hitler kept him waiting until three a.m. Finally, in the Führer's private quarters, Speer had his farewell visit. He complimented Hitler on his decision to stay in Berlin. History emphasizes the last act, Speer observed, and the Führer's denouement in Berlin would be judged as heroic. Hitler displayed no interest in anything Speer said. The visit ended with Hitler examining Speer with cold, protuberant eyes, then extending a limp hand. He expressed no gratitude for what Speer had done for Germany, no good wishes for his family. All that he said in a barely audible voice was, "So you're leaving. Good. *Auf Wiedersehen.*"

As he fled Berlin, Speer was convinced that Hitler would soon be dead, probably by his own hand. He headed for the next most powerful Nazi, Heinrich Himmler, who was holed up in a hospital in Hohenlychen, about sixty miles north of Berlin. A few days later, Speer learned that the Führer had died, bypassing all likely heirs and naming Dönitz as successor. At the news he wept. Speer then headed for Plön, where Dönitz had temporarily set up his government. There, the admiral named Speer minister of economics and production. The government moved to Flensburg, where Speer found himself a player in the tragicomic death scene of Nazi Germany. While there, he kept a plane standing by to whisk him off to Greenland, if that seemed desirable. Instead, when the Allies came on May 24, he was arrested.

To the very end, he had been unable to turn his back on Hitler. And he had never found the right moment to deliver his brave the-war-is-lost speech to the German people.

At three p.m., the escort guard took Speer to the visitors' room, where Flächsner was waiting behind the wire mesh. Speer spoke quietly, guiding his lawyer through his defense strategy—how, for example, they should play the mistreatment of conscript workers and the visit to the death camp. Understatement and contrition were to be the watchwords. He had one strong, persuasive case that Flächsner must hammer at: Here was a man who stood up to Hitler and his diabolic orders, fully aware that others had been shot for just such disobedience. The judges must see him as a man who risked his life to salvage his nation's future. And he had an even more compelling story to tell. Speer's voice dropped to a whisper. Did Flächsner know that Speer had once tried to assassinate Hitler?

28

To THE MEN ON CELLBLOCK C, New Year's Day was indistinguishable from all others. As Dr. Pfluecker made his daily rounds, Joachim von Ribbentrop pestered the old physician with questions he could not answer. How soon before the prosecution rested its case? When would the defense start? Should he mention the secret protocol he had arranged with the Soviet Union in 1939? Would that risk turning the Russian judges against him? Did Pfluecker think he had a good lawyer? Ribbentrop also asked the doctor why he was always tired. Pfluecker was not surprised. This insomniac never fell asleep before three a.m. and was awake by six. Pfluecker had given him sleeping pills, but Ribbentrop complained that the pills were destroying his mind.

Would the doctor please tell Colonel Andrus that he needed Fräulein Blank again? Ribbentrop said. His former secretary, Margarete Blank, was a prisoner in the women's wing, being held as a material witness. The month before, Ribbentrop had pleaded that he needed her to take dictation. How could he be expected to write out eight years of German foreign policy with a pad and pencil? The colonel had arranged to have Fräulein Blank brought down to Ribbentrop's cluttered cell; but Ribbentrop had abruptly dismissed her without explanation a few hours later. Now he needed her again. Ribbentrop's nickname among the prison staff was "the Mad Hatter."

When Dr. Pfluecker got up to leave, Ribbentrop barely noticed. He was too busy rummaging through the documents that littered his cell, desperate to find something proving the secret protocols he had engineered with Stalin. The pact with the Soviet Union had marked the acme of his career. It was one of the rare times that he had been able to sell Hitler on a foreign policy. The idea had struck Ribbentrop in March 1939, while he was reading a speech by Stalin in which the Soviet dictator maintained that he did not intend to pull the capitalists' chestnuts out of the fire. Ribbentrop read this line as a slap at Great Britain and France. He approached Hitler with the unthinkable—that the Nazis and the Communists might find common ground. Less than five months later, the pact that jolted the world was signed. Germany and the Soviet Union agreed on the spheres where each would dominate, and Stalin, in effect, gave Hitler the green light for the invasion of Poland.

How close Ribbentrop had come to missing his eminent role in the Third Reich. He might as easily have become a concert violinist. He had shown great musical promise as a child. He might have become a Canadian citizen. At age seventeen, he had emigrated to Canada to seek his fortune and only returned home when Germany went to war in 1914. He won a commission, and afterward courted Anneliese Henkell, daughter of a champagne magnate. He went to work as a salesman for his in-laws and benefited from his one genuine talent, a knack for languages, which served him well in foreign markets. When he was thirty-two, he had himself adopted by an aunt whose husband had been knighted. Thus, plain old Joachim Ribbentrop became Joachim von Ribbentrop.

He had not entered Hitler's orbit until 1932, when he managed to get an appointment with the rising political star. His qualifications to be foreign minister of a great nation were slender to invisible. Ribbentrop's formal schooling had ended at age sixteen. Yet, in a dazzling display of name-dropping, he persuaded Hitler that he knew all the best people in Europe. Göring took an instant dislike to the upstart. Hitler insisted that Ribbentrop could be invaluable since he knew Lord so-and-so and Lady so-and-so. Göring replied that it was true. Unfortunately, they all knew Ribbentrop.

Göring had spotted Ribbentrop for what he was, a parvenu whose intelligence was no match for his ambition. When Göring learned that Hitler intended to appoint this "champagne salesman" to a high diplomatic post, he urged Hitler to make it Rome. Any Nazi could get by in that sister fascist state. Instead, Hitler sent Ribbentrop to the Court of Saint James's. At dinner parties, Ribbentrop launched monologues aping Hitler's words and mannerisms, but without the magnetism. Soon, the word was out. The German ambassador to Great Britain was a boor and a bore.

The opinion, however, was not unanimous. Ribbentrop was welcomed in one corner of English society, among the Nazi sympathizers, Hitler admirers, anti-Semites, and the peace-at-any-price set. Reports circulated that Ambassador von Ribbentrop sent red roses every day to Wallis Simpson, the king's mistress and intended wife, who would cost Edward VIII his throne. Ribbentrop was rumored to be having an affair with the woman and paying her to influence the king in favor of Germany.

Down the corridor from Ribbentrop at Nuremberg, cell 10 was occupied by the man who inadvertently helped elevate him to foreign minister in 1938. Konstantin von Neurath, at the time, held the post himself. Neurath had been present at the Hossbach Conference, where Hitler baldly spelled out his intention to make war. Neurath was horrified, and said so. Thereafter, Hitler wanted someone more pliant in the Foreign Office, a diplomatic errand boy to deliver his foreign policies, not to resist them. Joachim von Ribbentrop fit perfectly.

In his new job, Ribbentrop substituted energy and ambition for competence and intelligence. During fourteen-hour days, he swelled the Foreign Office bureaucracy from 2,300 to over 10,000. His single original triumph had indeed been the Soviet-German pact, and now he was desperate to produce a copy of its secret clauses so that he could demonstrate the duplicity of the Russians and their unfitness to judge him as a war criminal.

He was seeing his lawyer, Dr. Fritz Sauter, today, and he hoped that Sauter might have found a copy. They met in the visitors' room, with Sauter, at six feet five inches, towering over his thin, haggard client. Before the war, Sauter had joined the Nazi party, drawn by its promises of national unity; but he had been thrown out for defending Jews and Communists in court. He was a famous advocate in Germany, and Walther Funk and Baldur von Schirach had also hired him. Sauter possessed an ego to match Ribbentrop's. During the visit, he treated Ribbentrop as he had on every other occasion, with professional coolness. He informed his client that he had not been able to unearth the secret passages of the German-Soviet nonaggression pact.

When Ribbentrop returned to his cell, he demanded to see the duty officer. He wanted a message delivered to Colonel Andrus at once. Fritz Sauter was to be fired as his defense counsel. It was New Year's Day, and Sauter had failed to wish him a happy New Year.

29

ON JANUARY 2, the staff returned to the Palace of Justice, flashing ID cards before red-cheeked guards who stood stamping their feet in the nine-degree Fahrenheit cold. At ten a.m., Justice Geoffrey Lawrence reconvened the International Military Tribunal. Sir Geoffrey's pink, cherubic countenance glowed after a vacation spent at his beloved Hill Farm in Wiltshire among his pedigreed cows and horses. Back in November, when the trial had opened, this Dickensian figure of plain speech and plain interests had been judged a mediocrity. Now, his simplicity was seen as the attribute of an uncluttered mind, a secure ego, and a strong if understated will. His evenhanded treatment of prosecution and defense alike had begun to persuade the defendants that room 600 might be a genuine arena for truth seeking and not necessarily the anteroom to the gallows.

Colonel Storey reopened the criminal-organization case, presenting evidence against the Gestapo and making a botch of it. Storey's idea of prosecuting was to introduce documents wholesale, the more the better, as though the sheer weight of the paper would ultimately tip the scales. When he became lost in this swamp of his own making, he might read the same document twice or prove the same point with five different documents. Sir Geoffrey, his patience wearing thin, strove to keep Storey on track. Storey kept piling on evidence the way a stoker shovels coal. As his assistants watched their efforts aborted in a feckless execution, they took to calling Storey "the Butcher of Nuremberg."

To the court's relief, a fresh face took the stand after lunch. Lieutenant Whitney Harris was a thirty-three-year-old navy officer and lawyer whose film-star handsomeness belied a serious character. He was conscientious, driven, and rarely seen among the habitués of the Grand Hotel. Harris had won this courtroom appearance for his work on the Ernst Kaltenbrunner case. As the day's session drew to a close, Harris was describing "the ninth crime for which Kaltenbrunner is responsible": that he had ordered the mass liquidation of prisoners at Dachau and other camps only days before they would have been liberated by the advancing Allies.

The following morning, John Harlan Amen replaced Harris at the stand. Amen had seized the spotlight for the direct examination of the next witness, SS General Otto Ohlendorf—yet Ohlendorf was in this court only because of Harris's initiative. Harris had interrogated him in order to obtain evidence against Kaltenbrunner. Ohlendorf, short, mousy, thirty-eight years old, had been a ranking member of the SD, the Sicherheitsdienst, the SS component that carried out intelligence, covert operations, and liquidations. Harris had begun his interrogation with routine questions, asking Ohlendorf's date of birth, place of birth, and SD assignments. One answer piqued his curiosity. Ohlendorf said that he served with the SD except for one year in 1941 when he headed Einsatzgruppe D in the East. Knowing the murderous reputation of the *Einsatzgruppen*, Harris had fired a question from the blue: "How many people did you kill?" The answer, delivered matter-of-factly, staggered him.

Harris then asked Ohlendorf how he had come to be given the *Einsatzgruppe* assignment? He had been trained in economics and the law at the universities of Göttingen and Leipzig and had a law degree, Ohlendorf explained—suitable background for his first SD assignment, economic intelligence. But he annoyed Heinrich Himmler by complaining about the mass killings of Jews in Poland. Ohlendorf, Himmler concluded, was obviously, "a product of too much education." With exquisite malice, he assigned Ohlendorf to head Einsatzgruppe D. As they talked, Harris concluded that this man should not merely be providing background for the Kaltenbrunner case: he belonged on the stand testifying directly against him. When Colonel Amen saw a copy of Harris's interrogation, he had claimed Ohlendorf for his own.

The witness walked to the stand wearing an unpressed gray suit. Amen's opening questions were calculatedly dull, queries about Kaltenbrunner's place in the RSHA organization chart, how long Ohlendorf had known his chief, what their relationship was. Then, abruptly, Amen asked how many people Einsatzgruppe D had killed. "In the year between June 1941 and June 1942 the *Einsatz* troops reported ninety thousand people liquidated," Ohlendorf answered. Did that include men, women, and children? Amen wanted to know. Yes, Ohlendorf replied. Amen next asked if mass shooting was the only method of execution. No, it was not, Ohlendorf explained. Reichsführer Himmler had noted that shooting women and children placed a terrible strain on the *Einsatz* personnel, especially family men. Therefore, beginning in 1942, women and children were gassed instead in closed vans. How many men did it take to kill ninety thousand people? Amen asked. His *Einsatzgruppe*, Ohlendorf said, had a strength of five hundred men. Walther Funk closed his eyes as Ohlendorf began explaining how the dead victims' gold and jewelry were shipped off the to Reich Ministry of Finance.

During the defense attorneys' turn to cross-examine, Sir David Maxwell-Fyfe listened attentively. He was famous for his own traplike cross-examining and was surprised at how the Germans still failed to get the point of it. Kaltenbrunner's lawyer, Kurt Kauffmann, kept hammering at Ohlendorf, trying to get him to admit that Kaltenbrunner had no authority to issue orders to concentration camps. Didn't such orders go directly from Himmler to the head of the Gestapo, Heinrich Müller, bypassing Kaltenbrunner? Ohlendorf replied that Kaltenbrunner fit directly into the chain of command. He was Müller's superior; hence he could relay orders from Himmler or initiate his own. Kauffmann, Sir David knew, had committed a classic cross-examination blunder: he had asked a question to which he did not know the answer.

The next defense examiner was Egon Kuboschok, substituting this day for Speer's attorney, Fritz Sauter. Since Ohlendorf considered himself primarily an intelligence officer, did he know, Kuboschok asked, that Albert Speer had taken actions to sabotage Hitler's scorched-earth orders? Ohlendorf answered that he did. Did Ohlendorf know, further, that Speer had tried to turn Heinrich Himmler over to the Allies at the end of the war? Ohlendorf's heretofore expressionless face registered amusement. He had never heard of such a thing, he said. Did Ohlendorf know, Kubuschok went on, that the Twentieth of July plotters had wanted Speer in their government? That he did know, Ohlendorf admitted. Finally, Kuboschok asked if the witness knew that Speer had planned an attempt on Hitler's life toward the end of the war. Excited whispers swept the courtroom. Göring turned around and glared at Speer. No, Ohlendorf said skeptically, he had never heard of such a plan.

Albert Speer listened, satisfied. Kuboschok had been less skillful than Sauter would have been. Still, the seeds of Speer's defense strategy had been planted.

Justice Lawrence called a brief adjournment. Instantly Göring was clambering over the chairs, thrusting his face next to Speer's. How dare he break up their united front against the prosecution? Göring shouted. What united front? Speer answered, turning away, as the guards pulled Göring back to his seat.

When the session resumed, an unasked question hung heavily in the air. It was posed, unexpectedly, by a defense counsel, sixty-four-year-old Ludwig Babel, who had the daunting task of defending the SS. Ohlendorf's cool recitation had so astonished Babel that he felt compelled to ask: "But did you have no scruples about the nature of these orders?" "Yes, of course," Ohlendorf answered. Then how was it that he had carried them out? Ohlendorf seemed surprised at the question. "Because it is inconceivable to me that a subordinate would not obey orders given by leaders of the state," he replied. Babel gazed at the witness for some time, then sat down wordlessly.

Francis Biddle had seen a name crop up from time to time, and had written in the margin of the document he now held, "Who is he?" The name was Adolf Eichmann. This afternoon, Biddle's curiosity was satisfied. An American prosecutor, Smith Brookhart, had begun questioning the next witness, an SS colleague of Otto Ohlendorf's named Dieter Wisliceny. Brookhart elicited from Wisliceny that in August 1942 he had gone to see Adolf Eichmann, head of Department IVA4 of the RSHA, the section dealing with Jewish matters. Wisliceny told Eichmann that he was being pressured by Slovakian officials to find out what had happened to seventeen thousand of their Jews deported to Poland. The Slovakians wanted to visit them and see how they were faring. Eichmann finally admitted that such a visit was impossible. The Jews were dead. How could that be? Wisliceny wanted to know. Extermination of the Jews was official policy, passed down from the Führer to Himmler to the RSHA, Eichmann explained. A disbelieving Wisliceny asked to see the order. He testified that Eichmann then took a document from his safe and showed it to him. This, Wisliceny said, was the first time he had heard of the Final Solution.

Smith Brookhart shifted the questioning to Kaltenbrunner. Kaltenbrunner had not been RSHA chief when the Final Solution began, he noted. But, he asked Wisliceny, after Kaltenbrunner took over, was there any change in the extermination policy? "There was no diminution or change of any kind," the witness answered. Did Kaltenbrunner know personally his subordinate who directed the Final Solution? There was no doubt of it, Wisliceny said. Kaltenbrunner and Eichmann were fellow townsmen from Austria. Kaltenbrunner's father had been the lawyer for the electrical firm managed by Eichmann's father. Their sons had gone to school together. Whenever Kaltenbrunner called his RSHA staff to Berlin, Wisliceny remembered, he had greeted Eichmann with special warmth, inquiring about his wife and children.

Late in the afternoon, Brookhart posed his last question. "Did Eichmann say anything at that time as to the number of Jews that had been killed?"

"He said he would leap laughing into the grave," Wisliceny answered, "because the feeling that he had five million people on his conscience would be for him a source of extraordinary satisfaction."

30

THE PRESS BAR WAS CROWDED, noisy, and smoke-filled. Still, the crush of reporters had thinned considerably since the trial's opening. The papers back home were no longer giving heavy daily play to a trial that, no matter how sensational the evidence, had already gone on for six weeks. Reporters had begun scrambling for fresh angles. Hal Burson, twenty-four-year-old bureau chief for the Armed Forces Network, had gone to Colonel Andrus with an idea. Burson wanted to get into cellblock C posing as a member of the guard detachment. "Son," Colonel Andrus told him, "this is serious business," and turned him down. Since he could not get into the cellblock himself, Burson cultivated the guards as sources. His resulting report revealed that the sphinxlike Jodl was the least popular prisoner. Keitel was the neatest. Hess and Ribbentrop ran neck-and-neck for sloppiest. One of the most popular prisoners was Speer. And, hands down, the GI favorite was Göring.

An Australian journalist had asked Andrus if he might query the defendants about their dreams. Andrus had taken up the request with the psychiatrist, Kelley, who put him off. The question would upset the prisoners, Kelley said. What he omitted was that the stuff of dreams was precisely the material he wanted saved for the book he and Gilbert planned to write. The persistent Australian then went to the defense lawyers and asked them if they knew what their clients dreamed about. Eight of the defendants, they reported, confessed to recurrent and frightening dreams about Colonel Andrus.

31

REPORTERS CHECKING the bulletin board Friday, January 4, found the prosecution taking on the German High Command. Of all the organizations indicted, conviction of this group seemed most difficult. Six years of war movies, newsreels, books, and Allied propaganda had made names like the Gestapo and the SS synonymous with fear and horror. But the High Command? These were generals, admirals, the men who direct wars that politicians begin, in Germany as in any nation. The prosecution had to prove not only that these professionals waged war, but that they had played a hand in starting it, and then fought it criminally. The prosecutor of the High Command was to be Colonel Telford Taylor.

The assignment was not one that Taylor would have chosen. He had come to Nuremberg via the Ultra codebreaking operation at Bletchley in England, one of numerous lawyers subsequently stockpiled by Jackson in the Palace of Justice. At Nuremberg, he had thus far occupied himself with an untaxing job as Jackson's liaison to the Russians. Since the High Command case was virtually going begging, Taylor had taken it for lack of anything better. At the same time, he made a compensating arrangement. The prison was full of lesser Nazis to be tried after the big fish. To prosecute at these subsequent trials, Robert Jackson had spotted a capable successor in Telford Taylor. The prospect of following Jackson as chief prosecutor provided Taylor the incentive for staying on and taking over the thankless, if challenging, High Command case.

From the moment Taylor approached the stand his performance attracted attention. He was an arresting presence—slim, wavy-haired, handsome, with the air of a poet in uniform. On the Nuremberg social circuit, Taylor had the reputation of a Renaissance man: tennis player, pianist, clarinetist, composer, writer, bridge expert, dancer. Only his self-protective air of detachment put some people off. He neither possessed nor sought the common touch.

His powers of reason held the court spellbound as he traced the corruption and transformation of an honorable officer corps into an unsoldierly, dishonorable tool of Hitler. He was, as a colleague put it, "smart in the way lawyers judge smartness. He had a keen memory, could recall precedents and marshal his case with a logic that marched." His only peer in court in the mastery of language was Jackson. Taylor had set himself a minimum objective. It might be impossible to prove the entire High Command guilty, but he was determined to convince the tribunal that individual German generals could be war criminals.

Monday morning, January 7, dawned bright and cold. Colonel Taylor resumed the prosecution, asking the court's permission to read a document into the record. As he did so, Otto Nelte, Field Marshal Keitel's lawyer, threw a quick glance at his client. The old soldier sat expressionless, like someone standing on a track who did not hear the train coming. "General Anton Dostler, on or about 24 March 1944, in the vicinity of La Spezia, Italy, contrary to the laws of war," Taylor read, "did order to be shot summarily, a group of United States Army personnel. . . ."

OSS people in the court knew the story. A fifteen-man team had slipped ashore behind the lines in northern Italy to blow up a railroad tunnel. The men were in uniform on a legitimate military mission when they were captured. On Dostler's orders, they had been shot without a trial. Dostler had defended his action by saying that he was carrying out the Commando Order, signed by Field Marshal Keitel. Taylor pointed out that Dostler had been tried by a military court in Italy and executed the month before.

Taylor went to the prosecution table and picked up another document, 551 PS, which he said would disprove the constant defense refrain that even Hitler's vilest wishes had to be obeyed on pain of punishment, including death. As the Allies gained a foothold in France after D-Day, German generals in Supreme Command West asked if the Commando Order still remained effective. The reply came back stating that it was "fully in force." Any Allied troops found operating beyond the battle perimeter, and any captured parachutists, were to be shot. Furthermore, Supreme Command West was to report daily how many of these "saboteurs" had been liquidated. This directive too had been issued by Field Marshal Keitel. Keitel and his ilk, Taylor went on, would have the court believe that failure to carry out the Führer's wishes was not an option: they must shoot or be shot, as it were. That was untrue. The paybook of every German soldier made clear that to carry out, knowingly, an illegal order was a crime. Perhaps the bravest German soldier of all, Field Marshal Erwin Rommel, on receiving the reaffirmed Commando Order, had simply burned it.

As soon as the court adjourned that afternoon, Captain Gilbert sped from the dock to the court reporters' room. He was looking for a statement against the High Command made that day by a witness named Erich von dem Bach-Zelewski, a forty-six-year-old general in the Waffen SS, the military arm of Himmler's empire. The reporter who had taken the testimony flipped through his notes, rolled a sheet of paper into a typewriter, and typed out the passage Gilbert wanted: "I am of the opinion when, for years and for decades, the doctrine is practiced that the Slavic race is an inferior race, and the Jews are not even human, then such an explosion was inevitable." The "explosion" that Bach-Zelewski had referred to was his role in putting down guerrilla resistance in Russia.

On the stand, Bach-Zelewski had been an unlikely-looking villain, tall, thin, blue-eyed, with the genial air of a popular schoolteacher. He nevertheless had won a reputation for ruthlessness in catching guerrilla fighters and executing them, along with thousands of hostages. Hitler had once called Bach-Zelewski "the model partisan fighter." The defense on cross-examination tried to have Bach-Zelewski establish that only outfits like his own SS—not soldiers in the regular army—had slaughtered people en masse. But the witness had spread guilt over the whole German war machine.

When Gilbert had heard Bach-Zelewski say in court that the Jew was not even considered human, something clicked into place. He took the statement the court reporter had typed out for him and went back to his office. There he dug out the notes he had taken the week before on Otto Ohlendorf's testimony and Wisliceny's account of Adolf Eichmann's macabre boast of sending millions of Jews to their deaths.

The search for the "why" of ingeniously organized, routinely administered mass murder carried out by presumably civilized people consumed Gilbert. His visit to the condemned men at Dachau had furnished one piece of the puzzle: a culture that fostered unthinking obedience. Ohlendorf's testimony had confirmed it. Bach-Zelewski's statement today provided a second piece, one that had been much on Gilbert's mind of late. Ordinary Germans would not kill innocent human beings. But what if Germans had been bombarded for years, as Bach-Zelewski pointed out, with propaganda that the Slav or the Jew was not a true human, but a corruption of the race, responsible for Germany's woes? What if this attitude was the official government position? What if the very laws of the land denied to Jews rights available to the lowliest German—the right to work, to own property, to marry freely, even to hold citizenship? Then a personality conditioned to unquestioning obedience, told to rid society of such pestilential vermin, could find the rationale to do it. These two factors explained much of the "why," Gilbert concluded. Still, there had to be more.

32

THE PROSECUTION CASE against the organizations had ended. Their defense would take place later. Next on the court's schedule was the prosecution of individual defendants. On January 8, documents incriminating the first batch—Göring, Hess, Ribbentrop, and Keitel—fell like a blizzard. The following morning, as the defendants were leaving the exercise yard, Keitel clicked his heels and turned aside to let Hermann Göring precede him into the cellblock. He intended to tell his lawyer, Otto Nelte, when they met this evening, how Göring could help him.

Keitel looked forward to Nelte's coming, as much for the break in the monotony as anything else. With the days now so short, it was virtually impossible to read or write a letter after supper. They were left in semidarkness to sit and brood until nine p.m., when it was time to go to bed, and when, perversely, the guards would shine the hated spotlights into their cells. The only time a pair of eyes was not peering at them was when they sat on the toilet in the alcove, when only their feet were visible. Life for them was reduced to the court proceedings on weekdays and solitude during nights and weekends, broken only by meetings with their lawyers, visits from Kelley and Gilbert, and a few minutes in the exercise yard. Keitel even looked forward to the weekly cold shower, in spite of the embarrassing rectal examinations.

Otto Nelte was one of the former Nazis on the defense team, a tax lawyer who had found the party tie useful in his practice. As they met in the visitors' room, Nelte asked Keitel if it was true that during the earlier interrogations he had authenticated his signature on the Commando Order. Keitel nodded. What choice had he had? The Prussian code of honor compelled him to speak the truth. What did Keitel think Göring could do for him? Nelte wanted to know. Keitel explained that he had once begged Göring to get him a frontline command. Even as a field marshal, he would have been content to lead a single division—anything to escape daily humiliation by the Führer. If Göring would testify in court that Keitel had made the request, Keitel reasoned, it would prove that he had not been a willing member of Hitler's court. As they parted, Nelte asked if Keitel had any word to pass along to his wife, who was now in Nuremberg with Jodl's wife. The shame he had brought onto his family was, Keitel said, his heaviest cross. Just ask her to pray for him, he told the lawyer.

Frau Keitel, though her husband was too much the Prussian ever to blame her, was partly responsible for his present fate. In 1934, Keitel had come close to his dream. After his father died, he had wanted nothing so desperately as to leave the army and become lord of the family estate in Helmscherode, Braunschweig. Lisa, a brewer's daughter, had been adamant. Why would she want to be a farmer's wife when she could be a general's lady? Keitel thus stayed in the army, and was as shocked as his fellow officers when Hitler named him chief of staff of the OKW, the high command. When Hitler once described

Keitel as having "the brains of a movie usher," another officer asked why the Führer had made him the highest-ranking figure in the German military. Because the man was "loyal as a dog," Hitler replied.

Keitel, so imposing, so military in bearing, served another purpose. In 1938, at Berchtesgaden, while Hitler was bullying Austrian chancellor Kurt von Schuschnigg to hand over his country, he loudly summoned Keitel from an anteroom. Was the German army in a state of invasion readiness? the Führer demanded. It was, Keitel replied, standing there in full dress uniform, every inch the soldier. The unspoken message had not been lost on Schuschnigg.

Hitler had been only a corporal in World War I, yet Keitel found himself mesmerized by the Führer's military genius. No matter what arguments his generals raised, Hitler could throw back Moltke or Schlieffen or Clausewitz. Keitel readily confessed that, in military matters, "I was the pupil, and the Führer the master."

After the visit with his lawyer, Keitel was marched back to his cell. All was deathly silent but for the bolt slamming behind him. He took off his clothes, folded them neatly, and laid them on the stone floor —they were allowed no hooks or hangers. Keitel asked the guard if he might sit up in bed this night since he had a painful boil on his neck. He had not reported it to Dr. Pfluecker. He never reported his ailments. His stoicism, however, was conditioned rather than natural, and purchased at a high price. His current blood pressure was 180 over 100. He had once confided to Major Kelley that he considered killing himself three times during the war. Kelley had written of Keitel, "At present, he has nothing to live for. Consequently, he is one of the most profound suicide risks."

The defense counsels had found a hangout, a surviving tavern near the courthouse, Gasthaus zum Stern. There, Otto Nelte repaired after his meeting with his client. A failing wood fire was being coaxed to life as he entered. Its meager warmth felt good. Nelte spied only one of his colleagues at this late hour—Ludwig Babel. The tavernkeeper brought a stein to Nelte. German beer was one thing that had survived the war intact, Babel said. Nelte spoke wearily. He wished to God that the Dostler affidavit had never surfaced. How, he wondered, was he to save the man who had issued the Commando Order when a German general had already been shot for obeying it?

33

THE PROSECUTORS HAD GONE AFTER the defendants in the front row, one by one, like ducks in a shooting gallery. January 9 was Alfred Rosenberg's turn. While Streicher worked the anti-Semitic gutter, Rosenberg sought to elevate anti-Semitism to a respectable philosophy. He reveled in Nazi titles that seemed out of comic opera, such as Deputy Führer for the Supervision of the Entire Ideological Training and Education of the Party, and Commissioner for Safeguarding the National Socialist Philosophy for Party and State. He was on trial for his later roles as minister for the Occupied Eastern Territories and chief of Einstab Rosenberg, the art-looting operation.

Major Douglas Kelley sat in the visitors' gallery, from which he could watch his colleague, Gustav Gilbert, hovering around the dock. As Kelley studied Rosenberg, handsome in a lifeless sort of way, his hair parted and combed in a pompadour familiar to any American teenager of that era, he remembered his first visit to the man's cell. Rosenberg had spoken to him of his book *The Myth of the Twentieth Century*. The word *myth* was a poor translation; *legend* would have been better, since Rosenberg propounded a semimystical theory of the blood superiority of the German race. On its publication in 1934, a quarter of a million copies of the book had sold. Its principal feature, however, seemed to be unreadability. The book was written in the dense, tortured style of much German philosophy. Hitler had leafed through it. Göring had never touched it. The propaganda minister, Josef Goebbels, called *Myth of the Twentieth Century* "an ideological belch." Goebbels, however, knew his countrymen. If they could not comprehend Rosenberg, then they would think the man must be profound.

Kelley had taken a young American interpreter with him on that early visit. Rosenberg asked if Kelley knew what a U-boat crewman did as soon as he crawled, filthy and oil-stained, out of the engine room to his bunk? He reached for his copy of *The Myth*, Rosenberg explained. Kelley asked the interpreter to translate a passage from Rosenberg's copy. The Nazi started to hand over the dog-eared book. But first, he asked the soldier's religion. Catholic, the interpreter replied. Rosenberg pulled the book back. "This young man is working for his country," he said. "He is a good soldier and a good Catholic. If he were to read my book, he would renounce the church immediately. I do not want to be responsible for that."

As Kelley had left the cell that day, Rosenberg had handed him a sheaf of papers written in longhand. It was a memorandum, he said, of great potential value to the United States—a plan for "the settlement of American Negroes in Africa." He had done the required calculations, Rosenberg wrote, and if America did not follow his advice, "in 150 years there will be no more Americans, only an unholy mongrelization."

The summation against Rosenberg this day was being delivered by a new face. Walter Brudno's appearance in court represented the triumph of talent over rank. Brudno was a rarity at Nuremberg—a lawyer without a commission, a private first class in a sea of brass. Though impressive in appearance and able, Brudno had been sidetracked by his superiors—and this included practically everyone—until Jackson spotted him. The chief prosecutor solved Brudno's hierarchical problem with a pragmatic stroke: he had had the army discharge Brudno, in effect promoting him to civilian. The fact that this was Brudno's maiden voyage, however, had not spared him Sir Geoffrey Lawrence's sharp tongue. The justice, rimless glasses perched at the tip of his nose, remarked, "Mr. Brudno, you have referred us to *The Myth of the Twentieth Century* on several occasions." "Yes, your honor," Brudno said, nodding. "We don't want to hear about it anymore." It was the voice of an English headmaster, prim yet not to be brooked.

Lawrence's impartiality had at first confused the defendants. Even his entrances into the courtroom signaled his attachment to fair play. Clad in a black robe and striped pants, he would bow first to the prosecution and then to the defense before taking his seat. By now, the attitude toward him of the defendants and their lawyers approached worship. Their respect heightened on learning that

Lawrence had won the Distinguished Service Order as a gunner in the First World War. Hans Fritzsche, the radio propagandist on trial, listened to Sir Geoffrey's precise, economical speech with awe. He particularly admired the man's gift for maintaining total authority without ever raising his voice. Fritzsche remarked to his countrymen that Lawrence was "so English, so un-German."

As Brudno wrapped up his summation, Douglas Kelley's eyes remained on Rosenberg. A foolish man, a pompous man, and, in the philosophical rubbish he had peddled, a muddled mind. But a capital case? Kelley wondered. Granted, the prosecution had proved that Rosenberg oversaw the wholesale theft of art and furnishings from Jewish homes in subjugated countries. But he had never killed anyone. In his role as minister for the Occupied Eastern Territories, he had actually tried to prevent the wholesale butchery carried out in the Soviet Union. His authority, however, had quickly been undermined by more brutal SS figures. As Kelley studied the face in the dock, he asked himself who had helped indoctrinate these butchers to their murderous hatred. He thought of Lord Acton's words: "The greatest crime is homicide. The accomplice is no better than the assassin. The theorist is the worst."

34

HOWARD K. SMITH HAD a fresh idea for a broadcast. Back home, women had filled countless jobs as the men went off to war—the Rosie the Riveter phenomenon. Here at Nuremberg, Smith had observed that easily half of the six hundred American staff members were women, employed not only as secretaries but as researchers, interpreters, and translators. Two lawyers on the American prosecution staff were women. In his report, Smith told America about WAC Major Catherine Falvey, who was going home to run for the Massachusetts state legislature. He described Harriet Zetterberg, a brilliant thirty-year-old law review graduate of the University of Wisconsin, known for preparing masterful briefs. What passed unnoticed, except perhaps by Zetterberg, was that she did not appear before the court. That role was reserved for the men on the staff. She was married to another prosecution lawyer, Daniel Margolies; because of the ban on spouses, the couple posed as unmarried and "living in sin" in a room at the Grand Hotel.

On the morning of January 10, as the defendants were marched from the prison to the courthouse, Captain Gilbert walked alongside Hans Frank to provide moral support. The twenty-one defendants formed four imprecise, sometimes shifting cliques—the unrepentant, dominated by Göring; the indignant, headed by Schacht; the confused, typified by Sauckel; and the penitents, led by Speer and Frank.

In the courtroom, Major William Baldwin, a glider veteran out of the OSS, began the Frank prosecution by introducing entries from the diaries Frank had kept while he was governor-general of Poland. "In September of 1941," Baldwin read from document 233 PS, "defendant Frank's own chief medical officer reported to him the appalling Polish health conditions. I read now from page forty-six of the diary. 'The Poles now have about 600 calories allotted to them, while the normal requirement for a human being is 2,200. . . . The number of Poles with communicable diseases has reached forty percent. . . . This situation presents a serious danger for the soldiers of the Reich coming into the Government-General.' " Yet, Baldwin went on, "In August 1942, Frank approved a new plan which called for a much larger contribution of foodstuffs to Germany at the expense of the Poles. I quote again from the diary, page thirty. 'Before the German people suffer starvation, the occupied territories and their people shall be exposed to starvation. This means a sixfold increase over that of last year's contributions by Poland. The new demand will be fulfilled exclusively at the expense of the foreign population. It must be done cold-bloodedly and without pity.' "

Captain Gilbert, standing to the left side of the dock, studied Frank. Baldwin's arguments were striking like hammer blows. Gilbert could virtually see the man buckle. Gilbert feared that this pounding might cause Frank to recant and seek sympathy and understanding in the camp of the diehards—in the Göring wing.

Friday, January 11, Harriet Zetterberg and her husband, Daniel Margolies, eagerly entered the courtroom. The couple had spent the Christmas break tracking down a physician, Dr. Franz Blaha, in

Czechoslovakia. Blaha's experiences, the prosecution believed, could incriminate several defendants. The doctor was testifying today as Tom Dodd's prosecution witness.

Early in the war, Blaha had been arrested by the Nazis and committed to Dachau, where, as a physician, he was ordered to carry out typhoid experiments on healthy patients. He refused and was banished to the autopsy room. By the end of the war, Blaha had performed twelve thousand autopsies. What struck Margolies and Zetterberg as the doctor took the stand was the innate dignity the man had managed to preserve. His face was deeply creviced, his eyes tired, the voice convincing by its very calmness.

The effect of the *Nacht und Nebel* decree had previously been described only in documentary evidence. Keitel's instructions when he issued the order read, "Intimidation can only be achieved either by capital punishment or through measures by which the relatives of the prisoners and the population cannot learn the fate of the criminals." Dodd asked Blaha to describe firsthand what happened to people spirited from their homes under the decree. The victims he had seen, Blaha testified, were shot in front of the Dachau crematoria to speed up the process of their obliteration. As the Germans liked to put it, this was where "we turn them into fog."

Dodd asked Blaha if he had ever seen any of the defendants in the dock at Dachau. The question was critical. Most of them had denied any knowledge of concentration camp operations. Blaha pointed and intoned the names, "Rosenberg, Frick, Funk, Sauckel." Another face had arrested Blaha's attention from the moment he arrived in court. There in the dock was his shy, studious boyhood chum, Arthur Zajtich. Zajtich had left Czechoslovakia for Austria and become a rising Nazi, Frank's apprentice in ruling Poland and later a power in his own right as Reich commissioner of the Netherlands. Blaha's friend had long since changed his name to Seyss-Inquart.

35

ON JANUARY 12, the prison had taken on its Saturday-afternoon aura, with the drama of the courtroom temporarily suspended and life reduced to the limits of a concrete cube. Weekends produced Gustav

Gilbert's most profitable visits, with the defendants' loneliness deepest and their guard down. As the psychologist entered the cellblock, a POW trusty was coming out, lugging a sack that once held army flour. Gilbert was by now familiar with the undercurrents of prison life. The sack, he knew, contained used coffee grounds salvaged from the kitchen, and was being smuggled out of the prison for sale in Nuremberg. He encountered the prison librarian, Otto Streng, another trusty, rolling a cartload of books from cell to cell. Gilbert asked Streng if he had anything for Speer. Streng handed him a single volume. Gilbert noted the title, *Memoirs of a German Painter*, by Ludwig Richter.

In cell 17, Speer eagerly awaited Gilbert's visit. He was determined to break Göring's hold over his fellow defendants, particularly after the way Göring had attacked him when the lawyer Kuboschok claimed that Speer had planned to assassinate Hitler. Speer understood clearly what the prosecutors and the bench hoped for from the defendants—not Göring's bid for unified defiance, but individual confession and remorse. Speer was trying to bring the more pliable defendants along with him onto that course. He had high hopes for the youth leader, Baldur von Schirach. Schirach was now talking about writing a denunciation of Hitler. This malleable man had to be kept away from Göring, Speer believed. Earlier, Frank too had seemed to be safely in the penitents' corner. But, after the prosecution mauled him, Frank had been wondering aloud why he should forsake his old comrades. Maybe he ought to make his last stand with Göring rather than with people who despised him. Speer marveled at Göring's capacity to intimidate and dominate without possessing a shred of real power. That was what he wanted to talk about to Gilbert.

Speer had long been familiar with Göring's bullying and bluster. Late in the war, he had shown Göring a still experimental jet aircraft. Göring immediately rushed to Hitler with the news. Hitler became ecstatic. How many of these planes could the Luftwaffe have operational, and how soon? Hitler wanted to know. At least five hundred, almost immediately, Göring assured him. He made the claim knowing that Speer was nowhere near ready to begin production. When the jets failed to appear in the sky quickly enough, Hitler raged, and Göring placed the blame on Speer.

The weak Kaltenbrunner might also be enlisted as a penitent,

Speer believed. And Speer would much rather have him as an ally than as an adversary. Only Kaltenbrunner knew what had really happened to Speer in the days after the Twentieth of July plot. Speer was so adroit that, though he served the Nazi regime, he had still managed to retain the respect of the conspirators. After the plot failed, Kaltenbrunner came to see him. He spoke in a tone of cordial menace. In a safe at Bendlerstrasse, the High Command headquarters, Kaltenbrunner said, his people had found a description of the government the plotters intended to install. He took out an organization chart and handed it to Speer. In a box labeled "Armaments," Speer's name appeared in neatly printed letters. Speer quickly pointed out a penciled notation alongside the box that read, "If possible." The plotters might have wanted him, but he had wanted no part of them, he said. Speer denied knowing about the plot. With that, Kaltenbrunner gave him an enigmatic smile and left.

The next day, Speer summoned his senior staff to a "loyalty meeting." In past speeches he had shunned party bombast. This day, however, he ladled it on like a *Gauleiter*. He praised Hitler's leadership to the skies and expressed his undying faith in the "Führer's greatness." He expected the same loyalty to Germany's leader, he said, from anyone who worked for him.

In the wake of the plot, nearly five thousand Germans were executed, many with far less connection to it than Speer. Hitler, of course, knew what Kaltenbrunner knew. That Speer's life was spared could only be explained by the rarest of Hitler's emotions: he felt genuine affection for Albert Speer. Would the whimpering giant in cell 26 keep quiet about Speer's eager display of loyalty after the plot? Speer could only hope so.

On Gilbert's arrival, Speer greeted the psychologist warmly in fluent, though heavily accented, English. Gilbert had observed the effect of Speer's language facility. When interpreters were occasionally stuck for a word, Speer would scribble his suggestion on a piece of paper and pass it along to the glass-enclosed interpreters' booth. His meaning, the interpreters agreed, was invariably the closest. In more than one sense, Gilbert concluded, Speer and his captors spoke the same language.

Gilbert handed Speer the library book. A rapport had grown between the two men. After his previous visit, the psychologist had written, "Speer is apparently sincere in his insistence that he is not trying to save his neck by this stand, since he is the only one who admitted a common guilt in his supporting the regime even *before* the trial started."

Speer thumbed idly through the book, all the while commenting to Gilbert on how cowardly he had been in the past. He hated Göring. Yet, with the others, he had celebrated the man's birthdays. Here in prison, he had finally broken free. Most of the defendants, however, were still in Göring's thrall. Frank was wavering. Speer and Göring were openly wrestling for Schirach's soul. "You know," Speer said, "it is not a good idea to let the defendants eat and work together. That is how Göring keeps whipping them into line."

After Gilbert left the cellblock, he pondered Speer's point and decided to suggest a new arrangement to Colonel Andrus.

36

CAPTAIN DREXEL SPRECHER GAVE the attractive German cashier in the cafeteria a practiced eye before he paid for his coffee and pastry. He took a seat at a nearby table. Sprecher was thirty-one, a tall, broad-shouldered, open-faced American whose boundless energy fueled a life of hard work and hard play. He had never given the nonfraternization rule the slightest respect, even when it was in force. Just coming out of an unhappy marriage and a divorce, Sprecher had dated German girls from his first week in Nuremberg.

He had brought with him to the cafeteria papers relating to his latest case. Sprecher had been deeply disappointed when Robert Ley's suicide cheated him out of his first major prosecution. Thereafter, he had been assigned Hans Fritzsche, the propagandist, who, Sprecher knew, hardly belonged in the dock with Adolf Hitler's chief lieutenants. As Sprecher's succinct, masterful briefs continued to please Jackson, the lawyer was sent after more challenging game, Baldur von Schirach. Schirach, as the former leader of the Hitler Youth, hoped to pass himself off as little more than the German equivalent of the national director of the Boy Scouts. Sprecher was developing a far darker record.

The letters he reviewed over his coffee both amused and exasperated him. American descendants of the signers of the Declaration of Independence were writing to the court, pleading for clemency for Baldur von Schirach! The accused Nazi war criminal was, in fact, three-quarters American. Schirach's grandfather had emigrated to America, served as a major in the Union army, lost a leg at Bull Run, and was an honorary pallbearer at the funeral of Abraham Lincoln. The grandfather married an American heiress and then returned to Germany. Schirach's father had also married an American woman who traced her forebears to a signer of the Declaration of Independence —hence the DAR support.

Sprecher believed Schirach, like Speer and Frick, to be a traitor to his class. Schirach's father had been director of the National Theater in Weimar, and young Baldur grew up in a world of poetry, theater, and music. The economic disaster that followed World War I, however, cost the senior Schirach his job. As the family's fortunes plunged, Baldur began reading such anti-Semitic tracts as Henry Ford's *The International Jew*, and by age eighteen he had become that rarity, a cultured storm trooper.

Sprecher had studied his quarry in the courtroom. There was a softness about Schirach; the flabby body and smooth face suggested too many cream pastries. Between his position as a youth leader and his appearance, Schirach was inevitably subjected to speculation about homosexuality. Marriage and four children had not insulated him from suspicion. One courtroom observer thought Schirach exuded "a whiff of the kind of scoutmaster who winds up in the Sunday newspapers."

In 1933, Hitler had named Schirach, then twenty-six years old, leader of German youth. From this post, he wove a net that snared nearly every German boy and girl. At age ten, boys were inducted into the Jungvolk and the girls into the Jungmädel. By age fourteen, the boys became full-blown Hitler Jugend and the girls entered the Bund Deutscher Mädel. At eighteen, the boys became party members. By 1939, Schirach's fiefdom numbered nine million young people, presumably pursuing health, beauty, and culture. "Every German boy who dies at the front is dying for Mozart," Schirach liked to say.

Sprecher recognized that heading a movement of robust, marching, singing boys and girls could hardly be viewed as a war crime; he hoped to convict Schirach on the basis of the ultimate purpose of all his efforts. Schirach was charged with conspiracy to commit aggression, and the very songs the Hitler Youth sang on Alpine hikes rang with aggressive intent:

> If all the world lies in ruins,
> What the devil do we care?
> We will still go on marching,
> For today Germany belongs to us,
> And tomorrow the world.

Sprecher's strategy was to add the evidence proving conspiracy to a still blacker count against Schirach: count four, crimes against humanity. In 1940, Hitler had pulled Schirach out of the army, where he had served for six months, and made him *Gauleiter* of Vienna. For the youth leader, now thirty-three, this was at last a grown-up's job, and with enviable perquisites, including a magnificent villa with seventeen servants.

When Reinhard Heydrich, Kaltenbrunner's predecessor as head of the RSHA security organization, was assassinated in Czechoslovakia, Schirach sent a "Dear Martin" letter to Hitler's secretary, Bormann. He had an idea that he wanted Bormann to put before the Führer. Everybody knew the British had masterminded the Heydrich killing. The Czechs were otherwise happy under German occupation and the British were simply trying to stir up trouble, Schirach pointed out. He had a plan: "A sudden violent air attack on a British cultural town would be most effective as 'The Revenge of Heydrich.'" Sprecher intended to introduce this document. It should have considerable effect on the British justices.

Sprecher hoped to convict Schirach not simply for song lyrics and a braggadocio memo. Soon after becoming *Gauleiter* of Vienna, Schirach informed Hitler that there were sixty thousand Jews in Vienna unfit for work. At the same time, the city faced an acute housing shortage. He needed relief. Hitler ordered that Schirach deport his Jews to the government-general of Poland. Schirach later boasted, "If anyone reproaches me with having driven from this city . . . tens of thousands into the ghettos of the East, I will reply, I see this as an act contributing to European culture." Schirach's cultural contribution resulted in the death of these tens of thousands of Jews in Auschwitz.

Thus soft-looking, cultivated Baldur von Schirach had taken an action worthy of an SS brute. That was the case Sprecher hoped to make: that Schirach had helped shape a generation of Germans to carry out barbarities, with himself as a model.

Shortly after concluding the prosecution of Schirach, Drexel Sprecher received a visitor in his office, Wolfe Frank, star of the language division. Given the English he spoke, Frank could have passed himself off as a lord. He was actually a German Jew born in Munich who had fled to England during the thirties. He had acquired his aristocratic enunciation during five years as a British army officer.

Wolfe Frank asked Sprecher if he had ever known a titled old German woman in Switzerland before the war. Sprecher remembered that in his student travels he had visited a distant relative in Zurich. The woman had turned out to be a minor member of the German nobility. What he remembered most was a picture of Hitler hanging on her wall. Though Sprecher came from solid small-town Republican stock, college had turned him into a "semi-Socialist," and he was shocked at the woman's choice of a hero. Why, he had asked, did she keep Hitler's photograph? "This man," she said, "will restore Germany."

Wolfe Frank explained that he had recently been visited by a woman, the Countess Faber-Castell. She had heard on the radio about Sprecher's prosecuting Baldur von Schirach, and his name sounded familiar. Could this be the same young man who had visited her mother in Zurich ten years before? If so, she hoped that Sprecher would call on her and her husband. She had given Wolfe Frank an address in the country some ten miles from Nuremberg.

Like most of the staff, Drexel Sprecher fled the bleak city every free weekend. And his curiosity had been piqued by the Faber-Castell invitation. Still, he was an Allied prosecutor. He knew nothing of the politics of these people, and he remembered the photograph of Hitler in Zurich. He decided it was best not to go alone and took with him Wolfe Frank as well as Bill Daldwin, the prosecutor of Hans Frank. The sky was a bright, hard blue as their canvas-topped jeep took them through rolling hills and great forested stretches of Franconia. They arrived at a rustic-elegant *Jagthaus*, the Faber-Castells' hunting lodge.

They were met by the Countess Nina and her husband, Roland Faber-Castell.

Sprecher's reticence soon began to melt in the bonhomie of the Faber-Castell home. They had no resentment over the U.S. occupation forces taking over their castle in Stein to house the press, Roland Faber-Castell said. The Nazis had done much the same, turning the castle to their purposes. As for his politics, Roland explained that he had barely escaped arrest after the Twentieth of July plot because of his known opposition to the Nazis. He had already been denazified by the American occupation authorities and was now busy rebuilding his business empire.

An attractive, talented thirty-year-old, Nina Faber-Castell entertained her guests by singing and playing her own songs on the piano. She noted, impishly, that Minister Goebbels had once called on her to compliment her on her talent. Roland Faber-Castell invited Sprecher to join him on a walk around the grounds. Tall pines shattered the sun's rays and scattered them over patches of snow and ice. Sprecher was thinking of similar winters in his native Wisconsin, when suddenly they came upon a scene of utter devastation. Hundreds of great trees had been snapped off at the base and splintered into virtual matchwood, their wounds still fresh and white. Allied bombers, Faber-Castell noted wryly, did not always hit their intended targets.

Hours later, after good food, good talk, and good drink, the visitors prepared to leave. On the drive back, an air of well-being settled over the three men. This afternoon's entertainment had not been the catered hospitality of the Grand Hotel or the seized comforts of a confiscated villa. The *Jagthaus* was a real home of sophisticated, amusing, friendly people. Sprecher was also relieved by the enlightened politics of his hosts. But then, one never seemed to meet a Nazi in Germany these days, except for the few in the dock at Nuremberg.

37

THE FIRST TIME Otto Kranzbuehler had shown up at the courthouse gate, the guards had been alarmed. Admiral Dönitz's lawyer was wearing the full naval uniform of the defeated enemy. The dashing thirty-nine-year-old Kranzbuehler was a *Flottenrichter*, a fleet judge, in the German navy. Admiral Dönitz believed that he had fought the war at sea as cleanly as the men of any other nation. A fellow naval officer, he had concluded, could best make that case.

Major Neave had located Kranzbuehler in the legal office of a German minesweeping unit which the British allowed to function to clear ports on the North and Baltic seas. At Nuremberg, Kranzbuehler had insisted on his right to wear the uniform, since it was the Allies who had kept him on active duty. He also hoped by appearing in uniform to register the point that most Germans had simply fought for their country; this was the role in which he intended to cast his client, Dönitz.

The hallways of the courthouse were virtually deserted this Sunday afternoon as Kranzbuehler made his way to the now-familiar mesh cages of the visitors' room. The next day, January 14, the prosecution would begin its case against Dönitz, and Kranzbuehler had come to discuss last-minute strategies. His client was already waiting. Dönitz was not an easy client; the moment the man opened his thin lips, any suggestion of the kindly grandfather vanished. His voice had the whine of a dentist's drill. He retained the habit of command, unbroken by his months of confinement. Kranzbuehler was thoroughly aware of the stories told about Dönitz in the German navy. Dönitz's twenty-one-year-old son, Peter, had been lost aboard one of the submarines in his father's wolf-pack fleet, one of twenty-five thousand German submariners out of forty thousand who perished. In May 1944, another son, Klaus, was killed aboard a reconnaissance ship looking for signs of the Allied invasion buildup along the English coast. When an aide brought him the news, Dönitz said nothing and kept working at his desk. He went home to tell his wife and then informed her that she was to accompany him for a luncheon date with the Japanese ambassador. Not a word was spoken during the lunch about their loss. The moment the lunch was over, Dönitz's wife collapsed.

Kranzbuehler had gone to the document room days before to obtain copies of the evidence the prosecution expected to introduce against Dönitz. Here in the visitors' room, he went over them with the admiral, who snapped out the objections Kranzbuehler should raise in court. The *Laconia* Order was going to be the most troublesome, the lawyer said. The order, issued by Dönitz after one of his subs sank the British transport *Laconia* in 1942, had a particularly harsh ring. It forbade German naval vessels to pick up survivors, even to help them into lifeboats or give them food and water. Dönitz had ended the order: "Be hard. Remember, the enemy has no regard for women and children when he bombs German cities."

The only reason he had issued the order, Dönitz told Kranzbuehler, was that American aircraft had attacked his submarines while the crews were trying to rescue the *Laconia*'s survivors. He knew for a fact that the American navy operated essentially under the same conditions as the *Laconia* Order. Yes, Kranzbuehler said, he of course intended to make this point on cross-examination. But the admiral had to understand, right or wrong, fair or not, this court would not entertain a defense of tu quoque.

The prosecution could also be expected to introduce evidence that Dönitz, beyond being simply a professional sailor, had been a staunch supporter of Hitler and Nazism. The day after the Twentieth of July attempt on Hitler's life, Dönitz had gone on the radio. "An insane clique of generals, which has nothing to do with our brave armed forces," he had said, "instigated this cowardly attempt at murder. . . . If these scoundrels think removal of the Führer can free us from our hard but inexorable struggle, they are wrong." That was not the speech he was concerned about, Dönitz said. Did the Americans have the address he had made on the struggle against Jewry? In it he had said, "I would rather eat dirt than have my grandson grow up in the Jewish spirit and faith." Fifty-two copies of the speech had been run off. Fifty-one had been destroyed. Did the prosecution have the last copy? Dönitz asked. They seemed to have everything else. Kranzbuehler said that he did not know.

As they finished, Dönitz asked if his lawyer knew why he was being tried. Before Kranzbuehler could reply, the admiral answered. They could not try Krupp, so they had gone after his son, Alfried. Since they could not try Himmler, they had settled for Kaltenbrunner. They could not try Goebbels, so they had indicted Fritzsche. And they could not try Hitler, so they had settled on him, as the Führer's successor. His indictment, Dönitz said, was "an example of American humor."

The British had felt all along that the Americans were hogging the stage. They particularly believed that the German navy was their game. They, after all, had fought the real fight against the *Kriegsmarine*. Thus, on Monday, January 14, Barrister-at-Law H. J. Phillimore opened the prosecution case against Grand Admiral Karl Dönitz. Dönitz was charged with complicity in waging aggressive warfare and with crimes committed during the war. As Phillimore introduced the issue of the *Laconia* Order, Major Airey Neave listened with bitter memories. A friend of his, as well as the man's wife and baby, had drowned when the ship went down. The prosecutor next moved to Dönitz's role in passing along Keitel's Commando Order to the German navy. As a result, captured British commandos had been shot without trial.

So far, the evidence against the admiral had dealt only with military actions, and had raised questions of how cruelly or fairly any war could be fought. The next phase of the prosecution, however, moved Dönitz into a less savory realm. He had stoutly maintained to his interrogators that he knew nothing of the horrors of the concentration camps. The British prosecutor introduced documents proving that Dönitz had personally requested twelve thousand camp inmates to work in navy shipyards.

On cross-examination, Kranzbuehler countered the charges as skillfully as the evidence permitted. Still, when the day was over and he retreated to the Nuremberg home where he was boarding, he faced a cross-examination of self. He had been a career legal officer, in the navy since 1934. He sat as a judge at court-martials and had sought to dispense justice within the law. He was mortified by the revelations of room 600. Had he known nothing of what had gone on? In that case, he must be an idiot. Had he been part of it? In that case, he must be a criminal. Had he known, yet done nothing? In that case, he must be a coward. The choices—idiot, criminal, or coward—all left Kranzbuehler depressed.

38

FEW COULD MISS the symmetry. On January 16, Robert Kempner opened the prosecution case against Wilhelm Frick, the man who had turned Hitlerian grudges into German law. Frick had headed the Ministry of the Interior, from which Kempner had been fired. Frick had promulgated the laws that drove Kempner from Germany. But for Frick, Kempner would not be standing in this courtroom this day as an American citizen and as his antagonist. The only things that had pried Kempner from a life he would happily have lived out in Germany were the deeds of the defendants. If anyone in the courtroom fit the German stereotype—ostentatiously learned, brusque, and didactic—it was Robert Kempner. A heavy accent completed the image.

The psychiatrist, Major Kelley, had found the sixty-nine-year-old Frick the most colorless of the defendants. Day after day, Frick sat in the dock looking, with his expressionless face, lifeless eyes, and incongruous checked sport jacket, like a professor whose courses students assiduously avoided. Frick's proudest achievement had been to make Adolf Hitler a German. Hitler had renounced his Austrian citizenship in 1925 to pursue his political star in Germany. His German citizenship application was initially turned down because he had been convicted of treason after the 1923 Munich putsch, his failed attempt to topple the Bavarian government. Frick tried another tack. Anyone named to an official post in Germany was automatically entitled to citizenship. Frick used his influence as a member of the Reichstag to have Hitler appointed constable of a small town called Hildburghausen. Hitler was offended and tore up the appointment. Other gambits failed, but Frick persevered. In February of 1932, he finally managed to have Hitler named a councilor for the state of Braunschweig. Less than a year later, Hitler became Germany's chancellor.

As early as 1924, Frick had introduced two then-shocking bills, one barring Jews from holding public office and another forbidding mixed marriages with Jews. He was merely trying to correct an imbalance, he had argued. The Jew was too powerful. Nearly half of the physicians in Germany were Jews, as were over half of the lawyers and eighty percent of theater directors. To support the proposed ban on intermarriage, Frick read accounts of lurid Jewish sex crimes from a new newspaper, *Der Stürmer*, published by one Julius Streicher.

In those early years, Frick was looked upon simply as another Nazi crank. By 1933, however, Hitler was in power and Frick became minister of the interior. That March, within a month after the Reichstag fire, which Hitler blamed on the Communists, Frick signed the Enabling Law giving Hitler the right to promulgate any measure without the Reichstag's approval. Frick further signed a decree entitled "Securing the Unity of Party and State," which established that the Nazi party controlled the German government and not the other way around. Hitler's authority was now total. Frick had served his Führer well. He had given the patina of legality to despotism.

Still, a Jew might have continued to live in Germany but for Frick's subsequent acts. Kempner began reciting the decrees ratified at the 1935 Congress of the Nazi Party in Nuremberg. Jews were deprived of their citizenship. No matter that twelve thousand of them had died for Germany in World War I and countless others had won Iron Crosses. Their German identity was effaced. Not only marriages, but sexual relations between Jews and Gentiles became a crime. Year by year, the noose tightened. Jews were denied employment, first in journalism, then in medicine, then in dentistry, then in law. They were forbidden to own property. Some decrees seemed a parody. Any Jew with a non-Jewish first name was to assume the name Israel if male and Sara if female. Jews were forbidden to keep canaries. In 1943, Frick signed a decree placing the Jews completely outside the law. You could do what you wanted to a Jew without fear of punishment. The process had begun in Nuremberg; hence this codified persecution became known collectively as the Nuremberg Laws. When the first laws were promulgated, there had been ten thousand Jews in Nuremberg. At the end of the war there were ten.

Kempner's courtroom style was too similar to his adversaries' for some of the Allies—too Teutonic, too dogmatic. Still, prosecutors at the British table whispered their relief that, for once, a lawyer on the American side had displayed a sense of historical perspective. The British prosecutors, in their black coats and striped trousers, formed a small, select corps, skilled in their profession and steeped in the historical context of each case. By contrast, as Howard K. Smith noted in a broadcast: "The weakest feature of the case has been Justice Jackson's staff . . . their briefs are written for them by assistants and many appear not to have read them over before entering the courtroom. They were probably quite skilled at defending railroads or prosecuting gangsters back home. But with a few brilliant exceptions, they have shown absolutely no knowledge of Nazism." Janet Flanner, in her January 5 piece for *The New Yorker*, noted the succinct, reasoned cases the British prosecutors made. But the Americans, she wrote, had managed to make frightful war crimes "dull and incoherent." Katy Walch, a British researcher working for the Americans, confided to a fellow Briton, "You see, they haven't had a classical education."

Jackson's huge staff was suffering from the inefficiencies of scale. For all the prosecutor's other strengths, administration was not among them. He was spending almost no time in the courtroom these days; instead, he willingly delegated the prosecution to assistants, who ran competing duchies. Jackson also recognized, too late, that he had made a fundamental mistake. The small corps of British prosecutors constituted a legal elite. Jackson, instead, had taken on phalanxes of American lawyers of mixed talents from the military. Most were civilians in uniform. They would acquire the requisite points for discharge, and within days would be on their way home, with hardly enough time to show their successors where the PX was, much less the intricacies of cases in progress. Jackson found himself begging people not to leave in the middle of a prosecution. Only 13 of his 150 original lawyers were still with him by January. Jackson complained that his staff was melting away.

Equally aggravating for him were reports from the courtroom of Justice Biddle's behavior on the bench. Biddle could be heard, in stage whispers, denigrating the performance of his countrymen. Poor preparation. Sloppy organization. Amateurish examination. In Jackson's view, Biddle, who months before had been lucky to get a job, had become haughty and full of himself.

At one point during the Frick prosecution, the justices noticed a wave of whispering that swept through the dock. A note was being passed from hand to hand. Hans Fritzsche had written that Major Gerecke was going home: the defendants must do something. The St. Louis chaplain had not seen his wife for more than two years. His soldier sons had made it home, while the aging Gerecke was still abroad eight months after the war had ended. He had indeed decided that it was time to leave.

Back in his cell, later that afternoon, Fritzsche wrote a letter addressed to "Mrs. Reverend Henry Gerecke, St. Louis, Missouri." "Your husband has been taking religious care of the undersigned for more than half a year," Fritzsche began. "We have heard that you wish to see him back home. Because we have wives and children, we understand this wish. Nevertheless, we beg you to put off this desire to have your family once more around you. We cannot lose your husband. No one else can break through the walls that have built up around us, both spiritual and material. We shall be deeply indebted to you. . . ." Fritzsche finished the letter and asked the officer of the day if he might have it circulated among the Protestant defendants.

When Colonel Andrus read Fritzsche's petition, signed by all the Germans, his reaction was instantaneous. The last thing he needed was to break in a new chaplain. He sent a copy of the petition to Gerecke. When the chaplain read it, he fell on his knees and prayed for guidance. If these men facing death needed him, surely his wife must understand.

39

LATE SATURDAY AFTERNOON, January 19, Captain Gilbert sat glassy-eyed, listening to the man who had influenced the political formation of Baldur von Schirach and Wilhelm Frick. He found his visits to Julius Streicher's cell an ordeal. Still, if he was to understand the impulses of the Nazi psyche, he had to understand one of its molders, this squat, coarse, hook-nosed, bullet-headed figure sitting on the cot opposite him. The floor of the cell was littered with Streicher's sketches. He would draw anything—a guard's face, his mess kit, even the toilet bowl. At the end of the day, he threw all the drawings out. The work, Gilbert had to admit, was good, and he wondered at the incongruity of artistic sensibility in so crude a man.

For Gilbert, the worst part of dealing with Streicher was to be patronized. "Circumcision was the most amazing stroke of genius," Streicher was saying. "It wasn't just for sanitary reasons, you can be sure. It was to assure racial consciousness. Do you know what the poet

Heine said about circumcision? You can wipe away baptism, but you cannot wipe away circumcision. Diabolical, isn't it?" As he spoke, Streicher popped a wad of gum. He supported this latest addiction by trading the guards his autograph for the gum. As Streicher talked, Gilbert was reminded of Walther Funk's complaint. He had already been punished enough, the banker said, since every day in court he had to sit next to Julius Streicher.

Fritzsche considered Streicher's *Der Stürmer* an embarrassing rag, and Gilbert, after reading a few issues, understood why. In one article, Streicher had written, "The male sperm in cohabitation is partially or completely absorbed by the female and thus enters her bloodstream. One single cohabitation of a Jew with an Aryan woman is sufficient to poison her blood forever . . . never again will she be able to bear pure Aryan children." Jews, Streicher had written, believed it was morally acceptable to violate a Gentile girl as young as three years old. Jews believed that Christ's mother was a whore. Jews believed that they had the right to take a Christian's money. Streicher had once lectured an audience of professors about a divining rod he had perfected for distinguishing between Jews and Gentiles. He had also amassed an impressive collection of pornography; he had bought it from Jews, he said, and kept it to show the kind of filth they read.

Gilbert marveled that this vulgar man had once been the most powerful figure in Nuremberg, as *Gauleiter* of Franconia, the part of Bavaria within which the city lay. Streicher had begun his professional life as a schoolteacher. He enlisted during the First World War, and by constantly volunteering for the most dangerous missions had won the Iron Cross first class and a battlefield commission. Streicher told Gilbert about the brightest moment in his life. He had formed his own right-wing party after the war. In 1922, he heard Hitler deliver a three-hour oration in Munich. He elbowed his way to the speaker's platform and offered the two thousand members of his group to Adolf Hitler "as a gift."

Streicher had ridden high until his libels against Göring's manhood led to the investigation and condemnation of his seamy business and sexual practices. Göring told the other defendants, "At least we did one good thing. We got that prick Streicher kicked out of office." Streicher indeed had had no power after his 1940 fall. *Der Stürmer* had been not a government organ but a private journal owned by

Streicher, and during the war years the paper's circulation dropped from over a million to fifteen thousand.

Part of Gilbert's problem, as he dealt with inmates like Hess, Rosenberg, and Streicher, was to find the line between true paranoia and culturally conditioned pseudoparanoia. In short, were these people crazy or had they been caught up in a crazy world? As Streicher discoursed on the nature of Jewish sperm, Gilbert had little doubt in this particular case. The larger question was whether the prosecution would be able to slip a noose over this neckless head. Could a fanatic be hanged for publishing racial rubbish?

40

SATURDAY, JANUARY 26, a night of numbing cold, with the temperature at ten degrees Fahrenheit, Maxwell-Fyfe held a soiree. On the drive out to Sir David's house in suburban Zirndorf, the British compound, Justice Jackson's staff car rolled past now-familiar sights: a stack of bathrooms, the tubs exposed, where a bomb had neatly blown off the side of an apartment house; a British plane hanging precariously from the steeple of the church into which it had crashed.

Sir David's party was to celebrate the birthday of Robert Burns. Scottishness ran deep in Sir David's being. He enjoyed the fact that his villa at 7 Goethestrasse was located on land where one of his Scottish ancestors had commanded a regiment during the Thirty Years War. On Sundays he would give his bodyguard the slip and retrace the ebb and flow of that long-ago battle. Though his father had been a poor schoolmaster and he himself a scholarship boy, his attachment to the past had bred in Sir David a deep conservatism. He had been elected to Parliament as a Conservative in 1935, and still held his seat. His celebrity at Nuremberg was burnished by the fact that his wife, Sylvia, was the sister of the actor Rex Harrison.

The party was clearly a roaring success. At a signal from the host, Scottish bagpipers in full Highland regalia marched in, accompanying the haggis Maxwell-Fyfe had ordered flown in from Scotland. After dinner a quartet of British prosecutors singled out the energetic Drexel

Sprecher for one of the parodies that had become a staple of Nuremberg entertaining:

They sang, to the tune of "Old Man River":

> Old man Sprecher, dat old man Sprecher,
> His hands keep wavin',
> He keeps us slavin',
> He keeps on hollerin',
> And we keep follerin'
> . . . along!

Sir Norman Birkett buttonholed Biddle's aide, Herb Wechsler, and violated a cardinal rule of Nuremberg social life by talking shop. The standards of the IMT, Sir Norman informed Wechsler, did not begin to compare with those of the high courts of England. Birkett also explained how much more elevated the Nuremberg bench would be had he been named president. Wechsler was uncomfortable. He tried to steer Birkett off the subject, only to have Sir Norman ask confidentially, Did Wechsler know that Lawrence took young ladies for long rides? And did he know that the British prosecutors referred to the American judges on the bench as Piddle and Barker? Wechsler knew of Birkett's fame in the British courts. Still, his behavior suggested an insecure personality lacking the easy confidence that comes naturally to the wellborn. A minute later, the gangly, wild-thatched jurist excused himself and was off charming a knot of guests with a sonorous recitation of Shakespeare. Wechsler liked that Birkett much better.

41

CAPTAIN GILBERT HAD CONSIDERED escaping for the weekend. The psychologist was emotionally burned out after months of standing in court all day and making nightly and weekend cell visits. He was worried, however, about the stability of Hess and Ribbentrop. Weekend or not, he decided, he would have to see them.

Hess did not stand as required when Gilbert entered the cell that Saturday afternoon. He never stood for anyone, including Colonel

Andrus. On his previous visit, Gilbert had sensed a deterioration in Hess's mental condition. For a time after his electric November 30 announcement that his memory had returned, Hess had stopped reading novels in the courtroom; his performance on the number-memory test had improved. But now he was reading in court again. At first, the guards had yanked the books from his hands, but after a time, Justice Lawrence told them not to bother. He feared that, with no other distraction, Hess might disrupt the proceedings by worse antics.

This day, Gilbert again administered the number-recall test. Hess slipped from a recall of eight digits forward and seven backward the previous time, to five forward and four backward today. He had difficulty remembering witnesses who had testified just days before. Gilbert left the cell and proceeded to the prison office to write his assessment. "The current apathy and beginnings of real and ostensible memory failure," Gilbert wrote, were "part of a negativistic pattern of reaction to the final smashing of the ideology which had supported his ego and now faces him with an intolerable choice between accepting a share of the guilt of Nazism or rejecting his Führer. He'll probably end up by rejecting reality again."

Major Kelley appeared at the door. They needed to talk, he said, leading Gilbert out to the empty exercise yard. As a friend and partner, Kelley went on, he wanted to warn Gilbert that his disdain for the military mind was becoming obvious to the colonel. It was hard, Gilbert replied, to have his work constantly second-guessed by a layman, but he would try to be more respectful. What Kelley left unsaid was that Andrus had suggested getting rid of Gilbert. Kelley had talked him out of it. The psychiatrist expected to be leaving Nuremberg soon, and Gilbert would be his sole pipeline to the data vital to their project.

Shortly after Gilbert left, Hess received another visitor, the court's liaison man, British major Airey Neave. Neave arrived in the midst of a minor tumult. Hess had just flung his mess kit, full of food, at a junior officer who dared peer into his cell. Why, Hess asked Neave, had he been left without a lawyer for a week? The major explained, as he had several times already, that Hess's counsel, Gunther von Rohrscheidt, had slipped on the ice and broken his leg. Very well, Hess said, he would defend himself. This was precisely the outcome

Neave had been sent to forestall. Hess defending himself would turn the trial into a circus, the judges feared. He and Hess could talk the matter over again tomorrow, Neave said, buying time.

As soon as Neave was gone, Hess demanded a pencil and paper from his guard. He was going to write a letter to the members of the court, he said. He had no faith in Rohrscheidt. He wanted him dismissed.

All correspondence from the defendants to the court had to pass through Colonel Andrus's hands. The colonel too had come into his office on Saturday, and he had just read Gilbert's latest evaluation of Hess as "passive suggestible . . . a gullible simpleton. Like the typical hysterical personality, he is incapable of facing reality and avoids frustration by developing a functional disorder, in this case, hysterical amnesia." The colonel was eager to read what this "passive suggestible" personality had written to the IMT. "I draw the attention of the court," Hess's letter read, "to the fact that I have now been a whole week without a defending counsel, while I have not been permitted the right to which the statute entitles me of pleading my own case. In consequence, I was prevented from questioning even a single witness of all those who came forward during this period, although again, I was entitled by the statute to do this." It hardly seemed the letter of a "gullible simpleton," Andrus thought. He forwarded it to Sir Geoffrey Lawrence's chamber.

42

ON SUNDAY, January 27, the day after the Hess visit, Gilbert went to see his other problem patient, Joachim von Ribbentrop. Sauckel and Kaltenbrunner collected stamps. Keitel played solitaire. Göring slept. Ribbentrop fidgeted. Gilbert found the man a windmill of unfocused energy, pacing his cell, scribbling furiously on a sheet of paper, wadding it up and flinging it to the floor, badgering the guards, the doctors, his lawyer, and then forgetting what he wanted of them. He was driving his current counsel, Fritz Sauter, mad. They would adopt a line of defense, and the next day Ribbentrop would deny that he had agreed to it. Ribbentrop would demand a certain witness and then, as soon as Sauter had arranged for the witness's appearance, would reject that person. "The man," Sauter concluded, "is impossible to defend." In Gilbert's view, the erratic behavior reflected a collapsed ego, one that had had the supporting timbers yanked away.

Gilbert tried to associate this Ribbentrop with the man described in an affidavit made by one of the former foreign minister's subordinates: "He would enter a room as though he were descending from a cloud and then suddenly, with a start of surprise, notice that others—mere humans—were also in the room. He would require his entire staff to line up at an airport and wait for five or six hours, even in the rain, until his plane arrived. He would appear and greet us with a frozen smile, raise his hand in the Heil Hitler salute, and be driven off. He was extremely theatrical. We called him the movie actor. He treated us like dogs." This was the same unkempt, ash-gray figure now stretched on his cot, complaining to Gilbert about another insomniac night.

He had a headache, Ribbentrop said. For how long? Gilbert wanted to know. On and off, for five years. Ribbentrop could cite the precise date when the problem began: July 28, 1941, six days after Germany invaded Russia. His diplomatic masterpiece had been the nonaggression pact between Germany and the Soviet Union. Hitler's action had left the treaty in shreds. For once, Ribbentrop had decided that he had to speak his mind. He told the Führer that he had opposed war with the Soviets all along; the outcome of the invasion was now beyond their control. Hitler flew into a rage, shrieking at Ribbentrop, abusing him until the foreign minister was left cowering and trembling. Ribbentrop was going to give him a stroke, Hitler screamed. Never, never must he oppose him on anything. After the tirade, Ribbentrop took to his sickbed for days. His right arm and leg became temporarily paralyzed. He never again stood up to Hitler. That was when the headaches had begun.

Ribbentrop's adjutant, Baron Gustav Steengracht von Moyland, had witnessed the triggering incident. When interrogated at Nuremberg, he had explained that Ribbentrop's uncharacteristic opposition had also made Hitler sick. The event provided Steengracht von Moyland insight into the darker caves of the Führer's personality. "The basic trait of his character," the baron told his interrogator, "was probably lack of confidence. Experts and decent people who tried to influence Hitler were engaged in a vain task. On the other hand, irresponsible creatures who incited him to take violent measures found him extremely accessible. These men were seen as strong, whereas the behavior of anyone halfway normal was condemned as weak or defeatist." Steengracht von Moyland's words resounded in Gilbert's mind as Ribbentrop described the incident of five years before. By sensibly objecting to the invasion of Russia, Ribbentrop had stepped out of the sycophant chorus into the role of sensible counselor. The move apparently had touched a nerve of Hitler's self-doubt and ignited the tantrum.

Gilbert had one more visit. Baldur von Schirach needed propping up to keep him in the penitents' camp. On entering the cell, Gilbert mentioned his visit to Ribbentrop. Schirach sneered and repeated the story of Ribbentrop's shameless acquisition of the aristocratic *von*. "Do you know what Goebbels said about Ribbentrop?" Schirach asked. "He was a husk without a kernel. He bought his name. He married his money. He swindled his way into office." Gilbert looked at this fop and wondered who was more reprehensible, the climber who clawed his way up or the patrician who stooped down to enjoy the fruits of Nazism.

43

THE TRIAL HAD NOT BEEN under way for more than an hour on Monday morning, January 28, when Sir Geoffrey appeared to be slipping into a coma. Charles Dubost, the deputy French prosecutor, was droning away on the stand. During the war, Dubost had been a judge by day and a Resistance leader by night, adept at blowing up trains and bridges. Now, the man had about him a weariness reflected throughout much of the French delegation. The chief French judge, Henri Donnedieu de Vabres, looked magnificent, with his medieval dress, massive hunched shoulders, long gray hair, and drooping mustache— but he never said anything, never asked a question. Donnedieu de Vabres was driven about town in an ancient black Citroën, and was frequently seen standing disconsolately beside it while his chauffeur repaired a breakdown. Airey Neave, who admired the French, thought perhaps their mood reflected the exhausted state of their country. The French staff had not been paid for almost three months.

The entire bench appeared on the verge of sleep as the next witness recited what appeared to be the entire inventory of goods stolen from France during five years of Nazi occupation. Göring nudged Hess. "I'm glad for every bottle of cognac and every cigar we took from them," he said. Hess answered, "Maybe if you hadn't taken all those things, you wouldn't be sitting here now." "Listen, Rudolf," Göring went on, "you don't smoke and you don't drink. And here you are, stuck with me all the same."

Dubost called on a parade of listless concentration camp victims to testify. Sir Geoffrey roused himself, "Monsieur Dubost," he asked, "are you proposing to call still more witnesses on the camps?" Yes, the prosecutor said sheepishly.

Suddenly, the torpor in the room lifted. Something about the woman in the tailored dark blue suit approaching the stand commanded attention. Marie Claude Vaillant-Couturier, age thirty-three, stood erect, her hair pulled back tightly, her face free of makeup, exuding dignity. She had taken leave of her post as a deputy in the French constituent assembly to testify. Dubost began drawing out her story. When France fell, Vaillant-Couturier had been an antifascist journalist, she testified. In 1942, she was arrested, interrogated, and ordered to sign a false confession. "I refused to sign it," she told the court. "The German officer threatened me. I told him I was not afraid of being shot. He told me, 'We have means at our disposal far worse than being shot.'" Soon afterward, Vaillant-Couturier found herself packed on a train with 230 other Frenchwomen en route to Auschwitz. They were given neither food nor drink throughout the journey.

Vaillant-Couturier was assigned to a sewing block at the camp. "We lived right where the trains stopped," she said. "They ran practically right up to the gas chamber. Consequently, we saw the unsealing of the cars and the soldiers letting men, women, and children out. We saw old couples forced to part from each other, mothers forced to abandon their young children. All these people were unaware of the fate awaiting them. To make their arrival more pleasant, an orchestra composed of pretty girls in white blouses and navy blue skirts played during the selection process, gay tunes from *The Merry Widow* and *The Tales of Hoffmann*. Those selected for the gas chamber, old people, mothers, and small children, were escorted immediately to a red brick building.

"All my life," the witness went on, "I will remember Annette Epaux. I saw her on a truck that was taking people to the gas chamber. She had her arms around another French woman. When the truck started she called to me, 'Think of my little boy, if you ever get back to France.' Then they began singing the 'Marseillaise.' " The court-room was quiet, but for the simultaneous interpreters echoing Vaillant-Couturier's words behind their glass enclosures.

As Dubost urged her gently on, the woman's head bowed. Her voice became barely audible. "One night, we were awakened by hor-rible cries," she said. "The next day we learned that the Nazis had run out of gas and the children had been hurled into the furnaces alive." Dubost asked her how many of the 230 Frenchwomen in her train survived Auschwitz. Forty-nine, Vaillant-Couturier answered.

After she was dismissed, the woman walked past the dock and stopped within feet of Hermann Göring. This was a moment that would never come her way again, she knew. As she wrote later, "I wanted to see them up close. I wanted to see the expressions on their faces. I looked at each of them in turn. They looked like ordinary people with a normal, human side, which somehow didn't surprise me. At Auschwitz, one of the SS used to bring sugar to a five-year-old gypsy boy after he gassed the boy's mother and sister."

During the midday break, Otto Kranzbuehler unexpectedly appeared in the doorway of the attic lunchroom, his ashen face contrasting sharply with his navy blue uniform. He looked at his client, Admiral Dönitz. "Didn't anybody know anything about these things?" he asked. Dönitz shrugged and went on eating. Göring looked up. "You know how it is," he said, "even in a battalion, the battalion commander doesn't know what's going on at the front. The higher up you are, the less you see of what's going on below." Kranzbuehler shook his head and left.

44

AFTER THE COURT ADJOURNED that day, Otto Streng, the librarian, brought Albert Speer *The Autobiography of Benvenuto Cellini*, as the prisoner had requested. But Speer had difficulty concentrating. The Vaillant-Couturier testimony had sent the court reeling, and he recognized one thing clearly. Of all the areas of evidence, association with the concentration camps was the most damning. He had done well so far, he believed, threading his way through the minefield of guilt. His lawyer had planted his two most attractive defenses in evidence, the Hitler assassination attempt and Speer's resistance to the Führer's scorched-earth directives. The nature of the relationship with Sauckel, as to who was superior to whom, was still up in the air. But a proven connection to the camps could be fatal. Speer had hard thinking to do.

The witness on the morning of January 29 was François Boix, a tall, lean, intense man. Boix had survived the Mauthausen concentration camp because he was a professional photographer. His testimony had begun the day before, following Marie Vaillant-Couturier's appearance. He had testified about a Mauthausen escapee who had been led to the gallows while a band played a ballad. Boix's reappearance today promised no letup in the grim chronicle of camp life.

Charles Dubost asked if Boix had ever seen any defendant in the dock at Mauthausen. "Speer," the witness replied. During the interrogation phase, Speer had admitted to being at Mauthausen, but only on the periphery, to consider construction of a railhead. Dubost asked Boix when he had seen the munitions chief. In 1943, Boix answered: "I did not see him myself, but the head of the identification department took a roll of film with his Leica, which I developed. I recognized Speer and some SS leaders." Dubost pressed on: "You saw Speer in the pictures you developed?" "Yes," Boix answered. "Afterward, I had to write his name and the date on the print." Some of the pictures, Boix said, had been taken at the Mauthausen quarry, where inmates were worked to death carrying out stones and "parachuted" to the bottom for the guards' amusement. "There are even pictures which show him congratulating Franz Ziereis, the commandant of Mauthausen, with a handshake," Boix added. All told, he said, he had seen Speer in thirty-six shots.

Documents introduced after Boix's appearance established that Speer had worked with Heinrich Himmler to obtain camp inmates for arms production. Minutes read from a meeting of the Central Planning Board recorded Speer's words: "There is nothing to be said against the SS taking drastic steps and putting known slackers into concentration camps. There is no alternative." A memo from the files of the SS was read into the record: "Albert Speer has been enrolled as an SS man on my staff by my order," signed "Heinrich Himmler, *Reichsführer.*"

A proud Harriet Zetterberg sat at the prosecution table. The evidence placing Speer at Mauthausen and in contact with Himmler was the fruit of her research.

As the court adjourned, Speer recognized that the day had been a disaster. He had been placed squarely at Mauthausen and in association with the commandant, Ziereis, a sadist known to take pleasure in carrying out executions personally. To be linked as well to Himmler was to be stained ineradicably. For the first time, Albert Speer felt brushed by the wingtip of the angel of death.

45

ROSE KORB WAS SORTING through the mail and came across something she thought the colonel might enjoy. Andrus spread it on his desk, a child's watercolor of snowflakes descending on a field of yellow and blue flowers. "Ah yes," he said, "done by the Himmler brat." To the Allies, Heinrich Himmler, after Hitler, had been the most chilling figure in the Nazi pantheon. It was Himmler who had rendered the Führer's abstract manias into the tangible solutions of Zyklon B gas and the crematoria. After Himmler's suicide, his wife had been arrested and she was now in the colonel's jail, held as a material witness. That left the problem of what to do with Himmler's daughter. Andrus had gone to some pains to find a still-operating school, and had her enrolled there. He had also given the child a watercolor set. She responded with presents addressed to "Dearest Colonel Andrus," one being a cotton snowman which Andrus kept on his desk. Still, it was not wise to be thought too soft, hence the colonel's references to "the brat."

The colonel's main concern this morning was not a Nazi off-spring, but Major Kelley's impending departure. All along, Andrus had felt a better rapport with the gregarious Kelley than with the reserved Gilbert, though both men's contact with the press made him nervous. A few weeks before, *Stars and Stripes* had broken the hushed-up story of Dr. Leonardo Conti's October suicide. Through his intelligence network, Andrus learned that Kelley had been talking to reporters. His sources further informed him that Kelley was "misappropriating" official files. This information had been followed by Kelley's abrupt announcement that he was going home on points.

Andrus had also learned about the Kelley-Gilbert book collaboration from Boris Polevoi, the *Pravda* correspondent. Polevoi had assiduously cultivated Gilbert, who he knew had access to the defendants. Gilbert had put off Polevoi time and again, saying it was against Andrus's regulations for him to talk to reporters. Finally, after Polevoi's endless pressure, Gilbert had blurted out, "I can't. I'm saving all that for a book." Polevoi thereupon began pressing Andrus for inside stories, and inevitably revealed his awareness of the book project.

On learning of Kelley's impending departure, Gilbert cornered the major and expressed his own surprise. Kelley explained that he was going home to pursue a new interest; he was going to write a book on racial prejudice. But what about their project? a stunned Gilbert asked. Kelley put an arm around Gilbert's shoulder. "Look, Gus," he said, "there's been a big fall-off in the public's interest in this trial." Gilbert asked Kelley where he could reach him after his discharge. He did not know, Kelley said; but he would be in touch.

On February 6, Major Douglas Kelley flew from airfield Y28 to the nearest port of embarkation. After he was gone, Gilbert discovered that Kelley had taken all the handwritten originals of the autobiographies they had asked the defendants to write. He had also taken a copy of all of Gilbert's notes on his cell visits. What Gilbert did not yet know was that Kelley had already approached the American publisher Simon and Schuster about a book of his own on the twenty-one men in the cells at Nuremberg.

46

THE DAY KELLEY LEFT, the prosecution opened the case of the stolen art treasures. Janet Flanner, Paris correspondent for *The New Yorker*, had eagerly awaited the moment. She had managed to obtain, on the eve of the case, a document that recorded Hermann Göring's lecture to an audience of *Gauleiter*s on how to treat conquered France. "What happens to the French is of complete indifference to me," Göring had told the party leaders. "Maxim's must have the best food for us but not for the French. . . . I intend to plunder in France, and profitably. There will be such inflation in Paris that everything will go for smash. The franc will not be worth more than a well-known type of paper used for a certain purpose." Göring was, Flanner had to admit, a man of his word. It began on June 21, 1940. Göring, in his sky-blue field marshal's uniform, had accompanied Hitler to the forest of Compiègne. Here the Germans savored the sweet revenge of having the French surrender in the very railway car where the Germans had been forced to capitulate in 1918. Afterward, Göring slipped away to the Jeu de Paume in the Louvre Museum, where he covetously eyed the works of Rubens, Fragonard, Velázquez, and the Cranachs, elder and younger. The *Reichsmarschall* and Hitler, both considering themselves connoisseurs, came up with a scheme through which Germany would become the "protector" of Europe's art treasures. The key was Alfred Rosenberg. Was Rosenberg not party chief for ideological training and education? Three months after the conquest of France, Hitler gave Rosenberg a simple, sweeping power, the right to confiscate art anywhere in occupied Europe.

Alfred Rosenberg was not really a German. He had been born in Reval, Estonia, into a German-speaking family. In gossip-ridden party circles, word spread that Rosenberg was not even an ethnic German. Supposedly, his artisan ancestors had simply taken the Germanic name of the local landowner. Rosenberg had not set foot in Germany until he was twenty-five years old. Though he rose spectacularly in the party, he knew that philistines mocked his intellectual aspirations; they joked behind his back about his *Myth of the Twentieth Century*. The new assignment gave Rosenberg the opportunity to show the Führer a man of action as well as a philosopher. He created Einstab Rosenberg to carry out his new art mission. His operatives followed simple procedures. If a desired painting, sculpture, or carving belonged to foreign Aryans, the owners were compelled to sell it. If it belonged to Jews, it was merely taken. The latter task was facilitated by the fact that thousands of French Jews had fled or been driven from their homes. Their property was declared "ownerless," and Einstab Rosenberg had an obligation to store it in safe places in the Reich. Rosenberg's proudest report to the Führer described 69,619 Jewish apartments in Paris emptied of their contents, filling 29,984 freight cars with art and fine furniture. Every Parisian moving company had to be hired to finish the job.

The prosecution possessed a document written by a Dr. Hermann Bunjes revealing how Göring benefited from Einstab Rosenberg. Dr. Bunjes, an art historian, had been engaged as Göring's personal agent in France. Seven months after the fall of Paris, Göring ordered Bunjes to meet him on his arrival at the Jeu de Paume. As Göring went through, he would tap his baton on the works to be sent to Germany. An uncomfortable Bunjes pointed out that French officials bitterly objected to the Einstab Rosenberg operations. This was Bunjes's first meeting with Göring, and the words came hesitantly. He sensed Göring's annoyance and sought to bolster his argument by pointing out that Rosenberg's activities contravened the Hague Convention on Land Warfare. Göring blew up, his voice echoing throughout the museum. "My orders are final! These art objects in the Jeu de Paume are to be taken to Germany immediately. Those for me are to be loaded into two railroad cars and attached to my private train." Bunjes went on manfully pointing out that even German army lawyers objected to these confiscations. "My dear Bunjes," Göring said, "let me worry about that. Don't you know I outrank any jurist in Germany?"

Göring had always contended that he was merely holding the works of art until a gallery could be erected for the German people; further, he clearly meant to pay for everything. But, as he once put it, "My collector's passion got the better of me." His major collecting rival had been the Führer, who had first crack. But Hitler's taste was much narrower than the *Reichsmarschall*'s. Göring was thus able to keep the works of artists whom Hitler considered degenerate—Chagall, Grosz, Klee, van Gogh, Cézanne, Gauguin, and Picasso. Göring also acquired works of Goya, Van Dyck, Hals, Velázquez, Titian, Raphael, and Fragonard. He once complimented Rosenberg on his performance and told him, "I have now obtained by purchase, presents, bequests, and barter, the greatest private collection in Europe."

It all came out in the prosecution case. And few, even in the dock, accepted Göring's claims that he had paid for much of the art. An assistant prosecutor, Thomas Lambert, listening to the evidence of Göring's looting, told a colleague, "There are now three grades of larceny: petty, grand, and glorious."

47

THE MOMENT WAS SWEET for Burt Andrus. After months of bureaucratic maneuvering, the colonel had finally managed to have his sketches approved as the official symbol of the IMT. The shield with the scales of justice dominating a broken swastika and fallen Nazi eagle now appeared on letterheads, as a shoulder patch on uniforms, as a pin for women's blouses, and in a dozen other uses. And here in his office stood the one Russian who had conquered the Americans, Nikitchenko's enchanting interpreter, Tania Giliarevskaya, seeking more information on the new insignia.

The seductive Tania also begged the colonel to add another name to the guest list for his Saturday soiree. Andrus's opera-dinner parties had become a feature of the social scene. He had established a reputation as an energetic and attentive host. It pleased him to have a U.S. Supreme Court justice, eminent English jurists, and bemedaled generals of four nations at his table. On February 9, he was throwing a party in honor of the Soviets who had arrived for their phase of the prosecution. Both Russian judges had accepted, Sir David and Lady Maxwell-Fyfe were coming, and so were a half dozen attractive women from the IMT staff. It was so convenient to entertain graciously here. The army provided the transportation, the dinner was written off as official entertainment, and Special Services produced the opera tickets.

The man Giliarevskaya wanted the colonel to invite was Major General Alexandrov. The gesture would please General Nikitchenko, she said. Andrus found the woman impossible to deny. Of course, he said, the general was welcome—though in Andrus's opinion, Alexandrov, not Comrade Rasumov, was probably the NKVD man on the scene, and merely wanted to come to keep an eye on his countrymen. Giliarevskaya thanked the colonel profusely and left with sample letterheads, shoulder patches, and a pin for herself, all depicting the colonel's insignia.

Despite the obstacles of politics and nationality, Tania and Major Bob Stewart had been seeing each other. Most of the time, their romance savored of forbidden fruit; but the forbidden nature also produced deep stresses. Jim Rowe, Stewart's colleague on the judges' staff, had taken the handsome major aside and warned him about how the Soviet security apparatus, the NKVD, worked. The woman was likely a plant, spying on the Americans through Stewart. It depressed Stewart to have to imagine himself and Tania as pawns in the games of nations and not simply as two human beings in love. Yet he could not entirely dismiss Rowe's warning. American intelligence was not without its own resources, and Rowe informed Stewart that Tania was married to a Russian general and had a child.

The colonel's party was a success. A performance of Verdi's *Ballo in Maschera* was followed by a night of dancing at the Grand. The young women whom Andrus had invited were especially grateful. Her invitation confirmed Katy Walch's good opinion of the colonel, and while dancing with Nikitchenko, the researcher picked up some intelligence of her own. In the coming days, the Russian prosecution expected to drop a blockbuster on the courtroom.

48

ON MONDAY MORNING, February 11, a Soviet prosecutor, General N. D. Zorya, was attempting to establish that Germany's invasion of the Soviet Union represented criminal aggression in violation of a binding peace pact. He read into the record an affidavit taken in Moscow from German field marshal Friedrich Paulus, who had surrendered at Stalingrad. In the statement, Paulus swore that he had had personal knowledge of Germany's aggressive intent.

The very mention of Paulus stirred bitter memories for the Germans. Jodl, Speer, Dönitz, even Göring—any of the shrewder minds in the dock—had recognized after the defeat at Stalingrad in 1943 that the war could not be won. The Germans had suffered horrific losses. Flags flew at half mast for three days of national mourning. The people were told that Field Marshal Paulus had fallen in battle with his troops. Actually, Paulus had gone over to the Russians after surrendering, and he subsequently broadcast speeches urging German soldiers to give up the hopeless struggle. His name became synonymous with treachery. But from Paulus's standpoint, he was no traitor. His Sixth Army had been surrounded. Hitler promised that Göring's Luftwaffe would come to Paulus's relief, but the planes never came. Still, Hitler had ordered the field marshal to fight on to the last man. In Paulus's judgment, Hitler had condemned 300,000 Germans to starvation, sickness, freezing cold, and ultimately to death or Russian captivity. He could find no reason to remain loyal to such a leader.

Otto Stahmer, Göring's lawyer, objected. Stahmer was a big, formidable man whose manner commanded authority. The Paulus affidavit was merely a piece of paper coerced from a traitor general by the Communists, Stahmer said. It proved nothing. If Paulus was such an important witness, let the prosecution produce him so that the defense could cross-examine him, or else they should withdraw this worthless evidence.

The Soviet chief prosecutor, Roman Rudenko, rose, a barely concealed smile on his face. He would indeed like to call Field Marshal Paulus as a witness, Rudenko told the court. In fact, he could produce him that afternoon. The three-alarm signal rang throughout the building. Reporters came barreling out of the pressroom, the cafeteria, the PX, jamming the entrance to room 600. Sir Geoffrey Lawrence asked if he was hearing correctly. The Soviet prosecutor replied that Paulus had been secretly flown in to Nuremberg and was now waiting in Rudenko's quarters.

As Sir Geoffrey called the court to order, a white-helmeted guard opened the door and a lone figure appeared, lean, dignified, wearing a dark blue suit that could not conceal the bearing of a soldier. In the visitors' gallery, Russian VIP guests leaned forward eagerly, among them Marshal Georgi Zhukov and the novelist Ilya Ehrenburg. Boris

Polevoi, the *Pravda* correspondent, studied Friedrich Paulus with particular interest. Polevoi had been in Stalingrad on the fateful day of the surrender. He remembered a young Soviet officer, pale and sweating in the midst of the Russian winter, standing before a destroyed building. The officer had been told that Paulus was trapped in the basement, and he was to go down and bring the field marshal out. Suspicious wires protruded from the basement stairway. The Russian descended warily. Minutes later, a gaunt, stooped figure, his cap and fur-lined greatcoat frosted with snow, had come up the stairs. He drew a revolver from his coat while the Russians stood frozen. He flung the weapon at their feet. Field Marshal Paulus had surrendered.

Hans Fritzsche too had been at Stalingrad. He had gone there to report to the German people on radio the heroic stand their sons were making. He had been appalled at the frightful conditions, the lack of food and medicine, the frozen hillocks of bodies dotting the fields. On his departure, he had bidden Paulus good-bye and seen defeat written in the man's eyes.

In the interpreters' booth, Lieutenant Peter Uiberall adjusted his earphones with a shaking hand. Thus far, Uiberall had been working in the Dostert operation testing other interpreter candidates, and this was his first stint behind a microphone. As Paulus began to testify, Uiberall was much relieved. The field marshal's speech was calm, slow, deliberate.

Until now, the defendants had expressed their contempt for the Soviet prosecution by ignoring the proceedings and reading novels concealed behind official papers. But this day, their attention was riveted. Roman Rudenko conducted the questioning. He first established that a Russo-German nonaggression pact had been in force between August 1939 and June 1941. What, he asked, had General Paulus been doing during that period? In September 1940, Paulus explained, he had been named a deputy chief of the general staff. What were his duties? He had been specifically assigned to develop an operation ultimately known as Barbarossa, a surprise attack on the Soviet Union. "Who of these defendants," Rudenko asked, "was an active participant in initiating the war of aggression against the Soviet Union?" Paulus surveyed the dock. "As I observed them," he said, "they were the chief of the OKW, Keitel, the chief of operations, Jodl, and Göring, as commander in chief of the air force."

As Justice Lawrence declared a recess, a ruckus broke out in the dock. Göring was shouting to Stahmer, "Ask that dirty pig if he knows he's a traitor. Ask Paulus if he's taken out Russian citizenship papers!" At the other end of the dock, Fritzsche was telling Schacht, "You see, that's the tragedy of the German people, right there. Poor Paulus was caught between the devil and his duty. If a man like that could betray his country, there must have been something wrong with the country."

49

PAULUS RETURNED ON FEBRUARY 12 for cross-examination. Keitel leaned toward Ribbentrop and said, "Just think of it. Paulus was supposed to take Jodl's place. If he had, Paulus would be up here instead of Jodl." Jodl knew it too, and throughout the hours of Paulus's cross-examination, the caprices of fate taunted him.

His American custodians found Alfred Jodl impenetrable, encased in glacial reserve. He made clear to Gilbert during cell visits that the psychologist's attentions were unwelcome. He was emotionally self-sufficient, and his practical mind could project his probable fate in this court as clearly as it had worked out Hitler's military operations.

Like Keitel, Jodl was a member of the militarist caste and inclined to deprecate upstart politicians. Thus, his eventual veneration of Hitler had come as a surprise to himself. In 1939, just before the Polish campaign, Jodl, on Keitel's recommendation, had been named operations chief of the general staff. Thereafter he had stood virtually at the Führer's elbow. As he witnessed Hitler's successful bluff in sending German troops into the presumably demilitarized Rhineland, the bloodless conquest of Austria, the humbling of Chamberlain at Munich, the easy early victories in Poland and France, he had been seduced. "It is all well and good for me as a member of the privileged class to look down my nose on the Austrian corporal," he once wrote. "But that would show not how lowborn he is, but how petty I am."

His analytical mind, however, could not be turned off when Hitler began to fail. As early as 1942, after Hitler had committed Germany to a two-front war, Jodl knew that his country could not win. He came to realize that the blunders of genius could be as colossal as its victories. The exhilaration of the early years vanished. Life under

Hitler's thumb, on the endless round from Berlin to the Wolf's Lair in Rastenburg to Berchtesgaden, became for Jodl a "cross between a monastery and a concentration camp."

In August of 1942, Hitler became infuriated by the lack of progress of Field Marshal Wilhelm List in the Caucasus campaign. He dispatched Jodl to goad the hesitant List onward. On his return from the front, Jodl reported that List's behavior was militarily correct. He himself had seen the snow-clogged mountain passes that List was operating in, and agreed that it was impossible to carry out Hitler's orders. Hitler leaned over the map table, eyes bulging. "I didn't send you, Jodl, to hear you report on all the difficulties," he began. "You were supposed to represent my view! That was your job! Instead you come back completely under the influence of the frontline commanders. You are nothing but their megaphone! I didn't need to send you there for that."

After the List affair, Hitler decided to replace Jodl with Paulus as operations chief, just as soon as Paulus conquered Stalingrad. Jodl too was eager for the change. How preferable that would have been, he thought, as he watched Paulus being cross-examined: Paulus up here, an indicted war criminal, and he, Alfred Jodl, permitted an honorable soldier's death alongside his men.

50

RAY D'ADDARIO, the signal corps photographer, received word to bring his camera to Justice Jackson's office. On his arrival, Mrs. Douglas informed him that today, February 13, was Jackson's birthday. She had planned a little surprise party, quietly putting out the word for the judges and senior staff to stop by the office as soon as court adjourned. First, she wanted D'Addario to take the justice's picture. Jackson protested modestly, but began clearing the debris from his desk while D'Addario set up the camera. The photographer was just about to shoot when Mrs. Douglas started combing Jackson's hair. D'Addario thought this would make an appealing picture, and clicked off several frames before shooting the justice alone.

That evening, Francis Biddle wrote to his wife, Katherine, that he was still the power behind the bench. "This is not an able crowd," he wrote. "Lawrence never has a thought of his own . . . though he does make an admirable presiding officer. The French add almost nothing.

"As Bob's birthday is today," he continued, "they had a cake for him with presents and jokes. But we all thought the affair really stuffy . . . too much spontaneous preparation, little piercing cries of delight by Mrs. Douglas, rouged to the eyes and trying to do a 'grand dame.' "
Among the staff, the closeness of Jackson and his secretary was well known. The rumor was that Jackson had an unhappy domestic situation back home. While Biddle was caustic, others who dealt with Elsie Douglas found the woman charming and capable. To Jackson, Elsie was just right, professionally indispensable and his trusted confidante. And she was sensitive to appearances. Ray D'Addario received a call from Mrs. Douglas the day after the party. Any photographs of her combing the justice's hair were to be destroyed, including the negatives, she instructed him.

51

ON THE MORNING OF FEBRUARY 14 the defendants welcomed the opportunity to walk and chat briefly in the exercise yard before being marched off to the courtroom. Schirach, because he received newspapers from American relatives, was always asked what was happening in the world outside. His news this morning threw a pall over the group. The Japanese "Tiger of Malaya," General Tomoyuki Yamashita, had just been executed for war crimes. Hans Frank mentioned the news to Göring to see how the "strongman" took it. Frank was annoyed that Göring still expected him to approach from behind and take his place at Göring's left, as though they were walking in the court of the Reich Chancellery rather than in a prison yard. "So what," Göring said of Yamashita's end. "You should brace yourself for a death with dignity. We will be martyrs. Even if it takes fifty years, the German people will recognize us as heroes. They'll put our bones in marble caskets in a great national shrine." Frank looked dubious. Still, Göring's bravado had its appeal to waverers like himself. Breast-beating, groveling before the victors, and self-flagellation were barely preferable to Göring's proud defiance. Often Göring made much sense, Frank thought, as when he reminded Keitel, Schacht, and Schirach that their wives, along with his Emmy, had been arrested. "You see," Göring lectured, "they are just as bad as the Gestapo. Don't let them pretend they're democratic. What do women and children have to do with all this?"

The case announced on the bulletin board that day made all uncomfortable but the Russians. They had insisted on charging the Germans with the Katyn massacre, the murder of thousands of Polish POWs in a forest near Smolensk in Russia. The Americans and British had hoped against hope that the Soviet Union would drop the charge. All Katyn did was to call attention to the ambiguous position of Russians sitting in judgment of others on charges of aggression and wartime atrocities. The Soviets had snatched almost half of Poland through their pact with Hitler. They had attacked Finland, annexed Estonia, Latvia, and Lithuania, and seized Bessarabia from Romania. No one denied that once they had gone to war the Russian armies and people had suffered monstrous atrocities at the hands of the Germans. There was so much evidence of this that the Western Allies believed it was both unnecessary and foolish to bring up the shaky Katyn charge.

Colonel Y. V. Pokrovsky, Rudenko's deputy, began introducing document USSR 34, the report of an Extraordinary Soviet State Commission claiming that the Nazis had murdered over eleven thousand Poles in the Katyn forest. Göring and Hess ostentatiously ripped off their earphones. Schirach chuckled in derision. The defendants' scorn had some justification, the Western lawyers knew. The prosecution had in hand strong evidence suggesting that the Russians, not the Nazis, had murdered the Poles. They appeared to be seizing a chance to palm off on the Nazis a war crime of their own. Robert Jackson was dismayed. The Russians were playing right into the defendants' hands. Doubts over Katyn could color the entire prosecution case.

On Saturday, Captain Gilbert was told to report to Colonel Andrus as soon as court adjourned. Gilbert made his way down to Andrus's first-floor office, glad to be wearing the colonel's new shoulder patch. On his arrival, Andrus handed him a new regulation growing out of Göring's disruptive behavior, particularly during the Paulus testimony.

He already knew what Gilbert was going to say, Andrus observed. This new rule would have a bad psychological effect on the defendants' morale. But Sir Geoffrey was on his back. Göring was a threat to the dignity of the proceedings. Gilbert finished reading the document, hard pressed to conceal his delight. This was essentially the isolation plan that Speer had urged on Gilbert and that he had recommended to the colonel weeks before. The colonel's proposal was necessary, Gilbert agreed. Good, Andrus said, because he expected the psychologist to work out the details and deliver the news.

Gilbert knew that Andrus's animus toward Göring bordered on an obsession. The colonel suspected Göring of being homosexual, though there was no proof. He told people that Göring wore rouge and lipstick and painted his toenails, basing the charge on the fact that Göring had brought to Nuremberg a leather case full of male toiletries. Gilbert found the colonel's easy aspersions unhelpful, and preferred to seek understanding of the Göring character in cell visits and in studying the man's dossier.

In the latter, he would find early clues to Göring's persona. Göring's father had been German consul general in Haiti at the time the mother came back to Germany to give birth to Hermann. Almost immediately, she returned to her husband, leaving the infant in the care of a friend. She did not see her son again for three years. According to the dossier, Göring's earliest memory was of his mother's return. She had opened her arms to embrace the child, who rushed at her and beat her in the face with his small fists. A person's first memory, Gilbert believed, was psychologically significant. In Göring's case, the memory revealed an ego, even at that tender age, offended at not being the center of his mother's universe. Gilbert also came across Frau Göring's early estimate of her son. "Hermann," she had said, "will either become a great man or a criminal." She was right, Gilbert thought; he had become both.

Upon leaving Andrus this Saturday, Gilbert returned to his office to begin what he considered an agreeable task—reducing the influence of the inmate Hermann Göring.

Andrus felt that his endurance had been tested to the limit. The wishes of Justice Lawrence—the reasonable requests of a civil man—did not upset him. But the memo he now held was from a deliberate tormentor. General Leroy Watson had continued to pull surprise inspections of the prison. In the latest—on Saturday, February 16—refuse had been found in the exercise yard, a guard was posted in the wrong place, a German civilian had a key to the ammo room. The report ended with Watson's customary officiousness: "You will report to my office Monday, February 18, with your explanation of these deficiencies."

What did they expect? Andrus complained. They sent him green kids. His personnel turnover had reached over 600 percent for enlisted men and 125 percent for officers. And the 21 defendants on cellblock C were not his only responsibility. He had 250 more prisoners in nine separate categories of confinement. Though he had been allotted four officers for his operations staff, he had only two. When replacements finally arrived, Watson had blithely informed Andrus that he was overstaffed and took the new men for himself.

Burton Andrus was a proud man, a professional. He knew that the one fatal reputation a soldier could acquire was to be labeled a whiner. For over twenty-seven years, he had taken his army assignments and carried them out without complaint. The Nuremberg job was a man-killer, the pressure unrelenting. He was on call virtually twenty-four hours a day, seven days a week. For reasons he could not fathom, he was being hounded by a man who wanted to break him and was coming close to succeeding. Andrus decided to do something he would never before have contemplated. He had a cousin, General Clint Andrus, at First Army headquarters, to whom he wrote a personal letter describing his treatment at the hands of Leroy Watson. He needed help, he said, before he was driven from his post and had an honorable career end in undeserved disgrace.

The defendants were taken to the prison basement for their weekly shower and strip search. In the meantime, their cells were searched and sprayed for vermin. Gus Gilbert decided to break the news on their return to the cellblock. He had the duty officer line them up in the corridor. The privilege of speaking to each other had been abused, he explained, particularly in recent outbursts in the courtroom. Henceforth, by order of Colonel Andrus, they were going to be assigned a new dining arrangement. Gilbert knew that the closest they came to normal socializing was in the lunchroom in the courthouse attic, time which they treasured. In the future, however, they would have lunch there in six separated dining spaces. Gilbert had designed the breakup to work to the prosecution's advantage. To what he called the "youth lunchroom" he assigned Speer, Fritzsche, Schirach, and Funk. His strategy was to have Speer and Fritzsche wean the other two from Göring's influence. Next, he set up an "elders' lunchroom," to include Papen, Neurath, Schacht, and Dönitz. The dynamic here was to have the others work on the admiral's loyalty to Hitler. To the next room, he assigned Frank, Seyss-Inquart, Keitel, and Sauckel. His hope was that Frank might crack the loyalty of his companions. Raeder, Streicher, Hess, and Ribbentrop were to dine together. Streicher's odious presence, Gilbert believed, would neutralize them. Jodl, Frick, Kaltenbrunner, and Rosenberg were put together because their lack of affinity might defuse any mischief. Hermann Göring was to dine alone. Göring cursed at the news.

That afternoon, Dr. Pfluecker visited the defendants to see who might be needing a sleeping pill that night. The doctor virtually clicked his heels as he entered each cell. In Pfluecker's mind, he was still in the presence of his superiors. He told Göring that the new lunch plan was shameful and added, "We Germans must stick together in good times and bad."

That evening, Lieutenant Tex Wheelis came on duty after having a few beers at the Snake Pit, one of the 27th Regiment's clubs. On learning of the new regulation, Wheelis stopped by Göring's cell. Tex Wheelis was controversial, a man whose brash camaraderie split people between admirers and detractors. He and Göring got along famously. Recently, Wheelis had had his picture taken with Göring, who inscribed it "To the great Texas hunter." One night at the bar of the Grand, Wheelis had shown a handsome silver watch to his friends. He turned it over and revealed the engraved signature of Hermann Göring. Göring had given it to him as a gift, he boasted.

This Saturday night, Wheelis told Göring how sorry he was about the unfair policy on the new lunch arrangement. But, the *Reichsmarschall* should be aware, he had a friend in Tex Wheelis.

On Sunday, February 17, Captain Gilbert visited Baldur von Schirach, a possible convert to repentance. He asked Schirach what had made him an anti-Semite. "Henry Ford," he answered. "In my youth, I moved in aristocratic circles and never came into contact with Jews." At age seventeen, he read Ford's book, *The International Jew*, and became an anti-Semite overnight. He thought he had discovered a great truth to guide his life. It was, he said, a form of perverted idealism, and had been his downfall. Nothing could have been more idealistic than his creation of the Hitler Youth, he had believed. Now he was regarded as the breeder of little Nazi monsters.

His wife's idealism, he told Gilbert, had even done him in with Hitler. He had married Henriette, the surprisingly refined daughter of the hustler photographer and Nazi court jester, Heinrich Hoffmann. As the wife of a prominent Nazi, Henriette had enjoyed freedom to travel abroad. In 1943, while in Lisbon, she picked up a copy of *Life* magazine and was horrified to read in it about Nazi atrocities. She went on to Amsterdam and watched from her hotel window as the Gestapo conducted a roundup of Dutch Jews. She saw them clubbed, kicked, and robbed of their valuables. She made up her mind. She must warn the Führer of this barbaric behavior.

The opportunity came that June when she and Baldur were invited to join Hitler at his retreat in Berchtesgaden. At what seemed an appropriate moment, Henriette gave Hitler an impassioned description of what she had read about in *Life* and witnessed with her own eyes in Amsterdam. "Pure sentimentality," Hitler said dismissively. He wished to hear no more of it. Thereafter, for the rest of the stay, Baldur von Schirach could do nothing right. When he began to describe his plans for refurbishing Vienna after the war, Hitler shrieked that Vienna must never be allowed to compete with Berlin. The couple left after two days and were never invited to Berchtesgaden again.

After the German surrender Schirach threw away his uniform, took the name Richard Falk, and disappeared into Austria. He could not believe his good fortune when he learned, over the BBC, that Baldur von Schirach was dead. He found a room in the Austrian town of Schwaz and began work on a mystery novel, *The Secrets of Myrna Loy*. But when he heard that Nazi leaders were being placed under arrest, he gave himself up to the Americans. He did so, he said, "in order to answer for my actions before an international court." At the same time, he volunteered to reeducate German youth in the ways of democracy.

Gilbert asked him if his turning over sixty thousand Viennese Jews to the SS had been another act of idealism. He had genuinely believed, Schirach said, that these people were being resettled in the East. That, Gilbert knew, was a lie. Schirach had been on the distribution list for Heydrich's and later Kaltenbrunner's weekly extermination reports.

This Sunday afternoon, Gilbert particularly wanted Schirach's reaction to the new segregation plan. He reminded Schirach that he was one of those who had been misbehaving in the dock, especially during the Katyn case. Instead of defending himself, Schirach collapsed in syrupy apology. That was precisely what worried Gilbert. The man seemed to surrender to the influence of the last person who talked to him. Schirach said he was pleased with the new dining arrangement. At least it placed him beyond Göring's reach.

Gilbert heard the same reaction in virtually all the cells. He had not realized how much they all feared Göring. Most relieved was Speer, who looked upon the separation as a personal victory, since he had originally planted the idea with Gilbert. As for Göring, Gilbert found him bewildered, like a prankish schoolboy surprised to find himself expelled. "Don't you see," he pleaded to Gilbert, "all this joking and horseplay is just comic relief. We've got to let off a little steam. If I didn't pep them up, some of them would simply collapse.

"Don't you think, in the loneliness of this cell, I reproach myself?" he went on. "Don't you think I wish my life had taken a different road instead of ending up like this?" Gilbert listened, surprised at the unaccustomed humility. As he prepared to leave, Göring begged him to change the arrangement at least so that he did not have to eat alone. He began to berate Andrus. "Just because I am the number-one Nazi in this group doesn't make me the most dangerous. The colonel ought to bear in mind that he is dealing with a historic figure. Right or wrong, we are historic personalities. And he is a nobody!"

Gilbert left the cell feeling that never had he been more right than in assigning Göring the solitary position.

52

ROMAN RUDENKO WAS NO FOOL, and when the Soviet prosecutor
seemed to be one, it was usually because of actions—such as the raising of the Katyn issue—forced on him by Moscow. It pained Rudenko
to realize that his people, who had suffered so incomparably at the
hands of the Nazis, had failed thus far to win commensurate sympathy
among the other Allies. Nikitchenko had tipped him off that the alternate American justice, Parker, even scoffed at "exaggerated Soviet
claims" of atrocities. Rudenko vowed to reverse that perception in the
days remaining to the Soviet prosecution.

The lack of understanding was explained in part by the Russians'
poorly concealed conviction that they had won the war alone. At the
press bar, *Pravda*'s man, Boris Polevoi, liked to toast "the Soviet people, who singlehandedly broke the backbone of the Nazi beast." To
Robert Jackson, the Russians at Nuremberg failed to win sympathy
because their heroism and suffering were so often demeaned by Communist claptrap. He winced as his Soviet counterparts claimed that
"Nazism was the child of capitalism," implying that not only Nazism,
but capitalism, was on trial in Nuremberg.

On Monday afternoon, February 18, Rudenko launched his effort
to make known the truth of the Soviet ordeal. The opening salvo was
to be a film entitled *Documentary Evidence of the German Fascist Invaders*. The film opened with the camera silently panning a snowy Russian
landscape. It moved in on a huddled form, lying in the snow, a small
boy. In his outstretched hand a live dove fluttered. The narrator explained that the child had been shot because he refused to give up the
dove to an SS man. From this single death, the film cut to a city square
filled with bodies stacked as evenly as Christmas trees. A close-up
revealed bloody bandages on dead Soviet soldiers. The narrator read
from a captured document the words of a German commander: "I
once again inform you that hereafter each officer has the right to shoot
prisoners of war." The scene lent meaning to a cold statistic: of 5.7
million Soviet POWs taken by the Germans, 3.7 million died in
captivity.

Long shots of acres of bodies were interspersed with close-ups of
weeping mothers gently patting the faces of their dead children. Cap-

tured German films showed naked women herded into a ditch, forced to lie down as German guards shot them and then smiled for the camera. Gus Gilbert studied the faces in the dock. All but Göring, who pretended to be reading a book, watched openmouthed.

The judges had heard testimony on Auschwitz; now they saw film. Thousands of neatly sorted pairs of shoes, hundreds of battered suitcases with names stenciled on the sides, mounds of human hair turned gray by the Zyklon B gas passed silently across the screen. The film lasted for forty-five minutes. Judge Parker, who had found the Russian claims exaggerated, asked to be excused. He was not feeling well.

Rudenko spent the next five days producing eyewitnesses and survivors. One man described the fate of the people of the village of Kholmetz. A German army officer had ordered the villagers to dig up mines in a road with farm tools. All were killed. Another Soviet prosecutor presented evidence, entitled "Crimes Against Culture and Scientific Treasures." In Kharkov, the Germans had gone into the city's library and used the books as bricks to firm up a muddy road for their armored vehicles. At Yasnaya Polyana, the estate of Leo Tolstoy, a German officer used the author's books as firewood. When told there was plenty of wood around, he replied that he preferred the light of Russian literature. The home of Tchaikovsky was used by the Germans as a motorcycle garage and heated by burning the composer's manuscripts. Using the Germans' own reports, the Russians proved that these were not isolated incidents, but the product of a deliberate policy to obliterate Russian culture.

The testimony, after six straight days, became repetitious. Points already proved were proved again and again. Still, a change had come over the court, as though the justices recognized that something more than law was at work here. The Russians needed this outpouring as a catharsis, the opportunity to say at last to the world, This was our sorrow. Instead of cutting witnesses short or, as so often, demanding to know the relevance of the testimony, Sir Geoffrey let them vent their pain uninterrupted.

For the Americans, with their nation spared, the reasons for Soviet bitterness and truculence became more understandable. As one American prosecutor put it, what the Germans had done in the Soviet Union was tantamount to rounding up all the Democratic or Republican leaders in Detroit and shooting them; or going into a school in the Bronx and sending all the Jewish children to a death camp. It was the equivalent of an enemy invader's embarking on a deliberate campaign to destroy every trace of American culture between New York City and Chicago, and using the Lincoln Memorial as a latrine.

Back in the cellblock, Gilbert sought reactions to the film. The usually glib Hans Fritzsche, face pale, cheek muscles twitching, said, "I am drowning in filth, I am choking in it. . . . I cannot go on. This has become a form of daily execution."

Gilbert reminded Göring of his blasé behavior in court. "Anybody can make an atrocity film," Göring answered. "You only have to take the corpses out of the grave and show a tractor shoving them back again. I am not a callous monster who has no use for human life," he went on. "It's not that atrocities make no impression on me. But I've seen so much already. Thousands of maimed and half-burned bodies in the First World War. The starvation. I don't have to see a film to be horrified." Göring turned the conversation to the new dining arrangement. How did the other defendants feel about his being left alone? he wanted to know. Gilbert said that he had heard nothing but satisfaction expressed so far.

53

THE INTERRUPTION ANNOYED Justice Jackson. He was already late to the courthouse this morning. He hated all the fuss over security. Nevertheless, Moritz Fuchs, his bodyguard, told the driver he had better stop. Up ahead was a roadblock and a jeep full of GIs armed with tommy guns. Recognizing the passengers, the young lieutenant at the roadblock saluted and waved them through.

The gateway to the Palace of Justice bristled with machine guns. Sandbags and gun emplacements had been thrown up around the entrance. M-4 Sherman tanks frowned in front of the iron fence. The Nuremberg military district was under a major alert. The cause of this activity was a report from a German named Max Manlin, ex-Gestapo, in the pay of General Watson's counterintelligence unit. Manlin provided a steady stream of intelligence of imminent uprisings, jailbreaks, sightings of Martin Bormann, and rumors that Eva Braun was still alive. This time, Manlin had persuaded General Watson to expect a breakout from Stalag D-13, followed by an attempt to rescue the defendants. D-13 was a POW camp, located north of Nuremberg, holding twenty thousand hardened SS veterans.

Boris Polevoi approached Colonel Andrus during the recess that morning and asked why the courthouse looked like a fortress under siege. Today's measures were purely psychological, to reassure people, particularly the women working in the palace who had heard the rumors of an SS breakout, Andrus explained. "Every possibility of escape from my prison has been eliminated," he said. How could the colonel be so confident? Polevoi wanted to know. Andrus began to tell him how the prison worked, from the twenty-four-hour watch on each cell to the rectal examinations. Polevoi was impressed.

54

HEINRICH HOFFMANN'S SUPERVISOR, Richard Heller, the young navy lieutenant who had toured Bavaria with the photographer, had gone home on points. But not before Hoffmann had landed, quite firmly, on his feet. He was driven daily from his lodgings at Countess Kalnoky's Witness House to the courthouse. He had amassed so many thousands of photographs to classify that his employment was guaranteed indefinitely. Did the prosecution require a shot of Hjalmar Schacht, preferably smiling, standing next to Hitler? Hoffmann would produce it. Did they need a photograph of Kaltenbrunner at Mauthausen? Hoffmann would find one. His room 158 on the second floor of the Palace of Justice witnessed a parade of GIs seeking photos of Hitler with Göring, with Eva Braun, or with his dog Blondi. Hoffmann would also sketch quick, deft likenesses of his visitors. In return, he acquired a store of whiskey, cigarettes, soap, gum, chocolates, and nylons. He managed to persuade the Americans that he needed an assistant, and was allowed to hire Helga, a buxom, blue-eyed nineteen-year-old with straw-blond hair who doted on "Herr Professor Hoffmann." The color returned to his cheeks and he started to grow a paunch.

Countess Kalnoky found herself, against her will, yielding to Hoffmann's cheapjack charm. The man was generous; he would return

to the house with his pockets stuffed with precious soap for her and
PX candy for her children. Hoffmann's presence in the house was
not, however, without tense moments. The prosecutors occasionally
boarded concentration camp witnesses there who were horrified to
learn the identity of their fellow guest. Hoffmann seemed barely
thrown off his stride by their accusing stares in the dining room. He
would introduce himself and explain away his role in the regime with
his pet rationalization: "The camera has no politics." He would spin
amusing stories about life in the Nazi court, usually with Göring or
Ribbentrop as the butt. Guests laughed in spite of themselves.

One afternoon, Hoffmann invited Kalnoky to his room. He had
something he wanted to show her, he said. He took out some watercolor landscapes. Did she know who had done them? he asked. The
countess found them undistinguished and said she had no idea who
the painter was. "My friend," Hoffmann said, "Adolf Hitler. You
know," he went on, "they show the other side of his personality."
What other side? she asked. "The calm, gentle side," Hoffmann answered.

55

ON FEBRUARY 23, Katy Walch, the Defense Rebuttal researcher, was
delighted to find herself at General Rudenko's party to celebrate Red
Army Day. Walch's situation was typical of that of young British
women at Nuremberg who had worked or studied in Germany before
the war and spoke the language. Walch had first gone there during
the mid-thirties as an au pair in the castle of a German count in the
SS. That was how she had found herself one Sunday as the croquet
partner of the count's guest, Reichsführer Heinrich Himmler. What
she remembered most vividly about this trifling man was that he had
cheated, sneaking his ball through the wicket with his foot. His hosts
had merely turned a blind eye and gushed at what a wonderful player
the *Reichsführer* was.

During the Russians' party, Walch found herself taken aside by
Tania Giliarevskaya, Nikitchenko's interpreter. The two women had
grown friendly. The beautiful Russian rarely visited the Defense Rebuttal office without wheedling copies of *Mademoiselle* from Katy. She

confided to Walch that she was desperate. Why? Katy asked. Tania looked furtively around the room, and whispered. She had taken great risks in seeing Major Robert Stewart. She was afraid something terrible was about to happen.

56

ON ENTERING THE COURTHOUSE on March 6, Boris Polevoi ran into young Oleg Troyanovsky, the interpreter, who had returned for the Russian prosecution. An alarmed Troyanovsky was carrying an armful of newspapers. "What's going on?" Polevoi asked. "Look at this," Troyanovsky said, holding up an English paper headlined SIR WINSTON CALLS FOR UNITED FRONT AGAINST SOVIET UNION. Troyanovsky next showed Polevoi the American GI newspaper, *Stars and Stripes.* UNITE TO STOP RUSSIANS, CHURCHILL WARNS, the headline read. The former British prime minister had made a speech the day before at a small college in Fulton, Missouri, claiming, "From Stettin in the Baltic to Trieste on the Adriatic, an iron curtain has descended across the continent." Churchill had pronounced the death of the wartime alliance and was calling for Western resistance to Communist expansion.

That day, with the completion of the Soviet presentation, the prosecution rested its case. While the moment should have sounded a chord of doom for the defendants, it was, by a quirk of fate, ending on a note of hope. True, the Allied prosecutors had achieved what they had set out to do. The four counts in the indictment had been proven indisputably and repeatedly, mostly through documentary evidence that the Germans had generated themselves. The charges had been lent flesh-and-blood believability by the testimony of thirty-three prosecution witnesses. Not the slightest doubt could remain that Nazi Germany had planned and waged aggressive war, that it had fought that conflict with flagrant disregard for the rules of warfare, and that, independent of any military necessity, it had committed mass murder on an inconceivable scale. Yet, that morning, an undercurrent of excitement coursed through the dock as the defense counsels held up their newspapers so that their clients could read the Churchill headlines. Knowing smiles flashed from defendant to defendant.

At the morning recess, it was as if a dam had broken. The defense lawyers rushed to their clients, and a cheerful babble ensued. Göring virtually did a jig in the dock. "What did I tell you?" he said. "Last summer I couldn't even hope to live till autumn. And now, I'll probably live through winter, summer, and spring and many times over. Mark my word. They'll be fighting among themselves before sentences can be pronounced on us." The washed-out, wrung-out Ribbentrop suddenly displayed his old hauteur. "I always expected it," he said. "Churchill is no fool. He knows we Germans are closer to him than the Reds." Hess dropped his catatonic stare and leaned over to Göring. "You will yet be the führer of Germany," he predicted.

That evening, Janet Flanner spotted a table of Russians in the press club bar and expressed her disappointment over Churchill's speech. She found them unperturbed. Boris Polevoi said with a shrug, "We've heard so many thousands of harsh capitalist words already. A few more from Churchill can't hurt us."

In cellblock C, Dr. Pfluecker made a happy observation on his final rounds. That night there were fewer requests for sleeping pills.

57

COLONEL LEON DOSTERT DEPARTED Nuremberg, leaving Alfred Steer, now promoted to full navy commander, as head of the Language Division. Steer was happy to see the man go. He had worked as deputy to the temperamental Dostert since the trial began. In Steer's eyes, Dostert was a manipulative opportunist, a peacock who used people below him while shamelessly ingratiating himself with those above. One of his pet boasts to Steer upon returning from meetings with the top brass was: "I have just seduced Justice so-and-so, or General so-and-so."

Steer, thirty-three, an energetic amalgam of man of action and scholar, with a Ph.D. from the University of Pennsylvania, had inherited a crushing responsibility. Though simultaneous interpretation was complex and just born at Nuremberg, it had quickly been taken for granted. Justice Birkett enjoyed exercising his talent for invective against the interpreters. A speech in the vigorous, masculine Russian of the prosecutor, Rudenko, had been rendered into English by an effete interpreter whom Birkett complained sounded like "a 'refayned' decaying cleric, a latecomer making an apology at the vicarage garden party rather than the prosecutor of major war crimes." Gruff German generals were interpreted by young women with chirpy little voices, diminishing the power of the witnesses' testimony. On one occasion, after the aristocratic Erwin Lahousen had been interpreted by a barely educated German-American, Birkett asked, "And what language was that?" "Brooklynese," Steer answered.

The interpreters also faced linguistic booby traps. Germans had a tendency to begin speaking with "*Ja.*" Interpreted literally, the utterance could amount to an admission of guilt. "Did you realize that what you were doing was criminal?" a prosecutor might ask. "*Ja,*" the witness would reply, meaning not "Yes," but a space-filler, more accurately translated as "Well . . ."

What his critics should know, Steer thought, was how many candidates he rejected. The Pentagon shipped him batches of new interpreters, mostly ill-prepared. When he heard clumsy, made-up cognates such as *judgify* or *tribunalize,* he knew he did not have a linguist. The rejects were consigned to an area called "Siberia," performing menial tasks until they could be shipped back to the States. And when all else ran smoothly, someone was always tripping over the cables that snaked through the courtroom, plunging the interpreting system into silence.

The defense was due to begin its case on March 8. Two days before, Hans Laternser, a lawyer defending Nazi organizations, stormed into Steer's office. "Don't you understand, we must be ready soon," Laternser complained, "and you have many documents you have not yet translated for us." Steer explained the demands on his operation, the shortage of personnel, the lack of funds. But, Laternser pointed out, they had the best interpreter in all Europe right here in Colonel Andrus's prison. Who was that? Steer asked. Paul Otto Schmidt, who was being held as a material witness, Laternser answered.

Schmidt had been Hitler's personal interpreter, present at every critical meeting Hitler had held with foreign leaders. When, in September of 1939, the British ambassador delivered his government's

ultimatum to Germany—get out of Poland or face war—it was Paul
Schmidt who had translated the message for Hitler. The beleagured
Steer went to Colonel Andrus and explained the jewel he held. Andrus
agreed that Steer could use Schmidt. But the prisoner would have to
be placed in a secure area under armed guard.

The interpreters stood around the room like fellow violinists who had
come to hear Heifetz. The center of attention was a tall, pale man
needing a shave and wearing a shabby suit jacket over an undershirt.
Steer had put together a team of stenographers to work in relays—
the only way to keep up with Paul Schmidt's output. The man picked
up a document in English from a stack, and, while pacing back and
forth, sight-translated it into German, then into French. Most translators worked best in one direction. But with Schmidt, it made no
difference. He went as easily from English to German as he did from
German to English, and did the same with other languages. He
stopped only long enough to go to the bathroom or to refuel with
Cokes and sandwiches.

After virtual nonstop round-the-clock days, Schmidt was taken
back to his cell, exhausted, clutching the packs of cigarettes with which
Steer had rewarded him. He slumped onto his cot. He had tried to
make Colonel Andrus understand. He had not become a party member until 1943, and then only because his lack of membership was
becoming conspicuous in the circle around Hitler. This translating
performance for the court, he hoped, would earn his way out of prison.
Yet he was still being held as a common criminal.

CHAPTER III

THE DEFENSE

1

THE BACK OF WINTER had been broken. The days were turning longer and warmer, and weeds had begun to sprout in the ruins. Newly arrived GIs made what now amounted to a pilgrimage out to Zeppelin Field, where they posed before Brownie cameras, making mock Nazi salutes from the platform where Hitler had roused the multitudes.

On the evening of March 7, several defense attorneys gathered at the Gasthaus zum Stern to drink beer and discuss the opening of their case the next day. They spoke like athletes who had been trained in a strange new sport and who would be taking the field for the first time. The Anglo-Saxon forms of law still fitted them like a poorly tailored suit. Even the point of the trial still puzzled them. Was it an honest effort to elicit guilt or innocence? Or was it a victor's spectacle? Admittedly, Sir Geoffrey's fairness was beyond question. The Germans were given access to the same documents as their opponents. They were allowed virtually unlimited time to confer with their clients. They were well paid—by the Allies. But why? Why would victors go through this protracted and costly exercise? It fit nothing in the Germans' experience.

Something in the courtroom was different. The regulars sensed it instantly. The witness stand, which until now had stood midway between the bench and the dock, had been moved during the night. The Russian judges had been outraged to learn that the defendants would testify from the same box as their accusers. Sir Geoffrey had found a last-minute compromise. Instead of replacing the box, he suggested that they simply move it away from the bench and closer to the dock so that the Russians would not find the nearness of the defendants so offensive.

The visitors' gallery was filled to overflowing. Göring, dark star of Nazism, was expected to take the stand as the first defense witness.

Instead, the first person Otto Stahmer called was Luftwaffe General Karl B. Bodenschatz, an old flying pal from Göring's Richthofen squadron, and later the *Reichsmarschall*'s liaison to Hitler. Bodenschatz's testimony was intended to establish that after 1943 Göring had stood discredited before Hitler and no longer exercised any significant power. Field Marshal Erhard Milch, the former plane production chief, followed. A barely suppressed ripple of laughter ran through the prosecution table as one of the attorneys reminded the others, sotto voce, of the status Milch had held in Göring's estimation. Göring had described Milch as "a fart out of my asshole."

The trial recessed and resumed Monday morning, with Stahmer continuing to call witnesses. It was not until the afternoon of Wednesday, March 13, that Göring would take the stand.

Dr. Pfluecker came to see Göring the night before. He found his patient agitated, sitting at his table, a dog-eared sheet of paper in his hand, talking out loud. Hans Fritzsche, as a professional broadcaster, had analyzed the failings of previous German witnesses and had written out advice which he entitled "Suggestions for Speakers." The Germans were often mistranslated, Fritzsche noted, because they used long sentences with the verb at the end, and because they spoke too fast. They should speak slowly, use short sentences, and move the subject and verb as close together as possible. They should pause between thoughts to give the interpreter time to catch up. Göring was now memorizing Fritzsche's advice.

He greeted his visitor gratefully. Dr. Pfluecker's attentions always buoyed him. He asked if he might have a stronger sedative that night. He doubted that he would sleep a wink. Pfluecker reminded him of the difference between natural sleep and drugged sleep. He must be alert the next day, Pfluecker cautioned. Göring settled for his regular pill.

If Paul Schmidt was the best that the Nuremberg interpreters had ever witnessed, Wolfe Frank ran a close second. Peter Uiberall had not expected a linguist when the dashing figure in the beribboned uniform of a British army captain first came to be tested. Frank spoke English with an upper-class accent, and, like Schmidt, could move flawlessly back and forth between English and German. The son of a

Jewish BMW plant manager, Frank had escaped to England in the late thirties. He had passed up the safe language positions offered him, and had volunteered for the commandos. At Nuremberg, he had set for himself one objective: to be the sole interpreter for English and German, with no relief, when Hermann Göring took the stand. Commander Steer could find no reason to deny him.

At 2:30 p.m., Stahmer, in his lilac university robe, rose from the defense counsel table and called his witness. Göring began to make his way to the small door that opened from the dock onto the courtroom floor. His dove-gray uniform was freshly pressed, but hung poorly. He had lost seventy-six pounds in captivity. The little door opened, revealing Göring's polished yellow boots, the pants bloused over the top. Around his neck he wore a wine-red scarf, suggesting his days as an air ace. He moved with a determined stride toward the witness box, clutching a thick purple folder. His face was flushed as Justice Lawrence asked, "Will you repeat this oath after me: I swear to God almighty and omniscient that I will speak the pure truth and will withhold or add nothing." Göring raised his right hand, trembling visibly, and repeated the oath in a quavering voice.

Did Göring believe that the Nazi party had come to power legally? Stahmer asked. The pages of his opened notebook shook in his hand. The sound of his voice, uncertain at first, gradually reassured him. It became more sonorous, precise in articulation, with the *r*s rolled vigorously. Göring proceeded to give a well-organized history of the rise of Nazism, barely glancing at his notes. "Once we came to power," he said, "we were determined to hold on to it under all circumstances. . . . We did not want to leave this any longer to chance, to elections and parliamentary majorities. . . ." The words were ice water flung in the face of the court. No apology, no evasion, no softening marked his recital. Once in the saddle, he explained, the party had intended to eliminate the Reichstag, to dissolve the regional parliaments, to end individual rights. The answer had taken twenty minutes, an annoyed Jackson noted, and Lawrence had never interfered.

Stahmer cued Göring to explain where the idea had come from to combine the ceremonial head of state and the head of government

in one person, Adolf Hitler. That was simple, Göring explained. They
had taken their example from the similar dual roles of the president
of the United States. Concentration camps? Stahmer asked. Göring
described in detail why and how he had started them. How could the
party rule until it had established order? And how could it maintain
order with its deadly enemies, particularly the Communists, running
free? "It was a question of removing danger," Göring said. "Only one
course was available, protective custody." And as for the name *concentration camp*, it had originated not with the Nazis, but with the foreign
press. The Nazis had just accepted it. He spoke for over two hours,
moving from stage fright to confidence to obvious relish in his own
performance.

Janet Flanner left the courthouse stunned. She sat in the press bus,
silent, digesting the meaning of Göring's debut. On arriving at the
Stein castle, she began writing her column for *The New Yorker*. She
had witnessed, she wrote, "one of the best brains of the period of
history when good brains are rare." Göring, she concluded, however,
was "a brain without a conscience."

Howard Smith had gone from the courtroom down to the pressroom, pondering the afternoon's significance. Hermann Göring in the
witness stand had far outperformed the dissolute *Reichsmarschall* whom
Smith remembered from the early years. "When a clever man is facing
death and has nothing to lose," Smith told his radio audience, "it
concentrates his mind marvelously."

Gustav Gilbert accompanied the defendants on their walk back to the
cellblock. Göring had to be restrained from bursting out ahead of the
pack. The guards also had to stop the others from gripping his hand
and treating him like an athlete who had just saved the game. Dönitz
turned to Speer. "You could see, even the judges were impressed," he
said. Speer had to agree. Gilbert later stopped by Göring's cell. The
man was sitting on his bed, his supper untouched. He could not eat a
thing, he told Gilbert. He was too excited. "It was a strain for me,"
Göring went on, "especially the first ten minutes when I couldn't
make my hands stop shaking." He was, however, looking forward to
tomorrow.

———————

Sir Norman Birkett sat in the study of his villa, also reviewing the day. Sir Geoffrey Lawrence's behavior had shocked him. Hermann Göring's so-called testimony had been a farce. The man had simply been allowed uncontested ownership of the court for as long as he chose to speak. Birkett intended to urge Lawrence to put some decent limits on Göring's tongue before the next day's session.

Göring was back on the witness stand at ten the next morning. The Nazi regime, he said with Stahmer's light prodding, was being vilified for imposing rigid obedience on its followers. In the prosecution's argument, this pyramid of unthinking submission from the top downward ended in places like Auschwitz and Mauthausen. But the *Führerprinzip*—the leadership principle—was merely sound management, Göring asserted: "Authority from above downward and responsibility from the bottom upward." Was this concept adopted only by power-crazed Nazis? Göring asked. "I should like to mention some parallels," he said. "The *Führerprinzip* is the same principle on which the Catholic church and the government of the USSR are both based." He nodded in the direction of the Soviet prosecution.

So far, he had not equivocated. But when Stahmer put the next question to him, the audience braced for an evasion. "To what extent did you participate in issuing the Nuremberg Laws of 1935?" Stahmer asked. Göring barely paused. "In my capacity as president of the Reichstag, I promulgated those laws, here in Nuremberg, where the Reichstag was meeting at the time."

During the lunch break, a dismayed Gilbert passed from the "youth room" to the "elders' room" to the other rooms, feeling the buoyed morale. The only bright patch was Hans Frank's feisty outburst. As they filed back down to the courtroom, Frank looked to Göring and said, "Well done, *Herr Reichsmarschall.* It's too bad you weren't thrown into jail years ago."

Göring waited until the third and final day of his direct examination to rebut the prosecution charges against the Luftwaffe. The world had been horrified at the German bombing of Rotterdam *after* the Netherlands had surrendered. It was true, Göring said, he had sent a squadron to bomb Rotterdam. But when the Germans learned that surrender negotiations were under way, they fired red flares into the sky to ward off their bombers. The first group did not understand the signal and, unfortunately, struck the target. The two groups behind did understand and turned back. Rotterdam had not been an atrocity, Göring argued. It had been a tragic error.

Göring next dealt head-on with the issue of how he had acquired his art treasures. "I decided that after the war, or at some time when it seemed appropriate to me, I would found an art gallery, either through purchase, or gifts, or through inheritance, and present this art to the German people." For the first time since he had taken the stand, the snickering from the audience was audible.

It was late in the afternoon Friday, March 15. Göring had been testifying for five hours. After the first day, he had no longer bothered to bring the purple file folder. In the final question, Stahmer asked if Germany had behaved any differently than her Allies in observing the rules of civilized conflict. Instruments like the Geneva and Hague conventions, Göring said, had been overrun by modern warfare. "At this point, I should like to say the very words which one of our greatest, most important and strongest opponents, the British prime minister Winston Churchill, used: 'In the struggle for life and death, there is, in the end, no legality.'" Sir Geoffrey adjourned the court. Hermann Göring had spoken, virtually without interruption and largely without notes, for over two and a half days. His cross-examination would begin after the weekend.

The Göring testimony had been brilliant enough, without his flinging Churchill's words in their faces, Maxwell-Fyfe believed. A message was fired off to Whitehall to find out where or when Sir Winston might have said such a thing. The closest, the Foreign Office replied, was a speech Churchill made in 1940 while still first lord of the Admiralty. "There could be no justice, if in a mortal struggle, the aggressor tramples down every sentiment of humanity, and if those who resist remain entangled in the tatters of violated legal convention." Göring had the words wrong, but the sentiment was uncomfortably close.

2

WAR CRIMES CERTAINLY PRODUCED strange bedfellows, Drexel Sprecher thought, as he took another game, nineteen to twenty-one. He was in the hunting lodge of a rich German industrialist playing Ping-Pong with Paul Schmidt, Adolf Hitler's personal interpreter, while Rudolf Diels, who had once headed the Gestapo under Hermann Göring, awaited his turn. In the meantime, his host, Roland Faber-Castell, was seated in a deep leather chair chatting with Fritz Sauter, counsel for Funk and Schirach. Sprecher rarely missed a weekend at his cousin Nina's country retreat. He never knew who would be the Faber-Castells' guests, since they cut across the upper spectrum of German society. Paul Schmidt was personally indebted to Sprecher, who had managed to spring him from the Nuremberg jail in part because of Schmidt's translating services to the IMT.

Sprecher had been astonished to find Diels here, and curious to talk to him. Göring's performance was on everybody's mind, and Diels had known the man when the Nazi regime was young. But it was a custom at the Faber-Castells' not to discuss the trial—or, as the host put it, not to speak of rope in the house of a condemned man. In Diels's case, what once had seemed bad luck turned out to be his salvation. When Göring realized that the Gestapo had become an international scandal, he let the insatiable Himmler have it. Diels, more a political policeman than a political assassin, was soon shoved aside in favor of Himmler's own men. Diels then went into conventional police work as head of the Cologne constabulary. He was at Nuremberg waiting to be called as a witness.

Drexel Sprecher was a valued guest at the lodge. Having a well-situated American friend was virtually every German's desire. Besides, Sprecher, amiable and an excellent conversationalist, was good company. As a guest, he left his prosecutor's hat at the court. His presence here with former Nazis and a defense lawyer would likely have shocked his courthouse colleagues, so he chose to say nothing about the nature of his weekend escapes. When he went back to Nuremberg, he put on the prosecutor's hat and applied to convicting Nazis the same energy that he put into pleasure. He knew that when the present trial was over, he would not be going home. After the top defendants were tried, a new court was to be constituted for the lesser fry—hundreds of defendants such as Einsatzgruppe D commander Otto Ohlendorf. Telford Taylor had already been picked by Justice Jackson as the chief prosecutor for these "subsequent proceedings," and Drexel Sprecher was to be his leading deputy.

Sprecher's cousin Nina came in, her cheeks red from a walk around the grounds. She reminded Roland of how lovely it was outdoors and suggested that he and Drexel might want to take a walk. The gesture almost seemed scripted, and as the two men moved into the woods, Sprecher realized that the house rule was about to be broken. After pointing out how his bomb-shattered trees were being removed, Faber-Castell suddenly asked Sprecher if Nazi industrialists were likely to be tried at these subsequent proceedings. Yes, Sprecher answered. "That is wrong," the German said. "They were only businessmen, like me." "Yes, and they were only too willing to use slave labor in their businesses," Sprecher countered. "They confiscated foreign property. They helped put Hitler into power, my friend." This was a Sprecher that Faber-Castell had not heard before. "I'm not sure, under the circumstances, that anyone else would have behaved differently," the German observed. "Will you be prosecuting these cases?" He probably would, Sprecher answered.

That night after dinner Sprecher found himself enjoying a cigar with Fritz Sauter and Rudolf Diels. He respected Sauter. The lawyer admitted that he had been a party member for five years. When, however, Communists and anti-Nazis had asked him to defend them, what else could he do? He took their cases and, consequently, was thrown out of the party. He was delighted to have been fired as the exasperating Ribbentrop's lawyer before the IMT, he said, since he was already stretched thin with his two other clients.

Diels finally raised the unspoken subject on everyone's mind—the Göring testimony. Diels said that Heinrich Hoffmann, who like himself was staying at the Witness House, had stopped making Göring the butt of his jokes. The Allies' error, Diels went on, had been to equate Göring's hedonism with softness of intellect. Justice Jackson would have to be very good indeed to catch this corpulent fox, he concluded.

3

Sir Norman Birkett had written to a colleague back home, "The first really great dramatic moment of this trial will come when Göring is cross-examined by the American prosecutor, Jackson. It will be a duel to the death between the representative of all that is worthwhile in civilization and the last important surviving protagonist of all that was evil. In a sense, the whole result of the trial depends on that duel."

On Sunday evening, March 17, Robert Jackson, at home on Lindenstrasse, was making last-minute preparations for the duel. The conservatory was again quilted with piles of documents he expected to employ. He had gathered his son, Bill, Elsie Douglas, and Whitney Harris, the prosecutor who had unearthed Otto Ohlendorf, to review strategy. He knew, Jackson said, that Göring could not beat the charges. The evidence was too overwhelming. "But he's showman enough to make a farce of it or go over the heads of the tribunal to the German people," Jackson said. That he intended to stop. But what was the best approach? His staff had developed two possible lines of questioning. The first was a series of rifle shots, intended to hit Göring with specific charges—for instance, that he had forced the Jews to pay for Kristallnacht, that he had signed anti-Semitic legislation, and that he had played a role in the execution of downed airmen. The other strategy was to employ heavy artillery and bombard Göring with sweeping questions, forcing him to accept his leading role in destroying German democracy, in arming Germany for war, in planning Nazi aggressions. By the time the group broke up late that evening, Robert Jackson had still not decided which weapon would best sink Hermann Göring.

The courtroom was packed as it had not been since opening day. Most of the morning was consumed by the defense counsels, finishing up Göring's direct examination, asking questions of him designed to absolve their clients. Göring readily obliged, manfully assuming responsibility for virtually everything. Meanwhile, the visitors fussed impatiently like fight fans compelled to endure lightweights before the main bout.

Not until 12:10 p.m. did Justice Lawrence ask, "Do the chief prosecutors wish to cross-examine?" Jackson moved to the prosecution stand with confident pugnacity. Behind him, to one side, sat Whitney Harris with a file box of folders neatly tabbed for quick retrieval. Jackson unbuttoned his morning coat and shoved his hands into his back pockets. He studied Göring in the witness stand. Göring stared back like an air ace gauging the enemy before a dogfight. "You are perhaps aware that you are the only living man who can expound to us the true purposes of the Nazi party and the inner workings of its leadership," Jackson said. He had made his decision earlier that morning. He was going to hit Göring first with artillery rather than rifle fire. Maxwell-Fyfe, a legendary cross-examiner, heard Jackson's bland query with surprise. It was not how he would have begun—but Jackson, no doubt, had a hidden strategy.

"I am perfectly aware of that," Göring answered. Jackson next asked if it was not true that the Nazis had intended to overthrow the Weimar Republic. "That was my firm intention," Göring answered, unblinking. When Jackson asked him if it was also true that on taking power the Nazis abolished democratic government, Göring responded, "We found it no longer necessary."

Jackson asked Göring if it was not true that people were thrown into concentration camps without recourse to the courts. Göring began a lengthy answer, but Jackson interrupted, trying to limit him to yes or no. Göring shot back that he needed to explain. Jackson shut him off. Any such amplification, he said, could be brought out on redirect examination by Göring's counsel. He started asking Göring another question, when he saw Biddle lean over and whisper to Lawrence. Sir Geoffrey nodded, then stopped Jackson in mid-query. "Mr. Jackson," he said, "the tribunal thinks the witness ought to be allowed to make what explanation he thinks right in answer to this question." Jackson flushed angrily. This ruling was contrary to cross-examination custom, Jackson knew, and he was convinced that Biddle was pulling Lawrence's strings. The prosecutor impatiently tapped his pen on the stand as Göring was allowed virtually to lecture the court at will.

Jackson next asked, "Now, was the leadership principle supported and adopted by you in Germany because you believed that no people are capable of self-government, or that you believed that some may be, but not the German people: or for that matter whether some of us are capable of using our own system but it should not be used in Germany?" Not only Göring, but the judges looked baffled. He did not understand the question, the witness said, but he would attempt to answer it anyway. Sir David Maxwell-Fyfe became increasingly mystified. Ten minutes into the cross-examination, he could still discern no overarching strategy in Jackson's approach.

Göring appeared to be enjoying himself, a prizefighter who has yet to feel his opponent's glove. He was also shrewdly exploiting an advantage. Between Jackson's long-winded questions and Wolfe Frank's translations, Göring had ample time to frame his answers, especially since he understood the questions in English before they were translated. Jackson was deprived of the cross-examiner's classic tactic: he could not "crowd" the witness with quick, hard, successive questions.

As Sir Lawrence adjourned for lunch, a journalist in the press gallery gestured toward Jackson and whispered, "Saved by the bell." Jackson's deputy prosecutors, who had come to watch their champion, filed out of the courtroom eyeing each other uneasily.

When the court resumed after lunch, Jackson began questioning Göring about the Nazi invasion of the Soviet Union. The charge of "conspiracy to commit aggression" had been eagerly embraced by him as far back as the earliest Bernays proposal. The Soviet example, however, was poorly chosen, in Göring's case. The defendant was able to point out, persuasively, that he had opposed Hitler on the invasion of the Soviet Union. Jackson kept plodding on, like an animal in a maze chasing the uncatchable, giving Göring further opportunity to demonstrate that if there had been a conspiracy to invade Russia, he had not been a supporter of it.

Throughout the afternoon, Göring continued to respond adroitly, displaying a phenomenal memory and, thanks to the court's indulgence, having all the time in the world to exercise it. At the end of the day, Maxwell-Fyfe came over to Jackson, his hand outstretched, and said, "Well done. All our worries are over about the conspiracy count." It was a courteous gesture. What Maxwell-Fyfe could not say was that Jackson, after four years on the Supreme Court and years spent amid the legal bureaucracy of the Justice Department, had been too long out of the gladiatorial arena. The cross-examiner in him was rusty.

Airey Neave had dinner that night at Justice Birkett's villa. He enjoyed the association with this mercurial, proud, witty man; and Birkett wanted company with whom he could comfortably discuss the day's events. Neave, serious, intelligent, and discreet, would do nicely. Birkett feared, he said, that the great duel was being lost by the forces of right, and that once lost, the momentum might never be reversed. Göring's performance was bound to give the other defendants heart. Jackson had great rhetorical power, but he had not the slightest notion as to how the cross-examination game was played. His reading from documents left no time for the lightning questions that stunned and threw a witness off balance. Not once had Jackson employed the deadliest gambit at which all good cross-examiners excel—luring the witness toward a waiting pit, then forcing him into it with an answer that cannot be evaded.

Jackson, and no doubt all of them, had made a miscalculation, Airey Neave observed. They had allowed Göring's bluster and buffoonery to obscure a simple fact. Hermann Göring's brain was a formidable instrument. He had graduated from the military academy at Gross Lichterfelde, Germany's West Point or Sandhurst, summa cum laude. Another point, Neave added: Göring was a murderer and a bastard—but he was a brave bastard and that came through in court.

Granting all that, Birkett said, Jackson had operated under a severe handicap. Lawrence's ruling that Göring's answers would not be curtailed had been outrageous. The witness, not the prosecutor or even the bench, was in control of the court.

The private verdict became public that night. Hal Burson sat next to his announcer in the broadcast booth, listening to him read the script Burson had written for the Armed Forces Network: "As the day ended with the suspense of a Pulitzer prize–winning play's second act, the talk among correspondents at Nuremberg boiled down to a single comment: Göring, so far, has had his own way. Someone is going to have to stop him."

The duel did not resume immediately the next morning. Göring's lawyer, Stahmer, had won the court's permission to squeeze in a witness named Birger Dahlerus, a Swedish businessman called to testify that Göring had not wanted war with England. Not until midafternoon did the Göring-Jackson combat renew. At one point, Jackson quoted from a document designed to show that Göring had violated the Treaty of Versailles by planning "the liberation of the Rhineland." Göring possessed a copy of the same report. He pointed out that Jackson had mistranslated it. The document dealt not with the Rhineland, but with the Rhine River. And it spoke not of "liberation," but of "clearing" the river of impediments to navigation in case of mobilization. Göring, it turned out, was right.

Still, were these actions not intended as part of a plan to rearm the Rhineland? Jackson asked. All countries made contingency plans, Göring answered. But weren't these plans "kept entirely secret from foreign powers"? Jackson asked. Göring snapped back, "I do not think I can recall reading beforehand the publication of the mobilization preparations of the United States." Jackson looked to the bench. "I respectfully submit to the tribunal that this witness is not being responsive in his examination! . . . It is perfectly futile to spend our time if we cannot have responsive answers to our questions. . . . This witness, it seems to me, is adopting, in the witness box, and in the dock, an arrogant and contemptuous attitude toward the tribunal which is giving him the trial which he never gave a living soul, nor dead ones either." Sir Geoffrey looked to Biddle. He upheld the decision to let the witness have his say. Jackson appeared on the point of apoplexy. Biddle whispered to Lawrence that this was probably a good point to adjourn for the day.

Jackson saw no point in delaying further. The source of his torment had to be confronted. He did not bother to return to his office but went straight to Biddle's chambers. There he found both Biddle and Parker. Biddle greeted him calmly and offered a seat. He preferred to stand, Jackson said. He could come to no other conclusion, he began, than that Biddle was deliberately trying to thwart him. He had not left the U.S. Supreme Court to come here and be sabotaged by his own countrymen. "I'd better resign and go home," Jackson announced. No, Biddle said. He understood that Bob was under tremendous strain. He and Parker both knew it. They had enormous admiration for the difficult job he was doing. The decisions on Göring were not personal. They were designed only to give the man no alibis when the trial ended. And that goal would best serve them all, the judges and the prosecution. Jackson left, hardly mollified.

Biddle invited Colonel Harlan Amen to dinner that night. Jackson was surrounded by yes-men like the pliant Bob Storey, Amen charged, people who were not going to tell him he was making a mess of it. He doesn't prepare properly, doesn't master his material before he goes into court. Göring had proved it today, tripping Bob up on the Rhineland business. Biddle remained quietly discreet, as Amen went on inventorying his boss's failings.

That night, writing to his wife, Biddle held nothing back. "Jackson's cross-examination, on the whole, has been futile and weak," he wrote. "Göring listens to every question, takes his time, answers well. Bob doesn't listen to the answers, depends on his notes, always a sign of weakness. He hasn't *absorbed* his case." And Biddle could not suppress his role. To the world Sir Geoffrey Lawrence might seem the master of the courtroom. Biddle did not contest that public impression. But, he told Katherine, "I do really run this show and have won on every point."

Sir Norman Birkett had a visitor, the British chief prosecutor, Sir David Maxwell-Fyfe. The meeting brought together possibly the two ablest cross-examiners in Britain. The purpose of his visit, Sir David said, was to advise Birkett that Bob Jackson was in a terrible emotional state. The man might have his failings as a courtroom adversary; but with that eloquent opening address and his prominent position as chief American prosecutor of the Nazi leaders, Jackson was the moral heart of the trial. His departure, or his perceived failure, would be a disaster.

Jackson's plight was not entirely his own fault, Birkett pointed out. He and Maxwell-Fyfe would be hard-pressed to defeat a clever defendant in cross-examination who could say whatever he wanted for as long as he wished. And Birkett agreed that it was not simply Jackson's reputation at stake. If Göring was allowed to run riot, what had started as a trial would end as a circus. Worse still, people might start to believe his cunning rationalizations. Lawrence must make clear that no further irrelevancies in answering questions would be tolerated, Birkett said. He was going to draft a statement to that effect to be read by Sir Geoffrey in court tomorrow. That should get the cross-examination back on track. And it certainly ought to restore Jackson's confidence.

Birkett and Sir Geoffrey arrived in the Judges' Room before the others. The president of the court looked over Birkett's draft and agreed that it was a splendid idea. But when Biddle saw it, he asked Sir Geoffrey how it would look for the chief justice to shut off a man on trial for his life. Worse still, how would it look if he were seen as reversing his earlier decision? Lawrence glanced at his watch. It was time for them to repair to the courtroom. Birkett's proposal was forgotten.

Göring had ended the previous day's questioning with the riposte that he did not recall the United States publicizing its mobilization plans. Jackson resumed his questioning with a complaint about Göring's reply. If left unchallenged, Jackson said, Göring's gibe would mislead the world as to the openness of American society. Sir Norman Birkett listened in dismay. Another Birkett rule of cross-examination was that a witness's flip answers should be left to wither of neglect. Jackson instead launched into a drawn-out explanation of the alternatives facing him, either to allow Göring's impertinence to stand or to rebut it.
    Biddle also listened in disbelief. Jackson was turning a molehill into a legal Mount Everest. Lawrence tried to move Jackson along by agreeing that Göring's remark had been irrelevant and that the court would so consider it. But that was not enough. The remark may be irrelevant, Jackson went on; but it was already in the record. Biddle whispered loudly to Parker, "How silly." Did Jackson want Göring's words stricken from the record? Lawrence asked.
    That was not what he wanted, Jackson replied. He wanted the witness held to yes or no answers. Was the prosecution saying that a witness could make no explanation of any kind to his answer? Sir Geoffrey asked. "I think that is the rule of cross-examination under ordinary circumstances," Jackson said. Jackson was making far too much of Göring's glib retort, Lawrence advised: "Certainly it would be wiser to ignore a statement of that sort . . . the counsel for the prosecution does not have to answer every irrelevant observation made

in cross-examination." The defendant, Lawrence ruled, "may make a short explanation" and is not confined simply to answering yes or no.

Jackson went on to the next issue. He took a sheaf of documents in hand. They were decrees, he said, signed by Göring in his various roles. Had he not issued a decree that a Jew could sell a business only with government permission? Göring said yes. Did Göring sign a decree that Jews might not own retail businesses, sell handicrafts, or form co-ops? Again Göring agreed. Jackson kept up the steady drumfire. Did Göring order Jews to surrender all their jewelry and gold to the government? Sequester Jewish property in Poland? Bar Jews from compensation for damage caused by German forces? At long last, Birkett thought, Jackson sounded like a cross-examiner.

Göring put one hand over the other to stop the trembling. Was it not true, Jackson pressed on, that on July 31, 1941, Göring signed the decree directing Reinhard Heydrich to plan a solution to the Jewish question? Göring protested that the document was in no way correctly translated. He then cleverly offered to read it himself. The word *Endlösung*, he said, had been rendered as "final solution" when it should have been "complete solution." He thereby robbed the document of the incriminating semantic power that "final solution" had already acquired. Actually, the phrase had been accurately translated in the first place. Jackson, a lawyer, not a linguist, did not pursue the matter.

The prosecutor moved the questioning to *Kristallnacht*, November 9, 1938, when storm troopers and Nazi hooligans looted and destroyed 815 Jewish shops and 76 synagogues and arrested twenty thousand Jews, of whom thirty-six died. *Kristallnacht* had allegedly been ignited by a report a few days before that a third secretary in the German Embassy in Paris, Ernst vom Rath, had been murdered by a seventeen-year-old German Jewish refugee, Herschel Grynszpan.

Jackson began reading into the record the grim inventory of destruction. His facts came from a report submitted to Göring the day after the rampage. Göring had then called a meeting at his air ministry, of Goebbels, Funk, Heydrich, and a man from the insurance industry, to discuss damage claims. Jackson read a verbatim exchange between Göring and the insurance representative. This man had pointed out that many goods in the burned-out Jewish shops had been there on consignment from non-Jewish suppliers. To which Göring said to Heydrich, "I wished you had killed two hundred Jews instead of destroying such valuables." Göring next announced that he was going to deny the Jews the right to insurance claims for their losses. That would save the insurance industry millions, he said. "All of a sudden an angel, in my somewhat corpulent shape, appears before you," he had told the insurance official. "I should like to go fifty-fifty with you."

Jackson threw at Göring the exact words he had used at the close of that meeting nearly eight years before: "I demand that German Jewry shall for their abominable crimes make a contribution of a billion marks. That will work. The pigs will not commit a second murder so quickly. I would not like to be a Jew in Germany." Was that a correct quote? Jackson asked. Göring answered gloomily that it was.

Jackson next nailed Göring with documentary proof of his art looting and his role in the wholesale pillaging of foodstuffs and resources from the Soviet Union. He finally had Göring reeling. A drumfire of hard, specific charges revealed the defendant as a coarse, venal, anti-Semitic co-architect of the worst evils of Nazism. Göring at last seemed to teeter on the edge of the pit.

And then Jackson let him get away. He began accusing Göring's Luftwaffe of destroying the house of the American ambassador during the bombing of Warsaw. The charge stood so dwarflike next to the horrors of mass murder, slave labor, and diabolical medical experiments heard in this courtroom, that it appeared as if Jackson were, willy-nilly, reading a list of pro forma questions prepared by some junior aide. To prove the bombing charge, Jackson introduced alleged Luftwaffe aerial photographs. Göring was allowed to examine them. The cocksureness returned. Before he became a World War I air ace, Göring had been an aerial photographer. He showed that, from the angle of the photographs, they were likely taken from a steeple, not an airplane. He turned them over. The backs of the photographs were blank—no date, no place, no identification, no authentication; unacceptable evidence in virtually any court of law.

Jackson moved on to questions about the execution of Allied fliers. But his queries were posed prosaically and with little follow-through, again as though he were merely reading down a list rather than stalking his quarry for the kill. The three days of Jackson versus Göring ended on a limp exchange over the authenticity of a signature on a minor order.

Francis Biddle wrote Katherine that Bob Jackson looked "beaten, full of a sense of failure. . . . I know he has it in for me. . . . I have repeatedly asked Bob to the house, but he never comes and I am afraid we are no longer friends." He believed Jackson's grievance stemmed from their reversed roles, he wrote. Now it was Jackson the courtroom supplicant and Biddle judging on high from the bench.

Whatever the ultimate verdict of the bench in room 600, the verdict at the Grand was clear. Göring had proved a brilliant villain, and Jackson a flawed hero. Barbara Pinion, an evidence researcher, echoed the grudging sentiments of the workaday staff. Göring at least knew what he believed. "The other defendants were always putting the blame on someone else. Not old Hermann," she observed.

4

TECH SERGEANT HAL BURSON'S REPORTS were broadcast daily from a powerful fifty-thousand-watt transmitter to over fifty outlets, in virtually every post in Germany where GIs were stationed. The Armed Forces Network had sent Burson to cover the trial to give American troops a sense of why they were in this country and, as a by-product, to expose the Germans to the truth of Nazism.

Burson sought occasionally to take the pulse of the man in the rubble by patronizing German bars. There he studied the face of defeat. German men had a hangdog, emasculated manner. Too many were dependent on their women, who worked for the victors or provided a service to which the men could only turn a blind eye. One story that Burson had not reported had occurred at Club 21 that spring. There, talk was not of legal fine points as in room 600, but of the going rate for a carton of cigarettes or a fräulein. That night, all eyes had turned to a pair of black GIs who suddenly appeared in the doorway. From a far corner, a voice in the accents of the South called out, "You boys better get out that door before it has time to hit your black asses." The two blacks held their ground. A half dozen whites sauntered belligerently toward them. The melee that followed spilled into the street, where more blacks were waiting. Three jeeploads of club-swinging MPs were required to break up the fracas.

Racial incidents had multiplied ever since a black unit had arrived in Nuremberg. Gunther Sadel, General Watson's young counterintelligence agent, had quickly become caught up in America's exported biases. Black soldiers wanted Sadel's coveted social passes for their German girlfriends. Ordinarily, the passes were printed on pink paper, but the printer had run out of pink stock. Sadel thus had the passes printed on yellow paper. An immediate cry went up from the blacks, with liberal journalists joining in. The army, obviously, had come up with a scheme for identifying and discriminating against German women who dated blacks. General Watson ordered Sadel to scour Germany and come up with pink paper.

The racial clashes bothered Gustav Gilbert as he tried to piece together his analysis of sanctioned mass murder. He had already concluded that, beyond an obedient people, the next requirement for this kind of crime was a belief in the inferiority of one's victims. He had had a discussion on this point recently with Göring. Göring had asked him about the black officers occasionally seen in the visitors' gallery. Could they command troops in combat? Göring wanted to know. Could they ride in the same buses as whites? Gilbert had just spent three days in court watching Robert Jackson prosecute Göring for crimes against humanity, specifically for issuing anti-Semitic edicts. Jim Crow and the Nuremberg Laws—was it not just a difference of degree?

5

THE NEXT PROSECUTOR to cross-examine Göring would be Sir David Maxwell-Fyfe. On the eve of his court appearance, Sir David stayed up into the early-morning hours preparing himself, determined to break through Göring's armor plating of ego and brains. The elements of cross-examination were as natural to the Scot as breathing, beginning with rule one: Ask only questions to which the answer is known.

The Russians, unfamiliar with the technique, were likely to ask, "I show you document 819 PS. Is your impression positive or negative?" They made Sir David cringe. The objective was not to elicit information, but to get incriminating facts into the record. Rule two: Abandon a losing line of questioning. Jackson had ploddingly followed his script, at times clear off the track. Sir David accepted that he was going up against an adversary of cutting wit. Thus, rule three: Ignore the clever asides, the sallies and impertinences. Hang on to the essentials like a bulldog with his teeth buried in the enemy's throat. A trial, in the end, was a contest, theater, a debating match, a game—deadly enough, but a game all the same. Jackson had depended on moral outrage. Sir David intended to outplay his opponents.

He further intended to pick the right fight. By now, in room 600, the extermination of ten thousand Hungarian Gypsies was merely a statistic. Maxwell-Fyfe intended to lead off with an issue that the men on the bench could feel and grasp. He was convinced that he had found his opening in the fate of the RAF fliers who had escaped from Stalag Luft III. For the British chief judge and his alternate, these were not heaped, anonymous corpses bulldozed into a ditch—they were sons, neighbors, classmates, brothers.

At 4:50 p.m. on the afternoon of March 20, Maxwell-Fyfe took the prosecutor's stand, a time when people had begun looking at their watches, not a propitious moment for courtroom pyrotechnics. Still, he plunged in for the half hour remaining. He looked up from his papers into the broad face in the witness stand. Göring's set smile and hard eyes seemed to be saying, "I handled the American, and I shall do the same with you."

The Sagan affair had begun on March 14, 1944, when seventy-six RAF POWs managed to burrow their way out of Stalag Luft III, at Sagan in Silesia. Hitler, at his Berchtesgaden retreat, became furious on getting the news. The escape was the third from Sagan in two weeks, he yelled at Keitel, and the tenth recent POW breakout overall. "Dozens of officers have escaped," he went on. "They are an enormous source of danger. You, Keitel, don't realize that in view of six million foreigners who are prisoners and working in Germany, these officers are leaders who could organize an uprising." On their recapture, Hitler ordered, the Sagan escapees were to be turned over to Himmler's secret police for "special treatment."

Twenty of them had been retaken within two hours and returned to Sagan before Hitler's tirade. Three were never accounted for, and three eventually made it to Sweden. The remaining fifty were caught in various parts of Germany. They were loaded aboard trucks and told that they were being returned to Luft III. They were let out at remote places to urinate, at which time Gestapo agents shot them. Their bodies were cremated and their ashes displayed at Sagan as an example to other would-be heros. One of the murdered fliers was Roger Bushel, a criminal-law silk from the Old Bailey, a close friend of Khaki Roberts of the British prosecution staff.

Thursday morning, March 21, Maxwell-Fyfe resumed his cross-examination. Sagan had been a crime known to Göring's chief subordinates, Sir David noted. "I am suggesting to you that it is absolutely impossible that in these circumstances, you knew nothing about it."

"Field Marshal Milch was here as a witness," Göring answered, "and, regrettably, was not asked about these points."

Maxwell-Fyfe's memory was as good as Göring's. "Oh, yes he was," the prosecutor shot back. "Milch took the same line as you, that he knew nothing about it. . . . Both you and Milch are now trying to shift the responsibility onto the shoulders of your junior officers." The attack on his honor jarred Göring. "That is untrue," he shouted. "You did nothing to prevent these men from being shot," Sir David snapped back. "You cooperated in this foul series of murders."

Maxwell-Fyfe was "crowding" Göring, barely waiting for the answers to be translated before firing the next question. Göring's sneers and brittle asides were nowhere evident. Beads of sweat glistened on his brow. The simultaneous interpreters flashed their warning lights to indicate that they were barely able to keep pace with the prosecutor. Justice Lawrence tapped his pencil, signaling Maxwell-Fyfe to slow down. Sir David knew exactly what he was doing, and he was not going to relent. He was deliberately flustering the witness. "I did not hear about this incident until after it occurred," Göring insisted. In fact, he had been on leave at the time of the Sagan escape.

The prey had been led to the pit. Sir David tumbled him into it. True, the *Reichsmarschall* had been on leave until March 29, 1944, he

said, reading from his personnel files. But the executions of the Sagan
fifty had gone on until April 13.

Justice Lawrence adjourned for lunch. During the break, Airey
Neave, twice escaped from German prison camps himself, approached
Maxwell-Fyfe, smiling broadly. "You've got him," Neave said. "I
know how that must feel to you," Sir David answered.

That afternoon, Göring returned to the witness stand palming a
card in his hand. On one side he had written, "Speak slower. Pause,"
and on the other, "Stand firm." As Maxwell-Fyfe approached, the
press gallery watched as if savoring a gifted stage performer. The reporters loved the prosecutor's Old Bailey locutions: a reasonably uttered, "Now, I want to be perfectly fair," followed by a bald accusation
of murder. "Let me remind you of the affidavit of Hoettl of the
RSHA," Maxwell-Fyfe began. "He says that approximately four million Jews have been killed in the concentration camps, while an additional two million met death in other ways. . . . Are you telling this
tribunal that a minister with your power in the Reich could remain
ignorant that this was going on?"

"These things were kept secret from me," Göring said. "I might
add that, in my opinion, not even the Führer knew the extent of what
was going on." The victim again stood on the edge of the pit. Was
Hitler innocent? He was going to read, Sir David said, from the Führer's comments to the Hungarian leader, Admiral Horthy. "The
Jews," Hitler had told Horthy, "have been treated as germs with
which a healthy body had been infected." "What else could that
mean?" Maxwell-Fyfe asked. Without waiting for an answer, he began
quoting from a report made to Göring in 1942: "There are only a few
Jews left alive. Tens of thousands have been disposed of," the report
read. Göring insisted that he had only known of "a policy of emigration, not liquidation of the Jews." The answer rang so hollow that the
old cross-examiner knew that this was the precise moment to stop.
With a nod to the president of the court, Sir David resumed his seat.
The Russian, Rudenko, took over, and the Frenchman, Champetier
de Ribes, completed Göring's cross-examination the following day.

That Friday evening, as Captain Gilbert made his rounds, he
found Göring in an edgy state. "I didn't cut a very pretty figure, did
I?" he said. Gilbert was quick to agree. Göring packed his meerschaum

pipe and puffed rapidly. "Don't forget," he continued, "I had the best legal brains of America, England, France, and Russia against me. And there I was, all alone. I bet even the prosecutors think I did well. Did you hear anything?" Gilbert did not respond. "Did you see Rudenko," Göring went on, "he was more nervous than I was. . . . I gave him a good dig when he asked me why I didn't refuse to obey Hitler's orders. I told him, if I did, I certainly would not have to worry about my health!" That, Göring explained, was the code in dictatorships for liquidation. He laughed with his old bravado. "Rudenko understood me, all right." The odd mixture of anxiety and egotism intrigued Gilbert. Which, in the days to come, he wondered, would take the upper hand in the soul of Hermann Göring?

Fellow prosecutors flocked to Maxwell-Fyfe's office, heaping praise on his performance. "Hermann Göring," Sir David said, "was the most formidable witness I ever examined."

6

Rudolf Hess's defense was scheduled to follow Göring's. The prosecutors were making bets as to whether this erratic figure would take the stand himself. It had been only four months since Hess had told the court that he had faked amnesia for tactical purposes and "henceforth my memory will again respond to the outside world." Captain Gilbert believed Hess's memory was genuinely faltering again.

Hess had acquired a new lawyer since firing Gunther von Rohrscheidt, whom he had accused of failing to defend him vigorously. His attorney now was Alfred Seidl, ex-Nazi, ex–army officer, and also Hans Frank's counsel. The guessing game about Hess's intentions finally appeared to be resolved when Seidl predicted to a reporter for the British Sunday *Express* that his client would take the stand. Seidl also took advantage of the interview to lay the foundation for an insanity defense. Hess was having difficulties, Seidl claimed. "He may be slow in answering questions . . . his mind is wandering and he may not be very lucid. . . . Anything can happen. I hope there will not be a scene."

Gustav Gilbert visited Hess on Sunday, March 23, the day before he was to testify. The deep-set eyes seemed to rove unanchored beneath the massive black brows. A permanent grimace cut above his blue-bearded chin like a thin scar. Hess's sudden, pointless bursts of laughter unnerved the psychologist. Just as suddenly, the laugh would stop and Hess would shoot a look of menace at his visitor. A few days before, Gilbert had brought Hess news of his old mentor, Professor Karl Haushofer, the man who had first influenced him to fly to Scotland. Professor Haushofer and his wife were dead, Gilbert had reported. They had recently gone into the garden of their home and drunk arsenic sweetened with a liqueur. When Frau Haushofer did not die immediately, she hanged herself. Gilbert reminded Hess that Haushofer was supposed to have been a witness for him. He vaguely remembered the name, Hess said. Then he added with a cackle, "I hope none of my other witnesses leave me in the lurch by preferring death." Hess mentioned another witness he wanted called—his brother, Alfred. Gilbert wondered, was this another Hess joke? Alfred Hess was insane. Gilbert had difficulty envisioning Hess as a power on any nation's stage. Yet, he was familiar enough with the man's history to know that this rattling husk had once been a serious figure. There was even a time when a self-conscious, socially insecure Adolf Hitler had used Hess as his liaison to Germany's aristocrats and wealthy industrialists.

Rudolf Hess had not lived in Germany until he was fourteen. His father had been a successful export-import merchant living in Egypt, where Rudolf was born. Hess still waxed rhapsodic over the land of his birth. "What a paradise it was," he wrote to his wife from prison. "I will never be completely free of the garden of Ibrahimieh, with its flowers and its scents and all the indecipherable, imponderable influences of the place."

The First World War had saved him from unwanted entry into his father's business. He wrote his mother, "Share my joy. I am in the infantry." Also in the List Regiment, in which Hess served, was a runner whom he never met, Corporal Adolf Hitler. Hess, however, left the infantry and finished the war as a pilot, infected with a love of flying that never deserted him. He first heard the former corporal of his old regiment speak in the backroom of the tiny Sternacher Tavern in Munich. Less than a dozen people had come to hear Hitler prophesy: "The banner of our movement shall one day wave over the Reichstag in Berlin, indeed, in every German home!" Hess had concluded that he was listening either to the country's savior or to a madman. He decided to enroll as the sixteenth member of the Nazi party on July 1, 1920.

When Hitler's 1923 putsch from the Munich Bürgerbraukeller failed to bring down the Bavarian government, Hess happily followed his Führer into Landsberg prison. The months in this comfortable minimum-security fortress, under house arrest really, became the making of Rudolf Hess. Later deprecators liked to say that Hess's chief service to Hitler had been to type *Mein Kampf.* Not true. The two men influenced each other, and it was Hess who brought into Hitler's orbit the geopoliticist Professor Karl Haushofer. Hess neither typed nor took dictation at Landsberg. He fed Hitler ideas, one of which was lebensraum, "living space," later used to justify Germany's attempts to absorb its neighbors.

On his release from prison, Hess became Hitler's secretary. When the Nazis took power, he was named deputy führer, and *Reichsminister* without portfolio. While a Goebbels or a Göring battled officials for positions bathed in public light, Hess worked tirelessly at unsung tasks. He became, in effect, the party's control over the German bureaucracy. No domestic public law, decree, or rule could be issued without first passing through Hess's hands. No act desired by the Nazis could be denied by the government. It was as if a Republican or Democratic national chairman were to take control over the Washington government apparatus.

As he rose in power, Hess could finally indulge the peculiar drives that pulsed beneath his conventional exterior. His marriage was already an odd, arid affair. As his wife, the former Ilse Proehl, described him, "Rudolf rarely smiled, did not smoke, despised alcohol and had no patience with young people enjoying dancing and social life. . . ." Their only child had been born ten years after a marriage that reportedly had been ordered by Hitler.

Hess took up vegetarianism and nature cures. He established a hospital for quack treatments rejected by the medical profession. He irritated Hitler by bringing his own health foods to dinner meetings. In the mid-thirties, Hess invited the Führer to his new home in Isartal, a fashionable Munich suburb. Party legend had it that this visit cost

Hess the position of successor to Hitler. The Führer was said to have found Hess's home in such unremitting bad taste that he decided no such person could ever lead Germany. That was the moment, allegedly, when Hitler turned to Göring as his successor. Thereafter, year by year, Hess had found himself outfoxed by craftier, tougher players. The flight to Scotland, his last desperate bid for influence, had followed.

Now he sat in a jail cell with a psychologist testing how many numbers he could remember. He gave up on four forward and three backward. Gilbert asked if he had made a decision about testifying in his own defense. No, he said, he would not testify. He did not want to be embarrassed by his bad memory. And he did not want to be questioned by people he disliked.

Alfred Seidl was relieved by his client's decision. But what was Seidl to do this Monday morning to defend Hess? A diversionary feint was the best strategy, he concluded. He came into the court with three copies of a "document book" which he shared with the bench and the prosecution. The book proved to be a paste-up of articles and newspaper stories criticizing the Treaty of Versailles. Seidl and the prosecution argued as to the admissibility of this material, until Lawrence could stand it no longer. However unjust the defense might find the treaty, Sir Geoffrey asked, was Seidl saying that it justified the war the Nazis started and the horrors that followed?

Seidl next sought to introduce the recently unearthed secret protocol from the German-Soviet nonaggression pact under which the two countries divided up Poland and allowed the Russians to seize the Baltics. His intent was to demonstrate the unfitness of the Soviets to sit in judgment on Rudolf Hess or any other German. Seidl eventually managed to get the treaty introduced, where it lay inert, neither supported nor rebutted. Two witnesses were called to prove that an overseas organization once under Hess's direction had not been a spy agency. With this limp performance, Hess's defense ended. Since the defendant had not taken the stand, he could not be cross-examined.

The shrewder lawyers recognized Hess's nonappearance as a remarkable instance of passive resistance, of being crazy like a fox. The eccentric in the rumpled tweed suit in the dock may have sat out the war, but he had been a charter Nazi, the planter of the aggressive seed of lebensraum. In his role in the issuance of the Nuremberg Laws for the Protection of Blood and Honor, Hess had been among those who had lit the fuse for the future Holocaust. His silence, however, spared him the cross-examination that Göring had gone through on the Jewish question or any other damning matters.

7

CAPTAIN GILBERT HAD BEEN UNEASY ever since Major Kelley had departed, particularly since Kelley had left no address where he could be reached. When in mid-March he received a letter from Kelley, Gilbert's apprehension was hardly relieved. The trial was evidently going to drag on much longer than any of them had expected, Kelley wrote. Consequently, he might go ahead with a Nuremberg book of his own—in addition, of course, to their joint project, in which his interest had revived. By the way, would Gus please forward to him transcripts of the trial as it progressed? Gilbert experienced the sinking sensation of a man whose partner was going in to collect the reward while he was still out chasing the desperadoes.

Kelley's letter also had the effect of sharpening Gilbert's sense of guilt. The trial's conclusion was indeed nowhere in sight. His wife, Matty, had watched her friends' husbands come home from the war and renew normal lives, yet she was still alone, making do on Gilbert's modest captain's pay. Lately, as the dreary, broken city pressed down on him, Gilbert thought increasingly of leaving and taking his wife and child to the warmth and sunshine of California. But the counterforce was still stronger. As he put it bluntly in a letter to Kelley, "I want to see them hang," a sentiment no one had ever heard this seemingly reserved professional utter aloud in Nuremberg.

Gilbert told Kelley that he, too, might write a book of his own, a Nuremberg diary. And he was sorry, but the administration had clamped down on trial transcripts. He was allowed only one copy, and consequently would not be able to oblige Kelley. He closed saying that he was delighted to know that Doug was still at work on their material.

He could not leave Nuremberg, not yet. Not when such possibilities beckoned as the one now open to him. He was going off to meet Göring's wife. No one Kelley could talk to in the United States could match that kind of raw material.

Emmy Sonnemann Göring was the *Reichsmarschall*'s second wife, a bosomy, warmhearted, generous woman who had never managed entirely to escape the shadow of the first wife. Göring's first marriage had been a fairy tale besmirched by scandal and tragedy. Among his desultory attempts to find employment after the Great War, Göring had worked for a time as an air taxi pilot in Sweden. On one job, he landed on the estate of a Swedish nobleman and there met Carin von Kantzow, a rich and beautiful baroness. Carin was married and the mother of an eight-year-old son, but love conquered discretion. She scandalized Swedish society by running off with Göring to Munich. There Hermann, now thirty, tried unsuccessfully to resume the life of a student. They were spared destitution only because Carin's husband, believing his wife was merely having a fling, supported her and her lover. The prudish Hitler, however, disapproved of the affair and put pressure on his disciple to get married, which Göring did in 1923, as soon as Carin's divorce came through.

On November 9 of that year, a cold and blustery day, Hitler and a band of two thousand Nazis, banners snapping, marched on Munich intent on toppling the Bavarian government. In the front rank, next to Hitler, strode Hermann Göring, his voice lifted in a Brownshirt marching song. As they reached the center of town, shots rang out from the police. Göring toppled to the ground, struck in the groin by a bullet ricocheting off the pavement. It was then that storm troopers carried him into the Jewish home where two sisters stopped the bleeding and saved Göring's life.

As soon as she could move him, Carin spirited Hermann to Austria, beyond the reach of German authorities. In a hospital, his wound suppurating, delirious with pain, Göring was given morphine twice daily. He soon became addicted. He and Carin drifted through Italy, then went back to Sweden, living on her money. Hermann was unable to hold a job. He became violent and had to be forcibly restrained from jumping out of an apartment window. He failed in a drug withdrawal clinic, and Carin was forced to commit him to an asylum.

There, in solitary confinement, he stormed about shrieking, "I am not insane. This is all part of a Jewish plot!" Hermann Göring had touched bottom.

Eventually, he was weaned from his addiction, and in 1926 returned to Germany with Carin to begin life anew. He begged Hitler to put him on the slate for the next elections of the Reichstag. Hitler saw in this desperate failure a salvageable wreck, and agreed. In June of 1928, Göring won one of twelve Nazi seats. His wily mind seized the possibilities. Göring asked for the party's transportation portfolio. He was soon taking fat bribes to steer government contracts to favored aircraft manufacturers. He went on the payrolls of the Heinkel and BMW companies as a "consultant." Lufthansa provided him an office and secretary. A steel magnate furnished his luxurious new apartment on Berlin's swank Badenschestrasse. The beautiful, aristocratic Carin became a leading Berlin socialite.

In October 1931, Göring's world again collapsed. Carin, always troubled by a weak heart, died. He tearfully confessed to her niece that all his boasting, his striving, his admitted megalomania, had had one root—his resolve to give Carin a life as good as the one she had abandoned for him.

Within nine months, he was consoling himself with Emmy Sonnemann, a pretty, good-natured, thirty-seven-year-old blond actress separated from her actor husband. Emmy was unsophisticated, undemanding, apolitical, and apparently had not a jealous bone in her body. Göring's first gift to her was a photograph of his late wife. After a nearly four-year affair, Göring married Emmy in 1935. He had in the meantime become the second-ranking figure in the state after Hitler. He lived like an Aryan pasha. He built a palatial estate northeast of Berlin on a bluff overlooking the city—his fifth home, including two castles. He built the estate with government funds and called it Carinhall. He also named his two yachts after his first wife. Emmy did not object.

Emmy had numerous Jewish friends in the theater, and as the anti-Semitic decrees of the thirties began to wreck their lives, she asked her husband to intervene. Her special pleading put Göring on the spot with his regime. Still, he helped occasionally, enriching himself along the way by taking a bribe to get a Jew out of a concentration

camp or secure a passport. He did perform one act of common de-
cency: he arranged for the two Jewish sisters who had saved his life
after the failed putsch to get out of Germany with their money. When
General Karl Bodenschatz had testified in Göring's defense before the
IMT, Stahmer had made sure that Bodenschatz got that fact into the
record.

In 1937, Göring suffered an excruciating toothache. Hitler sent
him to his personal dentist, who prescribed a new drug, a morphine
derivative called paracodeine. Göring was to take six of the little pills
a day until the pain stopped. The pain did stop, but Göring continued
to take the paracodeine. Within a few months, he was up to thirty
pills a day.

In 1938, Emmy presented Göring with his first child, a daughter,
Edda. There was something about his vanity, his figure swollen from
too much rich living, that prompted endless gibes about Göring's po-
tency. Fellow Nazis joked behind his back that a Göring aide had
fathered the child and that Edda stood for *Es dankt der Adjutant*, "All
thanks to the adjutant." Streicher had savored the rumors and had
gone public in *Der Stürmer* with his claim that Göring's daughter was
not conceived by him. Göring's best defense was the child. Edda had
a debatable asset for a little girl: she looked just like Hermann Göring.

Emmy Göring's fortunes had followed a roller-coaster course since
the war's end. Early in her husband's incarceration at Nuremberg,
Ensign Bill Jackson had tracked her to one of her homes, a lodge near
Rosenheim in Bavaria. Jackson was hunting for documentary evidence.
The door was answered by an ample Nordic woman of middle age,
cautiously cordial. Jackson informed Emmy that he was required to
search the house. She made no objection. Jackson unearthed no useful
documents, but in the cellar he uncovered magnums of champagne
and cases of cognac and scotch. In the attic he discovered humidors
filled with Havana cigars and a cache of Lucky Strike cigarettes in the
green packages that Americans had not seen since before the war. He
opened a steamer trunk and felt like a pirate discovering buried treasure. The trunk was crammed with silks, furs, jewels, and boxes of
gold coins. Jackson left the contents undisturbed and bade good-bye
to Frau Göring.

Weeks later, Emmy Göring was arrested and put into Straubing prison. Little Edda was sent to an orphanage. Emmy remained confined for five months, until February 1946. By then, Allied occupation officials feared that her plight might arouse sympathy for Göring. They released her. But Emmy could not return to any of her opulent residences. Instead, she, Edda, and a niece went to live in a shack in Sackdilling forest near Neuhaus, with no running water, electricity, or heat. It was here that Gus Gilbert was traveling to see her.

He arrived on March 23, armed with a sympathetic manner, cigarettes for the mother, and candy for the child. They sat in a primitive kitchen while Emmy tried to play the gracious hostess, and her niece served tea. As Edda happily scampered off with her candy, Emmy said, referring to Hitler, "Can you imagine that madman ordering that child shot?" It was the opening Gilbert had wanted. What he hoped to have by the time he left Sackdilling were weapons to break through Göring's emotional defenses and get him to acknowledge guilt and renounce Hitler. Emmy spoke bitterly of the days after Göring left the Führerbunker in Berlin, how he and his family were to be executed because Hermann had been "disloyal." Göring had gone wild with rage, she said, cursing Hitler so savagely that she feared their guards would shoot him on the spot.

It amazed him, Gilbert said, in view of the fact that the whole world now knew Hitler was a monster, that her husband persisted in remaining loyal to his memory. "The only reason I can imagine," Gilbert offered, "is that he does it just to spite a foreign court trying to judge him."

One had to understand Hermann's sense of honor, Emmy said. Today, Germany was full of hypocrites saying they had never supported Hitler and that they had been forced to join the party. "It's sickening," she said. "And Hermann wants to show that he, at least, is not backtracking like a coward." But wasn't her husband putting himself in a terrible light by this blind loyalty? Didn't it look as though he condoned Hitler's murderous policies? She took out a frayed handkerchief and wiped her eyes. "He is a fanatic on the subject of loyalty," she said. "That is the one thing on which we cannot agree. Loyalty to a man who would murder my child?

"Hitler must have been insane," she went on. Hermann had ad-

mitted as much to her. He told her it would have been far better had
Hitler been killed in 1938 in an auto accident. He would then have
died a great German.

On his return to Nuremberg on Sunday night, bearing a letter from
Emmy and a postcard from Edda, Gilbert went directly to Göring's
cell. Göring grabbed the letter and the postcard. He joked a bit about
Hess's phantom defense of the previous week. Gilbert then mentioned
his recent visit. Emmy was distressed, he said, by Göring's stubborn
fealty to a man "who ordered you arrested and shot at the end, and
little Edda too." Göring shrugged. He did not believe Hitler had ever
ordered him shot. "That was the work of that dirty swine Bormann,"
he said. Gilbert pressed on. His wife was desperate to see him, if only
for a few minutes. She wanted to talk him out of his misguided notion
of loyalty. "My wife can influence me in lots of things," he said, "but
as far as my basic code? Nothing can sway me." These matters were
in the realm of men, he declared. "It's not a woman's affair."

A tired Gilbert rose to leave. It had been a long weekend. He
bade Göring good night and went to the prison office, where he wrote:
"Göring's medieval egotistical sense of values is complete down to the
'chivalrous' attitude toward women, which conceals its narcissistic purpose behind a façade of condescending protective indulgence and allows no womanly humanitarian values to interfere with that purpose."

Gilbert's visit had nevertheless unsettled Göring. The psychologist's
words had forced him to consider the posture he had taken. But the
alternative to defiance was the belly-crawling contrition of a Speer or
a Frank, and that was not for Hermann Göring. He was fidgeting on
the edge of his cot, glaring angrily at the ever-present face in the
square porthole. Colonel Andrus had recently added a new security
measure; all chairs were taken from the cells during the night.
PFC Vincent Traina was leaning on the little shelf-door that hung
outward from the port. Göring came up to the door and ordered, "Get
me my chair!" The guard, jolted from his reveries, seized the blackjack
off the wall, rapped Göring's hand, and told him to sit down. Göring
began cursing and shrieking, "I have rights!" The guard flung the door
open, went in, and again ordered Göring to sit. Göring continued a
torrent of abuse. Traina beat him on his shoulder and then on his

upraised hands with the blackjack. Fritzsche, from the opposite side of the corridor, shouted for help. The duty officer came running, and led Traina out of the cell. What was going on? the officer wanted to know. Göring claimed that instead of giving him the chair when he asked for it, Traina had sat in it and made fun of him. Fritzsche called from across the way that what Göring said was true.

The puzzled officer looked to Göring. "You know me, Lieutenant," Göring said to him with melting sincerity. "Sure you know him," Traina broke in. "He's a Nazi killer and I'm just a GI." The fracas was duly reported to Colonel Andrus. His sentinel, Andrus ruled after an investigation, had "acted quite properly."

Riling his keepers was not a policy Hermann Göring could afford. He needed not antagonists but friends, like Tex Wheelis. He had already given Wheelis a handsome watch. Within the next few days, he managed to have a gold cigarette case extracted from his luggage in the baggage room, and he gave it to the lieutenant.

8

JOACHIM VON RIBBENTROP, once foreign minister of the Third Reich, was scheduled to begin his defense Tuesday, March 26. The week before, Ribbentrop's new lawyer, Martin Horn, had cornered Captain Gilbert during a midmorning recess. Horn, a young man with slicked-back black hair and a superior air, asked Gilbert if he had noticed anything strange lately in his client. The doctor no doubt knew, Horn said, that Ribbentrop had sent a letter to the tribunal offering to have himself tortured to death in expiation for Nazi atrocities. Yes, Gilbert said, he was familiar with the letter. Clearly, Horn went on, the man was suffering a nervous breakdown. Gilbert smelled an insanity plea and excused himself.

Horn found Ribbentrop as exasperating as had his predecessor, Fritz Sauter. The defendant's attention could not be focused long enough to proceed from A to B, before he was shooting off to Z, Horn complained. Ribbentrop paced constantly in his cell, rifling through disordered papers for the one document that would save him, and which he could never find. Horn had tested the insanity ploy because his client seemed to him a plausible candidate.

The night before Ribbentrop was to begin his defense, Colonel Andrus visited the cellblock. He looked into Ribbentrop's cell, but did not tarry. The mess and the odor repelled this spit-and-polish soldier. He asked only how Ribbentrop was sleeping. Ribbentrop ceased his dithering long enough to say, "You Americans certainly have better drugs than we Germans." Andrus agreed and walked on. He had discussed Ribbentrop's insomnia with the POW doctor, Ludwig Pfluecker. Andrus was afraid that if Ribbentrop hoarded sleeping pills, he might kill himself. If he took them, they could make him lethargic in the courtroom. The colonel feared a headline, DRUGGED PRISONER DRAGGED TO NUREMBERG DOCK. Pfluecker had come up with the solution—placebos compacted of baking soda provided by the mess hall. Thereafter, Ribbentrop slept like a lamb.

That evening, Ribbentrop was led to the visitors' room for a final conference with Horn before his defense opened the next day. As they faced each other through the chicken wire, Horn handed a single sheet of paper to the guard to check before passing it through the slot to his client. Earlier, Ribbentrop had written a note to Göring asking that he testify in his behalf. Göring had attended Hitler's key foreign policy sessions, and the *Reichsmarshall* could attest that the foreign minister had always tried for peaceful diplomatic solutions, Ribbentrop believed. He snatched at the letter. Göring had drawn a line through Ribbentrop's request and had written at the bottom, "I am only aware that Ribbentrop advised in favor of war."

Drexel Sprecher, making his own last-minute preparations to rebut the Ribbentrop defense, was discussing strategy with Colonel Harlan Amen over dinner at the Grand. Amen had been drinking heavily, which had no visible effect on his mind or his pugnacity. Sprecher was surprised to find himself working with Amen. His usual immediate superior was Amen's rival, Colonel Robert Storey.

The night after Jackson's cross-examination of Hermann Göring, Sprecher had talked with the chief prosecutor about the upcoming Ribbentrop case. He had been at work for some time on the rebuttal, and assumed that he would be helping Jackson prepare to cross-examine Ribbentrop. He found Jackson miserable with a head cold, impatient and irritable. Colonel Amen would be handling the cross-examination of Ribbentrop, Jackson informed Sprecher. Sprecher started to express his disappointment, when Jackson cut him off. That was all there was to it, he said. Sprecher wondered why Jackson was leaving the ring. Had the Göring experience shaken him that badly?

Ribbentrop, breaking the rules, jumped out of his bed after lights-out. A radio in the prison office was blaring American pop tunes. The guards playing basketball in the gym next to the exercise yard never stopped shouting. Even the thump of the ball on the gym floor could be heard in the cellblock. Ribbentrop yelled at his guard. They must cease all this racket. Tomorrow, he was going on trial for his life. The guard ordered him to shut up and go back to bed.

For Ribbentrop, driven to distraction by "Deep in the Heart of Texas," classical music had always been his greatest consolation. Ribbentrop thought of his violin as "the comrade who never let me down." Its song had given him solace after his mother's early death. The violin had quelled his adolescent passions. And when the war news was at its worst, he had played. But the sweetest notes for him had sounded in the wilds of Canada, his paradise lost.

Ribbentrop had gone to Canada in his youth in pursuit of a girl. He had lost the girl but had fallen in love with the country. Of course, Canadians could be rough. He had learned his English in England, and the Canadians were always mocking his "la-de-da" accent. They played tricks on him. Every time he went to put on his British tweed jacket, he would find the pockets full of stones, until finally he had to throw away the shapeless garment. It was just their unsophisticated sense of humor, he had concluded. He had stayed on, holding several jobs along the way—bank clerk in Montreal, draftsman for a construction company, newspaper reporter in New York. In 1914, the war broke out. He was back in Canada by then, intending to make it his home. He had only one kidney and could easily have avoided military service. But the pull of the fatherland proved too strong. Ribbentrop returned to Germany and to war.

Boris Polevoi leaned over the shoulder of Russia's famed cartoonist, Boris Yesimov. Polevoi watched, impressed at how quickly the artist caught Ribbentrop—the frightened, searching eyes, the shabby

clothes, the look of an unemployed salesman with no job prospects.
"You made the suit too baggy," Polevoi observed. "Don't worry," said
Yesimov with a smile. "It will straighten out when they hang him."

"He always reminded me of impending doom," Howard Smith
remarked. "In the old days, he looked handsome, even strong. He'd
come into the reception room saying things like, '*Meine Herren*, our
abundant patience is exhausted. An hour ago, the Wehrmacht crossed
the Russian border.' We were actually afraid of Ribbentrop in those
days."

Justice Lawrence called the court to order. Martin Horn's first
witness, Baron Gustav Steengracht von Moyland, was bald, distinguished, wearing a dark gray suit with a bloused handkerchief in his
breast pocket. The baron had run the Foreign Office while Ribbentrop
was running after Hitler. In the witness box he performed a useful if
humiliating function for his old chief. Ribbentrop had repeatedly told
him, the witness testified, that Adolf Hitler needed no foreign minister. He, Ribbentrop, was merely the Führer's traveling secretary.

Fräulein Margarete Blank, Ribbentrop's personal secretary, followed next. Horn asked what her boss's attitude was toward Adolf
Hitler? "Herr von Ribbentrop always showed the greatest admiration
and veneration for the Führer," she said. "To enjoy Hitler's confidence was his chief aim in life. In carrying out the role set him by
the Führer, Herr von Ribbentrop showed utter disregard for his
own interests." The prosecutors could barely contain their laughter.
Maxwell-Fyfe whispered to an associate, "Don't they ever rehearse a
witness?" No prosecutor asked to cross-examine Fräulein Blank. What
she had said could scarcely be improved upon.

On April 1, Ribbentrop took the stand. After direct examination
by Horn, Colonel Harlan Amen went after the witness with his customary ankle-biting ferocity. But it was Sir David Maxwell-Fyfe whom
the audience had crowded the visitors' gallery to watch. Ribbentrop,
during Horn's direct examination, had protested his innocence of
Hitler's aggressive intentions. He had in his hand, Sir David said, a
document dated March 15, 1939, surrendering the remaining independent part of Czechoslovakia to Germany. "Will you agree that the
document was obtained from Czechoslovakia's president by the most
intolerable threats of aggression?" the prosecutor asked. "No," Rib-

bentrop answered. But what further pressure could you put on the head of a country, Sir David asked, than to threaten that you would march in, in overwhelming strength, and also bomb Prague? "War, for instance," Ribbentrop answered primly. "War!" Sir David said in a moan of disbelief. "What is that *but* war?" Hjalmar Schacht leaned over to Gilbert standing near the dock. "Ribbentrop should be hanged for stupidity," he whispered. "There is no greater crime."

Ribbentrop had tried to pass off his rank as a general in the SS as merely honorary and foisted on him by Hitler. Sir David read from an application demonstrating that Ribbentrop had asked to join the SS three years before Hitler appointed him to any office. Furthermore, the papers established that he had applied for admission to the "Totenkopf," the Death's-Head Division, which ran the concentration camps. "Are you saying that you did not know that concentration camps were being carried on in an enormous scale?" Sir David asked. "I knew nothing about that," Ribbentrop answered. Maxwell-Fyfe asked that a map of Germany furled behind the witness box be unveiled. He then proceeded to read off the list of Ribbentrop's several homes. "These red dots on the map are concentration camps," he pointed out. Did Ribbentrop see how close five of his homes were to the camps? Maxwell-Fyfe snapped his folder shut, concluding his cross-examination.

The next day, Ribbentrop faced the French and Russian cross-examiners. Was it possible that Herr von Ribbentrop knew nothing of the extermination of the Jews? French prosecutor Edgar Faure began. Faure then read a memorandum prepared by Paul Schmidt, Hitler's interpreter, reporting a meeting between the Führer, Ribbentrop, and Admiral Miklós Horthy, the regent of Hungary. Hitler was quoted as demanding that Horthy hand over all the Jews in his country. Faure read Ribbentrop's words from the Schmidt account: "The foreign minister declared that the Jews were either to be exterminated or sent to concentration camps. There was no other alternative." "Did you say that?" Faure asked. Ribbentrop pouted. "Not in those words," he replied.

During Rudenko's turn, the Russian asked Ribbentrop, "Do you consider the seizure of Czechoslovakia an act of aggression?" "No," Ribbentrop answered. "Poland?" "No." "Denmark?" "No." "Norway?" "No." "Greece?" "No." "The Soviet Union?" "No." Ribbentrop was dismissed and returned to the dock. "You were not even interesting," Göring muttered.

Young Bill Jackson was in the Palace of Justice coffee shop when a guard approached to tell him that a woman wanted to see him. She had said she was Frau von Ribbentrop. Jackson told the guard to bring her to his office.

She was tall, dignified, refined. Gertrud von Ribbentrop explained that she had come to Nuremberg to see her husband. She hoped Mr. Jackson would help her. No family visits were permitted, Jackson explained; but he asked if he might otherwise be useful. Yes, she said, she wanted someone to tell Joachim that he should make out his will.

9

EIGHTEEN-YEAR-OLD PFC BILL GLENNY entered the cellblock singing. "Someday my grandchildren will ask me, Grandpa, what did you do in the war? And whatever else can I tell them? I opened and closed the cell door!" The parody had been written by another guard to the tune of "If I Had the Wings of an Angel." Glenny wailed the closing lyric, "Oh, if I had the bars of a captain, or the leaves of a major in gold, I would fly from this Nuremberg prison, and forever be quit of this hole!" Glenny relieved his predecessor and began a two-hour stint of watching Wilhelm Keitel play solitaire.

It was likely the worst job in Nuremberg, bracketed on one side by stupefying boredom and on the other by Colonel Andrus's ceaseless pressures. Virtually every combat veteran was long since gone from the prison staff. Glenny typified the men Andrus was now getting, young postwar draftees. On reporting for duty, he had been lectured, along with a half dozen other newcomers, by the colonel personally. They had been sitting in a room, chairs tilted back, telling jokes, until an officer with a pencil mustache, a riding crop, and a shining helmet appeared. The lieutenant accompanying him barked "Ten-shun!" Chairs clattered as the men jumped to their feet and, with barely an amenity, Colonel Andrus began to speak in staccato bursts: "You will never take your eye off the prisoner for more than two seconds. You will never allow a prisoner in bed to turn his back on you. You will never allow the prisoner to speak to another prisoner." To Glenny, the rules sounded farfetched, and the performance struck him as overacted.

Colonel Andrus had long ago given up trying to make the ISD into an elite unit. As he wrote to a friend after the latest batch of replacements arrived, "Some of the draftees are rubbish. Some of the officers shouldn't even have been enlisted men." But at least he now understood why all his requests for more and better-qualified personnel were rejected, even though the ISD was twenty percent below strength. General Lucian Truscott, now commanding the Third Army, always skimmed off the best new troops. "I get the slops they don't want," Andrus wrote. The implication was clear to him: the Americans, as they stiffened toward the Russians, were softening toward the Germans. Weak replacements were no accident. The army's apparent policy was to get seasoned, possibly vengeful soldiers out of Germany and replace them with GIs who had not seen the war and would get along well with the German people. "General Truscott," Andrus ended his letter, "is not in sympathy with the trial and hopes it will fail." Burt Andrus had been an army observer in London during the blitz. He remembered talking with a chambermaid cleaning his hotel room. She had lost her husband and a son at Dunkirk, and her home in the bombing. He himself had seen Dachau. How could people forget it all so soon? he wondered.

Admittedly, he leaned hard on his men, but he was merely passing along the pressure he took from above. Andrus was still summarily called in by General Leroy Watson and blamed for every theft, rape, or brawl in Nuremberg remotely attributable to his men. The colonel's letter of complaint to his cousin, General Clint Andrus, had been bucked up to headquarters for U.S. forces in the European theater. The chief of staff had written back saying that if the colonel could not get along with General Watson, perhaps he should ask to be relieved. This, Andrus felt, would have been an ignominious end to his career.

10

If Colonel Andrus had a model prisoner, it was Field Marshal Keitel, the man who never complained. This stoicism, however, won Keitel little credit among his countrymen. Göring described him as "a sergeant's mind in a field marshal's body." When Captain Gilbert once suggested to Keitel that he write his memoirs, Keitel asked what profit there would be in facing up to his life. It seemed to him an unbroken chain of misery; his youngest daughter dead of tuberculosis in 1940; one son killed and two more missing in Russia; his home destroyed in an air raid; his wife a virtual widow surviving on the charity of friends. In the end, the man for whom all the sacrifices had been made, all the humiliations swallowed, had repaid him with scorn. Hitler had written in his final testament that Keitel and the High Command were responsible for Germany's defeat.

During the war, Keitel had occasionally tried to salvage scraps of honor. He knew that the Wehrmacht intelligence chief, Admiral Wilhelm Canaris, was a patriot. Yet, Canaris had been among the nearly five thousand Germans executed in the orgy of vengeance following the Twentieth of July plot. Keitel had quietly slipped money to the Canaris family. But that was hardly redemption.

Early in the trial, his lawyer, Otto Nelte, a fifty-nine-year-old pragmatist, had tried to convince Keitel to confess. Even if they found him guilty, a soul-baring admission could mitigate his sentence, Nelte had argued. Keitel had agreed to consider the idea. But first he needed to consult with Göring, which he did in the exercise yard. Out of the question, Göring had told him. They had to present a united front. After a sleepless night, Keitel had told Nelte no—that because Göring had objected, he could not confess. Even in Nuremberg, he still obeyed orders.

Lackey, parrot, bootlicker, patsy, fall guy, weakling, messenger boy—all these gibes he had endured. What respect could such a man hope to retrieve? Admittedly, Keitel still cut an imposing figure as he walked, shoulders squared, to the witness box to begin his defense on April 3. His outward bearing, however, seemed merely to mock the craven interior man his colleagues knew. Maxwell-Fyfe waited his turn to cross-examine Keitel like a lion resting between feedings.

Keitel's lawyer rose from the defense table. Nelte's intention was to follow the Göring example, to ask his client questions eliciting full, self-serving answers, since Sir Geoffrey appeared content to let the defendants have their say. Who had been responsible for the sins laid at the feet of the German armed forces? Nelte asked. Keitel paused, then spoke firmly. "As a German officer, I consider it my duty to answer for all I have done," he said. "It will not always be possible to separate guilt from the threads of destiny. . . . But the men in the front lines, their officers and noncommissioned officers at the front, cannot be charged with guilt while the highest leaders reject responsibility. That is wrong and unworthy." The defendants in the dock sat up. The judges leaned forward. This was a Keitel none of them had expected to hear.

Nelte pointed out that Keitel's name appeared on the most odious orders. "What," the lawyer asked, "can you say in your defense?" "I bear the responsibility for whatever resulted from those orders. Furthermore, I bear the moral as well as the legal responsibility." Nelte raised an issue that to British eyes was the soul of dishonor, Keitel's role in passing along Hitler's order to execute the escaped Sagan RAF fliers. He had initially tried to avoid reporting the escape to Hitler, Keitel said, because he knew the Führer would react vengefully. But Himmler had already informed Hitler. Keitel thereafter argued against the Führer's determination to have the escapees shot, which merely made him the target of Hitler's wrath. He did at least talk Hitler out of shooting the men who had already been returned to Stalag Luft III, he explained. But in the end, he admitted, he had caved in to Hitler's demand for death.

General Jodl, in the back row of the dock, watched his old comrade with a flicker of sympathy. He remembered the day perfectly. He had known that Keitel was not the man to stand up to Hitler on this matter. He also knew instantly that this atrocity could never be explained away. Jodl had, in fact, told Keitel when the British arrested them in May 1945, "It is the Stalag Luft III business."

Keitel's defense entered its fourth day. On Saturday, April 6, Roman Rudenko led off the cross-examination. Rudenko relished the moment. To the Soviet prosecutor, Keitel's sudden nobility was poor recompense for the suffering the man's orders had inflicted on the Soviet people. He read from document R-98, the Reprisal Order, issued by Keitel, under which fifty Soviet hostages had been shot for every German soldier killed by partisans. Rudenko quoted Keitel: "One must bear in mind that in the countries affected, human life has absolutely no value." Had he signed the order containing this statement? Rudenko asked. Keitel answered yes. Rudenko asked if he considered this a proper order. Sweat beaded Keitel's brow. He had originally called for shooting five to ten hostages, he explained, but Hitler had upped the figure to fifty. Rudenko read from the same document. "The troops are, therefore, authorized and ordered to take any measures without restriction, even against women and children." Did not "any kind of measures" include murder? "Yes," Keitel admitted, barely audible, "but not of women and children."

Sir David Maxwell-Fyfe rose to continue the cross-examination. He questioned Keitel about Robert Paul Evans, a British seaman, age twenty. Evans had ridden a torpedo into a Norwegian fjord in an attempt to destroy the German battleship *Tirpitz*. "You have told us," Maxwell-Fyfe said, "that you have been a soldier for forty-one years. What in the name of all military tradition had that boy done wrong by operating a torpedo to attack a battleship?" Was this not a remarkable act of courage? "There is nothing wrong," Keitel agreed. "I recognize that it is right, a perfectly permissible attack." All the same, Robert Paul Evans on his capture had not been treated as a brave adversary, Sir David noted. He had been shot under Keitel's Commando Order. "What I want to understand is this," he went on. "You were a field marshal, standing in the boots of Blücher, Gneisenau, and Moltke. How did you tolerate all these young men being murdered?" He had explained, if not justified, his failure to resist Hitler in previous testimony, Keitel said. He could not go back and change that. But, he concluded, "I know that these incidents occurred and I know the consequences." Much of what he had gone along with, he said, was "against the inner voice of my conscience."

Sir David seized on the phrase. "Can you tell the tribunal the three worst things you had to do which were against the inner voice of your conscience?" It was a wild stab, the kind of self incriminating question that a defendant usually dodges. Keitel, instead, spoke calmly, looking straight ahead as though examining his face in an unseen mirror. First, he said, were "the orders given for the conduct of the war in the East, which were contrary to the accepted usages of warfare." He paused and cleared his throat. "The question of the fifty RAF fliers. And, worst of all, the *Nacht und Nebel* decree. . . . I personally thought that to deport individuals secretly was much crueler than a death sentence." Maxwell-Fyfe had no further questions. Keitel's expression suggested a man from whom a heavy burden had finally been lifted.

As Keitel made his way back to the dock, Göring leaned toward him and hissed, "Why didn't you say anything about how the Allies treated our saboteurs? You bungled it!" Keitel simply resumed his seat. Göring's was a minority opinion. The men in the dock, the judges on the bench, the prosecutors at their table, all had come to the same conclusion. The man who left the witness box was better than the man who had entered it.

11

TELFORD TAYLOR HAD BEEN in Washington since mid-February, acting virtually as a recruiting sergeant. After the prosecution had rested its case, a mass exodus of staff had taken place. Colonel Robert Storey, in his fifties, too long away from home, had left. Jackson had been hard put to hold on to his next in line, the colorful Tom Dodd. Dodd was, underneath the raconteur and party lover, a family man who wrote to his wife every day and also longed to go home. Jackson had to beg him to stay.

Telford Taylor himself had thought hard about his own future. He was a man of acknowledged brilliance, certainly the most intellectual figure on the American side. Bobbie Hardy, his researcher, found Taylor, at age thirty-eight, "too young to be so wise." He was, she believed, "the most incisive mind I ever dealt with. He could pierce to the heart of your argument before you could explain it." On March 29, Jackson formally appointed Colonel Taylor to succeed him as chief counsel for the subsequent trials of hundreds of concentration camp operators, Nazi "scientists," and assorted butchers to be tried after the main trial ended. For a former government lawyer whose military service had been confined largely to code work, Taylor's rank of full colonel was already impressive. Still, if he was going to stay on, with some civilian lawyers earning a handsome ten thousand dollars per annum in Nuremberg, he wanted more inducement. He wanted a star. Thus, Telford Taylor was promoted to general that spring, an occurrence that momentarily united Colonel Andrus and General Watson. Watson, a West Pointer, and Andrus, with nearly twenty-eight years in the army, resented that a uniformed civilian, in effect, had won the rank regular soldiers spent a lifetime pursuing.

Back in Washington, the newly minted general was having little luck signing up lawyers. It was now peacetime. The men had come home and were not eager to leave again. Taylor informed Jackson of the one recruitment incentive that would work; he could persuade lawyers to sign on if they could bring their families.

That spring, the army at long last lifted the ban on spouses. Francis Biddle immediately sent for Katherine, who arrived in April with Elzie Wechsler, wife of Biddle's chief aide, Herb Wechsler. Biddle left the quarters he had shared with Judge Parker and their aides on Hebelstrasse and took one of the handsomest houses still standing, the Villa Conradti, bumping Frau Conradti, who became his housekeeper.

Katherine Biddle found Nuremberg abounding in ironies. As she explored the city by day and comforted her emotionally starved Francis by night, she tried to capture their singular existence. She sat in the library overlooking a green field and began writing "Love Song in an Occupied Country."

> More alone than survivors on a storm wracked island,
> Everywhere surrounded by alien sounds and faces,
> Alien earth and bread,
> Heart looks into heart to find its recognition.
> Love thrusts out the broken city,
> The shapes at the gabled windows.
> What lies in the unmarked mound under the leaves?
> Turn to me where the pallet is thin
> And the feather quilt smells of foreign herbs,
> The linen is rough and cold.

No longer alien or lost,
Your breast is all that I ask of home,
And your need of it my arms hold.

The departure of the Biddles for the Villa Conradti sharpened the loneliness of Major Robert Stewart, Judge Parker's aide. Back at their shared house on Hebelstrasse, Biddle had been Stewart's understanding ally in his daring romance with Tania Giliarevskaya. Now, Tania was gone. Overnight she had simply disappeared back into the maw of Russia. The researcher who had befriended her, Katy Walch, had approached a Soviet officer at the Grand Hotel and demanded to know what had happened to her. "Tania?" he said. "What Tania? We have many Tanias."

Robert Jackson virtually disappeared from the court once the defense case began. His subordinates had, however, warned him that the bench was allowing the defense to introduce a deluge of irrelevant documents, bogging down the trial interminably. And so Jackson returned on April 9 to make a heated criticism of the court's permissiveness. The great majority of these documents, he argued, were useless, a waste of the court's and the translators' time. Jackson was becoming increasingly bitter, convinced that he had been ill used by the bench. Geoffrey Lawrence's vaunted "fair play," he told his staff, was letting the court get out of hand. Maybe the man could run a trial, but he seemed to have no grasp of what was happening historically in this room. Lawrence was refereeing a great moral contest as if it were a cricket match, even bending the rules to give the foreign team a break. Jackson was merely disappointed with Lawrence, but furious over Francis Biddle. Once the man had been his friend. Now, through the lens of repeated rejections in court, he saw only a puffed-up ego—a man who, when he wasn't flaunting his French, was aping an English lord, chewing his mustache and saying things like " 'Shtirring times, indeed. Shtirring times.' "

Francis Biddle returned to his chambers as soon as court adjourned, eager to be whisked home where his wife waited for him. His secretary advised him, however, that Justice Jackson was demanding to see him and Parker immediately.

Sir Geoffrey Lawrence was always ruling against him, Jackson said testily, pacing, hands jammed into his pockets. Lawrence had just done so again on his request to limit the defense to relevant documents. He was fully aware that Biddle controlled Lawrence like a puppeteer. Did Biddle realize what he was doing? Jackson asked. He was demoralizing people who were working night and day to bring justice to a wounded world. Biddle sat behind his desk, fingertips pressed together, presenting the exterior coolness produced by five generations of good breeding. Parker sat, hands folded across his paunch, studying Jackson over the tops of his glasses, his round face pained. Jackson went on: He had said it before and he would say it again. If he and his people were to be continuously overruled, while the bench stood the law on its head to favor the defendants, then he might as well go home. With that, Jackson stormed out.

12

To CAPTAIN GILBERT, Ernst Kaltenbrunner was among the most detestable defendants. Kaltenbrunner's guilt was immediate and personal. Alone among them, he had set his hands directly on the levers of extermination. As chief of the RSHA, the Reich Central Security Office, serving directly under Himmler, Kaltenbrunner had been responsible for the SD and the Gestapo, which had dispatched people to the camps. Adolf Eichmann, now understood to be the engineer of extermination, and who had managed to slip through the Allied dragnet, was a Kaltenbrunner subordinate and friend. In cell visits to the others, Gilbert strove to maintain his posture of professionalism, and, with his little gifts of cigars or candy, even to appear sympathetic. But to be in Kaltenbrunner's presence was akin to sitting with the murderer of one's mother, one's wife, one's child. Still, Gilbert had an obligation to the court to monitor the mental state of every defendant. He also had at his disposal in Kaltenbrunner an executive of mass murder to dissect for his book. And so, early Thursday morning, April 11, the day Kaltenbrunner's defense was to begin, Gilbert stopped by cell 26.

The prisoner seemed in reasonably good emotional condition, except for a slight hesitation in his speech traceable to his stroke. Kaltenbrunner mouthed the same rationalizations that Gilbert had heard from him before. His relationship to the concentration camps existed only on organization charts. Others had run them at Himmler's direction. He had occupied himself solely with intelligence matters. He had never issued an order for anyone's death. He had never seen a death camp. He had not known they existed.

Kaltenbrunner's lawyer, Kurt Kauffmann, forty-four years old, spare, tall, had the hot eye of the fanatic. As soon as his client was sworn in, he plunged ahead. "You are aware that you are under extremely serious charges," he said. "The prosecution connects your name with the Gestapo terror and the atrocities of the concentration camps. I now ask you, do you assume responsibility for the counts as charged?"

The lawyers at the prosecution table looked on with admiration. Few of the Germans seemed to have grasped the dynamics of the Anglo-Saxon adversarial system, the duel of wits between lawyers. Kauffmann appeared to have absorbed a defense fundamental: Get the worst out under direct examination on your own terms. Steal the cross-examiner's thunder. Kaltenbrunner answered that, technically, he accepted responsibility for actions carried out in his domain. "I know the hatred of the world is directed against me," he went on, now that Himmler, Gestapo chief Heinrich Müller, and Oswald Pohl, who ran the concentration camps, were all dead. But his liability was solely technical. These men had been the actual evildoers. Kauffmann asked about his client's signature on thousands of orders sending people to the camps and to their death. "Not once in my whole life did I ever see or sign a single protective custody order," Kaltenbrunner answered. The signatures Kauffmann was referring to were facsimiles, or had been typewritten. "You will admit this statement of yours is not very credible. It is a monstrosity," Kauffmann observed.

Kauffmann read into the record from a document indicating that Kaltenbrunner had ordered the execution of a team of OSS agents captured in uniform behind the lines. He asked his client to explain. "Completely out of the question," Kaltenbrunner answered. Such behavior would have been "a crime against the laws of warfare."

Kauffmann referred to earlier testimony by a prosecution witness, a camp guard, who had sworn that Kaltenbrunner watched while the gas chamber was demonstrated on Mauthausen inmates. "I never saw a gas chamber," Kaltenbrunner answered. "I did not know they existed at Mauthausen. . . . I never set foot in the detention camp at Mauthausen—that is, the concentration camp proper." Under Kauffmann's relentless pounding, Kaltenbrunner began shrieking his answers.

Kauffmann finished his direct examination and yielded to the prosecution. Sir David Maxwell-Fyfe and the other prosecutors recognized that they had overestimated their man. It was not that Kauffmann had picked up the subtleties of the adversarial system. He had learned only the prosecutorial side of it. Maxwell-Fyfe himself could not have done a better job of incriminating Ernst Kaltenbrunner.

During cross-examination, a voice reached from the grave to condemn Kaltenbrunner. The RSHA chief had heard earlier, to his relief, that the Mauthausen commandant, Fritz Ziereis, had died in a shoot-out at the end of the war. But John Harlan Amen produced a deathbed confession that Ziereis had made implicating Kaltenbrunner in the plan to suffocate surviving Mauthausen inmates in a sealed-off tunnel and in other atrocities.

The prosecution also questioned Kaltenbrunner about earlier testimony that placed him at Mauthausen, where, reportedly, he had witnessed demonstration executions by shooting, hanging, and gassing.

As the cross-examination ended and Kaltenbrunner returned to the dock, he passed Captain Gilbert. "I saw your people holding their sides with laughter," he said. "Please extend my congratulations to them for finding me such a stupid attorney."

13

GUNTHER SADEL, of General Watson's counterintelligence unit, enjoyed sitting in the visitors' gallery watching Kaltenbrunner laid bare. Such men had destroyed Sadel's family, parting his Jewish father and Gentile mother, and forcing Sadel to flee to America with his father seven years before. When he arrived at Nuremberg, he had had no idea if his mother was dead or alive.

On learning of this situation, Watson had told Sadel to cut himself a set of orders, take a jeep, go to Berlin, and look for her. Sadel had found Berlin no less devastated than Nuremberg, except that its state pained him more. Berlin had been home. He located the apartment house—scarred but still standing—where he had grown up. He walked to the third floor and there on the door was a tarnished plate with "Sadel" inscribed on it. His mother answered the bell.

Watson, on learning the news, had done the sort of thing that would inspire Sadel to walk through fire for him. The general had ordered Sadel's mother to Nuremberg as a "witness," entitling her to government transportation, rations, and living accommodations.

Sadel was summoned from the visitors' gallery during the Kaltenbrunner testimony to take on a new assignment for the general, one no odder than a dozen others the young PFC had already performed—setting up the social pass system, tracking down rumors of prison breaks, finding a pedigreed dog for an American reporter, and slipping a German into Andrus's jail as a "material witness" to spy for Watson. Sadel's latest task, the general told him, involved the daughter of the novelist Thomas Mann. Erika Mann, who was covering the trial, was rumored to be a lesbian and living with a Frenchwoman. Watson did not give a damn, he said, about the woman's love life. But she was well connected, and he was responsible for security. Watson suspected that another reporter was playing Peeping Tom on her apartment. Sadel was to stop it.

14

LIEUTENANT COMMANDER WHITNEY HARRIS COULD scarcely believe his good fortune. The British, he learned, had in custody Rudolf Franz Ferdinand Hoess, whose name was similar to that of the sometime amnesiac already in the dock, Rudolf Hess. Harris arranged to have Hoess transferred to Nuremberg, where he interrogated him for three days. What Hoess revealed was staggering, even by Nuremberg standards. But what to do with the information? Harris wondered. The prosecution case had already ended. Then, incredibly, Kaltenbrunner applied to have Hoess appear as a witness in his defense. Why he had done so was a mystery, unless he hoped to diminish his own guilt by comparison with someone whose deeds were even blacker. Rudolf Hoess had been the commandant of Auschwitz.

In the end, as in the case of Einsatzgruppe D commander Otto Ohlendorf, Whitney Harris was deprived of the full reward of his enterprise. If there was any cross-examining of Hoess to be done, John Harlan Amen would do it. That was how it worked in the big law firms, Harris suspected. Unsung young men did the plowing and the sowing; the older partners came along and reaped the harvest.

Rudolf Hoess's family, devout Catholics, had intended him for the priesthood. His father was stern, unapproachable, a godlike figure in young Rudolf's mind. The elder Hoess had made his son feel that his every misdeed wounded him personally. Rudolf had protected himself by gradually withdrawing from involvement with other people where he might run afoul of his father's strictures. He did not, however, become a priest. Instead, early in the Hitler regime, Hoess became a professional concentration camp administrator, starting at Dachau in 1934.

Whitney Harris watched from the sidelines, still struck by the ordinariness of this civil service cipher, as Hoess took the stand. Kurt Kauffmann, Kaltenbrunner's lawyer, invited Hoess to tell his story. In the summer of 1941, Hoess began, he was commandant at Auschwitz, a new concentration camp built on farmland in Poland. He was enlarging the camp to accommodate 100,000 prisoners, whom he expected to employ in agriculture. Instead, he explained, "I had to go to Himmler in Berlin where he imparted to me the following: 'The Führer has ordered the Final Solution, the *Endlösung,* of the Jewish question. We, the SS, have to execute it.' " Auschwitz had been picked because it was well situated for transportation and isolated enough for secrecy. Hoess still did not fully understand what he was supposed to do. Shortly afterward, Obersturmbannführer Adolf Eichmann came and explained Hoess's new duties in greater detail. He would get a better idea, Eichmann told him, by visiting a camp at Treblinka, near Warsaw.

In the course of Hoess's recital, only one point made was of any possible value to the defendant for whom he had been called. Kurt Kauffmann elicited that while Hoess was commandant of Auschwitz, Ernst Kaltenbrunner had never visited the camp. For the prosecution, this admission was a cheap price to pay for the coming right to cross-examine Hoess.

John Harlan Amen replaced Kauffmann at the stand and read aloud from the affidavit Whitney Harris had taken from Hoess describing his visit to Treblinka. In it, Hoess explained that he had been unimpressed by the Treblinka operation. It had taken the commandant there six months to eliminate eighty thousand Jews using monoxide gas. Hoess had a better idea. One of his Auschwitz guards had accidentally taken a whiff of Zyklon B, a chemical disinfectant used in the camp laundry. The man had passed out instantly. If a little of the chemical killed lice, enough should kill humans, Hoess and his staff reasoned. He tested the Zyklon B on Soviet prisoners of war locked in a room, and it worked. The substance was dropped from a hole in the ceiling, reacted instantly with oxygen in the air, and within three to fifteen minutes, the victims were dead.

Hoess outdid Treblinka tenfold. He built gas chambers to accommodate two thousand inmates at a time, compared to Treblinka's two hundred. He had two large crematoria built with four double ovens heated by coke. With these facilities, "It was possible to get rid of ten thousand people in twenty-four hours," Hoess affirmed. But that peak had been reached only once, in 1944, "when train delays caused five transports to arrive all in one day."

Hoess had overcome other deficiencies spotted at Treblinka. There, the prisoners realized what was happening to them, which created control problems. At Auschwitz, Hoess worked out a less stressful system. Freight cars would pull up to a railhead, where the passengers were unloaded. Upon delivery of their human cargo, train crews and guards were sent away, replaced by camp personnel sworn to secrecy; any revelation of what went on at Auschwitz was punishable by death. The new arrivals were then marched past SS doctors, who judged their fitness to work. The able-bodied, averaging twenty-five percent of a shipment, were taken into the camp and issued black-and-white-striped uniforms. Those unfit to work—the old, the sick, and those "of tender years," as Hoess described them—were taken directly to the gas chambers. They were ordered to undress and told not to forget where they had left their clothes, while they went in to take a shower. The chambers actually had showerheads, pipes, and drains. Usually the ruse worked. As Hoess wrote in a poem:

In the spring of '42 many blossoming people walked under
      the blossoming fruit trees of the old farmstead,
To their death, without premonition.

These innovations enabled Hoess to dispose of some two and a half million people during his tenure at Auschwitz.

After reading the affidavit, Amen asked Hoess how many people it had taken to kill two thousand persons a day. Hoess explained that he had had a staff of approximately three thousand men. He also made clear that he had not tolerated gratuitous cruelty. His men were there to exterminate people, not to torment them. Any misconduct by guards was punished by detention, transfer, and, if serious enough, by whipping. No guards, however, were compelled to kill. If they protested, they would simply be assigned to other duties.

At the end of the day, Captain Gilbert went to Hoess's cell on the second tier of the prison. The man jumped to his feet, but otherwise his face retained the same expression of ennui that the courtroom spectators had seen. "I suppose you want to know if my thoughts and habits are normal," Hoess said. "What do you think?" Gilbert asked. "I am entirely normal," Hoess answered. "Even while doing this extermination work, I led a perfectly normal family life." Gilbert invited the man to go on. Hoess did admit to one peculiarity: "I always felt happiest alone. . . . I was always self-sufficient. I never had close relationships, even in my youth. I never had a friend." He could watch people enjoying themselves, he said, but he could never join in. He had enjoyed most the period after the war, when he was a fugitive hiding on a farm with horses as his sole companions. "No," he went on, "I never had any need for friends. I never had any real intimacy with my parents, with my sisters."

Gilbert asked Hoess whether the Jews he had murdered had deserved their fate. He had never in his life heard anything else, Hoess explained. His whole political and educational formation had taught him that the Jew was Germany's enemy. He had never considered that there might be another side to the question, because he had never heard another side. Even so, it did not matter. He was an SS man. "We were all so trained to obey orders without thinking that the thought of disobeying never occurred to anybody. . . . I never gave much thought to whether it was wrong. It just seemed a necessity."

For Gilbert, it had all fallen into place at last. The puzzle of "why" was complete. He sat in his half-lit office in the courthouse, eyes fixed on a wall papered with duty rosters and the colonel's regulations. Gilbert's knowledge of German history was sufficient to tell him that Hitler had not invented anti-Semitism or the cult of obedience. At the beginning of the nineteenth century, the philosopher Johann Gottlieb Fichte had preached from the University of Berlin that Latins and Jews were decadent. Later, Georg Wilhelm Friedrich Hegel, from the same professorial chair, had glorified the state and ridiculed the pursuit of individual human happiness. Periods of "happiness" were the fetid pools of history, Hegel taught. War and heroes, absolved of conventional considerations of morality, were like cleansing winds that swept a nation to greatness. Another early thinker, Heinrich von Treitschke, had taught young Germans, "It does not matter what you think, as long as you obey." Adolf Hitler had merely sown his seed in receptive earth.

Today, in room 600, Gilbert had seen it all converge in one insignificant human being. Talking to the condemned SS prisoners at Dachau, he had concluded that institutionalized slaughter demanded a culture that placed obedience above thinking. "The thought of disobeying an order would simply never occur to anybody," Hoess had said. In the earlier testimony of Otto Ohlendorf, as he coolly explained how his Einsatzgruppe D shot ninety thousand people, the second piece of the puzzle had slipped into place: You can do it when you are persuaded that you are killing not people but pernicious, subhuman creatures. The indoctrination film *The Eternal Jew*, shown to German troops, had depicted Jews as rats infesting and infecting the nation. "We took it for granted we had to protect Germany from the Jews," Hoess had told Gilbert.

But these two forces, blind obedience and race hatred, while sufficient to account for the assembly-line slaughterers, still did not explain the architects and engineers of the Final Solution, such educated, even sophisticated men as Ohlendorf and Hoess. The final piece had been provided to Gilbert by the latter, the man who "never had a friend," who preferred the company of horses to that of people. Gilbert began writing: Rudolf Hoess was "outwardly normal, but lacked something essential to normality, the quality of empathy, the capacity to feel with our fellow man." Hoess had described the millions at Auschwitz not as people, but as "shadows passing before me." Combine unthinking obedience, racism, and a disconnection from the kinship of mankind, and you could produce an Auschwitz commandant.

His arriving at a solution that satisfied the mind served only to depress Gilbert's spirits. Every society had its authority-ridden personalities. Bigots exist all over. And schizoids, dead to normal feeling, walk the streets every day. The latent ingredients could be found everywhere. The distinction in Nazi Germany had been that these people had not functioned on the margins of society. They had run it.

15

COLONEL ANDRUS STUDIED the invitation with mixed astonishment, curiosity, wariness, and not a little pleasure. The press corps was inviting him to a party to celebrate his birthday at the Faber-Castell castle in Stein. The colonel's relations with the press had scarcely improved over the months. The stories reporters wheedled out of his staff got him into hot water with the court. Recently, *Stars and Stripes* had carried what appeared to be an interview with Hermann Göring, for which Andrus had caught hell from Justice Lawrence. Actually, an enterprising reporter had managed to get Otto Stahmer to slip a list of questions to his client.

To Andrus, the best way to get one's hand bitten was to feed the press. For their part, the reporters regarded Andrus with frustration. As much as the cells, sentries, and walls of the prison, he stood between them and the stories they wanted most—direct interviews with the defendants. Their invitation, Andrus thought, might be part of a softening-up operation. On the other hand, he personally had enjoyed a good press. In most stories, he was portrayed as an American archetype, the broncobuster who could break the toughest Nazi, the no-nonsense jailer of Nuremberg. He decided to accept the invitation.

The date set was April 15, the day after Rudolf Hoess completed his testimony.

The colonel found the press bar crowded with faces he recognized from the courtroom. Boris Polevoi, an admirer, threw a welcoming arm around the colonel. A correspondent from Chicago joshed Andrus about an article reporting that he used profanity in dealing with his prisoners. Andrus had a theory about cussing that he would share with them, he said. Swearing fit two occasions: "When you can't get people to believe you unless you get mad, and when you deal with a select group of sophisticates, like you people, who find a well-placed 'son of a bitch' amusing." The crowd laughed, and the colonel beamed. He was off to a good start.

The talk turned to the Hoess testimony. An English reporter asked what the moral difference was if you gassed people on the ground or cooked them from the air. Look at the firestorms in Hamburg and Dresden. Some 600,000 Germans had died in air raids, twenty times more than in Britain. Arthur "Bomber" Harris, British author of the level-the-cities strategy, had as much blood on his hands as a Rudolf Hoess. The Americans had better not be so bloody high-minded either, the Englishman went on. Look at Hiroshima and Nagasaki.

Andrus said that he was a simple soldier and had no intention of getting enmeshed in ethical dilemmas. An American reporter offered an answer. He had not noticed any Allied bombs dropped on Germany since the war ended, the reporter said. But did anyone believe that the slaughter of the Jews would have stopped if Germany had won the war? Besides, how many SS men had died pushing helpless people into gas chambers? Over sixty thousand Allied airmen had lost their lives pounding Germany into surrender.

The reporters went virtually down the cellblock, asking the colonel about each defendant's quirks. Andrus avoided personal observations and confined himself to describing his rigid security measures. As the evening ended, he concluded that they were not such a bad lot. He had enjoyed his birthday party.

16

HANS FRANK'S DEFENSE represented something of a personal investment to Captain Gilbert. He did not want Frank or any of them
absolved. What he hoped for on the stand was admission of wrong,
remorse, repentance. To Frank's credit, he had been virtually the first
to stand up to Göring's bullyragging. His reborn Catholicism, with
its promises of an afterlife, seemed to have given him reason to die,
if not to live. But the man was subject to manic swings. In one recent
visit, Frank had told Gilbert, "Today is Palm Sunday and I swore by
the crucifix that I will tell the truth and expose the sin as my last act
on earth. Let the chips fall where they may." But the very next day,
after a recess in the Hoess testimony, Gilbert had overheard Frank
tell Rosenberg, "They are trying to pin the murder of two thousand
Jews a day in Auschwitz on Kaltenbrunner. What about the thirty
thousand people killed in the bombing of Hamburg in a few hours?
How about the eighty thousand deaths from the atomic bombing of
Japan? Is that justice?" Frank's spine, Gilbert feared, was malleable.

Two days before Frank's defense was to begin, Gilbert had found
the man in his cell close to tears. He had read in a newspaper of the
death at Auschwitz of a Dr. Jacoby. He realized that this victim had
been his father's dearest friend in Munich, "a fine, kindly, upright old
man." After listening to Hoess, it had sunk in; Jacoby had been one
of that nameless herd extinguished daily at Auschwitz. "And I had
done nothing to stop it," Frank cried. "No, I didn't kill him myself.
But the things I said, and the things Rosenberg said, made those horrors possible. I have decided I must expiate my guilt." Gilbert had left
the cell with no idea which side this unstable figure would come down
on when he took the stand.

Hans Frank was sworn in on the morning of April 18. His lawyer,
Alfred Seidl, small, fussy, unimpressive, had been dubbed "Mickey
Mouse" by Göring. "Did you," Seidl asked, "ever participate in the
annihilation of the Jews?" In truth, Frank could evade. He had run
no death camps. He had risked going back to Germany from Poland
to make speeches supporting the rule of law. He had hated Himmler.
Auschwitz had not been in the part of Poland under his control. And

he had a gift for rationalizing his behavior. "I say, yes," Frank responded, his voice tremulous. "And the reason I say yes," he continued, "is because having lived through the five months of this trial, and particularly after having heard the testimony of the witness Hoess, my conscience does not allow me to throw the responsibility solely on minor people. I myself have never installed an extermination camp for Jews . . . but we have fought against Jewry for years; and we have indulged in the most horrible utterances. My own diary bears witness against me. Therefore, it is my duty to answer your question with yes." He paused, then spoke with quiet force. "A thousand years will pass and still Germany's guilt will not have been erased."

Gus Gilbert heard the answer with something that fleetingly approached admiration.

Waiting for the elevator, Frank looked around at his countrymen. Who was with him? Who reviled him? Hans Fritzsche, the old radio propagandist, edged his way toward him. Fritzsche was a reasonable man, one of those most shamed by the revelations of atrocities. "According to your own diary," Fritzsche said, "you not only smelled what was going on, you knew what was going on. It would have been more honest if you said so, instead of trying to hide among the millions of our people, hanging them"—he mimicked Frank's witness-stand emotion—"with one thousand years of guilt!" Fritzsche spun away. Frank was stung. He had felt cleansed by his unburdening. But Fritzsche, whom he regarded as a friend, had turned on him. What were the others thinking?

17

JUSTICE JACKSON WAS DELIGHTED to get away from Nuremberg and spend a few days in the baroque splendor of Prague, to which the Czechoslovakian president, Edvard Beneš, had invited him. He had left in mid-April, and entrusted direction of the American cross-examination to John Harlan Amen. In Prague, Jackson attended the trial of Karl Hermann Frank, the "Butcher of Lidice," no relation to Hans Frank. This Frank, among other crimes, had presided over the razing of the Czech city and the execution of all its male inhabitants in retribution for the assassination of Reinhard Heydrich. The trial was over quickly. Frank's execution was set for May 22, less than five weeks after the trial's beginning.

The swiftness of Czech justice heightened Jackson's concern over the seemingly interminable character of the Nuremberg trial. He had believed at one time that the case would be wrapped up by Christmas. Four months later, the end was still nowhere in sight, thanks in part to the limitless latitude Lawrence was granting the defense. The longer the trial dragged on, Jackson feared, the less sharp would be the bite of its judgments. Moral outrage, even over the Nazis' enormities, could not be sustained at a befitting level indefinitely.

While in Prague, Jackson was treated royally by the Czech government, a welcome sensation after the pressures and irritations of Nuremberg. Lately, a new source of friction had added to his discontent. He was being sniped at by colleagues on the Supreme Court. Jackson was not surprised that his archfoe, Justice Hugo Black, had ridiculed the IMT, calling it a "serious failure" and blaming the chief prosecutor. But his Washington agent, Charlie Horsky, had recently reported more dismaying news. Good, gray, upright Chief Justice Harlan Fiske Stone was telling intimates that Bob had gotten himself into a nasty business. The Nuremberg trial, according to America's ranking jurist, was nothing but "a high-grade lynching." To Jackson, returning to the Palace of Justice held out scant appeal.

The court went into Easter recess on April 19, and was not to resume until Tuesday, April 23. Captain Gilbert by now moved like a blinkered workhorse, permitting himself virtually no life outside the cells and the courtroom. The day before the recess, Gilbert had spoken at length with Göring on the nature of war. "Of course, the people don't want war," Göring told him. "Why would some poor slob on a farm want to risk his life in a war when the best he can get out of it is to come back in one piece? The common people don't want war; not in Russia, not in England, not in America, not for that matter in Germany. It's the leaders who determine the policy . . . and the people can always be made to do the leaders' bidding. All you have to do is tell them they are being attacked and denounce the pacifists for lack of patriotism. It works the same way in any country." Gilbert wondered what was the point of discussing morality with a man who understood the world with such crystalline cynicism.

On April 22, Harlan Stone, the chief justice, while reading a dissenting opinion in the U.S. Supreme Court, collapsed and died. Jackson's friends were instantly on the transatlantic telephone with one message. If he wanted to succeed Stone as chief justice, he must come home at once. Jackson conferred with people he trusted—Elsie Douglas, his son, Bill, a few others. Bob Jackson was a romantic with a realistic streak. He wanted the chief judgeship desperately. It would make his return to the court a triumph instead of a chore. But how could he walk out on the unfinished business in Nuremberg to lobby for a job in Washington? It was unseemly. If he gave an interview to the press, if he went to visit the troops, Marble Room pundits already had it that he was laying pipe for a run for the presidency. The month before, James Farley, the manager of two of Franklin Roosevelt's presidential victories, had been among the VIPs who flocked to the visitors' gallery. According to the Nuremberg party circuit, Farley had obviously come to sound out Jackson about a White House bid.

Columnist Drew Pearson broke a story claiming that Justices William O. Douglas and Hugo Black had threatened to quit the court if Truman named Jackson as chief justice. No denials were heard from either man. Jackson could not openly express his hunger for the job. He could only stay in Nuremberg and hope for Harry Truman's nod.

18

THE COUNTESS INGE KALNOKY OFTEN FELT herself playing the role of animal tamer, keeping congenital enemies apart. Under the roof of the Witness House she lodged camp survivors and former Gestapo agents, members of the anti-Hitler resistance and intimates of the Führer, such as Heinrich Hoffmann. The most unsympathetic of the guests turned out to be a huge-bodied, half-blind giant with thick glasses, Hans Bernd Gisevius, whose natural pose was arrogance and whose native language was sarcasm. Kalnoky, however, extended her considerable charm even to Gisevius. The effort was part of her desire to think better of her fellow Germans. She was sickened by the way they groveled before the Americans, denounced and spied on each other. Even Gisevius, so ready to demolish his intellectual inferiors, scraped before every American second lieutenant who stopped by the Witness House. And, Kalnoky was honest enough to admit, she did the same.

However dismissive of her other guests, Gisevius treated Kalnoky with rare chivalry. He revealed to her that he had been a member of the early Gestapo, was ousted in a power play, and wound up in the *Abwehr*—military intelligence. He was now feted by the Americans, he pointed out, because he had been a spy for the OSS during the war and part of the Twentieth of July plot. He had been called to Nuremberg as a defense witness for his former boss, onetime Nazi minister of the interior Wilhelm Frick. It struck Kalnoky as odd that this former Allied spy, this member of the anti-Hitler resistance, was to be a witness for a Nazi. Gisevius answered slyly that he did not know how useful he would be to Frick.

Among the defendants in the dock, Wilhelm Frick was the invisible man, his only distinguishing feature being the incongruous checkered sport jacket he wore every day. His lawyer, Otto Pannenbecker, had had to scramble desperately to find anyone who could help his client. Frick certainly could not help himself. The man was capable only of parroting stale Nazi dogma; thus Pannenbecker had no intention of putting him on the stand. Gisevius had been a long shot. Since he had worked for Frick, he might at least be able to establish that the man had exercised no real power, since he had lost it all to smarter, more ruthless Nazis.

Gisevius testified on April 24. Pannenbecker went through the direct examination and yielded to the American prosecutor. All eyes turned to Robert Jackson, who had grown tired of behind-the-back critics whispering that he had lost his taste for combat. By the end of Jackson's cross-examination, Gisevius had happily admitted that Hermann Göring had ordered a subordinate to murder Gregor Strasser, a rival to Hitler in the Nazi party; that Kaltenbrunner was more dangerous as chief of the RSHA than the dread Reinhard Heydrich; and that Field Marshal Keitel had been kept fully informed of the emergence of death factories in the East. Of the man he had supposedly come to defend, Gisevius said that the Twentieth of July plotters would certainly have had Frick on the list of Nazis to dispose of, had they succeeded. By the end of the testimony, Göring was on his feet cursing the perfidy and stupidity of Pannenbecker for calling Gisevius as a defense witness. The *Reichsmarschall* had to be dragged away and shoved into the elevator.

Hans Gisevius rose from the witness stand with ponderous importance. He had enjoyed himself enormously.

19

HANS FRANK HAD BEEN the keeper of a secret, and he was now writing about it in the memoir that occupied his hours in cell 15. It had all started in 1930, before the Nazis took power. Frank, then Hitler's youthful lawyer, had been summoned to the Führer's home. A distraught Hitler showed him a letter and spoke of a "disgusting blackmail plot." Frank was surprised to learn that Hitler had a half-nephew living in England. William Patrick Hitler, the son of Hitler's halfbrother, Alois, had written to say that it would benefit Uncle Adolf if certain rumors circulating in the press were not confirmed. The rumors were that Adolf Hitler had Jewish blood. Hitler viewed William's letter as a veiled threat of exposure. The conversation left Frank with legs trembling, since he lived in fear of his own Jewish ancestry's being exposed. To Frank's astonishment, Hitler asked him to make a confidential investigation of his family tree.

What he discovered, Frank now revealed in his memoirs, was that Hitler's paternal grandmother, Maria Anna Schicklgruber, had worked in Graz, Austria, as a cook in the home of a Jewish family named Frankenberger. At age forty-two, still unmarried, Maria Anna gave birth to a son. No father was indicated on the baptismal record. She named the child Alois Schicklgruber, and this Alois grew up to become Adolf Hitler's father.

Maria Anna's employers had a son, Frank wrote, and "On behalf of this son, then about nineteen years old, Frankenberger paid a maintenance allowance for Alois Schicklgruber from the time of the child's birth until his fourteenth year." The implication seemed fairly straightforward. The son of the household, not for the first time in history, had impregnated the maid. During his investigation, Frank discovered correspondence between the Frankenbergers and Maria Anna "betraying on both sides the tacit acknowledgment that Schicklgruber's illegitimate child had been engendered under circumstances which made the Frankenbergers responsible for his maintenance."

When the child was five, Maria Anna married a mill worker named Johann Georg Hiedler. The Frankenbergers' support payments nevertheless continued. The new husband showed no interest in legitimizing his wife's child. Young Alois himself later changed his name from Schicklgruber to Hitler, the spelling of Hiedler having been mangled by a priest on an official record.

In his memoir, Frank described his fear of reporting his findings to Hitler. For if the Frankenberger youth had indeed fathered Alois, then Adolf Hitler was one-quarter Jewish. To Frank's amazement, Hitler did not tear off his head. He denied nothing, including the Frankenbergers' support payments for his father. He appeared to know all about this background and seemed to have dispatched Frank only to find out how much others knew. As for the putative Jewish grandfather, Hitler had an explanation. It was Johann Hiedler who had been having an illicit relationship with Maria Anna. When she became pregnant, she accused the Frankenberger son only in order to extract money from the family. According to Hitler, "The Jew paid without going to court probably because he could not face the publicity that a legal settlement might have entailed." Given the choice of being the heir of Jews or of a blackmailer, Hitler had chosen a blackmailer.

The lawyerly Frank had deduced the only possibilities: either the Frankenberger youth was indeed the father, making Hitler one-quarter Jewish; or Johann Hiedler was the father, making Hitler one hundred percent Gentile; or Maria Anna had been involved with both men and did not know herself who had fathered her child. At the close of the entry, Frank wrote: "The possibility cannot be dismissed . . . that Hitler was one-quarter Jewish."

To Frank, the irresistible question was how this uncertain ancestry might have shaped Hitler's murderous anti-Semitism. Streicher's ravings in *Der Stürmer* always had a rich old Jew seducing an innocent

German maiden. Oddly, in *Mein Kampf*, Hitler had a "black-haired Jewish youth" lurking in wait to corrupt her. And among the Nuremberg Laws, Hitler, at one point, had insisted on a peculiar clause: any Aryan female under the age of forty-five—three years older than his grandmother had been when she gave birth—was forbidden from working as a servant in a Jewish home.

Frank found other startling parallels in *Mein Kampf*. Mixed-race children, Hitler wrote, "beginning in the third generation . . . invariably reveal their mixed breeding by one infallible signal. In all critical moments in which the racially pure make correct, that is, clear decisions, the racially mixed person will become uncertain, that is, he will arrive at half measures." *Mein Kampf* repeatedly condemned "half measures" and "halfheartedness." Hitler's decisions, whether right or wrong, had been certain and unhesitating. He was deaf to anyone who sought to temper them with contradicting facts or pleas for moderation. The way to prove that he did not suffer from third-generational indecision that would expose him as racially mixed—part Jew—was to overcompensate, to be more decisive, more certain, and more anti-Semitic than anyone else.

Herb Wechsler, Jim Rowe, Adrian Fisher, and Bob Stewart acted as law clerks to the court, helping the judges determine, for each defendant, which charges had been proven and which disproved. With the prosecution and the defense of a half dozen defendants completed, this staff began preparing draft verdicts. The premier question, because it dealt with the most monstrous crime, was to determine who bore responsibility for the Final Solution. In the carloads of documents, the one piece of paper that forever eluded the prosecution was a direct written order from Hitler setting the machinery in motion. Hitler's managerial style did not help. He had been an intuitive leader, no respecter of organization charts, likely to issue oral orders to whoever sprang into his mind or his vision. Consequently, Nazi Germany was a clutter of competing, overlapping fiefdoms.

As nearly as the court could determine, the phrase "final solution" had first been used by Hitler himself in 1935. In a talk on the Nuremberg Laws, he had said that if the nation's statutes were inadequate to deal with the Jewish question, "the problem must be handed over to the National Socialist party for a final solution." In November of 1938 Hitler ordered Göring, as his deputy, to devise a solution for the "Jewish question." On January 24, 1939, Göring delegated the assignment to Reinhard Heydrich, then head of the RSHA. Himmler entered the picture with the testimony of Rudolf Hoess. Hoess had stated that in June of 1941, Himmler told him that the Führer had ordered the final solution of the Jewish question through extermination.

On July 31, 1941, Göring sent an order to Heydrich that read, "Complementing the task assigned to you on January 24, 1939, which dealt with carrying out by emigration and evacuation a solution of the Jewish problem, I hereby charge you with making all preparations . . . I request furthermore, that you send me an overall plan . . . for the desired final solution of the Jewish question." With exterminations already under way at Treblinka, Auschwitz, and other camps, Reinhard Heydrich, on January 20, 1942, called a meeting of fourteen party and government bureaucrats at the old Interpol headquarters in the Berlin suburb of Wannsee. Heydrich had one item on his agenda. Referring to Göring's order, he said that Europe was to be cleared of its eleven million Jews. They were to be sent to the East, where those able would work until decimated "by natural reduction." The rest would be subject to "special treatment." The witness Dieter Wisliceny had testified that in July or August of 1942, Eichmann showed him a written order from Himmler calling for the Final Solution.

The judges could conclude from this tangled skein the following: The original order for a final solution had been passed from Hitler to Göring to Heydrich. But Göring could argue that his orders mentioned only "emigration and evacuation." The actual killing order appeared to have been given orally from Hitler to Himmler, and was initially applicable to Polish Jews. Once this plan was in operation, Heydrich called together the bureaucratic apparatus to apply the final solution to the whole of Europe. Hitler, Himmler, and Heydrich were dead. Of the survivors, Göring and Kaltenbrunner, Heydrich's successor, could be tied directly to the solution of extermination.

As for guilty knowledge, Josef Goebbels had written in his diary, "Göring perfectly realizes what is in store for us if we show any weakness in this war. On the Jewish question especially, we have taken a position from which there is no escape." The passage made two points clear: the leading Nazis understood the incriminating nature of the Final Solution, and their determination to fight to the bitter end had little to do with ideological conviction and much to do with saving their own skins.

20

MONDAY MORNING, April 29, the courtroom was packed with secretaries, researchers, and others eager to satisfy their curiosity. What sort of a woman would marry Julius Streicher, a man who washed his face in the toilet bowl, who talked dirty to children, who told Colonel Andrus that Eisenhower was a Jew and that Jackson had changed his name from Jacobson, who claimed the destruction of the dirigible *Hindenburg* had been a Jewish plot, and who was treated even by his fellow defendants like spit on the sidewalk? Streicher's counsel, Hans Marx, had called Frau Streicher to testify in her husband's defense.

The previous Friday, Streicher had made a perfect ass of himself on the stand. He beamed foolishly, as if glorying in the attention. He interrupted Marx so often that the lawyer asked the court if he might be relieved of the case. The British cross-examiner, the aristocratic Mervyn Griffith-Jones, tore Streicher apart with a rapier tongue. At one point Griffith-Jones noted that Streicher, in *Der Stürmer*, had referred to the Jews as "a nation of bloodsuckers and extortionists," and asked, "Do you think that's preaching race hatred?" "No," Streicher answered. "It is not preaching hatred. It is just a statement of fact."

Adele Streicher turned out to be an attractive blonde in her late thirties, at least twenty years younger than her husband. She moved gracefully, spoke sensibly and with undeniable charm. Her devotion to Streicher was evident; and, in this moment with his life in the balance, she served him well. In January 1940, she had come to work as secretary to Julius Streicher at his dairy farm in Pleikershof near Nuremberg, she testified. By then, he was already out of power and, she made clear, he had spent virtually the entire war doing "peasant" work, breaking stones, cutting wood, feeding cattle. As she left the stand, carriage erect, General Jodl, not noted for his spontaneity, remarked, "Wondrous are the ways of love."

When Adele Streicher left the courthouse, she went directly to the Nuremberg home of Dr. Pfluecker. Pfluecker had managed to get word to his family to take her in after the Americans had turned over Streicher's Pleikershof farm to displaced Jews. She eventually managed to get herself arrested for her unrelenting and vocal anti-Semitism.

21

"IF WE CAN'T CONVICT Hjalmar Schacht, we can't convict anybody on the industrial side," Justice Jackson told General Telford Taylor. Taylor listened in dismay. Jackson was such a fine man, a gifted man. Yet, here in Nuremberg, his judgment seemed to be clouded by unremitting tensions. He was obviously still smarting from the early defeat when he had been prevented from bringing the arms maker Alfried Krupp to trial in place of Krupp's semi-senile father. What was so crucial about the industrialist case? Taylor wondered. The industrialists, Jackson believed, had conspired to put Hitler into power. They had conspired to rearm Germany, and for what purpose but to wage aggressive war? Condemnation and punishment of the industrialists was key if the conspiracy strategy was to hang together.

Taylor, possibly the ablest American legal mind at Nuremberg, was by now convinced that the conspiracy theory had become obsolete. What was the point of taking up the IMT's time to convict the defendants of conspiring to commit aggression when ample evidence existed to convict them of actually committing aggression? Taylor sometimes found Jackson's rigid judgments and righteous posture hard to take. Yet he knew there was little he could do to dissuade the man. Jackson, determined to claim Schacht's scalp, had decided to go into the pit again for the cross-examination. He had chosen, Taylor believed, an elusive target.

In all these months in court, Hjalmar Schacht had assumed a pose that suggested he was trying to avoid being contaminated by his colleagues in the dock. Back in the fall, Schacht had told an interrogator, Lieutenant Nicholas Doman, "Young man, do you know why I am here?" Of course, Doman had replied. Schacht, wagging a finger, had said, "No, you do not. I am here because Justice Jackson wants an innocent man among these defendants who can be acquitted to prove this is a fair trial." On April 30, Schacht sat in the witness box, not as one facing his accusers, but as one eager to share his brilliant insights with lesser mortals.

This turn-of-the-century man, his steel-gray hair parted in the middle, his collar stiff, his neck corded, cut an unlikely romantic figure. At the age of sixty-four, however, with a daughter from an earlier marriage already forty, Schacht had won the hand of Nanci Vogler, a beautiful woman thirty years his junior. He had fathered his last child at sixty-six. Now sixty-nine, he was, according to the test, the most intelligent man on trial.

It cannot have harmed Schacht that of all the defendants, he was the only one to testify in English. He had been born Horace Greeley Hjalmar Schacht, named after the crusading American journalist. Schacht's father had lived in America for several years, and had even become an American citizen before resettling in Germany. Schacht was considered the financial wizard chiefly responsible for bringing Germany's catastrophic inflation under control in the twenties. On coming to power, Hitler had shrewdly named Schacht president of the Reichsbank, and later, minister of the economy.

During cross-examination, Jackson intended to destroy Schacht's denials that he helped plan and carry out aggressive warfare. The prosecution had a 1934 decree signed by Hitler and naming Schacht secret plenipotentiary general for the war economy. Jackson further had proof that Schacht's schemes had indeed financed Germany's rearmament, that he had made speeches praising Hitler, that he had called people who patronized Jewish shops "traitors," and that he had contributed money to the Nazi party. Jackson introduced photos showing Schacht marching with leading Nazis, giving the Nazi salute, and sitting next to Hitler.

The Nazis, however, had inadvertently provided Schacht with a powerful defense against Jackson's onslaughts. Schacht had not been part of the Twentieth of July plot against Hitler. When approached by the conspirators, he had stalled, saying he would have to know

more about their new government. Nevertheless, after the attempt, he
had been arrested and ended up at Dachau. Trying to convict a man
of war crimes who had been liberated by American troops after spending ten months in a concentration camp tested Jackson's prosecutorial
gifts to the utmost.

22

WINTER HAD SUITED the trial. The leaden skies, gray rubble, and wan
faces in the dock blended in melancholy harmony. Now, spring had
come. In the old town, people emerged from their caves and pitched
tents, or rigged shelters from charred timbers, corrugated sheets of
tin, and empty U.S. Army crates. On the outskirts, farmers poured
liquid manure from oxcarts onto thirsty fields. Anglers from the IMT,
like Sir David Maxwell-Fyfe, fished a Pegnitz River teeming with
trout. The windows of the courtroom were thrown open and the stagnant air gave way to the fragrance of hawthorn. Spring mocked the
trial, made it seem out of step with a world being reborn.

On Saturday, May 4, a lovely night, the best boxes at the Nuremberg opera house were reserved for prominent members of the IMT,
come to hear a newly arrived ensemble. The group had originally
numbered thirty-five musicians and first played together in the ghetto
of Kaunas, Lithuania, soon after the Nazi occupation. Their music
had saved them, at least some of them. The Germans had them
perform at labor roundups and executions. Later, they had toured
concentration camps. Only the twelve playing tonight had survived
the war.

The performance began lightly enough, with a standard romantic
repertoire—Leoncavallo, Meyerbeer, and Rossini. Toward the close,
the ensemble performed a song evoking a different world:

Ghetto, I will never forget you,
Dark and crooked streets,
Death looms from every corner.
No home. No parents, hungry, forgotten by God and man.
Where is your wife, your child, your family?
Where to? Why? What for?

For the staff of the IMT, more than the torrent of words and numbing statistics they heard day in, day out, the music plumbed a feeling not yet touched—the incomprehension of a doomed yet innocent people.

Tom Dodd was again the toast of the Marble Room. His performance in court the day before had made his staying on in Nuremberg worthwhile. With the support of the anonymous staffers who prepared his appearances, he had shattered the defense of Walther Funk. Round, soft, weeping, dark-jowled Funk might have seemed an unworthy adversary, a preposterous war criminal. His weak bladder had gotten Funk out of the German army during World War I. At Nuremberg, he often had to be led from the courtroom to the men's room. To the guards he was "the pisser." This unlikely figure, however, had been indicted on all four counts.

The winding trail that had led Funk to the Nuremberg dock had begun at what seemed a moment of success. Hitler had summoned him during a Berlin performance of *La Bohème* and said, almost as though he could not believe it himself, "I'll have to make you the minister of economy after all." Thus Funk had succeeded the old wizard Schacht. He was, in fact, bright and capable. But Funk was known best in party circles as a bon vivant who savored fine cigars, good scotch, risqué stories, and all-night revelry. Though he was married and liked to play the lecher, Funk discreetly chose his own sex for his most intimate companionship.

The worst thing he had done was to draft a law in the thirties barring Jews from operating retail businesses, a blow that had doomed tens of thousands to poverty or flight. What hovered over Funk at Nuremberg, however, was something more tangibly horrifying. After the conquest of Frankfurt, a U.S. army film unit had made a motion picture of unusual deposits in the vaults of the Reichsbank—heaps of diamonds, pearls, gold eyeglass frames, gold rings, gold earrings, gold watches, and gold teeth. The vault looked more like a hock shop than part of a bank. The prosecution had shown the film in court.

Earlier in Mondorf, in a fit of remorse, Funk had admitted to Colonel Andrus that he knew how the valuables, including the gold teeth, had found their way into his bank. Once the trial began, however, Funk had denied any knowledge of these deposits. In cross-examining him, Dodd read from an affidavit given by Emil Puhl, Funk's assistant at the Reichsbank. Puhl claimed that Heinrich Himmler had arranged with Funk to accept valuables collected by the SS in the East. When Puhl asked Funk the source of these valuables, Funk had told him to stop asking questions. Puhl further deposed that he and Funk had gone to the vaults from time to time to see the accumulation of this trove.

On the stand, Funk insisted that Puhl's affidavit was a lie. Why did they not produce the man himself? Funk protested. Puhl would clear his old chief. Dodd pressed the witness on his continued denial of the nature of the SS deposits. "Many people deposited valuables, although the bank was not required to look into them," Funk said petulantly. "Nobody," Dodd observed, "ever deposited his gold teeth in a bank."

Emil Puhl did, in fact, testify days later, only to incriminate Funk. There had been seventy-seven SS deposits of valuables, he told the court. Funk knew about them, and they were, he said, *Schweinerei*— they smelled bad from the start.

23

ON MAY 8, General Alfred Jodl watched from the dock, listening to Grand Admiral Karl Dönitz being sworn in. The date held a stinging memory for Jodl. Just over one year before, Dönitz had dispatched him to a French boys' school in Rheims with orders to employ every possible delaying tactic before signing Germany's surrender. Jodl's icy reception by the victors had opened his eyes to a bitter truth. The German military were not regarded as defeated yet honorable adversaries, but as pariahs.

During the lunch break, Captain Gilbert reminded Admiral Dönitz that this was the date celebrating the defeat of the Nazis. "Why do you think I'm sitting here?" Dönitz responded. Still, his truculence had waned in recent months. When Major Neave first delivered the indictments, Dönitz had scrawled on his, "Typical American humor!" Later, the revelations had begun to weigh on him. Gilbert had overheard Dönitz say in the elders' lunchroom, "I was furious with the idea of being dragged to the trial in the beginning, because I knew nothing about these atrocities. But, after all this evidence, the double-dealing, the dirty business in the East, I am satisfied there was good reason to get to the bottom of it." Get to the bottom of it, yes. But not necessarily at the cost of Karl Dönitz's neck. He still argued his own innocence.

Dönitz's lawyer, Flottenrichter Otto Kranzbuehler, was a familiar figure around the courthouse, as the only German permitted to wear his full uniform. Navy blue flattered Kranzbuehler, a good-looking man much admired by the women in court. As a career naval officer, he looked upon the Dönitz case as a defense not simply of the admiral, but of the German navy, to which the lawyer had given eleven years of his own life. To Kranzbuehler, the most dangerous piece of paper in the prosecution's hands was the *Laconia* Order, which his client had issued to the submarine fleet on September 17, 1942. The order—not to rescue survivors of sunken ships, and not to give them food or water—had applied to merchant vessels as well as warships. Subsequently, one German U-boat captain had spent five hours hunting down and machine-gunning the survivors of the Greek steamer *Peleos*. The *Laconia* Order had figured significantly in Dönitz's indictment for "crimes against persons and property on the high seas."

His task, Kranzbuehler knew, was to educate the judges as to what lay behind the admiral's seemingly heartless directive. The facts were that the *Laconia*, a well-armed British merchantman sailing the South Atlantic, had been sunk by submarine U-156. After the ship went down, the U-boat captain found the sea full of survivors. He wired Dönitz for instructions. Dönitz dispatched two more submarines to aid in a rescue operation. The three subs took survivors aboard until they were full, and towed the rest in lifeboats toward land. During this rescue operation, the U-156 flew a large Red Cross flag.

To the disbelief of the submariners, an American Liberator bomber arrived on the scene and began attacking the U-156. The submarine took a hit amidships. Crowded lifeboats were sunk. The attack was reported to Dönitz, who now ordered the U-156 to put all survivors back into lifeboats and break off the rescue. However, he ordered the other two vessels to continue to bring their survivors to port. Hitler was enraged by what he regarded as Dönitz's misguided compassion. He demanded that the safety of the U-boats must take priority over all else. Thus it was that Dönitz had subsequently issued the aid-no-survivors order.

Otto Kranzbuehler had read and reread the tu quoque prohibition of the London Charter. It said in effect that even though the Allies might have committed wrongs, this fact did not excuse the Germans. There had to be a way around this provision. If only he could get a high-ranking Allied officer to testify that the war on the high seas had been fought the same way on both sides, he might save Dönitz. Five weeks before, Kranzbuehler had petitioned the court to allow him to seek an affidavit from Admiral Chester Nimitz, commander of the U.S. Pacific fleet. "I in no way wish to prove or even maintain that the American admiralty in its U-boat warfare against Japan broke international law," Kranzbuehler argued. "On the contrary, I am of the opinion that it acted strictly in accordance with international law." He was not saying that we Germans did wrong, but so did you; rather, he was saying, you did right, and so did we.

The British, French, and Russian judges were ready to reject these legal acrobatics out of hand; but Francis Biddle was intrigued by Kranzbuehler's ingenuity. He used his accustomed influence over Lawrence to win approval for the lawyer's petition. At the time, the move had confirmed Dönitz's good judgment in enlisting not just a navy man, but a resourceful one, as his defense counsel. Nevertheless, Dönitz was getting discouraged. Weeks had passed. He would soon face cross-examination by Maxwell-Fyfe, and still no affidavit from Nimitz had arrived.

During these weeks, Kranzbuehler had not been idle. Sixty-seven German U-boat captains were still imprisoned in England in Camp 18 in Featherstone Park. Kranzbuehler had dispatched an assistant to the camp with a statement averring that Admiral Dönitz had never ordered his crews to kill survivors. They had been directed not to rescue them. All sixty-seven captains had signed the statement, and Kranzbuehler had managed to have it accepted into evidence.

Captain Heinz Eck had commanded the submarine that shot up survivors of the sunken Greek steamer *Peleos*. Nothing could have served Eck better during his own war-crimes trial than to have claimed that he had acted under Dönitz's orders. Kranzbuehler instead managed to obtain a deposition from Eck, just before his execution, in which the U-boat captain admitted that he had acted on his own.

On Thursday, May 9, the cross-examination began. Still Kranzbuehler had no word from Nimitz. Maxwell-Fyfe read from Dönitz's speeches, exposing him as a rabid anti-Semite. Sir David proved that Dönitz was well aware of the existence of concentration camps. Had he not requested twelve thousand inmates to work in his shipyards? And Dönitz was the man whom Adolf Hitler had found most worthy to succeed him, a successor who mouthed praises of the dead leader until Nazi Germany's last gasp.

During a recess on the last day of the prosecution's counterattack, Dönitz watched an unknown American naval officer leave the visitors' gallery and approach Kranzbuehler. He saw his lawyer nod and smile. Kranzbuehler immediately reported to Dönitz. They might soon have good news from America.

The day after Dönitz's defense ended, Admiral Nimitz had gone to his office at the Navy Department in Washington. It was a Saturday afternoon, and the crusty admiral was in sports clothes, an informality that did not ease the task of Commander Joseph Broderick of the judge advocate general's office. Broderick read from a list of questions provided by Kranzbuehler. "Did U.S. submarines in the Pacific attack merchantmen without warning?" Broderick asked. Yes, Nimitz said without hesitation, except for hospital ships. Under whose authority? the lawyer asked. By order of the highest naval authority, the chief of naval operations, dated December 7, 1941, Nimitz responded. Did American submarines rescue survivors? Broderick went on. U.S. submarines did not rescue survivors, Nimitz said, if such action would place the submarine at risk. The deposition was soon on its way to Kranzbuehler, who introduced it into evidence.

The night of Dönitz's appearance in court, Katherine Biddle had hosted a combination VE-day celebration and sixtieth-birthday party for her husband at a grand house reserved for VIP entertainment, the Villa Schickedanz. Jim Rowe, Biddle's clerk, had put aside his work on a draft of the Göring verdict to come to the party. Rowe was a man's man, a thirty-seven-year-old frontier intellectual out of Montana, a reformed two-fisted drinker. He had been Oliver Wendell Holmes's law clerk, an insider at the FDR White House, a war hero who had pulled strings to get into, not out of, combat. Rowe's respect mattered to other men. Earlier in the day, Biddle had received a letter from Rowe. "I confess to thinking many years ago," Rowe had written, "that you were just a dilettante, a Philadelphia gentleman, a Grotonian, and a Harvard man who was amusing yourself by being a New Deal liberal." But, Rowe went on, he had studied Biddle closely at Nuremberg and concluded, "Well done, Francis. You have measured up." Biddle, like any son of privilege, wondered in the privacy of his soul how much he had earned and how much he had merely inherited. Rowe's birthday message provided an answer he prized.

24

Colonel Burton Andrus left the courthouse Friday night, May 10, concerned about the appearance of the courtroom guards. Their uniforms were rumpled. Sharp, hard creases had vanished. His subordinate in charge of the guard detail had reminded the colonel that the men stood for hours in a poorly ventilated room wearing olive drab wool jackets and trousers, bathed in their own sweat. That afternoon Andrus had Rose Korb type out an order: as of the following week, the ISD would switch to summer khakis. He asked her to run off the directive and circulate it before she left for the day.

That night, Andrus attended a dinner party at the residence of a British prosecutor. By eleven p.m. he was home in bed. He was jarred from his sleep at dawn by someone banging on his door. He answered it to find a captain from the army's Criminal Investigation Division. Rose Korb, the officer informed him, was being questioned about a shooting.

Korb had looked forward to that Friday night. Two friends working for *Stars and Stripes*, Sergeants William Timmons and Paul Skelton, were in Nuremberg, eager to do the town. Korb had finished the colonel's assignment and gone home to Girls' Town to dress for the evening. At eight p.m., the two GIs picked her up in a jeep. They drove to the enlisted men's favorite, the Stork Club, upstairs over the

Nuremberg Opera House. At 11:45 p.m., after a night of singing and jitterbugging, Korb was ready to go home. The colonel expected her in the office early on Saturday morning. By now, her party included another GI and two British women. The six piled into the jeep and headed for Girls' Town. They were proceeding down Morgenstrasse past a park, a favorite trysting place for GIs and their German girlfriends, when a blurred figure stepped out of the shadows. Three shots rang out. Timmons managed to bring the wobbling jeep to a halt and then toppled forward. In the back, Shelton was also slumped over. Both men died soon afterward of gunshot wounds to the chest.

Rose Korb was distraught and red-eyed by the time Colonel Andrus arrived at the Nuremberg headquarters of the Criminal Investigation Division. The CID men had been terrible, she said, asking her the most intimate questions, making it seem as if she had been involved in a sordid affair that had ended in murder. She was also being hounded by reporters eager for a sensational story during a slow news cycle.

The CID chief told Andrus that he had a dragnet out combing every building and ruin in a four-mile-square area of Nuremberg. It could have been an ambush by "werewolves," he thought. Nazi diehards. His men had already arrested six Germans, but he had no real evidence connecting them to the crime.

Colonel Andrus obtained Rose Korb's release and took the young woman back to her apartment building. He confined Korb to quarters to protect her from the relentless pursuit of the press. A few days later, she informed the colonel that she had had enough of international justice. She was going home.

The investigation went on, with fifty Nuremberg police joining one hundred American MPs. In the end, the investigators suspected that the killing had nothing to do with vengeful Germans. The sketchy but more promising lead was one the U.S. Army was uneager to confirm. The volatile relations between American blacks and whites appeared finally to have exploded. According to witnesses in the park, the killings had most likely been committed by an unidentified black GI for uncertain motives—possibly a dispute over a German girlfriend, possibly mistaken identity, possibly racial hatred. The crime was never solved.

25

REPORTERS HAD OBSERVED the odd relationship for months. Two for-mer commanders of the German navy sitting side by side in the second row of the dock, day after day, barely exchanging a glance. Seventy-year-old Grand Admiral Erich Raeder had been a cart-before-the-horse defendant. He had been indicted, along with the propagandist Hans Fritzsche, at the insistence of the Russians because they too wanted to produce war criminals, and these were the best they could unearth. Thereafter, prosecution researchers had to scramble to find evidence to match the charges. The case finally prepared alleged that Raeder had violated the Treaty of Versailles by building up the German navy, that he had been present at the Hossbach Conference, where Hitler laid out his aggressive intentions, and that he had been party to the plan to invade Norway. The most curious document in the prosecution's possession was the "Moscow Statement," which Raeder had made while in Russian captivity. Several defendants, the prosecutors knew, would not enjoy having its contents revealed in court.

The Moscow Statement surfaced on May 20, when deputy Soviet prosecutor Colonel Y. V. Pokrovsky introduced it during cross-examination. Pokrovsky got Raeder to agree that he had given the statement freely, without coercion. The reason behind the coolness between Dönitz and Raeder immediately became apparent. Pokrovsky, quoting from the document, read Raeder's opinion of Dönitz: He was "conceited," and "hardly qualified" to head the German navy. By call-ing for continued resistance after he succeeded Hitler, Dönitz had "made a fool of himself." Dönitz reddened visibly as Pokrovsky read from a speech Dönitz had once given to the Hitler Youth. After that speech, Raeder had said in his statement, Dönitz "was ridiculed in all circles and earned himself the title of 'Hitlerboy Dönitz.'"

Göring fared scarcely better. Raeder's statement said of the *Reichsmarschall*, "Göring had a disastrous effect on the German Reich. His main peculiarities were unimaginable vanity, and immeasurable ambition . . . he was outstanding in his greed, wastefulness and soft, unsoldierly manner." Field Marshal Keitel, in Raeder's words, was "a man of unimaginable weakness . . . the Führer could treat him as badly as he wished and Keitel took it."

Raeder was unconcerned by the bridges he had burned with these exposures in court. When the day ended, he told Gilbert, "Naturally, I will be hanged or shot. I flatter myself to think I will be shot. I have no desire to serve a prison sentence at my age."

26

CAPTAIN GILBERT WAS APPREHENSIVE as Baldur von Schirach took the stand on the morning of May 23. If Gilbert had made one strategic contribution to this trial, he believed, it had been to split up the defendants, and to isolate Göring so that the others would be free of his intimidation. Gilbert had particularly wanted Schirach and Speer together during lunches at the "youth table," where Speer's strength and shrewdness might influence Schirach's naïveté and weakness. Schirach was capable of extraordinary self-delusion, Gilbert knew. The man saw himself, because of family ties and his command of English, almost as one of the Americans. He had once explained to the cell guard, Emilio DiPalma, "You see, our Hitler Youth was the same as your Boy Scouts." To which DiPalma, a combat veteran, replied, "I never saw a Boy Scout take apart an automatic rifle and reassemble it in one minute flat."

Göring had stayed in his cell this morning, complaining of sciatica. His absence should help buck up Schirach's resolve, Gilbert believed. Still, he was not sure what to expect from this educated patrician who admitted that his political philosophy could be shaped by the likes of Julius Streicher. Schirach went to the witness box, the wunderkind of the Hitler circle—and now, at thirty-nine, the youngest major war criminal.

While Schirach was testifying, Robert Jackson found himself facing another Russian enigma. Rudenko came to his office asking permission to remove a body from Nuremberg to Leipzig in the Soviet Zone. Who was it, and what had happened? Jackson asked. The dead man was General N. D. Zorya, the prosecutor who had introduced Field Marshal Paulus's testimony. Zorya had accidentally shot himself while cleaning his gun, Rudenko explained. Jackson was relieved that Rudenko was not reporting another American shooting of a Russian, as had occurred outside the Grand Hotel in December. He decided to bypass the army's Criminal Investigation Division, and sent two of his people out to the Russian compound in suburban Erlenstegen to check the story quietly. They subsequently informed Jackson that it was highly unlikely that a Russian general would be cleaning his own gun, particularly with the muzzle pointed between his eyes. But what to do? Jackson had no idea why the Russians had not simply spirited the general's body out of Nuremberg themselves. His principal objective here was to keep this trial moving, not to trigger an international incident. The general's demise was strictly an internal Russian matter, he decided, and gave Rudenko permission to move the body. The alliance was indeed under stress, and Jackson had no desire to aggravate it further.

Schirach's counsel began his second day of direct examination by deliberately raising his client's worst offenses. He drew an admission that Schirach knew about the mass exterminations in the East. He referred to the testimony of Rudolf Hoess and asked Schirach to comment. Those millions of murders were not committed by Hoess, Schirach said, in a firm voice: "Hoess was only the executioner. The murder was ordered by Adolf Hitler." The defendants looked toward the witness box as if controlled by a single string. "It was my guilt, which I will have to carry before God and the German nation, that I educated the youth of our people . . . for a man who for many years I considered impeccable as a leader and as a head of state. . . . I educated German youth for a man who committed murders a millionfold." Gilbert, to whom Schirach's repentance was something of a cause, felt agreeably relieved.

Tom Dodd, in his cross-examination, however, did not spare Schirach. He forced him to admit that he had recommended the spite bombing of an English cultural town in reprisal for the Heydrich assassination, and that he had evacuated from Vienna sixty thousand Jews who were later murdered. Yet, however briefly, Baldur von Schirach had displayed a spine that few had believed he possessed.

Back in the cellblock, Gilbert sought out Albert Speer's reaction. Speer said that he was delighted to see Göring's united front collaps-

ing, as first Keitel, then Frank, and now Schirach had accepted personal guilt and condemned the regime. He and Schirach, Speer said, had become *Duzfreund:* they used the familiar *du* in addressing each other. Of more immediate concern to Speer than Schirach, however, was the testimony of the next defendant due on the stand, Fritz Sauckel.

27

ROBERT SERVATIUS HURRIED through the cavernous halls of the Palace of Justice to the visitors' room, where he was to have a last-minute meeting with his client. The fifty-two-year-old Servatius had won a reputation in court for being logical and reasonable, and for cutting to the marrow of an issue. A sophisticate who had lived and studied in England, Paris, and Moscow, he had never succumbed to the lure of the Nazi party. As one reporter saw him, Servatius was a first-rate lawyer with a third-rate client. Servatius had no particular affection for Sauckel either. But he had come out of six years in the German army as an overage officer, and Nuremberg offered him an opportunity once again to make his mark in his profession. Servatius wanted this final meeting because Fritz Sauckel, he had found, required close supervision. He sat down opposite Sauckel on the other side of the mesh screen and went directly to the point. He was going to throw the toughest possible questions at Sauckel concerning the forced labor program, he explained. Better he should do it than the prosecution. Did Sauckel understand? Sauckel nodded eagerly. And do not babble, Servatius warned. Speak slowly. Use short sentences. Give the interpreters a chance to keep pace.

On Tuesday, May 28, Fritz Sauckel approached the witness box, bouncing on the balls of his feet like a referee at a boxing match. Servatius began quoting Sauckel's words at a meeting of the Central Planning Board. Sauckel had boasted there that, when necessary, his agents resorted to shanghaiing foreign workers. Explain this statement, Servatius asked. Sauckel looked stunned, as though a parent had delivered an unexpected slap. His speech revealed a provincial, uneducated German. Servatius shook his head in despair. Sauckel was pausing between every word, sounding like a zombie. Justice Lawrence interrupted the witness. "I do not know the German language," he said, "but it might make some sense for the defendant to pause at the end of the sentence rather than on every syllable."

Servatius asked Sauckel what he meant when he had said that, if the French failed to come up with enough workers, "we might have to put a prefect up against a wall." This time, Sauckel spewed out the answer so rapidly that Lawrence had to tell him to slow down. As the day wore on, however, Servatius made some headway, getting into the record evidence that his client had issued directives calling for decent treatment of workers and that Sauckel himself controlled no police or troops but depended on others to carry out his roundups.

The subject foremost on everyone's mind was broached the next day. "What was the relationship of your office to Speer's?" Servatius asked. At last, Sauckel spoke clearly and directly. "My office had to meet the demands made by Speer."

A worse moment for Speer occurred two days later, when Servatius called as a witness Max Timm, a Sauckel deputy. The lawyer asked the witness, "Could Speer give orders to Sauckel?" Timm gave a rambling answer. Servatius pressed harder. "Could Albert Speer give orders and instructions and did he give them?" "Yes," Timm answered.

Ironically, it was Sauckel's stunning ineptness that might present the greatest danger to Speer. Sauckel had been a terrible witness, losing control of himself, screeching hysterically at times, missing every opportunity his lawyer gave him to win the court's sympathy by admitting at least some guilt. Instead, he continued defending his behavior in outworn Nazi clichés. Often he simply missed the point of a question. Speer's problem was that people might not believe that so pathetic a creature could have been his equal, much less superior to him in the forced labor program.

28

FEW NOTICED THE FLOWERS on the witness box the morning of June 3 until General Alfred Jodl took the stand. Underneath the small glass vase of pink and white phlox, a note in a familiar hand read, "Calm,

calm, oh so calm, my dear. Do not lose your temper." Jodl smiled briefly at his wife, Luise, in the visitors' gallery, then resumed his customary mask. As secretary to her husband's lawyer, Franz Exner, Frau Jodl was occasionally able to get into court to see Alfred. She had arrived early this morning to boost his spirits.

In the beginning, Alfred Jodl had not figured on all the Allied war-criminal lists. But the Russians had insisted; they wanted him indicted for transmitting to German armies in Russia Hitler's orders for virtually unrestricted barbarism. The Americans had eventually settled on him to round out the list of defendants in keeping with the philosophy of collective guilt that Jackson favored: thus, Göring represented the Nazi leadership and the Luftwaffe, Schacht the industrialists, Keitel the general staff, Dönitz the navy, Kaltenbrunner the SS, and Jodl the army.

On the stand, Jodl's defense was that he tempered Hitler's worst impulses. "Among officers who dared look the Führer squarely in the face and speak in a tone and manner that made listeners hold their breath because they feared catastrophe," he testified, "among these few officers, I myself belonged." It was true. Unlike Keitel, who would be nodding before he knew what the Führer was saying, Jodl did speak out. He had been shunned by Hitler for months after his mission to the Caucasus, where he had defended the behavior of General List. He protested to Hitler when some eighty American POWs were murdered by SS troops near the Belgian village of Malmédy during the Battle of the Bulge.

Jodl had confessed to Gilbert, in a rare moment of self-revelation, that he often despised the Führer. "The things that made me hate Hitler," he said, "were his contempt for the middle class, with which I identified myself, his suspicion and contempt for the nobility, to which I was married, and his hatred of the general staff, of which I was a member." Jodl was the model officer, unafraid to undergo fire whether in the face of the enemy or a megalomaniac leader. But, as the prosecution was bent on proving, Jodl also displayed the other face of the German militarist—indiscriminate obedience once an order was given.

If Maxwell-Fyfe was the cross-examining scourge of the defendants, his countryman Geoffrey Dorling Roberts was close behind. "Khaki" Roberts was a huge man swathed in yards of double-breasted serge who had won his blue for rugby and played for England. He had a large mustache and large square teeth that he flashed at his prey in smiles of exuberant contempt. Some of his colleagues found Roberts bombastic; the defendants found him unnerving. Was it true that Hitler had wanted to drop Germany from the Geneva Convention, which governed the conduct of warfare, and that Jodl had resisted the move? Roberts asked. Jodl warily agreed. But what was Jodl's reason? Roberts shot back. Was it not as described in document D 606? He then proceeded to quote Jodl's words from the minutes of a meeting with Hitler: "Adherence to the accepted obligations [of the convention] does not in any way demand that we should have to impose on ourselves any limitations which will interfere with the conduct of the war." Jodl shifted uneasily as Roberts continued quoting him. "For instance, if the British sink a hospital ship, this must be used for propaganda purposes. That, of course, in no way prevents our sinking an English hospital ship at once as a reprisal and then expressing our regret that it was a mistake." Roberts asked Jodl to justify such hypocrisy. Jodl tried to explain that this was the only kind of reasoning that worked with Hitler. Legal or moral arguments for observing the Geneva Convention would only have inflamed him.

Wasn't Jodl's claim that he opposed brutal orders equally hypocritical? Roberts asked. He turned to a document signed by Jodl ordering troops in the East to punish guerrilla actions "not by legal prosecution of the guilty, but by such terror as to eradicate every inclination to resist," and by using "draconian methods." Barely pausing for Jodl's answer, Roberts attacked again. Were those not Jodl's words, uttered just before the Blitz? "Terror attacks against English centers of population . . . will paralyze the will of the people to resist." And after the plot against Hitler, didn't Jodl make a speech to staff officers in which he said, "The twentieth of July was the blackest day that Germany has yet seen and will remain so for all time"? "Why," Roberts asked, "was it such a black day for Germany when someone tried to assassinate a man who you now admit was a murderer?" Before Jodl could complete his response, Roberts shouted, "Do you still say that you are an honorable soldier, a truthful man?" Without waiting for a reply, Roberts turned his back on the witness and returned to the prosecution table.

29

ON JUNE 6, President Truman named Fred Vinson, his treasury secretary, as chief justice of the Supreme Court. Robert Jackson took the loss of the post he coveted without complaint—yet some of his associates thought they saw deep disappointment in the man.

30

ARTHUR SEYSS-INQUART SAT next to Albert Speer in the dock. While Speer drew attention, Seyss-Inquart, with rimless glasses, pale skin, mouse-brown hair, and a defeated air, went practically unseen. The man had a keen mind as measured on Gilbert's intelligence test, and was capable of perceptions rare in the Nazi mentality. After the Auschwitz commandant, Rudolf Hoess, had appeared in court, Dönitz and Göring made the point that Hoess was a southern German. A Prussian could never have done such things, they claimed. Gilbert had asked Seyss-Inquart's opinion. "The south German has the imagination and the emotionality to subscribe to a fanatic idea," Seyss-Inquart had explained. "But he is inhibited from excess by his natural humaneness. The Prussian, on the other hand, lacks the imagination to think in terms of abstract racial and political theories. But if he is told to do something, he does it." Hitler's genius, Seyss-Inquart concluded, was that he had "amalgamated emotionalism with authoritarianism." Hoess offered the perfect example.

On June 10, a limping Seyss-Inquart, crippled in a long-ago mountaineering accident, approached the stand. As his testimony unfolded, the contradictions amazed the court—the mild manner, the terrible deeds, the quiet speech, the horrific record. The subjects raised by his counsel on direct examination merely positioned the witness in the gunsights for his cross-examiner. Seyss-Inquart emerged as a man who had sold out Austria to Hitler's Reich, who apprenticed in Poland under Hans Frank, who brutalized his own fiefdom of occupied Holland. Under what Seyss-Inquart regarded as his firm but humane rule, 41,000 Dutch had been shot as hostages, 50,000 died of starvation, and fifty-six percent of Dutch Jews perished.

Seyss-Inquart had neither lied nor pleaded in his testimony, but had assumed a fatalist's resignation. When he rode down the elevator that day with Hans Fritzsche, Seyss-Inquart observed that it did not matter how he behaved: "Whatever I say, my rope is being woven from Dutch hemp."

Someone had described Franz von Papen as "an aristocrat who looked like an actor playing an aristocrat." Papen had managed to maintain that appearance through all these months in jail. On June 14, as he left the prison to begin his defense, his diplomat's aplomb and splendid appearance concealed his anxiety. He emerged from his cell, hair combed back in silver strands, face handsomely planed, blue pin-striped suit sharply creased. In the courthouse basement, he fluffed the snow-white handkerchief in his breast pocket and waited to board the elevator. "Think of it, excellency, if it weren't for you," Hermann Göring said, "none of us would be here." Papen recognized the truth in Göring's gibe. He had served briefly as chancellor of Germany in 1932, and then advised President von Hindenburg to replace him and make Hitler chancellor. Hitler had later remarked, "I shall never forget it, Herr von Papen." Papen had been indicted on counts one and two as part of the cabal that brought the Nazis to power. As he emerged from the elevator, his eyes went immediately to the defense counsel's table, where he was relieved to see one of the more admired lawyers, his son, also Franz von Papen, waiting to defend him.

31

TOM DODD HAD BEEN preparing himself for the Albert Speer cross-examination, when Speer asked if he might see the deputy prosecutor in the visitors' room. Speer told Dodd that Hermann Göring was his chief rival for the soul of the defendants. Göring stood for truculent defiance. Speer stood for admission of Nazi guilt. Göring had been cross-examined by Jackson, the chief Nuremberg prosecutor. But Speer was going to be questioned by a subordinate. With all due respect to Dodd, would not this difference be noticed by the other defendants? And would it not put Speer, in their eyes, in an inferior status to Göring, thus making it more difficult for Speer to win them to his side? Dodd was perplexed by Speer's peculiar measure of status. He nevertheless took up the matter with Jackson and recommended that the chief prosecutor take over Speer's cross-examination. If it made the man feel more important, if it made him a more cooperative and useful witness, why not? He had no ego stake in the assignment, Dodd said. Jackson agreed.

When word of the change got out, some of the prosecution staff became suspicious. Speer sat in court every day. He could not be unaware that Dodd was a tough, skilled, dangerous prosecutor. Jackson's performance in the adversarial arena was of another caliber, and Speer knew it.

Suspense mounted as the day approached for Speer to take the stand. The man presented an anomaly—an indicted war criminal who could easily have walked straight from the dock to dinner with the judges at the Grand. Speer tested the court's powers of objectivity. Could they discern the fine fault line of guilt between this brilliant, attractive figure and the lumpen Fritz Sauckel? Or, as one reporter put it, when babies born to women on forced labor transports had been thrown from the train, who was most responsible—Sauckel, who had conscripted the women, or Speer, who had demanded them as workers?

Speer had recently confided to Captain Gilbert that his lawyer, Hans Flächsner, tried to talk him out of confessing to war crimes that might incur the ultimate penalty. He was not going to hide the truth just to wangle a life sentence, Speer had told Gilbert, "and hate myself for the rest of my life." He had seen that Gilbert was favorably impressed.

On June 20, the eve of his defense, Speer mentally reviewed his assets one last time. What hard truths had he been telling Hitler when others pretended the war could still be won? What action had he taken when Hitler ordered Germany destroyed in a pointless Armageddon?

What heroic solution had he plotted while others still trembled in the Führer's presence? He and Flächsner had gone through it all, rehearsing the questions that would elicit the most beneficial answers.

At breakfast on June 21, Dr. Pfluecker brought Speer a tranquilizing pill in case he felt he needed it on the stand. Speer put the pill in the pocket of his newly pressed dark gray suit. He felt the smoothness of his freshly shaved chin, adjusted his tie, and stood waiting for the guard to unbolt the door.

Speer had instructed Flächsner to get the Sauckel business out of the way quickly. He must not carry his heaviest cross any longer than necessary. And he must not appear to be shifting blame for conscript labor. To seem to be ducking responsibility would tarnish himself worse than Sauckel. Thus, early in the direct examination, Flächsner asked Speer if he disapproved of Sauckel's recruitment of labor. On the contrary, Speer answered, "I was grateful to Sauckel for every worker he provided me with. Often when we failed to meet armament quotas because of a shortage of workers, I would blame Sauckel." He felt calm and controlled as he spoke. He had taken Dr. Pfluecker's pill.

Flächsner noted that Sauckel had claimed he worked for Speer. Would the witness please comment? It was the question at the heart of the matter. Speer hesitated as if contemplating icy water, then plunged in. "Of course, I expected Sauckel to meet, above all, the demands of war production," he said. But he did not control Sauckel, as proved by the fact that he did not get all the workers he requested.

Sauckel was jumping up and down, trying to signal his lawyer, Robert Servatius. He had told his interrogators months ago that Speer actually stockpiled workers, hoarding more than he could possibly use. Servatius whispered to Sauckel to be patient.

Flächsner asked Speer if Göring, as head of the Four Year Plan, had been included in manpower meetings. "I wouldn't have had any use for him," Speer said. "After all, we had practical work to do."

The morning session ended. Among those in the visitors' gallery that day was Lady Sylvia, the wife of Sir David Maxwell-Fyfe. During the lunch hour, she ran into the junior British prosecutor Mervyn Griffith-Jones in her husband's office. She was much impressed by

Herr Speer, Lady Sylvia said. Here was the sort of man Germany was going to need in the years ahead. Griffith-Jones went to a closet and brought out a ten-foot length of telephone wire. He showed her bloodstains on it. This was a whip used on conscript laborers at the Krupp arms works, he told her, a plant in Speer's munitions empire.

Speer had saved the afternoon session for his masterstroke. Since he held a "technical" ministry, Flächsner asked, "Do you wish to limit your responsibility to your sphere of work?" "No," Speer answered, "this war has brought an inconceivable catastrophe. Therefore, it is my unquestionable duty to assume my share of responsibility for the disaster of the German people. . . . I, as an important member of the leadership of the Reich, share in the total responsibility." The statement—so at odds with the whining, self-pitying, hand-wringing moral blindness of a Ribbentrop, a Kaltenbrunner, a Sauckel—clearly pleased the court.

Speer went on. By March of 1945, he said, "Hitler intended, deliberately, to destroy the means of life for his own people if the war were lost. I have no intention of using my actions during that phase of the war to help me in my personal defense." But he wanted those who sat in judgment on him to understand that period. Though Hitler was ordering German industry razed, Speer explained, he had made the perilous decision to thwart the Führer and to preserve a base on which a defeated people could rebuild their country. He made sure that the court understood the high price of such defiance. Hitler had had eight officers shot for failing to blow up the bridge over the Rhine at Remagen, Speer pointed out.

He chose to read himself, rather than have his lawyer read, a memorandum he sent to Hitler in March 1945. "Nobody has the right to destroy industrial plants, coal mines, electric plants, and other fa-cilities. . . . We have no right at this stage of the war to carry out destruction which might affect the life of the people." Other defen-dants had condemned Hitler—Frank with strident emotionalism, Schirach with abject apology—but Speer did so with manly com-posure.

Earlier in the trial, during Otto Ohlendorf's testimony back in January, Speer's lawyer had briefly mentioned his scheme to assassi-nate Hitler. Speer said that he now wanted to discuss that issue in some detail, not to cast himself in a heroic light, but only to show

how thoroughly he had become convinced of Adolf Hitler's insane destructiveness. "I am most unwilling to describe the details because there is always something repellent about such matters," he began. He would only do so, he went on, "if it was the tribunal's wish." Sir Geoffrey could barely conceal his eagerness. "The court would like to hear the details," he announced.

Speer explained that he knew of an air-intake shaft in the Reich Chancellery garden that ventilated the Führerbunker below. The shaft was covered by a grate at ground level, hidden behind shrubs. In February of 1945, he confided to the head of his munitions department, Dieter Stahl, that there was only one way to end the war. He asked Stahl to procure a poison gas which he intended to drop into the ventilating system. When Speer revisited the site in March, he found a twelve-foot chimney protecting the ventilator. From that point on, he banished all further thoughts of killing Adolf Hitler.

For his closing, Speer took the rhetorical high ground. "The sacrifices which were made on both sides after January 1945 were senseless," he said. "The dead of this period will be the accusers of the man responsible for the continuation of that struggle." That man was Adolf Hitler.

Captain Gilbert had been much moved this day by Albert Speer's contrition. He stopped by the man's cell that night and found him deathly pale, stretched out on his cot, holding his stomach. He was exhausted, Speer explained, and he was suffering painful cramps. "That was quite a strain," he said, "but I'm glad I got it out of my system. I spoke the truth and that's all there was to it."

On Friday afternoon, June 21, the courtroom filled as spectators gathered to watch Robert Jackson cross-examine Speer. Arkady Poltorak, a Russian documents specialist, wandered to the windows behind the bench. Poltorak pulled aside the heavy drapes and looked out on a sun-drenched street. He came back to the Russian prosecutors' table. "I'd like to tear those curtains down," he announced. "I want to throw those windows open and let sunbeams and street noises in here so that those criminal bastards can feel the pulse of life and know it's still going on in spite of all their efforts."

"Attention! All rise," the marshal called out. "The tribunal will now enter." Jackson took his place at the prosecutor's stand. "Will you tell me," he asked Speer, "whether you were a member of the SS?" "No," Speer answered, "I was not a member of the SS." Jackson went on: "You filled out an application at one time, or one was filled out for you and you never went through with it, I believe. Or something like that." Jackson trailed off, to the surprise of those at the prosecution table. They had documents that proved indisputably that Speer had been a member of the SS. Jackson, however, did not press the matter.

He asked Speer about German production of poison gas. Yes, Speer explained, three factories had been working on a gas of extraordinary lethality, but when he learned Hitler might actually use it, Speer claimed, he ordered production stopped. Jackson asked Speer about German experiments with the atom bomb. "We had not got as far as that," Speer answered, "because the finest minds we had in atomic research had emigrated to America." No one had to be told who most of these scientists were and why they had fled Germany.

"Is it not a fact," Jackson asked, "that in the circle around Hitler there was almost no one who would stand up and tell him that the war was lost, except yourself?" Jaws dropped among the British prosecutors. "That is correct to a certain extent," Speer answered modestly.

"Well, now I am going to give you some information about the Krupp labor camp and I am going to ask you some questions about it," Jackson said. "And I am not attempting to say that you were personally responsible for these conditions." He proceeded to read into the record from affidavits of Krupp conscript workers describing the horrors they had endured. The evidence seemed to dangle in the air without point, since the prosecutor had exonerated the witness of any responsibility in advance. Jackson then read from a document about steel whips used on workers at the Krupp works, the kind Maxwell-Fyfe's wife had just been shown. Speer mumbled something about there being no rubber truncheons available. "So the guards probably had something like this . . ." Jackson asked no further questions about steel whips. He moved instead to Hitler's scorched-earth policy. "You wanted to see Germany have a chance to restore her life.

Is that not a fact?" he asked. "Whereas Hitler took the position that if he couldn't survive, he didn't care whether Germany survived or not?" Speer found no reason to disagree.

The questioning turned to Speer's final visit to Hitler. Speer knew that Jackson was treading near a weak patch in the fabric of his defense. He had said earlier that he had planned to assassinate Hitler. Yet, after that, he had taken enormous risks to fly into doomed Berlin to see the Führer in the bunker. Why? Jackson asked. "I felt," said Speer, "that it was my duty not to run away like a coward, but to stand up to him again."

That was a new twist. Speer's visit had but one purpose, to bid a final farewell to his leader. At the time, he had been hurt by Hitler, who dismissed him with a weak handshake and no expression of gratitude or friendship.

Jackson accepted the present reply and went on to another area. "This policy of driving Germany to destruction after the war was lost had come to weigh on you to such a point that you were a party to several plots, were you not?" Speer had been a party to no plots, but again saw no reason to disagree with Jackson. The prosecutor reached his final question. "You as a member of the government and a leader in this period acknowledge a responsibility for its large policies but not for the details that occurred in their execution. Is that a fair statement of your position?" "Yes, indeed," Speer answered. He could not have phrased it more profitably himself.

A deputy Russian prosecutor, M. Y. Raginsky, was scorching in his cross-examination of Speer. But unremitting hostility and a hunger for vengeance were expected of the Soviets. As Speer's defense ended and he left the stand, his stomach pains ended as well.

Airey Neave left the courtroom much dismayed. He had expected the Sauckel-Speer controversy to turn on social class, the mailed fist for one defendant and the velvet glove for the other. His fears, he believed, had been borne out. Speer had performed brilliantly. The man was not being charged with destroying or saving Germany's industrial base. He was not being accused of trying or failing to assassinate Hitler. Yet he had managed to make these issues the keystones of his defense. As for the assassination story, how far had it gone? Speer had talked to numerous Allied interrogators before being taken to Nuremberg, always putting himself in the best possible light. Yet he had never uttered a word about a plan to kill Hitler to any of them.

Yet Neave was enough of a lawyer to detach his personal doubts from the positive impact of Speer's performance before the court. Speer had accepted his share of responsibility for slave labor; he had declared Hitler guilty of the senseless deaths of thousands on both sides for his insane continuation of a lost war. Indeed, Speer held Hitler responsible for starting the war, yet asserted that he too must bear a quota of personal guilt for this "disaster." And he had tried to thwart Hitler's scorched-earth orders and claimed to have planned to assassinate the man.

The admirable side of Speer's character appeared to have touched Jackson. The American prosecutor had made no attempt to question Speer about his awareness of the extermination of the Jews, which Himmler had described at a conference that Speer attended. Nor had he dealt with Speer's presence at the Mauthausen concentration camp. Speer had been allowed to talk of the production miracles he had performed, testimony that virtually cried out for cross-examination on the role slave labor played in these feats. He had not been asked.

Neave, then, was hardly surprised at the account that appeared in the *Daily Telegraph* after Speer's defense. The London paper's stance reflected the majority opinion reported out of Nuremberg. Speer had delivered "a tremendous indictment which might well stand for the German people and posterity as the most important and dramatic event of the trial."

32

BY THE END OF JUNE, reporters could easily get a room in the dormitories at the Stein Castle. The Nuremberg story had slipped to the back pages. The names of the only two defendants left to testify struck no fearsome images. Konstantin von Neurath and Hans Fritzsche sat next to each other in the far corner of the dock, rarely among those pointed out to curious spectators. Neurath, at seventy-three the oldest defendant, was exhibiting incipient senility. He had been Ribbentrop's predecessor as foreign minister and, like Papen and Schacht, had lent a patina of respectability to the Hitler regime.

Neurath's sin, as Maxwell-Fyfe put it in his cross-examination, was to have been foreign minister while Germany was "breaking only one treaty at a time." In 1939, Hitler named him Protector of Bohemia and Moravia in Czechoslovakia, nominally above the SS and Gestapo. But these organizations carried out their grim work ignoring this gentleman of the old school. A handful of reporters in the press gallery suffered hours of Neurath's rambling rationalizations, and then his defense ended.

Hans Fritzsche was the second defendant provided by the Russians. As with Raeder, the prosecution had been put in the position of working backward, of having the man first and then having to rustle up evidence to convict him. Fritzsche had headed the radio division in the Nazi Propaganda Ministry, and had been a popular commentator himself. Drexel Sprecher had applied his notable energy over several months trying to prove that Fritzsche used his broadcasts "to advocate, encourage, and incite" war crimes, particularly offenses against the Jews. But in a confidential memorandum, Sprecher admitted that the evidence was "utterly inadequate . . . to establish that Fritzsche had any intimate connection with the claims mentioned in counts three and four."

On the 166th day of the trial, Fritzsche left the stand. The last man in the dock had completed his defense.

It was Sir Geoffrey Lawrence's pleasure to take an evening stroll with his wife through the park near his home. This evening was particularly agreeable, with poppies and peonies somehow prospering in neglected beds. The Soviet documents man, Arkady Poltorak, and Lev Shenin, an assistant prosecutor, had also chosen the park for a walk. On seeing the justice and his wife approach, Poltorak mentioned to his companion that this might be a good chance to ask Sir Geoffrey if he intended to reopen the issue of the Katyn massacre. Shenin looked horrified. Didn't Poltorak know one of the cardinal rules of the IMT? One must never talk shop to Sir Geoffrey outside the court. Then what did one talk to him about? Poltorak asked. His horses, of course, Shenin replied, his dogs, his cows.

The Western judges had thought it foolish of the Soviet government to insist on introducing the Katyn massacre during the prosecution phase. Now, at the close of the defense phase, they had no choice but to allow the Germans to rebut the charge. The basic facts were clear enough. Sometime after the defeat of Poland, approximately 11,000 of her soldiers, including 8,300 officers, had disappeared. In February 1943, a German communications regiment stumbled onto the un-marked graves of 4,800 of these men in the Katyn forest near Smo-lensk. At issue was the question of which side, the Russians or the Germans, had killed these men.

For two days, July 1 and 2, forensic experts battled in room 600. Guilt turned on fixing the date when the Poles had died. The Russians claimed the deaths occurred in the autumn of 1941, after the Soviet Union had been invaded and while the Germans occupied the Katyn forest. The Germans claimed the Poles had died earlier, in 1940, when the Russians still held this territory.

In the end, the Germans had the better of it. Among their most persuasive evidence was the fact that all letters from the Poles had ceased after April 1940, at which time the Russians controlled the forest. The judges, except for Nikitchenko, were dismayed that the issue had ever arisen. To conclude that the Russians themselves had shot thousands of Poles would dilute the horror of the crimes of the Nazis. What was the court to do with this moral morass? Their re-sponsibility, they decided, was not to place blame on one of the coun-tries, but to determine if a certain charge against German war criminals was proved. They simply took the position that the Russian accusation against the Germans lacked sufficient evidence, and let the Katyn issue drop.

33

As HE HEADED for the Judges' Room this July morning, Justice Jackson felt better than he had in months. The next time he spoke in the courtroom, it would be in the realm where he was master, delivering the American prosecution's closing speech. The night before, he had withdrawn alone to his room with pen and legal pad to start forming his thoughts. For now, however, he had to resolve a debate over the time the defense attorneys would be allotted for their summations. He was painfully familiar with the stupefying lengths to which they could go, and the Germans were asking for unlimited time. If the trial did not end soon, he feared, its moral force would seep away. Jackson had polled his fellow prosecutors, and they agreed that three days was ample time for the defense to sum up its case. He was bringing this recommendation to the judges this morning.

Francis Biddle was coolly aloof, Sir Geoffrey seemed impatient, and the French judges' expressions revealed nothing. Only the two Russians were openly sympathetic to Jackson. Finally, Sir Geoffrey ruled. He had given the defendants not the slightest reason to attack the fairness of this trial thus far. He was not about to give them that opportunity now by gagging them. Biddle nodded. Otto Stahmer, Sir Geoffrey said, as spokesman for the defense, had asked for one day per defendant. If that meant a summation lasting three weeks, so be it.

Jackson forced himself to attend court on July 4, the day the defense summations began; his worst fears were confirmed. The defense lawyers had flooded the Language Division with documents to translate —many of them of dubious relevance—on a scale unknown since the opening of the trial. This morning, a few glassy-eyed reporters studied the floor and ceiling as Otto Stahmer explained why Hermann Göring was innocent. "When by the advent of the Renaissance and the Reformation," Stahmer droned on, "the spiritual basis of the medieval order was broken, this development into a universal world peace was reversed. Life, formerly tending toward stagnation and tranquillity . . ." Jackson could take no more and left. Stahmer was beginning his client's defense in the sixteenth century.

The posters had long since become faded and tattered—some 200,000 of them, bearing the photograph of Martin Bormann, plastered on walls, trees, telephone poles, and boxcars all over Germany. Bormann was a wanted man. As the Führer's secretary, he had exercised only borrowed power, but he had wielded it with ingenious malice. He had been particularly energetic in transmitting orders to shoot captured Allied fliers. His proximity to Hitler and his rabid hatred of Jews and

Slavs meant that he had full knowledge of the regime's foulest crimes. The problem with the Bormann case was that the man had disappeared in the last days of the war. The prosecution, nevertheless, wanted Bormann indicted, and the court had agreed. On July 6, the defense summations were interrupted so that the court could try Bormann in absentia.

Göring had made something of a cottage industry out of locating Bormann. He told Theodore Fenstermacher, a prosecutor who grilled him in the visitors' room, that Bormann was "a left-wing Nazi and had fled to the Soviet Union." "Mark my words," Göring had said, "he'll show up as the head of a Soviet-dominated puppet government." Navy lieutenant Thomas F. Lambert, Jr., who had had the semisurreal task of prosecuting Bormann, also interrogated Göring on the missing defendant's whereabouts. Bormann, Göring said with breezy assurance, was in Argentina, protected by President Juan Perón. Questioned later still, Göring confided to Fenstermacher that Bormann was in Spain with Generalissimo Franco. Fenstermacher described these conflicting accounts to Colonel Andrus. "Don't you know the man will do anything to get out of his cell?" Andrus explained.

Hans Fritzsche claimed to have been with Bormann on May 1, 1945, the day of his disappearance, when both men fled the Führerbunker. They were moving behind a tank with other fleeing Nazis when it exploded, probably from a shell hit. Fritzsche believed Bormann had been killed outright, but had not seen his body.

In January, during the prosecution phase, Lieutenant Lambert had submitted evidence displaying the heights and depths of Bormann's malice. He signed or issued orders that expelled millions of European Jews from their homes, forbade prosecution of German civilians who lynched downed Allied fliers, and barred the use of coffins to bury Soviet war prisoners. On July 6, Friedrich Bergold, the German lawyer given the task of defending Bormann, took virtually the only course left him—he declared his client dead.

After the Bormann hiatus, the defense summations resumed before a virtually empty courtroom, save for the captive audience of judges and defendants. Only during the remarks of Schacht's attorney,

Rudolf Dix, did the court come to life. Dix gestured toward Kalten-brunner, former head of the RSHA, and then toward Schacht, once a prisoner in Dachau. "It is surely a rare and grotesque picture to see a jailer and a prisoner sharing a bench in the dock," Dix noted. The court had seen for itself the shocking behavior of Judge Roland Freisler in the film shown of the People's Court. During the Nazi era, Dix defended Schacht as an enemy of the regime before Freisler, he explained. And now he was defending Schacht before the Allies as a war criminal. Need he say anything else in his client's defense? Schacht's situation summoned up the story of Seneca, Dix said, who had been put on trial by Nero for treason—and who then, when Nero died, had been placed on trial "for complicity in Nero's misgoverning and cruelties."

Colonel Andrus took advantage of the dog days to get his newly arrived wife, Katharine, and his daughter Kitty settled in Nuremberg. Kitty, the youngest of the colonel's four children, fresh from an American high school, soon received a practical European education. She became friendly with Hedda, the Andruses' maid, who was eager to improve her English. They were the same age, and Kitty Andrus listened agog at the living Hedda had done. The German girl had served as a nurse in the amputation ward of a military hospital. Her pilot fiancé had been killed on his first mission. She had watched from a hospital window as her city turned to ashes during the heaviest RAF raid of the war. The only time the maid's English faltered was when Kitty asked if Hedda had attended the Zeppelin Field rallies during Party Days. She did not understand, Hedda said, and returned to her work.

Two voluble men sat drinking in the Marble Room. Lieutenant Tex Wheelis was telling Captain John Vonetes, the American housing officer, how well he got along with the defendants. Hermann Göring was a friend of his, Wheelis claimed. The *Reichsmarschall* had given him this watch with his facsimile signature, the lieutenant noted, flashing it before Vonetes. He also had Göring's Mont Blanc pen with the name engraved on the cap, and photographs of the *Reichsmarschall* with personal inscriptions. There was only one thing wrong with prison duty in Nuremberg, Wheelis confided. What was that? Vonetes wanted to know. "It's the guy I have to work for," Wheelis answered. Vonetes knew Colonel Andrus, he said, but made no other comment.

Robert Jackson worked with the fervor of a man doing what he had been put on earth to do. In the waning days of July, he spared himself the agony of hearing the lawyers for Kaltenbrunner, Sauckel, Frick, Funk, the lot of them, excusing and explaining their clients' crimes. Instead, he stayed home in his study and worked on his closing speech. In the rough draft, so far, he hit Göring on virtually every page. He denounced the industrialists, thus preparing the ground for Telford Taylor's subsequent prosecutions of them after his own departure. Above all, he wanted the speech to proclaim to the world that the Nazi conspiracy to conquer, exploit, and exterminate had been proved.

These passages formed the muscle and sinew of his text. But he enjoyed just as well playing with language, trying out and testing aloud, in his rich baritone, the lyrics of condemnation: "Ribbentrop, that salesman of deception"; "Rosenberg, Nazism's intellectual high priest"; "Kaltenbrunner, the grand inquisitor"; "fanatical Frank" and "Streicher, the venomous vulgarian"; "Schirach, poisoner of youth"; "Sauckel, cruelest slaver since the pharaohs"; and "Funk, banker of gold teeth, the most ghoulish collateral in history." He asked Elsie Douglas to find a volume of Shakespeare. He wanted those lines between Gloucester and Lady Anne from *Richard III*, perfect for his peroration.

The defense summations ground on for a full three weeks, an arid stretch epitomized by Flottenrichter Kranzbuehler's dropping a 105-page "Closing Defense for the Defendant Dönitz" on the translations unit. The last summation was delivered by Alfred Seidl for Rudolf Hess, on July 25. Next, the prosecution would have its final word.

34

THE MORNING OF JULY 26, the defendants left their cells to hear the prosecution summation. Men in straits similar to their own, they knew, were faring badly. They had just learned the fate of Karl Her-

mann Frank, whose trial Justice Jackson had witnessed in Prague.
Frank, who had erased Lidice and slaughtered its men, had gone to
the gallows. Of seventy-seven Waffen SS troops convicted for murdering American POWs near Malmédy, forty-three had been sentenced to death.

Robert Jackson took advantage of the drive to the courthouse to
make last-minute revisions to his speech. His fellow passengers included his ever-present bodyguard, Sergeant Moritz Fuchs. Young
Fuchs had recently confided his post-trial hopes to Jackson. Before
the war, the sergeant had been an engineering student at Purdue.
But after the revelations heard day after day in room 600, and after
meeting the German Catholic stigmatic Teresa Neumann, Fuchs
found the prospect of a life spent at a drafting table unappealing. He
had told Jackson that he intended to enter the priesthood. Jackson
found the young soldier's decision moving, an affirmation of the moral
awakening that he hoped the trial would prompt well beyond room
600.
    The car slowed to a halt. Elsie Douglas checked Jackson's ap-
pearance one last time as the party entered the courthouse.

The American prosecutor conferred briefly with his son, Bill, who
was posted behind him holding relevant documents, as Sir Geoffrey
called the court to order. Robert Jackson was to speak first. Sir
Hartley Shawcross, supplanting Maxwell-Fyfe on this key occasion,
would succeed Jackson, followed by Auguste Champetier for France
and, finally, Roman Rudenko for the Soviet Union. The visitors'
gallery and the press area were once again thronged. The ex post
facto issue had to be dealt with early, Jackson began, not necessarily
to persuade the court, but to satisfy world opinion. Naturally, the
defendants' "dislike for the law which condemns them is not original,"
he noted. "It has been remarked before, 'No thief e'er felt the halter
draw with good opinion of the law.' " He had staked his prosecution
on the conspiracy theory, and he pronounced it proven beyond a
doubt in the written and uttered words of the conspirators themselves.
    He pointed to Schacht, sitting in his customary pose, legs crossed,

arms folded, head turned away, the picture of a man much put-upon. The absence of German industrialists in the dock still displeased Jackson; but Schacht would do. "Twenty days after the seizure of power, Schacht was host to Hitler, Göring, and some twenty leading industrialists," Jackson noted. He described the financier as "a Brahmin among the untouchables. . . . He could not bear to mingle with the Nazis socially, but never could he afford to separate from them politically. . . . Schacht always fought for his position in a regime he now affects to despise."

Only Göring came in for more killing fire. The *Reichsmarschall*, with perverse pride, stopped counting after Jackson's references to him surpassed forty. Jackson indicted the other defendants in turn: "the zealot Hess," "Keitel, the willing tool," and "Dönitz, the legatee of defeat." He accused the stolid philosopher Rosenberg of adding "boredom to the list of Nazi atrocities."

Albert Speer listened with a surface calm. Jackson's cross-examination of him the month before had been solicitous, even gentle, and, so far, the prosecutor had omitted Speer from his catalogue of villains. Suddenly, Jackson was quoting Speer. As Speer himself had said on the stand, Jackson noted, "the sacrifices which were made on both sides after January 1945 were without sense." And Speer had made clear that the monster responsible for these squandered lives was Adolf Hitler. Yes, Jackson had used Speer's words, but not against him. Was it possible to dream of acquittal?

Elsie Douglas had located the passage from Shakespeare that Bob wanted and listened intently as he approached his peroration. "These defendants now ask the tribunal to say that they are not guilty of planning, executing, or conspiring to commit this long list of crimes and wrongs," he began. "They stand before the record of this trial as blood-stained Gloucester stood by the body of his slain king. He begged of the widow, as they beg of you: 'Say I slew them not.' And the queen replied, 'Then say they are not slain. But dead they are . . .' If you were to say of these men that they are not guilty, it would be as true to say that there has been no war, there are no slain, there has been no crime."

The hush in the courtroom was complete. Jackson gathered up his papers and returned to the prosecution table. Neave and Justice

Birkett exchanged nods. Jackson might have his superiors in the thrust and parry of the game. But in finding the words that captured the majesty of justice, they had just witnessed the master.

In the "elders'" lunchroom, Franz von Papen grumbled to Gilbert that Jackson had ignored their defenses. The old diplomat, usually the soul of reserve, complained, "Why have we been sitting here for eight months? The prosecution still insisted on calling us liars and murderers."

Julius Streicher approached Gilbert. He was now ready to join the Jews in their fight for a homeland, he wanted the psychologist to know. He had read of recent rioting in Palestine. "Anybody who can fight and resist and stick together, and stick to their guns, for such people I can only have the greatest respect," he said. "Even if Hitler was living now, he too would admit they are a scrappy race. I'm ready to join and help them in their fight. I am not joking! The Jews will dominate the world. And I would be happy to help lead them to victory. I have studied them so long that I suppose I have adopted their characteristics. I'll make a proposition. Let me address a gathering at Madison Square Garden in New York. It will be a sensation!" Jodl and Rosenberg, overhearing Streicher, burst out into laughter.

Streicher's little speech suggested the ironies in the life of this coarse anti-Semite. Whenever a synagogue in Franconia had been desecrated or a rabbi turned out of his home, Streicher, as *Gauleiter*, had all books and manuscripts slated for destruction brought to him first. From them he selected the rarest, most valuable items for the library of *Der Stürmer*. Thus, with the war ended and with so much Jewish scholarship in ashes, the premier Jew-baiter had rescued a priceless collection of Judaica from the flames.

The lawyer in Hans Frank had picked up on something in Jackson's summation that the rest of his lunch partners had missed. He pointed out that, no matter how unrelenting the prosecutor's condemnation, he had not called for the death penalty.

In the afternoon session, Justice Lawrence called on the patrician Labourite Sir Hartley Shawcross. In a summation approaching Jackson's in eloquence, Sir Hartley called not simply for the defendants' conviction but for the death of them all. The French and Russian prosecutors also closed by demanding capital punishment.

Only the defense of the Nazi organizations and brief final statements by the defendants remained. Colonel John Harlan Amen's interrogations unit, its work done, had disbanded. Robert Jackson felt sufficiently comfortable to turn the direction of the prosecution temporarily over to Tom Dodd while he went home to remind the U.S. Supreme Court that he was still a member. In the courthouse, the climate of argument began to yield to a climate of judgment.

35

EMMY GÖRING HAD WRITTEN to Sir Geoffrey begging to be allowed to visit her husband. Lawrence had bucked the letter to Burt Andrus with a note saying, "The tribunal has no objection." Her request was a matter of prison security and thus entirely up to the colonel. Her appeal seemed a simple enough human cry. Why not let her come? But what if something went wrong? If, somehow, in spite of all his precautions, she brought Göring a plan for a breakout, or slipped him a concealed weapon, or poison? If he lost the court's prize catch, whose fault would it be? Certainly not that of the august British jurist; it would be Burt Andrus's neck. He had already been reprimanded by General Watson because of Frau Göring. A few days before, Watson's counterintelligence people had tailed the chaplain, Major Gerecke, on an errand of mercy to her cabin, and Andrus, as the minister's superior, had taken the rap. Even more baffling to Andrus, Robert Kempner, a Jew fired by Göring from the Prussian police and driven from Germany by the Nuremberg Laws, was known to be visiting Emmy laden with PX luxuries. What was Kempner trying to prove by showing kindness to his persecutor's wife? he wondered. Burt Andrus was not trying to prove anything. He knew his duty, and he knew the price if he failed. His mind was made up. He was going to deny Emmy Göring's request.

The colonel loved one part of the job. The stream of famous names drawn to Nuremberg was beginning to pick up again as the trial approached judgment day. They all wanted front-row seats in the gallery and visits to the prison. Lord Maugham, the leading British jurist and brother of the novelist Somerset Maugham, came to Nuremberg. Virgil Thomson and Charles Munch, figures from the world of music, came. So did former mayor of New York Fiorello LaGuardia, as well as actresses Rita Hayworth and Marlene Dietrich. *Pravda*'s Boris Polevoi flirted with Dietrich in the visitors' gallery, not knowing who she was. And Andrus noticed that somehow the itineraries of congressmen and government officials who visited Nuremberg always ended up at resorts in Garmisch-Partenkirchen.

The justices made an exception to their overall prohibition and allowed Andrus to take a few select journalists through cellblock C. Helmet gleaming, his riding crop tucked into place, he led them through the barrier of locks and sentries into the jail. Among the reporters was Andy Logan, age twenty-four, who had literally stepped from college onto the staff of *The New Yorker* and had managed a Nuremberg assignment to be with her prosecutor husband. Logan found most of the cells' inhabitants taciturn and Göring determinedly mute. But Albert Speer charmed the press people, behaving as though he were their delighted host, asking which papers they represented, answering their questions volubly. Logan also cast a journalist's eye over the colonel. Here was a man in his element, interspersing explanations of security measures with the history of each prisoner as the visitors passed by the cells. Forgotten for the moment were the pressures, collisions, and rivalries that plagued him daily. Colonel Andrus, the Nuremberg jailer, cut quite a figure.

36

ON JULY 30, the defense of seven indicted Nazi organizations—the Nazi party leadership, the Reich cabinet, the SS, the Gestapo, the SD, the SA, and the High Command—began. As in December, when the prosecution made its case against them, the Palace of Justice mail room was again inundated. The court had ordered notices placed throughout Germany describing how affected parties could apply to testify; over 313,000 people responded. From these, 603 members of the indicted groups were brought to Nuremberg and screened as potential witnesses. In the end, the tribunal took affidavits from ninety of them. Over and over, they expressed the same words or sentiments: "As a member of the SS, I was never expected to perform a dishonorable act. Never was I commanded to commit a crime."

Justice Francis Biddle heard the organization cases with scarcely concealed impatience. He recognized the neat logic of the prosecution: individuals conspire to evil intent; they create organizations to achieve their ends; therefore, both the individuals and the organizations are criminal. Appealing symmetry, Biddle thought, but poor law. Conviction of the Nazi party leadership alone would automatically brand over 600,000 Germans as war criminals. Yet the culpability of a *Reichsleiter* like Rosenberg and that of a block leader who had done little more than collect dues were hardly comparable. To Biddle, the prosecution of the organization cases was a result of Bob Jackson's righteous streak.

The organizations' defense continued uneventfully until August 20, when the courtroom suddenly crackled with anticipation. The press and visitors' galleries were again packed. Hermann Göring was returning to the witness stand.

During the SS case, the prosecution had cross-examined a witness named Wolfram Sievers, head of the German Ancestral Heritage Society. Sievers had described an arrangement he had made with the SS, under which the latter would kill "Jewish-Bolshevik" commissars and send him their skulls for scientific study. In the course of his testimony, Sievers implicated Göring as president of the Reich Research Council. Göring's lawyer, Otto Stahmer, persuaded his client that he had to disprove his complicity. Thus, Göring testified again. Had he ever given an order for medical experiments on humans? Stahmer asked the *Reichsmarschall*. Did he know Dr. Rascher, who performed the research on human guinea pigs at Dachau for the Luftwaffe? Did Göring order freezing experiments to be conducted on inmates? As president of the Reich Research Council, had he ordered studies carried out on germ warfare? Göring denied it all.

On arriving in the dock this morning, the *Reichsmarshall* had noticed that Justice Jackson was absent—which likely boded cross-examination by Maxwell-Fyfe. Sir David indeed rose, as Stahmer yielded the witness. He led the questioning to experiments on cold-weather clothing worn by fliers. "You have been a practical airman yourself, with a very gallant record of service in the air in the last war," he began. Given this personal interest, was it possible "you don't remember about experiments on these concentration camp detainees for testing air clothing?" He wore so many hats, Göring said. Tens of thousands of orders had been issued in his name. Even though Mr. Jackson, in his summation, had accused him of having his "fat fingers in every pie," he could not possibly have known of all medical experiments carried out in the Third Reich.

Maxwell-Fyfe produced a document containing correspondence between Heinrich Himmler and Field Marshal Erhard Milch, Göring's deputy. In one letter, Milch thanked Himmler for Dr. Rascher's work on problems confronted in flying at high altitudes. One test involved putting a Jewish inmate at a simulated height of 29,000 feet without oxygen. The subject had expired after thirteen minutes. Was it possible that a high-ranking, close associate like Milch could have knowledge of these deadly experiments, while Göring had not? Sir David asked. Göring explained that matters under his control had been classified as "very important," "important," and "routine." Experiments reviewed by the Luftwaffe Medical Inspectorate fell into the lowest category and were not brought to his attention. Sir David found the answer sufficiently incriminating and let it stand.

Russian prosecutor Major General Alexandrov followed Maxwell-Fyfe. Alexandrov called upon Walter Schreiber, a fifty-three-year-old German army doctor, and asked him to describe a medical conference the German had attended near Berlin in 1943. At this meeting, Schreiber said, a Dr. Kramer discussed experiments carried out for the Luftwaffe at Dachau, particularly tests on the warmth retention of various items of flying gear. The tests were performed by dropping inmates into freezing water. "Please tell the court what the defendant Göring had to do with such experiments," Alexandrov asked. Dr. Kramer had explained to them, Schreiber said, "that Göring had ordered these experiments, and that Reichsführer Himmler had kindly made available the subjects for the experiments." As he left the dock, Göring muttered at his lawyer. Stahmer had urged the gamble, but Göring had lost.

On August 30, the court heard final testimony on the indicted organizations, the last evidence to be presented before the IMT. The next day, each individual defendant would have fifteen minutes for a final statement. The judges would then retire to deliberate their fates.

37

JIM ROWE CAME into Francis Biddle's office and asked if he might speak privately with the American justice. Biddle admired the Montanan as a first-rate legal mind and a get-it-done administrator. During the war, Rowe's carrier, the *Sewanee*, had been among the first hit by Japanese kamikazes. With most of the firefighting crew killed outright, Rowe had grabbed a hose and braved the flames to save his men. He had won eight battle stars in the Pacific. Rowe's opinions carried weight with Biddle.

They had a security problem, Rowe said. Somebody was rifling Biddle's office at night. It could be thieves, an aggressive journalist, someone acting for the defense. The courthouse was a sieve. Just this morning, Rowe had found, lying around in the Language Division, the French translation of a secret session of the justices. He calculated that, between secretaries, translators, interpreters, typists, proofreaders, mimeograph operators, and other technical staff, fourteen people saw classified documents intended only for the eyes of the justices and their immediate aides. "If you're interested in hearing what the verdicts are going to be," Rowe said, "just sit in the lobby of the Grand Hotel." The leaks had to be stopped. Once the innermost deliberations of the judges fell into the hands of the press, the work of the court would be seriously compromised.

What did Rowe suggest? Biddle asked. First, Rowe answered, kick all the interpreters out of the judges' private meetings, except for one Russian. Biddle himself could handle the French. In the meantime, Rowe would devise a system to keep the judges' private sessions secure.

For two months, the justices' aides had been evaluating the evidence and preparing preliminary verdicts. Birkett, the great pen on the bench, had completed an early draft of the final judgment. The justices had met to review Birkett's fifty-thousand-word effort while the last defendant, Hans Fritzsche, was still on the stand. They had immediately grasped a nettle in the case: the conspiracy theory. The prosecution was relying on the Hossbach conference of November 1937 and other evidence to prove that several of the defendants conspired to launch an aggressive war. The French judge, Donnedieu de Vabres, who never asked a question in court and rarely uttered a word in their private sessions, finally spoke out. A conspiracy, Donnedieu de Vabres said, connotes participation among more-or-less-equal parties. The defendants themselves would be the first to laugh at the notion of Streicher, Funk, Frick, Sauckel, and Ribbentrop as Hitler's conspiratorial peers. It was ridiculous, the Frenchman said. By pursuing this mad idea of conspiracy, going back to events taking place in a sovereign country over the course of twenty years, they were feeding the critics who decried ex post facto justice. Judge these men by what they have done, Donnedieu de Vabres cautioned, not by what they allegedly planned to do. Drop the conspiracy charge.

But, Sir Geoffrey countered, Article 6 of the charter specifically included the crime of conspiracy. And they were bound by the charter.

Biddle spoke to the chief judge like a professor confronting an obtuse pupil. Because a statute described a crime, must they say the crime was committed? Could they not say of the conspiracy charge, "not proved," and save a lot of grief? The guilty would be convicted anyway, for the *commission* of crimes. There was little point in attempting to establish that a conspiracy to conquer the world had already been in place in some Munich beer hall in 1919. They should limit the conspiracy charge to events occurring after 1937, Biddle urged. Donnedieu de Vabres objected. If they accepted that the *Führerprinzip* meant ironbound obedience to the leader, then the idea of true conspirators made no sense either before or after 1937. He wanted conspiracy dropped.

Sir Norman Birkett paced agitatedly. He too had originally disliked the conspiracy charge, he said. But, as the trial unfolded, he had come to see Jackson's larger objective. If individuals were convicted only for individual acts, the trial would never rise above the level of an ordinary criminal prosecution. What they wanted to present to the world was the condemnation of a regime deliberately embarked on war. To drop conspiracy was to lose the trial's moral grandeur.

38

WHAT GÖRING AND COMPANY TALK ABOUT IN THEIR CELLS, the headline promised in the Sunday, August 25, London *Express*. "Hitler's Stomach Cause of All the Trouble," "When Ribbentrop Wanted a Medal," "Why Hitler Delayed Marriage," the subheads read. The *Express*'s source was Dr. Douglas Kelley, described as "Chief Psychiatrist at the Nuremberg Trials." The article included quotations from Göring, Hess, and Ribbentrop, divulging heretofore unrevealed secrets from inside the Reich and the Nuremberg prison. Colonel Andrus held the clipping like a contaminated object. The man he so admired, Sir Geoffrey Lawrence, had sent it to him with a note reading, "We shouldn't want any more of this, Colonel."

Andrus tossed the clipping at Gustav Gilbert and asked what he knew about it. Gilbert answered that he knew nothing about the origins of the Kelley story. Did Gilbert know that his psychiatrist friend was on the lecture circuit back in the States, criticizing the trial? the colonel asked. He intended to investigate this business, and he expected Gilbert's cooperation.

To Gilbert, even more alarming news had come earlier. Since Kelley appeared to have struck off on his own, Gilbert had started to shape his cell-visit notes, which he had taken as the prison psychologist, into his own book, tentatively entitled *Nuremberg Diary*. He had engaged a literary agent, who had negotiated a contract with the publisher Farrar, Straus. The agent had recently cabled Gilbert to tell him that Kelley was negotiating with Simon and Schuster. It had become a race, with Kelley holding the better post position. He was already in the States. He had completed whatever research he intended to use, while Gilbert was still making cell visits over 3,500 miles away. Farrar, Straus had informed Gilbert that they could not get his book out before March 1947. The best card that Gilbert held was a half-finished manuscript. He gave it to a friend returning to the States and asked him to take it to his agent. His hope was to demonstrate that he was well ahead of his rival and that it would be a mistake for Simon and Schuster to try to beat Gus Gilbert.

———————

Colonel Andrus sent a report to Sir Geoffrey explaining that Major Kelley had left Nuremberg on February 7, "under a cloud, as the impression had been gained that he was subordinating all his professional duties to an effort to gather information to publish for personal gain." In pursuit of this objective, "He has gone so far as to misappropriate in part official files of the tribunal."

Of course, the colonel had never been entirely comfortable with Gustav Gilbert either. The army recently had assigned Lieutenant Colonel W. H. Dunn as prison psychiatrist, and Andrus sent Justice Jackson a note saying that Gilbert was therefore of no further use to the ISD. He would keep the man, but only if Jackson insisted.

39

On August 31, a Saturday session, the defendants were to make their final statements before the verdicts were handed down. Most spent the night before honing their thoughts with their lawyers in the visitors' room. Hess remained in his cell writing to his wife. "You most certainly heard over the radio," he wrote, "that there has been another 'miracle' and I have completely recovered my mind. Or they may tell you that I have lost my reason or suffer from an 'idée fixe.' I hope you will see the humorous side of all this. Karl [Haushofer] once wrote that for the sake of a great cause one must be able to suffer the strain of seeming to one's own people, for a time, to be a traitor. To that I would add, or seem to be crazy. . . . I will face fate with . . . the same imperturbability with which I shall receive the verdict."

At the end of the block, in cell 17, Albert Speer concluded that honesty had proved to be the best defense after all. The more he admitted to himself the truth of his seduction by Hitler and the perversion of his talents in the service of Nazism, the easier it became to accept guilt and abandon denials. Not only did the truth relieve him of the baggage of self-deception, but it freed his mind to see beyond his own small fate. The same grasp of technology that he had once applied to pumping more tanks out of factories, he now applied to predicting the human condition in the atomic age. That was what he would devote his fifteen minutes to—not to saving the hide of Albert Speer, but to suggesting a path of hope for mankind into this new world.

After a brief chat, Jodl gave his lawyer, Franz Exner, a letter for his wife. Since he could occasionally see Luise in court, Jodl was judged one of the luckier defendants. But having her witness his humiliation also sharpened his pain. Underneath the indecipherable countenance, he was a confused man. Alfred Jodl genuinely did not understand why he was on trial. "I cannot rid myself of the conviction that I have not merited this fate," he wrote his wife. Still, if the worst came to pass, "Death will find here no broken, penitent victim, but a proud man who can look him coldly in the eye. . . . Yet, in my heart of hearts, I do not believe that this will be my sentence." He watched Exner disappear with the letter, hoping, however painful it would be, that Luise would appear in court when he spoke the next day.

The town was aswarm with journalism's luminous names—Joseph Alsop, Walter Lippmann, Harold Nicolson, and Rebecca West among them. Francis Biddle was delighted to have West back in town. During her July Nuremberg stint, he had set his sights on the writer and succeeded. They had gone off together for four days in Prague. Now, with West back to cover the trial's denouement, she became his houseguest at the Villa Conradti. On the eve of the defendants' final speeches, Biddle threw a cocktail party in West's honor. The guests were surprised to find this woman, who wrote so poetically at times and so scathingly at others, a small, dowdy figure. Still, they gathered like bees around the queen to hear her facile sketches of the men in the dock: She called Julius Streicher "a man a sane Germany would have sent to an asylum long ago." Of Göring: "When he's in a good humor he resembles the madam of a brothel." She loved Sir Geoffrey Lawrence, with that "voice of a silvery querulousness that flays without drawing a drop of blood."

After she retired to the Biddle guest room, West jotted down notes on the world of her Nuremberg hosts. The Britishers reminded her of life in some Kiplingesque "colonial hill station," where people insisted on traditional conduct and dress out of fear of going native.

As for the Americans, she wrote: "It is as if all the employees of the New York Telephone Company were transported to such a town as Toledo, Ohio, which by some melancholy visitation had been deprived of its amenities, and were forced to live there for ten months, during which they all had particular reasons for wanting to do something else, under an ordinance which forbade them any intercourse with the native Toledans. . . ."

The defendants were to make their final statements in the order in which they had been indicted. As Göring moved to the middle of the dock, a guard dangled before him a microphone suspended from a pole. He did not fail those who had grudgingly come to admire his belligerent consistency. This had been a poor excuse for a trial, Göring began: "The statements of defendants were accepted as true when they supported the prosecution. They were treated as perjury when they refuted the indictment." Why was he in the dock being treated as a common criminal? Let his judges have no illusions. "Since the three greatest powers on earth, together with other nations, fought against us, we finally were conquered by tremendous enemy superiority." Justice had nothing to do with this trial.

Hess was next. He asked the chief judge if he might remain seated, "because of the state of my health." He spoke in a reedy voice of his days in England: "The people around me during my imprisonment acted toward me in a way which led me to conclude that these people somehow were acting in an abnormal state of mind. . . . Some of the new ones who came to me in place of those who had been changed had strange eyes. They were glassy like eyes in a dream." The judges exchanged uneasy glances. Hess's lawyer, Seidl, looked as though he wanted to disappear. Hess went on. "In the spring of 1942, I had a visitor. . . . This visitor also had these strange eyes." Hess switched suddenly to the Moscow show trials of 1938. "One got the impression that these defendants, through a means unknown up until now, had been transported into an abnormal state of mind. . . ." Göring jammed Hess with his elbow and told him to stop. "Shut up," Hess shot back. Sir Geoffrey reminded the defendant that he had exceeded his fifteen minutes. "It was my pleasure that many years of my life were spent in working under the greatest son which my people produced in its thousand-year history," Hess concluded, folding his arms and sitting back, chin uplifted.

Major Airey Neave watched from the visitors' gallery. He had measured these men since the day he had delivered their indictments. Some had grown. Some had not. Ribbentrop, the next defendant, was among the latter. What Germany had attempted, the former foreign minister said, was what Great Britain had done in sweeping a fifth of the globe under her wing of empire, what America had done in occupying the New World, what Russia had done in spreading her dominion from Europe to Asia. A trace of the old hauteur appeared as Ribbentrop finished his statement and sat down.

As a soldier himself, Neave had been appalled at Keitel's prostitution of the warrior's code of honor. But Keitel was one who had grown, Neave believed. He detected a serenity in the man today. His tragedy, Keitel told the court, was that "the best I had to give as a soldier, obedience and loyalty, was exploited for purposes which could not be recognized at the time . . . and that I did not see that there is a limit set even for a soldier's performance of his duty. That is my fate."

Frank had moved the court during his earlier testimony with his fervent indictment of Nazism. Today he began, "On this witness stand, I said that a thousand years would not suffice to erase the guilt brought upon our people because of Hitler's conduct of this war." That debt "has already been completely wiped out." It was canceled by the mass crimes "which have been and still are being committed against Germans by Russians, Poles, and Czechs." Frank had recanted. At the last minute, a man who might have helped Germany shed the destructive myths of its past had instead chosen to poison the future.

Walther Funk wept and passed himself off as little more than a bank teller. Sauckel described having spent Christmas with the conscript workers he was accused of exploiting. Jodl justified German reprisals against "partisans who used every means which they considered expedient." Seyss-Inquart devoted his time to inventorying the health, insurance, and infant welfare programs he had introduced into Holland. Justice Biddle wrote in the margin of a document, "I am always struck by the apparently sincere and passionate idealism of so many of these defendants. But what ideals!"

Speer's steady, confident voice compelled silence in the courtroom. What would be Hitler's place in history? he asked. "After this trial the German people will condemn him as the originator of their misery and despise him." Dictatorship? "The German people will learn from these happenings not only to hate dictatorship . . . but to fear it." How could so advanced, so cultured, so sophisticated a nation as Germany have fallen under Hitler's demonic sway? The explanation was modern communications, Speer explained—the radio, the telephone, the teleprinter. No longer did a leader have to delegate authority afar to subordinates exercising independent judgment. Given modern communications, a Hitler could rule directly and personally through puppets. "Thus, the more technical the world becomes, the more individual freedom and the self-rule of mankind becomes essential."

Neave had long meditated on the relative guilt of Speer versus Sauckel. There was, in his mind, no possible confusion as to who had been superior and who subordinate in Hitler's court. Sauckel had been pathetic in his final plea today, as at every other point in the trial. Yet, Neave wondered, on what basis would the court judge their respective guilt, on substance or style, on class prejudice or hard evidence?

"This war has ended on the note of radio-controlled rockets, aircraft approaching the speed of sound, submarines and torpedoes which can find their own targets, atom bombs and the horrible prospect of chemical warfare," Speer went on. "In five to ten years, this kind of warfare will offer the possibility of firing rockets from continent to continent with uncanny precision. Through the smashing of the atom, it will be possible to destroy a million people in New York City in a matter of seconds with a rocket serviced by perhaps ten men. . . . A new large-scale war will end with the destruction of human culture and civilization. That is why this trial must contribute to the prevention of such wars in the future . . . a nation believing in its future will never perish. May God protect Germany and the culture of the West."

In the hush that followed, Neave sensed that the spectators had listened to Speer not as a man pleading for his life, but as one who had something valuable to tell them, someone with a vision born of redemption, after immersion in evil. They had heard what they wanted and even more: Hitler would be despised by posterity. Democracy must prevail over despotism. Life on earth had become infinitely more perilous. And heeding the lessons of this historic tribunal could save mankind from suicidal aggressions in an atomic age. After today, the world would likely remember Albert Speer more for his sensibilities as a human being than for his crimes as a Nazi. In truth, Neave noted, Speer had said not a word about himself or his guilt.

Hans Fritzsche concluded the statements of the defendants. Sir Geoffrey adjourned the court. The last of ninety-four witnesses had been heard, the last of over four thousand documents entered into evidence. The next time the defendants filed into room 600, it would be to learn their fates.

CHAPTER IV

JUDGMENT DAY

1

EVERYONE AT THE COURTHOUSE had a story about the Germans. Ted Fenstermacher, the prosecutor who had questioned Göring about Bormann, struck up a conversation with an ex-soldier in an Afrika Korps cap, one of thousands of jobless men haunting the streets. The veteran waved his arm across the panorama of ruin and remarked what a shame it was—the bombing had been so unnecessary, so near the war's end and against a city of no military importance. Fenstermacher asked how long it would take to rebuild Nuremberg. "Oh, ten, maybe twenty years," the soldier had answered. "But with a man like the Führer, we could do it in five."

2

ON MONDAY, September 2, the justices met to begin final debate on the verdicts. Jim Rowe briefed them on security measures he had devised. The phones would be disconnected while they deliberated. Any waste paper, unwanted notes, or unused copies of documents were to be placed in special bags to be burned. To protect the judges during this tense period, General Watson's office was arranging bulletproof cars for them. When Rowe had finished, Sir Geoffrey reminded his colleagues of their ultimate responsibility, and read aloud from Article 27 of the charter: "to impose upon a defendant, on conviction, death or such other punishment as shall be determined to be just."

They were still haunted by the fragility of this instrument, this International Military Tribunal. Was their jurisdiction rooted in any principle higher than the notion that might makes right? What authority did an American have to pass judgment on a German for a crime committed in Poland? If the issue was crimes committed during the war, why were only Germans on trial? What about war criminals among the Germans' allies, the Italians? Or, for that matter, crimes committed by their enemies, now their judges? And still more troublesome, what of the argument that the laws had been invented after the fact to fit the acts? Even now, after all these months, the judges hungered for assurances of legitimacy.

Rowe and his colleague Adrian "Butch" Fisher had ransacked the archives to put the justices' consciences at ease on the ex post facto issue. Biddle read to his colleagues a brief his aides had prepared. Going back to the adoption of the first of the Hague Conventions in 1899, they had pointed out, military courts had tried and punished individuals for violating the rules of warfare. Yet, these agreements did not define these violations as "crimes," or provide for enforcement or a court to try offenders or specify punishments. Still, no one questioned the legitimacy of such trials. Just since they had been sitting, military courts had meted out punishment to the German general Anton Dostler in Italy, to six German civilians who had murdered downed American fliers, to SS guards at Dachau, and to the killers of American GIs at Malmédy. What was the IMT but the extension of this precedent to the highest level?

John Parker raised the question of the alternates' role in determining the verdicts. Were they again to be the IMT's fifth wheel? Sir Geoffrey had already consulted with the other principal judges and decided that, on test votes, all eight judges would vote. On final votes, only the four principals would take part. Nikitchenko again proposed that two out of four votes be sufficient to convict. He was overruled. Three of four votes would be required for a finding of guilty.

If Burton Andrus had learned anything in twenty-eight years in the military, it was that idle troops are trouble-prone troops. One diversion he had authorized was use of the gym next to the exercise yard for the Twenty-seventh Infantry Regiment basketball league. Andrus had also picked up enough from the Kelleys and Gilberts of his acquaintance to know that he had to find something to occupy the anxious men on cellblock C, since Sir Geoffrey had informed him that deciding the verdicts could take a month. He thereupon devised the social hour. Unoccupied cell 32 was converted into a club room, stocked with playing cards, chess sets, and other games. Each defendant was allowed to host two parties there to which he could invite three other defendants. That meant forty-two chances for the Germans to get out and enjoy rare, normal companionship. The social hour became an instant success. Even Streicher, Kaltenbrunner, and the dull Frick received invitations. But, Andrus noted, the games were never touched. The defendants talked. They never stopped talking.

Early in the judges' deliberations, Henri Donnedieu de Vabres raised a question. If the judgment was death, might they not consider the firing squad for the military defendants? Nikitchenko objected. The bullet was the fate of honorable adversaries, not of butchers. For once, the Russian prevailed. Death sentences, the court decided, must be carried out by hanging. With the last of the ground rules set, they began to vote on the verdicts.

Biddle's secretary, Dorothy Owens, spent more time typing the judgment on Göring than it took for the court to reach it. Hess, however, was a more complex case. Was he a healthy, normal personality? Obviously not. Yet Hess understood the difference between right and wrong and the consequences of his acts, the medical experts had concluded. The judges also had to confront another anomaly. Hess had clearly been a leading Nazi, one who helped Hitler shape his warped philosophy. He was at least a co-inventor of the concept of lebensraum, Hitler's rationale for aggressions intended to increase Germany's living space. Hess had a role in the issuance of the Nuremberg Laws. He had been third in line, after Göring, in the Nazi dynasty. Yet Hess had launched a peace mission, however quixotic, and had spent most of the war in British prisons. The key question, according to Biddle, was why Hess had gone to Scotland. If it was a sincere bid for peace, that fact should be mitigating. If it was a cunning tactic to get Britain out of the war and facilitate the defeat of the Soviet Union, then he had played another role in the conspiracy of aggression.

Sir Geoffrey looked to Nikitchenko. The Russian had made his government's position clear. The Soviet Union wanted Rudolf Hess's head. The man's Scottish adventure had obviously been intended to isolate the Soviets for the kill. Lawrence therefore assumed that Nikitchenko would favor a guilty verdict on all counts, and the death penalty for Hess. Yet when it came to the vote, Nikitchenko hesitated. In the preliminary deliberations, he indeed favored death. But with a deadlock looming, he feared the others might seek to compromise on too lenient a level. He had reexamined this defendant, he said, and would not vote for Hess's death, but could support a life sentence. His decision stunned his colleagues. Biddle had grown fond of Nikitchenko as an amusing and appealing friend. But this stand, flying in the face of Moscow's demands, showed courage of a high order. They went to a vote.

How were they to judge the crimes of Ribbentrop, the spineless messenger boy for Hitler's foreign policies? The law clerks' memorandum summarized the worst of his behavior. He had ordered his ambassadors serving in the capitals of Germany's allies, Italy and Romania, to speed up the deportation of Jews to the East, knowing the fate awaiting them. He had urged that downed Allied fliers be turned over to lynch mobs. The only sympathy shown to Ribbentrop was a recognition of his fecklessness. As they went to a vote, Sir Norman Birkett remarked, "The mainspring of this man's life has been broken."

During the first week of deliberations, the halls of the Palace of Justice rang with an incongruous sound, the peal of children's laughter. Colonel Andrus had finally decided it was safe to allow the defendants family visits. The justices agreed, and asked the army to provide travel permits, transportation, and meals in a special canteen in the courthouse for the visitors.

Emma Schwabenland, an American civilian employee who managed the visitors' center, moved briskly, matching defendants with wives and children. She admired the colonel for allowing the visits, but was disappointed that he had insisted on keeping up the mesh wire. He had been adamant. No touching, no kissing, no hand-holding. That was how weapons and means of suicide were delivered.

The little girl with the thin legs and her father's broad face stood on a chair reciting poems and singing songs her mother had taught her for the occasion. Nearly a year and a half had passed since Hermann Göring had seen his wife and his daughter, Edda. Emmy, so vivacious in the past, looked as faded as the old print dress she wore. Her eyes darted nervously at the guards posted around the visitors' room. She continually twisted her handkerchief while little Edda burbled. "Daddy," she asked, "when you come home, will you wear all your medals in the bathtub like everybody says you do? I want to see them all covered with soapsuds."

Hans Frank awaited his family with a divided heart. Brigitte had written to him of their hand-to-mouth existence, of their children begging on the streets. When she told them that they would be able to visit their father, the eldest girl, Siegried, responded, "Oh, they haven't shot him yet?" Frank's wife, his onetime queen of Poland, had been plump and fashionable during the war, troubled only by his liaison with Lilli Gau. The woman coming to him now was thin, hard-faced, and shabby. His children approached uneasily.

Hjalmar Schacht sat as he did in the dock, erect, aloof, but with the satisfied smile of an old man who knows he has surprised his audience. His wife, an art expert thirty years his junior, was undeniably striking. Smiling at him were his two scrubbed, blond daughters, four and five years old.

Rosenberg's wife spoke to him, while his daughter waited in the hallway. Chaplain Henry Gerecke tried to talk to her there. The girl was thirteen and precociously pretty. Would she like to pray with him? Gerecke asked. "Don't give me that prayer crap," the girl answered. A startled Gerecke asked if there was anything else he might do for her. "Yes," she said, "how about a cigarette?"

With the visits over, a weeping Emmy Göring approached Emma Schwabenland. "Do you think the court will send my husband to an island, like Elba?" she asked. "Maybe I could join him there."

Back in the cellblock, the unvisited defendants waited. The Russians claimed they had been unable to find Frau Raeder, who lived in the Soviet Zone of Berlin. Hess refused to see visitors. "I am being held illegally," he had told Colonel Andrus, "and I do not wish my family to see me in this state of indignity." Keitel said he had disgraced himself and therefore could not face his wife.

As the justices considered the conspiracy charge against Wilhelm Keitel, Birkett pointed out that they were facing a paradox. Could a military robot like Keitel be considered a conspirator, one who schemed with Hitler to invent aggressions? Keitel's defense was a soldier's duty to obey. He virtually admitted that he did no thinking. Biddle thumbed through his copy of the charter. Here it was: Article 8. Following superior orders was not a permitted defense, "but may be considered in mitigation of punishment." They went to a vote on Keitel.

Guessing had become an obsessive game at the Stein Castle. The reporters gathered around the bar tended to agree on the "orders are orders" defense: It was not going to work for the staff chief of the German military; however much a lackey, Keitel would be convicted. Jodl, the thoroughgoing soldier, however, would not, they believed.

The justices polished off Kaltenbrunner quickly. The only argument centered on count one—whether he was significant enough to have conspired with Hitler to launch a war.

Alfred Rosenberg presented a trickier case. Up to his final statement, Rosenberg continued to embrace the National Socialist philosophy he had midwifed. He had also burglarized the art of a continent for Hitler's and Göring's personal enrichment, but not for his own. His defense counsel had proved that Rosenberg condemned the atrocities in the East, where he governed in name only. Rosenberg had, in effect, argued that he had tried to do the devil's work humanely. The judges' challenge was to determine how much he had succeeded in that inherent contradiction. Rosenberg was a fool and a bore, Biddle believed, but should that cost a man his life? On September 10, the vote for Rosenberg's conviction and execution stood at two to one. Biddle held the deciding vote and told the others he would have to sleep on it.

They found Hans Frank oddly tragic. Cultured, brilliant, he had struck a Faustian bargain—his conscience for riches and power—and lost all. His remorse seemed genuine. The Cracow opportunist had become the Nuremberg penitent, almost ecstatic in his sackcloth and ashes, even if his final statement could have been more contrite. When the emerging liberal force on the bench, Donnedieu de Vabres, suggested sparing Frank's life, Biddle was receptive. Nikitchenko insisted on hanging. Given his influence with Lawrence, Biddle again found a man's survival could depend on his nod.

Tex Wheelis leaned into the porthole, chatting with Hermann Göring while the cell guard stood aside. Göring congratulated Wheelis on his recent promotion to first lieutenant. Göring had two large suitcases, a small valise, and a hatbox in the baggage room. As the duty officer in the cellblock this day, Wheelis had the key. From this luggage, Göring's third gift to Wheelis had been retrieved, a pair of fine gray gloves.

PFC Bill Glenny watched the easy camaraderie, puzzled. The first Sunday that Glenny had escorted Göring to church service, he had blithely sat down next to him in the front row. The *Reichsmarschall* glared at him with such malevolence that Glenny fled to the back of the chapel. Thereafter, every time he was in Göring's presence, he felt the man's unnerving stare. Glenny, ordinarily a cocky soldier, was annoyed that he let this prisoner intimidate him. He was particularly upset that he lacked only Göring's signature for a full set of defendant autographs. Hess did not count. Hess gave autographs to no one. As the trial drew to its finale, the value of these signatures kept rising like a commodity in a seller's market. A complete set might fetch two hundred dollars. Most of the defendants would comply for a couple of cigarettes, and Streicher for a pack of gum.

One morning, Glenny worked up his courage. He had a sheet of paper and a pen ready. He thrust them through the square porthole. "Hermann," he said, "I want your autograph." Again, Göring gave him a chilling look, but seized the pen and scrawled his name. He flung the paper back at Glenny and said, "In fifty years, that will be priceless." Young Glenny had never found anything of the clown or buffoon in Hermann Göring.

A conspiracy is a chain. That was what the Anglo-Saxons had taught him, Nikitchenko said. Therefore, Julius Streicher should be found guilty of count one, conspiracy to commit aggression, and count four, crimes against humanity. Streicher had marched alongside Hitler from the beginning. Streicher's mouthpiece of race venom, *Der Stürmer*, taught millions of Germans that it was not simply right but necessary to hate the Jew and kill him. Streicher provided the motive for ordinary Germans to carry out mass murder the way other nations produced alarm clocks. *Der Stürmer*, the Russian argued, had paved the way to Auschwitz. Chief Justice Lawrence was receptive to Nikitchenko's rationale. Biddle listened until he could take no more. "It's preposterous to convict a little Jew-baiter like Streicher," he said, "simply because he was a friend of Hitler, or a *Gauleiter* or a Nazi." They were here to decide points of law, not to convict a man because to do so fit an exaggerated notion of conspiracy. Lawrence called for a vote.

Walther Funk was disposed of quickly, and the deliberations moved on to Hjalmar Schacht. Biddle took this opportunity to prove that his disagreements with Jackson were not personal. He knew Jackson was eager for a conviction of Schacht as a representative of the industrialist-financier class that had helped put Hitler into power. Biddle aligned himself with Nikitchenko, favoring conviction of Schacht on count one. Donnedieu de Vabres, however, wanted to acquit Schacht, as did Lawrence. John Parker did not have a counting vote, but suggested a way to break the stalemate. The justices, he said, should take into account Schacht's profession: "Herr Schacht was a banker and therefore a man of character."

Jim Rowe had worked out a system with the chief of the Language Division, Commander Alfred Steer, to keep the verdicts secret until judgment day. They took over a former German army barracks in nearby Furth. Steer recruited translators, typists, and others willing to be sequestered. A separate mess hall and dormitories were set up for the volunteers. No phones were permitted. Pages were handed to typists in random order, and the defendants' sentences were left blank until the last minute. A company of U.S. infantry posted guards outside the barracks around the clock.

Arthur Seyss-Inquart's best defense was faceless anonymity. Still, Seyss-Inquart filled a place in the mosaic of conspiracy, both as an Austrian who schemed to hand over his country to Germany, and as an occupation czar who brought untold suffering to Holland. The vote went quickly.

In naval matters, Francis Biddle was disposed to defer to Jim Rowe's firsthand experience over his own theorizing, and Rowe recommended acquittal for Grand Admiral Karl Dönitz. The man was unsympathetic—a rigid Nazi, a rabid anti-Semite, and Hitler's handpicked heir to boot—but he had to be judged for his acts, not his personality or politics. Admittedly, the order not to pick up defenseless survivors of sunken ships sounded brutal; but Kranzbuehler had been more right than he knew. Not only had the American navy fought no differently than the German fleet had, Rowe explained, but the Americans he served with fought the sea war more ruthlessly than the Germans. If the admiral was convicted, everything that Göring had been saying would be confirmed. "We'd be punishing Dönitz not for starting a war, but for losing one." These arguments were fresh in Biddle's mind as the court debated Dönitz's case.

What about the *Laconia* Order, and those helpless survivors clinging to lifeboats while German submariners cold-bloodedly machine-gunned them? Judge Parker asked. The perpetrator of that crime, Lieutenant Eck, had already been executed, Biddle pointed out. And Dönitz had never ordered survivors shot; he ordered that they not be rescued. But what about Dönitz's willingness to use twelve thousand of Himmler's concentration camp slaves to build ships? And his passing along the Commando Order? Nikitchenko asked. Now they were on firm ground, were they not? Sir Geoffrey brought them to a vote, with two quickly for condemnation. Once again, Biddle found that he could tip the scales.

Forget about the Hitler Youth business, Nikitchenko urged, as they took up the case of Baldur von Schirach. Let them concentrate on Schirach the *Gauleiter* of Vienna. Could there be any other punishment than his own death for a man who turned over sixty thousand Viennese Jews to certain slaughter? And, Sir Geoffrey added, Schirach was a villain who, to avenge the assassination of Reinhard Heydrich, wanted to bomb a center of English culture. Lawrence, too, favored the death penalty. Far too excessive, Donnedieu de Vabres protested. Twenty years would do. Biddle agreed. Sir Geoffrey decided that they would reconsider the case and vote again later.

Nikitchenko led the assault against Grand Admiral Raeder, the Russians' prize catch. Since the other Soviet contribution, Hans Fritzsche, was embarrassingly low-level and a possible candidate for acquittal, Nikitchenko wanted death for the admiral. Would not life imprisonment be harsh enough for a man over seventy? Sir Geoffrey asked. "Twenty years," Donnedieu de Vabres said. No, Nikitchenko insisted. Raeder had been present at the Hossbach Conference when Hitler unveiled his decision to launch the war, yet he had stayed on as chief of the German navy. Raeder spoke of honor, yet applied the infamous Commando Order to brave men captured in uniform, who were then executed. Either General Nikitchenko would have to come down, or Justice Donnedieu de Vabres would have to come up, Sir Geoffrey observed, or they were deadlocked.

The intelligence report from Third Army headquarters had alarmed Colonel Andrus. He directed his deputy, Major Teich, to muster the entire ISD in the exercise yard at 0900 hours on Friday, September 13.

Somehow the idea had circulated that they were past the worst of it, the colonel began. That was dead wrong. They were entering the most sensitive stage of their mission, from this moment until the sentences were carried out. He read from the Third Army report: "A very definite effort has been made on the part of certain persons to organize some means of either the liberation of some of the defendants now before the tribunal or for some other way of insuring that they escape the consequences of their acts." Men died in jailbreaks, he warned, and not just prisoners. Until the defendants walked out of this prison or were carried out, the ISD was not slackening its efforts.

Jodl's case again raised the question in Donnedieu de Vabres's mind. Could soldiers initiate a war or only fight it, question orders or only follow them? And again, if they found Jodl guilty and handed down the maximum sentence, should it be the firing squad or the rope? That had already been decided, Sir Geoffrey pointed out. They must deal with Keitel and Jodl identically, and if the judgment was death, the method was hanging.

During the deliberations over Sauckel, Sir Norman Birkett observed that of course the man was a boor; but should one hang for lack of breeding? Speer's fate sparked a more fierce debate. Francis Biddle was deeply troubled by Speer. He read from an analysis that Butch Fisher had prepared: "Sauckel had never had responsibility for any major policy decisions, but was always used to execute policies which had been decided on by more powerful men such as Göring and Speer." Furthermore, Speer acted with "complete ruthlessness and unfeeling efficiency in the application of a program which took

five million into slave labor and countless numbers to their death."
Speer always got his way over Sauckel, Fisher's analysis went on. "The
violence used in recruiting was largely in response to Speer's high
labor demands." Biddle set the paper aside. There was no doubt in
his mind. Speer's penalty must be death. Nikitchenko immediately
concurred. Only one more vote was needed.

Sir Geoffrey was troubled. What of the evidence that this man
had stood up to Hitler's scorched-earth madness, even considered as-
sassinating the tyrant? What about the man's obvious remorse and the
character and wisdom displayed in his final plea? These were not the
points at issue, Nikitchenko argued; they must consider only Speer's
commission of crimes as described in his indictment. Donnedieu de
Vabres argued that Speer deserved fifteen years. Another impasse.
They would vote again tomorrow, Sir Geoffrey ruled.

The principals let the alternates decide Hans Fritzsche's fate.
Propaganda had been a principal Nazi weapon, Lieutenant Colonel
Volchkov argued, and Fritzsche had wielded it over German radio
with deadly results. His "racial spittle," his contempt for Russians
and Slavs as subhumans, had sanctioned the deaths of Soviet POWs
and civilians in the millions. Judge Parker observed that Volchkov's
rhetoric was fine, but his law was weak. "Adolf Hitler wouldn't
have wasted five minutes with Hans Fritzsche," Parker noted. "The
man's here because Josef Goebbels is dead." Biddle concurred. Volchkov reddened angrily. What was the difference between the despised
Streicher and Fritzsche, he asked, except for a bit of polish in the
latter? Both championed racial hatred. They went to a vote on
Fritzsche.

Francis Biddle could not sleep. He had gladly exercised his intellectual
authority over his colleagues these past months. But now, particularly
in the verdicts of Frank, Speer, and Rosenberg, his persuasiveness
could determine who lived and who died. Speer's case continued to
trouble Biddle. The man's prostitution of his talent and intelligence
was appalling. If Biddle chose to, he could probably work on Lawrence
for the decisive death vote. Should he? The struggle in Biddle's soul
raged all night, until, at dawn, he made up his mind and at last fell
asleep.

The last votes—on the deferred cases—were taken on Thursday, September 26. The verdicts would be handed down within days.

On Friday, four unfamiliar officers checked into the Grand Hotel: Brigadier General Roy V. Rickard, U.S. Army, Brigadier Edmund Paton Walsh of Great Britain, Major General Georgi Malkov of the Soviet Union, and Brigadier General Pierre Morel of France. They formed the Quadripartite Commission for the Detention of War Criminals. They had come to Nuremberg to plan and supervise executions.

3

ROBERT JACKSON HAD RETURNED to Nuremberg on September 18, accompanied by Colonel Robert Storey, who wanted to watch the final curtain drop, and by his Washington liaison man, Charles Horsky. The chief U.S. prosecutor stepped into a backlog of administrative headaches. Reporters complained that only a pool would be allowed to cover executions. The recently arrived Quadripartite Commission wanted seats not in the visitors' gallery but on the courtroom floor when the verdicts were delivered. That struck Jackson as having the hangman sit in court holding a noose. The commission would occupy the gallery with the other visitors, he decided.

Sir Geoffrey summoned Colonel Andrus to review the special precautions the colonel was taking for judgment day. Andrus explained that final family visits would take place on September 28. Thereafter, relatives were to leave Nuremberg. On September 30, when the verdicts were to be handed down, Andrus would have a doctor in the basement, in addition to two guards who would be standing by in the elevator with a stretcher and a straitjacket in case any defendant went berserk. Another doctor and a nurse would be stationed in the visitors' gallery. After the men returned to the cellblock, he intended to implement new cell assignments: third tier, term sentences; second tier, life sentences; first tier, death sentences.

Justice Lawrence did not want the defendants passing through the usual gauntlet of gawkers on their way to lunch on judgment day. Andrus understood. He would send the prisoners back down by the elevator to eat in the basement. And Lawrence wanted no cameras in the courtroom when the men were sentenced. This was to be a civilized occasion, he warned.

Reporters at the press bar continued making bets on the verdicts. The latest tally showed four journalists predicting death for Schacht, eleven for Speer, thirty-two for Kaltenbrunner. The odds on Jodl's survival had risen over the past hours.

4

MONDAY, SEPTEMBER 30, broke sunny and clear. Bullet-proof cars arrived at the courthouse, sirens wailing, led by jeeps spiked with machine guns. The eight justices exited between protective files of armed infantry; a thousand troops circled the building, and sharpshooters stood silhouetted on surrounding rooftops.

In the Judges' Room, the two Frenchmen donned their gowns and placed ruffled jabots around their necks. Nikitchenko's and Volchkov's chocolate-brown uniforms displayed razor-edge creases. Biddle had abandoned natty waistcoats and bow ties in favor of a dark gray suit and robe. His mood was equally somber. He dreaded entering the courtroom this morning and facing the men in the dock. Lawrence appeared unruffled, his voice cool as he went over their final instructions. He would lead off, reading the passages of the judgment describing Nazism's rise to power. Donnedieu de Vabres and his alternate, Falco, would trace Germany's aggressions, country by country. Lawrence deliberately chose Biddle to handle the conspiracy charge. Biddle had been its harshest critic, and Lawrence wanted the court to present a united front. He selected mild John Parker to recite the most horrifying passages of the judgment, the crimes against humanity. The court's findings would echo more credibly from this placid American than from the implacable Russians. The Soviets would deliver the judgment on slave labor and Nazi organizations.

Lawrence picked up a thick black notebook. The others fell in behind him as he headed for the small door that opened onto the bench in room 600.

The visitors shifted restlessly as the voices of the judges droned on hour after hour, in effect recapping the history of an age. Not until four p.m. did Lieutenant Colonel Volchkov announce the verdicts on the indicted organizations: the Nazi party leadership, "Criminal"; the SS, "Criminal." The Gestapo and the SD, "Criminal." That league of Brownshirt bullies, the SA, was acquitted for having lost significance after the thirties, as was the Reich cabinet. The High Command was not judged criminal since, as Justice Lawrence explained, so few officers were involved that individual trials were preferable to a blanket judgment.

The court's guilty verdicts meant that anyone who was a member of the convicted organizations after 1939 was, automatically, a war criminal. Biddle, however, had successfully lobbied for exemptions for anyone drafted into membership or who had no knowledge of the organization's criminal purposes. While the trial was under way, however, U.S. occupation authorities had set up German-run denazification courts to review the status of over 3.5 million organization members. These bodies and subsequent war-crimes courts took into account a former Nazi's membership in a convicted organization in determining guilt or in barring that person from certain posts and rights of citizenship. Similar machinery was employed in other occupation zones. No member of a convicted organization, however, was punished solely on the strength of the IMT verdicts. To Biddle and other critics, the organization cases had largely been a pointless exercise.

The following morning, October 1, Colonel Andrus addressed the defendants gathered in the corridor of the cellblock. He spoke firmly but not unkindly. "You men have a duty to yourselves, to the German people, and to posterity, to face this day with dignity and manliness," he said. "I expect you to go into that courtroom, stand at attention, listen to your sentence, and then retire. You may be assured that there will be people to assist you after you have moved out of the sight of the general public."

The verdicts would be delivered first, the chief judge announced, followed by sentencing. The twenty-one men in the dock were to remain seated while they heard the judgments on the four counts applicable to them—conspiracy to commit aggression, the commission of aggression, crimes in the conduct of warfare, and crimes against humanity. Lawyers, researchers, and off-duty translators sat packed shoulder to shoulder at the prosecution tables. Movie cameras whirred and still cameras clicked in fluorescent lighting that gave the defendants a corpse's pallor.

"The defendant, Hermann Göring, was the moving force for aggressive war, second only to Adolf Hitler," Sir Geoffrey began. Göring created the Gestapo and concentration camps, before releasing them to Himmler. He signed the harshest anti-Semitic decrees. "He directed Himmler and Heydrich to 'bring about a complete solution of the Jewish question in the German sphere of influence in Europe.'" And, Sir Geoffrey added, he was a thief.

Göring, his uniform immaculate but drooping around the neck, his hair neatly combed, ground a fist into his jowl as Lawrence spoke. There was nothing to be said in mitigation, Lawrence concluded. The tribunal found Hermann Göring guilty on all four counts of the indictment.

Rudolf Hess refused to put on his earphones and rocked back and forth as Lawrence began to read his verdict. It was true, the justice said, that this man acted abnormally and suffered from lapses of memory. "But there is nothing to show that he does not realize the nature of the charges against him or is incapable of defending himself." Nevertheless, he had not participated in the physical abominations of the Reich, and therefore the tribunal found him, on the charge of crimes against humanity, not guilty. Hess, however, had been part of the original Nazi collusion, outranked only by Hitler and Göring. He had signed decrees dismembering Czechoslovakia and Poland. Hess was guilty on counts one and two: conspiracy to commit and the commission of aggression.

In the press gallery, *Newsweek*'s correspondent, James P. O'Donnell, jotted down impressions of the next defendant. "Ribbentrop . . . in worst shape of any man on dock . . . looks as if noose already around neck . . . sweating." The tribunal found the former foreign minister guilty on all four counts.

Field Marshal Keitel sat up like a cadet as his name was called. "Superior orders, even to a soldier, cannot be considered in mitigation where crimes so shocking and extensive have been committed," the justice read. "Guilty on all four counts."

Kaltenbrunner wore his customary hangman's scowl. Witnesses had placed him at Mauthausen, the judge read, and "testified that he had seen prisoners killed by the various methods of execution, hanging, shooting, gassing . . ." Guilty on counts three and four.

Nikitchenko read the judgment on Rosenberg: "21,903 art objects seized in the West," "stripping Eastern Territories of raw materials," "cleansing the occupied territories of Jews." Guilty on all four counts.

Hans Frank listened to Biddle read his verdict with the curiosity of a lawyer following an interesting case. It began well enough. "Most of the criminal program charged against Frank was put into effect through the police. Frank had jurisdictional difficulties with Himmler. . . . Hitler resolved many of these disputes in favor of Himmler. . . . It may also be true that some of the criminal policies did not originate with Frank." Did he dare hope? Biddle read on, "But, on taking over as governor-general of occupied Poland, Frank had said, 'The Poles will become the slaves of the Greater German World Empire.' " The defendant had cooperated in every brutal policy, Biddle continued. When he took over the government-general, there were two and a half million Polish Jews. When he left there were 100,000. Guilty on counts three and four.

The torpid Frick, onetime minister of the interior, the man who arranged Hitler's German citizenship, was found guilty of three of four counts.

Streicher nibbled on K-rations as Sir Geoffrey resumed reading the judgment, citing passages from *Der Stürmer*. "Streicher's incitement to murder and extermination," the justice said, ". . . clearly constitutes persecution on political and racial grounds . . . and constitutes a crime against humanity." Guilty on count four.

Walther Funk sank almost below the dock as Nikitchenko revived images of steel boxes full of gold teeth in the Reichsbank vaults. But "Funk was never a dominant figure in the various programs in which he participated." The judge's words hinted at mitigation of sentence, though Funk was found guilty on three counts.

Robert Jackson believed the next defendant was the linchpin required to hold the conspiracy case together. He had told his staff this morning that he regarded Hjalmar Schacht as the most contemptible individual on trial. "Schacht had freedom of choice. He could have gone with or against the Nazis. He did more to bring them to power than any other single individual." He was not alone in this sentiment. William L. Shirer, in the press gallery for CBS, had observed Nazi Germany longer than any of them. Shirer was convinced that the regime could not have risen without Schacht's misapplied genius.

Francis Biddle read the verdict. Hjalmar Schacht was acquitted on all counts. Jackson might well believe that it was Biddle, out to thwart him again on the conspiracy case. In fact, Schacht had escaped only through a two-to-two voting deadlock. Biddle had voted with Nikitchenko for conviction.

The courtroom was abuzz at an acquittal. After ten guilty verdicts in a row, it had begun to seem that the trial was indeed an elaborate exercise in vengeance. Schacht, from the outset, had cockily predicted his exoneration. He accepted it now as his due, without a trace of emotion.

Admiral Dönitz's prospects also looked brighter as Donnedieu de Vabres began: "The tribunal is not prepared to hold Dönitz guilty for his conduct of submarine warfare against armed British merchantmen. Nor was he guilty of ordering the killing of survivors." The tribunal accepted the position taken in the affidavit of Admiral Nimitz: the German navy had acted no differently from the American navy. Göring turned and smiled at the admiral. But Donnedieu de Vabres was not finished: Dönitz, however, had set up zones in which his U-boats could sink anything in sight, a clear violation of the Treaty of London on naval warfare. Dönitz's anger was visible. He had made part of the Atlantic a sinking zone; but the Americans had made the whole Pacific a sinking zone. The French judge continued. Dönitz had also passed along the Commando Order and sought to use concentration camp labor in shipbuilding. He was guilty of counts two and three, commission of aggression and military atrocities. His predecessor as chief of the navy, Grand Admiral Raeder, was judged guilty of counts one, two, and three.

Just days before, Biddle had received a letter from Baldur von Schirach's wife, Henrietta. "Our children love America," she had written in English. "It is their grandparents' country. They have a merry imagination of the ice cream and Walt Disney movies. The flags, the history, are as familiar to them as their own. Do I have to tell my children now that this America let your father die the most disgraceful death a man can find?" Biddle, reading the verdict, could well ask how many children among the sixty thousand Jews Schirach had shipped to the East had dreamed of ice cream and the movies of Walt Disney. The man, however, was too trifling to be convicted as a major conspirator. The court found him guilty on count four, crimes against humanity.

"Sauckel argues that he is not responsible for the excesses in the administration of the slave labor program," Biddle read. "He says that the total number of workers to be obtained was set by demands from agriculture and industry. . . . He testifies that insofar as he had any authority, he was constantly urging humane treatment. . . . There is no doubt, however," the judge went on, "that Sauckel had overall responsibility for the slave labor program, which he had carried out under terrible conditions of cruelty and suffering." Guilty on counts three and four.

The final odds on Jodl at the press bar the night before had been three to one for acquittal. He sat in defiant dignity as the court, with Donnedieu de Vabres reading, recounted his guilt in drafting plans for aggressive warfare and in passing along the Commando and Commissar orders. "He cannot now shield himself behind the myth of soldierly obedience at all costs," the judge concluded. Jodl was guilty on all four counts.

Suave Konstantin von Neurath, a gleaming white handkerchief in place, Ribbentrop's predecessor as foreign minister, had helped bring the Nazis to power and supinely signed death orders put in front of him by the SS in Czechoslovakia, the court concluded. Guilty on all four counts. Seyss-Inquart, professorial Reich commissar of the Netherlands, who sent 65,000 Dutch Jews to die, was declared guilty on three of four counts.

Robert Jackson watched Speer, usually so cool, looking tortured, his face a mass of blotches. If he could acquit one defendant, Jackson had concluded, it would be this man. "Speer's activities do not amount to . . . preparing wars of aggression," Biddle declared. Not guilty of counts one and two. As for atrocities against soldiers and civilians— counts three and four—"Speer knew when he made demands on Sauckel that they would be supplied by foreign laborers serving under compulsion . . . he used concentration camp labor in the industries under his control." He used Russian POWs in arms industries in likely violation of the Geneva Convention.

To Airey Neave, it seemed that the court had found Speer's guilt equal to Sauckel's, until the judge read, "Speer himself had no direct administrative responsibility for the program . . . he did not obtain administrative control over Sauckel . . . he was not directly concerned with the cruelty in the administration of the slave labor program. . . . He carried out his opposition to Hitler's scorched-earth program . . . at considerable personal risk." Speer was guilty on counts three and four. The chief burden for enslaving five million foreign workers had, however, been placed on the narrow shoulders of Fritz Sauckel. If any sentences less than death were to be handed down, Speer had reason to hope.

Two more acquittals followed. Franz von Papen, the former chancellor who had made the deal whereby Hitler succeeded to the post, was found innocent. Hans Fritzsche, third-rung radio propagandist, was also acquitted. Göring whispered to Hess that this insignificant fellow had no business in the dock with them anyway. Martin Bormann was convicted in absentia.

Sir Geoffrey adjourned the court at 1:45 p.m. They would reconvene for sentencing after lunch.

5

DURING THE BREAK, Robert Jackson took General Lucius Clay, General Eisenhower's deputy, and Ambassador Robert Murphy to lunch in the VIP dining room. He was furious at Schacht's acquittal, Jackson said. Not only did it wreck his conspiracy case; Schacht's release proved what the Russians had been saying all along—that the Western powers would never convict a capitalist. But didn't the acquittals establish the court as a legitimate bar of justice? his companions suggested. In Schacht's case, Jackson observed, it had taken a subversion of justice to achieve the appearance of it. As he left the dining room, reporters ambushed him, pressing for his reaction. As far as he was concerned, Jackson said, the unfortunate escape of Schacht, Papen, and the German High Command had been facilitated by the American judge. However, it would not be helpful to relations among the Allies to attribute this criticism to him. Those remarks, he said, were off the record.

The freed men stood in the pressroom, hemmed in by shouting reporters who urged cigarettes, candy, and drinks on them. Tom Dodd presented Schacht with a box of Havana cigars. Rebecca West watched with disgust. In Schacht and Papen she saw two sly old foxes who had gotten away with something approaching murder. A German policeman elbowed his way to the ex-defendants to announce that Dr. Wilhelm Hoegner, minister president of Bavaria, had issued a warrant for their arrest. They were still to be tried by a German court for the commission of war crimes. He also warned that an ugly mob was outside waiting for them. Schacht asked Colonel Andrus if he would allow them to stay in prison a few more days, until it was safe to leave. Andrus agreed.

An American reporter asked Karl Haensel, a defense lawyer, why Germans should be so unhappy that three of their own had escaped punishment. It was more than seeing people who had prospered during the regime going free, Haensel explained. Guilty verdicts, by fixing guilt on individuals, in effect absolved the German people. The more personal guilt, the less collective guilt.

A British reporter buttonholed the star interpreter, Wolfe Frank. Would Frank be handling the afternoon session? the reporter asked. "Yes," Frank answered. "I've been practicing my '*Tod durch den Strang* [death by the rope]' for days."

At 2:50 p.m. the justices' door opened, and Sir Geoffrey Lawrence emerged. At his nod, the others took their seats. Simultaneously, Hermann Göring, flanked by two white-helmeted guards, entered from the sliding door behind the dock. Göring's face looked deathly pale, even powdered. Sir Geoffrey began to read: "Defendant Hermann Göring, on the counts of the indictment on which you have been convicted, the International Military Tribunal sentences you—" Göring was waving his arms for Lawrence to stop. His earphones were dead, he said. Two GI technicians rushed to the dock. Lawrence looked on in despair: with effort, one achieved a frame of mind to condemn men, only to have the decorum shattered by an errant piece of wire. Göring indicated that all was well. Lawrence began again: "The International Military Tribunal sentences you to death by hanging." Göring, expressionless, dropped the headset, turned on his heels, and disappeared into the elevator.

Rudolf Hess swayed aimlessly, his eyes fixed on the ceiling, again refusing to put on earphones. "The tribunal sentences you to imprisonment for life," Sir Geoffrey announced. Nikitchenko fingered a ten-thousand-word dissent he intended to issue to the press as soon as the court adjourned. In it, he disowned Hess's life sentence, though he had voted for it. It would be difficult to make his overlords in Moscow understand the bargains struck in the Judges' Room—but the voting had been in secret, and the vehemence of his dissenting opinion might save his neck back home. His dissent also reviled the acquittals, especially of Schacht. The capitalists had underwritten the war of aggression, his dissent argued, and Schacht was the quintessential capitalist.

When Lawrence sentenced Joachim von Ribbentrop to hang, the man slumped, as if taking a body blow. Wilhelm Keitel heard his death sentence and nodded curtly, a subordinate who has just received an order.

"*Tod durch den Strang,*" death by the rope, Kaltenbrunner heard through his earphones. The same fate befell Alfred Rosenberg. When Biddle had gone to bed on the night of September 10, the fate of Rosenberg had lain in his hands. The next morning, he cast the vote that condemned him.

Hans Frank moved like a sleepwalker, banging into the dock chairs as he came forward. He heard his death sentence and held out his hands in wordless supplication. Wilhelm Frick heard the same sentence with impassivity. Julius Streicher virtually trotted forward, spread his legs wide, and stuck out his chin. "*Tod durch den Strang,*" Wolfe Frank translated over the interpreters' circuit.

The roll of death was finally broken. Walther Funk and Admiral Raeder received life sentences, and Admiral Dönitz ten years.

Henrietta von Schirach and Heinrich Hoffmann huddled by the radio in the Witness House to hear the broadcast of the trial. She held her father's hand as her husband's fate was announced. "The tribunal sentences you to twenty years' imprisonment," Justice Lawrence said. "He's going to live," Henrietta cried, jumping up and embracing her father. "Anything as long as he does not have to die!"

The remaining defendants stood in the basement, watching the men already sentenced exit from the elevator in handcuffs, some silent, some denouncing their verdicts. The acquittals of Schacht and Papen, men of his station, had heartened Albert Speer. He watched Fritz Sauckel enter the elevator; the man was back in barely a minute, bearing the expression of a terrified animal. "Death," Speer heard a guard say of Sauckel's sentence. Three more defendants and it would be Speer's turn.

General Jodl heard his death penalty, tore off the earphones, and stalked out. Konstantin von Neurath received fifteen years; Arthur Seyss-Inquart, death.

Speer entered the elevator. On seeing him emerge, Francis Biddle felt his gloom lift. Speer's fate had also been in his hands that sleepless night. The vote for Speer's death had been deadlocked at two to two, with Biddle and Nikitchenko in favor. Albert Speer, Biddle had finally concluded, was impressionable, idealistic, and prone to hero worship. The next morning, he changed his vote. "The tribunal sentences you," Sir Geoffrey announced, "to twenty years' imprisonment."

As the elevator descended, Speer felt as if he had been snatched from the edge of an abyss. But as the cold metal of the handcuffs encased his wrists and he was marched back to the cellblock, his mood began to shift. Yes, truth and contrition had succeeded in defeating the hangman. But twenty years? He would be an old man before he was free. Schacht and Papen had been acquitted. Lies, smoke screens, and dissembling might have worked better after all.

In the courtroom, the missing Martin Bormann was sentenced to death in absentia. After 315 days, the work of the tribunal was complete. The war-crimes trial had ended.

The press gallery erupted in pandemonium, with correspondents pushing and spilling over each other in a race for the telephones and telegraph office. The floor of the courtroom became a curious amalgam of handshaking, backslapping, and smiling faces in one quarter, and grim expressions and listless retreats elsewhere. Before wellwishers could descend on him, Robert Jackson slumped down in his seat, wondering what they had achieved. Had they merely routed a pack of villains? Or had they contributed to the march of civilization? Had they placed future aggressors on notice? Or would a bellicose mankind learn nothing? That jury was still out.

6

UNCERTAINTY COMPOUNDED the anxiety of the condemned eleven. The Allied Control Council, which governed Germany, had ruled that the executions were to be carried out fifteen days after sentencing. But did the ACC mean exactly fifteen days later, or at some point after fifteen days had elapsed? The defense lawyers were consequently unable to tell their clients exactly when they could expect to die.

Jodl had warned his wife in his last letter not to do anything "to fill my stupid old heart with hopes. Let it quietly swing itself away." Nevertheless, as soon as she learned Alfred's fate, Luise sent a telegram to the now-out-of-power Winston Churchill. "You have always been proud of being a soldier," it read. "You were the mast, when, in deadly peril, England kept the flag flying. May I, as the daughter of a Britishborn mother, appeal to you as a soldier, to give your voice of support for the life of my husband, Colonel General Jodl, who, like yourself, did nothing but fight for his country to the last." She dispatched similar pleas to General Eisenhower and Field Marshal Montgomery, asking how an officer who honorably signed Germany's surrender at Rheims could possibly "be treated like a common criminal."

Marguerite Higgins filed the story to the New York *Herald Tribune* from the courthouse telegraph room. Colonel Andrus, she reported, had switched all cell assignments to deprive the prisoners of access to old hiding places. Her story was not entirely accurate. The colonel had dispatched the men given jail terms to the upper tiers. But the condemned men were still in their same cells on what the guards now called Death Row.

Higgins returned to the press bar to find a new debate under way. Who was dying for what? Keitel for the general staff? Jodl for the German army? Kaltenbrunner for Himmler? As for the convictions of crazy Hess and Admiral Raeder, weren't they a sop to the Russians? Who was Sauckel dying for? a correspondent for the left-wing American paper *PM* asked: "the working stiffs of the world"? How could anyone lay the case against Sauckel alongside the case against Speer, and give one man death and the other twenty years? Wasn't it Speer who had cried at Adolf Hitler's death? Wasn't Speer at Mauthausen? Didn't he probably hear that grisly speech in which Himmler described the slaughter of the Jews? What about that pathetic sod, Streicher, what was he dying for? a British reporter asked. For incitement to murder, a companion answered. But that was the same thing Fritzsche had been accused of, and he went free.

A United Press reporter tracked down General Eisenhower at a castle in Ayrshire, Scotland. On the whole, he was pleased with the verdicts, Ike said, although "I was a little astonished that they found it so easy to convict military men."

"If the war had gone the other way, General," the reporter asked, "do you think they would have hanged you?"

"Such thoughts you have, young man," Ike answered.

The corridors of the Palace of Justice were eerily silent, as the staff fled as from a sinking ship. By noon of the day after the verdicts, the British delegation, luggage in hand, had assembled at Y28 for the flight back to England. Sir Geoffrey deflected reporters' questions about the verdicts and shifted the conversation to his pleasure at returning to Hill Farm in Wiltshire. His conversion over the past months from an anonymous entity to a figure of near-universal admiration did not interest him. It had never occurred to him that it could be otherwise.

Surely honors of some kind, even a peerage, must flow from this service, Sir Norman Birkett believed. But what kind and for whom? Was it possible that his behind-the-scenes contributions could somehow shine through the official role of Sir Geoffrey Lawrence?

By the time Robert Jackson's plane reached the mid-Atlantic, he was experiencing profound contentment. He looked around at the others who had helped him survive the ordeal—Bill, Elsie Douglas, his colleagues—and assessed the past year. Whatever the failures, the enemies, the aggravations and defeats, the balance was clear. He had been told that his opening speech would live in the annals of courtroom eloquence, and he tended to believe it. As he later reported in a letter to Whitney Harris, "The hard months at Nuremberg were well spent in the most important, enduring work of my life."

As he dismantled his office, Francis Biddle confessed to Jim Rowe a sense that the great adventures of his life were over, and that all that remained was the commentary.

The French and the Russians soon left too. The government of the latter took the position that the Western Allies had been too lenient on the Nazi gangsters who escaped death. But the Russians who had carried on the day-to-day courtroom battle left with satisfaction that they had set before the world the depths of their people's wartime agony. Nikitchenko, Rudenko, and a handful of others also had earned the respect, even the affection, of their Western colleagues. The Russians' departure, however, had an eye-for-an-eye quality, avenging the Germans' conduct in the Soviet Union. When the U.S. Army went to reclaim the houses where the Soviets had lived, they found them stripped of everything movable—furniture, light fixtures, bathtubs and toilet bowls, and every spoon, dish, cup, and saucer. It was all loaded aboard trucks, headed for the Soviet Zone.

7

On October 1, Lieutenant Tex Wheelis was appointed property officer in charge of the defendants' baggage room. Four days later, Hermann Göring requested a meeting with his defense counsel, Otto

Stahmer. Göring brought with him into room 57 a blue briefcase. It was a gift for his lawyer, Göring told the guard. The guard immediately summoned Major Teich, who recognized the briefcase from the baggage room. He examined it, found it empty, and allowed Stahmer to keep it. Teich, however, did not remember anyone's obtaining the required written permission for Göring to enter the baggage room to get Stahmer's gift. Someone else must have retrieved it for him.

Soon afterward, Stahmer got word to Emmy Göring in her cabin in Sackdilling that he had been able to arrange one last visit with Hermann. She was logged into the visitors' room at 2:45 p.m. Minutes later, Göring appeared in handcuffs. His first questions were about Edda. Did she know of the sentence? Did she understand what it meant? Yes, Emmy answered, Edda knew that her father was going to die. There was something worse than dying, Göring told her. It was the form of death these foreigners had imposed on him. "They can murder me," he told her, "but they have no right to judge me. That I deny them." Surely they would not hang him, Emmy said, as the visit ended. They could not hang Hermann Göring. They would take him away and intern him on an island, like Napoleon, she believed. He doubted that, Göring said. But of one thing she could be sure: "They will not hang me."

Gustav Gilbert wanted out. After the sentencing on October 1, he had waited in cellblock C to get the condemned men's reactions. It was the logical end of his work, the circle completed. After that, he could not get home soon enough. By sending his partial manuscript to New York, he had managed to kill off Douglas Kelley's bid to Simon and Schuster. But Kelley would no doubt find another publisher, and Gilbert was determined to beat him into print. He had submitted a request for his release to Colonel Andrus, who had forwarded it to Jackson before the latter's departure. Jackson had refused Gilbert, telling the puzzled psychologist that he wanted him to stay on as one of his "representatives." From that point, Gilbert found it impossible to continue wearing his mask of cool professionalism. He told a United Press reporter, "Hermann Göring's front of bravery is all baloney. They're all cowards, every one of them, including Göring. They're all trembling in their cells right now. The front they put up in court was all bravado. They don't find death as easy to take as it was to dish it out."

The heaviest emotional burden they now bore, he knew, was not knowing when they would die. In the meantime, sixteen of the defendants had appealed to the Allied Control Council, their last hope for clemency. The London Charter granted the ACC power to reduce, even to commute, sentences. Robert Servatius, Sauckel's lawyer, appealed to the ACC to consider the illogic of his client's death sentence. "Sauckel had nothing to do with concentration camp labor," Servatius petitioned; "that was an enterprise between Speer and Himmler. . . . Sauckel remained an outsider among the Nazi elite. Speer was a close friend of Hitler." Keitel had petitioned the ACC that he be shot. Göring, Frank, and Streicher did not want appeals, but their lawyers filed anyway. On October 9, the ACC met in closed session for three and a half hours. The four members, one from each of the occupying powers, weighed the appeals on two scales: Was there any political advantage to the Allies in reducing a sentence? Had the defendant rendered useful service to the prosecution? They made their decisions but chose not to inform the prisoners immediately.

On October 10, Colonel Andrus returned from a short trip to Belgium. The stream of what he called "tourists" waiting to visit his "zoo" had not abated. As time grew short, the famous and curious were eager to come to cellblock C. And the press continued to hound him. Was it true that Rosenberg had managed to commit suicide, that Hess had drafted a scheme for the Fourth Reich? The Quadripartite Commission, in charge of planning the executions, questioned him about his arrangements for a hangman. He explained that Master Sergeant John C. Woods was coming down from Landsberg. A thoroughgoing professional, Woods had "dropped" 347 men in a fifteen-year army career, most recently the Dachau SS murderers whom Captain Gilbert had interviewed over Christmas.

The colonel obtained fresh briefings on the prisoners' mental health from Lieutenant Colonel William Dunn, his current prison psychiatrist, and on their physical condition from Dr. Pfluecker and an army physician, First Lieutenant Charles J. Roska. Several of the condemned men, they reported, were taking cold morning showers, and most were joining in the exercise period permitted in the cellblock corridor—except for Göring, who never left his cell. You could not force hygiene and health on a man about to die, the colonel observed.

Hans Frank remained Father Sixtus O'Connor's prize convert. Frank might have partially reneged on his renunciation of the Nazi regime, but he had held faithful to his return to the church. In her last letter, his wife, Brigitte, had informed Frank that she and the children were living in a cold-water flat and that all their possessions had been confiscated. His present circumstances were such a mockery of the respectability and prestige he had sought all his life that he had no quarrel with his death sentence. An end to thinking and feeling was, he told the priest, a gift. In the time left him, Frank worked desperately to finish his memoirs. He had completed 1,090 pencil-written pages. Father O'Connor promised that he would smuggle the manuscript out to Frank's wife, if he had to carry it himself.

The army censor scanned the letter from Rudolf Hess to his wife, the first written since his sentencing. "I am greatly surprised," he wrote, "for I had reckoned with the death sentence." He reiterated his reasons for not seeing her "through a wire net with guards on both sides . . . it is beneath our dignity. Nevertheless," he told her, "I find myself in a state of most perfect calm, disturbed only by the thought that I cannot transfer my state to comrades who cannot feel the same way." He closed by saying, "In accordance with my refusal on principle to recognize the court, I paid no attention—ostentatiously—when the judgment in my case was announced. . . . As a matter of fact, it was quite long before I discovered, accidentally, what the sentence had been." The letter was one of dozens from Hess that the censor had cleared. And like all the others, this one struck him as a model of rationality.

Keitel pleaded with Dr. Pfluecker to use his influence to stop the mournful music. Every night the SS organist played *"Schlafe, mein Kindchen, schlaf ein"*—"Sleep My Little One, Sleep." Keitel, too, after initial resistance, had also begun an autobiography and felt himself drowning in melancholy memory. The song recalled his lost sons, dead or missing in the invasion of the Soviet Union which their father had helped launch. How fortunate it would have been, Keitel noted in his memoir, if he had been permitted a hero's death that steaming twentieth of July when the bomb intended for Hitler went off in the Wolf's Lair in Rastenburg. Later, after the war, he had been left unguarded for hours on end by his captors. How easy suicide would have been then, how preferable to this "Via Dolorosa to Nuremberg," he wrote.

How much more fortunate Erwin Rommel had been. In October 1944, Hitler learned that Germany's noblest soldier had supposedly supported the Twentieth of July plotters. Hitler told Keitel that they had only two options. The first was to arrest Rommel and court-martial him. That would be a terrible blow to the German people, who revered Rommel, Keitel said. The only other course, Hitler said, was to inform Rommel of what lay in store for him, should he fail to do "the right thing."

Keitel sent two generals, Wilhelm Burgdorf and Ernst Maisel, to Rommel's home near Ulm, where the field marshal was recuperating from a skull fracture suffered when his staff car had been strafed. They carried with them a vial of poison. They explained Rommel's choices to him, and promised protection for his family and a state funeral if he did what was expected.

On October 15, 1944, Keitel wrote his wife, "Rommel has died after all from the multiple skull injuries he received in a car accident. It is a heavy blow and a loss of a commander well favored by the gods." In an official announcement to the German people, Keitel told the same lie.

Pfluecker promised that he would speak to Colonel Andrus about the organist. Alone in his cell, Keitel understood fully, at last, the old proverb "Hell is truth seen too late." He had served evil with the same soldierly devotion with which he would have served good. His crime was that he had made no distinction.

8

COLONEL ANDRUS DELIVERED the news to the prisoners after morning church services on Sunday, October 13. The ACC had rejected all appeals for clemency. Before leaving Nuremberg, Justice Jackson had notified the commission that none of the defendants had provided service to the prosecution meriting mitigation. And clemency offered no political dividends, the ACC itself had concluded.

After seeing the prisoners, Andrus left for the airport, accompanied by his daughter Kitty. It was hardly an ideal time to be leaving Nuremberg. The hour of execution had to be imminent. Still, the Grand Duchy of Luxembourg had invited the colonel to receive the Order of the Oak Wreath Crown for his earlier direction of the prison at Mondorf. Kitty was to be presented to the grand duchess at a reception honoring her father. He had known little enough reward in this job, his wife had said, and he must not miss this trip. In any case, Andrus would be back the next day.

The day before, he had checked the latest psychiatric reports on his wards. Lieutenant Colonel Dunn had warned of potential difficulty with Sauckel and Ribbentrop; he described the latter as "a house that was not built of very good material originally and was now in the process of disintegration." As for Göring, Dunn reported, "He will face his sentence bolstered by his egocentricity, bravado, and showmanship. Göring will seize any opportunity to go out fighting."

Alfred Jodl received the word of the ACC decision with customary stoicism, outwardly at least. He knew of Luise's efforts, another dream to be dashed. Winston Churchill had replied that he had received her communication "and passed it to Attlee, the prime minister." Montgomery had reacted similarly. Her telegram to Eisenhower had been returned with a note, "Addressee has left town. No forwarding address given."

Jodl welcomed the arrival of the prison barber. As the POW trusty shaved him, he asked Jodl about a faded photograph on the table, a young woman holding an infant. That was him with his mother, Jodl answered. "It's too bad I didn't die then. Look how much grief I would have been spared. Frankly I don't know why I lived anyway."

On Sunday evening, Gilbert made a last visit to the prison, asking the condemned men how they felt about the denial of their appeals. Sauckel displayed the most palpable fear of dying. He had always done what he was told to the best of his ability, he told the psychologist.

How could he now be a condemned criminal? Yet, as Gilbert discussed the collapse of Sauckel's appeal, a ray of reality appeared to penetrate that modest intelligence. "We have an old saying, Doctor," Sauckel said. "The dogs will always catch the slowest one."

Julius Streicher spoke again of his mounting admiration for the Jews. Of course, Gilbert must know about his people's celebration of Purim, he said. Imagine the irony of that event; Haman, the cruel minister of Xerxes, and his ten sons, marched to the same gallows where the Persian had intended to hang the Jews. Streicher continued to astonish Gilbert with his biblical erudition.

Göring lay stretched on his cot, apathetic yet curiously alert about certain matters. He questioned Gilbert closely on one point. Was there absolutely no possibility that he would be allowed to face a firing squad? None, Gilbert answered. It was just as well, Göring said. He had heard the Americans were poor shots. His rounds completed, Gustav Gilbert left cellblock C for the last time.

Monday, October 14, the cellblock bustled with the customary morning routine for all but Göring, who still had his cell cleaned by a POW trusty. He lingered in the corridor, talking to Tex Wheelis, while the others mopped their cells. The guards liked having Lieutenant Wheelis on duty. His supervision was marked by an amiable laxity. Göring next spoke quietly and intently to Dr. Pfluecker until the guards locked him up again.

In his cell, Göring could slip his hand into the cavity where the flush pipe entered his toilet bowl. There he would find the cold, hard, reassuring tip of the cartridge. Inside was a glass vial of cyanide. How the cartridge had traveled from the baggage room to its present hiding place was known only to him and a probably unwitting accomplice. It was most likely Tex Wheelis who had retrieved from that room the gifts Göring had given the soldier and possibly other items, including the blue briefcase that Göring had presented to Stahmer.

9

COLONEL ANDRUS returned from Luxembourg Monday afternoon to find Master Sergeant John C. Woods, the Third Army executioner, waiting in his office. The sergeant had come by his trade while serving as a witness at a hanging. When the executioner had asked for a volunteer, Woods came forward and discovered his calling. The pot-bellied, ruby-faced forty-three-year-old commanded a certain awe wherever he served; this had engendered in the man a coarse confidence that grated on Andrus. Woods said that he had been told he would do the job on Wednesday, the sixteenth. True, Andrus said. The Quadripartite Commission was meeting at this moment to determine the exact hour and the disposition of bodies and personal effects.

Andrus reminded Woods that secrecy was vital. They did not want to trigger any fuss by the Germans—demonstrations, escape attempts, or uprisings. Woods explained that he had managed to get his team and equipment into town unobserved, traveling from Landsberg by back roads during the night, avoiding the reporters who had virtually staked out the city. His crew was now waiting at the Nuremberg military district headquarters. He had two boys in his five-man team, Woods said, who had never dropped anybody before; but he had been training them hard for three weeks.

Andrus slid open a desk drawer and handed Woods a sheet of paper, a list of the height and weight of the eleven condemned men. Woods had heard that Göring was enormous; but, he noticed, the prisoner who had weighed 262 pounds on his capture was down to 186. A basketball game would be under way tonight in the makeshift gym next to the exercise yard, Andrus said. That was the best time to slip into the yard. The noise of the game would help cover Woods's arrival.

That evening near eight p.m., the prisoners heard a commotion at the far end of the block. Word passed quickly that Colonel Andrus had ordered a surprise inspection. He wanted the cells turned inside out. Göring had to remove the capsule from the toilet. There was only one other place to conceal it temporarily during the inspection: in his rectum. Arriving at cell 5, First Lieutenant John W. West went through Göring's box of personal belongings, checked the underside of the table, the window ledge, and the toilet bowl. He looked under the bed, lifted the mattress, took it out into the corridor, shook it vigorously, inspected it, found no tears, and placed it back on the cot.

Göring waited until lights out. Once in bed, he could remove the cartridge, manage to work a tear in the mattress, and slip the cartridge into it.

The gym was dirty, the air foul, and the ceiling too low for set shots. "You boys go on, finish your game," an unfamiliar master sergeant drawled as he stood, arms folded, watching from the doorway. Woods estimated the dimensions of the gym at about eighty by thirty feet, plenty of room for his needs. He turned and left. Minutes later, the GIs heard vehicles pull up alongside the gym. They continued playing, the ball beating a thumping cadence against the wooden floor, counterpointed by their shouting. Woods and his assistants remained by their trucks, smoking, until the players headed for the showers in the prison basement. When the last of them was out of sight, Woods gave a signal and his men dropped the tailgates.

Willi Krug, on the third tier, was awakened after midnight by hammering and the sound of voices, but soon fell back asleep. Dr. Pfluecker heard the noise too, as did Albert Speer, whose speculations sent a chill down his spine.

While his men assembled the portable equipment, Sergeant Woods ran his hands over the ropes, waxed and flexed them until he was satisfied that he had achieved the right elasticity. He should have tested them with weights first, but could find none in the prison. He began weaving the nooses. By the time he finished, the hammering was stilled.

He observed his crew's handiwork with satisfaction. Three gallows stood in the middle of the gym, painted black, eight feet high, each approached by thirteen wooden steps. The front three sides below the landing were of wood; a black drape covered the back end. Woods mounted the first gallows and shifted his weight, testing its stability. A metal hook hung from the crossbar. Woods attached a noose to the hook. A lever jutted from the floor. Woods yanked it. The trapdoor opened with a metallic screech. He gave the lever a drop of oil. He repeated the ritual at each of the scaffolds.

One more task remained. His men strung a black curtain at one end of the gym, and behind it placed coffins and stretchers taken from the trucks. By the time they finished, dawn was washing away the dark of night. They piled into their vehicles and drove out of the prison yard. The whining motors awakened Willi Krug again. This time he decided to get up.

10

THE DAY BEGAN like any other in the fixed round of their lives. Krug collected the washbasins; the prisoners cleaned their cells and break-fasted on oatmeal and coffee. Rosenberg wanted a complaint brought to the colonel's attention. The nights were getting cold again, and he simply could not sleep with his hands outside the blankets. For all the surface calm, they kept asking Krug, was this the day?

The POW barber came to Hermann Göring's cell first, as usual. The escort guard handed him a blade, which the barber inserted into Göring's razor. The escort and the cell guard chatted animatedly about baseball. Something important in the sport was happening that night, Göring gathered. As the barber was leaving, Göring asked him, could this be the day?

The cell doors were thrown open for morning exercise—several brisk turns around the corridor, guard and prisoner shackled together. Once the men were locked up again, the librarian, Otto Streng, per-formed his other role, jailhouse mailman. Streicher received one letter, Ribbentrop five, Jodl seven, and Frank nine. Sauckel received none. Frank asked, with childlike eagerness, if he was the winner this morn-ing. Several asked Streng if this was the day.

On days when the evidence in court had been horrifying, a smell of shame clung to the cellblock. On a day brightened by a hopeful decision from the bench, a whiff of the old arrogance permeated the corridor. Today, cellblock C was electric.

Ribbentrop complained of insomnia to the army physician, First Lieutenant Roska. Roska reminded him that Dr. Pfluecker would bring the usual sedatives that evening. The former foreign minister wanted to read to the doctor a letter he had just written to his wife: "Millions have fallen. The Reich is destroyed and our people lie pros-trate. Is it not right that I too should fall? I am perfectly composed and will hold my head high, whatever happens. I will see you in another world." What did the doctor think of that? Ribbentrop wanted to know. Roska was impressed that this "disintegrating personality," whom he had been told especially to watch, had revealed unexpected dignity. It was a fine letter, the doctor said.

Roska interrupted Keitel in the midst of work on his memoirs. He was struck by the sparkling cleanliness the field marshal had some-how achieved in a jail cell. Keitel was downcast but told the doctor he felt fine and went back to his writing. Tomorrow would be October 16. Five years ago, to the day, he had drafted the Reprisal Order. "A human life in unsettled countries frequently counts for nothing," he had written, and then he had gone on to order the execution of fifty hostages for the death of a single German soldier. That and similar orders had led him to this cell, where his own life now counted for nothing.

Chaplain Gerecke and Father O'Connor sat in the prison office keeping their minds occupied by discussing the World Series game to be played that night. Gerecke was ready to put ten dollars on his hometown St. Louis Cardinals. O'Connor, ordinarily a Dodger fan, settled for the Boston Red Sox. Dr. Pfluecker listened, understanding nothing. A guard arrived and informed the chaplains and Pfluecker that the colonel wanted to see them in his office.

Andrus was subdued. He had just received word from the Quad-ripartite Commission. The condemned men were to be awakened at 11:45 this evening. They would receive their last meal and then be taken to the gym, where the executions would begin after midnight. Could they be told now? Pfluecker asked. No, Andrus said. Until they were awakened tonight, all was to proceed normally, even to distrib-uting sleeping pills for those who used them. Not a word he had uttered in this room, he warned, was to be repeated. Though Pfluecker was a German and still technically a POW, Andrus's trust in him was total.

That afternoon, Father O'Connor visited the cells of Frank, Kalten-brunner, and Seyss-Inquart to ask if they would like to make their confessions and take Communion. He read the alarm in their eyes, and to their inevitable questions, pretended that he had no infor-mation.

Dr. Pfluecker asked the corporal of the guard, Sergeant Denzil

Edie, to accompany him to Göring's cell. He wanted to give Göring a light sedative, he said. Edie accompanied the doctor to cell 5 and watched Pfluecker take Göring's pulse and give him a small white pill. Göring prodded the doctor for the latest word. The colonel's warning rang fresh in Pfluecker's ears. Still, Pfluecker thought, he must do something to help. All he dared say was, "This night might prove to be very short." He did not want to do anything to draw attention to himself by varying his usual routine, Göring said. But he had to remain alert. How could he, if he took his usual sleeping pills? Pfluecker promised to find a way. Immediately upon Pfluecker's departure, Göring called to Otto Streng for some stationery. On the librarian's return, Göring seated himself at the flimsy table and began writing, in a bold, vigorous hand:

> To the Allied Control Council:
> I would have had no objection to being shot. However, I will not facilitate execution of Germany's *Reichsmarschall* by hanging! For the sake of Germany, I cannot permit this. Moreover, I feel no moral obligation to submit to my enemies' punishment. For this reason, I have chosen to die like the great Hannibal.

He signed his name with a flourish.

Hermann Göring saw himself as a man of honor. Certain people in this prison had shown him kindness at some risk to themselves, especially Wheelis and Dr. Pfluecker. He owed them something. He took another sheet of paper and began:

"To the Commandant: I have had the poison capsule with me ever since the beginning of my imprisonment." He went on to explain that he had brought three capsules into Mondorf, the first deliberately left to be found in his clothes, another hidden in a container of skin cream still in his toiletry case in the baggage room. The third capsule, he said, he had hidden "here in the cell so well that in spite of repeated and thorough searches, it could not be found." While he was in the courtroom, he said, he had hidden the capsule in his boots. "None of those responsible for the searches is to be blamed," he ended, "for it was practically impossible to find the capsule. It would have been pure coincidence." He signed the letter, then decided to add another line. There was one person he did not have to protect. "Dr. Gilbert," he wrote, was the one who "told me that the control council had refused my petition to change the method of execution to shooting."

The next letter was to his wife.

> My one and only sweetheart, after serious consideration and sincere prayer to the Lord, I have decided to take my own life, lest I be executed in so terrible a fashion by my enemies. . . . My life came to an end when I bade you farewell for the last time. Ever since then, I have felt wonderfully at peace with myself and consider my death a deliverance. I take it as a sign from God that throughout all the months of my imprisonment, I was left with the means which now set me free of my temporal existence and that they were never found. . . . All my thoughts are with you and Edda and my dearest ones. My last heartbeats are for our great and eternal love.

He penned a quick note to Chaplain Gerecke asking his forgiveness, but saying, "for political reasons, I had to act this way."

He placed the four letters in an envelope and put them under his blanket. For reasons known only to himself, he had dated them October 11, 1946—clearly incorrect, since Gilbert had not talked to him about the ACC decision until October 13.

Kingsbury Smith, correspondent for the International News Service, recognized that he had been deeded a title to history. Smith was one of eight pool reporters chosen by lot to witness the executions. His instructions were to present himself at eight p.m. at the visitors' room, where, over the past eleven months, the defendants had met with their lawyers and more recently bade good-bye to their families. When Smith arrived, he found correspondents for Tass and *Pravda* chatting with Colonel Andrus. The other pool correspondents, representing French and British papers, arrived soon afterward. The colonel announced that the pool was to be given a tour of cellblock C. After that, the journalists would be held incommunicado until the hour of the executions. They were to take no photographs in the gym. The Third Army had sent down its own man from the Signal Corps in Frankfurt to serve as official photographer. They were fortunate to be allowed to cover the story at all. Justices Lawrence and Birkett, Andrus pointed out, had vigorously opposed any press presence at this "grue-some spectacle." But American officials feared creating future Bor-manns by allowing rumors to spread that Göring or Ribbentrop or Kaltenbrunner was still alive. The Americans wanted the press to con-firm the deaths to the world.

Dr. Pfluecker went to the prison dentist, Dr. Hoch, another POW trusty. Pfluecker had a problem. Every night, the guards watched him give Göring two sleeping pills, Seconal in a red capsule, which acted quickly but did not last long, and Amytal in a blue capsule, which produced deep sleep. He must not let Göring slip into a stupor this night. He asked Hoch to empty the blue capsule and fill it with sodium bicarbonate.

That evening, official word that the executions were imminent was passed to the press at the Faber-Castell castle. The reporters piled into buses for the trip to the Palace of Justice, where they were briefed by an army public information officer. They could expect no further news until after the hangings, he warned, which were scheduled to take place at an undisclosed hour on the sixteenth. They would get eyewitness accounts from the pool reporters. The correspondents be-gan crowding the windows, which offered a view of the lights burning in cellblock C. The officer warned them not to try to open the win-dows and lean out. Sentries had orders to shoot on sight.

In nearby buildings and bombed-out shells, journalists comman-deered vantage points. Dana, the German news service, had a three-man team, equipped with binoculars, posted in a roofless attic offering a view of the prison yard and gymnasium only two hundred yards away.

Göring impatiently surveyed the fleshy, kindly face of Chaplain Ge-recke. He had written a special devotional just for him, Gerecke said. Göring told him to leave it on his table. He would read it later. When would the executions take place? Göring asked. Gerecke ignored the question. Would Göring join him in prayer? No, Göring replied, he would watch the chaplain pray from his cot. "You'll never see your daughter, Edda, in heaven if you refuse the Lord's way of salvation," Gerecke warned, dropping to his knees. When the chaplain finished,

Göring asked again about the execution. He had a Christian duty not to let these men suffer the cruelty of not knowing, Göring said. Look at poor Sauckel; he was practically gibbering. Gerecke felt Göring's powerful will working on him. He insisted that he did not know and quickly left.

Göring heard the heavy door of the cellblock open and recognized the voice of Colonel Andrus above the hum of several others. The eight correspondents became silent at a signal from the colonel. They looked down a long, grayish corridor, the gloom broken only by eleven bare lights over eleven cell doors. Eleven cell guards leaned on the outer shelves peering in, frozen as if in a tableau. The press party started to follow Andrus, past the prison office, the baggage room, and the cells. In them they glimpsed men reading, pacing, smoking. Andrus then took the reporters to a tier in the prison where they were to remain until they were escorted to the gym after midnight.

As soon as Göring heard Andrus's party leave, he got up and retrieved his letters from beneath the blanket. He found the letter to the Allied Control Council and added a page. "I consider it in extremely bad taste," he wrote, "to present our deaths as a spectacle to the sensationalist press. . . . This finale is certainly in keeping with the baseness which the prosecution as well as the court have demonstrated. The whole thing is merely a show trial, a bad comedy. Personally, I shall die without this sensationalism and without an audience."

At 9:30 p.m., Dr. Pfluecker, in the company of the duty officer, Lieutenant Arthur McLinden, made his sleeping-pill rounds. They found Göring in his blue silk pajamas already in bed. Pfluecker gave Göring the blue and red capsules, which McLinden watched him take. McLinden noted the warm parting handshake of the two men. It had the quality of a farewell.

11

THE DANA NEWS CREW huddled in its attic perch, shivering in a wind-driven rain. Below them, Nurembergers hurried by, coats clutched to their throats, and a policeman stood beneath a feeble streetlamp, stamping his feet. The crew could make out people emerging from army staff cars in front of the courthouse. Dignitaries, the Germans guessed. The man with the binoculars swung them in a slow arc across the prison wall. Lights out, he reported, and checked his watch. The time was 9:35 p.m.

Among the passengers deposited at the Palace of Justice was Dr. Wilhelm Hoegner, minister president of Bavaria, chosen by the American occupation authorities as a German witness for the executions. Inside the courthouse, Hoegner was directed to a remote vaulted room, where the Quadripartite Commission had done its work, and where the witnesses were gathering. In addition to the eight pool reporters and four Quadripartite Commission members, thirty others would witness the final act of the trial, including doctors, chaplains, and German civil officials such as Hoegner. A stenographer from the Language Division had been assigned to capture the prisoners' last words. Colonel Andrus asked for the group's attention and began reading seating assignments in the gym.

The colonel had imposed a communications cutoff between the prison and the outside world. The only exception he had agreed to was one phone call to the prison office after each inning to give the score of the World Series. The Red Sox had tied up the game and Chaplain Gerecke, Father O'Connor, and a handful of guards impatiently awaited the next ring of the phone. The cellblock was otherwise still, the prisoners in bed, some already asleep.

Suddenly, shouts of "Corporal of the guard!" and heavy footsteps echoed down the empty corridor. Staff Sergeant Gregory Tymchyshyn came bursting into the prison office. "Chaplain, chaplain, there's something wrong with Göring!" Tymchyshyn shouted. Gerecke followed the sergeant to cell 5, where Göring was lying on his back, his right hand dangling over the side of the bed, his face a sickly green. Froth bubbled in one corner of his mouth as he breathed loudly and unnaturally. One eye was shut, the other open. Gerecke took his pulse. "Good Lord," he said, "this man is dying." Gerecke ordered a guard to fetch Dr. Pfluecker. The chaplain asked PFC Harold Johnson, the cell guard, what had happened. Johnson had seen Göring bring his arm to his face, fist clenched, as though shielding his eyes. Göring had then let his hand fall back. That was at exactly 10:44 p.m., the GI said. About three minutes later, Göring had started making choking noises. That was when he had shouted for the corporal of the guard.

Dr. Pfluecker arrived as Göring exhaled for the last time. The doctor took his pulse. There was nothing to be done, Pfluecker said. He had no experience with poisons. The army doctor, Lieutenant Roska, must be summoned. Pfluecker pulled back the blanket, revealing two envelopes resting on Göring's stomach. Captain Robert Starnes, the chief prison officer, arrived as Pfluecker was putting his head to Göring's chest to listen for the heartbeat. "Yes, he's dead," Pfluecker said, handing Starnes the two envelopes. Starnes felt something heavy in one, and extracted a cartridge, two and a half inches long, with a removable cap. In the other he found Göring's letters.

Dr. Roska arrived and made his way through the crowd outside Göring's cell. He was immediately struck by the odor of bitter almonds. He ran his finger around inside Göring's mouth and brought out tiny shards of glass. "Cyanide," Roska said.

Colonel Andrus was giving the witnesses the order of the executions when the call came. The colonel had better get over to the cellblock right away, Captain Starnes urged. Andrus ran all the way. Starnes met him and explained what had happened as they hurried to Göring's cell. The knot of people parted to let Andrus through. He stared at the face, now a concrete gray. With the one eye closed, Göring appeared to be winking at the colonel. Andrus glanced at his watch. It was 11:09 p.m. He told Starnes to have the guards wake up the other prisoners. He left the cell to phone the Quadripartite Commission. Starnes handed him the two envelopes and asked if the prisoners were still to be given their last meal. Andrus nodded and headed down the cellblock to the prison office. An incredulous General Rickard answered his call. The colonel heard a hurried conversation at the other end. Rickard came back on the line; the commission members were coming right over, he said.

The four officers arrived within minutes and cleared the cell of all but the two doctors. The Russian representative, General Georgi

Malkov, gave Göring a hard slap across the face. What was that for? Brigadier Paton Walsh asked. "You can't fake death," the Russian said. "The eyes always move. He's dead."

Andrus handed the envelopes with the cartridge and letters to General Rickard. The colonel had not read them, even the one addressed to him; he feared that doing so might incriminate him. He asked to be excused. It was his responsibility to inform the prisoners that their sentence was about to be carried out. General Rickard shouted after him that, as of now, he wanted them handcuffed.

The commission members pressed the doctors for details. Cyanide acted swiftly, Roska explained. It blocked the body's cells from taking oxygen. Death could occur in three to five minutes. The four men excused the doctors and began debating their alternatives. They considered having Göring brought to the gym on a stretcher, telling the witnesses that he had fainted, and then hanging the body. The idea was dismissed. Too many people already knew what had happened. The story would inevitably leak out and damage the credibility of the court. The sensible thing, they concluded, was to appoint a board to begin an immediate investigation, and to proceed with the executions.

General Rickard came out of the cell, looking for Colonel Andrus. He saw the prisoners, each handcuffed to a guard, sitting on their cots in their cells, the doors open. A last meal of sausage, potato salad, and fruit salad rested on their laps. Few touched the food. Rickard located Andrus. The two men found it difficult to look at each other; Andrus was mortified, and Rickard wanted to conceal his disbelief. Rickard told the colonel that he needed two senior officers from the ISD to serve on an investigating board. Andrus recommended Lieutenant Colonel W. H. Tweedy and Major Stanley Rosenthal. Rickard said that he himself would provide the board president, Colonel B. F. Hurless. One more thing. Andrus would have to tell the eight reporters in the pool what had happened.

The colonel returned to the tier where he had sequestered the reporters. He wore the shellacked green helmet and carried the riding crop. Only his tie was askew. "Göring is dead," he began. "He committed suicide by poisoning himself." They peppered him with questions. "The Quadripartite Commission is investigating," the colonel responded. "I have no further details." They made a reflexive bolt for the door, and then realized they were locked in. The executions would proceed on schedule, Andrus said. They would be taken to the gym at the appropriate time.

12

"THEY'RE COMING," the Dana man with the binoculars announced. He could make out a man between four guards and several unidentifiable officers following behind, coming from the jail. He stopped to wipe the lens of the binoculars. The rain had turned into a drizzle, still driven by a wind that whistled eerily through the ruins.

Colonel Andrus walked behind Joachim von Ribbentrop the thirty-five yards from the cellblock across the exercise yard to the gym. At the entrance, he removed his helmet and bowed stiffly. The German, his sparse gray hair whipped by the wind, returned the bow. To Andrus's relief, Ribbentrop had walked steadily, head held high, hands handcuffed behind him. The colonel remained outside the gym. He had been with these men too long to want to watch them die.

The time was 1:11 a.m. as Ribbentrop went through the door. He blinked in the harsh, unforgiving light. Two men from Master Sergeant Woods's detail removed his handcuffs and retied Ribbentrop's hands with a leather strap. Most witnesses sat at the tables; a few others stood against the wall. Ribbentrop was led to the gallows on the left. Woods's plan was to use two gallows and hold the third in reserve. An American army colonel stood at the foot of the steps and asked the prisoner to state his name. Ribbentrop did so in a firm voice, then mounted the stairs. Waiting for him at the top were Chaplain Gerecke and a stenographer, poised to record his last utterance. Another of Woods's men bound Ribbentrop's legs at the ankles with an army web belt. Ribbentrop was asked if he had anything to say. "My last wish," he said, "is that Germany realize its destiny and that an understanding be reached between East and West. I wish peace to the world." Woods slipped the noose over Ribbentrop's neck and a black hood over his head. He stepped back, and yanked the lever. The trapdoor opened with a crash and the body disappeared as down a mineshaft.

Two minutes later, Field Marshal Keitel stepped briskly up the stairs of the middle gallows as if he were mounting a reviewing stand. As he turned around to face the witnesses, he could see the rope in the gallows to his right twisting slowly. "More than two million soldiers went to their death for the fatherland before me," he said. "I now join my sons. *Deutschland über Alles!*"

After the trap was sprung on Keitel, the colonel in charge asked General Rickard if the witnesses might smoke while they waited for the doctors to pronounce the prisoners dead. Roska and a Russian physician disappeared behind the black curtain at the rear of Ribbentrop's scaffold, one carrying a flashlight, the other a stethoscope. The gym was quickly filled with smoke and the hum of subdued conversation. Kingsbury Smith, gesturing toward Keitel's gallows, said to a British reporter, "We've just witnessed history, probably the first professional soldier who wasn't able to hide behind his orders."

Fifteen minutes passed. The witnesses began to eye each other uneasily. They talked in hushed tones about the broken neck that was supposed to produce merciful, almost instant death. The doctors finally emerged. Ribbentrop was dead, Roska announced. Woods went behind the curtain and cut the rope with a large commando knife. Two GIs brought the body out on a stretcher and set it on top of a coffin behind the black curtain. The American colonel announced, "Cigarettes out, please, gentlemen," and gave the signal to bring in Kaltenbrunner, who was hanged while Father O'Connor, wearing a Franciscan habit, prayed next to him.

The doctors went under the middle gallows and pronounced Keitel dead. The British reporter leaned toward Kingsbury Smith and whispered, "That took forever."

Rosenberg died wordless. Frank faced his executioners with the beatific smile of a man happy to throw off the burden of life. Frick stumbled on the top step and had to be caught.

A commotion broke out at the entrance to the gym. Two GIs propelled a resistant Julius Streicher through the gym door. Back in his cell, the guards had had to force Streicher into his clothes. At the foot of the gallows, he refused to give the American colonel his name, screeching instead, "Heil Hitler!" "For the love of God, Julius," Father O'Connor pleaded, "tell them your name and get it over with." Streicher shouted, "*Purim Fest*, 1946," and then, turning to Sergeant

Woods, said, "Someday, the Bolsheviks will hang you!" After Strei-cher disappeared through the trapdoor, an eerie moan persisted. Woods descended the steps and vanished behind the curtain. Soon the moaning stopped.

Albert Speer, from his cell on the second tier, could hear the guards call out the names, one by one. This time it was "Sauckel." He heard the familiar thud of the prison door slamming shut.

Standing on the gallows, eyes darting wildly, Fritz Sauckel cried out, "I am dying an innocent man!" Jodl arrived with the collar of his tunic sticking up in the back. He licked his lips nervously as Woods slipped the hood over his head. The last to die was Arthur Seyss-Inquart, at 2:45 a.m.

Four GIs came into the gym bearing a stretcher covered by an army blanket. They set the stretcher down between the first two gal-lows. The American colonel asked the witnesses to come forward. As they did, he pulled off the blanket and revealed the corpse of Hermann Göring. Hoegner, the minister president of Bavaria, muttered, "The scoundrel. He should be hanged anyway." The British reporter whis-pered to Smith, "Only Germans can hate so, and then only one an-other."

Lieutenant Maurice McLaughlin, the Third Army photographer, stepped behind the curtain. No one was to doubt that these men were dead, the Quadripartite Commission had told him. McLaughlin in-serted the first flashbulb and began shooting Göring, one frontal, one left side, one right side, one naked. As he worked, he noticed bloody bruises about the mouths and noses of several of the bodies.

The reporters in the pressroom had been waiting throughout the night. Now, as dawn approached, the place was a shambles of paper cups half full of cold coffee, the remains of sandwiches, cigarette butts, and sleeping bodies coiled in corners or stretched out on tables. The last desultory card game had broken up long before. In the first few hours, the room had been a babel of speculation, interrupted by phone calls from bureau chiefs demanding to know why their reporters had not yet filed. When word raced through the pressroom that Dana, the German agency, had broken a story that all the war criminals had been executed, the pressure became unbearable. The correspondent of the London *News Chronicle* began pounding out a gripping eyewitness account of Hermann Göring mounting the gallows. One by one, others submitted their stories. The piece by the New York *Herald Tribune*'s correspondent produced an early-edition headline: 11 NAZI CHIEFS HANGED IN NUREMBERG PRISON: GOERING AND HENCHMEN PAY FOR WAR CRIMES. The AP's Thomas Reedy held out against repeated howling from his chief in New York that everybody was scooping him. Reedy resisted. As the hours passed, the pressroom had gradually died down. Suddenly, someone shouted, "Andrus is coming!" and the room shook itself back to life.

The colonel had spent the night with the investigating board trying to piece together Göring's last movements. He then had gone to his office to draft a statement. Finally, he braced himself for the inevitable confrontation with the press corps. He had been awake for nearly twenty-four hours. His skin was pale and mottled, his eyes redrimmed. He had a prepared statement, he announced. "Göring was not hanged," he began. "He committed suicide last night by taking cyanide of potassium. He was discovered at once by the sentinel who watched him make an odd noise and twitch. The sentinel called the doctor and chaplain. There were pieces of glass in his mouth and an odor of cyanide of potassium." Groans and shouts went up from several reporters who bolted for the phones and telegraph office to correct their stories. The rest continued pelting Andrus with questions. How good had the colonel's security been? Hadn't he said the prisoners couldn't breathe without his knowing it? Wasn't Göring the third prisoner he had lost? Andrus refused to answer questions.

Back in his office, he slumped into his chair. His conviction was that the suicide demonstrated Göring's cowardice, the man's inability to face his fate. But others, he knew, would simply conclude that the Nuremberg jailer had been outfoxed. He pulled himself together and began moving slowly down the corridor to go home and confront his own self-flagellating demons.

Later, Robert Jackson would issue a public statement praising Colonel Andrus as "a fine officer in a difficult task" who had been "diligent and intelligent and in all respects faithful to his trust." The colonel treasured the words.

It was still dark when two army six-by-six trucks pulled alongside the gym. The eleven coffins were quickly loaded. The trucks pulled away escorted by two unmarked cars bearing armed guards. By seven a.m., the small caravan had arrived at a forbidding gray stone building in East Munich's Ostfriedhof Cemetery. The German attendants had been alerted that the bodies of several American soldiers, killed during the war, would be arriving for cremation. Each coffin bore a label. The one marked "George Munger" held the body of Hermann Göring.

When the cremations were completed, including nooses and hoods, the ashes were taken to a white stucco villa in the Munich suburb of Solln. The house, which had once belonged to a wealthy merchant, was now the U.S. Army's European Theater Mortuary Number One. Shortly afterward, a group of army officers stood on the bank of the Contwentzbach, a stream running behind the house. They watched the mortuary staff bring down eleven aluminum cylinders. One by one the ashes were emptied into the water. The cylinders were chopped with axes and smashed flat with boot heels. The Contwentzbach carried the ashes into the Isar River, which conducted them to the Danube, which emptied them into the sea. The Quadripartite Commission had fulfilled its aim, to obliterate any corporeal trace of these men and any relic around which a shrine to Nazism might rise.

Master Sergeant John Woods was enjoying the glow of celebrity. Woods had been brought back to the Stein Castle to hold his first press conference. The coarse red face beamed. "I hanged those ten Nazis and I'm proud of it," he said. "I did a good job of it too. Everything clicked. I hanged 347 people and I never saw one go off better. I wasn't nervous. I haven't got any nerves. A fellow can't afford to have nerves in this business." What had he done immediately after the executions? a reporter asked. "Had me and my boys a stiff drink." He smiled. "We earned it."

Cecil Catling, veteran crime reporter for the *London Star*, asked Woods about reports that an unconscionable amount of time had elapsed before some of the men were pronounced dead—seventeen minutes for Ribbentrop, eighteen minutes for Jodl, a startling twenty-eight minutes for Keitel. He further had it on good authority, Catling said, that some of the men's faces were smashed. Woods looked briefly uncomfortable. Any noises heard from hanged men were reflex reactions, as any doctor could confirm, he said. And the blood? "Perfectly natural. That happens when the condemned man bites his tongue at the moment of the drop." Someone tossed the sergeant a noose and asked him to pose for photographs. He held the rope in powerful hands and smiled into the flashing lights.

What did Catling think of Woods's performance? his colleagues asked later. Rubbish, Catling said. The men had not been properly tied, nor had they been dropped from a sufficient height. He had witnessed enough hangings to know that they had not experienced the instant unconsciousness of a broken neck, but death by strangulation. Catling likely had it right. The army never used Master Sergeant Woods as a hangman again.

While the remaining prisoners awaited transfer to their new home, Spandau prison, a medieval fortress in Berlin, they were dispatched to clean up the recently vacated first-tier cells. Mess trays bearing the remains of the last meal still rested on cots and tables. Papers and bedding lay scattered about. Only Keitel's and Jodl's cells were immaculate, blankets neatly folded at the foot of each bed. Speer noticed that Seyss-Inquart had marked October 16 on his wall calendar with a penciled cross.

Speer, Schirach, and Hess were sent to mop the gym. Sunlight flooded through windows that had been blacked out during the executions. The light fell mercilessly on the wooden floor where the gallows had stood. They came upon a brown-red stain. Blood, Speer thought. He had difficulty maintaining his composure. Hess stood on the spot, clicked his heels, and raised his arm in the Nazi salute. Was it an act of mockery, madness, or sincerity? Speer wondered. With Hess, one never knew.

13

IN AMERICA AND EUROPE, those who had conducted the trial, the prosecutors and judges, watched their monumental effort disfigured at the last moment by a Nazi's cunning. The wrong headline had come out of Nuremberg—not JUSTICE TRIUMPHS, but GÖRING CHEATS HANGMAN. The trial had been intended to convict and punish the guilty, and, more loftily, to deter future aggressors. But it had had another objective: to force the German people to recognize the horrendous fruits of Hitler and Nazism. The day after the executions, John Stanton, *Time* magazine's Nuremberg correspondent, had gone into the streets to sample reactions. He found the Germans "suddenly straightened up. Men with eyes glistening stopped for excited talks with one another. . . . Germans who had avoided the eyes of Americans the night before, now looked at them frankly, with derisive smiles." Suddenly Göring was "our Hermann," the one who had "put one over" on Germany's conquerors. "Goering's dramatic gesture in death appeared to have helped these Germans forget his crimes," *The New York Times* editorialized. "The weapon that was to have been a weapon in the hands of democracy suddenly became one in the hands of unrepentant German nationalists."

A favorite Göring theme throughout the trial had been that the Soviet alliance with the West was a wartime shotgun marriage, doomed to failure. In death, he contributed to the breakup. Russian officials began speculating aloud that the Americans had connived to help Göring salvage his reputation and honor from ignominy.

Ten days after the executions, on October 26, the Quadripartite Commission released its public report on the suicide, a terse one-page statement. The commission fully endorsed the findings of its three-man investigating board. The members accepted Göring's claim that the cyanide capsule had always been in his possession. The commission accepted the investigating board's opinion that at various times Göring had secreted the capsule inside the toilet bowl, in his alimentary tract, and in the cavity of his umbilicus. The commission exonerated the cell guard on duty and all other prison personnel of negligence. "The security measures taken were proper in the peculiar conditions of the trial and were satisfactorily carried out," the commission's statement concluded.

The commission chose not to release the detailed top secret report of the investigators' findings. Nor did it reveal the existence of Göring's suicide notes. In their unpublished report, the investigators had described Göring as "clever and unrepentant . . . a subtle individual who outwitted his guards by clever maneuvering." The implication was that a round-the-clock detachment of approximately 120 men guarding one cellblock, carrying out strict regulations including constant surveillance and frequent searches, was no match for one crafty man locked in a cell.

As for the vaunted security, cell assignments had not been changed for a year. No rectal examinations had been made for six months. Göring had said in his note to the colonel that he had another cartridge concealed in a jar of face cream in his toiletry case. The investigating board found it, demonstrating that the defendants' baggage had never been thoroughly searched. PFC Bill Glenny later confided that many guards, like himself, had found the regulations— shining lights in sleeping men's faces, poking them if they slept facing the wall, forcing them to keep hands above the blankets, prohibiting conversation—to be "unrealistic," and had not uniformly enforced them.

Army laboratory tests confirmed that, at some point, the cartridge containing the fatal capsule had been secreted in Göring's rectum, since traces of fecal matter were found on it. The investigating board further determined that the cartridge could be temporarily hidden in the flush pipe of the toilet. And rips were found in Göring's mattress after the suicide which had not been there before.

The investigating board interrogated only five persons: Andrus; his deputy, Major Teich; Dr. Pfluecker; Dr. Roska; and Robert Starnes, the chief prison officer. Sworn statements were taken from thirty-four more prison personnel. Tex Wheelis's statement read: "I have had in my possession the key to the baggage room of the prison during the period 10 October 1946 to 15 October 1946 and can state positively that Göring received nothing from, nor had access to the baggage room during this period." It was a form statement identical to one signed by ten other officers who also had access to the baggage room. Neither Wheelis nor the other nine were questioned personally. The fact that two of three officers on the board were members of Andrus's staff left the impression that the ISD had investigated itself.

Those familiar with the ways of bureaucracies recognized what the army had done. Of course, an investigation had to be conducted; but the objective had not necessarily been to reveal the truth and punish the derelict. That, by extension, would be to rebuke the American army. British and French members of the Quadripartite Commission had no wish to embarrass brother officers. The only member likely to dispute the findings was the Soviet general, Malkov. And the commission's report was issued while he was conveniently away on business in Berlin.

Göring had made it easy for the commission. In his note to Andrus, he had explained how he had done it. Hence, a more penetrating inquiry was unnecessary. What would it have said about the U.S. Army had it been found that a POW trusty, or infinitely worse, a member of the American prison staff, had helped Hermann Göring commit suicide? Göring had neatly foreclosed that conclusion by exonerating everybody in advance. His access to the poison, he claimed, was the result of his own ingenuity. And the army accepted his explanation.

In Washington, Robert Jackson pondered the effect of Göring's dramatic exit on the work of the IMT. Undeniably, the suicide occupied center stage for the moment. But in time to come? The court had delivered its verdict on the accused with some dispatch, in less than a year. History would take far longer, he knew, to deliver its verdict on the IMT. The court's mission had been unprecedented—too novel, too far-reaching for contemporary judgment. Only time and its perspective could unveil the enduring meaning, if any, of those eleven months in room 600.

THE VERDICT
OF TIME

DID IT MATTER? Viewed through the lens of almost half a century, what was the significance of the events of Nuremberg 1945–1946? Did the trial, at the time, fairly judge the men brought before it? Did its grander objective of deterring aggression succeed? Did subsequent warmakers fear the measured fury of the law? Did Nuremberg bequeath permanent legal machinery for dealing with future war criminals?

The answers are not inspiring. The validity of the court is still debated. Criticisms that the IMT lacked jurisdiction, that it was imposing ex post facto law, and that it tried only the losers all contain seeds of truth. An editorial in *Fortune* magazine, written at the time, raised the point that, given the destructive power of the atomic bomb, it was futile to argue that there were "legal and proper as against illegal and improper" ways to kill hundreds of thousands of innocent people. The point is not easily gainsaid. Yet Nuremberg's defenders counter that the atomic bomb, however devastating, was used to end a war. The death factories operated by Nazi Germany exterminated people from nations already defeated. A war ending in German victory would certainly not have meant an end to mass murder, but its unfettered continuation.

The dilemma the victors faced at the time was simply to determine what to do after the Nazis had caused the deliberate deaths of some six million Jews and millions of others in killings divorced from any military necessity. Could the Allies merely walk away from murder so vast and so calculated? Critics, including Winston Churchill, continued to maintain, even after the trial, that the Nazi leaders should have been shot outright. That solution had a certain rough appeal. Yet, if it was wrong to punish people because the trial machinery was less than perfect, how could it be right to punish them with no trial at all? Senator Robert Taft, a conservative American leader of that era, and the British political scientist Harold Laski debated Nuremberg at Kenyon College in Ohio just days after the verdicts were handed down. Taft believed that "the trial of the vanquished by the victors cannot be impartial no matter how it is hedged about with the forms of law." He branded the death sentences "a miscarriage of justice that the American people will live to regret." A student in the audience asked, "What would you have done with these criminals?" Taft answered, "Life imprisonment, the same as Napoleon." "If it is proper to send a man to life in prison in an ex post facto proceeding," Laski retorted, "it is no more improper to hang him."

The IMT's legitimacy can be attacked on purist legal grounds. But once it was created, how fair a trial did the defendants receive? Germany was scoured to provide them with any German lawyer they wanted, including Nazis. The defense attorneys were paid and granted special privileges by the court. They were provided with secretarial, stenographic, and translation services, and with office space, at no cost. They enjoyed virtually unlimited time with their clients. They had access to all the documents in the hands of the prosecution. As Herbert Wechsler, Francis Biddle's aide, put it, "I just wish the average impecunious defendant in an American court could count on assistance as extensive in the preparation of his defense as those men enjoyed."

The wisdom of the individual verdicts can be debated endlessly. The indictment of Hans Fritzsche, a propagandist not even on the outer rim of the inner circle, was a pure concession to the Soviet Union. And Fritzsche was right; had Goebbels lived, Fritzsche would never have been tried. But Fritzsche was acquitted. More troublesome is the execution of Julius Streicher. Today, we are still debating whether violence in films and television induces violent behavior in audiences, and we do not have an answer. Was there a path that led from the rabid anti-Semitism of Streicher's *Der Stürmer* to the gas chambers at Auschwitz? Streicher and his works were loathsome. But one can ask, with Francis Biddle, is loathsomeness a capital offense?

Alfred Rosenberg's situation parallels Streicher's, to a point. Then they part. Streicher preached raw anti-Semitism. Rosenberg concocted a pseudosophisticated anti-Semitic philosophy. But Rosenberg was also the minister of the brutally subjugated Occupied Eastern Territories, where the lethal racial policies he had helped author were put into practice. Rosenberg did not disavow these policies, only their barbaric implementation.

Clearly, the most unfair verdict involved the treatment of Sauckel relative to that of Speer. Given the death and suffering inflicted by the forced labor system, few would argue that Sauckel should have been punished less severely, but rather that Speer should have been punished equally. Between slave trader and slave master, one discerns scant moral superiority. In sending Sauckel to die and allowing Speer to live, the court, consciously or unconsciously, made a class judgment.

Hjalmar Schacht may have felt unlucky when the Nazis clapped him into Dachau. The experience, however, saved him. Absent this badge of honor, and given Jackson's will to convict him, it is difficult to imagine that a lesser minister of economics, such as Walther Funk, would get life, while the man whose financial prowess enabled Hitler to come to power and rearm Germany would go free.

Many at Nuremberg believed Rudolf Hess insane and unfit for trial. Yet one cannot read the literally hundreds of letters that this man wrote, from the time of his internment in England in 1941, throughout the trial, and during the Spandau years, without concluding that here was a clear mind at work. If there was anything mad about Rudolf Hess it was his decision to act mad for nearly half a century. As for his guilt on the merits, if the conspiracy count had any validity, Hess, a founding Nazi, was certainly guilty.

But did the conspiracy count have validity? It was the charge least appreciated by the judges themselves; it required a tremendous stretch of the evidence to prove; and it risked ridicule because the defendants obviously had not been independent partners but henchmen in Hitler's thrall. And, viewed practically, the conspiracy charge was unnecessary. Had the Nazis conspired but never made war, obviously no trial would have ensued. As it turned out, not one defendant was charged only with conspiracy, and none was convicted solely of conspiracy. It was committing aggression, not scheming to commit it, that doomed them.

And the enormous effort invested in trying the organizations? When Murray Bernays first hatched the idea, its purpose was to provide a legal weapon against the thousands of rank-and-file who had knowingly and willingly done Hitler's dirtiest work. It is difficult to imagine an injured world simply turning away from an organization like the Gestapo, or from the assembly-line foremen who ran the death camps. At the time that Bernays's idea was accepted, however, no denazification machinery for reviewing low-level cases had yet been envisioned. The best that can be said is that, as it turned out, the trial of the organizations was not vital.

The military verdicts discomfited professional soldiers in nations other than Germany who could imagine themselves in Keitel's, Jodl's, Dönitz's, or Raeder's boots. Keitel was foredoomed by his position as chief of staff of the armed forces. But Jodl, had he managed to escape the major war criminals list, would likely not have paid with his life in the subsequent trials. In a later High Command case, six officers of equal or superior rank, though none so close to Hitler as Jodl, were convicted of the same offenses that had doomed him. Their sentences ranged from three years to life; and as the Allies began to commute sentences wholesale in the fifties, none of these men came close to serving a full life term.

It is difficult to reconcile Admiral Raeder's life sentence with one of ten years for Admiral Dönitz, except that Raeder had been Dönitz's superior until January 1943, and was thus responsible for his subordinate's acts as well as his own. Raeder had also been among the handful of top leaders to hear Hitler declare his aggressive intentions at the Hossbach Conference; and Raeder had stayed on after hearing it. In the end, the aging admiral served nine years of his life sentence.

The trial, in the final analysis, raises the distinction between law and justice. No saint or statesman lost his life or his freedom at Nuremberg. All the men who went to prison or mounted the gallows were willing, knowing, and energetic accomplices in a vast and malignant enterprise. They were all there for valid moral, if not technically perfect legal, reasons; but then, the murderer who gets off on a technicality has experienced law, not justice. The execution of a professional hate-monger like Julius Streicher, if legally debatable, does not begin to compare with the injustice done to a five-year-old sent to a gas chamber, an end encouraged by Streicher's race preachments. It can be argued that evil unpunished deprives us of a sense of moral symmetry in life, and that to punish evil has a healthy cathartic effect, confirming our belief in the ultimate triumph of good over evil. Nuremberg may have been flawed law, but it was satisfying justice.

But what of the long-term residue? Did the trial have any lasting impact beyond deciding the fate of twenty-one individuals? If so, were those effects salutary? The Nuremberg legacy is mixed. The one indisputable good to come out of the trial is that, to any sentient person, it documented beyond question Nazi Germany's crimes. To those old enough to remember personally the first horrifying film images of piles of pallid corpses being bulldozed into mass graves, it is hard to believe that this evidence of our eyes would ever be challenged. However, two generations have had time to grow up with no personal knowledge of World War II. Polls have shown that as many as twenty-two percent of all Americans doubt the Holocaust as historic fact. These people are prey to the revisionists—crackpots at best, masked racists at worst—who argue that the Holocaust is a Jewish-inspired hoax, that if people did die in concentration camps, they were few, not millions, and the causes were disease and wartime food shortages. One cannot know of the forty-two-volume transcript of the Nuremberg trial, the hundreds of official German documents, the Mauthausen "death books," the boastful reports of improved productivity in gas chambers and crematoria, the signed extermination orders, the films taken by German cameramen, the testimony of German witnesses like Ohlendorf and Hoess, in short the whole crushing weight of *German* evidence and not believe that it all happened, just as the Nazis themselves recorded it. Not a single defendant at Nuremberg ever denied that the mass killing had taken place, only that he had lacked personal knowledge and responsibility.

Another reward of Nuremberg was to destroy any Nazi dreams of martyrdom. Hermann Göring's predictions of grand statues in public squares and statuettes in every home never materialized. After World War II, no cries were heard about brave German soldiers stabbed in the back by homefront politicians, as were heard after World War I. The Third Reich was a foul creation, and the revelations at Nuremberg made that fact palpable.

Did Nuremberg contribute to a democratic Germany? Arguably yes, despite the disturbing emergence of neo-Nazis on the desperate edge of German political life today. Since World War II, no avowed Nazis have won significant public office in Germany. It cannot be assumed that the same flowering of democracy would have occurred had the Nazi leaders been shot out of hand, and had the revelations of the trial thus never become so public. Willy Brandt, who covered the trial as a journalist, managed to become West Germany's chancellor—a man who had turned his back not only on Nazism but on Germany itself in the Nazi era, and who had taken Norwegian citizenship. It is unlikely that Brandt could have come home and risen so high in a Germany spared the truths confirmed by the trial. He more likely would have been condemned as a traitor, not elected as leader.

But what of the brightest hope of the trial? Did it ever deter a single would-be aggressor? Did it lead to a permanent international tribunal where crimes against peace and crimes against humanity would be tried? Between 1945 and 1992, the world experienced twenty-four wars between nations, costing 6,623,000 civilian and military lives. Ninety-three civil wars, wars of independence, and insurgencies have cost 15,513,000 additional lives. Until 1993, no international instrument had been convened to try any aggressor or any perpetrator of war crimes in any of these 117 conflicts. Virtually all war-crimes trials that have occurred since Nuremberg were for offenses committed in World War II; and these trials have been conducted by individual nations, not international bodies. They have included the prosecution of Adolf Eichmann and John Demjanjuk in Israel and Klaus Barbie in France. In one of the few non–World War II trials, a U.S. military tribunal sentenced Lieutenant William Calley to life imprisonment for his role in the Vietnam My Lai massacre. But Calley's sentence was soon commuted.

Sites of savage depredations against the innocent can be found almost by sticking a pin in a map: in Algeria in the sixties; in Cambodia and Uganda in the seventies; in El Salvador, Nicaragua, and Beirut in the eighties; in the former Yugoslavia in the nineties. The two million to four million Cambodians exterminated by the Pol Pot regime between 1979 and 1981 proportionately exceeded the victims of the Holocaust in Europe. As for crimes against peace, the likelihood of anyone's being prosecuted for committing aggression has been even more remote than for committing atrocities. Aggression appears to be in the eye of the definer. The old Soviet Union crushed liberation movements in East Germany, Hungary, Czechoslovakia, and Poland, and invaded Afghanistan. America's critics would find elements of aggression in the U.S. interventions in Lebanon, the Dominican Republic, Cuba, Grenada, Panama, Libya, and Vietnam.

Less than a month after the executions at Nuremberg, the UN General Assembly unanimously adopted Resolution 95(I), affirming "the principles of International Law recognized by the Charter of the Nuremberg Tribunal and the judgment of the Tribunal." Until virtually yesterday, they remained no more than principles. They were never applied to any nation or individual. Then, in 1992, the ghost of Nuremberg began to stir. On October 6, the UN Security Council voted unanimously to establish a commission to collect evidence of war crimes in the former Yugoslavia. The actions, initially of Serbia and her irredentists, of annihilation, deportation, incarceration, and rape of the Muslims in Bosnia, under the chillingly familiar cry of "ethnic cleansing" (Hitler's call had been "to cleanse the world of Jewish poison"), outraged world opinion. On February 22, 1993, the UN Security Council again voted unanimously, this time to create an international war-crimes tribunal to prosecute atrocities perpetrated in the same region. Prosecution of aggression, however—the larger issue on which the legal pioneers of Nuremberg pinned their hopes —is left untouched by these actions.

Still, until this moment, the example of Nuremberg had remained what a philosopher called "a beautiful idea murdered by a gang of ugly facts." The recent UN initiatives raise cautious hopes that reports of this murder may have been exaggerated. By its very occurrence in the past, Nuremberg increases the prospects for effective war-crimes trials in our time. The denunciations that plagued that tribunal—that it was an ex post facto proceeding, that it lacked jurisdiction, that it amounted to victor's vengeance—need not be heard again. The world now has a legal precedent, set in the Palace of Justice almost half a century ago. Law that supersedes nations, and justice that penetrates frontiers may yet be achieved. But, history teaches us, not easily.

APPENDIX
The Göring Suicide: An Unclosed File

THE PRECISE DETAILS of Hermann Göring's suicide can no more be known than those of the perennially debated Kennedy and Lincoln assassinations. In all these cases, certain facts have vanished in the mist of history or have been lost to the grave. The reconstruction of Göring's suicide described here likely comes as close as the knowable evidence permits. My information has been drawn largely from files provided by the Berlin Documents Center, a key repository of material on the Nazi era. These files include the top secret report of the investigating board, which was not released at the time of the suicide, the testimony of witnesses on the scene, medical reports, and the original Göring suicide notes (all four of which were made available to the author). Ben E. Swearingen's *The Mystery of Hermann Goering's Suicide* is the most thorough study of the question to date, an admirable work of historical detection invaluable to anyone writing on this subject.

That the cyanide capsule initially entered the prison with Göring's luggage appears beyond dispute. It is not credible that he kept it in his cell throughout his captivity. It would have been foolhardy to do so, except during the very last hours. The baggage room, we know, had not been thoroughly searched, because the investigators did find another cyanide capsule there in Göring's belongings after his suicide. Cells and clothing had been searched, and fairly often, according to this author's interviews with guards and an examination of prison records. First Lieutenant John West carried out just such a search of Göring's cell and his personal possessions on October 14, 1946, the day before the man's death.

Though the prison logs do not show that Göring ever asked permission to visit the baggage room, we know that possessions of his were removed from time to time, as evidenced by the gifts he gave Lieutenant Wheelis and the blue briefcase he gave to his lawyer, Otto

Stahmer. These were obtained either by a prison officer who, like Wheelis, possessed the baggage-room key, or by Göring, who might have been admitted to the room without the visit's being logged as required.

Subsequent statements by Emmy Göring as to how her husband obtained the capsule are not helpful or convincing. On her last visit to her husband, on October 7, 1946, she asked if he had the capsule yet, to which Göring answered no. She never saw or spoke to him again. Immediately after the suicide she speculated to a reporter that "it must have been an American friend who did it." But twenty-eight years later she told Robert Kempner, the German-American prosecution staff member, that an unspecified friend *definitely* passed her husband the poison. Thus, her memory appeared to have improved over time. Later still, her daughter, Edda, hinted that someone had helped her father. A hearsay 1991 report has it that Klaus Riegele, a Göring nephew, admitted that it was Lieutenant Wheelis who gave his uncle the poison. This is possible, but not provable. Neither Göring's daughter, who was eight years old at the time of his death, nor his nephew could be any more certain of what had happened than their likely source, Emmy Göring, had been. Prison mates who might have known and lived to tell—Speer, Fritzsche, Pfluecker—all later wrote about their Nuremberg experiences, and it is unlikely that they would have omitted this book-selling bombshell from their accounts, had they known of it.

This author's conclusion is that Göring had conditioned a member of the prison staff, most likely Wheelis, to take items or pieces of luggage from the baggage room for him. And in the last such retrieval, Göring withdrew a hidden capsule. Alternatively, he himself could have been allowed into the baggage room, again most likely by Wheelis, and have been left there to his own devices. It is harder to believe that any American with access to the baggage room, including Wheelis, would knowingly have retrieved the capsule and have given it to Göring, thus enabling the major surviving war criminal of World War II to thwart justice. To have done so would have been a criminal act risking serious punishment. The character of Wheelis appears capable of foolishness, but not of criminality.

Why Göring dated his suicide notes October 11, 1946, remains a mystery. The date cannot be correct. It would have been reckless for Göring to have kept in his possession for five days letters revealing that he planned suicide. In two of the letters he makes reference to the decision on his appeal to the Allied Control Council, which he did not learn of until October 13. A further puzzle is why he felt the need to write the letter to Andrus saying that he had always had the capsule, unless it was to clear friends and to crow over outwitting his chief antagonist.

The years have produced a stream of explanations of the Göring suicide: the poison was hidden in his clay pipe, which he broke open on execution night; he hid it in his navel (which Dr. Roska declared physically impossible); he swallowed it (which the investigating board believed); and more bizarre solutions. Obviously, all hope of incontrovertible truth is lost when the only man in possession of it not only takes his secret to the grave, but releases a cloud of misinformation in his wake.

At least eleven prison personnel were in reasonably close contact with Göring the day he died. On other days, that number could reach as high as twenty-six. The possibilities are infinite. But the number is quickly thinned by probability. What actually happened may differ from the reconstruction offered here, but only in details that do not change the essential thrust—that the capsule was in the baggage room, and Göring managed to take it out or have it brought to him. The author, of course, assumes sole responsibility for the validity of this explanation.

AFTERMATH

What is known of the subsequent lives of principal figures in the trial:

Burton C. ANDRUS: Retired from the army; became a professor of geography and business administration at the University of Puget Sound in Tacoma, Washington; died in 1977, at the age of eighty-five. (In his final hours, he cried out, "Göring's just committed suicide. I must inform the Council.")

Roger BARRETT: Returned to practice law in Chicago.

Francis BIDDLE: Retired; wrote his autobiography, *In Brief Authority*; died in 1968 at age eighty-two.

Norman BIRKETT: Entered the House of Lords in 1947; died in 1962 at age seventy-nine.

Martin BORMANN: Remains were tentatively identified in Berlin in 1972; declared legally dead in 1973 by a West German court.

Walter BRUDNO: Returned to practice law in Texas.

Harold BURSON: Founded Burson Marsteller, a public-relations firm in New York.

Ray D'ADDARIO: Returned to Holyoke, Massachusetts; built a business in camera and gift shops.

Thomas DODD: Served as Connecticut Democratic member of the House of Representatives, 1953–1957; U.S. senator, 1959–1971; died, 1971.

Karl DÖNITZ: Served his ten-year sentence at Spandau prison; died in 1981 at the age of eighty-nine.

Leon DOSTERT: Returned to the language department of Georgetown University; reportedly developed the simultaneous-translation system for the United Nations.

Edgar FAURE: Became premier of France.

Theodore FENSTERMACHER: Returned to practice law in Cortland, N.Y.

Hans FRITZSCHE: After his acquittal at Nuremberg, was convicted by a German court; freed in 1950; died in 1953 at age fifty-three.

Moritz FUCHS: Ordained a Catholic priest in 1955.

Walther FUNK: After serving eleven years of a life sentence, released from Spandau in 1957 for reasons of poor health; died two years later at age sixty-nine.

Gustav GILBERT: Completed his book, *Nuremberg Diary*, which came out shortly after Douglas Kelley's book (see below); pursued a teaching and writing career in psychology; died in 1977 at age sixty-five.

Whitney HARRIS: Returned to practice law in St. Louis; wrote *Tyranny on Trial* on the Nuremberg trial.

Richard HELLER: Returned to practice law in New York City.

Rudolf HESS: Spent the rest of his life in Spandau prison; supposedly died by his own hand in 1987 at age ninety-three. (Hess's son believed he was murdered to prevent his divulging information on his flight to Scotland.)

Rudolf HOESS: Hanged by Polish authorities at Auschwitz in 1947.

Charles HORSKY: Continued to practice law in Washington, D.C.

Robert JACKSON: Returned to the U.S. Supreme Court; served until his death in 1954 at age sixty-two.

William E. JACKSON: Returned to practice law in New York City.

Ingeborg KALNOKY: Rejoined by her husband and emigrated to the United States.

Douglas KELLEY: His book, *22 Cells at Nuremberg*, was published shortly before Gustav Gilbert's book; he committed suicide on New Year's Day in 1957, reportedly with a cyanide capsule brought back from Nuremberg.

Robert KEMPNER: Returned to live in Germany; reportedly established a practice representing Jewish clients in Nazi restitution cases.

Daniel KILEY: Returned to become an award-winning architect, including the rebuilding of Pennsylvania Avenue in Washington, D.C.

Otto KRANZBUEHLER: Defended German industrialists in subsequent war-crimes trials; later developed a corporate law practice.

Thomas LAMBERT, Jr.: Became head of the American Trial Lawyers Association; taught law.

Geoffrey LAWRENCE: Elevated to the peerage for his work at Nuremberg, becoming Baron Oaksey; died in 1971.

Daniel MARGOLIES: Joined the U.S. State Department; worked on the German peace treaty.

David MAXWELL-FYFE: Elevated to the peerage, becoming Earl Kilmuir.

Airey NEAVE: Became a conservative member of Parliament; campaigned for the release of Rudolf Hess; became a key advisor to Prime Minister Margaret Thatcher; killed by an IRA car bomb in 1980.

Konstantin von NEURATH: Served seven years of a fifteen-year sentence; released for reasons of poor health in 1954; died two years later at age eighty-three.

Ion Timofeevich NIKITCHENKO: Nothing known beyond a Soviet report of his death several years after the trial.

Otto OHLENDORF: Convicted at a subsequent trial in Nuremberg; hanged with three other *Einsatzgruppen* commanders in 1951.

Friedrich PAULUS: Returned to the Soviet Union; went to live in East Germany in 1953; died in 1957.

Erich RAEDER: Served nine years of a life sentence; released in 1955 at age eighty; died in 1960 at age eighty-four.

James ROWE: Returned to practice law with fellow New Dealer Thomas Corcoran; participated in Democratic political campaigns; died in 1984.

Roman RUDENKO: Became chief prosecutor of the Soviet Union; prosecuted the American U-2 pilot, Gary Powers, shot down over the Soviet Union in 1960.

Gunther SADEL: Settled in Washington, D.C., and developed an insurance business.

Hjalmar SCHACHT: After his acquittal at Nuremberg, was sentenced to eight years by a German court; was cleared on appeal in 1950; died in 1970 at age ninety-three.

Baldur von SCHIRACH: Served his twenty-year sentence; released from Spandau prison in 1966; died in 1974 at age sixty-seven.

Robert SERVATIUS: Returned to private practice; defended Adolf Eichmann at the latter's war-crimes trial in Israel in 1961.

Sir Hartley SHAWCROSS: Left his career in Labour party politics; became a successful corporate lawyer.

Albert SPEER: Served his twenty-year sentence; released from Spandau prison in 1966; wrote two books on his life; died in 1981 at age seventy-six.

Drexel SPRECHER: Stayed on in Nuremberg to become, eventually, chief prosecutor at the subsequent trials; returned to the United

States in 1952 as a government lawyer; served as deputy chairman of the Democratic party.

Alfred STEER: Taught languages at Columbia University and the University of Georgia; authored several books on Goethe.

Robert STOREY: Became dean of the Southern Methodist Law Center and president of the American Bar Association.

Telford TAYLOR: After serving as chief prosecutor at subsequent Nuremberg proceedings, returned to the United States to practice law, teach, and write; in 1992, published his account of the major Nuremberg trial.

Peter UIBERALL: Served as a career officer in the U.S. Army.

Marie Claude VAILLANT-COUTURIER: Became a member of the French Senate.

Herbert WECHSLER: Returned to the Columbia University law faculty; taught and wrote.

Jack G. "Tex" WHEELIS: Served with the army in Korea and later as an ROTC instructor; died of a heart attack in 1954 at the age of forty-one.

John WOODS: Killed serving with the U.S. Army during the Korean War, reportedly in an accident involving a high-tension wire.

ACKNOWLEDGMENTS

EARLY IN WRITING the story of Nuremberg, I was fortunate enough to find, through the Nuremberg alumni directory, Drexel Sprecher, a prosecutor at the main trial and at the subsequent trials, and a scholar of those events ever since. Drex Sprecher was the soul of generosity in the time he granted me for extensive interviews, leads to other interviewees, and loans from his comprehensive personal Nuremberg library. He became not only a mainstay, but a good friend. Another indispensable contributor has been Colonel Burton Andrus, Jr. (USAF Ret.), son of the Nuremberg prison commandant, who for over forty-five years has maintained his father's personal files, an invaluable source. I owe Burt Andrus an unpayable debt of gratitude for opening those files to me. In them I was able to locate much material never before used. I am also grateful to Burt for introducing me to Duane J. Reed, chief of the special collections branch at the U.S. Air Force Academy library, who managed to locate Nuremberg-related photographs for me.

I owe a special debt to the distinguished broadcast journalist Howard K. Smith and his wife, Benedicte. Mr. Smith was generous in sharing his memories as one of the first newsmen on the scene at Nuremberg. Mrs. Smith obligingly ransacked their personal papers to produce her husband's broadcasts and letters from Nuremberg, a priceless trove. Harold Burson, who covered the trial for the Armed Forces Network, generously provided me with all his broadcasts for that period.

The Nuremberg lode at the National Archives in Washington amounts to thousands upon thousands of files. For helping me thread my way through that wealth of material and for pursuing my special requests, I am grateful for the cooperation of Robert Wolfe, Robin E. Cookson, and William Cunliffe of the archives' Captured German Records staff.

At the Library of Congress I again benefited from the wise guidance of my friend Margrit Krewson, of the German branch. As with my other books, Mrs. Krewson was again relentless in unearthing hard-to-locate materials for me.

My research took me to several other libraries and archives where people were unstinting of their time and expertise. These include Carolyn Davis and Karin D'Agostino at the Syracuse University Archives, where I worked with the papers of Francis Biddle, American justice on the Nuremberg tribunal; David Marwell, director of the Berlin Document Center, who provided me with heretofore unpublished Nuremberg material; Elizabeth Denier of the Franklin Delano Roosevelt Library, where the papers of James Rowe, a key Nuremberg figure, are held; Richard J. Sommers and his staff at the Military History Institute in Carlisle, Pennsylvania; Bernard Cavalcante of the Naval Historical Center, who helped me track missing persons; Father Julian Davies of the Franciscans, at Siena College, Albany, New York; the staff of the Columbia University Oral History Project; and Gunter Bischoff of the Eisenhower Center at the University of New Orleans.

Jean Hargrave of the New York State Library in Albany made available, under the most convenient conditions, the entire transcript of the trial. My college classmate Joan Barron, of the Guilderland, New York, Library, helped me track obscure but essential facts. Richard Waugh was similarly helpful at the Albany Public Library.

I owe special thanks to Ray D'Addario, a U.S. Army photographer at Nuremberg, who not only has amassed a valuable collection of trial photographs and films, but has an excellent private archive as well. Mr. D'Addario made all this material available to me. Dr. Charles Gilbert, son of the Nuremberg prison psychologist, Gustav Gilbert, took the trouble to locate his father's personal papers and gave me access to them, for which I am in his debt.

On a note of serendipity, my winter neighbor and friend in San Miguel de Allende, Mexico, Katherine Walch, turned out to have been a member of the Nuremberg prosecutor's staff and had gathered an impressive library over the years, including mimeographed transcripts used during the course of the trial. My deepest thanks go to her for the loan of this material and for her shared memories of Nuremberg. Also in San Miguel de Allende, Gloria Grant of the local *biblioteca* helped me with reference queries.

Father Moritz Fuchs, who served on the personal staff of chief Nuremberg prosecutor Justice Robert Jackson, spoke to me at length and risked lending me his irreplaceable collection of Nuremberg photographs. Ben E. Swearingen, author of the splendid book on Hermann Göring cited elsewhere, was also generous in answering my questions. In Germany, Dr. Klaus Kastner, vice president of the Nuremberg-Furth Court, proved invaluable, both by taking me through the courthouse where the trial took place and by sharing his boyhood memories of Nuremberg at the time of the trial.

My friends Richard Rosenbaum and Rena Button helped me in my requests for material from the archives of Yad Vashem in Jerusalem.

Dr. Guenter Bischof of the Eisenhower Center in New Orleans helped me to understand the postwar conditions in Germany; Captain John P. Bracken (USMC Ret.) provided useful material explaining the naval case at Nuremberg; and I much appreciate the curious sidelights about the defendants passed along to me by Angus Mclean Theurmer. Genya Markon of the Holocaust Museum in Washington kindly helped me to locate key photographs. I thank Dave Dynan of the Eighth Air Force Association, who led me to John "Marty" Shea, a World War II flier who proved a gold mine of information on the air raids that destroyed Nuremberg. Thomas and Renate Barker skillfully translated key documents for me.

I am grateful to Nan Graham, my editor at Viking Penguin, for sharing my enthusiasm for the project early on and for her sensitive and skillful editing of the manuscript, and my thanks to her assistant, Courtney Hodell. As ever, my friend and agent Clyde Taylor displayed his customary skill, concern, and judgment in representing me. Finally, my wholly inadequate gratitude goes to my wife, Sylvia, who not only struggled with the manuscript, but made valuable suggestions and original contributions to it.

Those persons who were good enough to grant me interviews are Margaret Allen, Burton C. Andrus, Jr., William Baldwin, Roger Barrett, Ruth Holden Bateman, Raymond Belanger, Barbara Pinion Bitter, Thomas Brown, Walter Brudno, Harold Burson, Albert Callan, Raymond D'Addario, Emilio DiPalma, Nicholas Doman, Arthur Donovan, Theodore Fenstermacher, Moritz Fuchs, Charles Gilbert, Matilda Gilbert, Robert Gilbert, William Glenny, Charles Gordon, Bobbie Hardy, Whitney Harris, Richard Heller, Charles Horsky, William Jackson, Klaus Kastner, Robert Keeler, Daniel Kiley, Thomas Lambert, Andy Logan, Daniel Margolies, David Marwell, Hans Nathan, David Pitcher, Dorothy Owens Reilly, Walter Rockler, Gunther Sadel, Peter Samulevich, John Martin Shea, Benedicte Smith, Howard K. Smith, Drexel Sprecher, Alfred Steer, Telford Taylor, Peter Uiberall, John Vonetes, Katherine Walch, Rolf Wartenberg, Herbert Wechsler, Katharine Williams, and Rose Korb Williams.

BIBLIOGRAPHY

BOOKS

ALEXANDER, Charles W., and Anne KEESHAN. *Justice at Nuremberg: A Pictorial Record of the Trial of Nazi War Criminals by the International Military Tribunal at Nuremberg, Germany, 1945–1946.* Marvel Press, 1946.

AMBROSE, Stephen E., and Guenter BISCHOF, eds. *Eisenhower and the German POWs: Facts Against Falsehood.* New Orleans: LSU Press, 1992.

ANDRUS, Burton C. *I Was the Nuremberg Jailer.* New York: Coward-McCann, 1969.

BACQUE, JAMES. *Other Losses: An Investigation into the Mass Deaths of German Prisoners at the Hands of the French and Americans after World War II.* Toronto: Stoddard, 1989.

BIDDLE, Francis. *In Brief Authority.* Garden City, N.Y.: Doubleday, 1962.

BROWN, Anthony Cave. *The Last Hero: Wild Bill Donovan.* New York: Times Books, 1982.

BULLOCK, Alan. *The Ribbentrop Memoirs.* London: Weidenfeld & Nicolson, 1953.

BYTWERK, Randall L. *Julius Streicher: The Man Who Persuaded a Nation to Hate Jews.* New York: Dorset Press, 1983.

CONOT, Robert E. *Justice at Nuremberg.* New York: Harper and Row, 1983.

COOPER, Robert W. *The Nuremberg Trial.* New York: Penguin Books, 1947.

COSTELLO, John. *Ten Days to Destiny.* New York: William Morrow, 1991.

CUMOLETTI, Henry V. *Crimes Against Humanity.* Gouverneur, N.Y.: MRS, 1989.

DASTRUP, Boyd L. *Crusade in Nuremberg: Military Occupation, 1945–49.* Westport, Conn.: Greenwood Press, 1985.

DAVIDSON, Eugene. *The Trial of the Germans.* London: Macmillan, 1966.

DÖNITZ, Karl. *Memoirs: Ten Years and Twenty Days.* Trans. R. H. Stevens. Annapolis, Md.: Naval Institute Press, 1959.

DREYFUSS, Allan. *These 21.* Stars and Stripes, 1946.

ELWYN-JONES, Lord. *In My Time: An Autobiography.* London: Weidenfeld & Nicolson, 1983.

FRITZSCHE, Hans. *The Sword in the Scales*, as told to Hildegard Springer. Trans. Diane Pike and Heinrich Fraenkel. London: Alan Wingate, 1953.

GASKIN, Hilary. *Eyewitness at Nuremberg*. London: Arms and Armour, 1990.

GERHART, EUGENE C. *America's Advocate: Robert H. Jackson*. New York: Bobbs-Merrill, 1958.

GILBERT, Gustav M., Ph.D. *Nuremberg Diary*. New York: Farrar, Straus, 1947.

———. *The Psychology of Dictatorship*. New York: The Ronald Press, 1950.

GLENDINNING, Victoria. *Rebecca West: A Life*. New York: Alfred A. Knopf, 1987.

HARRIS, Whitney R. *Tyranny on Trial*. Dallas: Southern Methodist University Press, 1954.

HECHT, Ingeborg. *Invisible Walls: A German Family Under the Nuremberg Laws*. Trans. J. Maxwell Brownjohn. New York: Harcourt Brace Jovanovich, 1984.

HIGHAM, Charles. *The Duchess of Windsor: The Secret Life*. New York: McGraw-Hill, 1988.

HYDE, H. Montgomery. *Lord Justice: The Life and Times of Lord Birkett of Ulverston*. New York: Random House, 1965.

IRVING, David. *Goering*. New York: William Morrow, 1989.

JACKSON, Robert H., and Eugene C. GERHARD. *America's Advocate*. Indianapolis and New York: Bobbs-Merrill, 1958.

KALNOKY, Ingeborg, with Ilona HERISKO. *The Witness House*. London: New English Library, 1975.

KEITEL, Wilhelm. *The Memoirs of Field Marshal Keitel*. Walter Gorlitz, ed. Trans. David Irving. New York: Stein & Day, 1966.

KELLEY, Douglas M., M.D. *22 Cells in Nuremberg*. New York: Greenberg, 1947.

KILMUIR (David MAXWELL-FYFE). *Political Adventure: The Memoirs of the Earl of Kilmuir*. London: Weidenfeld & Nicolson, 1964.

MANVELL, Roger, and Heinrich FRAENKEL. *Hess*. New York: Drake Publishers, 1973.

MASER, Werner. *Nuremberg: A Nation on Trial*. Trans. Richard Barry. New York: Charles Scribner's Sons, 1979.

MOSLEY, Leonard. *The Reich Marshal: A Biography of Hermann Goering*. Garden City, N.Y.: Doubleday, 1974.

NEAVE, Airey. *On Trial at Nuremberg*. Foreword by Rebecca West. Boston: Little, Brown, 1979.

POLEVOI, Boris. *The Final Reckoning: Nuremberg Diaries*. Moscow: Progress Publishers, 1978.

POLTORAK, Arkady. *The Nuremberg Epilogue*. Trans. David Skvirsky. Moscow: Progress Publishers, 1971.

POSNER, Gerald L. *Hitler's Children.* New York: Random House, 1991.

ROSENBAUM, Ron. *Travels with Dr. Death and Other Unusual Investigations.* New York: Penguin Books, 1991.

SHIRER, William L. *End of a Berlin Diary.* New York: Alfred A. Knopf, 1947.

SMITH, Bradley F. *Reaching Judgment at Nuremberg.* New York: Basic Books, 1977.

SPEER, Albert. *Inside the Third Reich.* New York: Avon, 1971.

———. *Spandau: The Secret Diaries.* New York: Pocket Books, 1977.

STOREY, Robert G. *The Final Judgment: From Pearl Harbor to Nuremberg.* San Antonio: Naylor, 1968.

SWEARINGEN, Ben E. *The Mystery of Hermann Goering's Suicide.* New York: Dell, 1985.

TAYLOR, Telford. *The Anatomy of the Nuremberg Trials: A Personal Memoir.* New York: Alfred A. Knopf, 1992.

TUSA, Ann, and John TUSA. *The Nuremberg Trial.* New York: Atheneum, 1984.

WECHSLER, Herbert. *Principles, Politics, and Fundamental Law.* Cambridge, Mass.: Harvard University Press, 1961.

WILLIAMS, Joseph H. *Captor-Captive.* Jacksonville, Fla.: Girtman Press, 1986.

YAHIL, Leni. *The Holocaust: The Fate of European Jewry 1932–45.* New York: Oxford University Press, 1991.

PERIODICALS

DANIEL, Raymond. " 'So What,' Say the Germans of Nuremberg." *New York Times Magazine*, December 3, 1945.

GERECKE, Henry F. "I Walked to the Gallows with the Nazi Chiefs." *Saturday Evening Post*, September 1, 1951.

HARRIS, MARTYN. "House Party." *The Spectator*, October 24, 1992.

KEMPNER, Robert M. W. "Impact of War on the German Mind." *New York Times Magazine*, October 6, 1946.

LOW, David. "Portrait of the Master Race in the Dock." *New York Times Magazine*, December 23, 1945.

PERSICO, Joseph E. "The Last Days of the Third Reich." *American Heritage*, April–May 1985.

PRENDERGAST, Mark. "Trial and Error." Interview with Dan Kiley. *North by Northeast* (Vermont Public Radio Magazine), July 1988.

TAYLOR, Telford. "The Nuremberg Trials." *Columbia Law Review*, vol. 55, April 1955.

WOLFE, Robert. "Putative Threat to National Security as a Nuremberg Defense for Genocide." *Annals of the American Academy of Political and Social Science*, July 1980.

ARCHIVAL AND LIBRARY SOURCES

BIDDLE, Francis. Papers. Syracuse University Library, Syracuse, N.Y.

FRANKLIN, Robert, Sr. Oral History, October 25, 1982. U.S. Army Military History Institute, Carlisle Barracks, Pa.

JACKSON, Justice Robert H. Interview by Harlan Phillips, February 1955. Oral History, Butler Library, Columbia University.

ROWE, James. Papers. Franklin Delano Roosevelt Library, Hyde Park, N.Y.

DOCUMENTS

Nuremberg: A History of U.S. Military Government. Issued by U.S. Forces European Theater, 1946.

Office of U.S. Chief of Counsel for Prosecution of Axis Criminality. *Nazi Conspiracy and Aggression,* vols. 1–8 and supplements A and B. U.S. Government Printing Office, Washington, D.C.

Report of Board of Proceedings in the Case of Hermann Goering Suicide, October 1946. Berlin Documents Center.

TOMASZEWSKA, Halina. Notes on interview with Lilli Gau, mistress of Hans Frank, September 6, 1945. Trans. from Polish. National Archives, Washington, D.C.

Trial of Major War Criminals Before the International Military Tribunal. 42 vols. U.S. Government Printing Office, Washington, D.C.

WALKER, Kenneth. "The Enemy Side of the Hill." *World War II German Military Studies,* vol. 1, July 30, 1949. U.S. Army Historical Division. National Archives, Washington, D.C.

FILMS

The following films were reviewed by the author: British Paramount News Reels, Nuremberg, 1945–1946; *Hitler's Final Solution: The Wannsee Conference,* screenplay by Paul Mommortz, directed by Heinz Schirk; *The Memory of Justice,* a documentary produced and directed by Marcel Ophuls, Stuyvesant Films, 1976.

SOURCE NOTES

SOURCE NOTES are keyed to the page number and a phrase occurring on that page. Citations from books, periodicals, and other attributed sources begin with the author's name, followed by page numbers. The source is fully identified in the bibliography. Where more than one work by the same author is cited, a distinguishing word from the appropriate title appears after the author's name. Sources not listed in the bibliography are identified in the note. The full names of interviewees cited can be found in the acknowledgments. Frequent sources cited are abbreviated as follows:

AFN   Armed Forces Network
BAP   Papers of Colonel Burton Andrus
BDC   Berlin Document Center
BIDP   Papers of Francis Biddle, Syracuse University
GGP   Papers of Gustav Gilbert
IMT   Trial of Major War Criminals before the International Military Tribunal, 42 volumes
JXO   Robert Jackson Oral History, Columbia University
RG 238 National Archives Collection, World War II War Crimes Records
ROWP   Papers of James Rowe, Franklin D. Roosevelt Library

Chapter I: Prelude to Judgment

3 *He had made this dawn descent every day:* Prison routine, BAP directives to staff August 13, 1945–October 15, 1946; interviews William Glenny, Emilio DiPalma.

4 *drag out the surrender:* German forces flee west, Persico, "The Last Days of the Third Reich," *American Heritage* April–May 1985, 66–73.

4 *died by the thousands:* Conditions in Allied POW camps, Ambrose and Bischof, draft manuscript, introduction 1–25. In 1989, a Canadian novelist, James Bacque, in a book entitled *Other Losses*, surprised World War II historians with claims that up to one million German prisoners of war died of mistreatment in American and other POW camps. Subsequent scholars have convincingly refuted Bacque's charges, which appear to have been based on misinterpretation of data and careless methodology. Ambrose and Bischof do suggest that the American victors were not wholly free of vindictiveness. General Lucius Clay is quoted as saying in 1945, "I feel that the Germans should suffer from hunger and from cold, as I believe such suffering is necessary to make them realize the consequences of a war which they caused." And between 56,000 and 78,000 German POWs did die in captivity, according to U.S. and German sources. However deplorable these deaths, they amounted to about one percent of German prisoners, roughly the same as the number of American POWs who died in German captivity.

6 *followed his lead:* Göring in World War I, Mosley 29–43; Irving 32. Prior to becoming an ace fighter pilot, Göring served a year as an aerial photographer.

8 *shooting the Nazi leaders:* Roosevelt position on war criminals, B. Smith 314. Secretary of War Henry Stimson also reports being told early in the war that President Roosevelt was "definitely in favor of execution without trial."

8 *Bob Jackson to prosecute:* Rosenman presents Truman's offer, JXO 1159.

9 *certificate of completion:* Jackson's legal training, Gerhart 32. Jackson read law in a Jamestown, N.Y., firm for a year, completed two years in one at Albany Law School, and received not a degree but a certificate of completion because he was still under twenty-one.

10 *"admire your intentions":* Jackson recruited for the New Deal, Gerhart 59–66.

10 *vice-presidential running mate:* Jackson political ambitions, Gerhart 122, 169, 199. Before the 1940 vice-presidential feeler, Jackson in 1937 did some speaking around New York State to test his prospects for a gubernatorial bid. He did not catch fire.

11 *when Stone left:* Jackson's hopes for the chief judgeship, Gerhart 231.

11 *study at Hickory Hill:* Jackson's home at Hickory Hill in northern Virginia, interview W. Jackson. This home later became the residence of Robert F. Kennedy and his family.

11 *He confided to Barkley:* Jackson's skepticism over war crimes, JXO 1181; IMT vol. 2, 130.

11 *laughably light sentences:* War-crimes history, Davidson 2, 3; Shirer 291; Tusa 19.

12 *"home before Christmas":* Jackson's acceptance of the post, Gerhart 32, 242, 253, 336; JXO 1163, 1577, 1656; interview W. Jackson.

12 *Axis war criminals:* Jackson appointed, White House Executive Order 9547 May 2, 1945; interview C. Horsky.

14 *rounding up war criminals:* Göring leaves Hitler; surrenders, Mosley 274, 310–11, 313, 317, 319–21; Irving 17, 19; Conot 32; interview R. Wartenberg.

15 *copy of Morgenthau's plan:* Stimson's reaction to the plan, Tusa 51, 54; B. Smith 23, 26; Conot 10.

17 *a criminal conspiracy, a gigantic plot:* Bernays proposal for conducting trials, B. Smith 27, 28; Tusa 54–55; Conot 12. Bernays wanted to consider the conspiracy as having begun well before the outbreak of war so that the Allies might try as criminal offenses the depredations against the Jews in Germany beginning with the Nazi accession to power in 1933.

17 *aggressive war a crime:* A new crime added to Bernays approach, Taylor 37.

18 *plan was full of holes:* Wechsler denigrates the Bernays proposal, Tusa 57; interview H. Wechsler. "Criminal conspiracy," such as Bernays proposed for war criminals and which Wechsler questioned, is defined in *Black's Law Dictionary*, 1933, as "a combination or agreement between two or more persons for accomplishing an unlawful end by unlawful means."

19 *to hire Murray Bernays:* Jackson meets Bernays, Taylor 48.

19 *"The Jew butcher of Cracow":* Capture of Frank, *New York Times* May 6, 1945; RG 238 Frank interrogation June 25, 1945; Maser 47.

19 *the motive force:* Frank's early life and relationship to Lilli Gau, RG 238 Frank interrogation June 25, 1945, Halina Tomaszewska transcript of interview of Lilli Gau, September 6, 1945; Davidson 427–28; Gilbert *Psychology* 138; Kelley 175; Posner 13–14.

22 *Frank began to rule:* Frank's early rule from Wawel Castle, RG 238 Frank interrogation June 26, 1945, September 6, 1945; IMT vol. 5, 78; Conot 214; Posner 19–20.

22 *Frank had a dark secret:* Frank background, Gilbert *Psychology* 37; Frank revealed in a July 7, 1945, interrogation by his American captors that his father was part Jewish and that his family name may have been Frankfurter.

24 *accepted Himmler's conditions:* Frank's conflicts with Himmler; his wife's corruption; son's visit, Posner 21–22; IMT vol. 10, 582, vol. 12, 132; RG 238 Tomaszewska transcript.

24 *he had been reborn:* Frank's resumption of the Lilli Gau affair; hopes for divorce; rule-of-law speeches, RG 238 Tomaszewska transcript, Frank interrogation September 10, 1945; IMT vol. 12, 153; Posner 24–25, 27–28, 30, 37.

25 *"We are on Mr. Roosevelt's list":* Frank and others cited as war criminals, Davidson 439.

25 *among other art treasures:* Frank flees Poland, RG 238 Frank interrogations September 10, 1945, October 8, 1945. The Da Vinci, *Lady with an Ermine*, which Frank stole, has long since made its way back from Germany to Cracow, where it now hangs in the Czartoryski Museum.

26 *face trial for war crimes:* Frank's capture by the Americans; suicide attempts, RG 238 Frank interrogations June 26, 1945, October 3, 1945; Conot 37; Maser 47.

28 *"I'll think about it":* Jackson hopes to recruit Donovan, JXO 1202, 1213; interview W. Jackson.

29 *After the surrender:* Jodl negotiates the German surrender, Persico, *American Heritage* April–May 1985, 66–73.

29 *Potemkin village government:* Dönitz succeeds Hitler, Persico *American Heritage* April–May 1985, 66–73; RG 238 Dönitz interrogation September 18, 1945.

29 *"the Rommel of the Seas":* Dönitz naval strategy, *London Times* May 2, 1945. While Dönitz's wolfpack strategy produced heavy Allied shipping losses, the price became exorbitant. With Allied intelligence and strategy breakthroughs the German submarine service suffered such heavy losses that the wolfpack strategy was essentially abandoned by February 1944.

30 *to mask his shock and outrage:* Dönitz and others arrested as war criminals, Associated Press May 23, 1945. Dönitz's surprise at his arrest is understandable considering the fact that shortly before his arrest he had been writing a long memorandum to Eisenhower describing his plans for rebuilding postwar Germany.

31 *Jackson began questioning Storey:* Storey's recruitment by Jackson; flight to London; Storey's description of Soviet war-crimes trials, B. Smith 322; Gerhart 115; JXO 1203, 1220, 1234, 1491.

32 *"Swarthy and ugly":* Jackson works with Maxwell-Fyfe, JXO 1240; Kilmuir 9.

32 *Nikitchenko, fifty years old:* Participants in the London meetings, Tusa 74–79; Poltorak 15, 153–54; Neave 235.

34 *"in every civilized code":* Jackson on the ex post facto problem, Tusa 81; Shirer 292.

34 *an alien court system:* Differences in Anglo-Saxon and Continental law, JXO 1564. With only two military men on the court (the two Russians, who were military legal officers) and only five military men among the defendants, why was the court called the International *Military* Tribunal? It was customary for breaches of the rules of warfare to be tried by military courts. But beyond custom, President Roosevelt had expressed a preference for a military court as one less likely to become entangled in legal technicalities and thus swifter in its justice (Tusa 61). And Jackson believed that the decisions of a military court would not create precedents that might subsequently be applied to American civilian courts (IMT vol. 3, 543). The rules of evidence eventually adopted by the IMT were, in fact, far less constrictive than those of an Anglo-Saxon court. Only two tests had to be met: Is the evidence relevant? Does it have probative (evidentiary) value? (IMT vol. 3, 543).

36 *tu quoque was inadmissible:* Jackson, Maxwell-Fyfe discussions on the *Führerprinzip;* ex post facto; tu quoque; superior orders defense; organization of the IMT, B. Smith 58; Conot 325; Tusa 132.

36 *After his denunciation:* Kaltenbrunner's capture; his reactions, RG 238 Kaltenbrunner dossier; Conot 95; Gilbert 255.

37 *to look for a trial site:* Jackson inspection of possible sites, B. Smith 134.

38 *treasure chest of his kingdom:* Descriptions of prewar Nuremberg, *Nuremberg: A History of U.S. Military Government* 1946; Poltorak 16; H. Smith broadcast December 18, 1945; Janet Flanner *The New Yorker* December 15, 1945; Neave 42.

38 *at the words of Adolf Hitler:* Nazi preferment of Nuremberg; rallies; issuance of anti-Semitic decrees, Poltorak 19; Davidson 310; *Nürnberg 1933–1945,* Staat Presse, Nuremberg 1990.

39 *"among the dead cities":* Destruction of Nuremberg, *History, 388th Bombardment Group (H)* U.S. Air Force History Office; interview J. Shea; Neave 44; *U.S. Strategic Bombing Survey* October 26, 1945; Dastrup 22–23; *Nuremberg: A History of U.S. Occupation* 6; Storey 87; Wechsler 139; Gerhart 1. Peter Uiberall, an army translations officer, recalled being so stunned at the totality of Nuremberg's destruction that he visited an air force intelligence unit housed in the Palace of Justice to ask what bombing strategy had been employed. He was shown a dotted map marking military targets and felt some relief that the destruction had not been deliberately indiscriminate. The result, however, was little different from carpet bombing.

39 *The Jackson party landed:* Jackson's inspection of Nuremberg and the courthouse, interviews W. Jackson, J. Vonetes; B. Smith 352; Conot 131; JXO 1300; Gerhart 334–35; *Life* September 3, 1945, 36; Neave 46.

41 *a knack for spotting significant documents:* Graebe's affidavit; organization of the documents operation, interview R. Barrett; IMT vol. 4, 253–57, vol. 2, 151–56; Storey 81–85.

42 *an urgent phone call:* Acquisition Rosenberg's papers, Davidson 126; *Washington Post* May 6, 1945; Conot 25; interview W. Baldwin.

42 *485 tons of diplomatic papers:* New caches of documents, Tusa 97.

43 *"my last will and testament":* General Hossbach's notes found, B. Smith 333; IMT vol. 2, 262–63, 269.

43 *a Frankfurt symposium:* Speer's early experiences upon capture, Conot 101–2, 253.

43 *the wunderkind:* Speer's arms-production achievements, Tusa 395; Davidson 484, 502; IMT vol. 16, 448.

44 *saving their skins through knowledge:* Speer's friendly interrogations, Neave 313; RG 238 *U.S. Strategic Bombing Survey Special Document* May 22–23, 1945.

45 *a major war criminal:* Speer's arrest, Conot 253.

46 *relieved to have Maxwell-Fyfe along:* Jackson's second visit to Nuremberg, Kilmuir 85. While the Labour party won the British parliamentary elections by a two-hundred-seat majority in the summer of 1945, the Conservative Sir David Maxwell-Fyfe managed to hold on to his seat in West Derby by 3,428 votes.

47 *trial of the Nazi war criminals should be held here:* Selection of Nuremberg, interviews J. Vonetes, D. Kiley; JXO 1303; "Backstage Battle at Nuremberg," *Saturday Evening Post,* January 19, 1946; Tusa 84.

47 *ready to sign an agreement:* London negotiations completed, RG 238 The London Agreement, August 8, 1945.

47 *who was to be tried:* Deciding the defendants, Poltorak 224–25; B. Smith 6, 30; Tusa 92–93.

48 *"I'm only a dreamer":* Departure of Murray Bernays, Conot 25; B. Smith 335; interview R. Barrett.

49 *He recognized Hermann Göring:* Flying the accused from Bad Mondorf to Nuremberg, BAP account by pilot, Lieutenant Robert G. Denson (undated); *Life* September 3, 1946; Andrus 62.

49 *had first gone under hostile fire:* Andrus's background, Neave 61; interview B. Andrus, Jr.; Andrus 15–16; BAP chief prosecutor's office personnel file of B. Andrus, Andrus letter to William Stebbins August 27, 1945.

50 *"I hate these Krauts":* Andrus's attitudes toward Germans, BAP Andrus letter to Marjorie D. Peck (undated).

50 *"lack of judgment":* Opinions of Andrus, Walker, 23; interview A. Steer.

51 *he intended to whip into line:* Andrus relations with Göring, Andrus 29–31, 34; Conot 31.

51 *left a cyanide capsule in his clothes:* Göring deceptions at Bad Mondorf, Andrus 32.

51 *"You are no longer soldiers":* Keitel and Jodl stripped of insignia, Davidson 353.

51 *something he had to get off his chest:* Funk and removal of gold teeth, Andrus 55.

51 *Anne Frank, who died:* Seyss-Inquart in Holland, Neave 168; Davidson 466.

52 *Andrus's total confidence:* Dr. Pfluecker's relations with Andrus, Fritzsche 51; Swearingen 100; BAP memorandum to staff September 2, 1945.

52 *"my name is Meir":* Göring boasts of air superiority, Swearingen 46.

53 *an office in the Pentagon:* Horsky as Jackson's Washington liaison, interview C. Horsky.

53 *The language problem:* testing and adapting the IBM simultaneous interpreting system, interviews C. Horsky, W. Jackson; Gaskin 43; Biddle 398; JXO 1318.

55 *Kiley arrived at the Palace of Justice:* Restoring the courthouse, interview D. Kiley; JXO 1298. Kiley tried to persuade Jackson to hold the trial in the Nuremberg opera house, arguing: "We could stage it in a dramatic, thrilling way, a sort of world stage, the defense on the stage and the judges around them." Jackson turned down the idea after one of his staff remarked, "Yes, the IMT presents Jackson's Follies."

56 *"I have been here before":* The prisoners are assigned cells, Kelley 11; Speer *Inside* 645; Neave 64; Maser 61; *Stars and Stripes* August 13, 1945; Andrus 84, 143; Conot 35; BAP memorandum to staff September 2, 1945; interview W. Glenny.

57 *on a field of azure:* The IMT symbol, BAP memorandum to Justice Jackson September 28, 1945; interviews R. D'Addario, R. Korb Williams.

57 *His visitor was Major Douglas Kelley:* Arrival of the prison psychiatrist, Andrus 35; BAP General Eisenhower message to Eastern Military District October 23, 1945, Andrus draft ms. 101.

58 *going to be a proud outfit:* The guards' responsibilities, interviews E. DiPalma, W. Glenny; Tusa 126; BAP Andrus orders September 2, September 11, November 10, 1945, Andrus letter to S. Schneider September 19, 1945.

60 *Göring had raged:* Göring's exemption from chores, Maser 91; Swearingen 69.

60 *What rank did he want:* Jackson meeting with Truman, JXO 1246.

61 *happily name Parker:* Parker as alternate judge, Biddle 372–73; *New York Times* October 16, 1991.

61 *a call from Francis Biddle:* Biddle-Jackson meeting, Gerhart 256; JXO 1322, 1324, 1326; Biddle 128, 364, 372; Conot 62; Tusa 229; Taylor 95.

63 *"Exercise is important":* Exercise yard rules, Kelley 166; Tusa 126; Maser 60; BAP Andrus order September 11, 1945.

64 *return to the cellblock:* First day in the exercise yard, Tusa 127; Fritzsche 20; AFN broadcast November 22, 1945.

65 *They entered Dambach:* Jackson's living quarters, JXO 1304, 1334, 1339; Storey 99; interviews W. Jackson, M. Fuchs, J. Vonetes; Taylor 216.

65 *People without a roof:* German opinions of the trial, JXO 1031.

65 *"The Tom Dewey of Brooklyn":* Background, John Harlan Amen, interviews W. Baldwin, W. Jackson, J. Vonetes; AFN broadcast March 27, 1946; Conot 38.

66 *Albert Göring was an engineer:* Göring's brother questioned, RG 238 A. Göring interrogation September 25, 1945.

66 *brother Hermann's attitudes:* Göring and the Jews, RG 238 A. Göring interrogation September 25, 1945; Mosley 230. Göring had an important Jewish figure in his growing-up. Hermann von Epenstein, a wealthy Jewish physician, owned Veldenstein Castle in Franconia, where the Göring family lived during Hermann's childhood. Epenstein was godfather to the Göring children and their mother's lover. Göring ultimately inherited the castle.

68 *Ribbentrop was ready to take responsibility:* Jackson questions Ribbentrop, RG 238 Ribbentrop interrogation October 5, 1945; interview T. Lambert; Neave 230, 239; Kelley 112. Ribbentrop's disconnection from reality is suggested in this passage from a letter he wrote to Winston Churchill at the end of the war (whom he addressed as "Vincent" Churchill): "I do not know, if the old and noble English custom of fair play is also applicable for a defeated foe. I also do not know if you wish to hear the political testament of a deceased man [Hitler]. But I could imagine that its contents might be adapted to heal wounds . . . [and] in this perilous epoch of our world be able to help bring about a better future for all people."

70 *Andrus had lost his first prisoner:* Conti suicide, Andrus 87; Neave 76.

70 *workmen ripped the bars out:* Tightened security after Conti's suicide, Swearingen 98; Andrus 25, 29; Tusa 133; interview W. Glenny; Speer *Spandau* 5.

71 *one of the most sensational flights:* Hess's flight to Scotland, Manvell 32, 80, 82, 88–89, 92, 102; Conot 46; Kelley 24.

74 *"a victim of hallucinations":* Hitler on the Hess flight, Manvell 107, 111, 112, 214.

74 *a disturbed mind:* Hess's internment in Britain, Gilbert, *Psychology* 124; Manvell 107, 109, 113–17, 119, 124–25, 128.

75 *the Russians insisted:* Why Hess was tried, Tusa 92; B. Smith 178.

75 *His best strategy:* Hess feigning amnesia, Manvell 135, 149. In June 1991, reports appeared that Hess had been lured to fly to Scotland by British intelligence. The claim was based on recently revealed KGB files which supposedly established that Hess had been in correspondence with the duke of Hamilton and that his letters had been intercepted by MI5. Thereafter, MI5 reportedly faked correspondence from Hamilton to Hess, without the duke's knowledge, that lured Hess to fly to Scotland for peace discussions. The matter is discussed in John Costello's *Ten Days to Destiny,* and the story appeared in the June 9, 1991, *New York Times.* While it is possible that the KGB had such information, its accuracy is questionable. Albrecht Haushofer's letter to the duke was indeed intercepted by British censors on November 2, 1940. And British intelligence apparently did hatch a plan—but a plan to put the duke and Haushofer (not Hess) together in Lisbon. As for Hess's being lured to England, he, by his own admission, had already made two attempts to fly to Scotland before the intelligence scheme was devised. Further, he never mentioned any correspondence between them on his meeting Hamilton or at any time during his captivity. Indeed, one of his early problems on parachuting into Scotland was to prove his identity, hardly necessary for a major Nazi presumably stepping into a British trap. In 1992, a year after the opening of the KGB files, the British released intelligence files that "contained nothing to support assertions, buttressed by KGB files . . . that British intelligence knew in advance that Hess was coming."

76 *Birkett was trapped:* Background and selection of Birkett for the IMT, Hyde 1–2, 472, 494; Neave 232–33; Conot 63–64; Biddle 380.

77 *His father had been lord chief justice:* Background and selection of Lawrence, B. Smith 4; Neave 231; Biddle 379; Tusa 112.

77 *product of two blue-blooded lines:* Biddle background, Biddle preface 4; Tusa 209; Neave 233; Conot 63–64.

78 *no intention of losing:* Biddle on the IMT's legitimacy, B. Smith 74; BIDP box 1 journal entry October 3, 1945.

78 *Lawrence to accept:* Lawrence over Biddle for the presidency of the court, B. Smith 3–4, 77; Kilmuir 90; BIDP box 1 journal entry October 10, 1945; JXD box 95. Biddle had already had experience with Nazi defendants. He was attorney general when eight German saboteurs were captured in the U.S. While the men might have been tried in a federal court (and likely would have received light sentences, since they were caught before they did anything beyond conspiring), President Roosevelt wanted them condemned to death and pressured the Justice Department to create a military tribunal. Biddle, ever eager to please Roosevelt, volunteered to prosecute. Six of the men were executed.

80 *"He's crazy":* Hess interrogated before Göring over his amnesia claim, Manvell 138; RG 238 Göring interrogation October 9, 1945; Davidson 301; Manvell 236.

81 *Hess was a fake:* Kelley 23, 26; Andrus 73; BAP Andrus memorandum "Suggestions to Major Kelley Concerning Interrogation of Hess" October 15, 1945.

81 *Sprecher had no business here:* The documents-versus-witnesses controversy, interview D. Sprecher.

82 *Biddle informed Neave:* Delivery of the indictments, Neave 64–226; Gilbert *Diary* 5; Speer *Inside* 642; Kilmuir 60.

86 *most of them were to keep talking:* Defendants' right to refuse interrogation after indictment, RG 238 interrogations Sauckel October 18, 1945, Frank October 19, 1945.

86 *"Man hat uns belogen und betrogen":* Gilbert volunteers for Nuremberg, GGP Gilbert speech draft (undated) "The men and women of defeated Germany," Gilbert letter to Kelley December 28, 1946; Conot 69; Gilbert *Diary* 3.

87 *Keitel had been interrogated:* Keitel signing and issuance of the Commando Order, RG 238 Keitel interrogation (date illegible); Davidson 381–83; IMT vol. 8, 547, vol. 9, 220, vol. 15, 321; Conot 307. The futility of trying to conduct modern warfare in civilized fashion is perhaps demonstrated in this excerpt from the *Handbook of Irregular Warfare* issued to British commandos and which Hitler used, in part, to justify the Commando Order:

> In the past we as a nation have not looked upon gangsters and their methods with favour; the time has now come when we are compelled to adopt some of their methods. . . . Remember you are not a wrestler trying to render your enemy helpless, you have to kill. And remember you are out to kill, not to hold him down until the referee has finished counting. . . . In finishing off an opponent use him as a weapon as it were, beating his head on the curb or any convenient stone. Do not forget that good weapons are often lying about ready at hand. A bottle with the bottom smashed off is more effective than a naked hand in gouging an opponent's face. . . . The vulnerable parts of the enemy are the heart, spine and privates. Kick him or knee him as hard as you can in the fork. While he is doubled up in pain get him on the ground and stamp his head in.

88 *"neither Bolshevism nor Czarism":* Issuance of the Reprisal and Commissar orders, IMT vol. 4, 438–39; Gilbert *Diary* 112; Maser 295.

89 *"I could never get away with this":* Keitel's unlikely rise, IMT vol. 10, 473; Gilbert *Psychology* 213; Gilbert *Diary* 25; RG 238 Keitel memoirs 147, 188, 231; Davidson 331, 333; Tusa 307; Cooper 124–25.

89 *"No enemy can be killed":* Keitel's blind obedience, IMT vol. 4, 473.

89 *"Thank God you're alive":* Keitel's loyalty to Hitler, RG 238 Keitel interrogation October 10, 1945.

90 *the psychiatrists' interpreter:* Andrus reaction to Gilbert, BAP draft Andrus ms. (no page shown).

90 *"if you have one German":* Kelley and Gilbert visit Göring, Kelley viii, 35–36, 71–73, 75.

91 *a study of the Nazis:* Kelley and Gilbert's book collaboration, GGP Gilbert letter to Kelley December 28, 1946.

91 *to choose the first witness:* Jackson and Donovan differ on strategy, interviews R. Barrett, H. Smith; Conot 150–51; JXO 1384–85.

92 *far less daunting:* Jackson's preference for documents, interview T. Taylor.

93 *the Judges' Room:* Who may defend the defendants, Gaskin 87; Neave 228, 237; Hyde 497, 498; Tusa 228.

94 *throw the Noak woman out:* Stahmer's anti-Semitism, RG 238 Frau Noak letter to U.S. occupation authorities October 1945; Otto Stahmer letter to Frau Utermoehlen January 14, 1945.

94 *Nazi defense lawyers:* Former Nazis may represent defendants, Neave 120–21, 228, 230.

94 *Allied war crimes:* Jodl raises tu quoque, B. Smith 210.

95 *Luise Jodl had been married:* Frau Jodl comes to Nuremberg; the Jodl marriage, interview H. Wechsler; Maser 192; Davidson 354; Kelley 122; Conot 94.

96 *"scornful laughter of God":* Frank rediscovers his faith; background of Father O'Connor, Gilbert *Diary* 20–21; Fritzsche 55; Tusa 235; Gerecke *Saturday Evening Post* September 1, 1951; interview R. Holden Bateman; Andrus 110.

98 *"Stand us against a wall":* Background Robert Ley, Gilbert *Diary* 7–8, 13, 33; Maser 47; Poltorak 32; Polevoi 118; Kelley 170; RG 238 Ley interrogation October 18, 1945.

99 *"I needed that":* Background Streicher; his troubles with Göring, Bytwerk 34, 40–43; Fritzsche 130; Conot 383–84; Maser 50; Neave 96.

100 *"He is sane":* Psychiatric examination of Streicher, Gilbert *Diary* 9–10; BAP Kelley report to Andrus January 4, 1946.

101 *"Ley has killed himself":* The Ley suicide, Andrus 88–89; BAP Lieutenant Paul H. Graven letter to Major Teich October 29, 1945; Gaskin 30; Kelley 73. Ley left a suicide note that read:

> Farewell. I can't stand this shame any longer. Physically, nothing is lacking. The food is good. It is warm in my cell. The Americans are correct and partially friendly. Spiritually, I have reading matter and write what-

ever I want. I receive paper and pencil. They do more for my health than necessary and I may smoke and receive tobacco and coffee. I may walk at least 20 minutes every day. Up to this point, everything is in order but the fact that I should be a criminal—this is what I can't stand.

101 *His jail . . . was now suicide-proof:* Tightened security, Swearingen 65; Polevoi 120.

102 *"six hundred people just to hang twenty-one":* Jackson-Biddle administrative quarrels, BIDP box 1 journal entry October 21, 1945; JXO 1364, 1368.

103 *staying on in Nuremberg:* Gilbert background, interviews R. Gilbert, C. Gilbert.

104 *to be a spy:* Gilbert's covert intelligence for Andrus, BAP Andrus letter to his wife January 24, 1946; GGP Kelley letter to Gilbert December 24, 1946.

105 *"only you showed independence":* Göring conversation with Dewitt C. Poole covering foreign policy, Soviet Union invasion, Göring's rise to power, RG 238 Göring interrogation November 6, 1945, Göring dossier; Irving 21–22, 44, 105, 408; Mosley 178, 204, 239, 275; IMT vol. 1, 35.

107 *burning of the Reichstag:* Göring's explanation, Irving 115–17; RG 238 Göring interrogation October 13, 1945.

107 *the world press began descending:* Press facilities, interviews H. Smith, A. Logan; Flanner *The New Yorker* October 26, 1946, 92; Polevoi 69–70, 81. Boris Polevoi, the *Pravda* correspondent at Nuremberg, complained that Soviet correspondents were not billeted in the castle, but in "the Russian Palace," cramped rooms previously occupied by workers from the pencil factory.

108 *a curtain had descended on civilization:* Day-to-day life in Nuremberg, interviews H. Smith, R. D'Addario, R. Keeler, C. Gordon, P. Uiberall, A. Donovan, B. Hardy; Cumoletti 89, 99–100; H. Smith broadcasts November 25, 1945, January 31, 1946.

109 *he wanted an equivalent vote:* Role of alternate justices, Conot 85; BIDP box 2 Biddle memorandum for the record November 14, 1945.

110 *"not a football match":* Jackson wants Krupp indicted, Hyde 496; IMT vol. 2, 1; Biddle 401; B. Smith 80; interview H. Wechsler.

111 *Speed was the acid test:* Setting up the simultaneous-interpretation system, interviews A. Steer, D. Kiley, P. Uiberall, T. Brown; Gaskin 38–39; Gerhart 358. In addition to the courtroom interpreters, court reporters took down the proceedings of the trial in shorthand, which was later transcribed. The U.S. Army Signal Corps recorded the trial on disks, magnetic tape, or wire recorders.

113 *organized bedlam:* Operation of the documents room, interviews R. Barrett, B. Pinion Bitter, T. Taylor, W. Brudno, R. Holden Bateman; Tusa 99, 215; Gaskin 51, 53.

115 *"Melancholy grandeur":* Jackson prepares for his opening address, Gerhart 304–305, 441; JXO 1389–96; interviews W. Jackson, H. Wechsler, D. Sprecher; IMT vol. 2, 130.

116 *"You are not here to convert anybody":* Chaplain Gerecke arrives, BAP Andrus draft ms. (undated); Tusa 235; Fritzsche 55; Gerecke *Saturday Evening Post* September 1, 1951.

116 *Gilbert was recording the answers:* The defendants take intelligence tests, Gilbert *Psychology* 107, 127, 143; Gilbert *Diary* 15, 30; Tusa 129–30. A score of 100 was considered average. University graduates would be expected to score in the 120–140 range. Gilbert recorded the following results for the defendants: Schacht 143; Seyss-Inquart 141; Göring 138; Dönitz 138; Papen 134; Raeder 134; Frank 130; Fritzsche 130; Schirach 130; Ribbentrop 129; Keitel 129; Speer 128; Jodl 127; Rosenberg 127; Neurath 125; Funk 124; Frick 124; Hess 120; Sauckel 118; Kaltenbrunner 113; Streicher 106.

118 *burned the Soviet files:* Rudenko background; complaints of destroyed Soviet documents, Conot 61; JXO 1539, 1550.

119 *"an officer of high standing":* Schacht courts Donovan; Jackson objects, Conot 151–52; interviews R. Holden Bateman, J. Vonetes; B. Smith 270–71; Swearingen 131–32.

120 *"I have the responsibility":* Jackson fires Donovan over trial strategy, Storey 98; Conot 150–51, 154–55; Brown 744; Harris xxxvi; JXO 1386–87; Gerhart 115; interviews T. Taylor, D. Sprecher.

121 *"I am in possession of certain information":* Speer tries to cut a deal, B. Smith 221; RG 238 Speer interrogation November 2, 1945.

123 *"a toast to the defendants":* Vyshinsky at a banquet; a Russo-American romance, Martyn Harris, "House Party," *The Spectator* October 24, 1992, 54; Kilmuir 107, 109; BIDP box 1 Biddle letter to son, Randolph, October 17, 1945; Biddle 376–77, 428.

124 *a national inferiority complex:* Jackson on Russian psychology, JXO 1558.

125 *Fear and stress:* Problems in the prison; Kaltenbrunner's illness, Davidson 531–33; B. Smith 292; Andrus 141; Kelley 134.

126 *"they think it's all propaganda":* Eve of the trial, Shirer 306, 313.

126 *He had come down with malaria:* Soviets seek to stall the trial opening, JXO 1375–83; Gerhart 509; Storey 111.

Chapter II: The Prosecution Case

132 *this dishrag in the dock:* Opening day, H. Smith broadcast November 20, 1945; J. Flanner *The New Yorker* January 5, 1946; IMT vol. 2, 30; Neave 243.

133 *"steak the day before they hang us":* The defendants during the first day, Fritzsche 73; Gilbert *Diary* 35–36.

134 *Donovan would be flying home:* The general's departure, JXO 1366–67.

134 *"This is history":* The gavel is stolen, interview R. D'Addario.

135 *"find myself a courthouse":* Jackson prepares to deliver opening speech, Shirer 301; Gerhart 353; Tusa 151.

135 *"not to make a speech":* The defendants enter pleas, Shirer 305; Tusa 150; Neave 245; IMT vol. 2, 98. The prepared statement that Göring twice attempted to deliver read:

> As *Reichsmarschall* of the Greater German Reich, I accept the political responsibility for all my own acts or for acts carried out on my orders. These acts were exclusively carried out for the welfare of the German people and because of my oath to the Führer. Although I am responsible for these acts only to the German people and can be tried only before a German court, I am at the same time prepared to give all the necessary information demanded of me by this court and to tell the whole truth without recognizing the jurisdiction of this court. I must, however, most strongly reject the accusation that my acts for which I accept full responsibility should be described as criminal. I must also reject the acceptance by me of responsibility for acts of other persons which were not known to me, of which, had I known them, I would have disapproved and which could not have been prevented by me anyway.

135 *"the first trial in history":* Jackson's opening address, IMT vol. 2, 98–102, 120, 154–55; Gerhart 363; *Life* December 10, 1945; JXO 1397–98.

138 *what must be their own fate:* Other executions and death sentences for war crimes, *New York Times* November 18, 22, 1945.

138 *"Murder hasn't been made a crime yet":* Shawcross and Rudenko opening speeches, Gilbert *Diary* 425–26; Tusa 179; Ophuls *Memory of Justice.*

139 *call him Tex:* Second Lieutenant Jack Wheelis is promoted, BAP Wheelis's transfer orders to Nuremberg September 26, 1945; personnel file, Jack Wheelis 0-1330498 November 22, 1945.

140 *Wheelis was a friend:* Göring courts Wheelis and other GIs, H. Smith broadcast November 27, 1945; Swearingen 198; Gilbert *Diary* 87; Gaskins 86.

141 *Smith finished his broadcast:* An evaluation of the trial, H. Smith broadcast November 27, 1945.

142 "Guten Morgen, Herr Reichsmarschall": Kempner prewar relations with Göring and Frick, Mosley 151, 324; *New York Times* October 6, 1946; Dreyfuss 26.

142 *directing the takeover by telephone:* Göring and the annexation of Austria, IMT vol. 2, 418.

143 *"I refer to document number 2430 PS":* Film, Nazi concentration camps, shown, IMT vol 2, 432–33; Neave 246; JXO 1407–8.

144 *no rank, no title:* Göring's cell marked, Polevoi 120.

145 *"These facts are the most fearful heritage":* Defendants' reactions to the concentration camp film, Gilbert *Diary* 43, 46–47; Maser 107.

146 *She seized the opportunity:* Operation of the Witness House, Kalnoky 1–10, 155–56.

146 *Lahousen marched to the witness stand:* Lahousen at the Witness House; subsequent testimony, Kalnoky 78–80; IMT vol. 2, 435, 449–50, vol. 3, 10, vol. 5, 33.

147 *"The order to liquidate":* Keitel orders execution of French generals, IMT vol. 2, 463–64, 474; Gilbert *Psychology* 228–29.

148 *amnesia would "interfere with his ability":* Hess's sanity hearing, BAP Report of Psychiatric Board to the IMT December 12, 1945; IMT vol. 1, 157, vol. 2, 493; Kelley 31, 35.

148 *"You probably won't be coming to court":* Gilbert warns Hess if he is found unfit for trial, Gilbert *Diary* 11, 51; Gilbert *Psychology* 129; Conot 159.

149 *"my memory will again respond":* Hess recants on amnesia, Shirer 319; Polevoi 89; IMT vol. 2, 478–79, 496; Gilbert *Diary* 51; Poltorak 50.

149 *"I decided to stop playing the game":* Doctors ponder authenticity of Hess's recovered memory, Kelley 52–53; Gilbert *Diary* 54.

150 *distinguish between right and wrong:* The court finds Hess can stand trial, IMT vol. 3, 1; BAP Report of Three Man Panel to IMT December 5, 1945. While the ten-doctor panel had concluded that Hess's condition would interfere with "his ability to conduct his defense," the court appears to have been influenced by an earlier report by a three-doctor panel which found:

> To the psychiatrist, the word insanity means the existence of unsoundness of mind of such a nature and degree as to prevent him from distinguishing between right and wrong and from adhering to the right . . . our examination revealed that Hess has no disorder of consciousness, understands perfectly everything that is said to him and therefore understands the nature of the proceedings against him.

150 *a bloodcurdling scream:* The noose trick, Fritzsche 44; Oral History, Colonel Robert Franklin, Sr., October 25, 1982, U.S. Army Military History Institute.

151 *"You are hereby informed":* Andrus wearies of complaints, BAP Andrus memorandum to "Persons concerned" December 3, 1945.

152 *"I wonder what facilities the Germans would provide":* Storey shows Birkett the defense counsels' resources, Storey 64, 101.

153 *"The nastiest person present":* David Low sketches, *New York Times Magazine* December 23, 1945.

155 *nor one so stupid:* Kaltenbrunner background; recovery from illness, RG 238 Kaltenbrunner dossier; IMT vol. 11, 233; Davidson 318, 321–22; Poltorak 80; Polevoi 265.

156 *"There goes the alliance":* East-West tensions mount, interview A. Callan.

157 *"I can't be held responsible":* Andrus's conflicts with Watson, Andrus 76; BAP Andrus message to Second Army HQ November 13, 1945.

158 *implementing the pass system:* Sadel establishes the social pass, interview G. Sadel.

158 *film from captured German newsreels: The Nazi Plan* screened in court, IMT vol. 3, 400–403, Conot 197; Poltorak 142; Gilbert *Diary* 66.

159 *"you filthy rogue":* Film of the People's Court, Ophuls *Memory of Justice;* H. Smith broadcast December 11, 1945; Cooper 30. In order to contrast Nazi-style justice with what Nazi defendants were receiving from the IMT, Robert Kempner arranged to have German government officials, politicians, teachers, clergymen, and judges visit the Nuremberg courtroom. Afterward, they were taken to a projection room where the Freisler People's Court film was shown.

160 *"if Hitler were to walk into this room":* Defendants' reaction to the film *The Nazi Plan,* Kelley 112–13; Gilbert *Psychology* 195.

160 *Dodd cut an impressive figure:* Dodd's first appearance in court, interviews T. Taylor, D. Margolies, W. Baldwin, W. Harris; IMT vol. 3, 403.

161 *"I had found a man":* Sauckel background, RG 238 Sauckel interrogations September 11, 12, 13, October 14, 1945.

162 *"We've taken heavy manpower losses":* Hitler makes Sauckel the labor czar, IMT vol. 19, 189, 196, vol. 14, 610, 622; Conot 142; RG 238 Sauckel interrogation September 12, 13, 19, 20, 21, 1945.

163 *"They fell on their knees":* Roundups of conscript workers, Conot 245–46.

166 *"I am really not responsible"*: Sauckel puts blame on Speer, Gilbert *Diary* 75.

167 *merriment of the Marble Room:* After-hours atmosphere, Neave 43, 53–54; Tusa 227–28; interviews J. Vonetes, G. Sadel, D. Owens Reilly, K. Walch.

168 *no reason to keep him locked up:* Hoffmann background; photography expedition, Poltorak 140; Polevoi 106; Conot 93; interview R. Heller.

169 *a man untouched by shame:* Hoffmann at the Witness House, Kalnoky 42–43.

170 *"six feet under"*: Andrus complains of press revelations, Reuters dispatch December 12, 1945; *London Daily Express* December 13, 1945; AFN broadcast November 23, 1945; interview H. Burson.

171 *"the money that bastard made"*: Göring on Hoffmann, Bullock 174.

171 *chief cause of Germany's defeat:* Göring and Ribbentrop mutual opinions, RG 238 Göring dossier; Gilbert *Diary* 13, 67; Tusa 241.

172 *a courtroom barometer:* Göring's dominance of the dock, H. Smith broadcast December 9, 1945.

172 *whisked the sheet from USA exhibit 254:* Dodd enters exhibits, IMT vol. 3, 516–17; interview R. Barrett.

173 *"among the clubs and kicks"*: Ghetto atrocity film shown, J. Flanner, *The New Yorker* January 5, 1946, 44.

175 *"Hitler got us into this"*: Defendants' reaction to ghetto atrocity film, IMT vol. 3, 536–37, 542, vol. 5, 200; Gilbert *Diary* 70–71.

176 *"my knees knocking"*: Frictions among Allied staffs, Gaskin 143; Neave 254; Kilmuir 101; Tusa 136. Wide discrepancies existed in pay scales. The American judge Biddle was paid at an annual rate of $15,000 and an American civilian staff lawyer about $7,000. Sir Geoffrey Lawrence's annual salary was closer to $2,000.

176 *"privatize, finalize, visualize"*: Birkett's disdain for the American staff, Hyde 515.

177 *"I accept Christ"*: Religious life in the cellblock, Fritzsche 125; Gerecke *Saturday Evening Post* September 1, 1951; Andrus 137.

178 *you could call him Meir:* Göring humiliated by Hitler, Mosley 289, 299; IMT vol. 15, 590.

178 *crush these "leftist" Nazis:* Göring and the Roehm purge, Gilbert *Diary* 79; Mosley 190–95. Göring at one point gave out the figure for deaths during the purge as seventy-two; but Himmler reportedly used the occasion to wipe out more than a hundred more of his enemies. After the slaughter, President Hindenburg sent Göring a telegram: "Accept my approval and gratitude for your successful action in suppressing the high treason."

181 *"those who merely did their bidding"*: German people react to indictment of Nazi organizations, AFN broadcast January 10, 1946; Davidson 556; RG 238 Kempner memorandum to Jackson January 23, 1946.

181 *went into convulsions and died:* Medical experiments, Gerhart 115, 371; Polevoi 147–49.

184 *"Hitler appears on the screen"*: Frank reflects on his relations with Hitler, Gilbert *Diary* 22, 82–83.

184 *"I decide the fate of criminals"*: Frank and the Roehm purge, Davidson 441; Gilbert *Psychology* 149; Posner 15.

187 *"They disappeared into the night and fog"*: Keitel issues the *Nacht und Nebel* decree, Davidson 338; Gilbert *Psychology* 228–32.

187 *"if we had disobeyed"*: Jodl defends obedience of orders, IMT vol. 19, 23, 26, 32; Gilbert *Diary* 28.

189 *"We didn't dare oppose the orders"*: Gilbert goes to Dachau; ponders impulses of mass murderers, interview R. Barrett; RG 238 Kaltenbrunner dossier; GGP Gilbert speech notes (undated); BAP Gilbert report to Andrus on Dachau visit January 3, 1946.

190 *His most vivid childhood memory:* Speer's early background, Speer *Inside* xiii, 32, 40; Conot 239.

191 *he won a commission:* Speer as Hitler's architect, Speer *Inside* 46, 52, 69, 71, 93–94, 137, 164, 166, 440; IMT vol. 16, 430.

192 *Dr. Todt had been killed:* Speer becomes armaments chief, Speer *Inside* 263–64; Conot 438; IMT vol. 16, 437.

193 *"These people must disappear"*: Speer's knowledge of slave labor conditions, concentration camps, and extermination, Conot 256, 437, 441; Speer *Inside* 474–75; IMT vol. 16, 444, 480.

194 *"The best have fallen"*: Speer resists Hitler's scorched-earth policy, Speer *Inside* 557, 592; Davidson 486; RG 238 U.S. Strategic Bombing Survey Special Report of Interrogation of Speer May 23, 1945.

195 *"So you're leaving. Good"*: Speer's farewell to Hitler; activities prior to capture, U.S. Strategic Bombing Survey Special Report May 23, 1945; Speer *Inside* 612, 615–17.

195 *Speer to the visitors' room:* Speer discusses strategy with his lawyer, BAP visitors' room log December 27, 1945.

196 *Ribbentrop pestered the old physician:* Ribbentrop behavior, Conot 53; IMT vol. 2, 254–55.

197 *He might have become a Canadian:* Early Ribbentrop background, Bullock 18, 109; Davidson 148; RG 238 Ribbentrop dossier.

197 *he persuaded Hitler:* Ribbentrop's rise to foreign minister, Conot 152; Higham 141; Davidson 151.

199 *failed to wish him a happy New Year:* Ribbentrop fires his lawyer, Neave 224.

199 *"the ninth crime":* Evidence against Kaltenbrunner, interview W. Harris; IMT vol 4, 306–7.

200 *"How many people did you kill":* W. Harris interrogates Ohlendorf, interview W. Harris; Wolfe, *Annals of the American Academy of Political Science* July 1980.

201 *"ninety thousand people liquidated":* Ohlendorf testimony, IMT vol. 4, 311, 319–23, 332.

201 *an attempt on Hitler's life:* Lawyer gives preview of Speer defense, IMT vol. 4, 343.

202 *"But did you have no scruples":* Ohlendorf's cross-examination, IMT vol. 4, 353–54.

203 *the Final Solution:* Witness Wisliceny sees a written order, IMT vol. 4, 357–60.

203 *"five million people on his conscience":* Emergence of Eichmann through Wisliceny's testimony, IMT vol. 4, 308, 355, 357–60, 371; B. Smith 115; Poltorak 344. Wisliceny testified that "the chief of the Security Police and the SD and the Inspector of Concentration Camps were entrusted with carrying out this so-called final solution. All Jewish men and women who were able to work were to be temporarily exempted from the so-called final solution and used for work in the concentration camps. The letter was signed by Himmler himself. I could not possibly be mistaken since Himmler's signature was well known to me."

203 *"this is serious business":* Dwindling press coverage, interview H. Burson; Andrus 173.

204 *taking on the German High Command:* Taylor for the prosecution; Taylor background, interviews T. Taylor, W. Rockler; IMT vol. 4, 390; Gaskin 133.

206 *"the Jews are not even human":* Testimony of Bach-Zelewski incriminates the Wehrmacht; interests Gilbert, Gilbert *Diary* 109, 114; IMT vol. 4, 451; Poltorak 126; GGP Gilbert speech notes (undated).

209 *"I was the pupil"*: Keitel's relationship to Hitler and rise to chief of staff, IMT vol. 9, 371, vol. 10, 600; Gilbert *Psychology* 208, 210; Davidson 341; Speer *Inside* 323; RG 238 Keitel interrogation October 1, 1945.

211 *"he would renounce the church"*: Rosenberg's *The Myth of the Twentieth Century*, Kelley 39, 47–48. Rosenberg's book appears to be one of the great unread German works of that era. In 1934, its year of publication, the book sold 250,000 copies. By the war's outbreak it had sold 1 million copies and, according to Rosenberg, was in the home of "every decent party member."

211 *"We don't want to hear about it"*: Brudno prosecution of Rosenberg, IMT vol. 5, 41; interview W. Brudno.

212 *she did not appear before the court:* Women at Nuremberg, H. Smith broadcast January 25, 1946.

213 *"cold-bloodedly and without pity"*: Baldwin begins Frank prosecution, interview W. Baldwin; IMT vol. 5, 82–83.

214 *spirited from their homes:* Dr. Blaha's testimony incriminates defendants, IMT vol. 5, 176–77, 181; interview D. Margolies.

216 *Kaltenbrunner knew what had really happened:* Speer's connection to the Twentieth of July plot, Speer *Inside* 501.

217 *"Göring keeps whipping them into line"*: Speer proposes splitting the defendants at lunchtime, Gilbert *Diary* 122.

218 *three-quarters American:* Sprecher prosecutes Schirach, Shirach background, interview Drexel Sprecher; Conot 421; IMT vol. 14, 363; Davidson 285. While membership in Schirach's Hitler Youth was technically voluntary, the pressures to join were formidable. An apprentice who was a member got a job more easily. Only members could win school prizes. In some districts, youths who did not want to be members had to sign a form, which singled them out as unpatriotic. In other areas, pressure was applied by setting a deadline beyond which the young person could never join.

219 *"The Revenge of Heydrich"*: Schirach proposes vengeance bombing; ships Jews from Vienna, Conot 423; IMT vol. 14, 491.

223 *"An insane clique of generals"*: Dönitz attacks the Twentieth of July plotters, RG 238 BBC intercept, Dönitz broadcast July 21, 1944; Posner 150.

224 *He was mortified:* Kranzbuehler contemplates his behavior during the Nazi era, Ophuls *Memory of Justice.*

225 *to make Adolf Hitler a German:* Frick's role in Hitler's citizenship, Davidson 264–65.

226 *Their German identity was effaced:* Frick's role in anti-Semitic decrees, Davidson 264, 267–68; IMT vol. 3, 523–25; Hecht 57, 63.

227 *"they haven't had a classical education"*: British judged better prosecutors, Neave 253; H. Smith broadcast January 17, 1946; J. Flanner *The New Yorker* January 5, 1946; interviews R. Barrett, D. Owens Reilly, K. Walch, H. Burson.

227 *his staff was melting away:* High American turnover, JXO 1402; Conot 283.

228 *"the most amazing stroke of genius"*: Gilbert visits Streicher; Streicher background, Gilbert *Diary* 117, 125; Davidson 47; Neave 94; Bytwerk 2, 5–6.

229 *"as a gift"*: Streicher's rise and fall, IMT vol. 12, 308; Bytwerk 8–15; RG 238 Streicher interrogation November 6, 1945.

232 *a deterioration in Hess's mental condition:* Gilbert believes amnesia has returned, Gilbert *Diary* 121, 130.

232 *What Kelley left unsaid:* Andrus wants to dismiss Gilbert, GGP Kelley letter to Gilbert December 24, 1946.

232 *he would defend himself:* Hess fires his lawyer, interview T. Fenstermacher; Neave 251.

233 *"I draw the attention"*: Hess complains about his lawyer, Neave 252; Hess's letter of January 30, 1946, to the court hardly suggests an addled mind:

> In the *New York Herald Tribune*, dated 27th January 1946, there is a report of an interview given by my former defending counsel, Dr. von Rohrscheidt. This contains a passage in which strictly confidential instructions given by me to Dr. von Rohrscheidt in respect of my defence, are given publicity, while at the same time it is emphasized that these were my instructions. This constitutes a breach of confidence and an offence against the secrecy to which an advocate is pledged; it is a grave professional offence, which in normal times would lead to denunciation before the governing Chamber of Lawyers. I therefore hereby place on record that I no longer have any confidence whatever in my former advocate. At the same time I draw the attention of the Court to the fact that I have now been a whole week without a defending counsel, while I have not been permitted to take advantage of the right to which the statute entitles me of pleading my own case. In consequence of this state of things, I was prevented from questioning even a single witness of all those who came forward during this period, although again I was entitled by the statute to do this.

234 *"He would enter a room"*: Ribbentrop, a problem client; his subservience to Hitler, Kelley 98; Poltorak 224; IMT vol. 10, 110; Gilbert *Diary* 130.

235 *"He bought his name"*: Schirach on Ribbentrop, Gilbert *Diary* 141; Tusa 299.

235 *he never said anything:* Description of Donnedieu de Vabres, Polevoi 294; J. Flanner *The New Yorker* March 30, 1946; Neave 234–35.

236 *goods stolen from France:* Opening of the French case; Göring's reaction, IMT vol. 5, 308–309, vol. 6, 184; Ophuls *Memory of Justice.*

236 *In 1942, she was arrested:* Testimony of Marie Claude Vaillant-Couturier on Auschwitz; Kranzbuehler's reaction, IMT vol. 6, 203–206, 215; Ophuls *Memory of Justice;* Poltorak 135.

238 *"I recognized Speer":* Boix's and other testimony damages Speer, IMT vol. 3, 440, 463–64, 492, vol. 6, 264, 269; H. Smith broadcast January 8, 1946.

240 Stars and Stripes *had broken the hushed-up story:* Conti suicide exposed, Swearingen 226–27.

240 *he was going home:* Kelley departs under conditions that Andrus questions, BAP Andrus memorandum February 7, 1946; GGP Gilbert letter to Kelley December 28, 1946, Gilbert letter to Dr. Lewis March 10, 1946.

240 *"I'm saving all that for a book":* Polevoi learns of the Gilbert-Kelley book project, Polevoi 185–86.

241 *"I intend to plunder in France":* Göring, Rosenberg, and prosecution of the art-looting operation, J. Flanner *The New Yorker* March 9, 1946; Mosley 253; Davidson 127; RG 238 Rosenberg dossier; IMT vol. 4, 90–91, vol. 9, 328.

242 *"My orders are final":* Rosenberg empties Jewish homes; Göring berates Bunjes, Davidson 138; RG 238 Bunjes letter to Dr. Turner February 5, 1941. Included in the art of the Old Masters that Göring amassed were works of Hals, Van Dyck, Goya, Velázquez, Rubens, Titian, Raphael, and Fragonard.

245 *Paulus stirred bitter memories:* Introduction of Paulus's affidavit, interview T. Taylor; Taylor 309; Tusa 195.

245 *a lone figure appeared:* Russians produce Paulus as a surprise witness, Polevoi 194, 196, 198–99; interview P. Uiberall; Poltorak 102–3; Fritzsche 116, 121; IMT vol. 7, 254–55, 261.

248 *"cross between a monastery and a concentration camp":* Jodl's background and troubled relationship with Hitler, Davidson 328, 343, 347–48; Tusa 498. Hitler's total conquest of Jodl in the early days is suggested in the general's diary entry for August 10, 1938:

> It is tragic that the Führer should have the whole nation behind him with the single exception of the Army generals. In my opinion it is only by action that they can now atone for their faults of lack of character and discipline. It is the same problem as in 1914. There is only one

undisciplined element in the Army—the generals, and in the last analysis this comes from the fact that they are arrogant. They have neither confidence nor discipline because they cannot recognize the Führer's genius.

248 *"This is not an able crowd"*: Biddle criticizes his colleagues and Jackson, BIDP Biddle letter to his wife, Katherine, February 13, 1946.

250 *"they are just as bad"*: Death of Yamashita; Göring criticizes arrest of Nazi wives, Poltorak 169; Gilbert *Diary* 55; GGP Gilbert memorandum to Andrus January 9, 1946.

250 *Doubts over Katyn could color the entire prosecution case:* The Russian prosecution presents the Katyn massacre, Conot 23; Tusa 113; Maser 109; IMT vol. 9, 3.

251 *The colonel suspected Göring:* Andrus's animus against Göring; wants to split defendants, Kelley 57–59, 61.

251 *"a great man or a criminal"*: childhood influences on Göring, Gilbert *Psychology* 84, 88.

252 *"your explanation of these deficiencies"*: Andrus-Watson clash, BAP Watson memorandum to Andrus February 14, 1946, Andrus memorandum for the record February 18, 1946, Andrus letter to General Clint Andrus February 20, 1946.

253 *Göring cursed at the news:* Gilbert announces new seating divisions for lunch, Gilbert *Diary* 158–59.

253 *"To the great Texas hunter"*: Wheelis befriends Göring, Swearingen 204; Mosley 204.

254 *Schirach could do nothing right:* Schirach becomes a Nazi anti-Semite; loses favor with Hitler over his wife's comments, IMT vol. 14, 308, 427–29; Gilbert *Diary* 23.

255 *"just comic relief"*: Defendants' reaction to separation; Göring complains, Gilbert *Diary* 155–56, 162; Kilmuir 69.

256 *"broke the backbone of the Nazi beast"*: Soviet boasts irk other Allies, Poltorak 5; Polevoi 175; Kilmuir 7.

256 *"the right to shoot prisoners of war"*: Soviet film, *Documentary Evidence of the German Fascist Invaders;* Nazi human and cultural atrocities in Russia, Polevoi 180; Tusa 198–99; IMT vol. 1, 48, vol. 8, 53, 75.

258 *"I've seen so much already"*: Göring and others react to Soviet atrocity film, Gilbert *Diary* 164, 171.

261 *"Unite to Stop Russians"*: Soviet correspondents learn of Iron Curtain speech, Polevoi 209–210. The *Stars and Stripes* enjoyed a great vogue in Nuremberg and elsewhere in Germany. The U.S. Military Government also sponsored a good, factual paper, *Die Neue Zeitung*, but the Germans had become so suspicious of any "official" news source that they far preferred the GIs' paper, assuming it to be an insider source.

262 *"Churchill is no fool":* Reaction of the defendants to the Iron Curtain speech, Polevoi 211; J. Flanner *The New Yorker* March 9, 1946.

263 *"And what language was that":* Simultaneous-interpretation problems, interviews A. Steer, P. Uiberall, T. Brown, D. Margolies; Hyde 521; Gaskins 47. On the witness stand and counsel's lectern were lights which would flash, yellow signaling the speaker to slow down, and red signaling the speaker to stop until the interpreter could catch up.

Chapter III: The Defense

268 *the first person Otto Stahmer called:* Göring's defense begins with Bodenschatz, IMT vol. 1, 1–4, 8–9.

269 *"Once we came to power":* Göring takes the stand, IMT vol. 9, 235, 250, 252–58.

270 *"one of the best brains":* Göring's performance wins grudging admiration, J. Flanner *The New Yorker* March 23, 1946; interview H. Smith; Gilbert *Diary* 194; Neave 257.

271 *"I promulgated those laws":* Göring defends the *Führerprinzip;* takes responsibility for the Nuremberg Laws, IMT vol. 1, 31, vol. 9, 263, 276; Gilbert *Diary* 197.

272 *Göring had been testifying for five hours:* Göring explains Rotterdam bombing, art thefts, cites Churchill, IMT vol. 9, 327, 340, 364; Gerhart 513.

274 *"They helped put Hitler into power":* Sprecher discusses Göring's defense and the case against the industrialists, interview D. Sprecher.

275 *"a duel to the death":* Birkett stresses the importance of Jackson's cross-examination of Göring, J. Flanner *The New Yorker* March 30, 1946; Hyde 509.

276 *"the witness ought to be allowed":* Jackson and the court clash over Göring's answers, JXO 1429, 1434; IMT vol. 9, 418–19.

278 *"Someone is going to have to stop him":* First round of cross-examination goes to Göring, Hyde 509–11; Neave 246, 248; AFN broadcast March 18, 1946.

279 *"an arrogant and contemptuous attitude":* Göring disputes translation of a document; angers Jackson, Tusa 281; IMT vol. 9, 507–508.

279 *"I'd better resign and go home":* Jackson confronts Biddle, Biddle 410; BIDP box 19 Biddle letter to his wife, Katherine, March 19, 1946.

281 *get the cross-examination back on track:* Birkett wants Göring reined in, Tusa 282; Hyde 512; Neave 255, 260. Maxwell-Fyfe, writing years later, said:

> I have been interested to see Birkett's comment that if the Tribunal had insisted on Goering answering the questions put to him without branching off into monologues "he would certainly have been much more under control, and the lost confidence of Mr. Justice Jackson would have been restored for the ultimate benefit of all concerned in the trial." Looking back, I am sure that Birkett's judgment was, for once, seriously at fault. If Goering—who, after all, was on trial for his life—could run rings round prosecuting counsel, that was a matter for counsel to put right without assistance from the Tribunal. Public opinion would not have tolerated—either at the time or subsequently—the constant interference of the judges on behalf of the prosecution.

281 *"it would be wiser to ignore a statement of that sort":* Jackson protests Göring gibe against the U.S., IMT vol. 9, 509–12.

282 *to plan a solution:* Jackson questions Göring on the Final Solution, IMT vol. 9, 517–19. Göring's shrewdness is demonstrated in an exchange between him and the prosecutor. On page 519, Jackson is questioning Göring over a decree in which Göring orders Heydrich to plan a *"Gesamtlösung"* and, later in the same document, an *"Endlösung."* The former translates as "complete solution" and the latter as "final solution." But Göring gives an answer making it appear that the translation of *both* words is "complete solution."

283 *"I would not like to be a Jew in Germany":* Jackson questions Göring on Kristallnacht, IMT vol. 9, 521, 532–33, 544.

284 *Jackson versus Göring ended:* Göring challenges the authenticity of photographs, IMT vol. 9, 565, 571.

284 *a brilliant villain:* Judgments on the Göring-Jackson confrontation, Tusa 290; Gerhart 399; interviews, T. Taylor, P. Uiberall, D. Margolies, B. Pinion Bitter, H. Smith.

284 *"You boys better get out":* GIs off duty; American race relations in Nuremberg, interviews H. Burson, R. Keeler, G. Sadel; Gilbert *Diary* 57. At the time of the trial, the U.S. military was still segregated by race. Not until 1948 did President Truman issue Executive Order 9981 integrating the armed forces.

286 *Sir David intended to outplay his opponents:* Maxwell-Fyfe prepares to cross-examine Göring, Ophuls *Memory of Justice;* JXO 1543; Biddle 410.

286 *"Dozens of officers have escaped":* Background, the Sagan case, Conot 309; Cooper 203; Elwyn-Jones 102; Neave 262.

287 *"You cooperated in this foul series of murders":* Maxwell-Fyfe questions Göring on the Sagan escape, IMT vol. 9, 579, 594–95, 614.

288 *"These things were kept secret from me"*: Maxwell-Fyfe questions Göring on extermination of the Jews, Gaskins 94; IMT vol. 9, 611, 619.

289 *"the most formidable witness I ever examined"*: Gilbert discusses the cross-examination with Göring, Gilbert *Diary* 208.

289 *"He may be slow in answering questions"*: Hess defense approaches; Hess's background, Conot 347; Manvell 17, 20, 27–28, 39; Posner 42; *Foreign Affairs* vol. 20, 1941.

291 *"Rudolf rarely smiled"*: Hess as third-ranking Nazi, Manvell 22, 37, 46–49, 52, 63; Posner 45; Kelley 21; Davidson 111. A typical example of the kind of errand Hess could perform through his connections on behalf of the socially insecure Hitler: the Nazis had purchased the Brown House in Munich as party headquarters and were having trouble paying for it. Hess went to see the powerful banker Fritz Thyssen about a loan. The Nazis kept the house; but the loan was never repaid.

292 *a remarkable instance of passive resistance:* Hess does not testify, Tusa 295, 299.

293 *"I want to see them hang"*: Gilbert's true feelings toward the defendants; his competition with Kelley, GGP Gilbert letters to Kelley March 13, April 5, April 13, 1946.

294 *a fairy tale besmirched:* Göring's fall and rise; marriage to Carin; addiction, Irving 39–40, 42, 46, 54–55, 63–64.

295 *"I am not insane"*: Göring is committed; recovers; elected to Reichstag, Irving 86–89, 90–95.

295 *He lived like an Aryan pasha:* Göring remarries, becomes addicted again, Irving 102, 104, 136–37; RG 238 Göring dossier; Mosley 213–14, 257.

297 *a shack in Sackdilling forest:* Emmy Göring's postwar odyssey; visit by Gilbert, interview W. Jackson; W. Jackson letter to author December 30, 1991; Posner 197; Davidson 101.

297 *"He is a fanatic on the subject of loyalty"*: Gilbert discusses with Emmy the Göring-Hitler relationship, Gilbert *Diary* 212–13.

298 *"It's not a woman's affair"*: Göring will not renounce Hitler, Gilbert *Diary* 213–14.

299 *"He's a Nazi killer"*: Göring's clash with a guard, Fritzsche 45; BAP statement of PFC Vincent Traina March 26, 1946.

299 *He needed not antagonists but friends:* Göring's gifts to Wheelis, Swearingen 146.

300 *"Ribbentrop advised in favor of war"*: Ribbentrop prepares for his defense, J. Flanner *The New Yorker* March 9, 1946; Gilbert *Diary* 195; Andrus 165; Davidson 87.

301 *Amen would be handling the cross-examination:* Jackson will not question Ribbentrop, interview D. Sprecher.

301 *intending to make it his home:* Ribbentrop in Canada, Bullock 5, 7, 9; Conot 51.

302 *"We were actually afraid of Ribbentrop":* Ribbentrop takes the stand, Poltorak 51; H. Smith broadcast November 24, 1945; IMT vol. 10, 347, 367, 386–87.

304 *"You were not even interesting":* French and Russian cross-examination of Ribbentrop, IMT vol. 10, 409, 426–28.

304 *he should make out his will:* Frau von Ribbentrop speaks with William Jackson, interview W. Jackson.

305 *"I get the slops they don't want":* Prison routine and Andrus's dissatisfaction with his personnel, interview W. Glenny; BAP Andrus draft manuscript 87. Andrus was in fact considerably short-handed. His table of organization called for 142 officers and men. At any given point, he averaged about 117, almost eighteen percent below strength.

306 *"a sergeant's mind":* Background Keitel; he rejects confession, Hyde 215; Kelley 123; Conot 259; Tusa 259.

307 *"I bear the responsibility":* Keitel admits blame on direct examination, IMT vol. 10, 470–71, 565, 628; Conot 310–11.

308 *"even against women and children":* Rudenko cross-examines Keitel on the Reprisal Order; Maxwell-Fyfe on the Commando Order, IMT vol. 10, 617, 623–25. During his testimony, Keitel gave an interesting inside observation on Hitler's leadership style: "[Hitler] made his accusations, objections and criticisms as a rule at people who were not present. I took the part of the absent person as a matter of principle because he could not defend himself. The result was that the accusations and criticisms were then aimed at me."

309 *"too young to be so wise":* Jackson losing staff; Taylor to succeed him in subsequent trials, JXO 1493; interviews E. Hardy, T. Taylor.

310 *"More alone than survivors":* Katherine Biddle writes on Nuremberg, BIDP box 19. General Joseph T. McNarney, commander of U.S. Forces European Theater, lifted the ban on civilian and military spouses coming into the U.S. occupation zone in mid-March 1946. The first spouses departed the United States on April 16.

312 *he might as well go home:* Jackson again threatens to leave, Neave 260; B. Smith 109; Conot 363.

313 *"this statement of yours is not very credible":* Defense lawyer Kauffmann questions Kaltenbrunner on concentration camps and atrocities, IMT vol. 11, 232, 243, 248–49, 324, 330–31, 532; Gilbert *Diary* 407. The prosecution, on cross-examination, introduced an affidavit made by two surviving Mauthausen inmates, "corpse carriers" who carried to the crematorium the bodies of fifteen people killed before Kaltenbrunner to demonstrate various extermination techniques.

316   *"The Führer has ordered the Final Solution":* Interrogation and background of Hoess, interview W. Harris; Gilbert *Psychology* 241.

318   *"To their death without premonition":* Hoess relates the history of Auschwitz on cross-examination, IMT vol. 10, 648, vol. 11, 398, 401, 404, 416–17. In his affidavit to Whitney Harris, Hoess described the effect of the gas used: "It was Zyklon [Cyclone] B, crystalline prussic acid which volatilized immediately upon contact with oxygen. The people became stunned with the first breath of it, and the killing took three to 15 minutes according to the weather and the number of those locked in."

319   *"I never gave much thought to whether it was wrong":* Gilbert visits Hoess, draws final conclusions on mass murderers, Gilbert *Diary* 258–59; GGP Gilbert speech notes (undated).

321   *He had enjoyed his birthday party:* Andrus meets the press socially at the Faber-Castell castle, BAP logbook entry April 15, 1946; Conot 20; B. Smith 299.

323   *"A thousand years will pass":* Frank's defense, Gilbert *Diary* 265, 280; IMT vol. 12, 2, 13, 19, 156; Fritzsche 199; Polevoi 301.

324   *"a high-grade lynching":* Jackson witnesses a Prague trial; is criticized by Supreme Court colleagues, Tusa 481; Gerhart 257, 259, 399–402, 436; Neave 246.

325   *and hope for Harry Truman's nod:* Death of Supreme Court Chief Justice Stone; Jackson's prospects to succeed him, IMT vol. 12, 97; Gerhart 258, 403; interview W. Jackson.

327   *He had enjoyed himself enormously:* Gisevius testimony damages Keitel and Göring, IMT vol. 12, 156, 169–70, 269; Kalnoky 178.

327   *a "disgusting blackmail plot":* Possibility of Hitler's Jewish ancestry, Rosenbaum 450–89; Davidson 429.

329   *who bore responsibility:* Tracing the Final Solution, Conot 259, 261; Davidson 75; B. Smith 176; IMT vol. 11, 50–51, 398; Film, *Hitler's Final Solution: The Wannsee Conference*; Maser 231; Wolfe *Annals of the American Academy of Political Science* July 1980; Swearingen 48. According to Ohlendorf, orders to the *Einsatzgruppen* to execute Jews reportedly went orally from Hitler to Himmler to Heydrich. Upon receiving this order, Bruno Stechenbach, then personnel chief of the RSHA, issued it in writing to *Einsatzgruppen* leaders in June of 1941, shortly before the attack on the Soviet Union.

332 *"Wondrous are the ways of love"*: Frau Streicher testifies in her husband's defense, Tusa 333; Davidson 45, 101; IMT vol. 12, 305, 307, 348, 388.

332 *"If we can't convict Hjalmar Schacht"*: Jackson's eagerness to convict the financier, interview T. Taylor.

333 *"do you know why I am here"*: Schacht background and defense testimony, interview N. Doman; Kelley 187; Posner 95, 100; IMT vol. 12, 417, 578, 584–85; H. Smith broadcast December 1, 1945. Schacht's imperturbable confidence is demonstrated by the fact that during his defense, he asked Speer to start designing a house for him to be built after the trial.

335 *"I'll have to make you the minister of economy"*: Funk background and rise, IMT vol. 13, 78, vol. 5, 160; Conot 402; Davidson 247–51.

336 *"Nobody . . . ever deposited his gold teeth in a bank"*: Funk on the stand, IMT vol. 13, 166, 169, 170–71; Conot 403; Davidson 250.

336 *"Why do you think I'm sitting here"*: Dönitz as Hitler's surrogate, Gilbert *Diary* 176, 299, 325.

337 *the most dangerous piece of paper*: Kranzbuehler seeks to defend the *Laconia* Order; prohibition of tu quoque, Davidson 403–405; B. Smith 249–50; IMT vol. 8, 625.

339 *the man whom Adolf Hitler had found most worthy*: Maxwell-Fyfe cross-examination hits Dönitz on anti-Semitism, concentration camps, and the Hitler succession, IMT vol. 13, 342, 392.

339 *questions provided by Kranzbuehler*: Nimitz affidavit aids Dönitz, IMT vol. 17, 377–80. Had Dönitz not been a rabid anti-Semite, not requested concentration camp labor for shipyards, and not passed along the Commando Order, it is unlikely he would have come to trial for his naval activities alone. A U.S. Navy captain, John P. Bracken, who advised on naval matters had made a report to Jackson on August 24, 1945, saying, in part: "Unless additional information implicating Doenitz in political as distinguished from military acts has been uncovered . . . it is believed there is insufficient evidence to convict him or to warrant his being tried."

341 *Both men died*: A potentially racially related double murder, interview R. Korb Williams; BAP logbook entries May 10, 13, 1946; BIDP box 19 Biddle letter to his wife, Katherine, May 17, 1946; *New York Times* May 12, 13, 14, 1946.

342 *The most curious document*: Introduction of Raeder's Moscow Statement damages Dönitz, Göring, and Keitel, Gilbert *Diary* 342, 346; Davidson 368–69.

344 *"murders a millionfold"*: Schirach takes the stand, IMT vol. 14, 361; Gilbert *Diary* 348–50. Schirach was fortunate that the prosecution failed to present evidence that he, along with Speer, had attended the 1943 meeting in Posen where Himmler spoke and left no doubt about what the Final Solution meant.

346 *"What was the relationship of your office to Speer's"*: Sauckel's defense; responsibility for slave labor, IMT vol. 14, 618, 620, 622, 626, vol. 15, 3, 6, 9, 55, 233.

347 *"The things that made me hate Hitler"*: Jodl almost escaped prosecution; his disillusionment with Hitler, Neave 314; Conot 27; Gilbert *Diary* 361.

348 *"an honorable soldier"*: Roberts's cross-examination hits Jodl on Geneva Convention, the Reprisal Order, terrorism against England, and loyalty to Hitler, IMT vol. 15, 506, 508–11; Davidson 350. While he was generally loyal, Jodl's occasional outspokenness toward Hitler could be breathtaking. After the Twentieth of July plot, Jodl spoke of a general he admired, named Bonin, who had been arrested by Hitler in 1934 on flimsy evidence. "You cannot be surprised, my Führer," Jodl said, "if you throw a man like Bonin into jail without any proof being found, and apparently only on the basis of rumor, that the spirit of July 20 dominates the General Staff."

349 *Truman named Fred Vinson:* Jackson misses out on chief judgeship, Conot 442; Biddle 411.

350 *"my rope is being woven from Dutch hemp"*: Seyss-Inquart analyzes the Germans; takes the stand, Gilbert *Diary* 286–87; Conot 446.

351 *Speer was going to be questioned by a subordinate:* Speer prefers Jackson to cross-examine, JXO 1448–49; Speer *Inside* 651.

352 *"I was grateful to Sauckel for every worker"*: Speer's lawyer tackles Speer-Sauckel controversy, IMT vol. 16, 429, 447, 456, 479.

353 *"We have no right at this stage of the war to carry out destruction"*: Speer describes actions to thwart Hitler's scorched-earth policy, IMT vol. 16, 489–90, 496, 499. Speer described the false reasons that the staff had to use to persuade Hitler to do what was right. As he testified: "I made him decide between the two situations: Firstly, if these industrial areas were lost, my armament potential would sink if they were not recaptured; and secondly, if they were recaptured, they would be of value to us only if we had not destroyed them."

354 *He asked Stahl to procure a poison gas:* Speer's plan to assassinate Hitler, IMT vol. 16, 494–95, 504.

355 *Jackson took his place at the prosecutor's stand:* Cross-examination of Speer, IMT vol. 16, 482, 514–15, 527, 563.

357 *"a tremendous indictment"*: Speer wins public acclaim, London *Daily Telegraph* June 20, 1946.

358 *Fritzsche left the stand:* Neurath and Fritzsche, the last defense cases, Conot 450; Davidson 168, 171, 175; Tusa 403–406.

359 *forensic experts battled in room 600:* Responsibility for Katyn massacre, IMT vol. 17, 337, 350; Biddle 416.

360 *ample time for the defense to sum up:* The court gives unlimited time for defense summations, interview D. Sprecher; JXO 1574; IMT vol. 17, 500.

360 *Bormann was a wanted man:* Göring "reveals" Bormann's whereabouts; Bormann tried in absentia, interviews T. Fenstermacher, T. Lambert; IMT vol. 2, 26, vol. 5, 304, vol. 19, 111; Neave 239; Taylor 465.

363 *"It's the guy I have to work for":* Wheelis's dislike of Andrus, interview J. Vonetes.

364 *he pronounced it proven beyond a doubt:* Jackson begins his summation; the conspiracy charge; the guilt of Schacht, IMT vol. 19, 392, 398, 400, 407, 415–17, 419, 428–29.

365 *"But dead they are":* Jackson ends his summation, IMT vol. 19, 432.

367 *for the death of them all:* Summations of other nations' prosecutors, Tusa 421, 423–24; Davidson 357; Neave 300; IMT vol. 19, 433, vol. 20, 1–14. Rudenko closed saying, "I appeal to the Tribunal to sentence all the defendants without exception to the supreme penalty, death. Such a verdict will be greeted with satisfaction by all progressive mankind."

367 *He was going to deny Emmy Göring's request:* Andrus initially opposes visits, Andrus 161; Mosley 347; BAP logbook entry August 3, 1946.

368 *take a few select journalists through:* Andrus escorts reporters through cellblock C, interview A. Logan.

369 *Biddle heard the organization cases:* Defense of the organizations begins; Biddle is skeptical, Neave 151. North of Nuremberg was Stalag D-13, a POW camp containing some 20,000 SS veterans, many of whom had submitted requests to be heard in defense of the organizations. Jackson dispatched Drexel Sprecher and three others to talk to these men. The POWs maintained, Sprecher reported back, that the SS was highly compartmentalized; most men were not assigned to concentration camps and they denied knowledge of the camp's operations. They had been, the POWs claimed, almost all infantrymen and artillerymen fighting with purely military units.

369 *Sievers implicated Göring:* Göring returns to testify in the organization case; Maxwell-Fyfe cross-examines, IMT vol. 21, 302–17; 524–25; 547.

372 *this mad idea of conspiracy:* The judges debate the conspiracy count, Biddle 465; BIDP box 1 Biddle letter to Wechsler July 10, 1946, box 14 minutes of judges' meeting August 14, 1946, box 19 memorandum Rowe to Biddle July 11, 1946; Neave 123–24, 128, 133; interview H. Wechsler.

374 *"see the humorous side of all this"*: Hess, Speer, et al. prepare their final statements, Manvell 172.

375 *"I do not believe that this will be my sentence"*: Jodl writes to his wife, Maser 237–38.

375 *they gathered like bees around the queen:* Rebecca West and Biddle, Taylor 548; Glendinning 193; Biddle 425; R. West, *The New Yorker* September 7, October 26, 1946.

376 *"conquered by tremendous enemy superiority"*: The defendants make final statements, IMT vol. 22, 365–410. Lawrence's scrupulous impartiality was again demonstrated when, in connection with threats the defense counsels had received, he announced:

> The Tribunal have been informed that the defendants' counsel have been receiving letters from Germans improperly criticizing their conduct as counsel in these proceedings. The Tribunal will protect counsel insofar as it is necessary so long as the Tribunal is in session, and it has no doubt that the Control Council will protect them thereafter against such attacks. In the opinion of the Tribunal, Defense Counsel have performed an important public duty in accordance with the high tradition of the legal profession, and the Tribunal thanks them for their assistance.

Chapter IV: Judgment Day

383 *still haunted by the fragility of this instrument:* The judges begin deliberating verdicts; confront the ex post facto criticism; ROWP box 44 Rowe memorandum to Biddle July 11, 1946; Taylor 10. Though forty-three death sentences were handed down against SS troops judged guilty of the murders of eighty-one American POWs near Malmédy, none was ever carried out. As a result of subsequent reviews and the desire to win German support during the Cold War, American officials substantially reduced most Malmédy sentences.

385 *they began to vote on the verdicts:* Göring, Hess, and Ribbentrop cases decided, B. Smith 177, 182, 184; Neave 316; IMT vol. 1, 282, vol. 5, 14–15, vol. 22, 532–33; ROWP box 44 Rowe notes on Hess deliberation (undated).

386 *safe to allow the defendants family visits:* Andrus approves, BIDP box 14 Andrus request to the tribunal September 2, 1946; Posner 12, 198; Conot 481; Andrus 182; Gerecke *Saturday Evening Post* September 1, 1951.

388 *he had struck a Faustian bargain:* Verdicts on Keitel, Kaltenbrunner, Frank, and Rosenberg, IMT vol. 1, 292; B. Smith 189, 193, 196. Donnedieu de Vabres was inclined to grant condemned military defendants death by the firing squad. Biddle was initially receptive. Nikitchenko argued vociferously for the rope, the position that, in the end, prevailed.

389 *Glenny watched the easy camaraderie:* The Göring-Wheelis relationship, Swearingen 146; interview W. Glenny.

389 *"a little Jew-baiter":* Verdicts on Streicher, Funk, and Schacht, IMT vol. 5, 118; B. Smith 173, 200, 206, 279; Neave 176; BIDP box 14 Biddle notes on court's meeting September 6, 1946.

390 *The vote went quickly:* verdicts on Seyss-Inquart, Dönitz, Schirach, Raeder, B. Smith 213, 238, 247, 254, 261–63; Davidson 382, 422.

392 *the ISD was not slackening its efforts:* Andrus alerts his men to a possible jailbreak, Andrus 157.

392 *should one hang for lack of breeding:* Verdicts on Frick, Jodl, Sauckel, Speer, Neurath, Papen, et al., B. Smith 207, 209, 211, 219, 222, 294–95; Neave 134, 199, 312.

393 *Biddle could not sleep:* Biddle ponders verdicts on Frank, Speer, and Rosenberg, B. Smith 222.

395 *Bullet-proof cars arrived at the courthouse:* Judgment day, Conot 492; Tusa 11; Poltorak 459.

396 *a pointless exercise:* Verdicts on the organizations, IMT vol. 22, 505–23. The entire Nazi party leadership was not found guilty. The cutoff point was *Ortsgruppenleiter. Amtsleiter* and below were exempt.

396 *"You men have a duty to yourselves":* Andrus addresses the defendants before judgment, Andrus 175.

397 *"second only to Adolf Hitler":* Individual verdicts handed down, IMT vol. 22, 526–80. In convicting Streicher of count four, crimes against humanity, the tribunal made a daring leap to connect words to acts. The judgment on him read: "In his speeches and articles, week after week, month after month, he infected the German mind with the virus of anti-Semitism and incited the German people to active persecution."

The tribunal was curiously dismissive of some of the most odious evidence against Speer. Acknowledging that Speer had used slave labor "in the industries under his control," the IMT concluded that he "attempted to use as few concentration camp workers as possible." The "few" numbered 30,000, thousands of whom were worked and starved to death. While the use of POWs in armaments production violated the Geneva Convention, Speer did employ Soviet prisoners, defending his actions with a technical argument— the Soviet Union was not a signatory to the Convention.

401 *He was furious at Schacht's acquittal:* Jackson insinuates that Biddle undermined the prosecution, JXO 1619. While not mentioning Biddle specifically, Jackson issued a public statement saying, "Our arguments for their conviction [Schacht and Papen] which seemed so convincing to all of us prosecutors seems not to have made a similar impression on the Tribunal."

402   *The more personal guilt, the less collective guilt:* Germans object to acquittals, B. Smith 300; Davidson 177; Cooper 271.

403   *"death by hanging":* Sentences handed down, Neave 311; Biddle 443, 476; IMT vol. 22, 588–90; Polevoi 315–16; Fritzsche 325; Speer *Spandau* 3. In his dissenting opinion, Nikitchenko also opposed the acquittals of Papen, Fritzsche, and particularly Schacht.

405   *Uncertainty compounded the anxiety:* An unclear execution date, BDC Board of Investigation Report 3. Some sources say that the executions were to be carried out fifteen days after sentencing. However, the Board of Investigation noted that "the charter which was furnished the accused prisoners provided that should execution be the sentence of the court, it will be carried into effect after the elapse of 15 days after the sentence was announced, *excluding Sundays.*" By this definition the executions could not have taken place before October 18, instead of October 16, when, in fact, they occurred.

405   *"treated like a common criminal":* Luise Jodl's appeals for clemency, Cooper 249; Maser 249.

405   *Higgins filed the story:* Cell transfers, *New York Herald Tribune* October 3, 1946.

406   *"so easy to convict military men":* Eisenhower on the verdicts, *New York Herald Tribune* October 3, 1946.

407   *"the most important, enduring work of my life":* Jackson reflects on the trial, Harris, introduction.

408   *"They will not hang me":* Stahmer given Göring's briefcase; Emmy visits Göring, BAP Andrus order on the prisoners' property November 23, 1945; BDC Report of Board of Proceedings October 1946; Mosley 352; Swearingen 25–26, 183.

408   *"They're all cowards":* Gilbert speaks out, *New York Times* October 3, 1946; BAP Andrus memorandum to General Rickard October 12, 1946.

409   *their last hope for clemency:* Appeals to the Allied Control Council, B. Smith 299; Conot 500–501; Maser 248–49; BIDP box 14 Biddle notes October 4, 1946.

410   *"I had reckoned with the death sentence":* Frank, Hess correspondence with spouses, Posner 37; Rosenbaum 460; Manvell 173, 176, 247.

411   *"the right thing":* Keitel's memoirs; his role in Rommel's death, BDC Report of Board of Proceedings October 1946; Maser 15–16, 53, 245; RG 238 Keitel interrogation September 28, 1945; Davidson 572. The repeated refrain of Keitel and the other military men was that they had no choice but to obey Hitler. Germany's Military Law Book, however, seems to allow for disobeying orders known to be unlawful. It reads:

1) If carrying out an order in the course of duty should violate a law, only the superior who gives the order is responsible. However, the subordinate who obeys it is punishable as a participant a) if he goes beyond the given order; or b) when he knows that the superior's order would have the purpose of leading to a military or other crime."

411 *Andrus delivered the news:* Clemency rejected; Göring defiant, Neave 299–300; Conot 503; BDC File 6a; BAP Lieutenant Colonel William Dunn report to Andrus August 28, 1946.

413 *Gilbert left cellblock C:* Gilbert's last visits; no firing squad for Göring, Maser 249; Swearingen 88; BDC Report of Board of Proceedings October 1946.

413 *a glass vial of cyanide:* Göring preparations for suicide; baggage room controls, interview W. Glenny; Swearingen 95, 211, 233; BDC Report of Board of Proceedings October 1946.

414 *His crew was now waiting:* Andrus meets the hangman; background Woods, *Buffalo* (New York) *Courier Express* October 19, 1946; Williams 66–70; BAP Andrus letter to G. Aitken March 15, 1968; BDC Report of Board of Proceedings October 1946; Andrus 187, 193, 198; interview R. Keeler.

414 *Word passed quickly:* The last cell inspection, BDC Report of Board of Proceedings statement of First Lieutenant West, statement of Lieutenant Roska October 16, 1946; Swearingen 249.

415 *Woods ran his hands over the ropes:* Preparation of the gallows, BAP Andrus draft ms. 71; Andrus 187, 193; Williams 64; Speer *Spandau* 9; Tusa 482; Kingsbury Smith, "The Execution of Nazi War Criminals, 16 October 1946"; *It Happened in 1946–1947*, edited by Clark Kinnard and Kingsbury Smith 641–48.

416 *The day began like any other:* The last day, *New York Times* October 16, 1946; Andrus 184, 187; Swearingen 253, 269; BDC Report of the Board of Proceedings October 1946; Bullock 200; Gilbert *Diary* 112.

417 *Father O'Connor visited the cells:* The priest offers to hear confessions; Dr. Pfluecker visits Göring, *New York Times* October 16, 1946; J. Powers *New York Sunday News* April 20, 1947.

418 *"This night might prove to be very short":* Dr. Pfluecker tips off Göring, Maser 250; Swearingen 153.

419 *He placed the four letters in an envelope:* Göring's suicide notes, Swearingen 220; BDC collection of last letters of the defendants. While some works on the trial refer to three Göring suicide notes, the Berlin Documents Center has four, all of which the author was permitted to see.

420   *He must not let Göring slip into a stupor:* Dr. Pfluecker arranges phony sleeping pills for Göring, Maser 250; BDC Report of Board of Proceedings October 1946 Exhibit AC.

420   *The reporters piled into buses:* The press prepares to cover the executions, Tusa 482; *New York Times* October 16, 1946; *Washington Post* October 15, 1946.

421   *eleven bare lights over eleven cell doors:* The press pool visits the jail; Göring adds to a letter, Taylor 608; Poltorak 467–69; Polevoi 317–21. The Göring letter to the Allied Control Council has a Roman I at the top. A loose page among the four suicide letters has a Roman II at the top. This latter page, in which Göring protests, "I consider it in extremely bad taste to present our death as a spectacle to the sensationalist press," strongly suggests that he added it to the letter to the ACC in response to Andrus's taking the press pool through the cellblock shortly before the executions.

422   *Lights out:* Activities outside the prison, Andrus 193; BDC Report of Board of Proceedings October 1946; interview R. Keeler.

422   *"there's something wrong with Göring":* Göring's suicide, J. Powers, *New York Sunday News* April 20, 1947; Swearingen 269, 283; Andrus 193; BDC Report of Board of Proceedings October 1946 statements of G. Tymchyshyn, H. Gerecke, H. Johnson, J. Carver, L. Pfluecker, C. Roska, R. Starnes. Pfluecker's behavior upon being called to Göring's cell strongly supports the conclusion that he knew Göring's intentions. Upon entering the cell, he said that Göring was dying and nothing could be done, because "I didn't have any experience with dying from poisoning." At this point no one had yet mentioned poisoning, though Pfluecker may have smelled cyanide, or he may have recognized poison symptoms, which contradict his claim of ignorance. In any case, he made no effort to revive Göring, though, at the time of Ley's suicide, he made vigorous efforts to revive that prisoner, including injections of Cardiozol and Lubulin, and he attempted artificial respiration.

423   *people parted to let Andrus through:* Andrus is notified of Göring's suicide; the Quadripartite Commission arrives, *Time* October 28, 1946; Andrus 191; Swearingen 79, 95; Gerecke *Saturday Evening Post* September 1, 1951.

424   *appoint a board:* The Quadripartite Commission examines alternatives; appoints a board, Andrus 192; Swearingen 93; interview K. Andrus Williams, BDC Report of Board of Proceedings Appointment of Board of Investigation October 15, 1946.

425   *The executions would proceed:* Andrus informs the prisoners; orders the last meal; tells the press pool of Göring's suicide, Tusa 484; *Life* October 28, 1946; Maser 250; Gerecke *Saturday Evening Post* September 1, 1951.

425   *Ribbentrop was led to the gallows:* The executions begin, *New York Herald Tribune* October 16, 1946; Andrus 194–96; BAP Andrus draft ms. 74; *It Happened in 1946–1947* Kinnard and Smith 641–48; *New York Times* October 16,

1946; *Life* October 28, 1946; Maser 252–53; Speer *Spandau* 9. Bureaucratic squabbles carried over even into the executions. Jackson had refused as unseemly a request by the Quadripartite Commission to be allowed to sit among the officers of the court on judgment day; he relegated the members to the visitors' gallery. When Whitney Harris arrived at the courthouse to witness the executions as Jackson's representative, he was refused entry by the Quadripartite Commission.

428 *"Göring was not hanged":* Andrus faces the full press corps, Swearingen 82–84; Tusa 484; Andrus 192; Interview K. Andrus Williams.

430 *raised his arm in the Nazi salute:* Speer and others clean the death house, Speer *Spandau* 10–11. The cremation and disposition of the condemned men's ashes were not fully revealed until the United Press broke the story on March 20, 1947. Even then, the editors included felt obliged to include an explanation:

> UP carries the following story, not to afford future German nationalists locations for shrines to late leading Nazis, but because the facts are increasingly generally known in Munich and it is understood that photographs of the disposal of the Nazi ashes are being offered for sale in the U.S. Thus the once-quadripartite secret is a secret no longer.

430 *The wrong headline:* Public reaction to the Göring suicide, *Time* October 28, 1946; Swearingen 123–24.

431 *The members accepted Göring's claim:* The public and secret reports of the Quadripartite Commission's investigation, BDC Report of Board of Proceedings "Findings" October 26, 1946, Report of Investigating Board to the Quadripartite Commission October 24, 1946 1–7, statement of J. West; Andrus 184; Swearingen 95, 107, 109, 214–15, 241. While Colonel Andrus fell under the blanket exoneration of the Quadripartite Commission (that "no individual or individuals be held responsible for the death by suicide of Hermann Goering"), he received personal vindication three months later. The War Department issued a statement saying:

> In response to queries from the press concerning the return to the United States of Colonel B. C. Andrus, formerly Commandant of the Nuremberg jail, the War Department stated today that Colonel Andrus's relief from duty at Nuremberg was in no way connected with the suicide of Hermann Goering. Colonel Andrus has had 31 months of overseas service and was eligible for return to the United States under the provisions of War Department policy for the rotation of personnel.

Epilogue

437 *The validity of the court is still debated:* The controversy, Gerhart 506; *Fortune* December 1945; *New York Times* October 6, 1946.

442   *the world experienced twenty-four wars:* Conflict and aggression continue, *World Military and Social Expenditures 1991* 22–25; World Priorities, Washington D.C., 1991; Conot 521; Maser 266; Tusa 488.

443   *never applied to any nation:* War crimes inaction through 1992, Taylor 637, 640.

INDEX

Roosevelt, Franklin D.: and Biddle, 77; death of, 7; desires summary execution of Nazis, 8, 462n; and Jackson, 10, 11; and war-crimes trials, 8, 15, 16, 18, 25, 464–65n, 469n

Rosenberg, Alfred, 25, 151, 416; and American blacks, 211; anti-Semitic doctrines, 210, 322, 438–39; arrested as war criminal, 30, 47; art-looting operation, 210, 212, 241–42, 243, 388; death sentence, 403; execution of, 426; files of, used as evidence, 42, 92; *The Myth of the Twentieth Century*, 210–11, 241, 480n; propaganda work, 158; prosecution case against, 210, 211, 212, 214; on slave labor program, 163; and Streicher, 366; verdicts against, 388, 398

Rosenman, Samuel, 7–9

Rosenthal, Stanley, 424

Roska, Charles J., 409, 416–17, 426; and Göring's suicide, 423, 424, 432, 447

Rotterdam, German bombing of, 271–72

Rowe, James, 244, 339–40, 451; and Biddle, 340, 371; and court security, 371, 383, 390; and verdict decisions, 384, 390–91

Royal Air Force (RAF), 39, 178; prisoners of war, shot by Germans, 286–88, 307

RSHA. *See* Reich Central Security Office

Rudenko, Roman A., 263, 407, 451; cross-examination of Göring, 288, 289; cross-examination of Keitel, 307–8; cross-examination of Ribbentrop, 303–4, Jackson and, 117–18, 124, 126, 343–44; opening and closing arguments, 138–39,

364, 491n; prosecution of Nazi atrocities in Soviet Union, 245, 246, 256, 257

SA (*Sturmabteilung*), 178, 179, 180, 184, 185, 396

Sadel, Gunther, 157, 158, 285, 314–315, 451

Sagan affair, 286–88, 307

Sauckel, Ernst Friedrich Christoph ("Fritz"), 214, 253; attempted escape during war, 164–65; conscription of slave labor, 25, 64, 162–64, 166, 345, 346, 352, 400, 439; death sentence, 404, 406, 409, 412–13; defense testimony, 345–46, 377, 378; displaced by Goebbels, 165; Dodd's prosecution of, 160, 163, 164, 166; execution of, 427, 439; as *Gauleiter* of Thuringia, 161–62; Hitler and, 161, 162, 165–66; persistent confusion at trial, 85, 160–61, 213, 346; Speer and, x, 85, 162, 163–64, 165, 167, 238, 346, 352, 401; verdicts against, 392, 400

Sauter, Fritz, 198, 199, 233–34, 273, 274, 299

Schacht, Hjalmar Horace Greeley, 151, 213, 250, 253, 451; acquittal of, 390, 399, 401–2, 403, 404, 439; aloofness from fellow defendants, 64, 332–33, 387; American background of, 51–52, 333; defense of, 362, 489n; imprisoned in Dachau, 52, 334, 439; IQ test results, 117; Jackson's prosecution of, 332, 333, 347, 364–65, 390, 401–2, 439; as minister of economy, 333; offers deal to Donovan, 119, 120, 121; as Reichsbank president, 52, 333; and Ribbentrop,